CW00739803

WOLF HALL

Also by Hilary Mantel

Bring Up the Bodies
Beyond Black
Every Day is Mother's Day
Vacant Possession
Eight Months on Ghazzah Street
Fludd
A Place of Greater Safety
A Change of Climate
An Experiment in Love
The Giant, O'Brien
Learning to Talk

NON-FICTION
Giving Up the Ghost

HILARY MANTEL

WOLF HALL

FOURTH ESTATE • *London*

First published in Great Britain in 2009 by
Fourth Estate
An imprint of HarperCollins*Publishers*
77–85 Fulham Palace Road
London W6 8JB
www.4thestate.co.uk

Copyright © Hilary Mantel 2009

First published in hardback in 2009
This hardback edition published in 2012

2

The right of Hilary Mantel to be identified as the author
of this work has been asserted by her in accordance
with the Copyright, Designs and Patents Act 1988

A catalogue record for this book is available from the British Library

ISBN 978-0-00-750977-5

All rights reserved. No part of this publication may be
reproduced, transmitted, or stored in a retrieval system,
in any form or by any means, without permission
in writing from Fourth Estate.

Typeset in Stempel Garamond by
G&M Designs Limited, Raunds, Northamptonshire

Endpapers taken from *De Ludo Scachorum* by Luca Pacioli
© Coronini Cronberg Foundation (Gorizia, Italy)

Printed in Great Britain by Clays Ltd, St Ives plc

MIX
Paper from
responsible sources
FSC™ C007454

FSC™ is a non-profit international organisation established to promote
the responsible management of the world's forests. Products carrying the
FSC label are independently certified to assure customers that they come
from forests that are managed to meet the social, economic and
ecological needs of present and future generations,
and other controlled sources.

Find out more about HarperCollins and the environment at
www.harpercollins.co.uk/green

To my singular friend
Mary Robertson this be given.

CONTENTS

CAST OF CHARACTERS

In Putney, 1500
Walter Cromwell, a blacksmith and brewer.
Thomas, his son.
Bet, his daughter.
Kat, his daughter.
Morgan Williams, Kat's husband.

At Austin Friars, from 1527
Thomas Cromwell, a lawyer.
Liz Wykys, his wife.
Gregory, their son.
Anne, their daughter.
Grace, their daughter.
Henry Wykys, Liz's father, a wool trader.
Mercy, his wife.
Johane Williamson, Liz's sister.
John Williamson, her husband.
Johane (Jo), their daughter.
Alice Wellyfed, Cromwell's niece, daughter of Bet Cromwell.
Richard Williams, later called Cromwell, son of Kat and Morgan.
Rafe Sadler, Cromwell's chief clerk, brought up at Austin
    Friars.

Thomas Avery, the household accountant.
Helen Barre, a poor woman taken in by the household.
Thurston, the cook.
Christophe, a servant.
Dick Purser, keeper of the guard dogs.

At Westminster
Thomas Wolsey, Archbishop of York, cardinal, papal legate,
    Lord Chancellor: Thomas Cromwell's patron.
George Cavendish, Wolsey's gentleman usher and later
    biographer.
Stephen Gardiner, Master of Trinity Hall, the cardinal's
    secretary, later Master Secretary to Henry VIII: Cromwell's
    most devoted enemy.
Thomas Wriothesley, Clerk of the Signet, diplomat, protégé of
    both Cromwell and Gardiner.
Richard Riche, lawyer, later Solicitor General.
Thomas Audley, lawyer, Speaker of the House of Commons,
    Lord Chancellor after Thomas More's resignation.

At Chelsea
Thomas More, lawyer and scholar, Lord Chancellor after
    Wolsey's fall.
Alice, his wife.
Sir John More, his aged father.
Margaret Roper, his eldest daughter, married to Will Roper.
Anne Cresacre, his daughter-in-law.
Henry Pattinson, a servant.

In the city
Humphrey Monmouth, merchant, imprisoned for sheltering
    William Tyndale, translator of the Bible into English.
John Petyt, merchant, imprisoned on suspicion of heresy.
Lucy, his wife.

John Parnell, merchant, embroiled in long-running legal dispute
  with Thomas More.
Little Bilney, scholar burned for heresy.
John Frith, scholar burned for heresy.
Antonio Bonvisi, merchant, from Lucca.
Stephen Vaughan, merchant at Antwerp, friend of
  Cromwell.

At court
Henry VIII.
Katherine of Aragon, his first wife, later known as Dowager
  Princess of Wales.
Mary, their daughter.
Anne Boleyn, his second wife.
Mary, her sister, widow of William Carey and Henry's ex-
  mistress.
Thomas Boleyn, her father, later Earl of Wiltshire and Lord
  Privy Seal: likes to be known as 'Monseigneur'.
George, her brother, later Lord Rochford.
Jane Rochford, George's wife.
Thomas Howard, Duke of Norfolk, Anne's uncle.
Mary Howard, his daughter.
Mary Shelton ⎫
Jane Seymour ⎭ ladies-in-waiting.
Charles Brandon, Duke of Suffolk, old friend of Henry,
  married to his sister Mary.
Henry Norris ⎫
Francis Bryan ⎪
Francis Weston ⎬ gentlemen attending the king.
William Brereton ⎪
Nicholas Carew ⎭
Mark Smeaton, a musician.
Henry Wyatt, a courtier.
Thomas Wyatt, his son.

Henry Fitzroy, Duke of Richmond, the king's illegitimate son.
Henry Percy, Earl of Northumberland.

The clergy
William Warham, aged Archbishop of Canterbury.
Cardinal Campeggio, papal envoy.
John Fisher, Bishop of Rochester, legal adviser to Katherine of
    Aragon.
Thomas Cranmer, Cambridge scholar, reforming Archbishop of
    Canterbury, succeeding Warham.
Hugh Latimer, reforming priest, later Bishop of Worcester.
Rowland Lee, friend of Cromwell, later Bishop of Coventry
    and Lichfield.

In Calais
Lord Berners, the Governor, a scholar and translator.
Lord Lisle, the incoming Governor.
Honor, his wife.
William Stafford, attached to the garrison.

At Hatfield
Lady Bryan, mother of Francis, in charge of the infant princess,
    Elizabeth.
Lady Anne Shelton, Anne Boleyn's aunt, in charge of the
    former princess, Mary.

The ambassadors
Eustache Chapuys, career diplomat from Savoy, London
    ambassador of Emperor Charles V.
Jean de Dinteville, an ambassador from Francis I.

The Yorkist claimants to the throne
Henry Courtenay, Marquis of Exeter, descended from a
    daughter of Edward IV.

Gertrude, his wife.
Margaret Pole, Countess of Salisbury, niece of Edward IV.
Lord Montague, her son.
Geoffrey Pole, her son.
Reginald Pole, her son.

The Seymour family at Wolf Hall
Old Sir John, who has an affair with the wife of his eldest son
   Edward.
Edward Seymour, his son.
Thomas Seymour, his son.
Jane, his daughter: at court.
Lizzie, his daughter, married to the Governor of Jersey.

William Butts, a physician.
Nikolaus Kratzer, an astronomer.
Hans Holbein, an artist.
Sexton, Wolsey's fool.
Elizabeth Barton, a prophetess.

The Tudors

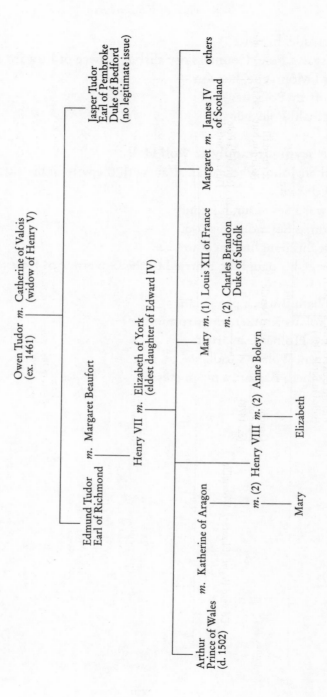

Owen Tudor *m.* Catherine of Valois
(ex. 1461)   (widow of Henry V)

Edmund Tudor
Earl of Richmond   *m.* Margaret Beaufort

Jasper Tudor
Earl of Pembroke
Duke of Bedford
(no legitimate issue)

Henry VII *m.* Elizabeth of York
(eldest daughter of Edward IV)

Arthur
Prince of Wales
(d. 1502)   *m.* Katherine of Aragon

m. (2) Henry VIII *m.* (2) Anne Boleyn

Mary   Elizabeth

Mary *m.* (1) Louis XII of France
     m. (2) Charles Brandon
              Duke of Suffolk

Margaret *m.* James IV
              of Scotland

others

The Yorkist Claimants

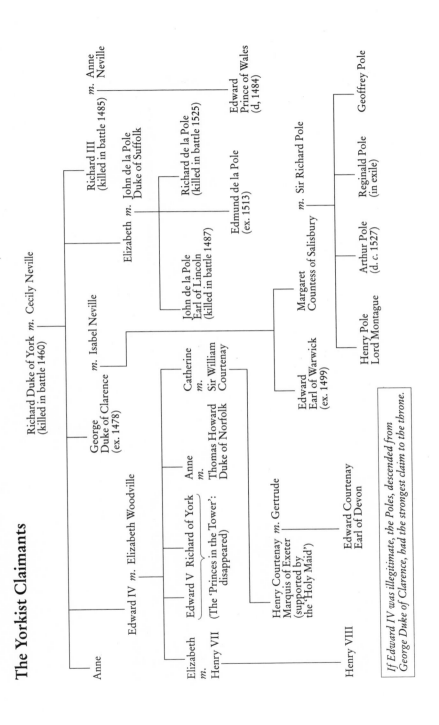

If *Edward IV was illegitimate, the Poles, descended from George Duke of Clarence, had the strongest claim to the throne.*

'There are three kinds of scenes, one called the tragic, second the comic, third the satyric. Their decorations are different and unalike each other in scheme. Tragic scenes are delineated with columns, pediments, statues and other objects suited to kings; comic scenes exhibit private dwellings, with balconies and views representing rows of windows, after the manner of ordinary dwellings; satyric scenes are decorated with trees, caverns, mountains and other rustic objects delineated in landscape style.'

VITRUVIUS, *De Architectura*, on the theatre, *c.*27BC

These be the names of the players:

Felicity	Cloaked Collusion
Liberty	Courtly Abusion
Measure	Folly
Magnificence	Adversity
Fancy	Poverty
Counterfeit Countenance	Despair
Crafty Conveyance	Mischief

Good Hope
Redress
Circumspection
Perseverance

Magnificence: an Interlude,
JOHN SKELTON, *c.*1520

xvii

PART ONE

I

Across the Narrow Sea
Putney, 1500

'So now get up.'

Felled, dazed, silent, he has fallen; knocked full length on the cobbles of the yard. His head turns sideways; his eyes are turned towards the gate, as if someone might arrive to help him out. One blow, properly placed, could kill him now.

Blood from the gash on his head – which was his father's first effort – is trickling across his face. Add to this, his left eye is blinded; but if he squints sideways, with his right eye he can see that the stitching of his father's boot is unravelling. The twine has sprung clear of the leather, and a hard knot in it has caught his eyebrow and opened another cut.

'So now get up!' Walter is roaring down at him, working out where to kick him next. He lifts his head an inch or two, and moves forward, on his belly, trying to do it without exposing his hands, on which Walter enjoys stamping. 'What are you, an eel?' his parent asks. He trots backwards, gathers pace, and aims another kick.

It knocks the last breath out of him; he thinks it may be his last. His forehead returns to the ground; he lies waiting, for Walter to jump on him. The dog, Bella, is barking, shut away in an outhouse. I'll miss my dog, he thinks. The yard smells of beer and blood. Someone is shouting, down on the riverbank. Nothing hurts, or perhaps it's that everything hurts, because there is no separate pain that he can pick out. But the cold strikes him, just in one place: just through his cheekbone as it rests on the cobbles.

'Look now, look now,' Walter bellows. He hops on one foot, as if he's dancing. 'Look what I've done. Burst my boot, kicking your head.'

Inch by inch. Inch by inch forward. Never mind if he calls you an eel or a worm or a snake. Head down, don't provoke him. His nose is clotted with blood and he has to open his mouth to breathe. His father's momentary distraction at the loss of his good boot allows him the leisure to vomit. 'That's right,' Walter yells. 'Spew everywhere.' Spew everywhere, on my good cobbles. 'Come on, boy, get up. Let's see you get up. By the blood of creeping Christ, stand on your feet.'

Creeping Christ? he thinks. What does he mean? His head turns sideways, his hair rests in his own vomit, the dog barks, Walter roars, and bells peal out across the water. He feels a sensation of movement, as if the filthy ground has become the Thames. It gives and sways beneath him; he lets out his breath, one great final gasp. You've done it this time, a voice tells Walter. But he closes his ears, or God closes them for him. He is pulled downstream, on a deep black tide.

The next thing he knows, it is almost noon, and he is propped in the doorway of Pegasus the Flying Horse. His sister Kat is coming from the kitchen with a rack of hot pies in her hands. When she sees him she almost drops them. Her mouth opens in astonishment. 'Look at you!'

'Kat, don't shout, it hurts me.'

She bawls for her husband: 'Morgan Williams!' She rotates on the spot, eyes wild, face flushed from the oven's heat. 'Take this tray, body of God, where are you all?'

He is shivering from head to foot, exactly like Bella did when she fell off the boat that time.

A girl runs in. 'The master's gone to town.'

'I know that, fool.' The sight of her brother had panicked the knowledge out of her. She thrusts the tray at the girl. 'If you leave them where the cats can get at them, I'll box your ears till you see stars.' Her hands empty, she clasps them for a moment in violent prayer. 'Fighting again, or was it your father?'

Yes, he says, vigorously nodding, making his nose drop gouts of blood: yes, he indicates himself, as if to say, Walter was here. Kat calls for a basin, for water, for water in a basin, for a cloth, for the devil to rise up, right now, and take away Walter his servant. 'Sit down before you fall down.' He tries to explain that he has just got up. Out of the yard. It could be an hour ago, it could even be a day, and for all he knows, today might be tomorrow; except that if he had lain there for a day, surely either Walter would have come and killed him, for being in the way, or his wounds would have clotted a bit, and by now he would be hurting all over and almost too stiff to move; from deep experience of Walter's fists and boots, he knows that the second day can be worse than the first. 'Sit. Don't talk,' Kat says.

When the basin comes, she stands over him and works away, dabbing at his closed eye, working in small circles round and round at his hairline. Her breathing is ragged and her free hand rests on his shoulder. She swears under her breath, and sometimes she cries, and rubs the back of his neck, whispering, 'There, hush, there,' as if it were he who were crying, though he isn't. He feels as if he is floating, and she is weighting him to earth; he would like to put his arms around her and his face in her apron, and rest there listening to her heartbeat. But he doesn't want to mess her up, get blood all down the front of her.

When Morgan Williams comes in, he is wearing his good town coat. He looks Welsh and pugnacious; it's clear he's heard the news. He stands by Kat, staring down, temporarily out of words; till he says, 'See!' He makes a fist, and jerks it three times in the air. 'That!' he says. 'That's what he'd get. Walter. That's what he'd get. From me.'

'Just stand back,' Kat advises. 'You don't want bits of Thomas on your London jacket.'

No more does he. He backs off. 'I wouldn't care, but look at you, boy. You could cripple the brute in a fair fight.'

'It never is a fair fight,' Kat says. 'He comes up behind you, right, Thomas? With something in his hand.'

'Looks like a glass bottle, in this case,' Morgan Williams says. 'Was it a bottle?'

He shakes his head. His nose bleeds again.

'Don't do that, brother,' Kat says. It's all over her hand; she wipes the blood clots down herself. What a mess, on her apron; he might as well have put his head there after all.

'I don't suppose you saw?' Morgan says. 'What he was wielding, exactly?'

'That's the value,' says Kat, 'of an approach from behind – you sorry loss to the magistrates' bench. Listen, Morgan, shall I tell you about my father? He'll pick up whatever's to hand. Which is sometimes a bottle, true. I've seen him do it to my mother. Even our little Bet, I've seen him hit her over the head. Also I've *not* seen him do it, which was worse, and that was because it was me about to be felled.'

'I wonder what I've married into,' Morgan Williams says.

But really, this is just something Morgan says; some men have a habitual sniffle, some women have a headache, and Morgan has this wonder. The boy doesn't listen to him; he thinks, if my father did that to my mother, so long dead, then maybe he killed her? No, surely he'd have been taken up for it; Putney's lawless, but you don't get away with murder. Kat's what he's got for a mother: crying for him, rubbing the back of his neck.

He shuts his eyes, to make the left eye equal with the right; he tries to open both. 'Kat,' he says, 'I have got an eye under there, have I? Because it can't see anything.' Yes, yes, yes, she says, while

6

Morgan Williams continues his interrogation of the facts; settles on a hard, moderately heavy, sharp object, but possibly not a *broken* bottle, otherwise Thomas would have seen its jagged edge, prior to Walter splitting his eyebrow open and aiming to blind him. He hears Morgan forming up this theory and would like to speak about the boot, the knot, the knot in the twine, but the effort of moving his mouth seems disproportionate to the reward. By and large he agrees with Morgan's conclusion; he tries to shrug, but it hurts so much, and he feels so crushed and disjointed, that he wonders if his neck is broken.

'Anyway,' Kat says, 'what were you doing, Tom, to set him off? He usually won't start up till after dark, if it's for no cause at all.'

'Yes,' Morgan Williams says, 'was there a cause?'

'Yesterday. I was fighting.'

'You were fighting yesterday? Who in the holy name were you fighting?'

'I don't know.' The name, along with the reason, has dropped out of his head; but it feels as if, in exiting, it has removed a jagged splinter of bone from his skull. He touches his scalp, carefully. Bottle? Possible.

'Oh,' Kat says, 'they're always fighting. Boys. Down by the river.'

'So let me be sure I have this right,' Morgan says. 'He comes home yesterday with his clothes torn and his knuckles skinned, and the old man says, what's this, been fighting? He waits a day, then hits him with a bottle. Then he knocks him down in the yard, kicks him all over, beats up and down his length with a plank of wood that comes to hand ...'

'Did he do that?'

'It's all over the parish! They were lining up on the wharf to tell me, they were shouting at me before the boat tied up. Morgan Williams, listen now, your wife's father has beaten Thomas and he's crawled dying to his sister's house, they've called the priest ... Did you call the priest?'

7

'Oh, you Williamses!' Kat says. 'You think you're such big people around here. People are lining up to tell you things. But why is that? It's because you believe anything.'

'But it's right!' Morgan yells. 'As good as right! Eh? If you leave out the priest. And that he's not dead yet.'

'You'll make that magistrates' bench for sure,' Kat says, 'with your close study of the difference between a corpse and my brother.'

'When I'm a magistrate, I'll have your father in the stocks. Fine him? You can't fine him enough. What's the point of fining a person who will only go and rob or swindle monies to the same value out of some innocent who crosses his path?'

He moans: tries to do it without intruding.

'There, there, there,' Kat whispers.

'I'd say the magistrates have had their bellyful,' Morgan says. 'If he's not watering his ale, he's running illegal beasts on the common, if he's not despoiling the common he's assaulting an officer of the peace, if he's not drunk he's dead drunk, and if he's not dead before his time there's no justice in this world.'

'Finished?' Kat says. She turns back to him. 'Tom, you'd better stay with us now. Morgan Williams, what do you say? He'll be good to do the heavy work, when he's healed up. He can do the figures for you, he can add and … what's the other thing? All right, don't laugh at me, how much time do you think I had for learning figures, with a father like that? If I can write my name, it's because Tom here taught me.'

'He won't,' he says. 'Like it.' He can only manage like this: short, simple, declarative sentences.

'Like? He should be ashamed,' Morgan says.

Kat says, 'Shame was left out when God made my dad.'

He says, 'Because. Just a mile away. He can easily.'

'Come after you? Just let him.' Morgan demonstrates his fist again: his little nervy Welsh punch.

* * *

8

After Kat had finished swabbing him and Morgan Williams had ceased boasting and reconstructing the assault, he lay up for an hour or two, to recover from it. During this time, Walter came to the door, with some of his acquaintance, and there was a certain amount of shouting and kicking of doors, though it came to him in a muffled way and he thought he might have dreamed it. The question in his mind now is, what am I going to do, I can't stay in Putney. Partly this is because his memory is coming back, for the day before yesterday and the earlier fight, and he thinks there might have been a knife in it somewhere; and whoever it was stuck in, it wasn't him, so was it by him? All this is unclear in his mind. What is clear is his thought about Walter: I've had enough of this. If he gets after me again I'm going to kill him, and if I kill him they'll hang me, and if they're going to hang me I want a better reason.

Below, the rise and fall of their voices. He can't pick out every word. Morgan says he's burnt his boats. Kat is repenting of her first offer, a post as pot-boy, general factotum and chucker-out; because, Morgan's saying, 'Walter will always be coming round here, won't he? And "Where's Tom, send him home, who paid the bloody priest to teach him to read and write, I did, and you're reaping the bloody benefit now, you leek-eating cunt."'

He comes downstairs. Morgan says cheerily, 'You're looking well, considering.'

The truth is about Morgan Williams – and he doesn't like him any the less for it – the truth is, this idea he has that one day he'll beat up his father-in-law, it's solely in his mind. In fact, he's frightened of Walter, like a good many people in Putney – and, for that matter, Mortlake and Wimbledon.

He says, 'I'm on my way, then.'

Kat says, 'You have to stay tonight. You know the second day is the worst.'

'Who's he going to hit when I'm gone?'

'Not our affair,' Kat says. 'Bet is married and got out of it, thank God.'

9

Morgan Williams says, 'If Walter was my father, I tell you, I'd take to the road.' He waits. 'As it happens, we've gathered some ready money.'

A pause.

'I'll pay you back.'

Morgan says, laughing, relieved, 'And how will you do that, Tom?'

He doesn't know. Breathing is difficult, but that doesn't mean anything, it's only because of the clotting inside his nose. It doesn't seem to be broken; he touches it, speculatively, and Kat says, careful, this is a clean apron. She's smiling a pained smile, she doesn't want him to go, and yet she's not going to contradict Morgan Williams, is she? The Williamses are big people, in Putney, in Wimbledon. Morgan dotes on her; he reminds her she's got girls to do the baking and mind the brewing, why doesn't she sit upstairs sewing like a lady, and praying for his success when he goes off to London to do a few deals in his town coat? Twice a day she could sweep through the Pegasus in a good dress and set in order anything that's wrong: that's his idea. And though as far as he can see she works as hard as ever she did when she was a child, he can see how she might like it, that Morgan would exhort her to sit down and be a lady.

'I'll pay you back,' he says. 'I might go and be a soldier. I could send you a fraction of my pay and I might get loot.'

Morgan says, 'But there isn't a war.'

'There'll be one somewhere,' Kat says.

'Or I could be a ship's boy. But, you know, Bella – do you think I should go back for her? She was screaming. He had her shut up.'

'So she wouldn't nip his toes?' Morgan says. He's satirical about Bella.

'I'd like her to come away with me.'

'I've heard of a ship's cat. Not of a ship's dog.'

'She's very small.'

'She'll not pass for a cat,' Morgan laughs. 'Anyway, you're too big all round for a ship's boy. They have to run up the rigging like little monkeys – have you ever seen a monkey, Tom? Soldier is more like it. Be honest, like father like son – you weren't last in line when God gave out fists.'

'Right,' Kat said. 'Shall we see if we understand this? One day my brother Tom goes out fighting. As punishment, his father creeps up behind and hits him with a whatever, but heavy, and probably sharp, and then, when he falls down, almost takes out his eye, exerts himself to kick in his ribs, beats him with a plank of wood that stands ready to hand, knocks in his face so that if I were not his own sister I'd barely recognise him: and my husband says, the answer to this, Thomas, is go for a soldier, go and find somebody you don't know, take out *his* eye and kick in his ribs, actually *kill* him, I suppose, and get paid for it.'

'May as well,' Morgan says, 'as go fighting by the river, without profit to anybody. Look at him – if it were up to me, I'd have a war just to employ him.'

Morgan takes out his purse. He puts down coins: chink, chink, chink, with enticing slowness.

He touches his cheekbone. It is bruised, intact: but so cold.

'Listen,' Kat says, 'we grew up here, there's probably people that would help Tom out –'

Morgan gives her a look: which says, eloquently, do you mean there are a lot of people would like to be on the wrong side of Walter Cromwell? Have him breaking their doors down? And she says, as if hearing his thought out loud, 'No. Maybe. Maybe, Tom, it would be for the best, do you think?'

He stands up. She says, 'Morgan, look at him, he shouldn't go tonight.'

'I should. An hour from now he'll have had a skinful and he'll be back. He'd set the place on fire if he thought I were in it.'

Morgan says, 'Have you got what you need for the road?'

He wants to turn to Kat and say, no.

11

But she's turned her face away and she's crying. She's not crying for him, because nobody, he thinks, will ever cry for him, God didn't cut him out that way. She's crying for her idea of what life should be like: Sunday after church, all the sisters, sisters-in-law, wives kissing and patting, swatting at each other's children and at the same time loving them and rubbing their little round heads, women comparing and swapping babies, and all the men gathering and talking business, wool, yarn, lengths, shipping, bloody Flemings, fishing rights, brewing, annual turnover, nice timely information, favour-for-favour, little sweeteners, little retainers, my attorney says ... That's what it should be like, married to Morgan Williams, with the Williamses being a big family in Putney ... But somehow it's not been like that. Walter has spoiled it all.

Carefully, stiffly, he straightens up. Every part of him hurts now. Not as badly as it will hurt tomorrow; on the third day the bruises come out and you have to start answering people's questions about why you've got them. By then he will be far from here, and presumably no one will hold him to account, because no one will know him or care. They'll think it's usual for him to have his face beaten in.

He picks up the money. He says, '*Hwyl, Morgan Williams. Diolch am yr arian.*' Thank you for the money. '*Gofalwch am Katheryn. Gofalwch am eich busnes. Wela i chi eto rhywbryd. Pob lwc.*'

Look after my sister. Look after your business. See you again sometime.

Morgan Williams stares.

He almost grins; would do, if it wouldn't split his face open. All those days he'd spent hanging around the Williamses' households: did they think he'd just come for his dinner?

'*Pob lwc,*' Morgan says slowly. Good luck.

He says, 'If I follow the river, is that as good as anything?'

'Where are you trying to get?'

'To the sea.'

For a moment, Morgan Williams looks sorry it has come to this. He says, 'You'll be all right, Tom? I tell you, if Bella comes looking for you, I won't send her home hungry. Kat will give her a pie.'

He has to make the money last. He could work his way down-river; but he is afraid that if he is seen, Walter will catch him, through his contacts and his friends, those kind of men who will do anything for a drink. What he thinks of, first, is slipping on to one of the smugglers' ships that go out of Barking, Tilbury. But then he thinks, France is where they have wars. A few people he talks to – he talks to strangers very easily – are of the same belief. Dover then. He gets on the road.

If you help load a cart you get a ride in it, as often as not. It gives him to think, how bad people are at loading carts. Men trying to walk straight ahead through a narrow gateway with a wide wooden chest. A simple rotation of the object solves a great many problems. And then horses, he's always been around horses, frightened horses too, because when in the morning Walter wasn't sleeping off the effects of the strong brew he kept for himself and his friends, he would turn to his second trade, farrier and blacksmith; and whether it was his sour breath, or his loud voice, or his general way of going on, even horses that were good to shoe would start to shake their heads and back away from the heat. Their hooves gripped in Walter's hands, they'd tremble; it was his job to hold their heads and talk to them, rubbing the velvet space between their ears, telling them how their mothers love them and talk about them still, and how Walter will soon be over.

He doesn't eat for a day or so; it hurts too much. But by the time he reaches Dover the big gash on his scalp has closed, and the tender parts inside, he trusts, have mended themselves: kidneys, lungs and heart.

He knows by the way people look at him that his face is still bruised. Morgan Williams had done an inventory of him before he left: teeth (miraculously) still in his head, and two eyes, miraculously seeing. Two arms, two legs: what more do you want?

He walks around the docks saying to people, do you know where there's a war just now?

Each man he asks stares at his face, steps back and says, 'You tell me!'

They are so pleased with this, they laugh at their own wit so much, that he continues asking, just to give people pleasure.

Surprisingly, he finds he will leave Dover richer than he arrived. He'd watched a man doing the three-card trick, and when he learned it he set up for himself. Because he's a boy, people stop to have a go. It's their loss.

He adds up what he's got and what he's spent. Deduct a small sum for a brief grapple with a lady of the night. Not the sort of thing you could do in Putney, Wimbledon or Mortlake. Not without the Williams family getting to know, and talking about you in Welsh.

He sees three elderly Lowlanders struggling with their bundles and moves to help them. The packages are soft and bulky, samples of woollen cloth. A port officer gives them trouble about their documents, shouting into their faces. He lounges behind the clerk, pretending to be a Lowland oaf, and tells the merchants by holding up his fingers what he thinks a fair bribe. 'Please,' says one of them, in effortful English to the clerk, 'will you take care of these English coins for me? I find them surplus.' Suddenly the clerk is all smiles. The Lowlanders are all smiles; they would have paid much more. When they board they say, 'The boy is with us.'

As they wait to cast off, they ask him his age. He says eighteen, but they laugh and say, child, you are never. He offers them fifteen, and they confer and decide that fifteen will do; they think he's younger, but they don't want to shame him. They ask what's happened to his face. There are several things he could say but he selects the truth. He doesn't want them to think he's some failed robber. They discuss it among themselves, and the one who can translate turns to him: 'We are saying, the English are cruel to their children. And cold-hearted. The child must stand if his father comes in the room. Always the child should say very correctly, "my father, sir", and "madam my mother".'

He is surprised. Are there people in the world who are not cruel to their children? For the first time, the weight in his chest shifts a little; he thinks, there could be other places, better. He talks; he tells them about Bella, and they look sorry, and they don't say anything stupid like, you can get another dog. He tells them about the Pegasus, and about his father's brewhouse and how Walter gets fined for bad beer at least twice a year. He tells them about how he gets fines for stealing wood, cutting down other people's trees, and about the too-many sheep he runs on the common. They are interested in that; they show the woollen samples and discuss among themselves the weight and the weave, turning to him from time to time to include and instruct him. They don't think much of English finished cloth generally, though these samples can make them change their mind … He loses the thread of the conversation when they try to tell him their reasons for going to Calais, and different people they know there.

He tells them about his father's blacksmith business, and the English-speaker says, interested, can you make a horseshoe? He mimes to them what it's like, hot metal and a bad-tempered father in a small space. They laugh; they like to see him telling a story. Good talker, one of them says. Before they dock, the most silent of them will stand up and make an oddly formal speech, at which one will nod, and which the other will translate. 'We are three brothers. This is our street. If ever you visit our town, there is a bed and hearth and food for you.'

Goodbye, he will say to them. Goodbye and good luck with your lives. *Hwyl,* cloth men. *Golfalwch eich busnes.* He is not stopping till he gets to a war.

The weather is cold but the sea is flat. Kat has given him a holy medal to wear. He has slung it around his neck with a cord. It makes a chill against the skin of his throat. He unloops it. He touches it with his lips, for luck. He drops it; it whispers into the water. He will remember his first sight of the open sea: a grey wrinkled vastness, like the residue of a dream.

II
Paternity
1527

So: Stephen Gardiner. Going out, as he's coming in. It's wet, and for a night in April, unseasonably warm, but Gardiner wears furs, which look like oily and dense black feathers; he stands now, ruffling them, gathering his clothes about his tall straight person like black angel's wings.

'Late,' Master Stephen says unpleasantly.

He is bland. 'Me, or your good self?'

'You.' He waits.

'Drunks on the river. The boatmen say it's the eve of one of their patron saints.'

'Did you offer a prayer to her?'

'I'll pray to anyone, Stephen, till I'm on dry land.'

'I'm surprised you didn't take an oar yourself. You must have done some river work, when you were a boy.'

Stephen sings always on one note. Your reprobate father. Your low birth. Stephen is supposedly some sort of semi-royal by-blow: brought up for payment, discreetly, as their own, by discreet people in a small town. They are wool-trade people, whom Master Stephen resents and wishes to forget; and since he himself knows everybody in the wool trade, he knows too much about his past for Stephen's comfort. The poor orphan boy!

Master Stephen resents everything about his own situation. He resents that he's the king's unacknowledged cousin. He resents that he was put into the church, though the church has done well by him. He resents the fact that someone else has late-night talks with the cardinal, to whom he is confidential secretary. He resents the fact that he's one of those tall men who are hollow-chested, not much weight behind him; he resents his knowledge that if they met on a dark night, Master Thos. Cromwell would be the one who walked away dusting off his hands and smiling.

'God bless you,' Gardiner says, passing into the night unseasonably warm.

Cromwell says, 'Thanks.'

The cardinal, writing, says without looking up, 'Thomas. Still raining? I expected you earlier.'

Boatman. River. Saint. He's been travelling since early morning and in the saddle for the best part of two weeks on the cardinal's business, and has now come down by stages – and not easy stages – from Yorkshire. He's been to his clerks at Gray's Inn and borrowed a change of linen. He's been east to the city, to hear what ships have come in and to check the whereabouts of an off-the-books consignment he is expecting. But he hasn't eaten, and hasn't been home yet.

The cardinal rises. He opens a door, speaks to his hovering servants. 'Cherries! What, no cherries? April, you say? Only April? We shall have sore work to placate my guest, then.' He sighs. 'Bring what you have. But it will never do, you know. Why am I so ill-served?'

Then the whole room is in motion: food, wine, fire built up. A man takes his wet outer garments with a solicitous murmur. All the cardinal's household servants are like this: comfortable, soft-footed, and kept permanently apologetic and teased. And all the cardinal's visitors are treated in the same way. If you had inter-

18

rupted him every night for ten years, and sat sulking and scowling at him on each occasion, you would still be his honoured
guest.

The servants efface themselves, melting away towards the
door. 'What else would you like?' the cardinal says.

'The sun to come out?'

'So late? You tax my powers.'

'Dawn would do.'

The cardinal inclines his head to the servants. 'I shall see to this
request myself,' he says gravely; and gravely they murmur, and
withdraw.

The cardinal joins his hands. He makes a great, deep, smiling
sigh, like a leopard settling in a warm spot. He regards his man of
business; his man of business regards him. The cardinal, at fifty-
five, is still as handsome as he was in his prime. Tonight he is
dressed not in his everyday scarlet, but in blackish purple and
fine white lace: like a humble bishop. His height impresses; his
belly, which should in justice belong to a more sedentary man, is
merely another princely aspect of his being, and on it, confid-
ingly, he often rests a large, white, beringed hand. A large head –
surely designed by God to support the papal tiara – is carried
superbly on broad shoulders: shoulders upon which rest (though
not at this moment) the great chain of Lord Chancellor of
England. The head inclines; the cardinal says, in those honeyed
tones, famous from here to Vienna, 'So now, tell me how was
Yorkshire.'

'Filthy.' He sits down. 'Weather. People. Manners. Morals.'

'Well, I suppose this is the place to complain. Though I am
already speaking to God about the weather.'

'Oh, and the food. Five miles inland, and no fresh fish.'

'And scant hope of a lemon, I suppose. What do they eat?'

'Londoners, when they can get them. You have never seen
such heathens. They're so high, low foreheads. Live in caves, yet
they pass for gentry in those parts.' He ought to go and look for

himself, the cardinal; he is Archbishop of York, but has never visited his see. 'And as for Your Grace's business –'

'I am listening,' the cardinal says. 'Indeed, I go further. I am captivated.'

As he listens, the cardinal's face creases into its affable, perpetually attentive folds. From time to time he notes down a figure that he is given. He sips from a glass of his very good wine and at length he says, 'Thomas ... what have you done, monstrous servant? An abbess is with child? Two, three abbesses? Or, let me see ... Have you set fire to Whitby, on a whim?'

In the case of his man Cromwell, the cardinal has two jokes, which sometimes unite to form one. The first is that he walks in demanding cherries in April and lettuce in December. The other is that he goes about the countryside committing outrages, and charging them to the cardinal's accounts. And the cardinal has other jokes, from time to time: as he requires them.

It is about ten o'clock. The flames of the wax candles bow civilly to the cardinal, and stand straight again. The rain – it has been raining since last September – splashes against the glass window. 'In Yorkshire,' he says, 'your project is disliked.'

The cardinal's project: having obtained the Pope's permission, he means to amalgamate some thirty small, ill-run monastic foundations with larger ones, and to divert the income of these foundations – decayed, but often very ancient – into revenue for the two colleges he is founding: Cardinal College, at Oxford, and a college in his home town of Ipswich, where he is well remembered as the scholar son of a prosperous and pious master butcher, a guild-man, a man who also kept a large and well-regulated inn, of the type used by the best travellers. The difficulty is ... No, in fact, there are several difficulties. The cardinal, a Bachelor of Arts at fifteen, a Bachelor of Theology by his mid-twenties, is learned in the law but does not like its delays; he cannot quite accept that real property cannot be changed into money, with the same speed and ease with which he changes a wafer into the body of Christ. When he once, as a test, explained to the cardinal just a minor point of the land law concerning – well, never mind, it was a minor point – he saw the cardinal break into a sweat and say, Thomas, what can I give you, to persuade you never to mention this to me again? Find a way, just do it, he would say when obstacles were raised; and when he heard of some small person obstructing his grand design, he would say, Thomas, give them some money to make them go away.

He has the leisure to think about this, because the cardinal is staring down at his desk, at the letter he has half-written. He looks up. 'Tom …' And then, 'No, never mind. Tell me why you are scowling in that way.'

'The people up there say they are going to kill me.'

'Really?' the cardinal says. His face says, I am astonished and disappointed. 'And will they kill you? Or what do you think?'

Behind the cardinal is a tapestry, hanging the length of the wall. King Solomon, his hands stretched into darkness, is greeting the Queen of Sheba.

'I think, if you're going to kill a man, do it. Don't write him a letter about it. Don't bluster and threaten and put him on his guard.'

'If you ever plan to be off your guard, let me know. It is something I should like to see. Do you know who … But I suppose they don't sign their letters. I shall not give up my project. I have personally and carefully selected these institutions, and His Holiness has approved them under seal. Those who object misunderstand my intention. No one is proposing to put old monks out on the roads.'

This is true. There can be relocation; there can be pensions, compensation. It can be negotiated, with goodwill on both sides. Bow to the inevitable, he urges. Deference to the lord cardinal. Regard his watchful and fatherly care; believe his keen eye is fixed on the ultimate good of the church. These are the phrases with which to negotiate. Poverty, chastity and obedience: these are what you stress when you tell some senile prior what to do. 'They don't misunderstand,' he says. 'They just want the proceeds themselves.'

'You will have to take an armed guard when next you go north.'

The cardinal, who thinks upon a Christian's last end, has had his tomb designed already, by a sculptor from Florence. His corpse will lie beneath the outspread wings of angels, in a sarcophagus of porphyry. The veined stone will be his monument, when his own veins are drained by the embalmer; when his limbs are set like marble, an inscription of his virtues will be picked out in gold. But the colleges are to be his breathing monument, working and living long after he is gone: poor boys, poor scholars, carrying into the world the cardinal's wit, his sense of wonder and of beauty, his instinct for decorum and pleasure, his finesse. No wonder he shakes his head. You don't generally have to give an armed guard to a lawyer. The cardinal hates any show of force. He thinks it unsubtle. Sometimes one of his people – Stephen Gardiner, let's say – will come to him denouncing some nest of heretics in the city. He will say earnestly, poor benighted souls. You pray for them, Stephen, and I'll pray for them, and we'll see if between us we can't bring them to a better state of mind. And tell them, mend their manners, or Thomas More will get hold of them and shut them in his cellar. And all we will hear is the sound of screaming.

'Now, Thomas.' He looks up. 'Do you have any Spanish?'

'A little. Military, you know. Rough.'

'You took service in the Spanish armies, I thought.'

'French.'

'Ah. Indeed. And no fraternising?'

'Not past a point. I can insult people in Castilian.'

'I shall bear that in mind,' the cardinal says. 'Your time may come. For now ... I was thinking that it would be good to have more friends in the queen's household.'

Spies, he means. To see how she will take the news. To see what Queen Catalina will say, in private and unleashed, when she has slipped the noose of the diplomatic Latin in which it will be broken to her that the king – after they have spent some twenty years together – would like to marry another lady. Any lady. Any well-connected princess whom he thinks might give him a son.

The cardinal's chin rests on his hand; with finger and thumb, he rubs his eyes. 'The king called me this morning,' he says, 'exceptionally early.'

'What did he want?'

'Pity. And at such an hour. I heard a dawn Mass with him, and he talked all through it. I love the king. God knows how I love him. But sometimes my faculty of commiseration is strained.' He raises his glass, looks over the rim. 'Picture to yourself, Tom. Imagine this. You are a man of some thirty-five years of age. You are in good health and of a hearty appetite, you have your bowels opened every day, your joints are supple, your bones support you, and in addition you are King of England. But.' He shakes his head. 'But! If only he wanted something simple. The Philosopher's Stone. The elixir of youth. One of those chests that occur in stories, full of gold pieces.'

'And when you take some out, it just fills up again?'

'Exactly. Now the chest of gold I have hopes of, and the elixir, all the rest. But where shall I begin looking for a son to rule his country after him?'

Behind the cardinal, moving a little in the draught, King Solomon bows, his face obscured. The Queen of Sheba – smiling, light-footed – reminds him of the young widow he lodged with when he lived in Antwerp. Since they had shared a bed, should he have married her? In honour, yes. But if he had married Anselma he couldn't have married Liz; and his children would be different children from the ones he has now.

'If you cannot find him a son,' he says, 'you must find him a piece of scripture. To ease his mind.'

The cardinal appears to be looking for it, on his desk. 'Well, Deuteronomy. Which positively recommends that a man should marry his deceased brother's wife. As he did.' The cardinal sighs. 'But he doesn't like Deuteronomy.'

Useless to say, why not? Useless to suggest that, if Deuteronomy orders you to marry your brother's relict, and Leviticus says don't, or you will not breed, you should try to live with the contradiction, and accept that the question of which takes priority was thrashed out in Rome, for a fat fee, by leading prelates, twenty years ago when the dispensations were issued, and delivered under papal seal.

'I don't see why he takes Leviticus to heart. He has a daughter living.'

'But I think it is generally understood, in the Scriptures, that "children" means "sons".'

The cardinal justifies the text, referring to the Hebrew; his voice is mild, lulling. He loves to instruct, where there is the will to be instructed. They have known each other some years now, and though the cardinal is very grand, formality has faded between them. 'I have a son,' he says. 'You know that, of course. God forgive me. A weakness of the flesh.'

The cardinal's son – Thomas Winter, they call him – seems inclined to scholarship and a quiet life; though his father may have other ideas. The cardinal has a daughter too, a young girl whom no one has seen. Rather pointedly, he has called her Dorothea, the gift of God; she is already placed in a convent, where she will pray for her parents.

'And you have a son,' the cardinal says. 'Or should I say, you have one son you give your name to. But I suspect there are some you don't know, running around on the banks of the Thames?'

'I hope not. I wasn't fifteen when I ran away.'

It amuses Wolsey, that he doesn't know his age. The cardinal peers down through the layers of society, to a stratum well below his own, as the butcher's beef-fed son; to a place where his servant is born, on a day unknown, in deep obscurity. His father was no doubt drunk at his birth; his mother, understandably, was preoccupied. Kat has assigned him a date; he is grateful for it.

'Well, fifteen ...' the cardinal says. 'But at fifteen I suppose you could do it? I know I could. Now I have a son, your boatman on the river has a son, your beggar on the street has a son, your would-be murderers in Yorkshire no doubt have sons who will be sworn to pursue you in the next generation, and you yourself, as we have agreed, have spawned a whole tribe of riverine brawlers – but the king, alone, has no son. Whose fault is that?'

'God's?'

'Nearer than God?'

'The queen?'

'More responsible for everything than the queen?'

He can't help a broad smile. 'Yourself, Your Grace.'

'Myself, My Grace. What am I going to do about it? I tell you what I might do. I might send Master Stephen to Rome to sound out the Curia. But then I need him here ...'

Wolsey looks at his expression, and laughs. Squabbling underlings! He knows quite well that, dissatisfied with their original parentage, they are fighting to be his favourite son. 'Whatever you think of Master Stephen, he is well grounded in canon law, and a very persuasive fellow, except when he tries to persuade you. I will tell you –' He breaks off; he leans forward, he puts his great lion's head in his hands, the head that would indeed have worn the papal tiara, if at the last election the right money had been paid out to the right people. 'I have begged him,' the cardinal says. 'Thomas, I sank to my knees and from that humble posture I tried to dissuade him. Majesty, I said, be guided by me. Nothing will ensue, if you wish to be rid of your wife, but a great deal of trouble and expense.'

'And he said ...?'

'He held up a finger. In warning. "Never," he said, "call that dear lady my wife, until you can show me why she is, and how it can be so. Till then, call her my sister, my dear sister. Since she was quite certainly my brother's wife, before going through a form of marriage with me."'

You will never draw from Wolsey a word that is disloyal to the king. 'What it is,' he says, 'it's …' he hesitates over the word, 'it's, in my opinion … preposterous. Though my opinion, of course, does not go out of this room. Oh, don't doubt it, there were those at the time who raised their eyebrows over the dispensation. And year by year there were persons who would murmur in the king's ear; he didn't listen, though now I must believe that he heard. But you know the king was the most uxorious of men. Any doubts were quashed.' He places a hand, softly and firmly, down on his desk. 'They were quashed and quashed.'

But there is no doubt of what Henry wants now. An annulment. A declaration that his marriage never existed. 'For eighteen years,' the cardinal says, 'he has been under a mistake. He has told his confessor that he has eighteen years' worth of sin to expiate.'

He waits, for some gratifying small reaction. His servant simply looks back at him: taking it for granted that the seal of the confessional is broken at the cardinal's convenience.

'So if you send Master Stephen to Rome,' he says, 'it will give the king's whim, if I may –'

The cardinal nods: you may so term it.

'– an international airing?'

'Master Stephen may go discreetly. As it were, for a private papal blessing.'

'You don't understand Rome.'

Wolsey can't contradict him. He has never felt the chill at the nape of the neck that makes you look over your shoulder when, passing from the Tiber's golden light, you move into some great bloc of shadow. By some fallen column, by some chaste ruin, the thieves of integrity wait, some bishop's whore, some nephew-of-a-nephew, some monied seducer with furred breath; he feels, sometimes, fortunate to have escaped that city with his soul intact.

'Put simply,' he says, 'the Pope's spies will guess what Stephen's about while he is still packing his vestments, and the cardinals and the secretaries will have time to fix their prices. If you must send him, give him a great deal of ready money. Those cardinals don't take promises; what they really like is a bag of gold to placate their bankers, because they're mostly run out of credit.' He shrugs. 'I know this.'

'I should send you,' the cardinal says, jolly. 'You could offer Pope Clement a loan.'

Why not? He knows the money markets; it could probably be arranged. If he were Clement, he would borrow heavily this year to hire in troops to ring his territories. It's probably too late; for the summer season's fighting, you need to be recruiting by Candlemas. He says, 'Will you not start the king's suit within your own jurisdiction? Make him take the first steps, then he will see if he really wants what he says he wants.'

'That is my intention. What I mean to do is to convene a small court here in London. We will approach him in a shocked fashion: King Harry, you appear to have lived all these years in an unlawful manner, with a woman not your wife. He hates – saving His Majesty – to appear in the wrong: which is where we must put him, very firmly. Possibly he will forget that the original scruples were his. Possibly he will shout at us, and hasten in a fit of indignation back to the queen. If not, then I must have the dispensation revoked, here or in Rome, and if I succeed in parting him from Katherine I shall marry him, smartly, to a French princess.'

No need to ask if the cardinal has any particular princess in mind. He has not one but two or three. He never lives in a single reality, but in a shifting, shadow-mesh of diplomatic possibilities. While he is doing his best to keep the king married to Queen Katherine and her Spanish-Imperial family, by begging Henry to forget his scruples, he will also plan for an alternative world, in which the king's scruples must be heeded, and the marriage to Katherine is void. Once that nullity is recognised – and the last eighteen years of sin and suffering wiped from the page – he will readjust the balance of Europe, allying England with France, forming a power bloc to oppose the young Emperor Charles, Katherine's nephew. And all outcomes are likely, all outcomes can be managed, even massaged into desirability: prayer and pressure, pressure and prayer, everything that comes to pass will pass by God's design, a design re-envisaged and redrawn, with helpful emendations, by the cardinal. He used to say, 'The king will do such-and-such.' Then he began to say, 'We will do such-and-such.' Now he says, 'This is what I will do.'

'But what will happen to the queen?' he asks. 'If he casts her off, where will she go?'

'Convents can be comfortable.'

'Perhaps she will go home to Spain.'

'No, I think not. It is another country now. It is – what? – twenty-seven years since she landed in England.' The cardinal sighs. 'I remember her, at her coming-in. Her ships, as you know, had been delayed by the weather, and she had been day upon day tossed in the Channel. The old king rode down the country, determined to meet her. She was then at Dogmersfield, at the Bishop of Bath's palace, and making slow progress towards London; it was November and, yes, it was raining. At his arriving, her household stood upon their Spanish manners: the princess must remained veiled, until her husband sees her on her wedding day. But you know the old king!'

He did not, of course; he was born on or about the date the old king, a renegade and a refugee all his life, fought his way to an unlikely throne. Wolsey talks as if he himself had witnessed everything, eye-witnessed it, and in a sense he has, for the recent past arranges itself only in the patterns acknowledged by his superior mind, and agreeable to his eye. He smiles. 'The old king, in his later years, the least thing could arouse his suspicion. He made some show of reining back to confer with his escort, and then he leapt – he was still a lean man – from the saddle, and told the Spanish to their faces, he would see her or else. My land and my laws, he said; we'll have no veils here. Why may I not see her, have I been cheated, is she deformed, is it that you are proposing to marry my son Arthur to a monster?'

Thomas thinks, he was being unnecessarily Welsh.

'Meanwhile her women had put the little creature into bed; or said they had, for they thought that in bed she would be safe against him. Not a bit. King Henry strode through the rooms, looking as if he had in mind to tear back the bedclothes. The women bundled her into some decency. He burst into the chamber. At the sight of her, he forgot his Latin. He stammered and backed out like a tongue-tied boy.' The cardinal chuckled. 'And then when she first danced at court – our poor prince Arthur sat smiling on the dais, but the little girl could hardly sit still in her chair – no one knew the Spanish dances, so she took to the floor with one of her ladies. I will never forget that turn of her head, that moment when her beautiful red hair slid over one shoulder … There was no man who saw it who didn't imagine – though the dance was in fact very sedate … Ah dear. She was sixteen.'

The cardinal looks into space and Thomas says, 'God forgive you?'

'God forgive us all. The old king was constantly taking his lust to confession. Prince Arthur died, then soon after the queen died, and when the old king found himself a widower he thought he might marry Katherine himself. But then …' He lifts his princely shoulders. 'They couldn't agree over the dowry, you know. The old fox, Ferdinand, her father. He would fox you out of any payment due. But our present Majesty was a boy of ten when he danced at his brother's wedding, and, in my belief, it was there and then that he set his heart on the bride.'

29

They sit and think for a bit. It's sad, they both know it's sad. The old king freezing her out, keeping her in the kingdom and keeping her poor, unwilling to miss the part of the dowry he said was still owing, and equally unwilling to pay her widow's portion and let her go. But then it's interesting too, the extensive diplomatic contacts the little girl picked up during those years, the expertise in playing off one interest against another. When Henry married her he was eighteen, guileless. His father was no sooner dead than he claimed Katherine for his own. She was older than he was, and years of anxiety had sobered her and taken something from her looks. But the real woman was less vivid than the vision in his mind; he was greedy for what his older brother had owned. He felt again the little tremor of her hand, as she had rested it on his arm when he was a boy of ten. It was as if she had trusted him, as if – he told his intimates – she had recognised that she was never meant to be Arthur's wife, except in name; her body was reserved for him, the second son, upon whom she turned her beautiful blue-grey eyes, her compliant smile. She always loved me, the king would say. Seven years or so of diplomacy, if you can call it that, kept me from her side. But now I need fear no one. Rome has dispensed. The papers are in order. The alliances are set in place. I have married a virgin, since my poor brother did not touch her; I have married an alliance, her Spanish relatives; but, above all, I have married for love.

And now? Gone. Or as good as gone: half a lifetime waiting to be expunged, eased from the record.

'Ah, well,' the cardinal says. 'What will be the outcome? The king expects his own way, but she, she will be hard to move.'

There is another story about Katherine, a different story. Henry went to France to have a little war; he left Katherine as regent. Down came the Scots; they were well beaten, and at Flodden the head of their king cut off. It was Katherine, that pink-and-white angel, who proposed to send the head in a bag by the first crossing, to cheer up her husband in his camp. They dissuaded her; told her it was, as a gesture, un-English. She sent, instead, a letter. And with it, the surcoat in which the Scottish king had died, which was stiffened, black and crackling with his pumped-out blood.

The fire dies, an ashy log subsiding; the cardinal, wrapped in his dreams, rises from his chair and personally kicks it. He stands looking down, twisting the rings on his fingers, lost in thought. He shakes himself and says, 'Long day. Go home. Don't dream of Yorkshiremen.'

Thomas Cromwell is now a little over forty years old. He is a man of strong build, not tall. Various expressions are available to his face, and one is readable: an expression of stifled amusement. His hair is dark, heavy and waving, and his small eyes, which are of very strong sight, light up in conversation: so the Spanish ambassador will tell us, quite soon. It is said he knows by heart the entire New Testament in Latin, and so as a servant of the cardinal is apt – ready with a text if abbots flounder. His speech is low and rapid, his manner assured; he is at home in courtroom or waterfront, bishop's palace or inn yard. He can draft a contract, train a falcon, draw a map, stop a street fight, furnish a house and fix a jury. He will quote you a nice point in the old authors, from Plato to Plautus and back again. He knows new poetry, and can say it in Italian. He works all hours, first up and last to bed. He makes money and he spends it. He will take a bet on anything.

He rises to leave, says, 'If you did have a word with God and the sun came out, then the king could ride out with his gentlemen, and if he were not so fretted and confined then his spirits would rise, and he might not be thinking about Leviticus, and your life would be easier.'

'You only partly understand him. He enjoys theology, almost as much as he enjoys riding out.'

He is at the door. Wolsey says, 'By the way, the talk at court … His Grace the Duke of Norfolk is complaining that I have raised

31

an evil spirit, and directed it to follow him about. If anyone mentions it to you … just deny it.'

He stands in the doorway, smiling slowly. The cardinal smiles too, as if to say, I have saved the good wine till last. Don't I know how to make you happy? Then the cardinal drops his head over his papers. He is a man who, in England's service, scarcely needs to sleep; four hours will refresh him, and he will be up when Westminster's bells have rung in another wet, smoky, lightless April day. 'Good night,' he says. 'God bless you, Tom.'

Outside his people are waiting with lights to take him home. He has a house in Stepney but tonight he is going to his town house. A hand on his arm: Rafe Sadler, a slight young man with pale eyes. 'How was Yorkshire?'

Rafe's smile flickers, the wind pulls the torch flame into a rainy blur.

'I haven't to speak of it; the cardinal fears it will give us bad dreams.'

Rafe frowns. In all his twenty-one years he has never had bad dreams; sleeping securely under the Cromwell roof since he was seven, first at Fenchurch Street and now at the Austin Friars, he has grown up with a tidy mind, and his night-time worries are all rational ones: thieves, loose dogs, sudden holes in the road.

'The Duke of Norfolk …' he says, then, 'no, never mind. Who's been asking for me while I've been away?'

The damp streets are deserted; the mist is creeping from the river. The stars are stifled in damp and cloud. Over the city lies the sweet, rotting odour of yesterday's unrecollected sins. Norfolk kneels, teeth chattering, beside his bed; the cardinal's late-night pen scratches, scratches, like a rat beneath his mattress. While Rafe, by his side, gives him a digest of the office news, he formulates his denial, for whom it may concern: 'His Grace the cardinal wholly rejects any imputation that he has sent an evil spirit to wait upon the Duke of Norfolk. He deprecates the suggestion in the strongest possible terms. No headless calf, no fallen angel in the shape of loll-tongued dog, no crawling pre-used winding sheet, no Lazarus nor animated cadaver has been sent by His Grace to pursue His Grace: nor is any such pursuit pending.'

Someone is screaming, down by the quays. The boatmen are singing. There is a faint, faraway splashing; perhaps they are drowning someone. 'My lord cardinal makes this statement without prejudice to his right to harass and distress my lord of Norfolk by means of any *fantasma* which he may in his wisdom elect: at any future date, and without notice given: subject only to the lord cardinal's views in the matter.'

This weather makes old scars ache. But he walks into his house as if it were midday: smiling, and imagining the trembling duke. It is one o'clock. Norfolk, in his mind, is still kneeling. A black-faced imp with a trident is pricking his calloused heels.

III
At Austin Friars
1527

Lizzie is still up. When she hears the servants let him in, she comes out with his little dog under her arm, fighting and squealing.

'Forget where you lived?'

He sighs.

'How was Yorkshire?'

He shrugs.

'The cardinal?'

He nods.

'Eaten?'

'Yes.'

'Tired?'

'Not really.'

'Drink?'

'Yes.'

'Rhenish?'

'Why not.'

The panelling has been painted. He walks into the subdued green and golden glow. 'Gregory –'

'Letter?'

'Of sorts.'

She gives him the letter and the dog, while she fetches the wine. She sits down, taking a cup herself.

'He greets us. As if there were only one of us. Bad Latin.'

'Ah, well,' she says.

'So, listen. He hopes you are well. Hopes I am well. Hopes his lovely sisters Anne and little Grace are well. He himself is well. And now no more for lack of time, your dutiful son, Gregory Cromwell.'

'Dutiful?' she says. 'Just that?'

'It's what they teach them.'

The dog Bella nibbles his fingertips, her round innocent eyes shining at him like alien moons. Liz looks well, if worn by her long day; wax tapers stand tall and straight behind her. She is wearing the string of pearls and garnets that he gave her at New Year.

'You're sweeter to look at than the cardinal,' he says.

'That's the smallest compliment a woman ever received.'

'And I've been working on it all the way from Yorkshire.' He shakes his head. 'Ah well!' He holds Bella up in the air; she kicks her legs in glee. 'How's business?'

Liz does a bit of silk-work. Tags for the seals on documents; fine net cauls for ladies at court. She has two girl apprentices in the house, and an eye on fashion; but she complains, as always, about the middlemen, and the price of thread. 'We should go to Genoa,' he says. 'I'll teach you to look the suppliers in the eye.'

'I'd like that. But you'll never get away from the cardinal.'

'He tried to persuade me tonight that I should get to know people in the queen's household. The Spanish-speakers.'

'Oh?'

'I told him my Spanish wasn't so good.'

'Not good?' She laughs. 'You weasel.'

'He doesn't have to know everything I know.'

'I've been visiting in Cheapside,' she says. She names one of her old friends, a master jeweller's wife. 'Would you like the news? A big emerald was ordered and a setting commissioned, for a ring, a woman's ring.' She shows him the emerald, big as her thumbnail.

'Which arrived, after a few anxious weeks, and they were cutting it in Antwerp.' Her fingers flick outwards. 'Shattered!'

'So who bears the loss?'

'The cutter says he was swindled and it was a hidden flaw in the base. The importer says, if it was so hidden, how could I be expected to know? The cutter says, so collect damages from your supplier …'

'They'll be at law for years. Can they get another?'

'They're trying. It must be the king, so we think. Nobody else in London would be in the market for a stone of that size. So who's it for? It isn't for the queen.'

The tiny Bella now lies back along his arm, her eyes blinking, her tail gently stirring. He thinks, I shall be curious to see if and when an emerald ring appears. The cardinal will tell me. The cardinal says, it's all very well, this business of holding the king off and angling after presents, but he will have her in his bed this summer, for sure, and by the autumn he'll be tired of her, and pension her off; if he doesn't, I will. If Wolsey's going to import a fertile French princess, he doesn't want her first weeks spoiled by scenes of spite with superseded concubines. The king, Wolsey thinks, ought to be more ruthless about his women.

Liz waits for a moment, till she knows she isn't going to get a hint. 'Now, about Gregory,' she says. 'Summer coming. Here, or away?'

Gregory is coming up thirteen. He's at Cambridge, with his tutor. He's sent his nephews, his sister Bet's sons, to school with him; it's something he is glad to do for the family. The summer is for their recreation; what would they do in the city? Gregory has little interest in his books so far, though he likes to be told stories, dragon stories, stories of green people who live in the woods; you can drag him squealing through a passage of Latin if you persuade him that over the page there's a sea serpent or a ghost. He likes to be in the woods and fields and he likes to hunt. He has plenty of growing to do, and we hope he will grow tall.

36

The king's maternal grandfather, as all old men will tell you, stood six foot four. (His father, however, was more the size of Morgan Williams.) The king stands six foot two, and the cardinal can look him in the eye. Henry likes to have about him men like his brother-in-law Charles Brandon, of a similar impressive height and breadth of padded shoulder. Height is not the fashion in the back alleys; and, obviously, not in Yorkshire.

He smiles. What he says about Gregory is, at least he isn't like I was, when I was his age; and when people say, what were you like? he says, oh, I used to stick knives in people. Gregory would never do that; so he doesn't mind – or minds less than people think – if he doesn't really get to grips with declensions and conjugations. When people tell him what Gregory has failed to do, he says, 'He's busy growing.' He understands his need to sleep; he never got much sleep himself, with Walter stamping around, and after he ran away he was always on the ship or on the road, and then he found himself in an army. The thing people don't understand about an army is its great, unpunctuated wastes of inaction: you have to scavenge for food, you are camped out somewhere with a rising water level because your mad capitaine says so, you are shifted abruptly in the middle of the night into some indefensible position, so you never really sleep, your equipment is defective, the gunners keep causing small unwanted explosions, the crossbowmen are either drunk or praying, the arrows are ordered up but not here yet, and your whole mind is occupied by a seething anxiety that things are going to go badly because *il principe*, or whatever little worshipfulness is in charge today, is not very good at the basic business of thinking. It didn't take him many winters to get out of fighting and into supply. In Italy, you could always fight in the summer, if you felt like it. If you wanted to go out.

'Asleep?' Liz says.

'No. But dreaming.'

'The Castile soap came. And your book from Germany. It was packaged as something else. I almost sent the boy away.'

In Yorkshire, which smelled of unwashed men, wearing sheepskins and sweating with anger, he had dreams about the Castile soap.

Later she says, 'So who is the lady?'

His hand, resting on her familiar but lovely left breast, removes itself in bewilderment. 'What?' Does she think he has taken up with some woman in Yorkshire? He falls on to his back and wonders how to persuade her this is not so; if necessary he'll take her there, and then she'll see.

'The emerald lady?' she says. 'I only ask because people say the king is wanting to do something very strange, and I can't really believe it. But that is the word in the city.'

Really? Rumour has advanced, in the fortnight while he has been north among the slope-heads.

'If he tries this,' she says, 'then half the people in the world will be against it.'

He had only thought, and Wolsey had only thought, that the Emperor and Spain would be against it. *Only* the Emperor. He smiles in the dark, hands behind his head. He doesn't say, which people, but waits for Liz to tell him. 'All women,' she says. 'All women everywhere in England. All women who have a daughter but no son. All women who have lost a child. All women who have lost any hope of having a child. All women who are forty.'

She puts her head on his shoulder. Too tired to speak, they lie side by side, in sheets of fine linen, under a quilt of yellow turkey satin. Their bodies breathe out the faint borrowed scent of sun and herbs. In Castilian, he remembers, he can insult people.

'Are you asleep now?'

'No. Thinking.'

'Thomas,' she says, sounding shocked, 'it's three o'clock.'

And then it is six. He dreams that all the women of England are in bed, jostling and pushing him out of it. So he gets up, to read his German book, before Liz can do anything about it.

It's not that she says anything; or only, when provoked, she says, 'My prayer book is good reading for me.' And indeed she does read her prayer book, taking it in her hand absently in the middle of the day – but only half stopping what she's doing – interspersing her murmured litany with household instructions; it was a wedding present, a book of hours, from her first husband, and he wrote her new married name in it, Elizabeth Williams. Sometimes, feeling jealous, he would like to write other things, contrarian sentiments: he knew Liz's first husband, but that doesn't mean he liked him. He has said, Liz, there's Tyndale's book, his New Testament, in the locked chest there, read it, here's the key; she says, you read it to me if you're so keen, and he says, it's in English, read it for yourself: that's the point, Lizzie. You read it, you'll be surprised what's not in it.

He'd thought this hint would draw her: seemingly not. He can't imagine himself reading to his household; he's not, like Thomas More, some sort of failed priest, a frustrated preacher. He never sees More – a star in another firmament, who acknowledges him with a grim nod – without wanting to ask him, what's wrong with you? Or what's wrong with me? Why does everything you know, and everything you've learned, confirm you in what you believed before? Whereas in my case, what I grew up with, and what I thought I believed, is chipped away a little and a little, a fragment then a piece and then a piece more. With every month that passes, the corners are knocked off the certainties of this world: and the next world too. Show me where it says, in the Bible, 'Purgatory'. Show me where it says relics, monks, nuns. Show me where it says 'Pope'.

He turns back to his German book. The king, with help from Thomas More, has written a book against Luther, for which the Pope has granted him the title of Defender of the Faith. It's not that he loves Brother Martin himself; he and the cardinal agree it would be better if Luther had never been born, or better if he had been born more subtle. Still, he keeps up with what's written, with what's smuggled through the Channel ports, and the little East Anglian inlets, the tidal creeks where a small boat with dubious cargo can be beached and pushed out again, by moonlight, to sea. He keeps the cardinal informed, so that when More and his clerical friends storm in, breathing hellfire about the newest heresy, the cardinal can make calming gestures, and say, 'Gentlemen, I am already informed.' Wolsey will burn books, but not men. He did so, only last October, at St Paul's Cross: a holocaust of the English language, and so much rag-rich paper consumed, and so much black printers' ink.

The Testament he keeps in the chest is the pirated edition from Antwerp, which is easier to get hold of than the proper German printing. He knows William Tyndale; before London got too hot for him, he lodged six months with Humphrey Monmouth, the master draper, in the city. He is a principled man, a hard man, and Thomas More calls him The Beast; he looks as if he has never laughed in his life, but then, what's there to laugh about, when you're driven from your native shore? His Testament is in octavo, nasty cheap paper: on the title page, where the printer's colophon and address should be, the words 'PRINTED IN UTOPIA'. He hopes Thomas More has seen one of these. He is tempted to show him, just to see his face.

He closes the new book. It's time to get on with the day. He knows he has not time to put the text into Latin himself, so it can be discreetly circulated; he should ask somebody to do it for him, for love or money. It is surprising how much love there is, these days, between those who read German.

By seven, he is shaved, breakfasted and wrapped beautifully in fresh unborrowed linen and dark fine wool. Sometimes, at this hour, he misses Liz's father; that good old man, who would always be up early, ready to drop a flat hand on his head and say, enjoy your day, Thomas, on my behalf.

He had liked old Wykys. He first came to him on a legal matter. In those days he was – what, twenty-six, twenty-seven? –

not long back from abroad, prone to start a sentence in one language and finish it in another. Wykys had been shrewd and had made a tidy fortune in the wool trade. He was a Putney man originally, but that wasn't why he employed him; it was because he came recommended and came cheap. At their first conference, as Wykys laid out the papers, he had said, 'You're Walter's lad, aren't you? So what happened? Because, by God, there was no one rougher than you were when you were a boy.'

He would have explained, if he'd known what sort of explanation Wykys would understand. I gave up fighting because, when I lived in Florence, I looked at frescoes every day? He said, 'I found an easier way to be.'

Latterly, Wykys had grown tired, let the business slide. He was still sending broadcloth to the north German market, when – in his opinion, with wool so long in the fleece these days, and good broadcloth hard to weave – he ought to be getting into kerseys, lighter cloth like that, exporting through Antwerp to Italy. But he listened – he was a good listener – to the old man's gripes, and said, 'Things are changing. Let me take you to the cloth fairs this year.'

Wykys knew he should show his face in Antwerp and Bergen op Zoom, but he didn't like the crossing. 'He'll be all right with me,' he told Mistress Wykys. 'I know a good family where we can stay.'

'Right, Thomas Cromwell,' she said. 'Make a note of this. No strange Dutch drinks. No women. No banned preachers in cellars. I know what you do.'

'I don't know if I can stay out of cellars.'

'Here's a bargain. You can take him to a sermon if you don't take him to a brothel.'

Mercy, he suspects, comes from a family where John Wycliffe's writings are preserved and quoted, where the scriptures in English have always been known; scraps of writing hoarded, forbidden verses locked in the head. These things come

down the generations, as eyes and noses come down, as meekness or the capacity for passion, as muscle power or the need to
take a risk. If you must take risks these days, better the preacher
than the whore; eschew Monsieur Breakbone, known in
Florence as the Neapolitan Fever, and in Naples, no doubt, as
Florence Rot. Good sense enforces abstinence – in any part of
Europe, these islands included. Our lives are limited in this way,
as the lives of our forefathers were not.

On the boat, he listened to the usual grievances from fellow
passengers: these bastard pilots, lanes not marked, English
monopolies. The merchants of the Hanse would rather their own
men brought the ships up to Gravesend: Germans are a pack of
thieves, but they know how to bring a boat upstream. Old
Wykys was queasy when they put out to sea. He stayed on deck,
making himself useful; you must have been a ship's boy, master,
one of the crew said. Once in Antwerp, they made their way to
the sign of the Holy Ghost. The servant opening the door
shouted 'It's Thomas come back to us,' as if he'd risen from the
dead. When the three old men came out, the three brothers from
the boat, they clucked, 'Thomas, our poor foundling, our
runaway, our little beaten-up friend. Welcome, come in and get
warm!'

Nowhere else but here is he still a runaway, still a little, beaten
boy.

Their wives, their daughters, their dogs covered him in kisses.
He left old Wykys by the fireside – it is surprising how international is the language of old men, swapping tips on salves for
aches, commiserating with petty wretchednesses and discussing
the whims and demands of their wives. The youngest brother
would translate, as usual: straight-faced, even when the terms
became anatomical.

He had gone out drinking with the three brothers' three sons.
'*Wat wil je?*' they teased him. 'The old man's business? His wife
when he dies?'

'No,' he said, surprising himself. 'I think I want his daughter.'

'Young?'

'A widow. Young enough.'

When he got back to London he knew he could turn the business around. Still, he needed to think of the day-to-day. 'I've seen your stock,' he said to Wykys. 'I've seen your accounts. Now show me your clerks.'

That was the key, of course, the key that would unlock profit. People are always the key, and if you can look them in the face you can be pretty sure if they're honest and up to the job. He tossed out the dubious chief clerk – saying, you go, or we go to law – and replaced him with a stammering junior, a boy he'd been told was stupid. Timid, was all he was; he looked over his work each night, mildly and wordlessly indicating each error and omission, and in four weeks the boy was both competent and keen, and had taken to following him about like a puppy. Four weeks invested, and a few days down at the docks, checking who was on the take: by the year end, Wykys was back in profit.

Wykys stumped away after he showed him the figures. 'Lizzie?' he yelled. 'Lizzie? Come downstairs.'

She came down.

'You want a new husband. Will he do?'

She stood and looked him up and down. 'Well, Father. You didn't pick him for his looks.' To him, her eyebrows raised, she said, 'Do you *want* a wife?'

'Should I leave you to talk it over?' old Wykys said. He seemed baffled: seemed to think they should sit down and write a contract there and then.

Almost, they did. Lizzie wanted children; he wanted a wife with city contacts and some money behind her. They were married in weeks. Gregory arrived within the year. Bawling, strong, one hour old, plucked from the cradle: he kissed the infant's fluffy skull and said, I shall be as tender to you as my father was not to me. For what's the point of breeding children, if each generation does not improve on what went before?

So this morning – waking early, brooding on what Liz said last night – he wonders, why should my wife worry about women who have no sons? Possibly it's something women do: spend time imagining what it's like to be each other.

One can learn from that, he thinks.

It's eight o'clock. Lizzie is down. Her hair is pushed under a linen cap and her sleeves turned back. 'Oh, Liz,' he says, laughing at her. 'You look like a baker's wife.'

'You mind your manners,' she says. 'Pot-boy.'

Rafe comes in: 'First back to my lord cardinal?' Where else, he says. He gathers his papers for the day. Pats his wife, kisses his dog. Goes out. The morning is drizzly but brightening, and before they reach York Place it is clear the cardinal has been as good as his word. A wash of sunlight lies over the river, pale as the flesh of a lemon.

PART TWO

I
Visitation
1529

They are taking apart the cardinal's house. Room by room, the king's men are stripping York Place of its owner. They are bundling up parchments and scrolls, missals and memoranda and the volumes of his personal accounts; they are taking even the ink and the quills. They are prising from the walls the boards on which the cardinal's coat of arms is painted.

They arrived on a Sunday, two vengeful grandees: the Duke of Norfolk a bright-eyed hawk, the Duke of Suffolk just as keen. They told the cardinal he was dismissed as Lord Chancellor, and demanded he hand over the Great Seal of England. He, Cromwell, touched the cardinal's arm. A hurried conference. The cardinal turned back to them, gracious: it appears a written request from the king is necessary; have you one? Oh: careless of you. It requires a lot of face to keep so calm; but then the cardinal has face.

'You want us to ride back to Windsor?' Charles Brandon is incredulous. 'For a piece of paper? When the situation's plain?'

That's like Suffolk; to think the letter of the law is some kind of luxury. He whispers to the cardinal again, and the cardinal says, 'No, I think we'd better tell them, Thomas ... not prolong the matter beyond its natural life ... My lords, my lawyer here says I can't give you the Seal, written request or not. He says that properly speaking I should only hand it to the Master of the Rolls. So you'd better bring him with you.'

He says, lightly, 'Be glad we told you, my lords. Otherwise it would have been three trips, wouldn't it?'

Norfolk grins. He likes a scrap. 'Am obliged, master,' he says.

When they go Wolsey turns and hugs him, his face gleeful. Though it is the last of their victories and they know it, it is important to show ingenuity; twenty-four hours is worth buying, when the king is so changeable. Besides, they enjoyed it. 'Master of the Rolls,' Wolsey says. 'Did you know that, or did you make it up?'

Monday morning the dukes are back. Their instructions are to turn out the occupants this very day, because the king wants to send in his own builders and furnishers and get the palace ready to hand over to the Lady Anne, who needs a London house of her own.

He's prepared to stand and argue the point: have I missed something? This palace belongs to the archdiocese of York. When was Lady Anne made an archbishop?

But the tide of men flooding in by the water stairs is sweeping them away. The two dukes have made themselves scarce, and there's nobody to argue with. What a terrible sight, someone says: Master Cromwell baulked of a fight. And now the cardinal's ready to go, but where? Over his customary scarlet, he is wearing a travelling cloak that belongs to someone else; they are confiscating his wardrobe piece by piece, so he has to grab what he can. It is autumn, and though he is a big man he feels the cold.

They are overturning chests and tipping out their contents. They scatter across the floor, letters from Popes, letters from the scholars of Europe: from Utrecht, from Paris, from Santiago de Compostela; from Erfurt, from Strassburg, from Rome. They are packing his gospels and taking them for the king's libraries. The texts are heavy to hold in the arms, and awkward as if they breathed; their pages are made of slunk vellum from stillborn calves, reveined by the illuminator in tints of lapis and leaf-green.

They take down the tapestries and leave the bare blank walls. They are rolled up, the woollen monarchs, Solomon and Sheba; as they are brought into coiled proximity, their eyes are filled by each other, and their tiny lungs breathe in the fibre of bellies and thighs. Down come the cardinal's hunting scenes, the scenes of secular pleasure: the sportive peasants splashing in ponds, the stags at bay, the hounds in cry, the spaniels held on leashes of silk and the mastiffs with their collars of spikes: the huntsmen with their studded belts and knives, the ladies on horseback with jaunty caps, the rush-fringed pond, the mild sheep at pasture, and the bluish feathered treetops, running away into a long plumed distance, to a scene of chalky bluffs and a white sailing sky.

The cardinal looks at the scavengers as they go about their work. 'Have we refreshments for our visitors?'

In the two great rooms that adjoin the gallery they have set up trestle tables. Each trestle is twenty feet long and they are bringing up more. In the Gilt Chamber they have laid out the cardinal's gold plate, his jewels and precious stones, and they are deciphering his inventories and calling out the weight of the plate. In the Council Chamber they are stacking his silver and parcel-gilt. Because everything is listed, down to the last dented pan from the kitchens, they have put baskets under the tables so they can throw in any item unlikely to catch the eye of the king. Sir William Gascoigne, the cardinal's treasurer, is moving constantly between the rooms, preoccupied, talking, directing the attention of the commissioners to any corner, any press and chest that he thinks they may have overlooked.

Behind him trots George Cavendish, the cardinal's gentleman usher; his face is raw and open with dismay. They bring out the cardinal's vestments, his copes. Stiff with embroidery, strewn with pearls, encrusted with gemstones, they seem to stand by themselves. The raiders knock down each one as if they are knocking down Thomas Becket. They itemise it, and having reduced it to its knees and broken its spine, they toss it into their travelling crates. Cavendish flinches: 'For God's sake, gentlemen, line those chests with a double thickness of cambric. Would you shred the fine work that has taken nuns a lifetime?' He turns: 'Master Cromwell, do you think we can get these people out before dark?'

'Only if we help them. If it's got to be done, we can make sure they do it properly.'

This is an indecent spectacle: the man who has ruled England, reduced. They have brought out bolts of fine holland, velvets and grosgrain, sarcenet and taffeta, scarlet by the yard: the scarlet silk in which he braves the summer heat of London, the crimson brocades that keep his blood warm when snow falls on Westminster and whisks in sleety eddies over the Thames. In public the cardinal wears red, just red, but in various weights, various weaves, various degrees of pigment and dye, but all of them the best of their kind, the best reds to be got for money. There have been days when, swaggering out, he would say, 'Right, Master Cromwell, price me by the yard!'

And he would say, 'Let me see,' and walk slowly around the cardinal; and saying 'May I?' he would pinch a sleeve between an expert forefinger and thumb; and standing back, he would view him, to estimate his girth – year on year, the cardinal expands – and so come up with a figure. The cardinal would clap his hands, delighted. 'Let the begrudgers behold us! On, on, on.' His procession would form up, his silver crosses, his sergeants-at-arms with their axes of gilt: for the cardinal went nowhere, in public, without a procession.

So day by day, at his request and to amuse him, he would put a value on his master. Now the king has sent an army of clerks to do it. But he would like to take away their pens by force and write across their inventories: *Thomas Wolsey is a man beyond price.*

'Now, Thomas,' the cardinal says, patting him. 'Everything I have, I have from the king. The king gave it to me, and if it pleases him to take York Place fully furnished, I am sure we own other houses, we have other roofs to shelter under. This is not Putney, you know.' The cardinal holds on to him. 'So I forbid you to hit anyone.' He affects to be pressing his arms by his sides, in smiling restraint. The cardinal's fingers tremble.

The treasurer Gascoigne comes in and says, 'I hear Your Grace is to go straight to the Tower.'

'Do you?' he says. 'Where did you hear that?'

'Sir William Gascoigne,' the cardinal says, measuring out his name, 'what do you suppose I have done that would make the king want to send me to the Tower?'

'It's like you,' he says to Gascoigne, 'to spread every story you're told. Is that all the comfort you've got to offer – walk in here with evil rumours? Nobody's going to the Tower. We're going' – and the household waits, breath held, as he improvises – 'to Esher. And your job,' he can't help giving Gascoigne a little shove in the chest, 'is to keep an eye on all these strangers and see that everything that's taken out of here gets where it's meant to go, and that nothing goes missing by the way, because if it does you'll be beating on the gates of the Tower and begging them to take you in, to get away from me.'

Various noises: mainly, from the back of the room, a sort of stifled cheer. It's hard to escape the feeling that this is a play, and the cardinal is in it: the Cardinal and his Attendants. And that it is a tragedy.

Cavendish tugs at him, anxious, sweating. 'But Master Cromwell, the house at Esher is an empty house, we haven't a pot, we haven't a knife or a spit, where will my lord cardinal sleep, I doubt we have a bed aired, we have neither linen nor firewood nor ... and how are we going to get there?'

'Sir William,' the cardinal says to Gascoigne, 'take no offence from Master Cromwell, who is, upon the occasion, blunt to a fault; but take what is said to heart. Since everything I have proceeds from the king, everything must be delivered back in good order.' He turns away, his lips twitching. Except when he teased the dukes yesterday, he hasn't smiled in a month. 'Tom,' he says, 'I've spent years teaching you not to talk like that.'

Cavendish says to him, 'They haven't seized my lord cardinal's barge yet. Nor his horses.'

'No?' He lays a hand on Cavendish's shoulder: 'We go upriver, as many as the barge will take. Horses can meet us at – at Putney, in fact – and then we will … borrow things. Come on, George Cavendish, exercise some ingenuity, we've done more difficult things in these last years than get the household to Esher.'

Is this true? He's never taken much notice of Cavendish, a sensitive sort of man who talks a lot about table napkins. But he's trying to think of a way to put some military backbone into him, and the best way lies in suggesting that they are brothers from some old campaign.

'Yes, yes,' Cavendish says, 'we'll order up the barge.'

Good, he says, and the cardinal says, Putney? and he tries to laugh. He says, well, Thomas, you told Gascoigne, you did; there's something about that man I never have liked, and he says, why did you keep him then? and the cardinal says, oh, well, one does, and again the cardinal says, Putney, eh?

He says, 'Whatever we face at journey's end, we shall not forget how nine years ago, for the meeting of two kings, Your Grace created a golden city in some sad damp fields in Picardy. Since then, Your Grace has only increased in wisdom and the king's esteem.'

He is speaking for everyone to hear; and he thinks, that occasion was about peace, notionally, whereas this occasion, we don't know what this is, it is the first day of a long or a short campaign; we had better dig in and hope our supply lines hold. 'I think we will manage to find some fire irons and soup kettles and whatever else George Cavendish thinks we can't do without. When I remember that Your Grace provisioned the king's great armies, that went to fight in France.'

'Yes,' the cardinal says, 'and we all know what you thought about our campaigns, Thomas.'

Cavendish says, 'What?' and the cardinal says, 'George, don't you call to mind what my man Cromwell said in the House of Commons, was it five years past, when we wanted a subsidy for the new war?'

'But he spoke against Your Grace!'

Gascoigne – who hangs doggedly to this conversation – says, 'You didn't advance yourself there, master, speaking against the king and my lord cardinal, because I do remember your speech, and I assure you so will others, and you bought yourself no favours there, Cromwell.'

He shrugs. 'I didn't mean to buy favour. We're not all like you, Gascoigne. I wanted the Commons to take some lessons from the last time. To cast their minds back.'

'You said we'd lose.'

'I said we'd be bankrupted. But I tell you, all our wars would have ended much worse without my lord cardinal to supply them.'

'In the year 1523 –' Gascoigne says.

'Must we refight this now?' says the cardinal.

'– the Duke of Suffolk was only fifty miles from Paris.'

'Yes,' he says, 'and do you know what fifty miles is, to a half-starved infantryman in winter, when he sleeps on wet ground and wakes up cold? Do you know what fifty miles is to a baggage train, with carts up to the axles in mud? And as for the glories of 1513 – God defend us.'

'Tournai! Thérouanne!' Gascoigne shouts. 'Are you blind to what occurred? Two French towns taken! The king so valiant in the field!'

If we were in the field now, he thinks, I'd spit at your feet. 'If you like the king so much, go and work for him. Or do you already?'

The cardinal clears his throat softly. 'We all do,' Cavendish says, and the cardinal says, 'Thomas, we are the works of his hand.'

When they get out to the cardinal's barge his flags are flying: the Tudor rose, the Cornish choughs. Cavendish says, wide-eyed, 'Look at all these little boats, waffeting up and down.' For a moment, the cardinal thinks the Londoners have turned out to wish him well. But as he enters the barge, there are sounds of hooting and booing from the boats; spectators crowd the bank, and though the cardinal's men keep them back, their intent is clear enough. When the oars begin to row upstream, and not downstream to the Tower, there are groans and shouted threats.

It is then that the cardinal collapses, falling into his seat, beginning to talk, and talks, talks, talks, all the way to Putney. 'Do they hate me so much? What have I done but promote their trades and show them my goodwill? Have I sown hatred? No. Persecuted none. Sought remedies every year when wheat was scarce. When the apprentices rioted, begged the king on my knees with tears in my eyes to spare the offenders, while they stood garlanded with the nooses that were to hang them.'

'The multitude,' Cavendish says, 'is always desirous of a change. They never see a great man set up but they must pull him down – for the novelty of the thing.'

'Fifteen years Chancellor. Twenty in his service. His father's before that. Never spared myself ... rising early, watching late ...'

'There, you see,' Cavendish says, 'what it is to serve a prince! We should be wary of their vacillations of temper.'

'Princes are not obliged to consistency,' he says. He thinks, I may forget myself, lean across and push you overboard.

The cardinal has not forgotten himself, far from it; he is looking back, back twenty years to the young king's accession. 'Put him to work, said some. But I said, no, he is a young man. Let him hunt, joust, and fly his hawks and falcons ...'

'Play instruments,' Cavendish says. 'Always plucking at something or other. And singing.'

'You make him sound like Nero.'

'Nero?' Cavendish jumps. 'I never said so.'

'The gentlest, wisest prince in Christendom,' says the cardinal. 'I will not hear a word against him from any man.'

'Nor shall you,' he says.

'But what I would do for him! Cross the Channel as lightly as a man might step across a stream of piss in the street.' The cardinal shakes his head. 'Waking and sleeping, on horseback or at my beads ... twenty years ...'

'Is it something to do with the English?' Cavendish asks earnestly. He's still thinking of the uproar back there when they embarked; and even now, people are running along the banks, making obscene signs and whistling. 'Tell us, Master Cromwell, you've been abroad. Are they particularly an ungrateful nation? It seems to me that they like change for the sake of it.'

'I don't think it's the English. I think it's just people. They always hope there may be something better.'

'But what do they get by the change?' Cavendish persists. 'One dog sated with meat is replaced by a hungrier dog who bites nearer the bone. Out goes the man grown fat with honour, and in comes a hungry and a lean man.'

He closes his eyes. The river shifts beneath them, dim figures in an allegory of Fortune. Decayed Magnificence sits in the centre. Cavendish, leaning at his right like a Virtuous Councillor, mutters words of superfluous and belated advice, to which the sorry magnate inclines his head; he, like a Tempter, is seated on the left, and the cardinal's great hand, with its knuckles of garnet and tourmaline, grips his own hand painfully. George would certainly go in the river, except that what he's saying, despite the platitudes, makes a bleak sense. And why? Stephen Gardiner, he thinks. It may not be proper to call the cardinal a dog grown fat, but Stephen is definitely hungry and lean, and has been promoted by the king to a place as his own private secretary. It is not unusual for the cardinal's staff to transfer in this way, after careful nurture in the Wolsey school of craft and diligence; but still, this places Stephen as the man who – if he manages his duties properly – may be closer than anyone to the king, except perhaps for the gentleman who attends him at his close-stool and hands him a diaper cloth. I wouldn't so much mind, he thinks, if Stephen got that job.

The cardinal closes his eyes. Tears are seeping from beneath his lids. 'For it is a truth,' says Cavendish, 'that fortune is inconstant, fickle and mutable ...'

All he has to do is to make a strangling motion, quickly, while the cardinal has his eyes shut. Cavendish, putting a hand to his throat, takes the point. And then they look at each other, sheepish. One of them has said too much; one of them has felt too much. It is not easy to know where the balance rests. His eyes scan the banks of the Thames. Still, the cardinal weeps and grips his hand.

As they move upriver, the littoral ceases to alarm. It is not because, in Putney, Englishmen are less fickle. It's just that they haven't heard yet.

The horses are waiting. The cardinal, in his capacity as a churchman, has always ridden a large strong mule; though, since he has hunted with kings for twenty years, his stable is the envy of every nobleman. Here the beast stands, twitching long ears, in its usual scarlet trappings, and by him Master Sexton, the cardinal's fool.

'What in God's name is he doing here?' he asks Cavendish.

Sexton comes forward and says something in the cardinal's ear; the cardinal laughs. 'Very good, Patch. Now, help me mount, there's a good fellow.'

But Patch – Master Sexton – is not up to the job. The cardinal seems weakened; he seems to feel the weight of his flesh hanging on his bones. He, Cromwell, slides from his saddle, nods to three of the stouter servants. 'Master Patch, hold Christopher's head.' When Patch pretends not to know that Christopher is the mule, and puts a headlock on the man next to him, he says, oh for Jesus' sake, Sexton, get out of the way, or I'll stuff you in a sack and drown you.

The man who's nearly had his head pulled off stands up, rubs his neck; says, thanks Master Cromwell, and hobbles forward to hold the bridle. He, Cromwell, with two others, hauls the cardinal into the saddle. The cardinal looks shamefaced. 'Thank you, Tom.' He laughs shakily. 'That's you told, Patch.'

They are ready to ride. Cavendish looks up. 'Saints protect us!' A single horseman is heading downhill at a gallop. 'An arrest!'

'By one man?'

'An outrider,' says Cavendish, and he says, Putney's rough but you don't have to send out scouts. Then someone shouts, 'It's Harry Norris.' Harry throws himself from his mount. Whatever he's come to do, he's in a lather about it. Harry Norris is one of the king's closest friends; he is, to be exact, the Groom of the Stool, the man who hands the diaper cloth.

Wolsey sees, immediately, that the king wouldn't send Norris to take him into custody. 'Now, Sir Henry, get your breath back. What can be so urgent?'

Norris says, beg pardon, my lord, my lord cardinal, sweeps off his feathered cap, wipes his face with his arm, smiles in his most engaging fashion. He speaks to the cardinal gracefully: the king has commanded him to ride after His Grace and overtake him, and speak words of comfort to him and give him this ring, which he knows well – a ring which he holds out, in the palm of his glove.

The cardinal scrambles from his mule and falls to the ground. He takes the ring and presses it to his lips. He's praying. Praying, thanking Norris, calling for blessings on his sovereign. 'I have nothing to send him. Nothing of value to send to the king.' He looks around him, as if his eye might light on something he can send; a tree? Norris tries to get him on his feet, ends up kneeling beside him, kneeling – this neat and charming man – in the Putney mud. The message he's giving the cardinal, it seems, is that the king only appears displeased, but is not really displeased; that he knows the cardinal has enemies; that he himself, Henricus Rex, is not one of them; that this show of force is only to satisfy those enemies; that he is able to recompense the cardinal with twice as much as has been taken from him.

The cardinal begins to cry. It's starting to rain, and the wind blows the rain across their faces. The cardinal speaks to Norris fast, in a low voice, and then he takes a chain from around his neck and tries to hang it around Norris's neck, and it gets tangled up in the fastenings of his riding cape and several people rush forward to help and fail, and Norris gets up and begins to brush himself down with one glove while clutching the chain in the other. 'Wear it,' the cardinal begs him, 'and when you look at it think of me, and commend me to the king.'

Cavendish jolts up, riding knee-to-knee. 'His reliquary!' George is upset, astonished. 'To part with it like this! It is a piece of the true Cross!'

'We'll get him another. I know a man in Pisa makes them ten for five florins and a round dozen for cash up front. And you get a certificate with St Peter's thumbprint, to say they're genuine.'

'For shame!' Cavendish says, and twitches his horse away.

Now Norris is backing away too, his message delivered, and they are trying to get the cardinal back on his mule. This time, four big men step forward, as if it were routine. The play has turned into some kind of low comic interlude; that, he thinks, is why Patch is here. He rides over and says, looking down from the saddle, 'Norris, can we have all this in writing?'

Norris smiles, says, 'Hardly, Master Cromwell; it's a confidential message to my lord cardinal. My master's words were meant only for him.'

'So what about this recompense you mention?'

Norris laughs – as he always does, to disarm hostility – and whispers, 'I think it might be figurative.'

'I think it might be, too.' Double the cardinal's worth? Not on Henry's income. 'Give us back what's been taken. We don't ask double.'

Norris's hand goes to the chain, now slung about his neck. 'But it all proceeds from the king. You can't call it theft.'

'I didn't call it theft.'

Norris nods, thoughtful. 'No more did you.'

'They shouldn't have taken the vestments. They belong to my lord as churchman. What will they have next? His benefices?'

'Esher – which is where you are going, are you not? – is of course one of the houses which my lord cardinal holds as Bishop of Winchester.'

'And?'

'He remains for the while in that estate and title, but … shall we say … it must come under the king's consideration? You know my lord cardinal is indicted under the statutes of praemunire, for asserting a foreign jurisdiction in the land.'

'Don't teach me the law.'

Norris inclines his head.

He thinks, since last spring, when things began to go wrong, I should have persuaded my lord cardinal to let me manage his revenues, and put some money away abroad where they can't get it; but then he would never admit that anything was wrong. Why did I let him rest so cheerful?

Norris's hand is on his horse's bridle. 'I was ever a person who admired your master,' he says, 'and I hope that in his adversity he will remember that.'

'I thought he wasn't in adversity? According to you.'

How simple it would be, if he were allowed to reach down and shake some straight answers out of Norris. But it's not simple; this is what the world and the cardinal conspire to teach him.

Christ, he thinks, by my age I ought to know. You don't get on by being original. You don't get on by being bright. You don't get on by being strong. You get on by being a subtle crook; somehow he thinks that's what Norris is, and he feels an irrational dislike taking root, and he tries to dismiss it, because he prefers his dislikes rational, but after all, these circumstances are extreme, the cardinal in the mud, the humiliating tussle to get him back in the saddle, the talking, talking on the barge, and worse, the talking, talking on his knees, as if Wolsey's unravelling, in a great unweaving of scarlet thread that might lead you back into a scarlet labyrinth, with a dying monster at its heart.

'Master Cromwell?' Norris says.

He can hardly say what he's thinking; so he looks down at Norris, his expression softened, and says, 'Thanks for this much comfort.'

'Well, take my lord cardinal out of the rain. I'll tell the king how I found him.'

'Tell him how you knelt in the mud together. He might be amused.'

'Yes.' Norris looks sad. 'You never know what will do it.'

It is at this point that Patch starts screaming. The cardinal, it seems – casting around for a gift – has given him to the king. Patch, he has often said, is worth a thousand pounds. He is to go with Norris, no time like the present; and it takes four more of the cardinal's men to subdue him to the purpose. He fights. He bites. He lashes out with fists and feet. Till he is thrown on to a baggage mule, stripped of its baggage; till he begins to cry, hiccupping, his ribs heaving, his stupid feet dangling, his coat torn and the feather in his hat broken off to a stub.

'But Patch,' the cardinal says, 'my dear fellow. You shall see me often, once the king and I understand each other again. My dear Patch, I will write you a letter, a letter of your own. I shall write it tonight,' he promises, 'and put my big seal on it. The king will cherish you; he is the kindest soul in Christendom.'

Patch wails on a single thin note, like someone taken by the Turks and impaled.

There, he says to Cavendish, he's more than one kind of fool. He shouldn't have drawn attention to himself, should he.

Esher: the cardinal dismounts under the shadow of old Bishop Wayneflete's keep, surmounted by octagonal towers. The gateway is set into a defensive wall topped with a walkway; stern enough at first sight, but the whole thing is built of brick, ornamented and prettily inlaid. 'You couldn't fortify it,' he says. Cavendish is silent. 'George, you're supposed to say, "But the need could never arise."'

The cardinal's not used the place since he built Hampton Court. They've sent messages ahead, but has anything been done? Make my lord comfortable, he says, and goes straight down to the kitchens. At Hampton Court, the kitchens have running water; here, nothing's running but the cooks' noses. Cavendish is right. In fact it is worse than he thinks. The larders are impoverished and such supplies as they have show signs of ill-keeping and plunder. There are weevils in the flour. There are mouse droppings where the pastry should be rolled. It is nearly Martinmas, and they have not even thought of salting their beef. The *batterie de cuisine* is an insult, and the stockpot is mildewed. There are a number of small boys sitting by the hearth, and, for cash down, they can be induced into scouring and scrubbing; children take readily to novelty, and the idea of cleaning, it seems, is novel to them.

My lord, he says, needs to eat and drink *now*; and he needs to eat and drink for … how long we don't know. This kitchen must be put in order for the winter ahead. He finds someone who can write, and dictates his orders. His eyes are fixed on the kitchen clerk. On his left hand he counts off the items: you do this, then this, then thirdly this. With his right hand, he breaks eggs into a basin, each one with a hard professional tap, and between his fingers the white drips, sticky and slow, from the yolk. 'How old is this egg? Change your supplier. I want a nutmeg. Nutmeg? Saffron?' They look at him as if he's speaking Greek. Patch's thin scream is still hurting his ears. Dusty angels look down on him as he pounds back to the hall.

It is late before they get the cardinal into any sort of bed worthy of the name. Where is his household steward? Where is his comptroller? By this time, he feels it is true that he and Cavendish are old survivors of a campaign. He stays up with Cavendish – not that there are beds, if they wanted them – working out what they need to keep the cardinal in reasonable comfort; they need plate, unless my lord's going to dine off dented pewter, they need bedsheets, table linen, firewood. 'I will send some people,' he says, 'to sort out the kitchens. They will be Italian. It will be violent at first, but then after three weeks it will work.'

Three weeks? He wants to set those children cleaning the copper. 'Can we get lemons?' he asks, just as Cavendish says, 'So who will be Chancellor now?'

I wonder, he thinks, are there rats down there? Cavendish says, 'Recall His Grace of Canterbury?'

Recall him – fifteen years after the cardinal chivvied him out of that office? 'No, Warham's too old.' And too stubborn, too unaccommodating to the king's wishes. 'And not the Duke of Suffolk' – because in his view Charles Brandon is no brighter than Christopher the mule, though better at fighting and fashion and generally showing off – 'not Suffolk, because the Duke of Norfolk won't have him.'

'And vice versa.' Cavendish nods. 'Bishop Tunstall?'

'No. Thomas More.'

'But, a layman and a commoner? And when he's so opposed in the matter of the king's marriage suit.'

He nods, yes, yes, it will be More. The king is known for putting out his conscience to high bidders. Perhaps he hopes to be saved from himself.

'If the king offers it – and I see that, as a gesture, he might – surely Thomas More won't accept?'

'He will.'

'Bet?' says Cavendish.

They agree the terms and shake hands on it. It takes their mind off the urgent problem, which is the rats, and the cold; which is the question of how they can pack a household staff of several hundred, retained at Westminster, into the much smaller space at Esher. The cardinal's staff, if you include his principal houses, and count them up from priests, law clerks, down to floor-sweepers and laundresses, is about six hundred souls. They expect three hundred following them immediately. 'As things stand, we'll have to break up the household,' Cavendish says. 'But we've no ready money for wages.'

'I'm damned if they're going unpaid,' he says, and Cavendish says, 'I think you are anyway. After what you said about the relic.'

He catches George's eye. They start to laugh. At least they've got something worthwhile to drink; the cellars are full, which is lucky, Cavendish says, because we'll need a drink over the next weeks. 'What do you think Norris *meant*?' George says. 'How can the king be in two minds? How can my lord cardinal be dismissed if he doesn't want to dismiss him? How can the king give way to my lord's enemies? Isn't the king master, over all the enemies?'

'You would think so.'

'Or is it *her*? It must be. He's frightened of her, you know. She's a witch.'

He says, don't be childish. George says, she is *so* a witch: the Duke of Norfolk says she is, and he's her uncle, he should know.

It's two o'clock, then it's three; sometimes it's freeing, to think you don't have to go to bed because there isn't a bed. He doesn't need to think of going home; there's no home to go to, he's got no family left. He'd rather be here drinking with Cavendish,

63

huddled in a corner of the great chamber at Esher, cold and tired and frightened of the future, than think about his family and what he's lost. 'Tomorrow,' he says, 'I'll get my clerks down from London and we'll try and make sense of what my lord still has by way of assets, which won't be easy as they've taken all the paperwork. His creditors won't be inclined to pay up when they know what's happened. But the French king pays him a pension, and if I remember it's always in arrears ... Maybe he'd like to send a bag of gold, pending my lord's return to favour. And you – you can go looting.'

Cavendish is hollow-faced and hollow-eyed when he throws him on to a fresh horse at first light. 'Call in some favours. There's hardly a gentleman in the realm that doesn't owe my lord cardinal something.'

It's late October, the sun a coin barely flipped above the horizon. 'Keep him cheerful,' Cavendish says. 'Keep him talking. Keep him talking about what Harry Norris said ...'

'Off you go. If you should see the coals on which St Lawrence was roasted, we could make good use of them here.'

'Oh, don't,' Cavendish begs. He has come far since yesterday, and is able to make jokes about holy martyrs; but he drank too much last night, and it hurts him to laugh. But not to laugh is painful too. George's head droops, the horse stirs beneath him, his eyes are full of bafflement. 'How did it come to this?' he asks. 'My lord cardinal kneeling in the dirt. How could it happen? How in the world could it?'

He says, 'Saffron. Raisins. Apples. And cats, get cats, huge starving ones. I don't know, George, where do cats come from? Oh, wait! Do you think we can get partridges?'

If we can get partridges we can slice the breasts, and braise them at the table. Whatever we can do that way, we will; and so, if we can help it, my lord won't be poisoned.

II

An Occult History of Britain
1521–1529

Once, in the days of time immemorial, there was a king of Greece who had thirty-three daughters. Each of these daughters rose up in revolt and murdered her husband. Perplexed as to how he had bred such rebels, but not wanting to kill his own flesh and blood, their princely father exiled them and set them adrift in a rudderless ship.

Their ship was provisioned for six months. By the end of this period, the winds and tides had carried them to the edge of the known earth. They landed on an island shrouded in mist. As it had no name, the eldest of the killers gave it hers: Albina.

When they hit shore, they were hungry and avid for male flesh. But there were no men to be found. The island was home only to demons.

The thirty-three princesses mated with the demons and gave birth to a race of giants, who in turn mated with their mothers and produced more of their own kind. These giants spread over the whole landmass of Britain. There were no priests, no churches and no laws. There was also no way of telling the time.

After eight centuries of rule, they were overthrown by Trojan Brutus.

The great-grandson of Aeneas, Brutus was born in Italy; his mother died in giving birth to him, and his father, by accident, he killed with an arrow. He fled his birthplace and became leader of a band of men who had been slaves in Troy. Together they embarked on a voyage north, and the vagaries of wind and tide drove them to Albina's coast, as the sisters had been driven before. When they landed they were forced to do battle with the giants, led by Gogmagog. The giants were defeated and their leader thrown into the sea.

Whichever way you look at it, it all begins in slaughter. Trojan Brutus and his descendants ruled till the coming of the Romans. Before London was called Lud's Town, it was called New Troy. And we were Trojans.

Some say the Tudors transcend this history, bloody and demonic as it is: that they descend from Brutus through the line of Constantine, son of St Helena, who was a Briton. Arthur, High King of Britain, was Constantine's grandson. He married up to three women, all called Guinevere, and his tomb is at Glastonbury, but you must understand that he is not really dead, only waiting his time to come again.

His blessed descendant, Prince Arthur of England, was born in the year 1486, eldest son of Henry, the first Tudor king. This Arthur married Katherine the princess of Aragon, died at fifteen and was buried in Worcester Cathedral. If he were alive now, he would be King of England. His younger brother Henry would likely be Archbishop of Canterbury, and would not (at least, we devoutly hope not) be in pursuit of a woman of whom the cardinal hears nothing good: a woman to whom, several years before the dukes walk in to despoil him, he will need to turn his attention; whose history, before ruin seizes him, he will need to comprehend.

Beneath every history, another history.

The lady appeared at court at the Christmas of 1521, dancing in a yellow dress. She was – what? – about twenty years old. Daughter of the diplomat, Thomas Boleyn, she has been brought up since childhood in the Burgundian court at Mechelen and Brussels, and more recently in Paris, moving in Queen Claude's train between the pretty chateaux of the Loire. Now she speaks her native tongue with a slight, unplaceable accent, strewing her sentences with French words when she pretends she can't think of the English. At Shrovetide, she dances in a court masque. The ladies are costumed as Virtues, and she takes the part of Perseverance. She dances gracefully but briskly, with an amused expression on her face, a hard, impersonal touch-me-not smile. Soon she has a little trail of petty gentlemen following her; and one not so petty gentleman. The rumour spreads that she is going to marry Harry Percy, the Earl of Northumberland's heir.

The cardinal hauls in her father. 'Sir Thomas Boleyn,' he says, 'speak to your daughter, or I will. We brought her back from France to marry her into Ireland, to the Butlers' heir. Why does she tarry?'

'The Butlers ...' Sir Thomas begins, and the cardinal says, 'Oh yes? The Butlers what? Any problem you have there, I'll fix the Butlers. What I want to know is, did you put her up to it? Conniving in corners with that foolish boy? Because, Sir Thomas, let me make myself plain: I won't have it. The king won't have it. It must be stopped.'

'I have scarcely been in England these last months. Your Grace cannot think that I am party to the scheme.'

'No? You would be surprised what I can think. Is this your best excuse? That you can't govern your own children?'

Sir Thomas is looking wry and holding out his hands. He's on the verge of saying, young people today ... But the cardinal stops him. The cardinal suspects – and has confided his suspicion – that the young woman is not enticed by the prospect of Kilkenny Castle and its frugal amenities, nor by the kind of social life that will be available to her when, on special occasions, she hacks on the poor dirt roads to Dublin.

'Who's that?' Boleyn says. 'In the corner there?'

The cardinal waves a hand. 'Just one of my legal people.'

'Send him out.'

The cardinal sighs.

'Is he taking notes of this conversation?'

'Are you, Thomas?' the cardinal calls. 'If so, stop it at once.'

Half the world is called Thomas. Afterwards, Boleyn will never be sure if it was him.

'Look now, my lord,' he says, his voice playing up and down the diplomat's scales: he is frank, a man of the world, and his smile says, now Wolsey, now Wolsey, you're a man of the world too. 'They're young.' He makes a gesture, designed to imperson-ate frankness. 'She caught the boy's eye. It's natural. I've had to break it to her. She knows it can't proceed. She knows her place.'

'Good,' the cardinal says, 'because it's below a Percy. I mean,' he adds, 'below, in the dynastic sense. I am not speaking of what one might do in a haystack on a warm night.'

'He doesn't accept it, the young man. They tell him to marry Mary Talbot, but ...' and Boleyn gives a little careless laugh, 'he doesn't care to marry Mary Talbot. He believes he is free to choose his wife.'

'Choose his –!' the cardinal breaks off. 'I never heard the like. He's not some ploughboy. He's the man who will have to hold the north for us, one of these days, and if he doesn't understand his position in the world then he must learn it or forfeit it. The match already made with Shrewsbury's daughter is a fit match for him, and a match made by me, and agreed by the king. And the Earl of Shrewsbury, I can tell you, doesn't take kindly to this sort of moonstruck clowning by a boy who's promised to his daughter.'

'The difficulty is ...' Boleyn allows a discreet diplomatic pause. 'I think that, Harry Percy and my daughter, they may have gone a little far in the matter.'

'What? You mean we *are* speaking of a haystack and a warm night?'

From the shadows he watches; he thinks Boleyn is the coldest, smoothest man he has ever seen.

'From what they tell me, they have pledged themselves before witnesses. How can it be undone, then?'

The cardinal smashes his fist on the table. 'I'll tell you how. I shall get his father down from the borders, and if the prodigal defies him, he will be tossed out of his heirdom on his prodigal snout. The earl has other sons, and better. And if you don't want the Butler marriage called off, and your lady daughter shrivelling unmarriageable down in Sussex and costing you bed and board for the rest of her life, you will forget any talk of pledges, and witnesses – who are they, these witnesses? I know those kind of witnesses who never show their faces when I send for them. So never let me hear it. Pledges. Witnesses. Contracts. God in Heaven!'

Boleyn is still smiling. He is a poised, slender man; it takes the effort of every finely tuned muscle in his body to keep the smile on his face.

'I do not ask you,' says Wolsey, relentless, 'whether in this matter you have sought the advice of your relatives in the Howard family. I should be reluctant to think that it was with their agreement that you launched yourself on this scheme. I should be sorry to hear the Duke of Norfolk was apprised of this: oh, very sorry indeed. So let me not hear it, eh? Go and ask your relatives for some *good* advice. Marry the girl into Ireland before the Butlers hear any rumour that she's spoiled goods. Not that I'd mention it. But the court does talk.'

Sir Thomas has two spots of angry red on his cheekbones. He says, 'Finished, my lord cardinal?'

'Yes. Go.'

Boleyn turns, in a sweep of dark silks. Are those tears of temper in his eyes? The light is dim, but he, Cromwell, is of very strong sight. 'Oh, a moment, Sir Thomas ...' the cardinal says. His voice loops across the room and pulls his victim back. 'Now,

Sir Thomas, remember your ancestry. The Percy family comprise, I do think, the noblest in the land. Whereas, notwithstanding your remarkable good fortune in marrying a Howard, the Boleyns were in trade once, were they not? A person of your name was Lord Mayor of London, not so? Or have I mixed up your line with some Boleyns more distinguished?'

Sir Thomas's face has drained; the scarlet spots have vanished from his cheeks, and he is almost fainting with rage. As he quits the room, he whispers, 'Butcher's boy.' And as he passes the clerk – whose beefy hand lies idly on his desk – he sneers, 'Butcher's dog.'

The door bangs. The cardinal says, 'Come out, dog.' He sits laughing, with his elbows on his desk and his head in his hands. 'Mark and learn,' he says. 'You can never advance your own pedigree – and God knows, Tom, you were born in a more dishonourable estate than me – so the trick is always to keep them scraped up to their own standards. They made the rules; they cannot complain if I am the strictest enforcer. Percys above Boleyns. Who does he think he is?'

'Is it good policy to make people angry?'

'Oh, no. But it amuses me. My life is hard and I find I want amusement.' The cardinal casts on him a kindly eye; he suspects he may be this evening's further diversion, now that Boleyn has been torn into strips and dropped on the ground like orange peel. 'Who need one look up to? The Percys, the Staffords, the Howards, the Talbots: yes. Use a long stick to stir them, if you must. As for Boleyn – well, the king likes him, and he is an able man. Which is why I open all his letters, and have done for years.'

'So has your lordship heard – no, forgive me, it is not fit for your ears.'

'What?' says the cardinal.

'It is only rumour. I should not like to mislead Your Grace.'

'You cannot speak and not speak. You must tell me now.'

'It's only what the women are saying. The silk women. And the cloth merchants' wives.' He waits, smiling. 'Which is of no interest to you, I'm sure.'

Laughing, the cardinal pushes back his chair, and his shadow rises with him. Firelit, it leaps. His arm darts out, his reach is long, his hand is like the hand of God.

But when God closes his hand, his subject is across the room, back to the wall.

The cardinal gives ground. His shadow wavers. It wavers and comes to rest. He is still. The wall records the movement of his breath. His head inclines. In a halo of light he seems to pause, to examine his handful of nothing. He splays his fingers, his giant firelit hand. He places it flat on his desk. It vanishes, melted into the cloth of damask. He sits down again. His head is bowed; his face, half-dark.

He Thomas, also Tomos, Tommaso and Thomaes Cromwell, withdraws his past selves into his present body and edges back to where he was before. His single shadow slides against the wall, a visitor not sure of his welcome. Which of these Thomases saw the blow coming? There are moments when a memory moves right through you. You shy, you duck, you run; or else the past takes your fist and actuates it, without the intervention of will. Suppose you have a knife in your fist? That's how murder happens.

He says something, the cardinal says something. They break off. Two sentences go nowhere. The cardinal resumes his chair. He hesitates before him; he sits down. The cardinal says, 'I really would like the London gossip. But I wasn't planning to beat it out of you.'

The cardinal bows his head, frowns at a paper on his desk; he is allowing time for the difficult moment to pass, and when he speaks again his tone is measured and easy, like a man telling anecdotes after supper. 'When I was a child, my father had a friend – a customer, really – who was of a florid complexion.' He touches his sleeve, in illustration. 'Like this ... scarlet. Revell was his name, Miles Revell.' His hand drifts to rest again, palm downwards on the blackish damask. 'For some reason I used to believe ... though I dare say he was an honest citizen, and liked a glass of Rhenish ... I used to believe he was a drinker of blood. I don't know ... some story I suppose that I had heard from my nurse, or from some other silly child ... and then when my father's apprentices knew about it – only because I was foolish enough to whine and cry – they would shout out, "Here comes Revell for his cup of blood, run, Thomas Wolsey ..." I used to flee as if the devil were after me. Put the marketplace between us. I marvel that I didn't fall under a wagon. I used to run, and never look. Even today,' he says – he picks up a wax seal from the desk, turns it over, turns it over, puts it down – 'even today, when I see a fair, florid man – let us say, the Duke of Suffolk – I feel inclined to burst into tears.' He pauses. His gaze comes to rest. 'So, Thomas ... can't a cleric stand up, unless you think he's after your blood?' He picks up the seal again; he turns it over in his fingers; he averts his eyes; he begins to play with words. 'Would a bishop abash you? A parish clerk panic you? A deacon disconcert?'

He says, 'What is the word? I don't know in English ... an *estoc* ...'

Perhaps there is no English word for it: the short-bladed knife that, at close quarters, you push up under the ribs. The cardinal says, 'And this was ...?'

This was some twenty years ago. The lesson is learned and learned well. Night, ice, the still heart of Europe; a forest, lakes silver beneath a pattern of winter stars; a room, firelight, a shape slipping against the wall. He didn't see his assassin, but he saw his shadow move.

'All the same ...' says the cardinal. 'It's forty years since I saw Master Revell. He will be long dead, I suppose. And your man?' He hesitates. 'Long dead too?'

It is the most delicate way that can be contrived, to ask a man if he has killed someone.

'And in Hell, I should think. If your lordship pleases.'

That makes Wolsey smile; not the mention of Hell, but the bow to the breadth of his jurisdiction. 'So if you attacked the young Cromwell, you went straight to the fiery pit?'

'If you had seen him, my lord. He was too dirty for Purgatory. The Blood of the Lamb can do much, we are told, but I doubt if it could have wiped this fellow clean.'

'I am all for a spotless world,' Wolsey says. He looks sad. 'Have you made a good confession?'

'It was a long time ago.'

'Have you made a good confession?'

'My lord cardinal, I was a soldier.'

'Soldiers have hope of Heaven.'

He looks up into Wolsey's face. There's no knowing what he believes. He says, 'We all have that.' Soldiers, beggars, sailors, kings.

'So you were a ruffian in your youth,' the cardinal says. '*Ça ne fait rien.*' He broods. 'This dirty fellow who attacked you ... he was not, in fact, in holy orders?'

He smiles. 'I didn't ask.'

'These tricks of memory ...' the cardinal says. 'Thomas, I shall try not to move without giving you warning. And in that way we shall do very well together.'

But the cardinal looks him over; he is still puzzling. It is early in their association and his character, as invented by the cardinal, is at this stage a work in progress; in fact, perhaps it is this evening that sets it going? In the years to come, the cardinal will say, 'I often wonder, about the monastic ideal – especially as applied to the young. My servant Cromwell, for instance – his youth was secluded, spent almost entirely in fasting, prayer and study of the Church Fathers. That's why he's so wild nowadays.'

And when people say, is he? – recalling, as best they can, a man who seems peculiarly discreet; when they say, really? Your man Cromwell? the cardinal will shake his head and say, but I try to mend matters, of course. When he breaks the windows we just call in the glaziers and part with the cash. As for the procession of aggrieved young women ... Poor creatures, I pay them off ...

But tonight he is back to business; hands clasped on his desk, as if holding together the evening passed. 'Come now, Thomas, you were telling me of a rumour.'

'The women judge from orders to the silk merchants that the king has a new –' He breaks off and says, 'My lord, what do you call a whore when she is a knight's daughter?'

'Ah,' the cardinal says, entering into the problem. 'To her face, "my lady." Behind her back – well, what is her name? Which knight?'

He nods to where, ten minutes ago, Boleyn stood.

The cardinal looks alarmed. 'Why did you not speak up?'

'How could I have introduced the topic?'

The cardinal bows to the difficulty.

'But it is not the Boleyn lady new at court. Not Harry Percy's lady. It is her sister.'

'I see.' The cardinal drops back in his chair. 'Of course.'

Mary Boleyn is a kind little blonde, who is said to have been passed all around the French court before coming home to this one, scattering goodwill, her frowning little sister trotting always at her heels.

'Of course, I have followed the direction of His Majesty's eye,' the cardinal says. He nods to himself. 'Are they now close? Does the queen know? Or can't you say?'

He nods. The cardinal sighs. 'Katherine is a saint. Still, if I were a saint, and a queen, perhaps I would feel I could take no harm from Mary Boleyn. Presents, eh? What sort? Not lavish, you say? I am sorry for her then; she should seize her advantage while it lasts. It's not that our king has so many adventures, though they do say ... they say that when His Majesty was young, not yet king, it was Boleyn's wife who relieved him of his virgin state.'

'Elizabeth Boleyn?' He is not often surprised. 'This one's *mother*?'

'The same. Perhaps the king lacks imagination in that way. Not that I ever believed it … If we were at the other side, you know,' he gestures in the direction of Dover, 'we wouldn't even try to keep track of the women. My friend King François – they do say he once oozed up to the lady he'd been with the night before, gave her a formal kiss of the hand, asked her name, and wished they might be better friends.' He bobs his head, liking the success of his story. 'But Mary won't cause difficulties. She's an easy armful. The king could do worse.'

'But her family will want to get something out of it. What did they get before?'

'The chance to make themselves useful.' Wolsey breaks off and makes a note. He can imagine its content: what Boleyn can have, if he asks nicely. The cardinal looks up. 'So should I have been, in my interview with Sir Thomas – how shall I put it – more douce?'

'I don't think my lord could have been sweeter. Witness his face when he left us. The picture of soothed gratification.'

'Thomas, from now on, any London gossip,' he touches the damask cloth, 'bring it right here to me. Don't trouble about the source. Let the trouble be mine. And I promise never to assault you. Truly.'

'It is forgotten.'

'I doubt that. Not if you've carried the lesson all these years.' The cardinal sits back; he considers. 'At least she is married.' Mary Boleyn, he means. 'So if she whelps, he can acknowledge it or not, as he pleases. He has a boy from John Blount's daughter and he won't want too many.'

Too large a royal nursery can be encumbering to a king. The example of history and of other nations shows that the mothers fight for status, and try to get their brats induced somehow into the line of succession. The son Henry acknowledges is known as Henry Fitzroy; he is a handsome blond child made in the king's own image. His father has created him Duke of Somerset and Duke of Richmond; he is not yet ten years old, and the senior nobleman in England.

Queen Katherine, whose boys have all died, takes it patiently: that is to say, she suffers.

When he leaves the cardinal, he is miserably angry. When he thinks back to his earlier life – that boy half-dead on the cobbles in Putney – he feels no tenderness for him, just a faint impatience: why doesn't he get up? For his later self – still prone to getting into fights, or at least being in the place where a fight might occur – he feels something like contempt, washed with a queasy anxiety. That was the way of the world: a knife in the dark, a movement on the edge of vision, a series of warnings which have worked themselves into flesh. He has given the cardinal a shock, which is not his job; his job, as he has defined it at this time, is to feed the cardinal information and soothe his temper and understand him and embellish his jokes. What went wrong was an accident of timing only. If the cardinal had not moved so fast; if he had not been so edgy, not knowing how he could signal to him to be less despotic to Boleyn. The trouble with England, he thinks, is that it's so poor in gesture. We shall have to develop a hand signal for 'Back off, our prince is fucking this man's daughter.' He is surprised that the Italians have not done it. Though perhaps they have, and he just never caught on.

In the year 1529, my lord cardinal newly disgraced, he will think back to that evening.

He is at Esher; it is the lightless, fireless night, when the great man has gone to his (possibly damp) bed, and there is only

George Cavendish to keep his spirits alive. What happened next, he asked George, with Harry Percy and Anne Boleyn?

He knew the story only in the cardinal's chilly and dismissive rendition. But George said, 'I shall tell you how it was. Now. Stand up, Master Cromwell.' He does it. 'A little to the left. Now, which would you like to be? My lord cardinal, or the young heir?'

'Oh, I see, is it a play? You be the cardinal. I don't feel equal to it.'

Cavendish adjusts his position, turning him imperceptibly from the window, where night and bare trees are their audience. His gaze rests on the air, as if he were seeing the past: shadowy bodies, moving in this lightless room. 'Can you look troubled?' George asks. 'As if you were brooding upon mutinous speech, and yet dare not speak? No, no, not like that. You are youthful, gangling, your head drooping, you are blushing.' Cavendish sighs. 'I believe you never blushed in your life, Master Cromwell. Look.' Cavendish sets his hands, gently, on his upper arms. 'Let us change roles. Sit here. You be the cardinal.'

At once he sees Cavendish transformed. George twitches, he fumbles, he all but weeps; he becomes the quaking Harry Percy, a young man in love. 'Why should I not match with her?' he cries. 'Though she be but a simple maid –'

'Simple?' he says. 'Maid?'

George glares at him. 'The cardinal never said that!'

'Not at the time, I agree.'

'Now I am Harry Percy again. "Though she be but a simple maid, her father a mere knight, yet her lineage is good –"'

'She's some sort of cousin of the king's, isn't she?'

'Some sort of cousin?' Cavendish again breaks up his role, indignant. 'My lord cardinal would have their descent unfolded before him, all drawn up by the heralds.'

'So what shall I do?'

'Just pretend! Now: her forebears are not without merit, young Percy argues. But the stronger the boy argues, the more

77

my lord cardinal waxes into a temper. The boy says, we have made a contract of matrimony, which is as good as a true marriage ...'

'Does he? I mean, did he?'

'Yes, that was the sense of it. Good as a true marriage.'

'And what did my lord cardinal do there?'

'He said, good God, boy, what are you telling me? If you have involved yourself in any such false proceeding, the king must hear of it. I shall send for your father, and between us we will contrive to annul this folly of yours.'

'And Harry Percy said?'

'Not much. He hung his head.'

'I wonder the girl had any respect for him.'

'She didn't. She liked his title.'

'I see.'

'So then his father came down from the north – will you be the earl, or will you be the boy?'

'The boy. I know how to do it now.'

He jumps to his feet and imitates penitence. It seems they had a long talk in a long gallery, the earl and the cardinal; then they had a glass of wine. Something strong, it must have been. The earl stamped the length of the gallery, then sat down, Cavendish said, on a bench where the waiting-boys used to rest between orders. He called his heir to stand before him, and took him apart in front of the servants.

'"Sir,"' says Cavendish, '"thou hast always been a proud, presumptuous, disdainful and very unthrift waster." So that was a good start, wasn't it?'

'I like,' he says, 'the way you remember the exact words. Did you write them down at the time? Or do you use some licence?'

Cavendish looks sly. 'No one exceeds your own powers of memory,' he says. 'My lord cardinal asks for an accounting of something or other, and you have all the figures at your fingertips.'

'Perhaps I invent them.'

'Oh, I don't think so.' Cavendish is shocked. 'You couldn't do that for long.'

'It is a method of remembering. I learned it in Italy.'

'There are people, in this household and elsewhere, who would give much to know the whole of what you learned in Italy.'

He nods. Of course they would. 'But now, where were we? Harry Percy, who is as good as married, you say, to Lady Anne Boleyn, is standing before his father, and the father says …?'

'That if he comes into the title, he would be the death of his noble house – he would be the last earl of Northumberland there ever was. And "Praise be to God," he says, "I have more choice of boys …" And he stamped off. And the boy was left crying. He had his heart set on Lady Anne. But the cardinal married him to Mary Talbot, and now they're as miserable as dawn on Ash Wednesday. And the Lady Anne said – well, we all laughed at the time – she said that if she could work my lord cardinal any displeasure, she would do it. Can you think how we laughed? Some sallow chit, forgive me, a knight's daughter, to menace my lord cardinal! Her nose out of joint because she could not have an earl! But we could not know how she would rise and rise.'

He smiles.

'So tell me,' Cavendish says, 'what did we do wrong? I'll tell you. All along, we were misled, the cardinal, young Harry Percy, his father, you, me – because when the king said, Mistress Anne is not to marry into Northumberland, I think, I think, the king had his eye cast on her, all that long time ago.'

'While he was close with Mary, he was thinking about sister Anne?'

'Yes, yes!'

'I wonder,' he says, 'how it can be that, though all these people think they know the king's pleasure, the king finds himself at every turn impeded.' At every turn, thwarted: maddened and

79

baffled. The Lady Anne, whom he has chosen to amuse him, while the old wife is cast off and the new wife brought in, refuses to accommodate him at all. How can she refuse? Nobody knows.

Cavendish looks downcast because they have not continued the play. 'You must be tired,' he says.

'No, I'm just thinking. How has my lord cardinal …' Missed a trick, he wants to say. But that is not a respectful way to speak of a cardinal. He looks up. 'Go on. What happened next?'

In May 1527, feeling embattled and bad-tempered, the cardinal opens a court of inquiry at York Place, to look into the validity of the king's marriage. It's a secret court; the queen is not required to appear, or even be represented; she's not even supposed to know, but all Europe knows. It is Henry who is ordered to appear, and produce the dispensation that allowed him to marry his brother's widow. He does so, and he is confident that the court will find the document defective in some way. Wolsey is prepared to say that the marriage is open to doubt. But he does not know, he tells Henry, what the legatine court can do for him, beyond this preparatory step; since Katherine, surely, is bound to appeal to Rome.

Six times (to the world's knowledge) Katherine and the king have lived in hope of an heir. 'I remember the winter child,' Wolsey says. 'I suppose, Thomas, you would not be back in England then. The queen was taken unexpectedly with pains and the prince was born early, just at the turn of the year. When he was less than an hour old I held him in my arms, the sleet falling outside the windows, the chamber alive with firelight, the dark coming down by three o'clock, and the tracks of birds and beasts covered that night by the snow, every mark of the old world wiped out, and all our pain abolished. We called him the New Year's prince. We said he would be the richest, the most beautiful, the most devoted. The whole of London was lit up in celebration … He breathed fifty-two days, and I counted every one of them. I think that if he had lived, our king might have been – I do not say a better king, for that could hardly be – but a more contented Christian.'

The next child was a boy who died within an hour. In the year 1516 a daughter was born, the Princess Mary, small but vigorous. The year following, the queen miscarried a male child. Another small princess lived only a few days; her name would have been Elizabeth, after the king's own mother.

Sometimes, says the cardinal, the king speaks of his mother, Elizabeth Plantagenet, and tears stand in his eyes. She was, you know, a lady of great beauty and calm, so meek under the misfortunes God sent her. She and the old king were blessed with many children, and some of them died. But, says the king, my brother Arthur was born to my mother and father within a year of their marriage, and followed, in not too long a time, by another goodly son, which was me. So why have I been left, after twenty years, with one frail daughter whom any vagrant wind may destroy?

By now they are, this long-married couple, dragged down by the bewildered consciousness of sin. Perhaps, some people say, it would be a kindness to set them free? 'I doubt Katherine will think so,' the cardinal says. 'If the queen has a sin laid on her conscience, believe me, she will shrive it. If it takes the next twenty years.'

What have I done? Henry demands of the cardinal. What have I done, what has she done, what have we done together? There is no answer the cardinal can make, even though his heart bleeds for his most benevolent prince; there is no answer he can make, and he detects something not entirely sincere in the question; he thinks, though he will not say so, except in a small room alone with his man of business, that no rational man could worship a God so simply vengeful, and he believes the king is a rational man. 'Look at the examples before us,' he says. 'Dean Colet, that great scholar. Now he was one of twenty-two children, and the

81

only one to live past infancy. Some would suggest that to invite such attrition from above, Sir Henry Colet and his wife must have been monsters of iniquity, infamous through Christendom. But in fact, Sir Henry was Lord Mayor of London –'

'Twice.'

'– and made a very large fortune, so in no way was he slighted by the Almighty, I would say; but rather received every mark of divine favour.'

It's not the hand of God kills our children. It's disease and hunger and war, rat-bites and bad air and the miasma from plague pits; it's bad harvests like the harvest this year and last year; it's careless nurses. He says to Wolsey, 'What age is the queen now?'

'She will be forty-two, I suppose.'

'And the king says she can have no more children? My mother was fifty-two when I was born.'

The cardinal stares at him. 'Are you sure?' he says: and then he laughs, a merry, easy laugh that makes you think, it's good to be a prince of the church.

'Well, about that, anyway. Over fifty.' They were hazy about these things in the Cromwell family.

'And did she survive the ordeal? She did? I congratulate both of you. But don't tell people, will you?'

The living result of the queen's labours is the diminutive Mary – not really a whole princess, perhaps two-thirds of one. He has seen her when he has been at court with the cardinal, and thought she was about the size of his daughter Anne, who is two or three years younger.

Anne Cromwell is a tough little girl. She could eat a princess for breakfast. Like St Paul's God, she is no respecter of persons, and her eyes, small and steady as her father's, fall coldly on those who cross her; the family joke is, what London will be like when our Anne becomes Lord Mayor. Mary Tudor is a pale, clever doll with fox-coloured hair, who speaks with more gravity than the

average bishop. She was barely ten years old when her father sent
her to Ludlow to hold court as Princess of Wales. It was where
Katherine had been taken as a bride; where her husband Arthur
died; where she herself almost died in that year's epidemic, and
lay bereft, weakened and forgotten, till the old king's wife paid
out of her private purse to have her brought back to London, day
by painful day, in a litter. Katherine had hidden – she hides so
much – any grief at the parting with her daughter. She herself is
daughter of a reigning queen. Why should Mary not rule
England? She had taken it as a sign that the king was content.

But now she knows different.

As soon as the secret hearing is convened, Katherine's stored-up
grievances come pouring out. According to her, the whole business is the fault of the cardinal. 'I told you,' Wolsey said. 'I told
you it would be. Look for the hand of the king in it? Look for the
will of the king? No, she cannot do that. For the king, in her
eyes, is immaculate.'

Ever since Wolsey rose in the king's service, the queen claims,
he has been working to push her out of her rightful place as
Henry's confidante and adviser. He has used every means he can,
she says, to drive me from the king's side, so that I know nothing
of his projects, and so that he, the cardinal, should have the direction of all. He has prevented my meetings with the ambassador
of Spain. He has put spies in my household – my women are all
spies for him.

The cardinal says, wearily, I have never favoured the French,
nor the Emperor neither: I have favoured peace. I have not
stopped her seeing the Spanish ambassador, only made the quite
reasonable request that she should not see him alone, so that I
might have some check on what insinuations and lies he presents
to her. The ladies of her household are English gentlewomen
who have a right to wait upon their queen; after almost thirty
years in England, would she have nothing but Spaniards? As for

driving her from the king's side, how could I do that? For years his conversation was, 'The queen must see this,' and 'Katherine will like to hear of this, we must go to her straight away.' There never was a lady who knew better her husband's needs.

She knows them; for the first time, she doesn't want to comply with them.

Is a woman bound to wifely obedience, when the result will be to turn her out of the estate of wife? He, Cromwell, admires Katherine: he likes to see her moving about the royal palaces, as wide as she is high, stitched into gowns so bristling with gemstones that they look as if they are designed less for beauty than to withstand blows from a sword. Her auburn hair is faded and streaked with grey, tucked back under her gable hood like the modest wings of a city sparrow. Under her gowns she wears the habit of a Franciscan nun. Try always, Wolsey says, to find out what people wear under their clothes. At an earlier stage in life this would have surprised him; he had thought that under their clothes people wore their skin.

There are many precedents, the cardinal says, that can help the king in his current concerns. King Louis XII was allowed to set aside his first wife. Nearer home, his own sister Margaret, who had first married the King of Scotland, divorced her second husband and remarried. And the king's great friend Charles Brandon, who is now married to his youngest sister Mary, had an earlier alliance put aside in circumstances that hardly bear inquiry.

But set against that, the fact that the church is not in the business of breaking up established marriages or bastardising children. If the dispensation was technically defective, or in any other way defective, why can it not be mended with a new one? So Pope Clement may think, Wolsey says.

When he says this, the king shouts. He can shrug that off, the shouting; one grows accustomed, and he watches how the cardinal behaves, as the storm breaks over his head; half-smiling, civil, regretful, he waits for the calm that succeeds it. But Wolsey is becoming uneasy, waiting for Boleyn's daughter – not the easy armful, but the younger girl, the flat-chested one – to drop her coy negotiations and please the king. If she would do this, the king would take an easier view of life and talk less about his conscience; after all, how could he, in the middle of an amour? But some people suggest that she is bargaining with the king; some say that she wants to be the new wife; which is laughable, Wolsey says, but then the king is infatuated, so perhaps he doesn't demur, not to her face. He has drawn the cardinal's attention to the emerald ring Lady Anne now wears, and has told him the provenance and the price. The cardinal looked shocked.

After the Harry Percy debacle, the cardinal had got Anne sent down to her family house at Hever, but she had insinuated herself back to court somehow, among the queen's ladies, and now he never knows where she'll be, and whether Henry will disappear from his grasp because he's chasing her across country. He thinks of calling in her father, Sir Thomas, and telling him off again, but – even without mentioning the old rumour about Henry and Lady Boleyn – how can you explain to a man that as his first daughter was a whore, so his second one should be too: insinuating that it's some sort of family business he puts them into?

'Boleyn is not rich,' he says. 'I'd get him in. Cost it out for him. The credit side. The debit side.'

'Ah yes,' the cardinal says, 'but you are the master of practical solutions, whereas I, as a churchman, have to be careful not actively to recommend that my monarch embark on a studied course of adultery.' He moves the quills around on his desk, shuffles some papers. 'Thomas, if you are ever … How shall I put it?'

He cannot imagine what the cardinal might say next.

'If you are ever close to the king, if you should find, perhaps after I am gone …' It's not easy to speak of non-existence, even if you've already commissioned your tomb. Wolsey cannot imagine a world without Wolsey. 'Ah well. You know I would prefer you to his service, and never hold you back, but the difficulty is ...'

Putney, he means. It is the stark fact. And since he's not a churchman, there are no ecclesiastical titles to soften it, as they have softened the stark fact of Ipswich.

'I wonder,' Wolsey says, 'would you have patience with our sovereign lord? When it is midnight and he is up drinking and giggling with Brandon, or singing, and the day's papers not yet signed, and when you press him he says, I'm for my bed now, we're hunting tomorrow ... If your chance comes to serve, you will have to take him as he is, a pleasure-loving prince. And he will have to take you as you are, which is rather like one of those square-shaped fighting dogs that low men tow about on ropes. Not that you are without a fitful charm, Tom.'

The idea that he or anyone else might come to have Wolsey's hold over the king is about as likely as Anne Cromwell becoming Lord Mayor. But he doesn't altogether discount it. One has heard of Jeanne d'Arc; and it doesn't have to end in flames.

He goes home and tells Liz about the fighting dogs. She also thinks it strikingly apt. He doesn't tell her about the fitful charm, in case it's something only the cardinal can see.

The court of inquiry is just about to break up, leaving the matter for further advisement, when the news comes from Rome that the Emperor's Spanish and German troops, who have not been paid for months, have run wild through the Holy City paying themselves, plundering the treasuries and stoning the artworks. Dressed satirically in stolen vestments, they have raped the wives and virgins of Rome. They have tumbled to the ground statues and nuns, and smashed their heads on the pavements. A common soldier has stolen the head of the lance that opened the side of Christ, and has attached it to the shaft of his own murderous weapon. His comrades have torn up antique tombs and tipped out the human dust, to blow away in the wind. The Tiber brims with fresh bodies, the stabbed and the strangled bobbing against the shore. The most grievous news is that the Pope is taken prisoner. As the young Emperor, Charles, is nominally in charge of these troops, and presumably will assert his authority and take advantage of the situation, King Henry's matrimonial cause is set back. Charles is the nephew of Queen Katherine, and while he is in the Emperor's hands, Pope Clement is not likely to look favourably on any appeals passed up from the legate in England.

Thomas More says that the imperial troops, for their enjoyment, are roasting live babies on spits. Oh, he would! says Thomas Cromwell. Listen, soldiers don't do that. They're too busy carrying away everything they can turn into ready money.

Under his clothes, it is well known, More wears a jerkin of horsehair. He beats himself with a small scourge, of the type used by some religious orders. What lodges in his mind, Thomas Cromwell's, is that somebody makes these instruments of daily torture. Someone combs the horsehair into coarse tufts, knots them and chops the blunt ends, knowing that their purpose is to snap off under the skin and irritate it into weeping sores. Is it monks who make them, knotting and snipping in a fury of righteousness, chuckling at the thought of the pain they will cause to persons unknown? Are simple villagers paid – how, by the dozen? – for making flails with waxed knots? Does it keep farm workers busy during the slow winter months? When the money for their honest labour is put into their hands, do the makers think of the hands that will pick up the product?

We don't have to invite pain in, he thinks. It's waiting for us: sooner rather than later. Ask the virgins of Rome.

He thinks, also, that people ought to be found better jobs.

Let us, says the cardinal at this point, take a step back from the situation. He suffers some genuine alarm; it has always been clear to him that one of the secrets of stability in Europe is to have the papacy independent, and in the clutches of neither France nor the Emperor. But his nimble mind is already skipping towards some advantage for Henry.

Suppose, he says – for in this emergency, it will be to me that Pope Clement looks to hold Christendom together – suppose I were to cross the Channel, stop off in Calais to reassure our people there and suppress any unhelpful rumours, then travel into France and conduct face-to-face talks with their king, then progress to Avignon, where they know how to host a papal court, and where the butchers and the bakers, the candle-stick-makers and the keepers of lodgings and indeed the whores have lived in hope these many years. I would invite the cardinals to meet me, and set up a council, so that the business of church government could be carried on while His Holiness is suffering the Emperor's hospitality. If the business brought before this council were to include the king's private matter, would we be justified in keeping so Christian a monarch waiting on the resolution of military events in Italy? Might we not rule? It ought not to be beyond the wit of men or angels to send a message to Pope Clement, even in captivity, and the same men or angels will bring a message back – surely endorsing our ruling, for we will have heard the full facts. And when, of course, in due time – and how we all look for that day – Pope Clement is restored to perfect liberty, he will be so grateful for the good order kept in his absence that any little matter of signatures or seals will be a formality. *Voilà* – the King of England will be a bachelor.

Before this can happen the king has to talk to Katherine; he can't always be hunting somewhere else, while she waits for him, patient, implacable, his place set for supper in her private apartments. It is June, 1527; well barbered and curled, tall and still trim from certain angles, and wearing white silk, the king makes his way to his wife's apartments. He moves in a perfumed cloud made of the essence of roses: as if he owns all the roses, owns all the summer nights.

His voice is low, gentle, persuasive, and full of regret. If he were free, he says, if there were no impediment, it is she, above all women, that he would choose for his wife. The lack of sons wouldn't matter; God's will be done. He would like nothing better than to marry her all over again; lawfully, this time. But there it is: it can't be managed. She was his brother's wife. Their union has offended divine law.

You can hear what Katherine says. That wreck of a body, held together by lacing and stays, encloses a voice that you can hear as far as Calais: it resounds from here to Paris, from here to Madrid, to Rome. She is standing on her status, she is standing on her rights; the windows are rattled, from here to Constantinople.

What a woman she is, Thomas Cromwell remarks in Spanish: to no one in particular.

By mid-July the cardinal is making his preparations for the voyage across the Narrow Sea. The warm weather has brought sweating sickness to London, and the city is emptying. A few have gone down already and many more are imagining they have it, complaining of headaches and pains in their limbs. The gossip in the shops is all about pills and infusions, and friars in the streets are doing a lucrative trade in holy medals. This plague came to us in the year 1485, with the armies that brought us the first Henry Tudor. Now every few years it fills the graveyards. It kills in a day. Merry at breakfast, they say: dead by noon.

So the cardinal is relieved to be quitting the city, though he cannot embark without the entourage appropriate for a prince of the church. He must persuade King François of the efforts he should make, in Italy, to free Pope Clement by military action; he must assure François of the King of England's amity and assistance, but without committing any troops or funds. If God gives him a following wind, he will bring back not only an annulment, but a treaty of mutual aid between England and France, one which will make the young Emperor's large jaw quiver, and draw a tear from his narrow Habsburg eye.

So why is he not more cheerful, as he strides about his private chamber at York Place? 'What will I get, Cromwell, if I gain everything I ask? The queen, who does not like me, will be cast off and, if the king persists in his folly, the Boleyns brought in, who do not like me either; the girl has a spite against me, her father I've made a fool of for years, and her uncle, Norfolk, would see me dead in a ditch. Do you think this plague will be over by the time I return? They say these visitations are all from God, but I can't pretend to know his purposes. While I'm away you should get out of the city yourself.'

He sighs; is the cardinal his only work? No; he is just the patron who demands the most constant attendance. Business always increases. When he works for the cardinal, in London or elsewhere, he pays his own expenses and those of the staff he sends out on Wolsey business. The cardinal says, reimburse yourself, and trusts him to take a fair percentage on top; he doesn't quibble, because what is good for Thomas Cromwell is good for Thomas Wolsey – and vice versa. His legal practice is thriving, and he is able to lend money at interest, and arrange bigger loans, on the international market, taking a broker's fee. The market is volatile – the news from Italy is never good two days together – but as some men have an eye for horseflesh or cattle to be fattened, he has an eye for risk. A number of noblemen are indebted to him, not just for arranging loans, but for making their estates pay better. It is not a matter of exactions from tenants, but, in the first place, giving the landowner an accurate survey of land values, crop yield, water supply, built assets, and then assessing the potential of all these; next, putting in bright people as estate managers, and with them setting up an accounting system that makes yearly sense and can be audited. Among the city merchants, he is in demand for his advice on trading partners overseas. He has a sideline in arbitration, commercial disputes mostly, as his ability to assess the facts of a case and give a swift impartial decision is trusted here, in Calais and in Antwerp. If you and your opponent can at least concur on the need to save the costs and delays of a court hearing, then Cromwell is, for a fee, your man; and he has the pleasant privilege, often enough, of sending away both sides happy.

These are good days for him: every day a fight he can win. 'Still serving your Hebrew God, I see,' remarks Sir Thomas More. 'I mean, your idol Usury.' But when More, a scholar revered through Europe, wakes up in Chelsea to the prospect of morning prayers in Latin, he wakes up to a creator who speaks the swift patois of the markets; when More is settling in for a session of self-scourging, he and Rafe are sprinting to Lombard Street to get the day's exchange rates. Not that he sprints, quite; an old injury drags sometimes, and when he's tired a foot turns inward, as if he's walking back towards himself. People suggest it is the legacy of a summer with Cesare Borgia. He likes the stories they tell about him. But where's Cesare now? He's dead.

'Thomas Cromwell?' people say. 'That is an ingenious man. Do you know he has the whole of the New Testament by heart?' He is the very man if an argument about God breaks out; he is the very man for telling your tenants twelve good reasons why their rents are fair. He is the man to cut through some legal entanglement that's ensnared you for three generations, or talk your sniffling little daughter into the marriage she swears she will never make. With animals, women and timid litigants, his manner is gentle and easy; but he makes your creditors weep. He can converse with you about the Caesars or get you Venetian glassware at a very reasonable rate. Nobody can out-talk him, if he wants to talk. Nobody can better keep their head, when markets are falling and weeping men are standing on the street tearing up letters of credit. 'Liz,' he says one night, 'I believe that in a year or two we'll be rich.'

She is embroidering shirts for Gregory with a black-work design; it's the same one the queen uses, for she makes the king's shirts herself.

'If I were Katherine I'd leave the needle in them,' he says.

She grins. 'I know you would.'

Lizzie had grown silent and stern when he told her how the king had spoken, at the meeting with Katherine. He had told her they should separate, pending a judgment on their marriage; perhaps she would retire from court? Katherine had said no; she said that would not be possible; she said she would seek advice from canon lawyers, and that he, himself, should equip himself with better lawyers, and better priests; and then, after the shouting was done, the people with their ears pressed to the walls had heard Katherine crying. 'He doesn't like her crying.'

'Men say,' Liz reaches for her scissors, '"I can't endure it when women cry" – just as people say, "I can't endure this wet weather." As if it were nothing to do with the men at all, the crying. Just one of those things that happen.'

'I've never made you cry, have I?'

'Only with laughter,' she says.

Conversation fades into an easy silence; she is embroidering her own thoughts, he is plotting what to do with his money. He is supporting two young scholars, not belonging to the family, through Cambridge University; the gift blesses the giver. I could increase those endowments, he thinks, and – 'I suppose I should make a will,' he says.

She reaches out for his hand. 'Tom, don't die.'

'Good God, no, I'm not proposing it.'

He thinks, I may not be rich yet but I am lucky. Look how I got out from under Walter's boots, from Cesare's summer, and a score of bad nights in back alleys. Men, it is supposed, want to pass their wisdom to their sons; he would give a great deal to protect his own son from a quarter of what he knows. Where does Gregory's sweet nature come from? It must be the result of his mother's prayers. Richard Williams, Kat's boy, is sharp, keen and forward. Christopher, his sister Bet's boy, is clever and willing too. And then he has Rafe Sadler, whom he trusts as he would trust his son; it's not a dynasty, he thinks, but it's a start. And quiet moments like this are rare, because his house is full of people every day, people who want to be taken to the cardinal. There are artists looking for a subject. There are solemn Dutch scholars with books under their arms, and Lübeck merchants unwinding at length solemn Germanic jokes; there are musicians in transit tuning up strange instruments, and noisy conclaves of agents for the Italian banks; there are alchemists offering recipes and astrologers offering favourable fates, and lonely Polish fur traders who've wandered by to see if someone speaks their language; there are printers, engravers, translators and cipherers; and poets, garden designers, cabalists and geometricians. Where are they tonight?

'Hush,' Liz says. 'Listen to the house.'

At first, there is no sound. Then the timbers creak, breathe. In the chimneys, nesting birds shuffle. A breeze blows from the river, faintly shivering the tops of trees. They hear the sleeping breath of children, imagined from other rooms. 'Come to bed,' he says.

The king can't say that to his wife. Or, with any good effect, to the woman they say he loves.

Now the cardinal's many bags are packed for France; his entourage yields little in splendour to the one with which he crossed seven years ago to the Field of the Cloth of Gold. His itinerary is leisurely, before he embarks: Dartford, Rochester, Faversham, Canterbury for three or four days, prayers at the shrine of Becket.

So, Thomas, he says, if you know the king's had Anne, get a letter to me the very day. I'll only trust it if I hear it from you. How will you know it's happened? I should think you'll know by his face. And if you have not the honour of seeing it? Good point. I wish I had presented you; I should have taken the chance while I had it.

'If the king doesn't tire of Anne quickly,' he tells the cardinal, 'I don't see what you are to do. We know princes please themselves, and usually it's possible to put some gloss on their actions. But what case can you make for Boleyn's daughter? What does she bring him? No treaty. No land. No money. How are you to present it as a creditable match at all?'

Wolsey sits with his elbows on his desk, his fingers dabbing his closed lids. He takes a great breath, and begins to talk: he begins to talk about England.

You can't know Albion, he says, unless you can go back before Albion was thought of. You must go back before Caesar's legions, to the days when the bones of giant animals and men lay on the ground where one day London would be built. You must go back to the New Troy, the New Jerusalem, and the sins and crimes of the kings who rode under the tattered banners of Arthur and who married women who came out of the sea or hatched out of eggs, women with scales and fins and feathers; beside which, he says, the match with Anne looks less unusual. These are old stories, he says, but some people, let us remember, do believe them.

He speaks of the deaths of kings: of how the second Richard vanished into Pontefract Castle and was murdered there or starved; how the fourth Henry, the usurper, died of a leprosy which so scarred and contracted his body that it was the size of a mannikin or child. He talks of the fifth Henry's victories in France, and the price, not in money, to be paid for Agincourt. He talks of the French princess whom that great prince married; she was a sweet lady, but her father was insane and believed that he was made of glass. From this marriage – Fifth Henry and the Glass Princess – sprung another Henry who ruled an England dark as winter, cold, barren, calamitous. Edward Plantagenet, son of the Duke of York, came as the first sign of spring: he was a native of Aries, the sign under which the whole world was made.

When Edward was eighteen years old, he seized the kingdom, and he did it because of a sign he received. His troops were baffled and battle-weary, it was the darkest time of one of God's darkest years, and he had just heard the news that should have broken him: his father and his youngest brother had been captured, mocked and slaughtered by the Lancastrian forces. It was Candlemas; huddled in his tent with his generals, he prayed for the slaughtered souls. St Blaise's Day came: 3 February, black and icy. At ten in the morning, three suns rose in the sky: three blurred discs of silver, sparkling and hazy through particles of frost. Their garland of light spread over the sorry fields, over the sodden forests of the Welsh borderlands, over his demoralised and unpaid troops. His men knelt in prayer on the frozen ground. His knights genuflected to the sky. His whole life took wing and soared. In that wash of brilliant light he saw his future. When no one else could see, he could see: and that is what it means to be a king. At the Battle of Mortimer's Cross he took prisoner one Owen Tudor. He beheaded him in Hereford marketplace and set his head to rot on the market cross. An unknown woman brought a basin of water and washed the severed head; she combed its bloody hair.

From then on – St Blaise's Day, the three suns shining – every time he touched his sword he touched it to win. Three months later he was in London and he was king. But he never saw the future again, not clearly as he had that year. Dazzled, he stumbled through his kingship as through a mist. He was entirely the creature of astrologers, of holy men and fantasists. He didn't marry as he should, for foreign advantage, but became enmeshed in a series of half-made, half-broken promises to an unknown number of women. One of them was a Talbot girl, Eleanor by name, and what was special about her? It was said she was descended – in the female line – from a woman who was a swan.

And why did he fasten his affection, finally, on the widow of a Lancastrian knight? Was it because, as some people thought, her cold blonde beauty raised his pulse? It was not exactly that; it was that she claimed descent from the serpent woman, Melusine, whom you may see in old parchments, winding her coils about the Tree of Knowledge and presiding over the union of the moon and the sun. Melusine faked her life as an ordinary princess, a mortal, but one day her husband saw her naked and glimpsed her serpent's tail. As she slid from his grip she predicted that her children would found a dynasty that would reign for ever: power with no limit, guaranteed by the devil. She slid away, says the cardinal, and no one ever saw her again.

Some of the candles have gone out; Wolsey does not call for more lights. 'So you see,' he says, 'King Edward's advisers were planning to marry him to a French princess. As I … as I have intended. And look what happened instead. Look how he chose.'

'How long is that? Since Melusine?'

It is late; the whole great palace of York Place is quiet, the city sleeping; the river creeping in its channels, silting its banks. In these matters, the cardinal says, there is no measure of time; these spirits slip from our hands and through the ages, serpentine, mutable, sly.

'But the woman King Edward married – she brought, did she not, a claim to the throne of Castile? Very ancient, very obscure?'

The cardinal nods. 'That was the meaning of the three suns. The throne of England, the throne of France, the throne of Castile. So when our present king married Katherine, he was moving closer to his ancient rights. Not that anyone, I imagine, dared put it in those terms to Queen Isabella and King Ferdinand. But it is as well to remember, and mention from time to time, that our king is the ruler of three kingdoms. If each had their own.'

'By your account, my lord, our king's Plantagenet grandfather beheaded his Tudor great-grandfather.'

'A thing to know. But not to mention.'

'And the Boleyns? I thought they were merchants, but should I have known they had serpent fangs, or wings?'

'You are laughing at me, Master Cromwell.'

'Indeed not. But I want the best information, if you are leaving me to watch this situation for you.'

The cardinal talks then about killing. He talks about sin: about what's to be expiated. He talks about the sixth King Henry, murdered in the Tower; of King Richard, born under Scorpio, the sign of secret dealings, tribulation and vice. At Bosworth, where the Scorpian died, bad choices were made; the Duke of Norfolk fought on the losing side, and his heirs were turned out of their dukedom. They had to work hard, long and hard, to get it back. So do you wonder, he says, why the Norfolk that is now shakes sometimes, if the king is in a temper? It's because he thinks he will lose all he has, at an angry man's whim.

The cardinal sees his man make a mental note; and he speaks of the loose rattling bones under the paving of the Tower, those bones bricked into staircases and mulched into the Thames mud. He talks about King Edward's two vanished sons, the younger of them prone to stubborn resurrections that almost threw Henry Tudor out of his kingdom. He speaks of the coins the Pretender struck, stamped with their message to the Tudor king: 'Your days are numbered. You are weighed in the balance: and found wanting.'

He speaks of the fear that was then, of the return of civil war. Katherine was contracted to be married into England, had been called 'Princess of Wales' since she was three years old; but before her family would let her embark from Corunna, they exacted a price in blood and bone. They asked Henry to turn his attention to the chief Plantagenet claimant, the nephew of King Edward and wicked King Richard, whom he had held in the Tower since he was a child of ten. To gentle pressure, King Henry capitulated; the White Rose, aged twenty-four, was taken out into God's light and air, in order to have his head cut off. But there is always another White Rose; the Plantagenets breed, though not unsupervised. There will always be the need for more killing; one must, says the cardinal, have the stomach for it, I suppose, though I don't know I ever have; I am always ill when there is an execution. I pray for them, these old dead people. I even pray for wicked King Richard sometimes, though Thomas More tells me he is burning in Hell.

Wolsey looks down at his own hands, twists the rings on his fingers. 'I wonder,' he murmurs. 'Wonder which it is.' Those who envy the cardinal say he has a ring which enables its owner to fly, and allows him to encompass the death of his enemies. It detects poisons, renders ferocious beasts harmless, ensures the favour of princes, and protects against drowning.

'I suppose other people know, my lord. Because they have employed conjurers, to try to get it copied.'

'If I knew, I'd get it copied myself. I'd give one to you.'

'I picked up a snake once. In Italy.'

'Why did you do that?'

'For a bet.'

'Was it poisonous?'

'We didn't know. That was the point of the bet.'

'Did it bite you?'

'Of course.'

'Why of course?'

'It wouldn't be much of a story, would it? If I'd put it down unharmed, and away it slid?'

Unwillingly, the cardinal laughs. 'What will I do without you,' he says, 'among the double-tongued French?'

In the house at Austin Friars, Liz is in bed but she stirs in her sleep. She half wakes, says his name and inches into his arms. He kisses her hair and says, 'Our king's grandfather married a serpent.'

Liz murmurs, 'Am I awake or asleep?' A heartbeat, and she slides away from him, and turns over, throwing out an arm; he wonders what she will dream. He lies awake, thinking. All that Edward did, his battles, his conquests, he did with Medici money behind him; their letters of credit were more important than signs and wonders. If King Edward was, as many people say, not the son of his father at all, not the son of the Duke of York; if King Edward's mother, as some people do believe, had bred him from an honest English soldier, an archer called Blaybourne; then if Edward married a serpent woman, his offspring would be ... Unreliable, is the word that comes to mind. If all the old stories are to be believed, and some people, let us remember, do believe them, then our king is one part bastard archer, one part hidden serpent, one part Welsh, and all of him in debt to the Italian banks ... He too slides, drifts towards sleep. His accounting fails; the spectral world moves in, where pages of figures used to be. Try always, the cardinal says, to learn what people wear under their clothes, for it's not just their skin. Turn the king inside out, and you will find his scaly ancestors: his warm, solid, serpentine flesh.

When in Italy he had picked up a snake for a bet, he had to hold it till they counted ten. They counted, rather slowly, in the slower languages: *eins, zwei, drei* ... At four, the startled snake flicked its head and bit him. Between four and five he tightened his grip. Now some cried, 'Blood of Christ, drop it!' Some prayed and some swore, some just kept on counting. The snake looked sick; when they had all reached ten, and not before, he eased its coiled body gently to the ground, and let it slip away into its future.

There was no pain, but one could see clearly the puncture wound. On instinct, he tasted it, almost bit his own wrist. He noticed, surprised by it, the private, white, English flesh of his inner arm; he saw the narrow blue-green veins into which the snake had slipped the poison.

He collected his winnings. He waited to die, but he never did die. If anything, he got stronger, quick to hide and quick to strike. There was no Milanese quartermaster could out-bawl him, no bought-in Bernese capitaine who would not fall back before his grim reputation for blood first and bargaining later. Tonight is hot, it is July; he is asleep; he dreams. Somewhere in Italy, a snake has children. He calls his children Thomas; they carry in their heads pictures of the Thames, of muddy shallow banks beyond the reach of the tide, beyond the wash of the water.

Next morning when he wakes, Liz is still sleeping. The sheets are damp. She is warm and flushed, her face smooth like a young girl's. He kisses her hairline. She tastes of salt. She murmurs, 'Tell me when you are coming home.'

'Liz, I'm not going,' he says. 'I'm not going with Wolsey.' He leaves her. His barber comes to shave him. He sees his own eyes in a polished mirror. They look alive; serpent eyes. What a strange dream, he says to himself.

As he goes downstairs he thinks he sees Liz following him. He think he sees the flash of her white cap. He turns, and says, 'Liz, go back to bed ...' But she's not there. He is mistaken. He picks up his papers and goes to Gray's Inn.

It is recess. The business is not legal; the discussion is of texts, and the whereabouts of Tyndale (somewhere in Germany), and the immediate problem is a fellow lawyer (so who shall say he should not be there, visiting Gray's Inn?) called Thomas Bilney, who is a priest also, and a fellow of Trinity Hall. 'Little Bilney' he's called, on account of his short stature and worm-like attributes; he sits twisting on a bench, and talking about his mission to lepers.

'The scriptures, to me, are as honey,' says Little Bilney, swivelling his meagre bottom, and kicking his shrunken legs. 'I am drunk on the word of God.'

'For Christ's sake, man,' he says. 'Don't think you can crawl out of your hole because the cardinal is away. Because now the Bishop of London has his hands free, not to mention our friend in Chelsea.'

'Masses, fasting, vigils, pardons out of Purgatory … all useless,' Bilney says. 'This is revealed to me. All that remains, in effect, is to go to Rome and discuss it with His Holiness. I am sure he will come over to my way of thinking.'

'You think your viewpoint is original, do you?' he says gloomily. 'Still, at that, it may be, Father Bilney. If you think the Pope would welcome your advice in these matters.'

He goes out, saying, there's one who will jump into the fire, given an invitation. Masters, be careful there.

He doesn't take Rafe to these meetings. He will not draw any member of his household into dangerous company. The Cromwell household is as orthodox as any in London, and as pious. They must be, he says, irreproachable.

The rest of the day is nothing to remember. He would have been home early, if he had not arranged to meet up in the German enclave, the Steelyard, with a man from Rostock, who brought along a friend from Stettin, who offered to teach him some Polish.

It's worse than Welsh, he says at the end of the evening. I'll need a lot of practice. Come to my house, he says. Give us notice and we'll pickle some herring; otherwise, it's pot-luck.

There's something wrong when you arrive home at dusk but torches are burning. The air is sweet and you feel so well as you walk in, you feel young, unscarred. Then you see the dismayed faces; they turn away at the sight of you.

Mercy comes and stands before him, but here is no mercy. 'Say it,' he begs her.

She looks away when she says, I am so sorry.

He thinks it's Gregory; he thinks his son is dead. Then he half knows, because where is Liz? He begs her, 'Say it.'

'We looked for you. We said, Rafe, go and see if he's at Gray's Inn, bring him back, but the gatekeepers denied they'd seen you the whole day. Rafe said, trust me, I'll find him, if I go over the whole city: but not a sign of you.'

He remembers the morning: the damp sheets, her damp forehead. Liz, he thinks, didn't you fight? If I had seen your death coming, I would have taken him and beaten in his death's head; I would have crucified him against the wall.

The little girls are still up, though someone has put them into their nightdresses, as if it were any ordinary night. Their legs and feet are bare and their nightcaps, round lace bonnets made by their mother, are knotted under their chins with a resolute hand. Anne's face is like a stone. She has Grace's hand tucked in her fist. Grace looks up at him, dubious. She almost never sees him; why is he here? But she trusts him and lets him lift her, without protest, into his arms. Against his shoulder she tumbles at once into sleep, her arms flung around his neck, the crown of her head tucked beneath his chin. 'Now, Anne,' he says, 'we must take Grace to bed, because she is little. I know you are not ready to sleep yet, but you must go in beside her, because she may wake and feel cold.'

'I may feel cold,' Anne says.

Mercy walks before him to the children's room. Grace is put down without waking. Anne cries, but she cries in silence. I'll sit with them, Mercy says: but he says, 'I will.' He waits until Anne's tears stop flowing, and her hand slackens in his.

These things happen; but not to us.

'Now let me see Liz,' he says.

The room – which this morning was only their bedroom – is lively with the scent of the herbs they are burning against contagion. They have lit candles at her head and feet. They have bound up her jaw with linen, so already she does not look like herself. She looks like the dead; she looks fearless, and as if she could

judge you; she looks flatter and deader than people he has seen
on battlefields, with their guts spilled.

He goes down, to get an account of her deathbed; to deal with the
household. At ten this morning, Mercy said, she sat down: Jesu, I
am so weary. In the middle of the day's business. Not like me, is
it? she'd said. I said, it's not like you, Liz. I put my hand to her
forehead, and I said, Liz, my darling … I told her, lie down, get to
bed with you, you have to sweat this out. She said, no, give me a
few minutes, I'm dizzy, perhaps I need to eat a little something,
but we sat down at the table and she pushed her food away …
   He would like her to shorten her account, but he understands her
need to tell it over, moment by moment, to say it out loud. It is like
a package of words she is making, to hand to him: this is yours now.
   At midday Elizabeth lay down. She was shivering, though her
skin burned. She said, is Rafe in the house? Tell him to go and
find Thomas. And Rafe did go, and any number of people went,
and they didn't find you.
   At half past twelve, she said, tell Thomas to look after the children. And then what? She complained her head ached. But
nothing to me, no message? No; she said she was thirsty.
Nothing more. But then Liz, she never did say much.
   At one o'clock, she called for a priest. At two, she made her
confession. She said she had once picked up a snake, in Italy. The
priest said it was the fever speaking. He gave her absolution. And
he could not wait, Mercy said, he could not wait to get out of the
house, he was so afraid he might take the contagion and die.
   At three in the afternoon, she declined. At four, she put off the
burden of this life.
   I suppose, he says, she will want to be buried with her first
husband.
   Why should you think that?
   Because I came more lately. He walks away. There is no point in
writing the usual directions about mourning clothes, beadsmen,

candles. Like all the others touched by this sickness, Liz must be buried quickly. He will not be able to send for Gregory or call the family together. The rule is for the household to hang a bunch of straw outside the door as sign of infection, and then restrict entry for forty days, and go abroad as little as possible.

Mercy comes in and says, a fever, it could be any fever, we don't have to admit to the sweat … If we all stayed at home, London would come to a standstill.

'No,' he says. 'We must do it. My lord cardinal made these rules and it would not be proper for me to scant them.'

Mercy says, where were you anyway? He looks into her face; he says, you know Little Bilney? I was with him; I warned him, I said he will jump into the fire.

And later? Later I was learning Polish.

Of course. You would be, she says.

She doesn't expect to make sense of it. He never expects to make any better sense of it than it makes now. He knows the whole of the New Testament by heart, but find a text: find a text for this.

Later, when he thinks back to that morning, he will want to catch again that flash of her white cap: though when he turned, no one was there. He would like to picture her with the bustle and warmth of the household behind her, standing in the doorway, saying, 'Tell me when you are coming home.' But he can only picture her alone, at the door; and behind her is a waste-land, and a blue-tinged light.

He thinks of their wedding night; her trailing taffeta gown, her little wary gesture of hugging her elbows. Next day she said, 'That's all right then.'

And smiled. That's all she left him. Liz who never did say much.

For a month he is at home: he reads. He reads his Testament, but he knows what it says. He reads Petrarch whom he loves, reads how he defied the doctors: when they had given him up to fever he lived still, and when they came back in the morning, he was sitting up writing. The poet never trusted any doctor after that; but Liz left him too fast for physician's advice, good or bad, or for the apothecary with his cassia, his galingale, his wormwood, and his printed cards with prayers on.

He has got Niccolò Machiavelli's book, *Principalities*; it is a Latin edition, shoddily printed in Naples, which seems to have passed through many hands. He thinks of Niccolò on the battle-field; of Niccolò in the torture chamber. He feels he is in the torture chamber but he knows that one day he will find the door out, because it is he who has the key. Someone says to him, what is in your little book? and he says, a few aphorisms, a few truisms, nothing we didn't know before.

Whenever he looks up from his book, Rafe Sadler is there. Rafe is a slight boy, and the game with Richard and the others is to pretend not to see him, and say, 'I wonder where Rafe is?' They are as pleased with this joke as a bunch of three-year-olds might be. Rafe's eyes are blue, his hair is sandy-brown, and you couldn't take him for a Cromwell. But still he is a tribute to the man who brought him up: dogged, sardonic, quick on the uptake.

He and Rafe read a book about chess. It is a book printed before he was born, but it has pictures. They frown over them, perfecting their game. For what seems like hours, neither of them makes a move. 'I was a fool,' Rafe says, a forefinger resting on the head of a pawn. 'I should have found you. When they said you weren't at Gray's Inn, I should have known you were.'

'How could you have known? I'm not reliably where I shouldn't be. Are you moving that pawn, or just patting it?'

'*J'adoube.*' Rafe snatches his hand away.

For a long time they sit gazing at their pieces, at the configuration which locks them in place. They see it coming: stalemate. 'We're too good for each other.'

'Perhaps we ought to play against other people.'

'Later. When we can wipe out all-comers.'

Rafe says, 'Ah, wait!' He seizes his knight and makes it leap.
Then he looks at the result, aghast.

'Rafe, you are *foutu*.'

'Not necessarily.' Rafe rubs his forehead. 'You might yet do
something stupid.'

'Right. You live in hope.'

Voices murmur. Sunlight outside. He feels he could almost
sleep, but when he sleeps Liz Wykys comes back, cheerful and
brisk, and when he wakes he has to learn the lack of her all over
again.

From a distant room a child is crying. Footsteps overhead.
The crying stops. He picks up his king and looks at the base of it,
as if to see how it is made. He murmurs, *'J'adoube.'* He puts it
back where it was.

Anne Cromwell sits with him, as the rain falls, and writes her
beginner's Latin in her copy book. By St John's Day she knows
all common verbs. She is quicker than her brother and he tells her
so. 'Let me see,' he says, holding out his hand for her book. He
finds that she has written her name over and over, 'Anne
Cromwell, Anne Cromwell ...'

News comes from France of the cardinal's triumphs, parades,
public Masses and extempore Latin orations. It seems that, once
disembarked, he has stood on every high altar in Picardy and
granted the worshippers remission of their sins. That's a few
thousand Frenchmen free to start all over again.

The king is chiefly at Beaulieu, a house in Essex he has
recently bought from Sir Thomas Boleyn, whom he has made
Viscount Rochford. All day he hunts, undeterred by the wet
weather. In the evening he entertains. The Duke of Suffolk and
the Duke of Norfolk join him at private suppers, which they
share with the new viscount. The Duke of Suffolk is his old
friend and if the king said, knit me some wings so I may fly, he
would say, what colour? The Duke of Norfolk is, of course, chief

of the Howard family and Boleyn's brother-in-law: a sinewy little twitcher, always twitching after his own advantage.

He does not write to the cardinal to tell him that everybody in England is saying that the king means to marry Anne Boleyn. He doesn't have the news the cardinal wants, so he doesn't write at all. He gets his clerks to do it, to keep the cardinal updated on his legal affairs, his finances. Tell him we are all well here, he says. Tender him my respects and my duty. Tell him how much we would like to see his face.

No one else in their household falls sick. This year London has escaped lightly – or at least, everyone says so. Prayers of thanksgiving are offered in the city churches; or prayers of appeasement, perhaps one should call them? In the little conclaves that meet at night, God's purpose is interrogated. London knows that it sins. As the Bible tells us, 'A merchant shall hardly keep himself from doing wrong.' And elsewhere it is stated, 'He that maketh haste to be rich shall not be innocent.' It is a sure sign of troubled minds, the habit of quotation. 'Whom the Lord loveth he correcteth.'

By early September, the plague has run its course and the family is able to gather to pray for Liz. Now she can have the ceremonies that were denied her when she left them so suddenly. Black coats are given to twelve poor men of the parish, the same mourners who would have followed her coffin; and each man in the family has pledged seven years of Masses for her soul. On the day appointed, the weather clears briefly, and there is a chill in the air. 'The harvest is passed, the summer is ended, and we are not saved.'

The small child Grace wakes in the night and says that she sees her mother in her shroud. She does not cry like a child, noisy and hiccupping, but like a grown woman, weeping tears of dread.

'All the rivers run into the sea, but the seas are not yet full.'

* * *

Morgan Williams shrinks year by year. Today especially he looks small and grey and harassed, as he grips his arm and says, 'Why are the best taken? Ah, why are they?' Then, 'I know you were happy with her, Thomas.'

They are back at Austin Friars, a swarm of women and children and robust men whom mourning hardly takes out of their customary black, the garb of lawyers and merchants, of accountants and brokers. There is his sister, Bet Wellyfed; her two boys, her little daughter Alice. There is Kat; his sisters have their heads together, deciding who shall move in to help out Mercy with the girls, 'until you marry again, Tom.'

His nieces, two good little girls, still clutch their rosary beads. They stare around them, unsure what they must do next. Ignored, as the people talk over their heads, they lean against the wall, and flick their eyes at each other. Slowly, they slide down the wall, straight-backed, till they are the height of two-year-olds, and balancing on their heels. 'Alice! Johane!' someone snaps; slowly they rise, solemn-faced, to their proper heights. Grace approaches them; silently they trap her, take off her cap, shake out her blonde hair and begin to plait it. While the brothers-in-law talk about what the cardinal is doing in France, his attention strays towards her. Grace's eyes grow wide as her cousins draw her hair back tight. Her mouth opens in a silent gape, like a fish's mouth. When one squeak escapes her, it is Liz's sister, the elder Johane, who crosses the room and scoops her up. Watching Johane, he thinks, as he often has, how alike the sisters are: were.

His daughter Anne turns her back on the women, slides her arm into her uncle's. 'We're talking about the Low Countries trade,' Morgan tells her.

'One thing's for sure, Uncle, they won't be pleased in Antwerp if Wolsey signs a treaty with the French.'

'That's what we're saying to your father. But, oh, he will stick by his cardinal. Come, Thomas! You don't like the French any more than we do.'

He knows, as they do not, how much the cardinal needs the friendship of King François; without one of the major powers of Europe to speak for him, how will the king get his divorce?

'Treaty of Perpetual Peace? Let's think, when was the last Perpetual Peace? I give it three months.' It is his brother-in-law Wellyfed who speaks, laughing; and John Williamson, who is Johane's husband, asks will they take bets on it: three months, six? Then he remembers they're at a solemn occasion. 'Sorry, Tom,' he says, and breaks into a spasm of coughing.

Johane's voice cuts across it: 'If the old gamester keeps coughing like this, the winter will finish him off, and then I'll marry you, Tom.'

'Will you?'

'Oh, for sure. As long as I get the right piece of paper from Rome.'

The party smile and hide their smiles. They give each other knowing looks. Gregory says, why is that funny? You can't marry your wife's sister, can you? He and his boy cousins go off into a corner to talk about private subjects – Bet's boys Christopher and Will, Kat's boys Richard and Walter – why did they call that child Walter? Did they need a reminder of their father, lurking around after his death, to remind them not to get too happy? The family never meet but he thanks God that Walter's not with them any more. He tells himself he should have more kindness towards his father, but his kindness extends only to paying for Masses for his soul.

In the year before he came back to England for good, he had crossed and recrossed the sea, undecided; he had so many friends in Antwerp, besides good business contacts, and as the city expanded, which it did every year, it seemed more and more the right place to be. If he was homesick, it was for Italy: the light, the language, Tommaso as he'd been there. Venice had cured him of any nostalgia for the banks of the Thames. Florence and Milan had given him ideas more flexible than those of people who'd stayed at home. But something pulled at him – curiosity about who was dead and who'd been born, a desire to see his sisters again, and laugh – one can always laugh somehow – about their upbringing. He had written to Morgan Williams to say, I'm thinking of London next. But don't tell my father. Don't tell him I'm coming home.

During the early months they tried to coax him. Look, Walter's settled down, you wouldn't know him. He's eased back on the drink. Well, he knew it was killing him. He keeps out of the law courts these days. He's even served his turn as church-warden.

What? he said. And he didn't get drunk on the altar wine? He didn't make off with the candle funds?

Nothing they said could persuade him down to Putney. He waited more than a year, till he was married and a father. Then he felt safe to go.

It was more than twelve years he'd been out of England. He'd been taken aback by the change in people. He left them young and they had softened or sharpened into middle age. The lissom were lean now and dried out. The plump were plumper. Fine features had blurred and softened. Bright eyes were duller. There were some people he didn't recognise at all, not at first glance.

But he would have known Walter anywhere. As his father walked towards him he thought, I'm seeing myself, in twenty, thirty years, if I'm spared. They said that drink had nearly done for him, but he didn't look half-dead. He looked as he had always looked: as if he could knock you down, and might decide to do it. His short strong body had broadened and coarsened. His hair, thick and curling, had hardly a thread of grey. His glance was skewering; small eyes, bright and golden-brown. You need good eyes in a smithy, he used to say. You need good eyes wherever you are, or they'll rob you blind.

'Where've you been?' Walter said. Where once he would have sounded angry, he now sounded merely irritated. It was as if his son had been on a message to Mortlake, and had taken his time over it.

'Oh … here and there,' he said.

'You look like a foreigner.'

'I am a foreigner.'

'So what have you been doing?'

He could imagine himself saying, 'This and that.' He did say it.

'And what sort of this and that are you doing now?'

'I'm learning the law.'

'Law!' Walter said. 'If it weren't for the so-called law, we would be lords. Of the manor. And a whole lot of other manors round here.'

That is, he thinks, an interesting point to make. If you get to be a lord by fighting, shouting, being bigger, better, bolder and more shameless than the next man, Walter should be a lord. But it's worse than that; Walter thinks he's entitled. He'd heard it all his childhood: the Cromwells were a rich family once, we had estates. 'When, where?' he used to say. Walter would say, 'Somewhere in the north, up there!' and yell at him for quibbling. His father didn't like to be disbelieved even when he was telling you an outright lie. 'So how do we come to such a low place?' he would ask, and Walter would say it was because of lawyers and cheats and lawyers who are all cheats, and who thieve land away from its owners. Understand it if you can, Walter would say, for I can't – and I'm not stupid, boy. How dare they drag me into court and fine me for running beasts on the so-called common? If all had their own, that would be my common.

Now, if the family's land was in the north, how could that be? No point saying this – in fact, it's the quickest way to get a lesson from Walter's fist. 'But was there no money?' he'd persist. 'What happened to it?'

Just once, when he was sober, Walter had said something that sounded true, and was, by his lights, eloquent: I suppose, he said,

I suppose we pissed it away. I suppose once it's gone it's gone. I suppose fortune, when it's lost, it will never visit again.

He thought about it, over the years. On that day when he went back to Putney, he'd asked him, 'If ever the Cromwells were rich, and I were to go after what's left, would that content you?'

His tone was meant to be soothing but Walter was hard to soothe. 'Oh yes, and share it out, I suppose? You and bloody Morgan that you're so thick with. That's my money, if all have their own.'

'It would be family money.' What are we doing, he thought, quarrelling right off, rowing within five minutes over this non-existent wealth? 'You have a grandson now.' He added, not aloud, 'And you aren't coming anywhere near him.'

'Oh, I have those already,' Walter said. 'Grandsons. What is she, some Dutch girl?'

He told him about Liz Wykys. Admitting, therefore, that he had been in England long enough to marry and have a child. 'Caught yourself a rich widow,' Walter said, sniggering. 'I suppose that was more important than coming to see me. It would be. I suppose you thought I'd be dead. Lawyer, is it? You were always a talker. A slap in the mouth couldn't cure it.'

'But God knows you tried.'

'I suppose you don't admit to the smithy work now. Or helping your uncle John and sleeping among the turnip shavings.'

'Good God, father,' he'd said, 'they didn't eat turnips at Lambeth Palace. Cardinal Morton eat turnips! What are you thinking?'

When he was a little boy and his uncle John was a cook for the great man, he used to run away to Lambeth to the palace, because the chances of getting fed were better. He used to hang around by the entrance nearest the river – Morton hadn't built his big gateway then – and watch the people come and go, asking who was who and recognising them next time by the colours of their clothes and the animals and objects painted on their shields. 'Don't stand about,' people bellowed at him, 'make yourself useful.'

Other children than he made themselves useful in the kitchen by fetching and carrying, their small fingers employed in plucking songbirds and hulling strawberries. Each dinner time the household officers formed up in procession in the passages off the kitchens, and they carried in the tablecloths and the Principal Salt. His uncle John measured the loaves and if they were not just right they were tossed into a basket for the lower household. Those that passed his test he counted as they went in; standing by him, pretending to be his deputy, he learned to count. Into the great hall would go the meats and the cheeses, the sugared fruits and the spiced wafers, to the archbishop's table – he was not a cardinal then. When the scrapings and remnants came back they were divided up. First choice to the kitchen staff. Then to the almshouse and the hospital, the beggars at the gate. What wasn't fit for them would go down the line to the children and the pigs.

Each morning and evening the boys earned their keep by running up the back staircases with beer and bread to put in the cupboards for the young gentlemen who were the cardinal's pages. The pages were of good family. They would wait at table and so become intimate with great men. They would hear their talk and learn from it. When they were not at the table they were learning out of great volumes from their music masters and other masters, who passed up and down the house holding nosegays and pomanders, who spoke in Greek. One of the pages was pointed out to him: Master Thomas More, whom the archbishop himself says will be a great man, so deep his learning already and so pleasant his wit.

One day he brought a wheaten loaf and put it in the cupboard and lingered, and Master Thomas said, 'Why do you linger?' But he did not throw anything at him. 'What is in that great book?'

113

he asked, and Master Thomas replied, smiling, 'Words, words, just words.'

Master More is fourteen this year, someone says, and is to go to Oxford. He doesn't know where Oxford is, or whether he wants to go there or has just been sent. A boy can be sent; and Master Thomas is not yet a man.

Fourteen is twice seven. Am I seven? he asks. Don't just say yes. Tell me am I? His father says, for God's sake, Kat, make him up a birthday. Tell him anything, but keep him quiet.

When his father says, I'm sick of the sight of you, he leaves Putney and sets off to Lambeth. When Uncle John says, we have plenty of boys this week, and the devil finds work for idle hands, he sets off back to Putney. Sometimes he gets a present to take home. Sometimes it is a brace of pigeons with their feet tied together, and gaping bloody beaks. He walks along the riverbank whirling them about his head, and they look as if they are flying, till somebody shouts at him, stop that! He can't do anything without someone shouting. Is it any wonder, John says, when you are into any mischief going, prone to giving back answers and always reliably to be found where you shouldn't be?

In a small cold room off the kitchen passages there is a woman called Isabella, who makes marzipan figures, for the archbishop and his friends to make plays with after supper. Some of the figures are heroes, such as Prince Alexander, Prince Caesar. Some are saints; today I am making St Thomas, she says. One day she makes marzipan beasts and gives him a lion. You can eat it, she says; he would rather keep it, but Isabella says it will soon fall to pieces. She says, 'Haven't you got a mother?'

He learns to read from the scribbled orders for wheat flour or dried beans, for barley and for ducks' eggs, that come out of the stewards' pantries. For Walter, the point of being able to read is to take advantage of people who can't; for the same purpose one must learn to write. So his father sends him to the priest. But again he is always in the wrong, for priests have such strange rules; he should come to the lesson specially, not on his way from whatever else he is doing, not carrying a toad in a bag, or knives that want sharpening, and not cut and bruised either, from one of those doors (doors called Walter) that he is always walking into. The priest shouts, and forgets to feed him, so he takes off to Lambeth again.

On the days when he turns up in Putney, his father says, where by the sweet saints have you been: unless he's busy inside, on top of a stepmother. Some of the stepmothers last such a short time that his father's done with them and kicked them out by the time he gets home, but Kat and Bet tell him about them, screeching with laughter. Once when he comes in, dirty and wet, that day's stepmother says, 'Who does this boy belong to?' and tries to kick him out into the yard.

One day when he is nearly home he finds the first Bella lying in the street, and he sees that nobody wants her. She is no longer than a small-sized rat and so shocked and cold that she doesn't even cry. He carries her home in one hand, and in the other a small cheese wrapped in sage leaves.

The dog dies. His sister Bet says, you can get another. He looks in the street but never finds one. There are dogs, but they belong to somebody.

It can take a long time to get to Putney from Lambeth and sometimes he eats the present, if it's not raw. But if he only gets a cabbage, he kicks it and rolls it and thrashes it till it is utterly, utterly destroyed.

At Lambeth he follows the stewards around and when they say a number he remembers it; so people say, if you haven't time to write it down, just tell John's nephew. He will cast an eye on a sack of whatever's been ordered in, then warn his uncle to check if it's short weight.

At night at Lambeth, when it's still light and all the pots have been scoured, the boys go outside on to the cobbles and play at football. Their shouts rise into the air. They curse and barge into each other, and till somebody yells to stop, they fight with their fists and sometimes bite each other. From the open window above, the young gentlemen sing a part-song in the high careful voices they learn.

Sometimes the face of Master Thomas More appears. He waves to him, but Master Thomas looks down without recognition at the children below. He smiles impartially; his white scholar's hand draws close the shutter. The moon rises. The pages go to their truckle-beds. The kitchen children wrap themselves in sacking and sleep by the hearth.

He remembers one night in summer when the footballers had stood silent, looking up. It was dusk. The note from a single recorder wavered in the air, thin and piercing. A blackbird picked up the note, and sang from a bush by the water gate. A boatman whistled back from the river.

1527: when the cardinal comes back from France, he immediately begins ordering up banquets. French ambassadors are expected, to set the seal on his concordat. Nothing, he says, nothing, will be too good for these gentlemen.

The court leaves Beaulieu on 27 August. Soon afterwards, Henry meets the returned cardinal, face-to-face for the first time since early June. 'You will hear that the king's reception of me was cold,' Wolsey says, 'but I can tell you it was not. She – Lady Anne – was present … this is true.'

On the face of it, a large part of his mission has been a failure. The cardinals would not meet him at Avignon: made the excuse that they didn't want to go south in the heat. 'But now,' he says, 'I have a better plan. I will ask the Pope to send me a co-legate, and I will try the king's matter in England.'

While you were in France, he says, my wife Elizabeth died.

The cardinal looks up. His hands fly to his heart. His right hand creeps down to the crucifix he wears. He asks how it occurred. He listens. His thumb runs over the tortured body of God: over and over, as if it were any lump of metal. He bows his head. He murmurs, 'Whom the Lord loveth ...' They sit in silence. To break the silence, he begins to ask the cardinal unnecessary questions.

He scarcely needs an account of the tactics of the summer just past. The cardinal has promised to help finance a French army which will go into Italy and try to expel the Emperor. While this is happening, the Pope, who has lost not just the Vatican but the papal states, and seen Florence throw out his Medici relatives, will be grateful and obliged to King Henry. But as for any long-term rapprochement with the French – he, Cromwell, shares the scepticism of his friends in the city. If you have been in the street in Paris or Rouen, and seen a mother pull her child by the hand, and say, 'Stop that squalling, or I'll fetch an Englishman,' you are inclined to believe that any accord between the countries is formal and transient. The English will never be forgiven for the talent for destruction they have always displayed when they get off their own island. English armies laid waste to the land they moved through. As if systematically, they performed every action proscribed by the codes of chivalry, and broke every one of the laws of war. The battles were nothing; it was what they did between the battles that left its mark. They robbed and raped for forty miles around the line of their march. They burned the crops in the fields, and the houses with the people inside them. They took bribes in coin and in kind and when they were encamped in a district they made the people pay for every day on which they were left unmolested. They killed priests and hung them up naked in the marketplaces. As if they were infidels, they ransacked the churches, packed the chalices in their baggage, fuelled their cooking fires with precious books; they scattered relics and stripped altars. They found out the families of the dead and demanded that the living ransom them; if the living could not pay, they torched the corpses before their eyes, without ceremony, without a single prayer, disposing of the dead as one might the carcases of diseased cattle.

This being so, the kings may forgive each other; the people scarcely can. He does not say this to Wolsey, who has enough bad news waiting for him. During his absence, the king had sent his own envoy to Rome for secret negotiations. The cardinal had found it out; and it had come to nothing, of course. 'But if the king is less than frank with me, it does nothing to aid our cause.'

He has never before met with such double-dealing. The fact is, the king knows his case is weak in law. He knows this, but does not want to know it. In his own mind, he has convinced himself he was never married and so is now free to marry. Let us say, his will is convinced, but not his conscience. He knows canon law, and where he does not know it already he has made himself expert. Henry, as the younger brother, was brought up and trained for the church, and for the highest offices within it. 'If His Majesty's brother Arthur had lived,' Wolsey says, 'then His Majesty would have been the cardinal, and not me. Now there's a thought. Do you know, Thomas, I haven't had a day off since … since I was on the boat, I suppose. Since the day I was seasick, starting at Dover.'

They had once crossed the Narrow Sea together. The cardinal had lain below, calling on God, but he, being used to the voyage, spent the time on deck, making drawings of the sails and rigging, and of notional ships with notional rigging, and trying to persuade the captain – 'yourself not offended,' he said – that there was a way of going faster. The captain thought it over and said, 'When you fit out a merchant ship of your own, you can do it that way. Of course, any Christian vessel will think you're pirates, so don't look for help if you get in difficulties. Sailors,' he explained, 'don't like anything new.'

'Nor does anyone else,' he'd said. 'Not as far as I can see.'

There cannot be new things in England. There can be old things freshly presented, or new things that pretend to be old. To be trusted, new men must forge themselves an ancient pedigree, like Walter's, or enter into the service of ancient families. Don't try to go it alone, or they'll think you're pirates.

This summer, with the cardinal back on dry land, he remembers that voyage. He waits for the enemy to come alongside, and for the hand-to-hand fighting to begin.

But for now he goes down to the kitchens, to see how they are getting on with their masterpieces to impress the French envoys. They have got the steeple on their sugar-paste model of St Paul's, but they are having trouble with the cross and ball on top. He says, 'Make marzipan lions – the cardinal wants them.'

They roll their eyes and say, will it never end?

Since he returned from France their master has been uncharacteristically sour. It is not just the overt failures that make him grumble, but the dirty work behind the scenes. Squibs and slanders were printed against him and as fast as he could buy them up there was a new batch on the street. Every thief in France seemed to converge on his baggage train; at Compiègne, though he mounted a day-and-night guard on his gold plate, a little boy was found to be going up and down the back stairs, passing out the dishes to some great robber who had trained him up.

'What happened? Did you catch him?'

'The great robber was put in the pillory. The boy ran away. Then one night, some villain sneaked into my chamber, and carved a device by the window …' And next morning, a shaft of early sun, creeping through mist and rain, had picked out a gallows, from which dangled a cardinal's hat.

Once again the summer has been wet. He could swear it has never been light. The harvest will be ruined. The king and the cardinal exchange recipes for pills. The king lays down cares of state should he happen to sneeze, and prescribes for himself an easy day of music-making or strolling – if the rain abates – in his gardens. In the afternoon, he and Anne sometimes retire and are private. The gossip is that she allows him to undress her. In the evenings, good wine keeps the chills out, and Anne, who reads the Bible, points out strong scriptural commendations to him.

After supper he grows thoughtful, says he supposes the King of France is laughing at him; he supposes the Emperor is laughing too. After dark the king is sick with love. He is melancholy, sometimes unreachable. He drinks and sleeps heavily, sleeps alone; he wakes, and because he is a strong man and a young man still he is optimistic, clear-headed, ready for the new day. In daylight, his cause is hopeful.

The cardinal doesn't stop work if he's ill. He just goes on at his desk, sneezing, aching, and complaining.

In retrospect, it is easy to see where the cardinal's decline began, but at the time it was not easy. Look back, and you remember being at sea. The horizon dipped giddily, and the shoreline was lost in mist.

October comes, and his sisters and Mercy and Johane take his dead wife's clothes and cut them up carefully into new patterns. Nothing is wasted. Every good bit of cloth is made into something else.

At Christmas the court sings:

> As the holly groweth green
> And never changes hue
> So I am, and ever hath been,
> Unto my lady true.
>
> Green groweth the holly, so doth the ivy.
> Though winter blasts blow ever so high.
>
> As the holly groweth green,
> With ivy all alone,
> When flowers cannot be seen
> And green-wood leaves be gone,
> Green groweth the holly.

* * *

Spring, 1528: Thomas More, ambling along, genial, shabby. 'Just the man,' he says. 'Thomas, Thomas Cromwell. Just the man I want to see.'

He is genial, always genial; his shirt collar is grubby. 'Are you bound for Frankfurt this year, Master Cromwell? No? I thought the cardinal might send you to the fair, to get among the heretic booksellers. He is spending a deal of money buying up their writings, but the tide of filth never abates.'

More, in his pamphlets against Luther, calls the German shit. He says that his mouth is like the world's anus. You would not think that such words would proceed from Thomas More, but they do. No one has rendered the Latin tongue more obscene.

'Not really my business,' Cromwell says, 'heretics' books. Heretics abroad are dealt with abroad. The church being universal.'

'Oh, but once these Bible men get over to Antwerp, you know … What a town it is! No bishop, no university, no proper seat of learning, no proper authorities to stop the proliferation of so-called translations, translations of scripture which in my opinion are malicious and wilfully misleading … But you know that, of course, you spent some years there. And now Tyndale's been sighted in Hamburg, they say. You'd know him, wouldn't you, if you saw him?'

'So would the Bishop of London. You yourself, perhaps.'

'True. True.' More considers it. He chews his lip. 'And you'll say to me, well, it's not work for a lawyer, running after false translations. But I hope to get the means to proceed against the brothers for sedition, do you see?' *The brothers*, he says; his little joke; he drips with disdain. 'If there is a crime against the state, our treaties come into play, and I can have them extradited. To answer for themselves in a straiter jurisdiction.'

'Have you found sedition in Tyndale's writing?'

'Ah, Master Cromwell!' More rubs his hands together. 'I relish you, I do indeed. Now I feel as a nutmeg must do when it's grated. A lesser man – a lesser lawyer – would say, "I have read

Tyndale's work, and I find no fault there." But Cromwell won't be tripped – he casts it back, he asks me, rather, have *you* read Tyndale? And I admit it. I have studied the man. I have picked apart his so-called translations, and I have done it letter by letter. I read him, of course, I do. By licence. From my bishop.'

'It says in Ecclesiasticus, "he that toucheth pitch shall be defiled." Unless his name's Thomas More.'

'Well now, I knew you were a Bible reader! Most apt. But if a priest hears a confession, and the matter be wanton, does that make the priest a wanton fellow himself?' By way of diversion, More takes his hat off, and absently folds it up in his hands; he creases it in two; his bright, tired eyes glance around, as if he might be confuted from all sides. 'And I believe the Cardinal of York has himself licensed his young divines at Cardinal College to read the sectaries' pamphlets. Perhaps he includes you in his dispensations. Does he?'

It would be strange for him to include his lawyer; but then it's strange work for lawyers altogether. 'We have come around in a circle,' he says.

More beams at him. 'Well, after all, it's spring. We shall soon be dancing around the maypole. Good weather for a sea voyage. You could take the chance to do some wool-trade business, unless it's just men you're fleecing these days? And if the cardinal asked you to go to Frankfurt, I suppose you'd go? Now if he wants some little monastery knocked down, when he thinks it has good endowments, when he thinks the monks are old, Lord bless them, and a little wandering in their wits; when he thinks the barns are full and the ponds well stocked with fish, the cattle fat and the abbot old and lean … off you go, Thomas Cromwell. North, south, east or west. You and your little apprentices.'

If another man were saying this, he'd be trying to start a fight. When Thomas More says it, it leads to an invitation to dinner. 'Come out to Chelsea,' he says. 'The talk is excellent, and we shall like you to add to it. Our food is simple, but good.'

Tyndale says a boy washing dishes in the kitchen is as pleasing to the eye of God as a preacher in the pulpit or the apostle on the Galilee shore. Perhaps, he thinks, I won't mention Tyndale's opinion.

More pats his arm. 'Have you no plans to marry again, Thomas? No? Perhaps wise. My father always says, choosing a wife is like putting your hand into a bag full of writhing creatures, with one eel to six snakes. What are the chances you will pull out the eel?'

'Your father has married, what, three times?'

'Four.' He smiles. The smile is real. It crinkles the corner of his eyes. 'Your beadsman, Thomas,' he says, as he ambles away.

When More's first wife died, her successor was in the house before the corpse was cold. More would have been a priest, but human flesh called to him with its inconvenient demands. He did not want to be a bad priest, so he became a husband. He had fallen in love with a girl of sixteen, but her sister, at seventeen, was not yet married; he took the elder, so that her pride should not be hurt. He did not love her; she could not read or write; he hoped that might be amended, but seemingly not. He tried to get her to learn sermons by heart, but she grumbled and was stubborn in her ignorance; he took her home to her father, who suggested beating her, which made her so frightened that she swore she would complain no more. 'And she never did,' More will say. 'Though she didn't learn any sermons either.' It seems he thought the negotiations had been satisfactory: honour preserved all round. The stubborn woman gave him children, and when she died at twenty-four, he married a city widow, getting on in years and advanced in stubbornness: another one who couldn't read. There it is: if you are so lenient with yourself as to insist on living with a woman, then for the sake of your soul you should make it a woman you really don't like.

Cardinal Campeggio, whom the Pope is sending to England at Wolsey's request, was a married man before he was a priest. It makes him especially suitable to help Wolsey – who of course has no experience of marital problems – on the next stage of the journey to thwart the king in his heart's desire. Though the imperial army has withdrawn from Rome, a spring of negotiations has failed to yield any definite result. Stephen Gardiner has been in Rome, with a letter from the cardinal, praising the Lady Anne, trying to disabuse the Pope of any notion he may entertain that the king is being wilful and whimsical in his choice of bride. The cardinal had sat long over the letter listing her virtues, writing it in his own hand. 'Womanly modesty ... chastity ... can I say chastity?'

'You'd better.'

The cardinal looked up. 'Know something?' He hesitated, and returned to his letter. 'Apt to bear children? Well, her family is fertile. Loving and faithful daughter of the church ... Perhaps stretching a point ... they say she has the scriptures in French set up in her chamber, and lets her women read them, but I would have no positive knowledge of that ...'

'King François allows the Bible in French. She learned her scriptures there, I suppose.'

'Ah, but women, you see. Women reading the Bible, there's another point of contention. Does she know what Brother Martin thinks is a woman's place? We shouldn't mourn, he says, if our wife or daughter dies in childbirth – she's only doing what God made her for. Very harsh, Brother Martin, very intractable. And perhaps she is not a Bible-woman. Perhaps it is a slur on her. Perhaps it is just that she is out of patience with churchmen. I wish she did not blame me for her difficulties. Not blame me so very much.'

Lady Anne sends friendly messages to the cardinal, but he thinks she does not mean them. 'If,' Wolsey had said, 'I saw the prospect of an annulment for the king, I would go to the Vatican in person, have my veins opened and allow the documents to be written in my own blood. Do you think, if Anne knew that, it would content her? No, I didn't think so, but if you see any of the Boleyns, make them the offer. By the way, I suppose you know a person called Humphrey Monmouth? He is the man who had Tyndale in his house for six months, before he ran off to wherever. They say he sends him money still, but that can't possibly be true, as how would he know where to send? Monmouth … I am merely mentioning his name. Because … now why am I?' The cardinal had closed his eyes. 'Because I am merely mentioning it.'

The Bishop of London has already filled his own prisons. He is locking up Lutherans and sectaries in Newgate and the Fleet, with common criminals. There they remain until they recant and do public penance. If they relapse they will be burned; there are no second chances.

When Monmouth's house is raided, it is clear of all suspect writings. It's almost as if he was forewarned. There are neither books nor letters that link him to Tyndale and his friends. All the same, he is taken to the Tower. His family is terrified. Monmouth is a gentle and fatherly man, a master draper, well liked in his guild and the city at large. He loves the poor and buys cloth even when trade is bad, so the weavers may keep in work. No doubt the imprisonment is designed to break him; his business is tottering by the time he is released. They have to let him go, for lack of evidence, because you can't make anything of a heap of ashes in the hearth.

Monmouth himself would be a heap of ashes, if Thomas More had his way. 'Not come to see us yet, Master Cromwell?' he says. 'Still breaking dry bread in cellars? Come now, my tongue is sharper than you deserve. We must be friends, you know.'

It sounds like a threat. More moves away, shaking his head: 'We must be friends.'

Ashes, dry bread. England was always, the cardinal says, a miserable country, home to an outcast and abandoned people, who are working slowly towards their deliverance, and who are visited by God with special tribulations. If England lies under God's curse, or some evil spell, it has seemed for a time that the spell has been broken, by the golden king and his golden cardinal. But those golden years are over, and this winter the sea will freeze; the people who see it will remember it all their lives.

Johane has moved into the house at Austin Friars with her husband John Williamson and her daughter little Johane – Jo, the children call her, seeing she is too small for a full name. John Williamson is needed in the Cromwell business. 'Thomas,' says Johane, 'what exactly is your business these days?'

In this way she detains him in talk. 'Our business,' he says, 'is making people rich. There are many ways to do this and John is going to help me out with them.'

'But John won't have to deal with my lord cardinal, will he?'

The gossip is that people – people of influence – have complained to the king, and the king has complained to Wolsey, about the monastic houses he has closed down. They don't think of the good use to which the cardinal has put the assets; they don't think of his colleges, the scholars he maintains, the libraries he is founding. They're only interested in getting their own fingers in the spoils. And because they've been cut out of the business, they pretend to believe the monks have been left naked and lamenting in the road. They haven't. They've been transferred elsewhere, to bigger houses better run. Some of the younger ones have been let go, boys who have no calling to the life. Questioning them, he usually finds they know nothing, which makes nonsense of the abbeys' claims to be the light of learning. They can stumble through a Latin prayer, but when you say, 'Go on then, tell me what it means,' they say, 'Means, master?' as if they thought that words and their meanings were so loosely attached that the tether would snap at the first tug.

'Don't worry about what people say,' he tells Johane. 'I take responsibility for it, I do, alone.'

The cardinal has received the complaints with a supreme hauteur. He has grimly noted in his file the names of the complainers. Then he has taken out of his file the list, and handed it over to his man, with a tight smile. All he cares for are his new buildings, his banners flying, his coat of arms embossed on the brickwork, his Oxford scholars; he's plundering Cambridge to get the brightest young doctors over to Cardinal College. There was trouble before Easter, when the dean found six of the new men in possession of a number of forbidden books. Lock them up by all means, Wolsey said, lock them up and reason with them. If the weather is not too hot, or not too wet, I might come up and reason with them myself.

No use trying to explain this to Johane. She only wants to know her husband's not within arrow-shot of the slanders that are flying. 'You know what you're doing, I suppose.' Her eyes dart upwards. 'At least, Tom, you always look as if you do.'

Her voice, her footstep, her raised eyebrow, her pointed smile, everything reminds him of Liz. Sometimes he turns, thinking that Liz has come into the room.

The new arrangements confuse Grace. She knows her mother's first husband was called Tom Williams; they name him in their household prayers. Is Uncle Williamson therefore his son? she asks.

Johane tries to explain it. 'Save your breath,' Anne says. She taps her head. Her bright little fingers bounce from the seed pearls of her cap. 'Slow,' she says.

Later, he says to her, 'Grace isn't slow, just young.'

'I never remember I was as foolish as that.'

'They're all slow, except us? Is that right?'

Anne's face says, more or less, that is right. 'Why do people marry?'

'So there can be children.'

'Horses don't marry. But there are foals.'

'Most people,' he says, 'feel it increases their happiness.'

'Oh, yes, that,' Anne says. 'May I choose my husband?'

127

'Of course,' he says; meaning, up to a point.

'Then I choose Rafe.'

For a minute, for two minutes together, he feels his life might mend. Then he thinks, how could I ask Rafe to wait? He needs to set up his own household. Even five years from now, Anne would be a very young bride.

'I know,' she says. 'And time goes by so slowly.'

It's true; one always seems to be waiting for something. 'You seem to have thought it through,' he says. You don't have to spell out to her, keep this to yourself, because she knows to do that; you don't have to lead this female child through a conversation with the little shifts and demurs that most women demand. She's not like a flower, a nightingale: she's like … like a merchant adventurer, he thinks. A look in the eye to skewer your intentions, and a deal done with a slap of the palm.

She pulls off her cap; she twists the seed pearls in her fingers, and tugs at a strand of her dark hair, stretching it and pulling out its wave. She scoops up the rest of her hair, twists it and wraps it around her neck. 'I could do that twice,' she says, 'if my neck were smaller.' She sounds fretful. 'Grace thinks I cannot marry Rafe because we are related. She thinks everybody who lives in a house must be cousins.'

'You are not Rafe's cousin.'

'Are you sure?'

'I am sure. Anne … put your cap back on. What will your aunt say?'

She makes a face. It is a face imitative of her aunt Johane. 'Oh, Thomas,' she murmurs, 'you are always so sure!'

He raises a hand to cover his smile. For a moment Johane seems less worrying. 'Put your cap on,' he says mildly.

She squashes it back on to her head. She is so little, he thinks; but still, she'd be better suited by a helmet. 'How did Rafe come here?' she says.

* * *

He came here from Essex, because that's where his father happened to be at the time. His father Henry was a steward to Sir Edward Belknap, who was a cousin of the Grey family, and so related to the Marquis of Dorset, and the marquis was Wolsey's patron, when the cardinal was a scholar at Oxford. So yes, cousins come into it; and the fact that, when he had only been back in England for a year or two, he was already somehow in the cardinal's affinity, though he had never set eyes on the great man himself; already he, Cromwell, was a man useful to employ. He worked for the Dorset family on various of their tangled lawsuits. The old marchioness had him tracking down bed hangings and carpets for her. Send that. Be here. To her, all the world was a menial. If she wanted a lobster or a sturgeon, she ordered it up, and if she wanted good taste she ordered it in the same way. The marchioness would run her hand over Florentine silks, making little squeaks of pleasure. 'You bought it, Master Cromwell,' she would say. 'And very beautiful it is. Your next task is to work out how we pay for it.'

Somewhere in this maze of obligations and duties, he met Henry Sadler, and agreed to take his son into his household. 'Teach him all you know,' Henry proposed, a little fearfully. He arranged to collect Rafe on his way back from business in his part of the country, but he picked a bad day for it: mud and drenching rain, clouds chasing in from the coast. It was not much after two when he splashed up to the door, but the light was already failing; Henry Sadler said, can't you stay, you won't make it to London before they close the gates. I ought to try to get home tonight, he said. I have to be in court, and then there'll be my Lady Dorset's debt collectors to see off, and you know how that is ... Mistress Sadler glanced fearfully outside, and down at her child: from whom she must now part, trusting him, at the age of seven, to the weather and the roads.

This is not harsh, this is usual. But Rafe was so small that he almost thought it harsh. His baby curls had been cropped and his ginger hair stood up at the crown. His mother and father knelt down and patted him. Then they swaddled and pulled and knotted him into multiple layers of over-wrapped padding, so that his slight frame swelled into the likeness of a small barrel. He looked down at the child and out at the rain and thought, sometimes I should be warm and dry like other men; how do they contrive it while I never can? Mistress Sadler knelt and took her son's face in her hands. 'Remember everything we have told you,' she whispered. 'Say your prayers. Master Cromwell, please see he says his prayers.'

When she looked up he saw that her eyes were blurred with tears and he saw that the child could not bear it, and was shaking inside his vast wrappings and about to howl. He threw his cloak around himself. A scatter of raindrops flew from it, baptised the scene. 'Well, Rafe, what do you think? If you're man enough …' He held out his gauntleted hand. The child's hand slotted into it. 'Shall we see how far we get?'

We'll do this fast so you don't look back, he thought. The wind and rain drove the parents back from the open door. He threw Rafe into the saddle. The rain came at them horizontally. On the outskirts of London the wind dropped. He lived at Fenchurch Street then. At the door a servant held out his arms in an offer to take Rafe, but he said, 'We drowned men will stick together.'

The child had become a dead weight in his arms, shrinking flesh inside seven sodden layers of interwrapped wool. He stood Rafe before the fire; vapours rose from him. Roused by the warmth, he put up small frozen fingers and tentatively began to unpick, to unravel himself. What place is this, he said, in a distinct, polite tone.

'London,' he said. 'Fenchurch Street. Home.'

He took a linen towel and gently blotted from his face the journey just passed. He rubbed his head. Rafe's hair stood up in spikes. Liz came in. 'Heaven direct me: boy or hedgehog?' Rafe turned his face to her. He smiled. He slept on his feet.

* * *

When the sweat comes back this summer, 1528, people say, as they did last year, that you won't get it if you don't think about it. But how can you not? He sends the girls out of London; first to the Stepney house, and then beyond. This time the court is infected. Henry tries to outride the plague, moving from one hunting lodge to the next. Anne is sent to Hever. The fever breaks out there among the Boleyn family and the lady's father goes down first. He lives; her sister Mary's husband dies. Anne falls ill but within twenty-four hours she is reported back on her feet. Still, it can wreck a woman's looks. You don't know what outcome to pray for, he says to the cardinal.

The cardinal says, 'I am praying for Queen Katherine … and also for the dear Lady Anne. I am praying for King François's armies in Italy, that they may meet with success, and yet not so much success that they forget how they need their friend and ally King Henry. I am praying for the king's Majesty and all his coun-cillors, and for the beasts in the field, and for the Holy Father and the Curia, may their decisions be guided from above. I am praying for Martin Luther, and for all those infected with his heresy, and for all who combat him, most especially the Chancel-lor of the Duchy of Lancaster, our dear friend Thomas More. Against all common sense and observation, I am praying for a good harvest, and for the rain to stop. I am praying for every-body. I am praying for everything. That is what it is, to be a cardinal. Only when I say to the Lord, "Now, about Thomas Cromwell –" does God say to me, "Wolsey, what have I told you? Don't you know when to give up?"'

When the infection reaches Hampton Court, the cardinal seals himself off from the world. Only four servants are allowed to approach him. When he re-emerges, he does look as if he has been praying.

At the end of the summer, when the girls come back to London, they have grown and Grace's hair has been bleached by the sun. She is shy of him and he wonders if now she can only associate him with that night when he carried her to bed, after she had been told her mother was dead. Anne says, next summer, whatever happens, I prefer to stay with you. The sickness has left the city, but the cardinal's prayers have met with variable success. The harvest is poor; the French are losing badly in Italy and their commander has died of plague.

Autumn comes. Gregory goes back to his tutor; his reluctance is clear enough, though little about Gregory is clear to him. 'What is it,' he asks him, 'what's wrong?' The boy won't say. With other people, he is sunny and lively, but with his father guarded and polite, as if to keep a formal distance between them. He says to Johane, 'Is Gregory frightened of me?'

Quick as a needle into canvas, she darts at him. 'He's not a monk; has he cause?' Then she softens. 'Thomas, why should he be? You're a kind father; in fact, I think too much so.'

'If he doesn't want to go back to his tutor, I could send him to Antwerp to my friend Stephen Vaughan.'

'Gregory will never make a man of business.'

'No.' You can't see him beating out a deal on interest rates with one of the Fuggers' agents or some sniggering de Medici clerk. 'So what will I do with him?'

'I'll tell you what to do – when he is ready, marry him well. Gregory is a gentleman. Anyone can see that.'

Anne is eager to make a start with Greek. He is thinking who best to teach her, asking around. He wants someone congenial, whom he can talk to over supper, a young scholar who will live in the house. He regrets the choice of tutor he's made for his son and nephews, but he won't take them away at this point. The man is quarrelsome, and to be sure there was a sad episode when one of the boys set fire to his room, because he'd been reading in bed with a candle. 'It wouldn't be Gregory, would it?' he'd said, always hopeful; the master seemed to think he was treating it as a joke. And he's always sending him bills that he believes he's paid; I need a household accountant, he thinks.

He sits at his desk, piled high with drawings and plans from Ipswich and Cardinal College, with craftsmen's estimates and bills for Wolsey's planting schemes. He examines a scar in the palm of his hand; it is an old burn-mark, and it looks like a twist of rope. He thinks about Putney. He thinks about Walter. He thinks about the jittery sidestep of a skittish horse, the smell of the brewery. He thinks about the kitchen at Lambeth, and about the tow-headed boy who used to bring the eels. He remembers taking the eel-boy by the hair and dipping his head in a tub of water, and holding it under. He thinks, did I really do that? I wonder why. The cardinal's probably right, I am beyond redemption. The scar sometimes itches; it is as hard as a spur of bone. He thinks, I need an accountant. I need a Greek tutor. I need Johane, but who says I can have what I need?

He opens a letter. It is from a priest called Thomas Byrd. He is in want of money, and it seems the cardinal owes him some. He makes a note, to have it checked out and paid, then picks up the letter again. It mentions two men, two scholars, Clerke and Sumner. He knows the names. They are two of the six college men, the Oxford men who had the Lutheran books. Lock them up and reason with them, the cardinal had said. He holds the letter and glances away from it. He knows something bad is coming; its shadow moves on the wall.

He reads. Clerke and Sumner are dead. The cardinal should be told, the writer says. Having no other secure place, the Dean saw fit to shut them in the college cellars, the deep cold cellars intended for storing fish. Even in that silent place, secret, icy, the summer plague sought them out. They died in the dark and without a priest.

All summer we have prayed and not prayed hard enough. Had the cardinal simply forgotten his heretics? I must go and tell him, he thinks.

It is the first week in September. His suppressed grief becomes anger. But what can he do with anger? It also must be suppressed.

But when at last the year turns, and the cardinal says, Thomas, what shall I give you for a new-year gift?, he says, 'Give me Little Bilney.' And without waiting for the cardinal to answer he says, 'My lord, he has been in the Tower for a year. The Tower would frighten anyone, but Bilney is a timid man and not strong and I am afraid he is straitly kept, and my lord, you remember Sumner and Clerke and how they died. My lord, use your power, write letters, petition the king if you must. Let him go.'

The cardinal leans back. He puts his fingertips together. 'Thomas,' he says. 'My dear Thomas Cromwell. Very well. But Father Bilney must go back to Cambridge. He must give up his project of going to Rome and addressing the Pope to bring him to a right way of thinking. There are very deep vaults under the Vatican, and my arm will not be able to reach him there.'

It is at the tip of his tongue to say, 'You could not reach into the cellars of your own college.' But he stops himself. Heresy – his brush with it – is a little indulgence that the cardinal allows him. He is always glad to have the latest bad books filleted, and any gossip from the Steelyard, where the German merchants live. He is happy to turn over a text or two, and enjoy an after-supper debate. But for the cardinal, any contentious point must be wrapped around and around again with a fine filament of words, fine as split hairs. Any dangerous opinion must be so plumped out with laughing apologies that it is as fat and harmless as the cushions you lean on. It is true that when he was told of the deaths underground, my lord was moved to tears. 'How could I not have known?' he said. 'Those fine young men!'

He cries easily in recent months, though that does not mean his tears are less genuine; and indeed now he wipes away a tear, because he knows the story: Little Bilney at Gray's Inn, the man who spoke Polish, the futile messengers, the dazed children, Elizabeth Cromwell's face set in the fixed severity of death. He leans across his desk and says, 'Thomas, please don't despair. You still have your children. And in time you may wish to marry again.'

I am a child, he thinks, who cannot be consoled. The cardinal places his hand over his. The strange stones flicker in the light, showing their depths: a garnet like a blood bubble; a turquoise with a silver sheen; a diamond with a yellow-grey blink, like the eye of a cat.

He will never tell the cardinal about Mary Boleyn, though the impulse will arise. Wolsey might laugh, he might be scandalised. He has to smuggle him the content, without the context.

Autumn, 1528: he is at court on the cardinal's business. Mary is running towards him, her skirts lifted, showing a fine pair of green silk stockings. Is her sister Anne chasing her? He waits to see.

She stops abruptly. 'Ah, it's you!'

He wouldn't have thought Mary knew him. She puts one hand against the panelling, catching her breath, and the other against his shoulder, as if he were just part of the wall. Mary is still dazzlingly pretty; fair, soft-featured. 'My uncle, this morning,' she says. 'My uncle Norfolk. He was roaring against you. I said to my sister, who is this terrible man, and she said –'

'He's the one who looks like a wall?'

Mary takes her hand away. She laughs, blushes, and with a little heave of her bosom tries to get her breath back.

'What was my lord of Norfolk's complaint?'

'Oh ...' she flaps a hand to fan herself, 'he said, cardinals, legates, it was never merry in England when we had cardinals among us. He says the Cardinal of York is despoiling the noble houses, he says he will have all to rule himself, and the lords to be like schoolboys creeping in for a whipping. Not that you should take any notice of what I say ...'

She looks fragile, breathless still: but his eyes tell her to talk. She gives a little laugh and says, 'My brother George roared too. He said that the Cardinal of York was born in a hospital for paupers and he employs a man was born in the gutter. My lord

father said, come now, my dear boy, you lose nothing if you are
exact: not quite a gutter, but a brewer's yard, I believe, for he's
certainly no gentleman.' Mary takes a step back. 'You look a
gentleman. I like your grey velvet, where did you find that?'

'Italy.'

He has been promoted, from being the wall. Mary's hand
creeps back; absorbed, she strokes him. 'Could you get me
some? Though a bit sober for a woman, perhaps?'

Not for a widow, he thinks. The thought must show on his face
because Mary says, 'That's it, you see. William Carey's dead.'

He bows his head and is very correct; Mary alarms him. 'The
court misses him sadly. As you must yourself.'

A sigh. 'He was kind. Given the circumstances.'

'It must have been difficult for you.'

'When the king turned his mind to Anne, he thought that,
knowing how things are done in France, she might accept a … a
certain position, in the court. And in his heart, as he put it. He
said he would give up all other mistresses. The letters he has
written, in his own hand …'

'Really?'

The cardinal always says that you can never get the king to
write a letter himself. Even to another king. Even to the Pope.
Even when it might make a difference.

'Yes, since last summer. He writes and then sometimes, where
he would sign Henricus Rex …' She takes his hand, turns up his
palm, and with her forefinger traces a shape. 'Where he should
sign his name, instead he draws a heart – and he puts their initials
in it. Oh, you mustn't laugh …' She can't keep the smile off her
face. 'He says he is suffering.'

He wants to say, Mary, these letters, can you steal them for
me?

'My sister says, this is not France, and I am not a fool like you,
Mary. She knows I was Henry's mistress and she sees how I'm
left. And she takes a lesson from it.'

He is almost holding his breath: but she's reckless now, she will have her say.

'I tell you, they will ride over Hell to marry. They have vowed it. Anne says she will have him and she cares not if Katherine and every Spaniard is in the sea and drowned. What Henry wants he will have, and what Anne wants she will have, and I can say that, because I know them both, who better?' Her eyes are soft and welling with tears. 'So that is why,' she says, 'why I miss William Carey, because now she is everything, and I am to be swept out after supper like the old rushes. Now I'm no one's wife, they can say anything they like to me. My father says I'm a mouth to feed and my uncle Norfolk says I'm a whore.'

As if he didn't make you one. 'Are you short of money?'

'Oh, yes!' she says. 'Yes, yes, yes, and no one has even thought about that! No one has even asked me that before. I have children. You know that. I need ...' She presses her fingers against her mouth, to stop it trembling. 'If you saw my son ... well, why do you think I called him Henry? The king would have owned him as his son, just as he has owned Richmond, but my sister forbade it. He does what she says. She means to give him a prince herself, so she doesn't want mine in his nursery.'

Reports have been sent to the cardinal: Mary Boleyn's child is a healthy boy with red-gold hair and lively appetites. She has a daughter, older, but in the context that's not so interesting, a daughter. He says, 'What age is your son now, Lady Carey?'

'Three in March. My girl Catherine is five.' Again she touches her lips, in consternation. 'I'd forgotten ... your wife died. How could I forget?' How would you even know, he wonders, but she answers him at once. 'Anne knows everything about people who work for the cardinal. She asks questions and writes the answers in a book.' She looks up at him. 'And you have children?'

'Yes ... do you know, no one ever asks me that either?' He leans one shoulder against the panelling, and she moves an inch closer, and their faces soften, perhaps, from their habitual brave distress, and into the conspiracy of the bereft. 'I have a big boy,' he says, 'he's at Cambridge with a tutor. I have a little girl called Grace; she's pretty and she has fair hair, though I don't ... My wife was not a beauty, and I am as you see. And I have Anne, Anne wants to learn Greek.'

'Goodness,' she says. 'For a woman, you know ...'

'Yes, but she says, "Why should Thomas More's daughter have the pre-eminence?" She has such good words. And she uses them all.'

'You like her best.'

'Her grandmother lives with us, and my wife's sister, but it's not ... for Anne it's not the best arrangement. I could send her into some other household, but then ... well, her Greek ... and I hardly see her as it is.' It feels like the longest speech, unless to Wolsey, that he's made for some time. He says, 'Your father should be providing properly for you. I'll ask the cardinal to speak to him.' The cardinal will enjoy that, he thinks.

'But I need a new husband. To stop them calling me names. Can the cardinal get husbands?'

'The cardinal can do anything. What kind of husband would you like?'

She considers. 'One who will take care of my children. One who can stand up to my family. One who doesn't die.' She touches her fingertips together.

'You should ask for someone young and handsome too. Don't ask, don't get.'

'Really? I was brought up in the other tradition.'

Then you had a different upbringing from your sister, he thinks. 'In the masque, at York Place, do you remember ... were you Beauty, or Kindness?'

'Oh ...' she smiles, 'that must be, what, seven years ago? I don't remember. I've dressed up so many times.'

'Of course, you are still both.'

'That's all I used to care about. Dressing up. I remember Anne, though. She was Perseverance.'

He says, 'Her particular virtue may be tested.'

Cardinal Campeggio came here with a brief from Rome to obstruct. Obstruct and delay. Do anything, but avoid giving judgment.

'Anne is always writing letters, or writing in her little book. She walks up and down, up and down. When she sees my lord father she holds up a palm to him, don't dare speak … and when she sees me, she gives me a little pinch. Like …' Mary demonstrates an airy pinch, with the fingers of her left hand. 'Like that.' She strokes the fingers of her right hand along her throat, till she reaches the little pulsing dip above her collarbone. 'There,' she says. 'Sometimes I am bruised. She thinks to disfigure me.'

'I'll talk to the cardinal,' he says.

'Do.' She waits.

He needs to go. He has things to do.

'I no longer want to be a Boleyn,' she says. 'Or a Howard. If the king would recognise my boy it would be different, but as it is I don't want any more of these masques and parties and dressing up as Virtues. They have no virtues. It's all show. If they don't want to know me, I don't want to know them. I'd rather be a beggar.'

'Really … it doesn't have to come to that, Lady Carey.'

'Do you know what I want? I want a husband who upsets them. I want to marry a man who frightens them.'

There is a sudden light in her blue eyes. An idea has dawned. She rests one delicate finger on the grey velvet she so admires, and says softly, 'Don't ask, don't get.'

Thomas Howard for an uncle? Thomas Boleyn for a father? The king, in time, for a brother?

'They'd kill you,' he says.

He thinks he shouldn't enlarge on the statement: just let it stand as fact.

She laughs, bites her lip. 'Of course. Of course they would. What am I thinking? Anyway, I'm grateful for what you have done already. For an interval of peace this morning – because when they're shouting about you, they're not shouting about me. One day,' she says, 'Anne will want to talk to you. She'll send for you and you'll be flattered. She'll have a little job for you, or she'll want some advice. So before that happens, you can have my advice. Turn around and walk the other way.'

She kisses the tip of her forefinger and touches it to his lips.

The cardinal does not need him that night, so he goes home to Austin Friars. His feeling is to put distance between himself and any Boleyns at all. There are some men, possibly, who would be fascinated by a woman who had been a mistress to two kings, but he is not one of them. He thinks about sister Anne, why she should take any interest in him; possibly she has information through what Thomas More calls 'your evangelical fraternity', and yet this is puzzling: the Boleyns don't seem like a family who think much about their souls. Uncle Norfolk has priests to do that for him. He hates ideas and never reads a book. Brother George is interested in women, hunting, clothes, jewellery and tennis. Sir Thomas Boleyn, the charming diplomat, is interested only in himself.

He would like to tell somebody what occurred. There is no one he can tell, so he tells Rafe. 'I think you imagined it,' Rafe says severely. His pale eyes open wide at the story of the initials inside the heart, but he doesn't even smile. He confines his incredulity to the marriage proposal. 'She must have meant something else.'

He shrugs; it's hard to see what. 'The Duke of Norfolk would fall on us like a pack of wolves,' Rafe says. 'He would come round and set fire to our house.' He shakes his head.

'But the pinching. What remedy?'

'Armour. Evidently,' says Rafe.

'It might raise questions.'

'Nobody's looking at Mary these days.' He adds accusingly, 'Except you.'

With the arrival of the papal legate in London, the quasi-regal household of Anne Boleyn is broken up. The king does not want the issue confused; Cardinal Campeggio is here to deal with his qualms about his marriage to Katherine, which are quite separate, he will insist, from any feelings he may entertain about Lady Anne. She is packed off to Hever, and her sister goes with her. A rumour floats back to London, that Mary is pregnant. Rafe says, 'Saving your presence, master, are you sure you only leaned against the wall?' The dead husband's family says it can't be his child, and the king is denying it too. It's sad to see the alacrity with which people assume the king is lying. How does Anne like it? She'll have time to get over her sulks, while she's rusticated. 'Mary will be pinched black and blue,' Rafe says.

People all over town tell him the gossip, without knowing quite how interested he is. It makes him sad, it makes him dubious, it makes him wonder about the Boleyns. Everything that passed between himself and Mary he now sees, hears, differently. It makes his skin creep, to think that if he had been flattered, susceptible, if he had said yes to her, he might soon have become father to a baby that looked nothing like a Cromwell and very like a Tudor. As a trick, you must admire it. Mary may look like a doll but she's not stupid. When she ran down the gallery showing her green stockings, she had a sharp eye out for prey. To the Boleyns, other people are for using and discarding. The feelings of others mean nothing, or their reputations, their family name.

He smiles, at the thought of the Cromwells having a family name. Or any reputation to defend.

Whatever has happened, nothing comes of it. Perhaps Mary was mistaken, or the talk was simply malice; God knows, the family invite it. Perhaps there was a child, and she lost it. The story peters out, with no definite conclusion. There is no baby. It is like one of the cardinal's strange fairy tales, where nature itself is perverted and women are serpents and appear and disappear at will.

Queen Katherine had a child that disappeared. In the first year of her marriage to Henry, she miscarried, but the doctors said that she was carrying twins, and the cardinal himself remembers her at court with her bodices loosened and a secret smile on her face. She took to her rooms for her confinement; after a time, she emerged tight-laced, with a flat belly, and no baby.

It must be a Tudor speciality.

A little later, he hears that Anne has taken the wardship of her sister's son, Henry Carey. He wonders if she intends to poison him. Or eat him.

New Year 1529: Stephen Gardiner is in Rome, issuing certain threats to Pope Clement, on the king's behalf; the content of the threats has not been divulged to the cardinal. Clement is easily panicked at the best of times, and it is not surprising that, with Master Stephen breathing sulphur in his ear, he falls ill. They are saying that he is likely to die, and the cardinal's agents are around and about in Europe, taking soundings and counting heads, chinking their purses cheerfully. There would be a swift solution to the king's problem, if Wolsey were Pope. He grumbles a little about his possible eminence; the cardinal loves his country, its May garlands, its tender birdsong. In his nightmares he sees squat spitting Italians, a forest of nooses, a corpse-strewn plain. 'I shall want you to come with me, Thomas. You can stand by my side and move quick if any of those cardinals tries to stab me.'

He pictures his master stuck full of knives, as St Sebastian is stuck full of arrows. 'Why does the Pope have to be in Rome? Where is it written?'

A slow smile spreads over the cardinal's face. 'Bring the Holy See home. Why not?' He loves a bold plan. 'I couldn't bring it to

London, I suppose? If only I were Archbishop of Canterbury, I could hold my papal court at Lambeth Palace … but old Warham does hang on and on, he always baulks me …'

'Your Grace could move to your own see.'

'York is so remote. I couldn't have the papacy in Winchester, you don't think? Our ancient English capital? And nearer the king?'

What an unusual regime this will turn out to be. The king at supper, with the Pope, who is also his Lord Chancellor … Will the king have to hand him his napkin, and serve him first?

When news comes of Clement's recovery, the cardinal doesn't say, a glorious chance lost. He says, Thomas, what shall we do next? We must open the legatine court, it can be no longer delayed. He says, 'Go and find me a man called Anthony Poynes.'

He stands, arms folded, waiting for further and better particulars.

'Try the Isle of Wight. And fetch me Sir William Thomas, whom I believe you will find in Carmarthen – he's elderly, so tell your men to go slowly.'

'I don't employ anyone slow.' He nods. 'Still, I take the point. Don't kill the witnesses.'

The trial of the king's great matter is approaching. The king intends to show that when Queen Katherine came to him she was not a virgin, having consummated her marriage with his brother Arthur. To that end he is assembling the gentlemen who attended the royal couple after their wedding at Baynard's Castle, then later at Windsor, where the court moved in November that year, and later at Ludlow, where they were sent to play at Prince and Princess of Wales. 'Arthur,' Wolsey says, 'would have been about your age, Thomas, if he had lived.' The attendants, the witnesses, are at least a generation older. And so many years have gone by – twenty-eight, to be precise. How good can their memories be?

143

It should never have come to this – to this public and unseemly exposure. Cardinal Campeggio has implored Katherine to bow to the king's will, accept that her marriage is invalid and retire to a convent. Certainly, she says sweetly, she will become a nun: if the king will become a monk.

Meanwhile she presents reasons why the legatine court should not try the issue. It is still *sub judice* at Rome, for one thing. For another, she is a stranger, she says, in a strange country; she ignores the decades in which she's been intimate with every twist and turn of English policy. The judges, she claims, are biased against her; certainly, she has reason to believe it. Campeggio lays hand on heart, and assures her he would give an honest judgment, even if he were in fear of his life. Katherine finds him too intimate with his co-legate; anyone who has spent much time with Wolsey, she thinks, no longer knows what honesty is.

Who is advising Katherine? John Fisher, Bishop of Rochester. 'Do you know what I can't endure about that man?' the cardinal says. 'He's all skin and bone. I abhor your skeletal prelate. It makes the rest of us look bad. One looks … corporeal.'

He is in his corporeal pomp, his finest scarlet, when the king and queen are summoned before the two cardinals at Blackfriars. Everyone had supposed that Katherine would send a proxy, but instead she appears in person. The whole bench of bishops is assembled. The king answers to his name, in a full, echoing voice, speaking out of his big bejewelled chest. He, Cromwell, would have advised a motion of the hand, a murmur, a dip of the head to the court's authority. Most humility, in his view, is pretence; but the pretence can be winning.

The hall is packed. He and Rafe are far-off spectators. Afterwards, when the queen has made her statement – a few men have been seen to cry – they come out into the sunshine. Rafe says, 'If we had been nearer, we could have seen whether the king could meet her eye.'

'Yes. That is really all anyone needs to know.'

'I'm sorry to say it, but I believe Katherine.'

'Hush. Believe nobody.'

Something blots out the light. It is Stephen Gardiner, black and scowling, his aspect in no way improved by his trip to Rome.

'Master Stephen!' he says. 'How was your journey home? Never pleasant, is it, to come back empty-handed? I've been feeling sorry for you. I suppose you did your best, such as it is.'

Gardiner's scowl deepens. 'If this court can't give the king what he wants, your master will be finished. And then it is I who will feel sorry for you.'

'Except you won't.'

'Except I won't,' Gardiner concedes; and moves on.

The queen does not return for the sordid parts of the proceedings. Her counsel speaks for her; she has told her confessor how her nights with Arthur left her untouched, and she has given him permission to break the seal of the confessional and make her assertion public. She has spoken before the highest court there is, God's court; would she lie, to the damnation of her soul?

Besides, there is another point, which everyone has in mind. After Arthur died, she was presented to prospective bridegrooms – to the old king, as it may be, or to the young Prince Henry – as fresh meat. They could have brought a doctor, who would have looked at her. She would have been frightened, she would have cried; but she would have complied. Perhaps now she wishes it had been so; that they had brought in a strange man with cold hands. But they never asked her to prove what she claimed; perhaps people were not so shameless in those days. The dispensations for her marriage to Henry were meant to cover either case: she was/was not a virgin. The Spanish documents are different from the English documents, and that is where we should be now, among the subclauses, studying paper and ink, not squabbling in a court of law over a shred of skin and a splash of blood on a linen sheet.

If he had been her adviser, he would have kept the queen in court, however much she squealed. Because, would the witnesses have spoken, to her face, as they spoke behind her back? She would be ashamed to face them, gnarled and grizzled and each equipped with perfect recollection; but he would have had her greet them cordially, and declare she would never have recognised them, after so much time gone by; and ask if they have grandchildren, and whether the summer heat eases their elderly aches and pains? The greater shame would be theirs: would they not hesitate, would they not falter, under the steady gaze of the queen's honest eyes?

Without Katherine present, the trial becomes a bawdy entertainment. The Earl of Shrewsbury is before the court, a man who fought with the old king at Bosworth. He recalls his own long-ago wedding night, when he was, like Prince Arthur, a boy of fifteen; never had a woman before, he says, but did his duty to his bride. On Arthur's wedding night, he and the Earl of Oxford had taken the prince to Katherine's chamber. Yes, says the Marquis of Dorset, and I was there too; Katherine lay under the coverlet, the prince got into bed beside her. 'No one is willing to swear to having climbed in with them,' Rafe whispers. 'But I wonder they haven't found someone.'

The court must make do with evidence of what was said next morning. The prince, coming out of the bridal chamber, said he was thirsty and asked Sir Anthony Willoughby for a cup of ale. 'Last night I was in Spain,' he said. A little boy's crude joke, dragged back into the light; the boy has been, these thirty years, a corpse. How lonely it is to die young, to go down into the dark without any company! Maurice St John is not there with him, in his vault at Worcester Cathedral: nor Mr Cromer nor William Woodall, nor any of the men who heard him say, 'Masters, it is good pastime to have a wife.'

When they have listened to all this, and they come out into the air, he feels strangely cold. He puts a hand to his face, touches his cheekbone. Rafe says, 'It would be a poor sort of bridegroom who would come out in the morning and say, "Good day, masters. Nothing done!" He was boasting, wasn't he? That was all. They've forgotten what it's like to be fifteen.'

Even as the court is sitting, King François in Italy is losing a battle. Pope Clement is preparing to sign a new treaty with the Emperor, Queen Katherine's nephew. He doesn't know this when he says, 'This is a bad day's work. If we want Europe to laugh at us, they've every reason now.'

He looks sideways at Rafe, whose particular problem, clearly, is that he cannot imagine anyone, even a hasty fifteen-year-old, wanting to penetrate Katherine. It would be like copulation with a statue. Rafe, of course, has not heard the cardinal on the subject of the queen's former attractions. 'Well, I reserve judgment. Which is what the court will do. It's all they can do.' He says, 'Rafe, you are so much closer in these matters. I can't remember being fifteen.'

'Surely? Were you not fifteen or so when you fetched up in France?'

'Yes, I must have been.' Wolsey: 'Arthur would have been about your age, Thomas, if he had lived.' He remembers a woman in Dover, up against a wall; her small crushable bones, her young, bleak, pallid face. He feels a small sensation of panic, loss; what if the cardinal's joke isn't a joke, and the earth is strewn with his children, and he has never done right by them? It is the only honest thing to be done: look after your children. 'Rafe,' he says, 'do you know I haven't made my will? I said I would but I never did. I think I should go home and draft it.'

'Why?' Rafe looks amazed. 'Why now? The cardinal will want you.'

'Come home.' He takes Rafe's arm. On his left side, a hand touches his: fingers without flesh. A ghost walks: Arthur, studious and pale. King Henry, he thinks, you raised him; now you put him down.

* * *

July 1529: Thomas Cromwell of London, gentleman. Being whole in body and memory. To his son Gregory six hundred and sixty-six pounds thirteen shillings and four pence. And feather-beds, bolsters and the quilt of yellow turkey satin, the joined bed of Flanders work and the carved press and the cupboards, the silver and the silver gilt and twelve silver spoons. And leases of farms to be held for him by the executors till he comes to full age, and another two hundred pounds for him in gold at that date. Money to the executors for the upbringing and marriage portions of his daughter Anne, and his little daughter Grace. A marriage portion for his niece Alice Wellyfed; gowns, jackets and doublets to his nephews; to Mercy all sorts of household stuff and some silver and anything else the executors think she should have. Bequests to his dead wife's sister Johane, and her husband John Williamson, and a marriage portion to her daughter, also Johane. Money to his servants. Forty pounds to be divided between forty poor maidens on their marriage. Twenty pounds for mending the roads. Ten pounds towards feeding poor prisoners in the London gaols.

His body to be buried in the parish where he dies: or at the direction of his executors.

The residue of his estate to be spent on Masses for his parents.

To God his soul. To Rafe Sadler his books.

When the summer plague comes back, he says to Mercy and Johane, shall we send the children out?

In which direction, Johane says: not challenging him, just wanting to know.

Mercy says, can anyone outrun it? They take comfort from a belief that since the infection killed so many last year, it won't be so violent this year; which he does not think is necessarily true, and he thinks they seem to be endowing this plague with a human or at least bestial intelligence: the wolf comes down on the sheepfold, but not on the nights when the men with dogs are waiting for him. Unless they think the plague is more than bestial or human – that it is God behind it – God, up to his old tricks. When he hears the bad news from Italy, about Clement's new treaty with the Emperor, Wolsey bows his head and says, 'My Master is capricious.' He doesn't mean the king.

On the last day of July, Cardinal Campeggio adjourns the legatine court. It is, he says, the Roman holidays. News comes that the Duke of Suffolk, the king's great friend, has hammered the table before Wolsey, and threatened him to his face. They all know the court will never sit again. They all know the cardinal has failed.

That evening with Wolsey he believes, for the first time, that the cardinal will come down. If he falls, he thinks, I come down with him. His reputation is black. It is as if the cardinal's joke has been incarnated: as if he wades through streams of blood, leaving in his wake a trail of smashed glass and fires, of widows and orphans. Cromwell, people say: that's a bad man. The cardinal will not talk about what is happening in Italy, or what has happened in the legate's court. He says, 'They tell me the sweating sickness is back. What shall I do? Shall I die? I have fought four bouts with it. In the year … what year? … I think it was 1518 … now you will laugh, but it was so – when the sweat had finished with me, I looked like Bishop Fisher. My flesh was wasted. God picked me up and rattled my teeth.'

'Your Grace was wasted?' he says, trying to raise a smile. 'I wish you'd had your portrait made then.'

Bishop Fisher has said in court – just before the Roman holidays set in – that no power, human or divine, could dissolve the marriage of the king and queen. If there's one thing he'd like to teach Fisher, it's not to make grand overstatements. He has an idea of what the law can do, and it's different from what Bishop Fisher thinks.

Until now, every day till today, every evening till this, if you told Wolsey a thing was impossible, he'd just laugh. Tonight he says – when he can be brought to the point – my friend King François is beaten and I am beaten too. I don't know what to do. Plague or no plague, I think I may die.

'I must go home,' he says. 'But will you bless me?'

He kneels before him. Wolsey raises his hand, and then, as if he has forgotten what he's doing, lets it hover in mid-air. He says, 'Thomas, I am not ready to meet God.'

He looks up, smiling. 'Perhaps God is not ready to meet you.'

'I hope that you will be with me when I die.'

'But that will be at some distant date.'

He shakes his head. 'If you had seen how Suffolk set on me today. He, Norfolk, Thomas Boleyn, Thomas Lord Darcy, they have been waiting only for this, for my failure with this court, and now I hear they are devising a book of articles, they are drawing up a list of accusations, how I have reduced the nobility, and so forth – they are making a book called – what will they call it? – "Twenty Years of Insults"? They are brewing some stewpot into which they are pouring the dregs of every slight, as they conceive it, by which they mean every piece of truth I have told them …' He takes a great rattling breath, and looks at the ceiling, which is embossed with the Tudor rose.

'There will be no such stewpots in Your Grace's kitchen,' he says. He gets up. He looks at the cardinal, and all he can see is more work to be done.

'Liz Wykys,' Mercy says, 'wouldn't have wanted her girls dragged about the countryside. Especially as Anne, to my knowledge, cries if she does not see you.'

'Anne?' He is amazed. 'Anne cries?'

'What did you think?' Mercy asks, with some asperity. 'Do you think your children don't love you?'

He lets her make the decision. The girls stay at home. It's the wrong decision. Mercy hangs outside their door the signs of the sweating sickness. She says, how has this happened? We scour, we scrub the floors, I do not think you will find in the whole of London a cleaner house than ours. We say our prayers. I have never seen a child pray as Anne does. She prays as if she's going into battle.

Anne falls ill first. Mercy and Johane shout at her and shake her to keep her awake, since they say if you sleep you will die. But the pull of the sickness is stronger than they are, and she falls exhausted against the bolster, struggling for breath, and falls further, into black stillness, only her hand moving, the fingers clenching and unclenching. He takes it in his own and tries to still it, but it is like the hand of a soldier itching for a fight.

Later she rouses herself, asks for her mother. She asks for the copybook in which she has written her name. At dawn the fever breaks. Johane bursts into tears of relief, and Mercy sends her away to sleep. Anne struggles to sit up, she sees him clearly, she smiles, she says his name. They bring a basin of water strewn with rose petals, and wash her face; her finger reaches out, tentative, to push the petals below the water, so each of them becomes a vessel shipping water, a cup, a perfumed grail.

But when the sun comes up her fever rises again. He will not let them begin it again, the pinching and pummelling, the shaking; he gives her into God's hands, and asks God to be good to him. He talks to her but she makes no sign that she hears. He is not, himself, afraid of contagion. If the cardinal can survive this plague four times, I am sure I am in no danger, and if I die, I have made my will. He sits with her, watching her chest heaving, watching her fight and lose. He is not there when she dies – Grace has already taken sick, and he is seeing her put to bed. So he is out of the room, just, and when they usher him in, her stern little face has relaxed into sweetness. She looks passive, placid; her hand is already heavy, and heavy beyond his bearing.

He comes out of the room; he says, 'She was already learning Greek.' Of course, Mercy says: she was a wonderful child, and your true daughter. She leans against his shoulder and cries. She says, 'She was clever and good, and in her way, you know, she was beautiful.'

His thought had been: she was learning Greek: perhaps she knows it now.

Grace dies in his arms; she dies easily, as naturally as she was born. He eases her back against the damp sheet: a child of impossible perfection, her fingers uncurling like thin white leaves. I never knew her, he thinks; I never knew I had her. It has always seemed impossible to him that some act of his gave her life, some unthinking thing that he and Liz did, on some unmemorable night. They had intended the name to be Henry for a boy, Katherine for a girl, and, Liz had said, that will do honour to your Kat as well. But when he had seen her, swaddled, beautiful, finished and perfect, he had said quite another thing, and Liz had agreed. We cannot earn grace. We do not merit it.

He asks the priest if his elder daughter can be buried with her copybook, in which she has written her name: Anne Cromwell. The priest says he has never heard of such a thing. He is too tired and angry to fight.

His daughters are now in Purgatory, a country of slow fires and ridged ice. Where in the Gospels does it say 'Purgatory'?

Tyndale says, now abideth faith, hope and love, even these three; but the greatest of these is love.

Thomas More thinks it is a wicked mistranslation. He insists on 'charity'. He would chain you up, for a mistranslation. He would, for a difference in your Greek, kill you.

He wonders again if the dead need translators; perhaps in a moment, in a simple twist of unbecoming, they know everything they need to know.

Tyndale says, 'Love never falleth away.'

October comes in. Wolsey presides, as usual, over the meetings of the king's council. But in the law courts, as Michaelmas term opens, writs are moved against the cardinal. He is charged with success. He is charged with the exercise of power. Specifically, he is charged with asserting a foreign jurisdiction in the king's realm – that is to say, with exercising his role as papal legate. What they mean to say is this: he is *alter rex*. He is, he has always been, more imperious than the king. For that, if it is a crime, he is guilty.

So now they swagger into York Place, the Duke of Suffolk, the Duke of Norfolk: the two great peers of the realm. Suffolk, his blond beard bristling, looks like a pig among truffles; a florid man, he remembers, turns my lord cardinal sick. Norfolk looks apprehensive, and as he turns over the cardinal's possessions, it is clear that he expects to find wax figures, perhaps of himself, perhaps with long pins stuck through them. The cardinal has done his feats by a compact with the devil; that is his fixed opinion.

He, Cromwell, sends them away. They come back. They come back with further and higher commissions and better signatures, and they bring with them the Master of the Rolls. They take the Great Seal from my lord cardinal.

Norfolk glances sideways at him, and gives him a fleeting, ferrety grin. He doesn't know why.

'Come and see me,' the duke says.

'Why, my lord?'

Norfolk turns down his mouth. He never explains.

'When?'

'No hurry,' Norfolk says. 'Come when you've mended your manners.'

It is 19 October 1529.

III

Make or Mar

All Hallows 1529

Halloween: the world's edge seeps and bleeds. This is the time when the tally-keepers of Purgatory, its clerks and gaolers, listen in to the living, who are praying for the dead.

At this time of year, with their parish, he and Liz would keep vigil. They would pray for Henry Wykys, her father; for Liz's dead husband, Thomas Williams; for Walter Cromwell, and for distant cousins; for half-forgotten names, long-dead half-sisters and lost step-children.

Last night he kept the vigil alone. He lay awake, wishing Liz back; waiting for her to come and lie beside him. It's true he is at Esher with the cardinal, not at home at the Austin Friars. But, he thought, she'll know how to find me. She'll look for the cardinal, drawn through the space between worlds by incense and candle-light. Wherever the cardinal is, I will be.

At some point he must have slept. When daylight came, the room felt so empty it was empty even of him.

All Hallows Day: grief comes in waves. Now it threatens to capsize him. He doesn't believe that the dead come back; but that doesn't stop him from feeling the brush of their fingertips, wing-tips, against his shoulder. Since last night they have been less individual forms and faces than a solid aggregated mass, their flesh slapping and jostling together, their texture dense like sea creatures, their faces sick with an undersea sheen.

Now he stands in a window embrasure, Liz's prayer book in hand. His daughter Grace liked to look at it, and today he can feel the imprint of her small fingers under his own. These are Our Lady's prayers for the canonical hours, the pages illuminated by a dove, a vase of lilies. The office is Matins, and Mary kneels on a floor of chequered tiles. The angel greets her, and the words of his greeting are written on a scroll, which unfurls from his clasped hands as if his palms are speaking. His wings are coloured: heaven-blue.

He turns the page. The office is Lauds. Here is a picture of the Visitation. Mary, with her neat little belly, is greeted by her pregnant cousin, St Elizabeth. Their foreheads are high, their brows plucked, and they look surprised, as indeed they must be; one of them is a virgin, the other advanced in years. Spring flowers grow at their feet, and each of them wears an airy crown, made of gilt wires as fine as blonde hairs.

He turns a page. Grace, silent and small, turns the page with him. The office is Prime. The picture is the Nativity: a tiny white Jesus lies in the folds of his mother's cloak. The office is Sext: the Magi proffer jewelled cups; behind them is a city on a hill, a city in Italy, with its bell tower, its view of rising ground and its misty line of trees. The office is None: Joseph carries a basket of doves to the temple. The office is Vespers: a dagger sent by Herod makes a neat hole in a shocked infant. A woman throws up her hands in protest, or prayer: her eloquent, helpless palms. The infant corpse scatters three drops of blood, each one shaped like a tear. Each bloody tear is a precise vermilion.

He looks up. Like an after-image, the form of the tears swims in his eyes; the picture blurs. He blinks. Someone is walking towards him. It is George Cavendish. His hands wash together, his face is a mask of concern.

Let him not speak to me, he prays. Let George pass on.

'Master Cromwell,' he says, 'I believe you are crying. What is this? Is there bad news about our master?'

He tries to close Liz's book, but Cavendish reaches out for it. 'Ah, you are praying.' He looks amazed.

Cavendish cannot see his daughter's fingers touching the page, or his wife's hands holding the book. George simply looks at the pictures, upside down. He takes a deep breath and says, 'Thomas …?'

'I am crying for myself,' he says. 'I am going to lose everything, everything I have worked for, all my life, because I will go down with the cardinal – no, George, don't interrupt me – because I have done what he asked me to do, and been his friend, and the man at his right hand. If I had stuck to my work in the city, instead of hurtling about the countryside making enemies, I'd be a rich man – and you, George, I'd be inviting you out to my new country house, and asking your advice on furniture and flower beds. But look at me! I'm finished.'

George tries to speak: he utters a consolatory bleat.

'Unless,' he says. 'Unless, George. What do you think? I've sent my boy Rafe to Westminster.'

'What will he do there?'

But he is crying again. The ghosts are gathering, he feels cold, his position is irretrievable. In Italy he learned a memory system, so he can remember everything: every stage of how he got here. 'I think,' he says, 'I should go after him.'

'Please,' says Cavendish, 'not before dinner.'

'No?'

'Because we need to think how to pay off my lord's servants.'

A moment passes. He enfolds the prayer book to himself; he holds it in his arms. Cavendish has given him what he needs: an accountancy problem. 'George,' he says, 'you know my lord's chaplains have flocked here after him, all of them earning – what? – a hundred, two hundred pounds a year, out of his liberality? So,

I think … we will make the chaplains and the priests pay off the household servants, because what I think is, what I notice is, that his servants love my lord more than his priests do. So, now, let's go to dinner, and after dinner I will make the priests ashamed, and I will make them open their veins and bleed money. We need to give the household a quarter's wages at least, and a retainer. Against the day of my lord's restoration.'

'Well,' says George, 'if anyone can do it, you can.'

He finds himself smiling. Perhaps it's a grim smile, but he never thought he would smile today. He says, 'When that's done, I shall leave you. I shall be back as soon as I have made sure of a place in the Parliament.'

'But it meets in two days … How will you manage it now?'

'I don't know, but someone must speak for my lord. Or they will kill him.'

He sees the hurt and shock; he wants to take the words back; but it is true. He says, 'I can only try. I'll make or mar, before I see you again.'

George almost bows. 'Make or mar,' he murmurs. 'It was ever your common saying.'

Cavendish walks about the household, saying, Thomas Cromwell was reading a prayer book. Thomas Cromwell was crying. Only now does George realise how bad things are.

Once, in Thessaly, there was a poet called Simonides. He was commissioned to appear at a banquet, given by a man called Scopas, and recite a lyric in praise of his host. Poets have strange vagaries, and in his lyric Simonides incorporated verses in praise of Castor and Pollux, the Heavenly Twins. Scopas was sulky, and said he would pay only half the fee: 'As for the rest, get it from the Twins.'

A little later, a servant came into the hall. He whispered to Simonides; there were two young men outside, asking for him by name.

He rose and left the banqueting hall. He looked around for the two young men, but he could see no one.

As he turned back, to go and finish his dinner, he heard a terrible noise, of stone splitting and crumbling. He heard the cries of the dying, as the roof of the hall collapsed. Of all the diners, he was the only one left alive.

The bodies were so broken and disfigured that the relatives of the dead could not identify them. But Simonides was a remarkable man. Whatever he saw was imprinted on his mind. He led each of the relatives through the ruins; and pointing to the crushed remains, he said, there is your man. In linking the dead to their names, he worked from the seating plan in his head.

It is Cicero who tells us this story. He tells us how, on that day, Simonides invented the art of memory. He remembered the names, the faces, some sour and bloated, some blithe, some bored. He remembered exactly where everyone was sitting, at the moment the roof fell in.

PART THREE

I
Three-Card Trick
Winter 1529–Spring 1530

Johane: 'You say, "Rafe, go and find me a seat in the new Parliament." And off he goes, like a girl who's been told to bring the washing in.'

'It was harder than that,' Rafe says.

Johane says, 'How would you know?'

Seats in the Commons are, largely, in the gift of lords; of lords, bishops, the king himself. A scanty handful of electors, if pressured from above, usually do as they're told.

Rafe has got him Taunton. It's Wolsey terrain; they wouldn't have let him in if the king had not said yes, if Thomas Howard had not said yes. He had sent Rafe to London to scout the uncertain territory of the duke's intentions: to find out what lies behind that ferrety grin. '*Am obliged, Master.*'

Now he knows. 'The Duke of Norfolk,' Rafe says, 'believes my lord cardinal has buried treasure, and he thinks you know where it is.'

They talk alone. Rafe: 'He'll ask you to go and work for him.'

'Yes. Perhaps not in so many words.'

He watches Rafe's face as he weighs up the situation. Norfolk is already – unless you count the king's bastard son – the realm's premier nobleman. 'I assured him,' Rafe says, 'of your respect, your ... your reverence, your desire to be at his – erm –'

'Commandment?'

'More or less.'

'And what did he say?'

'He said, hmm.'

He laughs. 'And was that his tone?'

'It was his tone.'

'And his grim nod?'

'Yes.'

Very well. I dry my tears, those tears from All Hallows day. I sit with the cardinal, by the fire at Esher in a room with a smoking chimney. I say, my lord, do you think I would forsake you? I locate the man in charge of chimneys and hearths. I give him orders. I ride to London, to Blackfriars. The day is foggy, St Hubert's Day. Norfolk is waiting, to tell me he will be a good lord to me.

The duke is now approaching sixty years old, but concedes nothing to the calendar. Flint-faced and keen-eyed, he is lean as a gnawed bone and as cold as an axe head; his joints seem knitted together of supple chain links, and indeed he rattles a little as he moves, for his clothes conceal relics: in tiny jewelled cases he has shavings of skin and snippets of hair, and set into medallions he wears splinters of martyrs' bones. 'Marry!' he says, for an oath, and 'By the Mass!', and sometimes takes out one of his medals or charms from wherever it is hung about his person, and kisses it in a fervour, calling on some saint or martyr to stop his current rage getting the better of him. 'St Jude give me patience!' he will shout; probably he has mixed him up with Job, whom he heard about in a story when he was a little boy at the knee of his first priest. It is hard to imagine the duke as a little boy, or in any way younger or different from the self he presents now. He thinks the Bible a book unnecessary for laypeople, though he understands priests make some use of it. He thinks book-reading an affectation altogether, and wishes there were less of it at court. His niece is always reading, Anne Boleyn, which is perhaps why she is unmarried at the age of twenty-eight. He does not see why it's a gentleman's business to write letters; there are clerks for that.

Now he fixes an eye, red and fiery. 'Cromwell, I am content you are a burgess in the Parliament.'

He bows his head. 'My lord.'

'I spoke to the king for you and he is also content. You will take his instructions in the Commons. And mine.'

'Will they be the same, my lord?'

The duke scowls. He paces; he rattles a little; at last he bursts out, 'Damn it all, Cromwell, why are you such a ... *person*? It isn't as if you could afford to be.'

He waits, smiling. He knows what the duke means. He is a person, he is a presence. He knows how to edge blackly into a room so that you don't see him; but perhaps those days are over.

'Smile away,' says the duke. 'Wolsey's household is a nest of vipers. Not that ...' he touches a medal, flinching, 'God forbid I should ...'

Compare a prince of the church to a serpent. The duke wants the cardinal's money, and he wants the cardinal's place at the king's side: but then again, he doesn't want to burn in Hell. He walks across the room; he slaps his hands together; he rubs them; he turns. 'The king is preparing to quarrel with you, master. Oh yes. He will favour you with an interview because he wishes to understand the cardinal's affairs, but he has, you will learn, a very long and exact memory, and what he remembers, master, is when you were a burgess of the Parliament before this, and how you spoke against his war.'

'I hope he doesn't think still of invading France.'

'God damn you! What Englishman does not! We own France. We have to take back our own.' A muscle in his cheek jumps; he paces, agitated; he turns, he rubs his cheek; the twitch stops, and he says, in a voice perfectly matter-of-fact, 'Mind you, you're right.'

He waits. 'We can't win,' the duke says, 'but we have to fight as if we can. Hang the expense. Hang the waste – money, men, horses, ships. That's what's wrong with Wolsey, you see. Always at the treaty table. How can a butcher's son understand –'

'*La gloire?*'

'Are you a butcher's son?'

'A blacksmith's.'

'Are you really? Shoe a horse?'

He shrugs. 'If I were put to it, my lord. But I can't imagine –'

'You can't? What can you imagine? A battlefield, a camp, the night before a battle – can you imagine that?'

'I was a soldier myself.'

'Were you so? Not in any English army, I'll be bound. There, you see.' The duke grins, quite without animosity. 'I knew there was something about you. I knew I didn't like you, but I couldn't put my finger on it. Where were you?'

'Garigliano.'

'With?'

'The French.'

The duke whistles. 'Wrong side, lad.'

'So I noticed.'

'With the French,' he chuckles. 'With the French. And how did you scramble out of that disaster?'

'I went north. Got into ...' He's going to say money, but the duke wouldn't understand trading in money. 'Cloth,' he says. 'Silk, mostly. You know what the market is, with the soldier over there.'

'By the Mass, yes! Johnnie Freelance – he puts his money on his back. Those Switzers! Like a troupe of play-actors. Lace, stripes, fancy hats. Easy target, that's all. Longbowman?'

'Now and then.' He smiles. 'On the short side for that.'

'Me too. Now, Henry draws a bow. Very nice. Got the height for it. Got the arm. Still. We won't win many battles like that any more.'

'Then how about not fighting any? Negotiate, my lord. It's cheaper.'

'I tell you, Cromwell, you've got face, coming here.'

'My lord – you sent for me.'

'Did I?' Norfolk looks alarmed. 'It's come to that?'

The king's advisers are preparing no fewer than forty-four charges against the cardinal. They range from the violation of the statutes of praemunire – that is to say, the upholding of a foreign jurisdiction within the king's realm – to buying beef for his household at the same price as the king; from financial malfeasance to failing to halt the spread of Lutheran heresies.

The law of praemunire dates from another century. No one who is alive now quite knows what it means. From day to day it seems to mean what the king says it means. The matter is argued in every talking shop in Europe. Meanwhile, my lord cardinal sits, and sometimes mutters to himself, and sometimes speaks aloud, saying, 'Thomas, my colleges! Whatever happens to my person, my colleges must be saved. Go to the king. Whatever vengeance, for whatever imagined injury, he would like to wreak on me, he surely cannot mean to put out the light of learning?'

In exile at Esher, the cardinal paces and frets. The great mind which once revolved the affairs of Europe now cogitates ceaselessly on its own losses. He lapses into silent inactivity, brooding as the light fails; for God's sake, Thomas, Cavendish begs him, don't tell him you're coming if you're not.

I won't, he says, and I am coming, but sometimes I am held up. The House sits late and before I leave Westminster I have to gather up the letters and petitions to my lord cardinal, and talk with all the people who want to send messages but don't want them put into writing.

I understand, Cavendish says; but Thomas, he wails, you can't imagine what it's like here at Esher. What time is it? my lord cardinal says. What time will Cromwell be here? And in an hour, again: Cavendish, what time is it? He has us out with lights, and reporting on the weather; as if you, Cromwell, were a person to be impeded by hailstorms or ice. Then next he will ask, what if he has met with some accident on the road? The road from London is full of robbers; wasteland and heathland, as the light fails, are creeping with the agents of malefice. From that he will pass on to say, this world is full of snares and delusions, and into many of them I have fallen, miserable sinner that I am.

When he, Cromwell, finally throws off his riding cloak and collapses into a chair by the fire – *God's blood*, that smoking chimney – the cardinal is at him before he can draw breath. What said my lord of Suffolk? How looked my lord of Norfolk? The king, have you seen him, did he speak to you? And Lady Anne, is she in health and good looks? Have you worked any device to please her – because we must please her, you know?

He says, 'There is one short way to please that lady, and that is to crown her queen.' He closes his lips on the topic of Anne and has no more to say. Mary Boleyn says she has noticed him, but till recently Anne gave no sign of it. Her eyes passed over him on their way to someone who interested her more. They are black eyes, slightly protuberant, shiny like the beads of an abacus; they are shiny and always in motion, as she makes calculations of her own advantage. But Uncle Norfolk must have said to her, 'There goes the man who knows the cardinal's secrets,' because now when he comes into her sight her long neck darts; those shining black beads go click, click, as she looks him up and down and decides what use can be got out of him. He supposes she is in health, as the year creeps towards its end; not coughing like a sick horse, for instance, nor gone lame. He supposes she is in good looks, if that's what you like.

One night, just before Christmas, he arrives late at Esher and the cardinal is sitting alone, listening to a boy play the lute. He says, 'Mark, thank you, go now.' The boy bows to the cardinal; he favours him, barely, with the nod suitable for a burgess in the Parliament. As he withdraws from the room the cardinal says, 'Mark is very adept, and a pleasant boy – at York Place, he was one of my choristers. I think I shouldn't keep him here, but send him to the king. Or to Lady Anne, perhaps, as he is such a pretty young thing. Would she like him?'

The boy has lingered at the door to drink in his praises. A hard Cromwellian stare – the equivalent of a kick – sends him out. He wishes people would not ask him what the Lady Anne would and would not like.

The cardinal says, 'Does Lord Chancellor More send me any message?'

He drops a sheaf of papers on the table. 'You look ill, my lord.'

'Yes, I am ill. Thomas, what shall we do?'

'We shall bribe people,' he says. 'We shall be liberal and open-handed with the assets Your Grace has left – for you still have benefices to dispose of, you still have land. Listen, my lord – even if the king takes all you have, people will be asking, can the king truly bestow what belongs to the cardinal? No one to whom he makes a grant will be sure in their title, unless you confirm it. So you still have, my lord, you still have cards in your hand.'

'And after all, if he meant to bring a treason ...' his voice falters, 'if ...'

'If he meant to charge you with treason you would be in the Tower by now.'

'Indeed – and what use would I be to him, head in one place, body in another? This is how it is: the king thinks, by degrading me, to give a sharp lesson to the Pope. He thinks to indicate, I as King of England am master in my own house. Oh, but is he? Or is Lady Anne master, or Thomas Boleyn? A question not to be asked, not outside this room.'

The battle is, now, to get the king alone; to find out his intentions, if he knows them himself, and broker a deal. The cardinal
urgently needs ready cash, that's the first skirmish. Day after day,
he waits for an interview. The king extends a hand, takes from
him what letters he proffers, glancing at the cardinal's seal. He
does not look at him, saying merely an absent 'Thanks.' One day
he does look at him, and says, 'Master Cromwell, yes ... I cannot
talk about the cardinal.' And as he opens his mouth to speak, the
king says, 'Don't you understand? I cannot talk about him.' His
tone is gentle, puzzled. 'Another day,' he says. 'I will send for
you. I promise.'

When the cardinal asks him, 'How did the king look today?'
he says, he looks as if he does not sleep.

The cardinal laughs. 'If he does not sleep it is because he does
not hunt. This icy ground is too hard for the hounds' pads, they
cannot go out. It is lack of fresh air, Thomas. It is not his
conscience.'

Later, he will remember that night towards the end of December when he found the cardinal listening to music. He will run it
through his mind, twice and over again.

Because as he is leaving the cardinal, and contemplating again
the road, the night, he hears a boy's voice, speaking behind a half-
open door: it is Mark, the lute-player. '... so for my skill he says
he will prefer me to Lady Anne. And I shall be glad, because
what is the use of being here when any day the king may behead
the old fellow? I think he ought, for the cardinal is so proud.
Today is the first day he ever gave me a good word.'

A pause. Someone speaks, muffled; he cannot tell who. Then
the boy: 'Yes, for sure the lawyer will come down with him. I say
lawyer, but who is he? Nobody knows. They say he has killed men
with his own hands and never told it in confession. But those hard
kinds of men, they always weep when they see the hangman.'

He is in no doubt that it is his own execution Mark looks
forward to. Beyond the wall, the boy runs on: 'So when I am

with Lady Anne she is sure to notice me, and give me presents.' A giggle. 'And look on me with favour. Don't you think? Who knows where she may turn while she is still refusing the king?'

A pause. Then Mark: 'She is no maid. Not she.'

What an enchanting conversation: servants' talk. Again comes a muffled answer, and then Mark: 'Could she be at the French court, do you think, and come home a maid? Any more than her sister could? And Mary was every man's hackney.'

But this is nothing. He is disappointed. I had hopes of particulars; this is just the *on dit*. But still he hesitates, and doesn't move away.

'Besides, Tom Wyatt has had her, and everybody knows it, down in Kent. I have been down to Penshurst with the cardinal, and you know that palace is near to Hever, where the lady's family is, and the Wyatts' house an easy ride away.'

Witnesses? Dates?

But then, from the unseen person, 'Shh!' Again, a soft giggle.

One can do nothing with this. Except bear it in mind. The conversation is in Flemish: language of Mark's birthplace.

Christmas comes, and the king, with Queen Katherine, keeps it at Greenwich. Anne is at York Place; the king can come upriver to see her. Her company, the women say, is exacting; the king's visits are short, few and discreet.

At Esher the cardinal takes to his bed. Once he would never have done that, though he looks ill enough to justify it. He says, 'Nothing will happen while the king and Lady Anne are exchanging their New Year kisses. We are safe from incursions till Twelfth Night.' He turns his head, against his pillows. Says, vehement, 'Body of Christ, Cromwell. Go home.'

The house at the Austin Friars is decorated with wreaths of holly and ivy, of laurel and ribboned yew. The kitchen is busy, feeding the living, but they omit this year their usual songs and Christmas plays. No year has brought such devastation. His sister Kat, her husband Morgan Williams, have been plucked from this life as fast as his daughters were taken, one day walking and talking and next day cold as stones, tumbled into their Thames-side graves and dug in beyond reach of the tide, beyond sight and smell of the river; deaf now to the sound of Putney's cracked church bell, to the smell of wet ink, of hops, of malted barley, and the scent, still animal, of woollen bales; dead to the autumn aroma of pine resin and apple candles, of soul cakes baking. As the year ends two orphans are added to his house, Richard and the child Walter. Morgan Williams, he was a big talker, but he was shrewd in his own way, and he worked hard for his family. And Kat – well, latterly she understood her brother about as well as she understood the motions of the stars: 'I can never add you up, Thomas,' she'd say, which was his failure entirely, because who had taught her, except him, to count on her fingers, and puzzle out a tradesman's bill?

If he were to give himself a piece of advice for Christmas, he'd say, leave the cardinal now or you'll be out on the streets again with the three-card trick. But he only gives advice to those who are likely to take it.

They have a big gilded star at the Austin Friars, which they hang in their great hall on New Year's Eve. For a week it shines out, to welcome their guests at Epiphany. From summer onwards, he and Liz would be thinking of costumes for the Three Kings, coveting and hoarding scraps of any strange cloth they saw, any new trimmings; then from October, Liz would be sewing in secrecy, improving on last year's robes by patching them over with new shining panels, quilting a shoulder and weighting a hem, and building each year some fantastical new crowns. His part was to think what the gifts would be, that the kings had in their boxes. Once a king had dropped his casket in shock when the gift began to sing.

This year no one has the heart to hang up the star; but he visits it, in its lightless store room. He slides off the canvas sleeves that protect its rays, and checks that they are unchipped and unfaded. There will be better years, when they will hang it up again; though he cannot imagine them. He eases back the sleeves, pleased at how ingeniously they have been made and how exactly they fit. The Three Kings' robes are packed into a chest, as also the sheepskins for the children who will be sheep. The shepherds' crooks lean in a corner; from a peg hang angel's wings. He touches them. His finger comes away dusty. He shifts his candle out of danger, then lifts them from the peg and gently shakes them. They make a soft sound of hissing, and a faint amber perfume washes into the air. He hangs them back on the peg; passes over them the palm of his hand, to soothe them and still their shiver. He picks up his candle. He backs out and closes the door. He pinches out the light, turns the lock and gives the key to Johane.

He says to her, 'I wish we had a baby. It seems such a long time since there was a baby in the house.'

'Don't look at me,' Johane says.

He does, of course. He says, 'Does John Williamson not do his duty by you these days?'

She says, 'His duty is not my pleasure.'

As he walks away he thinks, that's a conversation I shouldn't have had.

On New Year's Day, when night falls, he is sitting at his writing table; he is writing letters for the cardinal, and sometimes he crosses the room to his counting board and pushes the counters about. It seems that in return for a formal guilty plea to the praemunire charges, the king will allow the cardinal his life, and a measure of liberty; but whatever money is left him, to maintain his state, will be a fraction of his former income. York Place has been taken already, Hampton Court is long gone, and the king is thinking of how to tax and rob the rich bishopric of Winchester.

Gregory comes in. 'I brought you lights. My aunt Johane said, go in to your father.'

Gregory sits. He waits. He fidgets. He sighs. He gets up. He crosses to his father's writing table and hovers in front of him. Then, as if someone had said, 'Make yourself useful,' he reaches out timidly and begins to tidy the papers.

He glances up at his son, while keeping his head down over his task. For the first time, perhaps, since Gregory was a baby, he notices his hands, and he is struck by what they have become: not childish paws, but the large, white untroubled hands of a gentleman's son. What is Gregory doing? He is putting the documents into a stack. On what principle is he doing it? He can't read them, they're the wrong way up. He's not filing them by subject. Is he filing them by date? For God's sake, what *is* he doing?

He needs to finish this sentence, with its many vital subclauses. He glances up again, and recognises Gregory's design. It is a system of holy simplicity: big papers on the bottom, small ones on top.

'Father …' Gregory says. He sighs. He crosses to the counting board. With a forefinger he inches the counters about. Then he scoops them together, picks them up and clicks them into a tidy pile.

He looks up at last. 'That was a calculation. It wasn't just where I dropped them.'

'Oh, sorry,' Gregory says politely. He sits down by the fire and tries not to disturb the air as he breathes.

The mildest eyes can be commanding; under his son's gaze, he asks, 'What is it?'

'Do you think you can stop writing?'

'A minute,' he says, holding up a delaying hand; he signs the letter, his usual form: 'your assured friend, Thomas Cromwell.' If Gregory is going to tell him that someone else in the house is mortally ill, or that he, Gregory, has offered himself in marriage to the laundry girl, or that London Bridge has fallen down, he must be ready to take it like a man; but he must sand and seal this. He looks up. 'Yes?'

Gregory turns his face away. Is he crying? It would not be surprising, would it, as he has cried himself, and in public? He crosses the room. He sits down opposite his son, by the hearth. He takes off his cap of velvet and runs his hands back through his hair.

For a long time no one speaks. He looks down at his own thick-fingered hands, scars and burn marks hidden in the palms. He thinks, gentleman? So you call yourself, but who do you hope to mislead? Only the people who have never seen you, or the people you keep distanced with courtesy, legal clients and your fellows in the Commons, colleagues at Gray's Inn, the household servants of courtiers, the courtiers themselves ... His mind strays to the next letter he must write. Then Gregory says, his voice small as if he had receded into the past, 'Do you remember that Christmas, when there was the giant in the pageant?'

'Here in the parish? I remember.'

'He said, "I am a giant, my name is Marlinspike." They said he was as tall as the Cornhill maypole. What's the Cornhill maypole?'

'They took it down. The year of the riots. Evil May Day, they called it. You were only a baby then.'

'Where's the maypole now?'

'The city has it in store.'

'Shall we have our star again next year?'

'If our fortunes look up.'

'Shall we be poor now the cardinal is down?'

'No.'

The little flames leap and flare, and Gregory looks into them. 'You remember the year I had my face dyed black, and I was wrapped in a black calfskin? When I was a devil in the Christmas play?'

'I do.' His face softens. 'I remember.'

Anne had wanted to be dyed, but her mother had said it was not suitable for a little girl. He wishes he had said that Anne must have her turn as a parish angel – even if, being dark, she had to wear one of the parish's yellow knitted wigs, which slipped sideways, or fell over the children's eyes.

The year that Grace was an angel, she had wings made of peacock feathers. He himself had contrived it. The other little girls were dowdy goose creatures, and their wings fell off if they caught them on the corners of the stable. But Grace stood glittering, her hair entwined with silver threads; her shoulders were trussed with a spreading, shivering glory, and the rustling air was perfumed as she breathed. Lizzie said, Thomas, there's no end to you, is there? She has the best wings the city has ever seen.

Gregory stands up; he comes to kiss him good night. For a moment his son leans against him, as if he were a child; or as if the past, the pictures in the fire, were an intoxication.

Once the boy has gone to bed he sweeps his papers out of the tidy stack he has made. He refolds them. He sorts them with the endorsement out, ready for filing. He thinks of Evil May Day. Gregory did not ask, why were there riots? The riots were against foreigners. He himself had not long been home.

As 1530 begins, he does not hold an Epiphany feast, because so many people, sensible of the cardinal's disgrace, would be obliged to refuse his invitation. Instead, he takes the young men to Gray's Inn, for the Twelfth Night revels. He regrets it almost at once; this year they are noisier, and more bawdy, than any he remembers.

The law students make a play about the cardinal. They make him flee from his palace at York Place, to his barge on the Thames. Some fellows flap dyed sheets, to impersonate the river, and then others run up and throw water on them from leather buckets. As the cardinal scrambles into his barge, there are hunting cries, and one benighted fool runs into the hall with a brace of otter hounds on a leash. Others come with nets and fishing rods, to haul the cardinal back to the bank.

The next scene shows the cardinal floundering in the mud at Putney, as he runs to his bolt-hole at Esher. The students halloo and cry as the cardinal weeps and holds up his hands in prayer. Of all the people who witnessed this, who, he wonders, has offered it up as a comedy? If he knew, or if he guessed, the worse for them.

The cardinal lies on his back, a crimson mountain; he flails his hands; he offers his bishopric of Winchester to anyone who can get him back on his mule. Some students, under a frame draped with donkey skins, enact the mule, which turns about and jokes in Latin, and farts in the cardinal's face. There is much wordplay about bishoprics and bishop's pricks, which might pass as witty if they were street-sweepers, but he thinks law students should do better. He rises from his place, displeased, and his household has no choice but to stand up with him and walk out.

He stops to have a word with some of the benchers: how was this allowed to go forward? The Cardinal of York is a sick man, he may die, how will you and your students stand then before your God? What sort of young men are you breeding here, who are so brave as to assail a great man who has fallen on evil times – whose favour, a few short weeks ago, they would have begged for?

The benchers follow him, apologising; but their voices are lost in the roars of laughter that billow out from the hall. His young household are lingering, casting glances back. The cardinal is offering his harem of forty virgins to anyone who will help him mount; he sits on the ground and laments, while a flaccid and serpentine member, knitted of red wool, flops out from under his robes.

Outside, lights burn thin in the icy air. 'Home,' he says. He hears Gregory whisper, 'We can only laugh if he permits us.'

'Well, after all,' he hears Rafe say, 'he is the man in charge.'

He falls back a step, to speak with them. 'Anyway, it was the wicked Borgia Pope, Alexander, who kept forty women. And none of them were virgins, I can tell you.'

Rafe touches his shoulder. Richard walks on his left, sticking close. 'You don't have to hold me up,' he says mildly. 'I'm not like the cardinal.' He stops. He laughs. He says, 'I suppose it was ...'

'Yes, it was quite entertaining,' Richard says. 'His Grace must have been five feet around his waist.'

The night is loud with the noise of bone rattles, and alive with the flames of torches. A troop of hobby horses clatters past them, singing, and a party of men wearing antlers, with bells at their heels. As they near home a boy dressed as an orange rolls past, with his friend, a lemon. 'Gregory Cromwell!' they call out, and to him as their senior they courteously raise, in lieu of hats, an upper slice of rind. 'God send you a good new year.'

'The same to you,' he calls. And, to the lemon: 'Tell your father to come and see me about that Cheapside lease.'

They get home. 'Go to bed,' he says. 'It's late.' He feels it best to add, 'God see you safe till morning.'

They leave him. He sits at his work table. He remembers Grace, at the end of her evening as an angel: standing in the fire-light, her face white with fatigue, her eyes glittering, and the eyes of her peacock's wings shining in the firelight, each like a topaz, golden, smoky. Liz said, 'Stand away from the fire, sweetheart, or your wings will catch alight.' His little girl backed off, into shadow; the feathers were the colours of ash and cinders as she moved towards the stairs, and he said, 'Grace, are you going to bed in your wings?'

'Till I say my prayers,' she said, darting a look over her shoulder. He followed her, afraid for her, afraid of fire and some other danger, but he did not know what. She walked up the staircase, her plumes rustling, her feathers fading to black.

Ah, Christ, he thinks, at least I'll never have to give her to anyone else. She's dead and I'll not have to sign her away to some purse-mouthed petty gent who wants her dowry. Grace would have wanted a title. She would have thought because she was

176

lovely he should buy her one: Lady Grace. I wish my daughter
Anne were here, he thinks, I wish Anne were here and promised
to Rafe Sadler. If Anne were older. If Rafe were younger. If Anne
were still alive.

Once more he bends his head over the cardinal's letters.
Wolsey is writing to the rulers of Europe, to ask them to support
him, vindicate him, fight his cause. He, Thomas Cromwell,
wishes the cardinal would not, or if he must, could the encryp-
tion be more tricky? Is it not treasonable for Wolsey to urge
them to obstruct the king's purpose? Henry would deem it is.
The cardinal is not asking them to make war on Henry, on his
behalf: he's merely asking them to withdraw their approval of a
king who very much likes to be liked.

He sits back in his chair, hands over his mouth, as if to disguise
his opinion from himself. He thinks, I am glad I love my lord
cardinal, because if I did not, and I were his enemy – let us say I
am Suffolk, let us say I am Norfolk, let us say I am the king – I
would be putting him on trial next week.

The door opens. 'Richard? You can't sleep? Well, I knew it.
The play was too exciting for you.'

It is easy to smile now, but Richard does not smile; his face is
in shadow. He says, 'Master, I have a question to put to you. Our
father is dead and you are our father now.'

Richard Williams, and Walter-named-after-Walter Williams:
these are his sons. 'Sit down,' he says.

'So shall we change our name to yours?'

'You surprise me. The way things are with me, the people
called Cromwell will be wanting to change their names to
Williams.'

'If I had your name, I should never disown it.'

'Would your father like it? You know he believed he had his
descent from Welsh princes.'

'Ah, he did. When he'd had a drink, he would say, who will
give me a shilling for my principality?'

177

'Even so, you have the Tudor name in your descent. By some accounts.'

'Don't,' Richard pleads. 'It makes beads of blood stand out on my forehead.'

'It's not that hard.' He laughs. 'Listen. The old king had an uncle, Jasper Tudor. Jasper had two bastard daughters, Joan and Helen. Helen was Gardiner's mother. Joan married William ap Evan – she was your grandmother.'

'Is that all? Why did my father make it sound so deep? But if I am the king's cousin,' Richard pauses, 'and Stephen Gardiner's cousin ... what good can it do me? We're not at court and not likely to be, now the cardinal ... well ...' He looks away. 'Sir ... when you were on your travels, did you ever think you would die?'

'Yes. Oh, yes.'

Richard looks at him: how did that feel?

'I felt,' he said, 'irritated. It seemed a waste, I suppose. To come so far. To cross the sea. To die for ...' He shrugs. 'God knows why.'

Richard says, 'Every day I light a candle for my father.'

'Does that help you?'

'No. I just do it.'

'Does he know you do it?'

'I can't imagine what he knows. I know the living must comfort each other.'

'This comforts me, Richard Cromwell.'

Richard gets up, kisses his cheek. 'Good night. *Cysga'n dawel.*'

Sleep well; it is the familiar form for those who are close to home. It is the usage for fathers, for brothers. It matters what name we choose, what name we make. The people lose their name who lie dead on the field of battle, the ordinary corpses of no lineage, with no herald to search for them and no chantry, no perpetual prayers. Morgan's bloodline won't be lost, he is sure of it, though he died in a busy year for death, when London was never out of black. He touches his throat, where the medal would have been, the holy medal that Kat gave him; his fingers are surprised not to find it there. For the first time he understands why he took it off and slid it into the sea. It was so that no living hand could take it. The waves took it, and the waves have it still.

The chimney at Esher continues to smoke. He goes to the Duke of Norfolk – who is always ready to see him – and asks him what is to be done about the cardinal's household.

In this matter, both dukes are helpful. 'Nothing is more malcontent,' says Norfolk, 'than a masterless man. Nothing more dangerous. Whatever one thinks of the Cardinal of York, he was always well served. Prefer them to me, send them in my direction. They will be my men.'

He directs a searching look at Cromwell. Who turns away. Knows himself coveted. Wears an expression like an heiress: sly, coy, cold.

He is arranging a loan for the duke. His foreign contacts are less than excited. The cardinal down, he says, the duke has risen, like the morning sun, and sitteth at Henry's right hand. Tommaso, they say, seriously, you are offering what as guarantee? Some old duke who may be dead tomorrow – they say he is choleric? You are offering a dukedom as security, in that barbaric island of yours, which is always breaking out into civil war? And another war coming, if your wilful king will set aside the Emperor's aunt, and install his whore as queen?

Still: he'll get terms. Somewhere.

Charles Brandon says, 'You here again, Master Cromwell, with your lists of names? Is there anyone you specially recommend to me?'

'Yes, but I am afraid he is a man of a lowly stamp, and more fit that I should confer with your kitchen steward –'

'No, tell me,' says the duke. He can't bear suspense.

179

'It's only the hearths and chimneys man, hardly a matter for Your Grace ...'

'I'll have him, I'll have him,' Charles Brandon says. 'I like a good fire.'

Thomas More, the Lord Chancellor, has put his signature first on all the articles against Wolsey. They say one strange allegation has been added at his behest. The cardinal is accused of whispering in the king's ear and breathing into his face; since the cardinal has the French pox, he intended to infect our monarch.

When he hears this he thinks, imagine living inside the Lord Chancellor's head. Imagine writing down such a charge and taking it to the printer, and circulating it through the court and through the realm, putting it out there to where people will believe anything; putting it out there, to the shepherds on the hills, to Tyndale's ploughboy, to the beggar on the roads and the patient beast in its byre or stall; out there to the bitter winter winds, and to the weak early sun, and the snowdrops in the London gardens.

It is a wan morning, low unbroken cloud; the light, filtering sparely through glass, is the colour of tarnished pewter. How brightly coloured the king is, like the king in a new pack of cards: how small his flat blue eye.

There is a crowd of gentlemen around Henry Tudor; they ignore his approach. Only Harry Norris smiles, gives him a polite good morning. At a signal from the king, the gentlemen retire to a distance; bright in their riding cloaks – it is a hunting morning – they flutter, eddy, cluster; they whisper, one to the other, and conduct a discourse in nods and shrugs.

The king glances out of the window. 'So,' he says, 'how is ...?' He seems reluctant to name the cardinal.

'He cannot be well till he has Your Majesty's favour.'

'Forty-four charges,' the king says. 'Forty-four, master.'

'Saving Your Majesty, there is an answer to each one, and given a hearing we would make them.'

'Could you make them here and now?'

'If Your Majesty would care to sit.'

'I heard you were a ready man.'

'Would I come here unprepared?'

He has spoken almost without thinking. The king smiles. That fine curl of the red lip. He has a pretty mouth, almost like a woman's; it is too small for his face. 'Another day I would put you to the test,' he says. 'But my lord Suffolk is waiting for me. Will the cloud lift, do you think? I wish I'd gone out before Mass.'

'I think it will clear,' he says. 'A good day to be chasing something.'

'Master Cromwell?' The king turns, he looks at him, astonished. 'You are not of Thomas More's opinion, are you?'

He waits. He cannot imagine what the king is going to say.

'*La chasse*. He thinks it barbaric.'

'Oh, I see. No, Your Majesty, I favour any sport that's cheaper than battle. It's rather that …' How can he put it? 'In some countries, they hunt the bear, and the wolf and the wild boar. We once had these animals in England, when we had our great forests.'

'My cousin France has boar to hunt. From time to time he says he will ship me some. But I feel …'

You feel he is taunting you.

'We usually say,' Henry looks straight at him, 'we usually say, we gentlemen, that the chase prepares us for war. Which brings us to a sticky point, Master Cromwell.'

'It does indeed,' he says, cheerful.

'You said, in the Parliament, some six years ago, that I could not afford a war.'

It was seven years: 1523. And how long has this audience lasted? Seven minutes? Seven minutes and he is sure already. There's no point backing off; do that and Henry will chase you down. Advance, and he may just falter. He says, 'No ruler in the history of the world has ever been able to afford a war. They're not affordable things. No prince ever says, "This is my budget;

181

so this is the kind of war I can have." You enter into one and it uses up all the money you've got, and then it breaks you and bankrupts you.'

'When I went into France in the year 1513 I captured the town of Thérouanne, which in your speech you called –'

'A doghole, Majesty.'

'A doghole,' the king repeats. 'How could you say so?'

He shrugs. 'I've been there.'

A flash of anger. 'And so have I, at the head of my army. Listen to me, master – you said I should not fight because the taxes would break the country. What is the country for, but to support its prince in his enterprise?'

'I believe I said – saving Your Majesty – we didn't have the gold to see you through a year's campaign. All the bullion in the country would be swallowed by the war. I have read there was a time when people exchanged leather tokens, for want of metal coins. I said we would be back to those days.'

'You said I was not to lead my troops. You said if I was taken, the country couldn't put up the ransom. So what do you want? You want a king who doesn't fight? You want me to huddle indoors like a sick girl?'

'That would be ideal, for fiscal purposes.'

The king takes a deep ragged breath. He's been shouting. Now – and it's a narrow thing – he decides to laugh. 'You advocate prudence. Prudence is a virtue. But there are other virtues that belong to princes.'

'Fortitude.'

'Yes. Cost that out.'

'It doesn't mean courage in battle.'

'Do you read me a lesson?'

'It means fixity of purpose. It means endurance. It means having the strength to live with what constrains you.'

Henry crosses the room. Stamp, stamp, stamp in his riding boots; he is ready for *la chasse*. He turns, rather slowly, to show his majesty to better effect: wide and square and bright. 'We will pursue this. What constrains me?'

'The distance,' he says. 'The harbours. The terrain, the people. The winter rains and the mud. When Your Majesty's ancestors fought in France, whole provinces were held by England. From there we could supply, we could provision. Now that we have only Calais, how can we support an army in the interior?'

The king stares out into the silver morning. He bites his lip. Is he in a slow fury, simmering, bubbling to boiling point? He turns, and his smile is sunny. 'I know,' he says. 'So when we next go into France, we will need a sea coast.'

Of course. We need to take Normandy. Or Brittany. That's all.

'Well reasoned,' the king says. 'I bear you no ill will. Only I suppose you have no experience in policy, or the direction of a campaign.'

He shakes his head. 'None.'

'You said – before, I mean, in this speech of yours to the Parliament – that there was one million pounds in gold in the realm.'

'I gave a round figure.'

'But how would you find that figure?'

'I trained in the Florentine banks. And in Venice.'

The king stares at him. 'Howard said you were a common soldier.'

'That too.'

'Anything else?'

'What would Your Majesty like me to be?'

The king looks him full in the face: a rare thing with him. He looks back; it is his habit. 'Master Cromwell, your reputation is bad.'

He inclines his head.

'You don't defend yourself?'

'Your Majesty is able to form his own opinion.'

'I can. I will.'

At the door, the guards part their spears; the gentlemen step aside and bow; Suffolk pounds in. Charles Brandon: he looks too hot in his clothes. 'You ready?' he says to the king. 'Oh, Cromwell.' He grins. 'How's your fat priest?'

The king flushes with displeasure. Brandon doesn't notice. 'You know,' he chuckles, 'they say the cardinal once rode out with his servant, and checked his horse at the head of a valley, where looking down he saw a very fair church and its lands about. He says to his servant, Robin, who owns that? I would that were my benefice! Robin says, It is, my lord, it is.'

His story meets with poor success, but he laughs at it himself.

He says, 'My lord, they tell that story all over Italy. Of this cardinal, or that.'

Brandon's face falls. 'What, the same story?'

'*Mutatis mutandis*. The servant isn't called Robin.'

The king meets his eye. He smiles.

Leaving, he pushes past the gentlemen, and who should he meet but the king's Secretary! 'Good morning, good morning!' he says. He doesn't often repeat things, but the moment seems to call for it.

Gardiner is rubbing his great blue hands together. 'Cold, no?' he says. 'And how was that, Cromwell? Unpleasant, I think?'

'On the contrary,' he says. 'Oh, and he's going out with Suffolk; you'll have to wait.' He walks on, but then turns. There is a pain like a dull bruise inside his chest. 'Gardiner, can't we drop this?'

'No,' Gardiner says. His drooping eyelids flicker. 'No, I don't see that we can.'

'Fine,' he says. He walks on. He thinks, you wait. You may have to wait a year or two, but you just wait.

Esher, two days later: he is hardly through the gateway when Cavendish comes hurtling across the courtyard. 'Master Cromwell! Yesterday the king –'

'Calmly, George,' he advises.

'– yesterday he sent us four cartloads of furnishings – come and see! Tapestry, plate, bed hangings – was it by your suit?'

Who knows? He hadn't asked for anything directly. If he had, he'd have been more specific. Not *that* hanging, but *this* hanging, which my lord likes; he likes goddesses, rather than virgin martyrs, so away with St Agnes, and let's have Venus in a grove. My lord likes Venetian glassware; take away these battered silver goblets.

He looks contemptuous as he inspects the new stuff. 'Only the best for you boys from Putney,' Wolsey says. 'It is possible,' he adds, almost apologising, 'that what the king appointed for me was not in fact what was sent. That inferior substitutions were made, by inferior persons.'

'That is entirely possible,' he says.

'Still. Even so. We are more comfortable for it.'

'The difficulty is,' Cavendish says, 'we need to move. This whole house needs to be scrubbed out and aired.'

'True,' the cardinal says. 'St Agnes, bless her, would be knocked over by the smell of the privies.'

'So will you make suit to the king's council?'

He sighs. 'George, what is the point? Listen. I'm not talking to Thomas Howard. I'm not talking to Brandon. I'm talking to *him*.'

The cardinal smiles. A fat paternal beam.

He is surprised – as they thrash out a financial settlement for the cardinal – at Henry's grasp of detail. Wolsey has always said that the king has a fine mind, as quick as his father's, but more comprehensive. The old king grew narrow as he aged; he kept a hard hand on England; there was no nobleman he did not hold by a debt or bond, and he said frankly that if he could not be loved he would be feared. Henry has a different nature, but what is it? Wolsey laughs and says, I should write you a handbook.

But as he walks in the gardens of the little lodge at Richmond, where the king has allowed him to remove, the cardinal's mind becomes clouded, he talks about prophecies, and about the downfall of the priests of England, which he says is foretold, and will now happen.

Even if you don't believe in omens – and he doesn't, personally – he can see the problem. For if the cardinal is guilty of a crime in asserting his jurisdiction as legate, are not all those clerics, from bishops downwards, who assented to his legacy, also guilty? He can't be the only person who's thinking about this; but mostly, his enemies can't see past the cardinal himself, his vast scarlet presence on the horizon; they fear it will loom up again, ready for revenge. 'These are bad times for proud prelates,' says Brandon, when next they meet. He sounds jaunty, a man whistling to keep his courage up. 'We need no cardinals in this realm.'

'And he,' the cardinal says, furious, 'he, Brandon, when he married the king's sister out of hand – when he married her in the first days of her widowhood, knowing the king intended her for another monarch – his head would have been parted from his body, if I, a simple cardinal, had not pleaded for him to the king.'

I, a simple cardinal.

'And what excuse did Brandon make?' the cardinal says. '"Oh, Your Majesty, your sister Mary cried. How she did cry and beg me to marry her myself! I never saw woman cry so!" So he dried her tears and got himself up to a dukedom! And now he talks as if he's held his title since the Garden of Eden. Listen, Thomas, if men of sound learning and good disposition come to me – as Bishop Tunstall comes, as Thomas More comes – and plead that the church must be reformed, why then I listen. But Brandon! To talk about proud prelates! What was he? The king's horsekeeper! And I've known horses with more wit.'

'My lord,' Cavendish pleads, 'be more temperate. And Charles Brandon, you know, was of an ancient family, a gentleman born.'

'Gentleman, he? A swaggering braggart. That's Brandon.' The cardinal sits down, exhausted. 'My head aches,' he says. 'Cromwell, go to court and bring me better news.'

Day by day he takes his instructions from Wolsey at Richmond, and rides to wherever the king is. He thinks of the king as a terrain into which he must advance, with no sea coast to supply him.

He understands what Henry has learned from his cardinal: his floating diplomacy, his science of ambiguity. He sees how the king has applied this science to the slow, trackless, dubious ruin of his minister. Every kindness, Henry matches with a cruelty, some further charge or forfeiture. Till the cardinal moans, 'I want to go away.'

'Winchester,' he suggests, to the dukes. 'My lord cardinal is willing to proceed to his palace there.'

'What, so near the king?' Brandon says. 'We are not fools to ourselves, Master Cromwell.'

Since he, the cardinal's man, is with Henry so often, rumours have run all over Europe that Wolsey is about to be recalled. The king is cutting a deal, people say, to have the church's wealth in exchange for Wolsey's return to favour. Rumours leak from the council chamber, from the privy chamber: the king does not like his new set-up. Norfolk is found ignorant; Suffolk is accused of having an annoying laugh.

He says, 'My lord won't go north. He is not ready for it.'

'But I want him north,' Howard says. 'Tell him to go. Tell him Norfolk says he must be on the road and out of here. Or – and tell him this – I will come where he is, and I will tear him with my teeth.'

'My lord.' He bows. 'May I substitute the word "bite"?'

Norfolk approaches him. He stands far too close. His eyes are bloodshot. Every sinew is jumping. He says, 'Substitute nothing, you misbegotten –' The duke stabs a forefinger into his shoulder. 'You … person,' he says; and again, 'you nobody from Hell, you whore-spawn, you cluster of evil, you lawyer.'

He stands there, pushing away, like a baker pressing the dimples into a batch of manchet loaves. Cromwell flesh is firm, dense and impermeable. The ducal finger just bounces off.

Before they left Esher, one of the cats that had been brought in to kill the vermin gave birth to a litter in the cardinal's own rooms. What presumption, in an animal! But wait – new life, in the cardinal's suite? Could that be an *omen*? One day, he fears, there will be an omen of another sort: a dead bird will fall down that smoking chimney, and then – oh, woe is us! – he'll never hear the last of it.

But for the while the cardinal is amused, and puts the kittens on a cushion in an open chest, and watches as they grow. One of them is black and hungry, with a coat like wool and yellow eyes. When it is weaned he brings it home. He takes it from under his coat, where it has been sleeping curled against his shoulder. 'Gregory, look.' He holds it out to his son. 'I am a giant, my name is Marlinspike.'

Gregory looks at him, wary, puzzled. His glance flinches; his hand pulls away. 'The dogs will kill it,' he says.

Marlinspike goes down to the kitchen, to grow stout and live out his beastly nature. There is a summer ahead, though he cannot imagine its pleasures; sometimes when he's walking in the garden he sees him, a half-grown cat, lolling watchful in an apple tree, or snoring on a wall in the sun.

Spring 1530: Antonio Bonvisi, the merchant, invites him to supper at his fine tall house on Bishopsgate. 'I won't be late,' he tells Richard, expecting that it will be the usual tense gathering, everyone cross and hungry: for even a rich Italian with an ingenious kitchen cannot find a hundred ways with smoked eel or salt cod. The merchants in Lent miss their mutton and malmsey, their nightly grunt in a featherbed with wife or mistress; from now till Good Friday their knives will be out for some cut-throat intelligence, some mean commercial advantage.

But it is a grander occasion than he thought; the Lord Chancellor is there, amongst a company of lawyers and aldermen. Humphrey Monmouth, whom More once locked up, is seated well away from the great man; More looks at his ease, holding the company captive with one of his stories about that great scholar Erasmus, his dear friend. But when he looks up and sees him, Cromwell, he falls silent halfway through a sentence; he casts his eyes down, and an opaque and stony look grows on his face.

'Did you want to talk about me?' he asks. 'You can do it while I'm here, Lord Chancellor. I have a thick skin.' He knocks back a glass of wine and laughs. 'Do you know what Brandon is saying? He can't fit my life together. My travels. The other day he called me a Jewish peddler.'

'And was that to your face?' his host asks politely.

'No. The king told me. But then my lord cardinal calls Brandon a horsekeeper.'

Humphrey Monmouth says, 'You have the entrée these days, Thomas. And what do you think, now you are a courtier?'

There are smiles around the table. Because, of course, the idea is so ridiculous, the situation so temporary. More's people are city people, no grander; but he is *sui generis*, a scholar and a wit. And More says, 'Perhaps we should not press the point. There are delicate issues here. There is a time to be silent.'

An elder of the drapers' guild leans across the table and warns, his voice low: 'Thomas More said, when he took his seat, that he won't discuss the cardinal, or the Lady either.'

He, Cromwell, looks around at the company. 'The king surprises me, though. What he will tolerate.'

'From you?' More says.

'I mean Brandon. They're going to hunt: he walks in and shouts, are you ready?'

'Your master the cardinal found it a constant battle,' Bonvisi says, 'in the early years of the reign. To stop the king's companions becoming too familiar with him.'

'He wanted only himself to be familiar,' More suggests. 'Though, of course, the king may raise up whom he will.'

'Up to a point, Thomas,' Bonvisi says; there is some laughter.

'And the king enjoys his friendships. That is good, surely?'

'A soft word, from you, Master Cromwell.'

'Not at all,' Monmouth says. 'Master Cromwell is known as one who does everything for his friends.'

'I think ...' More stops; he looks down at the table. 'In all truth, I am not sure if one can regard a prince as a friend.'

'But surely,' Bonvisi says, 'you've known Henry since he was a child.'

'Yes, but friendship should be less exhausting ... it should be restorative. Not like ...' More turns to him, for the first time, as if inviting comment. 'I sometimes feel it is like ... like Jacob wrestling with the angel.'

'And who knows,' he says, 'what that fight was about?'

'Yes, the text is silent. As with Cain and Abel. Who knows?'

He senses a little disquiet around the table, among the more pious, the less sportive; or just those keen for the next course. What will it be? Fish!

'When you speak to Henry,' More says, 'I beg you, speak to the good heart. Not the strong will.'

He would pursue it, but the aged draper waves for more wine, and asks him, 'How's your friend Stephen Vaughan? What's new in Antwerp?' The conversation is about trade then; it is about shipping, interest rates; it is no more than a background hum to unruly speculation. If you come into a room and say, this is what we're not talking about, it follows that you're talking about nothing else. If the Lord Chancellor weren't here it would be just import duties and bonded warehouses; we would not be thinking of the brooding scarlet cardinal, and our starved Lenten minds would not be occupied by the image of the king's fingers creeping over a resistant, quick-breathing and virginal bosom. He leans back and fixes his gaze on Thomas More. In time there is a natural pause in conversation, a lull; and after a quarter-hour in which he has not spoken, the Lord Chancellor breaks into it, his voice low and angry, his eyes on the remnants of what he has eaten. 'The Cardinal of York,' he says, 'has a greed that will never be appeased, for ruling over other men.'

'Lord Chancellor,' Bonvisi says, 'you are looking at your herring as if you hate it.'

Says the gracious guest, 'There's nothing wrong with the herring.'

He leans forward, ready for this fight; he means not to let it pass. 'The cardinal is a public man. So are you. Should he shrink from a public role?'

'Yes.' More looks up. 'Yes, I think, a little, he should. A little less evident appetite, perhaps.'

'It's late,' Monmouth says, 'to read the cardinal a lesson in humility.'

'His real friends have read it long ago, and been ignored.'

'And you count yourself his friend?' He sits back, arms folded. 'I'll tell him, Lord Chancellor, and by the blood of Christ he will find it a consolation, as he sits in exile and wonders why you have slandered him to the king.'

'Gentlemen …' Bonvisi rises in his chair, edgy.

'No,' he says, 'sit down. Let's have this straight. Thomas More here will tell you, I would have been a simple monk, but my father put me to the law. I would spend my life in church, if I had the choice. I am, as you know, indifferent to wealth. I am devoted to things of the spirit. The world's esteem is nothing to me.' He looks around the table. 'So how did he become Lord Chancellor? Was it an accident?'

The doors open; Bonvisi jumps to his feet; relief floods his face. 'Welcome, welcome,' he says. 'Gentlemen: the Emperor's ambassador.'

It is Eustache Chapuys, come in with the desserts; the new ambassador, as one calls him, though he has been in post since fall. He stands poised on the threshold, so they may know him and admire: a little crooked man, in a doublet slashed and puffed, blue satin billowing through black; beneath it, his little black spindly legs. 'I regret to be so late,' he says. He simpers. '*Les dépêches, toujours les dépêches.*'

'That's the ambassador's life.' He looks up and smiles. 'Thomas Cromwell.'

'Ah, *c'est le juif errant!*'

At once the ambassador apologises: whilst smiling around, as if bemused, at the success of his joke.

Sit down, sit down, says Bonvisi, and the servants bustle, the cloths are swept away, the company rearranges itself more informally, except for the Lord Chancellor, who goes on sitting where he's sitting. Preserved autumn fruits come in, and spiced wine, and Chapuys takes a place of honour beside More.

'We will speak French, gentlemen,' says Bonvisi.

French, as it happens, is the first language of the ambassador of the Empire and Spain; and like any other diplomat, he will never take the trouble to learn English, for how will that help him in his next posting? So kind, so kind, he says, as he eases himself back in the carved chair their host has vacated; his feet do not quite touch the floor. More rouses himself then; he and the ambassador put their heads together. He watches them; they glance back at him resentfully; but looking is free.

In a tiny moment when they pause, he cuts in. 'Monsieur Chapuys? You know, I was talking with the king recently about those events, so regrettable, when your master's troops plundered the Holy City. Perhaps you can advise us? We don't understand them even now.'

Chapuys shakes his head. 'Most regrettable events.'

'Thomas More thinks it was the secret Mohammedans in your army who ran wild – oh, and my own people, of course, the wandering Jews. But before this, he has said it was the Germans, the Lutherans, who raped the poor virgins and desecrated the shrines. In all cases, as the Lord Chancellor says, the Emperor must blame himself; but to whom should we attach blame? Are you able to help us out?'

'My dear Sir Chancellor!' The ambassador is shocked. His eyes turn towards Thomas More. 'Did you speak so, of my imperial master?' A glance flicked over his shoulder, and he drops into Latin.

The company, linguistically agile, sit and smile at him. He advises, pleasantly, 'If you wish to be half-secret, try Greek. *Allez*, Monsieur Chapuys, rattle away! The Lord Chancellor will understand you.'

The party breaks up soon after, the Lord Chancellor rising to go; but before he does, he makes a pronouncement to the company, in English. 'Master Cromwell's position,' he says, 'is indefensible, it seems to me. He is no friend to the church, as we all know, but he is friend to one priest. And that priest the most corrupt in Christendom.'

With the curtest of nods he takes his leave. Even Chapuys does not warrant more. The ambassador looks after him, dubious, biting his lip: as if to say, I looked for more help and friendship there. Everything Chapuys does, he notices, is like something an actor does. When he thinks, he casts his eyes down, places two fingers to his forehead. When he sorrows, he sighs. When he is perplexed, he wags his chin, he half-smiles. He is like a man who has wandered inadvertently into a play, who has found it to be a comedy, and decided to stay and see it through.

The supper is over; the company dwindle away, into the early dusk. 'Perhaps sooner than you would have liked?' he says, to Bonvisi.

'Thomas More is my old friend. You should not come here and bait him.'

'Oh, have I spoiled your party? You invited Monmouth; was that not to bait him?'

'No, Humphrey Monmouth is my friend too.'

'And I?'

'Of course.'

They have slid back naturally into Italian. 'Tell me something that intrigues me,' he says. 'I want to know about Thomas Wyatt.' Wyatt went to Italy, having attached himself to a diplomatic mission, rather suddenly: three years ago now. He had a disastrous time there, but that's for another evening; the question is, why did he run away from the English court in such haste?

'Ah. Wyatt and Lady Anne,' Bonvisi says. 'An old story, I'd have thought?'

Well, perhaps, he says, but he tells him about the boy Mark, the musician, who seems sure Wyatt's had her; if the story's bouncing around Europe, among servants and menials, what are the odds the king hasn't heard?

'A part of the art of ruling, I suppose, is to know when to shut your ears. And Wyatt is handsome,' Bonvisi says, 'in the English style, of course. He is tall, he is blond, my countrymen marvel at him; where do you breed such people? And so assured, of course. And a poet!'

He laughs at his friend because, like all the Italians, he can't say 'Wyatt': it comes out '*Guiett*', or something like that. There was a man called Hawkwood, a knight of Essex, used to rape and burn and murder in Italy, in the days of chivalry; the Italians called him *Acuto*, The Needle.

'Yes, but Anne ...' He senses, from his glimpses of her, that she is unlikely to be moved by anything so impermanent as beauty. 'These few years she has needed a husband, more than anything: a name, an establishment, a place from which she can stand and negotiate with the king. Now, Wyatt's married. What could he offer her?'

'Verses?' says the merchant. 'It wasn't diplomacy took him out of England. It was that she was torturing him. He no longer dared be in the same room with her. The same castle. The same country.' He shakes his head. 'Aren't the English odd?'

'Christ, aren't they?' he says.

'You must take care. The Lady's family, they are pushing a little against the limit of what can be done. They are saying, why wait for the Pope? Can we not make a marriage contract without him?'

'It would seem to be the way forward.'

'Try one of these sugared almonds.'

He smiles. Bonvisi says, 'Tommaso, I may give you some advice? The cardinal is finished.'

'Don't be so sure.'

'Yes, and if you did not love him, you would know it was true.'

'The cardinal has been nothing but good to me.'

'But he must go north.'

'The world will chase him. You ask the ambassadors. Ask Chapuys. Ask them who they report to. We have them at Esher, at Richmond. *Toujours les dépêches.* That's us.'

'But that is what he is accused of! Running a country within the country!'

He sighs. 'I know.'

'And what will you do about it?'

'Ask him to be more humble?'

Bonvisi laughs. 'Ah, Thomas. Please, you know when he goes north you will be a man without a master. That is the point. You are seeing the king, but it is only for now, while he works out how to give the cardinal a pay-off that will keep him quiet. But then?'

He hesitates. 'The king likes me.'

'The king is an inconstant lover.'

'Not to Anne.'

'That is where I must warn you. Oh, not because of Guiett … not because of any gossip, any light thing said … but because it must all end soon … she will give way, she is just a woman … think how foolish a man would have been if he had linked his fortunes to those of the Lady's sister, who came before her.'

'Yes, just think.'

He looks around the room. That's where the Lord Chancellor sat. On his left, the hungry merchants. On his right, the new ambassador. There, Humphrey Monmouth the heretic. There, Antonio Bonvisi. Here, Thomas Cromwell. And there are ghostly places set, for the Duke of Suffolk large and bland, for Norfolk jangling his holy medals and shouting 'By the Mass!' There is a place set for the king, and for the doughty little queen, famished in this penitential season, her belly quaking inside the stout armour of her robes. There is a place set for Lady Anne, glancing around with her restless black eyes, eating nothing, missing nothing, tugging at the pearls around her little neck. There is a place for William Tyndale, and one for the Pope; Clement looks at the candied quinces, too coarsely cut, and his Medici lip curls. And there sits Brother Martin Luther, greasy and fat: glowering at them all, and spitting out his fish-bones.

A servant comes in. 'Two young gentlemen are outside, master, asking for you by name.'

He looks up. 'Yes?'

'Master Richard Cromwell and Master Rafe. With servants from your household, waiting to take you home.'

He understands that the whole purpose of the evening has been to warn him: to warn him off. He will remember it, the fatal *placement*: if it proves fatal. That soft hiss and whisper, of stone destroying itself; that distant sound of walls sliding, of plaster crumbling, of rubble crashing on to fragile human skulls? That is the sound of the roof of Christendom, falling on the people below.

Bonvisi says, 'You have a private army, Tommaso. I suppose you have to watch your back.'

196

'You know I do.' His glance sweeps the room: one last look. 'Good night. It was a good supper. I liked the eels. Will you send your cook to see mine? I have a new sauce to brighten the season. One needs mace and ginger, some dried mint leaves chopped –'

His friend says, 'I beg of you. I implore you to be careful.'

'– a little, but a very little garlic –'

'Wherever you dine next, pray do not –'

'– and of breadcrumbs, a scant handful …'

'– sit down with the Boleyns.'

II

Entirely Beloved Cromwell
Spring–December 1530

He arrives early at York Place. The baited gulls, penned in their keeping yards, are crying out to their free brothers on the river, who wheel screaming and diving over the palace walls. The carmen are pushing up from the river goods incoming, and the courts smell of baking bread. Some children are bringing fresh rushes, tied in bundles, and they greet him by name. For their civility, he gives each of them a coin, and they stop to talk. 'So, you are going to the evil lady. She has bewitched the king, you know? Do you have a medal or a relic, master, to protect you?'

'I had a medal. But I lost it.'

'You should ask our cardinal,' one child says. 'He will give you another.'

The scent of the rushes is sharp and green; the morning is fine. The rooms of York Place are familiar to him, and as he passes through them towards the inner chambers he sees a half-familiar face and says, 'Mark?'

The boy detaches himself from the wall where he is leaning. 'You're about early. How are you?'

A sulky shrug.

'It must feel strange to be back here at York Place, now the world is so altered.'

'No.'

'You don't miss my lord cardinal?'

'No.'

'You are happy?'

'Yes.'

'My lord will be pleased to know.' To himself he says, as he moves away, you may never think of us, Mark, but we think of you. Or at least I do, I think of you calling me a felon and predicting my death. It is true that the cardinal always says, there are no safe places, there are no sealed rooms, you may as well stand on Cheapside shouting out your sins as confess to a priest anywhere in England. But when I spoke to the cardinal of killing, when I saw a shadow on the wall, there was no one to hear; so if Mark reckons I'm a murderer, that's only because he thinks I look like one.

Eight anterooms: in the last, where the cardinal should be, he finds Anne Boleyn. Look, there are Solomon and Sheba, unrolled again, back on the wall. There is a draught; Sheba eddies towards him, rosy, round, and he acknowledges her: Anselma, lady made of wool, I thought I'd never see you again.

He had sent word back to Antwerp, applied discreetly for news; Anselma was married, Stephen Vaughan said, and to a younger man, a banker. So if he drowns or anything, he said, let me know. Vaughan writes back: Thomas, come now, isn't England full of widows? And fresh young girls?

Sheba makes Anne look bad: sallow and sharp. She stands by the window, her fingers tugging and ripping at a sprig of rosemary. When she sees him, she drops it, and her hands dip back into her trailing sleeves.

In December, the king gave a banquet, to celebrate her father's elevation to be Earl of Wiltshire. The queen was elsewhere, and Anne sat where Katherine should sit. There was frost on the ground, frost in the atmosphere. They only heard of it, in the Wolsey household. The Duchess of Norfolk (who is always furious about something) was furious that her niece should have precedence. The Duchess of Suffolk, Henry's sister, refused to eat. Neither of these great ladies spoke to Boleyn's daughter. Nevertheless, Anne had taken her place as the first lady of the kingdom.

But now it's the end of Lent, and Henry has gone back to his wife; he hasn't the face to be with his concubine as we move towards the week of Christ's Passion. Her father is abroad, on diplomatic business; so is her brother George, now Lord Rochford; so is Thomas Wyatt, the poet whom she tortures. She's alone and bored at York Place; and she's reduced to sending for Thomas Cromwell, to see if he offers any amusement.

A flurry of little dogs – three of them – run away from her skirts, yapping, darting towards him. 'Don't let them out,' Anne says, and with practised and gentle hands he scoops them up – they are the kind of dogs, Bellas, with ragged ears and tiny wafting tails, that any merchant's wife would keep, across the Narrow Sea. By the time he has given them back to her, they have nibbled his fingers and his coat, licked his face and yearned towards him with goggling eyes: as if he were someone they had so much longed to meet.

Two of them he sets gently on the floor; the smallest he hands back to Anne. '*Vous êtes gentil*,' she says, 'and how my babies like you! I could not love, you know, those apes that Katherine keeps. *Les singes enchaînés*. Their little hands, their little necks fettered. My babies love me for myself.'

She's so small. Her bones are so delicate, her waist so narrow; if two law students make one cardinal, two Annes make one Katherine. Various women are sitting on low stools, sewing or rather pretending to sew. One of them is Mary Boleyn. She keeps her head down, as well she might. One of them is Mary Shelton, a bold pink-and-white Boleyn cousin, who looks him over, and – quite obviously – says to herself, Mother of God, is that the best Lady Carey thought she could get? Back in the shadows there is another girl, who has her face turned away, trying to hide. He does not know who she is, but he understands why she's looking fixedly at the floor. Anne seems to inspire it; now that he's put the dogs down, he's doing the same thing.

'*Alors*,' Anne says softly, 'suddenly, everything is about you. The king does not cease to quote Master Cromwell.' She pronounces it as if she can't manage the English: *Cremuel*. 'He is so right, he is at all points correct ... Also, let us not forget, Maître Cremuel makes us laugh.'

'I see the king does sometimes laugh. But you, madame? In your situation? As you find yourself?'

A black glance, over her shoulder. 'I suppose I seldom. Laugh. If I think. But I had not thought.'

'This is what your life has come to.'

Dusty fragments, dried leaves and stems, have fallen down her skirts. She stares out at the morning.

'Let me put it this way,' he says. 'Since my lord cardinal was reduced, how much progress have you seen in your cause?'

'None.'

'No one knows the workings of Christian countries like my lord cardinal. No one is more intimate with kings. Think how bound to you he would be, Lady Anne, if you were the means of erasing these misunderstandings and restoring him to the king's grace.'

She doesn't answer.

'Think,' he says. 'He is the only man in England who can obtain for you what you need.'

'Very well. Make his case. You have five minutes.'

'Otherwise, I can see you're really busy.'

Anne looks at him with dislike, and speaks in French. 'What do you know of how I occupy my hours?'

'My lady, are we having this conversation in English or French? Your choice entirely. But let's make it one or the other, yes?'

He sees a movement from the corner of his eye; the half-hidden girl has raised her face. She is plain and pale; she looks shocked.

'You are indifferent?' Anne says.

'Yes.'

'Very well. In French.'

He tells her again: the cardinal is the only man who can deliver a good verdict from the Pope. He is the only man who can deliver the king's conscience, and deliver it clean.

She listens. He will say that for her. He has always wondered how well women can hear, beneath the muffling folds of their veils and hoods, but Anne does give the impression that she is hearing what he has said. She waits him out, at least; she doesn't interrupt, until at last she does: so, she says, if the king wants it, and the cardinal wants it, he who was formerly the chief subject in the kingdom, then I must say, Master Cremuel, it is all taking a marvellous long while to come to pass!

From her corner her sister adds, barely audible, 'And she's not getting any younger.'

Not a stitch have the women added to their sewing since he has been in the room.

'One may resume?' he asks, persuading her. 'There is a moment left?'

'Oh yes,' Anne says. 'But a moment only: in Lent I ration my patience.'

He tells her to dismiss the slanderers who claim that the cardinal obstructed her cause. He tells her how it distresses the cardinal that the king should not have his heart's desire, which was ever the cardinal's desire too. He tells her how all the king's subjects repose their hopes in her, for an heir to the throne; and how he is sure they are right to do so. He reminds her of the many gracious letters she has written to the cardinal in times past: all of which he has on file.

202

'Very nice,' she says, when he stops. 'Very nice, Master Cremuel, but try again. One thing. One simple thing we asked of the cardinal, and he would not. *One simple thing.*'

'You know it was not simple.'

'Perhaps I am a simple person,' Anne says. 'Do you feel I am?'

'You may be. I hardly know you.'

The reply incenses her. He sees her sister smirk. You may go, Anne says: and Mary jumps up, and follows him out.

Once again Mary's cheeks are flushed, her lips are parted. She's brought her sewing with her, which he thinks is strange; but perhaps, if she leaves it behind, Anne pulls the stitches out. 'Out of breath again, Lady Carey?'

'We thought she might run up and slap you. Will you come again? Shelton and I can't wait.'

'She can stand it,' he says, and Mary says, indeed, she likes a skirmish with someone on her own level. What are you working there? he asks, and she shows him. It is Anne's new coat of arms. On everything, I suppose, he says, and she smiles broadly, oh yes, her petticoats, her handkerchiefs, her coifs and her veils; she has garments that no one ever wore before, just so she can have her arms sewn on, not to mention the wall hangings, the table napkins …

'And how are you?'

She looks down, glance swivelling away from him. 'Worn down. Frayed a little, you might say. Christmas was …'

'They quarrelled. So one hears.'

'First he quarrelled with Katherine. Then he came here for sympathy. Anne said, what! I told you not to argue with Katherine, you know you always lose. If he were not a king,' she says with relish, 'one could pity him. For the dog's life they lead him.'

'There have been rumours that Anne –'

'Yes, but she's not. I would be the first to know. If she thick-
ened by an inch, it would be me who let out her clothes. Besides,
she can't, because they don't. They haven't.'

'She'd tell you?'

'Of course – out of spite!' Still Mary will not meet his eyes.
But she seems to feel she owes him information. 'When they are
alone, she lets him unlace her bodice.'

'At least he doesn't call you to do it.'

'He pulls down her shift and kisses her breasts.'

'Good man if he can find them.'

Mary laughs; a boisterous, unsisterly laugh. It must be audible
within, because almost at once the door opens and the small
hiding girl manoeuvres herself around it. Her face is grave, her
reserve complete; her skin is so fine that it is almost translucent.
'Lady Carey,' she says, 'Lady Anne wants you.'

She speaks their names as if she is making introductions
between two cockroaches.

Mary snaps, oh, by the saints! and turns on her heel, whipping
her train behind her with the ease of long practice.

To his surprise, the small pale girl catches his glance; behind
the retreating back of Mary Boleyn, she raises her own eyes to
Heaven.

Walking away – eight antechambers back to the rest of his day –
he knows that Anne has stepped forward to a place where he can
see her, the morning light lying along the curve of her throat. He
sees the thin arch of her eyebrow, her smile, the turn of her head
on her long slender neck. He sees her speed, intelligence and
rigour. He didn't think she would help the cardinal, but what do
you lose by asking? He thinks, it is the first proposition I have
put to her; probably not the last.

There was a moment when Anne gave him all her attention:
her skewering dark glance. The king, too, knows how to look;
blue eyes, their mildness deceptive. Is this how they look at each

other? Or in some other way? For a second he understands it; then he doesn't. He stands by a window. A flock of starlings settles among the tight black buds of a bare tree. Then, like black buds unfolding, they open their wings; they flutter and sing, stirring everything into motion, air, wings, black notes in music. He becomes aware that he is watching them with pleasure: that something almost extinct, some small gesture towards the future, is ready to welcome the spring; in some spare, desperate way, he is looking forward to Easter, the end of Lenten fasting, the end of penitence. There is a world beyond this black world. There is a world of the possible. A world where Anne can be queen is a world where Cromwell can be Cromwell. He sees it; then he doesn't. The moment is fleeting. But insight cannot be taken back. You cannot return to the moment you were in before.

In Lent, there are butchers who will sell you red meat, if you know where to go. At Austin Friars he goes down to talk to his kitchen staff, and says to his chief man, 'The cardinal is sick, he is dispensed from Lent.'

His cook takes off his hat. 'By the Pope?'

'By me.' He runs his eye along the row of knives in their racks, the cleavers for splitting bones. He picks one up, looks at its edge, decides it needs sharpening and says, 'Do you think I look like a murderer? In your good opinion?'

A silence. After a while, Thurston proffers, 'At this moment, master, I would have to say …'

'No, but suppose I were making my way to Gray's Inn … Can you picture to yourself? Carrying a folio of papers and an inkhorn?'

'I do suppose a clerk would be carrying those.'

'So you can't picture it?'

Thurston takes off his hat again, and turns it inside out. He looks at it as if his brains might be inside it, or at least some prompt as to what to say next. 'I see how you would look like a lawyer. Not like a murderer, no. But if you will forgive me, master, you always look like a man who knows how to cut up a carcase.'

He has the kitchen make beef olives for the cardinal, stuffed with sage and marjoram, neatly trussed and placed side by side in trays, so that the cooks at Richmond need do nothing but bake them. Show me where it says in the Bible, a man shall not eat beef olives in March.

He thinks of Lady Anne, her unslaked appetite for a fight; the sad ladies about her. He sends those ladies some flat baskets of small tarts, made of preserved oranges and honey. To Anne herself he sends a dish of almond cream. It is flavoured with rose-water and decorated with the preserved petals of roses, and with candied violets. He is above riding across the country, carrying food himself; but not that much above it. It's not so many years since the Frescobaldi kitchen in Florence; or perhaps it is, but his memory is clear, exact. He was clarifying calf's-foot jelly, chatting away in his mixture of French, Tuscan and Putney, when somebody shouted, 'Tommaso, they want you upstairs.' His movements were unhurried as he nodded to a kitchen child, who brought him a basin of water. He washed his hands, dried them on a linen cloth. He took off his apron and hung it on a peg. For all he knows, it is there still.

He saw a young boy – younger than him – on hands and knees, scrubbing the steps. He sang as he worked:

> '*Scaramella va alla guerra*
> *Colla lancia et la rotella*
> *La zombero boro borombetta,*
> *La boro borombo …*'

'If you please, Giacomo,' he said. To let him pass, the boy moved aside, into the curve of the wall. A shift of the light wiped the curiosity from his face, blanking it, fading his past into the past, washing the future clean. *Scaramella is off to war …* But I've been to war, he thought.

He had gone upstairs. In his ears the roll and stutter of the song's military drum. He had gone upstairs and never come down again. In a corner of the Frescobaldi counting house, a table was waiting for him. *Scaramella fa la gala*, he hummed. He had taken his place. Sharpened a quill. His thoughts bubbled and swirled, Tuscan, Putney, Castilian oaths. But when he committed his thoughts to paper they came out in Latin and perfectly smooth.

Even before he walks in from the kitchens at Austin Friars, the women of the house know that he has been to see Anne.

'So,' Johane demands. 'Tall or short?'

'Neither.'

'I'd heard she was very tall. Sallow, is she not?'

'Yes, sallow.'

'They say she is graceful. Dances well.'

'We did not dance.'

Mercy says, 'But what do you think? A friend to the gospel?'

He shrugs. 'We did not pray.'

Alice, his little niece: 'What was she wearing?'

Ah, I can tell you that; he prices and sources her, hood to hem, foot to fingertip. For her headdress Anne affects the French style, the round hood flattering the fine bones of her face. He explains this, and though his tone is cool, mercantile, the women somehow do not appreciate it.

'You don't *like* her, do you?' Alice says, and he says it's not for him to have an opinion; or you either, Alice, he says, hugging her and making her giggle. The child Jo says, our master is in a good mood. This squirrel trim, Mercy says, and he says, Calabrian. Alice says, oh, Calabrian, and wrinkles her nose; Johane remarks, I must say, Thomas, it seems you got close.

'Are her teeth good?' Mercy says.

'For God's sake, woman: when she sinks them into me, I'll let you know.'

When the cardinal had heard that the Duke of Norfolk was coming out to Richmond to tear him with his teeth, he had laughed and said, 'Marry, Thomas, time to be going.'

But to go north, the cardinal needs funding. The problem is put to the king's council, who fall out, and continue the quarrel in his hearing. 'After all,' Charles Brandon says, 'one can't let an archbishop creep away to his enthronement like a servant who's stolen the spoons.'

'He's done more than steal the spoons,' Norfolk says. 'He's eaten the dinner that would have fed all England. He's filched the tablecloth, by God, and drunk the cellar dry.'

The king can be elusive. One day when he thinks he has an appointment to meet Henry, he gets Master Secretary instead. 'Sit down,' Gardiner says. 'Sit down and listen to me. Contain yourself in patience, while I put you straight on a few matters.'

He watches him ranging to and fro, Stephen the noonday devil. Gardiner is a man with bones loose-jointed, his lines flowing with menace; he has great hairy hands, and knuckles which crack when he folds his right fist into his left palm.

He takes away the menace conveyed, and the message. Pausing in the doorway, he says mildly, 'Your cousin sends greetings.'

Gardiner stares at him. His eyebrows bristle, like a dog's hackles. He thinks that Cromwell presumes –

'Not the king,' he says soothingly. 'Not His Majesty. I mean your cousin Richard Williams.'

Aghast, Gardiner says, 'That old tale!'

'Oh, come,' he says. 'It's no disgrace to be a royal bastard. Or so we think, in my family.'

'In your family? What grasp have they on propriety? I have no interest in this young person, recognise no kinship with him, and I will do nothing for him.'

'Truly, you don't need to. He calls himself Richard Cromwell now.' As he is going – really going, this time – he adds, 'Don't let it keep you awake, Stephen. I have been into the matter. You may be related to Richard, but you are not related to me.'

He smiles. Inside, he is beside himself with rage, running with it, as if his blood were thin and full of dilute venom like the uncoloured blood of a snake. As soon as he gets home to Austin Friars, he hugs Rafe Sadler and makes his hair stand up in spikes. 'Heaven direct me: boy or hedgehog? Rafe, Richard, I am feeling penitent.'

'It is the season,' Rafe says.

'I want,' he says, 'to become perfectly calm. I want to be able to get into the coop without ruffling the chickens' feathers. I want to be less like Uncle Norfolk, and more like Marlinspike.'

He has a long soothing talk in Welsh with Richard, who laughs at him because old words are fading from his memory, and he is forever sliding through bits of English, with a sly borderlands intonation. He gives his little nieces the pearl and coral bracelets he bought them weeks ago, but forgot to give. He goes down to the kitchen and makes suggestions, all of them cheerful.

He calls his household staff together, his clerks. 'We need to plan it,' he says, 'how the cardinal will be made comfortable on the road north. He wants to go slowly so the people can admire him. He needs to arrive in Peterborough for Holy Week, and from there shift by stages to Southwell, where he will plan his further progress to York. The archbishop's palace at Southwell has good rooms, but still we may need to get builders in …'

George Cavendish has told him that the cardinal has taken to spending time in prayer. There are some monks at Richmond whose company he has sought; they spell out to him the value of thorns in the flesh and salt in the wound, the merits of bread and water and the sombre delights of self-flagellation. 'Oh, that settles it,' he says, annoyed. 'We have to get him on the road. He'd be better off in Yorkshire.'

He says to Norfolk, 'Well, my lord, how shall we do this? Do you want him gone or not? Yes? Then come to the king with me.'

Norfolk grunts. Messages are sent. A day or so later, they find themselves together in an antechamber. They wait. Norfolk paces. 'Oh, by St Jude!' the duke says. 'Shall we get some fresh air? Or don't you lawyers need it?'

They stroll in the gardens; or, he strolls, the duke stamps. 'When do the flowers come out?' the duke says. 'When I was a boy, we never had flowers. It was Buckingham, you know, who brought in this knot garden sort of stuff. Oh dear, it was fancy!'

The Duke of Buckingham, keen gardener, had his head cut off for treason. That was 1521: less than ten years ago. It seems sad to mention it now, in the presence of the spring: singing from every bush, every bough.

A summons is received. As they proceed to their interview, the duke baulks and jibs; his eye rolls and his nostrils distend, his breath comes short. When the duke lays a hand on his shoulder, he is forced to slow his pace, and they scuffle along – he resisting his impulse to pull away – like two war veterans in a beggars' procession. *Scaramella va alla guerra ...* Norfolk's hand is trembling.

But it is only when they get into the presence that he fully understands how it rattles the old duke to be in a room with Henry Tudor. The gilded ebullience makes him shrink inside his clothes. Henry greets them cordially. He says it is a wonderful day and pretty much a wonderful world. He spins around the room, arms wide, reciting some verses of his own composition. He will talk about anything except the cardinal. Frustrated, Norfolk turns a dusky red, and begins to mutter. Dismissed, they are backing out. Henry calls, 'Oh, Cromwell ...'

He and the duke exchange glances. 'By the Mass ...' mutters the duke.

Hand behind his back, he indicates, be gone, my lord Norfolk, I'll catch up with you later.

Henry stands with arms folded, eyes on the ground. He says nothing till he, Cromwell, has come close. 'A thousand pounds?' Henry whispers.

It is on the tip of his tongue to say, that will be a start on the ten thousand which, to the best of my knowledge and belief, you have owed the Cardinal of York for a decade now.

He doesn't say it, of course. At such moments, Henry expects you to fall to your knees – duke, earl, commoner, light and heavy, old and young. He does it; scar tissue pulls; few of us, by our forties, are not carrying injuries.

The king signals, you can get up. He adds, his tone curious, 'The Duke of Norfolk shows you many marks of friendship and favour.'

The hand on the shoulder, he means: the minute and unexpected vibration of ducal palm against plebeian muscle and bone. 'The duke is careful to preserve all distinctions of rank.' Henry seems relieved.

An unwelcome thought creeps into his head: what if you, Henry Tudor, were to be taken ill and fall at my feet? Am I allowed to pick you up, or must I send for an earl to do it? Or a bishop?

Henry walks away. He turns and says, in a small voice, 'Every day I miss the Cardinal of York.' There is a pause. He whispers, take the money with our blessing. Don't tell the duke. Don't tell anyone. Ask your master to pray for me. Tell him it is the best I can do.

The thanks he makes, still from his kneeling situation, is eloquent and extensive. Henry looks at him bleakly and says, dear God, Master Cromwell, you can talk, can't you?

He goes out, face composed, fighting the impulse to smile broadly. *Scaramella fa la gala* ... 'Every day I miss the Cardinal of York.'

Norfolk says, what, what, what did he say? Oh, nothing, he says. Just some special hard words he wants me to convey to the cardinal.

* * *

211

The itinerary is drawn up. The cardinal's effects are put on coastal barges, to be taken to Hull and go overland from there. He himself has beaten the bargees down to a reasonable rate.

He tells Richard, you know, a thousand pounds isn't much when you have a cardinal to move. Richard asks, 'How much of your own money is sunk in this enterprise?'

Some debts should never be tallied, he says. 'I myself, I know what is owed me, but by God I know what I owe.'

To Cavendish he says, 'How many servants is he taking?'

'Only a hundred and sixty.'

'Only.' He nods. 'Right.'

Hendon. Royston. Huntingdon. Peterborough. He has men riding ahead, with precise instructions.

That last night, Wolsey gives him a package. Inside it is a small and hard object, a seal or ring. 'Open it when I'm gone.'

People keep walking in and out of the cardinal's private chamber, carrying chests and bundles of papers. Cavendish wanders through, holding a silver monstrance.

'You will come north?' the cardinal says.

'I'll come to fetch you, the minute the king summons you back.' He believes and does not believe that this will happen.

The cardinal gets to his feet. There is a constraint in the air. He, Cromwell, kneels for a blessing. The cardinal holds out a hand to be kissed. His turquoise ring is missing. The fact does not evade him. For a moment, the cardinal's hand rests on his shoulder, fingers spread, thumb in the hollow of his collarbone.

It is time he was gone. So much has been said between them that it is needless to add a marginal note. It is not for him now to gloss the text of their dealings, nor append a moral. This is not the occasion to embrace. If the cardinal has no more eloquence to offer, he surely has none. Before he has reached the door of the room the cardinal has turned back to the fireplace. He pulls his chair to the blaze, and raises a hand to shield his face; but his hand is not between himself and the fire, it is between himself and the closing door.

He makes for the courtyard. He falters; in a smoky recess where the light has extinguished itself, he leans against the wall. He is crying. He says to himself, let George Cavendish not come by and see me, and write it down and make it into a play.

He swears softly, in many languages: at life, at himself for giving way to its demands. Servants walk past, saying, 'Master Cromwell's horse is here for him! Master Cromwell's escort at the gate!' He waits till he is in command of himself, and exits, disbursing coins.

When he gets home, the servants ask him, are we to paint out the cardinal's coat of arms? No, by God, he says. On the contrary, repaint it. He stands back for a look. 'The choughs could look more lively. And we need a better scarlet for the hat.'

He hardly sleeps. He dreams of Liz. He wonders if she would know him, the man he vows that soon he will be: adamant, mild, a keeper of the king's peace.

Towards dawn, he dozes; he wakes up thinking, the cardinal just now will be mounting his horse; why am I not with him? It is 5 April. Johane meets him on the stairs; chastely, she kisses his cheek.

'Why does God test us?' she whispers.

He murmurs, 'I do not feel we will pass.'

He says, perhaps I should go up to Southwell myself? I'll go for you, Rafe says. He gives him a list. Have the whole of the archbishop's palace scrubbed out. My lord will be bringing his own bed. Draft in kitchen staff from the King's Arms. Check the stabling. Get in musicians. Last time I passed through I noticed some pigsties up against the palace wall. Find out the owner, pay him off and knock them down. Don't drink in the Crown; the ale is worse than my father's.

Richard says, 'Sir … it is time to let the cardinal go.'

213

'This is a tactical retreat, not a rout.'

They think he's gone but he's only gone into a back room. He skulks among the files. He hears Richard say, 'His heart is leading him.'

'It is an experienced heart.'

'But can a general organise a retreat when he doesn't know where the enemy is? The king is so double in this matter.'

'One could retreat straight into his arms.'

'Jesus. You think our master is double too?'

'Triple at least,' Rafe says. 'Look, there was no profit for him, ever, in deserting the old man – what would he get but the name of deserter? Perhaps something is to be got by sticking fast. For all of us.'

'Off you go then, swine-boy. Who else would think about the pigsties? Thomas More, for instance, would never think about them.'

'Or he would be exhorting the pig-keeper, my good man, Easter approacheth –'

'– hast thou prepared to receive Holy Communion?' Rafe laughs. 'By the way, Richard, hast thou?'

Richard says, 'I can get a piece of bread any day in the week.'

During Holy Week, reports come in from Peterborough: more people have crowded in to look at Wolsey than have been in that town in living memory. As the cardinal moves north he follows him on the map of these islands he keeps in his head. Stamford, Grantham, Newark; the travelling court arrives in Southwell on 28 April. He, Cromwell, writes to soothe him, he writes to warn him. He is afraid that the Boleyns, or Norfolk, or both, have found some way of implanting a spy in the cardinal's retinue.

The ambassador Chapuys, hurrying away from an audience with the king, has touched his sleeve, drawn him aside. 'Monsieur Cremuel, I thought to call at your house. We are neighbours, you know.'

'I should like to welcome you.'

'But people inform me you are often with the king now, which is pleasant, is it not? Your old master, I hear from him every week. He has become solicitous about the queen's health. He asks if she is in good spirits, and begs her to consider that soon she will be restored to the king's bosom. And bed.' Chapuys smiles. He is enjoying himself. 'The concubine will not help him. We know you have tried with her and failed. So now he turns back to the queen.'

He is forced to ask, 'And the queen says?'

'She says, I hope God in his mercy finds it possible to forgive the cardinal, for I never can.' Chapuys waits. He does not speak. The ambassador resumes: 'I think you are sensible of the tangle of wreckage that will be left if this divorce is granted, or, shall we say, somehow extorted from His Holiness? The Emperor, in defence of his aunt, may make war on England. Your merchant friends will lose their livelihoods, and many will lose their lives. Your Tudor king may go down, and the old nobility come into their own.'

'Why are you telling me this?'

'I am telling all Englishmen.'

'Door-to-door?'

He is meant to pass to the cardinal this message: that he has come to the end of his credit with the Emperor. What will that do but drive him into an appeal to the French king? Either way, treason lies.

He imagines the cardinal among the canons at Southwell, in his chair in the chapter house, presiding beneath the high vaulting like a prince at his ease in some forest glade, wreathed by carvings of leaves and flowers. They are so supple that it is as if the columns, the ribs have quickened, as if stone has burst into florid life; the capitals are decked with berries, finials are twisted stems, roses entangle the shafts, flowers and seeds flourish on one stalk; from the foliage, faces peers, the faces of dogs, of hares,

215

of goats. There are human faces, too, so lifelike that perhaps they can change their expression; perhaps they stare down, astonished, at the portly scarlet form of his patron; and perhaps in the silence of the night, when the canons are sleeping, the stone men whistle and sing.

In Italy he learned a memory system and furnished it with pictures. Some are drawn from wood and field, from hedgerow and copse: shy hiding animals, eyes bright in the undergrowth. Some are foxes and deer, some are griffins, dragons. Some are men and women: nuns, warriors, doctors of the church. In their hands he puts unlikely objects, St Ursula a crossbow, St Jerome a scythe, while Plato bears a soup ladle and Achilles a dozen damsons in a wooden bowl. It is no use hoping to remember with the help of common objects, familiar faces. One needs startling juxtapositions, images that are more or less peculiar, ridiculous, even indecent. When you have made the images, you place them about the world in locations you choose, each one with its parcel of words, of figures, which they will yield you on demand. At Greenwich, a shaven cat may peep at you from behind a cupboard; at the palace of Westminster, a snake may leer down from a beam and hiss your name.

Some of these images are flat, and you can walk on them. Some are clothed in skin and walk around in a room, but perhaps they are men with their heads on backwards, or with tufted tails like the leopards in coats of arms. Some scowl at you like Norfolk, or gape at you, like my lord Suffolk, with bewilderment. Some speak, some quack. He keeps them, in strict order, in the gallery of his mind's eye.

Perhaps it is because he is used to making these images that his head is peopled with the cast of a thousand plays, ten thousand interludes. It is because of this practice that he tends to glimpse his dead wife lurking in a stairwell, her white face upturned, or whisking around a corner of the Austin Friars, or the house at Stepney. Now the image is beginning to merge with that of her sister Johane, and everything that belonged to Liz is beginning to belong to her: her half-smile, her questioning glance, her way of being naked. Till he says, enough, and scrubs her out of his mind.

Rafe rides up the country with messages to Wolsey too secret to put into letters. He would go himself, but though Parliament is prorogued he cannot get away, because he is afraid of what might be said about Wolsey if he is not there to defend him; and at short notice the king might want him, or Lady Anne. 'And although I am not with you in person,' he writes, 'yet be assured I am, and during my life shall be, with your grace in heart, spirit, prayer and service ...'

The cardinal replies: he is 'mine own good, trusty and most assured refuge in this my calamity'. He is 'mine own entirely beloved Cromwell'.

He writes to ask for quails. He writes to ask for flower seeds. 'Seeds?' Johane says. 'He is planning to take root?'

Twilight finds the king melancholy. Another day of regress, in his campaign to be a married man again; he denies, of course, that he is married to the queen. 'Cromwell,' he says, 'I need to find my way to ownership of those ...' He looks sidelong, not wishing to say what he means. 'I understand there are legal difficulties. I do not pretend to understand them. And before you begin, I do not want them explained.'

The cardinal has endowed his Oxford college, as also the school at Ipswich, with land that will produce an income in perpetuity. Henry wants their silver and gold plate, their libraries, their yearly revenues and the land that produces the revenues; and he does not see why he should not have what he wants. The wealth of twenty-nine monasteries has gone into those foundations – suppressed by permission of the Pope, on condition that the proceeds were used for the colleges. But do you know, Henry says, I am beginning to care very little about the Pope and his permissions?

It is early summer. The evenings are long and the grass, the air, scented. You would think that a man like Henry, on a night like this, could go to whichever bed he pleases. The court is full of eager women. But after this interview he will walk in the garden with Lady Anne, her hand resting on his arm, deep in conversation; then he will go to his empty bed, and she, one presumes, to hers.

When the king asks him what he hears from the cardinal, he says that he misses the light of His Majesty's countenance; that preparations for his enthronement at York are in hand. 'Then why doesn't he get to York? It seems to me he delays and delays.' Henry glares at him. 'I will say this for you. You stick by your man.'

'I have never had anything from the cardinal other than kindness. Why would I not?'

'And you have no other master,' the king says. 'My lord Suffolk asks me, where does the fellow spring from? I tell him there are Cromwells in Leicestershire, Northamptonshire – landed people, or once they were. I suppose you are from some unfortunate branch of that family?'

'No.'

'You may not know your own forebears. I shall ask the heralds to look into it.'

'Your Majesty is kind. But they will have scant success.'

The king is exasperated. He is failing to take advantage of what is on offer: a pedigree, however meagre. 'My lord cardinal told me you were an orphan. He told me you were brought up in a monastery.'

'Ah. That was one of his little stories.'

'He told me little stories?' Several expressions chase each other across the king's face: annoyance, amusement, a wish to call back times past. 'I suppose he did. He told me that you had a loathing of those in the religious life. That was why he found you diligent in his work.'

'That was not the reason.' He looks up. 'May I speak?'

'Oh, for God's sake,' Henry cries. 'I wish someone would.'

He is startled. Then he understands. Henry wants a conversation, on any topic. One that's nothing to do with love, or hunting, or war. Now that Wolsey's gone, there's not much scope for it; unless you want to talk to a priest of some stripe. And if you send for a priest, what does it come back to? To love; to Anne; to what you want and can't have.

'If you ask me about the monks, I speak from experience, not prejudice, and though I have no doubt that some foundations are well governed, my experience has been of waste and corruption. May I suggest to Your Majesty that, if you wish to see a parade of the seven deadly sins, you do not organise a masque at court but call without notice at a monastery? I have seen monks who live like great lords, on the offerings of poor people who would rather buy a blessing than buy bread, and that is not Christian conduct. Nor do I take the monasteries to be the repositories of learning some believe they are. Was Grocyn a monk, or Colet, or Linacre, or any of our great scholars? They were university men. The monks take in children and use them as servants, they don't even teach them dog Latin. I don't grudge them some bodily comforts. It cannot always be Lent. What I cannot stomach is hypocrisy, fraud, idleness – their worn-out relics, their threadbare worship, and their lack of invention. When did anything good last come from a monastery? They do not invent, they only repeat, and what they repeat is corrupt. For hundreds of years the monks have held the pen, and what they have written is what we take to be our history, but I do not believe it really is. I believe they have suppressed the history they don't like, and written one that is favourable to Rome.'

Henry appears to look straight through him, to the wall behind. He waits. Henry says, 'Dogholes, then?'

He smiles.

Henry says, 'Our history ... As you know, I am gathering evidence. Manuscripts. Opinions. Comparisons, with how matters are ordered in other countries. Perhaps you would consult with those learned gentlemen. Put a little direction into their efforts. Talk to Dr Cranmer – he will tell you what is needed. I could make good use of the money that flows yearly to Rome. King François is richer by far than I am. I do not have a tenth of his subjects. He taxes them as he pleases. For my part, I must call Parliament. If I do not, there are riots.' He adds, bitterly, 'And riots if I do.'

'Take no lessons from King François,' he says. 'He likes war too much, and trade too little.'

Henry smiles faintly. 'You do not think so, but to me that is the remit of a king.'

'There is more tax to be raised when trade is good. And if taxes are resisted, there may be other ways.'

Henry nods. 'Very well. Begin with the colleges. Sit down with my lawyers.'

Harry Norris is there to show him out of the king's private rooms. Not smiling for once, rather stern, he says, 'I wouldn't be his tax collector.'

He thinks, are the most remarkable moments of my life to be spent under the scrutiny of Henry Norris?

'He killed his father's best men. Empson, Dudley. Didn't the cardinal get one of their houses?'

A spider scuttles from under a stool and presents him with a fact. 'Empson's house on Fleet Street. Granted the ninth of October, the first year of this reign.'

'This glorious reign,' Norris says: as if he were issuing a correction.

Gregory is fifteen as summer begins. He sits a horse beautifully, and there are good reports of his swordsmanship. His Greek ... well, his Greek is where it was.

But he has a problem. 'People in Cambridge are laughing at my greyhounds.'

'Why?' The black dogs are a matched pair. They have curving muscled necks and dainty feet; they keep their eyes lowered, mild and demure, till they sight prey.

'They say, why would you have dogs that people can't see at night? Only felons have dogs like that. They say I hunt in the forests, against the law. They say I hunt badgers, like a churl.'

'What do you want?' he asks. 'White ones, or some spots of colour?'

'Either would be correct.'

'I'll take your black dogs.' Not that he has time to go out, but Richard or Rafe will use them.

'But what if people laugh?'

'Really, Gregory,' Johane says. 'This is your father. I assure you, no one will dare laugh.'

When the weather is too wet to hunt, Gregory sits poring over *The Golden Legend*; he likes the lives of the saints. 'Some of these things are true,' he says, 'some not.' He reads *Le Morte d'Arthur*, and because it is the new edition they crowd around him, looking over his shoulder at the title page. 'Here beginneth the first book of the most noble and worthy prince King Arthur sometime King of Great Britain …' In the forefront of the picture, two couples embrace. On a high-stepping horse is a man with a mad hat, made of coiled tubes like fat serpents. Alice says, sir, did you wear a hat like that when you were young, and he says, I had a different colour for each day in the week, but mine were bigger.

Behind this man, a woman rides pillion. 'Do you think this represents Lady Anne?' Gregory asks. 'They say the king does not like to be parted from her, so he perches her up behind him like a farmer's wife.' The woman has big eyes, and looks sick from jolting; it might just be Anne. There is a small castle, not much taller than a man, with a plank for a drawbridge. The birds, circling above, look like flying daggers. Gregory says, 'Our king takes his descent from this Arthur. He was never really dead but waited in the forest biding his time, or possibly in a lake. He is several centuries old. Merlin is a wizard. He comes later. You will see. There are twenty-one chapters. If it keeps on raining I mean to read them all. Some of these things are true and some of them lies. But they are all good stories.'

When the king next calls him to court, he wants a message sent to Wolsey. A Breton merchant whose ship was seized by the English eight years ago is complaining he has not had the compensation promised. No one can find the paperwork. It was the cardinal who handled the case – will he remember it? 'I'm sure he will,' he says. 'That will be the ship with powdered pearls for ballast, the hold packed with unicorns' horns?'

God forbid! says Charles Brandon; but the king laughs and says, 'That will be the one.'

'If the sums are in doubt, or indeed the whole case, may I look after it?'

The king hesitates. 'I'm not sure you have a *locus standi* in the matter.'

It is at this moment that Brandon, quite unexpectedly, gives him a testimonial. 'Harry, let him. When this fellow has finished, the Breton will be paying you.'

Dukes revolve in their spheres. When they confer, it is not for pleasure in each other's society; they like to be surrounded by their own courts, by men who reflect them and are subservient to them. For pleasure, they are as likely to be found with a kennel-man as another duke; so it is that he spends an amiable hour with Brandon, looking over the king's hounds. It is not yet the season for hunting the hart, so the running dogs are well fed in their kennels; their musical barking rises into the evening air, and the tracking dogs, silent as they are trained to be, rise on their hind legs and watch, dripping saliva, the progress of their suppers. The kennel children are carrying baskets of bread and bones, buckets of offal and basins of pigs'-blood pottage. Charles Brandon inhales, appreciative: like a dowager in a rose garden.

A huntsman calls forward a favourite bitch, white patched with chestnut, Barbada, four years old. He straddles her and pulls back her head to show her eyes, clouded with a fine film. He will hate to kill her, but he doubts she will be much use this season. He, Cromwell, cups the bitch's jaw in his hand. 'You can draw off the membrane with a curved needle. I've seen it done. You need a steady hand and to be quick. She doesn't like it, but then she won't like to be blind.' He runs his hand over her ribs, feels the panicked throb of her little animal heart. 'The needle must be very fine. And just this length.' He shows them, between finger and thumb. 'Let me talk to your smith.'

Suffolk looks sideways at him. 'You're a useful sort of man.'

They walk away. The duke says, 'Look here. The problem is my wife.' He waits. 'I have always wanted Henry to have what he wants, I have always been loyal to him. Even when he was talking about cutting my head off because I'd married his sister. But now, what am I to do? Katherine is the queen. Surely? My wife was always a friend of hers. She's beginning to talk of, I don't know, I'd give my life for the queen, that sort of thing. And for Norfolk's niece to have precedence over my wife, who was Queen of France – we can't live with it. You see?'

He nods. I see. 'Besides,' the duke says, 'I hear Wyatt is due back from Calais.' Yes, and? 'I wonder if I ought to tell him. Tell Henry, I mean. Poor devil.'

'My lord, leave it alone,' he says. The duke lapses into what, in another man, you would call silent thought.

Summer: the king is hunting. If he wants him, he has to chase him, and if he is sent for, he goes. Henry visits, on his summer progress, his friends in Wiltshire, in Sussex, in Kent, or stays at his own houses, or the ones he has taken from the cardinal.

Sometimes, even now, the queen in her stout little person rides out with a bow, when the king hunts within one of his great parks, or in some lord's park, where the deer are driven to the archers. Lady Anne rides too – on separate occasions – and enjoys the pursuit. But there is a season to leave the ladies at home, and ride into the forest with the trackers and the running hounds; to rise before dawn when the light is clouded like a pearl; to consult with the huntsman, and then unharbour the chosen stag. You do not know where the chase will end, or when.

Harry Norris says to him, laughing, your turn soon, Master Cromwell, if he continues to favour you as he does. A word of advice: as the day begins, and you ride out, pick a ditch. Picture it in your mind. When he has worn out three good horses, when the horn is blowing for another chase, you will be dreaming of that ditch, you will imagine lying down in it: dead leaves and cool ditch-water will be all you desire.

He looks at Norris: his charming self-deprecation. He thinks, you were with my cardinal at Putney, when he fell on his knees in the dirt; did you offer the pictures in your head to the court, to the world, to the students of Gray's Inn? For if not you, then who?

In the forest you may find yourself lost, without companions. You may come to a river which is not on a map. You may lose sight of your quarry, and forget why you are there. You may meet a dwarf, or the living Christ, or an old enemy of yours; or a new enemy, one you do not know until you see his face appear between the rustling leaves, and see the glint of his dagger. You may find a woman asleep in a bower of leaves. For a moment, before you don't recognise her, you will think she is someone you know.

At Austin Friars, there is little chance to be alone, or alone with just one person. Every letter of the alphabet watches you. In the counting house there is young Thomas Avery, whom you are training up to take a grip on your private finances. Midway through the letters comes Marlinspike, strolling in the garden with his observant golden eyes. Towards the end of the alphabet comes Thomas Wriothesley pronounced Risley. He is a bright young man, twenty-five or so and well connected, son of York Herald, nephew to Garter King-at-Arms. In Wolsey's household he worked under your direction, then was carried away by Gardiner, as Master Secretary, to work for him. Now he is sometimes at court, sometimes at Austin Friars. He's Stephen's spy, the children say – Richard and Rafe.

Master Wriothesley is tall, with red-blond hair, but without the propensity of others of that complexion – the king, let's say – to grow pink when gratified, or mottled when crossed; he is always pale and cool, always his handsome self, always composed. At Trinity Hall he was a great actor in the students' plays, and he has certain affectations, a consciousness of himself, of how he appears; they mimic him behind his back, Richard and Rafe, and say, 'My name is Wri-oth-es-ley, but as I wish to spare you effort, you can call me Risley.' They say, he only complicates his name like that so he can come here and sign things, and use up our ink. They say, you know Gardiner, he is too angry to use long names, Gardiner just calls him 'you'. They are pleased with this joke and for a while, every time Mr W appears, they shout, 'It's you!'

Have mercy, he says, on Master Wriothesley. Cambridge men should have our respect.

He would like to ask them, Richard, Rafe, Master Wriothesley call me Risley: do I look like a murderer? There is a boy who says I do.

This year, there has been no summer plague. Londoners give thanks on their knees. On St John's Eve, the bonfires burn all night. At dawn, white lilies are carried in from the fields. The city daughters with shivering fingers weave them into drooping wreaths, to pin on the city's gates, and on city doors.

He thinks about that little girl like a white flower; the girl with Lady Anne, who manoeuvred herself around the door. It would have been easy to find out her name, except he didn't, because he was busy finding out secrets from Mary. Next time he sees her … but what's the use of thinking of it? She will come of some noble house. He had meant to write to Gregory and say, I have seen such a sweet girl, I will find out who she is and, if I steer our family adroitly in the next few years, perhaps you can marry her.

He has not written this. In his present precarious situation, it would be about as useful as the letters Gregory used to write to him: *Dear father, I hope you are well. I hope your dog is well. And now no more for lack of time.*

Lord Chancellor More says, 'Come and see me, and we'll talk about Wolsey's colleges. I feel sure the king will do something for the poor scholars. Do come. Come and see my roses before the heat spoils them. Come and see my new carpet.'

It is a muted, grey day; when he arrives at Chelsea, Master Secretary's barge is tied up, the Tudor flag limp in the sultry air. Beyond the gatehouse, the red-brick house, new-built, offers its bright facade to the river. He strolls towards it, through the mulberry trees. Standing in the porch, under the honeysuckle, Stephen Gardiner. The grounds at Chelsea are full of small pet animals, and as he approaches, and his host greets him, he sees that the Chancellor of England is holding a lop-eared rabbit with snowy fur; it hangs peacefully in his hands, like ermine mittens.

'Is your son-in-law Roper with us today?' Gardiner asks. 'A pity. I hoped to see him change his religion again. I wanted to witness it.'

'A garden tour?' More offers.

'I thought that we might see him sit down a friend of Luther, as formerly he was, yet come back to the church by the time they bring in the currants and gooseberries.'

226

'Will Roper is now settled,' More says, 'in the faith of England and of Rome.'

He says, 'It's not really a good year for soft fruit.'

More looks at him out of the tail of his eye; he smiles. He chats genially as he leads them into the house. Lolloping after them comes Henry Pattinson, a servant of More's he sometimes calls his fool, and to whom he allows licence. The man is a great brawler; normally you take in a fool to protect him, but in Pattinson's case it's the rest of the world needs protection. Is he really simple? There's something sly in More, he enjoys embarrassing people; it would be like him to have a fool that wasn't. Pattinson's supposed to have fallen from a church steeple and hit his head. At his waist, he wears a knotted string which he sometimes says is his rosary; sometimes he says it is his scourge. Sometimes he says it is the rope that should have saved him from his fall.

Entering the house, you meet the family hanging up. You see them painted life-size before you meet them in the flesh; and More, conscious of the double effect it makes, pauses, to let you survey them, to take them in. The favourite, Meg, sits at her father's feet with a book on her knee. Gathered loosely about the Lord Chancellor are his son John; his ward Anne Cresacre, who is John's wife; Margaret Giggs, who is also his ward; his aged father, Sir John More; his daughters Cicely and Elizabeth; Pattinson, with goggle eyes; and his wife Alice, with lowered head and wearing a cross, at the edge of the picture. Master Holbein has grouped them under his gaze, and fixed them for ever: as long as no moth consumes, no flame or mould or blight.

In real life there is something fraying about their host, a suspicion of unravelling weave; being at his leisure, he wears a simple wool gown. The new carpet, for their inspection, is stretched out on two trestle tables. The ground is not crimson but a blush colour: not rose madder, he thinks, but a red dye mixed with whey. 'My lord cardinal liked turkey carpets,' he murmurs. 'The

Doge once sent him sixty.' The wool is soft wool from mountain sheep, but none of them were black sheep; where the pattern is darkest the surface has already a brittle feel, from patchy dyeing, and with time and use it may flake away. He turns up the corner, runs his fingertips over the knots, counting them by the inch, in an easy accustomed action. 'This is the Ghiordes knot,' he says, 'but the pattern is from Pergamon – you see there within the octagons, the eight-pointed star?' He smooths down the corner, and walks away from it, turns back, says 'there' – he walks forward, puts a tender hand on the flaw, the interruption in the weave, the lozenge slightly distorted, warped out of true. At worst, the carpet is two carpets, pieced together. At best, it has been woven by the village's Pattinson, or patched together last year by Venetian slaves in a backstreet workshop. To be sure, he needs to turn the whole thing over. His host says, 'Not a good buy?'

It's beautiful, he says, not wanting to spoil his pleasure. But next time, he thinks, take me with you. His hand skims the surface, rich and soft. The flaw in the weave hardly matters. A turkey carpet is not on oath. There are some people in this world who like everything squared up and precise, and there are those who will allow some drift at the margins. He is both these kinds of person. He would not allow, for example, a careless ambiguity in a lease, but instinct tells him that sometimes a contract need not be drawn too tight. Leases, writs, statutes, all are written to be read, and each person reads them by the light of self-interest. More says, 'What do you think, gentlemen? Walk on it, or hang it on the wall?'

'Walk on it.'

'Thomas, your luxurious tastes!' And they laugh. You would think they were friends.

They go out to the aviary; they stand deep in talk, while finches flit and sing. A small grandchild toddles in; a woman in an apron shadows him, or her. The child points to the finches, makes sounds expressive of pleasure, flaps its arms. It eyes Stephen Gardiner; its small mouth turns down. The nurse swoops in, before tears ensue; how must it be, he asks Stephen, to have such effortless power over the young? Stephen scowls.

More takes him by the arm. 'Now, about the colleges,' he says. 'I have spoken to the king, and Master Secretary here has done his best – truly, he has. The king may refound Cardinal College in his name, but for Ipswich I see no hope, after all it is only … I am sorry to say this, Thomas, but it is only the birthplace of a man now disgraced, and so has no special claim on us.'

'It is a shame for the scholars.'

'It is, of course. Shall we go in to supper?'

In More's great hall, the conversation is exclusively in Latin, though More's wife Alice is their hostess and does not have a word of it. It is their custom to read a passage of scripture, by way of a grace. 'It is Meg's turn tonight,' More says.

He is keen to show off his darling. She takes the book, kissing it; over the interruptions of the fool, she reads in Greek. Gardiner sits with his eyes shut tight; he looks, not holy, but exasperated. He watches Margaret. She is perhaps twenty-five. She has a sleek, darting head, like the head of the little fox which More says he has tamed; all the same, he keeps it in a cage for safety.

The servants come in. It is Alice's eye they catch as they place the dishes; here, madam, and here? The family in the picture don't need servants, of course; they exist just by themselves, floating against the wall. 'Eat, eat,' says More. 'All except Alice, who will burst out of her corset.'

At her name she turns her head. 'That expression of painful surprise is not native to her,' More says. 'It is produced by scraping back her hair and driving in great ivory pins, to the peril of her skull. She believes her forehead is too low. It is, of course. Alice, Alice,' he says, 'remind me why I married you.'

'To keep house, Father,' Meg says in a low voice.

'Yes, yes,' More says. 'A glance at Alice frees me from stain of concupiscence.'

He is conscious of an oddity, as if time has performed some loop or snared itself in a noose; he has seen them on the wall as Hans froze them, and here they enact themselves, wearing their various expression of aloofness or amusement, benignity and grace: a happy family. He prefers their host as Hans painted him; the Thomas More on the wall, you can see that he's thinking, but not what he's thinking, and that's the way it should be. The painter has grouped them so skilfully that there's no space between the figures for anyone new. The outsider can only soak himself into the scene, as an unintended blot or stain; certainly, he thinks, Gardiner is a blot or stain. The Secretary waves his black sleeves; he argues vigorously with their host. What does St Paul mean when he says Jesus was made a little lower than the angels? Do Hollanders ever make jokes? What is the proper coat of arms of the Duke of Norfolk's heir? Is that thunder in the distance, or will this heat keep up? Just as in the painting, Alice has a little monkey on a gilt chain. In the painting it plays about her skirts. In life, it sits in her lap and clings to her like a child. Sometimes she lowers her head and talks to it, so that no one else can hear.

More takes no wine, though he serves it to his guests. There are several dishes, which all taste the same – flesh of some sort, with a gritty sauce like Thames mud – and then junkets, and a cheese which he says one of his daughters has made – one of his daughters, wards, step-daughters, one of the women of whom the house is full. 'Because one must keep them employed,' he says. 'They cannot always be at their books, and young women are prone to mischief and idleness.'

'For sure,' he mutters. 'They'll be fighting in the streets next.' His eyes are drawn unwillingly to the cheese; it is pitted and wobbling, like the face of a stable boy after a night out.

'Henry Pattinson is excitable tonight,' More says. 'Perhaps he should be bled. I hope his diet has not been too rich.'

'Oh,' says Gardiner, 'I have no anxieties on that score.'

Old John More – who must be eighty now – has come in for supper, and so they yield the conversation to him; he is fond of telling stories. 'Did you ever hear of Humphrey Duke of Gloucester and the beggar who claimed to be blind? Did you ever hear of the man who didn't know the Virgin Mary was a Jew?' Of such a sharp old lawyer one hopes for more, even in his dotage. Then he begins on anecdotes of foolish women, of which he has a vast collection, and even when he falls asleep, their host has more. Lady Alice sits scowling. Gardiner, who has heard all these stories before, is grinding his teeth.

'Look there at my daughter-in-law Anne,' More says. The girl lowers her eyes; her shoulders tense, as she waits for what is coming. 'Anne craved – shall I tell them, my dear? – she craved a pearl necklace. She did not cease to talk about it, you know how young girls are. So when I gave her a box that rattled, imagine her face. Imagine her face again when she opened it. What was inside? Dried peas!'

The girl takes a deep breath. She raises her face. He sees the effort it costs her. 'Father,' she says, 'don't forget to tell the story of the woman who didn't believe the world was round.'

'No, that's a good one,' More says.

When he looks at Alice, staring at her husband with painful concentration, he thinks, she still doesn't believe it.

After supper they talk about wicked King Richard. Many years ago Thomas More began to write a book about him. He could not decide whether to compose in English or Latin, so he has done both, though he has never finished it, or sent any part of it to the printer. Richard was born to be evil, More says; it was written on him from his birth. He shakes his head. 'Deeds of blood. Kings' games.'

'Dark days,' says the fool.

'Let them never come again.'

'Amen.' The fool points to the guests. 'Let these not come again either.'

There are people in London who say that John Howard, grandfather of the Norfolk that is now, was more than a little concerned in the disappearance of the children who went into the Tower and never came out again. The Londoners say – and he reckons the Londoners know – that it was on Howard's watch that the princes were last seen; though Thomas More thinks it was Constable Brakenbury who handed the keys to the killers. Brakenbury died at Bosworth; he can't come out of his grave and complain.

The fact is, Thomas More is thick with the Norfolk that is now, and keen to deny that his ancestor helped disappear anyone, let alone two children of royal blood. In his mind's eye he frames the present duke: in one dripping, sinewy hand he holds a small golden-haired corpse, and in the other hand the kind of little knife a man brings to table to cut his meat.

He comes back to himself: Gardiner, jabbing the air, is pressing the Lord Chancellor on his evidence. Presently the fool's grumbling and groaning become unbearable. 'Father,' Margaret says, 'please send Henry out.' More rises to scold him, take him by the arm. All eyes follow him. But Gardiner takes advantage of the lull. He leans in, speaks English in an undertone. 'About Master Wriothesley. Remind me. Is he working for me, or for you?'

'For you, I would have thought, now he is made a Clerk of the Signet. They assist Master Secretary, do they not?'

'Why is he always at your house?'

'He's not a bound apprentice. He may come and go.'

'I suppose he's tired of churchmen. He wants to know what he can learn from … whatever it is you call yourself, these days.'

'A person,' he says placidly. 'The Duke of Norfolk says I'm a person.'

'Master Wriothesley has his eye on his advantage.'

'I hope we all have that. Or why did God give us eyes?'

'He thinks of making his fortune. We all know that money sticks to your hands.'

Like the aphids to More's roses. 'No,' he sighs. 'It passes through them, alas. You know, Stephen, how I love luxury. Show me a carpet, and I'll walk on it.'

The fool scolded and ejected, More rejoins them. 'Alice, I have told you about drinking wine. Your nose is glowing.' Alice's face grows stiff, with dislike and a kind of fear. The younger women, who understand all that is said, bow their heads and examine their hands, fiddling with their rings and turning them to catch the light. Then something lands on the table with a thud, and Anne Cresacre, provoked into her native tongue, cries, 'Henry, stop that!' There is a gallery above with oriel windows; the fool, leaning through one of them, is peppering them with broken crusts. 'Don't flinch, masters,' he shouts. 'I am pelting you with God.'

He scores a hit on the old man, who wakes with a start. Sir John looks about him; with his napkin, he wipes dribble from his chin. 'Now, Henry,' More calls up. 'You have wakened my father. And you are blaspheming. And wasting bread.'

'Dear Lord, he should be whipped,' Alice snaps.

He looks around him; he feels something which he identifies as pity, a heavy stirring beneath the breastbone. He believes Alice has a good heart; continues to believe it even when, taking his leave, permitted to thank her in English, she raps out, 'Thomas Cromwell, why don't you marry again?'

'No one will have me, Lady Alice.'

'Nonsense. Your master may be down but you're not poor, are you? Got your money abroad, that's what I'm told. Got a good house, haven't you? Got the king's ear, my husband says. And from what my sisters in the city say, got everything in good working order.'

'Alice!' More says. Smiling, he takes her wrist, shakes her a little. Gardiner laughs: his deep bass chuckle, like laughter through a crack in the earth.

When they go out to Master Secretary's barge, the scent of the gardens is heavy in the air. 'More goes to bed at nine o'clock,' Stephen says.

'With Alice?'

'People say not.'

'You have spies in the house?'

Stephen doesn't answer.

It is dusk; lights bob in the river. 'Dear God, I am hungry,' Master Secretary complains. 'I wish I had kept back one of the fool's crusts. I wish I had laid hands on the white rabbit; I'd eat it raw.'

He says, 'You know, he daren't make himself plain.'

'Indeed he dare not,' Gardiner says. Beneath the canopy, he sits hunched into himself, as if he were cold. 'But we all know his opinions, which I think are fixed and impervious to argument. When he took office, he said he would not meddle with the divorce, and the king accepted that, but I wonder how long he will accept it.'

'I didn't mean, make himself plain to the king. I meant, to Alice.'

Gardiner laughs. 'True, if she understood what he said about her she'd send him down to the kitchens and have him plucked and roasted.'

'Suppose she died? He'd be sorry then.'

'He'd have another wife in the house before she was cold. Someone even uglier.'

He broods: foresees, vaguely, an opportunity for placing bets. 'That young woman,' he says. 'Anne Cresacre. She is an heiress, you know? An orphan?'

'There was some scandal, was there not?'

'After her father died her neighbours stole her, for their son to marry. The boy raped her. She was thirteen. This was in Yorkshire … that's how they go on there. My lord cardinal was furious when he heard of it. It was he who got her away. He put her under More's roof because he thought she'd be safe.'

'So she is.'

Not from humiliation. 'Since More's son married her, he lives off her lands. She has a hundred a year. You'd think she could have a string of pearls.'

'Do you think More is disappointed in his boy? He shows no talent for affairs. Still, I hear you have a boy like that. You'll be looking for an heiress for him soon.' He doesn't reply. It's true; John More, Gregory Cromwell, what have we done to our sons? Made them into idle young gentlemen – but who can blame us for wanting for them the ease we didn't have? One thing about More, he's never idled for an hour, he's passed his life reading, writing, talking towards what he believes is the good of the Christian commonwealth. Stephen says, 'Of course you may have other sons. Aren't you looking forward to the wife Alice will find you? She is warm in your praises.'

He feels afraid. It is like Mark, the lute player: people imagining what they cannot know. He is sure he and Johane have been secret. He says, 'Don't you ever think of marrying?'

A chill spreads over the waters. 'I am in holy orders.'

'Oh, come on, Stephen. You must have women. Don't you?'

The pause is so long, so silent, that he can hear the oars as they dip into the Thames, the little splash as they rise; he can hear the ripples in their wake. He can hear a dog barking, from the southern shore. The Secretary asks, 'What kind of Putney enquiry is that?'

The silence lasts till Westminster. But on the whole, not too bad a trip. As he mentions, disembarking, neither of them has thrown the other in the river. 'I'm waiting till the water's colder,' Gardiner says. 'And till I can tie weights to you. You have a trick of resurfacing, don't you? By the way, why am I bringing you to Westminster?'

235

'I am going to see Lady Anne.'

Gardiner is affronted. 'You didn't say so.'

'Should I report all my plans to you?'

He knows that is what Gardiner would prefer. The word is that the king is losing patience with his council. He shouts at them, 'The cardinal was a better man than any of you, for managing matters.' He thinks, if my lord cardinal comes back – which by a caprice of the king's he may, any time now – then you're all dead, Norfolk, Gardiner, More. Wolsey is a merciful man, but surely: only up to a point.

Mary Shelton is in attendance; she looks up, simpers. Anne is sumptuous in her nightgown of dark silk. Her hair is down, her delicate feet bare inside kidskin slippers. She is slumped in a chair, as if the day has beaten the spirit out of her. But still, as she looks up, her eyes are sparkling, hostile. 'Where've you been?'

'Utopia.'

'Oh.' She is interested. 'What passed?'

'Dame Alice has a little monkey that sits on her knee at table.'

'I hate them.'

'I know you do.'

He walks about. Anne lets him treat her fairly normally, except when she has a sudden, savage seizure of I-who-will-be-Queen, and slaps him down. She examines the toe of her slipper. 'They say that Thomas More is in love with his own daughter.'

'I think they may be right.'

Anne's sniggering laugh. 'Is she a pretty girl?'

'No. Learned though.'

'Did they talk about me?'

'They never mention you in that house.' He thinks, I should like to hear Alice's verdict.

'Then what was the talk?'

'The vices and follies of women.'

'I suppose you joined it? It's true, anyway. Most women are foolish. And vicious. I have seen it. I have lived among the women too long.'

He says, 'Norfolk and my lord your father are very busy seeing ambassadors. France, Venice, the Emperor's man – just in these last two days.'

He thinks, they are working to entrap my cardinal. I know it.

'I did not think you could afford such good information. Though they say you have spent a thousand pounds on the cardinal.'

'I expect to get it back. From here and there.'

'I suppose people are grateful to you. If they have received grants out of the cardinal's lands.'

He thinks, your brother George, Lord Rochford, your father Thomas, Earl of Wiltshire, haven't they got rich from the cardinal's fall? Look at what George is wearing these days, look at the money he spends on horses and girls; but I don't see much sign of gratitude from the Boleyns. He says, 'I just take my conveyancer's fee.'

She laughs. 'You look well on it.'

'Do you know, there are ways and ways … Sometimes people just tell me things.'

It is an invitation. Anne drops her head. She is on the verge of becoming one of those people. But perhaps not tonight. 'My father says, one can never be sure of that person, one can never tell who he's working for. I should have thought – but then I am only a woman – that it is perfectly obvious that you're working for yourself.'

That makes us alike, he thinks: but does not quite say.

Anne yawns, a little catlike yawn. 'You're tired,' he says. 'I shall go. By the way, why did you send for me?'

'We like to know where you are.'

'So why does your lord father not send for me, or your brother?'

She looks up. It may be late, but not too late for Anne's knowing smile. 'They do not think you would come.'

August: the cardinal writes to the king, a letter full of complaint, saying that he is being hounded by his creditors, 'wrapped in misery and dread' – but the stories that come back are different. He is holding dinners, and inviting all the local gentry. He is dispensing charity on his old princely scale, settling lawsuits, and sweet-talking estranged husbands and wives into sharing a roof again.

Call-Me-Risley was up in Southwell in June, with William Brereton of the king's privy chamber: getting the cardinal's signature on a petition Henry is circulating, which he means to send to the Pope. It's Norfolk's idea, to get the peers and bishops to sign up to this letter asking Clement to let the king have his freedom. It contains certain murky, unspecific threats, but Clement's used to being threatened – no one's better at spinning a question out, setting one party against the other, playing ends against the middle.

The cardinal looks well, according to Wriothesley. And his building work, it seems, has gone beyond repairs and a few renovations. He has been scouring the country for glaziers, joiners, and for plumbers; it is ominous when my lord decides to improve the sanitation. He never had a parish church but he built the tower higher; never lodged anywhere where he did not draw up drainage plans. Soon there will be earthworks, culverts and pipes laid. Next he will be installing fountains. Wherever he goes he is cheered by the people.

'The people?' Norfolk says. 'They'd cheer a Barbary ape. Who cares what they cheer? Hang 'em all.'

'But then who will you tax?' he says, and Norfolk looks at him fearfully, unsure if he's made a joke.

Rumours of the cardinal's popularity don't make him glad, they make him afraid. The king has given Wolsey a pardon, but if he was offended once, he can be offended again. If they could think up forty-four charges, then – if fantasy is unconstrained by truth – they can think up forty-four more.

He sees Norfolk and Gardiner with their heads together. They look up at him; they glare and don't speak.

Wriothesley stays with him, in his shadow and footsteps, writes his most confidential letters, those to the cardinal and the king. He never says, I am too tired. He never says, it is late. He remembers all that he is required to remember. Even Rafe is not more perfect.

It is time to bring the girls into the family business. Johane complains of her daughter's poor sewing, and it seems that, transferring the needle surreptitiously into her wrong hand, the child has devised an awkward little backstitch which you would be hard-pushed to imitate. She gets the job of sewing up his dispatches for the north.

September 1530: the cardinal leaves Southwell, travelling by easy stages to York. The next part of his progress becomes a triumphal procession. People from all over the countryside flock to him, ambushing him at wayside crosses so that he can lay his magical hands on their children; they call it 'confirmation', but it seems to be some older sacrament. They pour in by the thousand, to gape at him; and he prays for them all.

'The council has the cardinal under observation,' Gardiner says, swishing past him. 'They have had the ports closed.'

Norfolk says, 'Tell him if I ever see him again, I will chew him up, bones, flesh and gristle.' He writes it down just so and sends it up-country: 'bones, flesh and gristle.' He can hear the crunch and snap of the duke's teeth.

On 2 October the cardinal reaches his palace at Cawood, ten miles from York. His enthronement is planned for 7 November. News comes that he has called a convocation of the northern church; it is to meet at York the day after his enthronement. It is a signal of his independence; some may think it is a signal of revolt. He has not informed the king, he has not informed old Warham, Archbishop of Canterbury; he can hear the cardinal's voice, soft and amused, saying, now, Thomas, why do they need to know?

Norfolk calls him in. His face is crimson and he froths a little at the mouth as he starts to shout. He has been seeing his armourer for a fitting, and is still wearing sundry parts – his cuirass, his garde-reins – so that he looks like an iron pot wobbling to the boil. 'Does he think he can dig in up there and carve himself a kingdom? Cardinal's hat not enough for him, only a crown will do for Thomas bloody Wolsey the bleeding butcher's boy, and I tell you, I tell you …'

He drops his gaze in case the duke should stop to read his thoughts. He thinks, my lord would have made such an excellent king; so benign, so sure and suave in his dealings, so equitable, so swift and so discerning. His rule would have been the best rule, his servants the best servants; and how he would have enjoyed his state.

His glance follows the duke as he bobs and froths; but to his surprise, when the duke turns, he smites his own metalled thigh, and a tear – at the pain, or something else – bubbles into his eye. 'Ah, you think me a hard man, Cromwell. I am not such a hard man that I don't see how you are left. Do you know what I say? I say I don't know one man in England who would have done what you have done, for a man disgraced and fallen. The king says so. Even him, Chapuys, the Emperor's man, he says, you cannot fault what's-he-called. I say, it's a pity you ever saw Wolsey. It's a pity you don't work for me.'

'Well,' he says, 'we all want the same thing. For your niece to be queen. Can we not work together?'

Norfolk grunts. There is something amiss, in his view, with that word 'together', but he cannot articulate what it is. 'Do not forget your place.'

He bows. 'I am mindful of your lordship's continuing favour.'

'Look here, Cromwell, I wish you would come down and see me at home at Kenninghall, and talk to my lady wife. She's a woman of monstrous demands. She thinks I shouldn't keep a woman in the house, for my pleasant usage, you know? I say, where else should she be? Do you want me to disturb myself on a winter's night and venture out on the icy roads? I don't seem to be able to express myself correctly to her; do you think you could come down and put my case?' He says, hastily, 'Not now, of course. No. More urgent ... see my niece ...'

'How is she?'

'In my view,' Norfolk says, 'Anne's out for bloody murder. She wants the cardinal's guts in a dish to feed her spaniels, and his limbs nailed over the city gates of York.'

It is a dark morning and your eyes naturally turn towards Anne, but something shadowy is bobbing about, on the fringes of the circle of light. Anne says, 'Dr Cranmer is just back from Rome. He brings us no good news, of course.'

They know each other; Cranmer has worked from time to time for the cardinal, as indeed who has not? Now he is active in the king's case. They embrace cautiously: Cambridge scholar, person from Putney.

He says, 'Master, why would you not come to our college? To Cardinal College, I mean? His Grace was very sorry you would not. We would have made you comfortable.'

'I think he wanted more permanence,' Anne says, sneering.

'But with respect, Lady Anne, the king has almost said to me that he will take over the Oxford foundation himself.' He smiles. 'Perhaps it can be called after you?'

This morning Anne wears a crucifix on a gold chain. Sometimes her fingers pull at it impatiently, and then she tucks her hands back in her sleeves. It is so much a habit with her that people say she has something to hide, a deformity; but he thinks

241

she is a woman who doesn't like to show her hand. 'My uncle Norfolk says Wolsey goes about with eight hundred armed men at his back. They say he has letters from Katherine – is that true? They say Rome will issue a decree telling the king to separate from me.'

'That would be a clear mistake on Rome's part,' Cranmer says.

'Yes it would. Because he won't be *told*. Is he some parish clerk, the King of England? Or some child? This would not happen in France; their king keeps his churchmen under his hand. Master Tyndale says, "One king, one law, is God's ordinance in every realm." I have read his book, *The Obedience of a Christian Man*. I myself have shown it to the king and marked the passages that touch on his authority. The subject must obey his king as he would his God; do I have the sense of it? The Pope will learn his place.'

Cranmer looks at her with a half-smile; she's like a child who you're teaching to read, who dazzles you by sudden aptitude.

'Wait,' she says, 'I have something to show you.' She darts a look. 'Lady Carey …'

'Oh, please,' Mary says. 'Do not give it currency.'

Anne snaps her fingers. Mary Boleyn moves forward into the light, a flash of blonde hair. 'Give it,' Anne says. It is a paper, which she unfolds. 'I found this in my bed, would you believe? As it happened, it was a night when that sickly milk-faced creeper had turned down the sheet, and of course I could not get any sense out of her, she cries if you look at her sideways. So I cannot know who put it there.'

She unfolds a drawing. There are three figures. The central figure is the king. He is large and handsome, and to make sure you don't miss him he is wearing a crown. On either side of him is a woman; the one on the left has no head. 'That's the queen,' she says, 'Katherine. And that's me.' She laughs. 'Anne *sans tête*.'

Dr Cranmer holds out his hand for the paper. 'Give it to me, I'll destroy it.'

She crumples it in her fist. 'I can destroy it myself. There is a prophecy that a queen of England will be burned. But a prophecy does not frighten me, and even if it is true, I will run the risk.'

Mary stands, like a statue, in the position where Anne left her; her hands are joined, as if the paper were still between them. Oh, Christ, he thinks, to see her out of here; to take her to somewhere she could forget she is a Boleyn. She asked me once. I failed her. If she asked me again, I would fail her again.

Anne turns against the light. Her cheeks are hollow – how thin she is now – her eyes are alight. '*Ainsi sera,*' she says. 'Never mind who grudges it, it will happen. I mean to have him.'

On their way out, he and Dr Cranmer do not speak, till they see the little pale girl coming towards them, the sickly milk-faced creeper, carrying folded linen.

'I think this is the one who cries,' he says. 'So do not look at her sideways.'

'Master Cromwell,' she says, 'this may be a long winter. Send us some more of your orange tarts.'

'I haven't seen you for so long … What have you been doing, where have you been?'

'Sewing mostly.' She considers each question separately. 'Where I'm sent.'

'And spying, I think.'

She nods. 'I'm not very good at it.'

'I don't know. You're very small and unnoticeable.'

He means it as a compliment; she blinks, in acknowledgement. 'I don't speak French. So don't you, if you please. It gives me nothing to report.'

'Who are you spying for?'

'My brothers.'

'Do you know Dr Cranmer?'

'No,' she says; she thinks it's a real question.

'Now,' he instructs her, 'you must say who you are.'

'Oh. I see. I'm John Seymour's daughter. From Wolf Hall.'

He is surprised. 'I thought his daughters were with Queen Katherine.'

'Yes. Sometimes. Not now. I told you. I go where I'm sent.'

'But not where you are appreciated.'

'I am, in the one way. You see, Lady Anne will not refuse any of the queen's ladies who want to spend time with her.' She raises her eyes, a pale momentary brightness. 'Very few do.'

Every rising family needs information. With the king considering himself a bachelor, any little girl can hold the key to the future, and not all his money is on Anne. 'Well, good luck,' he says. 'I'll try to keep it in English.'

'I would be obliged.' She bows. 'Dr Cranmer.'

He turns to watch her as she patters off in the direction of Anne Boleyn. A small suspicion enters his mind, about the paper in the bed. But no, he thinks. That is not possible.

Dr Cranmer says, smiling, 'You have a wide acquaintance among the court ladies.'

'Not very wide. I still don't know which daughter that was, there are three at least. And I suppose Seymour's sons are ambitious.'

'I hardly know them.'

'The cardinal brought Edward up. He's sharp. And Tom Seymour is not such a fool as he pretends.'

'The father?'

'Stays in Wiltshire. We never see him.'

'One could envy him,' Dr Cranmer murmurs.

Country life. Rural felicity. A temptation he has never known. 'How long were you at Cambridge, before the king called you up?'

Cranmer smiles. 'Twenty-six years.'

They are both dressed for riding. 'You are going back to Cambridge today?'

'Not to stay. The family' – the Boleyns, he means – 'want to have me at hand. And you, Master Cromwell?'

'A private client. I can't make a living from Lady Anne's black looks.'

Boys wait with their horses. From various folds of his garments Dr Cranmer produces objects wrapped in cloth. One of them is a carrot cut carefully lengthways, and another a wizened apple, quartered. As if he were a child, fair-minded with a treat, he gives him two slices of carrot and half the apple, to feed to his own horse; as he does so, he says, 'You owe much to Anne Boleyn. More than perhaps you think. She has formed a good opinion of you. I'm not sure she cares to be your sister-in-law, mind ...'

The beasts bend their necks, nibbling, their ears flicking in appreciation. It is a moment of peace, like a benediction. He says, 'There are no secrets, are there?'

'No. No. Absolutely none.' The priest shakes his head. 'You asked why I would not come to your college.'

'I was making conversation.'

'Still ... as we heard it in Cambridge, you performed such labours for the foundation ... the students and Fellows all commend you ... no detail escapes Master Cromwell. Though to be sure, this comfort on which you pride yourselves ...' His tone, smooth and unemphatic, doesn't change. 'In the fish cellar? Where the students died?'

'My lord cardinal did not take that lightly.'

Cranmer says, lightly, 'Nor did I.'

'My lord was never a man to ride down another for his opinions. You would have been safe.'

'I assure you he would have found no heresy in me. Even the Sorbonne could not fault me. I have nothing to be afraid of.' A wan smile. 'But perhaps ... ah well ... perhaps I'm just a Cambridge man at heart.'

He says to Wriothesley, 'Is he? At all points orthodox?'

'It's hard to say. He doesn't like monks. You should get on.'

245

'Was he liked at Jesus College?'

'They say he was a severe examiner.'

'I suppose he doesn't miss much. Although. He thinks Anne is a virtuous lady.' He sighs. 'And what do we think?'

Call-Me-Risley snorts. He has just married – a connection of Gardiner's – but his relations with women are not, on the whole, gentle.

'He seems a melancholy sort of man,' he says. 'The kind who wants to live retired from the world.'

Wriothesley's fair eyebrows rise, almost imperceptibly. 'Did he tell you about the barmaid?'

When Cranmer comes to the house, he feeds him the delicate meat of the roe deer; they take supper privately, and he gets his story from him, slowly, slowly and easily. He asks the doctor where he comes from, and when he says, nowhere you know, he says, try me, I've been to most places.

'If you had been to Aslockton, you wouldn't know you were there. If a man goes fifteen miles to Nottingham, let him only spend the night away, and it vanishes clear from his mind.' His village has not even a church; only some poor cottages and his father's house, where his family has lived for three generations. .

'Your father is a gentleman?'

'He is indeed.' Cranmer sounds faintly shocked: what else could he be? 'The Tamworths of Lincolnshire are among my connections. The Cliftons of Clifton. The Molyneux family, of whom you will have heard. Or have you?'

'And you have much land?'

'If I had thought, I would have brought the ledgers.'

'Forgive me. We men of business ...'

Eyes rest on him, assessing. Cranmer nods. 'A small acreage. And I am not the eldest. But he brought me up well. Taught me horsemanship. He gave me my first bow. He gave me my first hawk to train.'

Dead, he thinks, the father long dead: still looking for his hand in the dark.

'When I was twelve he sent me to school. I suffered there. The master was harsh.'

'To you? Or others as well?'

'If I am honest, I only thought of myself. I was weak, no doubt. I suppose he sought out weakness. Schoolmasters do.'

'Could you not complain to your father?'

'I wonder now why I did not. But then he died. I was thirteen. Another year and my mother sent me to Cambridge. I was glad of the escape. To be from under his rod. Not that the flame of learning burnt bright. The east wind put it out. Oxford – Magdalen especially, where your cardinal was – it was everything in those days.'

He thinks, if you were born in Putney, you saw the river every day, and imagined it widening out to the sea. Even if you had never seen the ocean you had a picture of it in your head from what you had been told by foreign people who sometimes came upriver. You knew that one day you would go out into a world of marble pavements and peacocks, of hillsides buzzing with heat, the fragrance of crushed herbs rising around you as you walked. You planned for what your journeys would bring you: the touch of warm terracotta, the night sky of another climate, alien flowers, the stone-eyed gaze of other people's saints. But if you were born in Aslockton, in flat fields under a wide sky, you might just be able to imagine Cambridge: no further.

'A man from my college,' Dr Cranmer says tentatively, 'was told by the cardinal that as an infant you were stolen by pirates.'

He stares at him for a moment, then smiles in slow delight. 'How I miss my master. Now he has gone north, there is no one to invent me.'

Dr Cranmer, cautious: 'So it is not true? Because I wondered if there was doubt over whether you were baptised. I fear it could be a question, in such an event.'

'But the event never took place. Really. Pirates would have given me back.'

Dr Cranmer frowns. 'You were an unruly child?'

'If I'd known you then, I could have knocked down your schoolmaster for you.'

Cranmer has stopped eating; not that he has tasted much. He thinks, at some level of his being this man will always believe I am a heathen; I will never disabuse him now. He says, 'Do you miss your studies? Your life has been disrupted since the king made you an ambassador and had you tossed on the high seas.'

'In the Bay of Biscay, when I was coming from Spain, we had to bale out the ship. I heard the sailors' confessions.'

'They must have been something to hear.' He laughs. 'Shouted over the noise of the storm.'

After that strenuous journey – though the king was pleased with his embassy – Cranmer might have dropped back into his old life, except that he had mentioned, meeting Gardiner in passing, that the European universities might be polled on the king's case. You've tried the canon lawyers; now try the theologians. Why not? the king said; bring me Dr Cranmer and put him in charge of it. The Vatican said it had nothing against the idea, except that the divines should not be offered money: a merry caveat, coming from a Pope with the surname of de' Medici. To him, this initiative seems nearly futile – but he thinks of Anne Boleyn, he thinks of what her sister had said: she's not getting any younger. 'Look, you've found a hundred scholars, at a score of universities, and some say the king is right –'

'Most –'

'And if you find two hundred more, what will it matter? Clement isn't open to persuasion now. Only to pressure. And I don't mean moral pressure.'

'But it's not Clement we have to persuade of the king's case. It's all of Europe. All Christian men.'

'I'm afraid the Christian women may be harder still.'

Cranmer drops his eyes. 'I could never persuade my wife of anything. I would never have thought to try.' He pauses. 'We are two widowers, I think, Master Cromwell, and if we are to become colleagues, I must not leave you wondering, or at the mercy of stories that people will bring to you.'

The light is fading around them while he talks, and his voice, each murmur, each hesitation, trails away into the dusk. Outside the room where they sit, where the house is going on its nightly course, there is a banging and scraping, as if trestles were being moved, and a faint sound of cheering and whooping. But he ignores it, settles his attention on the priest. Joan, an orphan, he says, servant in a gentleman's house where he used to visit; no people of her own, no marriage portion; he pitied her. A whisper in a panelled room raises spirits from the fens, fetches the dead: Cambridge twilights, damp seeping from the marshes and rush lights burning in a bare swept room where an act of love takes place. I could not help but marry her, Dr Cranmer says, and indeed, how can a man help marrying? His college took away his fellowship, of course, you cannot have married fellows. And naturally she had to leave her place, and not knowing what else to do with her, he lodged her at the Dolphin, which is kept by some connections of his, some – he confesses, not without a downward glance – some relations of his, yes it is true that some of his people keep the Dolphin.

'It's nothing to be ashamed of. The Dolphin is a good house.'

Ah, you know it: and he bites his lip.

He studies Dr Cranmer: his way of blinking, the cautious finger he lays to his chin, his eloquent eyes and his pale praying hands. So Joan was not, he says, she was not, you see, a barmaid, whatever people say, and I know what they do say. She was a wife with a child in her belly, and he a poor scholar, preparing to live with her in honest poverty, but that didn't happen, in the event. He thought he might find a position as secretary to some gentleman, or as a tutor, or that he might earn a living by his pen, but all that scheming was to no avail. He thought they might move from Cambridge, even from England, but they didn't have to, in the end. He hoped some connection of his would do something for him, before the child was born: but when Joan died in labour, no one could do anything for him, not any more. 'If the child had lived I would have salvaged something. As it was, no one knew what to say to me. They did not know whether to condole with me on losing my wife, or congratulate me because Jesus College had taken me back. I took holy orders; why not? All that, my marriage, the child I thought I would have, my colleagues seemed to regard it as some sort of miscalculation. Like losing your way in the woods. You get home and never think of it again.'

'There are some strange cold people in this world. It is priests, I think. Saving your presence. Training themselves out of natural feeling. They mean it for the best, of course.'

'It was not a mistake. We did have a year. I think of her every day.'

The door opens; it is Alice bringing in lights. 'This is your daughter?'

Rather than explain his family, he says, 'This is my lovely Alice. This is not your job, Alice?'

She bobs, a small genuflection to a churchman. 'No, but Rafe and the others want to know what you are talking about so long. They are waiting to know if there will be a dispatch to the cardinal tonight. Jo is standing by with her needle and thread.'

'Tell them I will write in my own hand, and we will send it tomorrow. Jo may go to bed.'

'Oh, we are not going to bed. We are running Gregory's greyhounds up and down the hall and making a noise fit to wake the dead.'

'I can see why you don't want to break off.'

'Yes, it is excellent,' Alice says. 'We have the manners of scullery maids and no one will ever want to marry us. If our aunt

Mercy had behaved like us when she was a girl, she would have been knocked round the head till she bled from the ears.'

'Then we live in happy times,' he says.

When she has gone, and the door is closed behind her, Cranmer says, 'The children are not whipped?'

'We try to teach them by example, as Erasmus suggests, though we all like to race the dogs up and down and make a noise, so we are not doing very well in that regard.' He does not know if he should smile; he has Gregory; he has Alice, and Johane and the child Jo, and in the corner of his eye, at the periphery of his vision, the little pale girl who spies on the Boleyns. He has hawks in his mews who move towards the sound of his voice. What has this man?

'I think of the king's advisers,' Dr Cranmer says. 'The sort of men who are about him now.'

And he has the cardinal, if the cardinal still thinks well of him after all that has passed. If he dies, he has his son's sable hounds to lie at his feet.

'They are able men,' Cranmer says, 'who will do anything he wants, but it seems to me – I do not know how it seems to you – that they are utterly lacking in any understanding of his situation … any compunction or kindness. Any charity. Or love.'

'It is what makes me think he will bring the cardinal back.'

Cranmer studies his face. 'I am afraid that cannot happen now.'

He has a wish to speak, to express the bottled rage and pain he feels. He says, 'People have worked to make misunderstandings between us. To persuade the cardinal that I am not working for his interests, only for my own, that I have been bought out, that I see Anne every day –'

'Of course, you do see her …'

'How else can I know how to move next? My lord cannot know, he cannot understand, what it's like here now.'

Cranmer says gently, 'Should you not go to him? Your presence would dispel any doubt.'

'There is no time. The snare is set for him and I dare not move.'

There is a chill in the air; the summer birds have flown, and black-winged lawyers are gathering for the new term in the fields of Lincoln's Inn and Gray's. The hunting season – or at least, the season when the king hunts every day – will soon be over. Whatever is happening elsewhere, whatever deceits and frustrations, you can forget them in the field. The hunter is among the most innocent of men; living in the moment makes him feel pure. When he returns in the evening, his body aches, his mind is full of pictures of leaves and sky; he does not want to read documents. His miseries, his perplexities have receded, and they will stay away, provided – after food and wine, laughter and exchange of stories – he gets up at dawn to do it all over again.

But the winter king, less occupied, will begin to think about his conscience. He will begin to think about his pride. He will begin to prepare the prizes for those who can deliver him results.

It is an autumn day, whitish sun flitting behind the loosening, flickering leaves. They go into the butts. The king likes to do more than one thing at once: talk, direct arrows at a target. 'Here we will be alone,' he says, 'and I will be free to open my mind to you.'

In fact, the population of a small village – as it might be, Aslockton – is circulating around them. The king does not know what 'alone' means. Is he ever by himself, even in his dreams? 'Alone' means without Norfolk clattering after him. 'Alone' means without Charles Brandon, who in a summer fit of fury the king advised to make himself scarce and not come within fifty miles of the court. 'Alone' means just with my yeoman of the bow and his menials, alone with my gentlemen of the privy chamber, who are my select and private friends. Two of these gentlemen, unless he is with the queen, sleep at the foot of his bed; so they have been on duty for some years now.

When he sees Henry draw his bow, he thinks, I see now he is royal. At home or abroad, in wartime or peacetime, happy or aggrieved, the king likes to practise several times in the week, as an Englishman should; using his height, the beautiful trained muscles of his arms, shoulders and chest, he sends his arrows snapping straight to the eye of the target. Then he holds out his arm, for someone to unstrap and restrap the royal armguard; for someone to change his bow, and bring him a choice. A cringing slave hands a napkin, to mop his forehead, and picks it up from where the king has dropped it; and then, exasperated, one shot or two falling wide, the King of England snaps his fingers, for God to change the wind.

The king shouts, 'From various quarters I receive the advice that I should consider my marriage dissolved in the eyes of Christian Europe, and may remarry as I please. And soon.'

He doesn't shout back.

'But others say ...' The breeze blows, his words are carried off, towards Europe.

'I am one of the others.'

'Dear Jesus,' Henry says. 'I will be unmanned by it. How long do you suppose my patience lasts?'

He hesitates to say, you are still living with your wife. You share a roof, a court, wherever you move together, she on the queen's side, you on the king's; you told the cardinal she was your sister not your wife, but if today you do not shoot well, if the breeze is not in your favour or you find your eyes blurred by sudden tears, it is only sister Katherine whom you can tell; you can admit no weakness or failure to Anne Boleyn.

He has studied Henry through his practice round. He has taken up a bow at his invitation, which causes some consternation in the ranks of the gentlemen who stud the grass and lean against trees, wearing their fallen-fruit silks of mulberry, gold and plum. Though Henry shoots well, he has not the action of a born archer; the born archer lays his whole body into the bow.

Compare him with Richard Williams, Richard Cromwell as he is now. His grandfather ap Evan was an artist with the bow. He never saw him, but you can bet he had muscles like cords and every one in use from the heels up. Studying the king, he is satisfied that his great-grandfather was not the archer Blaybourne, as the story says, but Richard, Duke of York. His grandfather was royal; his mother was royal; he shoots like a gentleman amateur, and he is king through and through.

The king says, you have a good arm, a good eye. He says disparagingly, oh, at this distance. We have a match every Sunday, he says, my household. We go to Paul's for the sermon and then out to Moorfields, we meet up with our fellow guildsmen and destroy the butchers and the grocers, and then we have a dinner together. We have grudge matches with the vintners …

Henry turns to him, impulsive: what if I came with you one week? If I came in disguise? The commons would like it, would they not? I could shoot for you. A king should show himself, sometimes, don't you feel? It would be amusing, yes?

Not very, he thinks. He cannot swear to it, but he thinks there are tears in Henry's eyes. 'For sure we would win,' he says. It is what you would say to a child. 'The vintners would be roaring like bears.'

It begins to drizzle, and as they walk towards a sheltering clump of trees, a pattern of leaves shadows the king's face. He says, Nan threatens to leave me. She says that there are other men and she is wasting her youth.

Norfolk, panicking, that last week of October 1530: 'Listen. This fellow here,' he jerks his thumb, rudely, at Brandon – who is back at court, of course he is back – 'this fellow here, a few years ago, he charged at the king in the lists, and nearly killed him. Henry had not put his visor down, God alone knows why – but these things happen. My lord here ran his lance – bam! – into the king's headpiece, and the lance shattered – an inch, *one inch*, from his eye.'

Norfolk has hurt his right hand, by the force of his demonstration. Wincing, but furious, earnest, he presses on. 'One year later, Henry is following his hawk – it's that cut-up sort of country, flat, deceptive, you know it – he comes to a ditch, he drives in a pole to help him cross, the infernal instrument breaks, God rot it, and there's His Majesty face down and stunned in a foot of water and mud, and if some servant hadn't clawed him out, well, gentlemen, I shudder to think.'

He thinks, that's one question answered. In case of peril, you may pick him up. Fish him out. Whatever.

'Suppose he dies?' Norfolk demands. 'Supposing a fever carries him away or he comes off his horse and breaks his neck? Then what? His bastard, Richmond? I've nothing against him, he's a fine boy, and Anne says I should get him married to my daughter Mary, Anne's no fool, let's put a Howard everywhere, she says, everywhere the king looks. Now I have no quarrel with Richmond, except he was born out of wedlock. Can he reign? Ask yourselves this. How did the Tudors get the crown? By title? No. By force? Exactly. By God's grace they won the battle. The old king, he had such a fist as you will go many a mile to meet, he had great books into which he entered his grudges and he forgave, when? Never! That's how one rules, masters.' He turns to his audience, to the councillors waiting and watching and to the gentlemen of the court and the bedchamber; to Henry Norris, to his friend William Brereton, to Master Secretary Gardiner; to, incidentally, as it happens, Thomas Cromwell, who is increasingly where he shouldn't be. He says, 'The old king bred, and by the help of Heaven he bred sons. But when Arthur died, there were swords sharpened in Europe, and they were sharpened to carve up this kingdom. Henry that is now, he was a child, nine years old. If the old king had not staggered on a few more years, the wars would have been to fight all over again. A child cannot hold England. And a bastard child? God give me strength! And it's November again!'

It's hard to fault what the duke says. He understands it all; even that last cry, wrung from the duke's heart. It's November, and a year has passed since Howard and Brandon walked into York Place and demanded the cardinal's chain of office, and turned him out of his house.

There is a silence. Then someone coughs, someone sighs. Someone – probably Henry Norris – laughs. It is he who speaks. 'The king has one child born in wedlock.'

Norfolk turns. He flushes, a deep mottled purple. 'Mary?' he says. 'That talking shrimp?'

'She will grow up.'

'We are all waiting,' Suffolk says. 'She has now reached fourteen, has she not?'

'But her face,' Norfolk says, 'is the size of my thumbnail.' The duke shows off his digit to the company. 'A woman on the English throne, it flies in the face of nature.'

'Her grandmother was Queen of Castile.'

'She cannot lead an army.'

'Isabella did.'

Says the duke, 'Cromwell, why are you here? Listening to the talk of gentlemen?'

'My lord, when you shout, the beggars on the street can hear you. In Calais.'

Gardiner has turned to him; he is interested. 'So you think Mary can rule?'

He shrugs. 'It depends who advises her. It depends who she marries.'

Norfolk says, 'We have to act soon. Katherine has half the lawyers of Europe pushing paper for her. This dispensation. That dispensation. The other dispensation with the different bloody wording that they say they've got in Spain. It doesn't matter. This has gone beyond paper.'

'Why?' Suffolk says. 'Is your niece in foal?'

'No! More's the pity. Because if she were, he'd have to do something.'

'What?' Suffolk says.

'I don't know. Grant his own divorce?'

There is a shuffle, a grunt, a sigh. Some look at the duke; some look at their shoes. There's no man in the room who doesn't want Henry to have what he wants. Their lives and fortunes depend on it. He sees the path ahead: a tortuous path through a flat terrain, the horizon deceptively clear, the country intersected by ditches, and the present Tudor, a certain amount of mud bespattering his person and his face, fished gasping into clear air. He says, 'That good man who pulled the king out of the ditch, what was his name?'

Norfolk says, drily, 'Master Cromwell likes to hear of the deeds of those of low birth.'

He doesn't suppose any of them will know. But Norris says, 'I know. His name was Edmund Mody.'

Muddy, more like, Suffolk says. He yells with laughter. They stare at him.

It is All Souls' Day: as Norfolk puts it, November again. Alice and Jo have come to speak to him. They are leading Bella – the Bella that is now – on a ribbon of pink silk. He looks up: may I be of service to you two ladies?

Alice says, 'Master, it is more than two years since my aunt Elizabeth died, your lady wife. Will you write to the cardinal, and ask him to ask the Pope to let her out of Purgatory?'

He says, 'What about your aunt Kat? And your little cousins, my daughters?'

The children exchange glances. 'We don't think they have been there so long. Anne Cromwell was proud of her working of numbers and boasted that she was learning Greek. Grace was vain of her hair and used to state that she had wings, this was a lie.

We think perhaps they must suffer more. But the cardinal could try.'

Don't ask, don't get, he thinks.

Alice says, encouragingly, 'You have been so active in the cardinal's business that he would not refuse. And although the king does not favour the cardinal any more, surely the Pope favours him?'

'And I expect,' says Jo, 'that the cardinal writes to the Pope every day. Though I do not know who sews his letters. And I suppose the cardinal might send him a present for his trouble. Some money, I mean. Our aunt Mercy says that the Pope does nothing except on cash terms.'

'Come with me,' he says. They exchange glances. He sweeps them along before him. Bella's small legs race. Jo drops her lead, but still Bella runs behind.

Mercy and the elder Johane are sitting together. The silence is not companionable. Mercy is reading, murmuring the words to herself. Johane is staring at the wall, sewing in her lap. Mercy marks her place. 'What's this, an embassy?'

'Tell her,' he says. 'Jo, tell your mother what you have been asking me.'

Jo starts to cry. It is Alice who speaks up and puts their case. 'We want our aunt Liz to come out of Purgatory.'

'What have you been teaching them?' he asks.

Johane shrugs. 'Many grown persons believe what they believe.'

'Dear God, what is going on under this roof? These children believe the Pope can go down to the underworld with a bunch of keys. Whereas Richard denies the sacrament –'

'What?' Johane's mouth falls open. 'He does what?'

Mercy says, 'Richard is right. When the good Lord said, this is my body, he meant, this signifies my body. He did not license priests to be conjurers.'

'But he said, *it is.* He did not say, this is like my body, he said, *it is.* Can God lie? No. He is incapable of it.'

258

'God can do anything,' Alice says.

Johane stares at her. 'You little minx.'

'If my mother were here, she would slap you for that.'

'No fighting,' he says. 'Please?' The Austin Friars is like the world in little. These few years it's been more like a battlefield than a household; or like one of the tented encampments in which the survivors look in despair at their shattered limbs and spoiled expectations. But they are his to direct, these last hardened troops; if they are not to be flattened in the next charge it is he who must teach them the defensive art of facing both ways, faith and works, Pope and new brethren, Katherine and Anne. He looks at Mercy, who is smirking. He looks at Johane, a high colour in her cheeks. He turns away from Johane and his thoughts, which are not precisely theological. He says to the children, 'You have done nothing wrong.' But their faces are stricken, and he coaxes them: 'I shall give you a present, Jo, for sewing the cardinal's letters; and I shall give you a present, Alice, I am sure that we do not need a reason. I shall give you marmosets.'

They look at each other. Jo is tempted. 'Do you know where to get them?'

'I think so. I have been to the Lord Chancellor's house, and his wife has such a creature, and it sits on her knee and attends to everything she says.'

Alice says, 'They are not the fashion now.'

'Though we thank you,' says Mercy.

'Though we thank you,' Alice repeats. 'But marmosets are not seen at court since Lady Anne came up. To be fashionable, we should like Bella's puppies.'

'In time,' he says. 'Perhaps.' The room is full of undercurrents, some of which he does not understand. He picks up his dog, tucks her under his arm and goes off to see how to provide some more money for brother George Rochford. He sits Bella on his desk, to take a nap among his papers. She has been sucking the end of her ribbon, and attempting subtly to undo the knot at her throat.

On 1 November 1530, a commission for the cardinal's arrest is given to Harry Percy, the young Earl of Northumberland. The earl arrives at Cawood to arrest him, forty-eight hours before his planned arrival in York for his investiture. He is taken to Ponte-fract Castle under guard, from there to Doncaster, and from there to Sheffield Park, the home of the Earl of Shrewsbury. Here at Talbot's house he falls ill. On 26 November the Constable of the Tower arrives, with twenty-four men at arms, to escort him south. From there he travels to Leicester Abbey. Three days later he dies.

What was England, before Wolsey? A little offshore island, poor and cold.

George Cavendish comes to Austin Friars. He cries as he talks. Sometimes he dries his tears and moralises. But mostly he cries. 'We had not even finished our dinner,' he says. 'My lord was taking his dessert when young Harry Percy walked in. He was spattered with mud from the road, and he had the keys in his hands, he had taken them from the porter already, and set sentries on the stairs. My lord rose to his feet, he said, Harry, if I'd known, I'd have waited dinner for you. I fear we've almost finished the fish. Shall I pray for a miracle?

'I whispered to him, my lord, do not blaspheme. Then Harry Percy came forward: my lord, I arrest you for high treason.'

Cavendish waits. He waits for him to erupt in fury? But he puts his fingers together, joined as if he were praying. He thinks, Anne arranged this, and it must have given her an intense and secret pleasure; vengeance deferred, for herself, for her old lover, once berated by the cardinal and sent packing from the court. He says, 'How did he look? Harry Percy?'

'He was shaking from head to foot.'

'And my lord?'

'Demanded his warrant, his commission. Percy said, there are items in my instructions you may not see. So, said my lord, if you will not show it, I shall not surrender to you, so here's a pretty state of affairs, Harry. Come, George, my lord said to me, we will go into my rooms, and have some conference. They followed him on his heels, the earl's party, so I stood in the door and I barred the way. My lord cardinal walked into his chamber, mastering himself, and when he turned he said, Cavendish, look at my face: I am not afraid of any man alive.'

He, Cromwell, walks away so that he does not have to see the man's distress. He looks at the wall, at the panelling, at his new linenfold panelling, and runs his index finger across its grooves. 'When they took him from the house, the townspeople were assembled outside. They knelt in the road and wept. They asked God to send vengeance on Harry Percy.'

God need not trouble, he thinks: I shall take it in hand.

'We were riding south. The weather was closing in. At Doncaster it was late when we arrived. In the street the towns-folk were packed shoulder to shoulder, and each person holding up a candle against the dark. We thought they would disperse, but they stood all night in the road. And their candles burned down. And it was daylight, of a sort.'

'It must have put heart into him. Seeing the crowds.'

'Yes, but by then – I did not say, I should have told you – he had gone a week without eating.'

'Why? Why did he do that?'

'Some say he meant to destroy himself. I cannot believe it, a Christian soul ... I ordered him a dish of warden pears, roasted with spices – did I do right?'

'And he ate?'

'A little. But then he put his hand to his chest. He said, there is something cold inside me, cold and hard like a whetstone. And that was where it began.' Cavendish gets up. Now he too walks about the room. 'I called for an apothecary. He made a powder and I had him pour it into three cups. I drank off one. He, the apothecary, he drank another. Master Cromwell, I trusted nobody. My lord took his powder and presently the pain eased, and he said, there, it was wind, and we laughed, and I thought, tomorrow he will be better.'

'Then Kingston came.'

'Yes. How could we tell my lord, the Constable of the Tower is here to fetch you? My lord sat down on a packing case. He said, William Kingston? William Kingston? He kept on saying his name.'

And all that time a weight in his chest, a whetstone, a steel, a sharpening knife in his gut.

'I said to him, now take it cheerfully, my lord. You will come before the king and clear your name. And Kingston said the same, but my lord said, you are leading me into a fool's paradise. I know what is provided for me, and what death is prepared. That night we did not sleep. My lord voided black blood from his bowels. The next morning he was too weak to stand, and so we could not ride. But then we did ride. And so we came to Leicester.

'The days were very short, the light poor. On Monday morning at eight he woke. I was just then bringing in the small wax lights, and setting them along the cupboard. He said, whose is that shadow that leaps along the wall? And he cried your name. God forgive me, I said you were on the road. He said, the ways are treacherous. I said, you know Cromwell, the devil does not delay him – if he says he is on the road he will be here.'

'George, make this story short, I cannot bear it.'

But George must have his say: next morning at four, a bowl of chicken broth, but he would not eat it. Is this not a meatless day? He asked for the broth to be taken away. By now he had been ill for eight days, continually voiding his bowels, bleeding and in pain, and he said, believe me, death is the end of this.

Put my lord in a difficulty, and he will find a way; with his craft and cunning, he will find a way, an exit. Poison? If so, then by his own hand.

It was eight next morning when he drew his last breath. Around his bed, the click of rosary beads; outside the restive stamp of horses in their stalls, the thin winter moon shining down on the London road.

'He died in his sleep?' He would have wished him less pain. George says, no, he was speaking to the last. 'Did he speak of me again?'

Anything? A word?

I washed him, George says, laid him out for burial. 'I found, under his fine holland shirt, a belt of hair ... I am sorry to tell you, I know you are not a lover of these practices, but so it was. I think he never did this till he was at Richmond among the monks.'

'What became of it? This belt of hair?'

'The monks of Leicester kept it.'

'God Almighty! They'll make it pay.'

'Do you know, they could provide nothing better than a coffin of plain boards?' Only when he says this does George Cavendish give way; only at this point does he swear and say, by the passion of Christ, I heard them knocking it together. When I think of the Florentine sculptor and his tomb, the black marble, the bronze, the angels at his head and foot ... But I saw him dressed in his archbishop's robes, and I opened his fingers to put into his hand his crozier, just as I thought I would see him hold it when he was enthroned at York. It was only two days away. Our bags were packed and we were ready for the road; till Harry Percy walked in.

'You know, George,' he says, 'I begged him, be content with what you have clawed back from ruin, go to York, be glad to be alive ... In the course of things, he would have lived another ten years, I know he would.'

'We sent for the mayor and all the city officials, so that they could see him in his coffin, so there could be no false rumours that he was living and escaped to France. Some made remarks about his low birth, by God I wish you had been there –'

'I too.'

'For to your face, Master Cromwell, they had not done it, nor would they dare. When the light failed we kept vigil, with the tapers burning around his coffin, till four in the morning, which you know is the canonical hour. Then we heard Mass. At six we laid him in the crypt. There left him.'

Six in the morning, a Wednesday, the feast of St Andrew the Apostle. I, a simple cardinal. There left him and rode south, to find the king at Hampton Court. Who says to George, 'I would not for twenty thousand pounds that the cardinal had died.'

'Look, Cavendish,' he says, 'when you are asked what the cardinal said in his last days, tell them nothing.'

George raises his eyebrows. 'I already have. Told them nothing. The king questioned me. My lord Norfolk.'

'If you tell Norfolk anything, he will twist it into treason.'

'Still, as he is Lord Treasurer, he has paid me my back wages. I was three-quarters of the year in arrears.'

'What were you paid, George?'

'Ten pounds a year.'

'You should have come to me.'

These are the facts. These are the figures. If the Lord of the Underworld rose up tomorrow in the privy chamber, and offered a dead man back, fresh from the grave, fresh from the crypt, the miracle of Lazarus for £20,000 – Henry Tudor would be pushed to scrape it together. Norfolk as Lord Treasurer? Fine; it doesn't matter who holds the title, who holds the clanking keys to the empty chests.

'Do you know,' he says, 'if the cardinal could say, as he used to say to me, Thomas, what would you like for a New Year's gift, I would say, I would like sight of the nation's accounts.'

Cavendish hesitates; he begins to speak; he stops; he starts again. 'The king said certain things to me. At Hampton Court. "Three may keep counsel, if two are away."'

'It is a proverb, I think.'

'He said, "If I thought my cap knew my counsel, I would cast it into the fire."'

'I think that also is a proverb.'

'He means to say that he will not choose any adviser now: not my lord of Norfolk, nor Stephen Gardiner, or anyone, any person to be close to him, to be so close as the cardinal was.'

He nods. That seems a reasonable interpretation.

Cavendish looks ill. It is the strain of the long sleepless nights, of the vigil around the coffin. He is worried about various sums of money the cardinal had on the journey, which he did not have when he died. He is worried about how to get his own effects from Yorkshire to his home; apparently Norfolk has promised him a cart and a transport allowance. He, Cromwell, talks about this while he thinks about the king, and out of sight of George folds his fingers, one by one, tight into the palm of his hand. Mary Boleyn traced, in his palm, a certain shape; he thinks, Henry, I have your heart in my hand.

When Cavendish has gone, he goes to his secret drawer and takes out the package that the cardinal gave him on the day he began his journey north. He unwinds the thread that binds it. It snags, knots, he works at it patiently; before he had expected it, the turquoise ring rolls into his palm, cold as if it came from the tomb. He pictures the cardinal's hands, long-fingered, white and unscarred, steady for so many years on the wheel of the ship of state; but the ring fits as if it had been made for him.

The cardinal's scarlet clothes now lie folded and empty. They cannot be wasted. They will be cut up and become other garments. Who knows where they will get to over the years? Your eye will be taken by a crimson cushion or a patch of red on a banner or ensign. You will see a glimpse of them in a man's inner sleeve or in the flash of a whore's petticoat.

Another man would go to Leicester to see where he died and talk to the abbot. Another man would have trouble imagining it, but he has no trouble. The red of a carpet's ground, the flush of the robin's breast or the chaffinch, the red of a wax seal or the heart of the rose: implanted in his landscape, cered in his inner eye, and caught in the glint of a ruby, in the colour of blood, the cardinal is alive and speaking. Look at my face: I am not afraid of any man alive.

At Hampton Court in the great hall they perform an interlude; its name is 'The Cardinal's Descent into Hell'. It takes him back to last year, to Gray's Inn. Under the eye of the officials of the king's household, the carpenters have been working furiously and for bonus rates, erecting frames upon which to drape canvas cloths painted with scenes of torture. At the back of the hall, the screens are entirely hung with flames.

The entertainment is this: a vast scarlet figure, supine, is dragged across the floor, howling, by actors dressed as devils. There are four devils, one for each limb of the dead man. The devils wear masks. They have tridents with which they prick the cardinal, making him twitch and writhe and beg. He had hoped the cardinal died without pain but Cavendish had said no. He died conscious, talking of the king. He had started out of sleep and said, whose is that shadow on the wall?

The Duke of Norfolk walks around the hall chortling, 'Isn't it good, eh? It's good enough to be printed! By the Mass, that's what I shall do! I shall have it printed, so I can take it home with me, and at Christmas we can play it all over again.'

Anne sits laughing, pointing, applauding. He has never seen her like this before: lit up, glowing. Henry sits frozen by her side. Sometimes he laughs, but he thinks if you could get close you would see that his eyes are afraid. The cardinal rolls across the floor, kicking out at the demons, but they harry him, in their woolly suits of black, and cry, 'Come, Wolsey, we must fetch you to Hell, for our master Beelzebub is expecting you to supper.'

When the scarlet mountain pops up his head and asks, 'What wines does he serve?' he almost forgets himself and laughs. 'I'll have no English wine,' the dead man declares. 'None of that cats' piss my lord of Norfolk lays on.'

Anne crows; she points; she points to her uncle; the noise rises high to the roof beams with the smoke from the hearth, the laughing and chanting from the tables, the howling of the fat prelate. No, they assure him, the devil is a Frenchman, and there are catcalls and whistles, and songs break out. The devils now catch the cardinal's head in a noose. They haul him to his feet, but he fights them. The flailing punches are not all fake, and he hears their grunts, as the breath is knocked out of them. But there are four hangmen, and one great scarlet bag of nothingness, who chokes, who claws; the court cries, 'Let him down! Let him down alive!'

The actors throw up their hands; they prance back and let him fall. When he rolls on the ground, gasping, they thrust their forks into him and wind out lengths of scarlet woollen bowel.

The cardinal utters blasphemies. He utters farts, and fireworks blast out from corners of the hall. From the corner of his eye, he sees a woman run away, a hand over her mouth; but Uncle Norfolk marches about, pointing: 'Look, there his guts are wound out, as the hangman would draw them! Why, I'd pay to see this!'

Someone calls, 'Shame on you, Thomas Howard, you'd have sold your own soul to see Wolsey down.' Heads turn, and his head turns, and nobody knows who has spoken; but he thinks it might be, could it be, Thomas Wyatt? The gentlemen devils have dusted themselves down and got their breath back. Shouting 'Now!' they pounce; the cardinal is dragged off to Hell, which is located, it seems, behind the screens at the back of the hall.

He follows them behind the screens. Pages run out with linen towels for the actors, but the satanic influx knocks them aside. At least one of the children gets an elbow in the eye, and drops his bowl of steaming water on his feet. He sees the devils wrench off their masks, and toss them, swearing, into a corner; he watches as they try to claw off their knitted devil-coats. They turn to each other, laughing, and begin to pull them over each other's heads. 'It's like the shirt of Nessus,' George Boleyn says, as Norris wrenches him free.

George tosses his head to settle his hair back into place; his white skin has flared from contact with the rough wool. George and Henry Norris are the hand-devils, who seized the cardinal by his forepaws. The two foot-devils are still wrestling each other from their trappings. They are a boy called Francis Weston, and William Brereton, who – like Norris – is old enough to know better. They are so absorbed in themselves – cursing, laughing, calling for clean linen – that they do not notice who is watching them and anyway they do not care. They splash themselves and each other, they towel away their sweat, they rip the shirts from the pages' hands, they drop them over their heads. Still wearing their cloven hooves, they swagger out to take their bow.

In the centre of the space they have vacated, the cardinal lies inert, shielded from the hall by the screens; perhaps he is sleeping.

He walks up to the scarlet mound. He stops. He looks down. He waits. The actor opens one eye. 'This must be Hell,' he says. 'This must be Hell, if the Italian is here.'

The dead man pulls off his mask. It is Sexton, the fool: Master Patch. Master Patch, who screamed so hard, a year ago, when they wanted to part him from his master.

Patch holds out a hand, to be helped to his feet, but he does not take it. The man scrambles up by himself, cursing. He begins to pull off his scarlet, dragging and tearing at the cloth. He,

Cromwell, stands with his arms folded, his writing hand tucked into a hidden fist. The fool casts away his padding, fat pillows of wool. His body is scrawny, wasted, his chest furred with wiry hairs. He speaks: 'Why you come to my country, Italian? Why you no stay in your own country, ah?'

Sexton is a fool, but he's not soft in the head. He knows well he's not an Italian.

'You should have stayed over there,' Patch says, in his own London voice. 'Have your own walled town by now. Have a cathedral. Have your own marzipan cardinal to eat after dinner. Have it all for a year or two, eh, till a bigger brute comes along and knocks you off the trough?'

He picks up the costume Patch has cast off. Its red is the fiery, cheap, quick-fading scarlet of Brazil-wood dye, and it smells of alien sweat. 'How can you act this part?'

'I act what part I'm paid to act. And you?' He laughs: his shrill bark, which passes as mad. 'No wonder your humour's so bitter these days. Nobody's paying you, eh? Monsieur Cremuel, the retired mercenary.'

'Not so retired. I can fix you.'

'With that dagger you keep where once was your waist.' Patch springs away, he capers. He, Cromwell, leans against the wall; he watches him. He can hear a child sobbing, somewhere out of sight; perhaps it is the little boy who has been hit in the eye, now slapped again for dropping the bowl, or perhaps just for crying. Childhood was like that; you are punished, then punished again for protesting. So, one learns not to complain; it is a hard lesson, but one never lost.

Patch is trying out various postures, obscene gestures; as if preparing for some future performance. He says, 'I know what ditch you were spawned in, Tom, and it was a ditch not far from mine.' He turns to the hall where, unseen and beyond the dividing screen, the king, presumably, continues his pleasant day. Patch plants his legs apart, he sticks out his tongue. 'The fool has said in his heart, there is no Pope.' He turns his head; he grins. 'Come back in ten years, Master Cromwell, and tell me who's the fool then.'

'You're wasting your jokes on me, Patch. Wearing out your stock-in-trade.'

'Fools can say anything.'

'Not where my writ runs.'

'And where is that? Not even in the backyard where you were christened in a puddle. Come and meet me here, ten years today, if you're still alive.'

'You would have a fright if I was dead.'

'Because I'll stand still, and let you knock me down.'

'I could crack your skull against the wall now. They'd not miss you.'

'True,' Master Sexton says. 'They would roll me out in the morning and lay me on a dunghill. What's one fool? England is full of them.'

He is surprised there is any daylight left; he had thought it was deepest night. In these courts, Wolsey lingers; he built them. Turn any corner, and you will think you will see my lord, with a scroll of draughtsman's plans in his hands, his glee at his sixty turkey carpets, his hope to lodge and entertain the finest mirror-makers of Venice – 'Now, Thomas, you will add to your letter some Venetian endearments, some covert phrases that will suggest, in the local dialect and the most delicate way possible, that I pay top rates.'

And he will add that the people of England are welcoming to foreigners and that the climate of England is benign. That golden birds sing on golden branches, and a golden king sits on a hill of coins, singing a song of his own composition.

When he gets home to Austin Friars he walks into a space that feels strange and empty. It has taken hours to get back from Hampton Court and it is late. He looks at the place on the wall where the cardinal's arms blaze out: the scarlet hat, at his request, recently retouched. 'You can paint them out now,' he says.

'And what shall we paint else, sir?'

'Leave a blank.'

'We could have a pretty allegory?'

'I'm sure.' He turns and walks away. 'Leave a space.'

III
The Dead Complain of Their Burial
Christmastide 1530

The knocking at the gate comes after midnight. His watchman rouses the household, and when he goes downstairs – wearing a savage expression and in all other respects fully dressed – he finds Johane in her nightgown, her hair down, asking 'What is this about?' Richard, Rafe, the men of the household steer her aside; standing in the hall at Austin Friars is William Brereton of the privy chamber, with an armed escort. They have come to arrest me, he thinks. He walks up to Brereton. 'Good Christmas, William? Are you up early, or down late?'

Alice and Jo appear. He thinks of that night when Liz died, when his daughters stood forlorn and bewildered in their night-shifts, waiting for him to come home. Jo begins to cry. Mercy appears and sweeps the girls away. Gregory comes down, dressed to go out. 'Here if you want me,' he says diffidently.

'The king is at Greenwich,' Brereton says. 'He wants you now.' He has ordinary ways of showing his impatience: slapping his glove against his palm and tapping his foot.

'Go back to bed,' he tells his household. 'The king wouldn't order me to Greenwich to arrest me; it doesn't happen that way.' Though he hardly knows how it happens; he turns to Brereton. 'What does he want me for?'

272

Brereton's eyes are roaming around, to see how these people live.

'I really can't enlighten you.'

He looks at Richard, and sees how badly he wants to give this lordling a smack in the mouth. That would have been me, once, he thinks. But now I am as sweet as a May morning. They go out, Richard, Rafe, himself, his son, into the dark and the raw cold.

A party of link-men are waiting with lights. A barge is waiting at the nearest landing stairs. It is so far to the Palace of Placentia, the Thames so black, that they could be rowing along the River Styx. The boys sit opposite him, huddled, not talking, looking like one composite relative; though Rafe of course is not his relative. I'm getting like Dr Cranmer, he thinks: the Tamworths of Lincolnshire are among my connections, the Cliftons of Clifton, the Molyneux family, of whom you will have heard, or have you? He looks up at the stars but they seem dim and far away; which, he thinks, they probably are.

So what should he do? Should he try for some conversation with Brereton? The family's lands are in Staffordshire, Cheshire, on the Welsh borders. Sir Randal has died this year and his son has come into a fat inheritance, a thousand a year at least in Crown grants, another three hundred or so from local monasteries ... He is adding up in his head. It is none too soon to inherit; the man must be his own age, or nearly that. His father Walter would have got on with the Breretons, a quarrelsome crew, great disturbers of the peace. He recalls a proceeding against them in Star Chamber, would be fifteen years back ... It doesn't seem likely to furnish a topic. Nor does Brereton seem to want one.

Every journey ends; terminates, at some pier, some mist-shrouded wharf, where torches are waiting. They are to go at once to the king, deep into the palace, to his private rooms. Harry Norris is waiting for them; who else? 'How is he now?' Brereton says. Norris rolls his eyes.

'Well, Master Cromwell,' he says, 'we do meet under the strangest circumstances. Are these your sons?' He smiles, glancing around their faces. 'No, clearly not. Unless they have divers mothers.'

He names them: Master Rafe Sadler, Master Richard Cromwell, Master Gregory Cromwell. He sees a flicker of dismay on his son's face, and clarifies: 'This is my nephew. This, my son.'

'You only to go in,' Norris says. 'Come now, he is waiting.' Over his shoulder, he says, 'The king is afraid he may take cold. Will you look out the russet nightgown, the one with the sables?'

Brereton grunts some reply. Poor work, shaking out the furs, when you could be up in Chester, waking the populace, beating a drum around the city walls.

It is a spacious chamber with a high carved bed; his eye flickers over it. In the candlelight, the bed hangings are ink-black. The bed is empty. Henry sits on a velvet stool. He seems to be alone, but there is a dry scent in the room, a cinnamon warmth, that makes him think that the cardinal must be in the shadows, holding the pithed orange, packed with spices, that he always carried when he was among a press of people. The dead, for sure, would want to ward off the scent of the living; but what he can see, across the room, is not the cardinal's shadowy bulk, but a pale drifting oval that is the face of Thomas Cranmer.

The king turns his head towards him as he enters. 'Cromwell, my dead brother came to me in a dream.'

He does not answer. What is a sensible answer to this? He watches the king. He feels no temptation to laugh. The king says, 'During the twelve days, between Christmas Day and Epiphany, God permits the dead to walk. This is well known.'

He says gently, 'How did he look, your brother?'

'He looked as I remember him … but he was pale, very thin. There was a white fire around him, a light. But you know, Arthur

274

would have been in his forty-fifth year now. Is that your age, Master Cromwell?'

'About,' he says.

'I am good at telling people's ages. I wonder who Arthur would have looked like, if he had lived. My father, probably. Now, I am like my grandfather.'

He thinks the king will say, who are you like? But no: he has established that he has no ancestors.

'He died at Ludlow. In winter. The roads impenetrable. They had to take his coffin in an ox-cart. A prince of England, to go in a cart. I cannot think that was well done.'

Now Brereton comes in, with the russet velvet, sable-lined. Henry stands up and sheds one layer of velvet, gains another, plusher and denser. The sable lining creeps down over his hands, as if he were a monster-king, growing his own fur. 'They buried him at Worcester,' he says. 'But it troubles me. I never saw him dead.'

Dr Cranmer says, from the shadows, 'The dead do not come back to complain of their burial. It is the living who are exercised about these matters.'

The king hugs his robe about him. 'I never saw his face till now in my dream. And his body, shining white.'

'But it is not his body,' Cranmer says. 'It is an image formed in Your Majesty's mind. Such images are *quasi corpora*, like bodies. Read Augustine.'

The king does not look as if he wants to send out for a book. 'In my dream he stood and looked at me. He looked sad, so sad. He seemed to say I stood in his place. He seemed to say, you have taken my kingdom, and you have used my wife. He has come back to make me ashamed.'

Cranmer says, faintly impatient, 'If Your Majesty's brother died before he could reign, that was God's will. As for your supposed marriage, we all know and believe that it was clean contrary to scripture. We know the man in Rome has no power to dispense from the law of God. That there was a sin, we acknowledge; but with God there is mercy enough.'

'Not for me,' Henry says. 'When I come to judgment my brother will plead against me. He has come back to make me ashamed and I must bear it.' The thought enrages him. 'I, I alone.'

Cranmer is about to speak; he catches his eye, imperceptibly shakes his head. 'Did your brother Arthur speak to you, in your dream?'

'No.'

'Did he make any sign?'

'No.'

'Then why believe he means Your Majesty anything but good? It seems to me you have read into his face what was not really there, which is a mistake we make with the dead. Listen to me.' He puts his hand upon the royal person, on his sleeve of russet velvet, on his arm, and he grasps it hard enough to make himself felt. 'You know the lawyers' saying *"Le mort saisit le vif"*? The dead grip the living. The prince dies but his power passes at the moment of his death, there is no lapse, no interregnum. If your brother visited you, it is not to make you ashamed, but to remind you that you are vested with the power of both the living and the dead. This is a sign to you to examine your kingship. And exert it.'

Henry looks up at him. He is thinking. He is stroking his sable cuff and his expression is lost. 'Is this possible?'

Again Cranmer begins to speak. Again he cuts him off. 'You know what is written on the tomb of Arthur?'

'*Rex quondam rexque futurus*. The former king is the future king.'

'Your father made it sure. A prince coming out of Wales, he made good the word given to his ancestors. Out of his lifetime's exile he came back and claimed his ancient right. But it is not enough to claim a country; it must be held. It must be held and made secure, in every generation. If your brother seems to say that you have taken his place, then he means you to become the king that he would have been. He himself cannot fulfil the prophecy, but he wills it to you. For him, the promise, and for you, the performance of it.'

The king's eyes move to Dr Cranmer, who says, stiffly, 'I cannot see anything against it. I still counsel against heeding dreams.'

'Oh, but,' he says, 'the dreams of kings are not like the dreams of other men.'

'You may be right.'

'But why now?' Henry says, reasonably enough. 'Why does he come back now? I have been king for twenty years.'

He bites back the temptation to say, because you are forty and he is telling you to grow up. How many times have you enacted the stories of Arthur – how many masques, how many pageants, how many companies of players with paper shields and wooden swords? 'Because this is the vital time,' he says. 'Because now is the time to become the ruler you should be, and to be sole and supreme head of your kingdom. Ask Lady Anne. She will tell you. She will say the same.'

'She does,' the king admits. 'She says we should no longer bow to Rome.'

'And should your father appear to you in a dream, take it just as you take this one. That he has come to strengthen your hand. No father wishes to see his son less powerful than himself.'

Henry slowly smiles. From the dream, from the night, from the night of shrouded terrors, from maggots and worms, he seems to uncurl, and stretch himself. He stands up. His face shines. The fire stripes his robe with light, and in its deep folds flicker ochre and fawn, colours of earth, of clay. 'Very well,' he says. 'I see. I understand it all now. I knew who to send for. I always know.' He turns and speaks into the darkness. 'Harry Norris? What time is it? Is it four o'clock? Have my chaplain robe for Mass.'

'Perhaps I could say Mass for you,' Dr Cranmer suggests, but Henry says, 'No, you are tired. I've kept you from your beds, gentlemen.'

It is as easy as that, as peremptory. They find themselves turned out. They pass the guards. They walk in silence, back to their people, the man Brereton shadowing them. At last, Dr Cranmer says, 'Neat work.'

He turns. Now he wants to laugh but he dare not laugh.

'A deft touch, "and should your father appear to you …" I take it you don't like to be roused too often in the small hours.'

'My household was alarmed.'

The doctor looks sorry then, as if he might have been frivolous. 'Of course,' he murmurs. 'Because I am not a married man, I do not think of these things.'

'I am not a married man, either.'

'No. I forgot.'

'You object to what I said?'

'It was perfect in every way. As if you had thought of it in advance.'

'How could I?'

'Indeed. You are a man of vigorous invention. Still … for the gospel, you know …'

'For the gospel, I count it a good night's work.'

'But I wonder,' Cranmer says, almost to himself. 'I wonder what you think the gospel is. Do you think it is a book of blank sheets on which Thomas Cromwell imprints his desires?'

He stops. He puts a hand on his arm and says, 'Dr Cranmer, look at me. Believe me. I am sincere. I cannot help it if God has given me a sinner's aspect. He must mean something by it.'

'I dare say.' Cranmer smiles. 'He has arranged your face on purpose to disconcert our enemies. And that hand of yours, to take a grip on circumstance – when you took the king's arm in your grasp, I winced myself. And Henry, he felt it.' He nods. 'You are a person of great force of will.'

Clerics can do this: speak about your character. Give verdicts: this one seems favourable, though the doctor, like a fortune-teller, has told him no more than he already knew. 'Come,' Cranmer says, 'your boys will be fretting to see you safe.'

Rafe, Gregory, Richard, cluster round him: what's happened? 'The king had a dream.'

'A dream?' Rafe is shocked. 'He got us out of bed for a dream?'

'Believe me,' Brereton says, 'he gets one out of bed for less than that.'

'Dr Cranmer and I agree that a king's dreams are not as other men's dreams.'

Gregory asks, 'Was it a bad dream?'

'Initially. He thought it was. It isn't now.'

They look at him, not understanding, but Gregory understands. 'When I was small I dreamed of demons. I thought they were under my bed, but you said, it can't be so, you don't get demons our side of the river, the guards won't let them over London Bridge.'

'So are you terrified,' Richard says, 'if you cross the river to Southwark?'

Gregory says, 'Southwark? What is Southwark?'

'Do you know,' Rafe says, in a schoolmaster's tone, 'there are times when I see a spark of something in Gregory. Not a blaze, to be sure. Just a spark.'

'That you should mock! With a beard like that.'

'Is that a beard?' Richard says. 'Those scant red bristles? I thought there was some negligence by the barber.'

They are hugging each other, wild with relief. Gregory says, 'We thought the king had committed him to some dungeon.'

Cranmer nods, tolerant, amused. 'Your children love you.'

Richard says, 'We cannot do without the man in charge.'

It will be many hours till dawn. It is like the lightless morning on which the cardinal died. There is a smell of snow in the air.

'I suspect he will want us again,' Cranmer says. 'When he has thought about what you have said to him and, shall we say, followed where his thoughts lead him?'

'Still, I shall go back to the city and show my face.' Change my clothes, he thinks, and wait for the next thing. To Brereton he says, 'You know where to find me. William.'

A nod, and he walks away. 'Dr Cranmer, tell the Lady we did a good night's work for her.' He throws his arm around his son's shoulder, whispers, 'Gregory, those Merlin stories you read – we are going to write some more.'

Gregory says, 'Oh, I didn't finish them. The sun came out.'

Later that day he walks back into a panelled chamber at Greenwich. It is the last day of 1530. He eases off his gloves, kidskin scented with amber. The fingers of his right hand touch the turquoise ring, settling it in place.

'The council is waiting,' the king says. He is laughing, as if at some personal triumph. 'Go and join them. They will give you your oath.'

Dr Cranmer is with the king; very pale, very silent. The doctor nods, to acknowledge him; and then, surprisingly, a smile floods his face, lighting up the whole afternoon.

An air of improvisation hangs over the next hour. The king does not want to wait and it is a matter of which councillors can be found at short notice. The dukes are in their own countries, holding their Christmas courts. Old Warham is with us, Archbishop of Canterbury. It is fifteen years since Wolsey kicked him out of his post as Lord Chancellor; or, as the cardinal always put it, relieved him of worldly office, so allowing him the opportunity, in his last years, to embrace a life of prayer. 'Well, Cromwell,' he says. 'You a councillor! What the world comes to!' His face is seamed, his eyes are dead-fish eyes. His hands shake a little as he proffers the holy book.

Thomas Boleyn is with us, Earl of Wiltshire, Lord Privy Seal. The Lord Chancellor is here; he thinks in irritation, why can More never get a proper shave? Can't he make time, shorten his whipping schedule? As More moves into the light, he sees that he is more dishevelled than usual, his face gaunt, plum-coloured stains under his eyes. 'What's happened to you?'

'You didn't hear. My father died.'

'That good old man,' he says. 'We will miss his wise counsel in the law.'

And his tedious stories. I don't think.

'He died in my arms.' More begins to cry; or rather, he seems to diminish, and his whole body to leak tears. He says, he was the light of my life, my father. We are not those great men, we are a shadow of what they were. Ask your people at Austin Friars to pray for him. 'It's strange, Thomas, but since he went, I feel my age. As if I were just a boy, till a few days ago. But God has snapped his fingers, and I see my best years are behind me.'

'You know, after Elizabeth died, my wife ...' And then, he wants to say, my daughters, my sister, my household decimated, my people never out of black, and now my cardinal lost ... But he will not admit, for even a moment, that sorrow has sapped his will. You cannot get another father, but he would hardly want to; as for wives, they are two-a-penny with Thomas More. 'You do not believe it now, but feeling will come back. For the world and all you must do in it.'

'You have had your losses, I know. Well, well.' The Lord Chancellor sniffs, he sighs, shakes his head. 'Let us do this necessary thing.'

It is More who begins to reads him the oath. He swears to give faithful counsel, in his speech to be plain, impartial, in his manner secret, in his allegiance true. He is getting on to wise counsel and discreet, when the door flies opens and Gardiner swoops in, like a crow that's spied a dead sheep. 'I don't think you can do this

281

without Master Secretary,' he says, and Warham says mildly, by the Blessed Rood, must we start swearing him all over again?

Thomas Boleyn is stroking his beard. His eye has fallen on the cardinal's ring, and his expression has moved from the shocked to the merely sardonic. 'If we do not know the procedure,' he says, 'I feel sure Thomas Cromwell has a note of it. Give him a year or two, and we may all find ourselves superfluous.'

'I am sure I shall not live to see it,' Warham says. 'Lord Chancellor, shall we get on? Oh, you poor man! Weeping again. I am very sorry for you. But death comes to us all.'

Dear God, he thinks, if that's the best you get from the Archbishop of Canterbury, I could do the job.

He swears to uphold the king's authorities. His pre-eminences, his jurisdictions. He swears to uphold his heirs and lawful successors, and he thinks of the bastard child Richmond, and Mary the talking shrimp, and the Duke of Norfolk showing off his thumbnail to the company. 'Well, that's done,' says the archbishop. 'And amen to it, for what choice have we? Shall we have a glass of wine warmed? This cold gets into the bones.'

Thomas More says, 'Now you are a member of the council, I hope you will tell the king what he ought to do, not merely what he can do. If the lion knew his own strength, it would be hard to rule him.'

Outside it is sleeting. Dark flakes fall into the waters of the Thames. England stretches away from him, low red sun on fields of snow.

He thinks back to the day York Place was wrecked. He and George Cavendish stood by as the chests were opened and the cardinal's vestments taken out. The copes were sewn in gold and silver thread, with patterns of golden stars, with birds, fishes, harts, lions, angels, flowers and Catherine wheels. When they were repacked and nailed into their travelling chests, the king's men delved into the boxes that held the albs and cottas, each folded, by an expert touch, into fine pleats. Passed hand to hand, weightless as resting angels, they glowed softly in the light; loose one, a man said, let us see the quality of it. Fingers tugged at the linen bands; here, let me, George Cavendish said. Freed, the cloth drifted against the air, dazzling white, fine as a moth's wing. When the lids of the vestments chests were raised there was the smell of cedar and spices, sombre, distant, desert-dry. But the floating angels had been packed away in lavender; London rain washed against the glass, and the scent of summer flooded the dim afternoon.

PART FOUR

I

Arrange Your Face

1531

Whether it is through pain or fear, or some defect of nature; whether because of the summer heat, or the sound of hunting horns winding into the distance, or the spinning of sparkling dust in empty rooms; or whether it is that the child has lost sleep, while from dawn onwards her father's decamping household was packed up around her; for whatever reason, she is shrunken into herself, and her eyes are the colour of ditchwater. Once, as he is going through the preliminary Latin politenesses, he sees her grip tighten on the back of her mother's chair. 'Madam, your daughter should sit.' In case a contest of wills should ensue, he picks up a stool and places it, with a decisive thud, by Katherine's skirts.

The queen leans back, rigid inside her boned bodice, to whisper to her daughter. The ladies of Italy, seemingly carefree, wore constructions of iron beneath their silks. It took infinite patience, not just in negotiation, to get them out of their clothes.

Mary drops her head to whisper back; she hints, in Castilian, that it is her woman's disorder. Two pairs of eyes rise to meet his. The girl's glance is almost unfocused; she sees him, he supposes, as a bulky mass of shadow, in a space welling with distress. Stand up straight, Katherine murmurs: like a princess of England. Braced against the chair back, Mary takes a deep breath. She turns to him her plain pinched face: hard as Norfolk's thumbnail.

It is early afternoon, very hot. The sun casts against the wall shifting squares of lilac and gold. The shrivelled fields of Windsor are laid out below them. The Thames shrinks from its banks.

The queen speaks in English. 'Do you know who this is? This is Master Cromwell. Who now writes all the laws.'

Caught awkwardly between languages, he says, 'Madam, shall we go on in English, or Latin?'

'Your cardinal would ask the same question. As if I were a stranger here. I will say to you, as I said to him, that I was first addressed as Princess of Wales when I was three years old. I was sixteen when I came here to marry my lord Arthur. I was a virgin and seventeen when he died. I was twenty-four years old when I became Queen of England, and I will say for the avoidance of doubt that I am at present aged forty-six, and still queen, and by now, I believe, a sort of Englishwoman. But I shall not repeat to you everything that I told the cardinal. I imagine he left you notes of these things.'

He feels he should bow. The queen says, 'Since the year began they have brought certain bills into Parliament. Until now Master Cromwell's talent was for moneylending, but now he finds he has a talent for legislation too – if you want a new law, just ask him. I hear that at night you take the drafts to your house in – where is your house?' She makes it sound like 'your dog-hole'.

Mary says, 'These laws are written against the church. I wonder that our lords allow it.'

'You know,' the queen says, 'that the Cardinal of York was accused under the praemunire laws of usurping your lord father's jurisdiction as ruler of England. Now Master Cromwell and his friends find all the clergy complicit in that crime, and ask them to pay a fine of more than one hundred thousand pounds.'

'Not a fine. We call it a benevolence.'

'I call it extortion.' She turns to her daughter. 'If you ask why the church is not defended, I can only tell you that there are noblemen in this land' – Suffolk, she means, Norfolk – 'who have been heard to say they will pull the power of the church down, that never again will they suffer – they use the word – a church-man to grow so great as our late legate. That we need no new Wolsey, I concur. With the attacks on the bishops, I do not concur. Wolsey was to me an enemy. That does not alter my feel-ings towards our Holy Mother the church.'

He thinks, Wolsey was to me a father and a friend. That does not alter my feelings towards our Holy Mother the church.

'You and Speaker Audley, you put your heads together by candlelight.' The queen mentions the Speaker's name as if she were saying 'your kitchen boy'. 'And when the morning comes you induce the king to describe himself as head of the church in England.'

'Whereas,' the child says, 'the Pope is head of the church everywhere, and from the throne of St Peter flows the lawfulness of all government. From no other source.'

'Lady Mary,' he says, 'will you not sit?' He catches her just as she folds at the knees, and eases her down on to the stool. 'It is just the heat,' he says, so she will not be ashamed. She turns up her eyes, shallow and grey, with a look of simple gratitude; and as soon as she is seated the look is replaced by an expression as stony as the wall of a town under siege.

'You say "induce",' he tells Katherine. 'But Your Highness, above anyone, knows that the king cannot be led.'

'But he may be enticed.' She turns to Mary, whose arms have crept over her belly. 'So your father the king is named head of the church, and to soothe the conscience of the bishops, they have caused this formula to be inserted: "as far as the law of Christ allows".'

'What does that mean?' Mary says. 'It means nothing.'

'Your Highness, it means everything.'

'Yes. It is very clever.'

'I beg you,' he says, 'to consider it in this way, that the king has merely defined a position previously held, one that ancient precedents –'

'– invented these last months –'

'– show as his right.'

Under her clumsy gable hood, Mary's forehead is slick with sweat. She says, 'What is defined can be redefined, yes?'

'Indeed,' her mother says. 'And redefined in favour of the church – if only I fall in with their wishes, and put myself out of the estate of queen and wife.'

The princess is right, he thinks. There is room for negotiation. 'Nothing here is irrevocable.'

'No, you wait to see what I will bring to your treaty table.' Katherine holds out her hands – little, stubby, puffy hands – to show that they are empty. 'Only Bishop Fisher defends me. Only he has been constant. Only he is able to tell the truth, which is that the House of Commons is full of heathens.' She sighs, her hands fall at her sides. 'And now under what persuasion has my husband ridden off without a farewell? He has not done so before. Never.'

'He means to hunt out of Chertsey for a few days.'

'With the woman,' Mary says. 'The person.'

'Then he will ride by way of Guildford to visit Lord Sandys – he wants to see his handsome new gallery at the Vyne.' His tone is easy, soothing, like the cardinal's; perhaps too much so? 'From there, depending on the weather, and the game, he will go to William Paulet at Basing.'

'I am to follow, when?'

'He will return in a fortnight, God willing.'

'A fortnight,' Mary says. 'Alone with the person.'

'Before then, madam, you are to go to another palace – he has chosen the More, in Hertfordshire, which you know is very comfortable.'

'Being the cardinal's house,' Mary says, 'it would be lavish.'

My own daughters, he thinks, would never have spoken so. 'Princess,' he says, 'will you, of your charity, cease to speak ill of a man who never did you harm?'

290

Mary blushes from neckline to hairline. 'I did not mean to fail in charity.'

'The late cardinal is your godfather. You owe him your prayers.'

Her eyes flicker towards him; she looks cowed. 'I pray to shorten his term in Purgatory …'

Katherine interrupts her. 'Send a box to Hertfordshire. Send a package. Do not seek to send me.'

'You shall have your whole court. The household is ready for two hundred.'

'I shall write to the king. You may carry the letter. My place is with him.'

'My advice,' he says, 'take this gently. Or he may …' He indicates the princess. His hands join and drift apart. Separate you.

The child is fighting down pain. Her mother is fighting down grief and anger, and disgust and fear. 'I expected this,' she says, 'but I did not expect he would send a man like you to tell me.' He frowns: does she think it would come better from Norfolk? 'They say you had a trade as a blacksmith; is that correct?'

Now she will say, shoe a horse?

'It was my father's trade.'

'I begin to understand you.' She nods. 'The blacksmith makes his own tools.'

Half a mile of chalk walls, a mirror for the glare, bounce at him a white heat. In the shadow of a gateway, Gregory and Rafe are jostling and pushing, insulting each other with culinary insults he has taught them: Sir, you are a fat Fleming, and spread butter on your bread. Sir, you are a Roman pauper, may your offspring eat snails. Master Wriothesley is leaning in the sun and watching them, with a lazy smile; butterflies garland his head.

'Oh, it's *you*,' he says. Wriothesley looks gratified. 'You look fit to be painted, Master Wriothesley. A doublet of azure, and a shaft of light precisely placed.'

'Sir? Katherine says?'

'She says our precedents are fake.'

Rafe: 'Does she understand that you and Dr Cranmer sat up all night over them?'

'Oh, wild times!' Gregory says. 'Seeing the dawn in, with Dr Cranmer!'

He throws an arm around Rafe's bony little shoulders and squeezes him; it is a liberation to be away from Katherine, from the girl flinching like a whipped bitch. 'Once I myself, with Giovannino – well, with some boys I knew –' He stops: what is this? I don't tell stories about myself.

'Please …' Wriothesley says.

'Well, we had a statue made, a smirking little god with wings, and then we beat it with hammers and chains to make it antique, and we hired a muleteer and drove it to Rome and sold it to a cardinal.' Such a hot day, when they were ushered into his presence: hazy, thunder in the distance, and white dust from building sites hanging in the air. 'I remember he had tears in his eyes when he paid us. "To think that on these charming little feet and these sweet pinions, the gaze of the Emperor Augustus may have rested." When the Portinari boys set off for Florence they were staggering under the weight of their purses.'

'And you?'

'I took my cut and stayed on to sell the mules.'

They head downhill through the inner courts. Emerging into the sun, he shades his eyes as if to see through the tangle of tree-tops that runs into the distance. 'I told the queen, let Henry go in peace. Or he might not let the princess move with her up-country.'

Wriothesley says, surprised, 'But it is decided. They are to be separated. Mary is to go to Richmond.'

He did not know. He hopes his hesitation is not perceptible. 'Of course. But the queen had not been told, and it was worth a try, yes?'

See how useful Master Wriothesley is. See how he brings us intelligence from Secretary Gardiner. Rafe says, 'It is harsh. To use the little girl against her mother.'

'Harsh, yes ... but the question is, have you picked your prince? Because that is what you do, you choose him, and you know what he is. And then, when you have chosen, you say yes to him – yes, that is possible, yes, that can be done. If you don't like Henry, you can go abroad and find another prince, but I tell you – if this were Italy, Katherine would be cold in her tomb.'

'But you swore,' Gregory says, 'that you respected the queen.'

'So I do. And I would respect her corpse.'

'You would not work her death, would you?'

He halts. He takes his son's arm, turns him to look into his face. 'Retrace our steps through this conversation.' Gregory pulls away. 'No, listen, Gregory. I said, you give way to the king's requests. You open the way to his desires. That is what a courtier does. Now, understand this: it is impossible that Henry should require me or any other person to harm the queen. What is he, a monster? Even now he has affection for her; how could he not? And he has a soul he hopes may be saved. He confesses every day to one or other of his chaplains. Do you think the Emperor does so much, or King Francis? Henry's heart, I assure you, is a heart full of feeling; and Henry's soul, I swear, is the most scrutinised soul in Christendom.'

Wriothesley says, 'Master Cromwell, he is your son, not an ambassador.'

He lets Gregory go. 'Shall we get on the river? There might be a breeze.'

In the Lower Ward, six couples of hunting dogs stir and yelp in the cages on wheels which are going to carry them across country. Tails waving, they are clambering over each other, twisting ears and nipping, their yaps and howls adding to the sense of near-panic that has taken over the castle. It's more like the evacuation

293

of a fort than the start of a summer progress. Sweating porters are heaving the king's furnishings on to carts. Two men with a studded chest have got wedged in a doorway. He thinks of himself on the road, a bruised child, loading wagons to get a lift. He wanders over. 'How did this happen, boys?'

He steadies one corner of the chest and backs them off into the shadows; adjusts the degree of rotation with a flip of his hand; a moment's fumbling and slipping, and they burst into the light, shouting 'Here she goes!' as if they had thought of it themselves. Be packing for the queen next, he says, for the cardinal's palace at the More, and they say, surprised, is that so, master, and what if the queen won't go? He says, then we will roll her up in a carpet and put her on your cart. He hands out coins: ease up, it's too hot to work so hard. He saunters back to the boys. A man leads up horses ready for harnessing to the hounds' wagons, and as soon as they catch their scent the dogs set up an excited barking, which can still be heard as they get on the water.

The river is brown, torpid; on the Eton bank, a group of list-less swans glides in and out of the weeds. Their boat bobs beneath them; he says, 'Is that not Sion Madoc?'

'Never forget a face, eh?'

'Not when it's ugly.'

'Have you seen yourself, *bach*?' The boatman has been eating an apple, core and all; fastidious, he flicks the pips over the side.

'How's your dad?'

'Dead.' Sion spits the stalk out. 'Any of these yours?'

'Me,' Gregory says.

'That's mine.' Sion nods to the opposite oar, a lump of a lad who reddens and looks away. 'Your dad used to shut up shop in this weather. Put the fire out and go fishing.'

'Lashing the water with his rod,' he says, 'and punching the lights out of the fish. Jump in and drag them gasping out of the green deep. Fingers through the gills: "What are you looking at, you scaly whoreson? Are you looking at me?"'

'He not being one to sit and enjoy the sunshine,' Madoc explains. 'I could tell you stories, about Walter Cromwell.'

Master Wriothesley's face is a study. He does not understand how much you can learn from boatmen, their argot blasphemous and rapid. At twelve he spoke it fluently, his mother tongue, and now it flows back into his mouth, something natural, something dirty. There are tags of Greek he has mastered, which he exchanges with Thomas Cranmer, with Call-Me-Risley: early language, unblighted, like tender fruit. But never does a Greek scholar pin back your ears as Sion does now, with Putney's opinion of the fucking Bullens. Henry goes to it with the mother, good luck to him. He goes to it with the sister, what's a king for? But it's got to stop somewhere. We're not beasts of the field. Sion calls Anne an eel, he calls her a slippery dipper from the slime, and he remembers what the cardinal had called her: my serpentine enemy. Sion says, she goes to it with her brother; he says, what, her brother George?

'Any brother she's got. Those kind keep it in the family. They do filthy French tricks, like –'

'Can you keep your voice down?' He looks around, as if spies might be swimming by the boat.

'– and that's how she trusts herself she don't give in to Henry, because if she lets him do it and she gets a boy he's, thanks very much, now clear off, girl – so she's oh, Your Highness, I never could allow – because she knows that very night her brother's inside her, licking her up to the lungs, and then he's, excuse me, sister, what shall I do with this big package – she says, oh, don't distress yourself, my lord brother, shove it up the back entry, it'll come to no harm there.'

Thanks, he says, I had no idea how they were managing.

The boys have got about one word in three. Sion gets a tip. It's worth anything, to be reacquainted with the Putney imagination. He will cherish Sion's simper: very unlike the real Anne.

Later, at home, Gregory says, 'Ought people to speak like that? And be paid for it?'

'He was speaking his mind.' He shrugs. 'So, if you want to know people's minds …'

'Call-Me-Risley is frightened of you. He says that when you were coming from Chelsea with Master Secretary, you threatened to throw him out of his own barge and drown him.'

That is not precisely his memory of the conversation.

'And does Call-Me think I would do it?'

'Yes. He thinks you would do anything.'

At New Year he had given Anne a present of silver forks with handles of rock crystal. He hopes she will use them to eat with, not to stick in people.

'From Venice!' She is pleased. She holds them up, so the handles catch and splinter the light.

He has brought another present, for her to pass on. It is wrapped in a piece of sky-blue silk. 'It is for the little girl who always cries.'

Anne's mouth opens a little. 'Don't you know?' Her eyes brim with black glee. 'Come, so I can tell you in your ear.' Her cheek brushes his. Her skin is faintly perfumed: amber, rose. 'Sir John Seymour? Dear Sir John? *Old* Sir John, as people call him?' Sir John is not, perhaps, more than a dozen years older than himself, but amiability can be ageing; with his sons Edward and Tom now the young men about court, he does give the impression of having eased into retirement. 'Now we understand why we never see him,' Anne murmurs. 'Now we know what he does down in the country.'

'Hunting, I thought.'

'Yes, and he has netted Catherine Fillol, Edward's wife. They were taken in the act, but I cannot find out where, whether in her bed, or his, or in a meadow, a hayloft – yes, cold, to be sure, but they were keeping each other warm. And now Sir John has confessed it all, man to man, telling his son to his face that he's had her every week since the wedding, so that's about two years and, say, six months, so …'

296

'You could round it off to a hundred and twenty times, assuming they abstain at the major feasts …'

'Adulterers don't stop for Lent.'

'Oh, and I thought they did.'

'She's had two babies, so allow respite for her lying-in … And they are boys, you know. So Edward is …' He imagines how Edward is. That pure hawk's profile. 'He is cutting them out of the family. They are to be bastards. She, Catherine Fillol, she's to be put in a convent. I think he should put her in a cage! He is asking for an annulment. As for dear Sir John, I think we will not see him at court soon.'

'Why are we whispering? I must be the last person in London to hear.'

'The king hasn't heard. And you know how proper he is. So if someone is to come to him joking about it, let it not be me or you.'

'And the daughter? Jane, is it?'

Anne sniggers. 'Pasty-face? Gone down to Wiltshire. Her best move would be to follow the sister-in-law into a nunnery. Her sister Lizzie married well, but no one wants Milksop, and now no one will.' Her eyes fall on his present; she says, suddenly anxious, jealous, 'What is it?'

'Only a book of needlework patterns.'

'As long as it is nothing to tax her wits. Why would you send her a present?'

'I feel sorry for her.' More now, of course.

'Oh. You don't like her, do you?' The correct answer is, no, my lady Anne, I only like you. 'Because, is it proper for you to send her a present?'

'It is not as if it is tales out of Boccaccio.'

She laughs. 'They could tell Boccaccio a tale, those sinners at Wolf Hall.'

* * *

Thomas Hitton, a priest, was burned just as February went out; taken up by Fisher, Bishop of Rochester, as a smuggler of Tyndale's scriptures. Soon afterwards, rising from the bishop's frugal table, a dozen guests had collapsed, vomiting, rigid with pain, and been taken, pale and almost pulseless, to their beds and the ministrations of the doctors. Dr Butts said the broth had done it; from testimony of the waiting-boys, it was the only dish they had tasted in common.

There are poisons nature herself brews, and he, before putting the bishop's cook to the torture, would have visited the kitchens and passed a skimmer over the stockpot. But no one else doubts there has been a crime.

Presently the cook admits to adding to the broth a white powder, which someone gave him. Who? Just a man. A stranger who had said it would be a good joke, to give Fisher and his guests a purge.

The king is beside himself: rage and fear. He blames heretics. Dr Butts, shaking his head, pulling his lower lip, says that poison is what Henry fears worse than Hell itself.

Would you put poison in a bishop's dinner because a stranger told you it would be a laugh? The cook won't say more, or perhaps he has reached a stage beyond saying. The interrogation has been mismanaged then, he says to Butts; I wonder why. The doctor, a man who loves the gospel, laughs sourly and says, 'If they wanted the man to talk, they should have called in Thomas More.'

The word is that the Lord Chancellor has become a master in the twin arts of stretching and compressing the servants of God. When heretics are taken, he stands by at the Tower while the torture is applied. It is reported that in his gatehouse at Chelsea he keeps suspects in the stocks, while he preaches at them and harries them: the name of your printer, the name of the master of the ship that brought these books into England. They say he uses the whip, the manacles and the torment-frame they call Skeffington's Daughter. It is a portable device, into which a man is folded, knees to chest, with a hoop of iron across his back; by means of a screw, the hoop is tightened until his ribs crack. It takes art to make sure the man does not suffocate: for if he does, everything he knows is lost.

Over the next week, two dinner guests die; Fisher himself rallies. It is possible, he thinks, that the cook did speak, but that what he said was not for the ears of the ordinary subject.

He goes to see Anne. A thorn between two roses, she is sitting with her cousin Mary Shelton, and her brother's wife Jane, Lady Rochford. 'My lady, do you know the king has devised a new form of death for Fisher's cook? He is to be boiled alive.'

Mary Shelton gives a little gasp, and flushes as if some gallant had pinched her. Jane Rochford drawls, '*Vere dignum et justum est, aequum et salutare.*' She translates for Mary: 'Apt.'

Anne's face wears no expression at all. Even a man as literate as he can find nothing there to read. 'How will they do it?'

'I did not ask about the mechanics. Would you like me to enquire? I think it will involve hoisting him up in chains, so that the crowd can see his skin peeling off and hear him screaming.'

To be fair to Anne, if you walked up to her and said, you are to be boiled, she would probably shrug: *c'est la vie.*

Fisher is in bed for a month. When he is up and about he looks like a walking corpse. The intercession of angels and saints has not sufficed to heal his sore gut and put the flesh back on his bones.

These are days of brutal truth from Tyndale. Saints are not your friends and they will not protect you. They cannot help you to salvation. You cannot engage them to your service with prayers and candles, as you might hire a man for the harvest. Christ's sacrifice was done on Calvary; it is not done in the Mass. Priests cannot help you to Heaven; you need no priest to stand between you and your God. No merits of yours can save you: only the merits of the living Christ.

March: Lucy Petyt, whose husband is a master grocer and a member of the Commons, comes to see him at Austin Friars. She is wearing black lambskin – imported, at a guess – and a modest grey worsted gown; Alice receives her gloves and surreptitiously slides in a finger to appraise the silk lining. He rises from his desk and takes her hands, drawing her to the fire and pressing upon her a cup of warm spiced wine. Her hands shake as she cradles the cup and she says, 'I wish John had this. This wine. This fire.'

It was snowing at dawn on the day of the raid on Lion's Quay, but soon a wintery sun was up, scouring windowpanes and casting the panelled rooms of city houses into sharp relief, ravines of shadows and cold floods of light. 'That is what I cannot get out of my mind,' Lucy says, 'the cold.' And More himself, his face muffled in furs, standing at the door with his officers, ready to search the warehouse and their own rooms. 'I was the first there,' she says, 'and I kept him hovering with pleas-antries – I called up, my dear, here is the Lord Chancellor come on parliamentary business.' The wine floods into her face, loosens her tongue. 'I kept saying, have you breakfasted, sir, are you sure, and the servants were weaving under his feet, impeding him' – she gives a little, mirthless, whooping laugh – 'and all the time John was stowing his papers behind a panel –'

'You did well, Lucy.'

'When they walked upstairs John was ready for him – oh, Lord Chancellor, welcome to my poor house – but the poor hapless man, he had cast his Testament under his desk, my eye went straight to it, I wonder their eyes didn't follow mine.'

An hour's search realised nothing; so are you sure, John, the Chancellor said, that you have none of these new books, because I was informed you had? (And Tyndale lying there, like a poison stain on the tiles.) I don't know who could have told you that, said John Petyt. I was proud of him, Lucy says, holding out her cup for more wine, I was proud that he spoke up. More said, it is true I have found nothing today, but you must go with these men. Mr Lieutenant, will you take him?

John Petyt is not a young man. At More's direction he sleeps on a pad of straw laid on the flagstones; visitors have been admitted only so that they can take back to his neighbours the news of how ill he looks. 'We have sent food and warm clothes,' Lucy says, 'and been turned away on the Lord Chancellor's orders.'

'There's a tariff for bribes. You pay the gaolers. You need ready money?'

'If I do I shall come to you.' She puts the cup down on his desk. 'He cannot lock us all up.'

'He has prisons enough.'

'For bodies, yes. But what are bodies? He can take our goods, but God will prosper us. He can close the booksellers, but still there will be books. They have their old bones, their glass saints in windows, their candles and shrines, but God has given us the printing press.' Her cheeks glow. She glances down to the drawings on his desk. 'What are these, Master Cromwell?'

'The plans for my garden. I am hoping to buy some of the houses at the back of here, I want the land.'

She smiles. 'A garden ... It is the first pleasant thing I have heard of in a while.'

'I hope you and John will come and enjoy it.'

'And this ... You are going to build a tennis court?'

'If I get the ground. And here, you see, I mean to plant an orchard.'

Tears well into her eyes. 'Speak to the king. We count on you.'

He hears a footstep: Johane's. Lucy's hand flies to her mouth. 'God forgive me ... For a moment I took you for your sister.'

'The mistake is made,' Johane says. 'And sometimes persists. Mistress Petyt, I am very sorry to hear your husband is in the Tower. But you have brought this on yourselves. You people were the first to throw calumnies at the late cardinal. But now I suppose you wish you had him back.'

Lucy goes out without a further word, only one long look over her shoulder. Outside he hears Mercy greet her; she will get a more sisterly word there. Johane walks to the fire and warms her hands. 'What does she think you can do for her?'

'Go to the king. Or to Lady Anne.'

'And will you? Do not,' she says, 'do not do it.' She scrubs away a tear with her knuckle; Lucy has upset her. 'More will not rack him. Word will get out, and the city would not have it. But he may die anyway.' She glances up at him. 'She is quite old, you know, Lucy Petyt. She ought not to wear grey. Do you see how her cheeks have fallen in? She won't have any more children.'

'I get the point,' he says.

Her hand clenches on her skirt. 'But what if he does? What if he does rack him? And he gives names?'

'What's that to me?' He turns away. 'He already knows my name.'

He speaks to Lady Anne. What can I do? she asks, and he says, you know how to please the king, I suppose; she laughs and says, what, my maidenhead for a grocer?

He speaks to the king when he is able, but the king gives him a blank stare and says the Lord Chancellor knows his business. Anne says, I have tried, I myself as you know have put Tyndale's books into his hand, his royal hand; could Tyndale, do you think, come back into this kingdom? In winter they negotiated, letters crossing the Channel. In spring, Stephen Vaughan, his man in Antwerp, set up a meeting: evening, the concealing dusk, a field outside the city walls. Cromwell's letter put into his hand, Tyndale wept: I want to come home, he said, I am sick of this, hunted city to city and house to house. I want to come home and if the king would just say yes, if he would say yes to the scriptures in our mother tongue, he can choose his translator, I will never write more. He can do with me what he pleases, torture me or kill me, but only let the people of England hear the gospel.

Henry has not said no. He had not said, never. Though Tyndale's translation and any other translation is banned, he may, one day, permit a translation to be made by a scholar he approves. How can he say less? He wants to please Anne.

But summer comes, and he, Cromwell, knows he has gone to the brink and must feel his way back. Henry is too timid, Tyndale too intransigent. His letters to Stephen sound a note of panic: abandon ship. He does not mean to sacrifice himself to Tyndale's truculence; dear God, he says, More, Tyndale, they deserve each other, these mules that pass for men. Tyndale will not come out in favour of Henry's divorce; nor, for that matter, will the monk Luther. You'd think they'd sacrifice a fine point of principle, to make a friend of the King of England: but no.

And when Henry demands, 'Who is Tyndale to judge me?' Tyndale snaps a message back, quick as word can fly: one Christian man may judge another.

'A cat may look at a king,' he says. He is cradling Marlinspike in his arms, and talking to Thomas Avery, the boy he's teaching his trade. Avery has been with Stephen Vaughan, so he can learn the practice among the merchants over there, but any boat may bring him to Austin Friars with his little bag, inside it a woollen jerkin, a few shirts. When he comes clattering in he shouts out for Mercy, for Johane, for the little girls, for whom he brings comfits and novelties from street traders. On Richard, on Rafe, on Gregory if he's about, he lands a few punches by way of saying I'm back, but always he keeps his bag tucked under his arm.

The boy follows him into his office. 'Did you never feel home-sick, master, when you were on your travels?'

He shrugs: I suppose if I'd had a home. He puts the cat down, opens the bag. He fishes up on his finger a string of rosary beads; for show, says Avery, and he says, good boy. Marlinspike leaps on to his desk; he peers into the bag, dabbing with a paw. 'The only mice in there are sugar ones.' The boy pulls the cat's ears,

303

tussles with him. 'We don't have any little pets in Master Vaughan's house.'

'He's all business, Stephen. And very stern, these days.'

'He says, Thomas Avery, what time did you get in last night? Have you written to your master? Been to Mass? As if he cares for the Mass! It's all but, how's your bowels?'

'Next spring you can come home.'

As they speak he is unrolling the jerkin. With a shake he turns it inside out, and with a small pair of scissors begins to slit open a seam. 'Neat stitching … Who did this?'

The boy hesitates; he colours. 'Jenneke.'

He draws out from the lining the thin, folded paper. Unwraps it: 'She must have good eyes.'

'She does.'

'And lovely eyes too?' He glances up, smiling. The boy looks him in the face. For a moment he seems startled, and as if he will speak; then he drops his gaze and turns away.

'Just tormenting you, Tom, don't take it to heart.' He is reading Tyndale's letter. 'If she is a good girl, and in Stephen's household, what harm?'

'What does Tyndale say?'

'You carried it without reading it?'

'I would rather not know. In case.'

In case you found yourself Thomas More's guest. He holds the letter in his left hand; his right hand curls loosely into a fist. 'Let him come near my people. I'll drag him out of his court at Westminster and beat his head on the cobbles till I knock into him some sense of the love of God and what it means.'

The boy grins and flops down on a stool. He, Cromwell, glances again at the letter. 'Tyndale says, he thinks he can never come back, even if my lady Anne were queen … a project he does nothing to aid, I must say. He says he would not trust a safe conduct, even if the king himself were to sign it, while Thomas More is alive and in office, because More says you need not keep a promise you have made to a heretic. Here. You may as well read. Our Lord Chancellor respects neither ignorance nor innocence.'

The boy flinches, but he takes the paper. What a world is this, where promises are not kept. He says gently, 'Tell me who is Jenneke. Do you want me to write to her father for you?'

'No.' Avery looks up, startled; he is frowning. 'No, she's an orphan. Master Vaughan keeps her at his own charge. We are all teaching her English.'

'No money to bring you, then?'

The boy looks confused. 'I suppose Stephen will give her a dowry.'

The day is too mild for a fire. The hour is too early for a candle. In lieu of burning, he tears up Tyndale's message. Marlinspike, his ears pricked, chews a fragment of it. 'Brother cat,' he says. 'He ever loved the scriptures.'

Scriptura sola. Only the gospel will guide and console you. No use praying to a carved post or lighting a candle to a painted face. Tyndale says 'gospel' means good news, it means singing, it means dancing: within limits, of course. Thomas Avery says, 'Can I truly come home next spring?'

John Petyt at the Tower is to be allowed to sleep in a bed: no chance, though, that he will go home to Lion's Quay.

Cranmer said to him, when they were talking late one night, St Augustine says we need not ask where our home is, because in the end we all come home to God.

Lent saps the spirits, as of course it is designed to do. Going in again to Anne, he finds the boy Mark, crouched over his lute and picking at something doleful; he flicks a finger against his head as he breezes past, and says, 'Cheer it up, can't you?'

Mark almost falls off his stool. It seems to him they are in a daze, these people, vulnerable to being startled, to being ambushed. Anne, waking out of her dream, says, 'What did you just do?'

'Hit Mark. Only,' he demonstrates, 'with one finger.'

Anne says, 'Mark? Who? Oh. Is that his name?'

This spring, 1531, he makes it his business to be cheerful. The cardinal was a great grumbler, but he always grumbled in some entertaining way. The more he complained, the more cheerful his man Cromwell became; that was the arrangement.

The king is a complainer too. He has a headache. The Duke of Suffolk is stupid. The weather is too warm for the time of year. The country is going to the dogs. He's anxious too; afraid of spells, and of people thinking bad thoughts about him in any specific or unspecific way. The more anxious the king becomes, the more tranquil becomes his new servant, the more hopeful, the more staunch. And the more the king snips and carps, the more do his petitioners seek out the company of Cromwell, so unfailing in his amiable courtesy.

At home, Jo comes to him looking perplexed. She is a young lady now, with a womanly frown, a soft crinkle of flesh on her forehead, which Johane her mother has too. 'Sir, how shall we paint our eggs at Easter?'

'How did you paint them last year?'

'Every year before this we gave them hats like the cardinal's.' She watches his face, to read back the effect of her words; it is his own habit exactly, and he thinks, not only your children are your children. 'Was it wrong?'

'Not at all. I wish I'd known. I would have taken him one. He would have liked it.'

Jo puts her soft little hand into his. It is still a child's hand, the skin scuffed over the knuckles, the nails bitten. 'I am of the king's council now,' he says. 'You can paint crowns if you like.'

This piece of folly with her mother, this ongoing folly, it has to stop. Johane knows it too. She used to make excuses, to be where he was. But now, if he's at Austin Friars, she's at the house in Stepney.

'Mercy knows,' she murmurs in passing.

The surprise is it took her so long, but there is a lesson here; you think people are always watching you, but that is guilt, making you jump at shadows. But finally, Mercy finds she has eyes in her head, and a tongue to speak, and picks a time when they can be alone. 'They tell me that the king has found a way around at least one of his stumbling blocks. I mean, the difficulty of how he can marry Lady Anne, when her sister Mary has been in his bed.'

'We have had all the best advice,' he says easily. 'Dr Cranmer at my recommendation sent to Venice, to a learned body of rabbis, to take opinions on the meaning of the ancient texts.'

'So it is not incest? Unless you have actually been married to one sister?'

'The divines say not.'

'How much did that cost?'

'Dr Cranmer wouldn't know. The priests and the scholars go to the negotiating table, then some less godly sort of man comes after them, with a bag of money. They don't have to meet each other, coming in or going out.'

'It hardly helps your case,' she says bluntly.

'There is no help in my case.'

'She wants to talk to you. Johane.'

'What's there to say? We all know –' We all know it can go nowhere. Even though her husband John Williamson is still coughing: one is always half listening for it, here and at Stepney, the annunciatory wheezing on a stairway or in the next room; one thing about John Williamson, he'll never take you by surprise. Dr Butts has recommended him country air, and keeping away from fumes and smoke. 'It was a moment of weakness,' he says. Then ... what? Another moment. 'God sees all. So they tell me.'

'You must listen to her.' Mercy's face, when she turns back, is incandescent. 'You owe her that.'

* * *

307

'The way it seems to me, it seems like part of the past.' Johane's voice is unsteady; with a little twitch of her fingers she settles her half-moon hood and drifts her veil, a cloud of silk, over one shoulder. 'For a long time, I didn't think Liz was really gone. I expected to see her walk in one day.'

It has been a constant temptation to him, to have Johane beautifully dressed, and he has dealt with it by, as Mercy says, *throwing* money at the London goldsmiths and mercers, so the women of Austin Friars are bywords among the city wives, who say behind their hands (but with a worshipful murmur, almost a genuflection), dear God, Thomas Cromwell, the money must be flowing in like the grace of God.

'So now I think,' she says, 'that what we did because she was dead, when we were shocked, when we were sorry, we have to leave off that now. I mean, we are still sorry. We will always be sorry.'

He understands her. Liz died in another age, when the cardinal was still in his pomp, and he was the cardinal's man. 'If,' she says, 'you would like to marry, Mercy has her list. But then, you probably have your own list. With nobody on it we know.'

'If, of course,' she says, 'if John Williamson had – God forgive me but every winter I think it is his last – then of course I, without question, I mean, at once, Thomas, as soon as decent, not clasping hands over his coffin … but then the church wouldn't allow it. The law wouldn't.'

'You never know,' he says.

She throws out her hands, words flood out of her. 'They say you intend to, what you intend, to break the bishops and make the king head of the church and take away his revenues from the Holy Father and give them to Henry, then Henry can declare the law if he likes and put off his wife as he likes and marry Lady Anne and he will say what is a sin and what not and who can be married. And the Princess Mary, God defend her, will be a bastard and after Henry the next king will be whatever child that lady gives him.'

'Johane ... when Parliament meets again, would you like to come down and tell them what you've just said? Because it would save a lot of time.'

'You can't,' she says, aghast. 'The Commons will not vote it. The Lords will not. Bishop Fisher will not allow it. Archbishop Warham. The Duke of Norfolk. Thomas More.'

'Fisher is ill. Warham is old. Norfolk, he said to me only the other day, "I am tired" – if you will permit his expression – "of fighting under the banner of Katherine's stained bedsheet, and if Arthur could enjoy her, or if he couldn't, who gives a – who cares any more?"' He is rapidly altering the duke's words, which were coarse in the extreme. '"Let my niece Anne come in," he said, "and do her worst."'

'What is her worst?' Johane's mouth is ajar; the duke's words will be rolling down Gracechurch Street, rolling to the river and across the bridge, till the painted ladies in Southwark are passing them mouth to mouth like ulcers; but that's the Howards for you, that's the Boleyns; with or without him, news of Anne's character will reach London and the world.

'She provokes the king's temper,' he says. 'He complains Katherine never in her life spoke to him as Anne does. Norfolk says she uses language to him you wouldn't use to a dog.'

'Jesu! I wonder he doesn't whip her.'

'Perhaps he will, when they're married. Look, if Katherine were to withdraw her suit from Rome, if she were to submit to judgment of her case in England, or if the Pope were to concede to the king's wishes, then all this – everything you've said, it won't happen, it will be just –' His hand makes a smooth, withdrawing motion, like the rolling up of a parchment. 'If Clement were to come to his desk one morning, not quite awake, and sign with his left hand some piece of paper he's not read, well, who could blame him? And then I leave him, we leave him, undisturbed, in possession of his revenues, in possession of his authority, because now Henry only wants one thing, and that is Anne in his bed; but time marches on and he is beginning to think, believe me, of other things he might want.'

'Yes. Like his own way.'

'He's a king. He's used to it.'

'And if the Pope is still stubborn?'

'He'll go begging for his revenue.'

'Will the king take the money of Christian people? The king is rich.'

'There you are wrong. The king is poor.'

'Oh. Does he know it?'

'I'm not sure he knows where his money comes from, or where it goes. While my lord cardinal was alive, he never wanted for a jewel in his hat or a horse or a handsome house. Henry Norris keeps his privy purse, but besides that he has too much of a hand in the revenue for my liking. Henry Norris,' he tells her before she can ask, 'is the bane of my life.' He is always, he does not add, with Anne when I need to see her alone.

'I suppose if Henry wants his supper, he can come here. Not this Henry Norris. I mean, Henry our pauper king.' She stands up; she sees herself in the glass; she ducks, as if shy of her own reflection, and arranges her face into an expression lighter, more curious and detached, less personal; he sees her do it, lift her eyebrows a fraction, curve up her lips at the corner. I could paint her, he thinks; if I had the skill. I have looked at her so long; but looking doesn't bring back the dead, the harder you look the faster and the further they go. He had never supposed Liz Wykys was smiling down from Heaven on what he was doing with her sister. No, he thinks, what I've done is push Liz into the dark; and something comes back to him, that Walter once said, that his mother used to say her prayers to a little carved saint she'd had in her bundle when she came down as a young woman from the north, and she used to turn it away before she got into bed with him. Walter had said, dear God, Thomas, it was St fucking Felicity if I'm not mistaken, and her face was to the wall for sure the night I got you.

Johane walks about the room. It is a large room and filled with light. 'All these things,' she says, 'these things we have now. The clock. That new chest you had Stephen send you from Flanders, the one with the carving of the birds and flowers, I heard with my own ears you say to Thomas Avery, oh, tell Stephen I want it, I don't care what it costs. All these painted pictures of people we don't know, all these, I don't know what, lutes and books of music, we never used to have them, when I was a girl I never used to look at myself in a mirror, but now I look at myself every day. And a comb, you gave me an ivory comb. I never had one of my own. Liz used to plait my hair and push it under my hood, and then I did hers, and if we didn't look how we ought to look, somebody soon told us.'

Why are we so attached to the severities of the past? Why are we so proud of ourselves for having endured our fathers and our mothers, the fireless days and the meatless days, the cold winters and the sharp tongues? It's not as if we had a choice. Even Liz, once when they were young, when she'd seen him early in the morning putting Gregory's shirt to warm before the fire, even Liz had said sharply, don't do that, he'll expect it every day.

He says, 'Liz – I mean, Johane …'

You've done that once too often, her face says.

'I want to be good to you. Tell me what I can give you.'

He waits for her to shout, as women do, do you think you can buy me, but she doesn't, she listens, and he thinks she is entranced, her face intent, her eyes on his, as she learns his theory about what money can buy. 'There was a man in Florence, a friar, Fra Savonarola, he induced all the people to think beauty was a sin. Some people think he was a magician and they fell under his spell for a season, they made fires in the streets and they threw in everything they liked, everything they had made or worked to buy, bolts of silk, and linen their mothers had embroidered for their marriage beds, books of poems written in the poet's hand, bonds and wills, rent-rolls, title deeds, dogs and cats, the shirts

311

from their backs, the rings from their fingers, women their veils, and do you know what was worst, Johane – they threw in their mirrors. So then they couldn't see their faces and know how they were different from the beasts in the field and the creatures screaming on the pyre. And when they had melted their mirrors they went home to their empty houses, and lay on the floor because they had burned their beds, and when they got up next day they were aching from the hard floor and there was no table for their breakfast because they'd used the table to feed the bonfire, and no stool to sit on because they'd chopped it into splinters, and there was no bread to eat because the bakers had thrown into the flames the basins and the yeast and the flour and the scales. And you know the worst of it? They were sober. Last night they took their wine-skins ...' He turns his arm, in a mime of a man lobbing something into a fire. 'So they were sober and their heads were clear, but they looked around and they had nothing to eat, nothing to drink and nothing to sit on.'

'But that wasn't the worst. You said the mirrors were the worst. Not to be able to look at yourself.'

'Yes. Well, so I think. I hope I can always look myself in the face. And you, Johane, you should always have a fine glass to see yourself. As you're a woman worth looking at.'

You could write a sonnet, Thomas Wyatt could write her a sonnet, and not make this effect ... She turns her head away, but through the thin film of her veil he can see her skin glow. Because women will coax: tell me, just tell me something, tell me your thoughts; and this he has done.

They part friends. They even manage without one last time for old time's sake. Not that they are parted, really, but now they are on different terms. Mercy says, 'Thomas, when you're cold and under a stone, you'll talk yourself out of your grave.'

The household is quiet, calm. The turmoil of the city is locked outside the gate; he is having the locks renewed, the chains reinforced. Jo brings him an Easter egg. 'Look, we have saved this one for you.' It is a white egg with no speckles. It is featureless, but a single curl, the colour of onion-skin, peeps out from under a lopsided crown. You pick your prince and you know what he is: or do you?

The child says, 'My mother sends a message: tell your uncle, for a present, I'd like a drinking cup made of the shell of a griffin's egg. It's a lion with the head and wings of a bird; it's died out now, so you can't get them any more.'

He says, 'Ask her what colour she wants.'

Jo plants a kiss on his cheek.

He looks into the glass and the whole bright room comes bouncing back to him: lutes, portraits, silk hangings. In Rome there was a banker called Agostino Chigi. In Siena, where he came from, they maintained he was the richest man in the world. When Agostino had the Pope around for dinner he fed him on gold plates. Then he looked at the aftermath – the sprawled, sated cardinals, the mess they left behind, the half-picked bones and fish skeletons, the oyster shells and the orange rinds – and he said, stuff it, let's save the washing-up.

The guests tossed their plates out of the open windows and straight into the Tiber. The soiled table linen flew after them, white napkins unfurling like greedy gulls diving for scraps. Peals of Roman laughter unfurled into the Roman night.

Chigi had netted the banks, and he had divers standing by for whatever escaped. Some sharp-eyed servant of his upper household stood by the bank when dawn came, and checked off the list, pricking with a pin each item retrieved as it came up from the deep.

1531: it is the summer of the comet. In the long dusk, beneath the curve of the rising moon and the light of the strange new star, black-robed gentlemen stroll arm in arm in the garden, speaking of salvation. They are Thomas Cranmer, Hugh Latimer, the priests and clerks of Anne's household detached and floated to

Austin Friars on a breeze of theological chit-chat: where did the church go wrong? How can we drift her into the right channel again? 'It would be a mistake,' he says, watching them from the window, 'to think any of those gentlemen agree one with the other on any point of the interpretation of scripture. Give them a season's respite from Thomas More, and they will fall to persecuting each other.'

Gregory is sitting on a cushion and playing with his dog. He is whisking her nose with a feather and she is sneezing to amuse him. 'Sir,' he says, 'why are your dogs always called Bella and always so small?'

Behind him at an oak table, Nikolaus Kratzer, the king's astronomer, sits with his astrolabe before him, his paper and ink. He puts down his pen and looks up. 'Master Cromwell,' he says lightly, 'either my calculations are wrong, or the universe is not as we think it.'

He says, 'Why are comets bad signs? Why not good signs? Why do they prefigure the fall of nations? Why not their rise?'

Kratzer is from Munich, a dark man of his own age with a long humorous mouth. He comes here for the company, for the good and learned conversation, some of it in his own language. The cardinal had been his patron, and he had made him a beautiful gold sundial. When he saw it the great man had flushed with pleasure. 'Nine faces, Nikolaus! Seven more than the Duke of Norfolk.'

In the year 1456 there was a comet like this one. Scholars recorded it, Pope Calixtus excommunicated it, and it may be that there are one or two old men alive who saw it. Its tail was noted down as sabre-shaped, and in that year the Turks laid siege to Belgrade. It is as well to take note of any portents the heavens may offer; the king seeks the best advice. The alignment of the planets in Pisces, in the autumn of 1524, was followed by great wars in Germany, the rise of Luther's sect, uprisings among common men and the deaths of 100,000 of the Emperor's subjects; also, three years of rain. The sack of Rome was foretold, full ten years before the event, by noises of battle in the air and under the ground: the clash of invisible armies, steel clattering against steel, and the spectral cries of dying men. He himself was not in Rome to hear it, but he has met many men who say they have a friend who knows a man who was.

He says, 'Well, if you can answer for reading the angles, I can check your workings.'

Gregory says, 'Dr Kratzer, where does the comet go, when we are not looking at it?'

The sun has declined; birdsong is hushed; the scent of the herb beds rises through the open window. Kratzer is still, a man trans-fixed by prayer or Gregory's question, gazing down at his papers with his long knuckly fingers joined. Down below in the garden, Dr Latimer glances up and waves to him. 'Hugh is hungry. Gregory, fetch our guests in.'

'I will run over the figures first.' Kratzer shakes his head. 'Luther says, God is above mathematics.'

Candles are brought in for Kratzer. The wood of the table is black in the dusk, and the light settles against it in trembling spheres. The scholar's lips move, like the lips of a monk at vespers; liquid figures spill from his pen. He, Cromwell, turns in the doorway and sees them. They flitter from the table, skim and melt into the corners of the room.

Thurston comes stumping up from the kitchens. 'I sometimes wonder what people think goes on here! Give some dinners, or we shall be undone. All these hunting gentlemen, and ladies too, they have sent us enough meat to feed an army.'

'Send it to the neighbours.'

'Suffolk is sending us a buck every day.'

'Monsieur Chapuys is our neighbour, he doesn't get many presents.'

'And Norfolk –'

'Give it out at the back gate. Ask the parish who's hungry.'

315

'But it is the butchering! The skinning, the quartering!'

'I'll come and give you a hand, shall I?'

'You can't do that!' Thurston wrings his apron.

'It will be a pleasure.' He eases off the cardinal's ring.

'Sit still! Sit still, and be a gentleman, sir. Indict something, can you not? Write a law! Sir, you must forget you ever knew these businesses.'

He sits back down again, with a heavy sigh. 'Are our benefactors getting letters of thanks? I had better sign them myself.'

'They are thanking and thanking,' Thurston says. 'A dozen of clerks scribbling away.'

'You must take on more kitchen boys.'

'And you more scribblers.'

If the king asks for him, he goes out of London to where the king is. August finds him in a group of courtiers watching Anne, standing in a pool of sunlight, dressed as Maid Marian and shooting at a target. 'William Brereton, good day,' he says. 'You are not in Cheshire?'

'Yes. Despite appearances, I am.'

I asked for that. 'Only I thought you would be hunting in your own country.'

Brereton scowls. 'Must I account to you for my movements?'

In her green glade, in her green silks, Anne is fretting and fuming. Her bow is not to her liking. In a temper, she casts it on the grass.

'She was the same in the nursery.' He turns to find Mary Boleyn at his side: an inch closer than anyone else would be.

'Where's Robin Hood?' His eyes are on Anne. 'I have dispatches.'

'He won't look at them till sundown.'

'He will not be occupied then?'

'She is selling herself by the inch. The gentlemen all say you are advising her. She wants a present in cash for every advance above her knee.'

'Not like you, Mary. One push backwards and, good girl, here's fourpence.'

'Well. You know. If kings are doing the pushing.' She laughs. 'Anne has very long legs. By the time he comes to her secret part he will be bankrupt. The French wars will be cheap, in comparison.'

Anne has knocked away Mistress Shelton's offer of another bow. She stalks towards them across the grass. The golden caul that holds her hair glitters with diamond points. 'What's this, Mary? Another assault on Master Cromwell's reputation?' There is some giggling from the group. 'Have you any good news for me?' she asks him. Her voice softens, and her look. She puts a hand on his arm. The giggling stops.

In a north-facing closet, out of the glare, she tells him, 'I have news for you, in fact. Gardiner is to get Winchester.'

Winchester was Wolsey's richest bishopric; he carries all the figures in his head. 'The preference may render him amenable.'

She smiles: a twist of her mouth. 'Not to me. He has worked to get rid of Katherine, but he would rather I did not replace her. Even to Henry he makes no secret of that. I wish he were not Secretary. You –'

'Too soon.'

She nods. 'Yes. Perhaps. You know they have burned Little Bilney? While we have been in the woods playing thieves.'

Bilney was taken before the Bishop of Norwich, caught preaching in the open fields and handing out to his audience pages of Tyndale's gospels. The day he was burned it was windy, and the wind kept blowing the flames away from him, so it was a long time before he died. 'Thomas More says he recanted when he was in the fire.'

'That is not what I hear from people who saw it.'

'He was a fool,' Anne says. She blushes, deep angry red. 'People must say whatever will keep them alive, till better times come. That is no sin. Would not you?' He is not often hesitant. 'Oh, come, you have thought about it.'

'Bilney put himself into the fire. I always said he would. He recanted before and was let go, so he could be granted no more mercy.'

Anne drops her eyes. 'How fortunate we are, that we never come to the end of God's.' She seems to shake herself. She stretches her arms. She smells of green leaves and lavender. In the dusk her diamonds are as cool as raindrops. 'The King of Outlaws will be home. We had better go and meet him.' She straightens her spine.

The harvest is getting in. The nights are violet and the comet shines over the stubble fields. The huntsmen call in the dogs. After Holy Cross Day the deer will be safe. When he was a child this was the time for the boys who had been living wild on the heath all summer to come home and make their peace with their fathers, stealing in on a harvest supper night when the parish was in drink. Since before Whitsun they had lived by scavenging and beggars' tricks, snaring birds and rabbits and cooking them in their iron pot, chasing any girls they saw back screaming to their houses, and on wet and cold nights sneaking into outhouses and barns, to keep warm by singing and telling riddles and jokes. When the season was over it was time for him to sell the cauldron, taking it door-to-door and talking up its merits. 'This pot is never empty,' he would claim. 'If you've only some fish-heads, throw them in and a halibut will swim up.'

'Is it holed?'

'This pot is sound, and if you don't believe me, madam, you can piss in it. Come, tell me what you will give me. There is no pot to equal this since Merlin was a boy. Toss in a mouse from your trap and the next thing you know it's a spiced boar's head with the apple ready in its mouth.'

'How old are you?' a woman asks him.

'That I couldn't say.'

'Come back next year, and we can lie in my feather bed.'

He hesitates. 'Next year I'm run away.'

'You're going on the road as a travelling show? With your pot?'

'No, I thought I'd be a robber on the heath. Or a bear-keeper's a steady job.'

The woman says, 'I hope it keeps fine for you.'

That night, after his bath, his supper, his singing, his dancing, the king wants a walk. He has country tastes, likes what you call hedge wine, nothing strong, but these days he knocks back his first drink quickly and nods to signal for more; so he needs Francis Weston's arm to steady him as he leaves the table. A heavy dew has fallen, and gentlemen with torches squelch over the grass. The king takes a few breaths of damp air. 'Gardiner,' he says. 'You don't get on.'

'I have no quarrel with him,' he says blandly.

'Then he has a quarrel with you.' The king vanishes into blackness; next he speaks from behind a torch flame, like God out of the burning bush. 'I can manage Stephen. I have his measure. He is the kind of robust servant I need, these days. I don't want men who are afraid of controversy.'

'Your Majesty should come inside. These night vapours are not healthy.'

'Spoken like the cardinal.' The king laughs.

He approaches on the king's left hand. Weston, who is young and lightly built, is showing signs of buckling at the knees. 'Lean on me, sir,' he advises. The king locks an arm around his neck, in a sort of wrestling hold. Bear-keeper's a steady job. For a moment he thinks the king is crying.

He didn't run away the next year, for bear-keeping or any other trade. It was next year that the Cornishmen came roaring up the country, rebels bent on burning London and taking the English king and bending him to their Cornish will. Fear went before their army, for they were known for burning ricks and ham-stringing cattle, for firing houses with the people inside, for slaughtering priests and eating babies and trampling altar bread.

The king lets him go abruptly. 'Away to our cold beds. Or is that only mine? Tomorrow you will hunt. If you are not well mounted we will provide. I will see if I can tire you out, though Wolsey said it was a thing impossible. You and Gardiner, you must learn to pull together. This winter you must be yoked to the plough.'

It is not oxen he wants, but brutes who will go head-to-head, injure and maim themselves in the battle for his favour. It's clear his chances with the king are better if he doesn't get on with Gardiner than if he does. Divide and rule. But then, he rules anyway.

Though Parliament has not been recalled, Michaelmas term is the busiest he has ever known. Fat files of the king's business arrive almost hourly, and the Austin Friars fills up with city merchants, monks and priests of various sorts, petitioners for five minutes of his time. As if they sense something, a shift of power, a coming spectacle, small groups of Londoners begin to gather outside his gate, pointing out the liveries of the men who come and go: the Duke of Norfolk's man, the Earl of Wiltshire's servant. He looks down on them from a window and feels he recognises them; they are sons of the men who every autumn stood around gossiping and warming themselves by the door of his father's forge. They are boys like the boy he used to be: restless, waiting for something to happen.

He looks down at them and arranges his face. Erasmus says that you must do this each morning before you leave your house: 'put on a mask, as it were.' He applies that to each place, each castle or inn or nobleman's seat, where he finds himself waking up. He sends some money to Erasmus, as the cardinal used to do. 'To buy him his gruel,' he used to say, 'and keep the poor soul in quills and ink.' Erasmus is surprised; he has heard only bad things of Thomas Cromwell.

From the day he was sworn into the king's council, he has had his face arranged. He has spent the early months of the year watching the faces of other people, to see when they register doubt, reservation, rebellion – to catch that fractional moment before they settle into the suave lineaments of the courtier, the facilitator, the yes-man. Rafe says to him, we cannot trust Wriothesley, and he laughs: I know where I am with Call-Me. He is well connected at court, but got his start in the cardinal's household: as who did not? But Gardiner was his master at Trinity Hall, and he has watched us both rise in the world. He has seen us put on muscle, two fighting dogs, and he cannot decide where to put his money. He says to Rafe, I might in his place feel the same; it was easy in my day, you just put your shirt on Wolsey. He has no fear of Wriothesley, or anyone like him. You can calculate the actions of unprincipled men. As long as you feed them they'll run at your heels. Less calculable, more dangerous, are men like Stephen Vaughan, men who write to you, as Vaughan does: Thomas Cromwell, I would do anything for you. Men who say they understand you, whose embrace is so tight and ungiving they will carry you over the abyss.

At Austin Friars he has beer and bread sent out to the men who stand at the gate: broth, as the mornings get sharper. Thurston says, well, if you aim to be feeding the whole district. It's only last month, he says, that you were complaining the larders were overflowing and the cellars were full. St Paul tells us we must know how to flourish in times of abasement and times of abundance, with a full stomach and an empty. He goes down to the kitchens to talk to the boys Thurston has taken on. They shout up with their names and what they can do, and gravely he notes their abilities in a book: Simon, can dress a salad and play a drum, Matthew, he can say his Pater Noster. All these *garzoni* must be trainable. One day they must be able to walk upstairs, as he did, and take a seat in the counting house. All must have warm and decent clothes, and be encouraged to wear them, not sell them, for he remembers from his days at Lambeth the profound cold of store rooms; in Wolsey's kitchens at Hampton Court, where the chimneys draw well and confine the heat, he has seen stray snowflakes drifting in the rafters and settling on sills.

When in the crisp mornings at dawn he comes out of his house with his entourage of clerks, the Londoners are already assembling. They drop back and watch him, neither friendly nor hostile. He calls out good morning to them and may God bless you, and some of them shout good morning back. They pull off their caps and, because he is a king's councillor, they stand bareheaded till he has gone by.

October: Monsieur Chapuys, the Emperor's ambassador, comes to Austin Friars to dine, and Stephen Gardiner is on the menu. 'No sooner appointed to Winchester, than sent abroad,' Chapuys says. 'And how do you think King Francis will like him? What can he do as a diplomat that Sir Thomas Boleyn cannot? Though I suppose he is *parti pris*. Being the lady's father. Gardiner more … ambivalent, you would say? More disinterested, that is the word. I cannot see what King Francis will get out of supporting the match, unless your king were to offer him – what? Money? Warships? Calais?'

At table with the household, Monsieur Chapuys has talked pleasantly of verse, portraiture, and his university years in Turin; turning to Rafe, whose French is excellent, he has spoken of falconry, as a thing likely to interest young men. 'You must go out with our master,' Rafe tells him. 'It is almost his only recreation these days.'

Monsieur Chapuys turns his bright little eyes upon him. 'He plays kings' games now.'

Rising from table, Chapuys praises the food, the music, the furnishings. One can see his brain turning, hear the little clicks, like the gins of an elaborate lock, as he encodes his opinions for his dispatches to his master the Emperor.

Afterwards, in his cabinet, the ambassador unleashes his questions; rattling on, not pausing for a reply. 'If the Bishop of Winchester is in France, how will Henry do without his Secretary? Master Stephen's embassy cannot be short. Perhaps this is your chance to creep closer, do you think? Tell me, is it true Gardiner is Henry's bastard cousin? And your boy Richard, also? Such things perplex the Emperor. To have a king who is so very little royal. It is perhaps no wonder he seeks to wed a poor gentlewoman.'

'I would not call Lady Anne poor.'

'True, the king has enriched her family.' Chapuys smirks. 'Is it usual in this country, to pay the girl for her services in advance?'

'Indeed it is – you should remember it – I should be sorry to see you chased down the street.'

'You advise her, Lady Anne?'

'I look over accounts. It is not much to do, for a dear friend.'

Chapuys laughs merrily. 'A friend! She is a witch, you know? She has put the king under an enchantment, so he risks everything – to be cast out of Christendom, to be damned. And I think he half knows it. I have seen him under her eye, his wits scattered and fleeing, his soul turning and twisting like a hare under the eye of a hawk. Perhaps she has enchanted you too.' Monsieur Chapuys leans forward and rests, on his own hand, his little monkey's paw. 'Break the enchantment, *mon cher ami*. You will not regret it. I serve a most liberal prince.'

November: Sir Henry Wyatt stands in the hall at Austin Friars; he looks at the blank space on the wall, where the cardinal's arms have been painted out. 'He has only been gone a year, Thomas. To me it seems more. They say that when you are an old man one year is the same as the next. I can tell you that is not true.'

Oh, come sir, the little girls shout, you are not so old you cannot tell a story. They tow him towards one of the new velvet armchairs and enthrone him. Sir Henry would be everyone's father, if they had their choice, everyone's grandfather. He has served in the treasury of this Henry, and the Henry before him; if the Tudors are poor, it's not his fault.

Alice and Jo have been out in the garden, trying to catch the cat. Sir Henry likes to see a cat honoured in a household; at the children's request, he will explain why.

'Once,' he begins, 'in this land of England, there arose a cruel tyrant by the name of Richard Plantagenet –'

'Oh, they were wicked folk of that name,' Alice bursts out. 'And do you know, there are still some of them left?'

There is laughter. 'Well, it is true,' Alice shouts, her cheeks burning.

'– and I, your servant Wyatt who relates this tale, was cast by this tyrant into a dungeon, to sleep upon the straw, a dungeon with but one small window, and that window barred ...'

Winter came on, Sir Henry says, and I had no fire; I had no food or water, for the guards forgot me. Richard Cromwell sits listening, chin on hand; he exchanges a look with Rafe; both of them glance at him, and he makes a little gesture, damping down the horror of the past. Sir Henry, they know, was not forgotten at the Tower. His guards laid white-hot knives against his flesh. They pulled out his teeth.

'So what must I do?' says Sir Henry. 'Lucky for me, my dungeon was damp. I drank the water that ran down the wall.'

'And for food?' Jo says. Her voice is low and thrilled.

'Ah, now we come to the best part of the tale.' One day, Sir Henry says, when I thought if I did not eat I was likely to die, I perceived that the light of my little window was blocked; looking up, what should I see, but the form of a cat, a black and white London cat. 'Now, Pusskins,' I said to her; and she mewed, and in doing so, she let fall her burden. And what had she brought me?

'A pigeon!' shouts Jo.

'Mistress, either you have been a prisoner yourself, or heard this tale before.'

The girls have forgotten that he does not have a cook, a spit, a fire; the young men drop their eyes, flinching from the mental picture of a prisoner tearing apart, with fettered hands, a mass of feathers swarming with bird-lice.

'Now, the next news I heard, lying on the straw, was the ringing of bells, and a cry in the streets, A Tudor! A Tudor! Without the cat's gift, I would not have lived to hear it, or hear the key turn in the lock, and King Henry himself cry, Wyatt, is that you? Come forth to your reward!'

Some forgivable exaggeration here. King Henry had not been in that cell, but King Richard had; it was he who oversaw the heating of the knife, and listened, his head tilted slightly, as Henry Wyatt screamed; who sidled away, fastidious, from the odour of burning flesh, and ordered the knife to be reheated, and applied again.

They say that Little Bilney, the night before he was burned, held his fingers in a candle flame, and called on Jesus to teach him how to endure the pain. That was not wise, to maim yourself before the event; wise or not, he thinks of it. 'Now, Sir Henry,' Mercy says, 'you must tell us the lion tale, because we won't sleep if we don't hear it.'

'Well, really that is my son's tale, he should be here.'

'If he were,' Richard says, 'the ladies would all be making goggle eyes at him, and sighing – yes you would, Alice – and they would not care about any lion tale.'

When Sir Henry was mended after his imprisonment he became a powerful man at court, and an admirer sent him a present of a lion cub. At Allington Castle I brought her up like my child, he says, till, as a girl will, she developed a mind of her own. One careless day, and mine the fault, she came out of her cage. Leontina, I called to her, stand till I lead you back; but then she crouched, quite silent, and sighted me, and her eyes were like fire. It was then I realised, he says, that I was not her father, for all that I had cherished her: I was her dinner.

Alice says, a hand to her mouth, 'Sir Henry, you thought your last hour had come.'

'Indeed I did, and so it had, if it had not been that my son Thomas chanced to step into the courtyard. In a second he saw my peril, and called out to her, Leontina, here to me; and she turned her head. In that moment, her glare distracted, I stepped back a pace, and another. Look at me, Thomas called. Now that day he was dressed very brightly, with long fluttering sleeves, and a loose gown the wind got inside, and his hair being fair, you know, which he wore long, he must have looked like a flame, I think, tall and flickering in the sun, and for a moment she stood, puzzling, and I stepped away, back and back ...'

Leontina turns; she crouches; leaving the father, she begins to stalk the son. You can see her padding feet and feel the stink of blood on her breath. (Meanwhile he, Henry Wyatt, in a cold lather of fear, backs off, backs away, in the direction of help.) In his soft enchanting voice, in loving murmurs, in the accents of prayer, Tom Wyatt speaks to the lion, asking St Francis to open her brutish heart to grace. Leontina watches. She listens. She opens her mouth. She roars: 'What does she say?'

'*Fee, fi, fo and fum, I smell the blood of an Englishman.*'

Tom Wyatt stands still as a statue. Grooms with nets creep across the court. Leontina is within feet of him, but once again she checks, listening. She stands, uncertain, ears twitching. He can see the pink drool from her jaw and smell her musty fur. She crouches back on her haunches. He scents her breath. She is ready to spring. He sees her muscles quiver, her jaw stretch; she leaps – but she spins in the air, an arrow stinging her ribs. She whirls, smashes at the barb, cries out, moans; another arrow thuds into her dense flank, and as she circles again, whining, the nets drop over her. Sir Henry, striding calmly towards her, places his third arrow in her throat.

Even as she dies she roars. She coughs blood and strikes out. One of the grooms bears her claw mark to this day. Her pelt can be seen on the wall at Allington. 'And you will come and visit me, young ladies,' Sir Henry says. 'And you can see what a brute she was.'

'Tom's prayers were not answered,' Richard says, smiling. 'St Francis did nothing about it, so far as I can see.'

'Sir Henry,' Jo pulls at his sleeve, 'you have not said the best part.'

'No. I forgot. So then my son Tom walks away, the hero of the hour, and is sick into a bush.'

The children release their breath. They all applaud. In its time the story had reached court, and the king – he was younger then, sweet in disposition – was a little awed by it. When he sees Tom even now, he will nod, and murmur to himself, 'Tom Wyatt. He can tame lions.'

When Sir Henry, who is fond of soft fruit, has eaten some fat brambles with yellow cream, he says, 'A word with you alone,' and they withdraw. If I were in your place, Sir Henry says, I'd ask him to make you Keeper of the Jewel House. 'From that post, when I had it, I found I had an overview of the revenue.'

'Ask him how?'

'Get Lady Anne to ask him.'

'Perhaps your son could help by asking Anne.'

Sir Henry laughs; or rather, he indicates with a little ahem that he knows a joke has been made. By the account of drinkers in Kent alehouses, and the backstairs servants at court (the musician Mark for one), Anne has done Thomas Wyatt all the favours a man might reasonably ask, even in a brothel.

'I mean to retire from court this year,' Sir Henry says. 'It's time I wrote my will. May I name you as executor?'

'You do me honour.'

'There is no one I'd rather trust with my affairs. You've the steadiest hand I know.'

He smiles, puzzled; nothing in his world seems steady to him.

'I understand you,' Wyatt says. 'I know our old fellow in scarlet nearly brought you down. But look at you, eating almonds, with all your teeth in your head, and your household around you, and your affairs prospering, and men like Norfolk speaking to you civil.' Whereas, he doesn't need to add, a year ago they were wiping their feet on you. Sir Henry breaks up, in his fingers, a cinnamon wafer, and dabs it on to his tongue, a careful, secular Eucharist. It is forty years, more, since the Tower, but his smashed-up jaw still stiffens and plagues him with pain. 'Thomas, I have something to ask you ... Will you keep an eye on my son? Be a father to him?'

'Tom is, what, twenty-eight? He may not like another father.'

'You cannot do worse than I did. I have much to regret, his marriage chiefly ... He was seventeen, he did not want it, it was I who wanted it, because her father was Baron Cobham, and I wanted to keep my place up among my neighbours in Kent. Tom was always good to look at, a kind boy and courteous as well, you'd have thought he would have done for the girl, but I don't know if she was faithful to him a month. So then, of course, he paid her in kind ... the place is full of his doxies, open a closet at Allington and some wench falls out of it. He roams off abroad and what comes of that? He ends up a prisoner in Italy, I shall never understand that affair. Since Italy he's had even less sense. Write you a piece of terza rima, of course, but sit down and work out where his money's gone ...' He rubs his chin. 'But there you have it. When all's said, there is no braver boy than my boy.'

'Will you come back now, and join the company? You know we take a holiday when you visit us.'

Sir Henry levers himself upright. He is a portly man, though he lives on pottage and mashes. 'Thomas, how did I get old?'

When they return to the hall it is to find a play in progress. Rafe is acting the part of Leontina and the household is roaring him on. It is not that the boys don't believe the lion tale; it is just that they like to put their own words to it. He extends a peremptory hand to Richard, who has been standing on a joint-stool, squealing. 'You are jealous of Tom Wyatt,' he says.

'Ah, don't be out of temper with us, master.' Rafe resumes human form and throws himself on to a bench. 'Tell us about Florence. Tell us what else you did, you and Giovannino.'

'I don't know if I should. You will make a play of it.'

Ah, do, they persuade him, and he looks around: Rafe encourages him with a purr. 'Are we sure Call-Me-Risley is not here? Well … when we had a day off, we used to take down buildings.'

'Take them down?' Henry Wyatt says. 'Did you so?'

'What I mean is, blow them up. But not without the owner's permission. Unless we thought they were crumbling and a danger to passers-by. We only charged for explosive materials. Not for our expertise.'

'Which was considerable, I suppose?'

'It's a lot of digging for a few seconds of excitement. But I knew some boys who went into it as a profession. In Florence,' he says, 'it was just what you might do for your recreation. Like fishing. It kept us out of trouble.' He hesitates. 'Well, no, it didn't. Not really.'

Richard says, 'Did Call-Me tell Gardiner? About your Cupid?'

'What do you think?'

The king had said to him, I hear you antiqued a statue. The king was laughing, but perhaps also making a note; laughing because the joke's against clerics, against cardinals, and he's in the mood for such a joke.

Secretary Gardiner: 'Statue, statute, not much difference.'

'One letter is everything, in legislating. But my precedents are not faked.'

'Stretched?' Gardiner says.

'Majesty, the Council of Constance granted your ancestor, Henry V, such control over the church in England as no other Christian king exercised in his realm.'

329

'The concessions were not applied. Not with consistency. Why is that?'

'I don't know. Incompetence?'

'But we have better councillors now?'

'Better kings, Your Majesty.'

Behind Henry's back, Gardiner makes a gargoyle face at him. He almost laughs.

The legal term closes. Anne says, come and eat a poor Advent supper with me. We'll use forks.

He goes, but he doesn't like the company. She has made pets of the king's friends, the gentlemen of his privy chamber: Henry Norris, William Brereton, those people, and her brother, of course, Lord Rochford. Anne is brittle in their company, and as ruthless with their compliments as a housewife snapping the necks of larks for the table. If her precise smile fades for a moment, they all lean forward, anxious to know how to please her. A bigger set of fools you would go far to seek.

For himself, he can go anywhere, he has been anywhere. Brought up on the table talk of the Frescobaldi family, the Portinari family, and latterly at the cardinal's table among the savants and wits, he is unlikely to find himself at a loss among the pretty people Anne gathers around her. God knows, they do their best, the gentlemen, to make him uncomfortable; he imports his own comfort, his calm, his exact and pointed conversation. Norris, who is a witty man, and not young, stultifies himself by keeping such company: and why? Proximity to Anne makes him tremble. It is almost a joke, but a joke that nobody tells.

After that first occasion, Norris follows him out, touches his sleeve, and brings him to a standstill, face to face. 'You don't see it, do you? Anne?'

He shakes his head.

'So what would be your idea? Some fat frau from your travels?'

'A woman I could love, would be a woman in whom the king has no interest at all.'

'If that is a piece of advice, tell it to your friend Wyatt's son.'

'Oh, I think young Wyatt has worked it out. He is a married man. He says to himself, from your deprivations make a verse. Don't we all grow wiser, from pinpricks to the *amour propre*?'

'Can you look at me,' Norris says, 'and think I grow wiser?'

He hands Norris his handkerchief. Norris mops his face and gives the handkerchief back. He thinks of St Veronica, swabbing with her veil the features of the suffering Christ; he wonders if, when he gets home, Henry's gentlemanly features will be imprinted on the cloth, and if so, will he hang the result on the wall? Norris turns away, with a little laugh: 'Weston – young Weston, you know – he is jealous of a boy she brings in to sing for us some nights. He is jealous of the man who comes in to mend the fire, or the maid who pulls her stockings off. Every time she looks at you, he keeps count, he says, there, there, do you see, she is looking at that fat butcher, she looked at him fifteen times in two hours.'

'It was the cardinal who was the fat butcher.'

'To Francis, one tradesman's the same as the next.'

'I quite see that. Give you good night.'

Night, Tom, Norris says, batting him on the shoulder, absent, distracted, almost as if they were equals, as if they were friends; his eyes are turned back to Anne, his steps are turned back to his rivals.

One tradesman the same as the next? Not in the real world. Any man with a steady hand and a cleaver can call himself a butcher: but without the smith, where does he get that cleaver? Without the man who works in metal, where are your hammers, your scythes, your sickles, scissors and planes? Your arms and armour, your arrowheads, your pikes and your guns? Where are your ships at sea and their anchors? Where are your grappling hooks, your nails, latches, hinges, pokers and tongs? Where are your spits, kettles, trivets, your harness rings, buckles and bits? Where are your knives?

He remembers the day they heard the Cornish army was coming. He was – what – twelve? He was in the forge. He had cleaned the big bellows and he was oiling the leather. Walter came over and looked at it. 'Wants caulking.'

'Right,' he said. (This was the kind of conversation he had with Walter.)

'It won't do itself.'

'I said, right, right, I'm doing it!'

He looked up. Their neighbour Owen Madoc stood in the doorway. 'They're on the march. Word's all down the river. Henry Tudor ready to fight. The queen and the little ones in the Tower.'

Walter wipes his mouth. 'How long?'

Madoc says, 'God knows. Those fuckers can fly.'

He straightens up. Into his hand has floated a four-pound hammer with an ash shaft.

The next few days they worked till they were ready to drop. Walter undertook body armour for his friends, and he to put an edge on anything that can cut, tear, lacerate rebel flesh. The men of Putney have no sympathy with these heathens. They pay their taxes: why not the Cornish? The women are afraid that the Cornishmen will outrage their honour. 'Our priest says they only do it to their sisters,' he says, 'so you'll be all right, our Bet. But then again, the priest says they have cold scaly members like the devil, so you might want the novelty.'

Bet throws something at him. He dodges. It's always the excuse for breakages, in that house: I threw it at Thomas. 'Well, I don't know what you like,' he says.

That week, rumours proliferate. The Cornishmen work under the ground, so their faces are black. They are half-blind and so you can catch them in a net. The king will give you a shilling for each you catch, two shillings if it's a big one. Just how big are they? Because they shoot arrows a yard long.

Now all household objects are seen in a new light. Skewers, spits, larding needles: anything for defence at close quarters. The neighbours are paying out to Walter's other business, the brewery, as if they think the Cornishmen mean to drink England dry. Owen Madoc comes in and commissions a hunting knife, hand-guard, blood gutter and twelve-inch blade. 'Twelve-inch?' he says. 'You'll be flailing around and cut your ear off.'

'You'll not be so pert when the Cornish seize you. They spit children like you and roast them on bonfires.'

'Can't you just slap them with an oar?'

'I'll slap your jaw shut,' Owen Madoc bellows. 'You little fucker, you had a bad name before you were born.'

He shows Owen Madoc the knife he has made for himself, slung on a cord under his shirt: its stub of blade, like a single, evil tooth. 'What do you think?'

'Christ,' Madoc says. 'Be careful who you leave it in.'

He says to his sister Kat – just resting his four-pound hammer on her windowsill at the Pegasus – why did I have a bad name before I was born?

Ask Morgan Williams, she says. He'll tell you. Oh, Tom, Tom, she says. She grabs his head and kisses it. You don't put yourself out there. Let *him* fight.

She hopes the Cornish will kill Walter. She doesn't say so, but he knows it.

When I am the man of this family, he says, things will be different, I can tell you.

Morgan tells him – blushing, for he is a very proper man – that boys used to follow his mother in the street, shouting 'Look at the old mare in foal!'

His sister Bet says, 'Another thing those Cornish have got, they have got a giant called Bolster, who's in love with St Agnes and he follows her around and the Cornish bear her image on their flags and so he's coming to London after them.'

'Bolster?' he sneers. 'I expect he's *that* big.'

'Oh, you will see,' Bet says. 'Then you won't be so quick with your answers.'

The women of the district, Morgan says, clucked around his mother pretending concern: what will it be when it's born, she's like the side of a house!

Then when he came into this world, bawling, with clenched fists and wet black curls, Walter and his friends reeled through Putney, singing. They shouted, 'Come and get it, girls!' and 'Barren wives served here!'

They never noted the date. He said to Morgan, I don't mind. I don't have a natal chart. So I don't have a fate.

As fate had it, there was no battle in Putney. For the outriders and escapees, the women were ready with bread knives and razors, the men to bludgeon them with shovels and mattocks, to hollow them with adzes and to spike them on butchers' steels. The big fight was at Blackheath instead: Cornishmen cut up into little pieces, minced by the Tudor in his military mincing machine. All of them safe: except from Walter.

His sister Bet says, 'You know that giant, Bolster? He hears that St Agnes is dead. He's cut his arm and in sorrow his blood has flowed into the sea. It's filled up a cave that can never be filled, which goes into a hole, which goes down beneath the bed of the sea and into the centre of the earth and into Hell. So he's dead.'

'Oh, good. Because I was really worried about Bolster.'

'Dead till next time,' his sister says.

So on a date unknown, he was born. At three years old, he was collecting kindling for the forge. 'See my little lad?' Walter would say, batting him fondly around the head. His fingers smelled of burning, and his palm was solid and black.

In recent years, of course, scholars have tried to give him a fate; men learned in reading the heavens have tried to work him back from what he is and how he is, to when he was born. Jupiter favourably aspected, indicating prosperity. Mercury rising, offering the faculty of quick and persuasive speech. Kratzer says, if Mars is not in Scorpio, I don't know my trade. His mother was fifty-two and they thought she could neither conceive nor deliver a child. She hid her powers and disguised him under draperies, deep inside her, for as long as she could contrive. He came out and they said, what is it?

In mid-December, James Bainham, a barrister of the Middle Temple, abjures his heresies before the Bishop of London. He has been tortured, the city says, More himself questioning him while the handle of the rack is turned and asking him to name other infected members of the Inns of Court. A few days later, a former monk and a leather-seller are burned together. The monk had run in consignments of books through the Norfolk ports and then, stupidly enough, through St Katharine's Dock, where the Lord Chancellor was waiting to seize them. The leather-seller had possession of Luther's *Liberty of a Christian Man*, the text copied out in his own hand. These are men he knows, the disgraced and broken Bainham, the monk Bayfield, John Tewkesbury, who God knows was no doctor of theology. That's how the year goes out, in a puff of smoke, a pall of human ash hanging over Smithfield.

On New Year's Day, he wakes before dawn to see Gregory at the foot of his bed. 'You'd better come. Tom Wyatt's been taken up.'

He is out of bed instantly; his first thought is that More has struck into the heart of Anne's circle. 'Where is he? They've not taken him to Chelsea?'

Gregory sounds mystified. 'Why would they take him to Chelsea?'

'The king cannot allow – it comes too near him – Anne has books, she has shown them to him – he himself has read Tyndale

– what next, is More going to arrest the king?' He reaches for a shirt.

'It's nothing to do with More. It's some fools taken up for making a riot in Westminster, they were in the street leaping over bonfires and took to smashing windows, you know how it goes …' Gregory's voice is weary. 'Then they go fighting the watch and they get locked up, and a message comes, will Master Cromwell go down and give the turnkey a New Year present?'

'Christ,' he says. He sits down on the bed, suddenly conscious of his nakedness, of feet, shins, thighs, cock, his pelt of body hair, bristling chin: and the sweat that has broken out across his shoulders. He pulls on his shirt. 'They'll have to take me as they find me,' he says. 'And I'll have my breakfast first.'

Gregory says, with light malice, 'You agreed to be a father to him. This is what being a father means.'

He stands up. 'Get Richard.'

'I'll come.'

'Come if you must, but I want Richard in case there's trouble.'

There is no trouble, only a bit of haggling. Dawn is breaking when the young gentlemen reel out into the air, haggard, battered, their clothes torn and dirty. 'Francis Weston,' he says, 'good morning, sir.' He thinks, if I'd known you were here, I'd have left you. 'Why are you not at court?'

'I am,' the boy says, on an outgust of sour breath. 'I am at Greenwich. I am not here. Do you understand?'

'Bilocation,' he says. 'Right.'

'Oh, Jesus. Oh, Jesus my Redeemer.' Thomas Wyatt stands in the bright snowy light, rubbing his head. 'Never again.'

'Till next year,' Richard says.

He turns, to see a last shambling figure fall out into the street. 'Francis Bryan,' he says. 'I should have known this enterprise would not be complete without you. Sir.'

Exposed to the first chill of the new year, Lady Anne's cousin shakes himself like a wet dog. 'By the tits of Holy Agnes, it's freezing.' His doublet is ripped and his shirt collar torn off, and he has only one shoe. He clutches at his hose to keep them up. Five years ago, he lost an eye in the joust; now he has lost his eyepatch, and the livid socket is on view. He looks around, with what ocular equipment remains. 'Cromwell? I don't remember you were with us last night.'

'I was in my bed and would be glad if I were there still.'

'Why not go back?' Risking dangerous slippage, he throws his hands out. 'Which of the city wives is waiting for you? Do you have one for each of the twelve days of Christmas?' He almost laughs, till Bryan adds, 'Don't you sectaries hold your women in common?'

'Wyatt,' he turns away, 'get him to cover himself, or his parts will be frostbitten. Bad enough to be without an eye.'

'Say thank you.' Thomas Wyatt bellows, and thumps his companions. 'Say thank you to Master Cromwell and pay him back what you owe him. Who else would be up so early on a holiday, and with his purse open? We could have been there till tomorrow.'

They do not look like men who have a shilling between them. 'Never mind,' he says. 'I'll put it on the account.'

II
'Alas, What Shall I Do For Love?'
Spring 1532

Time now to consider the compacts that hold the world together: the compact between ruler and ruled, and that between husband and wife. Both these arrangements rest on a sedulous devotion, the one to the interests of the other. The master and husband protect and provide; the wife and servant obey. Above masters, above husbands, God rules all. He counts up our petty rebellions, our human follies. He reaches out his long arm, hand bunched into a fist.

Imagine debating these matters with George, Lord Rochford. He is as witty a young man as any in England, polished and well read; but today what fascinates him is the flame-coloured satin that is pulled through his slashed velvet over-sleeve. He keeps coaxing the little puffs of fabric with a fingertip, pleating and nudging them and encouraging them to grow bigger, so that he looks like one of those jugglers who run balls down their arms.

It is time to say what England is, her scope and boundaries: not to count and measure her harbour defences and border walls, but to estimate her capacity for self-rule. It is time to say what a king is, and what trust and guardianship he owes his people: what protection from foreign incursions moral or physical, what freedom from the pretensions of those who would like to tell an Englishman how to speak to his God.

338

Parliament meets mid-January. The business of the early spring is breaking the resistance of the bishops to Henry's new order, putting in place legislation that – though for now it is held in suspension – will cut revenues to Rome, make his supremacy in the church no mere form of words. The Commons drafts a petition against the church courts, so arbitrary in their proceedings, so presumptuous in their claimed jurisdiction; it questions their jurisdiction, their very existence. The papers pass through many hands, but finally he himself works through the night with Rafe and Call-Me-Risley, scribbling amendments between the lines. He is flushing out the opposition: Gardiner, although he is the king's Secretary, feels obliged to lead his fellow prelates into the charge.

The king sends for Master Stephen. When he goes in, the hair on his neck is bristling and he is shrinking inside his skin like a mastiff being led towards a bear. The king has a high voice, for a big man, and it rises when he is angry to an ear-throbbing shriek. Are the clergy his subjects, or only half his subjects? Perhaps they are not his subjects at all, for how can they be, if they take an oath to obey and support the Pope? Should they not, he yells, be taking an oath to *me*?

When Stephen comes out he leans against the painted panelling. At his back a troupe of painted nymphs are frisking in a glade. He takes out a handkerchief but seems to have forgotten why; he twists it in his great paw, wrapping it around his knuckles like a bandage. Sweat trickles down his face.

He, Cromwell, calls for assistance. 'My lord the bishop is ill.' They bring a stool and Stephen glares at it, glares at him, then sits down with caution, as if he is not able to trust the joinery. 'I take it you heard him?'

Every word. 'If he does lock you up, I'll make sure you have some small comforts.'

Gardiner says, 'God damn you, Cromwell. Who are you? What office do you hold? You're nothing. Nothing.'

We have to win the debate, not just knock our enemies down. He has been to see Christopher St German, the aged jurist, whose word is respected all over Europe. The old man entertains him civilly at his house. There is no man in England, he says, who does not believe our church is in need of reform which grows more urgent by the year, and if the church cannot do it, then the king in Parliament must, and can. This is the conclusion I have come to, after some decades of studying the subject.

Of course, the old man says, Thomas More does not agree with me. Perhaps his time has passed. Utopia, after all, is not a place one can live.

When he meets the king, Henry rages about Gardiner: disloyalty, he shouts, ingratitude. Can he remain my Secretary, when he has set himself up in direct opposition to me? (This is the man whom Henry himself praised as a stout controversialist.) He sits quietly, watching Henry, trying by stillness to defuse the situation; to wrap the king in a blanketing silence, so that he, Henry, can listen to himself. It is a great thing, to be able to divert the wrath of the Lion of England. 'I think ...' he says softly, 'with Your Majesty's permission, what I think ... The Bishop of Winchester, as we know, likes arguing. But not with his king. He would not dare to do that for sport.' He pauses. 'So his views, though mistaken, are honestly held.'

'Indeed, but –' The king breaks off. Henry has heard his own voice, the voice he used to the cardinal when he brought him down. Gardiner is not Wolsey – if only in the sense that, if he is sacrificed, few will remember him with regret. And yet it suits him, for the moment, to have the snarling bishop still in his post; he has a care for Henry's reputation in Europe, and he says, 'Majesty, Stephen has served you as an ambassador to the limit of his powers, and it would be better to reconcile him, by honest persuasion, than to force his hand by the weight of your displeasure. It is the more pleasant course, and there is more honour in it.'

He watches Henry's face. He is alive to anything that concerns honour.

'Is that the advice you would always give?'

He smiles. 'No.'

'You are not wholly determined I should govern in a spirit of Christian meekness?'

'No.'

'I know you dislike Gardiner.'

'That is why Your Majesty should consider my advice.'

He thinks, you owe me, Stephen. The bill will come in by and by.

At his own house he meets with parliamentarians and gentlemen from the Inns of Court and the city livery companies; with Thomas Audley who is Mr Speaker, and his protégé Richard Riche, a golden-haired young man, pretty as a painted angel, who has an active, quick and secular mind; with Rowland Lee, a robust outspoken cleric, the least priestly man you would find in a long day's march. In these months, the ranks of his city friends are thinned by sickness and unnatural death. Thomas Somer, whom he has known for years, has died just after release from the Tower, where he was shut up for distributing the gospel in English; fond of fine clothes and fast horses, Somer was a man of irrepressible spirits, till at last he had his reckoning with the Lord Chancellor. John Petyt has been released but he is too sick to take any more part in the Commons. He visits him; he is confined to his chamber now. It is painful to hear him fighting for breath. The spring of 1532, the year's first warm weather, does nothing to ease him. I feel, he says, as if there is an iron hoop around my chest, and they are drawing it tighter. He says, Thomas, will you look after Luce when I die?

Sometimes, if he walks in the gardens with the burgesses or with Anne's chaplains, he feels the absence of Dr Cranmer at his right-hand side. He has been away since January, as the king's ambassador to the Emperor; on his travels, he will visit scholars in

Germany to canvass support for the king's divorce. He had said to him, 'What shall I do if, while you are away, the king has a dream?'

Cranmer had smiled. 'You worked it by yourself, last time. I was only there to nod it through.'

He sees the animal Marlinspike, his paws hanging as he drapes himself from a black bough. He points him out. 'Gentlemen, that was the cardinal's cat.' At the sight of the visitors Marlinspike darts along the boundary wall, and with a whisk of his tail disappears, into the unknown territory beyond.

Down in the kitchens at Austin Friars, the *garzoni* are learning to make spiced wafers. The process involves a good eye, exact timing and a steady hand. There are so many points at which it can go wrong. The mixture must have the right dropping consistency, the plates of the long-handled irons must be well greased and hot. When you press the plates together there is an animal shriek as they meet, and steam hisses into the air. If you panic and release the pressure you will have a claggy mess to scrape away. You must wait till the steam dies down, and then you start counting. If you miss a beat the smell of scorching permeates the air. A second divides the successes from the failures.

When he brings into the Commons a bill to suspend the payment of annates to Rome, he suggests a division of the House. This is far from usual, but amid shock and grumbling the members comply: for the bill to this side, against the bill to the other side. The king is present; he watches, he learns who is for him and who against, and at the end of the process he gives his councillor a grim nod of approval. In the Lords this tactic will not serve. The king has to go in person, three times, and argue his own case. The old aristocracy – proud families like the Exeter clan, with their own claim to the throne – are for Pope and Katherine and are not afraid to say so: or not yet. But he is identifying his enemies and, where he can, splitting them.

Once the kitchen boys have made a single commendable wafer, Thurston has them turn out a hundred more. It becomes second nature, the flick of the wrist with which one rolls the half-set wafer on to the handle of a wooden spoon and then flips it on to the drying rack to crisp. The successes – with time, they should all be successes – are stamped with the badges of the Tudors, and stacked by the dozen in the pretty inlaid boxes in which they will come to the table, each frail golden disk perfumed with rosewater. He sends a batch to Thomas Boleyn.

As father of the queen-to-be, Wiltshire thinks he deserves some special title, and has let it be known it would not be disagreeable to him to be known as Monseigneur. He confers with him, his son and their friends, then walks to see Anne, through the chambers at Whitehall. Month by month her state is greater, but he goes through with a bow from her people. At court and in the offices of Westminster he dresses not a whit above his gentleman's station, in loose jackets of Lemster wool so fine they flow like water, in purples and indigos so near black that it looks as if the night has bled into them; his cap of black velvet sits on his black hair, so that the only points of light are his darting eyes and the gestures of his solid, fleshy hands; those, and flashes of fire from Wolsey's turquoise ring.

At Whitehall – York Place, as it was – the builders are still in. For Christmas, the king had given Anne a bedroom. He led her to it himself, to see her gasp at the wall hangings, which were of cloth of silver and cloth of gold, the carved bed hung with crimson satin embroidered with images of flowers and children. Henry Norris had reported to him that Anne had failed to gasp; she had just looked around the room slowly, smiled, blinked. Then she had remembered what she ought to do; she pretended to feel faint at the honour, and it was only when she swayed and the king locked his arms around her that the gasp came. I do devoutly hope, Norris had said, that we shall all at least once in our lives cause a woman to utter that sound.

When Anne had expressed her thanks, kneeling, Henry had to leave, of course; to leave the shimmering room, trailing her by the hand, and go back to the New Year feast, to the public scrutiny of his expression: in the certainty that news of it would be conveyed all over Europe, by land and sea, in and out of cipher.

When at the end of his walk through the cardinal's old rooms he finds Anne sitting with her ladies, she already knows, or seems to know, what her father and brother have said. They think they are fixing her tactics, but she is her own best tactician, and able to think back and judge what has gone wrong; he admires anyone who can learn from mistakes. One day, the windows open to the wing-beats of nest-building birds, she says, 'You once told me that only the cardinal could set the king free. Do you know what I think now? I think Wolsey was the last person to do it. Because he was so proud, because he wanted to be Pope. If he had been more humble, Clement would have obliged him.'

'There may be something in that.'

'I suppose we should take a lesson,' Norris says.

They turn together. Anne says, 'Really, should we?' and he says, 'What lesson would that be?'

Norris is at a loss.

'None of us are likely to be cardinals,' Anne says. 'Even Thomas, who aspires to most things, would not aspire to that.'

'Oh? I wouldn't put money on it.' Norris slouches off, as only a silken gentleman can slouch, and leaves him behind with the women.

'So, Lady Anne,' he says, 'when you are reflecting on the late cardinal, do you take time to pray for his soul?'

'I think God has judged him, and my prayers, if I make them or if I do not, are of no effect.'

Mary Boleyn says, gently, 'He is teasing you, Anne.'

'If it were not for the cardinal, you would be married to Harry Percy.'

'At least,' she snaps, 'I would occupy the estate of wife, which is an honourable estate, but now –'

'Oh, but cousin,' Mary Shelton says, 'Harry Percy has gone mad. Everybody knows it. He is spending all his money.'

Mary Boleyn laughs. 'So he is, and my sister supposes it is his disappointment over her that is to blame.'

'My lady,' he turns to Anne, 'you would not like to be in Harry Percy's country. For you know he would do as those northern lords do, and keep you in a freezing turret up a winding stair, and only let you come down for your dinner. And just as you are seated, and they are bringing in a pudding made of oatmeal mixed with the blood of cattle they have got in a raid, my lord comes thundering in, swinging a sack – oh, sweetheart, you say, a present for me? and he says, aye, madam, if it please you, and opens the sack and into your lap rolls the severed head of a Scot.'

'Oh, that is horrible,' Mary Shelton whispers. 'Is that what they do?' Anne puts her hand to her mouth, laughing.

'And you know,' he says, 'that for your dinner you would prefer a lightly poached breast of chicken, sliced into a cream sauce with tarragon. And also a fine aged cheese imported by the ambassador of Spain, which he intended no doubt for the queen, but which somehow found its way to my house.'

'How could I be better served?' Anne asks. 'A band of men on the highway, waylaying Katherine's cheese.'

'Well, having staged such a coup, I must go ...' he gestures to the lute-player in the corner, 'and leave you with your goggle-eyed lover.'

Anne darts a look at the boy Mark. 'He does goggle. True.'

'Shall I send him off? The place is full of musicians.'

'Leave him,' Mary says. 'He's a sweet boy.'

Mary Boleyn stands up. 'I'll just ...'

'Now Lady Carey is going to have one of her conferences with Master Cromwell,' Mary Shelton says, in a tone of giving agreeable information.

Jane Rochford: 'She is going to offer him her virtue again.'

345

'Lady Carey, what can you not say before us all?' But Anne nods. He may go. Mary may go. Presumably Mary is to carry messages that she, Anne, is too delicate to convey direct.

Outside: 'Sometimes I need to breathe.' He waits. 'Jane and our brother George, you know they hate each other? He won't go to bed with her. If he is not with some other woman he sits up at night with Anne in her rooms. They play cards. They play Pope Julius till the dawn comes. Did you know the king pays her gambling debts? She needs more income, and a house of her own, a retreat, not too far from London, somewhere on the river –'

'Whose house has she in mind?'

'I don't think she means to turns anyone out.'

'Houses tend to belong to somebody.' Then a thought strikes him. He smiles.

She says, 'I told you to stay away from her, once. But now we cannot do without you. Even my father and my uncle say so. Nothing is done, nothing, without the king's favour, without his constant company, and nowadays when you are not with Henry he wants to know where you are.' She steps back, appraises him for a moment as if he were a stranger. 'My sister, too.'

'I want a job, Lady Carey. It isn't enough to be a councillor. I need an official place in the household.'

'I'll tell her.'

'I want a post in the Jewel House. Or the Exchequer.'

She nods. 'She made Tom Wyatt a poet. She made Harry Percy a madman. I'm sure she has some ideas about what to make you.'

A few days before Parliament met, Thomas Wyatt had come to apologise for getting him out of bed before dawn on New Year's Day. 'You have every right to be angry with me, but I've come to ask you not to be. You know how it is at New Year. Toasts are drunk, and the bowl goes round, and you must drain the bowl.'

He watches Wyatt as he walks about the room, too curious and restless and half-shy to sit down and make his amends face-to-face. He turns the painted globe of the world, and rests his forefinger on England. He stops to look at pictures, at a little altarpiece, and he turns, questioning; it was my wife's, he says, I keep it for her sake. Master Wyatt wears a jacket of a stiffened cream brocade trimmed with sables, which he probably cannot afford; he wears a doublet of tawny silk. He has tender blue eyes and a mane of golden hair, thinning now. Sometimes he puts his fingertips to his head, tentative, as if he still has his New Year headache; really, he is checking his hairline, to see if it has receded in the last five minutes. He stops and looks at himself in the mirror; he does this very often. Dear God, he says. Rolling about the streets with that crowd. I'm too old for such behaviour. But too young to lose my hair. Do you think women care about it? Much? Do you think if I grew a beard it would distract … No, probably not. But perhaps I will anyway. The king's beard looks well, does it not?

He says, 'Didn't your father give you any advice?'

'Oh yes. Drink off a bowl of milk before you go out. Stewed quinces in honey – do you think that works?'

He is trying not to laugh. He wants to take it seriously, his new post as Wyatt's father. He says, 'I mean, did he never advise you to stay away from women in whom the king is interested?'

'I did stay away. You remember I went to Italy? After that I was in Calais for a year. How much staying away can a man do?'

A question from his own life; he recognises it. Wyatt sits down on a small stool. He props his elbows on his knees. He holds his head, fingertips on his temples. He is listening to his own heartbeat; he is thinking; perhaps he is composing a verse? He looks up. 'My father says that now Wolsey is dead you're the cleverest man in England. So can you understand this, if I say it just once? If Anne is not a virgin, that's none of my doing.'

He pours him a glass of wine. 'Strong,' Wyatt says, after he has downed it. He looks into the depth of the glass, at his own fingers holding it. 'I must say more, I think.'

'If you must, say it here, and just once.'

'Is anyone hiding behind the arras? Somebody told me there are servants at Chelsea who report to you. No one's servants are safe, these days, there are spies everywhere.'

'Tell me in what day there were not spies,' he says. 'There was a child in More's house, Dick Purser, More took him in out of guilt after he was orphaned – I cannot say More killed the father outright, but he had him in the pillory and in the Tower, and it broke his health. Dick told the other boys he did not believe God was in the Communion host, so More had him whipped before the whole household. Now I have brought him here. What else could I do? I will take in any others he ill-treats.'

Smiling, Wyatt passes his hand over the Queen of Sheba: that is to say, over Anselma. The king has given him Wolsey's fine tapestry. Early in the year, when he went in to speak to him at Greenwich, the king had seen him raise his eyes to her in greeting, and had said, with a sideways smile, do you know this woman? I used to, he said, explaining himself, excusing himself; the king said, no matter, we all have our follies in youth, and you can't marry everyone, can you … He had said in a low voice, I have in mind that this belonged to the Cardinal of York, and then, more briskly, when you go home make a place for her; I think she should come to live with you.

He gives himself a glass of wine, and another to Wyatt; says, 'Gardiner has people outside the gate, watching who comes and goes. This is a city house, it is not a fortress – but if anybody's here who shouldn't be, my household does enjoy kicking them out. We quite like fighting. I'd prefer to put my past behind me, but I'm not allowed to. Uncle Norfolk keeps reminding me I was a common soldier, and not even in his army.'

'You call him that?' Wyatt laughs. 'Uncle Norfolk?'

'Between ourselves. But I don't need to remind you of what the Howards think is due to them. And you've grown up

Thomas Boleyn's neighbour, so you know not to cross him, whatever you feel about his daughter. I hope you don't feel anything – do you?'

'For two years,' Wyatt says, 'I was sick to my soul to think of any other man touching her. But what could I offer? I am a married man, and not the duke or prince she was fishing for, either. She liked me, I think, or she liked to have me in thrall to her, it amused her. We would be alone, she would let me kiss her, and I always thought … but that is Anne's tactic, you see, she says yes, yes, yes, then she says no.'

'And of course, you are such a gentleman.'

'What, I should have raped her? If she says stop she means it – Henry knows that. But then another day would come and again she would let me kiss her. Yes, yes, yes, no. The worst of it is her hinting, her boasting almost, that she says no to me but yes to others –'

'Who are?'

'Oh, names, names would spoil her pastime. It must be so arranged that every man you see, at court or down in Kent, you think, is he the one? Is it him, or him? So you are continually asking yourself why you've fallen short, why you can never please her, why you never get the chance.'

'I should think you write the best poems. You can comfort yourself there. His Majesty's verses can be a little repetitive, not to say self-centred.'

'That song of his, "Pastime With Good Company." When I hear it there is something inside me, like a little dog, that wants to howl.'

'True, the king is past forty. It is melancholy to hear him sing of the days when he was young and stupid.' He watches Wyatt. The young man looks dazed, as if he has a persistent pain between his eyes. He is claiming that Anne no longer torments him, but that's not how it looks. He says, brutal as a butcher, 'So how many lovers do you think she has had?'

Wyatt looks down at his feet. He looks at the ceiling. He says, 'A dozen? Or none? Or a hundred? Brandon tried to tell Henry she was soiled goods. But he sent Brandon away from court. Imagine if I tried. I doubt I'd get out of the room alive. Brandon forced himself to speak, because he thinks, come the day she gives in to Henry, what then? Will he not know?'

'Give her credit. She must have thought of that. Besides, the king is no judge of maidenheads. He admits as much. With Katherine, it took him twenty years to puzzle out his brother had been there before him.'

Wyatt laughs. 'When the day comes, or the night, Anne can hardly say that to him.'

'Listen. This is my view of the case. Anne does not concern herself with her wedding night because there is no cause for concern.' He wants to say, because Anne is not a carnal being, she is a calculating being, with a cold slick brain at work behind her hungry black eyes. 'I believe any woman who can say no to the King of England and keep on saying it, has the wit to say no to any number of men, including you, including Harry Percy, including anyone else she may choose to torment for her own sport while she is arranging her career in the way it suits her. So I think, yes, you've been made into a fool, but not quite in the way you thought.'

'That is meant as consolation?'

'It should console you. If you'd really been her lover I would fear for you. Henry believes in her virginity. What else can he believe? But he will prove jealous, once they're married.'

'As they will be? Married?'

'I am working hard with Parliament, believe me, and I think I can break the bishops. And after that, God knows ... Thomas More says that in the reign of King John when England was placed under an interdict by the Pope, the cattle didn't breed, the corn ceased to ripen, the grass stopped growing and birds fell out of the air. But if that starts to happens,' he smiles, 'I'm sure we can reverse our policy.'

'Anne has asked me: Cromwell, what does he really believe?'

'So you have conversations? And about me? Not just yes, yes, yes, no? I'm flattered.'

Wyatt looks unhappy. 'You couldn't be wrong? About Anne?'

'It's possible. For the moment I take her at her own valuation. It suits me. It suits us both.'

As Wyatt is leaving: 'You must come back soon. My girls have heard how handsome you are. You can keep your hat on, if you think they might be disillusioned.'

Wyatt is the king's regular tennis partner. Therefore he knows about humbled pride. He fetches up a smile.

'Your father told us all about the lion. The boys have made a play out of it. Perhaps you would like to come one day and take your own role?'

'Oh, the lion. Nowadays, I think back on it, and it doesn't seem to me like a thing I would do. Stand still, in the open, and draw it on.' He pauses. 'More like something you would do, Master Cromwell.'

Thomas More comes to Austin Friars. He refuses food, he refuses drink, though he looks in need of both.

The cardinal would not have taken no for an answer. He would have made him sit down and eat syllabub. Or, if it were the season, given him a large plate of strawberries and a very small spoon.

More says, 'In these last ten years the Turks have taken Belgrade. They have lit their campfires in the great library at Buda. It is only two years since they were at the gates of Vienna. Why would you want to make another breach in the walls of Christendom?'

'The King of England is not an infidel. Nor am I.'

'Are you not? I hardly know whether you pray to the god of Luther and the Germans, or some heathen god you met with on your travels, or some English deity of your own invention.

Perhaps your faith is for purchase. You would serve the Sultan if the price was right.'

Erasmus says, did nature ever create anything kinder, sweeter or more harmonious than the character of Thomas More?

He is silent. He sits at his desk – More has caught him at work – with his chin propped on his fists. It is a pose that shows him, probably, to some combative advantage.

The Lord Chancellor looks as if he might rend his garments: which could only improve them. One could pity him, but he decides not to. 'Master Cromwell, you think because you are a councillor you can negotiate with heretics, behind the king's back. You are wrong. I know about your letters that come and go to Stephen Vaughan, I know he has met with Tyndale.'

'Are you threatening me? I'm just interested.'

'Yes,' More says sadly. 'Yes, that is precisely what I am doing.'

He sees that the balance of power has shifted between them: not as officers of state, but as men.

When More leaves, Richard says to him, 'He ought not. Threaten you, I mean. Today, because of his office, he walks away, but tomorrow, who knows?'

He thinks, I was a child, nine or so, I ran off into London and saw an old woman suffer for her faith. The memory floods into his body and he walks away as if he sails on its tide, saying over his shoulder, 'Richard, see if the Lord Chancellor has his proper escort. If not, give him one, and try to put him on a boat back to Chelsea. We cannot have him wandering about London, haranguing anyone at whose gate he may arrive.'

He says the last bit in French, he does not know why. He thinks of Anne, her hand outstretched, drawing him towards her: *Maître Cremuel, à moi.*

He cannot remember the year but he remembers the late April weather, fat raindrops dappling the pale new leaves. He cannot remember the reason for Walter's temper, but he can remember the fear he felt in the pith of his being, and his heart banging against his ribs. In those days if he couldn't hide out with his uncle John at Lambeth he would get himself into the town and see who he could pick up with – see if he could earn a penny by running errands up and down to the quays, by carrying baskets or loading barrows. If you whistled for him, he came; lucky, he knows now, not to have got in with low-lifes who would lead him to be branded or whipped, or to be one of the small corpses fished out of the river. At that age you have no judgement. If somebody said, good sport over there, he followed the pointing finger. He had nothing against the old woman, but he had never seen a burning.

What's her crime? he said, and they said, she is a Loller. That's one who says the God on the altar is a piece of bread. What, he said, bread like the baker bakes? Let this child forward, they said. Let him be instructed, it will do him good to see up close, so he always goes to Mass after this and obeys his priest. They pushed him to the front of the crowd. Come here, sweetheart, stand with me, a woman said. She had a broad smile and wore a clean white cap. You get a pardon for your sins just for watching it, she said. Any that bring faggots to the burning, they get forty days' release from Purgatory.

When the Loller was led out between the officers the people jeered and shouted. He saw that she was a grandmother, perhaps the oldest person he had ever seen. The officers were nearly carrying her. She had no cap or veil. Her hair seemed to be torn out of her head in patches. People behind him said, no doubt she did that herself, in desperation at her sin. Behind the Loller came two monks, parading like fat grey rats, crosses in their pink paws. The woman in the clean cap squeezed his shoulder: like a mother might do, if you had one. Look at her, she said, eighty years old, and steeped in wickedness. A man said, not much fat on her bones, it won't take long unless the wind changes.

But what's her sin? he said.

I told you. She says the saints are but wooden posts.

353

Like that post they're chaining her to?

Aye, just like that.

The post will burn too.

They can get another next time, the woman said. She took her hand from his shoulder. She balled her two hands into fists and punched them in the air, and from the depth of her belly she let loose a scream, a halloo, in a shrill voice like a demon. The press of people took up the cry. They seethed and pushed forward for a view, they catcalled and whistled and stamped their feet. At the thought of the horrible thing he would see he felt hot and cold. He twisted to look up into the face of the woman who was his mother in this crowd. You watch, she said. With the gentlest brush of her fingers she turned his face to the spectacle. Pay attention now. The officers took chains and bound the old person to the stake.

The stake was on top of a pile of stones, and some gentlemen came, and priests, bishops perhaps, he did not know. They called out to the Loller to put off her heresies. He was close enough to see her lips moving but he could not hear what she said. What if she changes her mind now, will they let her go? Not they, the woman chuckled. Look, she is calling on Satan to help her. The gentlemen withdrew. The officers banked up wood and bales of straw around the Loller. The woman tapped him on the shoulder; let's hope it's damp, eh? This is a good view, last time I was at the back. The rain had stopped, the sun broken through. When the executioner came with a torch, it was pale in the sunshine, barely more than a slick movement, like the movement of eels in a bag. The monks were chanting and holding up a cross to the Loller, and it was only when they skipped backwards, at the first billow of smoke, that the crowd knew the fire was set.

They surged forward, roaring. Officers made a barrier with staves and shouted in great deep voices, back, back, back, and the crowd shrieked and fell back, and then came on again, roaring and chanting, as if it were a game. Eddies of smoke spoiled their view, and the crowd beat it aside, coughing. Smell her! they cried. Smell the old sow! He had held his breath, not to breathe her in. In the smoke the Loller was screaming. Now she calls on the saints! they said. The woman bent down and said in his ear, do you know that in the fire they bleed? Some people think they just shrivel up, but I've seen it before and I know.

By the time the smoke cleared and they could see again, the old woman was well ablaze. The crowd began cheering. They had said it would not take long but it did take long, or so it seemed to him, before the screaming stopped. Does nobody pray for her, he said, and the woman said, what's the point? Even after there was nothing left to scream, the fire was stoked. The officers trod around the margins, stamping out any wisps of straw that flew off, kicking back anything bigger.

When the crowd drifted home, chattering, you could tell the ones who'd been on the wrong side of the fire, because their faces were grey with wood-ash. He wanted to go home but again he thought of Walter, who had said that morning he was going to kill him by inches. He watched the officers strike with their iron bars at the human debris that was left. The chains retained the remnants of flesh, sucking and clinging. Approaching the men, he asked, how hot must the fire be, to burn bone? He expected them to have knowledge in the matter. But they didn't under-stand his question. People who are not smiths think all fires are the same. His father had taught him the colours of red: sunset red, cherry red, the bright yellow-red with no name unless its name is scarlet.

The Loller's skull was left on the ground, the long bones of her arms and legs. Her broken ribcage was not much bigger than a dog's. A man took an iron bar and thrust it through the hole where the woman's left eye had been. He scooped up the skull and positioned it on the stones, so it was looking at him. Then he hefted his bar and brought it down on the crown. Even before the blow landed he knew it was false, skewed. Shattered bone, like a star, flew away into the dirt, but the most part of the skull was intact. Jesus, the man said. Here, lad, do you want a go? One good swipe will stove her in.

Usually he said yes to any invitation. But now he backed away, his hands behind his back. God's blood, the man said, I wish I could afford to be choosy. Soon after that it came on to rain. The men wiped their hands, blew their noses and walked off the job. They threw down their iron bars amid what was left of the Loller. It was just splinters of bone now, and thick sludgy ash. He picked up one of the iron bars, in case he needed a weapon. He fingered its tapered end, which was cut like a chisel. He did not know how far he was from home, and whether Walter might come for him. He wondered how you kill a person by inches, whether by burning them or cutting them up. He should have asked the officers while they were here, for being servants of the city they would know.

The stink of the woman was still in the air. He wondered if she was in Hell now, or still about the streets, but he was not afraid of ghosts. They had put up a stand for the gentlemen, and though the canopy was taken down, it was high enough off the ground to crouch underneath for shelter. He prayed for the woman, thinking it could do no harm. He moved his lips as he prayed. Rainwater gathered above him and fell in great drops through the planking. He counted the time between drops and caught them in his cupped hand. He did this just for a pastime. Dusk fell. If it were an ordinary day he would have been hungry by now and gone looking for food.

In the twilight certain men came, and women too; he knew, because there were women, that they were not officers or people who would hurt him. They drew together, making a loose circle around the stake on its pile of stones. He ducked out from under the stand and approached them. You will be wondering what has happened here, he said. But they did not look up or speak to him.

They fell to their knees and he thought they were praying. I have prayed for her too, he said.

Have you? Good lad, one of the men said. He didn't even glance up. If he looks at me, he thought, he will see that I am not good, but a worthless boy who goes off with his dog and forgets to make the brine bath for the forge, so when Walter shouts where's the fucking slake-tub it's not there. With a sick lurch of his stomach he remembered what he'd not done and why he was to be killed. He almost cried out. As if he were in pain.

He saw now that the men and women were not praying. They were on their hands and knees. They were friends of the Loller, and they were scraping her up. One of the women knelt, her skirts spread, and held out an earthenware pot. His eyes were sharp even in the gloom, and out of the sludge and muck he picked a fragment of bone. Here's some, he said. The woman held out the bowl. Here's another.

One of the men stood apart, some way off. Why does he not help us? he said.

He is the watchman. He will whistle if the officers come.

Will they take us up?

Hurry, hurry, another man said.

When they had got a bowlful, the woman who was holding it said, 'Give me your hand.'

Trusting, he held it out to her. She dipped her fingers into the bowl. She placed on the back of his hand a smear of mud and grit, fat and ash. 'Joan Boughton,' she said.

Now, when he thinks back on this, he wonders at his own faulty memory. He has never forgotten the woman, whose last remnants he carried away as a greasy smudge on his own skin, but why is it that his life as a child doesn't seem to fit, one bit with the next? He can't remember how he got back home, and what Walter did instead of killing him by inches, or why he'd run off in the first place without making the brine. Perhaps, he thinks, I spilled the salt and I was too frightened to tell him. That

357

seems likely. One fear creates a dereliction, the offence brings on a greater fear, and there comes a point where the fear is too great and the human spirit just gives up and a child wanders off numb and directionless and ends up following a crowd and watching a killing.

He has never told anyone this story. He doesn't mind talking to Richard, to Rafe about his past – within reason – but he doesn't mean to give away pieces of himself. Chapuys comes to dinner very often and sits beside him, teasing out bits of his life story as he teases tender flesh from the bone.

Some tell me your father was Irish, Eustache says. He waits, poised.

It is the first I have heard of it, he says, but I grant you, he was a mystery even to himself. Chapuys sniffs; the Irish are a very violent people, he says. 'Tell me, is it true you fled from England at fifteen, having escaped from prison?'

'For sure,' he says. 'An angel struck off my chains.'

That will give him something to write home. 'I put the allegation to Cremuel, who answered me with a blasphemy, unfit for your Imperial ear.' Chapuys is never stuck for something to put in dispatches. If news is scant he sends the gossip. There is the gossip he picks up, from dubious sources, and the gossip he feeds him on purpose. As Chapuys doesn't speak English, he gets his news in French from Thomas More, in Italian from the merchant Antonio Bonvisi, and in God knows what – Latin? – from Stokesley, the Bishop of London, whose table he also honours. Chapuys is peddling the idea to his master the Emperor that the people of England are so disaffected by their king that, given encouragement by a few Spanish troops, they will rise in revolt. Chapuys is, of course, deeply misled. The English may favour Queen Katherine – broadly, it seems they do. They may mislike or fail to understand recent measures in the Parliament. But instinct tells him this; they will knit together against foreign interference. They like Katherine because they have forgotten she is Spanish, because she has been here for a long time. They are the same people who rioted against foreigners, on Evil May Day; the same people, narrow-hearted, stubborn, attached to their patch of ground. Only overwhelming force – a coalition, say, of Francis and the Emperor – will budge them. We cannot, of course, rule out the possibility that such a coalition may occur.

When dinner is over, he walks Chapuys back to his people, to his big solid boys, bodyguards, who lounge about, chatting in Flemish, often about him. Chapuys knows he has been in the Low Countries; does he think he doesn't understand the language? Or is this some elaborate double-bluff?

There were days, not too long past, days since Lizzie died, when he'd woken in the morning and had to decide, before he could speak to anybody, who he was and why. There were days when he'd woken from dreams of the dead and searching for them. When his waking self trembled, at the threshold of deliverance from his dreams.

But those days are not these days.

Sometimes, when Chapuys has finished digging up Walter's bones and making his own life unfamiliar to him, he feels almost impelled to speak in defence of his father, his childhood. But it is no use to justify yourself. It is no good to explain. It is weak to be anecdotal. It is wise to conceal the past even if there is nothing to conceal. A man's power is in the half-light, in the half-seen movements of his hand and the unguessed-at expression of his face. It is the absence of facts that frightens people: the gap you open, into which they pour their fears, fantasies, desires.

On 14 April 1532, the king appoints him Keeper of the Jewel House. From here, Henry Wyatt had said, you are able to take an overview of the king's income and outgoings.

The king shouts, as if to any courtier passing, 'Why should I not, tell me why should I not, employ the son of an honest blacksmith?'

359

He hides his smile, at this description of Walter; so much more flattering than any the Spanish ambassador has arrived at. The king says, 'What you are, I make you. I alone. Everything you are, everything you have, will come from me.'

The thought gives him a pleasure you can hardly grudge. Henry is so well disposed these days, so open-handed and amenable, that you must forgive him the occasional statement of his position, whether it is necessary or not. The cardinal used to say, the English will forgive a king anything, until he tries to tax them. He also used to say, it doesn't really matter what the title of the office is. Let any colleague on the council turn his back, he would turn again to find that I was doing his job.

He is in a Westminster office one day in April when Hugh Latimer walks in, just released from custody at Lambeth Palace. 'Well?' Hugh says. 'You might leave off your scribble, and give me your hand.'

He rises from his desk and embraces him, dusty black coat, sinew, bone. 'So you made Warham a pretty speech?'

'I made it extempore, in my fashion. It came fresh from my mouth as from the mouth of a babe. Perhaps the old fellow is losing his appetite for burnings now his own end is so near. He is shrivelling like a seedpod in the sun, when he moves you can hear his bones rattle. Anyway, I cannot account for it, but here you see me.'

'How did he keep you?'

'Bare walls my library. Fortunately, my brain is furnished with texts. He sent me off with a warning. Told me if I did not smell of the fire then I smelled of the frying pan. It has been said to me before. It must be ten years now, since I came up for heresy before the Scarlet Beast.' He laughs. 'But Wolsey, he gave me my preacher's licence back. And the kiss of peace. And my dinner. So? Are we any nearer a queen who loves the gospel?'

A shrug. 'We – they – are talking to the French. There is a treaty in the air. Francis has a gaggle of cardinals who might lend us their voices in Rome.'

Hugh snorts. 'Still waiting on Rome.'

'That is how it must be.'

'We will turn Henry. We will turn him to the gospel.'

'Perhaps. Not suddenly. A little and a little.'

'I am going to ask Bishop Stokesley to allow me to visit our brother Bainham. Will you come?'

Bainham is the barrister who was taken up by More last year and tortured. Just before Christmas he came before the Bishop of London. He abjured, and was free by February. He is a natural man; he wanted to live, how not? But once he was free his conscience would not let him sleep. One Sunday he walked into a crowded church and stood up before all the people, Tyndale's Bible in his hand, and spoke a profession of his faith. Now he is in the Tower waiting to know the date of his execution.

'So?' Latimer says. 'You will or you won't?'

'I should not give ammunition to the Lord Chancellor.'

I might sap Bainham's resolve, he thinks. Say to him, believe anything, brother, swear to it and cross your fingers behind your back. But then, it hardly matters what Bainham says now. Mercy will not operate for him, he must burn.

Hugh Latimer lopes away. The mercy of God operates for Hugh. The Lord walks with him, and steps with him into a wherry, to disembark under the shadow of the Tower; this being so, there is no need for Thomas Cromwell.

More says it does not matter if you lie to heretics, or trick them into a confession. They have no right to silence, even if they know speech will incriminate them; if they will not speak, then break their fingers, burn them with irons, hang them up by their wrists. It is legitimate, and indeed More goes further; it is blessed.

There is a group from the House of Commons who dine with priests at the Queen's Head tavern. The word comes from them, and spreads among the people of London, that anyone who supports the king's divorce will be damned. So devoted is God to the cause of these gentlemen, they say, that an angel attends the sittings of Parliament with a scroll, noting down who votes and how, and smudging a sooty mark against the names of those who fear Henry more than the Almighty.

At Greenwich, a friar called William Peto, the head in England of his branch of the Franciscan order, preaches a sermon before the king, in which he takes as his text and example the unfortunate Ahab, seventh king of Israel, who lived in a palace of ivory. Under the influence of the wicked Jezebel he built a pagan temple and gave the priests of Baal places in his retinue. The prophet Elijah told Ahab that the dogs would lick his blood, and so it came to pass, as you would imagine, since only the successful prophets are remembered. The dogs of Samaria licked Ahab's blood. All his male heirs perished. They lay unburied in the streets. Jezebel was thrown out of a window of her palace. Wild dogs tore her body into shreds.

Anne says, 'I am Jezebel. You, Thomas Cromwell, are the priests of Baal.' Her eyes are alight. 'As I am a woman, I am the means by which sin enters this world. I am the devil's gateway, the cursed ingress. I am the means by which Satan attacks the man, whom he was not bold enough to attack, except through me. Well, that is their view of the situation. My view is that there are too many priests with scant learning and smaller occupation. And I wish the Pope and the Emperor and all Spaniards were in the sea and drowned. And if anyone is to be thrown out of a palace window … *alors*, Thomas, I know who I would like to throw. Except the child Mary, the wild dogs would not find a scrap of flesh to gnaw, and Katherine, she is so fat she would bounce.'

When Thomas Avery comes home, he lowers to the flagstones the travelling chest in which he carries everything he owns, and rises with open arms to hug his master like a child. News of his government promotion has reached Antwerp. It seems Stephen Vaughan turned brick-red with pleasure and drank off a whole cup of wine without cutting it with water.

Come in, he says, there are fifty people here to see me but they can wait, come and tell me how is everyone across the sea. Thomas Avery starts talking at once. But inside the doorway of his room, he stops. He is looking at the tapestry given by the king. His eyes search it, then turn to his master's face, and then back to the tapestry. 'Who is that lady?'

'You can't guess?' He laughs. 'It is Sheba visiting Solomon. The king gave it to me. It was my lord cardinal's. He saw I liked it. And he likes to give presents.'

'It must be worth a fair sum.' Avery looks at it with respect, like the keen young accountant he is.

'Look,' he says to him, 'I have another present, what do you think of this? It is perhaps the only good thing ever to come out of a monastery. Brother Luca Pacioli. It took him thirty years to write.'

The book is bound in deepest green with a tooled border of gold, and its pages are edged in gilt, so that it blazes in the light. Its clasps are studded with blackish garnets, smooth, translucent. 'I hardly dare open it,' the boy says.

'Please. You will like it.'

It is *Summa de Arithmetica*. He unclasps it to find a woodcut of the author with a book before him, and a pair of compasses. 'This is a new printing?'

'Not quite, but my friends in Venice have just now remembered me. I was a child, of course, when Luca wrote it, and you were not even thought of.' His fingertips barely touch the page. 'Look, here he treats of geometry, do you see the figures? Here is where he says you don't go to bed until the books balance.'

'Master Vaughan quotes that maxim. It has caused me to sit up till dawn.'

'And I.' Many nights in many cities. 'Luca, you know, he was a poor man. He came out of Sansepulcro. He was a friend of artists and he became a perfect mathematician in Urbino, which is a little town up in the mountains, where Count Federigo the

363

great *condottiere* had his library of over a thousand books. He was magister at the university in Perugia, later in Milan. I wonder why such a man would remain a monk, but of course there have been practitioners of algebra and geometry who have been thrown into dungeons as magicians, so perhaps he thought the church would protect him ... I heard him lecture in Venice, it will be more than twenty years ago now, I was your age, I suppose. He spoke about proportion. Proportion in building, in music, in paintings, in justice, in the commonwealth, the state; about how rights should be balanced, the power of a prince and his subjects, how the wealthy citizen should keep his books straight and say his prayers and serve the poor. He spoke about how a printed page should look. How a law should read. Or a face, what makes it beautiful.'

'Will he tell me in this book?' Thomas Avery glances up again at the Queen of Sheba. 'I suppose they knew, who made the tapestry.'

'How is Jenneke?'

The boy turns the leaves with reverent fingers. 'It is a beautiful book. Your friends in Venice must admire you very much.'

So Jenneke is no more, he thinks. She is dead or she is in love with someone else. 'Sometimes,' he says, 'my friends in Italy send me new poems, but I think all the poems are in here ... Not that a page of figures is a verse, but anything that is precise is beautiful, anything that balances in all its parts, anything that is proportionate ... do you think so?'

He wonders at the power Sheba has to draw the boy's eyes. It is impossible he should have seen Anselma, ever met her, heard of her. I told Henry about her, he thinks. One of those afternoons when I told my king a little, and he told me a lot: how he shakes with desire when he thinks of Anne, how he has tried other women, tried them as an expedient to take the edge off lust, so that he can think and talk and act as a reasoning man, but how he has failed with them ... A strange admission, but he thinks it justifies him, he thinks it verifies the rightness of his pursuit, for I chase but one hind, he says, one strange deer timid and wild, and she leads me off the paths that other men have trod, and by myself into the depths of the wood.

'Now,' he says, 'we will put this book on your desk. So that you can be consoled by it when nothing seems to add up at all.'

He has great hopes of Thomas Avery. It's easy to employ some child who will total the columns and push them under your nose, get them initialled and then lock them in a chest. But what's the point of that? The page of an accounts book is there for your use, like a love poem. It's not there for you to nod and then dismiss it; it's there to open your heart to possibility. It's like the scriptures: it's there for you to think about, and initiate action. Love your neighbour. Study the market. Increase the spread of benevolence. Bring in better figures next year.

The date of James Bainham's execution is fixed for 30 April. He cannot go to the king, not with any hope of a pardon. Long ago Henry was given the title of Defender of the Faith; he is keen to show he deserves it still.

At Smithfield in the stand put up for the dignitaries he meets the Venetian ambassador, Carlo Capello. They exchange a bow. 'In what capacity are you here, Cromwell? As friend of this heretic, or by virtue of your position? In fact, what is your position? The devil alone knows.'

'And I am sure he will tell Your Excellency, when you next have a private talk.'

Wrapped in his sheet of flames, the dying man calls out, 'The Lord forgive Sir Thomas More.'

On 15 May, the bishops sign a document of submission to the king. They will not make new church legislation without the king's licence, and will submit all existing laws to a review by a commission which will include laymen – members of Parliament and the king's appointees. They will not meet in Convocation without the king's permission.

Next day, he stands in a gallery at Whitehall, which looks down on an inner court, a garden, where the king waits, and the Duke of Norfolk busies to and fro. Anne is in the gallery beside him. She is wearing a dark red gown of figured damask, so heavy that her tiny white shoulders seem to droop inside it. Sometimes – in a kind of fellowship of the imagination – he imagines resting his hand upon her shoulder and following with his thumb the scooped hollow between her collarbone and her throat; imagines with his forefinger tracking the line of her breast as it swells above her bodice, as a child follows a line of print.

She turns her head and half-smiles. 'Here he comes. He is not wearing the Lord Chancellor's chain. What can he have done with it?'

Thomas More looks round-shouldered and despondent. Norfolk looks tense. 'My uncle has been trying to arrange this for months,' Anne says. 'But the king will not be brought to it. He doesn't want to lose More. He wants to please everybody. You know how it is.'

'He knew Thomas More when he was young.'

'When I was young I knew sin.'

They turn, and smile at each other. 'Look now,' Anne says. 'Do you suppose that is the Seal of England, that he has got in that leather bag?'

When Wolsey gave up the Great Seal, he dragged out the process for two days. But now the king, in the private paradise below, is waiting with open hand.

'So who now?' Anne says. 'Last night he said, my Lord Chancellors are nothing but grief to me. Perhaps I shall do without one.'

'The lawyers will not like that. Somebody must rule the courts.'

'Then who do you say?'

'Put it in his mind to appoint Mr Speaker. Audley will do an honest job. Let the king try him in the role *pro tem*, if he will, and then if he does not like him he need not confirm it. But I think he will like him. Audley is a good lawyer and he is his own man, but he understands how to be useful. And he understands me, I think.'

'To think that someone does! Shall we go down?'

'You cannot resist it?'

'No more can you.'

They go down the inner staircase. Anne places her fingertips lightly on his arm. In the garden below, nightingales are hung in cages. Struck mute, they huddle against the sunlight. A fountain pit-patters into a basin. A scent of thyme rises from the herb-beds. From inside the palace, an unseen someone laughs. The sound is cut off as if a door had closed. He stoops and picks a sprig of the herb, bruises its scent into his palm. It takes him to another place, far from here. More makes his bow to Anne. She barely nods. She curtseys deeply to Henry, and arranges herself by his side, her eyes on the ground. Henry clutches her wrist; he wants to tell her something, or just be alone with her.

'Sir Thomas?' He offers his hand. More turns away. Then he thinks better of it; he turns back and takes it. His fingertips are ashy cold.

'What will you do now?'

'Write. Pray.'

'My recommendation would be write only a little, and pray a lot.'

'Now, is that a threat?' More is smiling.

'It may be. My turn, don't you think?'

When the king saw Anne, his face had lit up. His heart is ardent; in his councillor's hand, it burns to the touch.

He catches Gardiner at Westminster, in one of those smoky back courts where the sunlight never reaches. 'My lord bishop?'

Gardiner draws together his beetle brows.

'Lady Anne has asked me to think about a country house for her.'

'What is that to me?'

'Let me unfold to you,' he says, 'the way my thoughts proceed. It should be somewhere near the river, convenient for Hampton Court, and for her barge to Whitehall and Greenwich. Somewhere in good repair, as she has no patience, she will not wait. Somewhere with pretty gardens, well established … Then I think, what about Stephen's manor at Hanworth, that the king leased him when he became Master Secretary?'

Even in the dim light he can see the thoughts chasing each other through Stephen's brain. Oh my moat and my little bridges, my rose gardens and strawberry beds, my herb garden, my beehives, my ponds and orchard, oh my Italianate terracotta medallions, my intarsia, my gilding, my galleries, my seashell fountain, my deer park.

'It would be graceful in you to offer her the lease, before it becomes a royal command. A good deed to set against the bishops' stubbornness? Oh, come on, Stephen. You have other houses. It isn't as if you'll be sleeping under a haystack.'

'If I were,' the bishop says, 'I should expect one of your boys along with a ratting dog, to dig me out of my dreams.'

Gardiner's rodent pulses jump; his wet black eyes gleam. He is squeaking inside with indignation and stifled fury. But part of him may be relieved, when he thinks about it, that the bill has come in so early, and that he can meet its terms.

Gardiner is still Master Secretary, but he, Cromwell, now sees the king almost every day. If Henry wants advice, he can give it, or if the subject is outside his remit, he will find someone else who can. If the king has a complaint, he will say, leave it with me: if, by your royal favour, I may proceed? If the king is in a good humour he is ready to laugh, and if the king is miserable he is gentle and careful with him. The king has begun a course of dissimulation, which the Spanish ambassador, sharp-eyed as ever, has not failed to notice. 'He sees you in private, not in his presence chamber,' he says. 'He prefers if his nobles do not know how often he consults with you. If you were a smaller man, you could be brought in and out in a laundry basket. As it is, I think those so-spiteful privy chamber gentlemen cannot fail to tell their friends, who will mutter at your success, and circulate slanders against you, and plot to bring you down.' The ambassador smiles and says, 'If I may proffer an image which will appeal to you – do I hit the nail on the head?'

In a letter from Chapuys to the Emperor, one which happens to go by way of Mr Wriothesley, he learns of his own character. Call-Me reads it out to him: 'He says your antecedents are obscure, your youth reckless and wild, that you are a heretic of long standing, a disgrace to the office of councillor; but personally, he finds you a man of good cheer, liberal, open-handed, gracious …'

'I knew he liked me. I should ask him for a job.'

'He says that the way you got into the king's confidence, you promised you would make him the richest king England has ever had.'

He smiles.

Late in May, two fish of prodigal size are caught in the Thames, or rather they are washed up, dying, on the muddy shore. 'Am I expected to do something about it?' he says, when Johane brings the news in.

'No,' she says. 'At least, I don't think so. It's a portent, isn't it? It's an omen, that's all.'

In late July, he has a letter from Cranmer in Nuremberg. Before this he has written from the Low Countries, asking for advice on his commercial negotiations with the Emperor, matters in which he feels out of his depth; from towns along the Rhine, he has written hopefully that the Emperor must come to an accommodation with the Lutheran princes, as he needs their help against the Turks on the frontier. He writes of how he struggles to become an adept in England's usual diplomatic game: proffering the King of England's friendship, dangling promises of English gold, while actually failing to provide any.

But this letter is different. It is dictated, written in a clerk's hand. It talks of the workings of the holy spirit in the heart. Rafe reads it out to him, and points out, down at the bottom and running up the left margin, a few words in Cranmer's own script: 'Something has occurred. Not to be trusted to a letter. It may make a stir. Some would say I have been rash. I shall need your advice. Keep this secret.'

'Well,' Rafe says, 'let us run up and down Cheap: "Thomas Cranmer has a secret, we don't know what it is!"'

A week later Hans turns up at Austin Friars. He has rented a house in Maiden Lane and is staying at the Steelyard while it is fixed up for him. 'Let me see your new picture, Thomas,' he says, walking in. He stands before it. Folds his arms. Steps back a pace. 'You know these people? The likeness is good?'

Two Italian bankers, confederates, looking towards the viewer but longing to exchange glances; one in silks, one in fur; a vase of carnations, an astrolabe, a goldfinch, a glass through which the sand has half run; through an arched window, a ship rigged with silk, its sails translucent, drifting in a mirror sea. Hans turns away, pleased. 'How does he get that expression in the eye, so hard yet so sly?'

'How is Elsbeth?'

'Fat. Sad.'

'Is it surprising? You go home, give her a child, come away again.'

'I don't reckon to be a good husband. I just send the money home.'

'How long will you stay with us?'

Hans grunts, downs his cup of wine and talks about what he's left behind: talk about Basle, about the Swiss cantons and cities.

Riots and pitched battles. Images, not images. Statues, not statues. It is the body of God, it is not the body of God, it is sort-of the body of God. It is his blood, it is not his blood. Priests may marry, they may not. There are seven sacraments, there are three. The crucifix we creep to on our knees and reverence with our lips, or the crucifix we chop it up and burn it in the public square. 'I am no Pope-lover but I get tired of it. Erasmus has run off to Freiburg to the papists and now I have run off to you and Junker Heinrich. That's what Luther calls your king. "His Disgrace, the King of England."' He wipes his mouth. 'All I ask is to do some good work and be paid for it. And I prefer not to have my efforts wiped out by some sectary with a pail of whitewash.'

'You came here looking for peace and ease?' He shakes his head. 'Too late.'

'I was just going over London Bridge and I saw someone had attacked the Madonna's statue. Knocked off the baby's head.'

'That was done a while back. It would be that devil Cranmer. You know what he is when he's taken a drink.'

Hans grins. 'You miss him. Who would have thought you would be friends?'

'Old Warham is not well. If he dies this summer, Lady Anne will ask for Canterbury for my friend.'

Hans is surprised. 'Not Gardiner?'

'He's spoiled his chance with the king.'

'He is his own worst enemy.'

'I wouldn't say that.'

Hans laughs. 'It would be a great promotion for Dr Cranmer. He will not want it. Not he. So much pomp. He likes his books.'

'He will take it. It will be his duty. The best of us are forced against the grain.'

'What, you?'

'It is against the grain to have your old patron come and threaten me in my own house, and take it quietly. As I do. Have you been to Chelsea?'

'Yes. They are a sad household.'

'It was given out that he was resigning on grounds of ill health. So as not to embarrass anybody.'

'He says he has a pain here,' Hans rubs his chest, 'and it comes on him when he starts to write. But the others look well enough. The family on the wall.'

'You need not go to Chelsea for commissions now. The king has me at work at the Tower, we are restoring the fortifications. He has builders and painters and gilders in, we are stripping out the old royal apartments and making something finer, and I am going to build a new lodging for the queen. In this country, you see, the kings and queens lie at the Tower the night before they are crowned. When Anne's day comes there will be plenty of work for you. There will be pageants to design, banquets, and the city will be ordering gold and silver plate to present to the king. Talk to the Hanse merchants, they will want to make a show. Get them planning. Secure yourself the work before half the craftsmen in Europe are here.'

'Is she to have new jewels?'

'She is to have Katherine's. He has not lost all sense.'

'I would like to paint her. Anna Bolena.'

'I don't know. She may not want to be studied.'

'They say she is not beautiful.'

'No, perhaps she is not. You would not choose her as a model for a Primavera. Or a statue of the Virgin. Or a figure of Peace.'

'What then, Eve? Medusa?' Hans laughs. 'Don't answer.'

'She has great presence, *esprit* … You may not be able to put it in a painting.'

'I see you think I am limited.'

'Some subjects resist you, I feel sure.'

Richard comes in. 'Francis Bryan is here.'

'Lady Anne's cousin.' He stands up.

'You must go to Whitehall. Lady Anne is breaking up the furniture and smashing the mirrors.'

He swears under his breath. 'Take Master Holbein in to dinner.'

Francis Bryan is laughing so hard that his horse twitches under him, uneasy, and skitters sideways, to the danger of passers-by. By the time they get to Whitehall he has pieced this story together: Anne has just heard that Harry Percy's wife, Mary Talbot, is preparing to petition Parliament for a divorce. For two years, she says, her husband has not shared her bed, and when finally she asked him why, he said he could not carry on a pretence any longer; they were not really married, and never had been, since he was married to Anne Boleyn.

'My lady is enraged,' Bryan says. His eyepatch, sewn with jewels, winks as he giggles. 'She says Harry Percy will spoil everything for her. She cannot decide between striking him dead with one blow of a sword or teasing him apart over forty days of public torture, like they do in Italy.'

'Those stories are much exaggerated.'

He has never witnessed, or quite believed in, Lady Anne's uncontrolled outbursts of temper. When he is admitted she is pacing, her hands clasped, and she looks small and tense, as if someone has knitted her and drawn the stitches too tight. Three ladies – Jane Rochford, Mary Shelton, Mary Boleyn – are following her with their eyes. A small carpet, which perhaps ought to be on the wall, is crumpled on the floor. Jane Rochford says, 'We have swept up the broken glass.' Sir Thomas Boleyn, Monseigneur, sits at a table, a heap of papers before him. George sits by him on a stool. George has his head in his hands. His sleeves are only medium-puffed. The Duke of Norfolk is staring into the hearth, where a fire is laid but not lit, perhaps attempting through the power of his gaze to make the kindling spark.

'Shut the door, Francis,' George says, 'and don't let anybody else in.'

He is the only person in the room who is not a Howard.

'I suggest we pack Anne's bags and send her down to Kent,' Jane Rochford says. 'The king's anger, once roused –'

George: 'Say no more, or I may strike you.'

'It is my honest advice.' Jane Rochford, God protect her, is one of those women who doesn't know when to stop. 'Master Cromwell, the king has indicated there must be an inquiry. It must come before the council. It cannot be fudged this time. Harry Percy will give testimony unimpeded. The king cannot do all he has done, and all he means to do, for a woman who is concealing a secret marriage.'

'I wish I could divorce you,' George says. 'I wish you had a pre-contract, but Jesus, no chance of that, the fields were black with men running in the other direction.'

Monseigneur holds up a hand. 'Please.'

Mary Boleyn says, 'What is the use of calling in Master Cromwell, and not telling him what has already occurred? The king has already spoken to my lady sister.'

'I deny everything,' Anne says. It is as if the king is standing before her.

'Good,' he says. 'Good.'

'That the earl spoke to me of love, I allow. He wrote me verse, and I being then a young girl, and thinking no harm of it –'

He almost laughs. 'Verse? Harry Percy? Do you still have it?'

'No. Of course not. Nothing written.'

'That makes it easier,' he says gently. 'And of course there was no promise, or contract, or even talk of them.'

'And,' Mary says, 'no consummation of any kind. There could not be. My sister is a notorious virgin.'

'And how was the king, was he –'

'He walked out of the room,' Mary says, 'and left her standing.'

Monseigneur looks up. He clears his throat. 'In this exigency, there are a variety, and number of approaches, it seems to me, that one might –'

Norfolk explodes. He pounds up and down on the floor, like Satan in a Corpus Christi play. 'Oh, by the thrice-beshitten shroud of Lazarus! While you are selecting an approach, my lord, while you are taking a view, your lady daughter is slandered up and down the country, the king's mind is poisoned, and this family's fortune is unmaking before your eyes.'

'Harry Percy,' George says; he holds up his hands. 'Listen, will you let me speak? As I understand it, Harry Percy was persuaded once to forget his claims, so if he was fixed once –'

'Yes,' Anne says, 'but the cardinal fixed him, and most unfortunately the cardinal is dead.'

There is a silence: a silence sweet as music. He looks, smiling, at Anne, at Monseigneur, at Norfolk. If life is a chain of gold, sometimes God hangs a charm on it. To prolong the moment, he crosses the room and picks up the fallen hanging. Narrow loom. Indigo ground. Asymmetrical knot. Isfahan? Small animals march stiffly across it, weaving through knots of flowers. 'Look,' he says. 'Do you know what these are? Peacocks.'

Mary Shelton comes to peer over his shoulder. 'What are those snake things with legs?'

'Scorpions.'

'Mother Mary, do they not bite?'

'Sting.' He says, 'Lady Anne, if the Pope cannot stop you becoming queen, and I do not think he can, Harry Percy should not be in your way.'

'So shift him out of it,' Norfolk says.

'I can see why it would not be a good idea for you, as a family –'

'Do it,' Norfolk says. 'Beat his skull in.'

'Figuratively,' he says. 'My lord.'

Anne sits down. Her face is turned away from the women. Her little hands are drawn into fists. Monseigneur shuffles his papers. George, lost in thought, takes off his cap and plays with its jewelled pin, testing the point against the pad of his forefinger.

He has rolled the hanging up, and he presents it gently to Mary Shelton. 'Thank you,' she whispers, blushing as if he had proposed something intimate. George squeaks; he has succeeded in pricking himself. Uncle Norfolk says bitterly, 'You fool of a boy.'

Francis Bryan follows him out.

'Please feel you can leave me now, Sir Francis.'

'I thought I would go with you. I want to learn what you do.'

He checks his stride, slaps his hand flat into Bryan's chest, spins him sideways and hears the thud of his skull against the wall. 'In a hurry,' he says.

Someone calls his name. Master Wriothesley rounds a corner. 'Sign of Mark and the Lion. Five minutes' walk.'

Call-Me has had men following Harry Percy since he came to London. His concern has been that Anne's ill-wishers at court – the Duke of Suffolk and his wife, and those dreamers who believe Katherine will come back – have been meeting with the earl and encouraging him in a view of the past that would be useful, from their point of view. But seemingly no meetings have occurred: unless they are held in bath-houses on the Surrey bank.

Call-Me turns sharply down an alley, and they emerge into a dirty inn yard. He looks around; two hours with a broom and a willing heart, and you could make it respectable. Mr Wriothesley's handsome red-gold head shines like a beacon. St Mark, creaking above his head, is tonsured like a monk. The lion is small and blue and has a smiling face. Call-Me touches his arm: 'In there.' They are about to duck into a side door, when from above there is a shrill whistle. Two women lean out of a window, and with a whoop and a giggle flop their bare breasts over the sill. 'Jesu,' he says. 'More Howard ladies.'

Inside Mark and the Lion, various men in Percy livery are slumped over tables and lying under them. The Earl of Northumberland is drinking in a private room. It would be private, except there is a serving hatch through which faces keep leering. The earl sees him. 'Oh. I was half expecting you.' Tense, he runs his hands through his cropped hair, and it stands up in bristles all over his head.

He, Cromwell, goes to the hatch, holds up one finger to the spectators, and slams it in their face. But he is soft-voiced as ever when he sits down with the boy and says, 'Now, my lord, what is to be done here? How can I help you? You say you can't live with your wife. But she is as lovely a lady as any in this kingdom, if she has faults I never heard of them, so why can you not agree?'

But Harry Percy is not here to be handled like a timid falcon. He is here to shout and weep. 'If I could not agree with her on our wedding day, how can I agree now? She hates me because she knows we are not properly married. Why has only the king a conscience in the matter, why not I, if he doubts his marriage he shouts about it to the whole of Christendom, but when I doubt mine he sends the lowest man in his employ to sweet-talk me and tell me to go back home and make the best of it. Mary Talbot knows I was pledged to Anne, she knows where my heart lies and always will. I told the truth before, I said we had made a compact before witnesses and therefore neither of us was free. I swore it and the cardinal bullied me out of it; my father said he would strike me out of his line, but my father is dead and I am not afraid to speak the truth any more. Henry may be king but he is stealing another man's wife; Anne Boleyn is rightfully my wife, and how will he stand on the day of judgment, when he comes before God naked and stripped of his retinue?'

He hears him out. The slide and tumble into incoherence … true love … pledges … swore she would give her body to me, allowed me such freedom as only a betrothed woman would allow …

'My lord,' he says. 'You have said what you have to say. Now listen to me. You are a man whose money is almost spent. I am a man who knows how you have spent it. You are a man who has

377

borrowed all over Europe. I am a man who knows your credi-tors. One word from me, and your debts will be called in.'

'Oh, and what can they do?' Percy says. 'Bankers have no armies.'

'Neither have you armies, my lord, if your coffers are empty. Look at me now. Understand this. You hold your earldom from the king. Your task is to secure the north. Percys and Howards between them defend us against Scotland. Now suppose Percy cannot do it. Your men will not fight for a kind word –'

'They are my tenants, it is their duty to fight.'

'But my lord, they need supply, they need provision, they need arms, they need walls and forts in good repair. If you cannot ensure these things you are worse than useless. The king will take your title away, and your land, and your castles, and give them to someone who will do the job you cannot.'

'He will not. He respects all ancient titles. All ancient rights.'

'Then let's say I will.' Let's say I will rip your life apart. Me and my banker friends.

How can he explain to him? The world is not run from where he thinks. Not from his border fortresses, not even from White-hall. The world is run from Antwerp, from Florence, from places he has never imagined; from Lisbon, from where the ships with sails of silk drift west and are burned up in the sun. Not from castle walls, but from counting houses, not by the call of the bugle but by the click of the abacus, not by the grate and click of the mechanism of the gun but by the scrape of the pen on the page of the promissory note that pays for the gun and the gunsmith and the powder and shot.

'I picture you without money and title,' he says. 'I picture you in a hovel, wearing homespun, and bringing home a rabbit for the pot. I picture your lawful wife Anne Boleyn skinning and jointing this rabbit. I wish you every happiness.'

Harry Percy slumps over the table. Angry tears spring out of his eyes.

'You were never pre-contracted,' he says. 'Any silly promises you made had no effect in law. Whatever understanding you think you had, you didn't have it. And there is another matter, my lord. If ever you say one more word about Lady Anne's *freedom*' – he packs into one word a volume of disgust – 'then you will answer to me and the Howards and the Boleyns, and George Rochford will have no tender care of your person, and my lord Wiltshire will humble your pride, and as for the Duke of Norfolk, if he hears the slightest imputation against his niece's honour he will drag you out of whatever hole you are cowering in and bite your bollocks off. Now,' he says, resuming his former amiability, 'is that clear, my lord?' He crosses the room and opens the serving hatch again. 'You can peer in again now.' Faces appear; or, to be truthful, just bobbing foreheads, and eyes. In the doorway he pauses and turns back to the earl. 'And I will tell you this, for the avoidance of doubt. If you think Lady Anne loves you, you could not be more mistaken. She hates you. The only service you can do her now, short of dying, is to unsay what you said to your poor wife, and take any oath that is required of you, to clear her path to become Queen of England.'

On the way out he says to Wriothesley, 'I feel sorry for him really.' Call-Me laughs so hard he has to lean against the wall.

Next day he is early for the meeting of the king's council. The Duke of Norfolk takes his place at the head of the table, then shifts out of it when word comes that the king himself will preside. 'And Warham is here,' someone says: the door opens, nothing happens, then slowly very slowly the ancient prelate shuffles in. He takes his seat. His hands tremble as they rest on the cloth before him. His head trembles on his neck. His skin is parchment-coloured, like the drawing that Hans made of him. He looks around the table with a slow lizard blink.

He crosses the room and stands across the table from Warham, enquiring after his health, by way of a formality; it is clear he is dying. He says, 'This prophetess you harbour in your diocese. Eliza Barton. How is she getting on?'

Warham barely looks up. 'What is it you want, Cromwell? My commission found nothing against the girl. You know that.'

'I hear she is telling her followers that if the king marries Lady Anne he has only a year to reign.'

'I could not swear to that. I have not heard it with my own ears.'

'I understand Bishop Fisher has been to see her.'

'Well … or she to see him. One or the other. Why should he not? She is a blessed young woman.'

'Who is controlling her?'

Warham's head looks as if it will wobble off his shoulders. 'She may be unwise. She may be misled. After all, she is a simple country girl. But she has a gift, I am sure of it. When people come into her company, she can tell them at once what is troubling them. What sins are weighing on their conscience.'

'Indeed? I must go and see her. I wonder if she would know what's troubling me?'

'Peace,' Thomas Boleyn says. 'Harry Percy is here.'

The earl comes in between two of his minders. His eyes are red, and a whiff of stale vomit suggests he has resisted the efforts of his people to scrub him down. The king comes in. It is a warm day and he wears pale silks. Rubies cluster on his knuckles like bubbles of blood. He takes his seat. He rests his flat blue eye on Harry Percy.

Thomas Audley – standing in as Lord Chancellor – leads the earl through his denials. Pre-contracted? No. Promises of any kind? No carnal – I so regret to mention – knowledge? Upon my honour, no, no and no.

'Sad to say, we shall need more than your word of honour,' the king says. 'Matters have gone so far, my lord.'

Harry Percy looks panic-stricken. 'Then what more must I do?'

He says softly, 'Approach His Grace of Canterbury, my lord. He is holding out the Book.'

This, anyway, is what the old man is trying to do. Monseigneur tries to assist him, and Warham bats his hands away. Gripping the table, making the cloth slide, he hauls himself to his feet. 'Harry Percy, you have chopped and changed in this matter, you have asserted it, denied it, asserted it, now you are brought here to deny it again, but this time not only in the sight of men. Now … will you put your hand on this Bible, and swear before me and in the presence of the king and his council that you are free from unlawful knowledge of Lady Anne, and free from any marriage contract with her?'

Harry Percy rubs his eyes. He extends his hand. His voice shakes. 'I swear.'

'All done,' the Duke of Norfolk says. 'You'd wonder how the whole thing got about in the first place, wouldn't you?' He walks up to Harry Percy and grips him by the elbow. 'We shall hear no more of this, boy?'

The king says, 'Howard, you have heard him take his oath, cease to trouble him now. Some of you assist the archbishop, you see he is not well.' His mood softened, he smiles around at his councillors. 'Gentlemen, we will go to my private chapel, and see Harry Percy take Holy Communion to seal his oath. Then Lady Anne and I will spend the afternoon in reflection and prayer. I shall not want to be disturbed.'

Warham shuffles up to the king. 'Winchester is robing to say Mass for you. I am going home to my diocese.' With a murmur, Henry leans to kiss his ring. 'Henry,' the archbishop says, 'I have seen you promote within your own court and council persons whose principles and morals will hardly bear scrutiny. I have seen you deify your own will and appetite, to the sorrow and scandal of Christian people. I have been loyal to you, to the point of violation of my own conscience. I have done much for you, but now I have done the last thing I will ever do.'

※ ※ ※

At Austin Friars, Rafe is waiting for him. 'Yes?'

'Yes.'

'So now?'

'Now Harry Percy can borrow more money, and edge himself nearer his ruin. A progress which I shall be pleased to facilitate.' He sits down. 'I think one day I will have that earldom off him.'

'How would you do that, sir?' He shrugs: don't know. 'You would not want the Howards to have more sway in the borders than they do already.'

'No. No, possibly not.' He broods. 'Can you look out the papers about Warham's prophetess?'

While he waits, he opens the window and looks down into the garden. The pink of the roses in his arbours has been bleached out by the sun. I am sorry for Mary Talbot, he thinks; her life will not be easier after this. For a few days, a few days only, she instead of Anne was the talk of the king's court. He thinks of Harry Percy, walking in to arrest the cardinal, keys in his hand: the guard he set, around the dying man's bed.

He leans out of the window. I wonder if peach trees would be possible? Rafe brings in the bundle.

He cuts the tape and straightens out the letters and memoranda. This unsavoury business all started six years ago, at a broken-down chapel on the edge of Kentish marshland, when a statue of the Virgin began to attract pilgrims, and a young woman by name Elizabeth Barton started to put on shows for them. What did the statue do in the first place, to get attention? Move, probably: or weep blood. The girl is an orphan, brought up in the household of one of Warham's land agents. She has a sister, no other family. He says to Rafe, 'Nobody took any notice of her till she was twenty or so, and then she had some kind of illness, and when she got better she started to have visions, and speak in alien voices. She says she's seen St Peter at the gates of Heaven with his keys. She's seen St Michael weighing souls. If you ask her where your dead relatives are, she can tell you. If it's Heaven, she speaks in a high voice. If it's Hell, in a deep voice.'

'The effect could be comic,' Rafe says.

'Do you think so? What irreverent children I have brought up.' He reads, then looks up. 'She sometimes goes without food for nine days. Sometimes she falls suddenly to the ground. Not surprising, is it? She suffers spasms, torsions and trances. It sounds most displeasant. She was interviewed by my lord cardinal, but ...' his hand sifts the papers, 'nothing here, no record of the meeting. I wonder what happened. Probably he tried to get her to eat her dinner, she wouldn't have liked that. By this ...' he reads, '... she is in a convent in Canterbury. The broken-down chapel has got a new roof and money is rolling in to the local clergy. There are cures. The lame walk, the blind see. Candles light by themselves. The pilgrims are thick upon the roads. Why do I feel I have heard this story before? She has a flock of monks and priests about her, who direct the people's eyes heavenwards whilst picking their pockets. And we can presume it is these same monks and priests who have instructed her to hawk around her opinion on the subject of the king's marriage.'

'Thomas More has met her. As well as Fisher.'

'Yes, I keep that in mind. Oh, and ... look here ... Mary Magdalene has sent her a letter, illuminated in gold.'

'Can she read it?'

'Yes, it seems she can.' He looks up. 'What do you think? The king will endure being called names, if it is by a holy virgin. I suppose he is used to it. Anne berates him often enough.'

'Possibly he is afraid.'

Rafe has been to court with him; evidently, he understands Henry better than some people who have known him all his life. 'Indeed he is. He believes in simple maids who can talk to saints. He is disposed to believe in prophecies, whereas I ... I think we let it run for a time. See who visits her. Who makes offerings.

Certain noble ladies have been in touch with her, wanting their fortunes told and their mothers prayed out of Purgatory.'

'My lady Exeter,' Rafe says.

Henry Courtenay, Marquis of Exeter, is the king's nearest male relative, being a grandson of old King Edward; hence, useful to the Emperor, when he comes with his troops to boot out Henry and put a new king on the throne. 'If I were Exeter, I wouldn't let my wife dance attendance on some addle-witted girl who is feeding her fantasies that one day she will be queen.' He begins to refold the papers. 'This girl, you know, she claims she can raise the dead.'

At John Petyt's funeral, while the women are upstairs sitting with Lucy, he convenes an impromptu meeting downstairs at Lion's Quay, to talk to his fellow merchants about disorder in the city. Antonio Bonvisi, More's friend, excuses himself and says he will go home; 'The Trinity bless and prosper you,' he says, withdrawing and taking with him the mobile island of chill which has followed him since his unexpected arrival. 'You know,' he says, turning at the door, 'if there is a question of help for Mistress Petyt, I shall be glad –'

'No need. She is left wealthy.'

'But will the city let her take the business on?'

He cuts him off: 'I have that in hand.'

Bonvisi nods and goes out. 'Surprising he should show his face.' John Parnell, of the Drapers' Company, has a history of clashes with More. 'Master Cromwell, if you are taking charge of this, does it mean – do you have it in mind to speak to Lucy?'

'Me? No.'

Humphrey Monmouth says, 'Shall we have our meeting first, and broker marriages later? We are concerned, Master Cromwell, as you must be, as the king must be ... we are all, I think,' he looks around, 'we are all, now Bonvisi has left us, friendly to the cause for which our late brother Petyt was, in effect, a martyr, but it is for us to keep the peace, to disassociate ourselves from outbreaks of blasphemy ...'

In one city parish last Sunday, at the sacred moment of the elevation of the host, and just as the priest pronounced, *'hoc est enim corpus meum,'* there was an outbreak of chanting, *'hoc est corpus,* hocus pocus.' And in an adjacent parish, at the commemoration of the saints, where the priest requires us to remember our fellowship with the holy martyrs, *'cum Joanne, Stephano, Mathia, Barnaba, Ignatio, Alexandro, Marcellino, Petro ...'* some person had shouted out, 'and don't forget me and my cousin Kate, and Dick with his cockle-barrel on Leadenhall, and his sister Susan and her little dog Posset.'

He puts his hand over his mouth. 'If Posset needs a lawyer, you know where I am.'

'Master Cromwell,' says a crabbed elder from the Skinners' Company, 'you convened this gathering. Set us an example in gravity.'

'There are ballads made,' Monmouth says, 'about Lady Anne – the words are not repeatable in this company. Thomas Boleyn's servants complain they are called names on the street. Ordure thrown on their livery. Masters must keep a hand on their apprentices. Disloyal talk should be reported.'

'To whom?'

He says, 'Try me.'

He finds Johane at Austin Friars. She has made some excuse to stay at home: a summer cold. 'Ask me what secret I know,' he says.

For appearances' sake, she polishes the tip of her nose. 'Let me see. You know to a shilling what the king has in his treasury?'

'I know to the farthing. Not that. Ask me. Sweet sister.'

When she has guessed enough, he tells her, 'John Parnell is going to marry Luce.'

'What? And John Petyt not cold?' She turns away, to get over whatever she is feeling. 'Your brethren stick together. Parnell's household is not clean from sectaries. He has a servant in Bishop Stokesley's prison, so I hear.'

Richard Cromwell puts his head around the door. 'Master. The Tower. Bricks. Five shilling the thousand.'

'No.'

'Right.'

'You'd think she'd marry a safer sort of man.'

He goes to the door. 'Richard, come back.' Turns to Johane. 'I don't think she knows any.'

'Sir?'

'Get it down by sixpence, and check every batch. What you should do is choose a few in every load, and take a close interest in them.'

Johane in the room behind him: 'Anyway, you did the wise thing.'

'For instance, measure them ... Johane, did you think I'd get married out of some sort of inadvertence? By accident?'

'I'm sorry?' Richard says.

'Because if you keep measuring them, it throws brickmakers into a panic, and you'll see by their faces if they're trying any tricks.'

'I expect you have some lady in view. At court. The king has given you a new office –'

'Clerk of the Hanaper. Yes. A post in the chancery finances ... It hardly signs the flowery trail to a love affair.' Richard has gone, clattering downstairs. 'Do you know what I think?'

'You think you should wait. Till she, that woman, is queen.'

'I think it's the transport that pushes the cost up. Even by barge. I should have cleared some ground and built my own kilns.'

Sunday, 1 September, at Windsor: Anne kneels before the king to receive the title of Marquess of Pembroke. The Garter knights in their stalls watch her, the noble ladies of England flank her, and (the duchess having refused, and spat out an oath at the suggestion) Norfolk's daughter Mary bears her coronet on a cushion; the Howards and the Boleyns are *en fête*. Monseigneur caresses his beard, nods and smiles as he receives murmured congratulations from the French ambassador. Bishop Gardiner reads out Anne's new title. She is vivid in red velvet and ermine, and her black hair falls, virgin-style, in snaky locks to her waist. He, Cromwell, has organised the income from fifteen manors to support her dignity.

A *Te Deum* is sung. A sermon is preached. When the ceremony is over, and the women stoop to pick up her train, he sees a flash of blue, like a kingfisher, and glances up to see John Seymour's little daughter among the Howard ladies. A warhorse raises his head at the sound of trumpets, and great ladies look up and smile; but as the musicians play a flourish, and the procession leaves St George's Chapel, she keeps her pale face downturned, her eyes on her toes as if she fears tripping.

At the feast Anne sits beside Henry on the dais, and when she turns to speak to him her black lashes brush her cheeks. She is almost there now, almost there, her body taut like a bowstring, her skin dusted with gold, with tints of apricot and honey; when she smiles, which she does often, she shows small teeth, white and sharp. She is planning to commandeer Katherine's royal barge, she tells him, and have the device 'H&K' burned away, all Katherine's badges obliterated. The king has sent for Katherine's jewels, so she can wear them on the projected trip to France. He has spent an afternoon with her, two afternoons, three, in the fine September weather, with the king's goldsmith beside her making drawings, and he as master of the jewels adding suggestions; Anne wants new settings made. At first Katherine had refused to give up the jewels. She had said she could not part with the property of the Queen of England and put it into the hands of the disgrace of Christendom. It had taken a royal command to make her hand over the loot.

Anne refers everything to him; she says, laughing, 'Cromwell, you are my man.' The wind is set fair and the tide is running for him. He can feel the tug of it under his feet. His friend Audley must surely be confirmed as Chancellor; the king is getting used to him. Old courtiers have resigned, rather than serve Anne; the new comptroller of the household is Sir William Paulet, a friend of his from Wolsey days. So many of the new courtiers are his friends from Wolsey days. And the cardinal didn't employ fools.

After the Mass and Anne's installation, he attends the Bishop of Winchester as he disrobes, gets out of his canonicals into gear more suitable for secular celebrations. 'Are you going to dance?' he asks him. He sits on a stone window ledge, half-attentive to what is going on in the courts below, the musicians carrying in pipes and lutes, harps and rebecs, hautboys, viols and drums. 'You could cut a good figure. Or don't you dance now you're a bishop?'

Stephen's conversation is on a track of its own. 'You'd think it would be enough for any woman, wouldn't you, to be made a marquess in her own right? She'll give way to him now. Heir in the belly, please God, before Christmas.'

'Oh, you wish her success?'

'I wish his temper soothed. And some result out of this. Not to do it all for nothing.'

'Do you know what Chapuys is saying about you? That you keep two women in your household, dressed up as boys.'

'Do I?' He frowns. 'Better, I suppose, than two boys dressed up as women. Now that would be opprobrious.' Stephen gives a bark of laughter. They stroll together towards the feast. Trolly-lolly, the musicians sing. 'Pastime with good company, I love and shall until I die.' The soul is musical by nature, the philosophers say. The king calls up Thomas Wyatt to sing with him, and the musician Mark. 'Alas, what shall I do for love? For love, alas, what shall I do?'

'Anything he can think of,' Gardiner says. 'There is no limit, that I can see.'

He says, 'The king is good to those who think him good.' He floats it to the bishop, below the music.

'Well,' Gardiner says, 'if your mind is infinitely flexible. As yours, I see, would have to be.'

He speaks to Mistress Seymour. 'Look,' she says. She holds up her sleeves. The bright blue with which she has edged them, that kingfisher flash, is cut from the silk in which he wrapped her present of needlework patterns. How do matters stand now at Wolf Hall, he asks, as tactfully as he can: how do you ask after a family, in the wake of incest? She says in her clear little voice, 'Sir John is very well. But then Sir John is always very well.'

'And the rest of you?'

'Edward angry, Tom restless, my lady mother grinding her teeth and banging the doors. The harvest coming in, the apples on the bough, the maids in the dairy, our chaplain at his prayers, the hens laying, the lutes in tune, and Sir John … Sir John as always is very well. Why don't you make some business in Wiltshire and ride down to inspect us? Oh, and if the king gets a new wife, she will need matrons to attend her, and my sister Liz is coming to court. Her husband is the Governor of Jersey, you know him, Anthony Oughtred? I would rather go up-country to the queen, myself. But they say she is moving again, and her household is being reduced.'

'If I were your father … no …' he rephrases it, 'if I were to advise you, it would be to serve Lady Anne.'

'The marquess,' she says. 'Of course, it is good to be humble. She makes sure we are.'

'Just now it is difficult for her. I think she will soften, when she has her heart's desire.' Even as he says it, he knows it is not true.

Jane lowers her head, looks up at him from under her eyelids. 'That is my humble face. Do you think it will serve?'

He laughs. 'It would take you anywhere.'

When the dancers are resting, fanning themselves, from the galliards, pavanes and almanes, he and Wyatt sing the little soldiers' air: Scaramella to the war has gone, with his shield, his lance. It is melancholy, as songs are, whatever the words, when the light is failing and the human voice, unaccompanied, fades in the shadows of the room. Charles Brandon asks him, 'What is it about, that song, is it about a lady?'

'No, it is just about a boy who goes off to war.'

'What are his fortunes?'

Scaramella fa la gala. 'It's all one big holiday to him.'

'Those were better days,' the duke says. 'Soldiering.'

The king sings to the lute, his voice strong, true, plangent: 'As I Walked the Woods So Wild.' Some women weep, a little the worse for strong Italian wines.

At Canterbury, Archbishop Warham lies cold on a slab; coins of the realm are laid on his eyelids, as if to seal into his brain for eternity the image of his king. He is waiting to go down under the pavement of the cathedral, in the dank charnel vacancy by Becket's bones. Anne sits still as a statue, her eyes on her lover. Only her restless fingers move; she clutches on her lap one of her little dogs, and her hands run over and over its fur, twisting its curls. As the last note dies, candles are brought in.

October, and we are going to Calais – a train two thousand strong, stretched from Windsor to Greenwich, from Greenwich across the green fields of Kent to Canterbury: to a duke an entourage of forty, to a marquess thirty-five, to an earl twenty-four, while a viscount must scrape by with twenty, and he with Rafe and any clerks he can pack into the ships' rat-holes. The king is to meet his brother France, who intends to oblige him by speaking to the Pope in favour of his new marriage. François has offered to marry one of his three sons – *his three sons*, how God must love him – to the Pope's niece, Catherine de' Medici; he says he will make it a precondition of the match that Queen

Katherine is refused leave to appeal her case to Rome, and that his brother England is allowed to settle his marital affairs in his own jurisdiction, using his own bishops.

These two potent monarchs will see each other for the first time since the meeting called the Field of the Cloth of Gold, which the cardinal arranged. The king says the trip must cost less than that occasion, but when he is questioned on specifics he wants more of that and two of those – everything bigger, plusher, more lavish, and with more gilding. He is taking his own cooks and his own bed, his ministers and musicians, his horses, dogs and falcons, and his new marquess, whom Europe calls his concubine. He is taking the possible claimants to the throne, including the Yorkist Lord Montague, and the Lancastrian Nevilles, to show how tame they are and how secure are the Tudors. He is taking his gold plate, his linen, his pastry chefs and poultry-pickers and poison-taster, and he is even taking his own wine: which you might think is superfluous, but what do you know?

Rafe, helping him pack his papers: 'I understand that King Francis will speak to Rome for the king's cause. But I am not sure what he gets out of this treaty.'

'Wolsey always said that the making of a treaty is the treaty. It doesn't matter what the terms are, just that there are terms. It's the goodwill that matters. When that runs out, the treaty is broken, whatever the terms say.'

It is the processions that matter, the exchange of gifts, the royal games of bowls, the tilts, jousts and masques: these are not preliminaries to the process, they are the process itself. Anne, accustomed to the French court and French etiquette, sets out the difficulties in store. 'If the Pope were to visit him, then France could advance towards him, perhaps meeting him in a courtyard. But two monarchs meeting, once they are in sight, should take the same number of steps towards each other. And this works, unless one monarch – *hélas* – were to take very small steps, forcing the other to cover the ground.'

'By God,' Charles Brandon bursts out, 'such a man would be a knave. Would Francis do that?'

Anne looks at him, lids half-lowered. 'My lord Suffolk, is your lady wife ready for the journey?'

Suffolk reddens. 'My wife is a former Queen of France.'

'I am aware of it. François will be pleased to see her again. He thought her very beautiful. Though of course, she was young then.'

'My sister is beautiful still,' Henry says, pacific. But a tempest is boiling up inside Charles Brandon, and it breaks with a yell like a crack of thunder: 'You expect her to wait on you? On Boleyn's daughter? Pass you your gloves, madam, and serve you first at dinner? Make your mind up to it – that day will never come.'

Anne turns to Henry, her hand fastening on his arm. 'Before your face he humiliates me.'

'Charles,' Henry says, 'leave us now and come back when you are master of yourself. Not a moment before.' He sighs, makes a sign: Cromwell, go after him.

The Duke of Suffolk is seething and steaming. 'Fresh air, my lord,' he suggests.

Autumn has come already; there is a raw wind from the river. It lifts a flurry of sodden leaves, which flap in their path like the flags of some miniature army. 'I always think Windsor is a cold place. Don't you, my lord? I mean the situation, not just the castle?' His voice runs on, soothing, low. 'If I were the king, I would spend more time at the palace in Woking. You know it never snows there? At least, not once in twenty years.'

'If you were king?' Brandon stumps downhill. 'If Anne Boleyn can be queen, why not?'

'I take that back. I should have used a more humble expression.'

Brandon grunts. 'She will never appear, my wife, in the train of that harlot.'

'My lord, you had better think her chaste. We all do.'

'Her lady mother trained her up, and she was a great whore, let me tell you. Liz Boleyn, Liz Howard as was – she was the first to take Henry to bed. I know these things, I am his oldest friend. Seventeen, and he didn't know where to put it. His father kept him like a nun.'

'But none of us believe that story now. About Monseigneur's wife.'

'*Monseigneur!* Christ in Heaven.'

'He likes to be called that. It is no harm.'

'Her sister Mary trained her up, and Mary was trained in a brothel. Do you know what they do, in France? My lady wife told me. Well, not told me, but she wrote it down for me, in Latin. The man has a cock-stand, and she takes it in her mouth! Can you imagine such a thing? A woman who can do such a filthy proceeding, can you call that a virgin?'

'My lord … if your wife will not go to France, if you cannot persuade her … shall we say that she is ill? It would be something you could do for the king, whom you know is your friend. It would save him from –' He almost says, from the lady's harsh tongue. But he backs out of that sentence, and says something else. 'It would save face.'

Brandon nods. They are still heading towards the river, and he tries to check their pace because soon Anne will expect him back with news of an apology. When the duke turns to him, his face is a picture of misery. 'It's true, anyway. She is ill. Her beautiful little' – he makes a gesture, his hands cupping the air – 'all fallen away. I love her anyway. She's as thin as a wafer. I say to her, Mary, I will wake up one day, and I won't be able to find you, I'll take you for a thread in the bed linen.'

'I am so sorry,' he says.

He rubs his face. 'Ah, God. Go back to Harry, will you? Tell him we can't do this.'

'He will expect you to come to Calais, if your lady wife cannot.'

393

'I don't like to leave her, you see?'

'Anne is unforgiving,' he says. 'Hard to please, easy to offend. My lord, be guided by me.'

Brandon grunts. 'We all are. We must be. You do everything, Cromwell. You are everything now. We say, how did it happen? We ask ourselves.' The duke sniffs. 'We ask ourselves, but by the steaming blood of Christ we have no bloody answer.'

The steaming blood of Christ. It's an oath worthy of Thomas Howard, the senior duke. When did he become the interpreter of dukes, their explainers? He asks himself but he has no bloody answer. When he returns to the king and the queen-to-be, they are looking lovingly into each other's faces. 'The Duke of Suffolk begs pardon,' he says. Yes, yes, the king says. I'll see you tomorrow, but not too early. You would think they were already man and wife, a languorous night before them, filled with marital delights. You would think so, except he has Mary Boleyn's word for it that the marquisate has bought Henry only the right to caress her sister's inner thigh. Mary tells him this, and doesn't even put it in Latin. Whenever she spends time alone with the king, Anne reports back to her relations, no detail spared. You have to admire her; her measured exactness, her restraint. She uses her body like a soldier, conserving its resources; like one of the masters in the anatomy school at Padua, she divides it up and names every part, this my thigh, this my breast, this my tongue.

'Perhaps in Calais,' he says. 'Perhaps he will get what he wants then.'

'She will have to be sure.' Mary walks away. She stops and turns back, her face troubled. 'Anne says, Cromwell is my man. I don't like her to say that.'

In ensuing days, other questions emerge to torment the English party. Which royal lady will be hostess to Anne when they meet the French? Queen Eleanor will not – you cannot expect it, as she is the Emperor's sister, and family feeling is touched by His Disgrace's abandonment of Katherine. Francis's sister, the Queen of Navarre, pleads illness rather than receive the King of England's mistress. 'Is it the same illness that afflicts the poor Duchess of Suffolk?' Anne asks. Perhaps, Francis suggests, it would be appropriate if the new marquess were to be met by the Duchess of Vendôme, his own *maîtresse en titre*?

Henry is so angry that it gives him toothache. Dr Butts comes with his chest of specifics. A narcotic seems kindest, but when the king wakes he is still so mortified that for a few hours there seems no solution but to call the expedition off. Can they not comprehend, can they not grasp, that Anne is no man's mistress, but a king's bride-to-be? But to comprehend that is not in Francis's nature. He would never wait more than a week for a woman he wanted. Pattern of chivalry, he? Most Christian king? All he understands, Henry bellows, is rutting like a stag. But I tell you, when his rut is done, the other harts will put him down. Ask any hunter!

It is suggested, finally, that the solution will be to leave the future queen behind in Calais, on English soil where she can suffer no insult, while the king meets Francis in Boulogne. Calais, a small city, should be more easily contained than London, even if people line up at the harbourside to shout '*Putain!*' and 'Great Whore of England.' If they sing obscene songs, we will simply refuse to understand them.

At Canterbury, with the royal party in addition to the pilgrims from all nations, every house is packed from cellars to eaves. He and Rafe are lodged in some comfort and near the king, but there are lords in flea-bitten inns and knights in the back rooms of brothels, pilgrims forced into stables and outhouses and sleeping out under the stars. Luckily, the weather is mild for October. Any year before this, the king would have gone to pray at Becket's shrine and leave a rich offering. But Becket was a rebel against the Crown, not the sort of archbishop we like to encourage at the moment. In the cathedral the incense is still hanging in the air from Warham's interment, and prayers for his soul are a constant drone like the buzz of a thousand hives. Letters have gone to Cranmer, lying somewhere in Germany at the Emperor's travelling court. Anne has begun to refer to him as the Archbishop-Elect. No one knows how long he'll take getting home. With his secret, Rafe says.

Of course, he says, his secret, written down the side of the page.

Rafe visits the shrine. It is his first time. He comes back wide-eyed, saying it is covered in jewels the size of goose eggs.

'I know. Are they real, do you think?'

'They show you a skull, they say it's Becket's, it's smashed up by the knights but it's held together with a silver plate. For ready money, you can kiss it. They have a tray of his finger bones. They have his snotty handkerchief. And a bit of his boot. And a vial they shake up for you, they say it's his blood.'

'At Walsingham, they have a vial of the Virgin's milk.'

'Christ, I wonder what that is?' Rafe looks sick. 'The blood, you can tell it's water with some red soil in it. It floats about in clumps.'

'Well, pick up that goose quill, plucked from the pinions of the angel Gabriel, and we will write to Stephen Vaughan. We may have to set him on the road, to bring Thomas Cranmer home.'

'It can't be soon enough,' Rafe says. 'Just wait, master, till I wash Becket off my hands.'

Though he will not go to the shrine, the king wants to show himself to the people, Anne by his side. Leaving Mass, against all advice he walks out among the crowds, his guards standing back, his councillors around him. Anne's head darts, on the slender stem of her neck, turning to catch the comments that come her way. People stretch out their hands to touch the king.

Norfolk, at his elbow, stiff with apprehension, eyes everywhere: 'I don't care for this proceeding, Master Cromwell.' He himself, having once been quick with a knife, is alert for movements below the eyeline. But the nearest thing to a weapon is an outsize cross, wielded by a bunch of Franciscan monks. The crowd gives way to them, to a huddle of lay priests in their vestments, a contingent of Benedictines from the abbey, and in the midst of them a young woman in the habit of a Benedictine nun.

'Majesty?'

Henry turns. 'By God, this is the Holy Maid,' he says. The guards move in, but Henry holds up a hand. 'Let me see her.' She is a big girl, and not so young, perhaps twenty-eight; plain face, dusky, excited, with an urgent flush. She pushes towards the king, and for a second he sees him through her eyes: a blur of red-gold and flushed skin, a ready, priapic body, a hand like a ham that stretches out to take her by her nunly elbow. 'Madam, you have something to say to me?'

She tries to curtsey, but his grip won't let her. 'I am advised by Heaven,' she says, 'by the saints with whom I converse, that the heretics around you must be put into a great fire, and if you do not light that fire, then you yourself will burn.'

'Which heretics? Where are they? I do not keep heretics about my person.'

'Here is one.'

Anne shrinks against the king; against the scarlet and gold of his jacket she melts like wax.

'And if you enter into a form of marriage with this unworthy woman, you will not reign seven months.'

'Come, madam, seven months? Round it off, can you not? What sort of a prophet says "seven months"?'

'That is what Heaven tells me.'

'And when the seven months are up, who will replace me? Speak up, say who you would like to be king instead of me.'

The monks and priests are trying to draw her away; this was not part of their plan. 'Lord Montague, he is of the blood. The Marquis of Exeter, he is blood royal.' She in turn tries to pull away from the king. 'I see your lady mother,' she says, 'surrounded by pale fires.'

Henry drops her as if her flesh were hot. 'My mother? Where?'

'I have been looking for the Cardinal of York. I have searched Heaven, Hell and Purgatory, but the cardinal is not there.'

'Surely she is mad?' Anne says. 'She is mad and must be whipped. If she is not, she must be hanged.'

One of the priests says, 'Madam, she is a very holy person. Her speech is inspired.'

'Get her out of my way,' Anne says.

'Lightning will strike you,' the nun tells Henry. He laughs uncertainly.

Norfolk erupts into the group, teeth clenched, fist raised. 'Drag her back to her whorehouse, before she feels this, by God!' In the mêlée, one monk hits another with the cross; the Maid is drawn backwards, still prophesying; the noise from the crowd rises, and Henry grasps Anne by the arm and pulls her back the way they came. He himself follows the Maid, sticking close to the back of the group, till the crowd thins and he can tap one of the monks on the arm and ask to speak to her. 'I was a servant of Wolsey,' he says. 'I want to hear her message.'

Some consultation, and they let him through. 'Sir?' she says.

'Could you try again to find the cardinal? If I were to make an offering?'

She shrugs. One of the Franciscans says, 'It would have to be a substantial offering.'

'Your name is?'

'I am Father Risby.'

'I can no doubt meet your expectations. I am a wealthy man.'

'Would you want simply to locate the soul, to help your own prayers, or were you thinking in terms of a chantry, perhaps, an endowment?'

'Whatever you recommend. But of course I'd need to know he wasn't in Hell. There would be no point throwing away good Masses on a hopeless case.'

'I'll have to talk to Father Bocking,' the girl says.

'Father Bocking is this lady's spiritual director.'

He inclines his head. 'Come again and ask me,' the girl says. She turns and is lost in the crowd. He parts with some money there and then, to the entourage. For Father Bocking, whoever he may be. As it seems Father Bocking does the price list and keeps the accounts.

The nun has plunged the king into gloom. How would you feel if you were told you'd be struck by lightning? By evening he complains of a headache, a pain in his face and jaw. 'Go away,' he tells his doctors. 'You can never cure it, so why should you now? And you, madam,' he says to Anne, 'have your ladies put you to bed, I do not want chatter, I cannot stand piercing voices.'

Norfolk grumbles under his breath: the Tudor, always something the matter with him.

At Austin Friars, if anyone gets a sniffle or a sprain, the boys perform an interlude called 'If Norfolk were Doctor Butts'. Got a toothache? Pull them out! Trapped your finger? Hack your hand off! Pain in the head? Slice it off, you've got another.

Now Norfolk pauses, in backing out of the presence. 'Majesty, she didn't say the lightning would in fact kill you.'

'No more did she,' Brandon says cheerily.

'Not dead but dethroned, not dead but stricken and scorched, that's something to look forward to, is it?' Pitifully indicating his circumstances, the king barks for a servant to bring logs and a page to warm some wine. 'Am I to sit here, the King of England, with a miserable fire and nothing to drink?' He does look cold. He says, 'She saw my lady mother.'

'Your Majesty,' he says, cautious, 'you know that in the cathedral one of the windows has an image of your lady mother in glass? And would not the sun shine through, so it would seem as if she was in a dazzle of light? I think that is what the nun has seen.'

399

'You don't believe these visions?'

'I think perhaps she can't tell what she sees in the outside world from what is inside her head. Some people are like that. She is to be pitied, perhaps. Though not too much.'

The king frowns. 'But I loved my mother,' he says. Then: 'Buckingham set much store by visions. He had a friar who prophesied for him. Told him he would be king.' He does not need to add, Buckingham was a traitor and is more than ten years dead.

When the court sails for France he is in the king's party, on the *Swallow*. He stands on deck watching England recede, with the Duke of Richmond, Henry's bastard, excited to be on his first sea voyage, and to be in his father's company too. Fitzroy is a handsome boy of thirteen, fair-haired, tall for his age but slender: Henry as he must have been as a young prince, and endowed with a proper sense of himself and his own dignity. 'Master Cromwell,' he says, 'I have not seen you since the cardinal came down.' A moment's awkwardness. 'I am glad you prosper. Because it is said in the book called *The Courtier* that in men of base degree we often see high gifts of nature.'

'You read Italian, sir?'

'No, but parts of that book have been put into English for me. It is a very good book for me to read.' A pause. 'I wish' – he turns his head, lowering his voice – 'I wish the cardinal were not dead. Because now the Duke of Norfolk is my guardian.'

'And I hear Your Grace is to marry his daughter Mary.'

'Yes. I do not want to.'

'Why not?'

'I have seen her. She has no breasts.'

'But she has a good wit, my lord. And time may remedy the other matter, before you live together. If your people will translate for you that part of Castiglione's book that relates to gentlewomen and their qualities, I'm sure you will find that Mary Howard has all of them.'

Let's hope, he thinks, it won't turn out like Harry Percy's match, or George Boleyn's. For the girl's sake too; Castiglione says that everything that can be understood by men can be understood by women, that their apprehension is the same, their faculties, no doubt their loves and hates. Castiglione was in love with his wife Ippolita, but she died when he had only had her four years. He wrote a poem for her, an elegy, but he wrote it as if Ippolita was writing: the dead woman speaking to him.

In the ship's wake the gulls cry like lost souls. The king comes on deck and says his headache has cleared. He says, 'Majesty, we were talking of Castiglione's book. You have found time to read it?'

'Indeed. He extols *sprezzatura*. The art of doing everything gracefully and well, without the appearance of effort. A quality princes should cultivate, too.' He adds, rather dubious, 'King Francis has it.'

'Yes. But besides *sprezzatura* one must exhibit at all times a dignified public restraint. I was thinking I might commission a translation as a gift for my lord Norfolk.'

It must be in his mind, the picture of Thomas Howard in Canterbury, threatening to punch the holy nun. Henry grins. 'You should do it.'

'Well, if he would not take it as a reproach. Castiglione recommends that a man should not curl his hair nor pluck his eyebrows. And you know my lord does both.'

The princeling frowns at him. 'My lord of Norfolk?' Henry unleashes an unregal yell of laughter, neither dignified nor restrained. It is welcome to his ears. The ship's timbers creak. The king steadies himself with a hand on his shoulder. The wind stiffens the sails. The sun dances over the water. 'An hour and we will be in port.'

Calais, this outpost of England, her last hold on France, is a town where he has many friends, many customers, many clients. He knows it, Watergate and Lantern Gate, St Nicholas Church and Church of Our Lady, he knows its towers and bulwarks, its markets, courts and quays, Staple Inn where the Governor lodges, and the houses of the Whethill and Wingfield families, houses with shady gardens where gentlemen live in pleasant retreat from an England they claim they no longer understand. He knows the fortifications – crumbling – and beyond the city walls the lands of the Pale, its woods, villages and marshes, its sluices, dykes and canals. He knows the road to Boulogne, and the road to Gravelines, which is the Emperor's territory, and he knows that either monarch, Francis or Charles, could take this town with one determined push. The English have been here for two hundred years, but in the streets now you hear more French and Flemish spoken.

The Governor greets His Majesty; Lord Berners, old soldier and scholar, is the pattern of old-fashioned virtue, and if it were not for his limp, and his evident anxiety about the vast expenses he is about to incur, he would be straight out of the book called *The Courtier.* He has even arranged to lodge the king and the marquess in rooms with an interconnecting door. 'I think that will be very suitable, my lord,' he says. 'As long as there is a sturdy bolt on both sides.'

Because Mary told him, before they left dry land, 'Till now she wouldn't, but now she would, but he won't. He tells her he must be sure that if she gets a child it's born in wedlock.'

The monarchs are to meet for five days in Boulogne, then five days in Calais. Anne is aggrieved at the thought of being left behind. He can see by her restlessness that she knows this is a debatable land, where things might happen you cannot foretell. Meanwhile he has private business to transact. He leaves even Rafe behind, and slips away to an inn in a back court off Calkwell Street.

* * *

It is a low sort of place, and smells of wood smoke, fish and mould. On a side wall is a watery mirror through which he glimpses his own face, pale, only his eyes alive. For a moment it shocks him; you do not expect to see your own image in a hovel like this.

He sits at a table and waits. After five minutes there is a disturbance of the air at the back of the room. But nothing happens. He has anticipated they will keep him waiting; to pass the time, he runs over in his head the figures for last year's receipts to the king from the Duchy of Cornwall. He is about to move on to the figures submitted by the Chamberlain of Chester, when a dark shape materialises, and resolves itself into the person of an old man in a long gown. He totters forward, and in time two others follow him. You could change any one for the other: hollow coughs, long beards. According to some precedence which they negotiate by grunting, they take their seats on a bench opposite. He hates alchemists, and these look like alchemists to him: nameless splashes on their garments, watering eyes, vapour-induced sniffles. He greets them in French. They shudder, and one of them asks in Latin if they are not going to have anything to drink. He calls for the boy, and asks him without much hope what he suggests. 'Drink somewhere else?' the boy offers.

A jug of something vinegary comes. He lets the old men drink deeply before he asks, 'Which of you is Maître Camillo?'

They exchange glances. It takes them as long as it takes the Graiae to pass their single shared eye.

'Maître Camillo has gone to Venice.'

'Why?'

Some coughing. 'For consultations.'

'But he does mean to return to France?'

'Quite likely.'

'The thing you have, I want it for my master.'

A silence. How would it be, he thought, if I take the wine away till they say something useful? But one pre-empts him, snatching up the jug; his hand shakes, and the wine washes over the table. The others bleat with irritation.

'I thought you might bring drawings,' he says.

They look at each other. 'Oh, no.'

'But there are drawings?'

'Not as such.'

The spilt wine begins to soak into the splintered wood. They sit in miserable silence and watch this happen. One of them occupies himself in working his finger through a moth hole in his sleeve.

He shouts to the boy for a second jug. 'We do not wish to disoblige you,' the spokesman says. 'You must understand that Maître Camillo is, for now, under the protection of King Francis.'

'He intends to make a model for him?'

'That is possible.'

'A working model?'

'Any model would be, by its nature, a working model.'

'Should he find the terms of his employment in the least unsatisfactory, my master Henry would be happy to welcome him in England.'

There is another pause, till the jug is fetched and the boy has gone. This time, he does the pouring himself. The old men exchange glances again, and one says, 'The magister believes he would dislike the English climate. The fogs. And also, the whole island is covered with witches.'

The interview has been unsatisfactory. But one must begin somewhere. As he leaves he says to the boy, 'You might go and swab the table.'

'I may as well wait till they've upset the second jug, monsieur.'

'True. Take them in some food. What do you have?'

'Pottage. I wouldn't recommend it. It looks like what's left when a whore's washed her shift.'

'I never knew the Calais girls to wash anything. Can you read?'

'A little.'

'Write?'

'No, monsieur.'

'You should learn. Meanwhile use your eyes. If anyone else comes to talk to them, if they bring out any drawings, parchments, scrolls, anything of that kind, I want to know.'

The boy says, 'What is it, monsieur? What are they selling?'

He almost tells him. What harm could it do? But then in the end he can't think of the right words.

Part-way through the talks in Boulogne, he has a message that Francis would like to see him. Henry deliberates before giving him permission; face-to-face, monarchs should deal only with fellow monarchs, and lords and churchmen of high rank. Since they landed, Brandon and Howard, who were friendly enough on board ship, have been distant with him, as if to make it quite clear to the French that they accord him no status; he is some whim of Henry's, they pretend, a novelty councillor who will soon vanish in favour of a viscount, baron or bishop.

The French messenger tells him, 'This is not an audience.'

'No,' he says, 'I understand. Nothing of that sort.'

Francis sits waiting, attended only by a handful of courtiers, for what is not an audience. He is a beanpole of a man, his elbows and knees jutting at the air, his big bony feet restless inside vast padded slippers. 'Cremuel,' he says. 'Now, let me understand you. You are a Welshman.'

'No, Your Highness.'

Sorrowful dog eyes; they look him over, they look him over again. 'Not a Welshman.'

He sees the French king's difficulty. How has he got his passport to the court, if he is not from some family of humble Tudor retainers? 'It was the late cardinal who induced me into the king's business.'

'Yes, I know that,' Francis says, 'but I think to myself there is something else going on here.'

'That may be, Highness,' he says crisply, 'but it's certainly not being Welsh.'

Francis touches the tip of his pendulous nose, bending it further towards his chin. Choose your prince: you wouldn't like to look at this one every day. Henry is so wholesome, in his fleshy, scrubbed pink-and-whiteness. Francis says, his glance drifting away, 'They say you once fought for the honour of France.'

Garigliano: for a moment he lowers his eyes, as if he's remembering a very bad accident in the street: some mashing and irretrievable mangling of limbs. 'On a most unfortunate day.'

'Still … these things pass. Who now remembers Agincourt?'

He almost laughs. 'It is true,' he says. 'A generation or two, or three … four … and these things are nothing.'

Francis says, 'They say you are in very good standing with That Lady.' He sucks his lip. 'Tell me, I am curious, what does my brother king think? Does he think she is a maid? Myself, I never tried her. When she was here at court she was young, and as flat as a board. Her sister, however –'

He would like to stop him but you can't stop a king. His voice runs over naked Mary, chin to toes, and then flips her over like a griddle cake and does the other side, nape to heels. An attendant hands him a square of fine linen, and as he finishes he dabs the corner of his mouth: and hands the kerchief back.

'Well, enough,' Francis says. 'I see you will not admit to being Welsh, so that is the end of my theories.' The corners of his mouth turn up; his elbows work a little; his knees twitch; the not-audience is over. 'Monsieur Cremuel,' he says, 'we may not meet again. Your sudden fortunes may not last. So, come, give me your hand, like a soldier of France. And put me in your prayers.'

He bows. 'Your beadsman, sir.'

As he leaves, one of the courtiers steps forward, and murmuring, 'A gift from His Highness,' hands him a pair of embroidered gloves.

* * *

406

Another man, he supposes, would be pleased, and try them on. For his part, he pinches the fingers, and finds what he is looking for. Gently, he shakes the glove, his hand cupped.

He goes straight to Henry. He finds him in the sunshine, playing a game of bowls with some French lords. Henry can make a game of bowls as noisy as a tournament: whooping, groaning, shouting of odds, wails, oaths. The king looks up at him, his eyes saying, 'Well?' His eyes say, 'Alone,' the king's say, 'Later,' and not a word is spoken, but all the time the king keeps up his joking and backslapping, and he straightens up, watching his wood glide over the shorn grass, and points in his direction. 'You see this councillor of mine? I warn you, never play any game with him. For he will not respect your ancestry. He has no coat of arms and no name, but he believes he is bred to win.'

One of the French lords says, 'To lose gracefully is an art that every gentleman cultivates.'

'I hope to cultivate it too,' he says. 'If you see an example I might follow, please point it out.'

For they are all, he notices, intent on winning this game, on taking a piece of gold from the King of England. Gambling is not a vice, if you can afford to do it. Perhaps I could issue him with gaming tokens, he thinks, redeemable only if presented in person at some office in Westminster: with tortuous paperwork attached, and fees to clerks, and a special seal to be affixed. That would save us some money.

But the king's wood moves smoothly towards the marker ball. Henry is winning the game anyway. From the French, a spatter of polite applause.

When he and the king are alone, he says, 'Here's something you will like.'

Henry likes surprises. With a thick forefinger, his pink clean English nail, he nudges the ruby about on the back of his hand. 'It is a good stone,' he says. 'I am a judge of these things.' A pause. 'Who is the principal goldsmith here? Ask him to wait on me. It is a dark stone, Francis will know it again; I will wear it on my own finger before our meetings are done. France shall see how I am served.' He is in high good humour. 'However, I shall give you the value.' He nods, to dismiss him. 'Of course, you will compound with the goldsmith to put a higher valuation on it, and arrange to split the profit with him ... but I shall be liberal in the matter.'

Arrange your face.

The king laughs. 'Why would I trust a man with my business, if he could not manage his own? One day Francis will offer you a pension. You must take it. By the way, what did he ask you?'

'He asked if I were Welsh. It seemed a great question with him, I was sorry to be so disappointing.'

'Oh, you are not disappointing,' Henry says. 'But the moment you are, I will let you know.'

Two hours. Two kings. What do you know, Walter? He stands in the salty air, talking to his dead father.

When Francis comes back with his brother king to Calais, it is Anne who leads him out to dance after the evening's great feast. There is colour in her cheeks, and her eyes sparkle behind her gilded mask. When she lowers the mask and looks at the King of France, she wears a strange half-smile, not quite human, as if behind the mask were another mask. You can see his jaw drop; you can see him begin to drool. She entwines her fingers with his, and leads him to a window seat. They speak in French for an hour, whispering, his sleek dark head leaning towards her; sometimes they laugh, looking into each other's eyes. No doubt they are discussing the new alliance; he seems to think she has another treaty tucked down her bodice. Once Francis lifts her hand. She pulls back, half-resisting, and for one moment it seems he intends to lay her little fingers upon his unspeakable codpiece. Everyone knows that Francis has recently taken the mercury cure. But no one knows if it has worked.

Henry is dancing with the wives of Calais notables: gigue, saltarello. Charles Brandon, his sick wife forgotten, is making his partners scream by throwing them in the air so that their skirts fly up. But Henry's glance keeps straying down the hall to Anne, to Francis. His spine is stiff with his personal terror. His face expresses smiling agony.

Finally, he thinks, I must end this: can it be true, he wonders, that as a subject should, I really love my king?

He ferrets Norfolk out of the dark corner where he is hiding, for fear that he should be commanded to partner the Governor's wife. 'My lord, fetch your niece away. She has done enough diplomacy. Our king is jealous.'

'What? What the devil is his complaint now?' Yet Norfolk sees at a glance what is happening. He swears, and crosses the room – through the dancers, not round them. He takes Anne by her wrist, bending it back as if to snap it. 'By your leave, Highness. My lady, we shall dance.' He jerks her to her feet. Dance they do, though it bears no relation to any dance seen in any hall before this. On the duke's part, a thundering with demon hooves; on her part, a blanched caper, one arm held like a broken wing.

He looks across at Henry. The king's face expresses a sober, righteous satisfaction. Anne should be punished, and by whom except her kin? The French lords huddle together, sniggering. Francis looks on with narrowed eyes.

That night the king withdraws from company early, dismissing even the gentlemen of his privy chamber; only Henry Norris is in and out, trailed by an underling carrying wine, fruit, a large quilt, then a pan of coals; it has turned chilly. The women, in their turn, have become brisk and snappish. Anne's raised voice has been heard. Doors slam. As he is talking to Thomas Wyatt,

Mistress Shelton comes careering towards him. 'My lady wants a Bible!'

'Master Cromwell can recite the whole New Testament,' Wyatt says helpfully.

The girl looks agonised. 'I think she wants it to swear on.'

'In that case I'm no use to her.'

Wyatt catches her hands. 'Who's going to keep you warm tonight, young Shelton?' She pulls away from him, shoots off in pursuit of the scriptures. 'I'll tell you who. Henry Norris.'

He looks after the girl. 'She draws lots?'

'I have been lucky.'

'The king?'

'Perhaps.'

'Recently?'

'Anne would pull out their hearts and roast them.'

He feels he should not go far, in case Henry calls for him. He finds a corner for a game of chess with Edward Seymour. Between moves, 'Your sister Jane ...' he says.

'Odd little creature, isn't she?'

'What age would she be?'

'I don't know ... twenty or so? She walked around at Wolf Hall saying, "These are Thomas Cromwell's sleeves," and nobody knew what she was talking about.' He laughs. 'Very pleased with herself.'

'Has your father made a match for her?'

'There was some talk of –' He looks up. 'Why do you ask?'

'Just distracting you.'

Tom Seymour bursts through the door. 'Good e'en, grandfer,' he shouts at his brother. He knocks his cap off and ruffles his hair. 'There are women waiting for us.'

'My friend here advises not.' Edward dusts his cap. 'He says they're just the same as Englishwomen but dirtier.'

'Voice of experience?' Tom says.

Edward resettles his cap primly. 'How old would our sister Jane be?'

'Twenty-one, twenty-two. Why?'

Edward looks down at the board, reaches for his queen. He sees how he's trapped. He glances up in appreciation. 'How did you manage that?'

Later, he sits with a blank piece of paper before him. He means to write a letter to Cranmer and cast it to the four winds, send it searching through Europe. He picks up his pen but does not write. He revisits in his mind his conversation with Henry, about the ruby. His king imagines he would take part in a backstairs deceit, the kind that might have entertained him in the days when he antiqued cupids and sold them to cardinals. But to defend yourself against such accusations makes you seem guilty. If Henry does not fully trust him, is it surprising? A prince is alone: in his council chamber, in his bedchamber, and finally in Hell's antechamber, stripped – as Harry Percy said – for Judgment.

This visit has compacted the court's quarrels and intrigues, trapped them in the small space within the town's walls. The travellers have become as intimate with each other as cards in a pack: contiguous, but their paper eyes blind. He wonders where Tom Wyatt is, and in what sort of trouble. He doesn't think he can sleep: though not because he's worried about Wyatt. He goes to the window. The moon, as if disgraced, trails rags of black cloud.

In the gardens, torches burn in wall brackets, but he walks away from the light. The faint push and pull of the ocean is steady and insistent as his own heartbeat. He knows he shares this darkness, and within a moment there is a footstep, a rustle of skirts, a faint breathy gulp, a hand sliding on his arm. 'You,' Mary says.

'Me.'

'Do you know they unbolted the door between them?' She laughs, a merciless giggle. 'She is in his arms, naked as she was born. She can't change her mind now.'

411

'Tonight I thought they would quarrel.'

'They did. They like quarrelling. She claims Norfolk has broken her arm. Henry called her a Magdalene and some other names I forget, I think they were Roman ladies. Not Lucrece.'

'No. At least, I hope not. What did she want the Bible for?'

'To swear him. Before witnesses. Me. Norris. He made a binding promise. They are married in God's sight. And he swears he will marry her again in England and crown her queen when spring comes.'

He thinks of the nun, at Canterbury: if you enter into a form of marriage with this unworthy woman, you will not reign seven months.

'So now,' Mary says, 'it is just a question of whether he will find he is able to do the deed.'

'Mary.' He takes her hand. 'Don't frighten me.'

'Henry is timid. He thinks you expect a kingly performance. But if he is shy, Anne will know how to help.' She adds, carefully, 'I mean to say, I have advised her.' She slides her hand on to his shoulder. 'So now, what about us? It has been a weary struggle to bring them here. I think we have earned our recreation.'

No answer. 'You're not still frightened of my uncle Norfolk?'

'Mary, I am terrified of your uncle Norfolk.'

Still, that's not the reason, not the reason why he hesitates, not quite pulling away. Her lips brush his. She asks, 'What are you thinking?'

'I was thinking that if I were not the king's most dutiful servant, it would be possible to be on the next boat out.'

'Where would we go?'

He doesn't remember inviting a friend. 'East. Though I grant this would not be a good starting point.' East of the Boleyns, he thinks. East of everybody. He is thinking of the Middle Sea, not these northern waters; and one night especially, a warm midnight in a house in Larnaca: Venetian lights spilling out on to the dangerous waterfront, the slap of slave feet on tiles, a perfume of incense and coriander. He puts an arm around Mary, encountering something soft, totally unexpected: fox fur. 'Clever of you,' he says.

'Oh, we brought everything. Every stitch. In case we are here till winter.'

A glow of light on flesh. Her throat very white, very soft. All things seem possible, if the duke stays indoors. His fingertip teases out the fur till fur meets flesh. Her shoulder is warm, scented and a little damp. He can feel the bounce of her pulse.

A sound behind him. He turns, dagger in hand. Mary screams, pulls at his arm. The point of the weapon comes to rest against a man's doublet, under the breastbone. 'All right, all right,' says a sober, irritated English voice. 'Put that away.'

'Heavens,' Mary says. 'You almost murdered William Stafford.'

He backs the stranger into the light. When he sees his face, not till then, he draws back the blade. He doesn't know who Stafford is: somebody's horse-keeper? 'William, I thought you weren't coming,' Mary says.

'If I didn't, it seems you had a reserve.'

'You don't know what a woman's life is! You think you've fixed something with a man, and you haven't. He says he'll meet you, and he doesn't turn up.'

It is a cry from the heart. 'Give you good night,' he says. Mary turns as if to say, oh, don't go. 'Time I said my prayers.'

A wind has blown up from the Narrow Sea, snapping at the rigging in the harbour, rattling the windows inland. Tomorrow, he thinks, it may rain. He lights a candle and goes back to his letter. But his letter has no attraction for him. Leaves flurry from the gardens, from the orchards. Images move in the air beyond the glass, gulls blown like ghosts: a flash of his wife Elizabeth's white cap, as she follows him to the door on her last morning. Except that she didn't: she was sleeping, wrapped in damp linen, under the yellow turkey quilt. If he thinks of the fortune that brought him here he thinks equally of the fortune that brought him to that morning five years ago, going out of Austin Friars a married man, files of Wolsey's business under his arm: was he happy then? He doesn't know.

That night in Cyprus, long ago now, he had been on the verge of handing his resignation to his bank, or at least of asking them for letters of introduction to take him east. He was curious to see the Holy Land, its plant life and people, to kiss the stones where the disciples had walked, to bargain in the hidden quarters of strange cities and in black tents where veiled women scuttle like cockroaches into corners. That night his fortunes had been in equipoise. In the room behind him, as he looked out over the harbour lights, he heard a woman's throaty laughter, her soft '*al-hamdu lillah*' as she shook the ivory dice in her hand. He heard her spill them, heard them rattle and come to rest: 'What is it?'

East is high. West is low. Gambling is not a vice, if you can afford to do it.

'It is three and three.'

Is that low? You must say it is. Fate has not given him a shove, more of a gentle tap. 'I shall go home.'

'Not tonight, though. It is too late for the tide.'

Next day he felt the gods at his back, like a breeze. He turned back towards Europe. Home then was a narrow shuttered house on a quiet canal, Anselma kneeling, creamily naked under her trailing nightgown of green damask, its sheen blackish in candle-light; kneeling before the small silver altarpiece she kept in her room, which was precious to her, she had told him, the most precious thing I own. Excuse me just a moment, she had said to him; she prayed in her own language, now coaxing, now almost threatening, and she must have teased from her silver saints some flicker of grace, or perceived some deflection in their glinting rectitude, because she stood up and turned to him, saying, 'I'm ready now,' tugging apart the silk ties of her gown so that he could take her breasts in his hands.

III
Early Mass
November 1532

Rafe is standing over him, saying it is seven o'clock already. The king has gone to Mass.

He has slept in a bed of phantoms. 'We did not want to wake you. You never sleep late.'

The wind is a muted sigh in the chimneys. A handful of rain like gravel rattles against the window, swirls away, and is thrown back again. 'We may be in Calais for some time,' he says.

When Wolsey had gone to France, five years ago, he had asked him to watch the situation at court and to pass on a report of when the king and Anne went to bed. He had said, how will I know when it happens? The cardinal had said, 'I should think you'll know by his face.'

The wind has dropped and the rain respited by the time he reaches the church, but the streets have turned to mud, and the people waiting to see the lords come out still have their coats pulled over their heads, like a new race of walking decapitees. He pushes through the crowd, then threads and whispers his way through the gathered gentlemen: *s'il vous plaît, c'est urgent*, make way for a big sinner. They laugh and let him through.

Anne comes out on the Governor's arm. He looks tense – it seems his gout is troubling him – but he is attentive to her, murmuring pleasantries to which he gets no response; her expression is adjusted to a careful blankness. The king has a Wingfield lady on his arm, face uptilted, chattering. He is taking no notice of her at all. He looks large, broad, benign. His regal glance scans the crowd. It alights on him. The king smiles.

As he leaves the church, Henry puts on his hat. It is a big hat, a new hat. And in that hat there is a feather.

PART FIVE

I
Anna Regina
1533

The two children sit on a bench in the hall of Austin Friars. They are so small that their legs stick straight out in front of them, and as they are still in smocks one cannot tell their sex. Under their caps, their dimpled faces beam. That they look so fat and contented is a credit to the young woman, Helen Barre, who now unwinds the thread of her tale: daughter of a bankrupt small merchant out of Essex, wife of one Matthew Barre who beat her and deserted her, 'leaving me,' she says, indicating, 'with that one in my belly.'

The neighbours are always coming at him with parish problems. Unsafe cellar doors. A noisome goose house. A husband and wife who shout and bang pans all night, so the next house can't get to sleep. He tries not to fret if these things cut into his time, and he minds Helen less than a goose house. Mentally, he takes her out of cheap shrunken wool and re-dresses her in some figured velvet he saw yesterday, six shillings the yard. Her hands, he sees, are skinned and swollen from rough work; he supplies kid gloves.

'Though when I say he deserted me, it may be that he is dead. He was a great drinker and a brawler. A man who knew him told me he came off worst in a fight, and I should seek him at the bottom of the river. But someone else saw him on the quays at Tilbury, with a travelling bag. So which am I – wife or widow?'

'I will look into it. Though I think you would rather I didn't find him. How have you lived?'

'When he went first I was stitching for a sailmaker. Since I came up to London to search, I've been hiring out by the day. I have been in the laundry at a convent near Paul's, helping at the yearly wash of their bed linen. They find me a good worker, they say they will give me a pallet in the attics, but they won't take the children.'

Another instance of the church's charity. He runs up against them all the time. 'We cannot have you a slave to a set of hypocrite women. You must come here. I am sure you will be useful. The house is filling up all the time, and I am building, as you see.' She must be a good girl, he thinks, to turn her back on making a living in the obvious way; if she walked along the street, she wouldn't be short of offers. 'They tell me you would like to learn to read, so you can read the gospel.'

'Some women I met took me to what they call a night school. It was in a cellar at Broadgate. Before that, I knew Noah, the Three Kings, and father Abraham, but St Paul I had never heard of. At home on our farm we had pucks who used to turn the milk and blow up thunderstorms, but I am told they are not Christians. I wish we had stayed farming, for all that. My father was no hand at town life.' Her eyes, anxious, follow the children. They have launched themselves off the bench and toddled across the flag-stones to see the picture that is growing on the wall, and their every step causes her to hold her breath. The workman is a German, a young boy Hans recommended for a simple job, and he turns around – he speaks no English – to explain to the children what he is doing. A rose. Three lions, see them jump. Two black birds.

'Red,' the elder child cries.

'She knows colours,' Helen says, pink with pride. 'She is also beginning on one-two-three.'

The space where the arms of Wolsey used to be is being repainted with his own newly granted arms: *azure, on a fess*

420

between three lions rampant or, a rose gules, barbed vert, between two Cornish choughs proper. 'You see, Helen,' he says, 'those black birds were Wolsey's emblem.' He laughs. 'There are people who hoped they would never see them again.'

'There are other people, of our sort, who do not understand it.'

'You mean night school people?'

'They say, how can a man who loves the gospel, have loved such a man as that?'

'I never liked his haughty manners, you know, and his processions every day, the state he kept. And yet there was never a man more active in the service of England since England began. And also,' he says sadly, 'when you came into his confidence, he was a man of such grace and ease … Helen, can you come here today?' He is thinking of those nuns and the yearly wash of their bed linen. He is imagining the cardinal's appalled face. Laundry women followed his train as whores follow an army, hot from their hour-by-hour exertions. At York Place he had a bath made, deep enough for a man to stand up in it, the room heated by a stove such as you find in the Low Countries, and many a time he had negotiated business with the cardinal's bobbing, boiled-looking head. Henry has taken it over now, and splashes about in it with favoured gentlemen, who submit to being ducked under the water and half-drowned by their lord, if his mood takes him that way.

The painter offers the brush to the elder child. Helen glows. 'Careful, darling,' she says. A blob of blue is applied. You are a little adept, the painter says. *Gefällt es Ihnen, Herr Cromwell, sind Sie stolz darauf?'*

He says to Helen, he asks if I am pleased and proud. She says, if you are not, your friends will be proud for you.

I am always translating, he thinks: if not language to language, then person to person. Anne to Henry. Henry to Anne. Those days when he wants soothing, and she is as prickly as a holly bush. Those times – they do occur – when his gaze strays after another woman, and she follows it, and storms off to her own apartments. He, Cromwell, goes about like some public poet, carrying assurances of desire, each to each.

It is hardly three o'clock, and already the room is half-dark. He picks up the younger child, who flops against his shoulder and falls asleep with the speed at which someone pushed falls off a wall. 'Helen,' he says, 'this household is full of pert young men, and they will all put themselves forward in teaching you to read, bringing you presents and trying to sweeten your days. Do learn, and take the presents, and be happy here with us, but if anyone is too forward, you must tell me, or tell Rafe Sadler. He is the boy with the little red beard. Though I should not say boy.' It will be twenty years, soon, since he brought Rafe in from his father's house, a lowering, dark day like this, rain bucketing from the heavens, the child slumped against his shoulder as he carried him into his hall at Fenchurch Street.

The storms had kept them in Calais for ten days. Ships out of Boulogne were wrecked, Antwerp flooded, much of the countryside put under water. He would like to get messages to his friends, enquiring after their lives and property, but the roads are impassable, Calais itself a floating island upon which a happy monarch reigns. He goes to the king's lodgings to ask for an audience – business doesn't stop in bad weather – but he is told, 'The king cannot see you this morning. He and Lady Anne are composing some music for the harp.'

Rafe catches his eye and they walk away. 'Let us hope in time they have a little song to show for it.'

Thomas Wyatt and Henry Norris get drunk together in a low tavern. They swear eternal friendship. But their followers have a fight in the inn yard and roll each other in mud.

He never sets eyes on Mary Boleyn. Presumably she and Stafford have found some bolt-hole where they can compose together.

By candlelight, at noon, Lord Berners shows him his library, limping energetically from desk to desk, handling with care the old folios from which he has made his scholarly translations. Here is a romance of King Arthur: 'When I started reading it I almost gave up the project. It was clear to me it was too fantastical to be true. But little by little, as I read, you know, it appeared to me that there was a moral in this tale.' He does not say what it is. 'And here is Froissart done into English, which His Majesty himself bade me undertake. I could not do other, for he had just lent me five hundred pounds. Would you like to see my translations from the Italian? They are private ones, I have not sent them to the printer.'

He spends an afternoon with the manuscripts, and they discuss them at supper. Lord Berners holds a position, chancellor of the exchequer, which Henry has given him for life, but because he is not in London and attending to it, it does not bring him in much money, or the influence it should. 'I know you are a good man for business. Might you in confidence look over my accounts? They're not what you'd call in order.'

Lord Berners leaves him alone with the dog's breakfast that he calls his ledgers. An hour passes: the wind whistles across the rooftops, the candle flames tremble, hail batters the glass. He hears the scrape of his host's bad foot: an anxious face peers around the door. 'What joy?'

All he can find is money owing. This is what you get for devoting yourself to scholarship and serving the king across the sea, when you could be at court with sharp teeth and eyes and elbows, ready to seize your advantage. 'I wish you'd called on me earlier. There are always things that can be done.'

'Ah, but who knew you, Master Cromwell?' the old man says. 'One exchanged letters, yes. Wolsey's business, king's business. But I never knew you. It did not seem at all likely I should know you, until now.'

On the day they are finally ready to embark, the boy from the alchemists' inn turns up. 'You at last! What have you got for me?'

The boy displays his empty hands, and launches into English, of a sort. '*On dit* those magi have retoured to Paris.'

'Then I am disappointed.'

'You are hard to find, monsieur. I go to the place where *le roi Henri* and the *Grande Putain* are lodged, "*je cherche milord Cremuel*," and the persons there laughed at me and beat me.'

'That is because I am not a milord.'

'In that case, I do not know what a milord in your country looks like.' He offers the boy a coin for his efforts, and another for the beating, but he shakes his head. 'I thought to take service with you, monsieur. I have made up my mind to go travelling.'

'Your name is?'

'Christophe.'

'You have a family name?'

'*Ça ne fait rien.*'

'You have parents?'

A shrug.

'Your age?'

'What age would you say?'

'I know you can read. Can you fight?'

'There is much fighting *chez vous*?'

Christophe has his own squat build; he needs feeding up, but a year or two from now he will be hard to knock over. He puts him at fifteen, no more. 'You are in trouble with the law?'

'In France,' he says, disparagingly: as one might say, in far Cathay.

'You are a thief?'

The boy makes a jabbing motion, invisible knife in his fist.

'You left someone dead?'

'He didn't look well.'

He grins. 'You're sure you want Christophe for your name? You can change it now, but not later.'

'You understand me, monsieur.'

Christ, of course I do. You could be my son. Then he looks at him closely, to make sure that he isn't; that he isn't one of these brawling children the cardinal spoke of, whom he has left by the Thames, and not impossibly by other rivers, in other climes. But Christophe's eyes are a wide, untroubled blue. 'You are not afraid of the sea voyage?' he asks. 'In my house in London there are many French speakers. You'll soon be one of us.'

Now at Austin Friars, Christophe pursues him with questions. Those magi, what is it they have? Is it a carte of buried treasure? Is it – he flaps his arms – the instructions for one to make a flying machine? Is it a machine to *faire* great explosions, or a military dragon, breathes out fire?

He says, 'Have you ever heard of Cicero?'

'No. But I am prepared to hear of him. Till today I have never heard of Bishop Gardineur. *On dit* you have stole his strawberry beds and give them to the king's mistress, and now he intends …' the boy breaks off, and again gives his impression of a military dragon, 'to ruin you utterly and pursue you unto death.'

'And well beyond, if I know my man.'

There have been worse accounts of his situation. He wants to say, she is not a mistress, not any more, but the secret – though it must soon be an open secret – is not his to tell.

Twenty-fifth of January 1533, dawn, a chapel at Whitehall, his friend Rowland Lee as priest, Anne and Henry take their vows, confirm the contract they made in Calais: almost in secret, with no celebration, just a huddle of witnesses, the married pair both speechless except for the small admissions of intent forced out of them by the ceremony. Henry Norris is pale and sober: was it kind to make him witness it twice over, Anne being given to another man?

William Brereton is a witness, as he is in attendance in the king's privy chamber. 'Are you truly here?' he asks him. 'Or are you somewhere else? You gentlemen tell me you can bilocate, like great saints.'

Brereton glares. 'You've been writing letters up to Chester.'

'The king's business. How not?'

They must do this in a mutter, as Rowland joins the hands of bride and groom. 'I'll tell you just once. Keep away from my family's affairs. Or you'll come off worse, Master Cromwell, than you can imagine.'

Anne is attended by only one lady, her sister. As they leave – the king towing his wife, hand on her upper arm, towards a little harp music – Mary turns and gives him a sumptuous smile. She holds up her hand, thumb and finger an inch apart.

She had always said, I will be the first to know. It will be me who lets out her bodices.

He calls William Brereton back, politely; he says, you have made a mistake in threatening me.

He goes back to his office in Westminster. He wonders, does the king know yet? Probably not.

He sits down to his drafting. They bring in candles. He sees the shadow of his own hand moving across the paper, his own unconcealable fist unmasked by velvet glove. He wants nothing between himself and the weave of the paper, the black running line of ink, so he takes off his rings, Wolsey's turquoise and Francis's ruby – at New Year, the king slid it from his own finger and gave it back to him, in the setting the Calais gold-smith had made, and said, as rulers do, in a rush of confidence, now that will be a sign between us, Cromwell, send a paper with this and I shall know it comes from your hand even if you lack your seal.

A confidant of Henry's who was standing by – it was Nicholas Carew – had remarked, His Majesty's ring fits you without adjustment. He said, so it does.

He hesitates, his quill hovering. He writes, 'This realm of England is an Empire.' *This realm of England is an Empire, and so has been accepted in the world, governed by one Supreme Head and King ...*

At eleven o'clock, when the day has brightened as much as it will, he eats dinner with Cranmer in his lodging at Cannon Row, where he is living till his new dignity is conferred and he can move into Lambeth Palace. He has been practising his new signature, Thomas Elect of Canterbury. Soon he will dine in state, but today, like a threadbare scholar, he shoves his papers aside while some table linen is laid and they bring in the salt fish, over which he signs a grace.

'That won't improve it,' he says. 'Who's cooking for you? I'll send someone over.'

'So, is the marriage made?' It is like Cranmer to wait to be told: to work six hours in silent patience, head down over his books.

'Yes, Rowland was up to his office. He didn't wed her to Norris, or the king to her sister.' He shakes out his napkin. 'I know a thing. But you must coax it from me.'

He is hoping that Cranmer, by way of coaxing, will impart the secret he promised in his letter, the secret written down the side of the page. But it must have been some minor indiscretion, now forgotten. And because Canterbury Elect is occupied in poking uncertainly at scales and skin, he says, 'She, Anne, she is already having a child.'

Cranmer glances up. 'If you tell it in that tone, people will think you take the credit yourself.'

'Are you not astonished? Are you not pleased?'

'I wonder what fish this purports to be?' Cranmer says with mild interest. 'Naturally I am delighted. But I knew it, you see, because this marriage is clean – why would not God bless it with offspring? And with an heir?'

'Of course, with an heir. Look.' He takes out the papers he has been working on. Cranmer washes his fishy fingers and hunches towards the candle flame. 'So after Easter,' he says, reading, 'it will be against the law and the king's prerogative to make an appeal in any matter to the Pope. So there is Katherine's suit dead and buried. And I, Canterbury, can decide the king's cause in our own courts. Well, this has been long enough coming.'

He laughs. '*You* were long enough coming.' Cranmer was in Mantua when he heard of the honour the king intended for him. He began his journey circuitously: Stephen Vaughan met him at Lyons, and hustled him over the winter roads and through the snowdrifts of Picardy to the boat. 'Why did you delay? Doesn't every boy want to be an archbishop? Though not me, if I think back. What I wanted was my own bear.'

Cranmer looks at him, his expression speculative. 'I'm sure that could be arranged for you.'

Gregory has asked him, how will we know when Dr Cranmer is making a joke? He has told him, you won't, they are as rare as apple blossom in January. And now, for some weeks, he will be half-fearful that a bear will turn up at his door. As they part that day, Cranmer glances up from the table and says, 'Of course, I don't officially know.'

'About the child?'

'About the marriage. As I am to be judge in the matter of the king's old marriage, it would not be proper for me to hear that his new one has already taken place.'

'Right,' he says. 'What Rowland gets up to in the early hours of the morning is a matter for himself alone.' He leaves Cranmer with head bowed over the remains of their meal, as if studying to reassemble the fish.

As our severance from the Vatican is not yet complete, we cannot have a new archbishop unless the Pope appoints him. Delegates in Rome are empowered to say anything, promise anything, *pro tem*, to get Clement to agree. The king says, aghast, 'Do you know how much the papal bulls cost, for Canterbury? And that I shall have to pay for them? And you know how much it costs to install him?' He adds, 'It must be done properly, of course, nothing omitted, nothing scanted.'

'It will be the last money Your Majesty sends to Rome, if it rests with me.'

'And do you know,' the king says, as if he has discovered something astonishing, 'that Cranmer has not a penny of his own? He can contribute nothing.'

He borrows the money, on the Crown's behalf, from a rich Genovese he knows called Salvago. To persuade him into the loan, he sends around to his house an engraving which he knows Sebastian covets. It shows a young man standing in a garden, his eyes turned upwards to an empty window, at which it is to be hoped very soon a lady will appear; her scent hangs already in the air, and birds on the boughs look enquiringly into the vacancy, ready to sing. In his two hands the young man holds a book; it is a book shaped like a heart.

Cranmer sits on committees every day, in back rooms at Westminster. He is writing a paper for the king, to show that even if his brother's marriage to Katherine was not consummated, it does not affect the case for the annulment, for certainly they intended to be married, and that intention creates affinity; also, in the nights they spent together, it must have been their intention to make children, even if they did not go about it the right way. In order not to make a liar out of Henry or Katherine, one or the other, the committee men think up circumstances in which the match may have been partly consummated, or somewhat consummated, and to do this they have to imagine every disaster and shame that can occur between a man and a woman alone in a room in the dark. Do you like the work, he enquires; looking at their hunched and dusty persons, he judges them to have the experience they need. Cranmer in his writing keeps calling the queen 'the most serene Katherine', as if to separate her untroubled face, framed by a linen pillow, from the indignities being forced on her lower body: the boy's fumbling and scrabbling, the pawing at her thighs.

Meanwhile Anne, the hidden Queen of England, breaks free from her gentleman companions as she walks through a gallery at

Whitehall; she laughs as she breaks into a trot, almost a skip, and they reach out to contain her, as if she is dangerous, but she flings their hands away from her, laughing. 'Do you know, I have a great longing to eat apples? The king says it means I am having a baby, but I tell him no, no, it can't be that ...' She whirls around, around again. She flushes, tears bounce out of her eyes and seem to fly away from her like the waters of an unregulated fountain.

Thomas Wyatt pushes through the crowd. 'Anne ...' He snatches at her hands, he pulls her towards him. 'Anne, hush, sweetheart ... hush ...' She collapses into hiccupping sobs, folding herself against his shoulder. Wyatt holds her fast; his eyes travel around, as if he had found himself naked in the road, and is looking for some traveller to come along with a garment to cover his shame. Among the bystanders is Chapuys; the ambassador makes a rapid, purposeful exit, his little legs working, a sneer stamped on his face.

So that's the news sped to the Emperor. It would have been good if the old marriage were out, the new marriage in, confirmed to Europe before Anne's happy state were announced. But then, life is never perfect for the servant of a prince; as Thomas More used to say, we should not look to go to Heaven on feather beds.

Two days later he is alone with Anne; she is tucked into a window embrasure, eyes closed, basking like a cat in a scarce shaft of winter sun. She stretches out her hand to him, hardly knowing who he is; any man will do? He takes her fingertips. Her black eyes snap open. It's like a shop when the shutters are taken down: good morning, Master Cromwell, what can we sell each other today?

'I am tired of Mary,' she says. 'And I would like to be rid of her.'

Does she mean Katherine's daughter, the princess? 'She should be married,' she says, 'and out of my way. I never want to have to see her. I don't want to have to think about her. I have long imagined her married to some obscure person.'

He waits, still wondering.

'I don't suppose she would be a bad wife, for somebody who was prepared to keep her chained to the wall.'

'Ah. Mary your sister.'

'What did you think? Oh,' she laughs, 'you thought I meant Mary the king's bastard. Well, now you put it in my mind, she should be married too. What age is she?'

'Seventeen this year.'

'And still a dwarf?' Anne doesn't wait for an answer. 'I shall find some old gentleman for her, some very honourable feeble old gentleman, who will get no children on her and whom I will pay to stay away from court. But as for Lady Carey, what is to be done? She cannot marry you. We tease her that you are her choice. Some ladies have a secret preference for common men. We say, Mary, oh, how you long to repose in the arms of the blacksmith … even at the thought, you are growing hot.'

'Are you happy?' he asks her.

'Yes.' She drops her eyes, and her small hands rest on her ribcage. 'Yes, because of this. You see,' she says slowly, 'I was always desired. But now I am valued. And that is a different thing, I find.'

He pauses, to let her think her own thoughts: which he sees are precious to her. 'So,' she says, 'you have a nephew Richard, a Tudor of sorts, though I am sure I cannot understand how that came about.'

'I can draw out for you the tree of descent.'

She shakes her head, smiling. 'I wouldn't give you the trouble. Since this,' her fingers slip downwards, 'I wake up in the morning and I scarcely remember my name. I always wondered why women were foolish, and now I know.'

'You mentioned my nephew.'

'I have seen him with you. He looks a determined boy. He might do for her. What she wants are furs and jewels. You can give her those, can't you? And a child in the cradle every other

431

year. As for who fathers it, you can make your own household arrangements about that.'

'I thought,' he says, 'that your sister had an attachment?'

He doesn't want revenge: just clarification.

'Does she? Oh well, Mary's attachments ... usually passing and sometimes very odd – as you know, don't you.' It's not a question. 'Bring them to court, your children. Let's see them.'

He leaves her, eyes closing again, edging into marginal warmth, the small sort of sunbeam that is all February offers.

The king has given him lodgings within the old palace at Westminster, for when he works too late to get home. This being so, he has to walk mentally through his rooms at Austin Friars, picking up his memory images from where he has left them on windowsills and under stools and in the woollen petals of the flowers strewn in the tapestry at Anselma's feet. At the end of a long day he takes supper with Cranmer and with Rowland Lee, who stamps between the various working parties, urging them along. Sometimes Audley joins them, the Lord Chancellor, but they keep no state, just sit down like a bunch of inky students, and talk till it's Cranmer's bedtime. He wants to work them out, these people, test how far he can rely on them, and find out their weaknesses. Audley is a prudent lawyer who can sift a sentence like a cook sifting a sack of rice for grit. An eloquent speaker, he is tenacious of a point, and devoted to his career; now that he's Chancellor he aims to make an income to go with the office. As for what he believes, it's up for negotiation; he believes in Parliament, in the king's power exercised in Parliament, and in matters of faith ... let's say his convictions are flexible. As for Lee, he wonders if he believes in God at all – though it doesn't stop him having a bishopric in his sights. He says, 'Rowland, will you take Gregory into your household? I think Cambridge has done all that it can for him. And I admit that Gregory has done nothing for Cambridge.'

'I'll take him up the country with me,' Rowland says, 'when I go to have a row with the northern bishops. He is a good boy,

Gregory. Not the most forward, but I can understand that. We'll make him useful yet.'

'You don't intend him for the church?' Cranmer asks.

'I said,' growls Rowland, 'we'll make him useful.'

At Westminster his clerks are in and out, with news and gossip and paperwork, and he keeps Christophe with him, supposedly to look after his clothes, but really to make him laugh. He misses the music they have nightly at Austin Friars, and the women's voices, heard from other rooms.

He is at the Tower most days of the week, persuading the foremen to keep their men working through frost and rain; checking the paymaster's accounts, and making a new inventory of the king's jewels and plate. He calls on the Wardens of the Mint, and suggests a spot check on the weight of the king's coinage. 'What I should like to do,' he says, 'is make our English coins so sound that the merchants over the sea won't even bother weighing them.'

'Do you have authority for this?'

'Why, what are you hiding?'

He has written a memorandum for the king, setting out the sources of his yearly revenues, and detailing through which government offices they pass. It is remarkably concise. The king reads it and reads it again. He turns the paper over to see if anything convoluted and inexplicable is written on the back. But there is nothing more than meets his eye.

'It's not news,' he says, half-apologetic. 'The late cardinal carried it in his head. I shall keep calling at the Mint. If Your Majesty pleases.'

At the Tower he calls on a prisoner, John Frith. At his request, which does not count for nothing, the prisoner is cleanly kept above ground, with warm bedding, sufficient food, a supply of wine, paper, ink; though he has advised him to put away his writings if he hears the key in his lock. He stands by while the turnkey admits him, his eyes on the ground, not liking what he is going to see; but John Frith rises from his table, a gentle, slender young boy, a scholar in Greek, and says, Master Cromwell, I knew you would come.

When he takes Frith's hands he finds them all bones, cold and dry and with tell-tale traces of ink. He thinks, he cannot be so delicate, if he has lived so long. He was one of the scholars shut in the cellar at Wolsey's college, where the Bible men were held because there was no other secure place. When the summer plague struck underground, Frith lay in the dark with the corpses, till someone remembered to let him out.

'Master Frith,' he says, 'if I had been in London when you were taken –'

'But while you were in Calais, Thomas More was at work.'

'What made you come back into England? No, don't tell me. If you were going about Tyndale's work, I had better not know it. They say you have taken a wife, is that correct? In Antwerp? The one thing the king cannot abide – no, many things he cannot abide – but he hates married priests. And he hates Luther, and you have translated Luther into English.'

'You put the case so well, for my prosecution.'

'You must help me to help you. If I could get you an audience with the king ... you would have to be prepared, he is a most astute theologian ... do you think you could soften your answers, to accommodate him?'

The fire is built up but the room is still cold. You cannot get away from the mists and exhalations of the Thames. Frith says, his voice barely audible, 'Thomas More still has some credit with the king. And he has written him a letter, saying,' he manages to smile, 'that I am Wycliffe, Luther and Zwingli rolled together and tied up in string – one reformer stuffed inside another, as for a feast you might parcel a pheasant inside a chicken inside a goose. More means to dine on me, so do not injure your credit by asking for mercy. As for softening my answers ... I believe, and I will say before any tribunal –'

'Do not, John.'

'I will say before any tribunal what I will say before my last judge – the Eucharist is but bread, of penance we have no need, Purgatory is an invention ungrounded in scripture –'

'If some men come to you and say, come with us, Frith, you go with them. They will be my men.'

'You think you can take me out of the Tower?'

Tyndale's Bible says, with God shall nothing be unpossible. 'If not out of the Tower, then when you are taken to be questioned, that will be your chance. Be ready to take it.'

'But to what purpose?' Frith speaks kindly, as if speaking to a young pupil. 'You think you can keep me at your house and wait for the king to change his mind? I should have to break out of there, and walk to Paul's Cross, and say before the Londoners what I have already said.'

'Your witness cannot wait?'

'Not on Henry. I might wait till I was old.'

'They will burn you.'

'And you think I cannot bear the pain. You are right, I cannot. But they will give me no choice. As More says, it hardly makes a man a hero, to agree to stand and burn once he is chained to a stake. I have written books and I cannot unwrite them. I cannot unbelieve what I believe. I cannot unlive my life.'

He leaves him. Four o'clock: the river traffic sparse, a fine and penetrative vapour creeping between air and water.

Next day, a day of crisp blue cold, the king comes down in the royal barge to see the progress of the work, with the new French envoy; they are confidential, the king walking with a hand on de Dinteville's shoulder, or rather on his padding; the Frenchman is wearing so many layers that he seems broader than the door-ways, but he is still shivering. 'Our friend here must get some sport to warm his blood,' the king says, 'and he is a bungler with the bow – when we went into the butts last, he shook so much I thought he would shoot himself in the foot. He complains we are not serious falconers, so I have said he should go out with you, Cromwell.'

Is this a promise of time off? The king strolls away and leaves them. 'Not if it's cold like this,' the envoy says. 'I'm not standing in a field with the wind whistling, it will be the death of me. When shall we see the sun again?'

'Oh, about June. But the falcons will be moulting by then. I aim to have mine flying again in August, so *nil desperandum*, monsieur, we shall have some sport.'

'You wouldn't postpone this coronation, would you?' It's always so; after a little chaff and chat, out of his mouth pops an ambassador's purpose. 'Because when my master made the treaty, he didn't expect Henry to be flaunting his supposed wife and her big belly. If he were to keep her quietly, it would be a different matter.'

He shakes his head. There will be no postponement. Henry claims he has the support of the bishops, the nobles, judges, Parliament and the people; Anne's coronation is his chance to prove it. 'Never mind,' he says. 'Tomorrow we entertain the papal nuncio. You will see how my master will manage him.'

Henry calls down to them, from the walls, 'Come up here, sir, see the prospect of my river.'

'Do you wonder I shake?' the Frenchman says with passion. 'Do you wonder I tremble before him? My river. My city. My salvation, cut out and embroidered just for me. My personally tailored English god.' He swears under his breath, and begins to climb.

When the papal nuncio comes to Greenwich, Henry takes him by the hand and tells him frankly how his ungodly councillors torment him, and how he longs for a return of perfect amity with Pope Clement.

You could watch Henry every day for a decade and not see the same thing. Choose your prince: he admires Henry more and more. Sometimes he seems hapless, sometimes feckless, sometimes a child, sometimes master of his trade. Sometimes he seems an artist, in the way his eye ranges over his work; sometimes his hand moves and he doesn't seem to see it move. If he had been called to a lower station in life, he could have been a travelling player, and leader of his troupe.

At Anne's command, he brings his nephew to court, Gregory too; Rafe the king already knows, for he is always at his elbow. The king stands gazing for a long time at Richard. 'I see it. Indeed I do.'

There is nothing in Richard's face, as far as he can see, to show that he has Tudor blood, but the king is looking at him with the eye of a man who wants relatives. 'Your grandfather ap Evan the archer was a great servant to the king my father. You have a fine build. I should like to see you in the tilt yard. I should like to see you carry your colours in the joust.'

Richard bows. And then the king, because he is the essence of courtesy, turns to Gregory, and says, 'And you, Master Gregory, you are a very fine young man too.'

As the king walks away, Gregory's face opens in simple pleasure. He puts his hand on his arm, the place the king has touched, as if transferring regal grace to his fingertips. 'He is very splendid. He is so splendid. Beyond anything I ever thought. And to speak to me!' He turns to his father. 'How do you manage to speak to him every day?'

Richard gives him a sideways look. Gregory thumps him on the arm. 'Never mind your grandfather the archer, what would he say if he knew your father was *that* big?' He shows between finger and thumb the stature of Morgan Williams. 'I have been riding at the ring these many years. I have been riding at the Saracen's image and putting my lance just so, thud, right over his black Saracen's heart.'

'Yes,' Richard says patiently, 'but, squib, you will find a living knight a tougher proposition than a wooden infidel. You never think of the cost – armour of show quality, a stable of trained horses –'

'We can afford it,' he says. 'It seems our days as foot soldiers are behind us.'

That night at Austin Friars he asks Richard to come to speak with him alone after supper. Possibly he is at fault, in putting it as a business proposition, spelling out to him what Anne has suggested about his marriage. 'Build nothing on it. We have yet to get the king's approval.'

Richard says, 'But she doesn't know me.'

He waits, for objections; not knowing someone, is that an objection? 'I won't force you.'

Richard looks up. 'Are you sure?'

When have I, when have I ever forced anyone to do anything, he starts to say: but Richard cuts in, 'No, you don't, I agree, it's just that you are practised at persuading, and sometimes it's quite difficult, sir, to distinguish being persuaded by you from being knocked down in the street and stamped on.'

'I know Lady Carey is older than you, but she is very beautiful, I think the most beautiful woman at court, and she is not as witless as everyone thinks, and she has not got any of her sister's malice in her.' In a strange way, he thinks, she has been a good friend to me. 'And instead of being the king's unrecognised cousin, you would be his brother-in-law. We would all profit.'

'A title, perhaps. For me, and for you. Brilliant matches for Alice and Jo. What about Gregory? A countess at least for him.' Richard's voice is flat. Is he talking himself into it? It's hard to tell. With many people, most people perhaps, the book of their heart lies open to him, but there are times when it's easier to read outsiders than your own family. 'And Thomas Boleyn would be my father-in-law. And Uncle Norfolk would really be our uncle.'

'Imagine his face.'

'Oh, his face. Yes, one would go barefoot over hot coals to see his expression.'

'Think about it. Don't tell anybody.'

Richard goes out with a bob of the head but without another word. It seems he interprets 'don't tell anybody' as 'don't tell anybody but Rafe', because ten minutes later Rafe comes in, and stands looking at him, with his eyebrows raised. Red-headed people can look quite strained when they are raising eyebrows that aren't really there. He says, 'You need not tell Richard that Mary Boleyn once proposed herself to me. There's nothing between us. It won't be like Wolf Hall, if that's what you're thinking.'

'And what if the bride thinks different? I wonder you don't marry her to Gregory.'

'Gregory is too young. Richard is twenty-three, it is a good age to marry if you can afford it. And you have passed it – it's time you married too.'

'I'm going, before you find a Boleyn for me.' Rafe turns back and says softly, 'Only this, sir, and I think it is what gives Richard pause … all our lives and fortunes depend now on that lady, and as well as being mutable she is mortal, and the whole history of the king's marriage tells us a child in the womb is not an heir in the cradle.'

In March, news comes from Calais that Lord Berners has died. The afternoon in his library, the storm blowing outside: it seems when he looks back a haven of peace, the last hour he had to himself. He wants to make an offer for his books – a generous one, to help Lady Berners – but the folios seem to have jumped off their desks and walked, some in the direction of Francis Bryan, the old man's nephew, and some to another connection of his, Nicholas Carew. 'Would you forgive his debts,' he asks Henry, 'at least for his wife's lifetime? You know he leaves –'

'No sons.' Henry's mind has moved ahead: once I was in that unhappy state, no sons, but soon I shall have my heir.

He brings Anne some majolica bowls. The word *maschio* is painted on the outside, and inside are pictures of plump blond-haired babies, each with a coy little phallus. She laughs. The Italians say for a boy you have to keep warm, he tells her. Heat up your wine to heat up your blood. No cold fruit, no fish.

Jane Seymour says, 'Do you think it's already decided, what it will be, or does God decide later? Do you think it knows itself, what it is? Do you think if we could see inside you, we would be able to tell?'

'Jane, I wish you were still down in Wiltshire,' Mary Shelton says.

Anne says, 'You needn't cut me up, Mistress Seymour. It is a boy, and no one is to say or think otherwise.' She frowns, and you can see her bending, concentrating, the great force of her will.

'I'd like a baby,' Jane says.

'Watch yourself,' Lady Rochford tells her. 'If your belly shows, mistress, we'll have you bricked up alive.'

'In her family,' Anne says, 'they'd give her a bouquet. They don't know what continence means, down at Wolf Hall.'

Jane is flushed and trembling. 'I meant no harm.'

'Leave her,' Anne says. 'It's like baiting a fieldmouse.' She turns to him. 'Your bill is not passed yet. Tell me what is the delay.'

The bill, she means, to forbid appeals to Rome. He begins to explain to her the strength of the opposition, but she raises her eyebrows and says, 'My father is speaking for you in the Lords, and Norfolk. So who dare oppose us?'

'I shall have it through by Easter, depend upon it.'

'The woman we saw in Canterbury, they say her people are printing a book of her prophecies.'

'That may be, but I shall make sure no one reads it.'

'They say on St Catherine's Day last, while we were at Calais, she saw a vision of the so-called princess Mary crowned queen.' Her voice runs on, fluid, rapid, these are my enemies, this prophetess and those about her, Katherine who is plotting with

440

the Emperor, her daughter Mary the supposed heir, Mary's old governess Margaret Pole, Lady Salisbury, she and all her family are my enemies, her son Lord Montague, her son Reginald Pole who is abroad, people talk of his claim to the throne so why can he not be brought back, his loyalty examined? Henry Courtenay, the Marquis of Exeter, he believes he has a claim, but when my son is born that will put him out of his conceit. Lady Exeter, Gertrude, she is forever complaining that noblemen are being put down from their places by men of low birth, and you know who she means by that.

My lady, her sister says softly, do not distress yourself.

I am not distressed, Anne says. Her hand over the growing child, she says calmly, 'These people want me dead.'

The days are still short, the king's temper shorter. Chapuys bows and writhes before him, twisting and grimacing, as if he had in mind to ask Henry to dance. 'I have read with some perplexity certain conclusions reached by Dr Cranmer –'

'My archbishop,' the king says coldly; at great expense, the anointing has taken place.

'– conclusions regarding Queen Katherine –'

'Who? You mean my late brother's wife, the Princess of Wales?'

'– for Your Majesty knows that dispensations were issued in such form as to allow your own marriage to be valid, whether or no that former marriage was consummated.'

'I do not want to hear the word dispensation,' Henry says. 'I do not want to hear you mention what you call my marriage. The Pope has no power to make incest licit. I am no more Katherine's husband than you are.'

Chapuys bows.

'If the contract had not been void,' Henry says, patient for the last time, 'God would not have punished me with the loss of my children.'

'We do not know the blessed Katherine is beyond childbearing.' He looks up with a sly, delicate glance.

'Tell me, why do you think I do this?' The king sounds curious. 'Out of lust? Is that what you think?'

Kill a cardinal? Divide your country? Split the church? 'It seems extravagant,' Chapuys murmurs.

'But that is what you think. That is what you tell the Emperor. You are wrong. I am the steward of my country, sir, and if I now take a wife in a union blessed by God, it is to have a son by her.'

'But there is no guarantee that Your Majesty will have a son. Or any living children at all.'

'Why would I not?' Henry reddens. He is on his feet, shouting, angry tears spilling down his face. 'Am I not a man like other men? Am I not? Am I not?'

He is a game little terrier, the Emperor's man; but even he knows that when you've made a king cry it's time to back off. On the way out he says – dusting himself down, with his accustomed, self-deprecatory flutter – 'There is a distinction to be drawn between the welfare of the country and the welfare of the Tudor line. Or do you not think so?'

'So who is your preferred candidate for the throne? You favour Courtenay, or Pole?'

'You should not sneer at persons of royal blood.' Chapuys shakes out his sleeves. 'At least now I am officially informed of the lady's state, whereas before I could only deduce it from certain spectacles of folly I had witnessed ... Do you know how much you are staking, Cremuel, on the body of one woman? Let us hope no evil comes near her, eh?'

He takes the ambassador by the arm, wheels him around. 'What evil? Say what you mean.'

'If you would let go your grip on my jacket. Thank you. Very soon you resort to manhandling people, which shows, as they say, your breeding.' His words are full of bravado, but he is trembling. 'Look around you and see how by her pride and her presumption she offends your own nobility. Her own uncle has no stomach for her tricks. The king's oldest friends make excuses to stay away from court.'

'Wait till she's crowned,' he says. 'Watch them come running.'

On 12 April, Easter Sunday, Anne appears with the king at High Mass, and is prayed for as Queen of England. His bill went through Parliament just yesterday; he expects a modest reward, and before the royal party go in to break their fast, the king waves him over and gives him Lord Berners's old post, chancellor of the exchequer. 'Berners suggested you for it.' Henry smiles. He likes giving; like a child, he enjoys anticipating how pleased you will be.

During Mass, his mind had wandered through the city. What noisome goose houses have they waiting for him at home? What rows in the street, what babies left on church steps, what unruly apprentices with whom he will please have a word? Have Alice and Jo painted Easter eggs? They are too grown up now, but they are content to be the children of the house until the next generation comes along. It's time he put his mind to husbands for them. Anne, if she had lived, could be married by now, and to Rafe, as he is still not spoken for. He thinks of Helen Barre; how fast she gets on with her reading, how they cannot do without her at Austin Friars. He believes now that her husband is dead, and he thinks, I must talk to her, I must tell her she is free. She is too proper to show any pleasure, but who would not like to know that she is no longer subject to a man like that?

Through Mass, Henry keeps up a constant buzz of talk. He sorts papers and passes them up and down to his councillors; only at the consecration does he throw himself to his knees in a fever of reverence, as the miracle takes place and a wafer becomes God. As soon as the priest says, '*Ite, missa est*,' he whispers, come to me in my closet, alone.

First the assembled courtiers must make their bows to Anne. Her ladies sweep back and leave her alone in a little sunlit space. He watches them, watches the gentlemen and councillors, among whom, on this feast day, are many of the king's boyhood friends. He watches Sir Nicholas Carew in particular; nothing is wanting in his reverence to his new queen, but he cannot help a downturn of his mouth. Arrange your face, Nicholas Carew, your ancient family face. He hears Anne saying, these are my enemies: he adds Carew to the list.

Behind the chambers of state are the king's own rooms, which only his intimates see, where he is served by his gentlemen, and where he can be free of ambassadors and spies. This is Henry Norris's ground, and Norris gently congratulates him on his new appointment, and moves away, soft-footed.

'You know Cranmer is to convene a court to make a formal dissolution of the ...' Henry has said he does not want to hear any more about his marriage, so he will not even say the word. 'I have asked him to convene at the priory at Dunstable, because it is, what, ten, twelve miles to Ampthill, where *she* is lodged – so she can send her lawyers, if she likes. Or come to the court herself. I want you to go to see her, go secretly, just talk to her –'

Make sure she springs no surprises.

'Leave Rafe with me while you are gone.' At being so easily understood, the king relaxes into good humour. 'I can rely on him to say what Cromwell would say. You have a good boy there. And he is better than you are at keeping his face straight. I see you, when we sit in council, with your hand before your mouth. Sometimes, you know, I want to laugh myself.' He drops into a chair, covers his face as if to shade his eyes. He sees that, once again, the king is about to cry. 'Brandon says my sister is dying. There is no more the doctors can do for her. You know that fair hair she had once, hair like silver – my daughter had that. When she was seven she was the image of my sister, like a saint painted on a wall. Tell me, what am I to do with my daughter?'

He waits, till he knows it is a real question. 'Be good to her, sir. Conciliate her. She should not suffer.'

'But I must make her a bastard. I need to settle England on my lawful children.'

'Parliament will do it.'

'Yes.' He sniffs. Scrubs his tears away. 'After Anne is crowned. Cromwell, one thing, and then we will have our breakfast, because I am really very hungry. This project of a match for my cousin Richard …'

He thinks his way, rapidly, around the nobility of England. But no, he sees it's his Richard, Richard Cromwell. 'Lady Carey …' The king's voice softens. 'Well, I have thought it over, and I think, no. Or at least, not at this time.'

He nods. He understands his reason. When Anne understands it, she will spit nails.

'Sometimes it is a solace to me,' Henry says, 'not to have to talk and talk. You were born to understand me, perhaps.'

That is one view of their situations. He was six years or so in this world before Henry came into it, years of which he made good use. Henry takes off his embroidered cap, throws it down, runs his hands through his hair. Like Wyatt's golden mane, his hair is thinning, and it exposes the shape of his massive skull. For a moment he seems like a carved statue, like a simpler form of himself, or one of his own ancestors: one of the race of giants that roamed Britain, and left no trace of themselves except in the dreams of their petty descendants.

He goes back to Austin Friars as soon as he can get away. Surely he can have one day off? The crowds outside his gate have dispersed, as Thurston has fed them an Easter dinner. He goes out to the kitchen first, to give his man a slap on the head and a gold piece. 'A hundred open maws, I swear,' Thurston says. 'And by supper time they'll be round again.'

'It is a shame there should be beggars.'

'Beggars my arse. What comes out of this kitchen is so good, there are aldermen out there, with their hoods up so we don't know them. And I have a houseful here, whether you are with us

445

or not – I have Frenchmen, Germans, I have Florentiners, they all claim to know you and they all want their dinner to their own liking, I have their servants down here, pinch of that, soupçon of the other. We must feed fewer, or build another kitchen.'

'I'll get it in hand.'

'Master Rafe says for the Tower you have bought out the whole of a quarry in Normandy. He says the Frenchmen are all undermined, and dropping into holes in the ground.'

Such beautiful stone. The colour of butter. Four hundred men on the payroll, and anyone standing about instantly redeployed to the building work at Austin Friars. 'Thurston, don't let anybody put pinches or soupçons in our dinner.' He thinks, that's how Bishop Fisher nearly died; unless it was an unboiled stockpot after all. You could never fault Thurston's stockpot. He goes and views it, bubbling away. 'Where is Richard, do you know?'

'Chopping onions on the back step. Oh, you mean Master Richard? Upstairs. Eating. Where's anybody?'

He goes up. The Easter eggs, he sees, bear his own unmistakable features. Jo has painted his hat and his hair in one, so he seems to be wearing a cap with ear-flaps. She has given him at least two chins. 'Well, sir,' Gregory says, 'it is true you are getting stout. When Stephen Vaughan was here he could not believe you.'

'My master the cardinal waxed like the moon,' he says. 'It is a mystery, because he hardly sat down to dine but he would be leaping up to deal with some exigency, and even when he was at the table he could hardly eat for talking. I feel sorry for myself. I have not broken bread since last night.' He breaks it, and says, 'Hans wants to paint me.'

'I hope he can run fast,' Richard says.

'Richard –'

'Have your dinner.'

'My breakfast. No, never mind it. Come.'

'The happy bridegroom,' Gregory says, taunting.

'You,' his father threatens him, 'are going north with Rowland Lee. If you think I'm a hard man, wait till you meet Rowland.'

In his office, he says, 'How is your practice in the lists?'

'Good. Cromwells will knock down all-comers.'

He is afraid for his son; that he will fall, be maimed, be killed. Afraid for Richard too; these boys are the hope of his house. Richard says, 'So am I? The happy bridegroom?'

'The king says no. It is not because of my family, or your family – he calls you his cousin. He is, at this moment, his disposition to us, I would say it is excellent. But he needs Mary for himself. The child is due in late summer and he is afraid to touch Anne. And he does not wish to resume his celibate life.'

Richard looks up. 'He said this?'

'He left me to understand it. And as I understand it, I convey it to you, and we are both amazed, but we get over it.'

'I suppose if the sisters were more alike, one could begin to understand it.'

'I suppose,' he says, 'one could.'

'And he is the head of our church. No wonder foreigners laugh.'

'If he were a model of conduct in his private life, one would be … surprised … but for me, you see, I can only concern myself with his kingship. If he were oppressive, if he were to override Parliament, if he were to pay no heed to the Commons and govern only for himself … But he does not … so I cannot concern myself with how he behaves to his women.'

'But if he were not king …'

'Oh, I agree. You'd have him locked up. But again, Richard, leave aside Mary and he has behaved well enough. He hasn't filled a nursery with his bastards, as the Scottish kings do. There have been women, but who can name them? Only Richmond's mother, and the Boleyns. He has been discreet.'

'I dare say Katherine knew their names.'

'Who can say he will be a faithful husband? Will you?'

'I may not get the chance.'

'On the contrary, I have a wife for you. Thomas Murfyn's girl? A Lord Mayor's daughter is not a bad prospect. And your fortune will more than match hers, I will make sure of that. And Frances likes you. I know because I have asked her.'

'You have asked my wife to marry me?'

'Since I was dining there yesterday – no point in delay, was there?'

'Not really.' Richard laughs. He stretches back in his chair. His body – his capable, admirable body, which has impressed the king so much – is rinsed with relief. 'Frances. Good. I like Frances.'

Mercy approves. He cannot think how she would have taken to Lady Carey; he had not broached the topic with the women. She says, 'Don't leave it too long to make a match for Gregory. He is very young, I know. But some men never grow up until they have a son of their own.'

He hasn't thought about it, but it might be true. In that case, there's hope for the kingdom of England.

Two days later he is back at the Tower. The time goes quickly between Easter and Whit, when Anne will be crowned. He inspects her new apartments and orders in braziers to help dry out the plaster. He wants to get on with the frescoes – he wishes Hans would come down, but he is painting de Dinteville and says he needs to push on with it, as the ambassador is petitioning Francis for his recall, a whining letter on every boat. For the new queen we are not going to have those hunting scenes you see painted everywhere, or grim virgin saints with the instruments of their torture, but goddesses, doves, white falcons, canopies of green leaves. In the distance, cities seated on the hills: in the foreground, temples, groves, fallen columns and hot blue skies delineated, as within a frame, by borders of Vitruvian colours, quicksilver and cinnabar, burnt ochre, malachite, indigo and purple. He unrolls the sketches the craftsmen have made. Minerva's owl spreads her wings across a panel. A barefoot Diana fits an arrow to her bow. A white doe watches her from the trees. He scribbles a direction to the overseer: *Arrow to be picked out in gold. All goddesses have dark eyes.* Like a wingtip from the dark, dread brushes him: what if Anne dies? Henry will want another woman. He will bring her to these rooms. Her eyes may be blue. We will have to scour away the faces and paint them again, against the same cities, the same violet hills.

Outside he stops to watch a fight. A stonemason and the bricklayer's gaffer are swiping at each other with battens. He stands in the ring with the trowel men. 'What's it about?'

'Nuffing. Stone men have to fight brick men.'

'Like Lancaster and York?'

'Like that.'

'Have you ever heard of the field called Towton? The king tells me more than twenty thousand Englishmen died.'

The man gapes at him. 'Who were they fighting?'

'Each other.'

It was Palm Sunday, the year 1461. The armies of two kings met in the driving snow. King Edward the king's grandfather was the winner, if you can say there was a winner at all. Corpses made a bobbing bridge across the river. Uncounted numbers crawled away, rolled and tumbled in their own blood: some blinded, some disfigured, some maimed for life.

The child in Anne's womb is the guarantee of no more civil war. He is the beginning, the start of something, the promise of another country.

He walks into the fight. He bellows at them to stop. He gives them both a push and they bowl over backwards: two crumbly Englishmen, snappable bones, chalky teeth. Victors of Agincourt. He's glad Chapuys isn't there to see.

* * *

The trees are in full leaf when he rides into Bedfordshire, with a small train on unofficial business. Christophe rides beside him and pesters him: you have said you will tell me who is Cicero, and who is Reginald Pole.

'Cicero was a Roman.'

'A general?'

'No, he left that to others. As I, for example, might leave it to Norfolk.'

'Oh, Norferk.' Christophe subjects the duke to his peculiar pronunciation. 'He is one who pisses on your shadow.'

'Dear God, Christophe! I've heard of spitting on someone's shadow.'

'Yes, but we speak of Norferk. And Cicero?'

'We lawyers try to memorise all his speeches. If any man were walking around today with all of Cicero's wisdom in his head he would be …' He would be what? 'Cicero would be on the king's side,' he says.

Christophe is not much impressed. 'Pole, he is a general?'

'A priest. That is not quite true … He has offices in the church, but he has not been ordained.'

'Why not?'

'No doubt so he can marry. It is his blood that makes him dangerous. He is a Plantagenet. His brothers are here in this kingdom under our eye. But Reginald is abroad and we are afraid he is plotting with the Emperor.'

'Send one to kill him. I will go.'

'No, Christophe, I need you to stop the rain spoiling my hats.'

'As you wish.' Christophe shrugs. 'But I will kill a Pole when you require it, it will be my pleasure.'

The manor at Ampthill, once fortified, has airy towers and a splendid gatehouse. It stands on a hill with views over wooded countryside; it is a pleasant seat, the kind of house you'd visit after an illness to get your strength back. It was built with money gained in the French wars, in the days when the English used to win them.

To accord with Katherine's new status as Dowager Princess of Wales, Henry has trimmed her household, but still she is surrounded by chaplains and confessors, by household officers each with their own train of menials, by butlers and carvers, physicians, cooks, scullions, maltsters, harpers, lutenists, poultry keepers, gardeners, laundresses, apothecaries, and an entourage of wardrobe ladies, bedchamber ladies and their maids. But when he is ushered in she nods to her attendants to withdraw. No one had told her to expect him, but she must have spies on the road. Hence her nonchalant parade of occupation: a prayer book in her lap, and some sewing. He kneels to her, nods towards these encumbrances. 'Surely, madam, one or the other?'

'So, English today? Get up, Cromwell. We will not waste our time, as at our last interview, selecting which language to use. Because nowadays you are such a busy man.'

Formalities over, she says, 'First thing. I shall not attend your court at Dunstable. That is what you have come to find out, is it not? I do not recognise this court. My case is at Rome, awaiting the attention of the Holy Father.'

'Slow, isn't he?' He gives her a puzzled smile.

'I will wait.'

'But the king wishes to settle his affairs.'

'He has a man who will do it. I do not call him an archbishop.'

'Clement issued the bulls.'

'Clement was misled. Dr Cranmer is a heretic.'

'Perhaps you think the king is a heretic?'

'No. Only a schismatic.'

'If a general council of the church were called, His Majesty would submit to its judgment.'

'It will be too late, if he is excommunicate, and put outside the church.'

'We all hope – I am sure you do, madam – that day will never come.'

'*Nulla salus extra ecclesiam.* Outside the church there is no salvation. Even kings come to judgment. Henry knows it, and is afraid.'

'Madam, give way to him. For the present. Tomorrow, who knows? Do not cut off every chance of rapprochement.'

'I hear Thomas Boleyn's daughter is having a child.'

'Indeed, but …'

Katherine, above anyone, should know that guarantees nothing. She takes his meaning; thinks about it; nods. 'I see circumstances in which he might turn back to me. I have had much opportunity to study that lady's character, and she is neither patient nor kind.'

It doesn't matter; she only has to be lucky. 'In the event they have no children, you should think of your daughter Lady Mary. Conciliate him, madam. He may confirm her as his heir. And if you will give way, he will offer you every honour, and a great estate.'

'A great estate!' Katherine stands up. Her sewing slides from her skirts, the prayer book hits the floor with a fat leathery thump, and her silver thimble goes skittering across the boards and rolls into a corner. 'Before you make me any more preposterous offers, Master Cromwell, let me offer you a chapter from my history. After my lord Arthur died, I passed five years in poverty. I could not pay my servants. We bought in the cheapest food we could find, coarse food, stale food, yesterday's fish – any small merchant kept a better table than the daughter of Spain. The late King Henry would not let me go back to my father because he said he was owed money – he haggled over me like one of the doorstep women who sold us bad eggs. I put my faith in God, I did not despair, but I tasted the depth of humiliation.'

'So why would you want to taste it again?'

Face to face. They glare at each other. 'Assuming,' he says, 'humiliation is all the king intends.'

'Say it plainly.'

'If you are found out in treason the law will take its course with you, as if you were any other subject. Your nephew is threatening to invade us in your name.'

'That will not happen. Not in my name.'

'That is what I say, madam.' He softens his tone. 'I say the Emperor is busy with the Turks, he is not so fond of his aunt – saving your presence – that he will raise another army. But others say, oh, be quiet, Cromwell, what do you know? They say we must fortify our harbours, we must raise troops, we must put the country in a state of alert. Chapuys, as you know, continually agitates with Charles to blockade our ports and impound our goods and our merchant ships abroad. He urges war in every dispatch.'

'I have no knowledge of what Chapuys puts in his dispatches.'

It is a lie so staggering that he has to admire it. Having delivered it, Katherine seems weakened; she sinks down again into her chair, and before he can do it for her she wearily bends from the waist to pick up her sewing; her fingers are swollen, and bending seems to leave her breathless. She sits for a moment, recovering herself, and when she speaks again she is calm, deliberate. 'Master Cromwell, I know I have failed you. That is to say, I have failed your country, which by now is my country too. The king was a good husband to me, but I could not do that which is most necessary for a wife to do. Nevertheless, I was, I am, a wife – you see, do you, that it is impossible for me to believe that for twenty years I was a harlot? Now the truth is, I have brought England little good, but I would be loath to bring her any harm.'

'But you do, madam. You may not will it, but the harm is done.'

'England is not served by a lie.'

'That is what Dr Cranmer thinks. So he will annul your marriage, whether you come to the court or not.'

'Dr Cranmer will be excommunicated too. Does it not cause him a qualm? Is he so lost to everything?'

'This archbishop is the best guardian of the church, madam, that we have seen in many centuries.' He thinks of what Bainham said, before they burned him; in England there have been eight hundred years of mystification, just six years of truth and light; six years, since the gospel in English began to come into the kingdom. 'Cranmer is no heretic. He believes as the king believes. He will reform what needs reformation, that is all.'

'I know where this will end. You will take the church's lands and give them to the king.' She laughs. 'Oh, you are silent? You will. You mean to do it.' She sounds almost light-hearted, as people do sometimes when they're told they're dying. 'Master Cromwell, you may assure the king I will not bring an army against him. Tell him I pray for him daily. Some people, those who do not know him as I do, they say, "Oh, he will work his will, he will have his desire at any price." But I know that he needs to be on the side of the light. He is not a man like you, who just packs up his sins in his saddlebags and carries them from country to country, and when they grow too heavy whistles up a mule or two, and soon commands a train of them and a troop of muleteers. Henry may err, but he needs to be forgiven. I there-fore believe, and will continue to believe, that he will turn out of this path of error, in order to be at peace with himself. And peace is what we all wish for, I am sure.'

'What a placid end you make, madam. "Peace is what we all wish for." Like an abbess. You are quite sure by the way that you would not think of becoming an abbess?'

A smile. Quite a broad smile. 'I shall be sorry if I don't see you again. You are so much quicker in conversation than the dukes.'

'The dukes will be back.'

'I am braced. Is there news of my lady Suffolk?'

'The king says she is dying. Brandon has no heart for anything.'

'I can well believe it,' she murmurs. 'Her income as dowager queen of France dies with her, and that is the greater part of his revenue. Still, no doubt you will arrange him a loan, at some iniquitous rate of interest.' She looks up. 'My daughter will be curious to know I have seen you. She believes you were kind to her.'

He only remembers giving her a stool to sit on. Her life must be bleak, if she remembers that.

'Properly, she should have remained standing, awaiting a sign from me.'

Her own pain-racked little daughter. She may smile, but she doesn't yield an inch. Julius Caesar would have had more compunction. Hannibal.

'Tell me,' she says, testing the ground. 'The king would read a letter from me?'

Henry has taken to tearing her letters up unread, or burning them. He says they disgust him with their expressions of love. He does not have it in him to tell her this. 'Then rest for an hour,' she says, 'while I write it. Unless you will stay a night with us? I should be glad of company at supper.'

'Thank you, but I must start back, the council meets tomorrow. Besides, if I stayed, where would I put my mules? Not to mention my team of drivers.'

'Oh, the stables are half-empty. The king makes sure I am kept short of mounts. He thinks that I will give my household the slip and ride to the coast and escape on a ship to Flanders.'

'And will you?'

He has retrieved her thimble; he hands it back; she bounces it in her hand as if it were a die and she were ready to cast it.

'No. I shall stay here. Or go where I am sent. As the king wills. As a wife should.'

Until the excommunication, he thinks. That will free you from all bonds, as wife, as subject. 'This is yours too,' he says. He opens his palm; in it a needle, tip towards her.

* * *

The word is about town that Thomas More has fallen into poverty. He laughs about it with Master Secretary Gardiner. 'Alice was a rich widow when he married her,' Gardiner says. 'And he has land of his own; how can he be poor? And the daughters, he's married them well.'

'And he still has his pension from the king.' He is sifting through paperwork for Stephen, who is preparing to appear as leading counsel for Henry at Dunstable. He has filed away all the depositions from the Blackfriars hearings, which seem to have happened in another era.

'Angels defend us,' Gardiner says, 'is there anything you don't file?'

'If we keep on to the bottom of this chest I'll find your father's love letters to your mother.' He blows dust off the last batch. 'There you are.' The papers hit the table. 'Stephen, what can we do for John Frith? He was your pupil at Cambridge. Don't abandon him.'

But Gardiner shakes his head and busies himself with the documents, leafing through them, humming under his breath, exclaiming 'Well, who'd have known!' and 'Here's a nice point!'

He gets a boat down to Chelsea. The ex-Chancellor is at ease in his parlour, daughter Margaret translating from the Greek in a drone barely audible; as he approaches, he hears him pick her up on some error. 'Leave us, daughter,' More says, when he sees him. 'I won't have you in this devil's company.' But Margaret looks up and smiles, and More rises from his chair, a little stiff as if his back is bad, and offers a hand.

It is Reginald Pole, lying in Italy, who says he is a devil. The point is, he means it; it's not an image with him, as in a fable, but something he takes to be true, as he takes the gospel to be true.

'Well,' he says. 'We hear you can't come to the coronation because you can't afford a new coat. The Bishop of Winchester will buy you one himself if you'll show your face on the day.'

'Stephen? Will he?'

'I swear it.' He relishes the thought of going back to London and asking Gardiner for ten pounds. 'Or the guildsmen will make a collection, if you like, for a new hat and a doublet as well.'

'And how are you to appear?' Margaret speaks gently, as if she has been asked to mind two children for the afternoon.

'They are making something for me. I leave it to others. If I only avoid exciting mirth, it will be enough.'

Anne has said, you shall not dress like a lawyer on my coronation day. She has called out to Jane Rochford, taking notes like a clerk: Thomas must go into crimson. 'Mistress Roper,' he says, 'are you not yourself curious to see the queen crowned?'

Her father cuts in, talking over her: 'It is a day of shame for the women of England. One can hear them say on the streets – when the Emperor comes, wives shall have their rights again.'

'Father, I am sure they take care not to say that in Master Cromwell's hearing.'

He sighs. It's not much, to know that all the merry young whores are on your side. All the kept women, and the runaway daughters. Though now Anne is married, she sets herself up for an example. Already she has slapped Mary Shelton, Lady Carey tells him, for writing a riddle in her prayer book, and it was not even an indecent one. The queen sits very erect these days, child stirring in her belly, needlework in hand, and when Norris and Weston and their gentlemen friends come swarming into her apartments, she looks at them, when they lay compliments at her feet, as if they were strewing her hem with spiders. Unless you approach her with a Bible text in your mouth, better not approach her at all.

He says, 'Has the Maid been up to see you again? The prophetess?'

'She has,' Meg says, 'but we would not receive her.'

'I believe she has been to see Lady Exeter. At her invitation.'

'Lady Exeter is a foolish and ambitious woman,' More says.

'I understand the Maid told her that she would be Queen of England.'

'I repeat my comment.'

'Do you believe in her visions? Their holy nature, that is?'

'No. I think she is an impostor. She does it for attention.'

'Just that?'

'You don't know what young women will do. I have a house-ful of daughters.'

He pauses. 'You are blessed.'

Meg glances up; she recalls his losses, though she never heard Anne Cromwell demand, why should Mistress More have the pre-eminence? She says, 'There were holy maids before this. One at Ipswich. Only a little girl of twelve. She was of good family, and they say she did miracles, and she got nothing out of it, no personal profit, and she died young.'

'But then there was the Maid of Leominster,' More says, with gloomy relish. 'They say she is a whore at Calais now, and laughs with her clients after supper at all the tricks she worked on the believing people.'

So he does not like holy maids. But Bishop Fisher does. He has seen her often. He has dealings with her. As if taking the words out of his mouth, More says, 'Of course, Fisher, he has his own views.'

'Fisher believes she has raised the dead.' More lifts an eyebrow. 'But only for so long as it took for the corpse to make his confession and get absolution. And then he fell down and died again.'

More smiles. 'That sort of miracle.'

'Perhaps she is a witch,' Meg says. 'Do you think so? There are witches in the scriptures. I could cite you.'

Please don't. More says, 'Meg, did I show you where I put the letter?' She rises, marking with a thread her place in the Greek text. 'I have written to this maid, Barton ... Dame Elizabeth, we must call her, now she is a professed nun. I have advised her to

458

leave the realm in tranquillity, to cease to trouble the king with her prophecies, to avoid the company of great men and women, to listen to her spiritual advisers, and, in short, to stay at home and say her prayers.'

'As we all should, Sir Thomas. Following your example.' He nods, vigorously. 'Amen. And I suppose you kept a copy?'

'Get it, Meg. Otherwise he may never leave.'

More gives his daughter some rapid instructions. But he is satisfied that he is not ordering her to fabricate such a letter on the spot. 'I would leave,' he says, 'in time. I'm not going to miss the coronation. I've got my new clothes to wear. Will you not come and bear us company?'

'You'll be company for each other, in Hell.'

This is what you forget, this vehemence; his ability to make his twisted jokes, but not take them.

'The queen looks well,' he says. 'Your queen, I mean, not mine. She seems very comfortable at Ampthill. But you know that, of course.'

More says, unblinking, I have no correspondence with the, with the Princess Dowager. Good, he says, because I am watching two friars who have been carrying her letters abroad – I am beginning to think that whole order of the Franciscans is working against the king. If I take them and if I cannot persuade them, and you know I am very persuasive, into confirming my suspicion, I may have to hang them up by their wrists, and start a sort of contest between them, as to which one will emerge first into better sense. Of course, my own inclination would be to take them home, feed them and ply them with strong drink, but then, Sir Thomas, I have always looked up to you, and you have been my master in these proceedings.

He has to say it all before Margaret Roper comes back. He raps his fingers on the table, to make More sit up and pay attention. John Frith, he says. Ask to see Henry. He will welcome you like a lost child. Talk to him and ask him to meet Frith face-to-

459

face. I'm not asking you to agree with John – you think he's a
heretic, perhaps he is a heretic – I'm asking you to concede just
this, and to tell it to the king, that Frith is a pure soul, he is a fine
scholar, so let him live. If his doctrine is false and yours is true
you can talk him back to you, you are an eloquent man, you are
the great persuader of our age, not me – talk him back to Rome,
if you can. But if he dies you will never know, will you, if you
could have won his soul?

Margaret's footstep. 'Is this it, Father?'

'Give it to him.'

'There are copies of the copy, I suppose?'

'You would expect us,' the girl says, 'to take all reasonable care.'

'Your father and I were discussing monks and friars. How can
they be good subjects of the king, if they owe their allegiance to
the heads of their orders, who are abroad in other countries, and
who are themselves perhaps subjects of the King of France, or
the Emperor?'

'I suppose they are still Englishmen.'

'I meet few who behave as such. Your father will enlarge on
what I say.' He bows to her. He takes More's hand, holding its
shifting sinews in his own palm; scars vanish, it is surprising how
they do, and now his own hand is white, a gentleman's hand,
flesh running easily over the joints, though once he thought the
burn marks, the stripes that any smith picks up in the course of
business, would never fade.

He goes home. Helen Barre meets him. 'I've been fishing,' he
says. 'At Chelsea.'

'Catch More?'

'Not today.'

'Your robes came.'

'Yes?'

'Crimson.'

'Dear God.' He laughs. 'Helen –' She looks at him; she seems
to be waiting. 'I haven't found your husband.'

Her hands are plunged into the pocket of her apron. She shifts them, as if she were holding something; he sees that one of her hands is clutching the other. 'So you suppose he is dead?'

'It would be reasonable to think so. I have spoken with the man who saw him go into the river. He seems a good witness.'

'So I could marry again. If anybody wanted me.'

Helen's eyes rest on his face. She says nothing. Just stands. The moment seems to last a long time. Then: 'What happened to our picture? The one with the man holding his heart shaped like a book? Or do I mean his book shaped like a heart?'

'I gave it to a Genovese.'

'Why?'

'I needed to pay for an archbishop.'

She moves, reluctant, slow. She drags her eyes from his face. 'Hans is here. He has been waiting for you. He is angry. He says time is money.'

'I'll make it up to him.'

Hans is taking time off from his preparations for the coronation. He is building a living model of Mount Parnassus on Gracechurch Street, and today he has to put the Nine Muses through their paces, so he doesn't like being kept waiting by Thomas Cromwell. He is banging around in the next room. It seems he is moving the furniture.

They take Frith to the archbishop's palace at Croydon, to be examined by Cranmer. The new archbishop could have seen him at Lambeth; but the way to Croydon is longer, and lies through the woods. In the depth of these woods, they say to him, it would be a bad day for us if you were to give us the slip. For see how thick the trees are on the Wandsworth side. You could hide an army in there. We could spend two days searching there, more – and if you'd gone east, to Kent and the river, you'd be clear away before we got around to that side.

But Frith knows his road; he is going towards his death. They stand on the path, whistling, talking about the weather. One pisses, leisurely, against a tree. One follows the flight of a jay through the branches. But when they turn back, Frith is waiting, placid, for his journey to resume.

Four days. Fifty barges in procession, furnished by the city livery companies; two hours from the city to Blackwall, their rigging hung with bells and flags; a light but brisk breeze, as ordered from God in his prayers. Reverse order, anchor at the steps of Greenwich Palace, collect incoming queen in her own barge – Katherine's old one, rebadged, twenty-four oars: next her women, her guard, all the ornaments of the king's court, all those proud and noble souls who swore they'd sabotage the event. Boats packed with musicians; three hundred craft afloat, banners and pennants flying, the music ringing bank to bank, and each bank lined with Londoners. Downstream with the tide, led by an aquatic dragon spitting fire, and accompanied by wild men throwing fireworks. Sea-going ships discharge their ordnance in salute.

By the time they reach the Tower the sun is out. It looks as if the Thames is ablaze. Henry is waiting to greet Anne as she lands. He kisses her without formality, scooping back her gown, pinning it at her sides to show her belly to England.

Next, Henry makes knights: a shoal of Howards and Boleyns, their friends and followers. Anne rests.

Uncle Norfolk is missing the show. Henry has sent him to King Francis, to reaffirm the most cordial alliance between our two kingdoms. He is Earl Marshal and should be in charge of the coronation, but there is another Howard to step in as his deputy, and besides he, Thomas Cromwell, is running everything, including the weather.

He has conferred with Arthur Lord Lisle, who will preside at the coronation banquet: Arthur Plantagenet, a gentle relic of a former age. He is to go to Calais, directly this is over, to replace Lord Berners as Governor, and he, Cromwell, must brief him before he goes. Lisle has a long bony Plantagenet face, and he is tall like his father King Edward, who no doubt had many bastards, but none so distinguished as this elderly man, bending his creaky knee in obeisance before Boleyn's daughter. His wife Honor, his second wife, is twenty years his junior, small and delicate, a toy wife. She wears tawny silk, coral bracelets with gold hearts, and an expression of vigilant dissatisfaction, bordering on the peevish. She looks him up and down. 'I suppose you are Cromwell?' If a man spoke to you in that tone, you'd invite him to step outside and ask someone to hold your coat.

Day Two: bringing Anne to Westminster. He is up before first light, watching from the battlements as thin clouds disperse over the Bermondsey bank, and an early chill as clear as water is replaced by a steady, golden heat.

Her procession is led by the retinue of the French ambassador. The judges in scarlet follow, the Knights of the Bath in blue-violet of antique cut, then the bishops, Lord Chancellor Audley and his retinue, the great lords in crimson velvet. Sixteen knights carry Anne in a white litter hung with silver bells which ring at each step, at each breath; the queen is in white, her body shimmering in its strange skin, her face held in a conscious solemn smile, her hair loose beneath a circle of gems. After her, ladies on palfreys trapped with white velvet; and ancient dowagers in their chariots, their faces acidulated.

At every turn on the route there are pageants and living statues, recitations of her virtue and gifts of gold from city coffers, her white falcon emblem crowned and entwined with roses, and blossom mashed and minced under the treading feet of the stout sixteen, so scent rises like smoke. The route is hung with tapestries and banners, and at his orders the ground beneath the horses' hooves is gravelled to prevent slipping, and the crowds restrained behind rails in case of riots and crush;

every law officer London can muster is among the crowd, because he is determined that in time to come, when this is remembered and told to those who were not here, no one is going to say, oh, Queen Anne's coronation, that was the day I got my pocket picked. Fenchurch Street, Leadenhall, Cheap, Paul's Churchyard, Fleet, Temple Bar, Westminster Hall. So many fountains flowing with wine that it's hard to find one flowing with water. And looking down on them, the other Londoners, those monsters who live in the air, the city's uncounted population of stone men and women and beasts, and things that are neither human nor beasts, fanged rabbits and flying hares, four-legged birds and pinioned snakes, imps with bulging eyes and ducks' bills, men who are wreathed in leaves or have the heads of goats or rams; creatures with knotted coils and leather wings, with hairy ears and cloven feet, horned and roaring, feathered and scaled, some laughing, some singing, some pulling back their lips to show their teeth; lions and friars, donkeys and geese, devils with children crammed into their maws, all chewed up except for their helpless paddling feet; limestone or leaden, metalled or marbled, shrieking and sniggering above the populace, hooting and gurning and dry-heaving from buttresses, walls and roofs.

That night, the king permitting, he goes back to Austin Friars. He visits his neighbour Chapuys, who has secluded himself from the events of the day, bolting his shutters and stuffing his ears against the fanfares, the ceremonial cannon fire. He goes in a small satirical procession led by Thurston, taking the ambassador sweetmeats to ease his sulks, and some fine Italian wine sent to him by the Duke of Suffolk.

Chapuys greets him without a smile. 'Well, you have succeeded where the cardinal failed, Henry has what he wants at last. I say to my master, who is capable of looking at these things impartially, it is a pity from Henry's point of view that he did not take up Cromwell years ago. His affairs would have gone on much better.' He is about to say, the cardinal taught me every-thing, but Chapuys talks over him. 'When the cardinal came to a closed door he would flatter it – oh beautiful yielding door! Then he would try tricking it open. And you are just the same, just the same.' He pours himself some of the duke's present. 'But in the last resort, you just kick it in.'

The wine is one of those big, noble wines that Brandon favours, and Chapuys drinks appreciatively and says I don't understand it, nothing do I understand in this benighted country. Is Cranmer Pope now? Or is Henry Pope? Perhaps you are Pope? My men who were among the press today say they heard few voices raised for the concubine, and plenty who called upon God to bless Katherine, the rightful queen.

Did they? I don't know what city they were in.

Chapuys sniffs: they may well wonder. These days it is nothing but Frenchmen about the king, and she, Boleyn, she is half-French herself, and wholly bought by them; her entire family are in the pocket of Francis. But you, Thomas, you are not taken in by these Frenchmen, are you?

He reassures him: my dear friend, not for one instant.

Chapuys weeps; it's unlike him: all credit to the noble wine. 'I have failed my master the Emperor. I have failed Katherine.'

'Never mind.' He thinks, tomorrow is another battle, tomorrow is another world.

He is at the abbey by dawn. The procession is forming up by six. Henry will watch the coronation from a box screened by a lattice, sequestered in the painted stonework. When he puts his head in about eight o'clock the king is already sitting expectantly on a velvet cushion, and a kneeling servant is unpacking his breakfast. 'The French ambassador will be joining me,' Henry says; and he meets that gentleman as he is hurrying away.

'One hears you have been painted, Maître Cremuel. I too have been painted. You have seen the result?'

'Not yet. Hans is so occupied.' Even on this fine morning, here beneath fan vaulting the ambassador looks blue-tinged. 'Well,' he says, 'it appears that with the coronation of this queen, our two nations have reached a state of perfect amity. How to improve on perfection? I ask you, monsieur.'

The ambassador bows. 'Downhill from here?'

'Let's try, you know. To maintain a state of mutual usefulness. When our sovereigns are once again snapping at each other.'

'Another Calais meeting?'

'Perhaps in a year.'

'No sooner?'

'I will not put my king on the high seas for no cause.'

'We'll talk, Cremuel.' Flat-palmed, the ambassador taps him on the chest, over the heart.

Anne's procession forms up at nine. She is mantled in purple velvet, edged in ermine. She has seven hundred yards to walk, on the blue cloth that stretches to the altar, and her face is entranced. Far behind her, the dowager duchess of Norfolk, supporting her train; nearer, holding up the hem of her long robe, the Bishop of Winchester at one side, the Bishop of London at the other. Both of them, Gardiner and Stokesley, were king's men in the matter of the divorce; but now they look as if they wish they were far distant from the living object of his remarriage, who has a fine sheen of sweat on her high forehead, and whose compressed lips – by the time she reaches the altar – seem to have vanished into her face. Who says two bishops should hold up her hem? It's all written down in a great book, so old that one hardly dare touch it, breathe on it; Lisle seems to know it by heart. Perhaps it should be copied and printed, he thinks.

He makes a mental note, and then concentrates his will on Anne: Anne not to stumble, as she folds herself towards the ground to lie face-down in prayer before the altar, her attendants stepping forward to support her for the crucial twelve inches before belly hits sacred pavement. He finds himself praying: this child, his half-formed heart now beating against the stone floor, let him be sanctified by this moment, and let him be like his father's father, like his Tudor uncles; let him be hard, alert, watchful of opportunity, wringing use from the smallest turn of fortune. If Henry lives twenty years, Henry who is Wolsey's creation, and then leaves this child to succeed him, I can build my own prince: to the glorification of God and the commonwealth of England. Because I will not be too old. Look at Norfolk, already he is sixty, his father was seventy when he fought at Flodden. And I shall not be like Henry Wyatt and say, now I am retiring from affairs. Because what is there, but affairs?

Anne, shaky, is back on her feet. Cranmer, in a dense cloud of incense, is pressing into her hand the sceptre, the rod of ivory, and resting the crown of St Edward briefly on her head, before changing for a lighter and more bearable crown: a prestidigitation, his hands as supple as if he'd been shuffling crowns all his life. The prelate looks mildly excited, as if someone had offered him a cup of warm milk.

Anointed, Anna withdraws, incense billowing around her, swallowed into its murk: Anna Regina, to a bedchamber provided for her, to prepare for the feast in Westminster Hall. He pushes unceremoniously through the dignitaries – all you, all you who said you would not be here – and catches sight of Charles Brandon, Constable of England, mounted on his white horse and ready to ride into the hall among them. He is a huge, blazing presence, from which he withdraws his sight; Charles, he thinks, will not outlive me either. Back into the dimness, towards Henry. Only one thing checks him, the sight, whisking around a corner, of the hem of a scarlet robe; no doubt it is one of the judges, escaped from his procession.

The Venetian ambassador is blocking the entrance to Henry's box, but the king waves him aside, and says, 'Cromwell, did not my wife look well, did she not look beautiful? Will you go and see her, and give her ...' he looks around, for some likely present, then wrenches a diamond from his knuckle, 'will you give her this?' He kisses the ring. 'And this too?'

'I shall hope to convey the sentiment,' he says, and sighs, as if he were Cranmer.

The king laughs. His face is alight. 'This is my best,' he says. 'This is my best day.'

'Until the birth, Majesty,' says the Venetian, bowing.

It is Mary Howard, Norfolk's little daughter, who opens the door to him.

'No, you most certainly cannot come in,' she says. 'Utterly not. The queen is undressed.'

Richmond is right, he thinks; she has no breasts at all. Still. For fourteen. I'll charm this small Howard, he thinks, so he stands spinning words around her, complimenting her gown and her jewels, till he hears a voice from within, muffled like a voice from a tomb; and Mary Howard jumps and says, oh, all right, if she says so you can see her.

The bedcurtains are drawn close. He pulls them back. Anne is lying in her shift. She looks flat as a ghost, except for the shocking mound of her six-month child. In her ceremonial robes, her condition had hardly showed, and only that sacred instant, as she lay belly-down to stone, had connected him to her body, which now lies stretched out like a sacrifice: her breasts puffy beneath the linen, her swollen feet bare.

'Mother of God,' she says. 'Can you not leave Howard women alone? For an ugly man, you are very sure of yourself. Let me look at you.' She bobs her head up. 'Is that crimson? It's a very black crimson. Did you go against my orders?'

'Your cousin Francis Bryan says I look like a travelling bruise.'

'A contusion on the body politic.' Jane Rochford laughs.

'Can you do this?' he asks: almost doubting, almost tender. 'You are exhausted.'

'Oh, I think she will bear up.' There is no sisterly pride in Mary's voice. 'She was born for this, was she not?'

Jane Seymour: 'Is the king watching?'

'He is proud of her.' He speaks to Anne, stretched out on her catafalque. 'He says you have never looked more beautiful. He sends you this.'

Anne makes a little sound, a moan, poised between gratitude and boredom: oh, what, another diamond?

'And a kiss, which I said he had better bring in person.'

She shows no sign of taking the ring from him. It is almost irresistible, to place it on her belly and walk away. Instead he hands it to her sister. He says, 'The feast will wait for you, Highness. Come only when you feel ready.'

She levers herself upright, with a gasp. 'I am coming now.' Mary Howard leans forward and rubs her lower back, with an unpractised hand, a fluttering virginal motion as if she were stroking a bird. 'Oh, get away,' the anointed queen snaps. She looks sick. 'Where were you last evening? I wanted you. The streets cheered for me. I heard them. They say the people love Katherine, but really, it is just the women, they pity her. We will show them something better. They will love me, when this creature is out of me.'

Jane Rochford: 'Oh, but madam, they love Katherine because she is the daughter of two anointed sovereigns. Make your mind up to it, madam – they will never love you, any more than they love … Cromwell here. It is nothing to do with your merits. It is a point of fact. There is no use trying to evade it.'

'Perhaps enough,' Jane Seymour says. He turns to her and sees something surprising; she has grown up.

'Lady Carey,' Jane Rochford says, 'we must get your sister on her feet now and back in her robes, so see Master Cromwell out and enjoy your usual confabulation. This is not a day to break with tradition.'

At the door: 'Mary?' he says. Notices the dark stains under her eyes.

'Yes?' She speaks in a tone of 'yes, and what is it now?'

'I am sorry the marriage with my nephew did not come off.'

'Not that I was ever asked, of course.' She smiles tightly. 'I shall never see your house. And one hears so much of it.'

'What do you hear?'

'Oh … of chests bursting with gold pieces.'

'We would never allow that. We would get bigger chests.'

'They say it is the king's money.'

'It's all the king's money. His image is on it. Mary, look,' he takes her hand, 'I could not dissuade him from his liking for you. He –'

'How hard did you try?'

'I wish you were safe with us. Though of course it was not the great match you might expect, as the queen's sister.'

'I doubt there are many sisters who expect what I receive, nightly.'

She will get another child by Henry, he thinks. Anne will have it strangled in the cradle. 'Your friend William Stafford is at court. At least, I think he is still your friend?'

'Imagine how he likes my situation. Still, at least I get a kind word from my father. Monseigneur finds he needs me again. God forbid the king should ride a mare from any other stable.'

'This will end. He will free you. He will give you a settlement. A pension. I'll speak for you.'

'Does a dirty dishcloth get a pension?' Mary sways on the spot; she seems dazed with misery and fatigue; great tears swell in her eyes. He stands catching them, dabbing them away, whispering to her and soothing her, and wanting to be elsewhere. When he breaks free he gives her a backward glance, as she stands in the doorway, desolate. Something must be done for her, he thinks. She's losing her looks.

Henry watches from a gallery, high above Westminster Hall, as his queen takes her seat in the place of honour, her ladies around her, the flower of the court and the nobility of England. The king has fortified himself earlier, and is picking at a spice plate, dipping thin slices of apple into cinnamon. In the gallery with him, *encore les ambassadeurs*, Jean de Dinteville furred against the June chill, and his friend the Bishop of Lavaur, wrapped in a fine brocade gown.

'This has all been most impressive, Cremuel,' de Selve says; astute brown eyes study him, taking everything in. He takes in everything too: stitching and padding, studding and dyeing; he admires the deep mulberry of the bishop's brocade. They say these two Frenchmen favour the gospel, but favour at François's court extends no further than a small circle of scholars that the king, for his own vanity, wishes to patronise; he has never quite been able to grow his own Thomas More, his own Erasmus, which naturally piques his pride.

'Look at my wife the queen.' Henry leans over the gallery. He might as well be down there. 'She is worth the show, is she not?'

'I have had all the windows reglazed,' he says. 'The better to see her.'

'*Fiat lux*,' de Selve murmurs.

'She has done very well,' de Dinteville says. 'She must have been six hours on her feet today. One must congratulate Your Majesty on obtaining a queen who is as strong as a peasant woman. I mean no disrespect, of course.'

In Paris they are burning Lutherans. He would like to take it up with the envoys, but he cannot while the odour of roast swan and peacock drifts up from below.

'Messieurs,' he asks (music rising around them like a shallow tide, silver ripples of sound), 'do you know of the man Giulio Camillo? I hear he is at your master's court.'

De Selve and his friend exchange glances. This has thrown them. 'The man who builds the wooden box,' Jean murmurs. 'Oh yes.'

'It is a theatre,' he says.

De Selve nods. 'In which you yourself are the play.'

'Erasmus has written to us about it,' Henry says, over his shoulder. 'He is having the cabinetmakers create him little wooden shelves and drawers, one inside another. It is a memory system for the speeches of Cicero.'

'With your permission, he intends it as more than that. It is a theatre on the ancient Vitruvian plan. But it is not to put on plays. As my lord the bishop says, you as the owner of the theatre are to stand in the centre of it, and look up. Around you there is arrayed a system of human knowledge. Like a library, but as if – can you imagine a library in which each book contains another book, and a smaller book inside that? Yet it is more than that.'

The king slips into his mouth an aniseed comfit, and snaps down on it. 'Already there are too many books in the world. There are more every day. One man cannot hope to read them all.'

'I do not see how you understand so much about it,' de Selve says. 'All credit to you, Maître Cremuel. Giulio will only speak his own Italian dialect, and even in that he stammers.'

'If it pleases your master to spend his money,' Henry says. 'He is not a sorcerer, is he, this Giulio? I should not like Francis to fall into the hands of a sorcerer. By the way, Cromwell, I am sending Stephen back to France.'

Stephen Gardiner. So the French do not like doing business with Norferk. Not surprising. 'His mission will be of some duration?'

De Selve catches his eye. 'But who will do Master Secretary's job?'

'Oh, Cromwell will do it. Won't you?' Henry smiles.

He is hardly down into the body of the hall before Master Wriothesley intercepts him. This is a big day for the heralds and their officers, their children and their friends; fat fees coming their way. He says so, and Call-Me says, fat fees coming *your* way. He edges back against the screens, voice low; one could foresee this, he says, because Henry is tired of it, Winchester's grinding opposition to him every step of the way. He is tired of arguing; now he is a married man he looks for a little more *douceur.* With Anne? he says and Call-Me laughs: you know her better than me, if as they say she is a lady with a sharp tongue, then all the more he needs ministers who are kind to him. So devote yourself to keeping Stephen abroad, and in time he will confirm you in the post.

Christophe, dressed up for the afternoon, is hovering nearby and making signals to him. You will excuse me, he says, but Wriothesley touches his gown of crimson, as if for luck, and says, you are the master of the house and the master of the revels, you are the origin of the king's happiness, you have done what the cardinal could not, and much more besides. Even this – he gestures around him, to where the nobility of England, having already eaten their words, are working through twenty-three dishes – even this feast has been superbly managed. No one need call for anything, it is all at his hand before he thinks of it.

He inclines his head, Wriothesley walks away, and he beckons the boy. Christophe says, one tells me to impart nothing of confidence in the hearing of Call-Me, as Rafe says he go trit-trot to Gardineur with anything he can get. Now sir, I have a message, you must go quick to the archbishop. When the feast is done. He glances up to the dais where the archbishop sits beside Anne, under her canopy of state. Neither of them is eating, though Anne is pretending to; both of them are scanning the hall.

'I go trit-trot,' he says. He is taken with the phrase. 'Where?'

'His old lodging which he says you know. He wishes you to be secret. He says not to bring any person.'

'Well, you can come, Christophe. You're not a person.'

The boy grins.

He is apprehensive; does not quite like the thought of the abbey precincts, the drunken crowds at dusk, without somebody to watch his back. Unfortunately, a man cannot have two fronts.

They have almost reached Cranmer's lodging when fatigue enwraps his shoulders, an iron cloak. 'Pause for a moment,' he says to Christophe. He has hardly slept these last nights. He takes a breath, in shadow; here it is cold, and as he passes into the cloisters he is dipped in night. The rooms around are shuttered, empty, no sound from within. From behind him, an inchoate shouting from the Westminster streets, like the cries of those lost after a battle.

Cranmer looks up; he is already at his desk. 'These are days we will never forget,' he says. 'No one who has missed it would believe it. The king spoke warm words in your praise today. I think it was intended I should convey them.'

'I wonder why I ever gave any thought to the cost of brick-making for the Tower. It seems such a small item now. And tomorrow the jousts. Will you be there? My boy Richard is listed for the bouts on foot, fighting in single combat.'

'He will prevail,' Christophe declares. '*Biff*, and one is flat, never to rise again.'

'Hush,' Cranmer says. 'You are not here, child. Cromwell, please.'

He opens a low door at the back of the chamber. He dips his head, and framed by the doorway in the half light he sees a table, a stool, and on the stool a woman sitting, young, tranquil, her head bowed over a book. She looks up. '*Ich bitte Sie, ich brauch' eine Kerze.*'

'Christophe, a candle for her.'

The book before her he recognises; it is a tract of Luther's. 'May I?' he says, and picks it up.

He finds himself reading. His mind leaps along the lines. Is she some fugitive Cranmer is sheltering? Does he know the cost if

she is taken? He has time to read half a page, before the archbishop trickles in, like a late apology. 'This woman is …?'

Cranmer says, 'Margarete. My wife.'

'Dear God.' He slams Luther down on the table. 'What have
you done? Where did you find her? Germany, evidently. This is
why you were slow to return. I see it now. Why?'

Cranmer says meekly, 'I could not help it.'

'Do you know what the king will do to you when he finds you
out? The master executioner of Paris has devised a machine, with
a counterweighted beam – shall I draw it for you? – which when
a heretic is burned dips him into the fire and lifts him out again,
so that the people can see the stages of his agony. Now Henry
will be wanting one. Or he will get some device to tease your
head off your shoulders, over a period of forty days.'

The young woman looks up. *'Mein Onkel –'*

'Who is that?'

She names a theologian, Andreas Osiander: a Nuremberger, a
Lutheran. Her uncle and his friends, she says, and the learned
men of her town, they believe –

'It may be the belief in your country, madam, that a pastor
should have a wife, but not here. Did Dr Cranmer not warn you
of this?'

'Please,' Cranmer begs, 'tell me what she is saying. Does she
blame me? Is she wishing herself at home?'

'No. No, she says you are kind. What took hold of you, man?'

'I told you I had a secret.'

So you did. Down the side of the page. 'But to keep her here,
under the king's nose?'

'I have kept her in the country. But I could not refuse her wish
to see the celebrations.'

'She has been out on the streets?'

'Why not? No one knows her.'

True. The protection of the stranger in the city; one young
woman in a cheerful cap and gown, one pair of eyes among the

thousands of eyes: you can hide a tree in a forest. Cranmer approaches him. He holds out his hands, so lately smeared with the sacred oil; fine hands, long fingers, the pale rectangles of his palms crossed and recrossed by news of sea voyages and alliances. 'I asked you here as my friend. For I count you my chief friend, Cromwell, in this world.'

So there is nothing to do, in friendship, but to take these bony digits in his own. 'Very well. We will find a way. We will keep your lady secret. I only wonder that you did not leave her with her own family, till we can turn the king our way.'

Margarete is watching them, blue eyes flitting from face to face. She stands up. She pushes the table away from her; he watches her do it, and his heart lurches. Because he has seen a woman do this before, his own wife, and he has seen how she puts her palms down on the surface, to haul herself up. Margarete is tall, and the bulge of her belly juts above the table top.

'Jesus,' he says.

'I hope for a daughter,' the archbishop says.

'About when?' he asks Margarete.

Instead of answering, she takes his hand. She places it on her belly, pressing it down with her own. At one with the celebrations, the child is dancing: spanoletta, Estampie Royal. This is a perhaps a foot; this is a fist. 'You need a friend,' he says. 'A woman with you.'

Cranmer follows him as he pounds out of the room. 'About John Frith ...' he says.

'What?'

'Since he was brought to Croydon, I have seen him three times in private conversation. A worthy young man, a most gentle creature. I have spent hours, I regret not a second of it, but I cannot turn him from his path.'

'He should have run into the woods. That was his path.'

'We do not all ...' Cranmer drops his gaze. 'Forgive me, but we do not all see as many paths as you.'

'So you must hand him to Stokesley now, because he was taken in Stokesley's diocese.'

'I never thought, when the king gave me this dignity, when he insisted I occupy this seat, that among my first actions would be to come against a young man like John Frith, and to try to argue him out of his faith.'

Welcome to this world below. 'I cannot much longer delay,' Cranmer says.

'Nor can your wife.'

The streets around Austin Friars are almost deserted. Bonfires are starting up across the city, and the stars are obscured by smoke. His guards are on the gate: sober, he is pleased to note. He stops for a word; there is an art to being in a hurry but not showing it. Then he walks in and says, 'I want Mistress Barre.'

Most of his household have gone to see the bonfires, and they will be out till midnight, dancing. They have permission to do this; who should celebrate the new queen, if they do not? John Page comes out: something want doing, sir? William Brabazon, pen in hand, one of Wolsey's old crew: the king's business never stops. Thomas Avery, fresh from his accounts: there's always money flowing in, money flowing out. When Wolsey fell, his household deserted him, but Thomas Cromwell's servants stayed to see him through.

A door bangs overhead. Rafe comes down, boots clattering, hair sticking up. He looks flushed and confused. 'Sir?'

'I don't want you. Is Helen here, do you know?'

'Why?'

At that moment Helen appears. She is fastening up her hair under a clean cap. 'I need you to pack a bag and come with me.'

'For how long, sir?'

'I cannot say.'

'To go out of London?'

He thinks, I'll make some arrangement, the wives and daughters of men in the city, discreet women, they will find her servants, and a midwife, some competent woman who will put Cranmer's child into his hands. 'Perhaps for a short time.'

'The children –'

'We will take care of your children.'

She nods. Speeds away. You wish you had men in your service as swift as she. Rafe calls after her. 'Helen …' He looks irate. 'Where is she going, sir? You can't just drag her off into the night.'

'Oh, I can,' he says mildly.

'I need to know.'

'Believe me, you don't.' He relents. 'Or if you do, this is not the time – Rafe, I'm tired. I'm not going to argue.'

He could perhaps leave it to Christophe, and some of the more unquestioning members of his household, to take Helen from the warmth of Austin Friars to the chill of the abbey precincts; or he could leave it till the morning. But his mind is alive to the loneliness of Cranmer's wife, the strangeness of the city *en fête*, the deserted aspect of Cannon Row, where even in the shadow of the abbey robbers are bound to lurk. Even in the time of King Richard the district was home to gangs of thieves, who issued out by night at their pleasure, and when the dawn came swarmed back to claim the privilege of sanctuary, and no doubt to share the spoils with the clergy. I shall clean out that lot, he thinks. My men will be after them like ferrets down a hole.

Midnight: stone exhales a mossy breath, flagstones are slippery with the city's exhalations. Helen puts her hand into his. A servant admits them, eyes downcast; he slips him a coin to raise his eyes no higher. No sign of the archbishop: good. A lamp is lit. A door pushed ajar. Cranmer's wife is lying in a little cot. He says to Helen, 'Here is a lady who needs your compassion. You see her situation. She does not speak English. In any case, you need not ask her name.'

'Here is Helen,' he says. 'She has two children of her own. She will help you.'

Mistress Cranmer, her eyes closed, merely nods and smiles. But when Helen places a gentle hand on her, she reaches out and strokes it.

'Where is your husband?'

'*Er betet.*'

'I hope he is praying for me.'

The day of Frith's burning he is hunting with the king over the country outside Guildford. It is raining before dawn, a gusty, tugging wind bending the treetops: raining all over England, soaking the crops in the fields. Henry's mood is not to be dented. He sits down to write to Anne, left back at Windsor. After he has twirled his quill in his fingers, turned his paper about and about, he loses the will: you write it for me, Cromwell. I'll tell you what to put.

A tailor's apprentice is going to the stake with Frith: Andrew Hewitt.

Katherine used to have relics brought to her, Henry says, for when she was in labour with her children. A girdle of the Blessed Virgin. I hired it.

I don't think the queen will want that.

And special prayers to St Margaret. These are women's things. Best left to them, sir.

Later he will hear that Frith and the boy suffered, the wind blowing the flames away from them repeatedly. Death is a japester; call him and he will not come. He is a joker and he lurks in the dark, a black cloth over his face.

There are cases of the sweat in London. The king, who embodies all his people, has all the symptoms every day.

Now Henry stares at the rain falling. Cheering himself up, he says, it may abate, Jupiter is rising. Now, tell her, tell the queen …

He waits, his pen poised.

No, that's enough. Give it to me, Thomas, I will sign it.

He waits to see if the king will draw a heart. But the frivolities of courtship are over. Marriage is a serious business. *Henricus Rex.*

I think I have a stomach cramp, the king says. I think I have a headache. I feel queasy, and there are black spots before my eyes, that's a sign, isn't it?

If Your Majesty will rest a little, he says. And take courage.

You know what they say about the sweat. Merry at breakfast, dead by dinner. But do you know it can kill you in two hours?

He says, I have heard that some people die of fear.

By afternoon the sun is struggling out. Henry, laughing, spurs away his hunter under the dripping trees. At Smithfield Frith is being shovelled up, his youth, his grace, his learning and his beauty: a compaction of mud, grease, charred bone.

The king has two bodies. The first exists within the limits of his physical being; you can measure it, and often Henry does, his waist, his calf, his other parts. The second is his princely double, free-floating, untethered, weightless, which may be in more than one place at a time. Henry may be hunting in the forest, while his princely double makes laws. One fights, one prays for peace. One is wreathed in the mystery of his kingship: one is eating a duckling with sweet green peas.

The Pope now says his marriage to Anne is void. He will excommunicate him if he does not return to Katherine. Christendom will slough him off, body and soul, and his subjects will rise up and eject him, into ignominy, exile; no Christian hearth will shelter him, and when he dies his corpse will be dug with animal bones into a common pit.

He has taught Henry to call the Pope 'The Bishop of Rome'. To laugh when his name is mentioned. If it is uncertain laughter, it is better than his former genuflection.

Cranmer has invited the prophetess, Elizabeth Barton, to a meeting at his house in Kent. She has seen a vision of Mary, the former princess, as queen? Yes. Of Gertrude, Lady Exeter, as queen? Yes. He says gently, both cannot be true. The Maid says, I only report what I see. He writes that she is bouncing and full of confidence; she is used to dealing with archbishops, and she takes him for another Warham, hanging on her every word.

She is a mouse under the cat's paw.

Queen Katherine is on the move, her household much reduced, to the Bishop of Lincoln's palace at Buckden, an old red-brick house with a great hall and gardens that run out into copses and fields and so into the fenland landscape. September will bring her the first fruits of autumn, as October will bring the mists.

The king demands that Katherine give up for his coming child the robes in which the child Mary was christened. When he hears Katherine's answer, he, Thomas Cromwell, laughs. Nature wronged Katherine, he says, in not making her a man; she would have surpassed all the heroes of antiquity. A paper is put before her, in which she is addressed as 'Princess Dowager'; shocked, they show him how her pen has ripped through it, as she scores out the new title.

Rumours crop in the short summer nights. Dawn finds them like mushrooms in the damp grass. Members of Thomas Cromwell's household have been seeking a midwife in the small hours of the morning. He is hiding a woman at some country house of his, a foreign woman who has given him a daughter. Whatever you do, he says to Rafe, don't defend my honour. I have women like that all over the place.

They will believe it, Rafe says. The word in the city is that Thomas Cromwell has a prodigious …

Memory, he says. I have a very large ledger. A huge filing system, in which are recorded (under their name, and also under their offence) the details of people who have cut across me.

All the astrologers say that the king will have a son. But you are better not to deal with these people. A man came to him,

481

months ago, offering to make the king a philosopher's stone, and when he was told to make himself scarce he turned rude and contrary, as these alchemists do, and now gives it out that the king will die this year. Waiting in Saxony, he says, is the eldest son of the late King Edward. You thought him a rattling skeleton beneath the pavements of the Tower, only his murderers know where: you are deceived, for he is a man grown, and ready to claim his kingdom.

He counts it up: King Edward V, were he living, would be sixty-four this November coming. He's a bit late to the fight, he says.

He puts the alchemist in the Tower, to rethink his position.

No more from Paris. Whatever Maître Giulio's up to, he's very quiet about it.

Hans Holbein says, Thomas, I've got your hands done but I haven't paid much attention to your face. I promise this autumn I'll finish you off.

Suppose within every book there is another book, and within every letter on every page another volume constantly unfolding; but these volumes take no space on the desk. Suppose knowledge could be reduced to a quintessence, held within a picture, a sign, held within a place which is no place. Suppose the human skull were to become capacious, spaces opening inside it, humming chambers like beehives.

Lord Mountjoy, Katherine's Chamberlain, has sent him a list of all the necessities for the confinement of a Queen of England. It amuses him, the smooth and civil handover; the court and its ceremonies roll on, whoever the personnel, but it is clear Lord Mountjoy takes him as the man in charge of everything now.

He goes down to Greenwich and refurbishes the apartments, ready for Anne. Proclamations (undated) are prepared, to go out to the people of England and the rulers of Europe, announcing the birth of a prince. Just leave a little gap, he suggests, at the end of 'prince', so if need be you can squash in … But they look at him as if he's a traitor, so he leaves off.

When a woman withdraws to give birth the sun may be shining but the shutters of her room are closed so she can make her own weather. She is kept in the dark so she can dream. Her dreams drift her far away, from *terra firma* to a marshy tract of land, to a landing stage, to a river where a mist closes over the further bank, and earth and sky are inseparate; there she must embark towards life and death, a muffled figure in the stern directing the oars. In this vessel prayers are said that men never hear. Bargains are struck between a woman and her God. The river is tidal, and between one feather-stroke and the next, her tide may turn.

On 26 August 1533, a procession escorts the queen to her sealed rooms at Greenwich. Her husband kisses her, adieu and bon voyage, and she neither smiles nor speaks. She is very pale, very grand, a tiny jewelled head balanced on the swaying tent of her body, her steps small and circumspect, a prayer book in her hands. On the quay she turns her head: one lingering glance. She sees him; she sees the archbishop. One last look and then, her women steadying her elbows, she puts her foot into the boat.

II
Devil's Spit
Autumn and winter 1533

It is magnificent. At the moment of impact, the king's eyes are
open, his body braced for the *atteint*; he takes the blow perfectly,
its force absorbed by a body securely armoured, moving in the
right direction, moving at the right speed. His colour does not
alter. His voice does not shake.

'Healthy?' he says. 'Then I thank God for his favour to us. As
I thank you, my lords, for this comfortable intelligence.'

He thinks, Henry has been rehearsing. I suppose we all
have.

The king walks away towards his own rooms. Says over his
shoulder, 'Call her Elizabeth. Cancel the jousts.'

A bleat from a Boleyn: 'The other ceremonies as planned?'

No reply. Cranmer says, all as planned, till we hear different. I
am to stand godfather to the … the princess. He falters. He can
hardly believe it. For himself, he ordered a daughter, and he got a
daughter. His eyes follow Henry's retreating back. 'He did not
ask after the queen. He did not ask how she does.'

'It hardly matters, does it?' Edward Seymour, saying brutally
what everyone is thinking.

Then Henry, on his long solitary walk, stops, turns back. 'My
lord archbishop. Cromwell. But you only.'

In Henry's closet: 'Had you imagined this?'

Some would smile. He does not. The king drops into a chair. The urge arises to put a hand on his shoulder, as one does for any inconsolable being. He resists it; simply folds his fingers, protectively, into the fist which holds the king's heart. 'One day we will make a great marriage for her.'

'Poor scrap. Her own mother will wish her away.'

'Your Majesty is young enough,' Cranmer says. 'The queen is strong and her family are fertile. You can get another child soon. And perhaps God intends some peculiar blessing by this princess.'

'My dear friend, I am sure you are right.' Henry sounds dubious, but he looks around to take strength from his surroundings, as if God might have left some friendly message written on the wall: though there is only precedent for the hostile kind. He takes a breath and stands up and shakes out his sleeves. He smiles: and one can catch in flight, as if it were a bird with a strong-beating heart, the act of will that transforms a desolate wretch into the beacon of his nation.

He whispers to Cranmer later, 'It was like watching Lazarus get up.'

Soon Henry is striding about the palace at Greenwich, putting the celebrations under way. We are young enough, he says, and next time it will be a boy. One day we will make a great marriage for her. Believe me, God intends some peculiar blessing by this princess.

Boleyn faces brighten. It's Sunday, four in the afternoon. He goes and laughs a bit at the clerks who have 'prince' written on their proclamations, and who now have to squeeze extra letters in, then he goes back to working out the expenses for the new princess's household. He has advised that Gertrude, Lady Exeter, be among the child's godparents. Why should only the Maid have a vision of her? It will do her good to be seen by the whole court, smiling a forced smile and holding Anne's baby at the font.

* * *

The Maid herself, brought to London, is kept in a private house, where the beds are soft and the voices around her, the voices of Cromwell women, hardly disturb her prayers; where the key is turned in the oiled lock with a click as small as the snap of a bird's bone. 'Does she eat?' he asks Mercy, and she says, she eats as heartily as you: well, no, Thomas, perhaps not quite so heartily as you.

'I wonder what happened to her project of living on the Communion host?'

'They can't see her dining now, can they? Those priests and monks who set her on this course.'

Away from their scrutiny, the nun has started to act like an ordinary woman, acknowledging the simple claims of her body, like anyone who wants to live; but it may be too late. He likes it that Mercy doesn't say, ahh, the poor harmless soul. That she is not harmless by nature is clear when they have her over to Lambeth Palace to question her. You would think Lord Chancellor Audley, his chain of office hung about his splendid person, would be enough to subdue any country girl. Throw in the Archbishop of Canterbury, and you would imagine a young nun might feel some awe. Not a bit of it. The Maid treats Cranmer with condescension – as if he were a novice in the religious life. When he challenges her on any point and says, 'How do you know that?' she smiles pityingly and says, 'An angel told me.'

Audley brings Richard Riche with him to their second session, to take notes for them, and put any points that occur to him. He is Sir Richard now, knighted and promoted to Solicitor General. In his student days he was known for a sharp slanderous tongue, for irreverence to his seniors, for drinking and gaming for high stakes. But who would hold up his head, if people judged us by what we were like at twenty? Riche turns out to have a talent for drafting legislation which is second only to his own. His features, beneath his soft fair hair, are pinched with concentration; the boys call him Sir Purse. You'd never think, to see him precisely laying out his papers, that he was once the great disgrace of the Inner Temple. He says so, in an undertone, teasing him, while they wait for the girl to be brought in. Well, Master Cromwell! Riche says; what about you and that abbess in Halifax?

He knows better than to deny it: or any of those stories the cardinal told about him. 'Oh, that,' he says. 'It was nothing – they expect it in Yorkshire.'

He is afraid the girl may have caught the tail end of the exchange, because today, as she takes the chair they have placed for her, she gives him a particularly hard stare. She arranges her skirts, folds her arms and waits for them to entertain her. His niece Alice Wellyfed sits on a stool by the door: just there in case of fainting, or other upset. Though a glance at the Maid tells you she is no more likely to faint than Audley is.

'Shall I?' Riche says. 'Start?'

'Oh, why not?' Audley says. 'You are young and hearty.'

'These prophecies of yours – you are always changing the timing of the disaster you foresee, but I understood you said that the king would not reign one month after he married Lady Anne. Well, the months have passed, Lady Anne is crowned queen, and has given the king a fine daughter. So what do you say now?'

'I say in the eyes of the world he seems to be king. But in the eyes of God,' she shrugs, 'not any more. He is no more the real king than he,' she nods towards Cranmer, 'is really archbishop.'

Riche is not to be sidetracked. 'So it would be justified to raise rebellion against him? To depose him? To assassinate him? To put another in his place?'

'Well, what do you think?'

'And among the claimants your choice has fallen on the Courtenay family, not the Poles. Henry, Marquis of Exeter. Not Henry, Lord Montague.'

'Or,' he says sympathetically, 'do you get them mixed up?'

'Of course not.' She flushes. 'I have met both those gentle-men.'

Riche makes a note.

Audley says, 'Now Courtenay, that is Lord Exeter, descends from a daughter of King Edward. Lord Montague descends from King Edward's brother, the Duke of Clarence. How do you weigh their claims? Because if we are talking of true kings and false kings, some say Edward was a bastard his mother got by an archer. I wonder if you can cast any light?'

'Why would she?' Riche says.

Audley rolls his eyes. 'Because she talks to the saints on high. They'd know.'

He looks at Riche and it is as if he can read his thoughts: Niccolò's book says, the wise prince exterminates the envious, and if I, Riche, were king, those claimants and their families would be dead. The girl is braced for the next question: how is it she has seen two queens in her vision? 'I suppose it will sort itself out,' he says, 'in the fighting? It's good to have a few kings and queens in reserve, if you're going to start a war in a country.'

'It is not necessary to have a war,' the nun says. Oh? Sir Purse sits up: this is new. 'God is sending a plague on England instead. Henry will be dead in six months. So will she, Thomas Boleyn's daughter.'

'And me?'

'You too.'

'And all in this room? Except you, of course? All including Alice Wellyfed, who never did you harm?'

'All the women of your house are heretics, and the plague will rot them body and soul.'

'And what about the princess Elizabeth?'

She turns in her seat, to aim her words at Cranmer. 'They say when you christened her you warmed the water to spare her a shock. You should have poured it boiling.'

Oh, Christ in Heaven, Riche says. He throws his pen down. He is a tender young father, with a daughter in the cradle.

He drops a consoling hand on his, the Solicitor General's. You would think Alice would need consoling; but when the Maid condemned her to death, he had looked down the room at his niece to note that her face was the perfect picture of derision. He says to Riche, 'She didn't think it up herself, the boiling water. It is a thing they are saying on the streets.'

Cranmer huddles into himself; the Maid has bruised him, she has scored a point. He, Cromwell, says, 'I saw the princess yesterday. She is thriving, in spite of her ill-wishers.' His voice suggests calm: we must get the archbishop back in the saddle. He turns to the Maid: 'Tell me: did you locate the cardinal?'

'What?' Audley says.

'Dame Elizabeth said she would look out for my old master, on one of her excursions to Heaven, Hell and Purgatory, and I offered to pay her travelling expenses on the occasion. I gave her people a down-payment – I hope we see some progress?'

'Wolsey would have had another fifteen years of life,' the girl says. He nods: he has said the same himself. 'But then God cut him off, as an example. I have seen devils disputing for his soul.'

'You know the result?' he asks.

'There is no result. I searched for him all over. I thought God had extinguished him. Then one night I saw him.' A long, tactical hesitation. 'I saw his soul seated among the unborn.'

There is a silence. Cranmer shrinks in his seat. Riche gently nibbles the end of his pen. Audley twists a button on his sleeve, round and round till the thread tightens.

'If you like I can pray for him,' the Maid says. 'God usually answers my requests.'

'Formerly, when you had your advisers about you, Father Bocking and Father Gold and Father Risby and the rest, you would start bargaining at this point. I would propose a further sum for your goodwill, and your spiritual directors would drive it up.'

'Wait.' Cranmer lays a hand over his ribcage. 'Can we go back? Lord Chancellor?'

'We can go in any direction you choose, my lord archbishop. Three times round the mulberry bush …'

'You see devils?'

She nods.

'They appear how?'

'Birds.'

'A relief,' Audley says drily.

'No, sir. Lucifer stinks. His claws are deformed. He comes as a cockerel smeared in blood and shit.'

He looks up at Alice. He is ready to send her out. He thinks, what has been done to this woman?

Cranmer says, 'That must be disagreeable for you. But it is a characteristic of devils, I understand, to show themselves in more than one way.'

'Yes. They do it to deceive you. He comes as a young man.'

'Indeed?'

'Once he brought a woman. To my cell at night.' She pauses. 'Pawing her.'

Riche: 'He is known to have no shame.'

'No more than you.'

'And what then, Dame Elizabeth? After the pawing?'

'Pulled up her skirts.'

'And she didn't resist?' Riche says. 'You surprise me.'

Audley says, 'Prince Lucifer, I don't doubt he has a way with him.'

'Before my eyes, he had to do with her, on my bed.'

Riche makes a note. 'This woman, did you know her?' No answer. 'And the devil did not try the same with you? You can speak freely. It will not be held against you.'

'He came to sweet-talk me. Swaggering in his blue silk coat, it's the best he has. And new hose with diamonds down his legs.'

'Diamonds down his legs,' he says. 'Now that must have been a temptation?'

She shakes her head.

'But you are a fine young woman – good enough for any man, I'd say.'

She looks up; a flicker of a smile. 'I am not for Master Lucifer.'

'What did he say when you refused him?'

'He asked me to marry him.' Audley puts his head in his hands. 'I said I was vowed to chastity.'

'Was he not angry when you would not consent?'

'Oh yes. He spat in my face.'

'I would expect no better of him,' Riche says.

'I wiped his spit off with a napkin. It's black. It has the stench of Hell.'

'What is that like?'

'Like something rotting.'

'Where is it now, the napkin? I suppose you didn't send it to the laundry?'

'Dom Edward has it.'

'Does he show it to people? For money?'

'For offerings.'

'For money.'

Cranmer takes his face from his hands. 'Shall we pause?'

'A quarter hour?' Riche says.

Audley: 'I told you he was young and hearty.'

'Perhaps we will meet tomorrow,' Cranmer says. 'I need to pray. And a quarter of an hour will not do it.'

'But tomorrow is Sunday,' the nun says. 'There was a man who went out hunting on a Sunday and he fell down a bottomless pit into Hell. Imagine that.'

'How was it bottomless,' Riche asks, 'if Hell was there to receive him?'

'I wish I were going hunting,' Audley says. 'Christ knows, I'd take a chance on it.'

Alice rises from her stool and signals for her escort. The Maid gets to her feet. She is smiling broadly. She has made the archbishop flinch, and himself grow cold, and the Solicitor General all but weep with her talk of scalded babies. She thinks she is winning; but she is losing, losing, losing all the time. Alice puts a gentle hand on her arm, but the Maid shakes it off.

Outside, Richard Riche says, 'We should burn her.'

Cranmer says, 'Much as we may mislike her talk of the late cardinal appearing to her, and devils in her bedchamber, she speaks in this way because she has been taught to ape the claims of certain nuns who have gone before her, nuns whom Rome is pleased to recognise as saints. I cannot convict them of heresy, retrospectively. Nor have I evidence to try her for heresy.'

'Burned for treason, I meant.'

It is the woman's penalty; where a man is half-hanged and castrated, then slowly gutted by the executioner.

He says, 'There is no overt action. She has only expressed an intent.'

'Intent to raise rebellion, to depose the king, should that not be treason? Words have been construed as treasons, there are precedents, you know them.'

'I should be astonished,' Audley says, 'if they have escaped Cromwell's attention.'

It is as if they can smell the devil's spit; they are almost jostling each other to get into the air, which is mild, damp: a faint scent of leaves, a green-gold, rustling light. He can see that, in the years ahead, treason will take new and various forms. When the last treason act was made, no one could circulate their words in a printed book or bill, because printed books were not thought of. He feels a moment of jealousy towards the dead, to those who served kings in slower times than these; nowadays the products of some bought or poisoned brain can be disseminated through Europe in a month.

'I think new laws are needed,' Riche says.

'I have it in hand.'

'And I think this woman is too leniently kept. We are too soft. We are just playing with her.'

Cranmer walks away, shoulders stooped, his trailing habit brushing up the leaves. Audley turns to him, bright and resolute, a man keen to change the subject. 'So, the princess, you say she was well?'

The princess, unswaddled, had been placed on cushions at Anne's feet: an ugly, purple, grizzling knot of womankind, with an upstanding ruff of pale hair and a habit of kicking up her gown as if to display her most unfortunate feature. It seems stories have been put about that Anne's child was born with teeth, has six fingers on each hand, and is furred all over like a monkey, so her father has shown her off naked to the ambassadors, and her mother is keeping her on display in the hope of countering the rumours. The king has chosen Hatfield for her seat, and Anne says, 'It seems to me waste might be saved, and the proper order of things asserted, if Spanish Mary's household were broken up and she were to become a member of the household of the princess Elizabeth my daughter.'

'In the capacity of …?' The child is quiet; only, he notes, because she has crammed a fist into her maw, and is cannibalising herself.

'In the capacity of my daughter's servant. What else should she be? There can be no pretence at equality. Mary is a bastard.'

The brief respite is over; the princess sets up a screech that would bring out the dead. Anne's glance slides away sideways, and a sideways grin of infatuation takes over her whole face, and she leans down towards her daughter, but at once women swoop, flapping and bustling; the screaming creature is plucked up, wrapped up, swept away, and the queen's eyes follow pitifully as the fruit of her womb exits, in procession. He says gently, 'I think she was hungry.'

* * *

Saturday evening: supper at Austin Friars for Stephen Vaughan, so often in transit: William Butts, Hans, Kratzer, Call-Me Risley. Conversation is in various tongues and Rafe Sadler translates adroitly, smoothly, his head turning from side to side: high topics and low, statecraft and gossip, Zwingli's theology, Cranmer's wife. About the latter, it has not been possible to suppress the talk at the Steelyard and in the city; Vaughan says, 'Can Henry know and not know?'

'That is perfectly possible. He is a prince of very large capacities.'

Larger by the day, Wriothesley says, laughing; Dr Butts says, he is one of those men who must be active, and recently his leg is troubling him, that old injury; but think, is it likely that a man who has not spared himself on the hunting field and in the tilt yard should not get some injury by the time he is the king's age? He is forty-three this year, you know, and I should be glad, Kratzer, to have your view on what the planets suggest, for the later years of a man whose chart is so dominated by air and fire; by the by, did I not always warn of his moon in Aries (rash and hasty planet) in the house of marriage?

He says, impatient, we heard very little about the Aries moon when he was settled with Katherine for twenty years. It is not the stars that make us, Dr Butts, it is circumstance and *necessità*, the choices we make under pressure; our virtues make us, but virtues are not enough, we must deploy our vices at times. Or don't you agree?

He beckons to Christophe to fill their glasses. They talk about the Mint, where Vaughan is to have a position; about Calais, where Honor Lisle seems more busy in affairs than her husband the Governor. He thinks about Giulio Camillo in Paris, pacing and fretting between the wooden walls of his memory machine, while knowledge grows unseen and of itself in its cavities and concealed inner spaces. He thinks of the Holy Maid – by now established as not holy, and not a maid – no doubt at this moment sitting down to supper with his nieces. He thinks of his fellow interrogators: Cranmer on his knees in prayer, Sir Purse frowning over the day's transcripts, Audley – what will the Lord Chancellor be doing? Polishing his chain of office, he decides. He thinks of saying to Vaughan, below the conversation, was there not a girl in your house called Jenneke? What happened to her? But Wriothesley breaks in on his train of thought. 'When shall we see my master's portrait? You have been at work on it a while, Hans, it is time it came home. We are keen to see what you have made of him.'

'He is still busy with the French envoys,' Kratzer says. 'De Dinteville wants to take his picture home with him when he gets his recall ...'

There is some laughter at the expense of the French ambassador, always doing his packing and having to undo it again, as his master commands him to stay where he is. 'Anyway, I hope he does not take it too quick,' Hans says, 'because I mean to show it and get commissions off it. I want the king to see it, indeed I want to paint the king, do you think I can?'

'I will ask him,' he says easily. 'Let me choose the time.' He looks down the table to see Vaughan glow with pride, like Jupiter on a painted ceiling.

After they get up from the table his guests eat ginger comfits and candied fruits, and Kratzer makes some drawings. He draws the sun and the planets moving in their orbits according to the plan he has heard of from Father Copernicus. He shows how the world is turning on its axis, and nobody in the room denies it. Under your feet you can feel the tug and heft of it, the rocks groaning to tear away from their beds, the oceans tilting and slapping at their shores, the giddy lurch of Alpine passes, the forests of Germany ripping at their roots to be free. The world is not what it was when he and Vaughan were young, it is not what it was even in the cardinal's day.

The company has left when his niece Alice comes in, past his watchmen, wrapped up in a cloak; she is escorted by Thomas

Rotherham, one of his wards who lives in the house. 'Never fear, sir,' she says, 'Jo is sitting up with Dame Elizabeth, and nothing gets by Jo.'

Does it not? That child perpetually in tears over her spoiled sewing? That grubby little girl sometimes found rolling under a table with a wet dog, or chasing a peddler down the street? 'I would like to talk to you,' Alice says, 'if you have time for me?' Of course, he says, taking her arm, folding her hand in his; Thomas Rotherham turns pale – which puzzles him – and slides away.

Alice sits down in his office. She yawns. 'Excuse me – but she is hard work and the hours are long.' She tucks a strand of hair into her hood. 'She is ready to break,' she says. 'She is brave to your faces, but she cries at night, because she knows she is a fraud. And even while she is crying, she peeps under her eyelids to see what effect she is making.'

'I want it over with now,' he says. 'For all the trouble she has caused, we do not find ourselves an edifying spectacle, three or four of us learned in the law and the scriptures, convening day after day to try to trip one chit of a girl.'

'Why did you not bring her in before?'

'I didn't want her to shut the prophecy shop. I wanted to see who would come to her whistle. And Lady Exeter has, and Bishop Fisher. And a score of monks and foolish priests whose names I know, and a hundred perhaps whose names I don't know yet.'

'And will the king kill them all?'

'Very few, I hope.'

'You incline him to mercy?'

'I incline him to patience.'

'What will happen to her? Dame Eliza?'

'We will frame charges.'

'She will not go in a dungeon?'

'No, I shall move the king to treat her with consideration, he is always – he is usually – respectful of any person in the religious

496

life. But Alice,' he sees that she is dissolving into tears, 'I think this has all been too much for you.'

'No, not at all. We are soldiers in your army.'

'She has not been frightening you, talking about the devil's wicked offers?'

'No, it's Thomas Rotherham's offers ... he wants to marry me.'

'So that's what's wrong with him!' He is amused. 'Could he not ask himself?'

'He thought you would look at him in that way you have ... as if you were weighing him.'

Like a clipped coin? 'Alice, he owns a fat slice of Bedfordshire, and his manors prosper very nicely since I have been looking after them. And if you like each other, how could I object? You are a clever girl, Alice. Your mother,' he says softly, 'and your father, they would be very pleased with you, if they were able to see.'

This is why Alice is crying. She must ask her uncle's permission because this last year has left her orphaned. The day his sister Bet died, he was up-country with the king. Henry was receiving no messengers from London for fear of contagion, so she was dead and buried before he knew she was ill. When the news crept through at last, the king spoke to him with tenderness, a hand on his arm; he spoke of his own sister, the silver-haired lady like a princess in a book, removed from this life to gardens of Paradise, he had claimed, reserved for royal dead; for it is impossible, he had said, to think of that lady in any low place, any place of darkness, the barred charnel house of Purgatory with its flying cinders and sulphur reek, its boiling tar and roiling clouds of sleet.

'Alice,' he says, 'dry your tears, find Thomas Rotherham, and end his pain. You need not come to Lambeth tomorrow. Jo can come, if she is as formidable as you say.'

Alice turns in the doorway. 'I will see her again, though? Eliza Barton? I should like to see her before ...'

Before they kill her. Alice is no innocent in this world. Just as well. Look how the innocent end; used by the sin-sodden and the cynical, pulped to their purpose and ground under their heels.

He hears Alice running upstairs. He hears her calling, Thomas, Thomas ... It is a name that will bring half the house out, tumbling from their bedside prayers, from their very beds: yes, are you looking for me? He pulls his furred gown around him and goes outside to look at the stars. The precincts of his house are kept well lit; the gardens by torchlight are the site of excavations, trenches dug out for foundations, earth banked up into barrows and mounds. The vast timber frame of a new wing juts against the sky; in the middle distance, his new planting, a city orchard where Gregory, one day, will pick the fruit, and Alice, and Alice's sons. He has fruit trees already, but he wants cherries and plums like the ones he has eaten abroad, and late pears to use in the Tuscan fashion, to match their crisp metallic flesh with winter's salt cod. Then next year he means to make another garden at the hunting lodge he has at Canonbury, make it a retreat from the city, a summer house in the fields. He has work in hand at Stepney too, expansion; John Williamson is looking after the builders for him. Strange, but like a miracle the family's prosperity seems to have cured him of his killing cough. I like John Williamson, he thinks, why ever did I, with his wife ... Beyond the gate, cries and shouts, London never still or quiet; so many in the graveyards, but the living parading in the streets, drunken fighters pitching from London Bridge, sanctuary men stealing out to thieve, Southwark whores bawling out their prices like butchers selling dead flesh.

He goes inside. His desk draws him back. In a small chest he keeps his wife's book, her book of hours. Inside it are prayers on loose papers which she has inserted. Say the name of Christ a thousand times and it keeps fever away. But it doesn't, does it? The fever comes anyway and kills you. Beside the name of her first husband, Thomas Williams, she has written his own name, but she never, he notices, crossed Tom Williams out. She has recorded the births of her children, and he has written in beside them the dates of his daughters' deaths. He finds a space where he will note the marriages of his sisters' children: Richard to Frances Murfyn, Alice to his ward.

He thinks, perhaps I have got over Liz. It didn't seem possible that weight would ever shift from inside his chest, but it has lightened enough to let him get on with his life. I could marry again, he thinks, but is this not what people are always telling me? He says to himself, I never think of Johane Williamson now: not Johane as she was for me. Her body once had special meaning, but that meaning is now unmade; the flesh created beneath his fingertips, hallowed by desire, becomes just the ordinary substance of a city wife, a fading woman with no particular looks. He says to himself, I never think of Anselma now; she is just the woman in the tapestry, the woman in the weave.

He reaches for his pen. I have got over Liz, he says to himself. Surely? He hesitates, the quill in his hand, weighted by ink. He holds the pages down flat, and strikes out the name of her first husband. He thinks, I've meant to do that for years.

It is late. Upstairs he closes the shutter, where the moon gapes in hollow-eyed, like a drunk lost in the street. Christophe, folding garments, says, 'Is there loups? In this kingdom?'

'I think the wolves all died when the great forests were cut down. That howling you hear is only the Londoners.'

Sunday: in rose-tinted light they set out from Austin Friars, his men in their new livery of grey marbled cloth collecting the party from the city house where the nun has been held. It would be convenient, he thinks, if I had Master Secretary's barge, instead of making *ad hoc* arrangements when we have to cross the river. He has already heard Mass; Cranmer insists they all hear another. He watches the girl and sees her tears flow. Alice is right; she is at the end of her invention.

By nine o'clock she is unwinding the threads she has spent years ravelling up. She confesses in style, so hard and fast that Riche can hardly keep track, and she appeals to them as men of the world, as people with their way to make: 'You know how it is. You mention something and people are at you, what do you mean, what do you mean? You say you've had a vision and they won't leave you alone.'

'You can't disappoint people?' he says; she agrees, that's it, you can't. Once you start you have to keep going. If you try to go back they'll slaughter you.

She confesses that her visions are inventions. She never spoke to heavenly persons. Or raised the dead; that was all a fraud. She never had a hand in miracles. The letter from Mary Magdalene, Father Bocking wrote it, and a monk put gilding on the letters, in a minute she'll think of his name. The angels came out of her own invention, she seemed to see them but she knows now that they were just flashes of light against the wall. The voices she heard were not their voices, they were not distinct voices at all, just the sounds of her sisters singing in the chapel, or a woman in the road crying because she has been beaten and robbed, or perhaps the meaningless clatter of dishes from the kitchen; and those groans and cries, that seemed to come from the throats of the damned, it was someone above scraping a trestle across the floor, it was the whimper of a lost dog. 'I know now, sirs, that those saints were not real. Not in the way you are real.'

Something has broken inside her, and he wonders what that thing is.

She says, 'Is there any chance I could go home again to Kent?'

'I'll see what can be arranged.'

Hugh Latimer is sitting with them, and he gives him a hard look, as if he's making false promises. No, really, he says. Leave it with me.

Cranmer tells her gently, 'Before you can go anywhere, it will be necessary for you to make public acknowledgement of your imposture. Public confession.'

'She's not shy of crowds, are you?' These many years she's been on the road, a travelling show, and will be again, though now the nature of the show has changed; he means to display her, repentant, at Paul's Cross, and perhaps outside London too. He feels that she will take to the role of fraud, with the same relish with which she took to her role as saint.

He says to Riche, Niccolò tells us unarmed prophets always fail. He smiles and says, I mention this, Ricardo, because I know you like to have it by the book.

Cranmer leans forward and says to the Maid, these men about you, Edward Bocking and the rest, which of them were your lovers?

She is shocked: perhaps because the question has come from him, the sweetest of her interrogators. She just stares at him, as if one of them were stupid.

He says, murmuring, she may think lovers is not the word.

Enough. To Audley, to Latimer, to Riche, he says, 'I shall begin bringing in her followers, and her leaders. She has ruined many, if we care to press for their ruin. Fisher certainly, Margaret Pole perhaps, Gertrude and her husband for sure. Lady Mary the king's daughter, quite possibly. Thomas More no, Katherine no, but a fat haul of Franciscans.'

The court rises, if court is what you call it. Jo stands up. She has been sewing – or rather, unsewing, teasing out the pomegranate border from a crewel-work panel – these remnants of Katherine, of the dusty kingdom of Granada, linger in England still. She folds her work, dropping her scissors into her pocket, pinching up her sleeve and feeding her needle into the fabric for later use. She walks up to the prisoner and puts a hand on her arm. 'We must say adieu.'

'William Hawkhurst,' the girl says, 'I remember the name now. The monk who gilded the letter from Mary Magdalene.'

Richard Riche makes a note.

'Do not say any more today,' Jo advises.

'Will you come with me, mistress? Where I am going?'

'Nobody will come with you,' Jo says. 'I do not think you have the sense of it, Dame Eliza. You are going to the Tower, and I am going home to my dinner.'

This summer of 1533 has been a summer of cloudless days, of strawberry feasts in London gardens, the drone of fumbling bees, warm evenings to stroll under rose arbours and hear from the allées the sound of young gentlemen quarrelling over their bowls. The grain harvest is abundant even in the north. The trees are bowed under the weight of ripening fruit. As if he has decreed that the heat must continue, the king's court burns bright through the autumn. Monseigneur the queen's father shines like the sun, and around him spins a smaller but still blazing noonday planet, his son George Rochford. But it is Brandon who leads the dancing, galloping through the halls towing his new bride, whose age is fourteen. She is an heiress, and was betrothed to his son, but Charles thought an experienced man like him could turn her to better use.

The Seymours have put their family scandal behind them, and their fortunes are mending. Jane Seymour says to him, looking at her feet, 'Master Cromwell, my brother Edward smiled last week.'

'That was rash of him, what made him do so?'

'He heard his wife is sick. The wife he used to have. The one that my father, you know.'

'Is she likely to die?'

'Oh, very likely. Then he will get a new one. But he will keep her at his house in Elvetham, and never let her come within a mile of Wolf Hall. And when my father visits Elvetham, she will be locked in the linen room till he has gone again.'

Jane's sister Lizzie is at court with her husband, the Governor of Jersey, who is some connection of the new queen's. Lizzie comes packaged into her velvet and lace, her outlines as firm as her sister's are indefinite and blurred, her eyes bold and hazel and eloquent. Jane whispers in her wake; her eyes are the colour of water, where her thoughts slip past, like gilded fishes too small for hook or net.

It is Jane Rochford – whose mind, in his view, is underoccupied – who sees him watching the sisters. 'Lizzie Seymour must have a lover,' she says, 'it cannot be her husband who puts that glow in her cheeks, he is an old man. He was old when he was in the Scots wars.' The two sisters are just a little alike, she points out; they have the same habit of dipping their head and drawing in their underlip. 'Otherwise,' she says, smirking, 'you would think their mother had been up to the same tricks as her husband. She was a beauty in her day, you know, Margery Wentworth. And nobody knows what goes on down in Wiltshire.'

'I'm surprised you don't, Lady Rochford. You seem to know everyone's business.'

'You and me, we keep our eyes open.' She lowers her head, and says, as if directing the words inward, to her own body, 'I could keep my eyes open, if you like, in places you cannot go.'

Dear God, what does she want? It can't be money, surely? The question comes out colder than he means: 'Upon what possible inducement?'

She lifts her eyes to his. 'I should like your friendship.'

'No conditions attach to that.'

'I thought I might help you. Because your ally Lady Carey has gone down to Hever now to see her daughter. She is no longer wanted since Anne is back on duty in the bedchamber. Poor Mary.' She laughs. 'God dealt her a good enough hand but she never knew how to play it. Tell me, what will you do if the queen does not have another child?'

'There is no reason to fear it. Her mother had a child a year. Boleyn used to complain it kept him poor.'

'Have you ever observed that when a man gets a son he takes all the credit, and when he gets a daughter he blames his wife?

And if they do not breed at all, we say it is because her womb is barren. We do not say it is because his seed is bad.'

'It's the same in the gospels. The stony ground gets the blame.'

The stony places, the thorny unprofitable waste. Jane Rochford is childless after seven years of marriage. 'I believe my husband wishes I would die.' She says it lightly. He does not know how to answer. He has not asked for her confidence. 'If I do die,' she says, in the same bright tone, 'have my body opened. I ask you this in friendship. I am afraid of poison. My husband and his sister are closeted together for hours, and Anne knows all manner of poisons. She has boasted that she will give Mary a breakfast she will not recover from.' He waits. 'Mary the king's daughter, I mean. Though I am sure if it pleased Anne she would not scruple to make away with her own sister.' She glances up again. 'In your heart, if you are honest, you would like to know the things I know.'

She is lonely, he thinks, and breeding a savage heart, like Leontina in her cage. She imagines everything is about her, every glance or secret conversation. She is afraid the other women pity her, and she hates to be pitied. He says, 'What do you know of my heart?'

'I know where you have disposed it.'

'It is more than I know myself.'

'That is not uncommon among men. I can tell you who you love. Why do you not ask for her, if you want her? The Seymours are not rich. They will sell you Jane, and be glad of the bargain.'

'You are mistaken in the nature of my interest. I have young gentlemen in my house, I have wards, their marriages are my business.'

'Oh, fal la la,' she says. 'Sing another song. Tell it to infants in the nursery. Tell it to the House of Commons, you do most usually lie to them. But do not think you can deceive me.'

'For a lady who offers friendship, you have rough manners.'

'Get used to them, if you want my information. You go into Anne's rooms now, and what do you see? The queen at her prie-dieu. The queen sewing a smock for a beggar woman, wearing pearls the size of chickpeas.'

It is hard not to smile. The portrait is exact. Anne has Cranmer entranced. He thinks her the pattern of pious womanhood.

'So do you imagine that is what is really going on? Do you imagine she has given up communing with nimble young gentlemen? Riddles and verses and songs in praise of her, do you suppose she has given them up?'

'She has the king to praise her.'

'Not a good word will she hear from that quarter till her belly is big again.'

'And what will hinder that?'

'Nothing. If he is up to it.'

'Be careful.' He smiles.

'I never knew it was treason to say what passes in a prince's bed. All Europe talked about Katherine, what body part was put where, was she penetrated, and if she was did she know?' She sniggers. 'Harry's leg pains him at night. He is afraid the queen will kick him in the throes of her passion.' She puts her hand before her mouth, but the words creep out, narrow between her fingers. 'But if she lies still under him he says, what, madam, are you so little interested in making my heir?'

'I do not see what she is to do.'

'She says she gets no pleasure with him. And he – as he fought seven years to get her, he can hardly admit it has staled so soon. It was stale before they came from Calais, that is what I think.'

It's possible; maybe they were battle-weary, exhausted. Yet he gives her such magnificent presents. And they quarrel so much. Would they quarrel so much, if they were indifferent?

'So,' she goes on, 'between the kicking and the sore leg, and his lack of prowess, and her lack of desire, it will be a wonder if we ever have a Prince of Wales. Oh, he is good man enough, if he had

505

a new woman each week. If he craves novelty, who is to say she does not? Her own brother is in her service.'

He turns to look at her. 'God help you, Lady Rochford,' he says.

'To fetch his friends her way, I mean. What did you think I meant?' A little, grating laugh.

'Do you know what you mean yourself? You have been at court long enough, you know what games are played. It is no matter if any lady receives verses and compliments, even though she is married. She knows her husband writes verses elsewhere.'

'Oh, she knows that. At least, I know. There is not a minx within thirty miles who has not had a set of Rochford's verses. But if you think the gallantry stops at the bedchamber's door, you are more innocent than I took you for. You may be in love with Seymour's daughter, but you need not emulate her in having the wit of a sheep.'

He smiles. 'Sheep are maligned in that way. Shepherds say they can recognise each other. They answer to their names. They make friends for life.'

'And I will tell you who is in and out of everyone's bedchamber, it is that sneaking little boy Mark. He is the go-between for them all. My husband pays him in pearl buttons and comfit boxes and feathers for his hat.'

'Why, is Lord Rochford short of ready money?'

'You see an opportunity for usury?'

'How not?' At least, he thinks, there is one point on which we concur: pointless dislike of Mark. In Wolsey's house he had duties, teaching the choir children. Here he does nothing but stand about, wherever the court is, in greater or lesser proximity to the queen's apartments. 'Well, I can see no harm in the boy,' he says.

'He sticks like a burr to his betters. He does not know his place. He is a jumped-up nobody, taking his chance because the times are disordered.'

'I suppose you could say the same of me, Lady Rochford. And I am sure you do.'

Thomas Wyatt brings him baskets of cobnuts and filberts, bushels of Kentish apples, jolting up himself to Austin Friars on the carrier's cart. 'The venison follows,' he says, jumping down. 'I come with the fresh fruit, not the carcasses.' His hair smells of apples, his clothes are dusty from the road. 'Now you will have words with me,' he says, 'for risking a doublet worth –'

'The carrier's yearly earnings.'

Wyatt looks chastened. 'I forget you are my father.'

'I have rebuked you, so now we can fall to idle boyish talk.' Standing in a wash of chary autumn sun, he holds an apple in his hand. He pares it with a thin blade, and the peel whispers away from the flesh and lies among his papers, like the shadow of an apple, green on white paper and black ink. 'Did you see Lady Carey when you were in the country?'

'Mary Boleyn in the country. What dew-fresh pleasures spring to mind. I expect she's rutting in some hayloft.'

'Just that I want to keep hold of her, for the next time her sister is *hors de combat*.'

Wyatt sits down amid the files, an apple in his hand. 'Cromwell, suppose you'd been away from England for seven years? If you'd been like a knight in a story, lying under an enchantment? You would look around you and wonder, who are they, these people?'

This summer, Wyatt vowed, he would stay down in Kent. He would read and write on wet days, hunt when it is fine. But the fall comes, and the nights deepen, and Anne draws him back and back. His heart is true, he believes: and if she is false, it is difficult to pick where the falsehood lies. You cannot joke with Anne these days. You cannot laugh. You must think her perfect, or she will find some way to punish you.

'My old father talks about King Edward's days. He says, you see now why it's not good for the king to marry a subject, an Englishwoman?'

The trouble is, though Anne has remade the court, there are still people who knew her before, in the days when she came from France, when she set herself to seduce Harry Percy. They compete to tell stories of how she is not worthy. Or not human. How she is a snake. Or a swan. *Una candida cerva.* One single white doe, concealed in leaves of silver-grey; shivering, she hides in the trees, waiting for the lover who will turn her back from animal to goddess. 'Send me back to Italy,' Wyatt says. Her dark, her lustrous, her slanting eyes: she haunts me. She comes to me in my solitary bed at night.

'Solitary? I don't think so.'

Wyatt laughs. 'You're right. I take it where I can.'

'You drink too much. Water your wine.'

'It could have been different.'

'Everything could.'

'You never think about the past.'

'I never talk about it.'

Wyatt pleads, 'Send me away somewhere.'

'I will. When the king needs an ambassador.'

'Is it true that the Medici have offered for the Princess Mary's hand?'

'Not Princess Mary, you mean the Lady Mary. I have asked the king to think about it. But they are not grand enough for him. You know, if Gregory showed any interest in banking, I would look for a bride for him in Florence. It would be pleasant to have an Italian girl in the house.'

'Send me back there. Deploy me where I can be useful, to you or the king, as here I am useless and worse than useless to myself, and necessary to no one's pleasure.'

He says, 'Oh, by the bleached bones of Becket. Stop feeling sorry for yourself.'

Norfolk has his own view of the queen's friends. He rattles a little while he expresses it, his relics clinking, his grey disordered eyebrows working over wide-open eyes. These men, he says, these men who hang around with women! Norris, I thought better of him! And Henry Wyatt's son! Writing verse. Singing. Talk-talk-talking. 'What's the use of talking to women?' he asks earnestly. 'Cromwell, you don't talk to women, do you? I mean, what would be the topic? What would you find to say?'

I'll speak to Norfolk, he decides, when he comes back from France; ask him to incline Anne to caution. The French are meeting the Pope in Marseilles, and in default of his own attendance Henry must be represented by his most senior peer. Gardiner is already there. For me every day is like a holiday, he says to Tom Wyatt, when those two are away.

Wyatt says, 'I think Henry may have a new interest by then.'

In the days following he follows Henry's eyes, as they rest on various ladies of the court. Nothing in them, perhaps, except the speculative interest of any man; it's only Cranmer who thinks that if you look twice at a woman you have to marry her. He watches the king dancing with Lizzie Seymour, his hand lingering on her waist. He sees Anne watching, her expression cold, pinched.

Next day, he lends Edward Seymour some money on very favourable terms.

In the damp autumn mornings, when it is still half-light, his household are out early, in the damp and dripping woods. You don't get *torta di funghi* unless you pick the raw ingredients.

Richard Riche arrives at eight o'clock, his face astonished and alarmed. 'They stopped me at your gate, sir, and said, where's your bag of mushrooms? No one comes in here without mushrooms.' Riche's dignity is affronted. 'I don't think they would have asked the Lord Chancellor for mushrooms.'

'Oh, they would, Richard. But in an hour you will eat them with eggs baked in cream, and the Lord Chancellor will not. Shall we get down to work?'

Through September he has been rounding up the priests and monks who have been close to the Maid. He and Sir Purse sift the papers and conduct the interrogations. The clerics are no sooner under lock and key than they begin to deny her, and deny each other: I never believed in her, it was Father So-and-So who convinced me, I never wanted any trouble. As for their contacts with Exeter's wife, with Katherine, with Mary – each disclaims his own involvement and rushes to implicate his brother-in-Christ. The Maid's people have been in constant contact with the Exeter household. She herself has been at many of the chief monastic houses of the realm – Syon Abbey, the Charterhouse at Sheen, the Franciscan house at Richmond. He knows this because he has many contacts among disaffected monks. In every house there are a few, and he seeks out the most intelligent. Katherine herself has not met the nun. Why should she? She has Fisher to act as a go-between, and Gertrude, Lord Exeter's wife.

The king says, 'It is hard for me to believe Henry Courtenay would betray me. A Garter knight, a great man in the lists, my friend since I was a boy. Wolsey tried to part us, but I wouldn't have it.' He laughs. 'Brandon, do you remember Greenwich, that Christmas, which year was it? Remember the snowball fight?'

This is the whole difficulty of dealing with them, men who are always talking about ancient pedigrees, and boyhood friendships, and things that happened when you were still trading wool on the Antwerp exchange. You put the evidence under their noses, and they start getting teary over snowball fights. 'Look,' Henry says, 'it is Courtenay's wife that is to blame. When he knows the whole of her practices he will want to be rid of her. She is fickle and weak like all her sex, easily led into scheming.'

'So forgive her,' he says. 'Write her a pardon. Put these people under a debt of gratitude to you, if you want them to leave off their foolish sentiment towards Katherine.'

'You think you can buy hearts?' Charles Brandon says. He sounds as if he would be sad if the answer were yes.

He thinks, the heart is like any other organ, you can weigh it on a scale. 'It is not a price in money we are offering. I have enough to put the Courtenay family on trial, all Exeter's people. If we forbear to do it, we are offering their freedom and their lands. We are giving them a chance to recoup the honour of their name.'

Henry says, 'His grandfather left Crookback for my father's service.'

'If we forgive them they will play us for fools,' Charles says.

'I think not, my lord. Everything they do from now on, they do under my eye.'

'And the Poles, Lord Montague: what do you propose there?'

'He should not assume he will be pardoned.'

'Make him sweat, eh?' Charles says. 'I am not sure I like your way of dealing with noblemen.'

'They get their deserts,' the king says. 'Hush, my lord, I need to think.'

A pause. Brandon's position is too complicated for him to sustain. He wants to say, pay them out as traitors, Cromwell: but mind you butcher them respectfully. Suddenly his face clears. 'Ah, now I remember Greenwich. The snow was knee-deep that year. Ah, we were young then, Harry. You don't get snow any more, like you did when we were young.'

He gathers up his papers and begs to be excused. Reminiscence is setting in for the afternoon and there is work to be done. 'Rafe, ride over to West Horsley. Tell Exeter's wife the king thinks all women fickle and weak – though I should have thought he has plenty of evidence to the contrary. Tell her to set down in writing that she has not the wit of a flea. Tell her to claim

511

she is exceptionally easy to mislead, even for a woman. Tell her to grovel. Advise her on the wording. You know how to do it. Nothing can be too humble for Henry.'

This is the season for humility. The word from the talks in Marseilles is that King Francis has fallen at the Pope's feet and kissed his slippers. When the news comes, Henry bellows an obscenity and shreds the dispatch in his hands.

He collects up the pieces, lays it out on a table and reads it. 'Francis has kept faith with you after all,' he says. 'Surprisingly.' He has persuaded the Pope to suspend his bull of excommunication. England has a breathing space.

'I wish Pope Clement in his grave,' Henry says. 'God knows he is a man of filthy life, and he is always ailing, so he ought to die. Sometimes,' he says, 'I pray that Katherine might be translated into glory. Is that wrong?'

'If you snap your fingers, Majesty, a hundred priests will come running to tell you right from wrong.'

'It seems I prefer to hear it from you.' Henry broods, in a sulky twitching silence. 'If Clement dies, who will be the next rogue in office?'

'I've put my money on Alessandro Farnese.'

'Really?' Henry sits up. 'One lays bets?'

'But the odds are short. He has thrown about such bribes to the Roman mob all these years, that they will put the cardinals in terror when the time comes.'

'Remind me how many children has he.'

'Four I know of.'

The king is looking into the tapestry on the near wall, where white-shouldered women walk barefoot on a carpet of spring flowers. 'I may have another child soon.'

'The queen has spoken to you?'

'Not yet.' But he sees, we all do, the flare of colour in Anne's cheeks, the silk sleekness of her person, the tone of command ringing in her voice as she hands out favours and rewards to the people around her. This last week, there are more rewards than black looks, and Stephen Vaughan's wife, who is in the Bedchamber, says she has missed her courses. The king says, 'She has missed her ...' and then he stops, blushing like a schoolboy. He crosses the room, flings open his arms and embraces him, shining like a star, his great hands with their blazing rings seizing handfuls of the black velvet of his jacket. 'This time for sure. England is ours.'

Archaic, that cry from his heart: as if he were standing on the battlefield between the bloodied banners, the crown in a thorn bush, his enemies dead at his feet.

He disengages himself gently, smiling. He uncrumples the memorandum he had clenched in his fist when the king seized him; because is that not how men embrace, they knead each other with big fists, as if to knock each other down? Henry squeezes his arm and says, 'Thomas, it is like hugging a sea wall. What are you made of?' He takes the paper. He gapes. 'Is this what we must do this morning? This list?'

'Not more than fifty items. We shall soon work through.'

For the rest of the day he cannot stop smiling. Who cares for Clement and his bulls? He might as well stand on Cheap and let the populace pelt him. He might as well stand under the Christmas garlands – which we dust with flour in years when there is no snow – and sing, 'Hey nonny no, Fa-la-la, Under the trees so green-o.'

On a cold day towards the end of November the Maid and half a dozen of her principal supporters do penance at Paul's Cross. They stand shackled and barefoot in a whipping wind. The crowd is large and boisterous, the sermon lively, telling what the Maid did on her night walks when her sisters in religion were sleeping, and what lurid tales of devils she told to keep her followers in awe. Her confession is read out, at the end of which she asks the Londoners to pray for her, and begs for the king's mercy.

You wouldn't know her now, for the bonny girl they had at Lambeth. She looks haggard and ten years older. Not that she has been hurt, he would not countenance that for a woman, and in fact they have all talked without duress; the hard thing has been to stop them complicating the story by rumours and fantasies, so that half England is dragged into it. The one priest who had persistently lied, he had simply locked up with an informer; the man was detained for murder, and in no time at all Father Rich had set about saving his soul and interpreting to him the Maid's prophecies and impressing him with the names of important people he knew at court. Pitiful, really. But it has been necessary to put on this show, and next he will take it to Canterbury, so Dame Elizabeth can confess on her home ground. It is necessary to break the hold of these people who talk of the end times and threaten us with plagues and damnation. It is necessary to dispel the terror they create.

Thomas More is there, jostled among the city dignitaries; he is making towards him now, as the preachers step down and the prisoners are being led from the platform. More rubs his cold hands. He blows on them. 'Her crime is, she was made use of.'

He thinks, why did Alice let you out without your gloves? 'For all the testimony I have got,' he says, 'I still cannot understand how she arrived here, from the edge of the marshes to a public scaffold at Paul's. For sure she made no money out of it.'

'How will you frame the charges?' His tone is neutral, interested, lawyer-to-lawyer.

'The common law does not deal with women who say they can fly, or raise the dead. I shall put an act of attainder into Parliament. Treason charges for the principals. The accessories, life imprisonment, confiscation, fines. The king will be circumspect, I think. Even merciful. I am more interested in unravelling the plans of these people than in exacting penalties. I don't want a trial with scores of defendants and hundreds of witnesses, tying the courts up for years.'

More hesitates.

'Come on,' he says, 'you would have seen them off that way yourself, when you were Chancellor.'

'You may be right. I am clear anyway.' A pause. More says, 'Thomas. *In the name of Christ, you know that.*'

'As long as the king knows it. We must keep it firmly in his mind. A letter from you perhaps, enquiring after the princess Elizabeth.'

'I can do that.'

'Making it plain you accept her rights and title.'

'That is not a difficulty. The new marriage is made and must be accepted.'

'You don't think you could bring yourself to praise it?'

'Why does the king want other men to praise his wife?'

'Suppose you were to write an open letter. To say that you have seen the light in the matter of the king's natural jurisdiction over the church.' He looks across to where the prisoners are being loaded into the waiting carts. 'They are taking them back to the Tower now.' He pauses. 'You mustn't stand about. Come home with me to dinner.'

'No.' More shakes his head. 'I would rather be blown around on the river and go home hungry. If I could trust you only to put food in my mouth – but you will put words into it.'

He watches him melt into the crowd of home-going aldermen. He thinks, More is too proud to retreat from his position. He is afraid to lose his credibility with the scholars in Europe. We must find some way for him to do it, that doesn't depend on abjection. The sky has cleared now, to a flawless lapis blue. The London gardens are bright with berries. There is an obdurate winter ahead. But he feels a force ready to break, as spring breaks from the dead tree. As the word of God spreads, the people's eyes are opened to new truths. Until now, like Helen Barre, they knew Noah and the Flood, but not St Paul. They could count over the sorrows of our Blessed Mother, and say how the damned are carried down to Hell. But they did not know the manifold miracles and sayings of Christ, nor the words and deeds of the apostles, simple men who, like the poor of London, pursued simple wordless trades. The story is much bigger than they ever thought it was. He says to his nephew Richard, you cannot tell people just part of the tale and then stop, or just tell them the parts you choose. They have seen their religion painted on the walls of churches, or carved in stone, but now God's pen is poised, and he is ready to write his words in the books of their hearts.

But in these same streets Chapuys sees the stirrings of sedition, a city ready to open its gates to the Emperor. He was not at the sack of Rome but there are nights when he dreams of it as if he had been there: the black guts spilled on antique pavements, the half-dead draped in the fountains, the chiming of bells through the marsh fog, and the flames of arsonists' torches leaping along the walls. Rome has fallen and everything within it; it was not invaders but Pope Julius himself who knocked down old St Peter's, which had stood for twelve hundred years, the site where the Emperor Constantine himself had dug the first trench, twelve scoops of soil, one for each of the apostles; where the Christian martyrs, sewn into the skins of wild beasts, had been torn apart by dogs. Twenty-five feet he dug down to lay his new foundations, through a necropolis, through twelve centuries of fishbones and ash, his workmen's shovels powdering the skulls of saints. In the place where martyrs had bled, ghost-white boulders stood: marble, waiting for Michelangelo.

In the street he sees a priest carrying the host, no doubt to a dying Londoner; the passers-by uncover their heads and kneel, but a boy leans out of an upper window and jeers, 'Show us your Christ-is-Risen. Show us your Jack-in-the-Box.' He glances up; the boy's face, before it vanishes, is vivid with rage.

He says to Cranmer, these people want a good authority, one they can properly obey. For centuries Rome has asked them to believe what only children could believe. Surely they will find it more natural to obey an English king, who will exercise his powers under Parliament and under God.

Two days after he sees More shivering at the sermon, he conveys a pardon to Lady Exeter. It comes with some blistering words from the king, directed to her husband. It is St Catherine's Day: in honour of the saint who was threatened with martyrdom on a wheel, we all walk in circles to our destination. At least, that's the theory. He has never seen anyone over the age of twelve actually doing it.

There's a feeling of power in reserve, a power that drives right through the bone, like the shiver you sense in the shaft of an axe when you take it into your hand. You can strike, or you can not strike, and if you choose to hold back the blow, you can still feel inside you the resonance of the omitted thing.

Next day, at Hampton Court, the king's son the Duke of Richmond marries Norfolk's daughter Mary. Anne has arranged this marriage for the glorification of the Howards; also, to stop Henry marrying his bastard, to the boy's advantage, to some princess abroad. She has persuaded the king to waive the magnificent dower payment he would have expected and, triumphant in all her designs, she joins the dancing, her thin face flushed, her shining hair braided with dagger-tips of diamonds. Henry cannot take his eyes off her, and nor can he.

Richmond draws to him all other eyes, gambolling like a colt, showing off his wedding finery, turning, leaping, bouncing and strutting. Look at him, the older ladies say, and you will see how his father was once: that perfect glow, skin as thin as a girl's. 'Master Cromwell,' he demands, 'tell the king my father that I want to live with my wife. He says that I am to go back to my household and Mary is to stay with the queen.'

'He has a care for your health, my lord.'

'I am fifteen next.'

'It wants half a year till your birthday.'

The boy's blithe expression vanishes; a stony look takes over his face. 'Half a year is nothing. A man of fifteen is competent.'

'So we hear,' Lady Rochford says, standing idly by. 'The king your father brought witnesses to court to say his brother could do the deed at fifteen, and more than once a night.'

'It is also your bride's health that we need to think of.'

'Brandon's wife is younger than mine, and he has her.'

'Every time he sees her,' Lady Rochford says, 'if I judge by the startled expression on her face.'

Richmond is digging himself in for a long argument, entrenching himself behind precedent: it is his father's way of arguing. 'Did not my great-grandmother, Lady Margaret Beaufort, give birth at thirteen years, to the prince who would be Henry Tudor?'

Bosworth, the tattered standards, the bloody field; the stained sheet of maternity. Where do we all come from, he thinks, but this same hole and corner dealing: sweetheart, yield to me. 'I never heard it improved her health,' he says, 'or her temper. She had no children after.' Suddenly he is tired of the argument; he cuts it short, his voice tired and flat. 'Be reasonable, my lord. Once you've done it, you'll want to do it all the time. For about three years. That's the way it goes. And your father has other work in mind for you. He may send you to hold court in Dublin.'

Jane Rochford says, 'Be easy, my lamb. There are ways that can be contrived. A man may always meet a woman, if she is willing.'

'May I speak as your friend, Lady Rochford? You risk the king's displeasure if you meddle in this.'

'Oh,' she says easily, 'Henry will forgive anything to a pretty woman. They only seek to do what is natural.'

The boy says, 'Why should I live like a monk?'

'A monk? They go to it like goats. Master Cromwell here will tell you.'

'Perhaps,' Richmond says, 'it is madam the queen who wants to keep us apart. She doesn't mean the king to have a grandson in the cradle, before he has a son of his own.'

'But do you not know?' Jane Rochford turns to him. 'Has it not reached your ears that La Ana is *enceinte*?'

She gives her the name Chapuys gives her. He sees the boy's face open in blank dismay. Jane says, 'I fear by summer you will have lost your place, sweetheart. Once he has a son born in wedlock, you may tup to your heart's content. You will never reign, and your offspring will never inherit.'

It isn't often that you see a princeling's hopes destroyed, in the instant it takes to pinch out a candle flame: and with the same calculated movement, as if born of the neatness of habit. She has not even licked her fingers.

Richmond says, his face crumpling, 'It may be another girl.'

'It is almost treason to hope so,' Lady Rochford says. 'And if it is, she will have a third child, and a fourth. I thought she would not conceive again but I was wrong, Master Cromwell. She has proved herself now.'

Cranmer is in Canterbury, walking on a path of sand barefoot to his enthronement as primate of England. The ceremony done, he is sweeping out the priory of Christ Church, whose members gave so much encouragement to the false prophetess. It could be a long job, interviewing each monk, picking their stories apart. Rowland Lee storms into town to put some brawn into the business, and Gregory is in his train; so he sits in London reading a letter from his son, no longer nor more informative than his schoolboy letters: *And now no more for lack of time.*

He writes to Cranmer, be merciful to the community there, as nothing worse than misled. Spare the monk who gilded the Magdalene's letter. I suggest they give a present in cash to the king, three hundred pounds will please him. Clean out Christ Church and the whole diocese; Warham was archbishop for

519

thirty years, his family are entrenched, his bastard son is archdea-
con, take a new broom to them. Put in people from home: your
sad east Midlands clerks, formed under sober skies.

There is something beneath his desk, under his foot, the nature
of which he has avoided thinking about. He pushes his chair
back; it is half a shrew, a gift from Marlinspike. He picks it up
and thinks of Henry Wyatt, eating vermin in his cell. He thinks
of the cardinal, resplendent at Cardinal College. He throws the
shrew on the fire. The corpse fizzes and shrivels, bones gone
with an empty little pop. He picks up his pen and writes to
Cranmer, shake out those Oxford men from your diocese, and
put in Cambridge men we know.

He writes to his son, come home and spend the new year with
us.

December: in her frozen angularity, a blue light behind her cast
up from the snow, Margaret Pole looks as if she has stepped
from a church window, slivers of glass shaking from her gown;
in fact, those splinters are diamonds. He has made her come to
him, the countess, and now she looks at him from beneath her
heavy lids, she looks at him down her long Plantagenet nose,
and her greeting, ice-bright, flies out into the room. 'Cromwell.'
Just that.

She comes to business. 'The Princess Mary. Why must she quit
the house in Essex?'

'My lord Rochford wants it for his use. It's good hunting
country, you see. Mary is to join her royal sister's household, at
Hatfield. She will not need her own attendants there.'

'I offer to support my place in her household at my own
expense. You cannot prevent me from serving her.'

Try me. 'I am only the minister of the king's wishes, and you,
I suppose, are as anxious as I am to carry them out.'

'These are the wishes of the concubine. We do not believe, the
princess and I, that they are the king's own wishes.'

'You must stretch your credulity, madam.'

She looks down at him from her plinth: she is Clarence's daughter, old King Edward's niece. In her time, men like him knelt down to speak to women like her. 'I was in Katherine the queen's suite on the day she was married. To the princess, I stand as a second mother.'

'Blood of Christ, madam, you think she needs a second? The one she has will kill her.'

They stare at each other, across an abyss. 'Lady Margaret, if I may advise you ... your family's loyalty is suspect.'

'So you say. This is why you are parting me from Mary, as punishment. If you have matter enough to indict me, then send me to the Tower with Elizabeth Barton.'

'That would be much against the king's wishes. He reveres you, madam. Your ancestry, your great age.'

'He has no evidence.'

'In June last year, just after the queen was crowned, your son Lord Montague and your son Geoffrey Pole dined with Lady Mary. Then a scant two weeks later, Montague dined with her again. I wonder what they discussed?'

'Do you really?'

'No,' he says, smiling. 'The boy who carried in the dish of asparagus, that was my boy. The boy who sliced the apricots was mine too. They talked about the Emperor, about the invasion, how he might be brought to it. So you see, Lady Margaret, all your family owes much to my forbearance. I trust they will repay the king with future loyalty.'

He does not say, I mean to use your sons against their trouble-making brother abroad. He does not say, I have your son Geoffrey on my payroll. Geoffrey Pole is a violent, unstable man. You do not know how he will turn. He has paid him forty pounds this year to turn the Cromwell way.

The countess curls her lip. 'The princess will not leave her home quietly.'

'My lord of Norfolk intends to ride to Beaulieu, to tell her of the change in her circumstances. She may defy him, of course.'

He had advised the king, leave Mary in possession of her style as princess, do not diminish anything. Do not give her cousin the Emperor a reason to make war.

Henry had shouted, 'Will you go to the queen, and suggest to her that Mary keep her title? For I tell you, Master Cromwell, I am not going to do it. And if you put her in a great passion, as you will, and she falls ill and miscarries her child, you will be responsible! And I shall not incline to mercy!'

Outside the door of the presence chamber, he leans on the wall. He rolls his eyes and says to Rafe, 'God in Heaven, no wonder the cardinal was old before his time. If he thinks her pique will dislodge it, it cannot be stuck very fast. Last week I was his brother-in-arms, this week he is threatening me with a bloody end.'

Rafe says, 'It is a good thing you are not like the cardinal.'

Indeed. The cardinal expected the gratitude of his prince, in which matter he was bound to be disappointed. For all his capacities he was a man whose emotions would master him and wear him out. He, Cromwell, is no longer subject to vagaries of temperament, and he is almost never tired. Obstacles will be removed, tempers will be soothed, knots unknotted. Here at the close of the year 1533, his spirit is sturdy, his will strong, his front imperturbable. The courtiers see that he can shape events, mould them. He can contain the fears of other men, and give them a sense of solidity in a quaking world: this people, this dynasty, this miserable rainy island at the edge of the world.

By way of recreation at the end of the day, he is looking into Katherine's land holdings and judging what he can redistribute. Sir Nicholas Carew, who does not like him and does not like Anne, is amazed to receive from him a package of grants, including two fat Surrey manors to adjoin his existing holdings in the county. He seeks an interview to express his thanks; he has to ask

Richard, who keeps the Cromwell diary now, and Richard fits him in after two days. As the cardinal used to say, deference means making people wait.

When Carew comes in he is arranging his face. Chilly, self-absorbed, the complete courtier, he works at turning up the corners of his mouth. The result is a maidenly simper, incongruous above a luxuriant beard.

'Oh, I am sure you are deserving,' he says, shrugging it off. 'You are a boyhood friend of His Majesty and nothing gives him greater pleasure than to reward his old friends. Your wife is in touch with the Lady Mary, is she not? They are close? Ask her,' he says gently, 'to give the young woman good advice. Warn her to be conformable to the king in all things. His temper is short these days and I cannot answer for the consequences of defiance.'

Deuteronomy tells us, gifts blind the eyes of the wise. Carew is not particularly wise, in his opinion, but the principle holds good; and if not exactly blinded, at least he looks dazed. 'Call it an early Christmas present,' he tells him, smiling. He pushes the papers across his desk.

At Austin Friars they are cleaning out store rooms and building strong rooms. They will keep the feast at Stepney. The angel's wings are moved there; he wants to keep them, till there is another child in the house of the right size. He sees them going, shivering in their shroud of fine linen, and watches the Christmas star loaded on to a cart. Christophe asks, 'How would one work it, that savage machine that is all over points?'

He draws off one of the canvas sleeves, shows him the gilding. 'Jesus Maria,' the boy says. 'The star that guides us to Bethlehem. I thought it was an engine for torture.'

Norfolk goes down to Beaulieu to tell Lady Mary she must move to the manor at Hatfield, and be an attendant to the little princess, and live under the governance of Lady Anne Shelton, aunt to the queen. What ensues, he reports back in aggrieved tones.

'Aunt to the queen?' says Mary. 'There is but one queen, and that is my mother.'

'Lady Mary ...' Norfolk says, and the words make her burst into tears, and run to her room and lock herself in.

Suffolk goes up the country to Buckden, to convince Katherine to move to another house. She has heard that they mean to send her somewhere even damper than Buckden, and she says the damp will kill her, so she too shuts herself up, rattling the bolts into place and shouting at Suffolk in three languages to go away. She will go nowhere, she says, unless he is prepared to break down the door and bind her with ropes and carry her. Which Charles thinks is a little extreme.

Brandon sounds so sorry for himself when he writes back to London for instructions: a man with a bride of fourteen awaiting his attentions, to spend the holiday like this! When his letter is read out to the council, he, Cromwell, bursts out laughing. The sheer joy of it carries him into the new year.

There is a young woman walking the roads of the kingdom, saying she is the princess Mary, and that her father has turned her out to beg. She has been seen as far north as York and as far east as Lincoln, and simple people in these shires are lodging and feeding her and giving her money to see her on her way. He has people keeping an eye out for her, but they haven't caught her yet. He doesn't know what he would do with her if he did catch her. It is punishment enough, to take on the burden of a prophecy, and to be out unprotected on the winter roads. He pictures her, a dun-coloured, dwindling figure, tramping away towards the horizon over the flat muddy fields.

III
A Painter's Eye
1534

When Hans brings the finished portrait to Austin Friars he feels shy of it. He remembers when Walter would say, look me in the face, boy, when you tell me a lie.

He looks at the picture's lower edge, and allows his gaze to creep upwards. A quill, scissors, papers, his seal in a little bag, and a heavy volume, bound in blackish green: the leather tooled in gold, the pages gilt-edged. Hans had asked to see his Bible, rejected it as too plain, too thumbed. He had scoured the house and found the finest volume he owned on the desk of Thomas Avery. It is the monk Pacioli's work, the book on how to keep your books, sent to him by his kind friends in Venice.

He sees his painted hand, resting on the desk before him, holding a paper in a loose fist. It is uncanny, as if he had been pulled apart, to look at himself in sections, digit by digit. Hans has made his skin smooth as the skin of a courtesan, but the motion he has captured, that folding of the fingers, is as sure as that of a slaughterman's when he picks up the killing knife. He is wearing the cardinal's turquoise.

He had a turquoise ring of his own, one time, which Liz gave to him when Gregory was born. It was a ring in the shape of a heart.

He raises his eyes, to his own face. It does not much improve on the Easter egg which Jo painted. Hans had penned him in a little space, pushing a heavy table to fasten him in. He had time to think, while Hans drew him, and his thoughts took him far off, to another country. You cannot trace those thoughts behind his eyes.

He had asked to be painted in his garden. Hans said, the very notion makes me sweat. Can we keep it simple, yes?

He wears his winter clothes. Inside them, he seems made of a more impermeable substance than most men, more compacted. He could well be wearing armour. He foresees the day when he might have to. There are men in this realm and abroad (not only in Yorkshire now) who would stab him as soon as look at him.

I doubt, he thinks, they can hack through to the heart. The king had said, what are you made of?

He smiles. There is no trace of a smile on the face of his painted self.

'Right.' He sweeps into the next room. 'You can come and see it.'

They crowd in, jostling. There is a short, appraising silence. It lengthens. Alice says, 'He has made you look rather stout, Uncle. More than he need.'

Richard says, 'As Leonardo has demonstrated to us, a curved surface better deflects the impact of cannon balls.'

'I don't think you look like that,' Helen Barre says. 'I see that your features are true enough. But that is not the expression on your face.'

Rafe says, 'No, Helen, he saves it for men.'

Thomas Avery says, 'The Emperor's man is here, can he come in and have a look?'

'He is welcome, as always.'

Chapuys prances in. He positions himself before the painting; he skips forward; he leaps back. He is wearing marten furs over silks. 'Dear God,' Johane says behind her hand, 'he looks like a dancing monkey.'

'Oh no, I fear not,' Eustache says. 'Oh, no, no, no, no, no. Your Protestant painter has missed the mark this time. For one never thinks of you alone, Cremuel, but in company, studying the faces of other people, as if you yourself mean to paint them. You make other men think, not "what does he look like?" but "what do I look like?"' He whisks away, then swings around, as if to catch the likeness in the act of moving. 'Still. Looking at that, one would be loath to cross you. To that extent, I think Hans has achieved his aim.'

When Gregory comes home from Canterbury, he takes him in alone to see the painting, still in his riding coat, muddy from the road; he wants to hear his son's opinion, before the rest of the household get to him. He says, 'Your lady mother always said she didn't pick me for my looks. I was surprised, when the picture came, to find I was vain. I thought of myself as I was when I left Italy, twenty years ago. Before you were born.'

Gregory stands at his shoulder. His eyes rest on the portrait. He doesn't speak.

He is conscious that his son is taller than he is: not that it takes much. He steps sideways, though only in his mind, to see his boy with a painter's eye: a boy with fine white skin and hazel eyes, a slender angel of the second rank in a fresco dappled with damp, in some hill town far from here. He thinks of him as a page in a forest riding across vellum, dark curls crisp under a narrow band of gold; whereas the young men about him every day, the young men of Austin Friars, are muscled like fighting dogs, hair cropped to stubble, eyes sharp as sword points. He thinks, Gregory is all he should be. He is everything I have a right to hope for: his openness, his gentleness, the reserve and consideration with which he holds back his thoughts till he has framed them. He feels such tenderness for him he thinks he might cry.

He turns to the painting. 'I fear Mark was right.'

'Who is Mark?'

'A silly little boy who runs after George Boleyn. I once heard him say I looked like a murderer.'

Gregory says, 'Did you not know?'

527

PART SIX

I

Supremacy

1534

In the convivial days between Christmas and New Year, while the court is feasting and Charles Brandon is in the fens shouting at a door, he is rereading Marsiglio of Padua. In the year 1324 Marsiglio put to us forty-two propositions. When the feast of the Epiphany is past, he ambles along to put a few of them to Henry.

Some of these propositions the king knows, some are strange to him. Some are congenial, in his present situation; some have been denounced to him as heresy. It's a morning of brilliant, bone-chilling cold, the wind off the river like a knife in the face. We are breezing in to push our luck.

Marsiglio tells us that when Christ came into this world he came not as a ruler or a judge, but as a subject: subject to the state as he found it. He did not seek to rule, nor pass on to his disciples a mission to rule. He did not give power to one of his followers more than another; if you think he did, read again those verses about Peter. Christ did not make Popes. He did not give his followers the power to make laws or levy taxes, both of which churchmen have claimed as their right.

Henry says, 'I never remember the cardinal spoke of this.'

'Would you, if you were a cardinal?'

Since Christ did not induce his followers into earthly power, how can it be maintained that the princes of today derive their

531

power from the Pope? In fact, all priests are subjects, as Christ left them. It is for the prince to govern the bodies of his citizens, to say who is married and who can marry, who is a bastard and who legitimate.

Where does the prince get this power, and his power to enforce the law? He gets it through a legislative body, which acts on behalf of the citizens. It is from the will of the people, expressed in Parliament, that a king derives his kingship.

When he says this, Henry seems to be straining his ears, as if he might catch the sound of the people coming down the road to turn him out of his palace. He reassures him on the point: Marsiglio gives no legitimacy to rebels. Citizens may indeed band together to overthrow a despot, but he, Henry, is not a despot; he is a monarch who rules within the law. Henry likes the people to cheer him as he rides through London, but the wise prince is not always the most popular prince; he knows this.

He has other propositions to put to him. Christ did not bestow on his followers grants of land, or monopolies, offices, promotions. All these things are the business of the secular power. A man who has taken vows of poverty, how can he have property rights? How can monks be landlords?

The king says, 'Cromwell, with your facility for large numbers ...' He stares into the distance. His fingers pick at the silver lacing of his cuff.

'The legislative body,' he says, 'should provide for the maintenance of priests and bishops. After that, it should be able to use the church's wealth for the public good.'

'But how to free it,' Henry says. 'I suppose shrines can be broken.' Gem-studded himself, he thinks of the kind of wealth you can weigh. 'If there were any who dared.'

It is a characteristic of Henry, to run before you to where you were not quite going. He had meant to gentle him towards an intricate legal process of dispossession, repossession: the assertion of ancient sovereign rights, the taking back of what was always yours. He will remember that it was Henry who first suggested picking up a chisel and gouging the sapphire eyes out of saints. But he is willing to follow the king's thought. 'Christ taught us how to remember him. He left us bread and wine, body and blood. What more do we need? I cannot see where he asked for shrines to be set up, or instituted a trade in body parts, in hair and nails, or asked us to make plaster images and worship them.'

'Would you be able to estimate,' Henry says, 'even … no, I suppose you wouldn't.' He gets to his feet. 'Well, the sun shines, so …'

Better make hay. He sweeps the day's papers together. 'I can finish up.' Henry goes off to get into his double-padded riding coat. He thinks, we don't want our king to be the poor man of Europe. Spain and Portugal have treasure flowing in every year from the Americas. Where is our treasure?

Look around you.

His guess is, the clergy own a third of England. One day soon, Henry will ask him how the Crown can own it instead. It's like dealing with a child; one day you bring in a box, and the child asks, what is in there? Then it goes to sleep and forgets, but next day, it asks again. It doesn't rest until the box is open and the treats given out.

Parliament is about to reconvene. He says to the king, no parliament in history has worked as hard as I mean to work this one.

Henry says, 'Do what you have to do. I will back you.'

It's like hearing words you've waited all your life to hear. It's like hearing a perfect line of poetry, in a language you knew before you were born.

He goes home happy, but the cardinal is waiting for him in a corner. He is plump as a cushion in his scarlet robes and his face wears a martial and mutinous expression. Wolsey says, you know he will take the credit for your good ideas, and you the blame for his bad ones? When fortune turns against you, you will feel her lash: you always, he never.

He says, my dear Wolsey. (For now that cardinals are finished in this realm, he addresses him as a colleague, not a master.) My dear Wolsey, not entirely so – he didn't blame Charles Brandon for splintering a lance inside his helmet, he blamed himself for not putting his visor down.

The cardinal says, do you think this is a tilting ground? Do you think there are rules, protocols, judges to see fair play? One day, when you are still adjusting your harness, you will look up and see him thundering at you downhill.

The cardinal vanishes, with a chortle.

Even before the Commons convenes, his opponents meet to work out their tactics. Their meetings are not secret. Servants go in and out, and his method with the Pole conclaves bears repeating: there are young men in the Cromwell household not too proud to put on an apron and bring in a platter of halibut or a joint of beef. The gentlemen of England apply for places in his household now, for their sons and nephews and wards, thinking they will learn statecraft with him, how to write a secretary's hand and deal with translation from abroad, and what books one ought to read to be a courtier. He takes it seriously, the trust placed in him; he takes gently from the hands of these noisy young persons their daggers, their pens, and he talks to them, finding out behind the passion and pride of young men of fifteen or twenty what they are really worth, what they value and would value under duress. You learn nothing about men by snubbing them and crushing their pride. You must ask them what it is they can do in this world, that they alone can do.

The boys are astonished by the question, their souls pour out. Perhaps no one has talked to them before. Certainly not their fathers.

You introduce these boys, violent or unscholarly as they are, to humble occupations. They learn the psalms. They learn the use of a filleting blade and a paring knife; only then, for self-defence and in no formal lesson, they learn the *estoc*, the killing jerk under the ribs, the simple twist of the wrist that makes you sure. Christophe offers himself as instructor. These *messieurs*, he says, be sure they are dainty. They are cutting off the head of the stag or the tail of the rat, I know not what, to send home to their dear papa. Only you and me, master, and Richard Cremuel, we know how to stop some little fuckeur in his tracks, so that's the end of him, and he doesn't even squeak.

Before spring comes, some of the poor men who stand at his gate find their way inside it. The eyes and ears of the unlettered are as sharp as those of the gentry, and you need not be a scholar to have a good wit. Horseboys and kennelmen overhear the confidences of earls. A boy with kindling and bellows hears the sleepy secrets of early morning, when he goes in to light a fire.

On a day of strong sunlight, sudden and deceptive warmth, Call-Me-Risley strides into Austin Friars. He barks, 'Give you good morning, sir,' throws off his jacket, sits down to his desk and scrapes forward his stool. He picks up his quill and looks at the tip of it. 'Right, what do you have for me?' His eyes are glittering and the tips of his ears are pink.

'I think Gardiner must be back,' he says.

'How did you know?' Call-Me throws down his pen. He jumps up. He strides about. 'Why is he like he is? All this wrangling and jangling and throwing out questions when he doesn't care about the answers?'

'You liked it well enough when you were at Cambridge.'

'Oh, then,' Wriothesley says, with contempt for his young self. 'It's supposed to train our minds. I don't know.'

'My son claims it wore him out, the practice of scholarly disputation. He calls it the practice of futile argument.'

'Perhaps Gregory's not completely stupid.'

'I would be glad to think not.'

Call-Me blushes a deep red. 'I mean no offence, sir. You know Gregory's not like us. As the world goes, he is too good. But you don't have to be like Gardiner, either.'

'When the cardinal's advisers met, we would propose plans, there would perhaps be some dispute, but we would talk it through; then we would refine our plans, and implement them. The king's council doesn't work like that.'

'How could it? Norfolk? Charles Brandon? They'll fight you because of who you are. Even if they agree with you, they'll fight you. Even if they know you're right.'

'I suppose Gardiner has been threatening you.'

'With ruin.' He folds one fist into the other. 'I don't regard it.'

'But you should. Winchester is a powerful man and if he says he will ruin you that is what he means to do.'

'He calls me disloyal. He says while I was abroad I should have minded his interests, instead of yours.'

'My understanding is, you serve Master Secretary, whoever is acting in that capacity. If I,' he hesitates, 'if – Wriothesley, I make you this offer, if I am confirmed in the post, I will put you in charge at the Signet.'

'I will be chief clerk?' He sees Call-Me adding up the fees.

'So now, go to Gardiner, apologise, and get him to make you a better offer. Hedge your bets.'

His face alarmed, Call-Me hovers. 'Run, boy.' He scoops up his jacket and thrusts it at him. 'He's still Secretary. He can have his seals back. Only tell him, he has to come here and collect them in person.'

Call-Me laughs. He rubs his forehead, dazed, as if he's been in a fight. He throws on his coat. 'We're hopeless, aren't we?'

Inveterate scrappers. Wolves snapping over a carcase. Lions fighting over Christians.

The king calls him in, with Gardiner, to look through the bill he proposes to put into Parliament to secure the succession of Anne's children. The queen is with them; many private gentlemen see less of their wives, he thinks, than the king does. He rides, Anne rides. He hunts, Anne hunts. She takes his friends, and makes them into hers.

She has a habit of reading over Henry's shoulder; she does it now, her exploring hand sliding across his silky bulk, through the layers of his clothing, so that a tiny fingernail hooks itself beneath the embroidered collar of his shirt, and she raises the fabric just a breath, just a fraction, from pale royal skin; Henry's vast hand reaches to caress hers, an absent, dreamy motion, as if they were alone. The draft refers, time and again, and correctly it would seem, to '*your most dear and entirely beloved wife Queen Anne*'.

The Bishop of Winchester is gaping. As a man, he cannot unglue himself from the spectacle, yet as a bishop, it makes him clear his throat. Anne takes no notice; she carries on doing what she's doing, and reading out the bill, until she looks up, shocked: it mentions my death! '*If it should happen your said dear and entirely beloved wife Queen Anne to decease …*'

'I can't exclude the event,' he says. 'Parliament can do anything, madam, except what is against nature.'

She flushes. 'I shall not die of the child. I am strong.'

He doesn't remember that Liz lost her wits when she was carrying a child. If anything, she was ever more sober and frugal, and spent time making store-cupboard inventories. Anne the queen takes the draft out of Henry's hand. She shakes it in a passion. She is angry with the paper, jealous of the ink. She says, 'This bill provides that if I die, say I die now, say I die of a fever and I die undelivered, then he can put another queen in my place.'

'Sweetheart,' the king says, 'I cannot imagine another in your place. It is only notional. He must make provision for it.'

'Madam,' Gardiner says, 'if I may defend Cromwell, he envisages only the customary situation. You would not condemn His Majesty to a life as perpetual widower? And we know not the hour, do we?'

Anne takes no notice, it's as if Winchester had not spoken. 'And if she has a son, it says, that son will inherit. It says, *heirs male lawfully begotten.* Then what happens to my daughter and her claim?'

'Well,' Henry says, 'she is still a princess of England. If you look further down the paper, it says that …' He closes his eyes. God give me strength.

Gardiner springs to supply some: 'If the king never had a son, not in lawful matrimony with any woman, then your daughter would be queen. That is what Cromwell proposes.'

'But why must it be written like this? And where does it say that Spanish Mary is a bastard?'

'Lady Mary is out of the line of succession,' he says, 'so the inference is clear. We don't need to say more. You must forgive any coldness of expression. We try to write laws sparingly. And so that they are not personal.'

'By God,' Gardiner says with relish, 'if this isn't personal, what is?'

The king seems to have invited Stephen to this conference in order to snub him. Tomorrow, of course, it could go the other way; he could arrive to see Henry arm in arm with Winchester and strolling among the snowdrops. He says, 'We mean to seal this act with an oath. His Majesty's subjects to swear to uphold the succession to the throne, as laid out in this paper and ratified by Parliament.'

'An oath?' Gardiner says. 'What sort of legislation needs to be confirmed by an oath?'

'You will always find those who will say a parliament is misled, or bought, or in some way incapable of representing the commonwealth. Again, you will find those who will deny Parliament's competence to legislate in certain matters, saying they must be left to some other jurisdiction – to Rome, in effect. But I think that is a mistake. Rome has no legitimate voice in England. In my bill I mean to state a position. It is a modest one. I draft it, it may please Parliament to pass it, it may please the king to sign it. I shall then ask the country to endorse it.'

'So what will you do?' Stephen says, jeering. 'Have your boys from Austin Friars up and down the land, swearing every man Jack you dig out of an alehouse? Every man Jack and every Jill?'

'Why should I not swear them? Do you think because they are not bishops they are brutes? One Christian's oath is as good as another's. Look at any part of this kingdom, my lord bishop, and you will find dereliction, destitution. There are men and women on the roads. The sheep farmers are grown so great that the little man is knocked off his acres and the ploughboy is out of house and home. In a generation these people can learn to read. The ploughman can take up a book. Believe me, Gardiner, England can be otherwise.'

'I have made you angry,' Gardiner observes. 'Provoked, you mistake the question. I asked you not if their word is good, but how many of them you propose to swear. But of course, in the Commons you have brought in a bill against sheep –'

'Against the runners of sheep,' he says, smiling.

The king says, 'Gardiner, it is to help the common people – no grazier to run more than two thousand animals –'

The bishop cuts his king off as if he were a child. 'Two thousand, yes, so while your commissioners are rampaging through the shires counting sheep, perhaps they can swear the shepherds at the same time, eh? And these ploughboys of yours, in their preliterate condition? And any drabs they find in a ditch?'

He has to laugh. The bishop is so vehement. 'My lord, I will swear whoever is necessary to make the succession safe, and unite the country behind us. The king has his officers, his justices of the peace – and the lords of the council will be put on their honour to make this work, or I will know why.'

Henry says, 'The bishops will take the oath. I hope they will be conformable.'

'We want some new bishops,' Anne says. She names her friend Hugh Latimer. His friend, Rowland Lee. It seems after all she does have a list, which she carries in her head. Liz made preserves. Anne makes pastors.

'Latimer?' Stephen shakes his head, but he cannot accuse the queen, to her face, of loving heretics. 'Rowland Lee, to my certain knowledge, has never stood in a pulpit in his life. Some men come into the religious life only for ambition.'

'And have barely the grace to disguise it,' he says.

'I make the best of my road,' Stephen says. 'I was set upon it. By God, Cromwell, I walk it.'

He looks up at Anne. Her eyes sparkle with glee. Not a word is lost on her.

Henry says, 'My lord Winchester, you have been out of the country a great while, on your embassy.'

'I hope Your Majesty thinks it has been to his profit.'

'Indeed, but you have not been able to avoid neglecting your diocese.'

'As a pastor, you should mind your flock,' Anne says. 'Count them, perhaps.'

He bows. 'My flock is safe in fold.'

Short of kicking the bishop downstairs himself, or having him hauled out by the guards, the king can't do much more. 'All the same, feel free to attend to it,' Henry murmurs.

There is a feral stink that rises from the hide of a dog about to fight. It rises now into the room, and he sees Anne turn aside, fastidious, and Stephen put his hand to his chest, as if to ruffle up his fur, to warn of his size before he bares his teeth. 'I shall be back with Your Majesty within a week,' he says. His dulcet sentiment comes out as a snarl from the depth of his guts.

Henry bursts into laughter. 'Meanwhile we like Cromwell. Cromwell treats us very well.'

Once Winchester has gone, Anne hangs over the king again; her eyes flick sideways, as if she were drawing him into conspiracy. Anne's bodice is still tight-laced, only a slight fullness of her breasts indicating her condition. There has been no announcement; announcements are never made, women's bodies are uncertain things and mistakes can occur. But the whole court is sure she is carrying the heir, and she says so herself; apples are not mentioned this time, and all the foods she craved when she was carrying the princess revolt her, so the signs are good it will be a boy. This bill he will bring into the Commons is not, as she thinks, some anticipation of disaster, but a confirmation of her place in the world. She must be thirty-three this year. For how many years did he laugh at her flat chest and yellow skin? Even he can see her beauty, now she is queen. Her face seems sculpted in the purity of its lines, her skull small like a cat's; her throat has a mineral glitter, as if it were powdered with fool's gold.

Henry says, 'Stephen is a resolute ambassador, no doubt, but I cannot keep him near me. I have trusted him with my innermost councils, and now he turns.' He shakes his head. 'I hate ingratitude. I hate disloyalty. That is why I value a man like you. You were good to your old master in his trouble. Nothing could commend you more to me, than that.' He speaks as if he, personally, hadn't caused the trouble; as if Wolsey's fall were caused by a thunderbolt. 'Another who has disappointed me is Thomas More.'

Anne says, 'When you write your bill against the false prophetess Barton, put More in it, beside Fisher.'

He shakes his head. 'It won't run. Parliament won't have it. There is plenty of evidence against Fisher, and the Commons don't like him, he talks to them as if they were Turks. But More came to me even before Barton was arrested and showed me how he was clear in the matter.'

'But it will frighten him,' Anne says. 'I want him frightened. Fright may unmake a man. I have seen it occur.'

* * *

541

Three in the afternoon: candles brought in. He consults Richard's day-book: John Fisher is waiting. It is time to be enraged. He tries thinking about Gardiner, but he keeps laughing. 'Arrange your face,' Richard says.

'You'd never imagine that Stephen owed me money. I paid for his installation at Winchester.'

'Call it in, sir.'

'But I have already taken his house for the queen. He is still grieving. I had better not drive him to an extremity. I ought to leave him a way back.'

Bishop Fisher is seated, his skeletal hands resting on an ebony cane. 'Good evening, my lord,' he says. 'Why are you so gullible?'

The bishop seems surprised that they are not to start off with a prayer. Nevertheless, he murmurs a blessing.

'You had better ask the king's pardon. Beg the favour of it. Plead with him to consider your age and infirmities.'

'I do not know my offence. And, whatever you think, I am not in my second childhood.'

'But I believe you are. How else would you have given credence to this woman Barton? If you came across a puppet show in the street, would you not stand there cheering, and shout, "Look at their little wooden legs walking, look how they wave their arms? Hear them blow their trumpets". Would you not?'

'I don't think I ever saw a puppet show,' Fisher says sadly. 'At least, not one of the kind of which you speak.'

'But you're in one, my lord bishop! Look around you. It's all one great puppet show.'

'And yet so many did believe in her,' Fisher says mildly. 'Warham himself, Canterbury that was. A score, a hundred of devout and learned men. They attested her miracles. And why should she not voice her knowledge, being inspired? We know that before the Lord goes to work, he gives warning of himself through his servants, for it is stated by the prophet Amos ...'

'Don't prophet Amos me, man. She threatened the king. Foresaw his death.'

'Foreseeing it is not the same as desiring it, still less plotting it.'

'Ah, but she never foresaw anything that she didn't hope would happen. She sat down with the king's enemies and told them how it would be.'

'If you mean Lord Exeter,' the bishop says, 'he is already pardoned, of course, and so is Lady Gertrude. If they were guilty, the king would have proceeded.'

'That does not follow. Henry wishes for reconciliation. He finds it in him to be merciful. As he may be to you even yet, but you must admit your faults. Exeter has not been writing against the king, but you have.'

'Where? Show me.'

'Your hand is disguised, my lord, but not from me. Now you will publish no more.' Fisher's glance shoots upwards. Delicately, his bones move beneath his skin; his fist grips his cane, the handle of which is a gilded dolphin. 'Your printers abroad are working for me now. My friend Stephen Vaughan has offered them a better rate.'

'It is about the divorce you are hounding me,' Fisher says. 'It is not about Elizabeth Barton. It is because Queen Katherine asked my counsel and I gave it.'

'You say I am hounding you, when I ask you to keep within the law? Do not try to lead me away from your prophetess, or I will lead you where she is and lock you up next door to her. Would you have been so keen to believe her, if in one of her visions she had seen Anne crowned queen a year before it occurred, and Heaven smiling down on the event? In that case, I put it to you, you would have called her a witch.'

Fisher shakes his head; he retreats into bafflement. 'I always wondered, you know, it has puzzled me many a year, if in the gospels Mary Magdalene was the same Mary who was Martha's sister. Elizabeth Barton told me for a certainty she was. In the whole matter, she didn't hesitate.'

He laughs. 'Oh, she's familiar with these people. She's in and out of their houses. She's shared a bowl of pottage many a time with our Blessed Lady. Look now, my lord, holy simplicity was well enough in its day, but its day is over. We're at war. Just because the Emperor's soldiers aren't running down the street, don't deceive yourself – this is a war and you are in the enemy camp.'

The bishop is silent. He sways a little on his stool. Sniffs. 'I see why Wolsey retained you. You are a ruffian and so was he. I have been a priest forty years, and I have never seen such ungodly men as those who flourish today. Such evil councillors.'

'Fall ill,' he says. 'Take to your bed. That's what I recommend.'

The bill of attainder against the Maid and her allies is laid before the House of Lords on a Saturday morning, 21 February. Fisher's name is in it and so, at Henry's command, is More's. He goes to the Tower to see the woman Barton, to see if she has anything else to get off her conscience before her death is scheduled.

She has survived the winter, trailed across country to her outdoor confessions, standing exposed on scaffolds in the cutting wind. He brings a candle in with him, and finds her slumped on her stool like a badly tied bundle of rags; the air is both cold and stale. She looks up and says, as if they were resuming a conversation, 'Mary Magdalene told me I should die.'

Perhaps, he thinks, she has been talking to me in her head. 'Did she give you a date?'

'You'd find that helpful?' she asks. He wonders if she knows that Parliament, indignant over More's inclusion, could delay the bill against her till spring. 'I'm glad you've come, Master Cromwell. Nothing happens here.'

Not even his most prolonged, his most subtle interrogations had frightened her. To get Katherine pulled into it, he had tried every trick he knew: with no result. He says, 'You are fed properly, are you?'

'Oh yes. And my laundry done. But I miss it, when I used to go to Lambeth, see the archbishop, I liked that. Seeing the river. All the people bustling along, and the boats unloading. Do you know if I shall be burned? Lord Audley said I would be burned.' She speaks as if Audley were an old friend.

'I hope you can be spared that. It is for the king to say.'

'I go to Hell these nights,' she says. 'Master Lucifer shows me a chair. It is carved of human bones and padded with cushions of flame.'

'Is it for me?'

'Bless you, no. For the king.'

'Any sightings of Wolsey?'

'The cardinal's where I left him.' Seated among the unborn. She pauses; a long drifting pause. 'They say it can take an hour for the body to burn. Mother Mary will exalt me. I shall bathe in the flames, as one bathes in a fountain. To me, they will be cool.' She looks into his face but at his expression she turns away. 'Sometimes they pack gunpowder in the wood, don't they? Makes it quick then. How many will be going with me?'

Six. He names them. 'It could have been sixty. Do you know that? Your vanity brought them here.'

As he says it he thinks, it is also true that their vanity brought her: and he sees that she would have preferred sixty to die, to see Exeter and the Pole family pulled down to disgrace; it would have sealed her fame. That being so, why would she not name Katherine as party to the plot? What a triumph that would be for a prophet, to ruin a queen. There, he thinks, I shouldn't have been so subtle after all; I should have played on her greed to be infamous. 'Shall I not see you again?' she says. 'Or will you be there, when I suffer?'

'This throne,' he says. 'This chair of bones. It would be as well to keep it to yourself. Not to let the king hear of it.'

'I think he ought. He should have warning of what is waiting for him after death. And what can he do to me, worse than he already plans?'

'You don't want to plead your belly?'

She blushes. 'I'm not with child. You're laughing at me.'

'I would advise anyone to get a few more weeks of life, by any means they can. Say you have been ill-used on the road. Say your guards have dishonoured you.'

'But then I would have to say who did it, and they would be taken before a judge.'

He shakes his head, pitying her. 'When a guard despoils a prisoner, he doesn't leave her his name.'

Anyway, she doesn't like his idea, that's plain. He leaves her. The Tower is like a small town and its morning routine clatters on around him, the guards and the men from the Mint greet him, and the keeper of the king's beasts trots up to say it's dinner time – they eat early, the beasts – and does he want to see them fed? I take it very kindly, he says, waiving the pleasure; unbreakfasted himself, slightly nauseous, he can smell stale blood and from the direction of their cages hear their truffling grunts and smothered roars. High up on the walls above the river, out of sight, a man is whistling an old tune, and at the refrain breaks into song; he is a jolly forester, he sings. Which is most certainly untrue.

He looks around for his boatmen. He wonders whether the Maid is ill, and whether she will live to be killed. She was never harmed in his custody, only harassed; kept awake a night or two, but no longer than the king's business keeps him awake, and you don't, he thinks, find me confessing to anything. It's nine o'clock; by ten o'clock dinner, he has to be with Norfolk and Audley, who he hopes will not scream and smell, like the beasts. There is a tentative, icy sun; loops of vapour coil across the river, a scribble of mist.

At Westminster, the duke chases out the servants. 'If I want a drink I'll get it for myself. Go on, out, out you go. And shut the door! Any lurking at the keyhole, I'll skin you alive and salt you!' He turns, swearing under his breath, and takes his chair with a grunt. 'What if I begged him?' he says. 'What if I went down on my knees, said, Henry for the Lord's sake, take Thomas More out of the attainder?'

'What if we all begged him,' Audley says, 'on our knees?'

'Oh, and Cranmer too,' he says. 'We'll have him in. He's not to escape this delectable interlude.'

'The king swears,' Audley says, 'that if the bill is opposed, he will come before Parliament himself, both houses if need be, and insist.'

'He may have a fall,' the duke says. 'And in public. For God's sake, Cromwell, don't let him do it. He knew More was against him and he let him creep off to Chelsea to coddle his conscience. But it's my niece, I suppose, who wants him brought to book. She takes it personally. Women do.'

'I think the king takes it personally.'

'Which is weak,' Norfolk says, 'in my view. Why should he care how More judges him?'

Audley smiles uncertainly. 'You call the king weak?'

'*Call the king weak?*' The duke lurches forward and squawks into Audley's face, as if he were a talking magpie. 'What's this, Lord Chancellor, speaking up for yourself? You do usually wait till Cromwell speaks, and then it's chirrup-chirrup, yes-sir-no-sir, whatever you say, Tom Cromwell.'

The door opens and Call-Me-Risley appears, in part. 'By God,' says the duke, 'if I had a crossbow, I'd shoot your very head off. I said nobody was to come in here.'

'Will Roper is here. He has letters from his father-in-law. More wants to know what you will do for him, sir, as you have admitted that in law he has no case to answer.'

'Tell Will we are just now rehearsing how to beg the king to take More's name out of the bill.'

The duke knocks back his drink, the one he has poured himself. He bounces his goblet back on the table. 'Your cardinal used to say, Henry will give half his realm rather than be baulked, he will not be cheated of any part of his will.'

'But I reason … do not you, Lord Chancellor …'

'Oh, he does,' the duke says. 'Whatever you reason, Tom, he reasons. *Squawk, squawk.*'

Wriothesley looks startled. 'Could I bring Will in?'

'So we are united? On our knees to beg?'

'I won't do it unless Cranmer will,' the duke says. 'Why should a layman wear out his joints?'

'Shall we send for my lord Suffolk too?' Audley suggests.

'No. His boy is dying. His heir.' The duke scrubs his hand across his mouth. 'He wants just a month of his eighteenth birthday.' His fingers fidget for his holy medals, his relics. 'Brandon's got the one boy. So have I. So have you, Cromwell. And Thomas More. Just the one boy. God help Charles, he'll have to start breeding again with his new wife; that'll be a hardship to him, I'm sure.' He gives a bark of laughter. 'If I could pension my lady wife off, I could get a juicy fifteen-year-old too. But she won't go.'

It is too much for Audley. His face flushes. 'My lord, you have been married, and well married, these twenty years.'

'Do I not know it? It's like placing your person in a grizzled leather bag.' The duke's bony hand descends; he squeezes his shoulder. 'Get me a divorce, Cromwell, will you? You and my lord archbishop, come up with some grounds. I promise there'll be no murder done over it.'

'Where is murder done?' Wriothesley says.

'We're preparing to murder Thomas More, aren't we? Old Fisher, we're whetting the knife for him, eh?'

'God forbid.' The Lord Chancellor rises, sweeping his gown around him. 'These are not capital charges. More and the Bishop of Rochester, they are only accessories.'

'Which,' Wriothesley says, 'in all conscience is grave enough.'

Norfolk shrugs. 'Kill them now or later. More won't take your oath. Fisher won't.'

'I am quite sure they will,' Audley says. 'We shall use efficacious persuasions. No reasonable man will refuse to swear to the succession, for the safety of this realm.'

'So is Katherine to be sworn,' the duke says, 'to uphold the succession of my niece's infant? What about Mary – is she to be sworn? And if they will not, what do you propose? Draw them to Tyburn on a hurdle and hang them up kicking, for their relative the Emperor to see?'

He and Audley exchange a glance. Audley says, 'My lord, you shouldn't drink so much wine before noon.'

'Oh, *tweet, tweet*,' the duke says.

A week ago he had been up to Hatfield, to see the two royal ladies: the princess Elizabeth, and Lady Mary the king's daughter. 'Make sure you get the titles right,' he had said to Gregory as they rode.

Gregory had said, 'Already you are wishing you had brought Richard.'

He had not wanted to leave London during such a busy parliament, but the king persuaded him: two days and you can be back, I want your eye on things. The route out of the city was running with thaw water, and in copses shielded from the sun the standing pools were still iced. A weak sun blinked at them as they crossed into Hertfordshire, and here and there a ragged blackthorn blossomed, waving at him a petition against the length of winter.

'I used to come here years ago. It was Cardinal Morton's place, you know, and he would leave town when the law term was over and the weather was getting warm, and when I was nine or ten my uncle John used to pack me in a provisions cart with the best cheeses and the pies, in case anybody tried to steal them when we stopped.'

'Did you not have guards?'

'It was the guards he was afraid of.'

'*Quis custodiet ipsos custodes?*'

'Me, evidently.'

'What would you have done?'

'I don't know. Bitten them?'

The mellow brick frontage is smaller than he remembers, but that is what memory does. These pages and gentlemen running out, these grooms to lead away the horses, the warmed wine that awaits them, the noise and the fuss, it is a different sort of arrival from those of long ago. The portage of wood and water, the firing up the ranges, these tasks were beyond the strength or skill of a child, but he was unwilling to concede them, and worked alongside the men, grubby and hungry, till someone saw that he was about to fall over: or until he actually did.

Sir John Shelton is head of this strange household, but he has chosen a time when Sir John is from home; talk to the women, is his idea, rather than listen to Shelton after supper on the subjects of horses, dogs and his youthful exploits. But on the threshold, he almost changes his mind; coming downstairs at a rapid, creaking scuttle is Lady Bryan, mother of one-eyed Francis, who is in charge of the tiny princess. She is a woman of nearly seventy, well bedded into grand-maternity, and he can see her mouth moving before she is within range of his hearing: Her Grace slept till eleven, squalled till midnight, exhausted herself, poor little chicken! fell asleep an hour, woke up griz-zling, cheeks scarlet, suspicion of fever, Lady Shelton woken, physician aroused, teething already, a treacherous time! sooth-ing draught, settled by sun-up, woke at nine, took a feed ... 'Oh, Master Cromwell,' Lady Bryan says, 'this is never your son! Bless him! What a lovely tall young man! What a pretty face he has, he must get it from his mother. What age would he be now?'

'Of an age to talk, I believe.'

Lady Bryan turns to Gregory, her face aglow as if at the prospect of sharing a nursery rhyme with him. Lady Shelton sweeps in. 'Give you good day, masters.' A small hesitation: does the queen's aunt bow to the Master of the Jewel House? On the whole she thinks not. 'I expect Lady Bryan has given you a full account of her charge?'

'Indeed, and perhaps we could have an account of yours?'

'You will not see Lady Mary for yourself?'

'Yes, but forewarned ...'

'Indeed. I do not go armed, though my niece the queen recommends I use my fists on her.' Her eyes sweep over him, assessing; the air crackles with tension. How do women do that? One could learn it, perhaps; he feels, rather than sees, his son back off, till his regress is checked by the cupboard displaying the princess Elizabeth's already extensive collection of gold and silver plate. Lady Shelton says, 'I am charged that, if the Lady Mary does not obey me, I should, and here I quote you my niece's words, beat her and buffet her like the bastard she is.'

'Oh, Mother of God!' Lady Bryan moans. 'I was Mary's nurse too, and she was stubborn as an infant, so she'll not change now, buffet her as you may. You'd like to see the baby first, would you not? Come with me ...' She takes Gregory into custody, hand squeezing his elbow. On she rattles: you see, with a child of that age, a fever could be anything. It could be the start of the measles, God forbid. It could be the start of the smallpox. With a child of six months, you don't know what it could be the start of ... A pulse is beating in Lady Bryan's throat. As she chatters she licks her dry lips, and swallows.

He understands now why Henry wanted him here. The things that are happening cannot be put in a letter. He says to Lady Shelton, 'Do you mean the queen has written to you about Lady Mary, using these terms?'

'No. She has passed on a verbal instruction.' She sweeps ahead of him. 'Do you think I should implement it?'

'We will perhaps speak in private,' he murmurs.

'Yes, why not?' she says: a turn of her head, a little murmur back.

The child Elizabeth is wrapped tightly in layers, her fists hidden: just as well, she looks as if she would strike you. Ginger bristles poke from beneath her cap, and her eyes are vigilant; he has never seen an infant in the crib look so ready to take offence. Lady Bryan says, 'Do you think she looks like the king?'

He hesitates, trying to be fair to both parties. 'As much as a little maid ought.'

'Let us hope she doesn't share his girth,' Lady Shelton says. 'He fleshes out, does he not?'

'Only George Rochford says not.' Lady Bryan leans over the cradle. 'He says, she's every bit a Boleyn.'

'We know my niece lived some thirty years in chastity,' Lady Shelton says, 'but not even Anne could manage a virgin birth.'

'But the hair!' he says.

'I know,' Lady Bryan sighs. 'Saving Her Grace's dignity, and with all respect to His Majesty, you could show her at a fair as a pig-baby.' She pinches up the child's cap at the hairline, and her fingers work busily, trying to stuff the bristles out of sight. The child screws up her face and hiccups in protest.

Gregory frowns down at her: 'She could be anybody's.'

Lady Shelton raises a hand to hide her smile. 'You mean to say, Gregory, all babies look the same. Come, Master Cromwell.'

She takes him by the sleeve to lead him away. Lady Bryan is left reknotting the princess, who seems to have become loose in some particular. Over his shoulder, he says, 'For God's sake, Gregory.' People have gone to the Tower for saying less. He says to Lady Shelton, 'I don't see how Mary can be a bastard. Her parents were in good faith when they got her.'

She stops, an eyebrow raised. 'Would you say that to my niece the queen? To her face, I mean?'

'I already have.'

'And how did she take it?'

'Well, I tell you, Lady Shelton, if she had had an axe to hand, she would have essayed to cut off my head.'

'I tell you something in return, and you can carry it to my niece if you will. If Mary were indeed a bastard, and the bastard of the poorest landless gentleman that is in England, she should receive nothing but gentle treatment at my hands, for she is a good young woman, and you would need a heart of stone not to pity her situation.'

She is walking fast, her train sweeping over stone floors, into the body of the house. Mary's old servants are about, faces he has seen before; there are clean patches on their jackets where Mary's livery badge has been unpicked and replaced by the king's badge. He looks about and recognises everything. He stops at the foot of the great staircase. Never was he allowed to run up it; there was a back staircase for boys like him, carrying wood or coals. Once he broke the rules; and when he reached the top, a fist came out of the darkness and punched the side of his head. Cardinal Morton himself, lurking?

He touches the stone, cold as a tomb: vine leaves intertwined with some nameless flower. Lady Shelton looks at him smiling, quizzical: why does he hesitate? 'Perhaps we should change out of our riding clothes before we meet Lady Mary. She might feel slighted …'

'So she might if you delay. She will make something of it, in either case. I say I pity her, but oh, she is not easy! She graces neither our dinner table nor supper table, because she will not sit below the little princess. And my niece the queen has laid down that food must not be carried to her own room, except the little bread for breakfast we all take.'

She has led him to a closed door. 'Do they still call this the blue chamber?'

'Ah, your father has been here before,' she says to Gregory.

'He's been everywhere,' Gregory says.

She turns. 'See how you get on, gentlemen. By the way, she will not answer to "Lady Mary".'

It is a long room, it is almost empty of furniture, and the chill, like a ghost's ambassador, meets them on the threshold. The blue tapestries have been taken down and the plaster walls are naked. By an almost dead fire, Mary is sitting: huddled, tiny and pitifully young. Gregory whispers, 'She looks like Malekin.'

Poor Malekin, she is a spirit girl; she eats at night, lives on crumbs and apple peel. Sometimes, if you come down early and are quiet on the stairs, you find her sitting in the ashes.

Mary glances up; surprisingly, her little face brightens. 'Master Cromwell.' She gets to her feet, takes a step towards him and almost stumbles, her feet entangled in the hem of her dress. 'How long is it since I saw you at Windsor?'

'I hardly know,' he says gravely. 'The years have been good to you, madam.'

She giggles; she is now eighteen. She casts around her as if bewildered for the stool on which she was sitting. 'Gregory,' he says, and his son dives to catch the ex-princess, before she sits down on empty air. Gregory does it as if it were a dance step; he has his uses.

'I am sorry to keep you standing. You might,' she waves vaguely, 'sit down on that chest.'

'I think we are strong enough to stand. Though I do not think you are.' He sees Gregory glance at him, as if he has never heard this softened tone. 'They do not make you sit alone, and by this miserable fire, surely?'

'The man who brings the wood will not give me my title of princess.'

'Do you have to speak to him?'

'No. But it would be an evasion if I did not.'

That's right, he thinks: make life as hard as possible for yourself. 'Lady Shelton has told me about the difficulty in … the dinner difficulty. Suppose I were to send you a physician?'

'We have one here. Or rather, the child has.'

'I could send a more useful one. He might give you a regimen for your health, and lay it down that you were to take a large breakfast, in your own room.'

'Meat?' Mary says.

'In quantity.'

'But who would you send?'

'Dr Butts?'

Her face softens. 'I knew him at my court at Ludlow. When I was Princess of Wales. Which I still am. How is it I am put out of the succession, Master Cromwell? How is it lawful?'

'It is lawful if Parliament makes it so.'

'There is a law above Parliament. It is the law of God. Ask Bishop Fisher.'

'I find God's purposes obscure, and God knows I find Fisher no fit elucidator. By contrast, I find the will of Parliament plain.'

She bites her lip; now she will not look at him. 'I have heard Dr Butts is a heretic these days.'

'He believes as your father the king believes.'

He waits. She turns, her grey eyes fixed on his face. 'I will not call my lord father a heretic.'

'Good. It is better that these traps are tested, first, by your friends.'

'I do not see how you can be my friend, if you are also friend to the person, I mean the Marquess of Pembroke.' She will not give Anne her royal title.

'That lady stands in a place where she has no need of friends, only of servants.'

'Pole says you are Satan. My cousin Reginald Pole. Who lies abroad at Genoa. He says that when you were born, you were like any Christian soul, but that at some date the devil entered into you.'

'Did you know, Lady Mary, I came here when I was a boy, nine or ten? My uncle was a cook to Morton, and I was a poor snivelling lad who bundled the hawthorn twigs at dawn to light the ovens, and killed the chickens for the boiling house before the sun was up.' He speaks gravely. 'Would you suppose the devil had entered me by that date? Or was it earlier, around the time when other people are baptised? You understand it is of interest to me.'

Mary watches him, and she does it sideways; she still wears an old-style gable hood, and she seems to blink around it, like a horse whose headcloth has slipped. He says softly, 'I am not Satan. Your lord father is not a heretic.'

'And I am not a bastard, I suppose.'

'Indeed no.' He repeats what he told Anne Shelton: 'You were conceived in good faith. Your parents thought they were married. That does not mean their marriage was good. You can see the difference, I think?'

She rubs her forefinger under her nose. 'Yes, I can see the difference. But in fact the marriage was good.'

'The queen will be coming to visit her daughter soon. If you would simply greet her respectfully in the way you should greet your father's wife –'

'– except she is his concubine –'

'– then your father would take you back to court, you would have everything you lack now, and the warmth and comfort of society. Listen to me, I intend this for your good. The queen does not expect your friendship, only an outward show. Bite your tongue and bob her a curtsey. It will be done in a heartbeat, and it will change everything. Make terms with her before her new child is born. If she has a son, she will have no reason afterwards to conciliate you.'

'She is frightened of me,' Mary says, 'and she will still be frightened, even if she has a son. She is afraid I will make a marriage, and my own sons will threaten her.'

'Does anyone talk to you of marriage?'

A dry little laugh, incredulous. 'I was a baby at the breast when I was married into France. Then to the Emperor, into

France again, to the king, to his first son, to his second son, to his sons I have lost count of, and once again to the Emperor, or one of his cousins. I have been contracted in marriage till I am exhausted. One day I shall really do it.'

'But you will not marry Pole.'

She flinches, and he knows that it has been put to her: perhaps by her old governess Margaret Pole, perhaps by Chapuys, who stays up till dawn studying the tables of descent of the English aristocracy: strengthen her claim, put her beyond reproach, marry the half-Spanish Tudor back into the old Plantagenet line. He says, 'I have seen Pole. I knew him before he went out of the kingdom. He is not the man for you. Whatever husband you get, he will need a strong sword arm. Pole is like an old wife sitting by the fire, starting at Hob in the Corner and the Boneless Man. He has nothing but a little holy water in his veins, and they say he weeps copiously if his servant swats a fly.'

She smiles: but she slaps a hand over her mouth like a gag. 'That's right,' he says. 'You say nothing to anybody.'

She says, from behind her fingers, 'I can't see to read.'

'What, they keep you short of candles?'

'No, I mean my sight is failing. All the time my head aches.'

'You cry a good deal?' She nods. 'Dr Butts will bring a remedy. Till then, have someone read to you.'

'They do. They read me Tyndale's gospel. Do you know that Bishop Tunstall and Thomas More between them have identified two thousand errors in his so-called Testament? It is more heretical than the holy book of the Moslems.'

Fighting talk. But he sees that tears are welling up. 'All this can be put right.' She stumbles towards him and for a moment he thinks she will forget herself and lurch and sob against his riding coat. 'The doctor will be here in a day. Now you shall have a proper fire, and your supper. Wherever you like it served.'

'Let me see my mother.'

'Just now the king cannot permit it. But that may change.'

'My father loves me. It is only she, it is only that wretch of a woman, who poisons his mind.'

'Lady Shelton would be kind, if you would let her.'

'What is she, to be kind or not kind? I shall survive Anne Shelton, believe me. And her niece. And anyone else who sets themselves up against my title. Let them do their worst. I am young. I will wait them out.'

He takes his leave. Gregory follows him, his fascinated gaze trailing back to the girl who resumes her seat by the almost dead fire: who folds her hands, and begins the waiting, her expression set.

'All that rabbit fur she is bundled up in,' Gregory says. 'It looks as if it has been nibbled.'

'She's Henry's daughter for sure.'

'Why, does someone say she is not?'

He laughs. 'I didn't mean that. Imagine … if the old queen had been persuaded into adultery, it would have been easy to be rid of her, but how do you fault a woman who has never known but the one man?' He checks himself: it is hard even for the king's closest supporters to remember that Katherine is supposed to have been Prince Arthur's wife. 'Known two men, I should say.' He sweeps his eyes over his son. 'Mary never looked at you, Gregory.'

'Did you think she would?'

'Lady Bryan thinks you such a darling. Wouldn't it be in a young woman's nature?'

'I don't think she has a nature.'

'Get somebody to mend the fire. I'll order the supper. The king can't mean her to starve.'

'She likes you,' Gregory says. 'That's strange.'

He sees that his son is in earnest. 'Is it impossible? My daughters liked me, I think. Poor little Grace, I am never sure if she knew who I was.'

'She liked you when you made her the angel's wings. She said she was always going to keep them.' His son turns away; speaks as if he is afraid of him. 'Rafe says you will be the second man in the kingdom soon. He says you already are, except in title. He says the king will put you over the Lord Chancellor, and everybody. Over Norfolk, even.'

'Rafe is running ahead of himself. Listen, son, don't talk about Mary to anyone. Not even to Rafe.'

'Did I hear more than I should?'

'What do you think would happen if the king died tomorrow?'

'We should all be very sorry.'

'But who would rule?'

Gregory nods towards Lady Bryan, towards the infant in her cradle. 'Parliament says so. Or the queen's child that is not born yet.'

'But would that happen? In practice? An unborn child? Or a daughter not a year old? Anne as regent? It would suit the Boleyns, I grant you.'

'Then Fitzroy.'

'There is a Tudor who is better placed.'

Gregory's eyes turn back towards Lady Mary. 'Exactly,' he says. 'And look, Gregory, it's all very well planning what you will do in six months, what you will do in a year, but it's no good at all if you don't have a plan for tomorrow.'

After supper he sits talking to Lady Shelton. Lady Bryan has gone to bed, then come down again to chivvy them along. 'You'll be tired in the morning!'

'Yes,' Anne Shelton agrees, waving her away. 'In the morning there'll be no doing anything with us. We'll throw our breakfasts on the floor.'

They sit till the servants yawn off to another room, and the candles burn down, and they retreat into the house, to smaller and warmer rooms, to talk some more. You have given Mary good advice, she says, I hope she heeds it, I fear there are hard times ahead for her. She talks about her brother Thomas Boleyn, the most selfish man I ever knew, it is no wonder Anne is so grasping, all she has ever heard from him is talk of money, and how to gain a mean advantage over people, he would have sold those girls naked at a Barbary slave market if he had thought he would get a good price.

He imagines himself surrounded by his scimitared retainers, placing a bid for Mary Boleyn; he smiles, and returns his attention to her aunt. She tells him Boleyn secrets; he tells her no secrets, though she thinks he has.

Gregory is asleep when he comes in, but he turns over and says, 'Dear father, where have you been, to bed with Lady Shelton?'

These things happen: but not with Boleyns. 'What strange dreams you must have. Lady Shelton has been thirty years married.'

'I thought I could have sat with Mary after supper,' Gregory murmurs. 'If I didn't say the wrong thing. But then she is so sneery. I couldn't sit with such a sneery girl.' He flounces over in the feather bed, and falls asleep again.

When Fisher comes to his senses and asks pardon, the old bishop begs the king to consider that he is ill and infirm. The king indicates that the bill of attainder must take its course: but it is his habit, he says, to grant mercy to those who admit their fault.

The Maid is to be hanged. He says nothing of the chair of human bones. He tells Henry she has stopped prophesying, and hopes that at Tyburn, with the noose around her neck, she will not make a liar out of him.

When his councillors kneel before the king, and beg that Thomas More's name be taken out of the bill, Henry yields the point. Perhaps he has been waiting for this: to be persuaded. Anne is not present, or it might have gone otherwise.

They get up and go out, dusting themselves. He thinks he hears the cardinal laughing at them, from some invisible part of the room. Audley's dignity has not suffered, but the duke looks agitated; when he tried to get up, elderly knees had failed him, and he and Audley had lifted him by the elbows and set him on his feet. 'I thought I might be fixed there another hour,' he says. 'Entreating and entreating him.'

'The joke is,' he says to Audley, 'More's still being paid a pension from the treasury. I suppose that had better stop.'

'He has a breathing space now. I pray to God he'll see sense. Has he arranged his affairs?'

'Made over what he can to the children. So Roper tells me.'

'Oh, you lawyers!' the duke says. 'On the day I go down, who will look after me?'

Norfolk is sweating; he eases his pace, and Audley checks too, so they are dawdling along, and Cranmer comes behind like an afterthought. He turns back and takes his arm. He has been at every sitting of Parliament: the bench of bishops, otherwise, conspicuously underpopulated.

The Pope chooses this month, while he is rolling his great bills through Parliament, to give his judgment at last on Queen Katherine's marriage – a judgment so long delayed that he thought Clement meant to die in his indecision. The original dispensations, Clements finds, are sound; therefore the marriage is sound. The supporters of the Emperor let off fireworks in the streets of Rome. Henry is contemptuous, sardonic. He expresses these feelings by dancing. Anne can dance still, though her belly shows; she must take the summer quietly. He remembers the king's hand on Lizzie Seymour's waist. Nothing came of that, the young woman is no fool. Now it is little Mary Shelton he is whirling around, lifting her off her feet and tickling her and squeezing her and making her breathless with compliments. These things mean nothing; he sees Anne lift up her chin and avert her gaze and lean back in her chair, making some murmured comment, her expression arch; her veil brushing, for the briefest moment, against the jacket of that grinning cur

Francis Weston. It is clear Anne thinks Mary Shelton must be tolerated, kept sweet even. It's safest to keep the king among cousins, if no sister is on hand. Where is Mary Boleyn? Down in the country, perhaps longing like him for warmer weather.

And the summer arrives, with no intermission for spring, promptly on a Monday morning, like a new servant with a shining face: 13 April. They are at Lambeth – Audley, himself, the archbishop – the sun shining strongly through the windows. He stands looking down at the palace gardens. This is how the book *Utopia* begins: friends, talking in a garden. On the paths below, Hugh Latimer and some of the king's chaplains are play-fighting, pulling each other around like schoolboys, Hugh hanging around the necks of two of his clerical fellows so his feet swing off the floor. All they need is a football to make a proper holiday of it. 'Master More,' he says, 'why don't you go out and enjoy the sunshine? And we'll call for you again in half an hour, and put the oath to you again: and you'll give us a different answer, yes?'

He hears More's joints snap as he stands. 'Thomas Howard went on his knees for you!' he says. That seems like weeks ago. Late-night sittings and a fresh row every day have tired him, but sharpened his senses too, so he is aware that in the room behind him Cranmer is working himself into a terrible anxiety, and he wants More out of the room before the dam breaks.

'I don't know what you think a half-hour will do for me,' More says. His tone is easy, bantering. 'Of course, it might do something for you.'

More had asked to see a copy of the Act of Succession. Now Audley unrolls it; pointedly, he bends his head and begins reading, though he has read it a dozen times. 'Very well,' More says. 'But I trust I have made myself clear. I cannot swear, but I will not speak against your oath, and I will not try to dissuade anyone else from it.'

'That is not enough. And you know it is not.'

More nods. He meanders towards the door, careering first into the corner of the table, making Cranmer flinch, his arm darting out to steady the ink. The door closes after him.

'So?'

Audley rolls up the statute. Gently he taps it on the table, looking at the place where More had stood. Cranmer says, 'Look, this is my idea. What if we let him swear in secret? He swears, but we offer not to tell anybody? Or if he cannot take this oath, we ask him what oath he can take?'

He laughs.

'That would hardly meet the king's purpose,' Audley sighs. Tap, tap, tap. 'After all we did for him, and for Fisher. His name taken out of the attainder, Fisher fined instead of locked up for life, what more could they ask for? Our efforts flung back at us.'

'Oh well. Blessed are the peacemakers,' he says. He wants to strangle somebody.

Cranmer says, 'We will try again with More. At least, if he refuses, he should give his reasons.'

He swears under his breath, turns from the window. 'We know his reasons. All Europe knows them. He is against the divorce. He does not believe the king can be head of the church. But will he say that? Not he. I know him. Do you know what I hate? I hate to be part of this play, which is entirely devised by him. I hate the time it will take that could be better spent, I hate it that minds could be better employed, I hate to see our lives going by, because depend upon it, we will all be feeling our age before this pageant is played out. And what I hate most of all is that Master More sits in the audience and sniggers when I trip over my lines, for he has written all the parts. And written them these many years.'

Cranmer, like a waiting-boy, pours him a cup of wine, edges towards him. 'Here.'

In the archbishop's hand, the cup cannot help a sacramental character: not watered wine, but some equivocal mixture, this is my blood, this is like my blood, this is more or less somewhat like my blood, do this in commemoration of me. He hands the cup back. The north Germans make a strong liquor, *aquavitae*: a shot of that would be more use. 'Get More back,' he says.

A moment, and More stands in the doorway, sneezing gently. 'Come now,' Audley says, smiling, 'that's not how a hero arrives.'

'I assure you, I intend in no wise to be a hero,' More says. 'They have been cutting the grass.' He pinches his nose on another sneeze, and shambles towards them, hitching his gown on to his shoulder; he takes the chair placed for him. Before, he had refused to sit down.

'That's better,' Audley says. 'I knew the air would do you good.' He glances up, in invitation; but he, Cromwell, signals he will stay where he is, leaning by the window. 'I don't know,' Audley says, good-humoured. 'First one won't sit. Then t'other won't sit. Look,' he pushes a piece of paper towards More, 'these are the names of the priests we have seen today, who have sworn to the act, and set you an example. And you know all the members of Parliament are conformable. So why not you?'

More glances up, from under his eyebrows. 'This is not a comfortable place for any of us.'

'More comfortable than where you're going,' he says.

'Not Hell,' More says, smiling. 'I trust not.'

'So if taking the oath would damn you, what about all these?' He launches himself forward from the wall. He snatches the list of names from Audley, rolls it up and slaps it on to More's shoulder. 'Are they all damned?'

'I cannot speak for their consciences, only for my own. I know that, if I took your oath, I should be damned.'

'There are those who would envy your insight,' he says, 'into the workings of grace. But then, you and God have always been on familiar terms, not so? I wonder how you dare. You talk about your maker as if he were some neighbour you went fishing with on a Sunday afternoon.'

Audley leans forward. 'Let us be clear. You will not take the oath because your conscience advises you against it?'

'Yes.'

'Could you be a little more comprehensive in your answers?'

'No.'

'You object but you won't say why?'

'Yes.'

'Is it the matter of the statute you object to, or the form of the oath, or the business of oath-taking in itself?'

'I would rather not say.'

Cranmer ventures, 'Where it is a question of conscience, there must always be some doubt …'

'Oh, but this is no whim. I have made long and diligent consultation with myself. And in this matter I hear the voice of my conscience clearly.' He puts his head on one side, smiling. 'It is not so with you, my lord?'

'None the less, there must be some perplexity? For you must ask yourself, as you are a scholar and accustomed to controversy, to debate, how can so many learned men think on the one side, and I on the other? But one thing is certain, and it is that you owe a natural obedience to your king, as every subject does. Also, when you entered the king's council, long ago, you took a most particular oath, to obey him. So will not you do so?' Cranmer blinks. 'Set your doubts against that certainty, and swear.'

Audley sits back in his chair. Eyes closed. As if to say, we're not going to do better than that.

More says, 'When you were consecrated archbishop, appointed by the Pope, you swore your oath to Rome, but all day in your fist, they say, all through the ceremonies, you kept a little paper folded up, saying that you took the oath under protest. Is that not true? They say the paper was written by Master Cromwell here.'

Audley's eyes snap open: he thinks More has shown himself the way out. But More's face, smiling, is a mask of malice. 'I would not be such a juggler,' he says softly. 'I would not treat the Lord my God to such a puppet show, let alone the faithful of England. You say you have the majority. I say I have it. You say Parliament is behind you, and I say all the angels and saints are behind me, and all the company of the Christian dead, for as many generations as there have been since the church of Christ was founded, one body, undivided –'

'Oh, for Christ's sake!' he says. 'A lie is no less a lie because it is a thousand years old. Your undivided church has liked nothing better than persecuting its own members, burning them and hacking them apart when they stood by their own conscience, slashing their bellies open and feeding their guts to dogs. You call history to your aid, but what is history to you? It is a mirror that flatters Thomas More. But I have another mirror, I hold it up and it shows a vain and dangerous man, and when I turn it about it shows a killer, for you will drag down with you God knows how many, who will only have the suffering, and not your martyr's gratification. You are not a simple soul, so don't try to make this simple. You know I have respected you? You know I have respected you since I was a child? I would rather see my only son dead, I would rather see them cut off his head, than see you refuse this oath, and give comfort to every enemy of England.'

More looks up. For a fraction of a second, he meets his gaze, then turns away, coy. His low, amused murmur: he could kill him for that alone. 'Gregory is a goodly young man. Don't wish him away. If he has done badly, he will do better. I say the same of my own boy. What's the use of him? But he is worth more than a debating point.'

Cranmer, distressed, shakes his head. 'This is no debating point.'

'You speak of your son,' he says. 'What will happen to him? To your daughters?'

'I shall advise them to take the oath. I do not suppose them to share my scruples.'

'That is not what I mean, and you know it. It is the next generation you are betraying. You want the Emperor's foot on their neck? You are no Englishman.'

'You are barely that yourself,' More says. 'Fight for the French, eh, bank for the Italians? You were scarcely grown up in this realm before your boyhood transgressions drove you out of it, you ran away to escape gaol or a noose. No, I tell you what you are, Cromwell, you are an Italian through and through, and you have all their vices, all their passions.' He sits back in his chair: one mirthless grunt of laughter. 'This relentless bonhomie of yours. I knew it would wear out in the end. It is a coin that has changed hands so often. And now the small silver is worn out, and we see the base metal.'

Audley smirks. 'You seem not to have noted Master Cromwell's efforts at the Mint. His coinage is sound, or it is nothing.'

The Chancellor cannot help it, that he is a smirking sort of man; someone must keep calm. Cranmer is pale and sweating, and he can see the pulse galloping at More's temple. He says, 'We cannot let you go home. Still, it seems to me that you are not yourself today, so rather than commit you to the Tower, we could perhaps place you in the custody of the Abbot of Westminster ... Would that seem suitable to you, my lord of Canterbury?'

Cranmer nods. More says, 'Master Cromwell, I should not mock you, should I? You have shown yourself my most especial and tender friend.'

Audley nods to the guard at the door. More rises smoothly, as if the thought of custody has put a spring in his step; the effect is spoiled only by his usual grab at his garments, the scuffle as he shrugs himself together; and even then he seems to step backwards, and tread on his own feet. He thinks of Mary at Hatfield, rising from her stool and forgetting where she'd left it. After some fashion, More is bundled out of the room. 'Now he's got exactly what he wants,' he says.

He puts his palm against the glass of the window. He sees the smudge it makes, against the old flawed glass. A bank of cloud has come up over the river; the best of the day is behind them. Audley crosses the room to him. Hesitant, he stands at his shoulder. 'If only More would indicate which part of the oath he finds objectionable, it is possible something might be written to meet his objection.'

'You can forget that. If he indicates anything, he is done for. Silence is his only hope, and it is not much of a hope at that.'

'The king might accept some compromise,' Cranmer says. 'But I fear the queen will not. And indeed,' he says faintly, 'why should she?'

Audley puts a hand on his arm. 'My dear Cromwell. Who can understand More? His friend Erasmus told him to keep away from government, he told him he had not the stomach for it and he was right. He should never have accepted the office I now hold. He only did it to spite Wolsey, whom he hated.'

Cranmer says, 'He told him to keep away from theology too. Unless I am wrong?'

'How could you be? More publishes all his letters from his friends. Even when they reprove him, he makes a fine show of his humility and so turns it to his profit. He has lived in public. Every thought that passes through his mind he has committed to paper. He never kept anything private, till now.'

Audley reaches past him, opens the window. A torrent of birdsong crests on the edge of the sill and spills into the room, the liquid, fluent notes of the storm-thrush.

'I suppose he's writing an account of today,' he says. 'And sending it out of the kingdom to be printed. Depend upon it, in the eyes of Europe we will be the fools and the oppressors, and he will be the poor victim with the better turn of phrase.'

Audley pats his arm. He wants to console him. But who can begin to do it? He is the inconsolable Master Cromwell: the unknowable, the inconstruable, the probably indefeasible Master Cromwell.

Next day the king sends for him. He supposes it is to berate him for failing to get More to take the oath. 'Who will accompany me to this fiesta?' he enquires. 'Master Sadler?'

As soon as he enters the king's presence, Henry gestures with a peremptory sweep of his arm for his attendants to clear a space, and leave him alone in it. His face is like thunder. 'Cromwell, have I not been a good lord to you?'

He begins to talk ... gracious, and more than gracious ... own sad unworthiness ... if fallen short in any particular begs most gracious pardon ...

He can do this all day. He learned it from Wolsey.

Henry says, 'Because my lord archbishop thinks I have not done well by you. But,' he says, in the tone of one misunderstood, 'I am a prince known for my munificence.' The whole thing seems to puzzle him. 'You are to be Master Secretary. Rewards shall follow. I do not understand why I have not done this long ago. But tell me: when it was put to you, about the lords Cromwell that once were in England, you said you were nothing to them. Have you thought further?'

'To be honest, I never gave it another thought. I wouldn't wear another man's coat, or bear his arms. He might rise up from his grave and take issue with me.'

'My lord Norfolk says you enjoy being low-born. He says you have devised it so, to torment him.' Henry takes his arm. 'It would seem convenient to me,' he says, 'that wherever we go – though we shall not go far this summer, considering the queen's condition – you should have rooms provided for you next to mine, so we can speak whenever I need you; and where it is possible, rooms that communicate directly, so that I need no go-between.' He smiles towards the courtiers; they wash back, like a tide. 'God strike me,' Henry says, 'if I meant to neglect you. I know when I have a friend.'

Outside, Rafe says, 'God strike him … What terrible oaths he swears.' He hugs his master. 'This has been too long in coming. But listen, I have something to tell you when we get home.'

'Tell me now. Is it something good?'

A gentleman comes forward and says, 'Master Secretary, your barge is waiting to take you back to the city.'

'I should have a house on the river,' he says. 'Like More.'

'Oh, but leave Austin Friars? Think of the tennis court,' Rafe says. 'The gardens.'

The king has made his preparations in secret. Gardiner's arms have been burned off the paintwork. A flag with his coat of arms is raised beside the Tudor flag. He steps into his barge for the first time, and on the river, Rafe tells his news. The rocking of the boat beneath them is imperceptible. The flags are limp; it is a still morning, misty and dappled, and where the light touches flesh or linen or fresh leaves, there is a sheen like the sheen on an eggshell: the whole world luminous, its angles softened, its scent watery and green.

'I have been married half a year,' Rafe says, 'and no one knows, but you know now. I have married Helen Barre.'

'Oh, blood of Christ,' he says. 'Beneath my own roof. What did you do that for?'

Rafe sits mute while he says it all: she is a lovely nobody, a poor woman with no advantage to bring to you, you could have married an heiress. Wait till you tell your father! He will be outraged, he will say I have not looked after your interests. 'And suppose one day her husband turns up?'

'You told her she was free,' Rafe says. He is trembling.

'Which of us is free?'

He remembers what Helen had said: 'So I could marry again? If anybody wanted me?' He remembers how she had looked at him, a long look and full of meaning, only he did not read it. She might as well have turned somersaults, he would not have noticed, his mind had moved elsewhere; that conversation was over for him and he was on to something else. If I had wanted her for myself, and taken her, who could have reproached me for marrying a penniless laundress, even a beggar off the street? People would have said, so that was what Cromwell wanted, a beauty with supple flesh; no wonder he disdained the widows of the city. He doesn't need money, he doesn't need connections, he can afford to follow his appetites: he is Master Secretary now, and what next?

He stares down into the water, now brown, now clear as the light catches it, but always moving; the fish in its depths, the weeds, the drowned men with bony hands swimming. On the mud and shingle there are cast up belt buckles, fragments of glass, small warped coins with the kings' faces washed away. Once when he was a boy he found a horseshoe. A horse in the river? It seemed to him a very lucky find. But his father said, if horseshoes were lucky, boy, I would be the King of Cockaigne.

First he goes out to the kitchens to tell Thurston the news. 'Well,' the cook says easily, 'as you're doing the job anyway.' A chuckle. 'Bishop Gardiner will be burning up inside. His giblets will be sizzling in his own grease.' He whisks a bloodied cloth from a tray. 'See these quails? You get more meat on a wasp.'

'Malmsey?' he suggests. 'Seethe them?'

'What, three dozen? Waste of good wine. I'll do some for you, if you like. Come from Lord Lisle at Calais. When you write, tell him if he sends another batch, we want them fatter or not at all. Will you remember?'

'I'll make a note,' he says gravely. 'From now on I thought we might have the council meet here sometimes, when the king isn't sitting with us. We can give them dinner before.'

'Right.' Thurston titters. 'Norfolk could do with some flesh on his twiggy little legs.'

571

'Thurston, you needn't dirty your hands – you have enough staff. You could put on a gold chain, and strut about.'

'Is that what you'll be doing?' A wet poultry slap; then Thurston looks up at him, wiping pluck from his fingers. 'I think I'd rather keep my hand in. In case things take a down-turn. Not that I say they will. Remember the cardinal, though.'

He remembers Norfolk: tell him to go north, or I will come where he is and tear him with my teeth.

May I substitute the word 'bite'?

The saying comes to him, *homo homini lupus*, man is wolf to man.

'So,' he says to Rafe after supper, 'you've made your name, Master Sadler. You'll be held up as a prime example of how to waste your connections. Fathers will point you out to their sons.'

'I couldn't help it, sir.'

'How, not help it?'

Rafe says, as dry as he can manage, 'I am violently in love with her.'

'How does that feel? Is it like being violently angry?'

'I suppose. Maybe. In that you feel more alive.'

'I do not think I could feel any more alive than I am.'

He wonders if the cardinal was ever in love. But of course, why did he doubt? The all-consuming passion of Wolsey for Wolsey was hot enough to scorch all England. 'Tell me, that evening after the queen was crowned ...' He shakes his head, turns over some papers on his desk: letters from the mayor of Hull.

'I will tell you anything you ask,' Rafe says. 'I cannot imagine how I was not frank with you. But Helen, my wife, she thought it was better to be secret.'

'But now she is carrying a child, I suppose, so you must declare yourselves?'

Rafe blushes.

'That evening, when I came into Austin Friars looking for her, to take her to Cranmer's wife … and she came down,' his eyes move as if he were seeing it, 'she came down without her cap, and you after, with your hair sticking up, and you were angry with me for taking her away …'

'Well, yes,' Rafe says. His hand creeps up and he flattens his hair with his palm, as if that would help matters now. 'They were all gone out to the feasts. That was the first time I took her to bed, but it was no blame. By then she had promised herself to me.'

He thinks, I am glad I have not brought up in my house a young man without feeling, who only studies his advancement. If you are without impulses, you are, to a degree, without joy; under my protection, impulses are a thing Rafe can afford. 'Look, Rafe, this is a – well, God knows, a folly but not a disaster. Tell your father my promotion in the world will ensure yours. Of course, he will stamp and roar. It is what fathers are for. He will shout, I rue the day I parted with my boy to the debauched house of Cromwell. But we will bring him around. A little and a little.'

Till now the boy has been standing; he subsides on to a stool, hands on his head, head flung back; relief washes through his whole body. Was he so afraid? Of me? 'Look, when your father sets eyes on Helen, he'll understand, unless he's …' Unless he's what? You'd have to be dead and entombed not to notice: her bold and beautiful body, her mild eyes. 'We just need to get her out of that canvas apron she goes around in, and dress her up as Mistress Sadler. And of course you will want a house of your own. I will help you there. I shall miss the little children, I have grown fond of them, and Mercy too, we are all fond of them. If you want this new one to be the first child in your house, we can keep them here.'

'It is good of you. But Helen would never part with them. It is understood between us.'

So I shall never have any more children at Austin Friars, he thinks. Well, not unless I take time out of the king's business and go wooing: not unless, when a woman speaks to me, I actually listen. 'What will reconcile your father, and you can tell him this, is that from now on, when I am not with the king, you will be with him. Master Wriothesley will tease the diplomats and keep the ciphers, for it is sly work which will suit him, and Richard will be here to head the household when I am absent and drive my work forward, and you and I will attend on Henry, as sweet as two nursemaids, and cater to his whims.' He laughs. 'You are a gentleman born. He may promote you close to his person, to the privy chamber. Which would be useful to me.'

'I did not look for this to happen. I did not plan it.' Rafe drops his eyes. 'I know I can never take Helen with me to court.'

'Not as the world is now. And I do not think it will change in our lifetimes. But look, you have made your choice. You must never repent it.'

Rafe says, passionate, 'How could I think to keep a secret from you? You see everything, sir.'

'Ah. Only up to a point.'

When Rafe has gone he takes out his evening's work and begins on it, methodical, tapping the papers into place. His bills are passed but there is always another bill. When you are writing laws you are testing words to find their utmost power. Like spells, they have to make things happen in the real world, and like spells, they only work if people believe in them. If your law exacts a penalty, you must be able to enforce it – on the rich as well as the poor, the people on the Scottish borders and the Welsh marches, the men of Cornwall as well as the men of Sussex and Kent. He has written this oath, a test of loyalty to Henry, and he means to swear the men of every burgh and village, and all women of any consequence: widows with inheritances, landowners. His people will be tramping the wold and heath-land, pledging those who have barely heard of Anne Boleyn to uphold the succession of the child in her womb. If a man knows the king is called Henry, swear him; never mind if he confuses this king with his father or some Henry who came before. For princes like other men fade from the memory of common people; their features, on those coins he used to sift from the river silt, were no more than a slight irregularity under his finger-tips, and even when he had taken the coins home and scrubbed them he could not say who they might be; is this, he asked, Prince Caesar? Walter had said, let's see; then he had flipped the coin away from him in disgust, saying, it's but a tinny farthing from one of those kings who fought the French wars. Get out there and earn, he'd said, never mind Prince Caesar; Caesar was old when Adam was a lad.

He would chant, 'When Adam delved and Eve span, Who was then the gentleman?' Walter would chase him and hit him if he could catch him: there's a bloody rebel song for you, we know what to do with rebels here. They are dug into shallow graves, the Cornishmen who came up the country when he was a boy; but there are always more Cornishmen. And beneath Cornwall, beyond and beneath this whole realm of England, beneath the sodden marches of Wales and the rough territory of the Scots border, there is another landscape; there is a buried empire, where he fears his commissioners cannot reach. Who will swear the hobs and boggarts who live in the hedges and in hollow trees, and the wild men who hide in the woods? Who will swear the saints in their niches, and the spirits that cluster at holy wells rustling like fallen leaves, and the miscarried infants dug into unconsecrated ground: all those unseen dead who hover in winter around forges and village hearths, trying to warm their bare bones? For they too are his countrymen: the generations of the uncounted dead, breathing through the living, stealing their light from them, the bloodless ghosts of lord and knave, nun and whore, the ghosts of priest and friar who feed on living England, and suck the substance from the future.

575

He stares down at the papers on his desk, but his thoughts are far from here. My daughter Anne said, 'I choose Rafe.' He lowers his head into his hands and closes his eyes; Anne Cromwell stands before him, ten or eleven years old, broad and resolute like a man at arms, her small eyes unblinking, sure of her power to make her fate.

He rubs his eyes. Sifts his papers. What is this? A list. A meticulous clerk's hand, legible but making scant sense.

Two carpets. One cut in pieces.
7 sheets. 2 pillows. 1 bolster.
2 platters, 4 dishes, 2 saucers.
One small basin, weight 12lbs @ 4d the pound; my Lady
*   Prioress has it, paid 4 shillings.*

He turns the paper over, trying to find its origin. He sees that he is looking at the inventory of Elizabeth Barton's goods, left behind at her nunnery. All this is forfeit to the king, the personal property of a traitor: a piece of plank which serves as a table, three pillowcases, two candlesticks, a coat valued at five shillings. An old mantle has been given in charity to the youngest nun in her convent. Another nun, a Dame Alice, has received a bed-cover.

He had said to More, prophecy didn't make her rich. He makes a memorandum to himself: 'Dame Elizabeth Barton to have money to fee the hangman.' She has five days to live. The last person she will see as she climbs the ladder is her executioner, holding out his paw. If she cannot pay her way at the last, she may suffer longer than she needs. She had imagined how long it takes to burn, but not how long it takes to choke at the end of a rope. In England there is no mercy for the poor. You pay for everything, even a broken neck.

Thomas More's family has taken the oath. He has seen them himself, and Alice has left him in no doubt that she holds him personally responsible for failing to talk her husband into conformity. 'Ask him what in the name of God he's about. Ask him, is it clever, does he think it is, to leave his wife without company, his son without advice, his daughters without protection, and all of us at the mercy of a man like Thomas Cromwell?'

'That's you told,' Meg had murmured, with half a smile. Head bowed, she had taken his hand between her own. 'My father has spoken very warmly of you. Of how you have been courteous to him and how you have been vehement – which he accounts no less a favour. He says he believes you understand him. As he understands you.'

'Meg? Surely you can look at me?'

Another face bowed under the weight of a gable hood: Meg twitches her veils about her, as if she were out in a gale and they would provide protection.

'I can hold the king off for a day or two. I don't believe he wishes to see your father in the Tower, every moment he looks for some sign of …'

'Surrender?'

'Support. And then … no honour would be too high.'

'I doubt the king can offer the sort of honour he cares for,' Will Roper says. 'Unfortunately. Come on, Meg, let's go home. We need to get your mother on the river before she starts a brawl.' Roper holds out his hand. 'We know you are not vengeful, sir. Though God knows, he has never been a friend to your friends.'

'There was a time you were a Bible man yourself.'

'Men may change opinions.'

'I agree entirely. Tell your father-in-law that.'

It was a sour note to part on. I shall not indulge More, he thinks, or his family, in any illusion that they *understand* me. How could that be, when my workings are hidden from myself?

He makes a note: Richard Cromwell to present himself to the Abbot of Westminster, to escort Sir Thomas More, prisoner, to the Tower.

Why do I hesitate?

Let's give him one more day.

It is 15 April 1534. He calls in a clerk to tidy and file his papers, ready for tomorrow, and lingers by the fire, chatting; it is midnight, and the candles are burned down. He takes one and goes upstairs; Christophe, snoring, sprawls across the foot of his wide and lonely bed. Dear God, he thinks, my life is ridiculous. 'Wake up,' he says, but in a whisper; when Christophe does not respond, he lays hands on him and rolls him up and down, as if he were the lid for a pie, till the boy wakes up, expostulating in gutter French. 'Oh by the hairy balls of Jesus.' He blinks violently. 'My good master, I didn't know it was you, I was dreaming I was a pastry. Forgive me, I am completely drunk, we have been celebrating the conjunction of the beautiful Helen with the fortunate Rafe.' He raises a forearm, curls up his fist, makes a gesture of the utmost lewdness; his arm falls limp across his body, his eyelids slide ineluctably towards his cheeks, and with a final hiccup he subsides into sleep.

He hauls the boy to his pallet. Christophe is heavy now, a rotund bulldog pup; he grunts, he mutters, but he does not wake again.

He lays aside his clothes and says his prayers. He puts his head on the pillow: *7 sheets 2 pillows 1 bolster.* He sleeps as soon as the candle is out. But his daughter Anne comes to him in a dream. She holds up her left hand, sorrowful, to show him she wears no wedding ring. She twists up her long hair and wraps it around her neck like a noose.

Midsummer: women hurry to the queen's apartments with clean linen folded over their arms. Their faces are blank and shocked and they walk so quickly you know not to stop them. Fires are lit within the queen's apartments to burn what has bled away. If there is anything to bury, the women keep it a secret between themselves.

That night, huddled in a window embrasure, the sky lit by stars like daggers, Henry will tell him, it is Katherine I blame. I believe she ill-wishes me. The truth is her womb is diseased. All those years she deceived me – she couldn't carry a son, and she and her doctors knew it. She claims she still loves me, but she is destroying me. She comes in the night with her cold hands and her cold heart, and lies between me and the woman I love. She puts her hand on my member and her hand smells of the tomb.

The lords and ladies give the maids and midwives money, to say what sex the child was, but the women give different answers each time. Indeed, what would be worse: for Anne to have conceived another girl, or to have conceived and miscarried a boy?

Midsummer: bonfires are lit all over London, burning through the short nights. Dragons stalk the streets, puffing out smoke and clattering their mechanical wings.

II

The Map of Christendom

1534–1535

'Do you want Audley's post?' Henry asks him. 'It's yours if you say so.'

The summer is over. The Emperor has not come. Pope Clement is dead, and his judgments with him; the game is to play again, and he has left the door open, just a chink, for the next Bishop of Rome to hold a conversation with England. Personally, he would slam it shut; but these are not personal matters.

Now he thinks carefully: would it suit him to be Chancellor? It would be good to have a post in the legal hierarchy, so why not at the top? 'I have no wish to disturb Audley. If Your Majesty is satisfied with him, I am too.'

He remembers how the post tied Wolsey to London, when the king was elsewhere. The cardinal was active in the law courts; but we have lawyers enough.

Henry says, only tell me what you deem best. Abased, like a lover, he cannot think of the best presents. He says, Cranmer bids me, listen to Cromwell, and if he needs a post, a tax, an impost, a measure in Parliament or a royal proclamation, give it to him.

The post of Master of the Rolls is vacant. It is an ancient judicial office, it commands one of the kingdom's great secretariats. His predecessors will be those men, bishops for the most part, eminent in learning: those who lie down on their tombs, with their virtues in Latin engraved beneath. He is never more alive than when he twists the stem of this ripe fruit and snaps it from the tree.

'You were also right about Cardinal Farnese,' Henry says. 'Now we have a new Pope – Bishop of Rome, I should say – I have collected on my bets.'

'You see,' he says, smiling. 'Cranmer is right. Be advised by me.'

The court is amused to hear how the Romans have celebrated Pope Clement's death. They have broken into his tomb, and dragged his naked body through the streets.

The Master's house in Chancery Lane is the most curious house he has ever entered. It smells of must, mould and tallow, and behind its crooked facade it meanders back, a warren of little spaces with low doorways; were our forebears all dwarves, or were they not perfectly certain how to prop up a ceiling?

This house was founded three hundred years ago, by the Henry that was then; he built it as a refuge for Jews who wished to convert. If they took this step – advisable if they wished to be preserved from violence – they would forfeit all their possessions to the Crown. This being so, it was just that the Crown should house and feed them for their natural lives.

Christophe runs ahead of him, into the depths of the house. 'Look!' He trails his finger through a vast spider's web.

'You've broken up her home, you heartless boy.' He examines Ariane's crumbling prey: a leg, a wing. 'Let's be gone, before she comes back.'

Some fifty years after Henry had endowed the house, all Jews were expelled from the realm. Yet the refuge was never quite empty; even today two women live here. I shall call on them, he says.

Christophe is tapping the walls and beams, for all the world as if he knew what he was looking for. 'Wouldn't you run,' he says with relish, 'if someone tapped back?'

'Oh, Jesus!' Christophe crosses himself. 'I expect a hundred men have died here, Jews and Christians both.'

Behind this wainscot, it is true, he can sense the tiny bones of mice: a hundred generations, their articulated forefeet folded in eternal rest. Their descendants, thriving, he can smell in the air. This is a job for Marlinspike, he says, if we can catch him. The cardinal's cat is feral now, ranging at will through London gardens, lured by the scent of carp from the ponds of city monasteries, tempted – for all he knows – across the river, to be snuggled to the bosoms of whores, slack breasts rubbed with rose petals and ambergris; he imagines Marlinspike lolling, purring, declining to come home again. He says to Christophe, 'I wonder how I can be Master of the Rolls, if I am not master of a cat.'

'The Rolls have not paws to go walking.' Christophe is kicking a skirting. 'My foot go through it,' he says, demonstrating.

Will he leave the comforts of Austin Friars, for the tiny windows with their warped panes, the creaking passages, the ancient draughts? 'It will be a shorter journey to Westminster,' he says. His aim is bent there – Whitehall, Westminster and the river, Master Secretary's barge down to Greenwich or up to Hampton Court. I shall be back at Austin Friars often, he says to himself, almost every day. He is building a treasure room, a repository secure for any gold plate the king entrusts to him; whatever he deposits can quickly be turned into ready money. His treasure comes through the street on ordinary carts, to attract no attention, though there are vigilant outriders. The chalices are fitted into soft leather cases made for them. The bowls and dishes travel in canvas bags, interleaved with white woollen cloth at seven pence the yard. The jewels are swaddled in silk and packed into chests with new and shiny locks: and he has the keys. There are great pearls which gleam wet from the ocean, sapphires hot as India. There are jewels like the fruit you pick on a country afternoon: garnets like sloes, pink diamonds like rosehips. Alice says, 'For a handful of these I would, myself, overthrow any queen in Christendom.'

'What a good thing the king hasn't met you, Alice.'

Jo says, 'I would as soon have it in export licences. Or army contracts. Someone will make a fortune in the Irish wars. Beans, flour, malt, horseflesh …'

'I shall see what I can do for you,' he says.

At Austin Friars he holds the lease for ninety-nine years. His great-grandchildren will have it: some unknown Londoners. When they look at the documents his name will be there. His arms will be carved over the doorways. He rests his hand on the banister of the great staircase, looks up into the dust-mote glitter from a high window. When did I do this? At Hatfield, early in the year: looking up, listening for the sounds of Morton's household, long ago. If he himself went to Hatfield, must not Thomas More have gone up too? Perhaps it was his light footstep he expected, overhead?

He starts to think again, about that fist that came out of nowhere.

His first idea had been, move clerks and papers to the Rolls, then Austin Friars will become a home again. But for whom? He has taken out Liz's book of hours, and on the page where she kept the family listed he has made alterations, additions. Rafe will be moving out soon, to his new house in Hackney; and Richard is building in the same neighbourhood, with his wife Frances. Alice is marrying his ward Thomas Rotherham. Her brother Christopher is ordained and beneficed. Jo's wedding clothes are ordered; she is snapped up by his friend John ap Rice, a lawyer, a scholar, a man he admires and on whose loyalty he counts. I have done well for my folk, he thinks: not one of them poor, or unhappy, or uncertain of their place in this uncertain world. He hesitates, looking up into the light: now gold, now blue as a cloud passes. Whoever will come downstairs and claim him, must do it now. His daughter Anne with her thundering feet: Anne, he would say to her, couldn't we have felt mufflers over those hooves of yours? Grace skimming down like dust, drawn into a spiral, a lively swirl ... going nowhere, dispersing, gone.

Liz, come down.

But Liz keeps her silence; she neither stays nor goes. She is always with him and not with him. He turns away. So this house will become a place of business. As all his houses will become places of business. My home will be where my clerks and files are; otherwise, my home will be with the king, where he is.

Christophe says, 'Now we are removed to the Rolls House, I can tell you, *cher maître*, how I am happy that you did not leave me behind. For in your absence they would call me snail brain and turnip head.'

'*Alors* ...' he takes a view of Christophe, 'your head is indeed like a turnip. Thank you for attracting my attention to it.'

Installed at the Rolls, he takes a view of his situation: satisfactory. He has sold off his two Kent manors, but the king has given him one in Monmouthshire and he is buying another in Essex. He has his eye on plots in Hackney and Shoreditch, and is taking in leases on the properties around Austin Friars, which he intends to enfold in his building plans; and then, build a big wall around the lot. He has surveys to hand of a manor in Bedfordshire, one in Lincolnshire, and two Essex properties he intends to put in trust for Gregory. All this is small stuff. It's nothing to what he intends to have, or to what Henry will owe him.

Meanwhile, his outgoings would frighten a lesser man. If the king wants something done, you have to be able to staff the enterprise and fund it. It is hard to keep up with the spending of his noble councillors, and yet there are a crew of them who live at the pawn-shop and come to him month by month to patch the holes in their accounts. He knows when to let these debts run; there is more than one kind of currency in England. What he senses is a great net is spreading about him, a web of favours done and favours received. Those who want access to the king expect to pay for it, and no one has better access than he. And at the same time, the word is out: help Cromwell and he will help you. Be loyal, be diligent, be intelligent on his behalf; you will come into a reward. Those who commit their service to him will be promoted and protected. He is a good friend and master; this is said of him everywhere. Otherwise, it is the usual abuse. His father was a blacksmith, a crooked brewer, he was an Irishman, he was a criminal, he was a Jew, and he himself was just a wool-trader, he was a shearsman, and now he is a sorcerer: how else but by being a sorcerer would he get the reins of power in his hand? Chapuys writes to the Emperor about him; his early life remains a mystery, but he is excellent company, and he keeps his household and retainers in magnificent style. He is a master of language, Chapuys writes, a man of most eloquent address; though his French, he adds, is only *assez bien.*

He thinks, it's good enough for you. A nod and a wink will do for you.

These last months, the council has never been out of harness. A hard summer of negotiating has brought a treaty with the Scots. But Ireland is in revolt. Only Dublin Castle itself and the town of Waterford hold out for the king, while the rebel lords are offering their services and their harbours to the Emperor's troops. Among these isles it is the most wretched of territories, which does not pay the king what it costs him to garrison it; but he cannot turn his back on it, for fear of who else might come in. Law is barely respected there, for the Irish think you can buy off murder with money, and like the Welsh they cost out a man's life in cattle. The people are kept poor by imposts and seizures, by forfeitures and plain daylight robbery; the pious English abstain from meat on Wednesdays and Fridays, but the joke runs that the Irish are so godly they abstain every other day as well. Their great lords are brutal and imperious men, treacherous and fickle, inveterate feuders, extortionists and hostage takers, and their

585

allegiance to England they hold cheap, for they are loyal to nothing and prefer force of arms to law. As for the native chiefs, they recognise no natural limit to their claims. They say that on their land they own every ferny slope and lake, they own the heather, the meadow grass and the winds that riffle it; they own every beast and every man, and in times of scarcity they take the bread to feed their hunting dogs.

No wonder they don't want to be English. It would interrupt their status as slave-owners. The Duke of Norfolk still has serfs on his land, and even if the law courts move to free them the duke expects a fee from it. The king proposes to send Norfolk to Ireland, but he says he's spent enough futile months over there and the only way he'll go back is if they build a bridge so he can get home at the end of the week without getting his feet wet.

He and Norfolk fight in the council chamber. The duke rants, and he sits back and folds his arms and watches him ranting. You should have sent young Fitzroy to Dublin, he tells the council. An apprentice king – make a show, stage a spectacle, throw some money about.

Richard says to him, 'Perhaps we should go to Ireland, sir.'

'I think my campaigning days are over.'

'I would like to be in arms. Every man should be a soldier once in his life.'

'That is your grandfather speaking through you. Ap Evans the archer. Concentrate for now on making a show in the tournaments.'

Richard has proved a formidable man in the lists. It is more or less as Christophe says: *biff*, and they are flat. You would think the sport was in his nephew's blood, as it is in the blood of the lords who compete. He carries the Cromwell colours, and the king loves him for it, as he loves any man with flair and courage and physical strength. Increasingly, his bad leg forces him to sit with the spectators. When he is in pain he is panicked, you can see it in his eyes, and when he is recovering he is restless. Uncertainty about his own state of health makes him less inclined for the expense and trouble of organising a large tournament. When he does run a course, with his experience, his weight and height, his superb horses and the steel of his temperament, he is likely to win. But to avoid accidents, he prefers to run against opponents he knows.

Henry says, 'The Emperor, two or three years back when he was in Germany, did he not have an evil humour in his thigh? They say the weather didn't suit him. But then his dominions offer a change of climate. Whereas from one part of my kingdom to the next there is no change to be found.'

'Oh, I expect it's worse in Dublin.'

Henry looks out, hopeless, at the teeming rain. 'And when I ride out the people shout at me. They rise up out of ditches, and shout about Katherine, how I should take her back. How would they like it if I told them how to order their houses and wives and children?'

Even when the weather clears the king's fears do not diminish. 'She will escape and raise an army against me,' he says. 'Katherine. You do not know what she would do.'

'She told me she would not run.'

'And you think she never lies? I know she lies. I have proof of it. She lied about her own virginity.'

Oh, that, he thinks tiredly.

It seems Henry doesn't believe in the power of armed guards, in locks and keys. He thinks an angel recruited by the Emperor Charles will make them fall away. When he travels, he takes with him a great iron lock, which is affixed to his chamber door by a servant who goes with him for the purpose. His food is tasted for poison and his bed examined, last thing at night, for concealed weapons, such as needles; but even so, he is afraid he will be murdered as he sleeps.

* * *

Autumn: Thomas More is losing weight, a wiry little man emerging from what was never a superfluity of flesh. He lets Antonio Bonvisi send him food in. 'Not that you Lucchese know how to eat. I'd send it myself, but if he took ill, you know what people would say. He likes dishes of eggs. I don't know if he likes much else.'

A sigh. 'Milk puddings.'

He smiles. These are carnivorous days. 'No wonder he doesn't thrive.'

'I've known him for forty years,' Bonvisi says. 'A lifetime, Tommaso. You wouldn't hurt him, would you? Please assure me, if you can, that no one will hurt him.'

'Why do you think I'm no better than he is? Look, I have no need to put him under pressure. His family and friends will do it. Won't they?'

'Can't you just leave him there? Forget him?'

'Of course. If the king allows.'

He arranges for Meg Roper to visit. Father and daughter walk in the gardens, arm in arm. Sometimes he watches them from a window in the Lord Lieutenant's lodgings.

By November, this policy has failed. Turned back, really, and bitten his hand, like a dog that out of kindness you pick up in the street. Meg says, 'He has told me, and he has asked me to tell his friends, that he will have no more to do with oaths of any kind, and that if we hear he has sworn, we are to take it that he has been forced, by ill-usage and rough handling. And if a paper is shown to the council, with his signature on it, we are to understand it is not his hand.'

More is now required to swear to the Act of Supremacy, an act which draws together all the powers and dignities assumed by the king in the last two years. It doesn't, as some say, make the king head of the church. It states that he is head of the church, and always has been. If people don't like new ideas, let them have old ones. If they want precedents, he has precedents. A second enactment, which will come into force in the new year, defines the scope of treason. It will be a treasonable offence to deny Henry's titles or jurisdiction, to speak or write maliciously against him, to call him a heretic or a schismatic. This law will catch the friars who spread panic and say the Spanish are landing with the next tide to seize the throne for the Lady Mary. It will catch the priests who in their sermons rant against the king's authority and say he is dragging his subjects after him to Hell. Is it much for a monarch to ask, that a subject keep a civil tongue in his head?

This is new, people say to him, this treason by words, and he says, no, be assured, it is old. It casts into statute law what the judges in their wisdom have already defined as common law. It is a measure for clarification. I am all for clarity.

Upon More's refusal of this second oath, a bill is brought in against him, forfeiting his goods to the Crown. He now has no hope of release; or rather, the hope lies in himself. It is his duty to visit him, tell him he will no longer be allowed visitors, or strolls in the gardens.

'Nothing to see, this time of year.' More casts a glance at the sky, a narrow strip of grey through the high window. 'I can still have my books? Write letters?'

'For now.'

'And John Wood, he stays with me?'

His servant. 'Yes, of course.'

'He brings me a little news from time to time. They say the sweating sickness has broken out among the king's troops in Ireland. So late in the year, too.'

Plague has also broken out; he's not going to tell More that, or that the whole Irish campaign is a debacle and a money sink and that he wishes he had done as Richard said and gone out there himself.

'The sweat takes off so many,' More says, 'and so swiftly, and in their prime too. And if you survive it, you are in no condition to fight the wild Irish, that's for sure. I remember when Meg took it, she nearly died. Have you had it? No, you're never ill, are you?' He is chattering pointlessly, then he looks up. 'Tell me, what do you hear from Antwerp? They say Tyndale is there. They say he lives straitly. He dare not stray beyond the English merchants' house. They say he is in prison, almost as I am.'

It is true, or partly true. Tyndale has laboured in poverty and obscurity, and now his world has shrunk to a little room; while outside in the city, under the Emperor's laws, printers are branded and have their eyes put out, and brothers and sisters are killed for their faith, the men beheaded, the women buried alive. More has a sticky web in Europe still, a web made of money; it is his belief that his men have followed Tyndale these many months, but all his ingenuity, and Stephen Vaughan's on the spot, have not been able to find out which of the Englishmen who pass through that busy town are More's agents. 'Tyndale would be safer in London,' More says. 'Under yourself, the protector of error. Now, look at Germany today. You see, Thomas, where heresy leads us. It leads us to Münster, does it not?'

Sectaries, anabaptists, have taken over the city of Münster. Your worst nightmares – when you wake, paralysed, and think you have died – are bliss compared with this. The burgomasters have been ejected from the council, and thieves and lunatics have taken their places, proclaiming that the end times have come and all must be rebaptised. Citizens who dissent have been driven beyond the walls, naked, to perish in the snow. Now the city is under siege from its own prince-bishop, who intends to starve it out. The defenders, they say, are for the most part the women and children left behind; they are held in dread by a tailor called Bockelson, who has crowned himself King of Jerusalem. It is rumoured that Bockelson's friends have instituted polygamy, as recommended in the Old Testament, and that some of the women have been hanged or drowned rather than submit to rape under cover of Abraham's law. These prophets engage in daylight robbery, in the name of holding goods in common. It is said they have seized the houses of the rich, burned their letters, slashed their pictures, mopped the floors with fine embroidery, and shredded the records of who owns what, so former times can never come back.

'Utopia,' he says. 'Is it not?'

'I hear they are burning the books from the city libraries. Erasmus has gone into the flames. What kind of devils would burn the gentle Erasmus? But no doubt, no doubt,' More nods, 'Münster will be restored to order. Philip the prince of Hesse, Luther's friend, I have no doubt he will lend the good bishop his cannon and his cannoneers, and one heretic will put down another. The brethren fall to scrapping, do you see? Like rabid dogs drooling in the streets, who tear out each other's entrails when they meet.'

'I tell you how Münster will end. Someone inside the city will surrender it.'

'You think so? You look as if you would offer me odds. But there, I was never much of a gambler. And now the king has all my money.'

'A man like that, a tailor, jumps up for a month or two –'

'A wool merchant, a blacksmith's son, he jumps up for a year or two ...'

He stands, picks up his cape: black wool, lambskin lining. More's eyes gleam, ah, look, I have you on the run. Now he murmurs, as if it were a supper party, must you go? Stay a little, can't you? He lifts his chin. 'So I shall not see Meg again?'

The man's tone, the emptiness, the loss: it goes straight to his heart. He turns away, to keep his reply calm and trite. 'You have to say some words. That's all.'

'Ahh. Just words.'

'And if you don't want to say them I can put them to you in writing. Sign your name and the king will be happy. I will send my barge to row you back to Chelsea, and tie up at the wharf at the end of your own garden – not much to see, as you say, at this time of year, but think of the warm welcome within. Dame Alice is waiting – Alice's cooking, well, that alone would restore you; she is standing by your side watching you chew and the minute you wipe your mouth she picks you up in her arms and kisses away the mutton fat, why husband I have missed you! She bears you off to her bedchamber, locks the door and drops the key in her pocket and pulls off your clothes till there you are in your shirt and nothing but your little white legs sticking out – well, admit it, the woman is within her rights. Then next day – think of it – you rise before dawn, shuffle to your familiar cell and flog yourself, call for your bread and water, and by eight o'clock back in your hair shirt, and over it your old woollen gown, that blood-coloured one with the rent in ... feet up on a stool, and your only son bringing in your letters ... snapping the seal on your darling Erasmus ... Then when you have read your letters, you can hobble out – let's say it's a sunny day – and look at your caged birds, and your little fox in its pen, and you can say, I was a prisoner too, but no more, because Cromwell showed me I could be free ... Don't you want it? Don't you want to come out of this place?'

'You should write a play,' More says wonderingly.

He laughs. 'Perhaps I shall.'

'It's better than Chaucer. Words. Words. Just words.'

He turns. He stares at More. It's as if the light has changed. A window has opened on a strange country, where a cold wind from childhood blows. 'That book ... Was it a dictionary?'

More frowns. 'I'm sorry?'

'I came up the stairs at Lambeth – give me a moment ... I came running up the stairs, carrying your measure of small beer and your wheaten loaf, to keep you from being hungry if you woke in the night. It was seven in the evening. You were reading, and when you looked up you held your hands over the book,' he makes the shape of wings, 'as if you were protecting it. I asked you, Master More, what is in that great book? You said, words, words, just words.'

More tilts his head. 'This was when?'

'I believe I was seven.'

'Oh, nonsense,' More says genially. 'I didn't know you when you were seven. Why, you were ...' he frowns, 'you must have been ... and I was ...'

'About to go to Oxford. You don't remember. But why would you?' He shrugs. 'I thought you were laughing at me.'

'Oh, very probably I was,' More says. 'If indeed such a meeting took place. Now witness these present days, when you come here and laugh at me. Talking about Alice. And my little white legs.'

'I think it must have been a dictionary. You are sure you don't remember? Well ... my barge is waiting, and I don't want to keep the oars out in the cold.'

'The days are very long in here,' More says. 'The nights are longer. My chest is bad. My breathing is tight.'

'Back to Chelsea then, Dr Butts will visit, tut-tut Thomas More, what have you been doing to yourself? Hold your nose and drink off this foul mixture ...'

'Sometimes I think I shall not see morning.'

He opens the door. 'Martin?'

Martin is thirty, wiry, his fair hair under his cap already sparse: pleasant face with a crinkly smile. His native town is Colchester, his father a tailor, and he learned to read on Wycliffe's gospel, which his father hid in their roof under the thatch. This is a new England; an England where Martin can dust the old text down, and show it to his neighbours. He has brothers, all of them Bible men. His wife is just now confined with her third child, 'crawled into the straw,' as he puts it. 'Any news?'

'Not yet. But will you stand godfather? Thomas if it's a boy, or if it's a girl you name her, sir.'

A touch of palms and a smile. 'Grace,' he says. A money gift is understood; the child's start in life. He turns back to the sick man, who now slumps over his table. 'Sir Thomas says at night his breath comes short. Bring him some bolsters, cushions, whatever you can find, prop him up to ease him. I want him to have every opportunity to live to rethink his position, show loyalty to our king, and go home. And now, bid you both good afternoon.'

More looks up. 'I want to write a letter.'

'Of course. You shall have ink and paper.'

'I want to write to Meg.'

'Then send her a human word.'

More's letters are beyond the human. They may be addressed to his daughter, but they are written for his friends in Europe to read.

'Cromwell …?' More's voice calls him back. 'How is the queen?'

More is always correct, not like those who slip up and say 'Queen Katherine'. How is Anne? he means. But what could he tell him? He is on his way. He is out of the door. In the narrow window a blue dusk has replaced the grey.

He had heard her voice, from the next room: low, relentless. Henry yelping in indignation. 'Not me! Not *me*.'

In the antechamber, Thomas Boleyn, Monseigneur, his narrow face rigid. Some Boleyn hangers-on, exchanging glances: Francis Weston, Francis Bryan. In a corner, trying to make himself inconspicuous, the lutenist Mark Smeaton; what's he doing here? Not quite a family conclave: George Boleyn is in Paris, holding talks. An idea has been floated that the infant Elizabeth should marry a son of France; the Boleyns really think this is going to happen.

'Whatever can have occurred,' he says, 'to upset the queen?' His tone is astonished: as if she were the most placid of women.

Weston says, 'It's Lady Carey, she is – that is to say she finds herself –'

Bryan snorts. 'With a bellyful of bastard.'

'Ah. Didn't you know?' The shock around him is gratifying. He shrugs. 'I thought it a family matter.'

Bryan's eyepatch winks at him, today a jaundiced yellow. 'You must watch her very closely, Cromwell.'

'A matter in which I have failed,' Boleyn says. 'Evidently. She claims the child's father is William Stafford, and she has married him. You know this Stafford, do you?'

'Just about. Well,' he says cheerfully, 'shall we go in? Mark, we are not setting this affair to music, so take yourself off to where you can be useful.'

Only Henry Norris is attending the king: Jane Rochford, the queen. Henry's big face is white. 'You blame me, madam, for what I did before I even knew you.'

They have crowded in behind him. Henry says, 'My lord Wiltshire, can you not control either of your daughters?'

'Cromwell knew,' Bryan says. He snorts with laughter.

Monseigneur begins to talk, stumbling – he, Thomas Boleyn, diplomat famed for his silver-tongued finesse. Anne cuts him off: 'Why should she get a child by Stafford? I don't believe it's his. Why would he agree to marry her, unless for ambition – well, he has made a false move there, for he will never come to court again, nor will she. She can crawl on her knees to me. I care not. She can starve.'

If Anne were my wife, he thinks, I'd go out for the afternoon. She looks haggard, and she cannot stay still; you wouldn't trust her near a sharp knife. 'What to do?' Norris whispers. Jane Rochford is standing back against the tapestries, where nymphs entwine themselves in trees; the hem of her skirt is dipped in some fabulous stream, and her veil brushes a cloud, from which a goddess peeps. She lifts her face; her look is one of sober triumph.

I could have the archbishop fetched, he thinks. Anne wouldn't rage and stamp under his eyes. Now she has Norris by the sleeve; what is she doing? 'My sister has done this to spite me. She thinks she will sail about the court with her great belly, and pity me and laugh at me, because I have lost my own child.'

'I feel sure that, if the matter were to be viewed –' her father begins.

'Get out!' she says. 'Leave me, and tell her – Mistress Stafford – that she has forfeited any claim on my family. I don't know her. She is no longer a Boleyn.'

'Wiltshire, go.' Henry adds, in the tone in which a schoolboy is promised a whipping, 'I shall speak to you later.'

He says to the king, innocent, 'Majesty, shall we do no business today?' Henry laughs.

Lady Rochford runs beside him. He does not slow his pace so she has to pick up her skirts. 'Did you really know, Master Secretary? Or did you say that just to see their faces?'

'You are too good for me. You see through all my ploys.'

'Lucky I see through Lady Carey's.'

'It was you who detected her?' Who else, he thinks? With her husband George away she has no one to spy on.

Mary's bed is strewn with silks – flame, orange, carnation – as if a fire has broken out in the mattress. Across stools and a window seat trail lawn smocks, entangled ribbons and unpaired gloves. Are those the same green stockings she once revealed to the knee, running full-tilt towards him on the day she proposed marriage?

He stands in the doorway. 'William Stafford, eh?'

She straightens up, her cheeks flushed, a velvet slipper in her hand. Now the secret is out, she has loosened her bodice. Her eyes slide past him. 'Good girl, Jane, bring that here.'

'Excuse me, Master.' It is Jane Seymour, tiptoeing past him with an armful of folded laundry. Then a boy after her, bumping a yellow leather chest. 'Just here, Mark.'

'Behold me, Master Secretary,' Smeaton says. 'I'm making myself useful.'

Jane kneels before the chest and swings it opens. 'Cambric to line it?'

'Never mind cambric. Where's my other shoe?'

'Best be gone,' Lady Rochford warns. 'If Uncle Norfolk sees you he'll take a stick to you. Your royal sister thinks the king has fathered your child. She says, why would it be William Stafford?'

Mary snorts. 'So much does she know. What would Anne know of taking a man for himself? You can tell her he loves me. You can tell her he cares for me and no one else does. No one else in this world.'

He leans down and whispers, 'Mistress Seymour, I did not think you were a friend of Lady Carey.'

'No one else will help her.' She keeps her head down; the nape of her neck flushes pink.

'Those bed hangings are mine,' Mary says. 'Pull them down.' Embroidered on them, he sees, are the arms of her husband Will Carey, dead what – seven years now? 'I can unpick the badges.' Of course: what use are a dead man and his devices? 'Where's my gilt basin, Rochford, have you got it?' She gives the yellow chest a kick; it is stamped all over with Anne's falcon badge. 'If they see me with this, they'll take it off me and tip my stuff in the road.'

'If you can wait an hour,' he says, 'I'll send someone with a chest for you.'

'Will it be stamped Thomas Cromwell? God save me, I haven't an hour. I know what!' She begins to haul the sheets off the bed. 'Make bundles!'

'For shame,' Jane Rochford says. 'And run off like a servant who's stolen the silver? Besides, you won't need these things down in Kent. Stafford has a farm or something, hasn't he? Some little manor? Still, you can sell them. You'll have to, I suppose.'

'My sweet brother will help me when he returns from France. He will not see me cut off.'

'I beg to differ. Lord Rochford will be sensible, as I am, that you have disgraced all your kin.'

Mary turns on her, arm sweeping out like a cat flashing claws. 'This is better than your wedding day, Rochford. It's like getting a houseful of presents. You can't love, you don't know what love is, and all you can do is envy those who do know, and rejoice in their troubles. You are a wretched unhappy woman whose husband loathes her, and I pity you, and I pity my sister Anne, I would not change places with her, I had rather be in the bed of an honest poor gentleman who cares only for me than be like the queen and only able to keep her man with old whore's tricks – yes, I know it is so, he has told Norris what she offers him, and it doesn't conduce to getting a child, I can tell you. And now she is afraid of every woman at court – have you looked at her, have you looked at her lately? Seven years she schemed to be queen, and God protect us from answered prayers. She thought it would be like her coronation every day.' Mary, breathless, reaches into the mill of her possessions and throws Jane Seymour a pair of sleeves. 'Take these, sweetheart, with my blessing. You have the only kind heart at court.'

Jane Rochford, in departing, slams the door.

'Let her go,' Jane Seymour murmurs. 'Forget her.'

'Good riddance!' Mary snaps. 'I must be glad she didn't pick my things over, and offer me a price.' In the silence, her words go crash, flap, rattling around the room like trapped birds who panic and shit down the walls: he has told Norris what she offers him. By night, her ingenious proceedings. He is rephrasing it: as, surely, one must? I'll bet Norris is all ears. Christ alive, these people! The boy Mark is standing, gapey-faced, behind the door. 'Mark, if you stand there like a landed fish I shall have you filleted and fried.' The boy flees.

When Mistress Seymour has tied the bundles they look like birds with broken wings. He takes them from her and reties them, not with silk tags but serviceable string. 'Do you always carry string, Master Secretary?'

Mary says, 'Oh, my book of love poems! Shelton has it.' She pitches from the room.

'She'll need that,' he says. 'No poems down in Kent.'

'Lady Rochford would tell her that sonnets don't keep you warm. Not,' Jane says, 'that I've ever had a sonnet. So I wouldn't really know.'

Liz, he thinks, take your dead hand off me. Do you grudge me this one little girl, so small, so thin, so plain? He turns. 'Jane –'

'Master Secretary?' She dips her knees and rolls sideways on to the mattress; she sits up, drags her skirts from under her, finds her footing: gripping the bedpost, she scrambles up, reaches above her head, and begins to unhook the hangings.

'Come down! I'll do that. I'll send a wagon after Mistress Stafford. She can't carry all she owns.'

'I can do it. Master Secretary doesn't deal with bed hangings.'

'Master Secretary deals with everything. I'm surprised I don't make the king's shirts.'

Jane sways gently above him. Her feet sink into the feathers. 'Queen Katherine does. Still.'

'The Dowager Katherine. Come down.'

She hops down to the rushes, giving her skirts a shake. 'Even now after all that has passed between them. She sent a new parcel last week.'

'I thought the king had forbidden her.'

'Anne says they should be torn up and used for, well, you know what for, in a jakes. He was angry. Possibly because he doesn't like the word "jakes".'

'No more does he.' The king deprecates coarse language, and not a few courtiers have been frozen out for telling some dirty story. 'Is it true what Mary says? That the queen is afraid?'

'For now he is sighing over Mistress Shelton. Well, you know that. You have observed.'

'But surely that is harmless? A king is obliged to be gallant, till he reaches the age when he puts on his long gown and sits by the fire with his chaplains.'

'Explain it to Anne, she doesn't see it. She wanted to send Shelton away. But her father and her brother would not have it. Because the Sheltons are their cousins, so if Henry is going to look elsewhere, they want it to be close to home. Incest is so popular these days! Uncle Norfolk said – I mean, His Grace –'

'It's all right,' he says, distracted, 'I call him that too.'

Jane puts a hand over her mouth. It is a child's hand, with tiny gleaming nails. 'I shall think of that when I am in the country and have nothing to amuse me. And then does he say, dear nephew Cromwell?'

'You are leaving court?' No doubt she has a husband in view: some country husband.

'I hope that when I have served another season I might be released.'

Mary rips into the room, snarling. She juggles two embroidered cushions above the bulk of her child, a bulk which now seems evident; she has a hand free for her gilt basin, in which is her poetry book. She throws down the cushions, opens her fist and scatters a handful of silver buttons, which rattle into the basin like dice. 'Shelton had these. Curse her for a magpie.'

'It is not as if the queen likes me,' Jane says. 'And it is a long time since I saw Wolf Hall.'

For the king's new-year gift he has commissioned from Hans a miniature on vellum, which shows Solomon on his throne receiving Sheba. It is to be an allegory, he explains, of the king receiving the fruits of the church and the homage of his people.

Hans gives him a withering look. 'I grasp the point.'

Hans prepares sketches. Solomon is seated in majesty. Sheba stands before him, unseen face raised, her back to the onlooker.

'In your own mind,' he says, 'can you see her face, even though it's hidden?'

'You pay for the back of her head, that's what you get!' Hans rubs his forehead. He relents. 'Not true. I can see her.'

'See her like a woman you meet in the street?'

'Not quite like that. More like someone you remember. Like some woman you used to know when you were a child.'

They are seated in front of the tapestry the king gave him. The painter's eyes stray to it. 'This woman on the wall. Wolsey had her, Henry had her, now you.'

'I assure you, she has no counterpart in real life.' Well, not unless Westminster has some very discreet and versatile whore.

'I know who she is.' Hans nods emphatically, lips pressed together, eyes bright and taunting, like a dog who steals a handkerchief so you will chase it. 'They talk about it in Antwerp. Why don't you go over and claim her?'

'She is married.' He is taken aback, to think that his private business is common talk.

'You think she would not come away with you?'

'It's years. I have changed.'

'*Ja.* Now you are rich.'

'But what would be said of me, if I enticed away a woman from her husband?'

Hans shrugs. They are so matter-of-fact, the Germans. More says the Lutherans fornicate in church. 'Besides,' Hans says, 'there is the matter of the –'

'The what?'

Hans shrugs: nothing. 'Nothing! You are going to hang me up by my hands till I confess?'

'I don't do that. I only threaten to do it.'

'I meant only,' Hans says soothingly, 'there is the matter of all the other women who want to marry you. The wives of England, they all keep secret books of whom they are going to have next

601

when they have poisoned their husbands. And you are the top of everyone's list.'

In his idle moments – in the week there are two or three – he has been picking through the records of the Rolls House. Though the Jews are forbidden the realm, you cannot know what human flotsam will be washed up by the tide of fortune, and only once, for a single month in these three hundred years, has the house been empty. He runs his eye over the accounts of the successive wardens, and he handles, curious, the receipts for their relief given by the dead inhabitants, written in Hebrew characters. Some of them spent fifty years within these walls, flinching from the Londoners outside. When he walks the crooked passages, he feels their footsteps under his.

He goes to see the two who remain. They are silent and vigilant women of indeterminate age, and the names they go by are Katherine Wheteley and Mary Cook.

'What do you do?' With your time, he means.

'We say our prayers.'

They watch him for evidence of his intentions, good or ill. Their faces say, we are two women with nothing left but our life stories. Why should we part with them to you?

He sends them presents of fowl but he wonders if they eat flesh from gentile hands. Towards Christmas, the prior of Christchurch in Canterbury sends him twelve Kentish apples, each one wrapped in grey linen, of a special kind that is good with wine. He takes these apples to the converts, with wine he has picked out. 'In the year 1353,' he says, 'there was only one person in the house. I am sorry to think she lived here without company. Her last domicile was the city of Exeter, but I wonder where before that? Her name was Claricia.'

'We know nothing of her,' says Katherine, or possibly Mary. 'It would be surprising if we did.' Her fingertip tests the apples. Possibly she does not recognise their rarity, or that they are the best present the prior could find. If you don't like them, he says, or if you do, I have stewing pears. Somebody sent me five hundred.

'A man who meant to get himself noticed,' says Katherine or Mary, and the other says, 'Five hundred pounds would have been better.'

The women laugh, but their laughter is cold. He sees he will never be on terms with them. He likes the name Claricia and he wishes he had suggested it for the gaoler's daughter. It is a name for a woman you might dream of: one you could see straight through.

When the king's new-year present is done Hans says, 'It is the first time I have made his portrait.'

'You shall make another soon, I hope.'

Hans knows he has an English bible, a translation almost ready. He puts a finger to his lips; too soon to talk about it, next year maybe. 'If you were to dedicate it to Henry,' Hans says, 'could he now refuse it? I will put him on the title page, displayed in glory, head of the church.' Hans paces, growls out a few figures. He is thinking of paper and printer's costs, estimating his profits. Lucas Cranach draws title pages for Luther. 'Those pictures of Martin and his wife, he has sold prints by the basketful. And Cranach makes everybody look like a pig.'

True. Even those silvery nudes he paints have sweet pig-faces, and labourer's feet, and gristly ears. 'But if I paint Henry, I must flatter, I suppose. Show him how he was five years ago. Or ten.'

'Stick to five. He will think you are mocking him.'

Hans draws his finger across his throat, buckles at the knees, thrusts out his tongue like a man hanged; it seems he envisages every method of execution.

'An easy majesty would be called for,' he says.

Hans beams. 'I can do it by the yard.'

The end of the year brings cold and a green aqueous light, washing across the Thames and the city. Letters fall to his desk with a soft shuffle like great snowflakes: doctors of theology from Germany, ambassadors from France, Mary Boleyn from her exile in Kent.

He breaks the seal. 'Listen to this,' he says to Richard. 'Mary wants money. She says, she knows she should not have been so hasty. She says, love overcame reason.'

'Love, was it?'

He reads. She does not regret for a minute she has taken on William Stafford. She could have had, she says, other husbands, with titles and wealth. But *'if I were at liberty and might choose, I ensure you, Master Secretary, I have tried so much honesty to be in him, that I had rather beg my bread with him than to be the greatest Queen christened.'*

She dare not write to her sister the queen. Or her father or her uncle or her brother. They are all so cruel. So she is writing to him … He wonders, did Stafford lean over her shoulder, while she was writing? Did she giggle and say, Thomas Cromwell, I once raised *his* hopes.

Richard says, 'I hardly remember how Mary and I were to be married.'

'That was in other days than these.' And Richard is happy; see how it has worked out; we can thrive without the Boleyns. But Christendom was overturned for the Boleyn marriage, to put the ginger pig in the cradle; what if it is true, what if Henry is sated, what if the enterprise is cursed? 'Get Wiltshire in.'

'Here to the Rolls?'

'He will come to the whistle.'

He will humiliate him – in his genial fashion – and make him give Mary an annuity. The girl worked for him, on her back, and now he must pension her. Richard will sit in the shadows and take notes. It will remind Boleyn of the old days: the old days now being approximately six, seven years back. Last week Chapuys said to him, in this kingdom now you are all the cardinal was, and more.

* * *

It is Christmas Eve when Alice More comes to see him. There is a thin sharp light, like the edge of an old knife, and in this light Alice looks old.

He greets her like a princess, and leads her into one of the chambers he has had repanelled and painted, where a great fire leaps up a rebuilt chimney. The air smells of pine boughs. 'You keep the feast here?' Alice has made an effort for him; pinned her hair back fiercely, under a bonnet sewn with seed pearls. 'Well! When I came here before it was a musty old place. My husband used to say,' and he notes the past tense, 'my husband used to say, lock Cromwell in a deep dungeon in the morning, and when you come back that night he'll be sitting on a plush cushion eating larks' tongues, and all the gaolers will owe him money.'

'Did he talk a lot about locking me in dungeons?'

'It was only talk.' She is uneasy. 'I thought you might take me to see the king. I know he's always courteous to women, and kind.'

He shakes his head. If he takes Alice to the king she will talk about when he used to come to Chelsea and walk in the gardens. She will upset him: agitate his mind, make him think about More, which at present he doesn't. 'He is very busy with the French envoys. He means to keep a large court this season. You will have to trust my judgement.'

'You have been good to us,' she says, reluctant. 'I ask myself why. You always have some trick.'

'Born tricky,' he says. 'Can't help it. Alice, why is your husband so stubborn?'

'I no more comprehend him than I do the Blessed Trinity.'

'Then what are we to do?'

'I think he'd give the king his reasons. In his private ear. If the king said beforehand that he would take away all penalties from him.'

'You mean, license him for treason? The king can't do it.'

'Holy Agnes! Thomas Cromwell, to tell the king what he can't do! I've seen a cock swagger in a barnyard, master, till a girl comes one day and wrings his neck.'

'It's the law of the land. The custom of the country.'

'I thought Henry was set over the law.'

'We don't live at Constantinople, Dame Alice. Though I say nothing against the Turk. We cheer on the infidels, these days. As long as they keep the Emperor's hands tied.'

'I don't have much money left,' she says. 'I have to find fifteen shillings every week for his keep. I worry he'll be cold.' She sniffs. 'Still, he could tell me so himself. He doesn't write to me. It's all her, her, his darling Meg. She's not *my* child. I wish his first wife were here, to tell me if she was born the way she is now. She's close, you know. Keeps her own counsel, and his. She tells me now he gave her his shirts to wash the blood out, that he wore a shirt of hair beneath his linen. He did so when we were married and I begged him to leave it off and I thought he had. But how would I know? He slept alone and drew the bolt on his door. If he had an itch I never knew it, he was perforce to scratch it himself. Well, whatever, it was between the two of them, and me no part of it.'

'Alice –'

'Don't think I have no tenderness for him. He didn't marry me to live like a eunuch. We have had dealings, one time or another.' She blushes, more angry than shy. 'And when that is true, you cannot help feeling it, if a man might be cold, if he might be hungry, his flesh being one with yours. You feel to him as you might a child.'

'Fetch him out, Alice, if it is within your power.'

'More in yours than mine.' She smiles sadly. 'Is your little man Gregory home for the season? I have sometimes said to my husband, I wish Gregory Cromwell were my boy. I could bake him in a sugar crust and eat him all up.'

* * *

606

Gregory comes home for Christmas, with a letter from Rowland Lee saying he is a treasure and can come back to his household any time. 'So must I back,' Gregory says, 'or am I finished being educated now?'

'I have a scheme for the new year to improve your French.'

'Rafe says I am being brought up like a prince.'

'For now, you are all I have to practise on.'

'My sweet father ...' Gregory picks up his little dog. He hugs her, and nuzzles the fur at the back of her neck. He waits. 'Rafe and Richard say that when my education is sufficient you mean to marry me to some old dowager with a great settlement and black teeth, and she will wear me out with lechery and rule me with her whims, and she will leave her estate away from the children she has and they will hate me and scheme against my life and one morning I shall be dead in my bed.'

The spaniel swivels in his son's arms, turns on him her mild, round, wondering eyes. 'They are making sport of you, Gregory. If I knew such a woman, I would marry her myself.'

Gregory nods. 'She would never rule you, sir. And I dare say she would have a good deer park, which would be convenient to hunt. And the children would be in fear of you, even if they were men grown.' He appears half-consoled. 'What's that map? Is it the Indies?'

'This is the Scots border,' he says gently. 'Harry Percy's country. Look, let me show you. These are parcels of his estates he has given away to his creditors. We cannot let it continue, because we can't leave our borders to chance.'

'They say he is sick.'

'Sick, or mad.' His tone is indifferent. 'He has no heir, and he and his wife never come together, so it is not likely he will. He has fallen out with his brothers, and he owes a deal of money to the king. So it would make sense to name the king his heir, would it not? He will be brought to see it.'

Gregory looks stricken. 'Take his earldom?'

'He can keep the style. We'll give him something to live on.'

'Is this because of the cardinal?'

Harry Percy stopped Wolsey at Cawood, as he was riding south. He came in, keys in his hand, spattered with mud from the road: my lord, I arrest you for high treason. Look at my face, the cardinal said: I am not afraid of any man alive.

He shrugs. 'Gregory, go and play. Take Bella and practise your French with her; she came to me from Lady Lisle in Calais. I won't be long. I have to settle the kingdom's bills.'

For Ireland at the next dispatch, brass cannon and iron shot, rammers and charging ladles, serpentine powder and four hundredweight of brimstone, five hundred yew bows and two barrels of bowstrings, two hundred each of spades, shovels, crowbars, pickaxes, horsehides, one hundred felling axes, one thousand horseshoes, eight thousand nails. The goldsmith Cornelys has not been paid for the cradle he made for the king's last child, the one that never saw the light; he claims for twenty shillings disbursed to Hans for painting Adam and Eve on the cradle, and he is owed for white satin, gold tassels and fringes, and the silver for modelling the apples in the garden of Eden.

He is talking to people in Florence about hiring a hundred arquebusiers for the Irish campaign. They don't down tools, like Englishmen do, if they have to fight in the woods or on rocky terrain.

The king says, a lucky new year to you, Cromwell. And more to follow. He thinks, luck has nothing to do with it. Of all his presents, Henry is most pleased with the Queen of Sheba, and with a unicorn's horn, and a device to squeeze oranges with a great gold 'H' on it.

Early in the new year the king gives him a title no one has ever held before: Vicegerent in Spirituals, his deputy in church affairs. Rumours that the religious houses will be put down have been running about the kingdom for three years and more. Now he has the power to visit, inspect and reform monasteries; to close them, if need be. There is hardly an abbey whose affairs he does not know, by virtue of his training under the cardinal and the letters that arrive day by day – some monks complaining of abuses and scandals and their superiors' disloyalty, others seeking offices within their communities, assuring him that a word in the right quarter will leave them forever in his debt.

He says to Chapuys, 'Were you ever at the cathedral in Chartres? You walk the labyrinth,' he says, 'set into the pavement, and it seems there is no sense in it. But if you follow it faithfully it leads you straight to the centre. Straight to where you should be.'

Officially, he and the ambassador are barely on speaking terms. Unofficially, Chapuys sends him a vat of good olive oil. He retaliates with capons. The ambassador himself arrives, followed by a retainer carrying a parmesan cheese.

Chapuys looks doleful and chilly. 'Your poor queen keeps the season meagrely at Kimbolton. She is so afraid of the heretic councillors about her husband that she has all her food cooked over the fire in her own room. And Kimbolton is more like a stable than a house.'

'Nonsense,' he says briskly. He hands the ambassador a warming glass of spiced wine. 'We only moved her from Buckden because she complained it was damp. Kimbolton is a very good house.'

'Ah, you say that because it has thick walls and a wide moat.' The scent of honey and cinnamon wafts into the room, logs crackle in the hearth, the green boughs decorating his hall diffuse their own resinous scent. 'And the Princess Mary is ill.'

'Oh, the Lady Mary is always ill.'

'The more cause to care for her!' But Chapuys softens his tone. 'If her mother could see her, it would be much comfort to them both.'

'Much comfort to their escape plans.'

'You are a heartless man.' Chapuys sips his wine. 'You know, the Emperor is ready to stand your friend.' A pause, heavy with significance; into which, the ambassador sighs. 'There are rumours that La Ana is distraught. That Henry is looking at another lady.'

He takes a breath and begins to talk. Henry has no time for other women. He is too busy counting his money. He is growing very close, he doesn't want Parliament to know his income. I have difficulty getting him to part with anything for the universities, or to pay his builders, or even for the poor. He only thinks of ordnance. Munitions. Shipbuilding. Beacons. Forts.

Chapuys turns down his mouth. He knows when he's being spun a line; if he didn't, where would be the pleasure in it? 'So I am to tell my master, am I, that the King of England is so set on war he has no time for love?'

'There will be no war unless your master makes it. Which, with the Turks at his heels, he scarcely has time to do. Oh, I know his coffers are bottomless. The Emperor could ruin us all if he liked.' He smiles. 'But what good would that do the Emperor?'

The fate of peoples is made like this, two men in small rooms. Forget the coronations, the conclaves of cardinals, the pomp and processions. This is how the world changes: a counter pushed across a table, a pen stroke that alters the force of a phrase, a woman's sigh as she passes and leaves on the air a trail of orange flower or rosewater; her hand pulling close the bed curtain, the discreet sigh of flesh against flesh. The king – lord of generalities – must now learn to labour over detail, led on by intelligent greed. As his prudent father's son, he knows all the families of England and what they have. He has registered their holdings in his head, down to the last watercourse and copse. Now the church's assets are to come under his control, he needs to know their worth. The law of who owns what – the law generally – has accreted a parasitic complexity – it is like a barnacled hull, a roof slimy with moss. But there are lawyers enough, and how much ability does it require, to scrape away as you are directed? Englishmen may be superstitious, they may be afraid of the future, they may not know what England is; but the skills of adding and subtraction are not scarce. Westminster has a thousand scratching pens, but Henry will need, he thinks, new men, new structures, new thinking. Meanwhile he, Cromwell, puts his commissioners on the road. *Valor ecclesiasticus.* I will do it in six months, he says. Such an exercise has never been attempted before, it is true, but he has already done much that no one else has even dreamed of.

One day at the beginning of spring he comes back from Westminster chilled. His face aches, as if his bones lie open to the weather, and nagging at his memory is that day when his father mashed him into the cobblestones: his sideways view of Walter's boot. He wants to get back to Austin Friars, because he has had stoves installed and the whole house is warm; the Chancery Lane house is only warm in patches. Besides, he wants to be behind his wall.

Richard says, 'Your eighteen-hour days, sir, can't continue for ever.'

'The cardinal did them.'

That night in his sleep he goes down to Kent. He is looking over the accounts of Bayham Abbey, which is to be closed by Wolsey's command. The hostile faces of the monks, hovering over him, cause him to swear and say to Rafe, pack these ledgers and get them on the mule, we'll examine them over our supper and a glass of white burgundy. It is high summer. On horseback, the mule plodding after them, they pick a route through the monastery's neglected vineyards, dipping with the track into a sylvan dimness, into the bowl of broad-leaved green at the valley bottom. He says to Rafe, we are like two caterpillars sliding through a salad. They ride out again into a flood of sunlight, and before them is the tower of Scotney Castle: its sandstone walls, gold stippled with grey, shimmer above its moat.

He wakes. He has dreamed of Kent, or been there? The ripple of the sunshine is still on his skin. He calls for Christophe.

Nothing happens. He lies still. No one comes. It is early: no sound from the house below. The shutters are closed, and the stars are struggling to get in, working themselves with steel points into the splinters of the wood. It occurs to him that he has not really called for Christophe, only dreamed he has.

Gregory's many tutors have presented him with a sheaf of bills. The cardinal stands at the foot of his bed, wearing his full pontificals. The cardinal becomes Christophe, opening the shutter, moving against the light. 'You have a fever, master?'

Surely he knows, one way or the other? Have I to do everything, know everything? 'Oh, it is the Italian one,' he says, as if that discounts it.

'So must we fetch an Italian doctor?' Christophe sounds dubious.

Rafe is here. The whole household is here. Charles Brandon is here, who he thinks is real, till Morgan Williams comes in, who is dead, and William Tyndale, who is in the English House at Antwerp and dare not venture. On the stairs he can hear the efficient, deathly clip of his father's steel-tipped boots.

Richard Cromwell roars, can we have quiet in here? When he roars, he sounds Welsh; he thinks, on an ordinary day I would never have noticed that. He closes his eyes. Ladies move behind his lids: transparent like little lizards, lashing their tails. The serpent queens of England, black-fanged and haughty, dragging their blood-soaked linen and their crackling skirts. They kill and eat their own children; this is well-known. They suck their marrow before they are even born.

Someone asks him if he wants to confess.

'Must I?'

'Yes, sir, or you will be thought a sectary.'

But my sins are my strength, he thinks; the sins I have done, that others have not even found the opportunity of committing.

I hug them close; they're mine. Besides, when I come to judgment I mean to come with a memorandum in my hand: I shall say to my Maker, I have fifty items here, possibly more.

'If I must confess, I'll have Rowland.'

Bishop Lee is in Wales, they tell him. It might take days.

Dr Butts comes, with other doctors, a swarm of them sent by the king. 'It is a fever I got in Italy,' he explains.

'Let's say it is.' Butts frowns down at him.

'If I am dying, get Gregory. I have things to tell him. But if I am not, don't interrupt his studies.'

'Cromwell,' Butts says, 'I couldn't kill you if I shot you through with cannon. The sea would refuse you. A shipwreck would wash you up.'

They talk about his heart; he overhears them. He feels they should not: the book of my heart is a private book, it is not an order book left on the counter for any passing clerk to scrawl in. They give him a draught to swallow. Shortly afterwards he returns to his ledgers. The lines keep slipping and the figures intermingling and as soon as he has totalled up one column the total unmakes itself and all sense is subtracted. But he keeps trying and trying and adding and adding, until the poison or the healing draught loosens its grip on him and he wakes. The pages of the ledgers are still before his eyes. Butts thinks he is resting as ordered, but in the privacy of his mind little stick figures with arms and legs of ink climb out of the ledgers and walk about. They are carrying firewood in for the kitchen range, but the venison that is trussed to butcher turns back into deer, who rub themselves in innocence on the bark of the trees. The songbirds for the fricassee refeather themselves, hopping back on to the branches not yet cut for firewood, and the honey for basting has gone back to the bee, and the bee has gone back to the hive. He can hear the noises of the house below, but it is some other house, in another country: the chink of coins changing hands, and the scrape of wooden chests over a stone floor. He can hear his own voice, telling some story in Tuscan, in Putney, in the French of the camp and the Latin of a barbarian. Perhaps this is Utopia? At the centre of that place, which is an island, there is a place called Amaurotum, the City of Dreams.

He is tired out from the effort of deciphering the world. Tired from the effort of smiling at the foe.

Thomas Avery comes up from the counting house. He sits by him and holds his hand. Hugh Latimer comes and says psalms. Cranmer comes and looks at him dubiously. Perhaps he is afraid that he will ask, in his fever, how is your wife Grete these days?

Christophe says to him, 'I wish your old master the cardinal were here to comfort you, sir. He was a comfortable man.'

'What do you know of him?'

'I robbed him, sir. Did you not know? I robbed his gold plate.'

He struggles to sit up. 'Christophe? You were the boy at Compiègne?'

'Certainly it was me. Up and down the stairs with buckets of hot water for the bath, and each time a gold cup in the empty bucket. I was sorry to rob him, for he was so *gentil*. "What, you again with your pail, Fabrice?" You must understand, Fabrice was my name in Compiègne. "Give this poor child his dinner," he said. I tasted apricots, which I never had before.'

'But did they not catch you?'

'My master was caught, a very great thief. They branded him. There was a hue and cry. But you see, master, I was meant for greater fortune.'

I remember, he says, I remember Calais, the alchemists, the memory machine. 'Giulio Camillo is making it for François so he will be the wisest king in the world, but the dolt will never learn how to use it.'

This is fantasy, Butts says, the fever rising, but Christophe says, no, I assure you, there is a man in Paris who has built a soul. It is a building but it is alive. The whole of it is lined with little shelves. On these shelves you find certain parchments, fragments of writing, they are in the nature of keys, which lead to a box which contains a key which contains another key, but these keys are not made of metal, or these enfolded boxes of wood.

Then what, frog-boy? someone says.

They are made of spirit. They are what we shall have left, if all the books are burned. They will enable us to remember not only the past, but the future, and to see all the forms and customs that will one day inhabit the earth.

Butts says, he is burning up. He thinks of Little Bilney, how he put a hand in the candle flame the night before he died, testing out the pain. It seared his shrinking flesh; in the night he whimpered like a child and sucked his raw hand, and in the morning the city councillors of Norwich dragged him to the pit where their forefathers had burned Lollards. Even when his face was burned away, they were still pushing into it the emblems and banners of popery: their fabric singed and fringes alight, their blank-eyed virgins cured like herring and curling in the smoke.

He asks, politely and in several languages, for water. Not too much, Butts says, a little and a little. He has heard of an island called Ormuz, the driest kingdom in the world, where there are no trees and no crop but salt. Stand at its centre, and you look over thirty miles in all directions of ashy plain: beyond which lies the seashore, encrusted with pearls.

His daughter Grace comes by night. She makes her own light, wrapped within her shining hair. She watches him, steady, unblinking, till it is morning, and when they open the shutter the stars are fading and the sun and moon hang together in a pale sky.

A week passes. He is better and he wants work brought in but the doctors forbid it. How will it go forward, he asks, and Richard says, sir, you have trained us all and we are your disciples, you have made a thinking machine that marches forward as if it were alive, you don't need to be tending it every minute of every day.

Still, Christophe says, they say le roi Henri is groaning as if he were in pain himself: oh, where is Cremuel?

A message is brought. Henry has said, I am coming to visit. It's an Italian fever, so I am sure not to take it.

He can hardly believe it. Henry ran away from Anne when she had the sweat: even at the height of his love for her.

He says, send Thurston up. They have been keeping him on a low diet, invalid food like turkey. Now, he says, we are going to plan – what? – a piglet, stuffed and roasted in the way I once saw it done at a papal banquet. You will need chopped chicken, lardo, and a goat's liver, minced fine. You will need fennel seeds, marjoram, mint, ginger, butter, sugar, walnuts, hen's eggs and some saffron. Some people put in cheese but we don't make the right kind here in London, besides I myself think it is unnecessary. If you're in trouble about any of this send out to Bonvisi's cook, he'll see you right.

He says, 'Send next door to prior George, tell him to keep his friars off the streets when the king comes, lest he reform them too soon.' It's his feeling that the whole process should go slowly, slowly, so people will see the justice of it; no need to spill the religious out on to the streets. The friars who live at his gates are a disgrace to their order, but they are good neighbours to him. They have given up their refectory, and from their chamber windows at night drifts the sound of merry supper parties. Any day you can join a crowd of them drinking at the Well with Two Buckets just outside his gates. The abbey church is more like a market, and a fleshmarket too. The district is full of young bachelors from the Italian merchant houses, who are serving their London year; he often entertains them, and when they leave his table (drained of market information) he knows they make a dash for the friars' precincts, where enterprising London girls are sheltering from the rain and waiting to make amiable terms.

* * *

It is 17 April when the king makes his visit. At dawn there are showers. By ten o'clock the air is mild as buttermilk. He is up and in a chair, from which he rises. My dear Cromwell: Henry kisses him firmly on both cheeks, takes him by the arms and (in case he thinks he is the only strong man in the kingdom) he sits him back, decisively, in his chair. 'You sit and give me no argument,' Henry says. 'Give me no argument for once, Master Secretary.'

The ladies of the house, Mercy and his sister-in-law Johane, are decked out like Walsingham madonnas on a feast day. They curtsey low, and Henry sways above them, informally attired, jacket of silver brocade, vast gold chain across his chest, his fists flashing with Indian emeralds. He has not wholly mastered the family relationships, for which no one can blame him. 'Master Secretary's sister?' he says to Johane. 'No, forgive me. I remember now that you lost your sister Bet at the same time my own lovely sister died.'

It is such a simple, human sentence, coming from a king; at the mention of their most recent loss, tears well into the eyes of the two women, and Henry, turning to one, then the other, with a careful forefinger dots them from their cheeks, and makes them smile. The little brides Alice and Jo he whirls up into the air as if they were butterflies, and kisses them on the mouth, saying he wishes he had known them when he was a boy. The sad truth is, do you not notice, Master Secretary, the older one gets, the lovelier the girls?

Then eighty will have its advantages, he says: every drab will be a pearl. Mercy says to the king, as if talking to a neighbour, give over, sir: you're no age. Henry stretches out his arms and displays himself before the company: 'Forty-five in July.'

He notes the incredulous hush. It does the job. Henry is gratified.

Henry walks around and looks at all his paintings and asks who the people are. He looks at Anselma, the Queen of Sheba, on the wall. He makes them laugh by picking up Bella and talking to her in Honor Lisle's atrocious French. 'Lady Lisle sent the queen a little creature even smaller. He tips his head to one side and his ears prick up, as if to say, why are you speaking to me? So she calls him Pourquoi.' When he speaks of Anne his voice drips uxorious sentiment: like clear honey. The women smile, pleased to see their king set such an example. 'You know him, Cromwell, you have seen him on her arm. She takes him everywhere. Sometimes,' and now he nods judiciously, 'I think she loves him better than me. Yes, I am second to the dog.'

He sits smiling, no appetite, watching as Henry eats from the silver dishes Hans has designed.

Henry speaks kindly to Richard, calling him cousin. He signals for him to stand by while he talks to his councillor, and for others to retreat a little way. What if King Francis this and Francis that, should I cross the sea myself to patch together some sort of deal, would you cross over yourself when you are on your feet again? What if the Irish, what if the Scots, what if it all gets out of hand and we have wars like in Germany and peasants crowning themselves, what if these false prophets, what if Charles overruns me and Katherine takes the field, she is of mettlesome temper and the people love her, God knows why for I do not.

If that happens, he says, I will be out of this chair and take the field, my own sword in my hand.

When the king has enjoyed his dinner he sits by him and talks softly about himself. The April day, fresh and showery, puts him in mind of the day his father died. He talks of his childhood: I lived at the palace at Eltham, I had a fool called Goose. When I was seven the Cornish rebels came up, led by a giant, do you remember that? My father sent me to the Tower to keep me safe. I said, let me out, I want to fight! I wasn't frightened of a giant from the west, but I was frightened of my grandmother Margaret Beaufort, because her face was like a death's head, and her grip on my wrist was like a skeleton's grip.

When we were young, he says, we were always told, your grandmother gave birth to your lord father the king when she was a little creature of thirteen years. Her past was like a sword she held over us. What, Harry, are you laughing in Lent? When I, at little more years than you, gave birth to the Tudor? What, Harry, are you dancing, what, Harry, are you playing at ball? Her life was all duty. She kept twelve paupers in her house at Woking and once she made me kneel down with a basin and wash their yellow feet, she's lucky I didn't throw up on them. She used to start praying every morning at five. When she knelt down at her prie-dieu she cried out from the pain in her knees. And whenever there was a celebration, a wedding or a birth, a pastime or an occasion of mirth, do you know what she did? Every time? Without failing? She wept.

And with her, it was all Prince Arthur. Her shining light and her creeping saint. 'When I became king instead, she lay down and died out of spite. And on her deathbed, do you know what she told me?' Henry snorts. 'Obey Bishop Fisher in all things! Pity she didn't tell Fisher to obey me!'

When the king has left with his gentlemen, Johane comes to sit with him. They talk quietly; though everything they say is fit to be overheard. 'Well, it came off sweetly.'

'We must give the kitchen a present.'

'The whole household did well. I am glad to have seen him.'

'Is he what you hoped?'

'I had not thought him so tender. I see why Katherine has fought so hard for him. I mean, not just to be queen, which she thinks is her right, but to have him for a husband. I would say he is a man very apt to be loved.'

Alice bursts in. 'Forty-five! I thought he was past that.'

'You would have bedded him for a handful of garnets,' Jo sneers. 'You said so.'

'Well, you for export licences!'

'Stop!' he says. 'You girls! If your husbands should hear you.'

'Our husbands know what we are,' Jo says. 'We are full of ourselves, aren't we? You don't come to Austin Friars to look for shy little maids. I wonder our uncle doesn't arm us.'

'Custom constrains me. Or I'd send you to Ireland.'

Johane watches them rampage away. When they are out of earshot, she checks over her shoulder and murmurs, you will not credit what I am going to say next.

'Try me.'

'Henry is frightened of you.'

He shakes his head. Who frightens the Lion of England?

'Yes, I swear to you. You should have seen his face, when you said you would take your sword in your hand.'

The Duke of Norfolk comes to visit him, clattering up from the yard where his servants hold his plumed horse. 'Liver, is it? My liver's shot to pieces. And these five years my muscles have been wasting. Look at that!' He sticks out a claw. 'I've tried every physician in the realm, but they don't know what ails me. Yet they never fail to send in their accounts.'

Norfolk, he knows it for a fact, would never pay anything so mere as a doctor's bill.

'And the colics and the gripes,' the duke says, 'they make my mortal life a Purgatory. Sometimes I'm at stool all night.'

'Your Grace should take life more easily,' Rafe says. Not bolt your food, he means. Not race about in a lather like a post horse.

'I intend to, believe me. My niece makes it clear she wants none of my company and none of my counsel. I'm for my house at Kenninghall, and Henry can find me there if he wants me. God restore you, Master Secretary. St Walter is good, I hear, if a job's getting too much for you. And St Ubald against the headache, he does the trick for me.' He gropes inside his jacket. 'Brought you a medal. Pope blessed it. Bishop of Rome, sorry.' He drops it on the table. 'Thought you might not have one.'

He is out of the door. Rafe picks up the medal. 'It's probably cursed.'

On the stairs they can hear the duke, his voice raised, plaintive: 'I thought he was nearly dead! They told me he was nearly dead …'

He says to Rafe, 'Seen him off.'

Rafe grins. 'Suffolk too.'

Henry has never remitted the fine of thirty thousand pounds he imposed when Suffolk married his sister. From time to time he remembers it, and this is one of those times; Brandon has had to give up his lands in Oxfordshire and Berkshire to pay his debts, and now he keeps small state down in the country.

He closes his eyes. It is bliss to think of: two dukes on the run from him.

His neighbour Chapuys comes in. 'I told my master in dispatches that the king has visited you. My master is amazed that the king would go to a private house, to one not even a lord. But I told him, you should see the work he gets out of Cromwell.'

'He should have such a servant,' he says. 'But Eustache, you are an old hypocrite, you know. You would dance on my grave.'

'My dear Thomas, you are always the only opponent.'

Thomas Avery smuggles in to him Luca Pacioli's book of chess puzzles. He has soon done all the puzzles, and drawn out some of his own on blank pages at the back. His letters are brought and he reviews the latest round of disasters. They say that the tailor at Münster, the King of Jerusalem with sixteen wives, has had a row with one of them and cut her head off in the marketplace.

He re-emerges into the world. Knock him down and he will get up. Death has called to inspect him, she has measured him, breathed into his face: walked away again. He is a little leaner, his clothes tell him; for a while he feels light, no longer grounded in the world, each day buoyant with possibilities. The Boleyns congratulate him heartily on his return to health, and so they should, for without him how would they be what they are now? Cranmer, when they meet, keeps leaning forward to pat his shoulder and squeeze his hand.

While he has been recovering, the king has cropped his hair. He has done this to disguise his increasing baldness, though it doesn't, not at all. His loyal councillors have done the same, and soon it becomes a mark of fellowship between them. 'By God, sir,' Master Wriothesley says, 'if I wasn't frightened of you before, I would be now.'

'But Call-Me,' he says, 'you were frightened of me before.'

There is no change in Richard's aspect; committed to the tilting ground, he keeps his hair cropped to fit under a helmet. The shorn Master Wriothesley looks more intelligent, if that were possible, and Rafe more determined and alert. Richard Riche has lost the vestiges of the boy he was. Suffolk's huge face has acquired a strange innocence. Monseigneur looks deceptively ascetic. As for Norfolk, no one notices the change. 'What sort of hair did he have before?' Rafe asks. Strips of iron-grey fortify his scalp, as if laid out by a military engineer.

The fashion spreads into the country. When Rowland Lee next pitches into the Rolls House, he thinks a cannonball is coming at him. His son's eyes look large and calm, a still golden colour. Your mother would have wept over your baby curls, he says, rubbing his head affectionately. Gregory says, 'Would she? I hardly remember her.'

As April goes out, four treacherous monks are put on trial. The oath has been offered them repeatedly, and refused. It is a year since the Maid was put to death. The king showed mercy to her followers; he is not now so disposed. It is the Charterhouse of London where the mischief originates, that austere house of men who sleep on straw; it is where Thomas More tried his vocation, before it was revealed to him that the world needed his talents. He, Cromwell, has visited the house, as he has visited the recalcitrant community at Syon. He has spoken gently, he has spoken bluntly, he has threatened and cajoled; he has sent enlightened clerics to argue the king's case, and he has interviewed the disaffected members of the community and set them to work against their brethren. It is all to no avail. Their response is, go away, go away and leave me to my sanctified death.

If they think that they will maintain to the end the equanimity of their prayer-lives, they are wrong, because the law demands the full traitor's penalty, the short spin in the wind and the conscious public disembowelling, a brazier alight for human entrails. It is the most horrible of all deaths, pain and rage and humiliation swallowed to the dregs, the fear so great that the strongest rebel is unmanned before the executioner with his knife can do the job; before each one dies he watches his fellows and, cut down from the rope, he crawls like an animal round and round on the bloody boards.

Wiltshire and George Boleyn are to represent the king at the spectacle, and Norfolk, who, grumbling, has been dragged up from the country and told to prepare for an embassy to France. Henry thinks of going himself to see the monks die, for the court will wear masks, edging on their high-stepping horses among the city officials and the ragged populace, who turn out by the hundred to see any such show. But the king's build makes it difficult to disguise him, and he fears there may be demonstrations in favour of Katherine, still a favourite with the more verminous portion of every crowd. Young Richmond shall stand in for me, his father decides; one day he may have to defend, in battle, his half-sister's title, so it becomes him to learn the sights and sounds of slaughter.

The boy comes to him at night, as the deaths are scheduled next day: 'Good Master Secretary, take my place.'

'Will you take mine, at my morning meeting with the king? Think of it like this,' he says, firm and pleasant. 'If you plead sickness, or fall off your horse tomorrow or vomit in front of your father-in-law, he'll never let you forget it. If you want him to let you into your bride's bed, prove yourself a man. Keep your eyes on the duke, and pattern your conduct on his.'

But Norfolk himself comes to him, when it is over, and says, Cromwell, I swear upon my life that one of the monks spoke when his heart was out. Jesus, he called, Jesus save us, poor Englishmen.

'No, my lord. It is not possible he should do so.'

'Do you know that for a fact?'

'I know it from experience.'

The duke quails. Let him think it, that his past deeds have included the pulling out of hearts. 'I dare say you're right.' Norfolk crosses himself. 'It must have been a voice from the crowd.'

The night before the monks met their end, he had signed a pass for Margaret Roper, the first in months. Surely, he thinks, for Meg to be with her father when traitors are being led out to their deaths; surely she will turn from her resolve, she will say to her father, come now, the king is in his killing vein, you must take the oath as I have done. Make a mental reservation, cross your fingers behind your back; only ask for Cromwell or any officer of the king, say the words, come home.

But his tactic fails. She and her father stood dry-eyed at a window as the traitors were brought out, still in their habits, and launched on their journey to Tyburn. I always forget, he thinks, how More neither pities himself nor takes pity on others. Because I would have protected my own girls from such a sight, I think he would too. But he uses Meg to harden his resolve. If she will not give way, he cannot; and she will not give way.

The following day he goes in to see More himself. The rain splashes and hisses from the stones underfoot; walls and water are indistinguishable, and around small corners a wind moans like a winter wind. When he has struggled out of his wet outer layers he stands chatting to the turnkey Martin, getting the news of his wife and new baby. How shall I find him, he asks at last and Martin says, have you ever noticed how he has one shoulder up and the other down?

It comes from overmuch writing, he says. One elbow on the desk, the other shoulder dropped. Well, whatever, Martin says: he looks like a little carved hunchback on a bench end.

More has grown his beard; he looks as one imagines the prophets of Münster to look, though he would abhor the comparison. 'Master Secretary, how does the king take the news from abroad? They say the Emperor's troops are on the move.'

'Yes, but to Tunis, I think.' He casts a glance at the rain. 'If you were the Emperor, wouldn't you pick Tunis, rather than London? Look, I haven't come to quarrel with you. Just to see if you are comfortable.'

More says, 'I hear you have sworn my fool, Henry Pattinson.' He laughs.

'Whereas the men who died yesterday had followed your example, and refused to swear.'

'Let me be clear. I am no example. I am just myself, alone. I say nothing against the act. I say nothing against the men that made it. I say nothing against the oath, or against any man that swears it.'

'Ah, yes,' he sits down on the chest where More keeps his possessions, 'but all this saying nothing, it won't do for a jury, you know. Should it come to a jury.'

'You have come to threaten me.'

'The Emperor's feats of arms shorten the king's temper. He means to send you a commission, who will want a straight answer as to his title.'

'Oh I'm sure your friends will be too good for me. Lord Audley? And Richard Riche? Listen. Ever since I came here I have been preparing for my death, at your hands – yes, yours – or at the hands of nature. All I require is peace and silence for my prayers.'

'You want to be a martyr.'

'No, what I want is to go home. I am weak, Thomas. I am weak as we all are. I want the king to take me as his servant, his loving subject, as I have never ceased to be.'

'I have never understood where the line is drawn, between sacrifice and self-slaughter.'

'Christ drew it.'

'You don't see anything wrong with the comparison?'

Silence. The loud, contentious, quality of More's silence. It's bouncing off the walls. More says he loves England, and he fears all England will be damned. He is offering some kind of bargain to his God, his God who loves slaughter: 'It is expedient that one man shall die for the people.' Well, I tell you, he says to himself. Bargain all you like. Consign yourself to the hangman if you must. The people don't give a fourpenny fuck. Today is 5 May. In two days' time the commission will visit you. We will ask you to sit, you will decline. You will stand before us looking like a desert father, and we snugly wrapped against the summer chill. I will say what I say. You will say what you say. And maybe I will concede you have won. I will walk away and leave you, the king's good subject if you say so, till your beard grows down to your knees and the spiders weave webs across your eyes.

Well, that's his plan. Events overtake it. He says to Richard, has any damnable bishop of Rome in the history of his pox-ridden jurisdiction ever done anything so stupidly ill-timed as this? Farnese has announced England is to have a new cardinal: Bishop Fisher. Henry is enraged. He swears he will send Fisher's head across the sea to meet his hat.

The third of June: himself to the Tower, with Wiltshire for the Boleyn interest, and Charles Brandon, looking as if he would as soon be fishing. Riche to make notes; Audley to make jokes. It's wet again, and Brandon says, this must be the worst summer ever, eh? Yes, he says, good thing His Majesty isn't superstitious. They laugh: Suffolk, a little uncertainly.

Some said the world would end in 1533. Last year had its adherents too. Why not this year? There is always somebody ready to claim that these are the end times, and nominate his neighbour as the Antichrist. The news from Münster is that the skies are falling fast. The besiegers are demanding unconditional surrender; the besieged are threatening mass suicide.

He leads the way. 'Christ, what a place,' Brandon says. Drips are spoiling his hat. 'Doesn't it oppress you?'

'Oh, we're always here.' Riche shrugs. 'One thing or another. Master Secretary is wanted at the Mint or the jewel house.'

Martin lets them in. More's head jerks up as they enter.

'It's yes or no today,' he says.

'Not even good day and how do you.' Somebody has given More a comb for his beard. 'Well, what do I hear from Antwerp? Do I hear Tyndale is taken?'

'That is not to the point,' the Lord Chancellor says. 'Answer to the oath. Answer to the statute. Is it a lawfully made statute?'

'They say he strayed outside and the Emperor's soldiers have seized him.'

He says coldly, 'Had you prior knowledge?'

Tyndale has been, not just taken, but betrayed. Someone tempted him out of his haven, and More knows who. He sees himself, a second self, enacting another rainy morning just like this: in which he crosses the room, hauls the prisoner to his feet, beats out of him the name of his agent. 'Now, Your Grace,' he says to Suffolk, 'you are wearing a violent expression, pray be calm.'

Me? Brandon says. Audley laughs. More says, 'Tyndale's devil will desert him now. The Emperor will burn him. And the king will not lift a finger to save him, because Tyndale would not support his new marriage.'

'Perhaps you think he showed sense there?' Riche says.

'You must speak,' Audley says, gently enough.

627

More is agitated, words tumbling over each other. He is ignoring Audley, speaking to him, Cromwell. 'You cannot compel me to put myself in hazard. For if I had an opinion against your Act of Supremacy, which I do not concede, then your oath would be a two-edged sword. I must put my body in peril if I say no to it, my soul if I say yes to it. Therefore I say nothing.'

'When you interrogated men you called heretics, you did not allow evasion. You compelled them to speak and racked them if they would not. If they were made to answer, why not you?'

'The cases are not the same. When I compel an answer from a heretic, I have the whole body of law behind me, the whole might of Christendom. What I am threatened with here is one particular law, one singular dispensation of recent make, recognised here but in no other country –'

He sees Riche make a note. He turns away. 'The end is the same. Fire for them. Axe for you.'

'If the king grants you that mercy,' Brandon says.

More quails; he curls up his fingers on the tabletop. He notices this, detached. So that's a way in. Put him in fear of the more lingering death. Even as he thinks it, he knows he will not do it; the notion is contaminating. 'On numbers I suppose you have me beat. But have you looked at a map lately? Christendom is not what it was.'

Riche says, 'Master Secretary, Fisher is more a man than this prisoner before us, for Fisher dissents and takes the consequences. Sir Thomas, I think you would be an overt traitor, if you dared.'

More says softly, 'Not so. It is not for me to thrust myself on God. It is for God to draw me to him.'

'We take note of your obstinacy,' Audley says. 'We spare you the methods you have used on others.' He stands up. 'It is the king's pleasure that we move to indictment and trial.'

'In the name of God! What ill can I effect from this place? I do nobody harm. I say none harm. I think none harm. If this be not enough to keep a man alive –'

He cuts in on him, incredulous. 'You do nobody harm? What about Bainham, you remember Bainham? You forfeited his goods, committed his poor wife to prison, saw him racked with your own eyes, you locked him in Bishop Stokesley's cellar, you had him back at your own house two days chained upright to a post, you sent him again to Stokesley, saw him beaten and abused for a week, and still your spite was not exhausted: you sent him back to the Tower and had him racked again, so that finally his body was so broken that they had to carry him in a chair when they took him to Smithfield to be burned alive. And you say, Thomas More, that you do no harm?'

Riche begins to gather More's papers from the table. It is suspected he has been passing letters to Fisher upstairs: which is not a bad thing, if collusion in Fisher's treason can be shown. More drops his hand on them, fingers spread; then shrugs, and yields them. 'Have them if you must. You read all I write.'

He says, 'Unless we hear soon of a change of heart, we must take away your pen and papers. And your books. I will send someone.'

More seems to shrink. He bites his lip. 'If you must take them, take them now.'

'For shame,' Suffolk says. 'Do you take us for porters, Master More?'

Anne says, 'It is all about me.' He bows. 'When finally you have out of More what troubles his singular conscience, you will find that what is at the root of it is that he will not bend his knee to my queenship.'

She is small and white and angry. Long fingers tip to tip, bending each other back; eyes bright.

Before they go further, he has to recall to Henry last year's disaster; remind him that he cannot always have his own way, just by asking for it. Last summer Lord Dacre, who is one of the northern lords, was indicted for treason, accused of collusion

629

with the Scots. Behind the accusation were the Clifford family, Dacre's hereditary enemies and rivals; behind them the Boleyns, for Dacre had been outspoken in support of the former queen. The stage was set in Westminster Hall, Norfolk presiding over the court, as High Steward of the kingdom: and Dacre to be judged, as was his right, by twenty fellow lords. And then ... mistakes were made. Possibly the whole thing was a miscalculation, an affair driven too fast and hard by the Boleyns. Possibly he had erred in not taking charge of the prosecution himself; he had thought it was best to stay in the background, as many titled men have a spite against him for being who he is, and will take a risk to work him displeasure. Or else Norfolk was the problem, losing control of the court ... Whatever the reason, the charges were thrown out, to an outpouring by the king of astonishment and rage. Dacre was taken straight back to the Tower by the king's guard, and he was sent in to strike some deal, which must, he knew, end with Dacre broken. At his trial Dacre had talked for seven hours, in his own defence; but he, Cromwell, can talk for a week. Dacre had admitted to misprision of treason, a lesser offence. He bought a royal pardon for £10,000. He was released to go north again, a pauper.

But the queen was sick with frustration; she wanted an example made. And affairs in France are not going her way; some say that at the mention of her name, François sniggers. She suspects, and she is right, that her man Cromwell is more interested in the friendship of the German princes than in an alliance with France; but she has to pick her time for that quarrel, and she says she will have no peace till Fisher is dead, till More is dead. So now she circles the room, agitated, less than regal, and she keeps veering towards Henry, touching his sleeve, touching his hand, and he brushes her away, each time, as if she were a fly. He, Cromwell, watches. They are not the same couple from day to day: sometimes doting, sometimes chilly and distanced. The billing and cooing, on the whole, is the more painful to watch.

'Fisher gives me no anxiety,' he says, 'his offence is clear. In More's case … morally, our cause is unimpeachable. No one is in doubt of his loyalty to Rome and his hatred of Your Majesty's title as head of the church. Legally, however, our case is slender, and More will use every legal, every procedural device open to him. This is not going to be easy.'

Henry stirs into life. 'Do I retain you for what is easy? Jesus pity my simplicity, I have promoted you to a place in this kingdom that no one, no one of your breeding has ever held in the whole of the history of this realm.' He drops his voice. 'Do you think it is for your personal beauty? The charm of your presence? I keep you, Master Cromwell, because you are as cunning as a bag of serpents. But do not be a viper in my bosom. You know my decision. Execute it.'

As he leaves, he is conscious of the silence falling behind him. Anne walking to the window. Henry staring at his feet.

So when Riche comes in, quivering with undisclosed secrets, he is inclined to swat him like a fly; but then he takes hold of himself, rubs his palms together instead: the merriest man in London. 'Well, Sir Purse, did you pack up the books? And how was he?'

'He drew the blind down. I asked him why, and he said, the goods are taken away, so now I am closing the shop.'

He can hardly bear it, to think of More sitting in the dark.

'Look, sir.' Riche has a folded paper. 'We had some conversation. I wrote it down.'

'Talk me through it.' He sits down. 'I am More. You are Riche.' Riche stares at him. 'Shall I close the shutter? Is this better played out in the dark?'

'I could not,' Riche says, hesitant, 'leave him without trying once again –'

'Quite. You have your way to make. But why would he talk to you, if he would not talk to me?'

631

'Because he has no time for me. He thinks I don't matter.'

'And you Solicitor General,' he says, mocking.

'So we were putting cases.'

'What, as if you were at Lincoln's Inn after supper?'

'To tell the truth I pitied him, sir. He craves conversation and you know he rattles away. I said to him, suppose Parliament were to pass an act saying that I, Richard Riche, were to be king. Would you not take me for king? And he laughed.'

'Well, you admit it is not likely.'

'So I pressed him on it; he said, yes, majestic Richard, I so take you, for Parliament can do it, and considering what they have done already I should hardly be surprised if I woke up in the reign of King Cromwell, for if a tailor can be King of Jerusalem I suppose a lad from the smithy can be King of England.'

Riche pauses: has he given offence? He beams at him. 'When I am King Cromwell, you shall be a duke. So, to the point, Purse … or isn't there one?'

'More said, well, you have put a case, I shall put you a higher case. Suppose Parliament were to pass an act saying God should not be God? I said, it would have no effect, for Parliament has no power to do it. Then he said, aye, well, young man, at least you recognise an absurdity. And there he stopped, and gave me a look, as if to say, let us deal in the real world now. I said to him, I will put you a middle case. You know our lord the king has been named by Parliament head of the church. Why will you not go with the vote, as you go with it when it makes me monarch? And he said – as if he were instructing some child – the cases are not alike. For one is a temporal jurisdiction, and Parliament can do it. The other is a spiritual jurisdiction, and is what Parliament cannot exercise, for the jurisdiction is out of this realm.'

He stares at Riche. 'Hang him for a papist,' he says.

'Yes, sir.'

'We know he thinks it. He has never stated it.'

'He said that a higher law governed this and all realms, and if Parliament trespassed on God's law …'

'On the Pope's law, he means – for he holds them the same, he couldn't deny that, could he? Why is he always examining his conscience, if not to check day and night that it is in accord with the church of Rome? That is his comfort, that is his guide. It seems to me, if he plainly denies Parliament its capacity, he denies the king his title. Which is treason. Still,' he shrugs, 'how far does it take us? Can we show the denial was malicious? He will say, I suppose, that it was just talk, to pass the time. That you were putting cases, and that anything said in that wise cannot be held against a man.'

'A jury won't understand that. They'll take him to mean what he said. After all, sir, he knew it wasn't some students' debate.'

'True. You don't hold those at the Tower.'

Riche offers the memorandum. 'I have written it down faithfully to the best of my recollection.'

'You don't have a witness?'

'They were in and out, packing up the books in a crate, he had a lot of books. You cannot blame me for carelessness, sir, for how was I to know he would talk to me at all?'

'I don't blame you.' He sighs. 'In fact, Purse, you are the apple of my eye. You'll stand behind this in court?'

Doubtful, Riche nods. 'Tell me you will, Richard. Or tell me you won't. Let's have it straight. Have the grace to say so now, if you think your courage might fail. If we lose another trial, we can kiss goodbye to our livelihoods. And all our work will be for nothing.'

'You see, he couldn't resist it, the chance to put me right,' Riche says. 'He will never let it drop, what I did as a boy. He uses me to make his sermon on. Well, let him make his next sermon on the block.'

The evening before Fisher is to die, he visits More. He takes a strong guard with him, but he leaves them in the outer chamber

633

and goes in alone. 'I've got used to the blind drawn,' More says, almost cheerfully. 'You don't mind sitting in the twilight?'

'You need not be afraid of the sun. There is none.'

'Wolsey used to boast that he could change the weather.' He chuckles. 'It's good of you to visit me, Thomas, now that we have no more to say. Or have we?'

'The guards will come for Bishop Fisher early tomorrow. I am afraid they will wake you.'

'I should be a poor Christian if I could not keep vigil with him.' His smile has seeped away. 'I hear the king has granted him mercy as to the manner of his death.'

'He being a very old man, and frail.'

More says, with tart pleasantness, 'I'm doing my best, you know. A man can only shrivel at his own rate.'

'Listen.' He reaches across the table, takes his hand, wrings it: harder than he meant. My blacksmith's grip, he thinks: he sees More flinch, feels his fingers, the skin dry as paper over the bones. 'Listen. When you come before the court, throw yourself at that instant on the king's mercy.'

More says, wonderingly, 'What good will that do me?'

'He is not a cruel man. You know that.'

'Do I? He used not to be. He had a sweet disposition. But then he changed the company he kept.'

'He is susceptible always to a plea for mercy. I do not say he will let you live, the oath unsworn. But he may grant you the same mercy as Fisher.'

'It is not so important, what happens to the body. I have led in some ways a blessed life. God has been good and not tested me. Now he does I cannot fail him. I have been vigilant over my heart, and I have not always liked what I have found there. If it comes into the hands of the hangman at the last, so be it. It will be in God's hands soon enough.'

'Will you think me sentimental, if I say I do not want to see you butchered?' No reply. 'Are you not afraid of the pain?'

'Oh yes, I am very much afraid, I am not a bold and robust man such as yourself, I cannot help but rehearse it in my mind. But I will only feel it for a moment, and God will not let me remember it afterwards.'

'I am glad I am not like you.'

'Undoubtedly. Or you would be sitting here.'

'I mean, my mind fixed on the next world. I realise you see no prospect of improving this one.'

'And you do?'

Almost a flippant question. A handful of hail smacks itself against the window. It startles them both; he gets up, restless. He would rather know what's outside, see the summer in its sad blowing wreckage, than cower behind the blind and wonder what the damage is. 'I once had every hope,' he says. 'The world corrupts me, I think. Or perhaps it's just the weather. It pulls me down and makes me think like you, that one should shrink inside, down and down to a little point of light, preserving one's solitary soul like a flame under a glass. The spectacles of pain and disgrace I see around me, the ignorance, the unthinking vice, the poverty and the lack of hope, and oh, the rain – the rain that falls on England and rots the grain, puts out the light in a man's eye and the light of learning too, for who can reason if Oxford is a giant puddle and Cambridge is washing away downstream, and who will enforce the laws if the judges are swimming for their lives? Last week the people were rioting in York. Why would they not, with wheat so scarce, and twice the price of last year? I must stir up the justices to make examples, I suppose, otherwise the whole of the north will be out with billhooks and pikes, and who will they slaughter but each other? I truly believe I should be a better man if the weather were better. I should be a better man if I lived in a commonwealth where the sun shone and the citizens were rich and free. If only that were true, Master More, you wouldn't have to pray for me nearly as hard as you do.'

'How you can talk,' More says. Words, words, just words. 'I do, of course, pray for you. I pray with all my heart that you will see that you are misled. When we meet in Heaven, as I hope we will, all our differences will be forgot. But for now, we cannot wish them away. Your task is to kill me. Mine is to keep alive. It is my role and my duty. All I own is the ground I stand on, and that ground is Thomas More. If you want it you will have to take it from me. You cannot reasonably believe I will yield it.'

'You will want pen and paper to write out your defence. I will grant you that.'

'You never give up trying, do you? No, Master Secretary, my defence is up here,' he taps his forehead, 'where it will stay safe from you.'

How strange the room is, how empty, without More's books: it is filling with shadows. 'Martin, a candle,' he calls.

'Will you be here tomorrow? For the bishop?'

He nods. Though he will not witness the moment of Fisher's death. The protocol is that the spectators bow their knee and doff their hats to mark the passing of the soul.

Martin brings a pricket candle. 'Anything else?' They pause while he sets it down. When he is gone, they still pause: the prisoner sits hunched over, looking into the flame. How does he know if More has begun on a silence, or on preparation for speech? There is a silence which precedes speech, there is a silence which is instead of speech. One need not break it with a statement, one can break it with a hesitation: *if ... as it may be ... if it were possible ...* He says, 'I would have left you, you know. To live out your life. To repent of your butcheries. If I were king.'

The light fades. It is as if the prisoner has withdrawn himself from the room, leaving barely a shape where he should be. A draught pulls at the candle flame. The bare table between them, clear now of More's driven scribblings, has taken on the aspect of an altar; and what is an altar for, but a sacrifice? More breaks his silence at last: 'If, at the end and after I am tried, if the king does

636

not grant, if the full rigour of the penalty ... Thomas, how is it done? You would think when a man's belly were slashed open he would die, with a great effusion of blood, but it seems it is not so ... Do they have some special implement, that they use to pith him while he is alive?'

'I am sorry you should think me expert.'

But had he not told Norfolk, as good as told him, that he had pulled out a man's heart?

He says, 'It is the executioner's mystery. It is kept secret, to keep us in awe.'

'Let me be killed cleanly. I ask nothing, but I ask that.' Swaying on his stool, he is seized, between one heartbeat and the next, in the grip of bodily agitation; he cries out, shudders from head to foot. His hand beats, weakly, at the clean tabletop; and when he leaves him, 'Martin, go in, give him some wine' – he is still crying out, shuddering, beating the table.

The next time he sees him will be in Westminster Hall.

On the day of the trial, rivers breach their banks; the Thames itself rises, bubbling like some river in Hell, and washes its flotsam over the quays.

It's England against Rome, he says. The living against the dead.

Norfolk will preside. He tells him how it will be. The early counts in the indictment will be thrown out: they concern sundry words spoken, at sundry times, about the act and the oath, and More's treasonable conspiracy with Fisher – letters went between the two of them, but it seems those letters are now destroyed. 'Then on the fourth count, we will hear the evidence of the Solicitor General. Now, Your Grace, this will divert More, because he cannot see young Riche without working himself into a fit about his derelictions when he was a boy –' The duke raises an eyebrow. 'Drinking. Fighting. Women. Dice.'

Norfolk rubs his bristly chin. 'I have noticed, a soft-looking lad like that, he always does fight. To make a point, you see.

Whereas we damned slab-faced old bruisers who are born with our armour on, there's no point we need to make.'

'Quite,' he says. 'We are the most pacific of men. My lord, please attend now. We don't want another mistake like Dacre. We would hardly survive it. The early counts will be thrown out. At the next, the jury will look alert. And I have given you a handsome jury.'

More will face his peers; Londoners, the merchants of the livery companies. They are experienced men, with all the city's prejudices. They have seen enough, as all Londoners have, of the church's rapacity and arrogance, and they do not take kindly to being told they are unfit to read the scriptures in their own tongue. They are men who know More and have known him these twenty years. They know how he widowed Lucy Petyt. They know how he wrecked Humphrey Monmouth's business, because Tyndale had been a guest at his house. They know how he has set spies in their households, among their apprentices whom they treat as sons, among the servants so familiar and homely that they hear every night their master's bedside prayers.

One name makes Audley hesitate: 'John Parnell? It might be taken wrong. You know he has been after More since he gave judgment against him in Chancery –'

'I know the case. More botched it, he didn't read the papers, too busy writing a billet-doux to Erasmus, or locking some poor Christian soul in his stocks at Chelsea. What do you want, Audley, do you want me to go to Wales for a jury, or up to Cumberland, or somewhere they think better of More? I must make do with London men, and unless I swear in a jury of newborns, I cannot wipe their memories clear.'

Audley shakes his head. 'I don't know, Cromwell.'

'Oh, he's a sharp fellow,' the duke says. 'When Wolsey came down, I said, mark him, he's a sharp fellow. You'd have to get up early in the morning to be ahead of him.'

* * *

The night before the trial, as he is going through his papers at the Austin Friars, a head appears around the door: a little, narrow London head with a close-shaved skull and a raw young face. 'Dick Purser. Come in.'

Dick Purser looks around the room. He keeps the snarling bandogs who guard the house by night, and he has not been in here before. 'Come here and sit. Don't be afraid.' He pours him some wine, into a thin Venetian glass that was the cardinal's. 'Try this. Wiltshire sent it to me, I don't make much of it myself.'

Dick takes the glass and juggles it dangerously. The liquid is pale as straw or summer light. He takes a gulp. 'Sir, can I come in your train to the trial?'

'It still smarts, does it?' Dick Purser was the boy whom More had whipped before the household at Chelsea, for saying the host was a piece of bread. He was a child then, he is not much more now; when he first came to Austin Friars, they say he cried in his sleep. 'Get yourself a livery coat,' he says. 'And remember to wash your hands and face in the morning. I don't want you to disgrace me.'

It is the word 'disgrace' that works on the child. 'I hardly minded the pain,' he says. 'We have all had, saving you sir, as much if not worse from our fathers.'

'True,' he says. 'My father beat me as if I were a sheet of metal.'

'It was that he laid my flesh bare. And the women looking on. Dame Alice. The young girls. I thought one of them might speak up for me, but when they saw me unbreached, I only disgusted them. It made them laugh. While the fellow was whipping me, they were laughing.'

In stories it is always the young girls, innocent girls, who stay the hand of the man with the rod or the axe. But we seem to have strayed into a different story: a child's thin buttocks dimpling against the cold, his skinny little balls, his shy prick shrinking to a button, while the ladies of the house giggle and the menservants jeer, and the thin weals spring out against his skin and bleed.

639

'It's done and forgotten now. Don't cry.' He comes from behind his desk. Dick Purser drops his shorn head against his shoulder and bawls, in shame, in relief, in triumph that soon he will have outlived his tormentor. More did John Purser to death, he harassed him for owning German books; he holds the boy, feeling the jump of his pulses, his stiff sinews, the ropes of his muscles, and makes sounds of comfort, as he did to his children when they were small, or as he does to a spaniel whose tail has been trodden on. Comfort is often, he finds, imparted at the cost of a flea or two.

'I will follow you to the death,' the boy declares. His arms, fists clenched, grip his master: knuckles knead his spine. He sniffs. 'I think I will look well in a livery coat. What time do we start?'

Early. With his staff he is at Westminster Hall before anybody else, vigilant for last-minute hitches. The court convenes around him, and when More is brought in, the hall is visibly shocked at his appearance. The Tower was never known to do a man good, but he startles them, with his lean person and his ragged white beard, looking more like a man of seventy than what he is. Audley whispers, 'He looks as if he has been badly handled.'

'And he says I never miss a trick.'

'Well, my conscience is clear,' the Lord Chancellor says breezily. 'He has had every consideration.'

John Parnell gives him a nod. Richard Riche, both court official and witness, gives him a smile. Audley asks for a seat for the prisoner, but More twitches to the edge of it: keyed up, combative.

He glances around to check that someone is taking notes for him.

Words, words, just words.

He thinks, I remembered you, Thomas More, but you didn't remember me. You never even saw me coming.

III
To Wolf Hall
July 1535

On the evening of More's death the weather clears, and he walks in the garden with Rafe and Richard. The sun shows itself, a silver haze between rags of cloud. The beaten-down herb beds are scentless, and a skittish wind pulls at their clothes, hitting the backs of their necks and then veering round to slap their faces.

Rafe says, it's like being at sea. They walk at either side of him, and close, as if there were danger from whales, pirates and mermaids.

It is five days since the trial. Since then, much business has supervened, but they cannot help rehearse its events, trading with each other the pictures in their heads: the Attorney General jotting a last note on the indictment; More sniggering when some clerk made a slip in his Latin; the cold smooth faces of the Boleyns, father and son, on the judges' bench. More had never raised his voice; he sat in the chair Audley had provided for him, attentive, head tipped a little to the left, picking away at his sleeve.

So Riche's surprise, when More turned on him, was visible; he had taken a step backwards, and steadied himself against a table. 'I know you of old, Riche, why would I open my mind to you?' More on his feet, his voice dripping contempt. 'I have known you since your youth, a gamer and a dicer, of no commendable fame even in your own house ...'

'By St Julian!' Justice Fitzjames had exclaimed; it was ever his oath. Under his breath, to him, Cromwell: 'Will he gain by this?'

The jury had not liked it: you never know what a jury will like. They took More's sudden animation to be shock and guilt, at being confronted with his own words. For sure, they all knew Riche's reputation. But are not drinking, dice and fighting more natural in a young man, on the whole, than fasting, beads and self-flagellation? It was Norfolk who had cut in on More's tirade, his voice dry: 'Leave aside the man's character. What do you say to the matter in hand? Did you speak those words?'

Was it then that Master More played a trick too many? He had pulled himself together, hauling his slipping gown on to his shoulder; the gown secured, he paused, he calmed himself, he fitted one fist into the other. 'I did not say what Riche alleges. Or if I did say it, I did not mean it with malice, therefore I am clear under the statute.'

He had watched an expression of derision cross Parnell's face. There's nothing harder than a London burgess who thinks he's being played for a fool. Audley or any of the lawyers could have put the jury right: it's just how we lawyers argue. But they don't want a lawyer's argument, they want the truth: did you say it, or didn't you? George Boleyn leans forward: can the prisoner let us have his own version of the conversation?

More turns, smiling, as if to say, a good point there, young master George. 'I made no note of it. I had no writing materials, you see. They had already taken them away. For if you remember, my lord Rochford, that was the very reason Riche came to me, to remove from me the means of recording.'

And he had paused again, and looked at the jury as if expecting applause; they looked back, faces like stones.

Was that the turning point? They might have trusted More, being, as he was, Lord Chancellor at one time, and Purse, as everybody knows, such a waster. You never know what a jury will think: though when he had convened them, of course he had been persuasive. He had spoken with them that morning: I do not know what his defence is, but I don't hold out hope we will be finished by noon; I hope you all had a good breakfast? When you retire, you must take your time, of course, but if you are gone more than twenty minutes by my reckoning, I will come in to see how you do. To put you out of doubt, on any points of law.

Fifteen minutes was all they needed.

Now, this evening in the garden, July 6, the feast day of St Godelva (a blameless young wife of Bruges, whose evil husband drowned her in a pond), he looks up at the sky, feeling a change in the air, a damp drift like autumn. The interlude of feeble sun is over. Clouds drift and mass in towers and battlements, blowing in from Essex, stacking up over the city, driven by the wind across the broad soaked fields, across the sodden pastureland and swollen rivers, across the dripping forests of the west and out over the sea to Ireland. Richard retrieves his hat from a lavender bed and knocks droplets from it, swearing softly. A spatter of rain hits their faces. 'Time to go in. I have letters to write.'

'You'll not work till all hours tonight.'

'No, grandfather Rafe. I shall get my bread and milk and say my Ave and so to bed. Can I take my dog up with me?'

'Indeed no! And have you scampering overhead till all hours?'

It's true he didn't sleep much last night. It had come to him, the wrong side of midnight, that More was no doubt asleep himself, not knowing that it was his last night on earth. It is not usual, till the morning, to prepare the condemned man; so, he had thought, any vigil I keep for him, I keep alone.

They hurry in; the wind bangs a door behind them. Rafe takes his arm. He says, this silence of More's, it was never really silence, was it? It was loud with his treason; it was quibbling as far as quibbles would serve him, it was demurs and cavils, suave ambiguities. It was fear of plain words, or the assertion that plain words pervert themselves; More's dictionary, against our dictionary. You can have a silence full of words. A lute retains, in its bowl, the notes it has played. The viol, in its strings, holds a concord. A shrivelled petal can hold its scent, a prayer can rattle with curses; an empty house, when the owners have gone out, can still be loud with ghosts.

Someone – probably not Christophe – has put on his desk a shining silver pot of cornflowers. The dusky blueness at the base of the crinkled petals reminds him of this morning's light; a late dawn for July, a sullen sky. By five, the Lieutenant of the Tower would have gone in to More.

Down below, he can hear a stream of messengers coming into the courtyard. There is much to do, tidying up after the dead man; after all, he thinks, I did it when I was a child, picking up after Morton's young gentlemen, and this is the last time I will have to do it; he pictures himself in the dawn, slopping into a leather jug the dregs of small beer, squeezing up the candle ends to take to the chandlery for remelting.

He can hear voices in the hall; never mind them: he returns to his letters. The Abbot of Rewley solicits a vacant post for his friend. The Mayor of York writes to him about weirs and fish traps; the Humber is running clean and sweet, he reads, so is the Ouse. A letter from Lord Lisle in Calais, relating some muddled tale of self-justification: he said, then I said, so he said.

Thomas More stands before him, more solid in death than he was in life. Perhaps he will always be here now: so agile of mind and so adamant, as he appeared in his final hour before the court. Audley was so happy with the guilty verdict that he began to pass sentence without asking the prisoner if he had anything to say; Fitzjames had to reach out and slap his arm, and More himself rose from his chair to halt him. He had much to say, and his voice was lively, his tone biting, and his eyes, his gestures, hardly those of a condemned man, in law already dead.

But there was nothing new in it: not new anyway to him. I follow my conscience, More said, you must follow yours. My conscience satisfies me – and now I will speech plainly – that your statute is faulty (and Norfolk roars at him) and that your authority baseless (Norfolk roars again: 'Now we see your malice plain'). Parnell had laughed, and the jury exchanged glances, nodding to each other; and while the whole of Westminster Hall murmured, More proffered again, speaking against the noise, his treasonable method of counting. My conscience holds with the majority, which makes me know it does not speak false. 'Against Henry's kingdom, I have all the kingdoms of Christendom. Against each one of your bishops, I have a hundred saints. Against your one parliament, I have all the general councils of the church, stretching back for a thousand years.'

Norfolk said, take him out. It is finished.

Now it is Tuesday, it is eight o'clock. The rain drums against the window. He breaks the seal of a letter from the Duke of Richmond. The boy complains that in Yorkshire where he is seated, he has no deer park, so can show his friends no sport. Oh, you poor tiny duke, he thinks, how can I relieve your pain? Gregory's dowager with the black teeth, the one he is going to marry; she has a deer park, so perhaps the princeling should divorce Norfolk's daughter and marry her instead? He flips aside Richmond's letter, tempted to file it on the floor; he passes on. The Emperor has left Sardinia with his fleet, sailing to Sicily. A priest at St Mary Woolchurch says Cromwell is a sectary and he is not frightened of him: fool. Harry Lord Morley sends him a greyhound. There is news of refugees pouring out of the Münster area, some of them heading for England.

Audley had said, 'Prisoner, the court will ask the king to make grace upon you, as to the manner of your death.' Audley had leaned across: Master Secretary, did you promise him anything? On my life, no: but surely the king will be good to him? Norfolk says, Cromwell, will you move him in that regard? He will take it from you; but if he will not, I myself will come and plead with him. What a marvel: Norfolk, asking for mercy? He had glanced up, to see More taken out, but he had vanished already, the tall halberdiers closing rank behind him: the boat for the Tower is waiting at the steps. It must feel like going home: the familiar room with the narrow window, the table empty of papers, the pricket candle, the drawn blind.

The window rattles; it startles him, and he thinks, I shall bolt the shutter. He is rising to do it when Rafe comes in with a book in his hand. 'It is his prayer book, that More had with him at the last.'

He examines it. Mercifully, no blood specks. He holds it up by the spine and lets the leaves fan out. 'I already did that,' Rafe says.

More has written his name in it. There are underlinings in the text: *Remember not the sins of my youth.* 'What a pity he remembered Richard Riche's.'

'Shall I have it sent to Dame Alice?'

'No. She might think she is one of the sins.' The woman has put up with enough. In his last letter, he didn't even say goodbye to her. He shuts the book. 'Send it to Meg. He probably meant it for her anyway.'

The whole house is rocking about him; wind in the eaves, wind in the chimneys, a piercing draught under every door. It's cold enough for a fire, Rafe says, shall I see to it? He shakes his head. 'Tell Richard, tomorrow morning, go to London Bridge and see the bridge-master. Mistress Roper will come to him and beg her father's head to bury it. The man should take what Meg offers and see she is not impeded. And keep his mouth shut.'

Once in Italy, when he was young, he had joined a burial party. It isn't something you volunteer for; you're just told. They had bound cloth across their mouths, and shovelled their comrades into unhallowed ground; walked away with the smell of putrefaction on their boots.

Which is worse, he thinks, to have your daughters dead before you, or to leave them to tidy away your remains?

'There's something ...' He frowns down at his papers. 'What have I forgotten, Rafe?'

'Your supper?'

'Later.'

'Lord Lisle?'

'I've dealt with Lord Lisle.' Dealt with the river Humber. With the slanderous priest from Mary Woolchurch; well, not dealt with him, but put him in the pending pile. He laughs. 'You know what I need? I need the memory machine.'

Giulio has quit Paris, they say. He has scuttled back to Italy and left the device half built. They say that before his flight for some weeks he had neither spoken nor eaten. His well-wishers say he has gone mad, awed by the capacities of his own creature: fallen into the abyss of the divine. His ill-wishers maintain that demons crawled out of the crannies and crevices of the device, and panicked him so that he ran off by night in his shirt with not even a crust and a lump of cheese for the journey, leaving all his books behind him and his magus's robes.

It is not impossible that Giulio has left writings behind in France. For a fee they might be obtained. It is not impossible to have him followed to Italy; but would there be any point? It is likely, he thinks, that we shall never know what his invention really was. A printing press that can write its own books? A mind that thinks about itself? If I don't have it, at least the King of France doesn't either.

He reaches for his pen. He yawns and puts it down and picks it up again. I shall be found dead at my desk, he thinks, like the poet Petrarch. The poet wrote many unsent letters: he wrote to Cicero, who died twelve hundred years before he was born. He wrote to Homer, who possibly never even existed; but I, I have enough to do with Lord Lisle, and the fish traps, and the Emperor's galleons tossing on the Middle Sea. Between one dip of the pen, Petrarch writes, 'between one dip of the pen and the next, the time passes: and I hurry, I drive myself, and I speed towards death. We are always dying – I while I write, you while you read, and others while they listen or block their ears; they are all dying.'

He picks up the next batch of letters. A man called Batcock wants a licence to import 100 tuns of woad. Harry Percy is sick again. The authorities in Yorkshire have rounded up their rioters, and divided them into those to be charged with affray and manslaughter, and those to be indicted for murder and rape. Rape? Since when do food riots involve rape? But I forget, this is Yorkshire.

'Rafe, bring me the king's itinerary. I'll check that and then I'm finished here. I think we might have some music before we go to bed.'

The court is riding west this summer, as far as Bristol. The king is ready to leave, despite the rain. They will depart from Windsor, then to Reading, Missenden, Abingdon, moving across Oxfordshire, their spirits lifting, we hope, with the distance from London; he says to Rafe, if the country air goes to work, the queen will return with a big belly. Rafe says, I wonder the king can stand the hope each time. It would wear out a lesser man.

'If we ourselves leave London on the eighteenth, we can aim to catch up with them at Sudely. Will that work?'

'Better leave a day earlier. Consider the state of the roads.'

'There won't be any short cuts, will there?' He will use no fords but bridges, and against his inclination he will stick to the main roads; better maps would help. Even in the cardinal's day he was asking himself, might this be a project we could under- take? There are maps, of a kind; castles stud their fields, their battlements prettily inked, their chases and parks marked by lines of bushy trees, with drawings of harts and bristling boar. It is no wonder Gregory mistook Northumbria for the Indies, for these maps are deficient in all practical respects; they do not, for example, tell you which way is north. It would be useful to know where the bridges are, and to have a note of the distance between them. It would be useful to know how far you are from the sea. But the trouble is, maps are always last year's. England is always remaking herself, her cliffs eroding, her sandbanks drifting, springs bubbling up in dead ground. They regroup themselves while we sleep, the landscapes through which we move, and even the histories that trail us; the faces of the dead fade into other faces, as a spine of hills into the mist.

When he was a small child, six years old or about that, his father's apprentice had been making nails from the scrap pile: just common old flat-heads, he'd said, for fastening coffin lids. The nail rods glowed in the fire, a lively orange. 'What for do we nail down the dead?'

The boy barely paused, tapping out each head with two neat strokes. 'It's so the horrible old buggers don't spring out and chase us.'

He knows different now. It's the living that turn and chase the dead. The long bones and skulls are tumbled from their shrouds, and words like stones thrust into their rattling mouths: we edit their writings, we rewrite their lives. Thomas More had spread the rumour that Little Bilney, chained to the stake, had recanted as the fire was set. It wasn't enough for him to take Bilney's life away; he had to take his death too.

Today, More was escorted to the scaffold by Humphrey Monmouth, serving his turn as Sheriff of London. Monmouth is too good a man to rejoice in the reversal of fortune. But perhaps we can rejoice for him?

More is at the block, he can see him now. He is wrapped in a rough grey cape that he remembers as belonging to his servant John Wood. He is speaking to the headsman, apparently making some quip to him, wiping the drizzle from his face and beard. He is shedding the cape, the hem of which is sodden with rainwater. He kneels at the block, his lips moving in his final prayer.

Like all the other witnesses, he swirls his own cloak about him and kneels. At the sickening sound of the axe on flesh he darts one glance upwards. The corpse seems to have leapt back from the stroke and folded itself like a stack of old clothes – inside which, he knows, its pulses are still beating. He makes the sign of the cross. The past moves heavily inside him, a shifting of ground.

'So, the king,' he says. 'From Gloucester, he strikes out to Thornbury. Then Nicholas Poynz's house at Iron Acton: does Poynz know what he's letting himself in for? From there to Bromham ...'

Just this last year a scholar, a foreigner, has written a chronicle of Britain, which omits King Arthur on the ground that he never existed. A good ground, if he can sustain it; but Gregory says, no, he is wrong. Because if he is right, what will happen to Avalon? What will happen to the sword in the stone?

He looks up. 'Rafe, are you happy?'

'With Helen?' Rafe blushes. 'Yes, sir. No man was ever happier.'

'I knew your father would come round, once he had seen her.'

'It is only thanks to you, sir.'

From Bromham – we are now in early September – towards Winchester. Then Bishop's Waltham, Alton, Alton to Farnham. He plots it out, across country. The object is to get the king back to Windsor for early October. He has his sketch map across the page, England in a drizzle of ink; his calendar, quickly jotted, running down it. 'I seem to have four, five days in hand. Ah well. Who says I never get a holiday?'

Before 'Bromham', he makes a dot in the margin, and draws a long arrow across the page. 'Now here, before we go to Winchester, we have time to spare, and what I think is, Rafe, we shall visit the Seymours.'

He writes it down.

Early September. Five days. Wolf Hall.

AUTHOR'S NOTE

In parts of medieval Europe, the official new year began on 25 March, Lady Day, which was believed to be the date when an angel announced to Mary that she was carrying the child Jesus. As early as 1522, Venice adopted 1 January as the start of the new year, and other European countries followed at intervals, though England did not catch up till 1752. In this book, as in most histories, the years are dated from 1 January, which was celebrated as one of the twelve days of Christmas and was the day on which gifts were exchanged.

The gentleman usher George Cavendish, after the death of Wolsey, retired to the country, and in 1554, when Mary came to the throne, began a book, 'Thomas Wolsey, late Cardinal, his Life and Death.' It has been published in many editions, and can be found online in an edition with original spelling. It is not always accurate, but it is a very touching, immediate and readable account of Wolsey's career and Thomas Cromwell's part in it. Its influence on Shakespeare is clear. Cavendish took four years to complete his book, and died just as Elizabeth came to the throne.

ACKNOWLEDGEMENTS

I should like to thank Delyth Neil for the Welsh, Leslie Wilson for the German, and a Norfolk lady for the Flemish. Guada Abale for lending me a song. Judith Flanders for helping me when I couldn't get to the British Library. Dr Christopher Haigh for inviting me to a splendid dinner in Wolsey's hall at Christ Church. Jan Rogers for sharing a pilgrimage to Canterbury and a drink at the Cranmer Arms at Aslockton. Gerald McEwen for driving me around and putting up with my preoccupations. My agent Bill Hamilton and my publishers for their support and encouragement. Above all, Dr Mary Robertson; her business as a scholar has been with the facts of Cromwell's life, but she has encouraged me and lent me her expertise through the production of this fiction, put up with my fumbling speculations and been kind enough to recognise the portrait I have produced. This book is dedicated to her, with my thanks and love.

BRING UP THE BODIES

Also by Hilary Mantel

Beyond Black
Every Day is Mother's Day
Vacant Possession
Eight Months on Ghazzah Street
Fludd
A Place of Greater Safety
A Change of Climate
An Experiment in Love
The Giant, O'Brien
Learning to Talk
Wolf Hall

NON-FICTION
Giving Up the Ghost

HILARY MANTEL

BRING UP
THE BODIES

FOURTH ESTATE • *London*

First published in Great Britain in 2012 by
Fourth Estate
An imprint of HarperCollins*Publishers*
77–85 Fulham Palace Road,
London W6 8JB
www.4thestate.co.uk

Copyright © Tertius Enterprises 2012

11

The right of Hilary Mantel to be identified as the author
of this work has been asserted by her in accordance
with the Copyright, Design and Patents Act 1988

A catalogue record for this book is available from the British Library

HB ISBN 978-0-00-731509-3
Limited edition HB ISBN 978-0-00-748559-8
TPB ISBN 978-0-00-735358-3

All rights reserved. No part of this publication may be
reproduced, transmitted, or stored in a retrieval system,
in any form or by any means, without permission
in writing from Fourth Estate.

Typeset in Stempel Garamond by
G&M Designs Limited, Raunds, Northamptonshire
Printed in Great Britain byClays Ltd, St Ives plc

Endpapers taken from portrait of Anne Boleyn © Getty Images

MIX
Paper from
responsible sources
FSC
www.fsc.org
FSC C007454

FSC™ is a non-profit international organisation established to promote
the responsible management of the world's forests. Products carrying the
FSC label are independently certified to assure customers that they come
from forests that are managed to meet the social, economic and
ecological needs of present and future generations,
and other controlled sources.

Find out more about HarperCollins and the environment at
www.harpercollins.co.uk/green

Once again to Mary Robertson:
after my right harty commendacions,
and with spede.

CONTENTS

CAST OF CHARACTERS

The Cromwell household

Thomas Cromwell, a blacksmith's son: now Secretary to the king, Master of the Rolls, Chancellor of Cambridge University, and deputy to the king as head of the church in England.

Gregory Cromwell, his son.

Richard Cromwell, his nephew.

Rafe Sadler, his chief clerk, brought up by Cromwell as his son.

Helen, Rafe's beautiful wife.

Thomas Avery, the household accountant.

Thurston, his master cook.

Christophe, a servant.

Dick Purser, keeper of the watchdogs.

Anthony, a jester.

The dead

Thomas Wolsey, cardinal, papal legate, Lord Chancellor: dismissed from office, arrested and died, 1530.

John Fisher, Bishop of Rochester: executed 1535.

Thomas More, Lord Chancellor after Wolsey: executed 1535.

Elizabeth, Anne and Grace Cromwell, Thomas Cromwell's wife
   and daughters, died 1527–28; also Katherine Williams and
   Elizabeth Wellyfed, his sisters.

The king's family
Henry VIII.
Anne Boleyn, his second wife.
Elizabeth, Anne's infant daughter, heir to the throne.
Henry Fitzroy, Duke of Richmond, the king's illegitimate son.

The king's other family
Katherine of Aragon, Henry's first wife, divorced and under
   house arrest at Kimbolton.
Mary, Henry's daughter by Katherine and the alternative heir to
   the throne: also under house arrest.
Maria de Salinas, a former lady-in-waiting to Katherine of
   Aragon.
Sir Edmund Bedingfield, Katherine's keeper.
Grace, his wife.

The Howard and Boleyn families
Thomas Howard, Duke of Norfolk, uncle to the queen:
   ferocious senior peer and an enemy of Cromwell.
Henry Howard, Earl of Surrey, his young son.
Thomas Boleyn, Earl of Wiltshire, the queen's father:
   'Monseigneur'.
George Boleyn, Lord Rochford, the queen's brother.
Jane, Lady Rochford, George's wife.
Mary Shelton, the queen's cousin.
And offstage: Mary Boleyn, the queen's sister, now married and
   living in the country, but formerly the king's mistress.

The Seymour family of Wolf Hall

Old Sir John, notorious for having had an affair with his daughter-in-law.

Lady Margery, his wife.

Edward Seymour, his eldest son.

Thomas Seymour, a younger son.

Jane Seymour, his daughter, lady-in-waiting to both Henry's queens.

Bess Seymour, her sister, married to Sir Anthony Oughtred, Governor of Jersey: then widowed.

The courtiers

Charles Brandon, Duke of Suffolk: widower of Henry VIII's sister Mary: a peer of limited intellect.

Thomas Wyatt, a gentleman of unlimited intellect: Cromwell's friend: widely suspected of being a lover of Anne Boleyn.

Harry Percy, Earl of Northumberland: a sick and indebted young nobleman, once betrothed to Anne Boleyn.

Francis Bryan, 'the Vicar of Hell', related to both the Boleyns and the Seymours.

Nicholas Carew, Master of the Horse: an enemy of the Boleyns.

William Fitzwilliam, Master Treasurer, also an enemy of the Boleyns.

Henry Norris, known as 'Gentle Norris', chief of the king's privy chamber.

Francis Weston, a reckless and extravagant young gentleman.

William Brereton, a hard-nosed and quarrelsome older gentleman.

Mark Smeaton, a suspiciously well-dressed musician.

Elizabeth, Lady Worcester, a lady-in-waiting to Anne Boleyn.

Hans Holbein, a painter.

The clerics
Thomas Cranmer, Archbishop of Canterbury: Cromwell's friend.
Stephen Gardiner, Bishop of Winchester: Cromwell's enemy.
Richard Sampson, legal adviser to the king in his matrimonial affairs.

The officers of state
Thomas Wriothesley, known as Call-Me-Risley, Clerk of the Signet.
Richard Riche, Solicitor General.
Thomas Audley, Lord Chancellor.

The ambassadors
Eustache Chapuys, ambassador of Emperor Charles V.
Jean de Dinteville, a French envoy.

The reformers
Humphrey Monmouth, wealthy merchant, friend of Cromwell and evangelical sympathiser: patron of William Tyndale, the Bible translator, now in prison in the Low Countries.
Robert Packington: a merchant of similar sympathies.
Stephen Vaughan, a merchant at Antwerp, friend and agent of Cromwell.

The 'old families' with claims to the throne
Margaret Pole, niece of King Edward IV, supporter of Katherine of Aragon and the Princess Mary.
Henry, Lord Montague, her son.
Henry Courtenay, Marquis of Exeter.
Gertrude, his ambitious wife.

At the Tower of London
Sir William Kingston, the constable.
Lady Kingston, his wife.
Edmund Walsingham, his deputy.
Lady Shelton, aunt of Anne Boleyn.
A French executioner.

The Tudors (simplified)

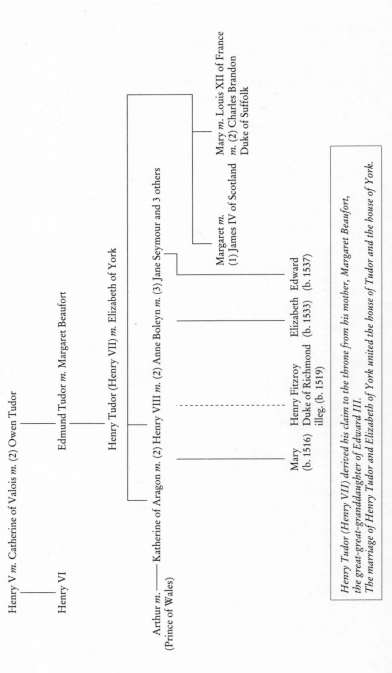

Henry V *m.* Catherine of Valois *m.* (2) Owen Tudor

Henry VI

Edmund Tudor *m.* Margaret Beaufort

Henry Tudor (Henry VII) *m.* Elizabeth of York

Arthur *m.* ——— Katherine of Aragon *m.* (2) Henry VIII *m.* (2) Anne Boleyn *m.* (3) Jane Seymour and 3 others
(Prince of Wales)

Mary   Henry Fitzroy   Elizabeth   Edward
(b. 1516)   Duke of Richmond   (b. 1533)   (b. 1537)
             illeg. (b. 1519)

Margaret *m.*
(1) James IV of Scotland

Mary *m.* Louis XII of France
m. (2) Charles Brandon
Duke of Suffolk

Henry Tudor (Henry VII) derived his claim to the throne from his mother, Margaret Beaufort, the great-great-granddaughter of Edward III.
The marriage of Henry Tudor and Elizabeth of York united the house of Tudor and the house of York.

Henry VIII's rivals from the House of York (simplified)

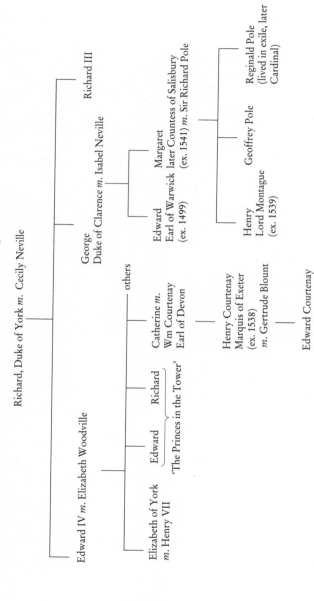

'Am I not a man like other men? Am I not? Am I not?'
HENRY VIII to Eustache Chapuys, Imperial ambassador

PART ONE

I
Falcons
Wiltshire, September 1535

His children are falling from the sky. He watches from horseback, acres of England stretching behind him; they drop, gilt-
winged, each with a blood-filled gaze. Grace Cromwell hovers in
thin air. She is silent when she takes her prey, silent as she glides
to his fist. But the sounds she makes then, the rustle of feathers
and the creak, the sigh and riffle of pinion, the small cluck-cluck
from her throat, these are sounds of recognition, intimate, daugh-
terly, almost disapproving. Her breast is gore-streaked and flesh
clings to her claws.

Later, Henry will say, 'Your girls flew well today.' The hawk
Anne Cromwell bounces on the glove of Rafe Sadler, who rides
by the king in easy conversation. They are tired; the sun is declining, and they ride back to Wolf Hall with the reins slack on the
necks of their mounts. Tomorrow his wife and two sisters will go
out. These dead women, their bones long sunk in London clay,
are now transmigrated. Weightless, they glide on the upper
currents of the air. They pity no one. They answer to no one.
Their lives are simple. When they look down they see nothing
but their prey, and the borrowed plumes of the hunters: they see
a flittering, flinching universe, a universe filled with their dinner.

All summer has been like this, a riot of dismemberment, fur
and feather flying; the beating off and the whipping in of hounds,

3

the coddling of tired horses, the nursing, by the gentlemen, of contusions, sprains and blisters. And for a few days at least, the sun has shone on Henry. Sometime before noon, clouds scudded in from the west and rain fell in big scented drops; but the sun re-emerged with a scorching heat, and now the sky is so clear you can see into Heaven and spy on what the saints are doing.

As they dismount, handing their horses to the grooms and waiting on the king, his mind is already moving to paperwork: to dispatches from Whitehall, galloped down by the post routes that are laid wherever the court shifts. At supper with the Seymours, he will defer to any stories his hosts wish to tell: to anything the king may venture, tousled and happy and amiable as he seems tonight. When the king has gone to bed, his working night will begin.

Though the day is over, Henry seems disinclined to go indoors. He stands looking about him, inhaling horse sweat, a broad, brick-red streak of sunburn across his forehead. Early in the day he lost his hat, so by custom all the hunting party were obliged to take off theirs. The king refused all offers of substitutes. As dusk steals over the woods and fields, servants will be out looking for the stir of the black plume against darkening grass, or the glint of his hunter's badge, a gold St Hubert with sapphire eyes.

Already you can feel the autumn. You know there will not be many more days like these; so let us stand, the horseboys of Wolf Hall swarming around us, Wiltshire and the western counties stretching into a haze of blue; let us stand, the king's hand on his shoulder, Henry's face earnest as he talks his way back through the landscape of the day, the green copses and rushing streams, the alders by the water's edge, the early haze that lifted by nine; the brief shower, the small wind that died and settled; the stillness, the afternoon heat.

'Sir, how are you not burned?' Rafe Sadler demands. A redhead like the king, he has turned a mottled, freckled pink, and even his eyes look sore. He, Thomas Cromwell, shrugs; he hangs an arm around Rafe's shoulders as they drift indoors. He went through the whole of Italy – the battlefield as well as the shaded arena of the counting house – without losing his London pallor. His ruffian childhood, the days on the river, the days in the fields: they left him as white as God made him. 'Cromwell has the skin of a lily,' the king pronounces. 'The only particular in which he resembles that or any other blossom.' Teasing him, they amble towards supper.

The king had left Whitehall the week of Thomas More's death, a miserable dripping week in July, the hoof prints of the royal entourage sinking deep into the mud as they tacked their way across to Windsor. Since then the progress has taken in a swathe of the western counties; the Cromwell aides, having finished up the king's business at the London end, met up with the royal train in mid-August. The king and his companions sleep sound in new houses of rosy brick, in old houses whose fortifications have crumbled away or been pulled down, and in fantasy castles like toys, castles never capable of fortification, with walls a cannon-ball would punch in as if they were paper. England has enjoyed fifty years of peace. This is the Tudors' covenant; peace is what they offer. Every household strives to put forward its best show for the king, and we've seen some panic-stricken plastering these last weeks, some speedy stonework, as his hosts hurry to display the Tudor rose beside their own devices. They search out and obliterate any trace of Katherine, the queen that was, smashing with hammers the pomegranates of Aragon, their splitting segments and their squashed and flying seeds. Instead – if there is no time for carving – the falcon of Anne Boleyn is crudely painted up on hatchments.

Hans has joined them on the progress, and made a drawing of Anne the queen, but it did not please her; how do you please her, these days? He has drawn Rafe Sadler, with his neat little beard and his set mouth, his fashionable hat a feathered disc balanced precariously on his cropped head. 'Made my nose very flat, Master Holbein,' Rafe says, and Hans says, 'And how, Master Sadler, is it in my power to fix your nose?'

'He broke it as a child,' he says, 'running at the ring. I picked him up myself from under the horse's feet, and a sorry bundle he was, crying for his mother.' He squeezes the boy's shoulder. 'Now, Rafe, take heart. I think you look very handsome. Remember what Hans did to me.'

Thomas Cromwell is now about fifty years old. He has a labourer's body, stocky, useful, running to fat. He has black hair, greying now, and because of his pale impermeable skin, which seems designed to resist rain as well as sun, people sneer that his father was an Irishman, though really he was a brewer and a blacksmith at Putney, a shearsman too, a man with a finger in every pie, a scrapper and brawler, a drunk and a bully, a man often hauled before the justices for punching someone, for cheating someone. How the son of such a man has achieved his present eminence is a question all Europe asks. Some say he came up with the Boleyns, the queen's family. Some say it was wholly through the late Cardinal Wolsey, his patron; Cromwell was in his confidence and made money for him and knew his secrets. Others say he haunts the company of sorcerers. He was out of the realm from boyhood, a hired soldier, a wool trader, a banker. No one knows where he has been and who he has met, and he is in no hurry to tell them. He never spares himself in the king's service, he knows his worth and merits and makes sure of his reward: offices, perquisites and title deeds, manor houses and farms. He has a way of getting his way, he has a method; he will charm a man or bribe him, coax him or threaten him, he will explain to a man where his true interests lie, and he will introduce that same man to aspects of himself he didn't know existed. Every day Master Secretary deals with grandees who, if they could, would destroy him with one vindictive swipe, as if he were a fly. Knowing this, he is distinguished by his courtesy, his calmness and his indefatigable attention to England's business. He is not in the habit of explaining himself. He is not in the habit of discussing his successes. But whenever good fortune has called on him, he has been there, planted on the threshold, ready to fling open the door to her timid scratch on the wood.

At home in his city house at Austin Friars, his portrait broods on the wall; he is wrapped in wool and fur, his hand clenched around a document as if he were throttling it. Hans had pushed a table back to trap him and said, Thomas, you mustn't laugh; and they had proceeded on that basis, Hans humming as he worked and he staring ferociously into the middle distance. When he saw the portrait finished he had said, 'Christ, I look like a murderer'; and his son Gregory said, didn't you know? Copies are being made for his friends, and for his admirers among the evangelicals in Germany. He will not part with the original – not now I've got used to it, he says – and so he comes into his hall to find versions of himself in various stages of becoming: a tentative outline, partly inked in. Where to begin with Cromwell? Some start with his sharp little eyes, some start with his hat. Some evade the issue and paint his seal and scissors, others pick out the turquoise ring given him by the cardinal. Wherever they begin, the final impact is the same: if he had a grievance against you, you wouldn't like to meet him at the dark of the moon. His father Walter used to say, 'My boy Thomas, give him a dirty look and he'll gouge your eye out. Trip him, and he'll cut off your leg. But if you don't cut across him, he's a very gentleman. And he'll stand anybody a drink.'

Hans has drawn the king, benign in summer silks, seated after supper with his hosts, the casements open to late birdsong, the first tapers coming in with the candied fruits. At each stage of his progress Henry stops in the principal house, with Anne the queen; his entourage beds down with the local gentlefolk. It is usual for the king's hosts, once at least in the visit, to entertain these peripheral hosts by way of thanks, which places a strain on the housekeeping arrangements. He has counted the provision carts rolling in; he has seen kitchens thrown into turmoil, and he himself has been down in the grey-green hour before dawn, when the brick ovens are swabbed out ready for the first batch of loaves, as carcasses are spitted, pots set on trivets, poultry plucked and jointed. His uncle was a cook to an archbishop, and as a child he hung about the Lambeth Palace kitchens; he knows this business inside out, and nothing about the king's comfort must be left to chance.

These days are perfect. The clear untroubled light picks out each berry shimmering in a hedge. Each leaf of a tree, the sun behind it, hangs like a golden pear. Riding westward in high summer, we have dipped into sylvan chases and crested the downs, emerging into that high country where, even across two counties, you can sense the shifting presence of the sea. In this part of England our forefathers the giants left their earthworks, their barrows and standing stones. We still have, every Englishman and woman, some drops of giant blood in our veins. In those ancient times, in a land undespoiled by sheep or plough, they hunted the wild boar and the elk. The forest stretched ahead for days. Sometimes antique weapons are unearthed: axes that, wielded with double fist, could cut down horse and rider. Think of the great limbs of those dead men, stirring under the soil. War was their nature, and war is always keen to come again. It's not just the past you think of, as you ride these fields. It's what's latent in the soil, what's breeding; it's the days to come, the wars unfought, the injuries and deaths that, like seeds, the soil of England is keeping warm. You would think, to look at Henry laughing, to look at Henry praying, to look at him leading his men through the forest path, that he sits as secure on his throne as he does on his horse. Looks can deceive. By night, he lies awake; he stares at the carved roof beams; he numbers his days. He says, 'Cromwell, Cromwell, what shall I do?' Cromwell, save me from the Emperor. Cromwell, save me from the Pope. Then he calls in his Archbishop of Canterbury, Thomas Cranmer, and demands to know, 'Is my soul damned?'

Back in London, the Emperor's ambassador, Eustache Chapuys, waits daily for news that the people of England have risen against their cruel and ungodly king. It is news that he dearly wishes to hear, and he would spend labour and hard cash to make it come true. His master, the Emperor Charles, is lord of the Low Countries as well as Spain and her lands beyond the seas; Charles is rich and, from time to time, he is angry that Henry Tudor has dared to set aside his aunt, Katherine, to marry a woman whom the people on the streets call a goggle-eyed whore. Chapuys is exhorting his master in urgent dispatches to invade England, to join with the realm's rebels, pretenders and malcontents, and to conquer this unholy island where the king by an act of Parliament has settled his own divorce and declared himself God. The Pope does not take it kindly, that he is laughed at in England and called mere 'Bishop of Rome', that his revenues are cut off and channelled into Henry's coffers. A bull of excommunication, drawn up but not yet promulgated, hovers over Henry, making him an outcast among the Christian kings of Europe: who are invited, indeed, encouraged, to step across the Narrow Sea or the Scots border, and help themselves to anything that's his. Perhaps the Emperor will come. Perhaps the King of France will come. Perhaps they will come together. It would be pleasant to say we are ready for them, but the reality is otherwise. In the case of an armed incursion we may have to dig up the giants' bones to knock them around the head with, as we are short of ordnance, short of powder, short of steel. This is not Thomas Cromwell's fault; as Chapuys says, grimacing, Henry's kingdom would be in better order if Cromwell had been put in charge five years ago.

If you would defend England, and he would – for he would take the field himself, his sword in his hand – you must know what England is. In the August heat, he has stood bare-headed by the carved tombs of ancestors, men armoured *cap à pie* in plate and chain links, their gauntleted hands joined and perched stiffly on their surcoats, their mailed feet resting on stone lions, griffins, greyhounds: stone men, steel men, their soft wives encased beside them like snails in their shells. We think time cannot touch the dead, but it touches their monuments, leaving them snub-nosed and stub-fingered from the accidents and attrition of time. A tiny dismembered foot (as of a kneeling cherub) emerges from a swathe of drapery; the tip of a severed thumb lies on a carved cushion. 'We must get our forefathers mended next year,' the lords of the western counties say: but their shields and support-ers, their achievements and bearings, are kept always paint-fresh, and in talk they embellish the deeds of their ancestors, who they were and what they held: the arms my forefather bore at Agincourt, the cup my forefather was given by John of Gaunt his own hand. If in the late wars of York and Lancaster, their fathers and grandfathers picked the wrong side, they keep quiet about it. A generation on, lapses must be forgiven, reputations remade; otherwise England cannot go forward, she will keep spiralling backwards into the dirty past.

He has no ancestors, of course: not the kind you'd boast about. There was once a noble family called Cromwell, and when he came up in the king's service the heralds had urged him for the sake of appearances to adopt their coat of arms; but I am none of theirs, he had said politely, and I do not want their achievements. He had run away from his father's fists when he was no older than fifteen; crossed the Channel, taken service in the French king's army. He had been fighting since he could walk; and if you're going to fight, why not be paid for it? There are more lucrative trades than soldiering, and he found them. So he decided not to hurry home.

And now, when his titled hosts want advice on the placement of a fountain, or a group of the Three Graces dancing, the king tells them, Cromwell here is your man; Cromwell, he has seen how they do things in Italy, and what will do for them will do for

10

Wiltshire. Sometimes the king departs a place with just his riding household, the queen left behind with her ladies and musicians, as Henry and his favoured few hunt hard across the country. And that is how they come to Wolf Hall, where old Sir John Seymour is waiting to welcome them, in the midst of his flourishing family.

'I don't know, Cromwell,' old Sir John says. He takes his arm, genial. 'All these falcons named for dead women … don't they dishearten you?'

'I'm never disheartened, Sir John. The world is too good to me.'

'You should marry again, and have another family. Perhaps you will find a bride while you are with us. In the forest of Savernake there are many fresh young women.'

I still have Gregory, he says, looking back over his shoulder for his son; he is always somehow anxious about Gregory. 'Ah,' Seymour says, 'boys are very well, but a man needs daughters too, daughters are a consolation. Look at Jane. Such a good girl.'

He looks at Jane Seymour, as her father directs him. He knows her well from the court, as she was lady-in-waiting to Katherine, the former queen, and to Anne, the queen that is now; she is a plain young woman with a silvery pallor, a habit of silence, and a trick of looking at men as if they represent an unpleasant surprise. She is wearing pearls, and white brocade embroidered with stiff little sprigs of carnations. He recognises considerable expenditure; leave the pearls aside, you couldn't turn her out like that for much under thirty pounds. No wonder she moves with gingerly concern, like a child who's been told not to spill something on herself.

The king says, 'Jane, now we see you at home with your people, are you less shy?' He takes her mouse-paw in his vast hand. 'At court we never get a word from her.'

Jane is looking up at him, blushing from her neck to her hairline. 'Did you ever see such a blush?' Henry asks. 'Never unless with a little maid of twelve.'

'I cannot claim to be twelve,' Jane says.

At supper the king sits next to Lady Margery, his hostess. She was a beauty in her day, and by the king's exquisite attention you would think she was one still; she has had ten children, and six of them are living, and three are in this room. Edward Seymour, the heir, has a long head, a serious expression, a clean fierce profile: a handsome man. He is well-read if not scholarly, applies himself wisely to any office he is given; he has been to war, and while he is waiting to fight again he acquits himself well in the hunting field and tilt yard. The cardinal, in his day, marked him out as better than the usual run of Seymours; and he himself, Thomas Cromwell, has sounded him out and found him in every respect the king's man. Tom Seymour, Edward's younger brother, is noisy and boisterous and more of interest to women; when he comes into the room, virgins giggle, and young matrons dip their heads and examine him from under their lashes.

Old Sir John is a man of notorious family feeling. Two, three years back, the gossip at court was all of how he had tupped his son's wife, not once in the heat of passion but repeatedly since she was a bride. The queen and her confidantes had spread the story about the court. 'We've worked it out at 120 times,' Anne had sniggered. 'Well, Thomas Cromwell has, and he's quick with figures. We suppose they abstained on a Sunday for shame's sake, and eased off in Lent.' The traitor wife gave birth to two boys, and when her conduct came to light Edward said he would not have them for his heirs, as he could not be sure if they were his sons or his half-brothers. The adulteress was locked up in a convent, and soon obliged him by dying; now he has a new wife, who cultivates a forbidding manner and keeps a bodkin in her pocket in case her father-in-law gets too close.

But it is forgiven, it is forgiven. The flesh is frail. This royal visit seals the old fellow's pardon. John Seymour has 1,300 acres including his deer park, most of the rest under sheep and worth two shilling per acre per year, bringing him in a clear twenty-five per cent on what the same acreage would make under the plough. The sheep are little black-faced animals interbred with Welsh mountain stock, gristly mutton but good enough wool. When at their arrival, the king (he is in bucolic vein) says, 'Cromwell, what would that beast weigh?' he says, without picking it up, 'Thirty pounds, sir.' Francis Weston, a young courtier, says with a sneer, 'Master Cromwell used to be a shearsman. He wouldn't be wrong.'

The king says, 'We would be a poor country without our wool trade. That Master Cromwell knows the business is not to his discredit.'

But Francis Weston smirks behind his hand.

Tomorrow Jane Seymour is to hunt with the king. 'I thought it was gentlemen only,' he hears Weston whisper. 'The queen would be angry if she knew.' He murmurs, make sure she doesn't know then, there's a good boy.

'At Wolf Hall we are all great hunters,' Sir John boasts, 'my daughters too, you think Jane is timid but put her in the saddle and I assure you, sirs, she is the goddess Diana. I never troubled my girls in the schoolroom, you know. Sir James here taught them all they needed.'

The priest at the foot of the table nods, beaming: an old fool with a white poll, a bleared eye. He, Cromwell, turns to him: 'And was it you taught them to dance, Sir James? All praise to you. I have seen Jane's sister Elizabeth at court, partnered with the king.'

'Ah, they had a master for that,' old Seymour chuckles. 'Master for dancing, master for music, that's enough for them. They don't want foreign tongues. They're not going anywhere.'

'I think otherwise, sir,' he says. 'I had my daughters taught equal with my son.'

Sometimes he likes to talk about them, Anne and Grace: gone seven years now. Tom Seymour laughs. 'What, you had them in the tilt yard with Gregory and young Master Sadler?'

13

He smiles. 'Except for that.'

Edward Seymour says, 'It is not uncommon for the daughters of a city household to learn their letters and a little beyond. You might have wanted them in the counting house. One hears of it. It would help them get good husbands, a merchant family would be glad of their training.'

'Imagine Master Cromwell's daughters,' Weston says. 'I dare not. I doubt a counting house could contain them. They would be a shrewd hand with a poleaxe, you would think. One look at them and a man's legs would go from under him. And I do not mean he would be stricken with love.'

Gregory stirs himself. He is such a dreamer you hardly think he has been following the conversation, but his tone is rippling with hurt. 'You insult my sisters and their memory, sir, and you never knew them. My sister Grace ...'

He sees Jane Seymour put out her little hand and touch Gregory's wrist: to save him, she will risk drawing the company's attention. 'I have lately,' she says, 'got some skill of the French tongue.'

'Have you, Jane?' Tom Seymour is smiling.

Jane dips her head. 'Mary Shelton is teaching me.'

'Mary Shelton is a kindly young woman,' the king says; and out of the corner of his eye, he sees Weston elbow his neighbour; they say Shelton has been kind to the king in bed.

'So you see,' Jane says to her brothers, 'we ladies, we do not spend all our time in idle calumny and scandal. Though God he knows, we have gossip enough to occupy a whole town of women.'

'Have you?' he says.

'We talk about who is in love with the queen. Who writes her verses.' She drops her eyes. 'I mean to say, who is in love with us all. This gentleman or that. We know all our suitors and we make inventory head to toe, they would blush if they knew. We say their acreage and how much they have a year, and then we decide if we will let them write us a sonnet. If we do not think they will keep us in fine style, we scorn their rhymes. It is cruel, I can tell you.'

He says, a little uneasy, it is no harm to write verses to ladies, even married ones, at court it is usual. Weston says, thank you for that kind word, Master Cromwell, we thought you might try and make us stop.

Tom Seymour leans forward, laughing. 'And who are your suitors, Jane?'

'If you want to know that, you must put on a gown, and take up your needlework, and come and join us.'

'Like Achilles among the women,' the king says. 'You must shave your fine beard, Seymour, and go and find out their lewd little secrets.' He is laughing, but he is not happy. 'Unless we find someone more maidenly for the task. Gregory, you are a pretty fellow, but I fear your great hands will give you away.'

'The blacksmith's grandson,' Weston says.

'That child Mark,' the king says. 'The musician, you know him? There is a smooth girlish countenance.'

'Oh,' Jane says, 'Mark's with us anyway. He's always loitering. We barely count him a man. If you want to know our secrets, ask Mark.'

The conversation canters off in some other direction; he thinks, I have never known Jane have anything to say for herself; he thinks, Weston is goading me, he knows that in Henry's presence I will not give him a check; he imagines what form the check may take, when he delivers it. Rafe Sadler looks at him out of the tail of his eye.

'So,' the king says to him, 'how will tomorrow be better than today?' To the supper table he explains, 'Master Cromwell cannot sleep unless he is amending something.'

'I will reform the conduct of Your Majesty's hat. And those clouds, before noon –'

'We wanted the shower. The rain cooled us.'

15

'God send Your Majesty no worse a drenching,' says Edward Seymour.

Henry rubs his stripe of sunburn. 'The cardinal, he reckoned he could change the weather. A good enough morning, he would say, but by ten it will be brighter. And it was.'

Henry does this sometimes; drops Wolsey's name into conversation, as if it were not he, but some other monarch, who had hounded the cardinal to death.

'Some men have a weather eye,' Tom Seymour says. 'That's all it is, sir. It's not special to cardinals.'

Henry nods, smiling. 'That's true, Tom. I should never have stood in awe of him, should I?'

'He was too proud, for a subject,' old Sir John says.

The king looks down the table at him, Thomas Cromwell. He loved the cardinal. Everyone here knows it. His expression is as carefully blank as a freshly painted wall.

After supper, old Sir John tells the story of Edgar the Peaceable. He was the ruler in these parts, many hundreds of years ago, before kings had numbers: when all maids were fair maids and all knights were gallant and life was simple and violent and usually brief. Edgar had in mind a bride for himself, and sent one of his earls to appraise her. The earl, who was both false and cunning, sent back word that her beauty had been much exaggerated by poets and painters; seen in real life, he said, she had a limp and a squint. His aim was to have the tender damsel for himself, and so he seduced and married her. Upon discovering the earl's treachery Edgar ambushed him, in a grove not far from here, and rammed a javelin into him, killing him with one blow.

'What a false knave he was, that earl!' says the king. 'He was paid out.'

'Call him rather a churl than an earl,' Tom Seymour says.

His brother sighs, as if distancing himself from the remark.

'And what did the lady say?' he asks; he, Cromwell. 'When she found the earl skewered?'

'The damsel married Edgar,' Sir John says. 'They married in the greenwood, and lived happily ever after.'

'I suppose she had no choice,' Lady Margery sighs. 'Women have to adapt themselves.'

'And the country folk say,' Sir John adds, 'that the false earl walks the woods still, groaning, and trying to pull the lance out of his belly.'

'Just imagine,' Jane Seymour says. 'Any night there is a moon, one might look out of the window and see him, tugging away and complaining all the while. Fortunately I do not believe in ghosts.'

'More fool you, sister,' Tom Seymour says. 'They'll creep up on you, my lass.'

'Still,' Henry says. He mimes a javelin throw: though in the restrained way one must, at a supper table. 'One clean blow. He must have had a good throwing arm, King Edgar.'

He says – he, Cromwell: 'I should like to know if this tale is written down, and if so, by whom, and was he on oath.'

The king says, 'Cromwell would have had the earl before a judge and jury.'

'Bless Your Majesty,' Sir John chuckles, 'I don't think they had them in those days.'

'Cromwell would have found one out.' Young Weston leans forward to make his point. 'He would dig out a jury, he would grub one from a mushroom patch. Then it would be all up with the earl, they would try him and march him out and hack off his head. They say that at Thomas More's trial, Master Secretary here followed the jury to their deliberations, and when they were seated he closed the door behind him and he laid down the law. "Let me put you out of doubt," he said to the jurymen. "Your task is to find Sir Thomas guilty, and you will have no dinner till you have done it." Then out he went and shut the door again and stood outside it with a hatchet in his hand, in case they broke out in search of a boiled pudding; and being Londoners, they care about their bellies above all things, and as soon as they felt them rumbling they cried, "Guilty! He is as guilty as guilty can be!"'

Eyes focus on him, Cromwell. Rafe Sadler, by his side, is tense with displeasure. 'It is a pretty tale,' Rafe tells Weston, 'but I ask you in turn, where is it written down? I think you will find my master is always correct in his dealings with a court of law.'

'You weren't there,' Francis Weston says. 'I heard it from one of those same jurymen. They cried, "Away with him, take out the traitor and bring us in a leg of mutton." And Thomas More was led to his death.'

'You sound as if you regret it,' Rafe says.

'Not I.' Weston holds up his hands. 'Anne the queen says, let More's death be a warning to all such traitors. Be their credit never so great, their treason never so veiled, Thomas Cromwell will find them out.'

There is a murmur of assent; for a moment, he thinks the company will turn to him and applaud. Then Lady Margery touches a finger to her lips, and nods towards the king. Seated at the head of the table, he has begun to incline to the right; his closed eyelids flutter, and his breathing is easeful and deep.

The company exchange smiles. 'Drunk with fresh air,' Tom Seymour whispers.

It makes a change from drunk with drink; the king, these days, calls for the wine jug more often than he did in his lean and sporting youth. He, Cromwell, watches as Henry tilts in his chair. First forward, as if to rest his forehead on the table. Then he starts and jerks backwards. A line of drool trickles down his beard.

This would be the moment for Harry Norris, the chief among the privy chamber gentlemen; Harry with his noiseless tread and his soft unjudging hand, murmuring his sovereign back to wakefulness. But Norris has gone across country, carrying the king's love letter to Anne. So what to do? Henry does not look like a tired child, as five years ago he might have done. He looks like any man in mid-life, lapsed into torpor after too heavy a meal; he looks bloated and puffy, and a vein is burst here and there, and even by candlelight you can see that his faded hair is greying. He, Cromwell, nods to young Weston. 'Francis, your gentlemanly touch is required.'

Weston pretends not to hear him. His eyes are on the king and his face wears an unguarded expression of distaste. Tom Seymour whispers, 'I think we should make a noise. To wake him naturally.'

'What sort of noise?' his brother Edward mouths.

Tom mimes holding his ribs.

Edward's eyebrows shoot up. 'You laugh if you dare. He'll think you're laughing at his drooling.'

The king begins to snore. He lurches to the left. He tilts dangerously over the arm of his chair.

Weston says, 'You do it, Cromwell. No man so great with him as you are.'

He shakes his head, smiling.

'God save His Majesty,' says Sir John, piously. 'He's not as young as he was.'

Jane rises. A stiff rustle from the carnation sprigs. She leans over the king's chair and taps the back of his hand: briskly, as if she were testing a cheese. Henry jumps and his eyes flick open. 'I wasn't asleep,' he says. 'Really. I was just resting my eyes.'

When the king has gone upstairs, Edward Seymour says, 'Master Secretary, time for my revenge.'

Leaning back, glass in hand: 'What I have done to you?'

'A game of chess. Calais. I know you remember.'

Late autumn, the year 1532: the night the king first went to bed with the queen that is now. Before she lay down for him Anne made him swear an oath on the Bible, that he would marry her as soon as they were back on English soil; but the storms trapped them in port, and the king made good use of the time, trying to get a son on her.

19

'You checkmated me, Master Cromwell,' Edward says. 'But only because you distracted me.'

'How did I?'

'You asked me about my sister Jane. Her age, and so on.'

'You thought I was interested in her.'

'And are you?' Edward smiles, to take the edge off the crude question. 'She is not spoken for yet, you know.'

'Set up the pieces,' he says. 'Would you like the board aligned as it was when you lost your train of thought?'

Edward looks at him, carefully expressionless. Incredible things are related of Cromwell's memory. He smiles to himself. He could set up the board, with only a little guesswork; he knows the type of game a man like Seymour plays. 'We should begin afresh,' he suggests. 'The world moves on. You are happy with Italian rules? I don't like these contests that drag out for a week.'

Their opening moves see some boldness on Edward's part. But then, a white pawn poised between his fingertips, Seymour leans back in his chair, frowning, and takes it into his head to talk about St Augustine; and from St Augustine moves to Martin Luther. 'It is a teaching that brings terror to the heart,' he says. 'That God would make us only to damn us. That his poor creatures, except some few of them, are born only for a struggle in this world and then eternal fire. Sometimes I fear it is true. But I find I hope it is not.'

'Fat Martin has modified his position. Or so I hear. And to our comfort.'

'What, more of us are saved? Or our good works are not entirely useless in God's sight?'

'I should not speak for him. You should read Philip Melanchthon. I will send you his new book. I hope he will visit us in England. We are talking to his people.'

Edward presses the pawn's little round head to his lips. He looks as if he might tap his teeth with it. 'Will the king allow that?'

'He would not let in Brother Martin himself. He does not like his name mentioned. But Philip is an easier man, and it would be good for us, it would be very good for us, if we were to come into some helpful alliance with the German princes who favour the gospel. It would give the Emperor a fright, if we had friends and allies in his own domains.'

'And that is all it means to you?' Edward's knight is skipping over the squares. 'Diplomacy?'

'I cherish diplomacy. It's cheap.'

'Yet they say you love the gospel yourself.'

'It is no secret.' He frowns. 'Do you really mean to do that, Edward? I see my way to your queen. And I should not like to take advantage of you again, and have you say I spoiled your game with small talk about the state of your soul.'

A skewed smile. 'And how is your queen these days?'

'Anne? She is at outs with me. I feel my head wobble on my shoulders when she stares at me hard. She has heard that once or twice I spoke favourably of Katherine, the queen that was.'

'And did you?'

'Only to admire her spirit. Which, anyone must admit, is steadfast in adversity. And again, the queen thinks I am too favourable to the Princess Mary – I mean to say, to Lady Mary, as we should call her now. The king loves his elder daughter still, he says he cannot help it – and it grieves Anne, because she wants the Princess Elizabeth to be the only daughter he knows. She thinks we are too soft towards Mary and that we should tax her to admit her mother was never married lawfully to the king, and that she is a bastard.'

Edward twiddles the white pawn in his fingers, looks at it dubiously, sets it down on its square. 'But is that not the state of affairs? I thought you had made her acknowledge it already.'

'We solve the question by not raising it. She knows she is put out of the succession, and I do not think I should force her beyond a point. As the Emperor is Katherine's nephew and Lady

21

Mary's cousin, I try not to provoke him. Charles holds us in the palm of his hand, do you see? But Anne does not understand the need to placate people. She thinks if she speaks sweetly to Henry, that is enough to do.'

'Whereas you must speak sweetly to Europe.' Edward laughs. His laugh has a rusty sound. His eyes say, you are being very frank, Master Cromwell: why?

'Besides,' his fingers hover over the black knight, 'I am grown too great for the queen's liking, since the king made me his deputy in church affairs. She hates Henry to listen to anyone but herself and her brother George and Monseigneur her father, and even her father gets the rough side of her tongue, and gets called lily-liver and timewaster.'

'How does he take that?' Edward looks down at the board. 'Oh.'

'Now take a careful look,' he urges. 'Do you want to play it out?'

'I resign. I think.' A sigh. 'Yes. I resign.'

He, Cromwell, sweeps the pieces aside, stifling a yawn. 'And I never mentioned your sister Jane, did I? So what's your excuse now?'

When he goes upstairs he sees Rafe and Gregory jumping around near the great window. They are capering and scuffling, eyes on something invisible at their feet. At first he thinks they are playing football without a ball. But then they leap up like dancers and back-heel the thing, and he sees that it is long and thin, a fallen man. They lean down to tweak and jab, to apply torsion. 'Ease off,' Gregory says, 'don't snap his neck yet, I need to see him suffer.'

Rafe looks up, and affects to wipe his brow. Gregory rests hands on knees, getting his breath back, then nudges the victim with his foot. 'This is Francis Weston. You think he is helping put the king to bed, but in fact we have him here in ghostly form. We stood around a corner and waited for him with a magic net.'

22

'We are punishing him,' Rafe leans down. 'Ho, sir, are you sorry now?' He spits on his palms. 'What next with him, Gregory?'

'Haul him up and out the window with him.'

'Careful,' he says. 'The king favours Weston.'

'Then he'll favour him when he's got a flat head,' Rafe says. They scuffle and push each other out of the way, trying to be the first to stamp Francis flat. Rafe opens a window and both stoop for leverage, hoisting the phantom across the sill. Gregory helps it over, unsnagging its jacket where it catches, and with one shove drops it head first on the cobbles. They peer out after it. 'He bounces,' Rafe observes, and then they dust off their hands, smiling at him. 'Give you good night, sir,' Rafe says.

Later, Gregory sits at the foot of the bed in his shirt, his hair tousled, his shoes kicked off, one bare foot idly scuffing the matting: 'So am I to be married? Am I to be married to Jane Seymour?'

'Early in the summer you thought I was going to marry you to an old dowager with a deer park.' People tease Gregory: Rafe Sadler, Thomas Wriothesley, the other young men of his house; his cousin, Richard Cromwell.

'Yes, but why were you talking to her brother this last hour? First it was chess then it was talk, talk, talk. They say you liked Jane yourself.'

'When?'

'Last year. You liked her last year.'

'If I did I've forgot.'

'George Boleyn's wife told me. Lady Rochford. She said, you may get a young stepmother from Wolf Hall, what will you think of that? So if you like Jane yourself,' Gregory frowns, 'she had better not be married to me.'

'Do you think I'd steal your bride? Like old Sir John?'

Once his head is on the pillow, he says, 'Hush, Gregory.' He closes his eyes. Gregory is a good boy, though all the Latin he has learned, all the sonorous periods of the great authors, have rolled through his head and out again, like stones. Still, you think of Thomas More's boy: offspring of a scholar all Europe admired, and poor young John can barely stumble through his Pater Noster. Gregory is a fine archer, a fine horseman, a shining star in the tilt yard, and his manners cannot be faulted. He speaks reverently to his superiors, not scuffling his feet or standing on one leg, and he is mild and polite with those below him. He knows how to bow to foreign diplomats in the manner of their own countries, sits at table without fidgeting or feeding spaniels, can neatly carve and joint any fowl if requested to serve his elders. He doesn't slouch around with his jacket off one shoulder, or look in windows to admire himself, or stare around in church, or interrupt old men, or finish their stories for them. If anyone sneezes, he says, 'Christ help you!'

Christ help you, sir or madam.

Gregory raises his head. 'Thomas More,' he says. 'The jury. Is that truly what happened?'

He had recognised young Weston's story: in a broad sense, even if he didn't assent to the detail. He closes his eyes. 'I didn't have a hatchet,' he says.

He is tired: he speaks to God; he says: God guide me. Sometimes when he is on the verge of sleep the cardinal's large scarlet presence flits across his inner eye. He wishes the dead man would prophesy. But his old patron speaks only of domestic matters, office matters. Where did I put that letter from the Duke of Norfolk? he will ask the cardinal; and next day, early, it will come to his hand.

He speaks inwardly: not to Wolsey, but to George Boleyn's wife. 'I have no wish to marry. I have no time. I was happy with my wife but Liz is dead and that part of my life is dead with her. Who in the name of God gave you, Lady Rochford, a licence to speculate about my intentions? Madam, I have no time for wooing. I am fifty. At my age, one would be the loser on a

24

long-term contract. If I want a woman, best to rent one by the hour.'

Yet he tries not to say 'at my age': not in his waking life. On a good day he thinks he has twenty years left. He often thinks he will see Henry out, though strictly it is not allowed to have that kind of thought; there is a law against speculating about the term of the king's life, though Henry has been a life-long student of inventive ways to die. There have been several hunting accidents. When he was still a minor the council forbade him to joust, but he did it anyway, face hidden by his helmet and his armour without device, proving himself again and again the strongest man on the field. In battle against the French he has taken the honours, and his nature, as he often mentions, is warlike; no doubt he would be known as Henry the Valiant, except Thomas Cromwell says he can't afford a war. Cost is not the whole consideration: what becomes of England if Henry dies? He was twenty years married to Katherine, this autumn it will be three with Anne, nothing to show but a daughter with each and a churchyard's worth of dead babies, some half-formed and christened in blood, some born alive but dead within hours, within days, within weeks at most. All the turmoil, the scandal, to make the second marriage, and still. Still Henry has no son to follow him. He has a bastard, Harry Duke of Richmond, a fine boy of sixteen: but what use to him is a bastard? What use is Anne's child, the infant Elizabeth? Some special mechanism may have to be created so Harry Richmond can reign, if anything but good should come to his father. He, Thomas Cromwell, stands very well with the young duke; but this dynasty, still new as kingship goes, is not secure enough to survive such a course. The Plantagenets were kings once and they think they will kings be again; they think the Tudors are an interlude. The old families of England are restless and ready to press their claim, especially since Henry broke with Rome; they bow the knee, but they are plotting. He can almost hear them, hidden among the trees.

You may find a bride in the forest, old Seymour had said. When he closes his eyes she slides behind them, veiled in cobwebs and splashed with dew. Her feet are bare, entwined in roots, her feather hair flies into the branches; her finger, beckoning, is a curled leaf. She points to him, as sleep overtakes him. His inner voice mocks him now: you thought you were going to get a holiday at Wolf Hall. You thought there would be nothing to do here except the usual business, war and peace, famine, traitorous connivance; a failing harvest, a stubborn populace; plague ravaging London, and the king losing his shirt at cards. You were prepared for that.

At the edge of his inner vision, behind his closed eyes, he senses something in the act of becoming. It will arrive with morning light; something shifting and breathing, its form disguised in a copse or grove.

Before he sleeps he thinks of the king's hat on a midnight tree, roosting like a bird from paradise.

Next day, so as not to tire the ladies, they cut short the day's sport, and return early to Wolf Hall.

For him, it is a chance to put off his riding clothes and get among the dispatches. He has hopes that the king will sit for an hour and listen to what he needs to tell him. But Henry says, 'Lady Jane, will you walk in the garden with me?'

She is at once on her feet; but frowning, as if trying to make sense of it. Her lips move, she all but repeats his words: Walk … Jane? … In the garden?

Oh yes, of course, honoured. Her hand, a petal, hovers above his sleeve; then it descends, and flesh grazes embroidery.

There are three gardens at Wolf Hall, and they call them the great paled garden, the old lady's garden and the young lady's garden. When he asks who they were, no one remembers; the old lady and the young lady are dust long ago, no difference between them now. He remembers his dream: the bride made of root fibre, the bride made of mould.

He reads. He writes. Something tugs at his attention. He gets up and glances from the window at the walks below. The panes are small and there is a wobble in the glass, so he has to crane his neck to get a proper view. He thinks, I could send my glaziers down, help the Seymours get a clearer idea of the world. He has a team of Hollanders who work for him at his various properties. They worked for the cardinal before him.

Henry and Jane are walking below. Henry is a massive figure and Jane is like a little jointed puppet, her head not up to the king's shoulders. A broad man, a high man, Henry dominates any room; he would do it even if God had not given him the gift of kingship.

Now Jane is behind a bush. Henry is nodding at her; he is speaking at her; he is impressing something on her, and he, Cromwell, watches, scratching his chin: is the king's head becoming bigger? Is that possible, in mid-life?

Hans will have noticed, he thinks, I'll ask him when I get back to London. Most likely I am under a mistake; probably it's just the glass.

Clouds are coming up. A heavy raindrop hits the pane; he blinks; the drop spreads, widens, trickles against the glazing bars. Jane bobs out into his sightline. Henry has her hand clamped firmly on his arm, trapping it with his other hand. He can see the king's mouth, still moving.

He resumes his seat. He reads that the builders working on the fortifications in Calais have downed tools and are demanding sixpence a day. That his new green velvet coat is coming down to Wiltshire by the next courier. That a Medici cardinal has been poisoned by his own brother. He yawns. He reads that hoarders on the Isle of Thanet are deliberately driving up the price of grain. Personally, he would hang hoarders, but the chief of them might be some little lordling who is promoting famine for fat profit, and so you have to tread carefully. Two years ago, at Southwark, seven Londoners were crushed to death in fighting for a dole of bread. It is a shame to England that the king's subjects should starve. He takes up his pen and makes a note.

Very soon – this is not a big house, you can hear everything – he hears a door below, and the king's voice, and a soft hum of solicitation around him ... wet feet, Majesty? He hears Henry's heavy tread approaching, but it seems Jane has melted away without a sound. No doubt her mother and her sisters have swept her aside, to hear all the king said to her.

As Henry comes in behind him, he pushes back his chair to rise. Henry waves a hand: carry on. 'Majesty, the Muscovites have taken three hundred miles of Polish territory. They say fifty thousand men are dead.'

'Oh,' Henry says.

'I hope they spare the libraries. The scholars. There are very fine scholars in Poland.'

'Mm? I hope so too.'

He returns to his dispatches. Plague in town and city ... the king is always very fearful of infection ... Letters from foreign rulers, wishing to know if it is true that Henry is planning to cut off the heads of all his bishops. Certainly not, he notes, we have excellent bishops now, all of them conformable to the king's wishes, all of them recognising him as head of the church in England; besides, what an uncivil question! How dare they imply that the King of England should account for himself to any foreign power? How dare they impugn his sovereign judgement? Bishop Fisher, it is true, is dead, and Thomas More, but Henry's treatment of them, before they drove him to an extremity, was mild to a fault; if they had not evinced a traitorous stubbornness, they would be alive now, alive like you and me.

He has written a lot of these letters, since July. He doesn't sound wholly convincing, even to himself; he finds himself repeating the same points, rather than advancing the argument into new territory. He needs new phrases ... Henry stumps about behind him. 'Majesty, the Imperial ambassador Chapuys asks may he ride up-country to visit your daughter, Lady Mary?'

'No,' Henry says.

He writes to Chapuys, *Wait, just wait, till I am back in London, when all will be arranged …*

No word from the king: just breathing, pacing, a creak from a cupboard where he rests and leans on it.

'Majesty, I hear the Lord Mayor of London scarcely leaves his house, he is so afflicted by migraine.'

'Mm?' Henry says.

'They are bleeding him. Is that what Your Majesty would advise?'

A pause. Henry focuses on him, with some effort. 'Bleeding him, I'm sorry, for what?'

This is strange. Much as he hates news of plague, Henry always enjoys hearing of other people's minor ailments. Admit to a sniffle or a colic, and he will make up a herbal potion with his own hands, and stand over you while you swallow it.

He puts down his pen. Turns to look his monarch in the face. It is clear that Henry's mind is back in the garden. The king is wearing an expression he has seen before, though on beast, rather than man. He looks stunned, like a veal calf knocked on the head by the butcher.

It is to be their last night at Wolf Hall. He comes down very early, his arms full of papers. Someone is up before him. Stock-still in the great hall, a pale presence in the milky light, Jane Seymour is dressed in her stiff finery. She does not turn her head to acknowledge him, but she sees him from the tail of her eye.

If he had any feeling for her, he cannot find traces of it now. The months run away from you like a flurry of autumn leaves bowling and skittering towards the winter; the summer has gone, Thomas More's daughter has got his head back off London Bridge and is keeping it, God knows, in a dish or bowl, and saying her prayers to it. He is not the same man he was last year, and he doesn't acknowledge that man's feelings; he is starting afresh, always new thoughts, new feelings. Jane, he begins to say, you'll be able to get out of your best gown, will you be glad to see us on the road …?

Jane is facing front, like a sentry. The clouds have blown away overnight. We may have one more fine day. The early sun touches the fields, rosy. Night vapours disperse. The forms of trees swim into particularity. The house is waking up. Unstalled horses tread and whinny. A back door slams. Footsteps creak above them. Jane hardly seems to breathe. No rise and fall discernible, of that flat bosom. He feels he should walk backwards, withdraw, fade back into the night, and leave her here in the moment she occupies: looking out into England.

II

Crows

London and Kimbolton, Autumn 1535

Stephen Gardiner! Coming in as he's going out, striding towards the king's chamber, a folio under one arm, the other flailing the air. Gardiner, Bishop of Winchester: blowing up like a thunderstorm, when for once we have a fine day.

When Stephen comes into a room, the furnishings shrink from him. Chairs scuttle backwards. Joint-stools flatten themselves like pissing bitches. The woollen Bible figures in the king's tapestries lift their hands to cover their ears.

At court you might expect him. Anticipate him. But here? While we are still hunting through the countryside and (notionally) taking our ease? 'This is a pleasure, my lord bishop,' he says. 'It does my heart good to see you looking so well. The court will progress to Winchester shortly, and I did not think to enjoy your company before that.'

'I have stolen a march on you, Cromwell.'

'Are we at war?'

The bishop's face says, you know we are. 'It was you who had me banished.'

'I? Never think it, Stephen. I have missed you every day. Besides, not banished. Rusticated.'

Gardiner licks his lips. 'You will see how I have spent my time in the country.'

31

When Gardiner lost the post of Mr Secretary – and lost it to him, Cromwell – it had been impressed on the bishop that a spell in his own diocese of Winchester might be advisable, for he had too often cut across the king and his second wife. As he had put it, 'My lord of Winchester, a considered statement on the king's supremacy might be welcome, just so that there can be no mistake about your loyalty. A firm declaration that he is head of the English church and, rightfully considered, always has been. An assertion, firmly stated, that the Pope is a foreign prince with no jurisdiction here. A written sermon, perhaps, or an open letter. To clear up any ambiguities in your opinions. To give a lead to other churchmen, and to disabuse ambassador Chapuys of the notion that you have been bought by the Emperor. You should make a statement to the whole of Christendom. In fact, why don't you go back to your diocese and write a book?'

Now here is Gardiner, patting a manuscript as if it were the cheek of a plump baby: 'The king will be pleased to read this. I have called it, *Of True Obedience.*'

'You had better let me see it before it goes to the printer.'

'The king himself will expound it to you. It shows why oaths to the papacy are of none effect, yet our oath to the king, as head of the church, is good. It emphasises most strongly that a king's authority is divine, and descends to him directly from God.'

'And not from a pope.'

'In no wise from a pope; it descends from God without intermediary, and it does not flow upwards from his subjects, as you once stated to him.'

'Did I? Flow upwards? There seems a difficulty there.'

'You brought the king a book to that effect, the book of Marsiglio of Padua, his forty-two articles. The king says you belaboured him with them till his head ached.'

'I should have made the matter shorter,' he says, smiling. 'In practice, Stephen, upwards, downwards – it hardly matters.

"Where the word of a king is, there is power, and who may say to him, what doest thou?"'

'Henry is not a tyrant,' Gardiner says stiffly. 'I rebut any notion that his regime is not lawfully grounded. If I were king, I would wish my authority to be legitimate wholly, to be respected universally and, if questioned, stoutly defended. Would not you?'

'If I were king ...'

He was going to say, if I were king I'd defenestrate you. Gardiner says, 'Why are you looking out of the window?'

He smiles absently. 'I wonder what Thomas More would say to your book?'

'Oh, he would much mislike it, but for his opinion I do not give a fig,' the bishop says heartily, 'since his brain was eaten out by kites, and his skull made a relic his daughter worships on her knees. Why did you let her take the head off London Bridge?'

'You know me, Stephen. The fluid of benevolence flows through my veins and sometimes overspills. But look, if you are so proud of your book, perhaps you should spend more time writing in the country?'

Gardiner scowls. 'You should write a book yourself. That would be something to see. You with your dog Latin and your little bit of Greek.'

'I would write it in English,' he says. 'A good language for all sorts of matters. Go in, Stephen, don't keep the king waiting. You will find him in a good humour. Harry Norris is with him today. Francis Weston.'

'Oh, that chattering coxcomb,' Stephen says. He makes a cuffing motion. 'Thank you for the intelligence.'

Does the phantom-self of Weston feel the slap? A gust of laughter sweeps out from Henry's rooms.

The fine weather did not much outlast their stay at Wolf Hall. They had hardly left the Savernake forest when they were enveloped in wet mist. In England it's been raining, more or less, for a

33

decade, and the harvest will be poor again. The price of wheat is forecast to rise to twenty shillings a quarter. So what will the labourer do this winter, the man who earns five or six pence a day? The profiteers have moved in already, not just on the Isle of Thanet, but through the shires. His men are on their tail.

It used to surprise the cardinal, that one Englishman would starve another and take the profit. But he would say, 'I have seen an English mercenary cut the throat of his comrade, and pull his blanket from under him while he's still twitching, and go through his pack and pocket a holy medal along with his money.'

'Ah, but he was a hired killer,' the cardinal would say. 'Such men have no soul to lose. But most Englishmen fear God.'

'The Italians think not. They say the road between England and Hell is worn bare from treading feet, and runs downhill all the way.'

Daily he ponders the mystery of his countrymen. He has seen killers, yes; but he has seen a hungry soldier give away a loaf to a woman, a woman who is nothing to him, and turn away with a shrug. It is better not to try people, not to force them to desperation. Make them prosper; out of superfluity, they will be generous. Full bellies breed gentle manners. The pinch of famine makes monsters.

When, some days after his meeting with Stephen Gardiner, the travelling court had reached Winchester, new bishops had been consecrated in the cathedral. 'My bishops', Anne called them: gospellers, reformers, men who see Anne as an opportunity. Who would have thought Hugh Latimer would be a bishop? You would rather have predicted he would be burned, shrivelled at Smithfield with the gospel in his mouth. But then, who would have thought that Thomas Cromwell would be anything at all? When Wolsey fell, you might have thought that as Wolsey's servant he was ruined. When his wife and daughters died, you might have thought his loss would kill him. But Henry has turned to him; Henry has sworn him in; Henry has put his time at his disposal and said, come, Master Cromwell, take my arm: through courtyards and throne rooms, his path in life is now made smooth and clear. As a young man he was always shouldering his way through crowds, pushing to the front to see the spectacle. But now crowds scatter as he walks through Westminster or the precincts of any of the king's palaces. Since he was sworn councillor, trestles and packing cases and loose dogs are swept from his path. Women still their whispering and tug down their sleeves and settle their rings on their fingers, since he was named Master of the Rolls. Kitchen debris and clerks' clutter and the footstools of the lowly are kicked into corners and out of sight, now that he is Master Secretary to the king. And no one except Stephen Gardiner corrects his Greek; not now he is Chancellor of Cambridge University.

Henry's summer, on the whole, has been a success: through Berkshire, Wiltshire and Somerset he has shown himself to the people on the roads, and (when the rain isn't bucketing down) they've stood by the roads and cheered. Why would they not? You cannot see Henry and not be amazed. Each time you see him you are struck afresh by him, as if it were the first time: a massive man, bull-necked, his hair receding, face fleshing out; blue eyes, and a small mouth that is almost coy. His height is six feet three inches, and every inch bespeaks power. His carriage, his person, are magnificent; his rages are terrifying, his vows and curses, his molten tears. But there are moments when his great body will stretch and ease itself, his brow clear; he will plump himself down next to you on a bench and talk to you like your brother. Like a brother might, if you had one. Or a father even, a father of an ideal sort: how are you? Not working too hard? Have you had your dinner? What did you dream last night?

The danger of a progress like this is that a king who sits at ordinary tables, on an ordinary chair, can be taken as an ordinary man. But Henry is not ordinary. What if his hair is receding and his belly advancing? The Emperor Charles, when he looks in the glass, would give a province to see the Tudor's visage instead of his own crooked countenance, his hook nose almost touching his chin. King Francis, a beanpole, would pawn his dauphin to have shoulders like the King of England. Any qualities they have, Henry reflects them back, double the size. If they are learned, he is twice learned. If merciful, he is the exemplar of mercy. If they are gallant, he is the pattern of knight errantry, from the biggest book of knights you can think of.

All the same: in village alehouses up and down England, they are blaming the king and Anne Boleyn for the weather: the concubine, the great whore. If the king would take back his lawful wife Katherine, the rain would stop. And indeed, who can doubt that everything would be different and better, if only England were ruled by village idiots and their drunken friends?

They move back towards London slowly, so that by the time the king arrives the city will be free from suspicion of plague. In cold chantry chapels under the gaze of wall-eyed virgins, the king prays alone. He doesn't like him to pray alone. He wants to know what he's praying for; his old master, Cardinal Wolsey, would have known.

His relations with the queen, as the summer draws to its official end, are chary, uncertain, and fraught with distrust. Anne Boleyn is now thirty-four years old, an elegant woman, with a refinement that makes mere prettiness seem redundant. Once sinuous, she has become angular. She retains her dark glitter, now rubbed a little, flaking in places. Her prominent dark eyes she uses to good effect, and in this fashion: she glances at a man's face, then her regard flits away, as if unconcerned, indifferent. There is a pause: as it might be, a breath. Then slowly, as if compelled, she turns her gaze back to him. Her eyes rest on his face. She examines this man. She examines him as if he is the only man in the world. She looks as if she is seeing him for the first time, and considering all sorts of uses for him, all sorts of possibilities which he has not even thought of himself. To her victim the moment seems to last an age, during which shivers run up his spine. Though in fact the trick is quick, cheap, effective and repeatable, it seems to the poor fellow that he is now distinguished among all men. He smirks. He preens himself. He grows a little taller. He grows a little more foolish.

He has seen Anne work her trick on lord and commoner, on the king himself. You watch as the man's mouth gapes a little and he becomes her creature. Almost always it works; it has never worked on him. He is not indifferent to women, God knows, just indifferent to Anne Boleyn. It galls her; he should have pretended. He has made her queen, she has made him minister; but they are uneasy now, each of them vigilant, watching each other for some slip that will betray real feeling, and so give advantage to the one or the other: as if only dissimulation will make them safe. But Anne is not good at hiding her feelings; she is the king's quicksilver darling, slipping and sliding from anger to laughter. There have been times this summer when she would smile secretly at him behind the king's back, or grimace to warn him that Henry was out of temper. At other times she would ignore him, turn her shoulder, her black eyes sweeping the room and resting elsewhere.

To understand this – if it bears understanding – we must go back to last spring, when Thomas More was still alive. Anne had called him in to talk of diplomacy: her object was a marriage contract, a French prince for her infant daughter Elizabeth. But the French proved skittish in negotiation. The truth is, even now they do not fully concede that Anne is queen, they are not convinced that her daughter is legitimate. Anne knows what lies behind their reluctance, and somehow it is his fault: his, Thomas Cromwell's. She had accused him openly of sabotaging her. He did not like the French and did not want the alliance, she claimed. Did he not shirk a chance to cross the sea for face-to-face talks? The French were all ready to negotiate, she says. 'And you were expected, Master Secretary. And you said you were ill, and my lord brother had to go.'

'And failed,' he had sighed. 'Very sadly.'

'I know you,' Anne said. 'You are never ill, are you, unless you wish to be? And besides, I perceive how things stand with you. You think that when you are in the city and not at the court you are not under our eye. But I know you are too friendly with the Emperor's man. I am aware Chapuys is your neighbour. But is that a reason why your servants should be always in and out of each other's houses?'

Anne was wearing, that day, rose pink and dove grey. The colours should have had a fresh maidenly charm; but all he could think of were stretched innards, umbles and tripes, grey-pink intestines looped out of a living body; he had a second batch of recalcitrant friars to be dispatched to Tyburn, to be slit up and gralloched by the hangman. They were traitors and deserved the death, but it is a death exceeding most in cruelty. The pearls around her long neck looked to him like little beads of fat, and as she argued she would reach up and tug them; he kept his eyes on her fingertips, nails flashing like tiny knives.

Still, as he says to Chapuys, while I am in Henry's favour, I doubt the queen can do me any harm. She has her spites, she has her little rages; she is volatile and Henry knows it. It was what fascinated the king, to find someone so different from those soft, kind blondes who drift through men's lives and leave not a mark behind. But now when Anne appears he sometimes looks harassed. You can see his gaze growing distant when she begins one of her rants, and if he were not such a gentleman he would pull his hat down over his ears.

No, he tells the ambassador, it's not Anne who bothers me; it's the men she collects about her. Her family: her father the Earl of Wiltshire, who likes to be known as 'Monseigneur', and her brother George, Lord Rochford, whom Henry has appointed to his privy chamber rota. George is one of the newer staff, because Henry likes to stick with men he is used to, who were his friends when he was young; from time to time the cardinal would sweep them out, but they would seep back like dirty water. Once they were young men of esprit, young men of élan. A quarter of a century has passed and they are grey or balding, flabby or paunchy, gone in the fetlock or missing some fingers, but still as arrogant as satraps and with the mental refinement of a gatepost. And now there is a new litter of pups, Weston and George Rochford and their ilk, whom Henry has taken up because he thinks they keep him young. These men – the old ones and the new – are with the king from his uprising to his downlying, and all his private hours in between. They are with him in his stool chamber, and when he cleans his teeth and spits into a silver basin; they swab him with towels and lace him into his doublet and hose; they know his person, each mole or freckle, each bristle in his beard, and they map the islands of his sweat when he comes from the tennis court and rips off his shirt. They know more than they should, as much as his laundress and his doctor, and they talk of what they know; they know when he visits the queen to try to bounce a son into her, or when, on a Friday (the day no Christian copulates) he dreams of a phantom woman and stains his sheets. They sell their knowledge at a high price: they want favours done, they want their own derelictions ignored, they think they are special and they want you to be aware of it. Ever since he, Cromwell, came up in Henry's service, he has been mollifying these men, flattering them, cajoling them, seeking always an easy way of working, a compromise; but sometimes, when for an hour they block him from access to his king, they can't keep the grins from their faces. I have probably, he thinks, gone as far as I can to accommodate them. Now they must accommodate me, or be removed.

The mornings are chilly now, and fat-bellied clouds bob after the royal party as they dawdle through Hampshire, the roads turning within days from dust to mud. Henry is reluctant to hurry back to business; I wish it were always August, he says. They are en route to Farnham, a small hunting party, when a report is galloped along the road: cases of plague have appeared in the town. Henry, brave on the battlefield, pales almost before their eyes and wrenches around his horse's head: where to? Anywhere will do, anywhere but Farnham.

He leans forward in the saddle, removing his hat as he speaks to the king. 'We can go before our time to Basing House, let me send a fast man to warn William Paulet. Then, so as not to burden him, to Elvetham for a day? Edward Seymour is at home, and I can hunt out supplies if he is unprovided.'

He drops back, letting Henry ride ahead. He says to Rafe, 'Send to Wolf Hall. Fetch Mistress Jane.'

'What, here?'

'She can ride. Tell old Seymour to put her on a good horse. I shall want her at Elvetham for Wednesday evening, any later will be too late.'

Rafe reins in, poised to turn. 'But. Sir. The Seymours will ask why Jane and why the hurry. And why we are going to Elvetham, when there are other houses nearby, the Westons at Sutton Place ...'

Drown or hang the Westons, he thinks. The Westons are no part of this plan. He smiles. 'Say they should do it because they love me.'

He sees Rafe thinking, so my master is going to ask for Jane Seymour after all. For himself or for Gregory?

He, Cromwell, had seen at Wolf Hall what Rafe could not see: silent Jane in his bed, pale and speechless Jane, that is what Henry dreams of now. You cannot account for a man's fantasies, and Henry is no lecher, he has not taken many mistresses. No harm if he, Cromwell, helps ease the king's way towards her. The king does not mistreat his bedfellows. He is not a man who hates a woman once he has had her. He will write her verses, and with prompting he will give her an income, he will advance her folk; there are many families who have decided, since Anne Boleyn came up in the world, that to bask in the sunshine of Henry's regard is an Englishwoman's highest vocation. If they play this carefully, Edward Seymour will rise within the court, and give him an ally where allies are scarce. At this stage, Edward needs advice. Because he, Cromwell, has better business sense than the Seymours. He will not let Jane sell herself cheap.

But what will Anne the queen do, if Henry takes as mistress a young woman she has laughed at since ever Jane waited upon her: whom she calls pasty-face and milksop? How will Anne counter meekness, and silence? Raging will hardly help her. She will have to ask herself what Jane can give the king, that at present he lacks. She will have to think it through. And it is always a pleasure to see Anne thinking.

When the two parties met after Wolf Hall – king's party and queen's party – Anne had been charming to him, laying her hand on his arm and chattering away in French about nothing very much. As if she had never mentioned, a few weeks before, that she would like to cut off his head; as if she was only making conversation. It is well to keep behind her in the hunting field. She is keen and quick but not too accurate. This summer she put a crossbow bolt in a straying cow. And Henry had to pay off the owner.

But look, never mind all this. Queens come and go. So recent history has shown us. Let us think about how to pay for England, her king's great charges, the cost of charity and the cost of justice, the cost of keeping her enemies beyond her shores.

From last year he has been sure of his answer: monks, that parasite class of men, are going to provide. Get out to the abbeys and convents through the realm, he had told his visitors, his inspectors: put to them the questions I will give you, eighty-six questions in all. Listen more than you speak, and when you have listened, ask to see the accounts. Talk to the monks and nuns about their lives and Rule. I am not interested where they think their own salvation lies, whether through Christ's precious blood only or through their own works and merits in part: well, yes, I am interested, but the chief matter is to know what assets they have. To know their rents and holdings, and whether, in the event it please the king as head of the church to take back what he owns, by what mechanism it is best to do it.

Don't expect a warm welcome, he says. They will rush to liquidate their assets ahead of your arrival. Take note of what relics they have or objects of local veneration, and how they exploit them, how much revenue they bring in by the year, for all that money is made off the back of superstitious pilgrims who would do better to stay at home and earn an honest living. Press them on their loyalty, what they think of Katherine, what they think of the Lady Mary, and how they regard the Pope; because if the mother houses of their orders are outside these shores, have they not a higher loyalty, as they might term it, to some foreign power? Put this to them and show them that they are at a disadvantage; it is not enough to assert their fidelity to the king, they must be ready to show it, and they can do that by making your work easy.

His men know better than to try to cheat him, but just to make sure he sends them out in pairs, one to watch the other. The abbeys' bursars will offer bribes, to understate their assets.

Thomas More, in his room in the Tower, had said to him, 'Where will you strike next, Cromwell? You are going to pull all England down.'

He had said, I pray to God, grant me life only as long as I use my power to build and not destroy. Among the ignorant it is said that the king is destroying the church. In fact he is renewing it. It will be a better country, believe me, once it is purged of liars and hypocrites. 'But you, unless you mend your manners towards Henry, will not be alive to see it.'

Nor was he. He doesn't regret what happened; his only regret is that More wouldn't see sense. He was offered an oath upholding Henry's supremacy in the church; this oath is a test of loyalty.

Not many things in life are simple, but this is simple. If you will not swear it, you indict yourself, by implication: traitor, rebel. More would not swear; then what could he do but die? What could he do but splash to the scaffold, on a day in July when the torrents never stopped, except for a brief hour in the evening and that too late for Thomas More; he died with his hose wet, splashed to the knees, and his feet paddling like a duck's. He doesn't exactly miss the man. It's just that sometimes, he forgets he's dead. It's as if they're deep in conversation, and suddenly the conversation stops, he says something and no answer comes back. As if they'd been walking along and More had dropped into a hole in the road, a pit as deep as a man, slopping with rainwater.

You do, in fact, hear of such accidents. Men have died, the track giving way under their feet. England needs better roads, and bridges that don't collapse. He is preparing a bill for Parliament to give employment to men without work, to get them waged and out mending the roads, making the harbours, building walls against the Emperor or any other opportunist. We could pay them, he calculated, if we levied an income tax on the rich; we could provide shelter, doctors if they needed them, their subsistence; we would all have the fruits of their work, and their employment would keep them from becoming bawds or pickpockets or highway robbers, all of which men will do if they see no other way to eat. What if their fathers before them were bawds, pickpockets or highway robbers? That signifies nothing. Look at him. Is he Walter Cromwell? In a generation everything can change.

As for the monks, he believes, like Martin Luther, that the monastic life is not necessary, not useful, not commanded of Christ. There's nothing imperishable about monasteries. They're not part of God's natural order. They rise and decay, like any other institutions, and sometimes their buildings fall down, or they are ruined by lax stewardship. Over the years any number of them have vanished or relocated or become swallowed into some other monastery. The number of monks is diminishing

43

naturally, because these days the good Christian man lives out in the world. Take Battle Abbey. Two hundred monks at the height of its fortunes, and now – what? – forty at most. Forty fat fellows sitting on a fortune. The same up and down the kingdom. Resources that could be freed, that could be put to better use. Why should money lie in coffers, when it could be put into circulation among the king's subjects?

His commissioners go out and send him back scandals; they send him monkish manuscripts, tales of ghosts and curses, meant to keep simple people in dread. The monks have relics that make it rain or make it stop, that inhibit the growth of weeds and cure diseases of cattle. They charge for the use of them, they do not give them free to their neighbours: old bones and chips of wood, bent nails from the crucifixion of Christ. He tells the king and queen what his men have found in Wiltshire at Maiden Bradley. 'The monks have part of God's coat, and some broken meats from the Last Supper. They have twigs that blossom on Christmas Day.'

'That last is possible,' Henry says reverently. 'Think of the Glastonbury thorn.'

'The prior has six children, and keeps his sons in his household as waiting men. He says in his defence he never meddled with married women, only with virgins. And then when he was tired of them or they were with child, he found them a husband. He claims he has a licence given under papal seal, allowing him to keep a whore.'

Anne giggles: 'And could he produce it?'

Henry is shocked. 'Away with him. Such men are a disgrace to their calling.'

But these tonsured fools are commonly worse than other men; does Henry not know that? There are some good monks, but after a few years of exposure to the monastic ideal, they tend to run away. They flee the cloisters and become actors in the world. In times past our forefathers with their billhooks and scythes attacked the monks and their servants with the fury they would bring against an occupying army. They broke down their walls and threatened to burn them out, and what they wanted were the monks' rent-rolls, the items of their servitude, and when they could get them they tore them and put them on bonfires, and they said, what we want is a little liberty: a little liberty, and to be treated like Englishmen, after the centuries we have been treated as beasts.

Darker reports come in. He, Cromwell, says to his visitors, just tell them this, and tell them loud: to each monk, one bed: to each bed, one monk. Is that so hard for them? The world-weary tell him, these sins are sure to happen, if you shut up men without recourse to women they will prey on the younger and weaker novices, they are men and it is only a man's nature. But aren't they supposed to rise above nature? What's the point of all the prayer and fasting, if it leaves them insufficient when the devil comes to tempt them?

The king concedes the waste, the mismanagement; it may be necessary, he says, to reform and regroup some of the smaller houses, for the cardinal himself did so when he was alive. But surely, the great houses, we can trust them to renew themselves?

Possibly, he says. He knows the king is devout and afraid of change. He wants the church reformed, he wants it pristine; he also wants money. But as a native of the sign Cancer, he proceeds crab-wise to his objective: a side-shuffle, a weaving motion. He, Cromwell, watches Henry, as his eyes pass over the figures he has been given. It's not a fortune, not for a king: not a king's ransom. By and by, Henry may want to think of the larger houses, the fatter priors basted in self-regard. Let us for now make a beginning. He says, I've sat at too many abbots' tables where the abbot nibbles raisins and dates, while for the monks it's herring again. He thinks, if I had my way I would free them all to lead a different life. They claim they're living the *vita apostolica*; but you didn't find the apostles feeling each other's bollocks. Those who want to go, let them go. Those monks who are ordained priest can be given benefices, do useful work in the parishes. Those under twenty-four, men and women both, can be sent back into the world. They are too young to bind themselves for life with vows.

He is thinking ahead: if the king had the monks' land, not just a little but the whole of it, he would be three times the man he is now. He need no longer go cap in hand to Parliament, wheedling for a subsidy. His son Gregory says to him, 'Sir, they say that if the Abbot of Glastonbury went to bed with the Abbess of Shaftesbury, their offspring would be the richest landowner in England.'

'Very likely,' he says, 'though have you seen the Abbess of Shaftesbury?'

Gregory looks worried. 'Should I have?'

Conversations with his son are like this: they dart off at angles, end up anywhere. He thinks of the grunts in which he and Walter communicated when he was a boy. 'You can look at her if you like. I must visit Shaftesbury soon, I have something to do there.'

The convent at Shaftesbury is where Wolsey placed his daughter. He says, 'Will you make a note for me, Gregory, a memorandum? Go and see Dorothea.'

Gregory longs to ask, who is Dorothea? He sees the questions chase each other across the boy's face; then at last: 'Is she pretty?'

'I don't know. Her father kept her close.' He laughs.

But he wipes the smile from his face when he reminds Henry: when monks are traitors, they are the most recalcitrant of that cursed breed. When you threaten them, 'I will make you suffer,' they reply that it is for suffering they were born. Some choose to starve in prison, or go praying to Tyburn and the attentions of the hangman. He said to them, as he said to Thomas More, this is not about your God, or my God, or about God at all. This is about, which will you have: Henry Tudor or Alessandro Farnese? The King of England at Whitehall, or some fantastically corrupt foreigner in the Vatican? They had turned their heads away; died speechless, their false hearts carved out of their chests.

When he rides at last into the gates of his city house at Austin Friars, his liveried servants bunch about him, in their long-skirted coats of grey marbled cloth. Gregory is on his right hand, and on his left Humphrey, keeper of his sporting spaniels, with whom he has had easy conversation on this last mile of the journey; behind him his falconers, Hugh and James and Roger, vigilant men alert for any jostling or threat. A crowd has formed outside his gate, expecting largesse. Humphrey and the rest have money to disburse. After supper tonight there will be the usual dole to the poor. Thurston, his chief cook, says they are feeding two hundred Londoners, twice a day.

He sees a man in the press, a little bowed man, scarcely making an effort to keep his feet. This man is weeping. He loses sight of him; he spots him again, his head bobbing, as if his tears were the tide and were carrying him towards the gate. He says, 'Humphrey, find out what ails that fellow.'

But then he forgets. His household are happy to see him, all his folk with shining faces, and a swarm of little dogs about his feet; he lifts them into his arms, writhing bodies and wafting tails, and asks them how they do. The servants cluster round Gregory, admiring him from hat to boots; all servants love him for his pleasant ways. 'The man in charge!' his nephew Richard says, and gives him a bone-crushing hug. Richard is a solid boy with the Cromwell eye, direct and brutal, and the Cromwell voice that can caress or contradict. He is afraid of nothing that walks the earth, and nothing that walks below it; if a demon turned up at Austin Friars, Richard would kick it downstairs on its hairy arse.

His smiling nieces, young married women now, have slackened the laces on their bodices to accommodate swelling bellies. He kisses them both, their bodies soft against his, their breath sweet, warmed by ginger comfits such as women in their condition use. He misses, for a moment ... what does he miss? The pliancy of gentle, willing flesh; the absent, inconsequential conversations of early morning. He has to be careful in any dealings with women, discreet. He should not give his ill-wishers the chance to defame him. Even the king is discreet; he doesn't want Europe to call him Harry Whoremaster. Perhaps he'd rather gaze at the unattainable, for now: Mistress Seymour.

At Elvetham Jane was like a flower, head drooping, modest as a drift of green-white hellebore. In her brother's house, the king had praised her to her family's face: 'A tender, modest, shame-faced maid, such as few be in our day.'

Thomas Seymour, keen as always to crash into the conversation and talk over his elder brother: 'For piety and modesty, I dare say Jane has few equals.'

He saw brother Edward hide a smile. Under his interested eye, Jane's family have begun – with a certain incredulity – to sense which way the wind is blowing. Thomas Seymour said, 'I could not brazen it out, even if I were the king I could not face it, inviting a lady like sister Jane to come to my bed. I wouldn't know how to begin. And would you, anyway? Why would you? It would be like kissing a stone. Rolling her about from one side of the mattress to the other, and your parts growing numb from cold.'

'A brother cannot picture his sister in a man's embrace,' Edward Seymour says. 'At least, no brother can who calls himself a Christian. Though they do say at court that George Boleyn –' He breaks off, frowning. 'And of course the king knows how to propose himself. How to offer himself. He knows how to do it, as a gallant gentleman. As you, brother, do not.'

It's hard to put down Tom Seymour. He just grins.

But Henry had not said much, before they rode away from Elvetham; made his hearty farewells, and never a word about the girl. Jane had whispered to him, 'Master Cromwell, why am I here?'

'Ask your brothers.'

'My brothers say, ask Cromwell.'

'So is it an utter mystery to you?'

'Yes. Unless I am to be married at last. Am I to be married to you?'

'I must forgo that prospect. I am too old for you, Jane. I could be your father.'

'Could you?' Jane says wonderingly. 'Well, stranger things have happened at Wolf Hall. I didn't even realise you knew my mother.'

A fleeting smile and she vanishes, leaving him looking after her. We could be married at that, he thinks; it would keep my mind agile, wondering how she might misconstrue me. Does she do it on purpose?

Though I can't have her till Henry's finished with her. And I once swore I would not take on his used women, did I not?

Perhaps, he had thought, I should scribble an aide-memoire for the Seymour boys, so they are clear on what presents Jane should and should not accept. The rule is simple: jewellery yes, money no. And till the deal is done, let her not take off any item of clothing in Henry's presence. Not even, he will advise, her gloves.

Unkind people describe his house as the Tower of Babel. It is said he has servants from every nation under the sun, except Scotland; so Scots keep applying to him, in hope. Gentlemen and even noblemen from here and abroad are pressing him to take their sons into his household, and he accepts all he thinks he can train. On any given day at Austin Friars a group of German scholars will be deploying the many varieties of their tongue, frowning over the letters of evangelists from their own territories. At dinner young Cambridge men exchange snippets of Greek; they are the scholars he has helped, now come to help him. Sometimes a company of Italian merchants come in for supper, and he chats with them in those languages he learned when he worked for the bankers in Florence and Venice. The retainers of his neighbour Chapuys loll about drinking at the expense of the Cromwell buttery, and gossip in Spanish, in Flemish. He himself speaks in French to Chapuys, as it is the ambassador's first language, and employs French of a more demotic sort to his boy Christophe, a squat little ruffian who followed him home from Calais, and who is never far from his side; he doesn't let him far from his side, because around Christophe fights break out.

There is a summer of gossip to catch up on, and accounts to go through, receipts and expenses of his houses and lands. But first he goes out to the kitchen to see his chief cook. It's that early-afternoon lull, dinner cleared, spits cleaned, pewter scoured and stacked, a smell of cinnamon and cloves, and Thurston standing solitary by a floured board, gazing at a ball of dough as if it were the head of the Baptist. As a shadow blocks his light, 'Inky fingers out!' the cook roars. Then, 'Ah. You, sir. Not before time. We had great venison pasties made against your coming, we had to give them out to your friends before they went bad. We'd have sent some up to you, only you move around so fast.'

He holds out his hands for inspection.

'I beg pardon,' Thurston says. 'But you see I have young Thomas Avery down here fresh from the account books, poking around the stores and wanting to weigh things. Then Master Rafe, look Thurston, we have some Danes coming, what can you make for Danes? Then Master Richard crashing in, Luther has sent his messengers, what sort of cakes do Germans like?'

He gives the dough a pinch. 'Is this for Germans?'

'Never mind what it is. If it works, you'll eat it.'

'Did they pick the quinces? It can't be long before we have frost. I can feel it in my bones.'

'Listen to you,' Thurston says. 'You sound like your own grandam.'

'You didn't know her. Or did you?'

50

Thurston chuckles. 'Parish drunk?'

Probably. What sort of woman could have suckled his father Walter Cromwell, and not turned to drink? Thurston says, as if it's just struck him, 'Mind you, a man has two grandams. Who were your mother's people, sir?'

'They were northerners.'

Thurston grins. 'Come out of a cave. You know young Francis Weston? He that waits on the king? His people are giving out that you're a Hebrew.' He grunts; he's heard that one before. 'Next time you're at court,' Thurston advises, 'take your cock out and put it on the table and see what he says to that.'

'I do that anyway,' he says. 'If the conversation flags.'

'Mind you …' Thurston hesitates. 'It's true, sir, you are a Hebrew because you lend money at interest.'

Mounting, in Weston's case. 'Anyway,' he says. He gives the dough another nip; it's a bit solid, is it not? 'What's new on the streets?'

'They're saying the old queen's sick.' Thurston waits. But his master has picked up a handful of currants and is eating them. 'She's sick at heart, I should think. They say she's put a curse on Anne Boleyn, so she won't have a boy. Or if she does have a boy, it won't be Henry's. They say Henry has other women and so Anne chases him around his chamber with a pair of shears, shouting she'll geld him. Queen Katherine used to shut her eyes like wives do, but Anne's not the same mettle and she swears he will suffer for it. So that would be a pretty revenge, wouldn't it?' Thurston cackles. 'She cuckolds Henry to pay him back, and puts her own bastard on the throne.'

They have busy, buzzing minds, the Londoners: minds like middens. 'Do they guess at who the father of this bastard will be?'

'Thomas Wyatt?' Thurston offers. 'Because she was known to favour him before she was queen. Or else her old lover Harry Percy –'

'Percy's in his own country, is he not?'

Thurston rolls his eyes. 'Distance don't stop her. If she wants him down from Northumberland she just whistles and whips him down on the wind. Not that she stops at Harry Percy. They say she has all the gentlemen of the king's privy chamber, one after another. She don't like delay so they all stand in a line frigging their members, till she shouts, "Next."'

'And in they troop,' he says. 'One and then another.' He laughs. Eats the final currant from his palm.

'Welcome home,' Thurston says. 'London, where we believe anything.'

'After she was crowned, I remember she called her whole household together, men and maids, and she sermonised them on how they should behave, no gambling except for tokens, no loose language and no flesh on show. It's slid a bit from there, I agree.'

'Sir,' Thurston says, 'you've got flour on your sleeve.'

'Well, I must go upstairs and sit down in council. Don't let supper be late.'

'When is it ever?' Thurston dusts him tenderly. 'When is it ever?'

This is his household council, not the king's; his familiar advisers, the young men, Rafe Sadler and Richard Cromwell, quick and ready with figures, quick to twist an argument, quick to seize a point. And also Gregory. His son.

This season young men carry their effects in soft pale leather bags, in imitation of the agents for the Fugger bank, who travel all over Europe and set the fashion. The bags are heart-shaped and so to him it always looks as if they are going wooing, but they swear they are not. Nephew Richard Cromwell sits down and gives the bags a sardonic glance. Richard is like his uncle, and keeps his effects close to his person. 'Here's Call-Me,' he says. 'Will you look at the feather in his hat?'

Thomas Wriothesley comes in, parting from his murmuring retainers; he is a tall and handsome young man with a head of burnished copper hair. A generation back, his family were called Writh, but they thought an elegant extension would give them consequence; they were heralds by office, so they were well-placed for reinvention, for the reworking of ordinary ancestors into something more knightly. The change does not go by without mockery; Thomas is known at Austin Friars as Call-Me-Risley. He has grown a trim beard recently, has fathered a son, and is accreting dignity each year. He drops his bag on the table and slides into his place. 'And how is Gregory?' he asks.

Gregory's face opens in delight; he admires Call-Me, and he hardly hears the note of condescension. 'Oh, I am well. I have been hunting all summer and now I will be back to William Fitzwilliam's household to join in his train, for he is a gentleman close to the king and my father thinks I can learn from him. Fitz is good to me.'

'Fitz.' Wriothesley snorts with amusement. 'You Cromwells!'

'Well,' Gregory says, 'he calls my father Crumb.'

'I suggest you don't take that up, Wriothesley,' he says amiably. 'Or at least, Crumb me behind my back. Though I've just been out to the kitchens and Crumb is nothing to what they call the queen.'

Richard Cromwell says, 'It's the women who keep the poison pot stirred. They don't like man-stealers. They think Anne should be punished.'

'When we left for the progress she was all elbows,' Gregory says, unexpectedly. 'Elbows and points and spikes. She looks more plush now.'

'So she does.' He is surprised the boy has noticed such a thing. The married men, experienced, watch Anne for signs of fattening as keenly as they watch their own wives. There are glances around the table. 'Well, we shall see. They have not been together the whole summer, but as I judge, enough.'

'It had better be enough,' Wriothesley says. 'The king will grow impatient with her. How many years has he waited, for a woman to do her duty? Anne promised him a son if he would wed her, and you wonder, would he do so much for her, if it were all to do again?'

Richard Riche joins them last, with a muttered apology. No heart-shaped bag for this Richard either, though once he would have been just the kind of young gallant to have five in different colours. What a change a decade brings! Riche was once the worst kind of law student, the kind with a file of pleas in mitigation to set against his sins; the kind who seeks out low taverns where lawyers are called vermin, and so is obliged in honour to start a fight; who arrives back at his lodgings in the Temple in the small hours stinking of cheap wine and with his jacket in shreds; the kind who halloos with a pack of terriers over Lincoln's Inn Fields. But Riche is sobered and subdued now, protégé of the Lord Chancellor Thomas Audley, and constantly to and fro between that dignitary and Thomas Cromwell. The boys call him Sir Purse; Purse is getting fatter, they say. The cares of office have fallen on him, the duties of the father of a growing family; once a golden boy, he looks to be covered by a faint patina of dust. Who would have thought he would be Solicitor General? But then he has a good lawyer's brain, and when you want a good lawyer, he is always at hand.

'Bishop Gardiner's book is not to your purpose,' Riche begins. 'Sir.'

'It is not wholly bad. On the king's powers, we concur.'

'Yes, but,' Riche says.

'I was moved to quote to Gardiner this text: "Where the word of a king is, there is power, and who shall say to him, what doest thou?"'

Riche raises his eyebrows. 'Parliament shall.'

Mr Wriothesley says, 'Trust Master Riche to know what Parliament can do.'

It was on the questions of Parliament's powers, it seems, that Riche tripped Thomas More, tripped and tipped him and perhaps betrayed him into treason. No one knows what was said in that room, in that cell; Riche had come out, pink-faced, hoping and half-suspecting that he had got enough, and gone straight from the Tower of London to him, to Thomas Cromwell. Who had said calmly, yes, this will do; we have him, thank you. Thank you, Purse, you did well.

Now Richard Cromwell leans towards him: 'Tell us, my little friend Purse: in your good opinion, can Parliament put an heir in the queen's belly?'

Riche blushes a little; he is nearly forty now, but because of his complexion he can still blush. 'I never said Parliament can do what God will not. I said it could do more than Thomas More would allow.'

'Martyr More,' he says. 'The word is in Rome that he and Fisher are to be made saints.' Mr Wriothesley laughs. 'I agree it is ridiculous,' he says. He darts a look at his nephew: enough now, say nothing more about the queen, her belly or any other part.

For he has confided to Richard Cromwell something at least of the events at Elvetham, at Edward Seymour's house. When the royal party was so suddenly diverted, Edward had stepped up and entertained them handsomely. But the king could not sleep that night, and sent the boy Weston to call him from his bed. A dancing candle flame, in a room of unfamiliar shape: 'Christ, what time is it?' Six o'clock, Weston said maliciously, and you are late.

In fact it was not four, the sky still dark. The shutter opened to let in air, Henry sat whispering to him, the planets their only witnesses: he had made sure that Weston was out of earshot, refused to speak till the door was shut. Just as well. 'Cromwell,' the king said, 'what if I. What if I were to fear, what if I were to begin to suspect, there is some flaw in my marriage to Anne, some impediment, something displeasing to Almighty God?'

He had felt the years roll away: he was the cardinal, listening to the same conversation: only the queen's name then was Katherine.

'But what impediment?' he had said, a little wearily. 'What could it be, sir?'

'I don't know,' the king had whispered. 'I don't know now but I may know. Was she not pre-contracted to Harry Percy?'

'No, sir. He swore not, on the Bible. Your Majesty heard him swear.'

'Ah, but you had been to see him, had you not, Cromwell, did you not trail him to some low inn and haul him up from his bench and pound his head with your fist?'

'No, sir. I would never so mistreat any peer of the realm, let alone the Earl of Northumberland.'

'Ah well. I am relieved to hear that. I may have got the details wrong. But that day the earl said what he thought I wanted him to say. He said that there was no union with Anne, no promise of marriage, let alone consummation. What if he lied?'

'On oath, sir?'

'But you are very frightening, Crumb. You would make a man forget his manners before God. What if he did lie? What if she made a contract with Percy amounting to a lawful marriage? If that were so, she cannot be married to me.'

He had kept silence, but he saw Henry's mind running; his own was darting like a startled deer. 'And I much suspect,' the king had whispered. 'I much suspect her with Thomas Wyatt.'

'No, sir,' he said, vehement even before he had time to think. Wyatt is his friend; his father, Sir Henry Wyatt, had charged him to make the boy's path smooth; Wyatt is not a boy any more, but never mind.

'You say no.' Henry leaned towards him. 'But did not Wyatt avoid the realm and go to Italy, because she would not favour him and he had no peace of mind while her image was before him?'

'Well, there you have it. You say it yourself, Majesty. She would not favour him. If she had, no doubt he'd have stayed.'

'But I cannot be sure,' Henry insists. 'Suppose she denied him then but favoured him some other time? Women are weak and easily conquered by flattery. Especially when men write verses to them, and there are some who say that Wyatt writes better verses than me, though I am the king.'

He blinks at him: four o'clock, sleepless; you could call it harmless vanity, God love him, if only it were not four o'clock. 'Majesty,' he says, 'put your mind at rest. If Wyatt had made any inroads on that lady's immaculate chastity, I feel sure he could not have resisted boasting about it. In verse, or common prose.'

Henry only grunts. But he looks up: Wyatt's well-dressed shade, silken, slides across the window, blocks the cold starlight. On your way, phantom: his mind brushes it before him; who can understand Wyatt, who absolve him? The king says, 'Well. Perhaps. Even if she did give way to Wyatt, it would be no impediment to my marriage, there can be no question of a contract between them since he himself was married as a boy and so not free to promise anything to Anne. But I tell you, it would be impediment to my trust in her. I would not take it kindly to have any woman lie to me, and say she came a virgin to my bed if she did not.'

Wolsey, where are you? You have heard all this before. Advise me now.

He stands up. He is easing this interview to an end. 'Shall I tell them to bring you something, sir? Something to help you sleep again for an hour or two?'

'I need something to sweeten my dreams. I wish I knew what it was. I have consulted Bishop Gardiner in this matter.'

He had tried to keep the shock off his face. Gone to Gardiner: behind my back?

'And Gardiner said,' Henry's face was the picture of desolation, 'he said there was doubt enough in the case, but that if the marriage were not good, if I were forced to put away Anne, I must return to Katherine. And I cannot do it, Cromwell. I am resolved that even if the whole of Christendom comes against me, I can never touch that stale old woman again.'

'Well,' he had said. He was looking at the floor, at Henry's large white naked feet. 'I think we can do better than that, sir. I do not pretend to follow Gardiner's reasoning, but then the bishop knows more canon law than me. I do not believe, however, you can be constrained or compelled in any matter, as you are master of your own household, and your own country, and of your own church. Perhaps Gardiner meant only to prepare Your Majesty for the obstacles others might raise.'

Or perhaps, he thought, he just meant to make you sweat and give you nightmares. Gardiner's like that. But Henry had sat up: 'I can do as it pleases me,' his monarch said. 'God would not allow my pleasure to be contrary to his design, nor my designs to be impeded by his will.' A shadow of cunning had crossed his face. 'And Gardiner himself said so.'

Henry yawned. It was a signal. 'Crumb, you don't look very dignified, bowing in a nightgown. Will you be ready to ride at seven, or shall we leave you behind and see you at supper?'

If you'll be ready, I'll be ready, he thinks, as he pads back to his bed. Come sunrise, will you forget we ever had this conversation? The court will be astir, the horses tossing their heads and sniffing the wind. By mid-morning we will be reunited with the queen's band; Anne will be chirruping atop her hunter; she will never know, unless her little friend Weston tells her, that last night at Elvetham the king sat gazing at his next mistress: Jane Seymour ignoring his pleading eyes, and placidly working her way through a chicken. Gregory had said, his eyes round: 'Doesn't Mistress Seymour eat a lot?'

And now the summer is over. Wolf Hall, Elvetham, fade into the dusk. His lips are sealed on the king's doubts and fears; it is autumn, he is at Austin Friars; with bowed head he listens to the court news, watches Riche's fingers twisting the silk tag on a document. 'Their households have been provoking each other in the streets,' his nephew Richard says. 'Thumbing of noses, curses, hands on daggers.'

'Sorry, who?' he says.

'Nicholas Carew's people. Scrapping with Lord Rochford's servants.'

'As long as they keep it away from the court,' he says sharply. The penalty for drawing a blade within the precincts of the royal court is amputation of the offending hand. What is the quarrel about, he begins to ask, then changes his question: 'What is their excuse?'

For picture Carew, one of Henry's old friends, one of his privy chamber gentlemen, and devoted to the queen that was. See him, an antique man with his long grave face, his cultivated air of having stepped straight from a book of knight-errantry. No surprise if Sir Nicholas, with his rigid sense of the fitness of things, has found it impossible to bend to George Boleyn's parvenu pretensions. Sir Nicholas is a papist to his steel-capped toes, and is offended to his marrow by George's support of reformed teaching. So an issue of principle lies between them; but what trivial event has sparked the quarrel into life? Did George and his evil company make a racket outside the chamber of Sir Nicholas, while he was at some solemn business like admiring himself in the looking glass? He stifles a smile. 'Rafe, have a word with both gentlemen. Tell them to leash their dogs.' He adds, 'You do right to mention it.' He is interested, always, to hear of divisions between the courtiers and how they arose.

Soon after his sister became queen, George Boleyn had called him in and given him some instruction, about how he should handle his career. The young man was flaunting a bejewelled gold chain, which he, Cromwell, weighed in his mind's eye; in his mind's eye he removed George's jacket, unstitched it, wound the fabric on to the bolt and priced it; once you have been in the cloth trade, you don't lose your eye for texture and drape, and if you are charged with raising revenue, you soon learn to estimate a man's worth.

Young Boleyn had kept him standing, while he occupied the room's single chair. 'Remember, Cromwell,' he began, 'that though you are of the king's council, you are not a gentleman born. You should confine yourself to speech where it is demanded of you, and for the rest, leave it alone. Do not meddle in the affairs of those set above you. His Majesty is pleased to bring you often into his presence, but remember who it was who placed you where he could see you.'

It's interesting, George Boleyn's version of his life. He had always supposed it was Wolsey who trained him up, Wolsey who promoted him, Wolsey who made him the man he is: but George says no, it was the Boleyns. Clearly, he has not been expressing proper gratitude. So he expresses it now, saying yes sir and no sir, and I see you are a man of singular good judgement for your years. Why, your father Monseigneur the Earl of Wiltshire, your uncle Thomas Howard Duke of Norfolk, they could not have instructed me better. 'I shall profit by this, I assure you sir, and from now on conduct myself more humble-wise.'

George was mollified. 'See you do.'

He smiles now, thinking of it; returns to the scribbled agenda. His son Gregory's eyes flit about the table, as he tries to pick up what isn't said: now cousin Richard Cromwell, now Call-Me-Risley, now his father, and the other gentlemen who have come in. Richard Riche frowns over his papers, Call-Me fiddles with his pen. Troubled men both, he thinks, Wriothesley and Riche, and alike in some ways, sidling around the peripheries of their own souls, tapping at the walls: oh, what is that hollow sound? But he has to produce to the king men of talent; and they are agile, they are tenacious, they are unsparing in their efforts for the Crown, and for themselves.

'One last thing,' he says, 'before we break up. My lord the Bishop of Winchester has so pleased the king that, at my urging, the king has sent him again to France as ambassador. It is thought his embassy will not be a short one.'

Slow smiles ripple around the table. He watches Call-Me. He was once a protégé of Stephen Gardiner. But he seems as joyful as the rest. Richard Riche turns pink, rises from the table and wrings his hand.

'Get him on the road,' Rafe says, 'and let him stay away. Gardiner is double in everything.'

'Double?' he says. 'He has a tongue like a three-pronged eel spear. First he is for the Pope, then Henry, then, mark what I say, he will be for the Pope again.'

'Can we trust him abroad?' Riche says.

'We can trust him only to know where his advantage lies. Which is with the king for now. And we can keep an eye on him, put some of our men in his train. Master Wriothesley, you can see to that, I think?'

Only Gregory seems dubious. 'My lord Winchester, an ambassador? Fitzwilliam tells me, an ambassador's first duty is to give no affront.'

He nods. 'And Stephen gives nothing but affront, does he?'

'Is not an ambassador supposed to be a cheerful fellow and affable? So Fitzwilliam tells me. He should be pleasant in any company, conversable and easy, and he should endear himself to his hosts. So he has chances to visit their homes, sit at their boards, become friendly with their wives and their heirs, and corrupt their household to his service.'

Rafe's eyebrows shoot up. 'Is that what Fitz teaches you?' The boys laugh.

'It's true,' he says. 'That is what an ambassador must do. So I hope Chapuys is not corrupting you, Gregory? If I had a wife, he would be sneaking sonnets to her, I know it, and bringing in bones for my dogs. Ah well ... Chapuys, he is pleasant company, you

61

Bring Up the Bodies

see. Not like Stephen Gardiner. But the truth is, Gregory, we need a stout ambassador for the French, a man full of spleen and spite. And Stephen has been among them before, and done himself credit. The French are hypocrites, pretending false friendship and demanding money as the price of it. You see,' he says, setting himself to educate his son. 'Just now the French have a plan to take the duchy of Milan from the Emperor, and they want us to subsidise them. And we must accommodate them, or seem to, for fear they will veer about and join with the Emperor and overwhelm us. So when the day comes that they say, "Deliver over the gold you have promised," we need that kind of ambassador, like Stephen, who will brazen it out and say, "Oh, the gold? Just take it out of what you already owe King Henry." King Francis will be spitting fire, yet in a manner we will have kept our word. You understand? We save our fiercest champions for the French court. Recall that my lord Norfolk was sometime ambassador there.'

Gregory dips his head. 'Any foreigner would fear Norfolk.'

'And any Englishman too. With good reason. Now the duke is like one of those giant cannon the Turks have. The blast is shocking but it needs three hours' cooling time before it can fire again. Whereas Bishop Gardiner, he can explode at ten-minute intervals, dawn to dusk.'

'But sir,' Gregory bursts out, 'if we promise them money, and we don't deliver it, what will they do?'

'By then, I hope, we will be firm friends with the Emperor again.' He sighs. 'It is an old game and it seems we must go on playing it, until I think of something better, or the king does. You have heard of the Emperor's recent victory at Tunis?'

'The whole world is talking of it,' Gregory says. 'Every Christian knight wishes he had been there.'

He shrugs. 'Time will tell how glorious it is. Barbarossa will soon find another base for his piracy. But with such a victory behind him, and the Turk quiet for the moment, the Emperor may turn on us and invade our shores.'

62

'But how do we stop him?' Gregory looks desperate. 'Must we not have Queen Katherine back?

Call-Me laughs. 'Gregory begins to perceive the difficulties of our trade, sir.'

'I liked it better when we talked of the present queen,' Gregory says in a low voice. 'And I got the credit for observing she was fatter.'

Call-Me says kindly, 'I should not laugh. You have the right of it, Gregory. All our labours, our sophistry, all our learning both acquired or pretended; the stratagems of state, the lawyers' decrees, the churchmen's curses, and the grave resolutions of judges, sacred and secular: all and each can be defeated by a woman's body, can they not? God should have made their bellies transparent, and saved us the hope and fear. But perhaps what grows in there has to grow in the dark.'

'They say that Katherine is ailing,' Richard Riche says. 'If she should die within the year, I wonder what world would be then?'

But look: we have sat here too long! Let's be up and out into the gardens of Austin Friars, Master Secretary's pride; he wants the plants he saw flowering abroad, he wants better fruit, so he nags the ambassadors to send him shoots and cuttings in the diplomatic bag. The keen young clerks stand by, ready to break a code, and all that tumbles out is a rootball, still pulsing with life after a journey through the straits of Dover.

He wants tender things to live, young men to thrive. So he has built a tennis court, a gift to Richard and Gregory and all the young men of his house. He is not quite beyond the game himself … if he could play a blind man, he says, or an opponent with one leg. Much of the game is tactics; his foot drags, he has to rely on cunning rather than speed. But he is proud of his building and glad to stand the expense. He has recently consulted with the king's keepers of tennis at Hampton Court, and had the measurements adjusted to those Henry prefers; the king has been to

Austin Friars to dine, so it is not unpossible that one day he may call in for an afternoon on the court.

In Italy, when he was a servant in Frescobaldi's household, the boys would go out in the hot evening and play games in the street. It was tennis of a kind, a *jeu de paume*, no racquets but just the hand; they would jostle and push and scream, bounce the ball off the walls and run it along a tailor's awning, till the master himself would come out and scold: 'If you boys don't respect my awning, I'll shear off your testicles and hang them over the doorway on a ribbon.' They would say sorry, master, sorry, and back off down the street, and play subdued in a back court. But half an hour later they would be back again, and he can still hear it in his dreams, the rattle as the ball's crude seam hit metal and skimmed into the air; he can feel the slap of leather against his palm. In those days, though he was carrying an injury he tried to run the stiffness off: this injury he'd got the other year, when he was at Garigliano with the French army. The *garzoni* would say, look Tommaso, how is it you got the wound in the back of the leg, were you running away? He would say, Mother of God, yes: I was only paid enough for running away, if you want me facing the front you have to pay me extra.

From this massacre the French scattered, and in those days he was French; the King of France paid his wages. He had crawled then limped, he and his comrades dragging their battered bodies as fast as they could from the victorious Spanish, trying to struggle back to ground not bogged with blood; they were wild Welsh bowmen and renegade Switzers, and a few English boys like himself, all of them more or less confused and penniless, gathering their wits in the aftermath of the rout, plotting a course, changing their nation and their names at need, washing up in the cities to the north, looking for the next battle or some safer trade.

At the back gate of a great house, a steward had interrogated him: 'French?'

'English.'

The man had rolled his eyes. 'So what can you do?'

'I can fight.'

'Evidently, not well enough.'

'I can cook.'

'We have no need of barbarous cuisine.'

'I can cast accounts.'

'This is a banking house. We are well supplied.'

'Tell me what you want done. I can do it.' (Already he boasts like an Italian.)

'We want a labourer. What is your name?'

'Hercules,' he says.

Against his better judgement, the man laughs. 'Come in, Ercole.'

Ercole limps in, over the threshold. The man bustles about his own duties. He sits down on a step, nearly weeping with pain. He looks around him. All he has is this floor. This floor is his world. He is hungry, he is thirsty, he is over seven hundred miles from home. But this floor can be improved. 'Jesus, Mary and Joseph!' he shouts. 'Water! Bucket! *Allez, allez!*'

They go. Quick they go. A pail arrives. He improves this floor. He improves this house. He does not improve it without resistance. They start him off in the kitchen, where as a foreigner he is ill-received, and where with the blades and spits and boiling water there is so much possibility for violence. But he is better at fighting than you would think: lacking in height, without skill or craft, but almost impossible to knock over. And what aids him is the fame of his countrymen, feared through Europe as brawlers and looters and rapists and thieves. As he cannot abuse his colleagues in their own language, he uses Putney. He teaches them terrible English oaths – 'By the bleeding nail-holes of Christ' – which they can use to relieve their feelings behind the backs of their masters. When the girl comes in the mornings, the herbs in her basket damp with dew, they step back, appreciate her and ask,

'Well, sweetheart, and how are you today?' When somebody interrupts a tricky task, they say, 'Why don't you fuck off out of here, or I'll boil your head in this pot.'

Before long he understood that fortune had brought him to the door of one of the city's ancient families, who not only dealt in money and silk, wool and wine, but also had great poets in their lineage. Francisco Frescobaldi, the master, came to the kitchen to talk to him. He did not share the general prejudice against Englishmen, rather he thought of them as lucky; although, he said, some of his ancestors had been brought close to ruin by the unpaid debts of kings of England long ago dead. He had little English himself and he said, we can always use your countrymen, there are many letters to write; you can write, I hope? When he, Tommaso or Ercole, had improved in Tuscan so much that he was able to express himself and make jokes, Frescobaldi had promised, one day I will call you to the counting house. I will make trial of you.

That day came. He was tried and he won. From Florence he went to Venice, to Rome: and when he dreams of those cities, as sometimes he does, a residual swagger trails him into his day, a trace of the young Italian he was. He thinks back to his younger self with no indulgence, but no blame either. He has always done what was needed to survive, and if his judgement of what was necessary was sometimes questionable … that is what it is to be young. Nowadays he takes poor scholars into his family. There's always a job for them, some niche where they can scribble away at tracts on good government or translations of the psalms. But he will also take in young men who are rough and wild, as he was rough and wild, because he knows if he is patient with them they will be loyal to him. Even now, he loves Frescobaldi like a father. Custom stales the intimacies of marriage, children grow truculent and rebel, but a good master gives more than he takes and his benevolence guides you through your life. Think of Wolsey. To his inner ear, the cardinal speaks. He says, I saw you, Crumb, when you were at Elvetham: scratching your balls in the dawn and wondering at the violence of the king's whims. If he wants a new wife, fix him one. I didn't, and I am dead.

Thurston's cake must have failed because it doesn't appear that evening at supper, but there is a very good jelly in the shape of a castle. 'Thurston has a licence to crenellate,' Richard Cromwell says, and immediately throws himself into a dispute with an Italian across the table: which is the best shape for a fort, circular or star-shaped?

The castle is made in stripes of red and white, the red a deep crimson and the white perfectly clear, so the walls seem to float. There are edible archers peeping from the battlements, shooting candied arrows. It even makes the Solicitor General smile. 'I wish my little girls could see it.'

'I'll send the moulds to your house. Though perhaps not a fort. A flower garden?' What pleases little girls? He's forgotten.

After supper, if there are no messengers pounding at the door, he will often steal an hour to be among his books. He keeps them at all his properties: at Austin Friars, at the Rolls House at Chancery Lane, at Stepney, at Hackney. There are books these days on all sorts of subjects. Books that advise you how to be a good prince, or a bad one. Poetry books and volumes that tell you how to keep accounts, books of phrases for use abroad, dictionaries, books that tell you how to wipe your sins clean and books that tell you how to preserve fish. His friend Andrew Boorde, the physician, is writing a book on beards; he is against them. He thinks of what Gardiner said: you should write a book yourself, that would be something to see.

If he did, it would be The Book Called Henry: how to read him, how to serve him, how best to preserve him. In his mind he writes the preamble. 'Who shall number the qualities, both public and private, of this most blessed of men? Among priests, he is devout: among soldiers, valiant: among scholars, erudite: among courtiers, most gentle and refined: and all these qualities, King Henry possesses in such a remarkable degree that the like was never seen since the world began.'

Erasmus says that you should praise a ruler even for qualities he does not have. For the flattery gives him to think. And the qualities he presently lacks, he might go to work on them.

He looks up as the door opens. It is his little Welsh boy, backing in: 'Ready for your candles, master?'

'Yes, more than ready.' The light shivers, then settles against dark wood like discs pared from a pearl. 'You see that stool,' he says. 'Sit on it.'

The boy flops down. The demands of the household have had him on the run since early morning. Why is it always little legs that have to save big legs? *Just run upstairs and fetch me ...* It flattered you, when you were young. You thought you were important, indeed essential. He used to hurtle around Putney, on errands for Walter. More fool him. Now it pleases him to say to a boy, take your ease. 'I used to speak a bit of Welsh when I was a boy. I can't now.'

He thinks, that's the bleat of the man of fifty: Welsh, tennis, I used to, I can't now. There are compensations: the head is better stored with information, the heart better proof against chips and fractures. Just now he is undertaking a survey of the queen's Welsh properties. For this and weightier reasons, he keeps a keen eye on the principality. 'Tell me your life,' he asks the child. 'Tell me how you came here.' With the boy's own bit of English, he pieces together his tale: arson, cattle raids, the usual borderlands story, ending in destitution, the making of orphans.

'Can you say the Pater Noster?' he asks.

'Pater Noster,' says the boy. 'Or, Our Father.'

'In Welsh?'

'No, sir. There are no prayers in Welsh.'

'Dear Jesus. I'll get a man on it.'

'Do, sir. Then I can pray for my father and mother.'

'Do you know John ap Rice? He was at supper with us tonight.'

'Married to your niece Johane, sir?'

The boy darts off. Little legs at work again. It's his aim that all the Welsh will speak English, but that can't be yet, and meanwhile they need God on their side. Brigands cover the whole principality, and bribe and threaten their way out of gaol; pirates savage the coasts. Those gentlemen with territory there, like Norris and Brereton of the king's privy chamber, seem resistant to his interest. They put their own dealings before the king's peace. They do not care to have their activities overseen. They do not care for justice: whereas he means to make an equal justice, from Essex to Anglesey, Cornwall to the Scots border.

Rice brings in with him a little velvet box, which he puts down on the desk: 'Present. You have to guess.'

He rattles it. Something like grains. His finger explores fragments, scaly, grey. Rice has been surveying abbeys for him. 'It wouldn't be St Apollonia's teeth?'

'Guess again.'

'Is it teeth from the comb of Mary Magdalene?'

Rice relents. 'St Edmund's nail parings.'

'Ah. Tip them in with the rest. The man must have had five hundred fingers.'

In the year 1257, an elephant died in the Tower menagerie and was buried in a pit near the chapel. But the following year he was dug up and his remains sent to Westminster Abbey. Now, what did they want at Westminster Abbey, with the remains of an elephant? If not to carve a ton of relics out of him, and make his animal bones into the bones of saints?

According to the custodians of holy relics, part of the power of these artefacts is that they are able to multiply. Bone, wood and stone have, like animals, the ability to breed, yet keep their intact nature; the offspring are in no wise inferior to the originals. So the crown of thorns blossoms. The cross of Christ puts out buds; it flourishes, like a living tree. Christ's seamless coat weaves copies of itself. Nails give birth to nails.

John ap Rice says, 'Reason cannot win against these people. You try to open their eyes. But ranged against you are statues of the virgin that weep tears of blood.'

'And they say I play tricks!' He broods. 'John, you must sit down and write. Your compatriots must have prayers.'

'They must have a Bible, sir, in their own tongue.'

'Let me first get the king's assured blessing for the English to have it.' It is his daily, covert crusade: for Henry to sponsor a great Bible, put it in every church. He is very close now and he thinks he can win Henry to it. His ideal would be a single country, single coinage, just one method of weighing and measuring, and above all one language that everybody owns. You don't have to go to Wales to be misunderstood. There are parts of this realm not fifty miles from London, where if you ask them to cook you a herring they give you a blank look instead. Only when you've pointed to the pan and impersonated a fish do they say, ah, now I see what you mean.

But his greatest ambition for England is this: the prince and his commonwealth should be in accord. He doesn't want the kingdom to be run like Walter's house in Putney, with fighting all the time and the sound of banging and shrieking day and night. He wants it to be a household where everybody knows what they have to do, and feels safe doing it. He says to Rice, 'Stephen Gardiner says I should write a book. What do you think? Perhaps I might if one day I retire. Till then, why should I give my secrets away?'

He remembers reading Machiavelli's book, shut up in the dark days after his wife's death: that book which now begins to make such a stir in the world, though it is more talked about than actually read. He had been confined to the house, he, Rafe, the immediate household, so as not to take fever into the city; turning the book over, he had said, you cannot really pluck out lessons from

Italian principalities and apply them to Wales and the northern border. We don't work the same way. The book seemed almost trite to him, nothing in it but abstractions – virtue, terror – and small particular instances of base conduct or flawed calculation. Perhaps he could improve on it, but he has no time; all he can do, when business is so pressing, is to toss phrases to clerks, poised with their pens for his dictation: '*I heartily commend me to you … your assured friend, your loving friend, your friend Thomas Cromwell.*' No fee attaches to the post of Secretary. The scope of the job is ill-defined and this suits him; whereas the Lord Chancellor has his circumscribed role, Mr Secretary can inquire into any office of state or corner of government. He has letters from throughout the shires, asking him to arbitrate in land disputes or lend his name to some stranger's cause. People he doesn't know send him tittle-tattle about their neighbours, monks send accounts of disloyal words spoken by their superiors, priests sift for him the utterances of their bishops. The affairs of the whole realm are whispered in his ear, and so plural are his offices under the Crown that the great business of England, parchment and roll awaiting stamp and signet, is pushed or pulled across his desk, to himself or from himself. His petitioners send him malmsey and muscatel, geldings, game and gold; gifts and grants and warrants, lucky charms and spells. They want favours and they expect to pay for them. This has been going on since first he came into the king's favour. He is rich.

And naturally, envy follows. His enemies dig out what they can, about his early life. 'So, I went down to Putney,' Gardiner had said. 'Or, to be accurate, I sent a man. They said down there, who'd have thought that Put-an-edge-on-it would have risen so high? We all thought he'd be hanged by now.'

His father would sharpen knives; people would hale him in the street: Tom, can you take this, ask your father can he do aught with it? And he'd scoop it up, whatever blunt instrument: leave it with me, he'll put an edge on it.

'It's a skill,' he told Gardiner. 'Honing a blade.'
'You've killed men. I know it.'
'Not in this jurisdiction.'
'Abroad doesn't count?'
'No court in Europe would convict a man who struck in self-defence.'
'But do you ask yourself why people want to kill you?'
He had laughed. 'Why, Stephen – much in this life is a mystery but that is no mystery at all. I was always first up in the morning. I was always the last man standing. I was always in the money. I always got the girl. Show me a heap, and I'm on top of it.'
'Or a whore,' Stephen murmured.
'You were young once. Have you been to the king with your findings?'
'He should know what kind of man he employs.' But then, Gardiner had broken off; he, Cromwell, approached him smiling. 'Do your worst, Stephen. Put your men on the road. Lay out money. Search Europe. You will not hear of any talent I possess, that England cannot use.' He had eased from within his coat an imaginary knife; he pressed it home, softly, easily, under Gardiner's ribs. 'Stephen, have I not begged you often and often to reconcile with me? And have you not refused?'
Credit to Gardiner, he didn't flinch. Only with a kind of creeping of his flesh, and a pull on his robe, eased himself away from the airy blade. 'The lad you knifed in Putney died,' he said. 'You did well to run, Cromwell. His family had a noose for you. Your father bought them off.'
He is amazed. 'What? Walter? Walter did?'
'He didn't pay much. They had other children.'
'Even so.' He had stood dumbfounded. Walter. Walter paid them off. Walter, who never gave him anything more than a kick.
Gardiner laughed. 'You see. I know things about your life you don't know yourself.'

* * *

It is late now; he will finish up at his desk, then go to his cabinet to read. Before him is an inventory from the abbey at Worcester. His men are thorough; everything is here, from a fireball to warm the hands to a mortar for crushing garlic. And a chasuble of changeable satin, an alb of cloth of gold, the Lamb of God cut out in black silk; an ivory comb, a brass lamp, three leather bottles and a scythe; psalm books, song books, six fox-nets with bells, two wheelbarrows, sundry shovels and spades, some relics of St Ursula and her eleven thousand virgins, together with St Oswald's mitre and a stack of trestle tables.

These are sounds of Austin Friars, in the autumn of 1535: the singing children rehearsing a motet, breaking off, beginning again. The voices of these children, small boys, calling out to each other from staircases, and nearer at hand the scrabbling of dogs' paws on the boards. The chink of gold pieces into a chest. The susurration, tapestry-muffled, of polyglot conversation. The whisper of ink across paper. Beyond the walls the noises of the city: the milling of the crowds at his gate, distant cries from the river. His inner monologue, running on, soft-voiced: it is in public rooms that he thinks of the cardinal, his footsteps echoing in lofty vaulted chambers. It is in private spaces that he thinks of his wife Elizabeth. She is a blur now in his mind, a whisk of skirts around a corner. That last morning of her life, as he left the house he thought he saw her following him, caught a flash of her white cap. He had half turned, saying to her, 'Go back to bed': but no one was there. By the time he came home that night her jaw was bound and there were candles at her head and feet.

It was only a year before his girls died of the same cause. In his house at Stepney he keeps in a locked box their necklaces of pearl and coral, Anne's copy books with her Latin exercises. And in the store room where they keep their play costumes for Christmas, he still has the wings made of peacock feathers that Grace wore in a parish play. After the play she walked upstairs, still in her wings; frost glittered at the window. I am going to say my prayers, she said: walking away from him, furled in her feathers, fading into dusk.

And now night falls on Austin Friars. Snap of bolts, click of key in lock, rattle of strong chain across wicket, and the great bar fallen across the main gate. The boy Dick Purser lets out the watchdogs. They pounce and race, they snap at the moonlight, they flop under the fruit trees, heads on paws and ears twitching. When the house is quiet – when all his houses are quiet – then dead people walk about on the stairs.

Anne the queen sends for him to her own chamber; it is after supper. Only a step for him, as at every major palace rooms are reserved for him now, near the king's. Just a staircase: and there, with the light of a sconce lapping at its gold trim, is the stiff new doublet of Mark Smeaton. Mark himself is lurking inside it.

What brings Mark here? He is without musical instruments as an excuse, and he is got up as gorgeously as any of the young lords who wait on Anne. Is there justice? he wonders. Mark does naught and gets more bonny each time I see him, and I do everything and get more grey and paunchy by the day.

Since unpleasantness usually ensues between them, it is in his mind to pass by with a nod, but Mark stands up straight and smiles: 'Lord Cromwell, how are you?'

'Ah, no,' he says. 'Still plain master.'

'It is a natural mistake. You seem every inch the lord. And surely, the king will do something for you soon.'

'Perhaps not. He needs me in the House of Commons.'

'Even so,' the boy murmurs, 'it would seem ungracious in him, when others are rewarded for much less service. Tell me, they say you have got music scholars in your house?'

A dozen or so merry little boys, saved from the cloister. They work at their books and practise their instruments, and at table they learn their manners; at supper they entertain his guests. They practise with the bow, and play fetch with the spaniels, and the littlest ones drag their hobby horses over the cobbles, and follow him about, sir, sir, sir, look at me, do you want to see me stand on my hands? 'They keep the household lively,' he says.

'If you should ever want someone to put a polish on their performance, think of me.'

'I will, Mark.' He thinks, I wouldn't trust you around my little boys.

'You will find the queen discontented,' the young man says. 'You know her brother Rochford has lately gone into France on a special embassy, and today he has sent a letter; it seems to be the common talk over there that Katherine has been writing to the Pope, asking him to put into effect that wicked sentence of excommunication he has pronounced against our master. And which would result in untold hurts and perils to our realm.' He nods, yes, yes, yes; he does not need Mark to tell him what excommunication is; can he not make it short? 'The queen is angry,' the boy says, 'for if this is so, Katherine is a plain traitor, and the queen wonders, why do we not act against her?'

'Suppose I tell you the reason, Mark? Would you take it in to her? It seems you could save me an hour or two.'

'If you would entrust me –' the boy begins; then sees his cold smile. He blushes.

'I'd trust you with a motet, Mark. Although.' He looks at him thoughtfully. 'It does seem to me that you must stand high in the queen's favour.'

'Master Secretary, I believe that I do.' Flattened, Mark is already bouncing back. 'It is we lesser men, often, who are most fit for royal confidence.'

'Well then. Baron Smeaton, eh, before long? I shall be the first to congratulate you. Even if I am still toiling on the benches of the Commons.'

* * *

With a whisk of her hand, Anne shoos away the ladies around her, who bob to him and whisper out. Her sister-in-law, George's wife, lingers: Anne says, 'Thank you, Lady Rochford, I shall not need you again tonight.'

Only her fool stays with her: a dwarf woman, peeping at him from behind the queen's chair. Anne's hair is loose beneath a cap of silver tissue shaped like a crescent moon. He makes a mental note of it; the women about him always enquire what Anne is wearing. This is how she receives her husband, the dark tresses displayed only for him, and incidentally for Cromwell, who is a tradesman's son and doesn't matter, any more than the boy Mark does.

She begins, as she often does, as if in the middle of a sentence. 'So I want you to go. Up-country to see her. Very secret. Only take the men you need. Here, you may read my brother Rochford's letter.' She flourishes it at her fingers' ends, then changes her mind, whips it back. 'Or ... no,' she says, and decides to sit on it instead. Perhaps, amid the news, it contains dispraise of Thomas Cromwell? 'I am very suspicious of Katherine, very suspicious. It seems they know in France what we only guess at. Your people are not vigilant, perhaps? My lord brother believes the queen is urging the Emperor to invade, as is the ambassador Chapuys, who by the way should be banished this kingdom.'

'Well, you know,' he says. 'We can't go throwing ambassadors out. Because then we don't get to know anything at all.'

Truth is, he is not afraid of Katherine's intrigues: the mood between France and the Empire is at the moment unremittingly hostile, and if open war breaks out, the Emperor will have no troops to spare for invading England. These things swing about in a week, and the Boleyn reading of any situation, he has noticed, is always a little behind the times, and influenced by the fact that they pretend to have special friends at the Valois court. Anne is still in pursuit of a royal marriage for her ginger little daughter. He used to admire her as a person who learned from her mistakes, who would pull back, re-calculate; but she has a streak of stubbornness to equal that of Katherine, the old queen, and it seems in this matter she will never learn. George Boleyn has been over to France again, intriguing for the match, but with no result. What's George Boleyn *for*? That's a question he asks himself. He says, 'Highness, the king could not compromise his honour by any ill-treatment of the queen that was. If it became known, it would be a personal embarrassment to him.'

Anne looks sceptical; she does not grasp the idea of embarrassment. The lights are low; her silver head bobs, glittering and small; the dwarf fusses and chuckles, muttering to herself out of sight; seated on her velvet cushions, Anne dangles her velvet slipper, like a child about to dip a toe in a stream. 'If I were Katherine, I too would intrigue. I would not forgive. I would do as she does.' She gives him a dangerous smile. 'You see, I know her mind. Though she is a Spaniard, I can put myself in her place. You would not see me meek, if Henry cast me off. I too would want war.' She takes a strand of hair between fingers and thumb, runs its length, thoughtful. 'However. The king believes she is ailing. She and her daughter both, they are always mewling, their stomachs are disordered or their teeth falling out, they have agues or rheum, they are up all night puking and down all day moaning, and all their pain is due to Anne Boleyn. So look. Do you, Cremuel, go and see her without warning. Then tell me if she is feigning, or no.'

She maintains, as an affectation, a skittish slur in her speech, the odd French intonation, her inability to say his name. There is a stir at the door: the king is coming in. He makes a reverence. Anne does not rise or curtsey; she says without preliminary, 'I have told him, Henry, to go.'

'I wish you would, Cromwell. And give us your own report. There is no one like you for seeing into the nature of things. When the Emperor wants a stick to beat me with, he says his aunt is dying, of neglect and cold, and shame. Well, she has servants. She has firewood.'

'And as for shame,' Anne says, 'she should die inside, when she thinks of the lies she has told.'

'Majesty,' he says, 'I shall ride at dawn and tomorrow send Rafe Sadler to you, if you permit, with the day's agenda.'

The king groans. 'No escape from your big lists?'

'No, sir, for if I gave you a respite you would forever have me on the road, on some pretext. Till I return, would you just ... sit on the situation?'

Anne shifts in her chair, brother George's letter under her. 'I shall do nothing without you,' Henry says. 'Take care, the roads are treacherous. I shall be your beadsman. Good night.'

He looks about the outer chamber, but Mark has vanished, and there is only a knot of matrons and maids: Mary Shelton, Jane Seymour and Elizabeth, the Earl of Worcester's wife. Who's missing? 'Where is Lady Rochford?' he says, smiling. 'Do I see her shape behind the arras?' He indicates Anne's chamber. 'Going to bed, I think. So you girls get her installed and then you will have the rest of the night for your ill behaviour.'

They giggle. Lady Worcester makes creepy motions with her finger. 'Nine of the clock, and here comes Harry Norris, bare beneath his shirt. Run, Mary Shelton. Run rather slowly ...'

'Who do you run from, Lady Worcester?'

'Thomas Cromwell, I could not possibly tell you. A married woman like myself?' Teasing, smiling, she creeps her fingers along his upper arm. 'We all know where Harry Norris would like to lie tonight. Shelton is only his bedwarmer for now. He has royal ambitions. He will tell anyone. He is sick with love for the queen.'

'I shall play cards,' Jane Seymour says. 'With myself, so there will be no undue losses. Master, is there any news of the Lady Katherine?'

'I have nothing to tell you. Sorry.'

Lady Worcester's glance follows him. She is a fine woman, careless and rather free-spending, no older than the queen. Her husband is away and he feels she too could run rather slowly, if he gave her the nod. But then, a countess. And he a humble master. And sworn to the road before sunrise.

They ride up-country towards Katherine without banner or display, a tight knot of armed men. It is a clear day and bitter cold. The brown tussocky land shows through layers of hard frost, and herons flap from frozen pools. Clouds stack and shift on the horizon, slate-grey and a mild deceptive rose; leading them from early afternoon is a silvered moon as mean as a clipped coin. Christophe rides beside him, growing more voluble and disgusted the further they travel from urban comfort. '*On dit* the king chose a hard country for Katherine. He hopes the mould will get into her bones and she will die.'

'He has no such thought. Kimbolton is an old house but very sound. She has every comfort. Her household costs the king four thousand pounds a year. It is no mean sum.'

He leaves Christophe to ponder that locution: no mean sum. At last the boy says, 'Spaniards are *merde*, anyway.'

'You watch the track and keep Jenny's feet out of holes. Any spills and I'll have you follow me home on a donkey.'

'*Hi-han*,' Christophe bellows, loud enough to make the men at arms turn in their saddles. 'French donkey,' he explains.

French fuckwit, one says, amiably enough. Riding beneath dark trees at the close of that first day's travel, they sing; it lifts the tired heart, and dispels spirits lurking in the verges; never underestimate the superstition of the average Englishman. As this year closes, the favourite will be variations on the song the king wrote himself, 'Pastime with good company/I love and shall until I die.' The variations are only mildly obscene, or he would feel obliged to check them.

The landlord of their inn is a harassed wisp of a man, who does his futile best to find out whom he is entertaining. His wife is a strong, discontented young woman, with angry blue eyes and a loud voice. He has brought his own travelling cook. 'What, my lord?' she says. 'You think we'd poison you?' He can hear her banging around in the kitchen, laying down what shall and shan't be done with her skillets.

She comes to his chamber late and asks, do you want anything? He says no, but she comes back: what, really, nothing? You might lower your voice, he says. This far from London, the king's deputy in church affairs can perhaps relax his caution? 'Stay, then,' he tells her. Noisy she may be, but safer than Lady Worcester.

He wakes before dawn, so suddenly that he doesn't know where he is. He can hear a woman's voice from below, and for a moment he thinks he is back at the sign of the Pegasus, with his sister Kat crashing about, and that it is the morning of his flight from his father: that all his life is before him. But cautiously, in the dark chamber without a candle, he moves each limb: no bruises; he is not cut; he remembers where he is and what he is, and moves into the warmth the woman's body has left, and dozes, an arm thrown across the bolster.

Soon he hears his landlady singing on the stairs. Twelve virgins went out on a May morning, it seems. And none of them came back. She has scooped up the money he left her. On her face, as she greets him, no sign of the night's transaction; but she comes out and speaks to him, her voice low, as they prepare to ride. Christophe, with a lordly air, pays the reckoning to their host. The day is milder and their progress swift and without event. Certain images will be all that remain from his ride into middle England. The holly berries burning in their bushes. The startled flight of a woodcock, flushed from almost beneath their hooves. The feeling of venturing into a watery place, where soil and marsh are the same colour and nothing is solid under your feet.

* * *

Kimbolton is a busy market town, but at twilight the streets are empty. They have made no great speed, but it is futile to wear out horses on a task that is important, but not urgent; Katherine will live or die at her own pace. Besides, it is good for him to get out to the country. Squeezed in London's alleys, edging horse or mule under her jetties and gables, the mean canvas of her sky pierced by broken roofs, one forgets what England is: how broad the fields, how wide the sky, how squalid and ignorant the populace. They pass a wayside cross that shows recent signs of excavation at its base. One of the men at arms says, 'They think the monks are burying their treasure. Hiding it from our master here.'

'So they are,' he says. 'But not under crosses. They're not that foolish.'

In the main street they draw rein at the church. 'What for?' says Christophe.

'I need a blessing,' he says.

'You need to make your confession, sir,' one of the men says.

Smiles are exchanged. It is harmless, no one thinks the worse of him: only that their own beds were cold. He has noticed this: that men who have not met him dislike him, but when they have met him, only some of them do. We could have put up at a monastery, one of his guard had complained; but no girls in a monastery, I suppose. He had turned in the saddle: 'You really think that?' Knowing laughter from the men.

In the church's frigid interior, his escort flap their arms across their bodies; they stamp their feet and cry 'Brr,' like bad actors. 'I'll whistle for a priest,' Christophe says.

'You will do no such thing.' But he grins; can imagine his young self saying it, and doing it too.

But there is no need to whistle. Some suspicious janitor is edging in with a light. No doubt a messenger is stumbling towards the great house with news: watch out, make ready, lords are here. It is decorous for Katherine to have some warning, he feels, but not too much. 'Imagine it,' Christophe says, 'we might burst in on her when she is plucking her whiskers. Which women of that age do.'

To Christophe, the former queen is a broken jade, a crone. He thinks, Katherine would be my age, or thereabouts. But life is harsher to women, particularly women who, like Katherine, have been blessed with many children and seen them die.

Silently the priest arrives at his elbow, a timid fellow who wants to show the church's treasures. 'Now you must be …' He runs through a list in his head. 'William Lord?'

'Ah. No.' This is some other William. A long explanation ensues. He cuts it short. 'As long as your bishop knows who you are.' Behind him is an image of St Edmund, the man with five hundred fingers; the saint's feet are pointed daintily, as if he is dancing. 'Hold up the lights,' he says. 'Is that a mermaid?'

'Yes, my lord.' A shadow of anxiety crosses the priest's face. 'Must she come down? Is she forbidden?'

He smiles. 'I just thought she's a long way from the sea.'

'She's stinking fish.' Christophe yells with laughter.

'Forgive the boy. He's no poet.'

A feeble smile from the priest. On an oak screen St Anne holds a book for the instruction of her little daughter, the Virgin Mary; St Michael the Archangel hacks away with a scimitar at a devil entwining his feet. 'Are you here to see the queen, sir? I mean,' the priest corrects himself, 'the Lady Katherine?'

This priest doesn't know me from Adam, he thinks. I could be any emissary. I could be Charles Brandon, Duke of Suffolk. I could be Thomas Howard, Duke of Norfolk. They have both tried on Katherine their scant persuasive powers and their best bully-boy tricks.

He doesn't give his name, but he leaves an offering. The priest's hand enfolds the coins as if to warm them. 'You will forgive my slip, my lord? Over the lady's title? I swear I meant no harm by it. For an old countryman such as I am, it is hard to keep up with the changes. By the time we have understood one report from London, it is contradicted by the next.'

'It's hard for us all,' he says, shrugging. 'You pray for Queen Anne every Sunday?'

'Of course, my lord.'

'And what do your parishioners say to that?'

The priest looks embarrassed. 'Well, sir, they are simple people. I would not pay heed to what they say. Though they are all very loyal,' he adds hastily. 'Very loyal.'

'No doubt. Will you please me now, and this Sunday in your prayers remember Tom Wolsey?'

The late cardinal? He sees the old fellow revising his ideas. This can't be Thomas Howard or Charles Brandon: for if you speak the name of Wolsey, they can hardly restrain themselves from spitting at your feet.

When they leave the church, the last light is vanishing into the sky, and a stray snowflake drifts along towards the south. They remount; it has been a long day; his clothes feel heavy on his back. He doesn't believe the dead need our prayers, nor can they use them. But anyone who knows the Bible as he does, knows that our God is a capricious God, and there's no harm in hedging your bets. When the woodcock flew up in its flash of reddish brown, his heart had knocked hard. As they rode he was aware of it, each beat a heavy wing-beat; as the bird found the conceal-ment of trees, its tracing of feathers inked out to black.

They arrive in the half-dark: a hallooing from the walls, and an answering shout from Christophe: 'Thomas Cremuel, Secretary to the king and Master of the Rolls.'

'How do we know you?' a sentry bellows. 'Show your colours.'

'Tell him show a light and let me in,' he says, 'or I'll show his backside my boot.'

He has to say these things, when he's up-country; it's expected of him, the king's common adviser.

The drawbridge must come down for them: an antique scrape, a creak and rattling of bolts and chains. At Kimbolton they lock in early: good. 'Remember,' he says to his party, 'do not make the priest's mistake. When you talk to her household she is the Dowager Princess of Wales.'

'What?' Christophe says.

'She is not the king's wife. She never was the king's wife. She is the wife of the king's deceased brother, Arthur, Prince of Wales.'

'Deceased means dead,' Christophe says. 'I know it.'

'She is not a queen, or former queen, as her second so-called marriage was not licit.'

'That is, not permissible,' Christophe says. 'She make the mistake of conjugation with both brothers, Arthur first then Henry.'

'And what are we to think of such a woman?' he says, smiling.

Flare of torches and, taking form out of dimness, Sir Edmund Bedingfield: Katherine's keeper. 'I think you might have warned us, Cromwell!'

'Grace, you didn't want warning of me, did you?' He kisses Lady Bedingfield. 'I didn't bring my supper. But there's a mule cart behind me, it will be here tomorrow. I have venison for your own table, and some almonds for the queen, and a sweet wine that Chapuys says she favours.'

'I am glad of anything that will tempt her appetite.' Grace Bedingfield leads the way into the great hall. In the firelight she stops and turns to him: 'Her doctor suspects she has a growth in her belly. But it may take a long course. When you would think she has suffered enough, poor lady.'

He hands his gloves, his riding coat, to Christophe. 'Will you wait upon her straight away?' Bedingfield asks. 'Though we were not expecting you, she may be. It is hard for us, because the townspeople favour her and word slips in with servants, you cannot prevent it, I believe they stand and signal from beyond the moat. I think she knows most of what goes on, who passes on the road.'

Two ladies, Spanish by their dress and well-advanced in age, press themselves against a plaster wall and look at him with resentment. He bows to them, and one remarks in her own tongue that this is the man who has sold the King of England's soul. The wall behind them is painted, he sees, with the fading figures of a scene from paradise: Adam and Eve, hand in hand, stroll among beasts so new to creation they have not yet learned their names. A small elephant with a rolling eye peeps shyly through the foliage. He has never seen an elephant, but understood them to be higher by far than a warhorse; perhaps it's not had time to grow yet. Branches bowed with fruit hang above its head.

'Well, you know the form,' Bedingfield says. 'She lives in that room and has her ladies – those ones – cook for her over the fire. You knock and go in, and if you call her Lady Katherine she kicks you out, and if you call her Your Highness she lets you stay. So I call her nothing. You, I call her. As if she were a girl that scrubs the steps.'

Katherine is sitting by the fire shrunk into a cape of very good ermines. The king will want that back, he thinks, if she dies. She glances up, and puts out a hand for him to kiss: unwilling, but more because of the chill, he thinks, than because she is reluctant to acknowledge him. She is jaundiced, and there is an invalid fug in the room – the faint animal scent of the furs, a vegetal stench of undrained cooking water, and the sour reek from a bowl with which a girl hurries away: containing, he suspects, the evacuated contents of the dowager's stomach. If she is ill in the night, perhaps she dreams of the gardens of the Alhambra, where she grew up: the marble pavements, the bubbling of crystal water into basins, the drag of a white peacock's tail and the scent of lemons. I could have brought her a lemon in my saddlebag, he thinks.

As if reading his thoughts, she speaks to him in Castilian. 'Master Cromwell, let us abandon this weary pretence that you do not speak my language.'

He nods. 'It has been hard in times past, standing by while your maids talked about me. "Jesu, isn't he ugly, do you think he has a hairy body like Satan?"'

'My maids said that?' Katherine seems amused. She withdraws her hand, out of his sight. 'They are long gone, those lively girls. Only old women remain, and a handful of licensed traitors.'

'Madam, those about you love you.'

'They report on me. All my words. They even listen in to my prayers. Well, master.' She raises her face to the light. 'How do you think I look? What will you say of me when the king asks you? I have not seen myself in a mirror these many months.' She pats her fur cap, pulls its lappets over her ears; laughs. 'The king used to call me an angel. He used to call me a flower. When my first son was born, it was the depths of winter. All England lay under snow. There were no flowers to be had, I thought. But Henry gave me six dozen roses made of the purest white silk. "White as your hand, my love," he said, and kissed my finger-tips.' A twitch beneath the ermine tells him where a bunched fist lies now. 'I keep them in a chest, the roses. They at least do not fade. Over the years I have given them to those who have done me some service.' She pauses; her lips move, a silent invocation: prayers for departed souls. 'Tell me, how is Boleyn's daughter? They say she prays a good deal, to her reformed God.'

'She has indeed a reputation for piety. As she has the approbation of the scholars and bishops.'

'They are using her. As she is using them. If they were true churchmen they would shrink from her in horror, as they would shrink from an infidel. But I expect she is praying for a son. She lost the last child, I am told. Ah well, I know how that is. I pity her from the bottom of my heart.'

'She and the king have hopes of another child soon.'

'What? Particular hope, or general hope?'

He pauses; nothing definite has been said; Gregory could be wrong. 'I thought she confided in you,' Katherine says sharply. She scans his face: is there some rift, some *froideur*? 'They say Henry pursues other women.' Katherine's finger strokes the fur: absently round and round, rubbing at the pelt. 'It is so soon. They have only been married such a little space. I suppose she looks at the women about her, and says to herself, always questioning, is it you, madam? Or you? It has always surprised me that those who are untrustworthy themselves are blind when placing their own trust. La Ana thinks she has friends. But if she does not give the king a son soon, they will turn on her.'

He nods. 'You may be right. Who will turn first?'

'Why should I alert her?' Katherine asks drily. 'They say that when she is crossed she carps like a common scold. I am not surprised. A queen, and she calls herself a queen, must live and suffer under the world's eye. No woman is above her but the Queen of Heaven, so she can look for no companionship in her troubles. If she suffers she suffers alone, and she needs a special grace to bear it. It appears Boleyn's daughter has not received this grace. I ask myself why that could be.'

She breaks off; her lips open and her flesh draws itself together, as if squirming away from her clothes. You are in pain, he starts to say, but she waves him to silence, it's nothing, nothing. 'Gentlemen about the king, who swear now they will lay down their lives for her smile, will soon offer their devotion to another. They used to offer that same devotion to me. It was because I was the king's wife, it was nothing to do with my person. But La Ana takes it as a tribute to her charms. And besides, it is not just the men she should fear. Her sister-in-law, Jane Rochford, now there is a vigilant young woman … when she served me she often brought secrets to me, love secrets, secrets I would perhaps rather not know, and I doubt her ears and eyes are less sharp nowadays.' Still her fingers work away, now massaging a spot near her breastbone. 'You wonder, how can Katherine, who is banished, know the workings of the court? That is for you to ponder.'

I don't have to ponder long, he thinks. It is Nicholas Carew's wife, a particular friend of yours. And it is Gertrude Courtenay, the Marquis of Exeter's wife; I caught her out in plotting last year, I should have locked her up. Perhaps even little Jane Seymour; though Jane has her own career to serve, since Wolf Hall. 'I know you have your sources,' he says. 'But should you trust them? They act in your name, but not in your best interests. Or those of your daughter.'

'Will you let the princess visit me? If you think she needs counsel to steady her, who better than I?'

'If it stood to me, madam ...'

'What harm can it do the king?'

'Put yourself in his place. I believe your ambassador Chapuys has written to Lady Mary, saying he can get her out of the country.'

'Never! Chapuys can have no such thought. I guarantee it in my own person.'

'The king thinks that perhaps Mary might corrupt her guards, and if permitted to make a journey to see you she might spur away, and take ship for the territories of her cousin the Emperor.'

It almost brings a smile to his lips, to think of the skinny, scared little princess embarking on such a desperate and criminal course of action. Katherine smiles too; a twisted, malicious smile. 'And then what? Does Henry fear my daughter will come riding back, with a foreign husband by her side, and turn him out of his kingdom? You can assure him, she has no such intention. I will answer for her, again, with my own person.'

'Your own person must do a good deal, madam. Guarantee this, answer for that. You have only one death to suffer.'

'I wish it might do Henry good. When my death arrives, in whatever manner, I hope to meet it in such a way as to set him an example when the time comes for his own.'

'I see. Do you think a lot about the king's death?'

'I think about his afterlife.'

'If you want to do his soul good, why do you continually obstruct him? It hardly makes him a better man. Do you never think that, if you had bowed to the king's wishes years ago, if you had entered a convent and allowed him to remarry, he would never have broken with Rome? There would have been no need. Sufficient doubt was cast upon your marriage for you to retire with a good grace. You would have been honoured by all. But now the titles you cling to are empty. Henry was a good son of Rome. You drove him to this extremity. You, not he, split Christendom. And I expect that you know that, and that you think about it in the silence of the night.'

There is a pause, while she turns the great pages of her volume of rage, and puts her finger on just the right word. 'What you say, Cromwell, is … contemptible.'

She's probably right, he thinks. But I will keep tormenting her, revealing her to herself, stripping her of any illusions, and I will do it for her daughter's sake: Mary is the future, the only grown child the king has, England's only prospect if God calls away Henry and the throne is suddenly empty. 'So you won't be giving me one of those silk roses,' he says. 'I thought you might.'

A long look. 'At least, as an enemy, you stand in plain sight. I wish my friends could bear to be as conspicuous. The English are a nation of hypocrites.'

'Ingrates,' he agrees. 'Natural liars. I've found it myself. I would rather the Italians. The Florentines, so modest. The Venetians, transparent in all their dealing. And your own race, the Spaniards. Such an honest people. They used to say of your royal father Ferdinand, that his open heart would undo him.'

'You are amusing yourself,' she says, 'at the expense of a dying woman.'

'You want a great deal of credit for dying. You offer guarantees on the one hand, you want privileges on the other.'

'A state such as mine, it usually buys kindness.'

'I am trying to be kind, but you do not see it. At the last, madam, can you not put your own will aside, and for the sake of your daughter, reconcile with the king? If you leave this world at odds with him, blame will be visited on her. And she is young and has her life to live.'

'He will not blame Mary. I know the king. He is not so mean a man.'

He is silent. She still loves her husband, he thinks: in some kink or crevice of her old leathern heart, she is still hoping for his footstep, his voice. And with his gift to her hand, how can she forget that he once loved her? After all, there must have been weeks of work in the silk roses, he must have ordered them long before he knew the child was a boy. 'We called him the New Year's prince,' Wolsey had said. 'He lived fifty-two days, and I counted every one.' England in winter: the pall of sliding snow, blanketing the fields and palace roofs, smothering tile and gable, slipping silent over window glass; feathering the rutted tracks, weighting the boughs of oak and yew, sealing the fishes under ice and freezing the bird to the branch. He imagines the cradle, curtained in crimson, gilded with the arms of England: the rockers huddled into their clothes: a brazier burning and the air fresh with the New Year scents of cinnamon and juniper. The roses brought to her triumphant bedside – how? In a gilded basket? In a long box like a coffin, a casket inlaid with polished shells? Or tumbled to her coverlet from a silk sheath embroidered with pomegranates? Two happy months pass. The child thrives. It is understood through the world that the Tudors have an heir. And then on the fifty-second day, a silence behind a curtain: a breath, not a breath. The women of the chamber snatch up the prince, crying in shock and fear; hopelessly crossing themselves, they cower by the cradle to pray.

'I will see what can be done,' he says. 'About your daughter. About a visit.' How perilous can it be to bring one little girl across country? 'I do think the king would permit it, if you would advise Lady Mary to be in all respect conformable to his will, and recognise him, as now she does not, as head of the church.'

'In that matter the Princess Mary must consult her own conscience.' She holds up a hand, palm towards him. 'I see you pity me, Cromwell. You should not. I have been prepared for death a long time. I believe that Almighty God will reward my efforts to serve him. And I shall see my little children again, who have gone before me.'

Your heart could break for her, he thinks: if it were not proof against breaking. She wants a martyr's death on the scaffold. Instead she will die in the Fens, alone: choke on her own vomit, like as not. He says, 'What about Lady Mary, is she also ready to die?'

'The Princess Mary has meditated on Christ's passion since she was an infant in the nursery. She will be ready when he calls.'

'You are an unnatural parent,' he says. 'What parent would risk a child's death?'

But he remembers Walter Cromwell. Walter used to jump on me with his big boots: on me, his only son. He gathers himself for one last effort. 'I have instanced to you, madam, a case where your stubbornness in setting yourself against the king and his council served only to bring about a result you most abhor. So you can be wrong, do you see? I ask you to consider that you may be wrong more than once. For the love of God, advise Mary to obey the king.'

'The Princess Mary,' she says, dully. She does not seem to have the breath for any further protest. He watches her for a moment, and prepares to withdraw. But then she looks up. 'I have wondered, master, in what language do you confess? Or do you not confess?'

'God knows our hearts, madam. There is no need for an idle formula, or for an intermediary.' No need for language either, he thinks: God is beyond translation.

* * *

He falls out of the door and almost into the arms of Katherine's keeper: 'Is my chamber ready?'

'But your supper ...'

'Send me up a bowl of broth. I am talked out. All I want is my bed.'

'Anything in it?' Bedingfield looks roguish.

So, his escort has informed on him. 'Just a pillow, Edmund.'

Grace Bedingfield is disappointed he has retired so early. She thought she would get all the court news; she resents being stuck out here with the silent Spaniards, a long winter ahead. He must repeat the king's instructions: utmost vigilance against the outside world. 'I don't mind if Chapuys's letters get through, it will keep her occupied working the cipher. She isn't important to the Emperor now, it's Mary he cares about. But no visitors, except under the king's seal or mine. Although –' He breaks off; he can see the day, next spring and if Katherine is still alive, when the Emperor's army is riding up-country, and it is necessary to snatch her out of their path and hold her hostage; it would be a poor show if Edmund refused to yield her. 'Look.' He shows his turquoise ring. 'You see this? The late cardinal gave it me, and I am known to wear it.'

'Is that it, the magic one?' Grace Bedingfield takes his hand. 'Melts stone walls, makes princesses fall in love with you?'

'This is the one. If any messenger brings you this, let him in.'

When he closes his eyes that night a vault rises above him, the carved roof of Kimbolton's church. A man ringing handbells. A swan, a lamb, a cripple with a stick, two lovers' hearts entwined. And a pomegranate tree. Katherine's emblem. That might have to go. He yawns. Chisel them into apples, that'll fix it. I'm too tired for unnecessary effort. He remembers the woman at the inn and feels guilty. He pulls a pillow towards him: just a pillow, Edmund.

When the innkeeper's wife spoke to him as they were mounting their horses, she had said, 'Send me a present. Send me a present from London, something you can't get here.' It will have to be something she can wear on her back, otherwise it will be vanished away by some light-fingered traveller. He will remember his obligation, but very likely by the time he returns to London he will have forgotten what she looked like. He had seen her by candlelight, and then the candle was out. When he saw her by daylight she could have been a different woman. Perhaps she was.

When he sleeps he dreams of the fruit of the Garden of Eden, outstretched in Eve's plump hand. He wakes momentarily: if the fruit is ripe, when did those boughs blossom? In what possible month, in what possible spring? Schoolmen will have addressed the question. A dozen furrowed generations. Tonsured heads bent. Chilblained fingers fumbling scrolls. It's the sort of silly question monks are made for. I'll ask Cranmer, he thinks: my archbishop. Why doesn't Henry ask Cranmer's advice, if he wants to be rid of Anne? It was Cranmer who divorced him from Katherine; he would never tell him he must go back to her stale bed.

But no, Henry cannot speak of his doubts in that quarter. Cranmer loves Anne, he thinks her the pattern of a Christian woman, the hope of good Bible readers all over Europe.

He sleeps again and dreams of the flowers made before the dawn of the world. They are made of white silk. There is no bush or stem to pluck them from. They lie on the bare uncreated ground.

He looks closely at Anne the queen, the day he brings back his report; she looks sleek, contented, and the benign domestic hum of their voices, as he approaches, tell him that she and Henry are in harmony. They are busy, their heads together. The king has his drawing instruments to hand: his compasses and pencils, his rules, inks and penknives. The table is covered in unscrolling plans, and in artificers' moulds and batons.

He makes them his reverence, and comes to the point: 'She is not well, and I believe it would be a kindness to let her have a visit from ambassador Chapuys.'

Anne shoots out of her chair. 'What, so he can intrigue with her more conveniently?'

'Her doctors suggest, madam, that she will soon be in her grave, and not able to work you any displeasure.'

'She would come out of it, flapping in her shroud, if she saw the chance to thwart me.'

Henry stretches out a hand: 'Sweetheart, Chapuys has never acknowledged you. But when Katherine is gone, and can no longer make trouble for us, I will make sure he bends his knee.'

'Nevertheless, I do not think he should go out of London. He encourages Katherine in her perversity, and she encourages her daughter.' She darts a glance at him. 'Cremuel, you agree, do you not? Mary should be brought to court and made to kneel before her father and swear the oath, and there on her knees she should beg pardon for her treasonous obstinacy, and acknowledge that my daughter, and not she, is heir to England.'

He indicates the plans. 'Not building, sir?'

Henry looks like a child caught with its fingers in the sugar box. He pushes one of the batons towards him. The designs, still novel to the English eye, are those he grew accustomed to in Italy: fluted urns and vases, mantled and winged, and the sightless heads of emperors and gods. These days the native flowers and trees, the winding stems and blossoms, are disdained for wreathed arms, for the laurels of victory, the shaft of the lictor's axe, the shaft of the spear. He sees that Anne's status is not served by simplicity; for more than seven years now, Henry has been adapting his taste to hers. Henry used to enjoy hedge wines, the fruits of the English summer, but now the wines he favours are heavy, perfumed, drowsy; his body is heavy, so sometimes he seems to block out the light. 'Are we building from the foundations?' he enquires. 'Or just a layer of ornamentation? Both cost money.'

'How ungracious you are,' Anne says. 'The king is sending you some oak for your own building at Hackney. And some for Master Sadler, for his new house.'

With a dip of his head he signals his thanks. But the king's mind is up-country, with the woman who still claims to be his wife. 'What use is Katherine's life to her, now?' Henry asks. 'I am sure she is tired of contention. God knows, I am tired of it. She were better to join the saints and holy martyrs.'

'They have waited for her long enough.' Anne laughs: too loudly.

'I picture the lady dying,' the king says. 'She will be making speeches and forgiving me. She is always forgiving me. It is she who needs forgiveness. For her blighted womb. For poisoning my children before they were born.'

He, Cromwell, flits his eyes to Anne. Surely now, if she has anything to tell, is the moment? But she turns away, leans down and scoops her spaniel Purkoy into her lap. She buries her face in his fur, and the little dog, startled from his sleep, whimpers and twists in her hands and watches Master Secretary bow himself out.

Outside waiting for him, George Boleyn's wife: her confiding hand, drawing him aside, her whisper. If someone said to Lady Rochford, 'It's raining,' she would turn it into a conspiracy; as she passed the news on, she would make it sound somehow indecent, unlikely, but sadly true.

'Well?' he says. 'Is she?'

'Ah. Has she said nothing still? Of course, the wise woman says nothing till she feels it quickening.' He regards her: stony-eyed. 'Yes,' she says at last, casting a nervous glance over her shoulder. 'She has been wrong before. But yes.'

'Does the king know?'

'You should tell him, Cromwell. Be the man with good news. Who knows, he might knight you on the spot.'

He is thinking, fetch me Rafe Sadler, fetch me Thomas Wriothesley, send a letter to Edward Seymour, whistle up my nephew Richard, cancel supper with Chapuys, but don't let our dishes go to waste: let's invite Sir Thomas Boleyn.

'I suppose it is to be expected,' Jane Rochford says. 'She was with the king for much of the summer, was she not? A week here, a week there. And when he was not with her, he would write her love letters, and send them by the hand of Harry Norris.'

'My lady, I must leave you, I have business.'

'I'm sure you have. Ah well. And you are usually such a good listener. You always attend to what I say. And I say that this summer he wrote her love letters, and sent them by the hand of Harry Norris.'

He is moving too fast to make much of her last sentence; though, as he will admit later, the detail will affix itself and adhere to certain sentences of his own, not yet formed. Phrases only. Elliptic. Conditional. As everything is conditional now. Anne blossoming as Katherine fails. He pictures them, their faces intent and skirts bunched, two little girls in a muddy track, playing teeter-totter with a plank balanced on a stone.

Thomas Seymour says at once, 'This is Jane's chance, now. He will hesitate no more, he will want a new bedfellow. He will not touch the queen till she gives birth. He cannot. There is too much to lose.'

He thinks, already perhaps the secret king of England has fingers, has a face. But I thought that before, he reminds himself. At her coronation, when Anne carried her belly so proudly; and after all, it was only a girl.

'I still don't see it,' says old Sir John, the adulterer. 'I don't see how he'd want Jane. Now if it were my daughter Bess. The king has danced with her. He liked her very well.'

'Bess is married,' Edward says.

Tom Seymour laughs. 'The more fit for his purpose.'

96

Edward is irate. 'Don't talk of Bess. Bess would not have him. Bess is not in question.'

'It could turn to good,' Sir John says, tentative. 'For until now Jane's never been any use to us.'

'True,' Edward says. 'Jane is as much use as a blancmange. Now let her earn her keep. The king will need a companion. But we do not push her in his way. Let it be as Cromwell here has advised. Henry has seen her. He has formed his intent. Now she must avoid him. No, she must repel him.'

'Oh, hoity-toity,' old Seymour says. 'If you can afford it.'

'Afford what's chaste, what's seemly?' Edward snaps. 'You never could. Be quiet, you old lecher. The king pretends to forget your crimes, but no one really forgets. You are pointed at: the old goat who stole his son's bride.'

'Yes, hold your peace, Father,' Tom says. 'We're talking to Cromwell.'

'One thing I am afraid of,' he says. 'Your sister loves her old mistress, Katherine. This is well known to the present queen, who spares no opportunity for harshness. If she sees that the king is looking at Jane, I am afraid she will be further persecuted. Anne is not one to sit by while her husband makes a – a companion – of another woman. Even if she thought it a temporary arrangement.'

'Jane will pay no heed,' Edward says. 'What though she gets a pinch or a slap? She will know how to bear herself patiently.'

'She will play him for some great reward,' says old Seymour.

Tom Seymour says, 'He made Anne a marquise before he had her.'

Edward's face is as grim as if he is ordering up an execution. 'You know what he made her. Marquise first. Queen thereafter.'

Parliament is prorogued, but London lawyers, flapping their black gowns like crows, settle to their winter term. The happy news seeps and leaks through the court. Anne lets out her bodices. Bets are laid. Pens scribble. Letters are folded. Seals pressed to wax. Horses are mounted. Ships set sail. The old families of England kneel and ask God why he favours the Tudors. King Francis frowns. Emperor Charles sucks his lip. King Henry dances.

The conversation at Elvetham, that early hour's confabulation: it is as if it had never been. The king's doubts about his marriage, it seems, have vanished.

Though in the desolate winter gardens, he has been seen walking with Jane.

Her family surround her; they call him in. 'What did he say, sister?' Edward Seymour demands. 'Tell me everything, everything he said.'

Jane says, 'He asked me if I would be his good mistress.'

They exchange glances. There is a difference between a mistress and a good mistress: does Jane know that? The first implies concubinage. The second, something less immediate: an exchange of tokens, a chaste and languorous admiration, a prolonged courtship … though it can't be very prolonged, of course, or Anne will have given birth and Jane will have missed her chance. The women cannot predict when the heir will see the light, and he can get no further with Anne's doctors.

'Look, Jane,' Edward tells her, 'this is no time to be shy. You must give us particulars.'

'He asked me if I would look kindly on him.'

'Kindly on him when?'

'For instance, if he wrote me a poem. Praising my beauty. So I said I would. I would thank him for it. I wouldn't laugh, even behind my hand. And I wouldn't raise any objection to any statements he might make in verse. Even if they were exaggerated. Because in poems it is usual to exaggerate.'

He, Cromwell, congratulates her. 'You have it covered from every angle, Mistress Seymour. You would have made a sharp lawyer.'

'You mean, if I had been born a man?' She frowns. 'But still, it is not likely, Master Secretary. The Seymours are not tradesmen.'

Edward Seymour says, 'Good mistress. Write you verse. Very well. Good so far. But if he attempts anything on your person, you must scream.'

Jane says, 'What if nobody came?'

He puts his hand on Edward's arm. He wants to stop this scene developing any further. 'Listen, Jane. Don't scream. Pray. Pray aloud, I mean. Mental prayer will not do it. Say a prayer with the Holy Virgin in it. Something that will appeal to His Majesty's piety and sense of honour.'

'I understand,' Jane says. 'Do you have a prayer book on your person, Master Secretary? Brothers? No matter. I will go and look for mine. I am sure I can find something that will fit the bill.'

In early December, he receives word from Katherine's doctors that she is eating better, though praying no less. Death has moved, perhaps, from the head of the bed to its foot. Her recent pains have eased and she is lucid; she uses the time to make her bequests. She leaves her daughter Mary a gold collar she brought from Spain, and her furs. She asks for five hundred masses to be said for her soul, and for a pilgrimage to be made to Walsingham.

Details of the dispositions make their way back to Whitehall. 'These furs,' Henry says, 'have you seen them, Cromwell? Are they any good? If they are, I want them sent down to me.'

Teeter-totter.

The women around Anne say, you would not think she was *enceinte*. In October she looked well enough, but now she seems to be losing flesh, rather than gaining. Jane Rochford tells him, 'You would almost think she is ashamed of her condition. And His Majesty is not attentive to her, as formerly he was attentive when her belly was big. Then, he could not do enough for her. He would cater to her whims and wait on her like a maid. I once

99

came in to find her feet in his lap, and he rubbing them like an ostler nursing some splay-hooved mare.'

'Rubbing doesn't help a splayed hoof,' he says, earnest. 'You have to trim it and fit a special shoe.'

Rochford stares at him. 'Have you been talking to Jane Seymour?'

'Why?'

'Never mind,' she says.

He has seen Anne's face as she watches the king, as she watches the king watching Jane. You expect black anger, and the enactment of it: scissored-up sewing, broken glass. Instead, her face is narrow; she holds her jewelled sleeve across her body, where the child is growing. 'I must not disturb myself,' she says. 'It could injure the prince.' She pulls her skirts aside when Jane passes. She huddles into herself, narrow shoulders shrinking; she looks cold as a doorstep orphan.

Teeter-totter.

The rumour in the country is that Master Secretary has brought a woman back from his recent trip to Hertfordshire, or Bedfordshire, and set her up in his house at Stepney, or at Austin Friars, or at King's Place in Hackney, which he is rebuilding for her in lavish style. She is the keeper of an inn, and her husband has been seized and locked up, for a new crime invented by Thomas Cromwell. The poor cuckold is to be charged and hanged at the next assize; though, by some reports, he has already been found dead in his prison, bludgeoned, poisoned, and with his throat cut.

III
Angels
Stepney and Greenwich,
Christmas 1535–New Year 1536

Christmas morning: he comes hurtling out in pursuit of whatever trouble is next. A huge toad blocks his path. 'Is that Matthew?'

From the amphibian mouth, a juvenile chortle. 'Simon. Merry Christmas, sir, how do you?'

He sighs. 'Overworked. Did you send your duties to your mother and father?'

The singing children go home in the summer. At Christmas, they are busy singing. 'Will you be going to see the king, sir?' Simon croaks. 'I bet their plays at court are not so good as ours. We are playing Robin Hood, and King Arthur is in it. I play Merlin's toad. Master Richard Cromwell plays the Pope and has a begging bowl. He cries "Mumpsimus sumpsimus, hocus pocus." We give him stones for alms. He threatens us with Hell.'

He pats Simon's warty skin. The toad clears his path with a ponderous hop.

Since his return from Kimbolton, London has closed around him: late autumn, her fading and melancholy evenings, her early dark. The sedate and ponderous arrangements of the court have enfolded him, entrapped him into desk-bound days prolonged by candlelight into desk-bound nights; sometimes he would give a king's ransom to see the sun. He is buying land in the lusher parts of England, but he has no leisure to visit it; so these farms, these ancient manors in their walled gardens, these watercourses with their little quays, these ponds with their gilded fish rising to the hook; these vineyards, flower gardens, arbours and walks, remain to him flat, each one a paper construct, a set of figures on a page of accounts: not sheep-nibbled margins, nor meadows where kine stand knee-deep in grass, not coppices nor groves where a white doe shivers, a hoof poised; but parchment domains, leases and freeholds delimited by inky clauses, not by ancient hedges or boundary stones. His acres are notional acres, sources of income, sources of dissatisfaction in the small hours, when he wakes up and his mind explores their geography: in these waking nights before sullen or frozen dawns, he thinks not of the freedom his holdings allow, but of the trampling intrusion of others, their easements and rights of way, their fences and vantage points, that allow them to impinge on his boundaries and interfere with his quiet possession of his future. Christ knows, he is no country boy: though where he grew up, in the streets near the quays, Putney Heath was at his back, a place to go missing. He spent long days there, running with his brethren, boys as rough as himself: all of them in flight from their fathers, from their belts and fists, and from the education they were threatened with if they ever stood still. But London pulled him to her urban gut; long before he sailed the Thames in Master Secretary's barge, he knew the currents and the tide, and he knew how much could be picked up, casually, at watermen's trades, by unloading boats and running crates in barrows uphill to the fine houses that lined the Strand, the houses of lords and bishops: the houses of men with whom, daily, he now sits down at the council board.

The winter court perambulates, its accustomed circuit: Greenwich and Eltham, the houses of Henry's childhood: Whitehall and Hampton Court, once the cardinal's houses. It is usual these days for the king, wherever the court resides, to dine alone in his private rooms. Outside the royal apartments, in the outer Watching Chamber or the Guard Chamber – in whatever that outer hall is named, in the palaces in which we find ourselves – there is a top table, where the Lord Chamberlain, head of the king's private household, holds court for the nobility. Uncle Norfolk sits at this table, when he is with us at court; so does Charles Brandon, Duke of Suffolk, and the queen's father, the Earl of Wiltshire. There is a table, somewhat lower in status, but served with due honour, for functionaries like himself, and for the old friends of the king who happen not to be peers. Nicholas Carew sits there, Master of the Horse; and William Fitzwilliam, Master Treasurer, who of course has known Henry since he was a boy. William Paulet, Master Comptroller, presides at the head of this board: and he wonders, until it is explained to him, at their habit of lifting their goblets (and their eyebrows) in a toast to someone not there. Till Paulet explains, half-embarrassed, 'We toast the man who sat here before me. Master Comptroller who was. Sir Henry Guildford, his blessed memory. You knew him, Cromwell, of course.'

Indeed: who did not know Guildford, that practised diplomat, that most studied of courtiers? A man of the king's own age, he had been Henry's right arm since he came to the throne, he an unpractised, well-meaning, optimistic prince of nineteen. Two glowing spirits, earnest in pursuit of glory and a good time, the master and servant had aged together. You would have backed Guildford to survive an earthquake; but he did not survive Anne Boleyn. His partisanship was clear: he loved Queen Katherine and said so. (And if I did not love her, he said, then propriety alone, and my Christian conscience, would compel me to back her case.) The king had excused him out of long friendship; only let us, he had pleaded, leave the matter unmentioned, the disagreement unstated. Do not mention Anne Boleyn. Make it possible for us to stay friends.

But silence had not been enough for Anne. The day I am queen, she had told Guildford, is the day you lose your job.

Madam, said Sir Henry Guildford: the day you become queen, is the day I resign.

And so he did. Henry said: Come on, man! Don't let a woman nag you out of your post! It's just women's jealousy and spite, ignore it.

But I fear for myself, Guildford said. For my family and my name.

Do not abandon me, said the king.

Blame your new wife, Henry Guildford said.

And so he quit the court. And went home to the country. 'And died,' says William Fitzwilliam, 'within a few short months. They say, of a broken heart.'

A sigh runs around the table. That's the way it takes men; life's work over, rural ennui stretching ahead: a procession of days, Sunday to Sunday, all without shape. What is there, without Henry? Without the radiance of his smile? It's like perpetual November, a life in the dark.

'Wherefore we remember him,' Sir Nicholas Carew says. 'Our old friend. And we drink a toast – Paulet here does not mind – to the man who would still be Master Comptroller, if the times were not out of joint.'

He has a gloomy way of making a toast, Sir Nicholas Carew. Levity is unknown to one so dignified. He, Cromwell, had been sitting at table for a week before Sir Nicholas deigned to turn a cold eye upon him, and nudge the mutton his way. But their relations have eased since then; after all, he, Cromwell, is an easy man to get along with. He sees that there is a camaraderie among men such as these, men who have lost out to the Boleyns: a defiant camaraderie, such as exists among those sectaries in Europe who are always expecting the end of the world, but who hope that, after the earth has been consumed by fire, they will be seated in glory: grilled a little, crisp at the edges and blackened in parts, but still, thanks be to God, alive for eternity, and seated at his right hand.

He knew Henry Guildford himself, as Paulet reminds him. It must be five years ago now that he had been entertained by him handsomely, at Leeds Castle down in Kent. It was only because Guildford wanted something, of course: a favour, from my lord cardinal. But still, he had learned from Guildford's table talk, from the way he ordered his household, from his prudence and discreet wit. More lately, he had learned from Guildford's example how Anne Boleyn could break a career; and how far they were from forgiving her, his companions at table. Men like Carew, he knows, tend to blame him, Cromwell, for Anne's rise in the world; he facilitated it, he broke the old marriage and let in the new. He does not expect them to soften to him, to include him in their companionship; he only wants them not to spit in his dinner. But Carew's stiffness bends a little, as he joins them in talk; sometimes the Master of the Horse swivels towards him his long, indeed somewhat equine head; sometimes he gives him a slow courser's blink and says, 'Well, Master Secretary, and how are you today?'

And as he searches for a reply that Nicholas will understand, William Fitzwilliam will catch his eye, and grin.

During December a landslide, an avalanche of papers has crossed his desk. Often he ends the day smarting and thwarted, because he has sent Henry vital and urgent messages and the gentlemen of the privy chamber have decided it's easier for them if they keep the business back till Henry's in the mood. Despite the good news he has had from the queen, Henry is testy, capricious. At any moment he may demand the oddest item of information, or pose questions with no answer. What's the market price of Berkshire wool? Do you speak Turkish? Why not? Who does speak Turkish? Who was the founder of the monastery at Hexham?

Seven shilling the sack, and rising, Majesty. No. Because I was never in those parts. I will find a man if one can be got. St Wilfred, sir. He closes his eyes. 'I believe the Scots razed it, and it was built up again in the time of the first Henry.'

'Why does Luther think,' the king demands, 'that I should come into conformity with his church? Should he not think of coming into conformity with me?'

About St Lucy's Day, Anne calls him in, taking him from the affairs of Cambridge University. But Lady Rochford is there to check him before he reaches her, put a hand on his arm. 'She is a sorry sight. She cannot stop blubbing. Have you not heard? Her little dog is dead. We could not face telling her. We had to ask the king himself to do it.'

Purkoy? Her favourite? Jane Rochford conducts him in, glances at Anne. Poor lady: her eyes are cried to slits. 'Do you know,' Lady Rochford murmurs, 'when she miscarried her last child, she did not shed a tear?'

The women skirt around Anne, keeping their distance as if she were barbed. He remembers what Gregory said: Anne is all elbows and points. You could not comfort her; even a hand extended, she would regard as a presumption, or a threat. Katherine is right. A queen is alone, whether in the loss of her husband, her spaniel or her child.

She turns her head: 'Cremuel.' She orders her women out: a vehement gesture, a child scaring crows. Unhurried, like bold corvines of some new and silky kind, the ladies gather their trains, flap languidly away; their voices, like voices from the air, trail behind them: their gossip broken off, their knowing cackles of laughter. Lady Rochford is the last to take wing, trailing her feathers, reluctant to yield the ground.

Now there is no one in the room but himself and Anne and her dwarf, humming in the corner, waggling her fingers before her face.

'I am so sorry,' he says, his eyes down. He knows better than to say, you can get another dog.

'They found him –' Anne throws out a hand, 'out there. Down in the courtyard. The window was open above. His neck was broken.'

She does not say, he must have fallen. Because clearly this is not what she thinks. 'Do you remember, you were here, that day my cousin Francis Bryan brought him from Calais? Francis walked in and I had Purkoy off his arm before you could blink. He was a creature who did no one harm. What monster would find it in their heart to pick him up and kill him?'

He wants to soothe her; she seems as torn, as injured, as if the attack had been on her person. 'Probably he crept out on the sill and then his paws slipped. Those little dogs, you expect them to fall on their feet like a cat, but they don't. I had a spaniel jumped out of my son's arms because she saw a mouse, and she snapped her leg. It's easily done.'

'What happened to her?'

He says gently, 'We could not mend her.' He glances up at the fool. She is grinning in her corner, and jerking her fists apart in a snapping motion. Why does Anne keep the thing? She should be sent to a hospital. Anne scrubs at her cheeks; all her fine French manners fallen away, she uses her knuckles, like a little girl. 'What is the news from Kimbolton?' She finds a handkerchief and blows her nose. 'They say Katherine could live six months.'

He does not know what to say. Perhaps she wants him to send a man to Kimbolton to drop Katherine from a height?

'The French ambassador complains he came twice to your house and you would not see him.'

'I was busy,' he shrugs.

'With?'

'I was playing bowls in the garden. Yes, twice. I practise constantly, because if I lose a game I am in a rage all day, and I go looking for papists to kick.'

Once, Anne would have laughed. Not now. 'I myself do not care for this ambassador. He does not give me his respect, as the envoy before did. None the less, you must be careful of him. You must do him all honour, because it is only King Francis who is keeping the Pope from our throats.'

Farnese as wolf. Snarling and dripping bloody drool. He is not sure she is in a mood to be talked to, but he will try. 'It is not for love of us that Francis helps us.'

'I know it is not for love.' She teases out her wet handkerchief, looking for a dry bit. 'Not for love of me, anyway. I am not such a fool.'

'It is only that he does not want the Emperor Charles to over-run us and make himself master of the world. And he does not like the bull of excommunication. He does not think it right that the Bishop of Rome or any priest should set himself up to deprive a king of his own country. But I wish France would see his own interest. It is a pity there is not a skilled man to open to him the advantages of doing as our sovereign lord has done, and taking the headship of his own church.'

'But there are not two Cremuels.' She manages a sour smile.

He waits. Does she know how the French now see her? They no longer believe she can influence Henry. They think she is a spent force. And though the whole of England has taken an oath to uphold her children, no one abroad believes that, if she fails to give Henry a son, the little Elizabeth can reign. As the French ambassador said to him (the last time he let him in): if the choice is between two females, why not prefer the elder? If Mary's blood is Spanish, at least it is royal. And at least she can walk straight and has control of her bowels.

From her corner the creature, the dwarf, comes shuffling towards Anne on her bottom; she pulls at her mistress's skirts. 'Get away, Mary,' Anne says. She laughs at his expression. 'Did you not know I have rebaptised my fool? The king's daughter is almost a dwarf, is she not? Even more squat than her mother. The French would be shocked if they saw her, I think a glimpse of her would scuttle their intentions. Oh, I know, Cremuel, I know what they are trying to do behind my back. They had my brother to and fro for talks, but they never meant to make a marriage with Elizabeth.' Ah, he thinks, she grasps it at last. 'They are trying for a match between the dauphin and the Spanish bastard. All the time they are smiling to my face and are working away behind my back. You knew this and you did not tell me.'

'Madam,' he murmurs, 'I tried.'

'It is as if I did not exist. As if my daughter had never been born. As if Katherine were still queen.' Her voice sharpens. 'I will not endure it.'

So what will you do? In the next breath she tells him. 'I have thought of a way. With Mary.' He waits. 'I might visit her,' she says. 'And not alone. With some gallant young gentlemen.'

'You do not lack for those.'

'Or why should you not visit her, Cremuel? You have some handsome boys in your train. Do you know the wretch has never had a compliment in her life?'

'From her father she has, I believe.'

'When a girl is eighteen, her father no longer counts with her. She craves other company. Believe me, I know, because once I was as foolish as any girl. A maiden of that age, she wants someone to write her a verse. Someone who turns his eyes to her and sighs when she enters the room. Admit now, this is what we have not tried. To flatter her, seduce her.'

'You want me to compromise her?'

'Between us we can contrive it. Do it yourself even, I care not, someone told me she liked you. And I should like to see Cremuel pretending to be in love.'

'It would be a foolish man who came near Mary. I think the king would kill him.'

'I am not suggesting he bed her. God save me, I would not impose it on any friend of mine. All that is needed is to have her make a fool of herself, and do it in public, so she loses her reputation.'

'No,' he says.

'What?'

'That is not my aim and those are not my methods.'

Anne flushes. Anger mottles her throat. She will do anything, he thinks. Anne has no limits. 'You will be sorry,' she says, 'for the way you speak to me. You think you are grown great and that you no longer need me.' Her voice is shaking. 'I know you are talking to the Seymours. You think it is secret but nothing is secret from me. It shocked me when I heard it, I can tell you, I did not think you would put your money on such a bad risk. What has Jane Seymour got but a maidenhead, and what use is a maidenhead, the morning after? Before the event she is the queen of his heart, and after it she is just another drab who could not keep her skirts down. Jane has neither looks nor wit. She will not hold Henry a week. She will be packed off to Wolf Hall and forgotten.'

'Perhaps so,' he says. There is a chance that she is right; he would not discount it. 'Madam, things were once happier between us. You used to listen to my advice. Let me advise you now. Drop your plans and schemes. Lay down the burden of them. Keep yourself in quietness till the child is born. Do not risk its wellbeing by agitating your mind. You have said yourself, strife and contention can mark a child even before it sees the light. Bend your mind to the king's desires. As for Jane, she is pale and inconspicuous, is she not? Pretend you do not see her. Turn your head from sights that are not for you.'

She leans forward in her chair, hands clenched on her knees. 'I will advise you, Cremuel. Make terms with me before my child is born. Even if it is a girl I will have another. Henry will never abandon me. He waited for me long enough. I have made the wait worth his while. And if he turns his back on me he will turn his back on the great and marvellous work done in this realm since I became queen – I mean the work for the gospel. Henry will never return to Rome. He will never bow his knee. Since my coronation there is a new England. It cannot subsist without me.'

Not so, madam, he thinks. If need be, I can separate you from history. He says, 'I hope we are not at odds. I give you homely advice, as friend to friend. You know I am, or I was, the father of a family. I always did counsel my wife to calmness at such a time. If there is anything I can do for you, tell me and I will do it.' He looks up at her. His eyes glitter. 'But do not threaten me, good madam. I find it uncomfortable.'

She snaps, 'Your comfort is not my concern. You must study your advantage, Master Secretary. Those who are made can be unmade.'

He says, 'I entirely agree.'

He bows himself out. He pities her; she is fighting with the women's weapons that are all she has. In the anteroom to her presence chamber, Lady Rochford is alone. 'Still snivelling?' she asks.

'I think she has gathered herself.'

'She is losing her looks, don't you think? Was she too much in the sun this summer? She is beginning to line.'

'I don't look at her, my lady. Well, no more than a subject ought.'

'Oh, you don't?' She is amused. 'Then I'll tell you. She looks every day of her age and more. Faces are not incidental. Our sins are written on them.'

'Jesus! What have I done?'

She laughs. 'Mr Secretary, that is what we all would like to know. But then, perhaps it is not always true. Mary Boleyn down in the country, I hear she blossoms like the month of May. Fair and plump, they say. How is it possible? A jade like Mary, through so many hands you can't find a stable lad who hasn't had her. But put the two side by side, and it is Anne who looks – how would you express it? Well-used.'

Chattering, the other ladies flock into the room. 'Have you left her alone?' says Mary Shelton: as if Anne ought not to be alone. She picks up her skirts and flits back to the inner chamber.

He takes his leave of Lady Rochford. But something is scuffling about his feet, impeding him. It is the dwarf woman, on all fours. She growls in her throat and makes as if to nip him. He just restrains himself from kicking her away.

He goes about his day. He wonders, how can it be for Lady Rochford, to be married to a man who humiliates her, preferring to be with his whores and making no secret of it? He has no means of answering the question, he admits; no point of entry into her feelings at all. He knows he doesn't like her hand on his arm. Misery seems to leak and seep from her pores. She laughs but her eyes never laugh; they flit from face to face, they take in everything.

The day Purkoy came from Calais to the court, he had held Francis Bryan by the sleeve: 'Where can I get one?' Ah, for your mistress, that one-eyed devil had enquired: fishing for gossip. No, he had said, smiling, just for myself.

Soon Calais was in an uproar. Letters flitting across the Narrow Sea. Master Secretary would like a pretty dog. Find him one, find him one quick, before someone else gets the credit. Lady Lisle, the governor's wife, wondered if she should part with her own dog. By one hand and another, a half-dozen spaniels were whisked in. Each was parti-coloured and smiling, with a feathered tail and delicate miniature feet. Not one of them was like Purkoy, with his ears pricked, his habit of interrogation. *Pourquoi?*

Good question.

Advent: first the fast and then the feast. In the store rooms, raisins, almonds, nutmegs, mace, cloves, liquorice, figs and ginger. The King of England's envoys are in Germany, holding talks with the League of Schmalkald, the confederation of Protestant princes. The Emperor is at Naples. Barbarossa is at Constantinople. The servant Anthony is in the great hall at Stepney, perched on a ladder and wearing a robe embroidered with the moon and stars. 'All right, Tom?' he shouts.

The Christmas star sways above his head. He, Cromwell, stands looking up at its silvered edges: sharp as blades.

It was only last month that Anthony joined the household, but it is hard to think of him as a beggar at the gate. When he had rode back from his visit to Katherine, the usual press of Londoners had gathered outside Austin Friars. They might not know him up-country, but they know him here. They come to stare at his servants, at his horses and their tack, at his colours flying; but today he rides in with an anonymous guard, a bunch of tired men coming from nowhere. 'Where've you been, Lord Cromwell?' a man bawls: as if he owes the Londoners an explanation. Sometimes he sees himself, in his mind's eye, dressed in filched cast-offs, a soldier from a broken army: a starving boy, a stranger, a gawper at his own gate.

They are about to pass into the courtyard, when he says, wait; a wan face bobs by his side; a little man has weaselled through the crowd, and catches at his stirrup. He is weeping, and so evidently harmless that no one even raises a hand to him; only he, Cromwell, feels his neck bristle: this is how you are trapped, your attention snared by some staged incident while the killer comes behind with the knife. But the men at arms are a wall at his back, and this bowed wretch is shaking so much that if he whipped out a blade he would peel his own knees. He leans down. 'Do I know you? I saw you here before.'

Tears trickle down the man's face. He has no visible teeth, a state that would upset anyone. 'God bless you, my lord. May he cherish you and increase your wealth.'

'Oh, he does.' He is tired of telling people he is not their lord.

'Give me a place,' the man begs. 'I am in rags, as you see. I will sleep with the dogs if it please you.'

'The dogs might not like it.'

One of his escort closes in: 'Shall I whip him off, sir?'

At this, the man sets up a fresh wailing. 'Oh, hush,' he says, as if to a child. The lament redoubles, the tears spurt as if he had a pump behind his nose. Perhaps he cried his teeth right out of his head? Is that possible?

'I am a masterless man,' the poor creature sobs. 'My dear lord was killed in an explosion.'

'God forgive us, what kind of explosion?' His attention is riveted: are people wasting gunpowder? We may need that if the Emperor comes.

The man is rocking himself, his arms clasped across his chest; his legs seem about to give way. He, Cromwell, reaches down and hauls him up by his sagging jerkin; he doesn't want him rolling on the ground and panicking the horses. 'Stand up. Give your name.'

A choked sob: 'Anthony.'

'What can you do, besides weep?'

'If it please you, I was much valued before … alas!' He breaks down entirely, wracked and swaying.

'Before the explosion,' he says patiently. 'Now, what was it you did? Water the orchard? Swill out the privies?'

'Alas,' the man wails. 'Neither of those. Nothing so useful.' His chest heaves. 'Sir, I was a jester.'

He lets go of his jerkin, stares at him, and begins to laugh. A disbelieving snigger runs from man to man through the crowd. His escort bow over their saddles, giggling.

The little man seems to bounce from his grip. He regains his balance and looks up at him. His cheeks are quite dry, and a sly smile has replaced the lineaments of despair. 'So,' he says, 'am I coming in?'

Now as Christmas approaches Anthony keeps the household open-mouthed with stories of the horrors that have come to people he knows, round and about the time of the Nativity: assault by innkeepers, stables catching fire, livestock wandering the hills. He does different voices for men and women, can make dogs talk impertinently to their masters, can mimic ambassador Chapuys and anyone else you name. 'Do you impersonate me?' he asks.

'You grudge me the opportunity,' Anthony says. 'A man could wish for a master who rolls his words around his mouth, or is always crossing himself and crying Jesu-Maria, or grinning, or frowning, or a man with a twitch. But you don't hum, or shuffle your feet or twirl your thumbs.'

'My father had a savage temper. I learned as a child to be still. If he noticed me, he hit me.'

'As for what is in there,' Anthony looks him in the eye, taps his forehead, 'as for what's in there, who knows? I may as well impersonate a shutter. A plank has more expression. A water butt.'

'I'll give you a good character, if you want a new master.'

'I'll get you in the end. When I learn to imitate a gatepost. A standing stone. A statue. There are statues who move their eyes. In the north country.'

'I have some of them in custody. In the strong rooms.'

'Can I have the key? I want to see if they are still moving their eyes, in the dark without their keepers.'

'Are you a papist, Anthony?'

'I may be. I like miracles. I have been a pilgrim in my time. But the fist of Cromwell is more proximate than the hand of God.'

On Christmas Eve Anthony sings 'Pastime With Good Company', in the person of the king and wearing a dish for a crown. He expands before your eyes, his meagre limbs fleshing out. The king has a silly voice, too high for a big man. It's something we pretend not to notice. But now he laughs at Anthony, his hand covering his mouth. When has Anthony seen the king? He seems to know his every gesture. I wouldn't be surprised, he thinks, if Anthony has been bustling about the court these many years, drawing a *per diem* and nobody asking what he's for or how he got on to the payroll. If he can imitate a king, he can easily imitate a busy useful fellow with places to be and business to see to.

Christmas Day comes. The bells peal at Dunstan's church. Snowflakes drift on the wind. Spaniels wear ribbons. It is Master Wriothesley who is first to arrive; he was a great actor when he was at Cambridge, and these last years he has been in charge of the plays in their household. 'Give me just a small role,' he had begged him. 'I could be a tree? Then I need not learn anything. Trees have an impromptu wit.'

'In the Indies,' Gregory says, 'trees can ambulate. They lift themselves up by their roots and if the wind blows they can move to a more sheltered spot.'

'Who told you that?'

'I'm afraid it was me,' says Call-Me-Risley. 'But he was so pleased to hear of it, I'm sure it was none harm.'

Wriothesley's pretty wife is dressed as Maid Marion, her hair loose and falling to her waist. Wriothesley is simpering in skirts, to which his toddling daughter clings. 'I've come as a virgin,' he says. 'They're so rare these days that they send unicorns out looking for them.'

'Go and change,' he says. 'I don't like it.' He lifts Master Wriothesley's veil. 'You're not very convincing, with that beard.'

Call-Me drops a curtsey. 'But I must have a disguise, sir.'

'We have a worm costume left,' Anthony says. 'Or you could be a giant striped rose.'

'St Uncumber was a virgin and grew a beard,' Gregory volunteers. 'The beard was to repulse her suitors and so guard her chastity. Women pray to her if they wish to be rid of their husbands.'

Call-Me goes to change. Worm or flower? 'You could be the worm in the bud,' Anthony suggests.

Rafe and his nephew Richard have come in; he sees them exchange a glance. He lifts Wriothesley's child in his arms, asks after her baby brother and admires her cap. 'Mistress, I have forgot your name.'

'I am called Elizabeth,' the child says.

Richard Cromwell says, 'Aren't you all, these days?'

I will win Call-Me, he thinks. I will win him away from Stephen Gardiner completely, and he will see where his true interest lies, and be loyal only to me and to his king.

When Richard Riche comes in with his wife he admires her new sleeves of russet satin. 'Robert Packington charged me six shillings,' she says, her tone outraged. 'And fourpence to line them.'

'Has Riche paid him?' He is laughing. 'You don't want to pay Packington. It only encourages him.'

When Packington himself arrives, it's with a grave face; it's clear he has something to say, and it's not just 'How do you?' His friend Humphrey Monmouth is by his side, a stalwart of the Drapers' Guild. 'William Tyndale is still in prison, and likely to be killed as I hear.' Packington hesitates, but clearly he must speak. 'I think of him in durance, as we enjoy our feast. What will you do for him, Thomas Cromwell?'

Packington is a gospel man, a reformer, one of his oldest friends. As a friend, he lays his difficulties before him: he himself cannot negotiate with the authorities in the Low Countries, he needs Henry's permission. And Henry will not grant it, as Tyndale would never give him a good opinion in the matter of his divorce. Like Martin Luther, Tyndale believes Henry's marriage to Katherine is valid, and no consideration of policy will sway him. You would think he would bend, to suit the King of England, to make a friend of him; but Tyndale is an obdurate man, plain and stubborn as a boulder.

'So must our brother burn? This is what you are telling me? A merry Christmas to you, Master Secretary.' He turns away. 'They say money follows you these days like a spaniel his master.'

He puts a hand on his arm: 'Rob –' Then pulls back, says heartily, 'They're not wrong.'

He knows what his friend thinks. Master Secretary is so powerful that he can move the king's conscience; and if he can, why does he not, unless he is too busy lining his pocket? He wants to ask, give me a day off, in Christ's name.

Monmouth says, 'You have not forgot our brothers whom Thomas More burned? And those he hounded to death? Those broken by months in prison?'

'He didn't break you. You lived to see More come down.'

'But his arm reached out of his grave,' Packington says. 'More had men everywhere, all about Tyndale. It was More's agents who betrayed him. If you cannot move the king, perhaps the queen can?'

'The queen needs help herself. And if you want to help her, tell your wives to curb their poisoned tongues.'

He moves away. Rafe's children – his stepchildren rather – are crying out to him to come and see their disguises. But the conversation, broken off, leaves a sour taste in his mouth that persists throughout the festival. Anthony pursues him with jokes, but he turns his eyes to the child dressed as an angel: it is Rafe's stepdaughter, the elder child of his wife Helen. She is wearing the peacock wings he made long ago for Grace.

Long ago? It is not ten years, not nearly ten. The feathers' eyes gleam; the day is dark, but banks of candles pick out threads of gold, the scarlet splash of holly berries bound on the wall, the points of the silver star. That night, as snowflakes float to earth, Gregory asks him, 'Where do the dead live now? Do we have Purgatory or not? They say it still exists, but no one knows where. They say we do no good by praying for the suffering souls. We cannot pray them out, as once we could.'

When his family died, he had done everything as was the custom in those days: offerings, masses. 'I don't know,' he says. 'The king will not allow preaching on Purgatory, it is so contentious. You can talk to Archbishop Cranmer.' A twist of his mouth. 'He'll tell you the latest thinking.'

'I take it very hard if I cannot pray for my mother. Or if they let me pray but say I am wasting my breath because nobody hears me.'

Imagine the silence now, in that place which is no-place, that anteroom to God where each hour is ten thousand years long. Once you imagined the souls held in a great net, a web spun by God, held safe till their release into his radiance. But if the net is

118

cut and the web broken, do they spill into freezing space, each year falling further into silence, until there is no trace of them at all?

He takes the child to a looking glass so she can see her wings. Her steps are tentative, she is in awe at herself. Mirrored, the peacock eyes speak to him. Do not forget us. As the year turns, we are here: a whisper, a touch, a feather's breath from you.

Four days later, Eustache Chapuys, the ambassador of Spain and the Holy Roman Empire, arrives in Stepney. He comes in to a warm welcome from the household, who approach him and wish him well in Latin and French. Chapuys is a Savoyard, speaks some Spanish but English hardly at all, though he is beginning to understand more than he speaks.

Back in the city their two households have been fraternising since a gusty autumn night when a fire started at the ambassador's lodging, and his wailing attendants, soot-blackened and carrying all they could salvage, came banging at the gates of Austin Friars. The ambassador lost his furniture and his wardrobe; one could not help laughing at the sight of him, wrapped in a scorched curtain with only a shirt beneath. His entourage spent the night on pallets on the floor of the hall, brother-in-law John Williamson having quit his chamber to allow the unexpected dignitary to occupy it. Next day the ambassador suffered the embarrassment of going into company in borrowed clothes too large for him; it was either that, or take the Cromwell livery, a spectacle from which an ambassador's career could never recover. He had set tailors to work at once. 'I don't know where we will replicate that violent flame-coloured silk you favour. But I'll put the word out in Venice.' Next day, he and Chapuys had walked over the ground together, under the blackened beams. The ambassador gave a low moan as he stirred with a stick the wet black sludge that had been his official papers. 'Do you think,' he had said, glancing up, 'that the Boleyns did this?'

The ambassador has never acknowledged Anne Boleyn, never been presented to her; he must forgo that pleasure, Henry has decreed, till he is ready to kiss her hand and call her queen. His allegiance is to the other queen, the exile at Kimbolton; but Henry says, Cromwell, sometime we will practise to bring Chapuys face to face with the truth. I should like to see what he would do, the king says, if he were put in Anne's path and could not avoid her.

Today the ambassador is wearing a startling hat. More like the sort that George Boleyn sports, than a hat for a grave councillor. 'What do you think, Cremuel?' He tilts it.

'Very becoming. I must get one of those.'

'Allow me to present you ...' Chapuys removes it from his head with a flourish, then reconsiders. 'No, it would not fit your big head. I shall have one made for you.' He takes his arm. '*Mon cher*, your household is a delight as always. But may we talk apart?'

In a private room, the ambassador attacks. 'They say that the king will command priests to marry.'

He is caught off-guard; but he does not mean to be jolted out of his good humour. 'There is some merit in it, for the avoiding of hypocrisy. But I can be clear with you, that will not happen. The king will not hear of it.' He looks closely at Chapuys; has he perhaps heard that Cranmer, Archbishop of Canterbury, has a secret wife? Surely he cannot know. If he did, he would denounce and ruin him. They hate Thomas Cranmer, these so-called Catholics, almost as much as they hate Thomas Cromwell. He indicates the best chair to the ambassador. 'Will you not sit and take a glass of claret?'

But Chapuys will not be diverted. 'I hear you are going to put all the monks and nuns out on the road.'

'From whom did you hear that?'

'From the mouths of the king's own subjects.'

'Listen to me, Monsieur. As my commissioners go about, I hear little from the monks but petitions to be let go. And nuns too, they cannot endure their bondage, they come to my men weeping and asking for their liberty. I have it in hand to pension the monks, or find them useful posts. If they are scholars they can be given stipends. If they are ordained priests, the parishes will use them. And the money the monks are sitting on, I should like to see some of that go to the parish priests. I do not know how it may be in your country, but some benefices only bring a man four or five shillings a year. Who will take on a cure of souls, for a sum that won't pay for his firewood? And when I have got the clergy an income they can live on, I mean to make each priest mentor to a poor scholar, so he helps him through the university. The next generation of priests will be learned, and they will instruct in their turn. Tell your master this. Tell him I mean good religion to increase, not wither.'

But Chapuys turns away. He is plucking nervously at his sleeve and his words fall over each other. 'I do not tell my master lies. I tell him what I see. I see a restless population, Cremuel, I see discontent, I see misery; I see famine, before the spring. You are buying corn from Flanders. Be thankful to the Emperor that he allows his territories to feed yours. That trade could be stopped, you know.'

'What would he gain by starving my countrymen?'

'He would gain this, that they would see how evilly they are governed, and how opprobrious are the king's proceedings. What are your envoys doing with the German princes? Talk, talk, talk, month after month. I know they hope to conclude some treaty with the Lutherans and import their practices here.'

'The king will not have the form of the Mass varied. He is clear on it.'

'Yet,' Chapuys stabs a finger in the air, 'the heretic Melanchthon has dedicated a book to him! You cannot hide a book, can you? No, deny it as you will, Henry will end by abolishing half the sacraments and making common cause with these heretics, on purpose to upset my master, who is their emperor and overlord.

121

Henry begins by mocking the Pope, and he will end up embracing the devil.'

'You appear to know him better than I do. Henry, I mean. Not the devil.'

He is amazed by the turn the conversation has taken. It is only ten days since he enjoyed a genial supper with the ambassador, and Chapuys assured him that the Emperor's only thought was for the realm's tranquillity. There was no talk of blockades then, no talk of starving England. 'Eustache,' he says, 'what has happened?'

Chapuys sits down abruptly, slumps forward with his elbows on his knees. His hat sinks lower, till he removes it altogether, and puts it on the table; not without a glance of regret. 'Thomas, I have heard from Kimbolton. They say the queen cannot keep her food down, she cannot even take water. In six nights she has not slept two hours together.' Chapuys grinds his fists into his eyes. 'I fear she cannot live more than a day or two. I do not want her to die alone, without anyone who loves her. I fear the king will not let me go. Will you let me go?'

The man's grief touches him; it comes from the heart, it is beyond his remit as envoy. 'We'll go to Greenwich and ask him,' he says. 'This very day. We'll go now. Put your hat back on.'

On the barge he says, 'That's a thaw wind.' Chapuys seems not to appreciate it. He huddles into himself, wrapped in layers of lambskin.

'The king intended to joust today,' he says.

Chapuys sniffs, 'In the snow?'

'He can have the field cleared.'

'No doubt by toiling monks.'

He has to laugh, at the ambassador's tenacity. 'We must hope the sport went forward, then Henry will be in a good humour. He has just come from the little princess at Eltham. You must ask after her health. And you must make her a New Year's gift, have you thought of it?'

The ambassador glowers at him. All he would give Elizabeth is a knock on the head.

'I am glad we are not iced up. Sometimes we cannot use the river for weeks. Have you seen it when it's frozen over?' No reply. 'Katherine is strong, you know. If there is no more snow and the king permits, you can ride tomorrow. She has been ill before and she has regained her ground. You will find her sitting up in bed and asking why you've come.'

'Why are you chattering?' Chapuys says gloomily. 'It is not like you.'

Why indeed? If Katherine dies it will be a great thing for England. Charles may be her fond nephew but he will not keep up a quarrel for a dead woman. The threat of war will vanish. It will be a new era. Only he hopes she does not suffer. There would be no point in that.

They tie up at the king's landing stage. Chapuys says, 'Your winters are so long. I wish I was still a young man in Italy.'

The snow is banked up on the quay, the fields are still blanketed. The ambassador received his education in Turin. You don't get this sort of wind there, shrieking around the towers like a soul in torment. 'You forget the swamps and the bad air, don't you?' he says. 'I'm like you, I only remember the sunshine.' He puts a hand under the ambassador's elbow to steer him on to dry land. Chapuys himself keeps a firm hold on his hat. Its tassels are damp and drooping, and the ambassador himself looks as if he might cry.

Harry Norris is the gentleman who greets them. 'Ah, "gentle Norris",' Chapuys whispers. 'One could do worse.'

Norris is, as always, the pattern of courtesy. 'We ran a few courses,' he says, in answer to enquiry. 'His Majesty had the best of it. You will find him cheerful. Now we are getting dressed for the masque.'

He never sees Norris but he remembers Wolsey stumbling from his own home before the king's men, fleeing to a cold empty house at Esher: the cardinal kneeling in the mud and gibbering his thanks, because the king by way of Norris had sent him a token of goodwill. Wolsey was kneeling to thank God, but it looked as if he were kneeling to Norris. It doesn't matter how Norris oils around him now; he can never wipe that scene from his mind's eye.

Inside the palace, a roaring heat, stampeding feet; musicians toting their instruments, upper servants bawling brutish orders at lower. When the king comes out to greet them, it is with the French ambassador at his side. Chapuys is taken aback. An effusive greeting is *de rigueur*; kiss-kiss. How smoothly, easily, Chapuys has slipped back into his persona; with what a courteous flourish he makes his reverence to His Majesty. Such a practised diplomat can even cajole his stiff knee joints; not for the first time, Chapuys reminds him of a dancing master. The remarkable hat he holds by his side.

'Merry Christmas, ambassador,' the king says. He adds hopefully, 'The French have already made me great gifts.'

'And the Emperor's gifts will be with Your Majesty at New Year,' Chapuys boasts. 'You will find them even more magnificent.'

The French ambassador eyes him. 'Merry Christmas, Cremuel. Not bowling today?'

'Today I am at your disposal, Monsieur.'

'I take my leave,' the Frenchman says. He looks sardonic; the king has already linked his arm with Chapuys's. 'Majesty, may I assure you in parting that my master King François has knit his heart to yours?' His glance sweeps over Chapuys. 'With the friendship of France, you may be assured you will reign unmolested, and need no longer fear Rome.'

'Unmolested?' he says: he, Cromwell. 'Well, ambassador, that's gracious of you.'

The Frenchman skims by him with a curt nod. Chapuys stiffens as French brocade grazes his own person; snatches his hat away, as if to save it from contamination. 'Shall I hold that for you?' Norris whispers.

But Chapuys has fastened his attention on the king. 'Katherine the queen ...' he begins.

'The Dowager Princess of Wales,' Henry says sternly. 'Yes, I hear the old woman is off her food again. Is that what you're here about?'

Harry Norris whispers, 'I have to dress up as a Moor. Will you excuse me, Mr Secretary?'

'Gladly, in this case,' he says. Norris melts away. For the next ten minutes he has to stand and hear the king lying fluently. The French, he says, have made him great promises, all of which he believes. The Duke of Milan is dead, both Charles and Francis claim the duchy, and unless they can resolve it there will be war. Of course, he is always a friend to the Emperor, but the French have promised him towns, they have promised him castles, a seaport even, so in duty to the commonweal he must think seriously about a formal alliance. However, he knows the Emperor has it in his power to make offers as good, if not better ...

'I will not dissemble with you,' Henry tells Chapuys. 'As an Englishman, I am always straight in my dealings. An Englishman never lies nor deceives, even for his own profit.'

'It seems,' Chapuys snaps, 'that you are too good to live. If you cannot mind your country's interests, I must mind them for you. They will not give you territory, whatever they say. May I remind you what poor friends the French have been to you these last months while you have not been able to feed your people? If it were not for the shipments of grain my master permits, your subjects would be corpses piled from here to the Scots border.'

Some exaggeration there. Lucky that Henry is in holiday humour. He likes feasts, pastimes, an hour in the lists, a masque in prospect; he likes even more the idea that his former wife is lying in the fens gasping her last. 'Come, Chapuys,' he says. 'We will have private conference in my chamber.' He draws the ambassador with him and, over his head, winks.

But Chapuys stops dead. The king must stop too. 'Majesty, we can speak of this hereafter. My mission now brooks no delay. I beg for permission to ride where the ... where Katherine is. And I implore you to allow her daughter to see her. It may be for the last time.'

'Oh, I could not be moving the Lady Mary around without my council's advice. And I see no hope of convening them today. The roads, you know. As for you, how do you propose to travel? Have you wings?' The king chuckles. He reasserts his grip and bears the ambassador away. A door closes. He, Cromwell, stands glaring at it. What further lies will be told behind it? Chapuys will have to bargain his mother's bones away to match these great offers Henry claims he has from the French.

He thinks, what would the cardinal do? Wolsey used to say, 'Never let me hear you claim, "You don't know what goes on behind closed doors." Find out.'

So. He is going to think of some reason to follow them in there. But here is Norris blocking his path. In his Moorish drapery, his face blacked, he is playful, smiling, but still vigilant. Prime Christmas game: let's fuck about with Cromwell. He is about to spin away Norris by his silken shoulder, when a small dragon comes waggling along. 'Who is in that dragon?' he asks.

Norris snorts. 'Francis Weston.' He pushes back his woolly wig to reveal his noble forehead. 'Said dragon is going to waggle waggle to the queen's apartments to beg for sweetmeats.'

He grins. 'You sound bitter, Harry Norris.'

Why would he not? He's served his time at the queen's door. On her threshold.

Norris says, 'She will play with him and pat his little rump. She's fond of puppy dogs.'

'Did you find out who killed Purkoy?'

126

'Don't say that,' the Moor beseeches. 'It was an accident.'

At his elbow, causing him to turn, is William Brereton. 'Where's that thrice-blasted dragon?' he enquires. 'I'm supposed to get after it.'

Brereton is dressed as an antique huntsman, wearing the skin of one of his victims. 'Is that real leopard skin, William? Where did you catch it, up in Chester?' He feels it critically. Brereton seems to be naked beneath it. 'Is that proper?' he asks.

Brereton snarls, 'It's the season of licence. If you were forced to impersonate an antique hunter, would you wear a jerkin?'

'As long as the queen is not treated to the sight of your *attributi*.'

The Moor giggles. 'He wouldn't be showing her anything she hasn't seen.'

He raises an eyebrow. 'Has she?'

Norris blushes easily, for a Moor. 'You know what I meant. Not William's. The king's.'

He holds up a hand. 'Please take note, I am not the one who introduced this topic. By the way, the dragon went in that direction.'

He remembers last year, Brereton swaggering through Whitehall, whistling like a stable boy; breaking off to say to him, 'I hear the king, when he does not like the papers you bring in to him, knocks you well about the pate.'

You'll be knocked, he had said to himself. Something in this man makes him feel he is a boy again, a sullen belligerent little ruffian fighting on the riverbank at Putney. He has heard it before, this rumour put about to demean him. Anyone who knows Henry knows it is impossible. He is the first gentleman of Europe, his courtesy unflawed. If he wants someone stricken, he employs a subject to do it; he would not sully his own hand. It is true they sometimes disagree. But if Henry were to touch him, he would walk away. There are princes in Europe who want him. They make him offers; he could have castles.

Now he watches Brereton, as he heads towards the queen's suite, bow slung over his furry shoulder. He turns to speak to Norris, but his voice is drowned out by a metallic clatter, a clash as of guardsmen: shouts of 'Make way for my lord the Duke of Suffolk.'

The duke's upper body is still armed; perhaps he has been out there in the yard, jousting by himself. His large face is flushed, his beard – more impressive year on year – spreads over his breast-plate. The valiant Moor steps forward to say, 'His Majesty is in conference with –' but Brandon knocks him aside, as if he were on a crusade.

He, Cromwell, follows on the duke's heels. If he had a net, he would drop it over him. Brandon bangs once on the king's door with his fist, then throws it open before him. 'Leave what you're doing, Majesty. You want to hear this, by God. You're quit of the old lady. She is on her deathbed. You will soon be a widower. Then you can get rid of the other one, and marry into France, by God, and lay your hands on Normandy as dowry ...' He notices Chapuys. 'Oh. Ambassador. Well, you can take yourself off. No use you staying for scraps. Go home and make your own Christmas, we don't want you here.'

Henry has turned white. 'Think what you are saying.' He approaches Brandon as if he might knock him down; which, if he had a poleaxe, he could. 'My wife is carrying a child. I am lawfully married.'

'Oh.' Charles blows out his cheeks. 'Yes, as far as that goes. But I thought you said –'

He, Cromwell, hurls himself towards the duke. Where in the name of Satan's sister did Charles get this notion? Marry into France? It must be the king's plan, as Brandon has none of his own. It looks as if Henry is carrying on two foreign policies: one he knows about and one he doesn't. He takes a grip on Brandon. He is a head shorter. He doesn't think he can move half a ton of idiot, still padded and partly armed. But it seems he can, he can

128

move him fast, fast, and try to get him out of earshot of the ambassador, whose face is astonished. Only when he has propelled Brandon across the presence chamber does he stop and demand, 'Suffolk, where do you get this from?'

'Ah, we noble lords know more than you do. The king makes plain to us his real intentions. You think you know all his secrets, but you are mistaken, Cromwell.'

'You heard what he said. Anne is carrying his child. You are mad if you think he will turn her out now.'

'He's mad if he thinks it's his.'

'What?' He pulls back from Brandon as if the breastplate were hot. 'If you know anything against the queen's honour, you are bound as a subject to speak plainly.'

Brandon wrenches his arm away. 'I spoke plain before and look where it got me. I told him about her and Wyatt, and he kicked me out of the court and back to the east country.'

'Drag Wyatt into this, and I'll kick you to China.'

The duke's face is congested with rage. How has it come to this? Only weeks ago, Brandon was asking him to be godfather to the son he has with his new little wife. But now the duke snarls, 'Get back to your abacus, Cromwell. You are only for fetching in money, when it comes to the affairs of nations you cannot deal, you are a common man of no status, and the king himself says so, you are not fit to talk to princes.'

Brandon's hand in his chest, shoving him back: once again, the duke is making for the king's person. It is Chapuys, frozen in dignity and sorrow, who imposes some order, stepping between the king and the heaving, boiling mass of the duke. 'I take my leave, Majesty. As always I find you a most gracious prince. If I am in time, as I trust I shall be, my master will be consoled to have news of his aunt's final hours from the hand of his own envoy.'

'I can do no less,' Henry says, sobered. 'God speed.'

'I ride at first light,' Chapuys tells him; rapidly, they walk away, through the morris men and the bobbing hobby horses, through a merman and his shoal, skirting round a castle that rumbles towards them, painted masonry on oiled wheels.

Outside on the quay Chapuys turns to him. Within his mind, oiled wheels must be revolving; what he has heard about the woman he calls the concubine, he will already be coding into dispatches. They cannot pretend between them that he did not hear; when Brandon bawls, trees fall in Germany. It would not be surprising if the ambassador were cawing in triumph: not at the thought of a French marriage, to be sure, but at the thought of Anne's eclipse.

But Chapuys keeps his countenance; he is very pale, very earnest. 'Cremuel,' he says, 'I note the duke's comments. About your person. About your position.' He clears his throat. 'For what it is worth, I am myself a man of humble origins. Though not perhaps so low …'

He knows Chapuys's history. His people are petty lawyers, two generations away from the soil.

'And again for what it is worth, I believe you are fit to deal. I would back you in any assemblage this side of Heaven. You are an eloquent and learned man. If I wanted an advocate to argue for my life, I would give you the brief.'

'You dazzle me, Eustache.'

'Go back to Henry. Move him that the princess might see her mother. A dying woman, what policy can it hurt, what interest …' One angry, dry sob breaks out of the poor man's throat. In a moment he recovers himself. He removes his hat, stares at it, as if he cannot think where he got it. 'I do not think I should wear this hat,' he says. 'It is more a Christmas hat, would you say? Still, I am loath to lose it, it is quite unique.'

'Give it to me. I will have it sent to your house and you can wear it on your return.' When you are out of mourning, he thinks. 'Look … I will not raise your hopes about Mary.'

'You being an Englishman, who never lies or deceives.' Chapuys gives a bark of laughter. 'Jesu-Maria!'

'The king will not permit any meeting that could strengthen Mary's spirit of disobedience.'

'Even if her mother is on her deathbed?'

'Especially then. We do not wants oaths, deathbed promises. You see that?'

He speaks to his bargemaster: I shall stay here and see how it goes with the dragon, whether he eats the hunter or what. Convey the ambassador up to London, he must prepare for a journey. 'But how will you get back yourself?' Chapuys says.

'Crawl, if Brandon has his way.' He puts his hand on the little man's shoulder. Says softly, 'This clears the way, you know? For an alliance with your master. Which will be very good for England and her trade, and is what you and I both want. Katherine has come between us.'

'And what about the French marriage?'

'There will be no French marriage. It is a fairy tale. Go. It will be dark in an hour. I hope you rest tonight.'

Already, twilight steals across the Thames; there are crepuscular deeps in the lapping waves, and a blue dusk creeps along the banks. He says to one of the boatmen, do you think the roads north will be open? God help me, sir, the man says: I only know the river, and anyway I've never stirred north of Enfield.

When he arrives back in Stepney torchlight spills out of the house, and the singing children, in a state of high excitement, are carolling in the garden; dogs are barking, black shapes bobbing against the snow, and a dozen mounds, ghostly white, tower over the frozen hedges. One, taller than the rest, wears a mitre; it has a stub of blue-tinged carrot for its nose, and a smaller stub for its cock. Gregory pitches towards him, a swirl of excitement: 'Look, sir, we have made the Pope out of snow.'

'First we made the Pope.' The glowing face beside him belongs to Dick Purser, the boy who keeps the watchdogs. 'We made the

Pope, sir, and then he looked harmless by himself and so we made a set of cardinals. Do you like them?'

His kitchen boys swarm about him, frosted and dripping. The whole household has turned out, or at least everyone under thirty. They have lit a bonfire – well away from the snowmen – and appear to be dancing around it, led by his boy Christophe.

Gregory gets his breath. 'We only did it for the better setting forth of the king's supremacy. I do not think it is wrong, because we can blow a trumpet then kick them flat, and cousin Richard said we may, and he himself moulded the Pope's head, and Master Wriothesley who was here looking for you thrust in the Pope's little member and laughed at it.'

'Such children you are!' he says. 'I like them very much. We will have the fanfare tomorrow when there's more light, shall we?'

'And can we fire a cannon?'

'Where would I get a cannon?'

'Speak to the king, sir.' Gregory is laughing; he knows the cannon is a step too far.

Dick Purser's sharp eye has fallen on the ambassador's hat. 'Might we borrow that? We have done ill with the Pope's tiara, because we did not know how it should look.'

He spins the hat in his hand. 'You're right, this is more the sort of thing Farnese wears. But no. This hat is a sacred charge. I have to answer to the Emperor for it. Now, let me go,' he says, laughing, 'I must write letters, we look for great changes soon.'

'Stephen Vaughan is here,' Gregory says.

'Is he? Ah. Good. I have a use for him.'

He tramps towards the house, firelight licking his heels. 'Pity Master Vaughan,' Gregory says. 'I think he came for his supper.'

'Stephen!' A hasty embrace. 'No time,' he says. 'Katherine is dying.'

'What?' his friend says. 'I heard nothing of this in Antwerp.'

Vaughan is always in transit. He is about to be in transit again. He is Cromwell's servant, he is the king's servant, he is the king's eyes and ears across the Narrow Sea; nothing passes with the Flemish merchants or the guilds at Calais that Stephen does not know and report. 'I am bound to say, Master Secretary, you keep a disorderly household. One might as well eat supper in a field.'

'You are in a field,' he says. 'More or less. Or you soon will be. You must get on the road.'

'But I am just off the ship!'

This is how Stephen manifests his friendship: constant complaints, carping and grumbles. He turns and issues orders: feed Vaughan, water Vaughan, bed down Vaughan, have a good horse ready to go at dawn. 'Don't fret, you can sleep the night. Then you must escort Chapuys up to Kimbolton. You speak the languages, Stephen! Nothing must pass in French or Spanish or Latin, but I know every word.'

'Ah. I see.' Stephen draws his person together.

'Because I think that if Katherine dies, Mary will be desperate to take ship for the Emperor's domains. He is her cousin, after all, and though she should not trust him, she cannot be convinced of that. And we can hardly chain her to the wall.'

'Keep her up-country. Keep her where there is no port in two days' ride.'

'If Chapuys saw an exit for her, she would fly on the wind and set to sea in a sieve.'

'Thomas.' Vaughan, a grave man, lays a hand upon him. 'What is all this agitation? It is not like you. You are afraid of being bested by a little girl?'

He would like to tell Vaughan what has passed, but how to convey the texture of it: the smoothness of Henry's lies, the solid weight of Brandon when he shoved him, dragged him, man-handled him away from the king; the raw wetness of the wind on his face, the taste of blood in his mouth. It will always be like this, he thinks. It will go on being like this. Advent, Lent, Whitsuntide. 'Look,' he sighs, 'I must go and write to Stephen Gardiner in France. If this is the end of Katherine, I must make sure he knows it from me.'

'No more grovelling to Frenchmen for our salvation,' Stephen says. Is that a grin? It is a wolfish one. Stephen is a merchant, and he values the Low Countries trade. When relations with the Emperor founder, England runs out of money. When the Emperor is on our side, we grow rich. 'We can patch all the quarrels,' Stephen says. 'Katherine was the cause of all. Her nephew will be as relieved as we are. He never wanted to invade us. And now he has enough to do with Milan. Let him scrap with the French if he must. Our king will be free. A free hand to do as he likes.'

That is what worries me, he thinks. This free hand. He makes his apologies to Stephen. Vaughan stops him. 'Thomas. You will wreck yourself with this pace you keep up. Do you ever consider, that half your years be spent?'

'Half? Stephen, I am fifty.'

'I forget.' A little laugh. 'Fifty already? I don't know you have changed much since ever I knew you.'

'That is an illusion,' he says. 'But I promise to take a rest, when you do.'

In his cabinet it is warm. He closes the shutters, insulating himself from the white glare without. He sits down to write to Gardiner, commending him. The king is very pleased with his embassy to France. He is sending funds.

He puts down his pen. Whatever possessed Charles Brandon? He knows there has been gossip that Anne's child is not Henry's. There has even been gossip that she is not with child at all, only pretending; and it is true she seems very uncertain when it will be born. But he had thought these rumours were blowing from France into England; and what would they know at the French court? He has dismissed it as empty malice. It is what Anne attracts; that is her misfortune, or one of them.

Under his hand there is a letter from Calais, from Lord Lisle. He feels exhausted at the thought of it. Lisle is telling him all about his Christmas Day, from his first waking in the frosty dawn. At some point in the festivities, Lord Lisle received an insult: the Mayor of Calais kept him waiting. So he, in his turn, kept the Mayor waiting ... and now both parties are writing to him: which is more important, Master Secretary, governor or mayor? Say it is me, say it is me!

Arthur Lord Lisle is the pleasantest man in the world; except, clearly, when the mayor cuts across him. But he is in debt to the king and has not paid a penny in seven years. He should perhaps do something about that; the treasurer of the king's chamber has sent him a note about it. And on that subject ... Harry Norris, by virtue of his position in the king's immediate household, by some custom the origin and use of which he has never fathomed, is in charge of the secret funds which the king has stashed in his principal houses, for use in some exigency; it is not clear what would free up these funds, or where they come from, or how much coin is stored, or who has access if Norris were to ... if Norris were to be off duty when the need arose. Or if Norris were to meet with some accident. Once again he lays down his quill. He starts to imagine accidents. He puts his head in his hands, fingertips over tired eyes. He sees Norris flying from his horse. Sees Norris tumbled in the mud. Says to himself, 'Get back to your abacus, Cromwell.'

His New Year gifts have started to come in already. A supporter in Ireland has sent him a roll of white Irish blankets and a flask of aqua vitae. He would like to swaddle himself in the blankets, drain the flask, roll over on the floor and sleep.

Ireland is quiet this Christmas, in greater peace than she has seen for forty years. Mainly he has brought this about by hanging people. Not many: just the right ones. It's an art, a necessary art; the Irish chiefs have been begging the Emperor to use the country as a landing stage, for his invasion of England.

He takes a breath. Lisle, mayor, insults, Lisle. Calais, Dublin, secret funds. He wants Chapuys to get to Kimbolton in time. But he doesn't want Katherine to rally. You should not desire, he knows, the death of any human creature. Death is your prince, you are not his patron; when you think he is engaged elsewhere, he will batter down your door, walk in and wipe his boots on you.

He sifts his papers. More chronicles of monks who sit in the alehouse all night and come reeling to the cloister at dawn; more priors found under hedges with prostitutes; more prayers, more pleas; tales of neglectful clergy who won't christen children or bury the dead. He sweeps them away. Enough. A stranger writes to him – an old man judging by his hand – to say that the conversion of the Mohammedans is imminent. But what sort of church can we offer them? Unless there is sweeping change soon, the letter says, the heathens will be in more darkness than before. And you are Vicar General, Master Cromwell, you are the king's vicegerent: what are you going to do about it?

He wonders, does the Turk work his people as hard as Henry works me? If I had been born an infidel I could have been a pirate. I could have sailed the Middle Sea.

As he turns up the next paper he almost laughs; some hand has laid before him a fat land grant, from the king to Charles Brandon. It is pastureland and woodland, furze and heath, and the manors sprinkled through it: Harry Percy, the Earl of Northumberland, has made over this land to the Crown in part payment of his massive debts. Harry Percy, he thinks: I told him I would bring him down for his part in destroying Wolsey. And by God, I have not broken sweat; with his manner of life he has destroyed himself. It only remains to take his earldom away, as I swore I would.

The door opens, discreetly; it is Rafe Sadler. He looks up, surprised. 'You should be with your household.'

'I heard you had been at court, sir. I thought there might be letters to write.'

'Go through these, but not tonight.' He bundles over the papers for the grants. 'Brandon may not get many such presents this New Year.' He tells Rafe what has passed: Suffolk's outburst, Chapuys's amazed face. He does not tell him what Suffolk said, about how he was not fit to deal in the affairs of his betters; he shakes his head and says, 'Charles Brandon, I was looking at him today ... you know how he used to be cried up as a handsome fellow? The king's own sister fell in love with him. But now, that big slab face of his ... he has no more grace than a dripping pan.'

Rafe pulls up a low stool and sits thinking, forearms laid on the desk, his head pillowed on them. They are used to each other's silent company. He inches a candle closer and frowns at some more papers, makes marginal marks. The king's face rises before him: not Henry as he was today, but Henry as he was at Wolf Hall, coming from the garden, his expression dazed, drops of rain on his jacket: and the pale circle of Jane Seymour's face by his side.

After a time he glances at Rafe: 'Are you all right down there, little man?'

Rafe says, 'This house always smells of apples.'

It is true; Great Place is set among orchards, and the summer seems to linger in the garrets where the fruit is stored. At Austin Friars the gardens are raw, saplings bound to stakes. But this is an old house; it was a cottage once, but it was built up for his own use by Sir Henry Colet, father of the learned Dean of St Paul's. When Sir Henry died Lady Christian lived out her days here, and then by Sir Henry's will the house devolved to the Mercers' Guild. He holds it on a fifty-year sub-lease, which should see him out, and Gregory in. Gregory's children can grow up wrapped in the aroma of baking, of honey and sliced apples, raisins and cloves. He says, 'Rafe. I must get Gregory married.'

'I'll make a memorandum,' Rafe says, and laughs.

A year ago, Rafe could not laugh. Thomas, his first child, had lived only a day or two after he was baptised. Rafe took it like a

Christian man, but it sobered him, and he was a sober young man already. Helen had children by her first husband, but had never lost one; she took it badly. Yet this year, after a long and harsh labour that frightened her, she has another son in the cradle, and they have called him Thomas too. May it bring him better fortune than his brother; reluctant as he was to come out and face the world, he seems strong, and Rafe has relaxed into fatherhood.

'Sir,' Rafe says. 'I have been wanting to ask. Is that your new hat?'

'No,' he says gravely. 'It is the hat of the ambassador of Spain and the Empire. Would you like to try it on?'

A commotion at the door. It is Christophe. He cannot enter in the ordinary way; he treats doors as his foe. His face is still black from the bonfire. 'A woman is here for you, sir. Very urgent. She will not be sent away.'

'What manner of woman?'

'Quite old. But not so old you would kick her downstairs. Not on a cold night like this.'

'Oh, for shame,' he says. 'Wash your face, Christophe.' He turns to Rafe. 'An unknown woman. Am I inky?'

'You'll do.'

In his great hall, waiting for him by the light of sconces, a lady who lifts her veil and speaks to him in Castilian: Maria, Lady Willoughby, once Maria de Salinas. He is aghast: how is this possible, he asks, she has come alone from her house in London, at night, in the snow?

She cuts him short. 'I come to you in desperation. I cannot get to the king. There is no time to lose. I must have a pass. You must give me a paper. Or when I arrive at Kimbolton they will not let me in.'

But he switches her to English; in any dealings with Katherine's friends, he wants witnesses. 'My lady, you cannot travel in this weather.'

'Here.' She fumbles for a letter. 'Read this, it is from the queen's physician, his own hand. My mistress is in pain and afraid and alone.'

He takes the paper. Some twenty-five years ago, when Katherine's entourage had first arrived in England, Thomas More had described them as hunchbacked pygmies, refugees from Hell. He cannot comment; he was still out of England himself, and far from the court, but it sounds like one of More's poetic exaggerations. This lady came a little later; she was Katherine's favourite; only her marriage to an Englishman had parted them. She was beautiful then, and now, a widow, she is beautiful still; she knows it and will use it, even when she is shrinking with misery and blue with cold. She swirls out of her cloak, and gives it to Rafe Sadler, as if he stood there for that purpose. She crosses the room and takes his hands. 'Mother of God, Thomas Cromwell, let me go. You will not refuse me this.'

He glances at Rafe. The boy is as immune to Spanish passion as he might be to a wet dog buffeting the door. 'You must understand, Lady Willoughby,' Rafe says coolly, 'that this is a family matter, not even a council matter. You may beseech Master Secretary all you like, but it is for the king to say who visits the dowager.'

'Look, my lady,' he says. 'The weather is filthy. Even if it thaws tonight, it will be worse up-country. I cannot guarantee your safety, even if I give you an escort. You might fall from your horse.'

'I will walk there!' she says. 'How will you stop me, Master Secretary? Keep me in chains? Will you have your black-faced peasant tie me up and lock me in a closet till the queen is dead?'

'You are ridiculous, madam,' Rafe says. He seems to feel some need to step in and protect him, Cromwell, from women's wiles. 'It is as Master Secretary says. You cannot ride in this weather. You are no longer young.'

Under her breath she utters a prayer, or curse. 'Thank you for your gallant reminder, Master Sadler, without your advice I might have thought myself sixteen. Ah, do you see, I am an Englishwoman now! I know how to say the opposite of what I mean.' A shadow of calculation crosses her face. 'The cardinal would have let me go.'

'Then what a pity he is not here to tell us about it.' But he takes the cloak from Rafe, places it around her shoulders. 'Go, then. I see you are determined. Chapuys is riding up there with a pass, so perhaps ...'

'I am sworn to be on the road at dawn. God turn his back on me, if I am not. I shall outpace Chapuys, he is not impelled as I am.'

'Even if you get there ... it is a harsh country and the roads barely worth the name. You might reach the castle itself and have a fall. Even under the walls.'

'What?' she says. 'Oh, I see.'

'Bedingfield has his orders. But he could not leave a lady in a snowdrift.'

She kisses him. 'Thomas Cromwell. God and the Emperor will requite you.'

He nods. 'I trust in God.'

She sweeps out. They can hear her voice raised in enquiry: 'What are these strange mounds of snow?'

'I hope they do not tell her,' he says to Rafe. 'She is a papist.'

'One never kisses me like that,' Christophe complains.

'Perhaps if you washed your face,' he says. He looks keenly at Rafe. 'You would not have let her go.'

'I would not,' Rafe says stiffly. 'The ruse would not have occurred to me. And even if it had ... no, I would not, I would have been afraid to cross the king.'

'That's why you will thrive and live to be old.' He shrugs. 'She will ride. Chapuys will ride. And Stephen Vaughan will watch them both. Are you coming tomorrow morning? Bring Helen and her daughters. Not the baby, it's too cold. We are going to have a fanfare, Gregory says, and then trample the papal court into the ground.'

'She loved the wings,' Rafe says. 'Our little girl. She wants to know if she can wear them every year.'

'I don't see why not. Till Gregory has a daughter big enough.'

They embrace. 'Try to sleep, sir.'

He knows Brandon's words will go round in his head when that head touches the pillow. 'When it comes to the affairs of nations you cannot deal, you are not fit to talk to princes.' Useless to swear vengeance on Duke Dripping Pan. He will undo himself, and perhaps for good this time, shouting around Greenwich that Henry is a cuckold. Surely even an old favourite cannot get away with that?

Besides, Brandon's right. A duke can represent his master at the court of a foreign king. Or a cardinal; even if he is low-born like Wolsey, his office in the church dignifies him. A bishop like Gardiner; he may be of dubious provenance, but by his office he is Stephen Winchester, incumbent of England's richest see. But Cremuel remains a nobody. The king gives him titles that no one abroad understands, and jobs that no one at home can do. He multiplies offices, duties pile on him: plain Master Cromwell goes out at morning, plain Master Cromwell comes in at night. Henry had offered him the Lord Chancellor's post; no, don't disturb Lord Audley, he had said. Audley does a good job; Audley, in fact, does as he's told. Perhaps, though, he should have agreed? He sighs, at the thought of wearing the chain. You cannot, surely, be both Lord Chancellor and Master Secretary? And he will not give up that post. It doesn't matter if it gives him a lesser status. It doesn't matter if the French don't comprehend. Let them judge by results. Brandon can make a racket, unreproved, near the royal person; he can slap the king on the back and call him Harry; he can chuckle with him over ancient jests and tilt-yard escapades. But chivalry's day is over. One day soon moss will grow in the tilt yard. The days of the moneylender have arrived, and the days of the swaggering privateer; banker sits down with banker, and kings are their waiting boys.

Last thing, he opens the shutter to say good night to the Pope. He hears a drip from a drainage spout above, he hears the deep groan as snow slides across the tiles above him, and falls in a clean sheet of white that for a second obliterates his view. His eyes follow it; with a little puff like white smoke, the fallen snow joins the trodden slush on the ground. He was right about the wind on the river. He draws the shutter closed. The thaw has begun. The great spoiler of souls, with his conclave, is left dripping in the dark.

At New Year he visits Rafe in his new house at Hackney, three storeys of brick and glass by St Augustine's church. On his first visit at summer's end, he had noted everything in place for Rafe's happy life: pots of basil on the kitchen sills, garden plots seeded and the bees in their hives, the doves in their cote and the frames in place for the roses that will climb them; the pale oak-panelled walls gleaming in expectation of paint.

Now the house is settled, bedded in, scenes from the gospels glowing on the wall: Christ as fisher of men, a startled steward tasting the good wine at Cana. In an upper room reached by the steep steps from the parlour, Helen reads Tyndale's gospel as her maids sew: '... by grace are ye saved.' St Paul may not suffer a woman to teach, but it is not exactly teaching. Helen has put off the poverty of her early life. The husband who beat her is dead, or gone so far away that we count him dead. She can become Sadler's wife, a rising man in Henry's service; she can become a serene hostess, a learned woman. But she cannot lose her history. One day the king will say, 'Sadler, why do you not bring your wife to court, is she very ugly?'

He will interrupt: 'No sir; very beautiful.' But Rafe will add, 'Helen is lowly born and does not know court manners.'

'Why did you wed her?' Henry will demand. And then his face will soften: Ah, I see, for love.

Now Helen takes his hands and wishes him a continuance of good fortune. 'I pray to God every day for you, for you were the origin of my happiness when you took me into your house. I pray him send you health and good luck and the king's listening ear.'

He kisses her and holds her close as if she were his daughter. His godson is howling in the next room.

On Twelfth Night the last marzipan moon is eaten up. The star is taken down, Anthony supervising. Its wicked points are fitted into their sleeves, and it is carried carefully to its store room. The peacock wings sigh into their linen shroud, and are hung on their peg behind the door.

Reports come from Vaughan that the old queen is better. Chapuys thinks so well of her that he is on the road back to London. He found her wasted, so weak that she could not sit up. But now she is eating again, taking comfort in the company of her friend Maria de Salinas; her gaolers were forced to admit this lady, after she suffered an accident under the very walls.

But later he, Cromwell, will hear of how on the evening of 6 January – just about the time, he thinks, that we were seeing our Christmas into store – Katherine grew restless. She felt herself failing, and during the night she told her chaplain that she would like to take communion: asking anxiously, what hour is it now? It is not yet four o'clock, he told her, but in case of urgency, the canonical hour can be advanced. Katherine waits it out, lips moving, a holy medal folded in her palm.

She will die that day, she says. She has studied death, many times anticipated it, and she is not shy at its approach. She dictates her wishes about her burial arrangements, which she does not expect to be observed. She asks for her household to be paid off, her debts to be settled.

At ten in the morning a priest anoints her, touching the holy oil to her eyelids and lips, her hands and feet. These lids will now

143

seal and not reopen, she will neither look nor see. These lips have finished their prayers. These hands will sign no more papers. These feet have finished their journey. By noon her breathing is stertorous, she is labouring to her end. At two o'clock, light cast into her chamber by the fields of snow, she resigns from life. As she draws her last breath, the sombre forms of her keepers close in. They are reluctant to disturb the aged chaplain, and the old women shuffling from her bedside. Before they have washed her, Bedingfield has put his fastest rider on the road.

8 January: the news arrives at court. It filters out from the king's rooms then runs riot up staircases to the rooms where the queen's maids are dressing, and through the cubby holes where kitchen boys huddle to doze, and along lanes and passages through the breweries and the cold rooms for keeping fish, and up again through the gardens to the galleries and bounces up to the carpeted chambers where Anne Boleyn sinks to her knees and says, 'At last God, not before time!' The musicians tune up for the celebrations.

Anne the queen wears yellow, as she did when she first appeared at court, dancing in a masque: the year, 1522. Everyone remembers it, or they say they do: Boleyn's second daughter with her bold dark eyes, her speed, her grace. The fashion for yellow had started among the wealthy in Basle; for a few months, if a draper could get hold of it, he could make a killing. And then suddenly it was everywhere, in sleeves and hose and even hair-bands for those who couldn't afford more than a sliver. By the time of Anne's debut it had slid down the scale abroad; in the domains of the Emperor, you'd see a woman in a brothel hoisting her fat dugs and tight-lacing her yellow bodice.

Does Anne know this? Today her gown is worth five times the one she wore when her father was her only banker. It is sewn over with pearls, so that she moves in a blur of primrose light. He says to Lady Rochford, do we call it a new colour, or an old colour come back? Will you be wearing it, my lady?

She says, I don't think it suits any complexion, myself. And Anne should stick to black.

On this happy occasion, Henry wants to show off the princess. You would think such a small child – she is now almost two and a half – would be looking about her for her nurse, but Elizabeth chuckles as she is passed hand-to-hand by the gentlemen, scuffing up their beards and batting at their hats. Her father bounces her in his arms. 'She looks forward to seeing her little brother, don't you, dumpling?'

There is a stir from the courtiers; all Europe knows Anne's condition, but it is the first time it has been mentioned in public. 'And I share her impatience,' the king says. 'It's been long enough to wait.'

Elizabeth's face is losing its baby roundness. Hail Princess Ferret Face. The older courtiers say they can see the king's father in her, and his brother, Prince Arthur. She has her mother's eyes though, busy and full in their orbits. He thinks Anne's eyes beautiful, though best when they gleam with interest, as a cat's do when she sees the whisk of some small creature's tail.

The king seizes back his darling and coos to her. 'Up to the sky!' he says, and tosses her up, then swoops her down and plants a kiss on her head.

Lady Rochford says, 'Henry has a tender heart, does he not? Of course, he is pleased with any child. I have seen him kiss a stranger's baby in much the same way.'

At the first sign of fractiousness the child is taken away, wrapped tight in furs. Anne's eyes follow her. Henry says, as if remembering his manners, 'We must accept that the country will mourn for the dowager.'

Anne says, 'They didn't know her. How can they mourn? What was she to them? A foreigner.'

'I suppose it is proper,' the king says, reluctant. 'As she was once given the title of queen.'

'Mistakenly,' Anne says. She is relentless.

145

The musicians strike up. The king tows Mary Shelton into the dance. Mary is laughing. She has been missing this last half hour, and now she's pink-cheeked, her eyes brilliant; no mistaking what she's been doing. He thinks, if old Bishop Fisher could see this kick-up, he would think the Antichrist has arrived. He is surprised to find himself, even for a moment, viewing the world through Bishop Fisher's eyes.

On London Bridge after his execution, Fisher's head remained in such a state of preservation that the Londoners began to talk of a miracle. Eventually he had the bridge keeper pull it down and drop it in a weighted sack into the Thames.

At Kimbolton, Katherine's body has been turned over to the embalmers. He imagines a rustle in the dark, a sigh, as the nation arranges itself to pray. 'She sent me a letter,' Henry says. He slides it from among the folds of his yellow jacket. 'I don't want it. Here, Cromwell, take it away.'

As he folds it he glances at it: '*And lastly I make this vow, that mine eyes desire you above all things.*'

After the dancing, Anne calls him in. She is sombre, dry, attentive: all business. 'I wish to make my thoughts known to Lady Mary the king's daughter.' He notes the respectful address. It isn't 'the Princess Mary'. But it isn't 'the Spanish bastard' either. 'Now that her mother is gone and cannot influence her,' Anne says, 'we may hope she will be less stiff in maintaining her errors. I have no need to conciliate her, God knows. But I think if I could put an end to the ill-feeling between the king and Mary, he would thank me for it.'

'He would be beholden to you, madam. And it would be an act of charity.'

'I wish to be a mother to her.' Anne flushes; it does sound unlikely. 'I do not expect her to call me "my lady mother", but I expect her to call me Your Highness. If she will conform herself to her father I shall be pleased to have her at court. She will have an honoured place, and not much below mine. I shall not expect a deep reverence from her, but the ordinary form of courtesy which royal persons use among themselves, within their families, the younger to the elder. Assure her, I shall not make her carry my train. She will not have to sit at table with her sister the Princess Elizabeth, so no question of her lower rank will arise. I think this is a fair offer.' He waits. 'If she will render me the respect which is my due, I shall not walk before her on ordinary occasions, but we will walk hand in hand.'

For one so tender about her dignities as Anne the queen, it is an unparalleled set of concessions. But he imagines Mary's face when it is put to her. He is glad he will not be there to see it in person.

He makes a respectful good night, but Anne calls him back. She says, in a low voice: 'Cremuel, this is my offer, I will go no further. I am resolved to make it and then I cannot be blamed. But I do not think she will take it, and then we will both be sorry, for we are condemned to fight till the breath goes out of our bodies. She is my death, and I am hers. So tell her, I shall make sure she does not live to laugh at me after I am gone.'

He goes to Chapuys's house to pay his condolences. The ambassador is wrapped in black. A draught is cutting through his rooms that seems to blow straight from the river, and his mood is one of self-reproach. 'How I wish I had not left her! But she seemed better. She sat up that morning and they dressed her hair. I had seen her eat some bread, a mouthful or two, I thought that was an advance. I rode away in hope, and within hours she was failing.'

'You must not blame yourself. Your master will know you did all you could. After all, you are sent here to watch the king, you cannot be too long from London in the winter.'

He thinks, I have been there since Katherine's trials began: a hundred scholars, a thousand lawyers, ten thousand hours of argument. Almost since the first word was spoken against her marriage, for the cardinal kept me informed; late at night with a glass of wine, he would talk about the king's great matter and how he saw it would work out.

Badly, he said.

'Oh, this fire,' Chapuys says. 'Do you call this a fire? Do you call this a climate?' Smoke from the wood eddies past them. 'Smoke and smells and no heat!'

'Get a stove. I've got stoves.'

'Oh, yes,' the ambassador moans, 'but then the servants stuff them with rubbish and they blow up. Or the chimneys fall apart and you have to send across the sea for a man to fix them. I know all about stoves.' He rubs his blue hands. 'I told her chaplain, you know. When she is on her deathbed, I said, ask her whether Prince Arthur left her a virgin or not. All the world must believe a declaration made by a dying woman. But he is an old man. In his grief and trouble he forgot. So now we will never be sure.'

That is a large admission, he thinks: that the truth may be other than what Katherine told us all these years. 'But do you know,' Chapuys says, 'before I left her, she said a troubling thing to me. She said, "It might be all my fault. That I stood out against the king, when I could have made an honourable withdrawal and let him marry again." I said to her, madam – because I was amazed – madam, what are you thinking, you have right on your side, the great weight of opinion, both lay and clerical – "Ah but," she said to me, "to the lawyers there was doubt in the case. And if I erred, then I drove the king, who does not brook opposition, to act according to his worse nature, and therefore I partly share in the guilt of his sin." I said to her, good madam, only the harshest authority would say so; let the king bear his own sins, let him answer for them. But she shook her head.' Chapuys shakes his, distressed, perplexed. 'All those deaths, the good Bishop Fisher, Thomas More, the sainted monks of the Charterhouse … "I am going out of life," she said, "dragging their corpses."'

He is silent. Chapuys crosses the room to his desk and opens a little inlaid box. 'Do you know what this is?'

He picks up the silk flower, carefully in case it falls to dust in his fingers. 'Yes. Her present from Henry. Her present when the New Year's prince was born.'

'It shows the king in a good light. I would not have believed him so tender. I am sure I would not have thought to do it.'

'You are a sad old bachelor, Eustache.'

'And you a sad old widower. What did you give your wife, when your lovely Gregory was born?'

'Oh, I suppose … a gold dish. A gold chalice. Something to set up on her shelf.' He hands back the silk flower. 'A city wife wants a present she can weigh.'

'Katherine gave me this rose as we parted,' Chapuys says. 'She said, it is all I have to bequeath. She told me, choose a flower from the coffer and go. I kissed her hand and took to the road.' He sighs. He drops the flower on his desk and slides his hands into his sleeves. 'They tell me the concubine is consulting diviners to tell the sex of her child, although she did that before and they all told her it was a boy. Well, the queen's death has altered the position of the concubine. But not perhaps in the way she would like.'

He lets that pass. He waits. Chapuys says, 'I am informed that Henry paraded his little bastard about the court when he heard the news.'

Elizabeth is a forward child, he tells the ambassador. But then you must remember that, when he was hardly a year older than his daughter is now, the young Henry rode through London, perched on the saddle of a warhorse, six feet from the ground and gripping the pommel with fat infant fists. You should not discount her, he tells Chapuys, just because she is young. The Tudors are warriors from their cradle.

'Ah, well, yes,' Chapuys flicks a speck of ash from his sleeve. 'Assuming she is a Tudor. Which some people do doubt. And the

149

hair proves nothing, Cremuel. Considering I could go out on the street and catch half a dozen redheads without a net.'

'So,' he says, laughing, 'you consider Anne's child could have been fathered by any passer-by?'

The ambassador hesitates. He does not like to admit he has been listening to French rumours. 'Anyway,' he sniffs, 'even if she is Henry's child, she is still a bastard.'

'I must leave you.' He stands up. 'Oh. I should have brought back your Christmas hat.'

'You may have custody of it.' Chapuys huddles into himself. 'I shall be in mourning for some time. But do not wear it, Thomas. You will stretch it out of shape.'

Call-Me-Risley comes straight from the king, with news of the funeral arrangements.

'I said to him, Majesty, you will bring the body to St Paul's? He said, she can be laid to rest in Peterborough, Peterborough is an ancient and honourable place and it will cost less. I was astonished. I persisted, I said to him, these things are done by precedent. Your Majesty's sister Mary, the Duke of Suffolk's wife, was taken to Paul's to lie in state. And do you not call Katherine your sister? And he said, ah but, my sister Mary was a royal lady, once married to the King of France.' Wriothesley frowns. 'And Katherine is not royal, he claims, though both her parents were sovereigns. The king said, she will have all she is entitled to as Dowager Princess of Wales. He said, where is the cloth of estate that was put over the hearse when Arthur died? It must be somewhere in the Wardrobe. It can be re-used.'

'That makes sense,' he says. 'The Prince of Wales's feathers. There wouldn't be time to weave a new one. Unless we keep her lingering above ground for it.'

'It appears that she asked for five hundred masses for her soul,' Wriothesley says. 'But I was not about to tell Henry that, because from day to day one never knows what he believes. Anyway, the trumpets blew. And he marched off to Mass. And the queen with him. And she was smiling. And he had a new gold chain.'

Wriothesley's tone suggests he is curious: just that. It passes no judgement on Henry.

'Well,' he says, 'if you're dead, Peterborough is as good a place as any.'

Richard Riche is up in Kimbolton taking an inventory, and has started a spat with Henry about Katherine's effects; not that Riche loved the old queen, but he loves the law. Henry wants her plate and her furs, but Riche says, Majesty, if you were never married to her, she was a *feme sole* not a *feme covert*, if you were not her husband you have no right to lay hands on her property.

He has been laughing over it. 'Henry will get the furs,' he says. 'Riche will find the king a way around it, believe me. You know what she should have done? Bundled them up and given them to Chapuys. There's a man who feels the chill.'

A message comes, for Anne the queen from the Lady Mary, in reply to her kind offer to be a mother to her. Mary says she has lost the best mother in the world and has no need for a substitute. As for fellowship with her father's concubine, she would not degrade herself. She would not hold hands with someone who has shaken paws with the devil.

He says, 'Perhaps the timing was awry. Perhaps she had heard of the dancing. And the yellow dress.'

Mary says she will obey her father, so far as her honour and her conscience allow. But that is all she will do. She will not make any statement or take any oath that requires her to recognise that her mother was not married to her father, or to accept a child of Anne Boleyn as heir of England.

Anne says, 'How does she dare? Why does she even think she can negotiate? If my child is a boy, I know what will happen to her. She had better make her peace with her father now, not come crying to him for mercy when it is too late.'

'It's good advice,' he says. 'I doubt she will take it.'

'Then I can do no more.'

'I honestly think you cannot.'

And he does not see what more he can do for Anne Boleyn. She is crowned, she is proclaimed, her name is written in the statutes, in the rolls: but if the people do not accept her as queen …

Katherine's funeral is planned for 29 January. The early bills are coming in, for the mourning attire and candles. The king continues elated. He is ordering up court entertainments. There is to be a tournament in the third week of the month and Gregory is down as a contestant. Already the boy is in a sweat of preparation. He keeps calling in his armourer, sending him off and calling him back again; changing his mind about his horse. 'Father, I hope I am not drawn against the king,' he says. 'Not that I fear him. But it will be hard work, trying to remember it is him, and also trying to forget it is him, trying your best to get a touch but please God no more than a touch. Suppose I should have the bad luck to unhorse him? Can you imagine if he came down, and to a novice like me?'

'I wouldn't worry,' he says. 'Henry was jousting before you could walk.'

'That's the whole difficulty, sir. He is not as quick as he was. So the gentlemen say. Norris says, he's lost his apprehension. Norris says you can't do it if you're not scared, and Henry is convinced he is the best, so he fears no opponent. And you should fear, Norris says. It keeps you sharp.'

'Next time,' he says, 'get drawn on the king's team at the start. That avoids the problem.'

'How would one do that?'

Oh, dear God. How would one do anything, Gregory? 'I'll have a word,' he says patiently.

'No, don't.' Gregory is upset. 'How would that stand with my honour? If you were there arranging matters? This is something

I must do for myself. I know you know everything, father. But you were never in the lists.'

He nods. As you please. His son clanks away. His tender son.

As the New Year begins, Jane Seymour continues her duties about the queen, unreadable expressions drifting across her face as if she were moving within a cloud. Mary Shelton tells him: 'The queen says that if Jane gives way to Henry he will be tired of her after a day, and if she does not give way he will be tired of her anyway. Then Jane will be sent back to Wolf Hall, and her family will lock her in a convent because she is no further use to them. And Jane says nothing.' Shelton laughs, but kindly enough. 'Jane does not feel it would be very different. As she is now in a portable convent, and bound by her own vows. She says, "Master Secretary thinks I would be very sinful to let the king hold my hand, though he begs me, 'Jane, give me your little paw.' And as Master Secretary is second only to the king in church affairs, and a very godly man, I take notice of what he says."'

One day Henry seizes Jane as she is passing and sits her on his knee. It is a sportive gesture, boyish, impetuous, no harm in it; so he says later, excusing himself sheepishly. Jane does not smile or speak. She sits calmly till she is released, as if the king were any joint-stool.

Christophe comes to him, whispering: 'Sir, they are saying on the streets that Katherine was murdered. They are saying that the king locked her in a room and starved her to death. They are saying that he sent her almonds, and she ate, and was poisoned. They are saying that you sent two murderers with knives, and that they cut out her heart, and that when it was inspected, your name was branded there in big black letters.'

'What? On her heart? "Thomas Cromwell"?'

Christophe hesitates. '*Alors* ... Perhaps just your initials.'

PART TWO

I
The Black Book
London, January–April 1536

When he hears the shout of 'Fire!' he turns over and swims back into his dream. He supposes the conflagration is a dream; it's the sort he has.

Then he wakes to Christophe bellowing in his ear. 'Get up! The queen is on fire.'

He is out of bed. The cold slices into him. Christophe yells, 'Quick, quick! She is totally incinderated.'

Moments later, when he arrives on the queen's floor, he finds the smell of singed cloth heavy in the air, and Anne surrounded by gibbering women, but unhurt, in a chair, wrapped in black silk, with a chalice of warmed wine in her hands. The cup jiggles, spills a little; Henry is tearful, hugging her, and his heir who is inside her. 'If only I had been with you, sweetheart. If only I had spent the night. I could have put you out of danger in an instant.'

On and on he goes. Thank the Lord God who watches over us. Thank the God who protects England. If only I. With a blanket, a quilt, stifling them. I, in an instant, beating out the flames.

Anne takes a gulp of her wine. 'It is over. I am not harmed. Please, my lord husband. Peace. Let me drink this.'

He sees, in a flash, how Henry irritates her; his solicitude, his doting, his clinging. And in the depth of a January night she can't disguise the irritation. She looks grey, her sleep broken. She turns

157

to him, Cromwell, and speaks in French. 'There is a prophecy that a queen of England will be burned. I did not think it meant in her own bed. It was an unattended candle. Or so one assumes.'

'By whom unattended?'

Anne shudders. She looks away.

'We had better take order,' he says to the king, 'that water be kept to hand, and one woman be appointed on every rota to check that all lights are extinguished about the queen. I cannot think why it is not the custom.'

All these things are written down in the Black Book, which comes from King Edward's time. It orders the household: orders everything, in fact, except the king's privy chamber, whose workings are not transparent.

'If only I had been with her,' says Henry. 'But, you see, our hopes being what they are ...'

The King of England cannot afford carnal relations with the woman carrying his child. The risk of miscarriage is too great. And for company he looks elsewhere too. Tonight you can see how Anne's body stiffens as she pulls away from her husband's hands, but in daylight hours, their position is reversed. He has watched Anne as she tries to draw the king into conversation. His abruptness, all too often. His turned shoulder. As if to deny his need of her. And yet his eyes follow her ...

He is irritated; these are women's things. And the fact that the queen's body, wrapped only in a damask nightgown, seems too narrow for that of a woman who will give birth in spring; that is a woman's thing too. The king says, 'The fire did not come very near her. It is the corner of the arras that is burned up. It is Absalom hanging in the tree. It is a very good piece and I would like you to ...'

'I'll get someone over from Brussels,' he says.

The fire has not touched King David's son. He hangs from the branches, strung up by his long hair: his eyes are wild and his mouth opens in a scream.

It is hours yet till daylight. The rooms of the palace seem hushed, as if they are waiting for an explanation. Guards patrol through the dark hours; where were they? Should not some woman have been with the queen, sleeping on a pallet at the foot of her bed? He says to Lady Rochford, 'I know the queen has enemies, but how were they allowed to come so near her?'

Jane Rochford is on her high horse; she thinks he is attempting to blame her. 'Look, Master Secretary. Shall I be plain with you?'

'I wish you would.'

'First, this is a household matter. It is not within your remit. Second, she was in no danger. Third, I do not know who lit the candle. Four, if I did I would not tell you.'

He waits.

'Five: no one else will tell you either.'

He waits.

'If, as it may happen, some person visits the queen after the lights are out, then it is an event over which we should draw a veil.'

'Some person.' He digests this. 'Some person for the purposes of arson, or for purposes of something else?'

'For the usual purposes of bedchambers,' she says. 'Not that I say there is such a person. I would not have any knowledge of it. The queen knows how to keep her secrets.'

'Jane,' he says, 'if the time comes when you wish to disburden your conscience, do not go to a priest, come to me. The priest will give you a penance, but I will give you a reward.'

What is the nature of the border between truth and lies? It is permeable and blurred because it is planted thick with rumour, confabulation, misunderstandings and twisted tales. Truth can break the gates down, truth can howl in the street; unless truth is pleasing, personable and easy to like, she is condemned to stay whimpering at the back door.

Tidying up after Katherine's death, he had been moved to explore some legends of her early life. Account books form a narrative as engaging as any tale of sea monsters or cannibals. Katherine had always said that, between the death of Arthur and her marriage to the young Prince Henry, she had been miserably neglected, wretchedly poor: eaten yesterday's fish, and so on. One had blamed the old king for it, but when you look at the books, you see he was generous enough. Katherine's household were cheating her. Her plate and jewels were leaking on to the market; in that she must have been complicit? She was lavish, he sees, and generous; regal, in other words, with no idea of living within her means.

You wonder what else you have always believed, believed without foundation. His father Walter had laid out money for him, or so Gardiner said: compensation, for the stab wound he inflicted, the injured family paid off. What if, he thinks, Walter didn't hate me? What if he was just exasperated with me, and showed it by kicking me around the brewery yard? What if I deserved it? Because I was always crowing, 'Item, I have a better head for drink than you; Item, I have a better head for everything. Item, I am prince of Putney and can wallop anybody from Wimbledon, let them come from Mortlake and I will mince them. Item, I am already one inch taller than you, look at the door where I have put a notch, go on, go on, father, go and stand against the wall.'

He writes:

Anthony's teeth.
Question: What happened to them?

Anthony's testimony, in answer to me, Thomas Cromwell: They were knocked out by his brutal father.

To Richard Cromwell: He was in a fortress besieged by the Pope. Abroad somewhere. Some year. Some Pope. The fortress was undermined and a charge planted. As he was standing in an unlucky spot, his teeth were blown clear out of his head.

To Thomas Wriothesley: When he was a sailor off Iceland his captain traded them for provisions with a man who could carve chessmen out of teeth. Did not understand the nature of the bargain until men in furs came to knock them out.

To Richard Riche: He lost them in a dispute with a man who impugned the powers of Parliament.

To Christophe: Somebody put a spell on him and they all fell out. Christophe says, 'I was told as a child about diabolists in England. There is a witch in every street. Practically.'

To Thurston: He had an enemy was a cook. And this enemy painted a batch of stone to look like hazelnuts, and invited him to a handful.

To Gregory: They were sucked out of his head by a great worm that crawled out of the ground and ate his wife. This was in Yorkshire, last year.

He draws a line under his conclusions. Says, 'Gregory, what should I do about the great worm?'

'Send a commission against it, sir,' the boy says. 'It must be put down. Bishop Rowland Lee would go up against it. Or Fitz.'

He gives his son a long look. 'You do know it's Arthur Cobbler's tales?'

Gregory gives him a long look back. 'Yes, I do know.' He sounds regretful. 'But it makes people so happy when I believe them. Mr Wriothesley, especially. Though now he has grown so grave. He used to amuse himself by holding my head under a water spout. But now he turns his eyes up to Heaven and says "the King's Majesty". Though he used to call him, His High Horridness. And imitate how he walks.' Gregory plants his fists on his hips and stamps across the room.

He raises a hand to cover his smile.

The day of the tournament comes. He is at Greenwich but excuses himself from the spectators' stand. The king had been at him that morning, as they sat side by side in his closet at early Mass: 'How much does the lordship of Ripon bring in? To the Archbishop of York?'

'A little over two hundred and sixty pounds, sir.'

'And what does Southwell bring in?'

'Scant one hundred and fifty pounds, sir.'

'Do you say so? I thought that it would be more.'

Henry is taking the closest interest in the finances of the bishops. Some people say, and he would not demur, that we should put the bishops on a fixed stipend and take the profits of their sees for the treasury. He has worked out that the money raised could pay for a standing army.

But this is not the time to put it to Henry. The king falls to his knees and prays to whatever saint guards knights in the lists. 'Majesty,' he says, 'if you run against my son Gregory, will you forbear to unhorse him? If you can help it?'

But the king says, 'I would not mind if little Gregory unhorsed me. Though it is unlikely, I would take it in good part. And we cannot help what we do, really. Once you are thundering down at a man, you cannot check.' He stops himself and says kindly, 'It is quite a rare event, you know, to bring your opponent down. It is not the sole aim of the contest. If you are concerned about what

162

showing he will make, you need not be. He is very able. He would not be a combatant otherwise. One cannot break a lance on a timid opponent, he must run at full pace against you. Besides, no one ever does badly. It is not allowed. You know how the heralds put it. As it might be, "Gregory Cromwell has jousted well, Henry Norris has jousted very well, but our Sovereign Lord the king has jousted best of all."'

'And have you, sir?' He smiles to take any sting from the words.

'I know you councillors think I should take to the spectators' bench. And I will, I promise, it has not escaped me that a man of my age is past his best. But you see, Crumb, it is hard to give up what you have worked at since you were a boy. There were some Italian visitors once, they were cheering us on, Brandon and myself, and they thought that Achilles and Hector had come back to life. So they said.'

But which is which? One dragged through the dust by the other ...

The king says, 'You turn your boy out beautifully, and your nephew Richard too. No nobleman could do more. They are a credit to your house.'

Gregory has done well. Gregory has done very well. Gregory has done best of all. 'I don't want him to be Achilles,' he says, 'I only want him not to be flattened.'

There is a correspondence between the score sheet and the human body, in that the paper has divisions marked off, for the head and the torso. A touch on the breastplate is recorded, but not fractured ribs. A touch on the helm is recorded, but not a cracked skull. You can pick up the score sheets afterwards and read back a record of the day, but the marks on paper do not tell you about the pain of a broken ankle or the efforts of a suffocating man not to vomit inside his helmet. As the combatants will always tell you, you really needed to see it, you had to be there.

Gregory was disappointed when his father had excused himself from watching. He pleaded a prior engagement with his papers. The Vatican is offering Henry three months to return to obedience, or the bull of excommunication against him will be printed and distributed through Europe, and every Christian hand will be against him. The Emperor's fleet is set for Algiers, with forty thousand armed men. The abbot of Fountains has been systematically robbing his own treasury, and entertains six whores, though presumably he needs a rest between. And the parliamentary session opens in a fortnight.

He had met an old knight once, in Venice, one of those men who had made a career of riding to tournaments all over Europe. The man had described his life to him, crossing frontiers with his band of esquires and his string of horses, always on the move from one prize to the next, till age and the accumulation of injuries put him out of the game. On his own now, he tried to pick up a living teaching young lords, enduring mockery and time-wasting; in my day, he had said, the young were taught manners, but now I find myself fettling horses and polishing breastplates for some little tosspot I wouldn't have let clean my boots in the old days; for look at me now, reduced to drinking with, what are you, an Englishman?

The knight was a Portuguese, but he spoke dog-Latin and a kind of German, interspersed with technicalities which are much the same in all languages. In the old days each tournament was a testing-ground. There was no display of idle luxury. Women, instead of simpering at you from gilded pavilions, were kept for afterwards. In those days the scoring was complex and the judges had no mercy on any infringement of the rules, so you could shatter all your lances but lose on points, you could flatten your opposer and come out not with a bag of gold but with a fine or a blot on your record. A breach of rules would trail you through Europe, so some infringements committed, let's say, in Lisbon, would catch up with you in Ferrara; a man's reputation would go before him, and in the end, he said, given a bad season, a run of ill-luck, reputation's all you've got; so don't you push your luck, he said, when fortune's star is shining, because the next minute, it isn't. Come to that, don't pay out good money for horoscopes. If things are going to go badly for you, is that what you need to know as you saddle up?

One drink in, the old knight talked as if everybody had followed his trade. You should set your squires, he said, at each end of the barrier, to make your horse swerve wide if he tries to cut the corner, or else you may catch your foot, easy done if there's no end-guard, bloody painful: have you ever done that? Some fools collect their boys in the middle, where the atteint will occur; but what's the use? Indeed, he agreed, what use at all: and wondered at that delicate word, *atteint*, for the brutal shock of contact. These spring-loaded shields, the old man said, have you seen them, they jump apart when they're hit? Babies' tricks. The old-time judges didn't need a device like that to tell them when a man had got a touch – no, they used their eyes, they had eyes in those days. Look, he said: there are three ways to fail. Horse can fail. Boys can fail. Nerve can fail.

You have to get your helmet on tightly so that you have a good line of sight. You keep your body square-on, and when you are about to strike, then and only then turn your head so that you have a full view of your opposer, and watch the iron tip of your lance straight on to your target. Some people veer away in the second before the clash. It is natural, but forget what is natural. Practise till you break your instinct. Given a chance you will always swerve. Your body wants to preserve itself and your instinct will try to avoid crashing your armoured warhorse and your armoured self into another man and horse coming at full gallop the other way. Some men don't swerve, but instead they close their eyes at the moment of impact. These men are of two kinds: the ones who know they do it and can't help it, and the ones who don't know they do it. Get your boys to watch you when you practise. Be neither of these kinds of men.

So how shall I improve, he said to the old knight, how shall I succeed? These were his instructions: you must sit easily in your saddle, as if you were riding out to take the air. Hold your reins loosely, but have your horse collected. In the *combat à plaisance*, with its fluttering flags, its garlands, its rebated swords and lances tipped with buffering coronals, ride as if you were out to kill. In the *combat à l'outrance*, kill as if it were a sport. Now look, the knight said, and slapped the table, here's what I've seen, more times than I care to count: your man braces himself for the atteint, and at that final moment, the urgency of desire undoes him: he tightens his muscles, he pulls in his lance-arm against his body, the tip tilts up, and he's off the mark; if you avoid one fault, avoid that. Carry your lance a little loose, so when you tense your frame and draw in your arm your point comes exactly on the target. But remember this above all: defeat your instinct. Your love of glory must conquer your will to survive; or why fight at all? Why not be a smith, a brewer, a wool merchant? Why are you in the contest, if not to win, and if not to win, then to die?

The next day he saw the knight again. He, Tommaso, was coming back from drinking with his friend Karl Heinz, and when they spotted the old man he was lying with his head on *terra firma*, his feet in the water; in Venice at dusk, it can so easily be the other way around. They pulled him on to the bank and turned him over. I know this man, he said. His friend said, who owns him? Nobody owns him, but he curses in German, therefore let us take him to the German House, for I myself am staying not at the Tuscan House but with a man who runs a foundry. Karl Heinz said, you are dealing in arms? and he said, no, altar cloths. Karl Heinz said, you are as likely to shit rubies as learn an Englishman's secrets.

As they were talking they were hauling the old man upright, and Karl Heinz said, they have cut his purse, look. A wonder they did not kill him. In a boat they took him to the Fondaco where the German merchants stay, and which was just then rebuilding after the fire. You can bed him down in the warehouse among the crates, he said. Find something to cover him, and give him food and drink when he wakes. He will live. He is an old man but tough. Here is money.

A whimsical Englishman, Karl Heinz said. He said, I myself have benefited from strangers who were angels in disguise.

There is a guard on the water gate, not set by the merchants but by the state, as the Venetians wish to know all that goes on within the houses of the nations. So more coins are passed, to the guard. They pull the old man out of the boat; he is half-awake now, flailing his arms and speaking something, perhaps Portuguese. They are dragging him in, under the portico, when Karl Heinz says, 'Thomas, have you seen our paintings? Here,' he says, 'you, guard, give us the benefit of holding up your torch, or must we pay you for that too?'

Light flares against the wall. Out of the brick blossoms a flow of silk, red silk or pooled blood. He sees a white curve, a slender moon, a sickle cut; as the light washes over the wall, he sees a woman's face, the curve of her cheek edged with gold. She is a goddess. 'Hold up the torch,' he says. On her blown and tangled hair there is a gilded crown. Behind her are the planets and stars. 'Who did you hire for this?' he asks.

Karl Heinz says, 'Giorgione is painting it for us, his friend Tiziano is painting the Rialto front, the Senate is paying their fees. But by God, they will milk it from us in commissions. Do you like her?'

The light touches her white flesh. It falters away from her, patching her with dark. The watchman lowers his torch and says, what, you think I am standing here all night for your pleasure in the gnawing cold? Which is an exaggeration, to get more money, but it is true that mist creeps over the bridges and walkways, and a chill wind has got up from the sea.

Parting from Karl Heinz, the moon herself a stone in the waters of the canal, he sees an expensive whore out late, her servants supporting her elbows, teetering over the cobbles on her high chopines. Her laughter rings on the air, and the fringed end of her yellow scarf snakes away from her white throat and into the mist. He watches her; she does not notice him. Then she is gone. Somewhere a door opens for her and somewhere a door is closed. Like the woman on the wall, she melts and is lost in the dark. The square is empty again; and he himself only a black shape against the brickwork, a fragment cut out of the night. If I ever need to vanish, he says, this is where I shall do it.

But that was long ago and in another country. Now Rafe Sadler is here with a message: he must return suddenly to Greenwich, to this raw morning, the rain just holding off. Where is Karl Heinz today? Dead probably. Since the night he saw the goddess growing on the wall, he has intended to commission one himself, though other purposes – making money and drafting legislation – have taken up his time.

'Rafe?'

Rafe stands in the doorway and does not speak. He looks up at the young man's face. His hand lets go his quill and ink splashes the paper. He stands up at once, wrapping his furred robe about him as if it will buffer him from what is to come. He says, 'Gregory?' and Rafe shakes his head.

Gregory is intact. He did not run a course.

The tournament is interrupted.

It is the king, Rafe says. It is Henry, he is dead.

Ah, he says.

He dries the ink with dust from the box of bone. Blood everywhere, no doubt, he says.

He keeps at hand a gift he was given once, a Turkish dagger made of iron, the sheath engraved with a pattern of sunflowers. Until now he had always thought of it as an ornament, a curio. He tucks it away amongst his garments.

* * *

He will recall, later, how difficult it was to get through the doorway, to turn his steps to the tilting ground. He feels weak, the backwash of the weakness that had made him drop the pen when he thought that Gregory was hurt. He says to himself, it is not Gregory; but his body is dazed, slow to catch up with the news, as if he himself had received a killing blow. Whether, now, to go forward to try to seize command, or to seize this moment, perhaps the last moment, to quit the scene: to make good an escape, before the ports are blocked, and to go where? Perhaps to Germany? Is there any principality, state, in which he would be safe from the reach of Emperor or Pope, or the new ruler of England, whoever that may be?

He has never backed off; or once, perhaps, from Walter when he was seven years old: but Walter came on. Since then: forward, forward, *en avant!* So his hesitation is not long, but afterwards he will have no recollection of how he arrived in a lofty and gilded tent, embroidered with the arms and devices of England, and standing over the corpse of King Henry VIII. Rafe says, the contests had not begun, he was running at the ring, the point of his lance scooped the eye of the circle. Then the horse stumbled under him, man and rider down, horse rolling with a scream and Henry beneath it. Now Gentle Norris is on his knees by the bier, praying, tears cascading down his cheeks. There is a blur of light on plate armour, helms hiding faces, iron jaws, frog mouths, the slits of visors. Someone says, the beast went down as if its leg were broke, no one was near the king, no one to blame. He seems to hear the appalling noise of it, the horse's roar of terror as it pitches, the screams from the spectators, the grating clatter of steel and hooves on steel as one huge animal entangles with another, warhorse and king collapsing together, metal driven into flesh, hoof into bone.

'Fetch a mirror,' he says, 'to hold to his lips. Fetch a feather to see if it stirs.'

The king has been manhandled out of his armour, but is still laced in his tournament jacket of wadded black, as if in mourning

169

for himself. There is no evident blood, so he asks, where was he hurt? Someone says, he knocked his head; but that is all the sense he can glean from the wailing and babbling that fills the tent. Feathers, mirrors, they intimate it has been done; tongues clamour like bell tongues, their eyes are like pebbles in their heads, one shocked and vacant face turns to another, oaths are uttered and prayers, and they move slowly, slowly; no one wants to carry the corpse inside, it is too much to take on oneself, it will be seen, it will be reported. It is a mistake to think that when the king dies his councillors shout, 'Long live the king.' Often the fact of the death is hidden for days. As this must be hidden ... Henry is waxen, and he sees the shocking tenderness of human flesh evicted from steel. He is lying on his back, all his magnificent height stretched on a piece of ocean-blue cloth. His limbs are straight. He looks uninjured. He touches his face. It is still warm. Fate has not spoiled him or mangled. He is intact, a present for the gods. They are taking him back as he was sent.

He opens his mouth and shouts. What do they mean, leaving the king lying here, untouched by Christian hand, as if he were already excommunicate? If this were any other fallen man they would be enticing his senses with rose petals and myrrh. They would be pulling his hair and tweaking his ears, burning a paper under his nose, wrenching open his jaw to trickle in holy water, blowing a horn next to his head. All this should be done and – he looks up and sees Thomas Howard, the Duke of Norfolk, running at him like a demon. Uncle Norfolk: uncle to the queen, premier nobleman of England. 'By God, Cromwell!' he snarls. And his import is clear. By God, I've got you now; by God, your presumptuous guts will be drawn: by God, before the day is over your head will be spiked.

Perhaps. But in the next seconds he, Cromwell, seems to body out and fill all the space around the fallen man. He sees himself, as if he were watching from the canvas above: his girth expands, even his height. So that he occupies more ground. So that he takes up more space, breathes more air, is planted and solid when Norfolk careers into him, twitching, trembling. So he is a fortress on a rock, serene, and Thomas Howard just bounces back from his walls, wincing, flinching, and blethering God knows what about God knows who. 'MY LORD NORFOLK!' he roars at him. 'My lord Norfolk, where is the queen?'

Norfolk is panting hard. 'On the floor. I told her. I myself. My place to do it. My place, am her uncle. Fallen in a fit. Fell down. Dwarf trying to pull her up. Kicked it away. Oh God Almighty!'

Now who governs, for Anne's unborn child? When Henry purposed to go to France, he said he would leave Anne as regent, but that was more than a year ago, and besides he never did go, and so we don't know if he would have done it; Anne had said to him, Cremuel, if I am regent, watch yourself, I will have your obedience or I will have your head. Anne as regent would have made short work of Katherine, of Mary: Katherine is passed beyond her reach, but Mary there for the killing. Uncle Norfolk, lurched down by the corpse for a quick prayer, has stumbled up again: 'No, no, no,' he is saying. 'No woman with a big belly. Such cannot rule. Anne cannot rule. Me, me, me.'

Gregory is pushing through the crowd. He has had the sense to fetch Fitzwilliam, Master Treasurer. 'The Princess Mary,' he says to Fitz. 'How to get her. I must have her. Or the realm is done for.'

Fitzwilliam is one of Henry's old friends, a man of his own age: too capable by nature, thank God, to panic and gibber. 'Her keepers are Boleyns,' Fitz says. 'I don't know if they'll yield her.'

Yes, and what a fool I was, he thinks, not to get among them and suborn them and advance-bribe them for an occasion such as this; I said I would send my ring for Katherine's deliverance, but for the princess I made no such arrangement. Let Mary remain in the hands of the Boleyns, and she is dead. Let her fall into the hands of the papists, they will set her up as queen, and I am dead. There will be civil war.

Courtiers are now pouring into the tent, all inventing how Henry died, all exclaiming, denying, lamenting; the noise rises, and he grips Fitz's arm: 'If this news gets up-country before we do, we will never see Mary alive.' Her guardians will not hang her up from the staircase, they will not stab her, but they will make sure she meets with an accident, a broken neck on the road. Then if Anne's unborn child is a girl, Elizabeth is queen, as we have no other.

Fitzwilliam says, 'Wait now, let me think. Where is Richmond?' The king's bastard, sixteen years old. He is a commodity, he is to be reckoned with, he is to be secured. Richmond is Norfolk's son-in-law. Norfolk must know where he is, Norfolk is best placed to lay hands on him, bargain with him, lock him up or turn him loose: but he, Cromwell, does not fear a bastard boy, and besides, the young man favours him, in all their dealings he has buttered him like a parsnip.

Norfolk is now buzzing from side to side, a maddened wasp, and as if he were a wasp the onlookers shrink from him, eddying away, then swaying back. The duke buzzes into him; he, Cromwell, bats the duke away. He stares down at Henry. He thinks he has seen, but it might be fantasy, a twitch of an eyelid. It is enough. He stands over Henry, like a figure on a tomb: a broad, mute, ugly guardian. He waits: then he sees that flicker again, he thinks he does. His heart lurches. He puts his hand on the king's chest, slapping it down, like a merchant closing a deal. Says calmly, 'The king is breathing.'

There is an unholy roar. It is something between a moan and a cheer and a wail of panic, a shout to God, a riposte to the devil.

Beneath the jacket, within the horsehair padding, a fibrillation, a quiver of life: his hand heavy and flat on the regal breast, he feels he is raising Lazarus. It is as if his palm, magnetised, is drawing life back into his prince. The king's respiration, though shallow, seems steady. He, Cromwell, has seen the future; he has seen England without Henry; he prays aloud, 'Long live the king.'

172

'Fetch the surgeons,' he says. 'Fetch Butts. Fetch any man with skill. If he dies again, they will not be blamed. My word on that. Get me Richard Cromwell my nephew. Fetch a stool for my lord Norfolk, he has had a shock.' He is tempted to add, throw a bucket of water on Gentle Norris: whose prayers, he has time to notice, are of a marked papist character.

The tent is now so crowded that it seems to have been picked up by its moorings, to be carried on men's heads. He takes a last look at Henry before his still form disappears under the ministrations of doctors and priests. He hears a long, retching gasp; but one has heard the same from corpses.

'Breathe,' Norfolk shouts. 'Let the king breathe!' And as if in obedience, the fallen man takes a deep, sucking, scraping breath. And then he swears. And then he tries to sit up.

And it is over.

But not entirely: not until he has studied the Boleyn expressions around. They look numb, bemused. Their faces are pinched in the bitter cold. Their great hour has passed, before they realised it has arrived. How have they all got here so fast? Where have they come from? he asks Fitz. Only then he realises that the light is fading. What felt like ten minutes has been two hours: two hours since Rafe stood in the doorway, and he dropped his pen on the page.

He says to Fitzwilliam, 'Of course, it never happened. Or if it did, it was an incident of no importance.'

For Chapuys and the other ambassadors, he will stick by his original version: the king fell, hit his head, and was unconscious for ten minutes. No, at no time did we think he was dead. After ten minutes he sat up. And now he is perfectly well.

The way I tell it, he says to Fitzwilliam, you would think that the blow on the head had improved him. That he actually set out to get it. That every monarch needs a blow on the head, from time to time.

Fitzwilliam is amused. 'A man's thoughts at such a time hardly bear scrutiny. I recall thinking, should we not send for the Lord Chancellor? But I don't know what I thought he was to do.'

'My thought,' he confesses, 'was, somebody get the Archbishop of Canterbury. I think I believed a king couldn't die without his supervision. Imagine trying to bustle Cranmer across the Thames. He would make you join him in a gospel reading first.'

What does the Black Book say? Nothing to the purpose. No one has made a plan for a king struck down between one moment and the next, one second mounted tall and riding full tilt, next second mashed into the ground. No one dares. No one dares think about it. Where protocol fails, it is war to the knife. He remembers Fitzwilliam beside him; Gregory in the crowd; Rafe by his side, and then Richard his nephew. Was it Richard who helped lever the king upright as he tried to sit, while the doctors cried, 'No, no, lie him down!' Henry had clasped his hands to his chest, as if to squeeze his own heart. He had struggled to rise, he had made inarticulate noises, that sounded like words but were not, as if the Holy Ghost had descended upon him and he was speaking in tongues. He had thought, panic darting through him, what if he never makes sense again? What does the Black Book say if a king is rendered simple? Outside he remembers the roaring of Henry's fallen horse, struggling to rise; but surely that cannot be what he heard, surely they had slaughtered it?

Then Henry himself was roaring. That night, the king rips the bandage from his head. The bruising, the swelling, is God's verdict on the day. He is determined to show himself to his court, to counter any rumours that he is mauled or dead. Anne approaches him, supported by her father, 'Monseigneur'. The earl is really supporting her, not pretending to. She looks white and frail; now her pregnancy shows. 'My lord,' she says, 'I pray, the whole of England prays, that you will never joust again.'

Henry beckons her to approach. Beckons her till her face is close to his own. His voice low and vehement: 'Why not geld me while you are at it? That would suit you, would it not, madam?'

Faces open in shock. The Boleyns have the sense to draw Anne backwards, backwards and away, Mistress Shelton and Jane Rochford flapping and tut-tutting, the whole Howard, Boleyn clan closing around her. Jane Seymour, alone of the ladies, does not move. She stands and looks at Henry and the king's eyes fly straight to her, a space opens around her and for a moment she stands in the vacancy, like a dancer left behind when the line moves on.

Later he is with Henry in his bedchamber, the king collapsed in a velvet chair. Henry says, when I was a boy, I was walking with my father in a gallery at Richmond, one night in summer about eleven of the clock, he had my arm in his and we were deep in talk or he was: and suddenly there was a great crashing and a splintering, the whole building gave a deep groan, and the floor fell away at our feet. I will remember it all my life, standing on the brink, and the world vanished from beneath us. But for a moment I did not know what I heard, whether it was the timbers splintering or our bones. Both of us by God's grace still stood on solid ground, and yet I had seen myself plummeting, down and down through the floor below till I hit the earth and smelled it, damp like the grave. Well … when I fell today, that was how it was. I heard voices. Very distant. I could not make out the words. I felt myself borne through the air. I did not see God. Or angels.

'I hope you were not disappointed when you woke. Only to see Thomas Cromwell.'

'You were never more welcome,' Henry says. 'Your own mother on the day you were born was no gladder to see you than I was today.'

The grooms of the chamber are here, going soft-footed about their usual duties, sprinkling the king's sheets with holy water.

'Steady,' Henry says crossly. 'Do you want me to take a chill? A drowning is not more efficacious than a drop.' He turns and says, low-voiced, 'Crumb, you know this never happened?'

He nods. What records are already made, he is in the process of expunging. Afterwards it will be known that on such a date, the king's horse stumbled. But God's hand plucked him from the ground and set him back laughing on his throne. Another item of note, for The Book Called Henry: knock him down and he bounces.

But the queen has a point. You've seen these jousters from the old king's time, limping about the court, the wincing and addle-pated survivors of the lists; men who've taken a blow on the head once too often, men who walk crooked, bent like a dog-leg brick. And all your skill counts for nothing when your day of reckoning comes. Horse can fail. Boys can fail. Nerve can fail.

That night he says to Richard Cromwell, 'It was a bad moment for me. How many men can say, as I must, "I am a man whose only friend is the King of England"? I have everything, you would think. And yet take Henry away and I have nothing.'

Richard sees the helpless truth of it. Says, 'Yes.' What else can he say?

Later he voices the same thought, in a cautious and modified form, to Fitzwilliam. Fitzwilliam looks at him: thoughtful, not without sympathy. 'I don't know, Crumb. You are not without support, you know.'

'Forgive me,' he says sceptically, 'but in what way does this support manifest?'

'I mean that you would have support, should you need it against the Boleyns.'

'Why should I? The queen and I are perfect friends.'

'That's not what you tell Chapuys.'

He inclines his head. Interesting, the people who talk to Chapuys; interesting too, what the ambassador chooses to pass on, from one party to another.

'Did you hear them?' Fitz says. His tone is disgusted. 'Outside the tent, when we thought the king was dead? Shouting "Boleyn, Boleyn!" Calling out their own name. Like cuckoos.'

He waits. Of course he heard them; what is the real question here? Fitz is close to the king. He was brought up at court with Henry since they were small boys, though his family is good gentry, not noble. He has been to war. Has had a crossbow bolt in him. Has been abroad on embassies, knows France, knows Calais, the English enclave there and its politics. He is of that select company, the Garter knights. He writes a good letter, to the point, neither abrupt nor circumlocutory, nor larded with flattery, nor cursory in expressions of regard. The cardinal liked him, and he is affable to Thomas Cromwell when they dine daily in the guard chamber. He is always affable: and now more so? 'What would have happened, Crumb, if the king had not come back to life? I shall never forget Howard pitching in, "Me, me, me!"'

'It is not a spectacle we will erase from our minds. As for ...' he hesitates, 'well, if the worst had been, the king's body dies but the body politic continues. It might be possible to convene a ruling council, made up from the law officers, and from those chief councillors that are now ...'

'... amongst whom, yourself ...'

'Myself, granted.' Myself in several capacities, he thinks: who more trusted, who closer, and not just Master Secretary but a law officer, Master of the Rolls? 'If Parliament were willing, we might bring together a body who would have ruled as regent till the queen was delivered, and perhaps with her permission during a minority ...'

'But you know Anne would give no such permission,' Fitz says.

'No, she would have all to rule herself. Though she would have to fight Uncle Norfolk. Between the two of them I do not know who I would back. The lady, I think.'

'God help the realm,' Fitzwilliam says, 'and all the men in it. Of the two, I would sooner have Thomas Howard. At least if it came to it, one could challenge him to come outside and fight. Let the lady be regent and the Boleyns would walk on our backs. We would be their living carpet. She would have "AB" sewn into our skins.' He rubs his chin. 'But so she will anyway. If she gives Harry a son.'

He is aware that Fitz is watching him. 'On the topic of sons,' he says, 'have I thanked you in proper form? Let me know if there is anything I can do for you. Gregory has thrived under your guidance.'

'The pleasure is mine. Send him back to me soon.'

I will, he thinks, and with the lease on a little abbey or two, when my new laws are passed. His desk is piled high with business for the new session of Parliament. Before many years are out he would like Gregory to have a seat beside him in the Commons. He must see all aspects of how the realm is governed. A term in Parliament is an exercise in frustration, it is a lesson in patience: whichever way you like to look at it. They commune of war, peace, strife, contention, debate, murmur, grudges, riches, poverty, truth, falsehood, justice, equity, oppression, treason, murder and the edification and continuance of the commonwealth; then do as their predecessors have done – that is, as well as they might – and leave off where they began.

After the king's accident, everything is the same, yet nothing is the same. He is still on the wrong side of the Boleyns, of Mary's supporters, the Duke of Norfolk, the Duke of Suffolk, and the absent Bishop of Winchester; not to mention the King of France, the Emperor, and the Bishop of Rome, otherwise known as the Pope. But the contest – every contest – is sharper now.

On the day of Katherine's funeral, he finds himself downcast. How close we hug our enemies! They are our familiars, our other selves. When she was sitting on a silk cushion at the Alhambra, a seven-year-old working her first embroidery, he was scrubbing roots in the kitchen at Lambeth Palace, under the eye of his uncle John, the cook.

So often in council he has taken Katherine's part, as if he were one of her appointed lawyers. 'You make this argument, my lords,' he has said, 'but the dowager princess will allege ...' And 'Katherine will refute you, thus.' Not because he favours her cause but because it saves time; as her opponent, he enters into her concerns, he judges her stratagems, he reaches every point before she does. It has long been a puzzle to Charles Brandon: 'Whose side is this fellow on?' he would demand.

But even now Katherine's cause is not considered settled, in Rome. Once the Vatican lawyers have started a case, they don't stop just because one of the parties is dead. Possibly, when all of us are dead, from some Vatican oubliette a skeleton secretary will rattle along, to consult his fellow skeletons on a point of canon law. They will chatter their teeth at each other; their absent eyes will turn down in the sockets, to see that their parchments have turned to dust motes in the light. Who took Katherine's virginity, her first husband or her second? For all eternity we will never know.

He says to Rafe, 'Who can understand the lives of women?'

'Or their deaths,' Rafe says.

He glances up. 'Not you! You don't think she was poisoned, do you?'

'It is rumoured,' Rafe says gravely, 'that the poison was introduced to her in some strong Welsh beer. A brew which, it seems, she had taken a delight in, these last few months.'

He catches Rafe's eye, and snorts with suppressed laughter. The dowager princess, swigging strong Welsh beer. 'From a leather tankard,' Rafe says. 'And think of her slapping it down on the table. And roaring "Fill it up."'

He hears running feet approaching. What now? A bang at the door, and his little Welsh boy appears, out of breath. 'Master, you are to go at once to the king. Fitzwilliam's people have come for you. I think somebody is dead.'

'What, somebody else?' he says. He picks up his sheaf of papers, throws them into a chest, turns the key on them and gives it to Rafe. From now on he leaves no secret unattended, no fresh ink exposed to the air. 'Who have I to raise this time?'

You know what it's like when a cart overturns in the street? Everybody you meet has witnessed it. They saw a man's leg sliced clean off. They saw a woman gasp her last. They saw the goods looted, thieves stealing from the back-end while the carter was crushed at the front. They heard a man roar out his last confession, while another whispered his last will and testament. And if all the people who say they were there had really been there, then the dregs of London would have drained to the one spot, the gaols emptied of thieves, the beds empty of whores, and all the lawyers standing on the shoulders of the butchers to get a better look.

Later that day, 29 January, he will be on his way to Greenwich, shocked, apprehensive, at the news Fitzwilliam's men had brought. People will tell him, 'I was there, I was there when Anne broke off her talk, I was there when she put down her book, her sewing, her lute, I was there when she broke off her merriment at the thought of Katherine lowered into the ground. I saw her face change. I saw her ladies close about her. I saw them sweep her to her chamber and bolt the door, and I saw the trail of blood left on the ground as she walked.'

We need not believe that. Not the trail of blood. They saw it in their minds perhaps. He will ask, what time did the queen's pains begin? But no one seemed able to tell him, despite their close knowledge of the incident. They have concentrated on the blood trail and left out the facts. It will take all day for the bad news to leak from the queen's bedside. Sometimes women do bleed but the child clings on and grows. Not this time. Katherine is too fresh in her tomb to lie quiet. She has reached out and shaken Anne's child free, so it is brought untimely into the world and no bigger than a rat.

At evening, outside the queen's suite, the dwarf sits on the flags, rocking and moaning. She is pretending to be in labour, someone says: unnecessarily. 'Can you not remove her?' he asks the women.

Jane Rochford says, 'It was a boy, Mr Secretary. She had carried it under four months, as we judge.'

Early October, then. We were still on progress. 'You will have a note of the itinerary,' Lady Rochford murmurs. 'Where was she then?'

'Does it matter?'

'I should think you would like to know. Oh, I know that plans were changed, sometimes on the instant. That sometimes she was with the king, sometimes not, that sometimes Norris was with her, and sometimes others of the gentlemen. But you are right, Master Secretary. It is of no moment. The doctors can be sure of very little. We cannot say when it was conceived. Who was here and who was there.'

'Perhaps we should leave it like that,' he says.

'So. Now that she has lost another chance, poor lady … what world will be?'

The dwarf scrambles to her feet. Watching him, holding his gaze, she pulls her skirts up. He is not quick enough to look away. She has shaved herself or someone has shaved her, and her parts are bald, like the parts of an old woman or a little child.

Later, before the king, holding Mary Shelton's hand, Jane Rochford is unsure of everything. 'The child had the appearance of a male,' she says, 'and of about fifteen weeks' gestation.'

'What do you mean, the appearance of?' the king demands. 'Could you not tell? Oh, get away, woman, you have never given birth, what do you know? It should have been matrons at her

181

bedside, what did you want there? Could not you Boleyns give way to someone more useful, must you be there in a crowd whenever disaster strikes?'

Lady Rochford's voice shakes, but she sticks to her point. 'Your Majesty may interview the doctors.'

'I have.'

'I only repeat their words.'

Mary Shelton bursts into tears. Henry looks at her and says humbly, 'Mistress Shelton, forgive me. Sweetheart, I did not mean to make you cry.'

Henry is in pain. His leg has been bound up by the surgeons, the leg he injured in the joust over ten years ago; it is prone to ulcerate, and it seems that the recent fall has opened a channel into his flesh. All his bravado has melted away; it is like the days when he dreamed of his brother Arthur, the days he was run ragged by the dead. It is the second child she has lost, he says that night, in private: though who knows, there could have been others, the women keep these things to themselves till their bellies show, we do not know how many of my heirs have bled away. What does God want of me now? What must I do to please him? I see he will not give me male children.

He, Cromwell, stands back while Thomas Cranmer, pale and smooth, takes charge of the king's bereavement. We much misconstrue our creator, the archbishop says, if we blame him for every accident of fallen nature.

I thought he regarded every sparrow that falls, the king says, truculent as a child. Then why does he not regard England?

Cranmer will have some reason. He hardly listens. He thinks of the women about Anne: wise as serpents, mild as doves. Already a certain line is being spun, about the day's events; it is spun in the queen's chamber. Anne Boleyn is not to blame for this misfortune. It is her uncle Thomas Howard, the Duke of Norfolk, who is at fault. When the king took his tumble, it was Norfolk who burst in on the queen, shouting that Henry was dead, and giving her such a shock that the unborn heart stopped.

And further: it is Henry's fault. It is because of the way he has been behaving, mooning over old Seymour's daughter, dropping letters in her place in chapel and sending her sweetmeats from his table. When the queen saw he loved another, she was struck to the quick. The sorrow she has taken has made her viscera revolt and reject the tender child.

Just be clear, Henry says coldly, when he stands at the foot of the lady's bed and hears this reading of events. Just be clear on this, madam. If any woman is to blame, it is the one I am looking at. I will speak to you when you are better. And now fare you well, because I am going to Whitehall to prepare for the Parliament, and you had better stay in bed till you are restored. Which I myself, I doubt I will ever be.

Then Anne shouts after him – or so Lady Rochford says – 'Stay, stay my lord, I will soon give you another child, and all the quicker now Katherine is dead ...'

'I do not see how that will speed the business.' Henry limps away. Then in his own rooms the privy chamber gentlemen move carefully about him, as if he were made of glass, making their preparations for departure. Henry is repenting now of his hasty pronouncement, because if the queen stays behind all the women must stay behind, and he will not be able to feast his eyes on his little bun-face, Jane. Further reasoning follows him, conveyed by Anne in a note perhaps: this lost foetus, conceived when Katherine was alive, is inferior to the conception that will follow, at some unknown date, but soon. For even if the child had lived and grown up, there would have been some who still doubted his claim; whereas now Henry is a widower, no one in Christendom can dispute that his marriage to Anne is licit, and any son they beget is heir to England.

'Well, what do you make of that chain of reasoning?' Henry demands. Leg stout with bandages, he heaves himself into a chair in his private rooms. 'No, do not confer, I want an answer from each of you, each Thomas alone.' He grimaces, though he means to smile. 'Do you know the confusion you cause among the French? They have made of you one composite counsellor, and in dispatches they call you Dr Chramuel.'

They exchange glances, he and Cranmer: the pork butcher and the angel. But the king does not wait for their advice, joint or several; he talks on, like a man sticking a dagger into himself to prove how much it hurts. 'If a king cannot have a son, if he cannot do that, it matters not what else he can do. The victories, the spoils of victory, the just laws he makes, the famous courts he holds, these are as nothing.'

It is true. To maintain the stability of the realm: this is the compact a king makes with his people. If he cannot have a son of his own, he must find an heir, name him before his country falls into doubt and confusion, faction and conspiracy. And who can Henry name, that will not be laughed at? The king says, 'When I remember what I did for the present queen, how I raised her from a gentleman's daughter … I cannot think now why I did it.' He looks at them as if to say, do you know, Dr Chramuel? 'It seems to me,' he is groping, perplexed, for the right phrases, 'it seems to me I was somehow dishonestly led into this marriage.'

He, Cromwell, eyes the other half of himself, as if through a mirror: Cranmer looks thrown. 'How, dishonestly?' the archbishop asks.

'I feel sure I was not in my clear mind then. Not as I am now.'

'But sir,' Cranmer says. 'Majesty. Saving Your Grace, your mind cannot be clear. You have suffered a great loss.'

Two, in fact, he thinks: today your son was born dead, and your first wife buried. No wonder you tremble.

'It seems to me I was seduced,' Henry says, 'that is to say, I was practised upon, perhaps by charms, perhaps by spells. Women do use such things. And if that were so, then the marriage would be null, would it not?'

184

Cranmer holds out his hands, like a man trying to send back the tide. He sees his queen vanishing into thin air: his queen who has done so much for true religion. 'Sir, sir ... Majesty ...'

'Oh, peace!' Henry says: as if it were Cranmer who had started it. 'Cromwell, when you were soldiering, did you ever hear of anything that would heal a leg like mine? I have knocked it again now and the surgeons say the foul humours must come out. They fear that the rot has got as far as the bone. But do not tell anybody. I would not like word to spread abroad. Will you send a page to find Thomas Vicary? I think he must bleed me. I need some relief. Give you good night.' He adds, almost under his breath, 'For I suppose even this day must end.'

Dr Chramuel goes out. In an antechamber, one of him turns to the other. 'He will be different tomorrow,' the archbishop says.

'Yes. A man in pain will say anything.'

'We should not heed it.'

'No.'

They are like two men crossing thin ice; leaning into each other, taking tiny, timid steps. As if that will do you any good, when it begins to crack on every side.

Cranmer says uncertainly, 'Grief for the child sways him. Would he wait so long for Anne, to throw her over so quickly? They will soon be perfect friends.'

'Besides,' he says. 'He is not a man to admit he was wrong. He may have his doubts about his marriage. But God help anyone else who raises them.'

'We must calm these doubts,' Cranmer says. 'Between us we must do it.'

'He would like to be the Emperor's friend. Now that Katherine is not there to cause ill-feeling between them. And so we must face the fact that the present queen is ...' He hesitates to say, superfluous; he hesitates to say, an obstacle to peace.

'She is in his way,' Cranmer says bluntly. 'But he will not sacrifice her? Surely he will not. Not to please Emperor Charles or any man. They need not think it. Rome need not think it. He will never revert.'

'No. Have some faith in our good master to maintain the church.'

Cranmer hears the words he has left unspoken: the king does not need Anne, to help him do that.

Although, he says to Cranmer. It is hard to remember the king, before Anne; hard to imagine him without her. She hovers around him. She reads over his shoulder. She gets into his dreams. Even when she's lying next to him it's not close enough for her. 'I tell you what we'll do,' he says. He squeezes Cranmer's arm. 'Let's give a dinner, shall we, and invite the Duke of Norfolk?'

Cranmer shrinks. 'Norfolk? Why would we?'

'For reconciliation,' he says breezily. 'I fear that on the day of the king's accident, I may have, um, slighted his pretensions. In a tent. When he raced in. Well-founded pretensions,' he adds reverently. 'For is he not our senior peer? No, I pity the duke from the bottom of my heart.'

'What did you do, Cromwell?' The archbishop is pale. 'What did you do in that tent? Did you lay violent hands upon him, as I hear you did recently with the Duke of Suffolk?'

'What, Brandon? I was only moving him.'

'When he was not of a mind to be moved.'

'It was for his own good. If I had left him there in the king's presence, Charles would have talked himself into the Tower. He was slandering the queen, you see.' And any slander, any doubt, he thinks, must come from Henry, out of his own mouth, and not from mine, or any other man's. 'Please, please,' he says, 'let us have a dinner. You must give it at Lambeth, Norfolk will not come to me, he will think I plan to put a sleeping draught in the claret and convey him on board ship to be sold into slavery. He will like to come to you. I will supply the venison. We will have jellies in the shape of the duke's major castles. It will be no cost to you. And no trouble to your cooks.'

186

Cranmer laughs. At last, he laughs. It has been a hard-fought campaign, to get him even to smile. 'As you wish, Thomas. We shall have a dinner.'

The archbishop sets his hands on his upper arms, kisses him right and left. The kiss of peace. He does not feel soothed, or assuaged, as he returns to his own rooms through the palace unnaturally quiet: no music from distant rooms, perhaps the murmur of prayer. He tries to imagine the lost child, the manikin, its limbs budding, its face old and wise.

Few men have seen such a thing. Certainly he has not. In Italy, once, he stood holding up a light for a surgeon, while in a sealed room draped in shadows he sliced a dead man apart to see what made him work. It was a fearful night, the stench of bowel and blood clogging the throat, and the artists who had jostled and bribed for a place tried to elbow him away: but he stood firm, for he had guaranteed to do so, he had said he would hold the light. And so he was among the elect of that company, the luminaries, who saw muscle stripped from bone. But he has never seen inside a woman, still less a gravid corpse; no surgeon, even for money, would perform that work for an audience.

He thinks of Katherine, embalmed and entombed. Her spirit cut free, and gone to seek out her first husband: wandering now, calling his name. Will Arthur be shocked to see her, she such a stout old woman, and he still a skinny child?

King Arthur of blessed memory could not have a son. And what happened after Arthur? We don't know. But we know his glory vanished from the world.

He thinks of Anne's chosen motto, painted up with her coat of arms: 'The Most Happy'.

He had said to Jane Rochford, 'How is my lady the queen?'

Rochford had said, 'Sitting up, lamenting.'

He had meant, has she lost much blood?

Katherine was not without sin, but now her sins are taken off her. They are all heaped upon Anne: the shadow who flits after her, the woman draped in night. The old queen dwells in the radiance of God's presence, her dead infants swaddled at her feet, but Anne dwells in this sinful world below, stewed in her childbed sweat, in her soiled sheet. But her hands and feet are cold and her heart is like a stone.

So here's the Duke of Norfolk, expecting to be fed. Dressed in his best, or at least what's good enough for Lambeth Palace, he looks like a piece of rope chewed by a dog, or a piece of gristle left on the side of a trencher. Bright fierce eyes under unruly brows. Hair an iron stubble. His person is meagre, sinewy, and he smells of horses and leather and the armourer's shop, and mysteriously of furnaces or perhaps of cooling ash: dust-dry, pungent. He fears no one alive except Henry Tudor, who could at a whim take his dukedom away, but he fears the dead. They say that at any of his houses at close of day you can hear him slamming the shutters and shooting the bolts, in case the late Cardinal Wolsey is blowing through a window or slithering up a stair. If Wolsey wanted Norfolk he would lie quiet inside a table top, breathing along the grain of the wood; he would ooze through a keyhole, or flop down a chimney with a soft flurry like a soot-stained dove.

When Anne Boleyn came up in the world, and she a niece of his illustrious family, the duke thought his troubles were over. Because he has troubles; the greatest nobleman has his rivals, his ill-wishers, his defamers. But he believed that, with Anne crowned in due time, he would be always at the king's right hand. It hasn't worked out like that, and the duke has become disaffected. The match hasn't brought the Howards the riches and honours he expected. Anne has taken the rewards for herself, and Thomas Cromwell has taken them. The duke thinks Anne should be guided by her male kin, but she won't be guided; in fact she has made it plain that she sees herself, and not the duke, as the head of the family now. Which is unnatural, in the duke's view: a woman cannot be head of anything, subordination and submission is her role. Let her be a queen and a rich woman, still she should know her place, or be taught it. Howard sometimes grumbles in public: not about Henry, but about Anne Boleyn. And he has found it expedient to spend his time in his own country, harassing his duchess, who often writes to Thomas Cromwell with complaints of his treatment of her. As if he, Thomas Cromwell, could turn the duke into one of the world's great lovers, or even into a semblance of a reasonable man.

But then when Anne's latest pregnancy was known, the duke had come to court, flanked by his smirking retainers and soon joined by his peculiar son. Surrey is a young man with a great conceit of himself as handsome, talented and lucky. But his face is lopsided, and he does himself no favours, in having his hair cut like a bowl. Hans Holbein admits he finds him a challenge. Surrey is here tonight at Lambeth, forfeiting an evening in the brothel. His eyes roam about the room; perhaps he thinks Cranmer keeps naked girls behind the arras.

'Well, now,' says the duke, rubbing his hands. 'When are you coming down to see me at Kenninghall, Thomas Cromwell? We have good hunting, by God, we have something to shoot at every season of the year. And we can get you a bedwarmer if you want one, a common woman of the type you like, we have a maidservant just now,' the duke sucks in his breath, 'you should see her titties.' His knotty fingers knead the air.

'Well, if she's yours,' he murmurs. 'I wouldn't like to deprive you.'

The duke shoots a glance at Cranmer. Perhaps one ought not to talk about women? But then, Cranmer's not a proper archbishop, not in Norfolk's view; he's some petty clerk Henry found in the fens one year, who promised to do anything he asked in return for a mitre and two good meals a day.

'By God, you look ill, Cranmer,' the duke says with gloomy relish. 'You look as if you can't keep the flesh on your bones. No more can I. Look at this.' The duke thrusts himself back from the table, elbowing a poor youth who stands ready with the wine jug. He stands up and parts his gown, thrusting out a skinny calf. 'What do you make of that?'

That's horrible, he agrees. It's humiliation, surely, that wears Thomas Howard to the bone? In company his niece interrupts him and talks over him. She laughs at his holy medals and the relics he wears, some of them very sacred. At table she leans towards him, says, Come, uncle, take a crumb from my hand, you are wasting away. 'And I am,' he says. 'I don't know how you do it, Cromwell. Look at you, all fleshed out in your gown, an ogre would eat you roasted.'

'Ah, well,' he says, smiling, 'that's the risk I run.'

'I think you drink some powder that you got in Italy. Keeps you sleek. I suppose you wouldn't part with the secret?'

'Eat up your jelly, my lord,' he says patiently. 'If I do hear of a powder I will get a sample for you. My only secret is that I sleep at night. I am at peace with my maker. And of course,' he adds, leaning back at his ease, 'I have no enemies.'

'What?' says the duke. His eyebrows shoot up into his hair. He serves himself some more of Thurston's jelly crenellations, the scarlet and the pale, the airy stone and the bloody brick. As he swills them around his mouth he opines on several topics. Chiefly Wiltshire, the queen's father. Who should have brought Anne up properly and with more attention to discipline. But no, he was too busy boasting about her in French, boasting about what she would become.

'Well, she did become,' says young Surrey. 'Didn't she, my lord father?'

'I think it's she who's wasting me away,' the duke says. 'She knows all about powders. They say she keeps poisoners in her house. You know what she did to old Bishop Fisher.'

'What did she do?' young Surrey says.

'Do you know nothing, boy? Fisher's cook was paid to put a powder in the broth. It nigh killed him.'

190

'That would have been no loss,' the boy says. 'He was a traitor.'

'Yes,' Norfolk says, 'but in those days his treason stood still to be proved. This is not Italy, boy. We have courts of law. Well, the old fellow pulled around, but he was never well after. Henry had the cook boiled alive.'

'But he never confessed,' he says: he, Cromwell. 'So we cannot say for sure the Boleyns did it.'

Norfolk snorts. 'They had motive. Mary had better watch herself.'

'I agree,' he says. 'Though I do not think poison is the chief danger to her.'

'What then?' Surrey says.

'Bad advice, my lord.'

'You think she should listen to you, Cromwell?' Young Surrey now lays down his knife and begins to complain. Noblemen, he laments, are not respected as they were in the days when England was great. The present king keeps about himself a collection of men of base degree, and no good will come of it. Cranmer creeps forward in his chair, as if to intervene, but Surrey gives him a glare that says, you're exactly who I mean, archbishop.

He nods to a boy to refill the young man's glass. 'You do not suit your talk to your audience, sir.'

'Why should I?' Surrey says.

'Thomas Wyatt says you are studying to write verse. I am fond of poems, as I passed my youth among the Italians. If you would favour me, I would like to read some.'

'No doubt you would,' Surrey says. 'But I keep them for my friends.'

When he gets home his son comes out to greet him. 'Have you heard what the queen is doing? She has risen from her childbed and things incredible are spoken of her. They say she was seen toasting cobnuts over the fire in her chamber, tossing them about in a latten pan, ready to make poisoned sweetmeats for the Lady Mary.'

'It would be someone else with the latten pan,' he says, smiling. 'A minion. Weston. That boy Mark.'

Gregory sticks stubbornly by his version: 'It was herself. Toasting. And the king came in, and frowned to see her at the occupation, for he didn't know what it meant, and he has suspicions of her, you see. What are you at, he asked, and Anne the queen said, oh my lord, I am but making sweetmeats to reward the poor women who stand at the gate and call out their greetings to me. The king said, is it even so, sweetheart? Then bless you. And so he was utterly misled, you see.'

'And where did this happen, Gregory? You see, she is at Greenwich, and the king at Whitehall.'

'No matter,' Gregory says cheerfully. 'In France witches can fly, latten pan and cobnuts and all. And that is where she learned it. In truth the whole Boleyn affinity are become witches, to witch up a boy for her, for the king fears he can give her none.'

His smile becomes pained. 'Do not spread this about the household.'

Gregory says happily, 'Too late, the household has spread it about me.'

He remembers Jane Rochford saying to him, it must be two years back: 'The queen has boasted she will give Katherine's daughter a breakfast she will not recover from.'

Merry at breakfast, dead by dinner. It was what they used to say about the sweating sickness, that killed his wife and daughters. And unnatural ends, when they occur, are usually swifter than that; they cut down at a stroke.

'I am going to my rooms,' he says. 'I have to draw up a paper. Do not let me be interrupted. Richard may come in if he will.'

'What about me, can I come in? For instance, if the house were on fire, you would like to hear of it?'

'Not from you. Why would I believe you?' He pats his son. Hurries off to his private room and shuts the door.

The meeting with Norfolk has, on the face of it, no pay-off. But. He takes his paper. At the top he writes:

THOMAS BOLEYN

This is the lady's father. He pictures him in his mind. An upright man, still lithe, proud of his looks, who pays great attention to turning himself out, just like his son George: a man to test the ingenuity of London goldsmiths, and to swivel around his fingers jewels which he says have been given him by foreign rulers. These many years he has served Henry as a diplomat, a trade for which he is fitted by his cold emollience. He is not a man wedded to action, Boleyn, but rather a man who stands by, smirking and stroking his beard; he thinks he looks enigmatic, but instead he looks as if he's pleasuring himself.

Still, he knew how to act when the chance presented itself, how to set his family climbing, climbing, to the highest branches of the tree. It's cold up there when the wind blows, the cutting wind of 1536.

As we know, his title of Earl of Wiltshire seems to him insufficient to indicate his special status, so he has invented for himself a French title, *Monseigneur*. And it gives him pleasure, to be so addressed. He lets it be known this title should be universally adopted. From whether the courtiers comply, you can tell a great deal about where they stand.

He writes:

Monseigneur: All the Boleyns. Their women. Their chaplains.
    Their servants.
All the Boleyn toadies in the privy chamber, that is to say,

Henry Norris
Francis Weston
William Brereton, etc.

But plain old 'Wiltshire', delivered in accents brisk:
The Duke of Norfolk.
Sir Nicholas Carew (of the privy chamber) who is cousin to
    Edward Seymour, and married to the sister of:
Sir Francis Bryan, cousin to the Boleyns, but cousin to the
    Seymours also, and friend of:
Mr Treasurer, William Fitzwilliam.

He looks at this list. He adds the names of two grandees:

The Marquis of Exeter, Henry Courtenay.
Henry Pole, Lord Montague.

These are the old families of England; they draw their claims from ancient lines; they smart, more than any of us, under the pretensions of the Boleyns.

He rolls up his paper. Norfolk, Carew, Fitz. Francis Bryan. The Courtenays, the Montagues, and their ilk. And Suffolk, who hates Anne. It is a set of names. You cannot take too much from it. These people are not necessarily friends of each other. They are just, to one degree and another, friends of the old dispensation and enemies of the Boleyns.

    He closes his eyes. He sits, his breathing calm. In his mind, a picture appears. A lofty hall. Into which he commands a table.

    The trestles are lugged up by menials.

    The top is fixed in place.

    Liveried officials unroll the cloth, tweaking and smoothing; like the king's tablecloth, it is blessed, its attendants murmuring a Latin formula as they stand back to take a view and even up the edges.

So much for the table. Now for somewhere for the guests to sit.

The servants scrape over the floor a weighty chair, the Howard coat of arms carved into its back. That's for the Duke of Norfolk, who lowers his bony bum. 'What have you got,' he asks plaintively, 'to tempt my appetite, Crumb?'

Now bring up another chair, he commands the servants. Set it down at my lord Norfolk's right hand.

This one is for Henry Courtenay, the Marquis of Exeter. Who says, 'Cromwell, my wife insisted on coming!'

'It does my heart good to see you, Lady Gertrude,' he says, bowing. 'Take your seat.' Until this dinner, he has always tried to avoid this rash and interfering woman. But now he puts on his polite face: 'Any friend of the Lady Mary is welcome to dine.'

'The Princess Mary,' Gertrude Courtenay snaps.

'As you will, my lady,' he sighs.

'Now here comes Henry Pole!' Norfolk exclaims. 'Will he steal my dinner?'

'There is food for all,' he says. 'Bring up another chair for Lord Montague. A fitting chair, for a man of royal blood.'

'We call it a throne,' Montague says. 'By the way, my mother is here.'

Lady Margaret Pole, the Countess of Salisbury. Rightful queen of England, according to some. King Henry has taken a wise course with her and all her family. He has honoured them, cherished them, kept them close. Much good it's done him: they still think the Tudors are usurpers, though the countess is fond of Princess Mary, whose childhood governor she was: honouring her more for her royal mother, Katherine, than for her father, whom she regards as the spawn of Welsh cattle-raiders.

Now the countess, in his mind, creaks to her place. She stares around her. 'You have a magnificent hall here, Cromwell,' she says, peeved.

'The rewards of vice,' says her son Montague.

He bows again. He will swallow any insult, at this point.

'Well,' Norfolk says, 'where's my first dish?'

'Patience, my lord,' he says.

He takes his own place, a humble three-legged stool, down at the end of the table. He gazes up at his betters. 'In a moment the platters will come in. But first, shall we say a grace?'

He glances up at the beams. Up there are carved and painted the faces of the dead: More, Fisher, the cardinal, Katherine the queen. Below them, the flower of living England. Let us hope the roof doesn't fall in.

The day after he, Thomas Cromwell, has exercised his imagination in this way, he feels the need to clarify his position, in the real world; and to add to the guest list. His daydream has not got as far as the actual feast, so he does not know what dishes he is going to offer. He must cook up something good, or the magnates will storm out, pulling off the cloth and kicking his servants.

So: he now speaks to the Seymours, privately yet plainly. 'As long as the king holds by the queen that is now, I will hold by her too. But if he rejects her, I must reconsider.'

'So you have no interest of your own in this?' Edward Seymour says sceptically.

'I represent the king's interests. That is what I am for.'

Edward knows he will get no further. 'Still ...' he says. Anne will soon be recovered from her mishap and Henry can have her back in bed, but it is clear that the prospect has not made him lose interest in Jane. The game has changed, and Jane must be repositioned. The challenge puts a glint in Seymour eyes. Now Anne has failed again, it is possible that Henry may wish to remarry. The whole court is talking of it. It is Anne Boleyn's former success that allows them to imagine it.

'You Seymours should not raise your hopes,' he says. 'He falls out with Anne and falls in again, and then he cannot do too much for her. That is how they have always been.'

Tom Seymour says, 'Why would one prefer a tough old hen to a plump little chick? What use is it?'

'Soup,' he says: but not so that Tom can hear.

The Seymours are in mourning, though not for the dowager Katherine. Anthony Oughtred is dead, the governor of Jersey, and Jane's sister Elizabeth is left a widow.

Tom Seymour says, 'If the king takes on Jane as his mistress, or whatever, we should look to make some great match for Bess.'

Edward says, 'Just stick to the matter in hand, brother.'

The brisk young widow comes to court, to help the family in their campaign. He'd thought they called her Lizzie, this young woman, but it seems that was just her husband's name for her, and to her family she's Bess. He is glad, though he doesn't know why. It is unreasonable of him to think other women shouldn't have his wife's name. Bess is no great beauty, and darker than her sister, but she has a confident vivacity that compels the eye. 'Be kind to Jane, Master Secretary,' Bess says. 'She is not proud, as some people think. They wonder why she doesn't speak to them, but it's only because she can't think what to say.'

'But she will speak to me.'

'She will listen.'

'An attractive quality in women.'

'An attractive quality in anyone. Wouldn't you say? Though Jane above all women looks to men to tell her what she should do.'

'Then does she do it?'

'Not necessarily.' She laughs. Her fingertips brush the back of his hand. 'Come. She is ready for you.'

Warmed by the sun of the King of England's desire, which maiden would not glow? Not Jane. She is in deeper black, it seems, than the rest of her family, and she volunteers that she has been praying for the soul of the late Katherine: not that she needs it, for surely, if any woman has gone straight to Heaven …

'Jane,' Edward Seymour says, 'I am warning you now and I want you to listen carefully and heed what I say. When you come into the king's presence, it must be as if no such woman as the late Katherine ever existed. If he hears her name in your mouth, he will cease his favour, upon the instant.'

'Look,' Tom Seymour says. 'Cromwell here wants to know, are you truly and entirely a virgin?'

He could blush for her. 'If you aren't, Mistress Jane,' he says, 'it can be managed. But you must tell us now.'

Her pale, oblivious regard: 'What?'

Tom Seymour: 'Jane, even you must understand the question.'

'Is it correct that no one has ever asked for you in marriage? No contract or understanding?' He feels desperate. 'Did you never like anybody, Jane?'

'I liked William Dormer. But he married Mary Sidney.' She looks up: one flash of those ice-blue eyes. 'I hear they're very miserable.'

'The Dormers didn't think we were good enough,' Tom says. 'But now look.'

He says, 'It is to your credit, Mistress Jane, that you have formed no attachments till your family were ready to marry you. For young women often do, and then it ends badly.' He feels that he should clarify the point. 'Men will tell you that they are so in love with you that it is making them ill. They will say they have stopped eating and sleeping. They say that they fear unless they can have you they will die. Then, the moment you give in, they get up and walk away and lose all interest. The next week they will pass you by as if they don't know you.'

'Did you do this, Master Secretary?' Jane asks.

He hesitates.

'Well?' Tom Seymour says. 'We would like to know.'

'I probably did. When I was young. I am telling you in case your brothers cannot bring themselves to tell you. It is not a pretty thing for a man to have to admit to his sister.'

'So you see,' Edward urges. 'You must not give in to the king.'

Jane says, 'Why would I want to do that?'

'His honeyed words –' Edward begins.

'His what?'

The Emperor's ambassador has been skulking indoors, and won't come out to meet Thomas Cromwell. He would not go up to Peterborough for Katherine's funeral because she was not being buried as a queen, and now he says he has to observe his mourning period. Finally, a meeting is arranged: the ambassador will happen to be coming back from Mass at the church of Austin Friars, while Thomas Cromwell, now in residence at the Rolls House at Chancery Lane, has called by to inspect his building work, extensions to his principal house nearby. 'Ambassador!' he cries: as if he were wildly surprised.

The bricks ready for use today were fired last summer, when the king was still on his progress through the western counties; the clay for them was dug the winter before, and the frost was breaking down the clumps while he, Cromwell, was trying to break down Thomas More. Waiting for Chapuys to appear, he has been haranguing the bricklayers' gaffer about water penetration, which he definitely does not want. Now he takes hold of Chapuys and steers him away from the noise and dust of the sawpit. Eustache is seething with questions; you can feel them, jumping and agitating in the muscles of his arm, buzzing in the weave of his garments. 'This Semer girl ...'

It is a lightless day, still, the air frigid. 'Today would be a good day to fish for pike,' he says.

The ambassador struggles to master his dismay. 'Surely your servants ... if you must have this fish ...'

'Ah, Eustache, I see you do not understand the sport. Have no fear, I will teach you. What could be better for the health than to be out from dawn to dusk, hours and hours on a muddy bank, with the trees dripping above, watching your own breath on the air, alone or with one good companion?'

Various ideas are fighting inside the ambassador's head. On the one hand, hours and hours with Cromwell: during which he might drop his guard, say anything. On the other hand, what good am I to my Imperial master if my knees seize up entirely, and I have to be carried to court in a litter? 'Could we not fish for it in the summer?' he asks, without much hope.

'I could not risk your person. A summer pike would pull you in.' He relents. 'The lady you mean is called Seymour. As in, "Ambassador, I would like to see more of you." Though some old folk pronounce it Semer.'

'I make no progress in this tongue,' the ambassador complains. 'Anyone may say his name any way he likes, different on different days. What I hear is, the family is ancient, and the woman herself not so young.'

'She served the dowager princess, you know. She was fond of Katherine. She lamented, in fact, what had befallen her. She is troubled about the Lady Mary, and they say she has sent her messages to be of good cheer. If the king continues his favour to her, she may be able to do Mary some good.'

'Mm.' The ambassador looks sceptical. 'I have heard this, and also that she is of a very meek and pious character. But I fear there may be a scorpion lurking under the honey. I would like to see Mistress Semer, can you arrange that? Not to meet her. To glimpse her.'

'I am surprised that you take so much interest. I should have thought you would be more interested in which French princess Henry will marry, should he dissolve his present arrangements.'

Now the ambassador is stretched tight on the ladder of terror. Better the devil you know? Better Anne Boleyn, than a new threat, a new treaty, a new alliance between France and England?

'But surely not!' he explodes. 'Cremuel, you told me that this was a fairy tale! You have expressed yourself a friend of my master, you will not countenance a French match?'

'Calmly, ambassador, calmly. I do not claim I can govern Henry. And after all, he may decide to continue with his present marriage, or if not, to live chaste.'

'You are laughing!' the ambassador accuses. 'Cremuel! You are laughing behind your hand.'

And so he is. The builders skirt around them, giving them space, rough London craftsmen with tools stuck in their belts. Penitent, he says, 'Do not get your hopes up. When the king and his woman have one of their reconciliations, it goes hard with anyone who has spoken out against her in the interim.'

'You would maintain her? You would support her?' The ambassador's whole body has stiffened, as if he had really been on that riverbank all day. 'She may be your co-religionist –'

'What?' He opens his eyes wide. 'My co-religionist? Like my master the king, I am a faithful son of the holy Catholic church. Only just now we are not in communion with the Pope.'

'Let me put it another way,' Chapuys says. He squints up at the grey London sky, as if seeking help from above. 'Let us say your ties to her are material, not spiritual. I understand that you have had preferment from her. I am aware of that.'

'Do not mistake me. I owe Anne nothing. I have preferment from the king, from no one else.'

'You have sometimes called her your dear friend. I remember occasions.'

'I have sometimes called you my dear friend. But you're not, are you?'

Chapuys digests the point. 'There is nothing I wish to see more,' he says, 'than peace between our nations. What could better mark an ambassador's success in his post, than a rapprochement after years of trouble? And now we have the opportunity.'

'Now Katherine is gone.'

Chapuys does not argue with that. He just winds his cloak closer about him. 'The king has got no good of the concubine, and will get none now. No power in Europe recognises his marriage. Even the heretics do not recognise it, though she has done her best to make friends of them. What profit can there be to you, in keeping matters as they are: the king unhappy, Parliament fretful, the nobility fractious, the whole country revolted by the woman's pretensions?'

Slow drops of rain have begun to fall: ponderous, icy. Chapuys glances up again irritably, as if God were undermining him at this crucial point. Taking a grip on the ambassador once more, he tows him over the rough ground towards shelter. The builders have put up a canopy, and he turns them out, saying, 'Give us a minute, boys, will you?' Chapuys huddles by the brazier, and grows confidential. 'I hear the king talks of witchcraft,' he whispers. 'He says that he was seduced into the marriage by certain charms and false practices. I see he does not confide in you. But he has spoken to his confessor. If this is so, if he entered into the match in a state of entrancement, then he might find he is not married at all, and free to take a new wife.'

He gazes over the ambassador's shoulder. Look, he says, this is how it will be: in a year these damp and freezing spaces will be inhabited rooms. His hand sketches the line of the jettied upper storeys, the glazed bays.

Inventories for this project: lime and sand, oak timbers and special cements, spades and shovels, baskets and ropes, tackets, pin nails, roof nails, lead pipes; tiles yellow and tiles blue, window locks, latches, bolts and hinges, iron door handles in the shape of roses; gilding, painting, 2 lb. of frankincense to perfume the new rooms; 6d per day per labourer, and the cost of candles for labour by night.

'My friend,' Chapuys says, 'Anne is desperate and dangerous. Strike first, before she strikes you. Remember how she brought down Wolsey.'

His past lies about him like a burnt house. He has been building, building, but it has taken him years to sweep up the mess.

At the Rolls House, he finds his son, who is packing to go away for the next phase of his education. 'Gregory, you know St Uncumber? You say that women pray to her to be rid of useless husbands. Now, is there a saint that men can pray to if they wish to be quit of their wives?'

'I don't think so.' Gregory is shocked. 'The women pray because they have no other means. A man can consult a cleric to find why the marriage is not licit. Or he can chase her away and pay her money to stay in a separate house. As the Duke of Norfolk pays his wife.'

He nods. 'That's very helpful, Gregory.'

Anne Boleyn comes up to Whitehall to celebrate the feast of St Matthias with the king. She has changed, all in a season. She is light, starved, she looks as she did in her days of waiting, those futile years of negotiations before he, Thomas Cromwell, came along and cut the knot. Her flamboyant liveliness has faded to something austere, narrow, almost nun-like. But she does not have a nun's composure. Her fingers play with the jewels at her girdle, tug at her sleeves, touch and retouch the jewels at her throat.

Lady Rochford says, 'She thought that when she was queen, she would take comfort in going over the days of her coronation, hour by hour. But she says she has forgotten them. When she tries to remember, it's as if it happened to someone else, and she wasn't there. She didn't tell me this, of course. She told brother George.'

From the queen's rooms comes a dispatch: a prophetess has told her that she will not bear Henry a son while his daughter Mary is alive.

You have to admire it, he says to his nephew. She is on the offensive. She is like a serpent, you do not know when she will strike.

He has always rated Anne highly as a strategist. He has never believed in her as a passionate, spontaneous woman. Everything she does is calculated, like everything he does. He notes, as he has these many years, the careful deployment of her flashing eyes. He wonders what it would take to make her panic.

The king sings:

> 'My most desire my hand may reach,
> My will is always at my hand;
> Me need not long for to beseech,
> Her that has power me to command.'

So he thinks. He can beseech and beseech, but it has no effect on Jane.

But the nation's business must go forward, and this is how: an act to give Wales members of Parliament, and make English the language of the law courts, and to cut from under them the powers of the lords of the Welsh marches. An act to dissolve the small monasteries, those houses worth under two hundred pounds a year. An act to set up a Court of Augmentations, a new body to deal with the inflow of revenue from these monasteries: Richard Riche to be its chancellor.

In March, Parliament knocks back his new poor law. It was too much for the Commons to digest, that rich men might have some duty to the poor; that if you get fat, as gentlemen of England do, on the wool trade, you have some responsibility to the men turned off the land, the labourers without labour, the sowers without a field. England needs roads, forts, harbours, bridges. Men need work. It's a shame to see them begging their bread, when honest labour could keep the realm secure. Can we not put them together, the hands and the task?

But Parliament cannot see how it is the state's job to create work. Are not these matters in God's hands, and is not poverty and dereliction part of his eternal order? To everything there is a season: a time to starve and a time to thieve. If rain falls for six months solid and rots the grain in the fields, there must be providence in it; for God knows his trade. It is an outrage to the rich and enterprising, to suggest that they should pay an income tax, only to put bread in the mouths of the workshy. And if Secretary Cromwell argues that famine provokes criminality: well, are there not hangmen enough?

The king himself comes to the Commons to argue for the law. He wants to be Henry the Beloved, a father to his people, a shepherd to his flock. But the Commons sit stony-faced on their benches and stare him out. The wreckage of the measure is comprehensive. 'It has ended up as an act for the whipping of beggars,' Richard Riche says. 'It is more against the poor than for them.'

'Perhaps we can bring it in again,' Henry says. 'In a better year. Do not lose heart, Master Secretary.'

So: there will be better years, will there? He will keep trying; sneak it past them when they're off their guard, start off the measure in the Lords and face down the opposition ... there are ways and ways with Parliament, but there are times he wishes he could kick the members back to their own shires, because he could get on faster without them. He says, 'If I were king, I would not take it so quietly. I would make them shake in their shoes.'

Richard Riche is Mr Speaker in this Parliament; he says nervously, 'Don't incense the king, sir. You know what More used to say. "If the lion knew his own strength, it were hard to rule him."'

'Thank you,' he says. 'That consoles me mightily, Sir Purse, a text from the grave from that blood-soaked hypocrite. Has he anything else to say about the situation? Because if so I'm going to get his head back off his daughter and boot it up and down Whitehall till he shuts up for good and all.' He bursts into laughter. 'The Commons. God rot them. Their heads are empty. They never think higher than their pockets.'

Still, if his fellows in Parliament are worried about their incomes, he is buoyant about his own. Though the lesser monastic houses are to be dissolved, they may apply for exemptions, and all these applications come to him, accompanied by a fee or a pension. The king will not keep all his new lands in his own name, but lease them out, so continual application is made to him, for this place or that, for manors, farms, pasture; each applicant offers him a little something, a one-off payment or an annuity, an annuity that will pass to Gregory in time. It's the way business has always been done, favours, sweeteners, a timely transfer of funds to secure attention, or a promise of split proceeds: just now there is so much business, so many transactions, so many offers he can hardly, in civility, decline. No man in England works harder than he does. Say what you like about Thomas Cromwell, he offers good value for what he takes. And he's always ready to lend: William Fitzwilliam, Sir Nicholas Carew, that ageing one-eyed reprobate Francis Bryan.

He gets Sir Francis round and gets him drunk. He, Cromwell, can trust himself; when he was young, he learned to drink with Germans. It's over a year since Francis Bryan quarrelled with George Boleyn: over what, Francis hardly remembers, but the grudge remains, and until his legs go from under him he is able to act out the more florid bits of the row, standing up and waving his arms. Of his cousin Anne he says, 'You like to know where you are with a woman. Is she a harlot, or a lady? Anne wants you to treat her like the Virgin Mary, but she also wants you to put your cash on the table, do the business and get out.'

Sir Francis is intermittently pious, as conspicuous sinners tend to be. Lent is here: 'It is time for you to enter into your yearly frenzy of penitence, is it not?'

Francis pushes up the patch on his blind eye, and rubs the scar tissue; it itches, he explains. 'Of course,' he says, 'Wyatt's had her.'

He, Thomas Cromwell, waits.

But then Francis puts his head down on the table, and begins to snore.

'The Vicar of Hell,' he says thoughtfully. He calls for boys to come in. 'Take Sir Francis home to his own people. But wrap him up warm, we may need his testimony in the days to come.'

He wonders exactly how much you'd have to leave on the table, for Anne. She's cost Henry his honour, his peace of mind. To him, Cromwell, she is just another trader. He admires the way she's laid out her goods. He personally doesn't want to buy; but there are customers enough.

Now Edward Seymour is promoted into the king's privy chamber, a singular mark of favour. And the king says to him, 'I think I should have young Rafe Sadler among my grooms. He is a gentleman born, and a pleasant young man to have near me, and I think it would help you, Cromwell, would it not? Only he is not for ever to be putting papers under my nose.'

Rafe's wife Helen bursts into tears when she hears the news. 'He will be away at court,' she says, 'for weeks at a time.'

He sits with her in the parlour at Brick Place, consoling her as best he can. 'This is the best thing that has ever happened for Rafe, I know,' she says. 'I am a fool to weep over it. But I cannot bear to be parted from him, nor he from me. When he is late I send men to look along the road. I wish we could be under the same roof every night we live.'

'He is a lucky man,' he says. 'And I don't mean just lucky in the king's favour. You are both of you lucky. To love so much.'

Henry used to sing a song, in his Katherine days:

'I hurt no man, I do no wrong,
I love true where I did marry.'

Rafe says, 'You need a steady nerve, to be always with Henry.'

'You have a steady nerve, Rafe.'

He could give him advice. Extracts from The Book Called Henry. As a child, a young man, praised for the sweetness of his nature and his golden looks, Henry grew up believing that all the world was his friend and everybody wanted him to be happy. So any pain, any delay, frustration or stroke of ill-luck seems to him an anomaly, an outrage. Any activity he finds wearying or displeasant, he will try honestly to turn into an amusement, and if he cannot find some thread of pleasure he will avoid it; this to him seems reasonable and natural. He has councillors employed to fry their brains on his behalf, and if he is out of temper it is probably their fault; they shouldn't block him or provoke him. He doesn't want people who say, 'No, but ...' He wants people who say, 'Yes, and ...' He doesn't like men who are pessimistic and sceptical, who turn down their mouths and cost out his brilliant projects with a scribble in the margin of their papers. So do the sums in your head where no one can see them. Do not expect consistency from him. Henry prides himself on understanding his councillors, their secret opinions and desires, but he is resolved that none of his councillors shall understand him. He is suspicious of any plan that doesn't originate with himself, or seem to. You can argue with him but you must be careful how and when. You are better to give way on every possible point until the vital point, and to pose yourself as one in need of guidance and instruction, rather than to maintain a fixed opinion from the start and let him think you believe you know better than he does. Be sinuous in argument and allow him escapes: don't corner him, don't back him against the wall. Remember that his mood depends on other people, so consider who has been with him since you were with him last. Remember he wants more than to be advised of his

208

power, he wants to be told he is right. He is never in error. It is only that other people commit errors on his behalf or deceive him with false information. Henry wants to be told that he is behaving well, in the sight of God and man. 'Cromwell,' he says, 'you know what we should try? Cromwell, would it not reflect well on my honour if I ...? Cromwell, would it not confound my enemies if ...?' And all these are the ideas you put to him last week. Never mind. You don't want the credit. You just want action.

But there is no need for these lessons. All his life Rafe has been training for this. A scrap of a boy, he is no athlete, he could never exercise himself in tilt or tournament, a stray breeze would whisk him out of the saddle. But he has the heft for this. He knows how to watch. He knows how to listen. He knows how to send a message encrypted, or a message so secret that no message appears to be there; a piece of information so solid that its meaning seems to be stamped out in the earth, yet its form so fragile that it seems to be conveyed by angels. Rafe knows his master; Henry is his master. But Cromwell is his father and his friend.

You can be merry with the king, you can share a joke with him. But as Thomas More used to say, it's like sporting with a tamed lion. You tousle its mane and pull its ears, but all the time you're thinking, those claws, those claws, those claws.

In Henry's new church, Lent is as raw and cold as ever it was under the Pope. Miserable, meatless days fray a man's temper. When Henry talks about Jane, he blinks, tears spring to his eyes. 'Her little hands, Crumb. Her little paws, like a child's. She has no guile in her. And she never speaks. And if she does I have to bend my head to hear what she says. And in the pause I can hear my heart. Her little bits of embroidery, her scraps of silk, her halcyon sleeves she cut out of the cloth some admirer gave her once, some poor boy struck with love for her ... and yet she has never succumbed. Her little sleeves, her seed pearl necklace ...

209

she has nothing ... she expects nothing ...' A tear at last sneaks from Henry's eye, meanders down his cheek and vanishes into the mottled grey and ginger of his beard.

Notice how he speaks of Jane: so humble, so shy. Even Archbishop Cranmer must recognise the portrait, the black reverse portrait of the present queen. All the riches of the New World would not sate her; while Jane is grateful for a smile.

I am going to write Jane a letter, Henry says. I am going to send her a purse, for she will need money for herself now she is removed from the queen's chamber.

Paper and quills are brought to his hand. He sits down and sighs and sets about it. The king's handwriting is square, the hand he learned as a child from his mother. He has never picked up speed; the more effort he puts into it, the more the letters seem to turn back on themselves. He takes pity on him: 'Sir, would you like to dictate it, and I will write for you?'

It would not be the first time he has written a love letter for Henry. Over their sovereign's bent head, Cranmer looks up and meets his eyes: full of accusation.

'Have a look,' Henry says. He doesn't offer it to Cranmer. 'She'll understand, yes, that I want her?'

He reads, trying to put himself in the place of a maiden lady. He looks up. 'It is very delicately expressed, sir. And she is very innocent.'

Henry takes the letter back and writes in a few reinforcing phrases.

It is the end of March. Mistress Seymour, stricken with panic, seeks an interview with Mr Secretary; it is set up by Sir Nicholas Carew, though Sir Nicholas himself is absent, not yet ready to commit himself to talks. Her widowed sister is with her. Bess gives him a searching glance; then drops her bright eyes.

'Here is my difficulty,' Jane says. She looks at him wildly; he thinks, maybe that's all she means to say: here is my difficulty.

She says, 'You can't … His Grace, His Majesty, you can't for one moment forget who he is, even though he demands you do. The more he says, "Jane I am your humble suitor," the less humble you know he is. And every moment you are thinking, what if he stops talking and I have to say something? I feel as if I'm standing on a pincushion, with the pins pointing up. I keep thinking, I'll get used to it, next time I'll be better, but when he comes in, "Jane, Jane …" I'm like a scalded cat. Though, have you ever seen a scalded cat, Master Secretary? I have not. But I think, if after this short time I'm so frightened of him –'

'He wants people to be frightened.' With the words arrives the truth of them. But Jane is too intent on her own struggles to hear what he has said.

'– if I'm frightened of him now, what will it be like to see him every day?' She breaks off. 'Oh. I suppose you know. You do see him, Master Secretary, most days. Still. Not the same, I suppose.'

'No, not the same,' he says.

He sees Bess, in sympathy, raise her eyes to her sister. 'But Master Cromwell,' Bess says, 'it cannot always be acts of Parliament and dispatches to ambassadors and revenue and Wales and monks and pirates and traitorous devices and Bibles and oaths and trusts and wards and leases and the price of wool and whether we should pray for the dead. There must sometimes be other topics.'

He is struck by her overview of his situation. It is as if she has understood his life. He is taken by an impulse to clasp her hand and ask her to marry him; even if they did not get on in bed, she seems to have a gift for précis that eludes most of his clerks.

'Well?' Jane says. 'Are there? Other topics?'

He can't think. He squashes his soft hat between his hands. 'Horses,' he says. 'Henry likes to know about trades and crafts, simple things. In my youth I learned to shoe a horse, he likes to know about that, the right shoe for the job, so he can confound his own smiths with secret knowledge. The archbishop, too, he is

211

a man who will ride any horse that comes to his hand, he is a timid man but horses like him, he learned to manage them when he was young. When he is tired of God and men we speak of these matters with the king.'

'And?' Bess says. 'You are together many hours.'

'Dogs, sometimes. Hunting dogs, their breeding and virtues. Fortresses. Building them. Artillery. The range of it. Cannon foundries. Dear God.' He runs his hand through his hair. 'We sometimes say, we will have a day out together, ride down to Kent, to the weald, to see the ironmasters there, study their operations, and propose them new ways of casting cannon. But we never do it. Something is always in our way.'

He feels irredeemably sad. As if he has been plunged into mourning. And at the same time he feels, if someone tossed a feather bed into the room (which is unlikely) he would throw Bess on to it, and have to do with her.

'Well, that's that,' Jane says, her tone resigned. 'I could not found a cannon to save my life. I am sorry to have taken your time, Master Secretary. You had better get back to Wales.'

He knows what she means.

Next day, the king's love letter is brought to Jane, with a heavy purse. It is a scene staged before witnesses. 'I must return this purse,' Jane says. (But she does not say it before she has weighed it, fondled it, in her tiny hand.) 'I must beg the king, if he wishes to make me a present of money, to send it again when I should contract an honourable marriage.'

Given the king's letter, she declares she had better not open it. For well she knows his heart, his gallant and ardent heart. For herself, her only possession is her womanly honour, her maidenhead. So – no, really – she had better not break the seal.

And then, before she returns it to the messenger, she holds it in her two hands: and places, on the seal, a chaste kiss.

'She kissed it!' Tom Seymour cries. 'What genius possessed her? First his seal. Next,' he sniggers, 'his sceptre!'

In a fit of joy, he knocks his brother Edward's hat off. He has been playing this joke for twenty years or more, and Edward has never been amused. But just this once, he fetches up a smile.

When the king gets the letter back from Jane, he listens closely to what his messenger has to tell him, and his face lights up. 'I see I was wrong to send it. Cromwell here has spoken to me of her innocence and her virtue, and with good reason, as it appears. From this point I will do nothing that will offend her honour. In fact, I shall only speak to her in the presence of her kin.'

If Edward Seymour's wife were to come to court, they could make a family party, with whom the king could take supper without any affront to Jane's modesty. Perhaps Edward should have a suite in the palace? Those rooms of mine at Greenwich, he reminds Henry, that communicate directly with yours: what if I were to move out and let the Seymours move in? Henry beams at him.

He has been studying the Seymour brothers intently since the visit to Wolf Hall. He will have to work with them; Henry's women come trailing families, he does not find his brides in the forest hiding under a leaf. Edward is grave, serious, yet he is ready to unfold his thoughts to you. Tom is close, that's what he thinks; close and cunning, brain busily working beneath that show of bonhomie. But it's perhaps not the best brain. Tom Seymour will give me no trouble, he thinks, and Edward I can carry with me. His mind is already moving ahead, to a time when the king indicates his pleasure. Gregory and the Emperor's ambassador, between them, have suggested the way forward. 'If he can annul twenty years with his true wife,' Chapuys has said to him, 'I am sure it is not beyond your wit to find some grounds to free him from his concubine. No one has ever believed the marriage was good in the first place, except those who are employed to say yes to him.'

He wonders, though, about the ambassador's 'no one'. No one in the Emperor's court, perhaps: but all England has sworn to the marriage. It is not a light matter, he tells his nephew Richard, to undo it legally, even if the king commanded it. We shall wait a little, we will not go to anyone, let them come to us.

He asks for a document to be drawn up, showing all grants to the Boleyns since 1524. 'Such a thing would be good to have at my hand, in case the king calls for it.'

He does not mean to take anything away. Rather, enhance their holdings. Load them with honours. Laugh at their jokes.

Though you must be careful what you laugh at. Master Sexton, the king's jester, has jested about Anne and called her a ribald. He thought he had licence, but Henry lumbered across the hall and clouted him, banged his head on the panelling and banished him the court. They say Nicholas Carew gave the man refuge, out of pity.

Anthony is aggrieved about Sexton. One jester does not like to hear of the downfall of another; especially, Anthony says, when his only vice is foresight. Oh, he says, you have been listening to the gossip in the kitchen. But the fool says, 'Henry kicks out the truth and Master Sexton with it. But these days it has a way of creeping under the bolted door and down the chimney. One day he will give in and invite it to stand by the hearth.'

William Fitzwilliam comes to the Rolls House and sits down with him. 'So how does the queen, Crumb? Still perfect friends, though you dine with the Seymours?'

He smiles.

Fitzwilliam jumps up, wrenches the door open to see no one is lurking, then sits down again, and resumes. 'Cast your mind back. This Boleyn courtship, this Boleyn marriage. How did the king look, in the eyes of grown men? Like one who only studies his own pleasures. Like a child, that is to say. To be so impassioned, to be so enslaved by a woman, who after all is made just as other women are – some said it was unmanly.'

'Did they? Well, I am shocked. We cannot have it said of Henry that he is not a man.'

'A man' – and Fitzwilliam stresses the word – 'a man should be governor of his passions. Henry shows much force of will but little wisdom. It harms him. She harms him. The harm will go on.'

It seems he will not name her, Anna Bolena, La Ana, the concubine. So, if she harms the king, would it be the act of a good Englishman to remove her? The possibility lies between them, approached but still unexplored. It is treason, of course, to speak against the present queen and her heirs; a treason from which the king alone is exempt, for he could not violate his own interest. He reminds Fitzwilliam of this: he adds, even if Henry speaks against her, do not be drawn.

'But what do we look for in a queen?' Fitzwilliam asks. 'She should have all the virtues of an ordinary woman, but she must have them to a high degree. She must be more modest, more humble, more discreet and more obedient even than they: so that she sets an example. There are those who ask themselves, is Anne Boleyn any of these things?'

He looks at Master Treasurer: go on.

'I think I can speak frankly to you, Cromwell,' Fitz says: and (after checking at the door once again) he does. 'A queen should be mild and pitiful. She should move the king to mercy – not drive him on to harshness.'

'You have some particular case in mind?'

Fitz was in Wolsey's household as a young man. No one knows what part Anne played in the fall of the cardinal; her hand was hidden in her sleeve. Wolsey knew he could hope for no mercy from her, and he received none. But Fitz seems to brush away the cardinal. He says, 'I hold no brief for Thomas More. He was not the adept in affairs of state that he thought he was. He thought he could sway the king, he thought he could control him, he thought that Henry was still a sweet young prince he could lead by the hand. But Henry is a king and he will be obeyed.'

'Yes, and?'

'And I wish that with More it could have ended another way. A scholar, a man who was Lord Chancellor, to drag him out in the rain and cut off his head ...'

He says, 'You know, sometimes I forget he's gone. There is some piece of news and I think, what will More say to this?'

Fitz glances up. 'You don't talk to him, do you?'

He laughs. 'I don't go to him for advice.' Though I do, of course, consult the cardinal: in the privacy of my short hours of sleep.

Fitz says, 'Thomas More scuttled his chances with Anne when he would not come to see her crowned. She would have seen him dead a year before it happened, if she could have proved treason on him.'

'But More was a clever lawyer. Amongst the other things he was.'

'The Princess Mary – the Lady Mary, I should say – she is no lawyer. A friendless girl.'

'Oh, I would think that her cousin the Emperor counts as her friend. And a very good friend to have, too.'

Fitz looks irritated. 'The Emperor is a great idol, set up in another country. Day by day, she needs a more proximate defender. She needs someone to push forward her interests. Stop this, Crumb – this dancing around the point.'

'Mary just needs to keep breathing,' he says. 'I am not often accused of dancing.'

Fitzwilliam stands up. 'Well now. A word to the wise.'

The feeling is that something is wrong in England and must be set right. It's not the laws that are wrong or the customs. It's something deeper.

Fitzwilliam leaves the room, then he comes back in. Says abruptly, 'If it is old Seymour's daughter next, there will be some jealousy among those who think their own noble house should be preferred – but after all, the Seymours are an ancient family, and he won't have this trouble with her. I mean, men running after her like dogs after a – well ... You just look at her, Seymour's little girl, and you know that nobody's ever pulled her skirts up.' This time he does go; but giving him, Cromwell, a sort of mock salute, a flourish in the direction of his hat.

Sir Nicholas Carew comes to see him. The very fibres of his beard are bristling with conspiracy. He half-expects the knight to wink as he sits down.

When it comes to it, Carew is surprisingly brisk. 'We want the concubine ousted. We know you want it too.'

'We?'

Carew looks up at him, from beneath bristling brows; like a man who has shot off his one crossbow bolt, he must now plod over the terrain, seeking friend or foe or just a place to hide for the night. Ponderously, he clarifies. 'My friends in this matter do comprise a good part of the ancient nobility of this nation, those of honourable lineage, and ...' He sees Cromwell's face and hurries on. 'I speak of those very near the throne, those in the line of old King Edward. Lord Exeter, the Courtenay family. Also Lord Montague and his brother Geoffrey Pole. Lady Margaret Pole, who as you know was governor to the Princess Mary.'

He casts up his eyes. 'Lady Mary.'

'If you must. We call her the princess.'

He nods. 'We will not let that stop us discussing her.'

'Those I have named,' Carew says, 'are the principal persons on whose behalf I speak, but as you will be aware, the most part of England would rejoice to see the king free of her.'

'I don't think the most part of England knows or cares.' Carew means, of course, the most part of *my* England, the England of ancient blood. Any other country, for Sir Nicholas, does not exist.

He says, 'I suppose Exeter's wife Gertrude is active in this matter.'

'She has been,' Carew leans forward to impart something very secret, 'in communication with Mary.'

'I know,' he sighs.

'You read their letters?'

'I read everybody's letters.' Including yours. 'But look,' he says, 'this smells of intrigue against the king himself, does it not?'

'In no wise. His honour is at the heart of it.'

He nods. Point taken. 'And so? What do you require of me?'

'We require you to join with us. We are content to have Seymour's girl crowned. The young woman is my kin, and she is known to favour true religion. We believe she will bring Henry back to Rome.'

'A cause close to my heart,' he murmurs.

Sir Nicholas leans forward. 'This is our difficulty, Cromwell. You are a Lutheran.'

He touches his jacket: round about his heart. 'No, sir, I am a banker. Luther condemns to Hell those who lend at interest. Is it likely that I should take his part?'

Sir Nicholas laughs heartily. 'I did not know. Where would we be, without Cromwell to lend us money?'

He asks, 'What is to happen to Anne Boleyn?'

'I don't know. Convent?'

So the bargain is struck and sealed: he, Cromwell, is to assist the old families, the true faithful; and afterwards, under the new regime, they will keep his services in consideration: his zeal in this matter may cause them to forget the blasphemies of these last three years, which otherwise would invite condign punishment.

'Just one thing, Cromwell.' Carew stands up. 'Don't keep me waiting next time. It ill becomes a man of your stamp to keep a man of my stamp kicking his heels in an anteroom.'

'Ah, was that the noise?' Though Carew wears the padded satin of the courtier, he always imagines him in show-armour: not the kind you fight in, the kind you buy from Italy to impress your friends. Heel-kicking would be a noisy business, then: clatter, clang. He looks up. 'I meant no slight, Sir Nicholas. From now we will make all speed. Consider me at your right hand, furnished for the fight.'

That's the sort of bombast Carew understands.

Now Fitzwilliam is talking to Carew. Carew is talking to his wife, who is Francis Bryan's sister. His wife is talking, or writing at least, to Mary to let her know that her prospects are improving by the hour, that La Ana may be displaced. At the very least, it's a way of keeping Mary quiet for the while. He doesn't want her to hear the rumours that Anne is launching fresh hostilities. She may panic, and try to escape; they say she has various absurd plans, like drugging the Boleyn women about her and spurring off by night. He has warned Chapuys, though not in so many words of course, that if Mary does escape Henry is likely to hold him responsible, and to have no regard for the protection of his diplomatic status. At the very least, he will be booted around like Sexton the jester. At worst, he may never see his native shores again.

Francis Bryan is keeping the Seymours at Wolf Hall abreast of events at court. Fitzwilliam and Carew are talking to the Marquis of Exeter, and Gertrude, his wife. Gertrude is talking over supper to the Imperial ambassador, and to the Pole family, who are as papist as they dare to be, who have teetered on the edge of treason these last four years. No one is talking to the French ambassador. But everyone is talking to him, Thomas Cromwell.

In sum, this is the question his new friends are asking: if Henry can retire one wife, and she a daughter of Spain, can he not give a pension to Boleyn's daughter and put her away in some country house, having found defects in the marriage documents? His casting off of Katherine, after twenty years of marriage, offended all Europe. The marriage with Anne is recognised nowhere but in this realm, and has not endured three years; he could annul it, as a folly. After all, he has his own church to do so, his own archbishop.

In his head he rehearses a request. 'Sir Nicholas? Sir William? Will you come to my humble house to dine?'

He does not really mean to ask them. Word would soon reach the queen. A coded glance is enough, a nod and a wink. But once again in his mind he sets the table.

Norfolk at the head. Montague and his sainted mother. Courtenay and his blasted wife. Sliding in behind them, our friend Monsieur Chapuys. 'Oh, dammit,' Norfolk sulks, 'now must we speak French?'

'I will translate,' he offers. But who's this clattering in? It's Duke Dishpan. 'Welcome, my lord Suffolk,' he says. 'Take a seat. Careful not to get crumbs in that great beard of yours.'

'If there were a crumb.' Norfolk is hungry.

Margaret Pole spears him with a glacial stare. 'You have set a table. You have given us all seats. You have given us no napery.'

'My apologies.' He calls for a servant. 'You wouldn't want to get your hands dirty.'

Margaret Pole shakes out her napkin. On it is imprinted the face of the dead Katherine.

A bawling comes from without, the direction of the buttery. Francis Bryan reels in, already a bottle to the good. '*Pastime with good company ...*' He crashes to his place.

Now he, Cromwell, nods to his menials. Extra stools are fetched. 'Squeeze them in,' he says.

Carew and Fitzwilliam enter. They take their places without a smile or a nod. They have come ready to the feast, their knives in their hands.

He looks around at his guests. All are prepared. A Latin grace; English would be his choice, but he will suit his company. Who cross themselves ostentatiously, in papist style. Who look at him, expectant.

He shouts for the waiters. The doors burst open. Sweating men heave the platters to the table. It seems the meat is fresh, in fact not slaughtered yet.

It is just a minor breach of etiquette. The company must sit and salivate.

The Boleyns are laid at his hand to be carved.

Now that Rafe is in the privy chamber, he has closer acquaintance with the musician, Mark Smeaton, who has been promoted among the grooms. When Mark first showed himself at the cardinal's door, he sloped up in patched boots and a canvas doublet that had belonged to a bigger man. The cardinal put him into worsted, but since he joined the royal household he goes in damask, perched on a fine gelding with a saddle of Spanish leather, the reins clutched in gold-fringed gloves. Where is the money coming from? Anne is recklessly generous, Rafe says. The gossip is that she has given Francis Weston a sum to keep his creditors at bay.

You can understand, Rafe says, that because now the king does not admire the queen so much, she is keen to have young men about her who hang on her words. Her rooms are busy thoroughfares, the privy chamber gentlemen constantly calling in on this errand or that, and lingering to play a game or share a song; where there is no message to carry, they invent one.

Those gentlemen who are less in the queen's favour are keen to talk to the newcomer and give him all the gossip. And some things he doesn't need to be told, he can see and hear for himself. Whispering and scuffling behind doors. Covert mockery of the king. Of his clothes, of his music. Hints of his shortcomings in bed. Where would those hints come from, but the queen?

There are some men who talk all the time about their horses. This is a steady mount but I used to have one speedier; that's a fine filly you have there, but you should see this bay I have my eye on. With Henry, it's ladies: he finds something to like in almost any female who crosses his path, and will scratch up a compliment for her, though she be plain and old and sour. With the young ones, he is enraptured twice a day: has she not the finest eyes, is not her throat white, her voice sweet, her hand shapely? Generally it's look and don't touch: the most he will venture, blushing slightly, 'Don't you think she must have pretty little duckies?'

One day Rafe hears Weston's voice in the next room, running on, amused, in imitation of the king: 'Has she not the wettest cunt you ever groped?' Giggles, complicit sniggers. And 'Hush! Cromwell's spy is about.'

Harry Norris has been absent from court lately, spending time on his own estates. When he is on duty, Rafe says, he tries to suppress the talk, sometimes seems angry at it; but sometimes he lets himself smile. They talk about the queen and they speculate …

Go on, Rafe, he says.

Rafe doesn't like telling this. He feels it is below him to be an eavesdropper. He thinks hard before he speaks. 'The queen needs to conceive another child quickly to please the king, but where is it to come from, they ask. Since Henry cannot be trusted to do the business, which of them is to do him a favour?'

'Did they come to any conclusion?'

Rafe rubs the crown of his head and makes his hair stand up. You know, he says, they would not really do it. None of them. The queen is sacred. It is too great a sin even for such lustful men as they be, and they are too much in fear of the king, surely, even though they mock him. Besides, she would not be so foolish.

'I ask you again, did they come to any conclusion?'

'I think it's every man for himself.'

He laughs. '*Sauve qui peut.*'

He hopes none of this will be needed. If he acts against Anne he hopes for a cleaner way. It's all foolish talk. But Rafe cannot unhear it, he cannot unknow it, there it is.

March weather, April weather, icy showers and splinters of sun; he meets Chapuys, indoors, this time.

'You seem pensive, Master Secretary. Come to the fire.'

He shakes away the raindrops from his hat. 'I have a weight on my mind.'

'Do you know, I think you only set up these meetings with me to annoy the French ambassador?'

'Oh yes,' he sighs, 'he is very jealous. In truth I would visit you more often, except that word always gets back to the queen. And she contrives to use it against me in one way or another.'

'I could wish you a more gracious mistress.' The ambassador's implicit question: how is that going, the getting of a new mistress? Chapuys has floated to him, could there not be a new treaty between our sovereigns? Something that would safeguard Mary, her interests, perhaps place her back in the line of succession, after any children Henry might have with a new wife? Assuming, of course, the present queen were gone?

'Ah, Lady Mary.' Lately he has taken to putting his hand to his hat when her name is mentioned. He can see the ambassador is touched by this, he can see him preparing to put it in dispatches. 'The king is willing to hold formal talks. It would please him to be united in friendship to the Emperor. So much he has said.'

'Now you must bring him to the point.'

'I have influence with the king but I cannot answer for him, no subject can. This is my difficulty. To succeed with him, one must anticipate his desires. But one then stands exposed, should he change his mind.'

Wolsey his master had advised, make him say what he wants, do not guess, for by guessing you may destroy yourself. But perhaps, since Wolsey's day, the king's unexpressed commands have become harder to ignore. He fills the room with a seething discontent, stares up into the sky when you ask him to sign a paper: as if he were expecting deliverance.

'You fear he will turn on you,' Chapuys says.

'He will, I suppose. One day.'

Sometimes he wakes in the night and thinks of it. There are courtiers who have honourably retired. He can think of instances. Of course, it is the other kind that loom larger, if you are wakeful around midnight. 'But if that day comes,' the ambassador says, 'what will you do?'

'What can I do? Arm myself with patience and leave the rest to God.' And hope the end is quick.

'Your piety does you credit,' Chapuys says. 'If fortune turns against you, you will need friends. The Emperor –'

'The Emperor would not spare a thought for me, Eustache. Or for any common man. No one raised a finger to help the cardinal.'

'The poor cardinal. I wish I had known him better.'

'Stop buttering me up,' he says sharply. 'Have done.'

Chapuys gives him a searching glance. The fire roars up. Vapours rise from his clothes. The rain patters at the window. He shivers. 'You are ill?' Chapuys enquires.

'No, I am not allowed to be. If I took to my bed the queen would turn me out of it and say I am faking. If you want to cheer me up, get out that Christmas hat of yours. It was a pity you had to put it away for mourning. Easter would be none too soon to see it again.'

'I think you are making jokes, Thomas, at the expense of my hat. I have heard that while it was in your custody it was derided, not only by your clerks but by your stable boys and dog-keepers.'

'The reverse is true. There were many applications to try it on. I wish that we may see it at all major feasts of the church.'

'Once again,' Chapuys says, 'your piety does you credit.'

* * *

He sends Gregory away to his friend Richard Southwell, to learn the art of speaking in public. It is good for him to get out of London, and to get away from the court, where the atmosphere is tense. All around him there are signs of unease, little huddles of courtiers that disperse at his approach. If he is to place all in hazard, and he thinks he is, then Gregory should not have to go through the pain and doubt, hour by hour. Let him hear the conclusion of events; he does not need to live through them. He has no time now to explain the world to the simple and the young. He has to watch the movements of cavalry and ordnance across Europe, and the ships on the seas, merchantmen and men of war: the influx of gold from the Americas to the treasury of the Emperor. Sometimes peace looks like war, you cannot tell them apart; sometimes these islands look very small. The word from Europe is that Mount Etna has erupted, and brought floods throughout Sicily. In Portugal there is a drought; and everywhere, envy and contention, fear of the future, fear of hunger or the fact of it, fear of God and doubt over how to placate him, and in what language. The news, when he gets it, is always a fortnight out of date: the posts are slow, the tides against him. Just as the work of fortifying Dover is coming to an end, the walls of Calais are falling down; frost has cracked the masonry and opened a fissure between Watergate and Lanterngate.

On Passion Sunday a sermon is preached in the king's chapel by Anne's almoner, John Skip. It appears to be an allegory; the force of it appears to be directed against him, Thomas Cromwell. He smiles broadly when those who attended explain it to him, sentence by sentence: his ill-wishers and well-wishers both. He is not a man to be knocked over by a sermon, or to feel himself persecuted by figures of speech.

Once when he was a boy he had been in a rage against his father Walter and he had rushed at him, intent to butt him in the belly with his head. But it was just before the Cornish rebels came swarming up the country, and as Putney reckoned it was in their line of march, Walter had been bashing out body armour for himself and his friends. So when he ran head-first, there was a bang, which he heard before he felt it. Walter was trying on one of his creations. 'That'll teach you,' his father said, phlegmatic.

He often thinks about it, that iron belly. And he thinks he has got one, without the inconvenience and weight of metal. 'Cromwell has plenty stomach,' his friends say; his enemies too. They mean he has appetite, gusto, attack: first thing in the morning or last thing at night, a bloody collop of meat would not disgust him, and if you wake him in the small hours he is hungry then too.

An inventory comes in, from Tilney Abbey: vestments of red turkey satin and white lawn, wrought with beasts in gold. Two altar cloths of white Bruges satin, with drops like spots of blood, made of red velvet. And the contents of the kitchen: weights, tongs and fire forks, flesh hooks.

Winter melts into spring. Parliament is dissolved. Easter Day: lamb with ginger sauce, a blessed absence of fish. He remembers the eggs the children used to paint, giving each speckled shell a cardinal's hat. He remembers his daughter Anne, her hot little hand cupped around the eggshell so the colour ran: 'Look! *Regardez!*' She was learning French that year. Then her amazed face; her curious tongue creeping out to lick the stain from her palm.

The Emperor is in Rome, and the word is that he has had a seven-hour meeting with the Pope; how much of that was devoted to plotting against England? Or did the Emperor speak up for his brother monarch? It is rumoured there will be an accord between the Emperor and the French: bad news for England, if so. Time to push on with negotiations. He sets up a meeting between Chapuys and Henry.

A letter is sent to him from Italy, which begins, 'Molto magnifico signor ...' He remembers Hercules, the labourer.

* * *

Two days after Easter, the Imperial ambassador is welcomed at court by George Boleyn. At the sight of glinting George, teeth and pearl buttons flashing, the ambassador's eye rolls like the eye of a startled horse. He has been received by George before, but he did not expect him today: rather one of his own friends, perhaps Carew. George addresses him at length in his elegant and courtly French. You will please to hear Mass with His Majesty and then, if you will do me the favour, it will be my pleasure to entertain you personally to ten o'clock dinner.

Chapuys is looking around: Cremuel, help!

He stands back, smiling, watching the operations of George. I'll miss him, he thinks, in the days when it is all over for him: when I kick him back to Kent, to count his sheep and take a homely interest in the grain harvest.

The king himself gives Chapuys a smile, a gracious word. He, Henry, sails to his private closet above. Chapuys disposes himself amid George's hangers-on. '*Judica me, Deus,*' intones the priest. 'Judge me, oh God, and separate my cause from the nation that is not holy: deliver me from the unjust and deceitful man.'

Chapuys now turns around and stabs him with a look. He grins. 'Why art thou sad, oh my soul?' asks the priest: in Latin of course.

As the ambassador shuffles towards the altar to receive the sacred host, the gentlemen around him, neat as practised dancers, hesitate half a pace and fall behind him. Chapuys falters; George's friends have surrounded him. He darts a glance over his shoulder. Where am I, what should I do?

At that moment, and exactly in his line of sight, Anne the queen sweeps down from her own private galleried space: head high, velvet and sables, rubies at her throat. Chapuys hesitates. He cannot go forward, for he is afraid to cross her path. He cannot go back, because George and his minions are pressing him. Anne turns her head. A pointed smile: and to the enemy, she makes a reverence, a gracious inclination of her jewelled neck. Chapuys screws up his eyes tight, and bows to the concubine.

After all these years! All these years he has picked his path, so that never, never was he brought face to face with her, never brought to this stark choice, to this damnable politesse. But what else could he do? It will soon be reported. It will get back to the Emperor. Let us hope and pray that Charles will understand.

All this shows on the ambassador's face. He, Cremuel, kneels and takes communion. God turns to paste on his tongue. While this process occurs, it is reverent to close the eyes; but on this singular occasion, God will forgive him for looking about. He sees George Boleyn, pink with pleasure. He sees Chapuys, white with humiliation. He sees Henry dazzle in gold as he descends, ponderous, from the gallery. The king's tread is deliberate, his step is slow; his face is blazing with solemn triumph.

Despite the best efforts of pearly George, as they leave the chapel the ambassador breaks away. He scurries towards him, then his hand fastens with a terrier grip. 'Cremuel! You knew this was planned. How could you so embarrass me?'

'It is for the best, I assure you.' He adds, sombre, thoughtful, 'What use as a diplomat would you be, Eustache, if you did not understand the character of princes? They do not think as other men think. To commoners' minds like ours, Henry seems perverse.'

Light dawns in the ambassador's eye. 'Ahh.' He lets out a long breath. He grasps, in that single moment, why Henry has forced him to make a public reverence to a queen whom he no longer wants. Henry is tenacious of his will, he is stubborn. Now he has carried his point: his second marriage has been acknowledged. Now, if he likes, he can let it go.

Chapuys draws his garments together, as if he feels a draught from the future. He whispers, 'Must I really dine with her brother?'

'Oh yes. You will find him a charming host. After all,' he raises a hand to hide his smile, 'has he not just enjoyed a triumph? He and his whole family?'

Chapuys huddles closer. 'I am shocked to see her. I have not seen her so close. She looks like a thin old woman. Was that Mistress Seymour, in the halcyon sleeves? She is very plain. What does Henry see in her?'

'He thinks she's stupid. He finds it restful.'

'Clearly he is enamoured. There must be something about her not evident to the stranger's eye.' The ambassador sniggers. 'No doubt she has a very fine *enigme*.'

'No one would know,' he says blankly. 'She is a virgin.'

'After so long at your court? Surely Henry is deluded.'

'Ambassador, keep this for later. Your host is here.'

Chapuys folds his hands over his heart. He makes George, Lord Rochford, a sweeping bow. Lord Rochford does the same. Arm in arm, they mince away. It sounds as if Lord Rochford is reciting verses in praise of the spring.

'Hm,' says Lord Audley: 'What a performance.' The weak sunshine glints from the Lord Chancellor's chain of office. 'Come on, my boy, let's go and gnaw a crust.' Audley chuckles. 'The poor ambassador. He looks like someone being carried by slavers to the Barbary coast. He does not know what country he will wake up in tomorrow.'

Nor do I, he thinks. You can rely on Audley to be jovial. He closes his eyes. Some hint, some intimation has reached him, that he has had the best of the day, though it is only ten o'clock. 'Crumb?' the Lord Chancellor says.

It is some time after dinner that it all begins to fall apart, and in the worst possible way. He has left Henry and the ambassador together in a window embrasure, to caress each other with words, to coo about an alliance, to make each other immodest proposi-tions. It is the king's change of colour he notices first. Pink and white to brick red. Then he hears Henry's voice, high-pitched, cutting: 'I think you presume too much, Chapuys. You say I acknowledge your master's right to rule in Milan: but perhaps the

King of France has as good a right, or better. Do not presume to know my policy, ambassador.'

Chapuys jumps back. He thinks of Jane Seymour's question: Master Secretary, have you ever seen a scalded cat?

The ambassador speaks: something low and supplicating. Henry raps back at him, 'You mean to say that what I took as a courtesy, from one Christian prince to the other, is really a bargaining position? You agree to bow to my wife the queen, and then you send me a bill?'

He, Cromwell, sees Chapuys hold up a placating hand. The ambassador is trying to interrupt, to limit the damage, but Henry talks over him, audible to the whole chamber, to the whole gaping assembly, and to those pressing in behind. 'Does your master not remember what I did for him, in his early troubles? When his Spanish subjects rose up against him? I kept the seas open for him. I lent him money. And what do I get back?'

A pause. Chapuys has to send his mind scurrying back, to the years before he was in post. 'The money?' he suggests weakly.

'Nothing but broken promises. Recall, if you will, how I helped him against the French. He promised me territory. Next thing I heard, he was making a treaty with Francis. Why should I trust a word he says?'

Chapuys draws himself up: as far as a little man can. 'Game little cockerel,' Audley says, in his ear.

But he, Cromwell, is not to be distracted. His eyes are fastened on the king. He hears Chapuys say, 'Majesty. That is not a question to be asked, by one prince of another.'

'Is it not?' Henry snarls. 'In times past, I would never have had to ask it. I take every brother prince to be honourable, as I am honourable. But sometimes, Monsieur, I suggest to you, our fond and natural assumptions must give way before bitter experience. I ask you, does your master take me for a fool?' Henry's voice swoops upwards; he bends at the waist, and his fingers make little paddling motions on his knees, as if he were trying to entice a child or a small dog. 'Henry!' he squeaks. 'Come to Charles! Come to your kind master!' He straightens up, almost spitting in his rage. 'The Emperor treats me like an infant. First he whips me, then he pets me, then it is the whip again. Tell him I am not an infant. Tell him I am an emperor in my own realm, and a man, and a father. Tell him to keep out of my family business. I have put up with his interference for too long. First he seeks to tell me who I can marry. Then he wants to show me how to manage my daughter. Tell him, I shall deal with Mary as I see fit, as a father does deal with a disobedient child. No matter who her mother is.'

The king's hand – in fact, dear God, his fist – makes crude contact with the ambassador's shoulder. His path cleared, Henry stamps out. An imperial performance. Except that his leg drags. He shouts over his shoulder, 'I require a profound and public apology.'

He, Cromwell, lets out his breath. The ambassador fizzes across the room, gibbering. Distraught, he seizes his arm. 'Cremuel, I do not know for what I am to apologise. I come here in good faith, I am tricked into coming face to face with that creature, I am forced to exchange compliments with her brother through a whole dinner, and then I am attacked by Henry. He wants my master, he needs my master, he is just playing the old game, trying to sell himself dear, pretending he might send troops to King Francis to fight in Italy – where are these troops? I do not see them, I have eyes, I do not see his army.'

'Peace, peace,' Audley soothes. 'We will do the apologising, Monsieur. Let him cool down. Never fear. Hold back your dispatches to your good master, do not write tonight. We will keep the talks going.'

Over Audley's shoulder, he sees Edward Seymour, gliding through the crowd. 'Ah, ambassador,' he says, with a suave confidence he does not feel. 'Here is an opportunity for you to meet –'

Edward springs forward, '*Mon cher ami ...*'

Black glances from Boleyns. Edward into the breach, armed with confident French. Sweeping Chapuys aside: none too soon. A stir at the door. The king is back, erupting into the midst of the gentlemen.

'Cromwell!' Henry stops before him. He is breathing hard. 'Make him understand. It is not for the Emperor to make conditions to me. It is for the Emperor to apologise, for threatening me with war.' His face congests. 'Cromwell, I know just what you have done. You have gone too far in this matter. What have you promised him? Whatever it is, you have no authority. You have put my honour in hazard. But what do I expect, how can a man like you understand the honour of princes? You have said, "Oh, I am sure of Henry, I have the king in my pocket." Don't deny it, Cromwell, I can hear you saying it. You mean to train me up, don't you? Like one of your boys at Austin Friars? Touch my cap when you come down of a morning and say "How do you, sir?" Walk through Whitehall half a pace behind you. Carry your folios, your inkhorn and your seal. And why not a crown, eh, brought behind you in a leather bag?' Henry is convulsing with rage. 'I really believe, Cromwell, that you think you are king, and I am the blacksmith's boy.'

He will never claim, later, that his heart did not turn over. He is not one to boast of a coolness no reasonable man would possess. Henry could, at any moment, gesture to his guards; he could find himself with cold metal at his ribs, and his day done.

But he steps back; he knows his face shows nothing, neither repentance nor regret nor fear. He thinks, you could never be the blacksmith's boy. Walter would not have had you in his forge. Brawn is not the whole story. In the flames you need a cool head, when sparks are flying to the rafters you must note when they fall on you and knock the fire away with one swat of your hard palm: a man who panics is no use in a shop full of molten metal. And now, his monarch's sweating face thrust into his, he remembers something his father told him: if you burn your hand, Tom, raise your hands and cross your wrists before you, and hold them so till you get to the water or the salve: I don't know how it works, but it confuses the pain, and then if you utter a prayer at the same time, you might get off not too bad.

He raises his palms. He crosses his wrists. Back you go, Henry. As if confused by the gesture – as if almost relieved to be stopped – the king ceases ranting: and he backs off a pace, turning his face away and so relieving him, Cromwell, of that bloodshot stare, of the indecent closeness of the popping blue whites of the king's eyes. He says, softly, 'God preserve you, Majesty. And now, will you excuse me?'

So: whether he will excuse or no, he walks away. He walks into the next room. You have heard the expression, 'My blood was boiling'? His blood is boiling. He crosses his wrists. He sits down on a chest and calls for a drink. When it is fetched he takes into his right hand the cool pewter cup, running the pads of his fingers around its curves: the wine is strong claret, he spills a drop, he blots it with his forefinger and for neatness touches it with his tongue, so it vanishes. He cannot say whether the trick has decreased the pain, as Walter said it would. But he is glad his father is with him. Someone must be.

He looks up. Chapuys's face is hovering over him: smiling, a mask of malice. 'My dear friend. I thought your last hour had come. Do you know, I thought you would forget yourself and hit him?'

He looks up and smiles. 'I never forget myself. What I do, I mean to do.'

'Though you may not mean what you say.'

He thinks, the ambassador has suffered cruelly, just for doing his job. In addition, I have injured his feelings, I have been ironical about his hat. Tomorrow I shall organise him a present, a horse, a horse of some magnificence, a horse for his own riding. I myself, before it departs my stables, will lift a hoof and check the shoe.

✻ ✻ ✻

The king's council meets next day. Wiltshire, or Monseigneur, is present: the Boleyns are sleek cats, lolling in their seats and preening their whiskers. Their kinsman, the Duke of Norfolk, looks ragged, unnerved; he stops him on the way in – stops him, Cromwell – 'All right, lad?'

Was ever the Master of the Rolls so addressed, by the Earl Marshal of England? In the council chamber Norfolk scuffles the stools about, creaks down on one that suits him. 'That's what he does, you know.' He flashes him a grin, a glimpse of fang. 'You're balanced just so, standing on your feet, then he blows the pavement from under you.'

He nods, smiling patiently. Henry comes in, sits like a great sulky baby on a chair at the head of the table. Meets no one's eye.

Now: he hopes his colleagues know their duties. He has told them often enough. Flatter Henry. Beseech Henry. Implore him to do what you know he must do anyway. So Henry feels he has a choice. So he feels a warm regard for himself, as if he is not consulting his own interests but yours.

Majesty, the councillors say. If it please you. To look favourably, for the sake of the realm and commonweal, on the Emperor's slavish overtures. On his whimpers and pleas.

This occupies fifteen minutes. At last, Henry says, well, if it is for the good of the commonweal, I will receive Chapuys, we will continue negotiations. I must swallow, I suppose, any personal insults I have received.

Norfolk leans forward. 'Think of it like a draught of medicine, Henry. Bitter. But for the sake of England, do not spit.'

The subject of physicians once raised, the marriage of the Lady Mary is discussed. She continues to complain, wherever the king moves her, of bad air, insufficient food, insufficient consideration of her privacy, of dolorous limb pains, headaches and heaviness of spirit. Her doctors have advised that congress with a man would be good for her health. If a young woman's vital spirits are bottled up, she becomes pale and thin, her appetite wanes, she begins to waste; marriage is an occupation for her, she forgets her minor ailments; her womb remains anchored and primed for use, and shows no tendency to go wandering about her body as if it had nothing better to do. In default of a man, the Lady Mary needs strenuous exercise on horseback; difficult, for someone under house arrest.

Henry clears his throat at last, and speaks. 'The Emperor, it is no secret, has discussed Mary with his own councillors. He would like her married out of this realm, to one of his relatives, within his own domains.' His lips tighten. 'In no wise will I suffer her to go out of the country; or indeed to go anywhere at all, while her behaviour to me is not what it ought to be.'

He, Cromwell, says, 'Her mother's death is still raw with her. I have no doubt she will see her duty, over these next weeks.'

'How pleasing to hear from you at last, Cromwell,' says Monseigneur with a smirk. 'You do most usually speak first, and last, and everywhere in the middle, so that we more modest councillors are obliged to speak sotto voce, if at all, and pass notes to each other. May we ask if this new reticence of yours relates, in any way, to yesterday's events? When His Majesty, if I do recall correctly, administered a check to your ambition?'

'Thank you for that,' the Lord Chancellor says, flatly. 'My lord Wiltshire.'

The king says, 'My lords, the subject is my daughter. I am sorry to have to recall you. Though I am far from sure she should be discussed in council.'

'Myself,' Norfolk says, 'I would go up-country to Mary and make her swear the oath, I would plant her hand on the gospel and hold it there flat, and if she would not take her oath to the king and to my niece's child, I would beat her head against the wall till it were as soft as a baked apple.'

'And thank you again,' Audley says. 'My lord Norfolk.'

'Anyway,' the king says sadly. 'We have not so many children that we can well afford to lose one out of the kingdom. I would rather not part with her. One day she will be a good daughter to me.'

The Boleyns sit back, smiling, hearing the king say he seeks no great foreign match for Mary, she is of no importance, a bastard whom one considers only out of charity. They are well content with the triumph afforded them yesterday by the Imperial ambassador; and they are showing their good taste by not boasting about it.

As soon as the meeting ends, he, Cromwell, is mobbed by the councillors: except for the Boleyns, who waft off in the other direction. The meeting has gone well; he has got everything he wants; Henry is back on course for a treaty with the Emperor: why then does he feel so restless, stifled? He elbows his colleagues aside, though in a mannerly fashion. He wants air. Henry passes him, he stops, he turns, he says, 'Master Secretary. Will you walk along with me?'

They walk. In silence. It is for the prince, not the minister, to introduce a topic.

He can wait.

Henry says, 'You know, I wish we would go down to the weald one day, as we have said, to talk to the ironmasters.'

He waits.

'I have had various drawings, mathematical drawings, and advices concerning how our ordnance can be improved, but to be truthful, I cannot make as much of it as you would.'

More humble, he thinks. A little more humble yet.

Henry says, 'You have been in the forest and met charcoal burners. I remember you said to me once, they be very poor men.'

He waits. Henry says, 'One must know the process from the beginning, I think, whether one is making armour or ordnance. It is no use demanding of a metal that it has certain properties, a certain temper, unless you know how it is made, and the difficulties your craftsman may encounter. Now, I have never been too

236

proud to sit down for an hour with the gauntlet maker, who armours my right hand. We must study, I think, every pin, every rivet.'

And? Yes?

He leaves the king to stumble on.

'And, well. And, so. You are my right hand, sir.'

He nods. Sir. How touching.

Henry says, 'So, to Kent, to the weald: will we go? Shall I choose a week? Two, three days should do it.'

He smiles. 'Not this summer, sir. You will be engaged otherwise. Besides, the ironmasters are like all of us. They must have a holiday. They must lie in the sun. They must pick apples.'

Henry looks at him, mild, beseeching, from the tail of his blue eye: give me a happy summer. He says, 'I cannot live as I have lived, Cromwell.'

He is here to take instructions. Get me Jane: Jane, so kind, who sighs across the palate like sweet butter. Deliver me from bitterness, from gall.

'I think I might go home,' he says. 'If you will permit. I have much to do if I am to set this affair in train, and I feel ...' His English deserts him. This sometimes happens. '*Un peu ...*' But his French deserts him too.

'But you are not ill? You will be back soon?'

'I shall seek a consultation with the canon lawyers,' he says. 'It may take some days, you know what they are. It will go no slower than I can help. I shall speak to the archbishop.'

'And perhaps to Harry Percy,' Henry says. 'You know how she ... the betrothal, the whatever, the relationship between them ... well, I think they were as good as married, were they not? And if that won't run ...' He rubs his beard. 'You know that I was, before I was with the queen, I was, on occasion, with her sister, her sister Mary, which –'

'Oh yes, sir. I remember Mary Boleyn.'

'– and it will be seen that, having been linked with kin so near to Anne, I could not make a valid marriage to her ... however, you will only use that if you have to, I do not want unnecessary ...'

He nods. You don't want history to make a liar of you. In public before your courtiers you had me state that you had never had to do with Mary Boleyn, while you sat there and nodded. You removed all impediments: Mary Boleyn, Harry Percy, you swept them aside. But now our requirements have changed, and the facts have changed behind us.

'So fare you well,' Henry says. 'Be very secret. I trust in your discretion, and your skill.'

How necessary, but how sad, to hear Henry apologise. He has developed a perverse respect for Norfolk, with his grunt of 'All right, lad?'

In an antechamber Mr Wriothesley is waiting for him. 'So do you have instructions, sir?'

'Well, I have hints.'

'Do you know when they might take form?'

He smiles. Call-Me says, 'I hear that in council the king declared he will seek to marry Lady Mary to a subject.'

Surely that's not what the meeting concluded? In a moment, he feels like himself again: hears himself laughing and saying, 'Oh for Christ's sake, Call-Me. Who told you that? Sometimes,' he says, 'I think it would save time and work if all the interested parties came to the council, including foreign ambassadors. The proceedings leak out anyway, and to save them mishearing and misconstruing they might as well hear everything at first hand.'

'I've got it wrong, then?' Wriothesley says. 'Because I thought, marrying her to a subject, to some low man, that was a plan thought up by the queen that is now?'

He shrugs. The young man gives him a glassy look. It will be some years before he understands why.

* * *

Edward Seymour seeks an interview with him. There is no doubt in his mind that the Seymours will come to his table, even if they have to sit under it and catch the crumbs.

Edward is tense, hurried, nervous. 'Master Secretary, taking the long view –'

'In this matter, a day would be a long view. Get your girl out of it, let Carew take her to his house down in Surrey.'

'Do not think I wish to know your secrets,' Edward says, picking his words. 'Do not think I wish to pry into matters that are not for me. But for my sister's sake I would like to have some indication –'

'Oh, I see, you want to know if she should order her wedding clothes?' Edward gives him an imploring look. He says soberly, 'We are going to seek an annulment. Just now I do not know on what grounds.'

'But they will fight,' Edward says. 'The Boleyns if they go down will take us with them. I have heard of serpents that, though they are dying, exude poison through their skins.'

'Did you ever pick up a snake?' he asks. 'I did once, in Italy.' He holds out his palms. 'I am unmarked.'

'Then we must be very secret,' Edward says. 'Anne must not know.'

'Well,' he says wryly, 'I do not think we can keep it from her for ever.'

But she will know all the sooner, if his new friends do not stop trapping him in anterooms, blocking his path and bowing to him; if they do not stop this whispering and eyebrow raising and digging each other with their elbows.

He says to Edward, I must go home and shut the door and consult with myself. The queen is plotting something, I know not what, something devious, something dark, perhaps so dark that she herself does not know what it is, and as yet is only dreaming of it: but I must be quick, I must dream it for her, I shall dream it into being.

According to Lady Rochford, Anne complains that since she rose from childbed Henry is always watching her; and not in the way he used to.

For a long time he has noticed Harry Norris watching the queen; and from some eminence, perched like a carved falcon over a doorway, he has seen himself watching Harry Norris.

For now, Anne seems oblivious to the wings that hover over her, to the eye that studies her path as she jinks and swerves. She chatters about her child Elizabeth, holding up on her fingers a tiny cap, a pretty ribboned cap, just come from the embroiderer.

Henry looks at her flatly as if to say, why are you showing me this, what is it to me?

Anne strokes the scrap of silk. He feels a needle point of pity, an instant of compunction. He studies the fine silk braid that edges the queen's sleeve. Some woman with the skills of his dead wife made that braid. He is looking very closely at the queen, he feels he knows her as a mother knows her child, or a child its mother. He knows every stitch in her bodice. He notes the rise and fall of her every breath. What is in your heart, madam? That is the last door to be opened. Now he stands on the threshold and the key is in his hand and he is almost afraid to fit it into the lock. Because what if it doesn't, what if it doesn't fit and he has to fumble there, with Henry's eyes on him, hear the impatient click of the royal tongue, as surely his master Wolsey once heard it?

Well, then. There was an occasion – in Bruges, was it? – when he had broken down a door. He wasn't in the habit of breaking doors, but he had a client who wanted results and wanted them today. Locks can be picked, but that's for the adept with time to spare. You don't need skill and you don't need time if you've got a shoulder and a boot. He thinks, I wasn't thirty then. I was a youth. Absently his right hand rubs his left shoulder, his forearm, as if remembering the bruises. He imagines himself entering Anne, not as a lover but as a lawyer, and rolled in his fist his papers, his writs; he imagines himself entering the heart of the queen. In its chambers he hears the click of his own boot heels.

At home, he takes from his chest the Book of Hours that belonged to his wife. It was given to her by her first husband Tom Williams, who was a good enough fellow, but not a man of substance like himself. Whenever he thinks of Tom Williams now it is as a blank, a faceless waiting man dressed in the Cromwell livery, holding his coat or perhaps his horse. Now that he can handle, at his whim, the finest texts in the king's library, the prayer book seems a poor thing; where is the gold leaf? Yet the essence of Elizabeth is in this book, his poor wife with her white cap, her blunt manner, her sideways smile and busy craftswoman's fingers. Once he had watched Liz making a silk braid. One end was pinned to the wall and on each finger of her raised hands she was spinning loops of thread, her fingers flying so fast he couldn't see how it worked. 'Slow down,' he said, 'so I can see how you do it,' but she'd laughed and said, 'I can't slow down, if I stopped to think how I was doing it I couldn't do it at all.'

II
Master of Phantoms
London, April–May 1536

'Come and sit with me a while.'

'Why?' Lady Worcester is wary.

'Because I have cakes.'

She smiles. 'I am greedy.'

'I even have a waiter to serve them.'

She eyes Christophe. 'This boy is a waiter?'

'Christophe, first Lady Worcester requires a cushion.'

The cushion is plump with down and embroidered with a pattern of hawks and flowers. She takes it in her two hands, strokes it absently, then positions it behind her and leans back. 'Oh, that's better,' she smiles. Pregnant, she rests a composed hand on her belly, like a Madonna in a painting. In this small room, its window open to mild spring air, he is holding a court of inquiry. He does not mind who comes in to see him, who is noticed as they come and go. Who would not pass the time with a man who has cakes? And Master Secretary is always pleasant and useful. 'Christophe, hand my lady a napkin, and go and sit in the sun for ten minutes. Close the door behind you.'

Lady Worcester – Elizabeth – watches the door close; then she leans forward and whispers, 'Master Secretary, I am in such trouble.'

'And this,' he indicates her person, 'cannot be easy. Is the queen jealous of your condition?'

'Well, she keeps me close to her, and she need not. She asks me each day how I do. I could not have a fonder mistress.' But her face shows doubt. 'In some ways it would be better if I were to go home to the country. As it is, kept before the court, I am pointed at by all.'

'Do you think then it is the queen herself who began the murmurs against you?'

'Who else?'

A rumour is going about the court that Lady Worcester's baby is not the earl's child. Perhaps it was spread out of malice; perhaps as someone's idea of a joke: perhaps because someone was bored. Her gentle brother, the courtier Anthony Browne, has stormed into her rooms to take her to task: 'I told him,' she says, 'don't pick on me. Why me?' As if sharing her indignation, the curd tart on her palm quakes in its pastry shell.

He frowns. 'Let me take you back a step. Is your family blaming you because people are talking about you, or because there is truth in what they say?'

Lady Worcester dabs her lips. 'You think I will confess, just for cakes?'

'Let me smooth this over for you. I should like to help you if I can. Has your husband reason to be angry?'

'Oh, men,' she says. 'They are always angry. They are so angry they can't count on their fingers.'

'So it could be the earl's?'

'If it is a strong boy I dare say he will own it.' The cakes are distracting her: 'That white one, is that almond cream?'

Lady Worcester's brother, Anthony Browne, is Fitzwilliam's half-brother. (All these people are related to each other. Luckily, the cardinal left him a chart, which he updates whenever there is a wedding.) Fitzwilliam and Browne and the aggrieved earl have been conferring in corners. And Fitzwilliam has said to him, can you find out, Crumb, for I am sure I cannot, what the devil is going on among the queen's waiting-women?

'And then there's the debts,' he says to her. 'You are in a sad place, my lady. You have borrowed from everyone. What did you buy? I know there are sweet young men about the king, witty young men too, always amorous and ready to write a lady a letter. Do you pay to be flattered?'

'No. To be complimented.'

'You should get that free.'

'I believe that is a gallant speech.' She licks her fingers. 'But you are a man of the world, Master Secretary, and you know that if you yourself wrote a woman a poem you would enclose a bill.'

He laughs. 'True. I know the value of my time. But I did not think your admirers were so miserly.'

'But they have so much to do, these boys!' She selects a candied violet, nibbles it. 'I do not know why we speak of idle youths. They are busy day and night, making their careers. They wouldn't send their account in. But you must buy them a jewel for their cap. Or some gilt buttons for a sleeve. Fee their tailor, perhaps.'

He thinks of Mark Smeaton, in his finery. 'Does the queen pay out in this way?'

'We call it patronage. We don't call it paying out.'

'I accept your correction.' Jesus, he thinks, a man could use a whore, and call it 'patronage'. Lady Worcester has dropped some raisins on the table and he feels the urge to pick them up and feed them to her; probably that would be all right with her. 'So when the queen is a patron, does she ever, does she ever patronise in private?'

'In private? How could I know?'

He nods. It's tennis, he thinks. That shot was too good for me. 'What does she wear, to patronise?'

'I have not myself seen her naked.'

'So you think, these flatterers, you don't think she goes to it with them?'

'Not in my sight or hearing.'

'But behind a closed door?'

'Doors are often closed. It is a common thing.'

'If I were to ask you to bear witness, would you repeat that on oath?'

She flicks a speck of cream away. 'That doors are often closed? I could go so far.'

'And what would be your fee for that?' He is smiling; his eyes rest on her face.

'I am a little afraid of my husband. Because I have borrowed money. He does not know, so please … hush.'

'Point your creditors in my direction. And for the future, if you need a compliment, draw on the bank of Cromwell. We look after our customers and our terms are generous. We are known for it.'

She puts down her napkin; picks a last primrose petal from the last cheese cake. She turns at the door. A thought has struck her. Her hand bunches her skirts. 'The king wants a reason to put her aside, yes? And the closed door will be enough? I would not wish her harm.'

She grasps the situation, at least partly. Caesar's wife must be above reproach. Suspicion would ruin the queen, a crumb or a sliver of truth would ruin her faster; you wouldn't need a bed sheet with a snail-trail left by Francis Weston or some other sonneteer. 'Put her aside,' he says. 'Yes, possibly. Unless these rumours prove to be misunderstandings. As I'm sure they will in your case. I am sure your husband will be contented when the child is born.'

Her face clears. 'So you will speak to him? But not about the debt? And speak to my brother? And William Fitzwilliam? You will persuade them to leave me alone, please? There is nothing I have done, that other ladies have not.'

'Mistress Shelton?' he says.

'That would be no news.'

246

'Mistress Seymour.'

'That would be news indeed.'

'Lady Rochford?'

She hesitates. 'Jane Rochford does not like the sport.'

'Why, is my lord Rochford inept?'

'Inept.' She seems to taste the word. 'I have not heard her describe it like that.' She smiles. 'But I have heard her describe it.'

Christophe is back. She sails past him, a woman disburdened. 'Oh, look at that,' Christophe says. 'She has picked all the petals off the top, and left the crumb.'

Christophe sits down to stuff his maw with the remnants. He craves honey, sugar. You can never mistake a boy who was brought up hungry. We are coming to the sweet season of the year, when the air is mild and the leaves pale, and lemon cakes are flavoured with lavender: egg custards, barely set, infused with a sprig of basil; elderflowers simmered in a sugar syrup and poured over halved strawberries.

St George's Day. All over England, cloth and paper dragons sway in noisy procession through the streets, and the dragon-slayer after them in his armour of tin, beating an old rusty sword on his shield. Virgins plait wreaths of leaves, and spring flowers are carried into church. In the hall at Austin Friars, Anthony has hung from the ceiling beams a beast with green scales, a rolling eye and a lolling tongue; it looks lascivious, and reminds him of something, but he can't remember what.

This is the day the Garter knights hold their chapter, where they elect a new knight if any member has died. The Garter is the most distinguished order of chivalry in Christendom: the King of France is a member, so is the King of Scots. So is Monseigneur the queen's father, and the king's bastard Harry Fitzroy. This year the meeting is at Greenwich. The foreign members will not attend, it is understood, and yet the chapter serves as a gathering of his new allies: William Fitzwilliam, Henry Courtenay the Marquis of

Exeter, my lord of Norfolk, and Charles Brandon, who seems to have forgiven him, Thomas Cromwell, for shoving him around the presence chamber: who now seeks him out and says, 'Cromwell, we have had our differences. But I always did say to Harry Tudor, now take note of Cromwell, let him not go down with his ingrate master, for Wolsey has taught him his tricks and he may be useful to you accordingly.'

'Did you so, my lord? I am much bound to you for that word.'

'Aye, well, we see the consequence, for now you are a rich man, are you not?' He chuckles. 'And so is Harry rich.'

'And I am always glad to bestow gratitude in the proper quarter. May I ask, who will my lord vote for in the Garter chapter?'

Brandon gives him a strenuous wink. 'Depend on me.'

There is one vacancy, caused by the death of Lord Bergavenny; there are two men who expect to have it. Anne has been pressing the merits of brother George. The other candidate is Nicholas Carew; and when soundings have been taken and the votes have been counted it is Sir Nicholas whose name is read out by the king. George's people are quick to limit the damage, to give out that they didn't expect anything: that Carew was promised the next vacancy, that King Francis himself asked the king three years ago to give it him. If the queen is displeased, she does not show it, and the king and George Boleyn have a project to discuss. The day after May Day, a royal party is to ride down to Dover to inspect the new work on the harbour, and George will accompany it in his capacity as Warden of the Cinque Ports: an office which he fills badly, in his, Cromwell's opinion. He himself plans to ride down with the king. He could even go over to Calais for a day or two, and order matters there; so he gives out, the rumour of his arrival serving to keep the garrison on the *qui vive*.

Harry Percy has come down from his own country for the Garter meeting, and is now at his house at Stoke Newington. That might be useful, he says to his nephew Richard, I might send someone to see him and sound him out, whether he might be prepared to give back word on this pre-contract business. Go myself, if I need to. But we must take this week hour by hour. Richard Sampson is waiting for him, Dean of the Chapel Royal, Doctor of Canon Law (Cambridge, Paris, Perugia, Siena): the king's proctor in his first divorce.

'Here is a pretty pickle,' is all the dean will say, laying down his folios in his precise way. There is a mule cart outside, groaning with further folios, well-wrapped to save them from adverse weather: the documents go all the way back to the king's first expressed dissatisfaction with his first queen. At which time, he says, to the dean, we were all young. Sampson laughs; it is a clerical laugh, like the creak of a vestment chest. 'I barely recall being young, but I suppose we were. And some of us carefree.'

They are going to try for nullity, see if Henry can be released. 'I hear Harry Percy bursts into tears at the sound of your name,' Sampson says.

'They much exaggerate. The earl and I have had many civil interchanges these last months.'

He keeps turning over papers from the first divorce, and finding the cardinal's hand, amending, suggesting, drawing arrows in the margin.

'Unless,' he says, 'Anne the queen would decide to enter religion. Then the marriage would be dissolved of itself.'

'I'm sure she would make an excellent abbess,' Sampson says politely. 'Have you sounded out my lord archbishop yet?'

Cranmer is away. He has been putting it off. 'I have to show him,' he tells the dean, 'that our cause, that is to say, the cause of the English Bible, will get on better without her. We want the living word of God to sound in the king's ears like music, not like Anne's ingrate whining.'

He says 'we', including the dean out of courtesy. He is not at all sure that, in his heart, Sampson is devoted to reform, but it is outward compliance that concerns him, and the dean is always cooperative.

'This little matter of sorcery.' Sampson clears his throat. 'The king does not mean us to pursue it seriously? If it could be proved that some unnatural means were used to draw him into the marriage, then of course his consent could not be free, the contract is of no effect; but surely, when he says he was seduced by charms, by spells, he was speaking, as it were, in figures? As a poet might speak of a lady's fairy charms, her wiles, her seductions ...? Oh, by the Mass,' the dean says mildly. 'Do not look at me in that way, Thomas Cromwell. It is a business I would rather not meddle in. I would rather have Harry Percy again, and between us beat him into sense. I would rather bring out the matter of Mary Boleyn, whose name, I must say, I hoped never to hear again.'

He shrugs. He sometimes thinks about Mary; what it would have been like, if he had taken her up on her offers. That night in Calais, he had been so close he could taste her breath, sweetmeats and spices, wine ... but of course, that night in Calais, any man with functioning tackle would have done for Mary. Gently, the dean breaks into his train of thought: 'May I suggest? Go and talk to the queen's father. Talk to Wiltshire. He's a reasonable man, we were at Bilbao together on embassy a few years back, I always found him to be reasonable. Get him to ask his daughter to go quietly. Save us all twenty years of grief.'

To 'Monseigneur', then: he has Wriothesley to take the record of the meeting. Anne's father brings his own folio, while brother George brings only his delightful self. He is always a sight to see: George likes his clothes braided and tasselled, stippled and striped and slashed. Today he wears white velvet over red silk, scarlet rippling from each gash. He is reminded of a picture he saw once in the Low Countries, of a saint being flayed alive. The skin of the man's calves was folded neatly over his ankles, like soft boots, and his face wore an expression of unblinking serenity.

He puts his papers down on the table. 'I will not waste words. You see the situation. Matters have come to the king's attention that, if he had always known them, would have prevented this pretensed marriage with Lady Anne.'

George says, 'I have spoken to the Earl of Northumberland. He stands by his oath. There was no pre-contract.'

'Then that is unfortunate,' he says. 'I do not see what I am to do. Perhaps you can help me, Lord Rochford, with some suggestions of your own?'

'We will help you to the Tower,' says George.

'Minute that,' he says to Wriothesley. 'My lord Wiltshire, may I recall some circumstances that your son here may be unaware of? In the matter of your daughter and Harry Percy, the late cardinal called you to account, warning you that there could be no match between them, for the lowness of your family and the high estate of the Percy line. And your answer was that you were not responsible for what Anne did, that you could not control your own children.'

Thomas Boleyn arranges his face, as a certain piece of knowledge dawns. 'So it was you, Cromwell. Scribbling in the shadows.'

'I never denied it, my lord. Now on that occasion you did not get much sympathy from the cardinal. Myself, being a father of a family, I understand how these things occur. You would hold to it, at the time, that your daughter and Harry Percy had gone far in the matter. By which you meant – as the cardinal was pleased to put it – a haystack and a warm night. You implied their liaison was consummated, and a true marriage.'

Boleyn smirks. 'But then, the king made known his feelings for my daughter.'

'So you rethought your position. As one does. I am asking you to rethink once more. It would be better for your daughter if she had in fact been married to Harry Percy. Then her marriage to the king could be proclaimed null. And the king would be left free to select another lady.'

A decade of self-aggrandisement, since his daughter flashed her cunny at the king, has made Boleyn rich and settled and confident. His era is drawing to a close, and he, Cromwell, sees him decide not to fight it. Women age, men like variety: it's an old story, and even an anointed queen cannot escape it to write her own ending. 'So. What about Anne?' her father says. No particular tenderness attaches to the question.

He says, as Carew did, 'Convent?'

'I should expect a generous settlement,' Boleyn says. 'For the family, I mean.'

'Wait,' George says. 'My lord father, enter into no undertakings with this man. Enter into no discussion.'

Wiltshire speaks coldly to his son. 'Sir. Calmly. Things are as they are. What if, Cromwell, she were to be left in possession of her estate as marchioness? And we, her family, remain in undisturbed possession of ours?'

'I think the king would prefer her to withdraw from the world. I am sure we could find some godly house, well-governed, where her beliefs and views will be comfortable.'

'I am disgusted,' George says. He edges away from his father.

He says, 'Minute Lord Rochford's disgust.'

Wriothesley's pen scratches.

'But our land?' Wiltshire says. 'Our offices of state? I could continue to serve the king as Lord Privy Seal, surely. And my son here, his dignities and titles –'

'Cromwell wants me out,' George shoots to his feet. 'That's the plain truth. He has never ceased to interfere with what I do in defence of the realm, he is writing to Dover, he is writing to Sandwich, his men are swarming everywhere, my letters are redirected to him, my orders are countermanded by him –'

'Oh, sit down,' Wriothesley says. He laughs: as much at his own wearied impertinence, as at George's face. 'Or of course, my lord, stand, if you please.'

Now Rochford does not know which to do. All he can do is reinforce that he is standing, by flouncing on the spot; he can pick up his hat; he can say, 'I pity you, Master Secretary. If you succeed in forcing out my sister, your new friends will make short work of you once she is gone, and if you do not succeed, and she and the king are reconciled, then I shall make short work of you. So whichever way you turn, Cromwell, you have overreached yourself this time.'

He says mildly, 'I only sought this interview, my lord Rochford, because you have influence with your sister, no man more. I am offering you your safety, in return for your kind help.'

The elder Boleyn closes his eyes. 'I'll talk to her. I'll talk to Anne.'

'And talk to your son here, because I will talk to him no more.'

Wiltshire says, 'I marvel, George, that you do not see where this is tending.'

'What?' George says. 'What, what?' He is still whatting as his father tows him away. On the threshold the elder Boleyn bows his head civilly. 'Master Secretary. Master Wriothesley.'

They watch them go out: father and son. 'That was interesting,' Wriothesley says. 'And where is it tending, sir?'

He reshuffles his papers.

'I remember,' Wriothesley says, 'a certain play at court, after the cardinal came down. I remember Sexton, the jester, dressed in scarlet robes, in the character of the cardinal, and how four devils bore him off to Hell, each seizing an extremity. And they were masked. And I wondered, was George –'

'Right forepaw,' he says.

'Ah,' says Call-Me-Risley.

'I went behind the screen at the back of the hall. I saw them pull off their hairy bodies, and Lord Rochford take off his mask. Why did you not follow me? You could have seen for yourself.'

Mr Wriothesley smiles. 'I did not care to go behind that scene. I feared you might confuse me with the players, and for ever after I would be tainted in your mind.'

He remembers it: an evening of feral stench, as the flower of chivalry became hunting dogs, baying for blood, the whole court hissing and jeering as the figure of the cardinal was dragged and bounced across the floor. Then a voice called out from the hall: 'Shame on you!' He asks Wriothesley, 'That was not you who spoke?'

'No.' Call-Me will not lie. 'I think perhaps it was Thomas Wyatt.'

'I believe it was. I have thought about it these many years. Look, Call-Me, I have to go and see the king. Shall we have a glass of wine first?'

Mr Wriothesley on his feet. Searching out a waiting boy. Light shines on the curve of a pewter jug, Gascon wine splashes into a cup. 'I gave Francis Bryan an import licence for this,' he says. 'Would be three months back. No palate, has he? I didn't know he'd be selling it back to the king's buttery.'

He goes to Henry, scattering guards, attendants, gentlemen; he is barely announced, so that Henry looks up, startled, from his music book. 'Thomas Boleyn sees his way. He is only anxious to retain his good name with Your Majesty. But I cannot get any cooperation from his son.'

'Why not?'

Because he's an idiot? 'I think he believes Your Majesty's mind can be changed.'

Henry is piqued. 'He ought to know me. George was a little lad of ten when he first came to court, he ought to know me. I do not change my mind.'

It's true, in the one way. Like a crab the king goes sideways to his destination, but then he sinks his pincers in. It is Jane Seymour who is pinched. 'I tell you what I think about Rochford,' Henry says. 'He is what, thirty-two now, but he is still called Wiltshire's son, he is still called the queen's brother, he does not feel he has come into his own, and he has no heir to follow him, not so much

254

as a daughter. I have done what I can for him. I have sent him abroad many a time to represent me. And that will cease, I suppose, because when he is no longer my brother, no one will take any notice of him. But he will not be a poor man. I may continue to favour him. Though not if he is obstructive. So he should be warned. Must I speak to him myself?'

Henry looks irritated. He should not have to manage this. Cromwell is supposed to manage it for him. Ease out the Boleyns, ease in the Seymours. His business is more kingly: praying for the success of his enterprises, and writing songs for Jane.

'Leave it a day or two, sir, and I will interview him apart from his father. I think in Lord Wiltshire's presence he feels the need to strut and posture.'

'Yes, I am not often wrong,' Henry says. 'Vanity, that's all it is. Now listen.' He sings:

'The daisy delectable,
The violet wan and blue.
I am not variable ...

'You perceive it is an old song that I am trying to rework. What pairs with blue? Apart from "new"?'

What else do you need, he thinks. He takes his leave. The galleries are lit by torches, from which figures melt away. The atmosphere at court, this Friday evening in April, reminds him of the public bath-houses they have in Rome. The air is thick and the swimming figures of other men glide past you – perhaps men you know, but you don't know them without their clothes. Your skin is hot then cold then hot again. The tiles are slippery beneath your feet. On each side of you are doors left ajar, just a few inches, and outside your line of sight, but very close to you, perversities are occurring, unnatural conjugations of bodies, men and women and men and men. You feel nauseous, from the sticky heat and what you know of human nature, and you wonder why you have come. But you have been told that a man must go to the bath-house at least once in his life, or he won't believe it when other people tell him what goes on.

'The truth is,' Mary Shelton says, 'I would have tried to see you, Master Secretary, even if you had not sent for me.' Her hand shakes; she takes a sip of wine, looks deeply into the bowl as if divining, then raises her eloquent eyes. 'I pray I never pass another day like this one. Nan Cobham wants to see you. Marjorie Horsman. All the women of the bedchamber.'

'Have you something to tell me? Or is it that you just want to cry on my papers and make the ink run?'

She puts down the cup and gives him her hands. He is moved by the gesture, it is like a child showing you her hands are clean. 'Shall we try to disentangle it?' he asks gently.

All day from the queen's rooms, shouting, slamming doors, running feet: hissed conversations in undertones. 'I wish I were gone from the court,' Shelton says. 'I wish myself in another place.' She slides her hands away. 'I should be married. Is that too much, to be married and have some children, while I am still young?'

'Now, do not be sorry for yourself. I thought you were marrying Harry Norris.'

'So did I.'

'I know that there was some falling out between you, but that would be a year ago now?'

'I suppose Lady Rochford told you. You should not listen, you know, she invents things. But yes, it was true, I quarrelled with Harry, or he quarrelled with me, and it was over young Weston coming to the queen's rooms in and out of season, and Harry thought he was casting his fancy to me. And so thought I. But I did not encourage Weston, I swear.'

He laughs. 'But Mary, you do encourage men. It is what you do. You cannot help it.'

'So Harry Norris said, I will give that puppy a kick in the ribs he will not forget. Though Harry is not that sort of man, to go around kicking puppies. And the queen my cousin said, no kicking in my chamber, if you please. Harry said, by your royal favour I will take him out to the courtyard and kick him, and –' she cannot help laugh, though shakily, miserably, '– and Francis standing there all the time, though they were talking about him as if he were absent. So Francis said, well, I should like to see you kick me, for at your great age, Norris, you will wobble over –'

'Mistress,' he says, 'can you make it short?'

'But they go on like this an hour or more, scrapping and digging and scratching around for favour. And my lady the queen is never weary of it, she eggs them on. Then Weston, he said, do not agitate yourself, gentle Norris, for I come not here for Mistress Shelton, I come for the sake of another, and you know who that is. And Anne said, no, tell me, I cannot guess. Is it Lady Worcester? Is it Lady Rochford? Come, tell us, Francis. Tell us who you love. And he said, madam, it is yourself.'

'And what did the queen say?'

'Oh, she defied him. She said, you must not say so, for my brother George will come and kick you too, for the honour of the Queen of England. And she was laughing. But then Harry Norris quarrelled with me, about Weston. And Weston quarrelled with him, about the queen. And both of them quarrelled with William Brereton.'

'Brereton? What had he to do with it?'

'Well, he happened to come in.' She frowns. 'I think it was then. Or it was some other time that he happened to come in. And the queen said, now, here is the man for me, Will is one who shoots his arrow straight. But she was tormenting them all. You cannot understand her. One moment she is reading out Master Tyndale's gospel. Next moment ...' She shrugs. 'She opens her lips and out slides the devil's tail.'

So then, by Shelton's account, a year passes. Harry Norris and Mistress Shelton are speaking again, and soon they have made it up and Harry is creeping to her bed. And all is as before. Until today: 29 April. 'This morning it began with Mark,' Mary Shelton says. 'You know how he hovers? He is always outside the queen's presence chamber. And as she goes by she does not speak to him but laughs and tugs his sleeve or knocks his elbow, and once she snapped off the feather in his cap.'

'I never heard of this as love play,' he says. 'Is it something they do in France?'

'And this morning she said, oh, look at this little doggie, and she tousled him and pulled his ears. And his silly eyes brimming. Then she said to him, why are you so sad, Mark, you have no business to be sad, you are here to entertain us. And he offered to kneel down, saying, "Madam –" and she cut him off. She said to him, oh for Mary's sweet sake, stand on your two feet, I do you favours in noticing you at all, what do you expect, do you think I should talk to you as if you were a gentleman? I cannot, Mark, because you are an inferior person. He said, no, no madam, I do not expect a word, a look suffices for me. So she waited. Because she expected him to praise the power of her glance. That her eyes are lodestones, and so on. But he did not, he just burst into tears, and "Farewell," he said, and walked away. Just turned his back on her. And she laughed. And so we went in to her chamber.'

'Take your time,' he says.

'Anne said, does he think I am some item from Paris Garden? That is, you know –'

'I know what Paris Garden is.'

She blushes. 'Of course you do. And Lady Rochford said, it were well if Mark were dropped from a height, like your dog Purkoy. Then the queen burst into tears. Then she struck Lady Rochford. And Lady Rochford said, do that again and I will buffet you back, you are no queen but a mere knight's daughter,

Master Secretary Cromwell has your measure, your day is over, madam.'

He says, 'Lady Rochford is getting ahead of herself.'

'Then Harry Norris came in.'

'I was wondering where he was.'

'He said, what is this commotion? Anne said, do me a good turn, take away my brother's wife and drown her, then he can have a fresh one who may do him some good. And Harry Norris was amazed. Anne said to him, did you not swear you would do anything I wanted? That you would walk barefoot to China for me? And Harry said, you know he is droll, he said, I think it was barefoot to Walsingham I offered. Yes, she said, and repent your sins there, because you look for dead men's shoes, if aught came to the king but good, you would look to have me.'

He wants to write down what Shelton says, but he dare not move in case she stops saying it.

'Then the queen turned to me, and said, Mistress Shelton, you perceive now why he does not marry you? He is in love with me. So he claims, and has claimed this long while. But he will not prove it, by putting Lady Rochford in a sack and carrying her to the riverbank, which I much desire. Then Lady Rochford ran out.'

'I think I understand why.'

Mary looks up. 'I know you are laughing at us. But it was horrible. For me it was. Because I thought that it was a jest between them that Harry Norris loved her, and then I saw it was not. I swear he had turned pale and he said to Anne, will you spill all your secrets or only some? And he walked away and he did not even bow to her, and she ran after him. And I do not know what she said, because we were all frozen like statues.'

Spill her secrets. All or only some. 'Who heard this?'

She shakes her head. 'Perhaps a dozen people. They could not help but hear it.'

And then, it appears, the queen was frantic. 'She looked at us ranged about her, and she wanted to get Norris back, she said a priest must be fetched, she said Harry must take an oath that he knew her to be chaste, a faithful good wife. She said he must take back everything said, and she would take it back too, and they would put their hands on the Bible in her chamber, and then everybody would know that it was idle talk. She is terrified Lady Rochford will go to the king.'

'I know Jane Rochford likes to carry bad news. But not such bad news as that.' Not to a husband. That his dear friend and his wife have discussed his death, with a view to how they will console themselves after.

It is treason. Possibly. To envisage the death of the king. The law recognises it: how short the step, from dreaming to desiring to encompassing. We call it 'imagining' his death: the thought is father to the deed, and the deed is born raw, ugly, premature. Mary Shelton does not know what she has witnessed. She thinks it is a lovers' quarrel. She thinks it is one incident in her own long career of love and love's misfortunes. 'I doubt,' she says dully, 'that Harry Norris will marry me now, or even trouble himself pretending he is going to marry me. If you had asked me last week has the queen given way to him, I would have told you no, but when I look at them now, it is clear such words have passed between them, such looks, and how can I know what deeds? I think ... I don't know what to think.'

'I'll marry you, Mary,' he says.

She laughs, in spite of herself. 'Master Secretary, you will not, you are always saying you will marry this lady and that, but we know you hold yourself a great prize.'

'Ah well. So it's back to Paris Garden.' He shrugs, he smiles; but he feels the need to be brisk with her, to hurry on. 'Now understand me, you must be discreet and silent. The thing you must do here – you and the other ladies – you must protect yourselves.'

Mary is struggling. 'It could not tend to bad, could it? If the king hears, he will know how to take it, yes? He may suppose it is all light words? No harm? It is all conjecture, perhaps I have spoken in haste, one cannot know that anything has passed between them, I could not swear it.' He thinks, but you will swear it; by and by you will. 'You see, Anne is my cousin.' The girl's voice falters. 'She has done everything for me –'

Even pushed you into the king's bed, he thinks, when she was carrying a child: to keep Henry in the family.

'What will happen to her?' Mary's eyes are solemn. 'Will he leave her? There is talk but Anne does not believe it.'

'She must stretch her credulity a little.'

'She says, I can always get him back, I know how. And you know she always has. But whatever has happened with Harry Norris, I will not continue with her, for I know she would take him from me and no scruple, if she has not already. And gentle-women cannot be on such terms. And Lady Rochford cannot continue. And Jane Seymour is removed, for – well, I will not say why. And Lady Worcester must go home for her lying-in this summer.'

He sees the young woman's eyes move, calculating, counting. To her, a problem is looming: a problem of staffing Anne's privy chamber. 'But I suppose England has enough ladies,' she says. 'It were well she began again. Yes, a new beginning. Lady Lisle in Calais looks to send her daughters over. I mean, her daughters from her first husband. They are pretty girls and I think they will do very well when they are trained.'

It is as if Anne Boleyn has entranced them, men and women both, so that they cannot see what is happening around them and cannot hear the meaning of their own words. They have lived in stupidity such a long season. 'So do you write to Honor Lisle,' Mary says, with perfect confidence. 'She will be for ever your debtor if she gets her girls at court.'

'And you? What will you do?'

'I'll take thought,' she says. She is never put down for long. That's why men like her. There will be other times, other men, other manners. She hops to her feet. She plants a kiss on his cheek.

It is Saturday evening.

Sunday: 'I wish you had been here this morning,' Lady Rochford says with relish. 'It was something to witness. The king and Anne in the great window together, so everybody in the courtyard below could see them. The king has heard about the quarrel she had with Norris yesterday. Well, the whole of England has heard of it. You could see the king was beside himself, his face was purple. She stood with her hands clasped at her breast ...' She shows him, clasping her own hands. 'You know, like Queen Esther, in the king's great tapestry?'

He can picture it easily, that richly textured scene, woven courtiers gathered about their distressed queen. One maid, as if unconcerned, carries a lute, perhaps en route to Esther's apartments; others gossip aside, the women's smooth faces uptilted, the men's heads inclined. Among these courtiers with their jewels and elaborate hats he has looked in vain for his own face. Perhaps he is somewhere else, plotting: a snapped skein, a broken end, an intractable knot of threads. 'Like Esther,' he says. 'Yes.'

'Anne must have sent for the little princess,' Lady Rochford says, 'because then a nurse heaved up with her, and Anne snatched her and held her up, as if to say, "Husband, how can you doubt this is your daughter?"'

'You are supposing that was his question. You could not hear what was said.' His voice is cold; he hears it himself, its coldness surprises him.

'Not from where I stood. But I doubt it bodes any good to her.'

'Did you not go to her, to comfort her? She being your mistress?'

'No. I went looking for you.' She checks herself, her tone suddenly sobered. 'We – her women – we want to speak out and save ourselves. We are afraid she is not honest and that we will be blamed for concealing it.'

'In the summer,' he says, 'not last summer but the one before, you said to me that you believed the queen was desperate to get a child, and was afraid the king could not give her one. You said he could not satisfy the queen. Will you repeat it now?'

'I'm surprised you don't have a note of our talk.'

'It was a long talk, and – with respect to you, my lady – more full of hints than particulars. I want to know what you would stand to, if you were to be put on oath before a court.'

'Who is to be tried?'

'That is what I am hoping to determine. With your kind help.'

He hears these phrases flow out of him. With your kind help. Yourself not offended. Saving his Majesty.

'You know it has come out about Norris and Weston,' she says. 'How they have declared their love for her. They are not the only ones.'

'You do not take it as just a form of courtesy?'

'For courtesy, you do not sneak around in the dark. On and off barges. Slipping through gates by torchlight. Bribes to the porters. It has been happening these two years and more. You cannot know who you have seen, where and when. You would be sharp if you could catch any of them.' She pauses, to be sure she has his attention. 'Let us say the court is at Greenwich. You see a certain gentleman, one who waits on the king. And you suppose his tour of duty is over, and you imagine him to be in the country; but then you are about your own duties with the queen, and you see him whisking around the corner. You think, why are you here? Norris, is that you? Many a time I have thought some one of them is at Westminster, and then I spy him at Richmond. Or he is supposed to be at Greenwich, and there he is at Hampton Court.'

'If they change their duties among themselves, it is no matter.'

'But I do not mean that. It is not the times, Master Secretary. It is the places. It is the queen's gallery, it is her antechamber, it is her threshold, and sometimes the garden stair, or a little gate left unlocked by some inadvertence.' She leans forward, and her fingertips brush his hand as it lies on his papers. 'I mean they come and go by night. And if anyone enquires why they should be there, they say they are on a private message from the king, they cannot say to whom.'

He nods. The privy chamber carry unwritten messages, it is one of their tasks. They come and go between the king and his peers, sometimes between the king and foreign ambassadors, and no doubt between the king and his wife. They do not brook questioning. They cannot be held to account.

Lady Rochford sits back. She says softly, 'Before they were married, she used to practise with Henry in the French fashion. You know what I mean.'

'I have no idea what you mean. Were you ever in France yourself?'

'No. I thought you were.'

'As a soldier. Among the military, the *ars amatoria* is not refined.'

She considers this. A hardness creeps into her voice. 'You wish to shame me out of saying what I must say, but I am no virgin girl, I see no reason not to speak. She induced Henry to put his seed otherwise than he should have. So now he berates her, that she caused him to do so.'

'Opportunities lost. I understand.' Seed gone to waste, slid away in some crevice of her body or down her throat. When he could have been seeing to her in the honest English way.

'He calls it a filthy proceeding. But God love him, Henry does not know where filth begins. My husband George is always with Anne. But I've told you that before.'

'He is her brother, I suppose it is natural.'

'Natural? Is that what you call it?'

'My lady, I know you would like it to be a crime to be a fond brother and a cold husband. But there is no statute that makes it so, and no precedent for your relief.' He hesitates. 'Do not think I am without sympathy for you.'

For what can a woman like Jane Rochford do when circumstances are against her? A widow well-provided can cut a figure in the world. A merchant's wife can with diligence and prudence take business matters into her hands, and squirrel away a store of gold. A labouring woman ill-used by a husband can enlist robust friends, who will stand outside her house all night and bang pans, till the unshaven churl tips out in his shirt to chase them off, and they pull up his shirt and mock his member. But a young married gentlewoman has no way to help herself. She has no more power than a donkey; all she can hope for is a master who spares the whip. 'You know,' he says, 'that your father Lord Morley is a scholar I hold in great esteem. Have you never advised with him?'

'What is the use?' She is scornful. 'When we married he said he was doing his best for me. It is what fathers say. He paid less mind to contracting me to Boleyn than he would to selling a hound puppy. If you think there's a warm kennel and a dish of broken meats, what more do you need to know? You don't ask the animal what it wants.'

'So you have never thought you might be released from your marriage?'

'No, Master Cromwell. My father went into everything thoroughly. Just as thoroughly as you would expect, of a friend of yours. No previous promise, no pre-contract, no shadow of one. Even you and Cranmer between you couldn't get us an annulment. On the wedding day we sat at our supper with our friends, and George told me, I am only doing this because my father says I must. That was good hearing, you will agree, for a girl of twenty who cherished hopes of love. And I defied him, I said the same back to him: I said, if my father did not enforce me, I would be far from you, sir. So then the light faded and we were put to bed.

He put his hand out and flipped my breast and said, I have seen plenty of these, and many better. He said, lie down, open your body, let us do our duty and make my father a grandfather, and then if we have a son we can live apart. I said to him, then do it if you think you can, pray God you may set seed tonight, and then you may take your dibber away and I need not look at it again.' A little laugh. 'But I am barren, you see. Or so I must believe. It may be that my husband's seed is bad or weak. God knows, he spends it in some dubious places. Oh, he is a gospeller, is George, St Matthew be his guide and St Luke protect him. No man as godly as George, the only fault he finds with God is that he made folk with too few orifices. If George could meet a woman with a quinny under her armpit, he would call out "Glory be" and set her up in a house and visit her every day, until the novelty wore off. Nothing is forbidden to George, you see. He'd go to it with a terrier bitch if she wagged her tail at him and said bow-wow.'

For once he is struck silent. He knows he will never get it out of his mind, the picture of George in a hairy grapple with a little ratting dog.

She says, 'I am afraid he has given me a disease and that is why I have never conceived a child. I think there is something destroying me from the inside. I think I might die of it one day.'

She had asked him once, if I die suddenly, have them cut open my corpse to look inside. In those days she thought Rochford might poison her; now she is sure he has done so. He murmurs, my lady, you have borne a great deal. He looks up. 'But this is not to the point. If George knows something about the queen that the king should be told, I can bring him to witness, but I cannot know he will speak out. I can hardly compel the brother against the sister.'

She says, 'I am not talking about his being a witness. I am telling you he spends time in her chamber. Alone with her. And the door closed.'

'In conversation?'

'I have been to the door and heard no voices.'

'Perhaps,' he says, 'they join in silent prayer.'

'I have seen them kiss.'

'A brother may kiss his sister.'

'He may not, not in that way.'

He picks up his pen. 'Lady Rochford, I cannot write down, "He kissed her in that way."'

'His tongue in her mouth. And her tongue in his.'

'You want me to record that?'

'If you fear you won't remember it.'

He thinks, if this comes out in a law court the city will be in an uproar, if it is mentioned in Parliament the bishops will be frigging themselves on their benches. He waits, his pen poised. 'Why would she do this, such a crime against nature?'

'The better to rule. Surely you see it? She is lucky with Elizabeth, the child is like her. But suppose she gets a boy and it has Weston's long face? Or it looks like Will Brereton, what might the king say to that? But they cannot call it a bastard if it looks like a Boleyn.'

Brereton too. He makes a note. He remembers how Brereton once joked with him he could be in two places at once: a chilly joke, a hostile joke, and now, he thinks, now at last, I laugh. Lady Rochford says, 'Why do you smile?'

'I have heard that in the queen's rooms, among her lovers, there was talk of the king's death. Did George ever join in with it?'

'It would kill Henry if he knew how they laugh at him. How his member is discussed.'

'I want you to think hard,' he says. 'Be sure of what you are doing. If you give evidence against your husband, in a court of law or to the council, you may find yourself a lonely woman in the years to come.'

Her face says, am I now so rich in friends? 'I will not bear the blame,' she says. 'You will, Master Secretary. I am thought a woman of no great wit or penetration. And you are what you are, a man of resource who spares no one. It will be thought that you drew the truth out of me, whether I was willing or no.'

It seems to him little more need be said. 'In order to sustain that notion, it will be necessary for you to contain your pleasure and feign distress. Once George is arrested, you must petition for mercy for him.'

'I can do that.' Jane Rochford puts out the tip of her tongue, as if the moment were sugared and she can taste it. 'I am safe, for the king will take no notice, I can guarantee.'

'Be advised by me. Talk to no one.'

'Be advised by me. Talk to Mark Smeaton.'

He tells her, 'I am going to my house at Stepney. I have asked Mark for supper.'

'Why not entertain him here?'

'There has been disturbance enough, don't you think?'

'Disturbance? Oh, I see,' she says.

He watches her out. The door does not close before Rafe and Call-Me-Risley are in the room with him. Pale and set, both of them steady: from which he knows they have not been eavesdropping. 'The king wishes inquiries to begin,' Wriothesley says. 'Utmost discretion, but all possible speed. He can no longer ignore the talk, after the incident. The quarrel. He has not approached Norris.'

'No,' Rafe says. 'They think, the gentlemen in the privy chamber, that it has all blown over. The queen has calmed herself, by all accounts. Tomorrow's jousts are to go ahead as usual.'

'I wonder,' he says, 'would you go to Richard Sampson, Rafe, and tell him that, *entre nous*, matters are out of our hands? It may not be necessary to sue for nullity after all. Or at least, I think the queen will be disposed to give way to anything the king requires of her. She has not much of a negotiating position left. I think we have Henry Norris within bow shot. Weston. Oh, and Brereton too.'

Rafe Sadler raises his eyebrows. 'I would have said the queen hardly knew him.'

'It seems he has the habit of walking in at the wrong moment.'

'You seem very calm, sir,' Call-Me says.

'Yes. Learn from it.'

'What does Lady Rochford say?'

He frowns. 'Rafe, before you go to Sampson, do you sit down there, at the head of the table. Pretend you are the king's council, meeting in privy session.'

'All of them, sir?'

'Norfolk and Fitzwilliam and all. Now, Call-Me. You are a lady of the queen's bedchamber. On your feet. May we have a curtsey? Thank you. Now, I am a page who fetches you a stool. And a cushion on it. Sit down and give the councillors a smile.'

'If you will,' Rafe says uncertainly. But then the spirit of the thing seizes him. He reaches forward and tickles Call-Me under the chin. 'What have you to tell us, delicate madam? Pray, divulge, and part your ruby lips.'

'This beautiful lady alleges,' he says – he, Cromwell, with a wave of his hand – 'that the queen is of light conditions. That her conduct gives rise to suspicion of evil-doing, of flouting of the laws of God, even if no one has witnessed actions contrary to statute.'

Rafe clears his throat. 'Some might say, madam, why did you not speak of this before?'

'Because it was treason to speak against the queen.' Mr Wriothesley is a ready man, and maidenly excuses flow from him. 'We had no choice but to shield her. What could we do, but reason with her, and persuade her to give up her light ways? And yet we could not. She kept us in awe. She is jealous of anyone who has an admirer. She wants to take him from her. She does not scruple to threaten anyone she thinks has erred, whether matron or maid, and she can ruin a woman that way, look at Elizabeth Worcester.'

269

'So now you can no longer forbear to speak out?' Rafe says.

'Now burst into tears, Wriothesley,' he instructs.

'Consider it done.' Call-Me dabs his cheek.

'What a play it makes.' He sighs. 'I wish now we could all take off our disguises and go home.'

He is thinking, Sion Madoc, a boatman on the river at Windsor: 'She goes to it with her brother.'

Thurston, his cook: 'They are standing in a line frigging their members.'

He remembers what Thomas Wyatt told him: 'That is Anne's tactic, she says yes, yes, yes, then she says no ... the worst of it is her hinting to me, her boasting almost, that she says no to me, but yes to others.'

He had asked Wyatt, how many lovers do you think she has had? And Wyatt had answered, 'A dozen? Or none? Or a hundred?'

He himself thought Anne cold, a woman who took her maidenhead to market and sold it for the best price. But this coldness – that was before she was wed. Before Henry heaved himself on top of her, and off again, and she was left, after he had stumbled back to his own apartments, with the bobbing circles of candlelight on the ceiling, the murmurs of her women, the basin of warm water and the cloth: and Lady Rochford's voice as she scrubs herself, 'Careful, madam, do not wash away a Prince of Wales.' Soon she is alone in the dark, with the scent of masculine sweat on the linen, and perhaps one useless maidservant turning and snuffling on a pallet: she is alone with the small sounds of river and palace. And she speaks, and no one answers, except the girl who mutters in her sleep: she prays, and no one answers; and she rolls on to her side, and smooths her hands over her thighs, and touches her own breasts.

So what if, one day, it's yes, yes, yes, yes, yes? To whoever happens to be standing by when the thread of her virtue snaps? Even if it's her brother?

He says to Rafe, to Call-Me, 'I have heard such matter today as I never thought to hear in a Christian country.'

They wait, the young gentlemen: their eyes on his face. Call-Me says, 'Am I still a lady, or shall I take my seat and pick up my pen?'

He thinks, what we do here in England, we send our children into other households when they are young, and so it is not rare for a brother and sister to meet, when they are grown, as if for the first time. Think how it must be then: this fascinating stranger whom you know, this mirror of you. You fall in love, just a little: for an hour, an afternoon. And then you make a joke of it; the residual drag of tenderness remains. It is a feeling that civilises men, and makes them behave better, to dependent women, than otherwise they might. But to go further, to trespass on forbidden flesh, to leap the great gap from a fleeting thought to action ... Priests tell you that temptation slides into sin and you cannot put a hair between. But surely that is not true. You kiss the woman's cheek, very well; then you bite her neck? You say, 'Sweet sister,' and then next minute you flip her back and cant her skirts up? Surely not. There is a room to be crossed and buttons to be undone. You don't sleepwalk into it. You don't fornicate inadvertently. You don't fail to see the other party, who she is. She doesn't hide her face.

But then, it may be that Jane Rochford is lying. She has cause.

'I am not often perplexed,' he says, 'about how to proceed, but I find I have to deal with a matter I hardly dare speak of. I can only partly describe it, so I do not know how to draw up a charge sheet. I feel like one of those men who shows a freak at a fair.'

At a fair the drunken churls throw down their money, and then they disdain what you offer. 'Call that a freak? That's nothing to my wife's mother!'

And all their fellows slap them on the back and chortle.

But then you say to them, well, neighbours, I showed you that only to test your mettle. Part with a penny more, and I shall show you what I have here in the back of the tent. It is a sight to make hardened men quail. And I guarantee that you have never seen devil's work like it.

And then they look. And then they throw up on their boots. And then you count the money. And lock it in your strongbox.

Mark at Stepney. 'He has brought his instrument,' Richard says. 'His lute.'

'Tell him to leave it without.'

If Mark was blithe before, he is suspicious now, tentative. On the threshold, 'I thought, sir, I was to entertain you?'

'Make no doubt of it.'

'I had thought there would be a great company, sir.'

'You know my nephew, Master Richard Cromwell?'

'Still, I am happy to play for you. Perhaps you want me to hear your singing children?'

'Not today. In the circumstances you might be tempted to overpraise them. But will you sit down, and take a cup of wine with us?'

'It would be a charity if you could put us in the way of a rebec player,' Richard says. 'We have but the one, and he is always running off to Farnham to see his family.'

'Poor boy,' he says in Flemish, 'I think he is homesick.'

Mark looks up. 'I did not know you spoke my language.'

'I know you did not. Or you would not have used it to be so disrespectful of me.'

'I am sure, sir, I never meant any harm.' Mark can't remember, what he's said or not said about his host. But his face shows he recalls the general tenor of it.

'You forecast I should be hanged.' He spreads his arms. 'Yet I live and breathe. But I am in a difficulty, and although you do not like me, I have no choice but to come to you. So I ask your charity.'

Mark sits, his lips slightly parted, his back rigid, and one foot pointing to the door, showing he would very much like to be out of it.

'You see.' He puts his palms together: as if Mark were a saint on a plinth. 'My master the king and my mistress the queen are at odds. Everybody knows it. Now, my dearest wish is to reconcile them. For the comfort of the whole realm.'

Give the boy this: he is not without spirit. 'But, Master Secretary, the word about the court is, you are keeping company with the queen's enemies.'

'For the better to find out their practices,' he says.

'If I could believe that.'

He sees Richard shift on his stool, impatient.

'These are bitter days,' he says. 'I do not remember such a time of tension and misery, not since the cardinal came down. In truth I do not blame you, Mark, if you find it hard to trust me, there is such ill-feeling at court that no one trusts anyone else. But I come to you because you are close to the queen, and the other gentlemen will not help me. I have the power to reward you, and will make sure you have everything you deserve, if only you can give me some window into the queen's desires. I need to know why she is so unhappy, and what I can do to remedy it. For it is unlikely she will conceive an heir, while her mind is unquiet. And if she could do that: ah, then all our tears would be dried.'

Mark looks up. 'Why, it is no wonder she is unhappy,' he says. 'She is in love.'

'With whom?'

'With me.'

He, Cromwell, leans forward, elbows on the table: then puts a hand up to cover his face.

'You are amazed,' Mark suggests.

That is only part of what he feels. I thought, he says to himself, that this would be difficult. But it is like picking flowers. He

273

lowers his hand and beams at the boy. 'Not so amazed as you might think. For I have watched you, and I have seen her gestures, her eloquent looks, her many indications of favour. And if these are shown in public, then what in private? And of course it is no surprise any woman would be drawn to you. You are a very handsome young man.'

'Though we thought you were a sodomite,' Richard says.

'Not I, sir!' Mark turns pink. 'I am as good a man as any of them.'

'So the queen would give a good account of you?' he asks, smiling. 'She has tried you and found you to her liking?'

The boy's glance slides away, like a piece of silk over glass. 'I cannot discuss it.'

'Of course not. But we must draw our own conclusions. She is not an inexperienced woman, I think, she would not be interested in a less than masterly performance.'

'We poor men,' Mark says, 'poor men born, are in no wise inferior in that way.'

'True,' he says. 'Though gentlemen keep that fact from ladies, if they can.'

'Otherwise,' Richard says, 'every duchess would be frolicking in a copse with a woodcutter.'

He cannot help laugh. 'Only there are so few duchesses and so many woodcutters. There must be competition between them, you would think.'

Mark looks at him as if he is profaning a sacred mystery. 'If you mean she has other lovers, I have never asked her, I would not ask her, but I know they are jealous of me.'

'Perhaps she has tried them and found them a disappointment,' Richard says. 'And Mark here takes the prize. I congratulate you, Mark.' With what open Cromwellian simplicity he leans forward and asks, 'How often?'

'It cannot be easy to steal the opportunity,' he suggests. 'Even though her ladies are complicit.'

'They are not my friends either,' Mark says. 'They would even deny what I have told you. They are friends of Weston, Norris, those lords. I am nothing to them, they ruffle my hair and call me waiting boy.'

'The queen is your only friend,' he says. 'But such a friend!' He pauses. 'At some point, it will be necessary for you to say who the others are. You have given us two names.' Mark looks up, shocked, at the change of tone. 'Now name them all. And answer Master Richard. How often?'

The boy has frozen under his gaze. But at least he enjoyed his moment in the sun. At least he can say he took Master Secretary by surprise: which few men can say, who are now living.

He waits for Mark. 'Well, perhaps you are right not to speak. Best to get it down in writing, no? I must say, Mark, my clerks will be as astonished as I am. Their fingers will tremble and they will blot the page. So will the council be astonished, when they hear of your successes. There will be many lords who envy you. You cannot expect their sympathy. "Smeaton, what is your secret?" they will demand. You will blush and say, ah, gentlemen, I cannot impart. But you will impart all, Mark, for they will make you. And you will do it freely, or do it enforced.'

He turns away from the boy, as Mark's face falls open in dismay, as his body begins to shake: five rash minutes of boasting, in one ungratified life and, like nervous tradesmen, the gods at once send in their account. Mark has lived in a story of his own devising, where the beautiful princess in her tower hears beyond her casement music of unearthly sweetness. She looks out and sees by moonlight the humble musician with his lute. But unless the musician turns out to be a prince in disguise, this story cannot end well. The doors open and ordinary faces crowd in, the surface of the dream is shattered: you are in Stepney on a warm night at the beginning of spring, the last birdsong is fading into the hush of twilight, somewhere a bolt rattles, a stool is scraped across the floor, a dog barks below the window and Thomas Cromwell says to you, 'We all want our supper, let's get on, here is the paper and the ink. Here is Master Wriothesley, he will write for us.'

'I can give no names,' the boy says.

'You mean, the queen has no lovers but you? So she tells you. But I think, Mark, she has been deceiving you. Which she could easily do, you must admit, if she has been deceiving the king.'

'No.' The poor boy shakes his head. 'I think she is chaste. I do not know how I came to say what I said.'

'Nor do I. No one had hurt you, had they? Or coerced you, or tricked you? You spoke freely. Master Richard is my witness.'

'I take it back.'

'I don't think so.'

There is a pause, while the room repositions itself, figures dispose themselves in the landscape of the evening. Master Secretary says, 'It's chilly, we should have a fire lit.'

Just an ordinary household request, and yet Mark thinks they mean to burn him. He jumps off his stool and makes for the door; perhaps the first bit of sense he's shown, but Christophe is there, broad and amiable, to head him off. 'Seat yourself, pretty boy,' Christophe says.

The wood is laid already. Such a long time it takes, to fan the spark. A little, welcome crackle, and the servant withdraws, wiping his hands on his apron, and Mark watches the door close after him, with a lost expression that may be envy, because he would rather be a kitchen hand now or a boy that scours privy pits. 'Oh, Mark,' Master Secretary says. 'Ambition is a sin. So I am told. Though I have never seen how it is different from using your talents, which the Bible commands we do. So here you are, and here I am, and both of us servants of the cardinal at one time. And if he could see us sitting here tonight, do you know, I don't think he would be the least surprised? Now, to business. Who did you displace in the queen's bed, was it Norris? Or perhaps you have a rota, like the queen's chamber servants?'

'I don't know. I take it back. I can give you no names.'

'It is a shame you should suffer alone, if others are culpable. And of course, they are more culpable than you, as they are gentlemen who the king has personally rewarded and made great, and all of them educated men, and some of them of mature years: whereas you are simple and young, and as much to be pitied as punished, I would say. Tell us now about your adultery with the queen and what you know of her dealings with other men, and then if your confession is prompt and full, clear and unsparing, it is possible that the king will show mercy.'

Mark is hardly hearing him. His limbs are trembling and his breathing is short, he is beginning to cry and to stumble over his words. Simplicity is best now, brisk questions requiring easy answers. Richard asks him, 'You see this person here?' Christophe points to himself, in case Mark is in doubt. 'Do you take him for a pleasant fellow?' Richard asks. 'Would you like to spend ten minutes alone with him?'

'Five would do it,' Christophe predicts.

He says, 'I explained to you, Mark, that Mr Wriothesley will write down what we say. But he will not necessarily write down what we do. You follow me? That will be just between us.'

Mark says, 'Mother Mary, help me.'

Mr Wriothesley says, 'We can take you to the Tower where there is a rack.'

'Wriothesley, may I have a word with you aside?' He waves Call-Me out of the room and on the threshold speaks in an undertone. 'It is better not to specify the nature of the pain. As Juvenal says, the mind is its own best torturer. Besides, you should not make empty threats. I will not rack him. I do not want him carried to his trial in a chair. And if I needed to rack a sad little fellow like this … what next? Stamping on dormice?'

'I am reproved,' Mr Wriothesley says.

He puts his hand on Wriothesley's arm. 'Never mind. You are doing very well.'

This is a business that tries the most experienced. He remembers that day in the forge when a hot iron had seared his skin. There was no choice of resisting the pain. His mouth dropped open and a scream flew out and hit the wall. His father ran to him and said 'Cross your hands,' and helped him to water and to salve, but afterwards Walter said to him, 'It's happened to us all. It's how you learn. You learn to do things the way your father taught you, and not by some foolish method you hit upon yourself half an hour ago.'

He thinks of this: re-entering the room, he asks Mark, 'Do you know you can learn from pain?'

But, he explains, the circumstances must be right. To learn, you must have a future: what if someone has chosen this pain for you and they are going to inflict it for as long as they like, and only stop once you're dead? You can make sense of your suffering, perhaps. You can offer it up for the struggling souls in Purgatory, if you believe in Purgatory. That might work for saints, whose souls are shining white. But not for Mark Smeaton, who is in mortal sin, a self-confessed adulterer. He says, 'No one wants your pain, Mark. It's no good to anyone, no one's interested in it. Not even God himself, and certainly not me. I have no use for your screams. I want words that make sense. Words I can transcribe. You have already spoken them and it will be easy enough to speak them again. So now what you do is your choice. It is your responsibility. You have done enough, by your own account, to damn you. Do not make sinners of us all.'

It may, even now, be necessary to impress on the boy's imagination the stages on the route ahead: the walk from the room of confinement to the place of suffering: the wait, as the rope is uncoiled or the guiltless iron is set to heat. In that space, every thought that occupies the mind is taken out and replaced by blind terror. Your body is emptied and filled up with dread. The feet stumble, the breath labours. The eyes and ears function but the head can't make sense of what is seen and heard. Time falsifies itself, moments becoming days. The faces of your torturers loom up like giants or they become impossibly distant, small, like dots. Words are spoken: bring him here, seat him, now it is time. They were words attached to other and common meanings, but if you survive this they will only ever have one meaning and the meaning is pain. The iron hisses as it is lifted from the flame. The rope doubles like a serpent, loops itself, and waits. It is too late for you. You will not speak now, because your tongue has swelled and filled your mouth and language has eaten itself. Later you will speak, when you are carried away from the machinery and set down on straw. I have endured it, you will say. I have come through. And pity and self-love will crack open your heart, so that at the first gesture of kindness – let us say, a blanket or a sip of wine – your heart will overflow, your tongue unstop. Out flow the words. You were not brought to this room to think, but to feel. And in the end you have felt too much for yourself.

But Mark will be spared this; for now he looks up: 'Master Secretary, will you tell me again what my confession must be? Clear and … what was it? There were four things but I have already forgot them.' In a thicket of words he is stuck fast, and the more he fights the deeper the thorns rip his flesh. If appropriate, a translation can be made for him, yet his English has always seemed good enough. 'But you understand me, sir, I cannot tell you what I do not know?'

'Can you not? Then you must be my guest tonight. Christophe, you can see to that, I think. In the morning, Mark, your own powers will surprise you. Your head will be clear and your memory perfect. You will see that it is not in your interests to protect the gentlemen who share your sin. Because if the position were reversed, believe me, they would not spare a thought for you.'

* * *

He watches Christophe lead Mark away by the hand, as one might lead a simpleton. He waves away Richard and Call-Me to their suppers. He had intended to join them, but he finds he wants nothing, or only a dish he ate as a boy, a simple salad of purslane, the leaves picked that morning and left wrapped in a damp cloth. He ate it then for want of better and it did not stave off hunger. Now it is enough. When the cardinal fell, he had found posts for many of his poor servants, taking in some himself; if Mark had been less insolent, he might have taken him in too. Then he would not be a ruined being, as now he is ruined. His affectations would have been kindly ridiculed, till he became more manly. His expertise would have been lent out to other households and he would have been shown how to value himself and cost out his time. He would been shown how to make money for himself, and put in the way of a wife: instead of spending his best years snuffling and scraping outside the apartments of a king's wife, and having her jog his elbow and snap the feather in his hat.

At midnight, after the whole household has retired, a message from the king comes, to say that he has called off this week's visit to Dover. The jousts, however, will go ahead. Norris is listed, and George Boleyn. They are drawn on opposite teams, one for the challengers, one for the defenders: perhaps they will damage each other.

He does not sleep. His thoughts race. He thinks, I never lay awake a night for love, though poets tells me that is the procedure. Now I lie awake for its opposite. But then, he does not hate Anne, he is indifferent to her. He does not even hate Francis Weston, any more than you hate a biting midge; you just wonder why it was created. He pities Mark, but then, he thinks, we take him for a boy: when I was as old as Mark is now, I had crossed the sea and the frontiers of Europe. I had lain screaming in a ditch and hauled myself out of it, and got myself on the road: not once but twice, once in flight from my father and once from the Spanish on the battlefield. When I was as old as Mark is now, or

Francis Weston, I had distinguished myself in the houses of the Portinari, the Frescobaldi, and long before I was the age of George Boleyn I had dealt for them in the exchanges of Europe; I had broken down doors in Antwerp; I had come home to England, a changed man. I had made over my language, and to my exultation, and unexpectedly, I spoke my native tongue with more fluency than when I went away; I commended me to the cardinal, and at the same time, I was marrying a wife, I was proving myself in the law courts, I would go into court and smile at the judges and talk, my expertise laggard to my presentation, and the judges were so happy that I smiled at them and didn't smack them round the head, that they saw the case my way, often as not. The things you think are the disasters in your life are not the disasters really. Almost anything can be turned around: out of every ditch, a path, if you can only see it.

He thinks of lawsuits he has never thought of in years. Whether the judgement was good. Whether he would have given it against himself.

He wonders if he will ever sleep, and what he will dream. It is only in his dreams that he is private. Thomas More used to say you should build yourself a retreat, a hermitage, within your own house. But that was More: able to slam the door in everyone's face. In truth you cannot separate them, your public being and your private self. More thought you could, but in the end he had men he called heretics dragged to his house in Chelsea, so he could persecute them conveniently in the bosom of his family. You can insist on separation, if you must: go to your cabinet and say, 'Leave me alone to read.' But outside the room, you can hear breathing and scuffling, as a seething discontent builds up, a rumble of expectation: he is a public man, he belongs to us, when will he come forth? You cannot blank it out, the shuffle of the feet of the body politic.

He turns over in bed and says a prayer. In the depth of the night, he hears screaming. It is more like the wail of a child's nightmare than a man's scream of pain, and he thinks, half-asleep, shouldn't some woman be doing something about that? Then he thinks, it must be Mark. What are they doing to him? I said do nothing yet.

But he does not stir. He does not think his household would go against his orders. He wonders if they are asleep in Greenwich. The armoury is too near the palace itself, and the hours before a joust are often alive with the tap of hammers. The beating, the shaping, the welding, the polishing in the polishing mill, these operations are complete; there is just some last-minute riveting, an oiling and easing, final adjustments to please the anxious combatants.

He wonders, why did I leave Mark that space to boast, to undo himself? I could have condensed the process; I could have told him what I wanted, and threatened him. But I encouraged him; I did it so that he would be complicit. If he told the truth about Anne, he is guilty. If he lied about Anne, he is hardly innocent. I was prepared, if necessary, to put him under duress. In France, torture is usual, as necessary as salt to meat; in Italy, it is a sport for the piazza. In England, the law does not countenance it. But it can be used, at a nod from the king: on a warrant. It is true there is a rack at the Tower. No one withstands it. No one. For most men, since the way it works is so obvious, a glimpse of it is enough.

He thinks, I will tell Mark that. It will make him feel better about himself.

He gathers the sheet about him. Next moment, Christophe comes in to wake him. His eyes seem to flinch from the light. He sits up. 'Oh, Jesus. I have not slept all night. Why was Mark screaming?'

The boy laughs. 'We locked him in with Christmas. I thought of it, myself. You remember when I first saw the star in its sleeves? I said, master, what is that machine that is all over points? I thought it was an engine for torture. Well, it is dark in Christmas.

He fell against the star and it impaled him. Then the peacock wings came out of their shroud and brushed his face with fingers. And he thought a phantom was shut up with him in the dark.'

He says, 'You must do without me for an hour.'

'You are not ill, God forbid?'

'No, just wretched with lack of sleep.'

'Pull the covers over your head, and lie as one dead,' Christophe advises. 'I shall come back in an hour with bread and ale.'

When Mark tumbles out of the room he is grey with shock. Feathers adhere to his clothes, not peacock feathers but fluff from the wings of parish seraphs, and smudged gilding from the Three Kings' robes. Names run out of his mouth so fluently that he has to check him; the boy's legs threaten to give way and Richard has to hold him up. He has never had this problem before, the problem of having frightened someone too much. 'Norris' is somewhere in the babble, 'Weston' is there, so far so likely: and then Mark names courtiers so fast that their names merge and fly, he hears Brereton and says, 'Write that down,' he swears he hears Carew, also Fitzwilliam, and Anne's almoner and the Archbishop of Canterbury; he is in there himself of course, and at one point the child alleges Anne has committed adultery with her own husband. 'Thomas Wyatt ...' Mark pipes ...

'No, not Wyatt.'

Christophe leans forward and flicks his knuckles against the side of the boy's head. Mark stops. He looks around, wonderingly, for the source of the pain. Then once again he is confessing and confessing. He has worked through the privy chamber from gentlemen to grooms and he is naming persons unknown, probably cooks and kitchen boys he knew in his former less exalted life.

'Put him back with the ghost,' he says, and Mark gives one scream, and is silent.

'You have had to do with the queen how many times?' he asks.

Mark says, 'A thousand.'

Christophe gives him a little slap.

'Three times or four.'

'Thank you.'

Mark says, 'What will happen to me?'

'That rests with the court who will try you.'

'What will happen to the queen?'

'That rests with the king.'

'Nothing good,' Wriothesley says: and laughs.

He turns. 'Call-Me. You're early today?'

'I could not sleep. A word, sir?'

So today the positions are reversed, it is Call-Me-Risley who is taking him aside, frowning. 'You will have to bring in Wyatt, sir. You take it too much to heart, this charge his father laid on you. If it comes to it, you cannot protect him. The court has talked for years about what he may have done with Anne. He stands first in suspicion.'

He nods. It is not easy to explain to a young man like Wriothesley why he values Wyatt. He wants to say, because, good fellows though you are, he is not like you or Richard Riche. He does not talk simply to hear his own voice, or pick arguments just to win them. He is not like George Boleyn: he does not write verses to six women in the hope of bundling one of them into a dark corner where he can slip his cock into her. He writes to warn and to chastise, and not to confess his need but to conceal it. He understands honour but does not boast of his own. He is perfectly equipped as a courtier, but he knows the small value of that. He has studied the world without despising it. He understands the world without rejecting it. He has no illusions but he has hopes. He does not sleepwalk through his life. His eyes are open, and his ears for sounds others miss.

But he decides to give Wriothesley an explanation he can follow. 'It is not Wyatt,' he says, 'who stands in my way with the king. It is not Wyatt who turns me out of the privy chamber when I need the king's signature. It is not he who is continually dropping slander against me like poison into Henry's ear.'

Mr Wriothesley looks at him speculatively. 'I see. It is not so much, who is guilty, as whose guilt is of service to you.' He smiles. 'I admire you, sir. You are deft in these matters, and without false compunction.'

He is not sure he wants Wriothesley to admire him. Not on those grounds. He says, 'It may be that any of these gentlemen who are named could disarm suspicion. Or if suspicion remained, they could by some appeal stay the king's hand. Call-Me, we are not priests. We don't want their sort of confession. We are lawyers. We want the truth little by little and only those parts of it we can use.'

Wriothesley nods. 'But still I say, bring in Thomas Wyatt. If you don't arrest him your new friends will. And I have been wondering, sir, forgive me if I am persistent, but what will happen afterwards with your new friends? If the Boleyns go down, and it seems they must, the supporters of the Princess Mary will take the credit. They will not thank you for the part you have played. They may speak you fair now, but they will never forgive you for Fisher and More. They will turn you out of office, and they may destroy you completely. Carew, the Courtenays, those people, they will have all to rule.'

'No. The king will have all to rule.'

'But they will persuade him and entice him. I mean Margaret Pole's children, the old noble houses – they take it as natural they should have sway and they mean to have it. They will undo all the good you have done these last five years. And also they say that Edward Seymour's sister, if he marries her, she will take him back to Rome.'

He grins. 'Well, Call-Me, who will you back in a fight, Thomas Cromwell or Mistress Seymour?'

But of course Call-Me is right. His new allies hold him cheap. They take their triumph as natural, and for a mere promise of forgiveness he is to follow them and work for them and repent everything he has done. He says, 'I do not claim I can tell the future, but I do know one or two things such folk are ignorant of.'

One can never be sure what Wriothesley is reporting to Gardiner. Hopefully, matter that will cause Gardiner to scratch his head in puzzlement, and quiver in alarm. He says, 'What do you hear from France? I understand there is much talk of the book that Winchester wrote, justifying the king's supremacy. The French believe he wrote it under duress. Does he allow people to think that?'

'I am sure –' Wriothesley begins.

He cuts him off. 'No matter. I find I like the picture it puts in my head, Gardiner whining how he is crushed.'

He thinks, let's see if that gets back. It is his contention that Call-Me forgets for weeks at a time that he is the bishop's servant. He is an edgy young man, tense, and Gardiner's bellowing makes him ill; Cromwell is a congenial master, and easy day-to-day. He has said to Rafe, I quite like Call-Me, you know. I am interested in his career. I like watching him. If I ever broke with him, Gardiner would send another spy, who might be worse.

'Now,' he says, turning back to the company, 'we had better get poor Mark to the Tower.' The boy has shrunk to his knees, and is begging not to be put back with Christmas. 'Give him a rest,' he says to Richard, 'in a room clear of phantoms. Offer him food. When he is coherent, take his formal statement, and have it well witnessed before he leaves here. If he proves difficult, leave him to Christophe and Master Wriothesley, it is business more fit for them than for you.' Cromwells do not exhaust themselves on menial work; if they once did, that day has passed. He says, 'If Mark tries to renege once he is out of here, they will know what to do at the Tower. Once you have his confession secure, and all the names you need, go down to the king at Greenwich. He will be expecting you. Trust the message to no one. Drop the word in his ear yourself.'

Richard pulls Mark Smeaton to his feet, handling him as one might handle a puppet: and with no more ill-will than one would spare for a marionette. Through his mind darts, unprompted, the image of old Bishop Fisher tottering to the scaffold, skeletal and obstinate.

It is already nine in the morning. The dews of May Day have burned from the grass. All over England, green boughs are carried in from the woods. He is hungry. He could eat a cut of mutton: with samphire, if any has been sent up from Kent. He needs to sit down for his barber. He has not perfected the art of dictating letters while being shaved. Perhaps I'll grow my beard, he thinks. It would save time. Only then, Hans would insist on committing another portrait against me.

At Greenwich by this time, they will be sanding the arena for the jousts. Christophe says, 'Will the king fight today? Will he fight the Lord Norris and slay him?'

No, he thinks, he will leave that to me. Past the workshops, the store rooms and the jetties, the natural haunt of men such as himself, the pages will be placing silk cushions for the ladies in the towers that overlook the tilt yard. Canvas and rope and tar give way to damask and fine linen. The oil and stench and din, the smell of the river, give way to the perfume of rosewater and the murmurings of the maids as they dress the queen for the day ahead. They sweep away the remnants of her small meal, the crumbs of white bread, the slices of sweet preserves. They bring her petticoats and kirtles and sleeves and she makes choice. She is laced and tied and trussed, she is polished and flounced and studded with gems.

The king – it would be three or four years back and to justify his first divorce – put out a book called *A Glass of the Truth*. Parts of it, they say, he wrote himself.

Now Anne Boleyn calls for her glass. She sees herself: her jaundiced skin, lean throat, collarbones like twin blades.

1 May 1536: this, surely, is the last day of knighthood. What happens after this – and such pageants will continue – will be no

more than a dead parade with banners, a contest of corpses. The king will leave the field. The day will end, broken off, snapped like a shinbone, spat out like smashed teeth. George Boleyn, brother to the queen, will enter the silken pavilion to disarm, laying aside the favours and tokens, the scraps of ribbon the ladies have given him to carry. When he lifts off his helmet he will hand it to his squire, and see the world with misted eyes, falcons emblazoned, leopards couchant, claws, talons, teeth: he will feel his head on his shoulders wobbling as soft as jelly.

Whitehall: that night, knowing Norris is in custody, he goes to the king. A snatched word with Rafe in an outer room: how is he?

'Well,' Rafe says, 'you would expect him to be storming about like Edgar the Peaceable, looking for someone to stick with a javelin.' They exchange a smile, remembering the supper table at Wolf Hall. 'But he is calm. Surprisingly so. As if he knew, long ago. In his heart. And by his express wish he is alone.'

Alone: but who would he be with? Useless to expect Gentle Norris whispering towards him. Norris was keeper of the king's private purse; now one imagines the king's money loose and rolling down the highway. The angels' harps are slashed, and discord is general; purse strings are cut, and the silk ties of garments snapped to spill flesh.

As he stands on his threshold, Henry turns his eyes: 'Crumb,' he says heavily. 'Come and sit.' He waves away the attentions of the groom who hovers by the door. He has wine and pours it himself. 'Your nephew will have told you what passed at the tilting ground.' He says softly, 'He is a good boy, Richard, is he not?' His gaze is distant, as if he would like to wander off the point. 'I was among the spectators today, not an actor at all. She of course was as ever: at ease among her women, her countenance very haughty, but then smiling and stopping to converse with this gentleman or that.' He sniggers, a flat, incredulous sound. 'Oh yes, she has had some conversation.'

Then the bouts began, the heralds calling out each rider. Henry Norris had some ill-luck. His horse, startled by something, jibbed and laid back its ears, danced and tried to shed its rider. (Horse can fail. Boys can fail. Nerve can fail.) The king sent a message down to Norris, advising him to retire; a substitute would be sent to him, one of the king's own string of fighting horses, still kept trimmed and tacked in case it should be his sudden pleasure to take the field.

'It was a usual courtesy,' Henry explains; and shifts in his chair, like one called to justify himself. He nods: of course, sir. Whether Norris did in fact return to the lists, he is unsure. It was mid-afternoon when Richard Cromwell made his way through the crowds to the gallery, and knelt before the king; and at a word, approached to whisper in his ear. 'He explained how the musician Mark was taken,' the king says. 'He had confessed all, your nephew said. What, confessed freely? I asked him. Your nephew said, nothing was done against Mark. Not a hair of his head harmed.'

He thinks, but I shall have to burn the peacock wings.

'And then ...' the king says. For a moment he baulks, as Norris's horse did: and falls silent.

He will not continue. But he, Cromwell, already knows what occurred. Upon hearing the word from Richard, the king rose from his place. His servants eddied about him. He signed to a page, 'Find out Henry Norris, and tell him I ride to Whitehall, now. I want his company.'

He gave no explanation. He did not tarry. He did not speak to the queen. But covered the miles back, Norris beside him: Norris puzzled, Norris astonished, Norris almost slipping from the saddle with fright. 'I taxed him with the matter,' Henry says. 'With the boy Mark's confession. He would say nothing, but of his innocence.' Again that flat, scornful little laugh. 'But since then, Master Treasurer has questioned him. Norris admits it, he says he loved her. But when Fitz put it to him that he is an adulterer, that he desired my death so he could marry her, he said no, no and no. You will put questions to him, Cromwell, but when you do, tell him again what I told him as we rode. There can be mercy. There may be mercy, if he confesses and names the others.'

'We have names from Mark Smeaton.'

'I would not trust him,' Henry says contemptuously. 'I would not trust some little fiddle-player with the lives of men I have called my friends. I await some corroboration of his story. We will see what the lady says when she is taken.'

'Their confessions will be enough, sir, surely. You know who is suspected. Let me take them all in ward.'

But Henry's mind has strayed. 'Cromwell, what does it mean, when a woman turns herself about and about in the bed? Offering herself, this way and that? What would put it into her head to do such a thing?'

There is only one answer. Experience, sir. Of men's desires and her own. He does not need to say it.

'One way is apt for the procreation of children,' Henry says. 'The man lies on her. Holy church sanctions it, on the permitted days. Some churchmen say that though it is a grievous thing for a brother to copulate with a sister, it is still more grievous should a woman sit astride a man, or should a man approach a woman as if she were a bitch. For these practices, and others I will not name, Sodom was destroyed. I fear that any Christian man or woman who is in thrall to such vices will incur a judgement: what do you say? Where would a woman, not bred in a whorehouse, get knowledge of such things?'

'Women talk among themselves,' he says. 'As men do.'

'But a sober, a godly matron, whose only duty is to get a child?'

'I suppose she might want to pique her good man's interest, sir. So he does not venture to Paris Garden or some other ill-reputed place. If, let's say, they were long married.'

'But three years? Is that long?'

'No, sir.'

'It is not even three.' For a moment the king has forgotten that we are not talking about himself, but about some notional, God-fearing Englishman, some forester or ploughman. 'Where would she get the idea?' he persists. 'How would she know the man would like it?'

He bites back the obvious answer: perhaps she talked to her sister, who was in your bed first. Because now the king has wandered away from Whitehall and back to the country, to the blunt-fingered cottar and his wife in apron and cap: the man who crosses himself and asks leave of the Pope before he pinches out the light and sombrely tups his spouse, her knees to the roof beams and his backside bobbing. Afterwards, this godly couple, they kneel by their bed: they join in prayer.

But one day when the cottar is about his employment, the woodsman's little apprentice sneaks in and takes out his tool: now Joan, he says, now Jenny, bend over the table and let me teach you a lesson your mother never taught you. And so she trembles; and so he teaches her; and when the honest cottar comes home and mounts her that night, she thinks with every thrust and grunt of a newer way of doing things, a sweeter way, a dirtier way, a way that makes her eyes widen with surprise and another man's name jerk out of her mouth. Sweet Robin, she says. Sweet Adam. And when her husband recalls that his own name is Henry, does that not cause him to scratch his pate?

It is dusk now, outside the king's windows; his kingdom is growing chilly, his councillor too. They need lights and a fire. He opens the door and at once the room is full of folk: around the king's person, the grooms dart and swerve like early swallows in the twilight. Henry barely notices their presence. He says, 'Cromwell, do you suppose the rumours did not come to me? When every ale wife knew them? I am a simple man, you see. Anne told me she was untouched and I chose to believe her. She

291

lied to me for seven years that she was a maid pure and chaste. If she could carry on such a deceit, what else might she be capable of? You can arrest her tomorrow. And her brother. Some of these acts alleged against her are not fit for discussion among decent people, lest they are moved by examples to sins they would not otherwise have dreamed to exist. I ask you and all my councillors to be close and discreet.'

'It is easy,' he says, 'to be deceived about a woman's history.'

For suppose Joan, suppose Jenny, had another life before her cottage life? You thought she grew up in a clearing at the other side of the wood. Now you hear, from reliable sources, that she came to womanhood in a harbour town, and danced naked on a table for sailors.

Did Anne, he will wonder later, understand what was coming? You would have thought that at Greenwich she would have been praying, or writing letters to her friends. Instead, if reports are true, she has walked blindly through her last morning, doing what she always used to do: she has been to the tennis courts, where she placed bets on the outcome of the matches. Late morning, a messenger came to ask her to appear before the king's council, sitting in His Majesty's absence: in the absence, too, of Master Secretary, who is busy elsewhere. The councillors told her that she would be charged with adultery with Henry Norris and Mark Smeaton: and with one other gentleman, for the moment unnamed. She must go to the Tower, pending proceedings against her. Her manner, Fitzwilliam tells him later, was incredulous and haughty. You cannot put a queen on trial, she said. Who is competent to try her? But then, when she was told that Mark and Henry Norris had confessed, she burst into tears.

From the council chamber, she is escorted to her own rooms, to dine. At two o'clock, he is heading there, with Audley the Lord Chancellor, and Fitzwilliam by his side. Mr Treasurer's affable face is creased with strain. 'I was not happy this morning in council, to hear her told so bluntly that Harry Norris has confessed. He confessed to me he loved her. He didn't confess to any act.'

'So what did you do, Fitz?' he asks him. 'Did you speak up?'

'No,' Audley says. 'He fidgeted and stared into the middle distance. Didn't you, Master Treasurer?'

'Cromwell!' It is Norfolk who is roaring, swatting his way through the throng of courtiers towards him. 'Now, Cromwell! I hear the singer has sung to your tune. What did you do to him? I wish I had been there. This will furnish a pretty ballad from the printer's shop. Henry fingering the lute, while the lutenist fingers his wife's quim.'

'If you hear of any such printer,' he says, 'tell me and I will close him down.'

Norfolk says, 'But listen to me, Cromwell. I do not intend this bag of bones to be the ruin of my noble house. If she has miscon-ducted herself, it must not bear on the Howards, only the Boleyns. And I don't need Wiltshire finished off. I just want his foolish title taken off him. *Monseigneur*, if you please.' The duke bares his teeth in glee. 'I want to see him diminished, after his pride these past years. You will recall that I never promoted this marriage. No, Cromwell, that was you. I always warned Henry Tudor of her character. Perhaps this will teach him that in the future he should listen to me.'

'My lord,' he says, 'do you have the warrant?'

Norfolk flourishes a parchment. When they enter Anne's rooms, her gentlemen servants are just rolling away the great tablecloth, and she is still seated under her canopy of estate. She is wearing crimson velvet and she turns – the bag of bones – the perfect ivory oval of her face. Hard to think she has eaten anything; there is a fretful silence in the room, strain visible on every face. They must wait, the councillors, until the rolling is performed, till the folding of the napery is accomplished, and the correct reverences made.

'So you are here, uncle,' she says. Her voice is small. One by one she acknowledges them. 'Lord Chancellor. Master Treasurer.' Other councillors are pushing in behind them. Many people, it seems, have dreamed of this moment; they have dreamed that Anne would plead with them on her knees. 'My lord Oxford,' she says. 'And William Sandys. How are you, Sir William?' It is as if she finds it soothing, to name them all. 'And you, Cremuel.' She leans forward. 'You know, I created you.'

'And he created you, madam,' Norfolk snaps. 'And be sure he repents him of it.'

'But I was sorry first,' Anne says. She laughs. 'And I am sorry more.'

'Ready to go?' Norfolk says.

'I do not know how to be ready,' she says simply.

'Just come with us,' he says: he, Cromwell. He holds out a hand.

'I would rather not go to the Tower.' The same small voice, empty of everything except politeness. 'I would rather go to see the king. Can I not be taken up to Whitehall?'

She knows the answer. Henry never says goodbye. Once, on a summer's day of still heat, he rode away from Windsor and left Katherine behind; he never saw her again.

She says, 'Surely, masters, you will not take me like this, as I stand? I have no necessities, not a change of shift, and I should have my women with me.'

'Your clothes will be brought to you,' he says. 'And women to serve you.'

'I had rather have my own ladies of my privy chamber.'

Glances are exchanged. She seems not to know it is these women who have given evidence against her, these women who crowd around Master Secretary everywhere he moves, keen to tell him anything he wants, desperate to protect themselves. 'Well, if I cannot have my choice ... some persons at least from my household. So I can keep my proper state.'

Fitz clears his throat. 'Madam, your household is to be dissolved.'

She flinches. 'Cremuel will find them places,' she says lightly. 'He is good about servants.'

Norfolk nudges the Lord Chancellor. 'Because he grew up with them, eh?' Audley turns his face away: he is always Cromwell's man.

'I do not think I shall come with any of you,' she says. 'I will go with William Paulet, if he is pleased to escort me, because in the council this morning you all abused me, but Paulet was a very gentleman.'

'By God,' Norfolk chuckles. 'Go with Paulet, is it? I'll lock you under my arm and drag you to the boat with your arse in the air. Is that what you want?'

With one accord, the councillors turn on him, and glare. 'Madam,' Audley says, 'be assured, you will be handled as befits your status.'

She stands. Gathers her crimson skirts, raising them, fastidious, as if she will not now touch the common ground. 'Where is my lord brother?'

Last seen at Whitehall, she is told: which is true, though by now the guards may have come for him. 'And my father Monseigneur? This is what I do not understand,' she says. 'Why is Monseigneur not here with me? Why does he not sit down with you gentlemen and resolve this?'

'No doubt there will be resolution hereafter.' The Lord Chancellor is almost purring. 'Everything will be provided to keep you in comfort. It is arranged.'

'But arranged for how long?'

No one answers her. Outside the chamber, William Kingston waits for her, the Constable of the Tower. Kingston is a huge man, the king's own build; he conducts himself nobly, but his office, and his appearance, have struck terror into the hearts of the strongest men. He remembers Wolsey, when Kingston went up-country to arrest him: the cardinal's legs went from under him, and he had to sit down on a chest to recover. We should have left Kingston at home, he whispers to Audley, and taken her ourselves. Audley murmurs, 'We could have, certainly; but don't you think, Master Secretary, that you're frightening enough on your own account?'

It amazes him, the Lord Chancellor's levity, as they pass into the open air. At the king's landing stage, the heads of stone beasts swim in the water, and so do their own shapes, the shapes of gentlemen, their forms broken by ripples, and the everted queen, flickering like a flame in a glass: around them, the dance of mild afternoon sunshine, and a flood of birdsong. He hands Anne into the barge, as Audley seems reluctant to touch her, and she shies away from Norfolk; and as if fishing his thoughts out of his mind, she whispers, 'Cremuel, you have never forgiven me for Wolsey.' Fitzwilliam gives him a glance, murmurs something he does not catch. Fitz was a favourite of the cardinal's in his day, and perhaps they are sharing a thought: now Anne Boleyn knows what it is like to be turned out of your house and put upon the river, your whole life receding with every stroke of the oars.

Norfolk takes a place opposite his niece, twitching and tutting. 'You see? You see now, madam! You see what happens, when you spurn your own family?'

'I do not think "spurn" is the word,' Audley says. 'She hardly did that.'

He gives Audley a black look. He has asked for discretion on the charges against brother George. He does not want Anne to start flailing about and knock someone out of the boat. He withdraws into himself. Watches the water. A company of halberdiers are their escort, and he admires each fine axe edge, the sharp gleam on their blades. From an armoury's point of view, they are surprisingly cheap to produce, halberds. But probably, as a weapon of war, they've had their day. He thinks of Italy, the battlefield, the forward push of pike. There is a powder house at the Tower and he likes to go in and talk to the firemasters. But perhaps that is a task for another day.

Anne says, 'Where is Charles Brandon? I am sure he is sorry not to have seen this.'

'He is with the king, I suppose,' Audley says. He turns to him and whispers, 'Poisoning his mind against your friend Wyatt. You have your work cut out there, Master Secretary.'

His eyes are on the far bank. 'Wyatt is too good a man to lose.'

The Lord Chancellor sniffs. 'Verses will not save him. Damn him, rather. We know he writes in riddles. But I think perhaps the king will feel they have been solved.'

He thinks not. There are codes so subtle that they change their whole meaning in half a line, or in a syllable, or in a pause, a caesura. He has prided himself, will pride himself, on asking Wyatt no questions that will force him to lie, though he may dissimulate. Anne should have dissimulated, Lady Rochford has explained to him: on her first night with the king she should have acted the virgin's part, lain rigid and weeping. 'But, Lady Rochford,' he had objected, 'faced with such fear, any man might falter. The king is not a rapist.'

Oh, well then, Lady Rochford had said. She should at least have flattered him. She should have acted like a woman who was getting a happy surprise.

He did not relish the topic; he sensed in Jane Rochford's tone the peculiar cruelty of women. They fight with the poor weapons God has bestowed – spite, guile, skill in deceit – and it is likely that in conversations between themselves they trespass in places where a man would never trust his footing. The king's body is borderless, fluent, like his realm: it is an island building itself or eroding itself, its substance washed out into the waters salt and fresh; it has its shores of polder, its marshy tracts, its reclaimed margins; it has tidal waters, emissions and effusions, quags that slough in and out of the conversation of Englishwomen, and dark mires where only priests should wade, rush lights in their hands.

On the river the breeze is cold; summer still weeks away. Anne is watching the water. She looks up and says, 'Where is the archbishop? Cranmer will defend me and so will all my bishops, they owe their promotion to me. Fetch Cranmer and he will swear I am a good woman.'

Norfolk leans forward and speaks into her face: 'A bishop would spit on you, niece.'

'I am the queen and if you do me harm, then a curse will come on you. No rain will fall till I am released.'

A soft groan from Fitzwilliam. The Lord Chancellor says, 'Madam, it is such foolish talk of curses and spells that has brought you here.'

'Oh? I thought you said I was a false wife, are you now saying I am a sorcerer too?'

Fitzwilliam says, 'It was none of us raised the subject of curses.'

'You cannot do anything against me. I will swear on oath I am true, and the king will listen. You can bring no witnesses. You do not even know how to charge me.'

'Charge you?' Norfolk says. 'Why charge you, I ask myself. It would save us trouble if we pitched you out and drowned you.'

Anne shrinks into herself. Huddled as far as she can get from her uncle, she looks the size of a child.

As the barge moors at the Court Gate he sees Kingston's deputy, Edmund Walsingham, scanning the river; in conversation with him, Richard Riche. 'Purse, what are you doing here?'

'I thought you might want me, sir.'

The queen steps on to dry land, steadies herself on Kingston's arm. Walsingham bows to her. He seems agitated; he looks around, wondering to which councillor he should address himself. 'Are we to fire the cannon?'

'That's usual,' Norfolk says, 'is it not? When a person of note comes in, at the king's pleasure. And she is of note, I suppose?'

'Yes, but a queen ...' the man says.

'Fire the cannon,' Norfolk demands. 'The Londoners ought to know.'

'I think they know already,' he says. 'Didn't my lord see them running along the banks?'

Anne looks up, scans the stonework above her head, the narrow loupe windows and the gratings. There are no human faces, just the flap of a raven's wing, and its voice above her, startling in its human quality. 'Is Harry Norris here?' she asks. 'Has he not cleared my name?'

'I fear not,' Kingston says. 'Nor his own.'

Something happens to Anne then, which later he will not quite understand. She seems to dissolve and slip from their grasp, from Kingston's hands and his, she seems to liquefy and elude them, and when she resolves herself once more into woman's form she is on hands and knees on the cobbles, her head thrown back, wailing.

Fitzwilliam, the Lord Chancellor, even her uncle, step back; Kingston frowns, his deputy shakes his head, Richard Riche looks stricken. He, Cromwell, takes hold of her – since no one else will do it – and sets her back on her feet. She weighs nothing, and as he lifts her, her wail breaks off, as if her breath had been stopped. Silent, she steadies herself against his shoulder, leans into him: intent, complicit, ready for the next thing they will do together, which is kill her.

As they turn back to the royal barge, Norfolk barks, 'Master Secretary? I need to see the king.'

'Alas,' he says, as if the regret were genuine: alas, that will not be possible. 'His Majesty has asked for peace and seclusion. Surely, my lord, in the circumstances you would do the same.'

'In the circumstances?' Norfolk echoes. The duke is dumb, at least for a minute, as they inch out into the central channel of the Thames: and he frowns, no doubt thinking of his own ill-used wife and the chances of her straying. A snort of derision is best, the duke decides: 'I tell you what, Master Secretary, I know you're friendly with my duchess, so what do you say? Cranmer can have us annulled, and she's yours for the asking. What, you won't have her? She comes with her own bedding and a riding mule, and she doesn't eat much. I'll make over forty shillings a year and we'll shake hands on it.'

'My lord, curb yourself,' Audley says fiercely. He is driven to the reproach of last resort: 'Remember your ancestry.'

'It's more than Cromwell can,' the duke sniggers. 'Now listen to me, Crumb. If I say I need to see the Tudor, no blacksmith's boy will say me nay.'

'He may weld you, my lord,' Richard Riche says. They had not noticed him slip aboard. 'He may take upon him to beat and reshape your head. Master Secretary has skills you have never imagined.'

A sort of giddiness has seized them, a reaction to the horrible sight they have left behind on the quay. 'He may pound you into a different shape entirely,' Audley says. 'You may wake up a duke and by noon you may be curved into a horseboy.'

'He may melt you,' Fitzwilliam says. 'You begin as a duke and end as a leaden drip.'

'You may live out your days as a trivet,' Riche says. 'Or a hinge.'

He thinks, you must laugh, Thomas Howard, you must laugh or burst into flames: which will it be? If you combust we can at least throw water on you. With a spasm, a shudder, the duke turns his back on them to master himself: 'Tell Henry,' he says. 'Tell him I renounce the wench. Tell him I no longer call her niece.'

He, Cromwell, says, 'You will have the chance to show loyalty. If it comes to a trial, you will preside over the court.'

'At least, we think that is the procedure,' Riche chips in. 'A queen has never come to trial before. What does the Lord Chancellor say?'

'I say nothing.' Audley holds up his palms. 'You and Wriothesley and Master Secretary have worked it all between you, as you usually do. Only – Cromwell, you will not put the Earl of Wiltshire among the judges?'

He smiles. 'Her father? No. I would not do that.'

'How will we charge Lord Rochford?' Fitzwilliam asks. 'If he is indeed to be charged?'

Norfolk says, 'It is the three for trial? Norris, Rochford, and the fiddle player?'

'Oh no, my lord,' he says calmly.

'There's more? By the Mass!'

'How many lovers has she had?' Audley says, with a keenness barely suppressed.

Riche says, 'Lord Chancellor, you have seen the king? I have seen him. He is pale and ill from the strain. That, in fact, is treason in itself, if any harm should happen to his royal body. Indeed, I think we may say harm has already occurred.'

If dogs could smell out treason, Riche would be a bloodhound, that prince among trufflers.

He says, 'I keep an open mind as to how these gentlemen are to be charged, whether with concealing a treason or with the offence itself. If they claim to be only a witness to the misdeeds of others they must say who those others are, they must earnestly and openly tell us what they know; but if they withhold names, we must suspect they are themselves among the guilty.'

The boom of the cannon catches them unawares, shuddering across the water; you feel the jolt inside, in your bones.

That evening a message comes to him from Kingston at the Tower. Write down everything she says and everything she does, he had told the constable, and Kingston – a dutiful, civil and prudent man, though sometimes obtuse – can be relied on for that. As the councillors walked away to the barge, Anne asked him, 'Master Kingston, shall I go into a dungeon?' No, madam, he had assured her, you shall have the chambers where you lay before your coronation.

At that, he reports, she fell into a storm of weeping, 'It is too good for me. Jesus have mercy on me.' Then she knelt down on the stones and prayed and wept, said the constable: then, most strangely, or so it seemed to him, she began to laugh.

Without a word, he passes the letter to Wriothesley. Who looks up from it, and when he speaks his tone is hushed. 'What has she done, Master Secretary? Perhaps something we have not yet imagined.'

He looks at him, exasperated. 'You are not going to begin on that witchcraft business?'

'No. But. If she says she is not worthy, she is saying she is guilty. Or so it seems to me. But I do not know guilty of what.'

'Remind me what I said. What kind of truth do we want? Did I say, the whole truth?'

'You said, only the truth we can use.'

'I reiterate the point. But you know, Call-Me, I shouldn't have to. You're quick on the uptake. Once should be enough.'

It is a warm evening, and he sits by an open window, his nephew Richard for company. Richard knows when to keep silence and when to talk; it is a family trait, he supposes. Rafe Sadler is the only other company he would have liked, and Rafe is with the king.

Richard looks up. 'I had a letter from Gregory.'

'Oh yes?'

'You know Gregory's letters.'

'"The sun is shining. We have had good hunting and great cheer. I am well, how are you? And now no more for lack of time."'

Richard nods. 'He doesn't change, Gregory. Though he does, I suppose. He wants to come here to you. He should be with you, he thinks.'

'I was trying to spare him.'

'I know. But perhaps you should let him. You cannot keep him a child.'

He broods. If his son is to become accustomed to the king's service, perhaps he should know what it involves. 'You can leave me,' he says to Richard. 'I might write to him.'

Richard pauses to shut out the night air. Outside the door his voice runs on, giving kindly commands: bring down my uncle's furred gown, he may want it, and take in to him more lights. He is sometimes surprised if he knows someone cares for him, cares enough to think of his bodily comfort: except for his servants, who are paid to do it. He wonders how the queen finds herself, amid her new Tower household: Lady Kingston has been set among her attendants, and though he has placed women of the Boleyn family around her, they might not be those she would have chosen for herself. They are women of experience, who will know how the tide is running. They will listen keenly to weeping and laughter, and any words like, 'It is too good for me.'

He believes he understands Anne, as Wriothesley does not. When she said the queen's lodgings were too good for her, she did not mean to admit her guilt, but to say this truth: I am not worthy, and I am not worthy because I have failed. One thing she set out to do, this side of salvation: get Henry and keep him. She has lost him to Jane Seymour, and no court of law will judge her more harshly than she judges herself. Since Henry rode away from her yesterday, she has been an impostor, like a child or a court fool, dressed in the costumes of a queen and now ordered to live in the queen's rooms. She knows adultery is a sin and treason a crime, but to be on the losing side is a greater fault than these.

Richard puts his head back in and says, 'Your letter, shall I write it for you? Save your eyes?'

He says, 'Anne is dead to herself. We shall have no trouble with her now.'

* * *

He has asked the king to keep to his privy chamber, admit as few people as possible. He has strictly instructed the guards to turn away petitioners, whether men or women. He does not want the king's judgement contaminated, as it can be, by the last person he talked to; he does not want Henry persuaded or cajoled or pushed off course. Henry seems inclined to obey him. These last years, the king has tended to retire from public view: at first because he wanted to be with his concubine Anne, and then because he wanted to be without her. Behind his privy chamber, he has his secret lodgings; and sometimes, after he has been put into his great bed and the bed has been blessed, after the candles have been snuffed, he pushes away the damask counterpane and slides from the mattress and pads into a secret chamber, where he creeps into another, unofficial bed, and sleeps like a natural man, naked and alone.

So it is in the muffled silence of these secret rooms, hung with tapestries of the Fall of Man, that the king says to him, 'Cranmer has sent a letter from Lambeth. Read it to me, Cromwell. I have had it read once, but do you read it again.'

He takes the paper. You can feel Cranmer shrinking as he writes, hoping the ink will run and the words blur. Anne the queen has favoured him, Anne has listened to him and promoted the cause of the gospel; Anne has made use of him, too, but Cranmer can never see that. '"*I am in such perplexity,*" he writes, "*that my mind is clean amazed; for I never had better opinion in woman, than I had in her.*"'

Henry interrupts him. 'See how we were all deceived.'

'"*... which maketh me to think,*" he reads, "*that she should not be culpable. And again, I think your Highness would not have gone so far, except she had surely been culpable.*"'

'Wait till he hears it all,' Henry says. 'He will not have heard the like. At least, I hope he has not. I do not think there has ever been an instance in the world like this.'

'"*Now I think that your Grace best knoweth, that next unto your Grace I was most bound unto her of all creatures living ...*"'

Henry breaks in again. 'But you will see he goes on to say, if she is culpable she should be punished without mercy, and held for an example. Seeing how I raised her from nothing. And further he says, that no one who loves the gospel will favour her, rather hate her.'

Cranmer adds, '*Wherefore I trust that your Grace will bear no less entire favour unto the truth of the gospel, than you did before forsomuch as your grace's favour to the gospel was not led by affection unto her, but by zeal unto the truth.*'

He, Cromwell, puts the letter down. That seems to cover everything. She cannot be guilty. But yet she must be guilty. We, her brethren, repudiate her.

He says, 'Sir, if you want Cranmer, send for him. You could comfort each other, and perhaps between you try to understand all this. I will tell your people to let him in. You look as if you need fresh air. Go down the stair into the privy garden. You will not be disturbed.'

'But I have not seen Jane,' Henry says. 'I want to look at her. We can bring her here?'

'Not yet, sir. Wait till the business is more forward. There are rumours on the streets, and crowds who want to see her, and ballads made, deriding her.'

'Ballads?' Henry is shocked. 'Find out the authors. They must be straitly punished. No, you are right, we must not bring Jane here until the air is pure. So you go to her, Cromwell. I want you to carry a certain token.' He produces from among his papers a tiny, jewelled book: the kind a woman keeps at her girdle, looped on a gold chain. 'It was my wife's,' he says. Then he checks himself and looks away in shame. 'I mean to say, it was Katherine's.'

He does not want to take the time to go down to Surrey to Carew's house, but it seems he must. It is a well-proportioned house put up some thirty years ago, its great hall especially splendid and much copied by gentlemen building their own houses.

305

He has been there before, with the cardinal in his time. It looks as though since then Carew has brought Italians in to replan the gardens. The gardeners doff their straw hats to him. The walks are coming into their early summer glory. Birds twitter from an aviary. The grass is shorn as close as velvet pile. Nymphs watch him with stone eyes.

Now that the business is tending one way and one way only, the Seymours have begun teaching Jane how to be a queen. 'This business you get up to with doors,' Edward Seymour says. Jane blinks at him. 'The way you hold the door still and slide yourself around it.'

'You told me to be discreet.' Jane lowers her eyes, to show him what discretion means.

'Now. Go out of the room,' Edward says. 'Come back in. Like a queen, Jane.'

Jane sneaks out. The door creaks behind her. In the hiatus, they look at each other. The door swings open. There is a long pause – as it might be, a regal pause. The doorway stands empty. Then Jane appears, inching around the corner. 'Is that better?'

'Do you know what I think?' he says. 'I think that from now on Jane won't be opening her own doors, so it doesn't matter.'

'My belief is,' Edward says, 'this modesty could pall. Look up at me, Jane. I want to see your expression.'

'But what makes you think,' Jane murmurs, 'that I want to see yours?'

In the gallery the whole family is assembled. The two brothers, prudent Edward and hasty Tom. Worthy Sir John, the old goat. Lady Margery, the noted beauty of her day, about whom John Skelton once penned a line: 'benign, courteous and meek', he called her. The meekness is not evident today: she looks grimly triumphant, like a woman who has squeezed success from life, though it's taken her nearly sixty years to do it.

Bess Seymour, the widowed sister, sails in. She has a parcel wrapped in linen in her hands. 'Master Secretary,' she says, with a reverence. She says to her brother, 'Here, Tom, hold this. Sit down, sister.'

Jane sits on a stool. You expect someone to hand her a slate and begin her on A.B.C. 'Now,' Bess says. 'Off with this.' For a moment, she looks as if she is attacking her sister: with a vigorous double-handed tug, she rips off her half-moon headdress, flips up its veil and bundles the whole into the waiting hands of her mother.

Jane in her white cap looks naked and pained, her face as small and wan as a face on a sickbed. 'Cap off too, and start again,' Bess orders. She drags at the knotted string under her sister's chin. 'What have you done with this, Jane? It looks as if you've been sucking it.' Lady Margery produces a pair of embroidery scissors. With a snip, Jane is freed. Her sister whisks the cap off and Jane's pale hair, a thin ribbon of light, streaks over her shoulder. Sir John ahems and looks away, the old hypocrite: as if he'd seen something beyond the male remit. The hair has a moment's freedom before Lady Margery plucks it up and wraps it around her hand, as unfeeling as if it were a hank of wool; Jane frowns as it is whipped up from her nape, coiled, and crammed under a newer, stiffer cap. 'We're going to pin this,' Bess says. She works, absorbed. 'More elegant, if you can stand it.'

'Never liked strings myself,' Lady Margery says.

'Thank you, Tom,' Bess says, and takes her parcel. She casts aside the wrappings. 'Cap tighter,' she decrees. Her mother pinches as directed, repins. The next moment a fabric box is crammed on Jane's head. Her eyes turn up, as if for help, and she utters one little bleat, as the wire frame bites into her scalp. 'Well, I am surprised,' Lady Margery says. 'You've got a bigger head than I thought, Jane.' Bess applies herself to bending the wire. Jane sits mute. 'That'll do,' Lady Margery says. 'It's got a bit of give in it. Push it down. Turn up the lappets. About chin level, Bess. That's how the old queen used to like it.' She stands back to assess her daughter, now imprisoned in an old-fashioned gable hood, the kind that hasn't been seen since Anne came up. Lady Margery sucks in her lips and studies her daughter. 'Tilting,' she pronounces.

'That's Jane, I think,' Tom Seymour says. 'Sit up straight, sister.'

Jane puts her hands to her head, gingerly, as if the construction might be hot. 'Leave it alone,' her mother snaps. 'You wore it before. You'll get used to it.'

From somewhere Bess produces a length of fine black veiling. 'Sit still.' She begins to pin it to the back of the box, her face absorbed. Ouch, that was my neck, Jane says, and Tom Seymour gives a heartless laugh; some private joke of his, too unseemly to share, but one can guess. 'I'm sorry to keep you, Master Secretary,' Bess says, 'but she has to get this right. We cannot have her reminding the king of, you know.'

Just take care, he thinks, uneasy: it is only four months since Katherine died, perhaps the king does not want to be reminded of her either.

'We have several more frames at our command,' Bess tells her sister, 'so if you really can't balance it, we can take the whole thing down and try again.'

Jane closed her eyes. 'I'm sure it will do.'

'How did you get them so quickly?' he asks.

'They have been put away,' Lady Margery says. 'In chests. By women like myself who knew they would be needed again. We shall not see the French fashions now, not for many a year, please God.'

Old Sir John says, 'The king has sent her jewels.'

'Things La Ana had no use for,' Tom Seymour says. 'But they will all come to her soon.'

Bess says, 'I suppose Anne will not want them, in her convent.'

Jane glances up: and now she does it, now she meets the eyes of her brothers, and pulls her gaze away again. It is always a surprise to hear her voice, so soft and so unpractised, its tone so at odds with what she has to say. 'I do not see how that can work, the convent. First Anne would claim that she was carrying the king's child. Then he would be forced to wait on her, without result, for there is never a result. After that she would think of new delays. And meanwhile none of us would be safe.'

Tom says, 'She knows Henry's secrets, I dare say. And would sell them to her friends the French.'

'Not that they are her friends,' Edward says. 'Not any more.'

'But she would try,' Jane says.

He sees them, closing ranks: a fine old English family. He asks Jane, 'Would you do anything you can, to ruin Anne Boleyn?' His tone implies no reproach; he's just interested.

Jane considers: but only for a moment. 'No one need contrive at her ruin. No one is guilty of it. She ruined herself. You cannot do what Anne Boleyn did, and live to be old.'

He must study Jane, now, the expression on her downturned face. When Henry courted Anne she looked squarely at the world, her chin tilted upwards, her shallow-set eyes like pools of darkness against the glow of her skin. But one searching glance is enough for Jane, and then she casts her eyes down. Her expression is withdrawn, brooding. He has seen it before. He has been looking at pictures these forty years. When he was a boy, before he ran away from England, a picture was a splayed cunt chalked on a wall, or a flat-eyed saint you studied while you yawned through Sunday Mass. But in Florence the masters had painted silver-faced virgins, demure, reluctant, whose fate moved within them, a slow reckoning in the blood; their eyes were turned inwards, to images of pain and glory. Has Jane seen such pictures? Is it possible that the masters drew from life, that they studied the face of some woman betrothed, some woman being walked by her kin to the church door? French hood, gable hood, it is not enough. If Jane could veil her face completely, she would do it, and hide her calculations from the world.

309

'Well now,' he says. He feels awkward, attracting attention back to himself. 'The reason I have come, the king has sent me with a gift.'

It is wrapped in silk. Jane looks up as she turns it over in her hands. 'You once gave me a gift, Master Cromwell. And in those days no one else did so. You may be sure I shall remember that, when it is in my power to do you good.'

Just in time to frown at this, Sir Nicholas Carew has made an entrance. He does not come into a room like lesser men, but rolls in, like a siege engine or some formidable hurling device: and now, halting before Cromwell, he looks as if he wishes to bombard him. 'I have heard about these ballads,' he says. 'Cannot you suppress them?'

'They're nothing personal,' he says. 'Just warmed-over libels from when Katherine was queen and Anne was the pretender.'

'The two cases are in no way alike. This virtuous lady, and that …' Words fail Carew; and indeed, her judicial status uncertain, the charges not yet framed, it is hard to describe Anne. If she is a traitor she is, pending the verdict of the court, technically dead; though at the Tower, Kingston reports, she eats heartily enough, and giggles, like Tom Seymour, over private jokes.

'The king is rewriting old songs,' he says. 'Reworking their references. A dark lady is taken out and a fair lady brought in. Jane knows how these things are managed. She was with the old queen. If Jane has no illusions, a little maid such as she, then you should get rid of yours, Sir Nicholas. You are too old for them.'

Jane sits unmoving with her present in her hands, still wrapped. 'It's all right to undo it, Jane,' her sister says kindly. 'Whatever it is, it's yours to keep.'

'I was listening to Master Secretary,' Jane says. 'One can learn a great deal from him.'

'Hardly apt lessons for you,' Edward Seymour says.

'I don't know. Ten years in the train of Master Secretary, and I might learn to stand up for myself.'

'Your happy destiny,' says Edward, 'is to be a queen, not a clerk.'

'So do you,' Jane says, 'give thanks to God I was born a woman?'

'We thank God on our knees daily,' Tom Seymour says, with leaden gallantry. It is new to him, to have this meek sister require compliments, and he is not swift to respond. He gives brother Edward a glance and a shrug: sorry, best I can do.

Jane unwraps her prize. She runs the chain through her fingers; it is as fine as one of her own hairs. She holds the tiny book in the palm of her hand and turns it over. In the gold and black enamel of its cover, initials are studded in rubies, and entwined: 'H' and 'A'.

'Think nothing of it, the stones can be replaced,' he says quickly. Jane hands him the object. Her face has fallen; she does not yet know how thrifty the king can be, this most magnificent prince. Henry should have warned me, he thinks. Beneath Anne's initial you can still distinguish the 'K'. He passes it to Nicholas Carew. 'You take note?'

The knight opens it, fumbling with the tiny clasp. 'Ah,' he says. 'A Latin prayer. Or a Bible verse?'

'If I may?' He takes it back. 'Here is the Book of Proverbs. "Who can find a good, a virtuous woman? Her price is beyond rubies."' Evidently it's not, he thinks: three presents, three wives, and only one jeweller's bill. He says to Jane, smiling, 'Do you know this woman who is mentioned here? Her clothing is silk and purple, says the author. I could tell you much more about her, from verses this page cannot contain.'

Edward Seymour says, 'You should have been a bishop, Cromwell.'

'Edward,' he says, 'I should have been Pope.'

He is taking his leave, when Carew crooks a peremptory finger. Oh, Lord Jesus, he breathes to himself, I am in trouble now, for not being humble enough. Carew motions him aside. But it is not to reproach him. 'The Princess Mary,' Carew murmurs, 'is very hopeful of a call to her father's side. What better remedy and comfort at such a time, for the king, than to have the child of his true marriage in his house?'

'Mary is better where she is. The subjects discussed here, in the council and on the street, are not fit for the ears of a young girl.'

Carew frowns. 'There may be something in that. But she looks to have messages from the king. Tokens.'

Tokens, he thinks; that can be arranged.

'There are ladies and gentlemen from the court,' Carew says, 'who wish to ride up-country to pay their respects, and if the princess is not to be conducted here, surely the terms of her confinement should be relaxed? It is hardly suitable, now, to have Boleyn women around her. Perhaps her old governor, the Countess of Salisbury ...'

Margaret Pole? That haggard papist battleaxe? But now is not the time to deliver hard truths to Sir Nicholas; that can wait. 'The king will dispose,' he says comfortably. 'It is a close family matter. He will know what is best for his daughter.'

By night, when the candles are lit, Henry leaks easy tears over Mary. But by daylight he sees her for what she is: disobedient, self-willed, still unbroken. When all this is tidied away, the king says, I shall turn my attention to my duties as father. I am sad that the Lady Mary and I have become estranged. After Anne, reconciliation will become possible. But, he adds, there will be certain conditions. To which, mark my words, my daughter Mary will adhere.

'One more thing,' Carew says. 'You must pull Wyatt in.'

Instead, he has Francis Bryan fetched. Francis comes in grinning: he thinks himself the untouchable man. His eye patch is decorated with a small winking emerald, which gives a sinister effect: one green eye, and the other ...

312

He examines it: says, 'Sir Francis, what colour are your eyes? I mean, your eye?'

'Red, generally,' Bryan says. 'But I try not to drink during Lent. Or Advent. Or on Fridays.' He sounds lugubrious. 'Why am I here? You know I'm on your side, don't you?'

'I only asked you to supper.'

'You asked Mark Smeaton to supper. And look where he is now.'

'It is not I who doubts you,' he says with a heavy, actor's sigh. (How he enjoys Sir Francis.) 'It is not I, but the world at large, who asks where your loyalties lie. You are, of course, the queen's kinsman.'

'I am Jane's kinsman too.' Bryan is still at ease, and he shows it by leaning back in his chair, his feet thrust out under the table. 'I hardly thought I should be interrogated.'

'I am talking to everyone who is close to the queen's family. And you are certainly close, you have been with them since the early days; did you not go to Rome, chasing the king's divorce, pressing the Boleyns' case with the best of them? But what should you fear? You are an old courtier, you know everything. Used wisely, wisely shared, knowledge may protect you.'

He waits. Bryan has sat up straight.

'And you want to please the king,' he says. 'All I ask is to be sure that, if you are put to it, you will give evidence on any point I require.'

He could swear that Francis sweats Gascon wine, his pores leaking that mouldy, ropey stuff he's been buying cheap and selling dear to the king's own cellars.

'Look, Crumb,' Bryan says. 'What I know is, Norris always imagined rutting with her.'

'And her brother, what did he imagine?'

Bryan shrugs. 'She was sent to France and they never knew each other till they were grown. I have known such things happen, have not you?'

'No, I cannot say I have. We never went in for incest where I grew up, God knows we had crimes enough and sins, but there were places our fantasy did not stretch.'

'You saw it in Italy, I wager. Only sometimes people see it and they don't dare name it.'

'I dare name anything,' he says calmly. 'As you will see. My imagination may lag behind each day's revelations, but I am working hard to catch up with them.'

'Now she is not queen,' Bryan says, 'because she is not, is she ... I can call her what she is, a hot minx, and where has she better opportunity, than with her family?'

He says, 'By that reasoning, do you think she goes to it with Uncle Norfolk? It could even be you, Sir Francis. If she has a mind to her relatives. You are a great gallant.'

'Oh, Christ,' Bryan says. 'Cromwell, you would not.'

'I only mention it. But as we are at one in this matter, or we appear to be, will you do me a service? You could ride over to Great Hallingbury, and prepare my friend Lord Morley for what is coming. It is not the sort of news you can break in a letter, not when the friend is elderly.'

'You think it's better face to face?' An incredulous laugh. 'My lord, I shall say, I come myself to spare you a shock – your daughter Jane will soon be a widow, because her husband is to be decapitated for incest.'

'No, the matter of incest we leave to the priests. It is for treason he will die. And we do not know the king will choose decapitation.'

'I do not believe I can do it.'

'But I do. I have great faith in you. Think of it as a diplomatic mission. You have performed those. Though I wonder how.'

'Sober,' Francis Bryan says. 'I shall need a drink for this one. And you know, I have a dread of Lord Morley. He is always pulling out some ancient manuscript, and saying, "Look here,

Francis!" and laughing heartily at the jokes in it. And you know my Latin, any schoolboy would be ashamed of it.'

'Don't wheedle,' he says. 'Saddle your horse. But before you ride to Essex, do me a further service. Go see your friend Nicholas Carew. Tell him I agree to his demands and I will talk to Wyatt. But warn him, tell him not to push me because I will not be pushed. Remind Carew that there may be more arrests, I am not yet able to say who. Or rather, if I am able, I am not willing. Understand, and make your friends understand, that I must have a free hand to deal. I am not their waiting boy.'

'Am I free to go?'

'Free as air,' he says, blandly. 'But what about supper?'

'You can eat mine,' Francis says.

Though the king's chamber is dark, the king says, 'We must look into a glass of truth. I think I am to blame, as what I suspected I did not own.'

Henry looks at Cranmer as if to say, it's your turn now: I admit my fault, so give me absolution. The archbishop looks harrowed; he does not know what Henry will say next, or if he can trust himself to respond. This is not a night for which Cambridge ever trained him. 'You were not remiss,' he tells the king. He darts a questioning look, like a long needle, at him, Cromwell. 'In these matters, surely the accusation should not come before the evidence.'

'You must bear in mind,' he says to Cranmer – for he is bland and easy and full of phrases – 'you must bear in mind that not I but the whole council examined the gentlemen who now stand accused. And the council called you in, laid the matter before you, and you did not demur. As you have said yourself, my lord archbishop, we would not have gone so far in the matter without grave consideration.'

'When I look back,' Henry says, 'so much falls into place. I was misled and betrayed. So many friends lost, friends and good servants, lost, alienated, exiled from court. And worse ... I think of Wolsey. The woman I called my wife practised against him with all her ingenuity, with every weapon of slyness and rancour.'

Which wife would that be? Both Katherine and Anne worked against the cardinal. 'I do not know why I have been so crossed,' Henry says. 'But does not Augustine call marriage "a mortal and slavish garment"?'

'Chrysostom,' Cranmer murmurs.

'But let that pass,' he, Cromwell, says hastily. 'If this marriage is dissolved, Majesty, Parliament will petition you to marry again.'

'I dare say it will. How may a man do his duty, to both his realm and to God? We sin even in the very act of generation. We must have offspring, and kings especially must, and yet we are warned against lust even in marriage, and some authorities say, do they not, that to love your wife immoderately is a kind of adultery?'

'Jerome,' Cranmer whispers: as if he would just as soon disown the saint. 'But there are many other teachings that are more comfortable, and that praise the married state.'

'Roses snatched from the thorns,' he says. 'The church does not offer much comfort to the married man, though Paul says we should love our wives. It is hard, Majesty, not to think marriage is sinful inherently, since the celibates have spent many centuries saying that they are better than we are. But they are not better. Repetition of false teachings does not make them true. You agree, Cranmer?'

Just kill me now, the archbishop's face says. Against all the laws of king and church, he is a married man; he married in Germany when he was among the reformers, he keeps Frau Grete secretly, he hides her in his country houses. Does Henry know? He must know. Will Henry say? No, because he is intent on his own plight. 'Now I cannot see why I ever wanted her,' the king says. 'That is why I think she has practised on me with charms and enchantments. She claims she loves me. Katherine claimed she loved me. They say love, and mean the opposite. I believe Anne has tried to undermine me at every turn. She was always unnatural. Think how she would taunt her uncle, my lord of Norfolk. Think how she would scorn her father. She would presume to censure my own conduct, and press on me advice in matters well beyond her understanding, and give me such words as no poor man would willingly hear from his wife.'

Cranmer says, 'She was bold, it is true. She knew it for a fault and would try to bridle herself.'

'Now she shall be bridled, by God.' Henry's tone is ferocious; but the next moment he has modulated it, to the plaintive accents of the victim. He opens his walnut writing box. 'Do you see this little book?' It is not really a book, or not yet, just a collection of loose leaves, tied together; there is no title page, but a sheet black with Henry's own laboured hand. 'It is a book in the making. I have written it. It is a play. It is a tragedy. It is my own case.' He offers it.

He says, 'Keep it sir, till we have more leisure to do justice to it.'

'But you ought to know,' the king insists. 'Her nature. How ill she has behaved to me, when I gave her everything. All men should know and be warned about what women are. Their appetites are unbounded. I believe she has committed adultery with a hundred men.'

Henry looks, for a moment, like a hunted creature: hounded by women's desire, dragged down and shredded. 'But her brother?' Cranmer says. He turns away. He will not look at the king. 'Is it likely?'

'I doubt she could resist him,' Henry says. 'Why spare? Why not drink the cup to the filthy dregs? And while she was indulging her own desires, she was killing mine. When I would approach her, only to do my duty, she would give me such a look

317

as would daunt any man. I know now why she did so. She wanted to be fresh for her lovers.'

The king sits. He begins to talk, to ramble. Anne took him by the hand, these ten years ago and more. She led him into the forest, and at the sylvan edge, where the broad light of day splinters and filters into green, he left his good judgement, his innocence. She drew him on all day, till he was trembling and exhausted, but he could not stop even to catch his breath, he could not go back, he had lost the path. All day he chased her, until the light faded, and he followed her by the light of torches: and then she turned on him, and stifled the torches, and left him alone in the dark.

The door opens softly: he looks up, and it is Rafe, where once it would have been Weston, perhaps. 'Majesty, my lord of Richmond is here to say good night. May he come in?'

Henry breaks off. 'Fitzroy. Of course.'

Henry's bastard is now a princeling of sixteen, though his fine skin, his open gaze, make him seem younger than his age. He has the red-gold hair of King Edward IV's line; he has a look of Prince Arthur too, Henry's elder brother who died. He is hesitant as he confronts his bull of a father, hovering in case he is unwanted. But Henry rises and embraces the boy, his face wet with tears. 'My little son,' he says, to the child who will soon make six foot. 'My only son.' The king is crying so hard now that he has to blot his face on his sleeve. 'She would have poisoned you,' he moans. 'Thank God that by the cunning of Master Secretary the plot was found out in time.'

'Thank you, Master Secretary,' the boy says formally. 'For finding out the plot.'

'She would have poisoned you and your sister Mary, both of you, and made that little blotch she spawned the heir to England. Or my throne would have passed to whatever she whelped next, God save me, if it lived. I doubt a child of hers could live. She was too wicked. God abandoned her. Pray for your father, pray God does not abandon me. I have sinned, I must have. The marriage was illicit.'

'What, this one was?' the boy says. 'This one as well?'

'Illicit and accursed.' Henry rocks the boy back and forth, gripping him ferociously, fists clenched behind his back: so, perhaps, does a bear crush her cubs. 'The marriage was outside God's law. Nothing could make it lawful. Neither of them was my wife, not this one and not the other, thank God she is in her grave now, and I do not have to listen to her snuffling and praying and entreating and meddling in my business. Do not tell me there were dispensations, I do not want to hear it, no Pope can dispense from the law of Heaven. How did she ever come near me, Anne Boleyn? Why did I ever look at her? Why did she blind my eyes? There are so many women in the world, so many fresh and young and virtuous women, so many good and kind women. Why have I been cursed with women who destroy the children in their own wombs?'

He lets the boy go, so abruptly that he staggers.

Henry sniffs. 'Go now, child. To your own guiltless bed. And you, Master Secretary, to your ... back to your own people.' The king blots his face with his handkerchief. 'I am too tired to confess tonight, my lord archbishop. You may go home too. But you will come again, and absolve me.'

It seems a comfortable idea. Cranmer hesitates: but he is not one to press for secrets. As they leave the chamber, Henry takes up his little book; absorbed, he turns the pages, and settles down to read his own story.

Outside the king's chamber he gives the signal to the hovering gentlemen. 'Go in and see if he wants anything.' Slow, reluctant, his body servants creep towards Henry in his lair: unsure of their welcome, unsure of everything. Pastime with good company: but where's the company now? It's cringing against the wall.

He takes his leave of Cranmer, embracing him, whispering: 'All will work for good.' Young Richmond touches his arm: 'Master Secretary, there is something I must tell you.'

He is tired. He was up at dawn writing letters into Europe. 'Is it urgent, my lord?'

'No. But it is important.'

Imagine having a master who knows the difference. 'Go ahead, my lord, I am all attention.'

'I want to tell you, I have had a woman now.'

'I hope that she was all you desired.'

The boy laughs uncertainly. 'Not really. She was a whore. My brother Surrey arranged it for me.' Norfolk's son, he means. By the light of a sconce, the boy's face flickers, gold to black to cross-hatched gold again, as if he were dipped in shadows. 'But this being so, I am a man, and I think Norfolk should let me live with my wife.'

Richmond has already been married off, to Norfolk's daughter, little Mary Howard. For reasons of his own, Norfolk has kept the children apart; if Anne had given Henry a son in wedlock, the bastard boy would be worthless to the king, and it has entered Norfolk's calculations that in that case, if his daughter was a virgin, he could perhaps marry her more usefully elsewhere.

But all those calculations are needless now. 'I'll speak to the duke for you,' he says. 'I think he will now be keen to fall in with your wishes.'

Richmond flushes: pleasure, embarrassment? The boy is no fool and knows his situation, which in a few days has improved beyond all measure. He, Cromwell, can hear the voice of Norfolk, as clear as if he were reasoning in the king's council: Katherine's daughter has been made a bastard already, Anne's daughter will follow, so all three of Henry's children are illegitimate. If that is so, why not prefer the male to the female?

'Master Secretary,' the boy says, 'the servants in my household are saying Elizabeth is not even the queen's child. They say she was smuggled into the bedchamber in a basket, and the queen's dead child carried out.'

'Why would she do that?' He is always curious to hear the reasoning of household servants.

'It is because, to be queen, she struck a bargain with the devil. But the devil always cheats you. He let her be queen, but he would not let her bear a live child.'

'You would think the devil would have sharpened her wit, though. If she was bringing in a baby in a basket, surely she would have brought in a boy?'

Richmond manages a miserable smile. 'Perhaps she laid hold of the only baby she could get. After all, people do not leave them in the street.'

They do, though. He is bringing in a bill to the new Parliament, to provide for the orphan boys of London. His idea is, look after the orphan boys, and they will look after the girls.

'Sometimes,' the boy says, 'I think about the cardinal. Do you ever think of him?' He sinks down to sit on a chest; and he, Cromwell, sits down with him. 'When I was a very little child, and very foolish as children are, I used to think the cardinal was my father.'

'The cardinal was your godfather.'

'Yes, but I thought ... Because he was so tender to me. He would visit me and carry me, and though he gave me great gifts of gold plate, he brought me a silk ball and also a doll, which you know, boys do like ...' he drops his head, 'when they are little children, and I am speaking of when I was still in a gown. I knew there was some secret about me, and I thought that was it, that I was a priest's son. When the king came he was a stranger to me. He brought me a sword.'

'And did you guess then that he was your father?'

'No,' says the boy. He opens his hands, to show his helpless nature, the nature he had as a little child. 'No. It had to be explained to me. Do not tell him, please. He would not understand.'

Of all the shocks the king has received, it could be the greatest, to know that his son did not recognise him. 'Has he many other children?' Richmond asks. He speaks, now, with the authority of a man of the world. 'I suppose he must have.'

'To my knowledge, he has no child who could hurt your claim. They said Mary Boleyn's son was his, but she was married at the time and the boy took her husband's name.'

'But I suppose he will marry Mistress Seymour now, when this marriage,' the boy stumbles over his words, 'when whatever is to happen, when it happens. And she will have a son, perhaps, because the Seymours are fertile stock.'

'If that occurs,' he says gently, 'you must stand ready, the first to congratulate the king. And you must be prepared all your life to place yourself at the service of this little prince. But on a more immediate matter, if I may advise ... if your living with your wife should be further delayed, it is best to find a kind and clean young woman and make an arrangement with her. Then when you part from her, pay her some small retainer so she does not talk about you.'

'Is that what you do, Master Secretary?' The question is ingenuous, but for a moment he wonders if the boy is spying for someone.

'It is better not discussed between gentlemen,' he says. 'And emulate your father the king, who in speaking of women is never coarse.' Violent, perhaps, he thinks: but never coarse. 'Be prudent and do not deal with whores. You must not catch a disease, like the French king. Then also, if your young woman gives you a child, you have its keeping and bringing up, and you know it is not another man's.'

'But you cannot be sure ...' Richmond breaks off. The realities of the world are tumbling in fast on this young man. 'If the king can be deceived, surely any man can be deceived. If married ladies are false, any gentleman could be bringing up another man's child.'

He smiles. 'But another gentleman would be bringing up his.'

He means to begin, when he has time to plan it, some form of registration, documentation to record baptisms so he can count the king's subjects and know who they are, or at least, who their mothers say they are: family name and paternity are two different things, but one must start somewhere. He scans the faces of the Londoners as he rides through the city, and he thinks of streets in other cities where he has lived or passed through, and he wonders. I could do with more children, he thinks. He has been continent in his living as far as it is reasonable for a man to be, but the cardinal used to invent scandals about him and his many concubines. Whenever some stout young felon was dragged to the gallows, the cardinal would say, 'There, Thomas, that will be one of yours.'

The boy yawns. 'I am so tired,' he says. 'Yet I have not been hunting today. So I don't know why.'

Richmond's servants are hovering: their badge a demi-lion rampant, their livery of blue and yellow faded in the failing light. Like nursemaids snatching up a child from muddy puddles, they want to sweep the young duke away from whatever Cromwell is plotting. There is a climate of fear and he has created it. Nobody knows how long the arrests will go on and who else will be taken. He feels even he does not know, and he is in charge of it. George Boleyn is lodged in the Tower. Weston and Brereton have been allowed a last night to sleep in the world, a few hours' grace to arrange their affairs; this time tomorrow the key will have turned on them: they could run, but where to? None of the men except Mark have been properly interrogated: that is to say, interrogated by him. But the scrapping for the spoils has begun. Norris had not been in ward for a day before the first letter came in, seeking a share of his offices and privileges, from a man who pleaded he had fourteen children. Fourteen hungry mouths: not to mention the man's own needs, and the snapping teeth of his lady wife.

* * *

Next day, early, he says to William Fitzwilliam, 'Come with me to the Tower to talk to Norris.'

Fitz says, 'No, you go. I cannot do it a second time. I have known him all my years. The first time nearly killed me.'

Gentle Norris: chief bottom-wiper to the king, spinner of silk threads, spider of spiders, black centre of the vast dripping web of court patronage: what a spry and amiable man he is, past forty but wearing it lightly. Norris is a man always in equipoise, a living illustration of the art of *sprezzatura*. No one has ever seen him ruffled. He has the air of a man who has not so much achieved success, as become resigned to it. He is as courteous to a dairy maid as to a duke; at least, for as long he has an audience. A master of the tournament ground, he breaks a lance with an air of apology, and when he counts the coin of the realm he washes his hands afterwards, in spring water scented with rose petals.

Nevertheless, Harry has grown rich, as those about the king cannot help but grow rich, however modestly they strive; when Harry snaps up some perquisite, it is as if he, your obedient serv-ant, were sweeping away from your sight something distasteful. And when he volunteers for some lucrative office, it is as if he is doing it out of a sense of duty, and to save lesser men the trouble.

But look at Gentle Norris now! It is a sad thing to see a strong man weep. He says so, as he sits down, and enquires after his keeping, whether he is being served with the food he likes and how he has slept. His manner is benign and easy. 'During the days of Christmas last, Master Norris, you impersonated a Moor, and William Brereton showed himself half-naked in the guise of a hunter or wild man of the woods, going towards the queen's chamber.'

'For God's sake, Cromwell,' Norris sniffs. 'Are you in earnest? You are asking me in all seriousness about what we did when we were costumed for a masque?'

'I counselled him, William Brereton, against exposing his person. Your retort was that the queen had seen it many a time.'

Norris reddens: as he did on the date in question. 'You mistake me on purpose. You know I meant that she is a married woman and so a man's ... a man's gear is no strange sight to her.'

'You know what you meant. I only know what you said. You must admit that such a remark would not strike the king's ear as innocent. On the same occasion as we were standing in conversation we saw Francis Weston, disguised. And you remarked he was going to the queen.'

'At least he wasn't naked,' Norris says. 'In a dragon suit, wasn't he?'

'He was not naked when we saw him, I agree. But what did you say next? You spoke to me of the queen's attraction to him. You were jealous, Harry. And you didn't deny it. Tell me what you know against Weston. It will be easier for you thereafter.'

Norris has pulled himself together and blown his nose. 'All you are alleging is some loose words capable of many interpretations. If you are seeking proofs of adultery, Cromwell, you will have to do better than this.'

'Oh, I don't know. By the nature of the thing, there is seldom a witness to the act. But we consider circumstances and opportunities and expressed desires, we consider weighty probabilities, and we consider confessions.'

'You will have no confession from me or Brereton either.'

'I wonder.'

'You will not put gentlemen to the torture, the king would not permit it.'

'There don't have to be formal arrangements.' He is on his feet, he slams his hand down on the table. 'I could put my thumbs in your eyes, and then you would sing "Green Grows the Holly" if I asked you to.' He sits down, resumes his former easy tone. 'Put yourself in my place. People will say I have tortured you anyway. They will say I have tortured Mark, they are already putting the word about. Though not a gossamer thread of him is snapped, I swear. I have Mark's free confession. He has given me names. Some of them surprised me. But I have mastered myself.'

'You are lying.' Norris looks away. 'You are trying to trick us into betraying, each man the other.'

'The king knows what to think. He does not ask for eyewitnesses. He knows your treason and the queen's.'

'Ask yourself,' Norris says, 'how likely is it, that I should so forget my honour, as to betray the king who has been so good to me and to place in such terrible danger a lady I revere? My family has served the King of England time out of mind. My great-grandfather served King Henry VI, that saintly man, God rest his soul. My grandfather served King Edward, and would have served his son if he had lived to reign, and after he was driven out of the realm by the scorpion Richard Plantagenet, he served Henry Tudor in exile, and served him still when he was crowned king. I have been at the side of Henry since I was a boy. I love him like a brother. Do you have a brother, Cromwell?'

'None living.' He looks at Norris, exasperated. He seems to think that with eloquence, with sincerity, with frankness, he can change what is happening. The whole court has seen him slobbering over the queen. How could he expect to go shopping with his eyes, and finger the goods no doubt, and not have an account to settle at the end of it?

He gets up, he walks away, he turns, he shakes his head: he sighs. 'Ah, for God's sake, Harry Norris. Have I to write it on the wall for you? The king must be rid of her. She cannot give him a son and he is out of love with her. He loves another lady and he cannot come at her unless Anne is removed. Now, is that simple enough for your simple tastes? Anne will not go quietly, she warned me of it once; she said, if ever Henry puts me aside, it will be war. So if she will not go, she must be pushed, and I must push her, who else? Do you recognise the situation? Will you take your mind back? In a like case, my old master Wolsey could not gratify the king, and then what? He was disgraced and driven to his death. Now I mean to learn from him, and I mean the king to be gratified in every respect. He is now a miserable cuckold, but he will forget it when he is a bridegroom again, and it will not be long.'

'I suppose the Seymours have the wedding feast ready.'

He grins. 'And Tom Seymour is having his hair curled. And on that wedding day, the king will be happy, I will be happy, all England will be happy, except Norris, for I fear he will be dead. I see no help for it, unless you confess and throw yourself on the king's mercy. He has promised mercy. And he keeps his promises. Mostly.'

'I rode with him from Greenwich,' Norris says, 'away from the tournament, all that long ride. Every stride he badgered me, what have you done, confess. I will tell you what I told him, that I am an innocent man. And what is worse,' and now he is losing his composure, he is irate, 'what is worse is that you and he both know it. Tell me this, why is it me? Why not Wyatt? Everyone suspects him with Anne, and has he ever directly denied it? Wyatt knew her before. He knew her in Kent. He knew her from her girlhood.'

'And so what of it? He knew her when she was a simple maid. What if he did meddle with her? It may be shameful but it is no treason. It is not like meddling with the king's wife, the Queen of England.'

'I am not ashamed of any dealings I have had with Anne.'

'Are you ashamed of your thoughts about her, perhaps? You told Fitzwilliam as much.'

'Did I?' Norris says bleakly. 'Is that what he took away, from what I said to him? That I am ashamed? And if I am, Cromwell, even if I am … you cannot make my thoughts a crime.'

He holds out his palms. 'If thoughts are intentions, if intentions are malign … if you did not have her unlawfully, and you say you did not, did you intend to have her lawfully, after the king's death? It is getting on six years since your wife died, why have you not married again?'

'Why haven't you?'

He nods. 'A good question. I ask myself. But I have not promised myself to a young woman, and then broken my promise, as you have. Mary Shelton has lost her honour to you –'

Norris laughs. 'To me? To the king, rather.'

'But the king was not in a position to marry her, and you were, and she had your pledge, and yet you dallied. Did you think the king would die, so you could marry Anne? Or did you expect her to dishonour her marriage vows during the king's life, and become your concubine? It is one or the other.'

'If I say either, you will damn me. You will damn me if I say nothing at all, taking my silence for agreement.'

'Francis Weston thinks you are guilty.'

'That Francis thinks anything, is news to me. Why would he …?' Norris breaks off. 'What, is he here? In the Tower?'

'He is in ward.'

Norris shakes his head. 'He is a boy. How can you do this to his people? I admit he is a careless, headstrong boy, he is known to be no favourite of mine, it is known we have cut across each other –'

'Ah, rivals in love.' He puts his hand to his heart.

'By no means.' Ah, Harry is ruffled now: he has flushed darkly, he is trembling with rage and fear.

'And what do you think to brother George?' he asks him. 'You may have been surprised to encounter rivalry from that quarter. I hope you were surprised. Though the morals of you gentlemen astonish me.'

'You do not trap me that way. Any man you name, I will say nothing against him and nothing for him. I have no opinion on George Boleyn.'

'What, no opinion on incest? If you take it so quietly and without objection, I am forced to conjecture there may be truth in it.'

'And if I were to say, I think there might be guilt in that case, you would say to me, "Why, Norris! Incest! How can you believe such an abomination? Is it a ploy to lead me away from your own guilt?"'

He looks at Norris with admiration. 'Not for nothing have you known me twenty years, Harry.'

'Oh, I have studied you,' Norris says. 'As I studied your master Wolsey before you.'

'That was politic in you. Such a great servant of the state.'

'And such a great traitor at the end.'

'I must take your mind back. I do not ask you to remember the manifold favours you received at the cardinal's hands. I only ask you to recall an entertainment, a certain interlude played at court. It was a play in which the late cardinal was set upon by demons and carried down to Hell.'

He sees Norris's eyes move, as the scene rises before him: the firelight, the heat, the baying spectators. Himself and Boleyn grasping the victim's hands, Brereton and Weston laying hold of him by his feet. The four of them tossing the scarlet figure, tumbling him and kicking him. Four men, who for a joke turned the cardinal into a beast; who took away his wit, his kindness and his grace, and made him a howling animal, grovelling on the boards and scrabbling with his paws.

It was not truly the cardinal, of course. It was the jester Sexton in a scarlet robe. But the audience catcalled as if it had been real, they yelled and shook their fists, they swore and mocked. Behind a screen the four devils pulled off their masks and their hairy jerkins, cursing and laughing. They saw Thomas Cromwell leaning against the panelling, silent, wrapped in a robe of mourning black.

Now, Norris gapes at him: 'And that is why? It was a play. It was an entertainment, as you said yourself. The cardinal was dead, he could not know. And while he was alive, was I not good to him in his trouble? Did I not, when he was exiled from court, ride after him, and come to him on Putney Heath with a token from the king's own hand?'

He nods. 'I concede that others behaved worse. But you see, none of you behaved like Christians. You behaved like savages instead, falling on his estates and possessions.'

He sees he need not continue. The indignation on Norris's face is replaced by a look of blank terror. At least, he thinks, the fellow has the wit to see what this is about: not one year's grudge or two, but a fat extract from the book of grief, kept since the cardinal came down. He says, 'Life pays you out, Norris. Don't you find? And,' he adds gently, 'it is not all about the cardinal, either. I would not want you to think I am without motives of my own.'

Norris raises his face. 'What has Mark Smeaton done to you?'

'Mark?' He laughs. 'I don't like the way he looks at me.'

Would Norris understand if he spelled it out? He needs guilty men. So he has found men who are guilty. Though perhaps not guilty as charged.

A silence falls. He sits, he waits, his eyes on the dying man. He is already thinking what he will do with Norris's offices, his Crown grants. He will try to oblige the humble applicants, like the man with fourteen children, who wants the keeping of a park at Windsor and a post in the administration of the castle. Norris's offices in Wales can be parcelled out to young Richmond, and that will bring the posts in effect back to the king and under his own supervision. And Rafe could have the Norris estate at Greenwich, he could house Helen and the children there when he has to be at court. And Edward Seymour has mentioned he would like Norris's house in Kew.

Harry Norris says, 'I assume you will not just lead us out to execution. There will be a process, a trial? Yes? I hope it will be quick. I suppose it will. The cardinal used to say, Cromwell will do in a week what will take another man a year, it is not worth your while to block him or oppose him. If you reach out to grip him he will not be there, he will have ridden twenty miles while you are pulling your boots on.' He looks up. 'If you intend to kill me in public, and mount a show, be quick. Or I may die of grief alone in this room.'

He shakes his head. 'You'll live.' He once thought it himself, that he might die of grief: for his wife, his daughters, his sisters, his father and master the cardinal. But the pulse, obdurate, keeps its rhythm. You think you cannot keep breathing, but your ribcage has other ideas, rising and falling, emitting sighs. You must thrive in spite of yourself; and so that you may do it, God takes out your heart of flesh, and gives you a heart of stone.

Norris touches his ribs. 'The pain is here. I felt it last night. I sat up, breathless. I durst not lie down again.'

'When he was brought down, the cardinal said the same. The pain was like a whetstone, he said. A whetstone, and the knife was drawn across it. And it ground away, till he was dead.'

He rises, picks up his papers: inclining his head, takes his leave. Henry Norris: left forepaw.

William Brereton. Gentleman of Cheshire. Servant in Wales to the young Duke of Richmond, and a bad servant too. A turbulent, arrogant, hard-as-nails man, from a turbulent line.

'Let's go back,' he says, 'let's go back to the cardinal's time, because I do remember someone of your household killed a man during a bowls match.'

'The game can get very heated,' Brereton says. 'You know yourself. You play, I hear.'

'And the cardinal thought, it is time for a reckoning; and your family were fined because they impeded the investigation. I ask myself, has anything changed since then? You think you can do anything because you are the Duke of Richmond's servant, and because Norfolk favours you –'

'The king himself favours me.'

He raises his eyebrows. 'Does he? Then you should complain to him. Because you are ill-lodged, are you not? Sadly for you,

the king is not here, so you must make do with me and my long
memory. But let us not cast back for instances. Look, for instance,
at the case of the Flintshire gentleman, John ap Eyton. That is so
recent you have not forgot it.'

'So that is why I am here,' Brereton says.

'Not entirely, but leave aside now your adultery with the
queen and concentrate on Eyton. The facts of the case are known
to you. There is a quarrel, blows exchanged, one of your household ends up dead, but the man Eyton is tried in due form before
a London jury, and is acquitted. Now, having no respect for either
law or justice, you swear revenge. You have the Welshman
abducted. Your servants hang him out of hand, all this – do not
interrupt me, man – all this with your permission and contriv-
ance. I give this as one instance. You think this is only one man
and he doesn't matter, but you see he does. You think a year or
more has passed and no one remembers, but I remember. You
believe the law should be what you would like it to be, and it is
on that principle that you conduct yourself in your holdings on
the marches of Wales, where the king's justice and the king's name
are brought into contempt every day. The place is a stronghold of
thieves.'

'You say I am a thief?'

'I say you consort with them. But your schemes end here.'

'You are judge and jury and hangman, is that it?'

'It is better justice than Eyton had.'

And Brereton says, 'I concede that.'

What a fall this is. Only days ago, he was petitioning Master
Secretary for spoils, when the abbey lands in Cheshire should be
given out. Now no doubt the words run through his head, the
words he used to Master Secretary when he complained of his
high-handed ways: I must tutor you in realities, he had said
coldly. We are not creatures of some lawyers' conclave at Gray's
Inn. In my own country, my family upholds the law, and the law
is what we care to uphold.

Now he, Master Secretary, asks, 'Do you think Weston has had to do with the queen?'

'Perhaps,' Brereton looks as if he hardly cares, one way or the other. 'I barely know him. He is young and foolish and good-looking, isn't he, and women regard these things? And she may be a queen but she is only a woman, who knows what she might be persuaded to?'

'You think women more foolish than men?'

'In general, yes. And weaker. In matters of love.'

'I note your opinion.'

'What about Wyatt, Cromwell? Where is he in this?'

'You are in no place,' he says, 'to put questions to me.' William Brereton; left hindpaw.

George Boleyn is well past thirty, but he still has the sheen we admire in the young, the sparkle and the clear gaze. It is hard to associate his pleasant person with the kind of bestial appetite of which his wife accuses him, and for a moment he looks at George and wonders if he can be guilty of any offences, except a certain pride and elation. With the graces of his person and mind, he could have floated and hovered above the court and its sordid machinations, a man of refinement moving in his own sphere: commissioning translations of the ancient poets, and causing them to be published in exquisite editions. He could have ridden pretty white horses that curvet and bow in front of ladies. Unfortunately, he liked to quarrel and brag, intrigue and snub. As we find him now, in his light circular room in the Martin Tower, we find him pacing, hungry for conflict, we ask ourselves, does he know why he is here? Or is that surprise still to come?

'You are perhaps not much to blame,' he says, as he takes his seat: he, Thomas Cromwell. 'Join me at this table,' he directs. 'One hears of prisoners wearing a path through stone, but I do not believe it can really happen. It would take three hundred years perhaps.'

Boleyn says, 'You are accusing me of some sort of collusion, concealment, concealing misconduct on my sister's part, but this charge will not stand, because there was no misconduct.'

'No, my lord, that is not the charge.'

'Then what?'

'That is not what you are accused of. Sir Francis Bryan, who is a man of great imaginative capacities –'

'Bryan!' Boleyn looks horrified. 'But you know he is an enemy of mine.' His words tumble over each other. 'What has he said, how can you credit anything he says?'

'Sir Francis has explained it all to me. And I begin to see it. How a man may hardly know his sister, and meet her as a grown woman. She is like himself, yet not. She is familiar, yet piques his interest. One day his brotherly embrace is a little longer than usual. The business progresses from there. Perhaps neither party feels they are doing anything wrong, till some frontier is crossed. But I myself am far too lacking in imagination to imagine what that frontier could be.' He pauses. 'Did it begin before her marriage, or after?'

Boleyn begins to tremble. It is shock; he can hardly speak. 'I refuse to answer this.'

'My lord, I am accustomed to dealing with those who refuse to answer.'

'Are you threatening me with the rack?'

'Well, now, I didn't rack Thomas More, did I? I sat in a room with him. A room here at the Tower, such as the one you occupy. I listened to the murmurs within his silence. Construction can be put on silence. It will be.'

George says: 'Henry killed his father's councillors. He killed the Duke of Buckingham. He destroyed the cardinal and harried him to his death, and struck the head off one of Europe's great scholars. Now he plans to kill his wife and her family and Norris who has been his closest friend. What makes you think it will be different with you, that are not the equal of any of these men?'

334

He says, 'It ill becomes anyone of your family to evoke the cardinal's name. Or Thomas More's, for that matter. Your lady sister burned for vengeance. She would say to me, what, Thomas More, is he not dead yet?'

'Who began this slander against me? It is not Francis Bryan, surely. Is it my wife? Yes. I should have known.'

'You make the assumption. I do not confirm it. You must have a guilty conscience towards her, if you think she has such cause to hate you.'

'And will you believe something so monstrous?' George begs. 'On the word of one woman?'

'There are other women who have been recipients of your gallantry. I will not bring them before a court if I can help it, I can do that much to protect them. You have always regarded women as disposable, my lord, and you cannot complain if in the end they think the same of you.'

'So am I to be put on trial for gallantry? Yes, they are jealous of me, you are all jealous, I have had some success with women.'

'You still call it success? You must think again.'

'I never heard it was a crime. To spend time with a willing lover.'

'You had better not say that in your defence. If one of your lovers is your sister ... the court will find it, what shall we say ... pert and bold. Lacking in gravity. What would save you now – I mean, what might preserve your life – would be a full statement of all you know about your sister's dealings with other men. Some suggest there are liaisons which would put yours in the shade, unnatural though it may be.'

'You are a Christian man, and you ask me this? To give evidence to kill my sister?'

He opens his hands. 'I ask nothing. I only point out what some would see as the way forward. I do not know whether the king would incline to mercy. He might let you live abroad, or he might grant you mercy as to the manner of your death. Or not. The traitor's penalty, as you know, is fearful and public; he dies in great pain and humiliation. I see you do know, you have witnessed it.'

Boleyn folds into himself: narrowing himself, arms across his body, as if to protect his guts from the butcher's knife, and he slumps to a stool; he thinks, you should have done that before, I told you to sit, you see how without touching you I have made you sit? He tells him softly, 'You profess the gospel, my lord, and that you are saved. But your actions do not suggest you are saved.'

'You may take your thumbprints off my soul,' George says. 'I discuss these matters with my chaplains.'

'Yes, so they tell me. I think you have become too assured of forgiveness, believing you have years ahead of you to sin and yet though God sees all he must be patient, like a waiting man: and you will notice him at last, and answer his suit, if only he will wait till you are old. Is that your case?'

'I will speak to my confessor about that.'

'I am your confessor now. Did you say, in the hearing of others, that the king was impotent?'

George sneers at him. 'He can do it when the weather is set fair.'

'In doing so, you called into question the parentage of the Princess Elizabeth. You will readily see this is treason, as she is the heir to England.'

'*Faute de mieux*, as far as you're concerned.'

'The king now believes he could not have a son from this marriage, as it was not lawful. He believes there were hidden impediments and that your sister was not frank about her past. He means to make a new marriage, which will be clean.'

'I marvel you explain yourself,' George says. 'You never did so before.'

'I do so for one reason – so that you can realise your situation and entertain no false hope. These chaplains you speak of, I will send them to you. They are fit company for you now.'

'God grants sons to every beggar,' George says. 'He grants them to the illicit union, as well as the blessed, to the whore as well as the queen. I wonder that the king can be so simple.'

'It is a holy simplicity,' he says. 'He is an anointed sovereign, and so very close to God.'

Boleyn scrutinises his expression, for levity or scorn: but he knows his face says nothing, he can rely on his face for that. You could look back through Boleyn's career, and say, 'There he went wrong, and there.' He was too proud, too singular, unwilling to bridle his whims or turn himself to use. He needs to learn to bend with the breeze, like his father; but the time he has to learn anything is running out fast. There is a time to stand on your dignity, but there is a time to abandon it in the interests of your safety. There is a time to smirk behind the hand of cards you have drawn, and there is a time to throw down your purse on the table and say, 'Thomas Cromwell, you win.'

George Boleyn, right forepaw.

By the time he gets to Francis Weston (right hindpaw) he has been approached by the young man's family and offered a great deal of money. Politely, he has refused them; in their circumstances he would do just the same, except that it is hard to imagine Gregory or any member of his household to be such a fool as this young man has been.

The Weston family go further: they approach the king himself. They will make an offering, they will make a benevolence, they will make a large and unconditional donation to the king's treasury. He discusses it with Fitzwilliam: 'I cannot advise His Majesty. It is possible that lesser charges can be brought. It depends how much His Majesty thinks his honour is touched.'

But the king is not disposed to be lenient. Fitzwilliam says grimly, 'If I were Weston's people, I would pay the money anyway. To ensure favour. Afterwards.'

That is the very approach he has settled on himself, thinking of the Boleyn family (those who survive) and the Howards. He will shake the ancestral oaks and gold coins will drop each season.

Even before he comes to the room where Weston is held, the young man knows what to expect; he knows who is gaoled with him; he knows or has a good idea of the charges; his gaolers must have babbled, because he, Cromwell, has cut off communication between the four men. A talkative gaoler can be useful; he can nudge a prisoner towards cooperation, towards acceptance, towards despair. Weston must guess his family's initiative has failed. You look at Cromwell and you think, if bribery won't do it, nothing else will. It's useless to protest or disclaim or contradict. Abasement might just do it, it's worth a try. 'I taunted you, sir,' Francis says. 'I belittled you. I am sorry I ever did so. You are the king's servant and it was proper for me to respect that.'

'Well, that is a handsome apology,' he says. 'Though you should beg forgiveness of the king and of Jesus Christ.'

Francis says, 'You know I am not long married.'

'And your wife left at home in the country. For obvious reasons.'

'Can I write to her? I have a son. He is not yet a year.' A silence. 'I wish my soul to be prayed for after I am dead.'

He would have thought God could make his own decisions, but Weston believes the creator may be pushed and coaxed and maybe bribed a little. As if following his thought, Weston says, 'I am in debt, Master Secretary. To the tune of a thousand pounds. I am sorry for it now.'

'No one expects a gallant young gentleman like yourself to be thrifty.' His tone is kindly, and Weston looks up. 'Of course, these debts are more than you could reasonably pay, and even set against the assets you will have when your father dies, they are a heavy burden. So your extravagance gives people to think, what expectations had young Weston?'

For a moment, the young man looks at him with a dumb, rebellious expression, as if he does not see why this should be brought against him: what have his debts to do with anything? He does not see where it is leading. Then he does. He, Cromwell, puts out a hand to grab his clothes, to stop him slumping forward in shock. 'A jury will easily grasp the point. We know the queen gave you money. How could you live as you did? It is easy to see. A thousand pounds is nothing to you, if you hoped to marry her once you had contrived the king's death.'

When he is sure that Weston can sit upright, he opens his fist and eases his grip. Mechanically, the boy reaches up and straightens his clothes, straightens the little ruff of his shirt collar.

'Your wife will be taken care of,' he tells him. 'Have no unease on that score. The king never extends animosity to widows. She will be cared for better, I dare say, than you ever cared for her.'

Weston looks up. 'I cannot fault your reasoning. I see how it will weigh when it is given in evidence. I have been a fool and you have stood by and seen it all. I know how I have undone myself. I cannot fault your conduct either, because I would have injured you if I could. And I know I have not lived a good … I have not lived … you see, I thought I should have another twenty years or more to live as I have, and then when I am old, forty-five or fifty, I should give to hospitals and endow a chantry, and God would see I was sorry.'

He nods. 'Well, Francis,' he says. 'We know not the hour, do we?'

'But Master Secretary, you know that whatever wrong I have done, I am not guilty in this matter of the queen. I see by your face you know it, and all the people will know it too when I am brought out to die, and the king will know it and think about it in his private hours. I shall be remembered, therefore. As the innocent are remembered.'

It would be cruel to disturb that belief; he looks to his death to give him greater fame than his life has done. All the years that

339

stretched before him, and no reason to believe that he meant to make any better use of them than he made of the first twenty-five; he himself says not. Brought up under the wing of his sovereign, a courtier since he was a child, from a family of courtiers: never a moment's doubt about his place in the world, never a moment's anxiety, never a moment's thankfulness for the great privilege of having been born Francis Weston, born in the eye of fortune, born to serve a great king and a great nation: he will leave nothing but his debt, and a tarnished name, and a son: and anyone can father a son, he says to himself: until he remembers why we are here and what all this is about. He says, 'Your wife has written for you to the king. Asking for mercy. You have a great many friends.'

'Much good they will do me.'

'I do not think you realise that at this juncture, many men would find themselves alone. It should cheer you. You should not be bitter, Francis. Fortune is fickle, every young adventurer knows that. Resign yourself. Regard Norris. No bitterness there.'

'Perhaps,' the young man blurts, 'perhaps Norris thinks he has no reason for bitterness. Perhaps his regrets are honest ones, and necessary. Perhaps he deserves to die, as I do not.'

'He is well paid out, you think, for meddling with the queen.'

'He is always in her company. It is not to discuss the gospel.'

He is, perhaps, on the verge of a denunciation. Norris had begun on some admission to William Fitzwilliam, but he bit it back. Perhaps the facts will come out now? He waits: sees the boy's head sink into his hands; then, impelled by something, he does not know what, he stands up, says, 'Francis, excuse me,' and walks out of the room.

Outside Wriothesley is waiting, with gentlemen of his household. They are leaning against the wall, sharing some joke. They stir at the sight of him, look expectant. 'Are we finished?' Wriothesley says. 'He has confessed?'

He shakes his head. 'Each man will give a good account of himself, but he will not absolve his fellows. Also, they will all say

"I am innocent," but they do not say, "She is innocent." They are not able. It may be she is, but none of them will give his word on it.'

It is just as Wyatt once told him: 'The worst of it is,' he had said, 'her hinting to me, her boasting almost, that she says no to me, but yes to others.'

'Well, you have no confessions,' Wriothesley says. 'Do you want us to get them?'

He gives Call-Me a look that knocks him back, so he steps on the foot of Richard Riche. 'What, Wriothesley, do you think I am too soft to the young?'

Riche rubs his foot. 'Shall we draw up specimen charges?'

'The more the merrier. Forgive me, I need a moment …'

Riche assumes he has gone out to piss. He does not know what caused him to break off from Weston and walk out. Perhaps it was when the boy said 'forty-five or fifty'. As if, past mid-life, there is a second childhood, a new phase of innocence. It touched him, perhaps, the simplicity of it. Or perhaps he just needed air. Let us say you are in a chamber, the windows sealed, you are conscious of the proximity of other bodies, of the declining light. In the room you put cases, you play games, you move your personnel around each other: notional bodies, hard as ivory, black as ebony, pushed on their paths across the squares. Then you say, I can't endure this any more, I must breathe: you burst out of the room and into a wild garden where the guilty are hanging from trees, no longer ivory, no longer ebony, but flesh; and their wild lamenting tongues proclaim their guilt as they die. In this matter, cause has been preceded by effect. What you dreamed has enacted itself. You reach for a blade but the blood is already shed. The lambs have butchered and eaten themselves. They have brought knives to the table, carved themselves, and picked their own bones clean.

* * *

May is blossoming even in the city streets. He takes flowers in to the ladies in the Tower. Christophe has to carry the bouquets. The boy is filling out and looks like a bull garlanded for sacrifice. He wonders what they did with their sacrifices, the pagans and the Jews of the Old Testament; surely they would not waste fresh meat, but give it to the poor?

Anne is housed in the suite of rooms that were redecorated for her coronation. He himself had overseen the work, and watched as goddesses, with their soft and brilliant dark eyes, blossomed on the walls. They bask in sunlit groves, under cypress trees; a white doe peeps through foliage, while the hunters head off in another direction, and hounds lollop ahead of them, making their hound music.

Lady Kingston rises to greet him, and he says, 'Sit down, dear madam ...' Where is Anne? Not here in her presence chamber.

'She is praying,' one of the Boleyn aunts says. 'So we left her to it.'

'She has been a while,' the other aunt says. 'Are we sure she hasn't got a man in there?'

The aunts giggle; he does not join them; Lady Kingston gives them a hard look.

The queen emerges from the little oratory; she has heard his voice. Sunlight strikes her face. It is true what Lady Rochford says, she has begun to line. If you did not know she was a woman who had held a king's heart in her hand, you would take her for a very ordinary person. He supposes there will always be a strained levity in her, a practised coyness. She will be one of those women who at fifty thinks she is still in the game: one of those tired old experts in innuendo, women who simper like maids and put their hand on your arm, who exchange glances with other women when a prospect like Tom Seymour heaves into view.

But of course, she will never be fifty. He wonders if this is the last time he will see her, before the courtroom. She sits down, in shadow, in the midst of the women. The Tower always feels damp from the river and even these new, bright rooms feel clammy. He asks if she would like furs brought in, and she says, 'Yes. Ermine. Also, I do not want these women. I should like women of my own choosing, not yours.'

'Lady Kingston attends you because –'

'Because she is your spy.'

'– because she is your hostess.'

'Am I then her guest? A guest is free to leave.'

'I thought you would like to have Mistress Orchard,' he says, 'as she is your old nurse. And I didn't think you would object to your aunts.'

'They have grudges against me, both of them. All I see and hear is sniggering and tutting.'

'Jesus! Do you expect applause?'

This is the trouble with the Boleyns: they hate their own kin. 'You will not speak in that way to me,' Anne says, 'when I am released.'

'I apologise. I spoke without thinking.'

'I do not know what the king means by holding me here. I suppose he does it to test me. It is some stratagem he has devised, yes?'

She does not really think that, so he does not answer.

'I should like to see my brother,' Anne says.

One aunt, Lady Shelton, looks up from her needlework. 'That is a foolish demand, in the circumstances.'

'Where is my father?' Anne says. 'I do not understand why he does not come to my aid.'

'He is lucky to be at liberty,' Lady Shelton says. 'Expect no help there. Thomas Boleyn always looked after himself first, and I know it, for I am his sister.'

Anne ignores her. 'And my bishops, where are they? I have nourished them, I have protected them, I have furthered the cause of religion, so why do they not go to the king for me?'

The other Boleyn aunt laughs. 'You expect bishops to intervene, to make excuses for your adultery?'

It is evident that, in this court, Anne has already been tried. He says to her, 'Help the king. Unless he is merciful your cause is lost, you can do nothing for yourself. But you may do something for your daughter Elizabeth. The more humbly you hold yourself, the more penitent you show yourself, the more patiently you bear with the process, the less bitterness will His Majesty feel when your name is raised hereafter.'

'Ah, the process,' Anne says, with a flash of her old sharpness. 'And what is this process to be?'

'The confessions of the gentlemen are now being compiled.'

'The what?' Anne says.

'You heard,' Lady Shelton says. 'They will not lie for you.'

'There may be other arrests, other charges, though by speaking out now, by being open with us, you could shorten the pain for all concerned. The gentlemen will come to trial together. For yourself and my lord your brother, since you are ennobled, you will be judged by your peers.'

'They have no witnesses. They can make any accusation, and I can say no to it.'

'That is true,' he concedes. 'Though it is not true about the witnesses. When you were at liberty, madam, your ladies were intimidated by you, forced to lie for you, but now they are emboldened.'

'I am sure they are.' She holds his gaze; her tone is scornful. 'In the way Seymour is emboldened. Tell her from me, God sees her tricks.'

He stands to take his leave. She unnerves him, the wild distress she is keeping in check, holding back but only just. There seems no point in prolonging the business, but he says, 'If the king begins a process to nullify your marriage, I may return, to take statements from you.'

'What?' she says. 'That too? Is it necessary? Murder will not be enough?'

He bows and turns away. 'No!' She fetches him back. She is on her feet, detaining him, timidly touching his arm; as if it is not her release she wants, so much as his good opinion. 'You do not believe these stories against me? I know in your heart you do not. Cremuel?'

It is a long moment. He feels himself on the edge of something unwelcome: superfluous knowledge, useless information. He turns, hesitates, and reaches out, tentative …

But then she raises her hands and clasps them at her breast, in the gesture Lady Rochford had showed him. Ah, Queen Esther, he thinks. She is not innocent; she can only mimic innocence. His hand drops to his side. He turns away. He knows her for a woman without remorse. He believes she would commit any sin or crime. He believes she is her father's daughter, that never since childhood has she taken any action, coaxed or coerced, that might damage her own interests. But in one gesture, she has damaged them now.

She has seen his face change. She steps back, puts her hands around her throat: like a strangler she closes them around her own flesh. 'I have only a little neck,' she says. 'It will be the work of a moment.'

Kingston hurries out to meet him; he wants to talk. 'She keeps doing that. Her hands around her neck. And laughing.' His honest gaoler's face is dismayed. 'I cannot see that it is any occasion for laughter. And there are other foolish sayings, which my wife has reported. She says, it will not stop raining till I am released. Or start raining. Or something.'

He casts a glance at the window and he sees only a summer shower. In a moment the sun will scorch the moisture from the stones. 'My wife tells her,' Kingston says, 'to leave off such foolish talk. She said to me, Master Kingston, shall I have justice? I said to her, madam, the poorest subject of the king has justice. But she just laughs,' Kingston says. 'And she orders her dinner. And she eats it with a good appetite. And she says verses. My wife cannot follow them. The queen says they are verses of Wyatt's. And she says, Oh, Wyatt, Thomas Wyatt, when shall I see you here with me?'

At Whitehall he hears Wyatt's voice and walks towards it, attendants wheeling after him; he has more attendants than ever he did, some of them people he has never seen before. Charles Brandon, Duke of Suffolk, Charles Brandon big as a house: he is blocking Wyatt's path, and they are yelling at one another. 'What are you doing?' he shouts, and Wyatt breaks off and says over his shoulder, 'Making peace.'

He laughs. Brandon stumps away, grinning behind his vast beard. Wyatt says, 'I have begged him, set aside your old enmity for me, or it will kill me, do you want that?' He looks after the duke with disgust. 'I suspect he does. This is his chance. He went to Henry long ago, blustering that he had suspicions of me with Anne.'

'Yes, but if you recall, Henry kicked him back to the east country.'

'Henry will listen now. He will find him easy to believe.'

He takes Wyatt by the arm. If he can move Charles Brandon, he can move anybody. 'I am not going to dispute in a public place. I sent for you to come to my house, you fool, not to go raging about in public view and making people say, What, Wyatt, is he still at large?'

Wyatt puts a hand over his. He takes in a deep breath, trying to calm himself. 'My father told me, get to the king, and stay with him day and night.'

'That is not possible. The king is seeing no one. You must come to me at the Rolls House, but then –'

'If I go to your house people will say I am arrested.'

He drops his voice. 'No friend of mine will suffer.'

'They are strange and sudden friends you have this month. Papist friends, Lady Mary's people, Chapuys. You make common cause with them now, but what about afterwards? What will happen if they abandon you before you abandon them?'

'Ah,' he says equably, 'so you think the whole house of Cromwell will come down? Trust me, will you? Well, you have no choice, really, have you?'

From Cromwell's house, to the Tower: Richard Cromwell as escort, and the whole thing done so lightly, in such a spirit of friendliness, that you would think they were going out for a day's hunting. 'Beg the constable to do all honour to Master Wyatt,' he tells Richard. And to Wyatt, 'It is the only place you are safe. Once you are in the Tower no one can question you without my permission.'

Wyatt says, 'If I go in I shall not come out. They want me sacrificed, your new friends.'

'They will not want to pay the price,' he says easily. 'You know me, Wyatt. I know how much everyone has, I know what they can afford. And not only in cash. I have your enemies weighed and assessed. I know what they will pay and what they will baulk at, and believe me, the grief they will expend if they cross me in this matter, it will bankrupt them of tears.'

When Wyatt and Richard have gone on their way, he says to Call-Me-Risley, frowning: 'Wyatt once said I was the cleverest man in England.'

'He didn't flatter,' Call-Me says. 'I learn much daily, from mere proximity.'

'No, it is him. Wyatt. He leaves us all behind. He writes himself and then he disclaims himself. He jots a verse on some scrap of paper, and slips it to you, when you are at supper or praying in the chapel. Then he slides a paper to some other person, and it is the same verse, but a word is different. Then that person says to you, did you see what Wyatt wrote? You say yes, but you are talking of different things. Another time you trap him and say, Wyatt, did you really do what you describe in this verse? He smiles and tells you, it is the story of some imaginary gentleman, no one we know; or he will say, this is not my story I write, it is yours, though you do not know it. He will say, this woman I describe here, the brunette, she is really a woman with fair hair, in disguise. He will declare, you must believe everything and nothing of what you read. You point to the page, you tax him: what about this line, is this true? He says, it is poet's truth. Besides, he claims, I am not free to write as I like. It is not the king, but metre that constrains me. And I would be plainer, he says, if I could: but I must keep to the rhyme.'

'Someone should take his verses to the printer,' Wriothesley says. 'That would fix them.'

'He would not consent to that. They are private communications.'

'If I were Wyatt,' Call-Me says, 'I would have made sure no one misconstrued me. I would have stayed away from Caesar's wife.'

'That is the wise course.' He smiles. 'But it is not for him. It is for people like you and me.'

When Wyatt writes, his lines fledge feathers, and unfolding this plumage they dive below their meaning and skim above it. They tell us that the rules of power and the rules of war are the same, the art is to deceive; and you will deceive, and be deceived in your turn, whether you are an ambassador or a suitor. Now, if a man's subject is deception, you are deceived if you think you grasp his meaning. You close your hand as it flies away. A statute is written to entrap meaning, a poem to escape it. A quill, sharpened, can stir and rustle like the pinions of angels. Angels are messengers. They are creatures with a mind and a will. We do not know for a fact that their plumage is like the plumage of falcons, crows, peacocks. They hardly visit men nowadays. Though in Rome he knew a man, a turnspit in the papal kitchens, who had come face to face with an angel in a passage dripping with chill, in a sunken store room of the Vatican where cardinals never tread; and people bought him drinks to make him talk about it. He said the angel's substance was heavy and smooth as marble, its expression distant and pitiless; its wings were carved from glass.

When the indictments come to his hand, he sees at once that, though the script is a clerk's, the king has been at work. He can hear the king's voice in every line: his outrage, jealousy, fear. It is not enough to say that she incited Norris to adultery with her in October 1533, nor Brereton in November the same year; Henry must imagine the 'base conversations and kisses, touchings, gifts'. It is not enough to cite her conduct with Francis Weston, in May 1534, or to allege that she lay down for Mark Smeaton, a man of low degree, in April last year; it is necessary to speak of the lovers' burning resentment of each other, of the queen's furious jealousy of any other woman they look at. It is not enough to say that she sinned with her own brother: one must imagine the kisses, presents, jewels that passed between them, and how they looked when she was 'alluring him with her tongue in the said George's mouth, and the said George's tongue in hers'. It is more like a conversation with Lady Rochford, or any other scandal-loving woman, than it is like a document one carries into court; but all the same, it has its merits, it makes a story, and it puts into the heads of those who will hear it certain pictures that will not easily be got out again. He says, 'You must add at every point, and to every offence, "and several days before and after". Or a similar phrase, that makes it clear the offences are numerous, perhaps more numerous than even the parties themselves recollect. For in that way,' he says, 'if there is specific denial of one date, one place, it will not be enough to injure the whole.'

And look what Anne has said! According to this paper, she has confessed, 'she would never love the king in her heart'.

Bring Up the Bodies

Never has. Does not now. And never could.

He frowns over the documents and then gives them out to be picked over. Objections are raised. Is Wyatt to be added? No, by no means. If he must be tried, he thinks, if the king goes so far, then he will be pulled away from this contaminated crew, and we will start again with a blank sheet; with this trial, with these defendants, there is no way but one, no exit, no direction except the scaffold.

And if there are discrepancies, visible to those who keep accounts of where the court resides on this day or that? He says, Brereton once told me he could be in two places at once. Come to think of it, so did Weston. Anne's lovers are phantom gentlemen, flitting by night with adulterous intent. They come and go by night, unchallenged. They skim over the river like midges, flicker against the dark, their doublets sewn with diamonds. The moon sees them, peering from her hood of bone, and Thames water reflects them, glimmering like fish, like pearls.

His new allies, the Courtenays and the Pole family, profess themselves unsurprised by the charges against Anne. The woman is a heretic and so is her brother. Heretics, it is well known, have no natural limits, no constraints, fear neither the law of the land nor the law of God. They see what they want and they take it. And those who (foolishly) have tolerated heretics, out of laziness or pity, then discover at last what their true nature is.

Henry Tudor will learn harsh lessons from this, the old families say. Perhaps Rome will stretch out a hand to him in his trouble? Perhaps, if he creeps on his knees, then after Anne is dead the Pope will forgive him, and take him back?

And I? he asks. Oh, well, you, Cromwell ... his new masters look at him with various expressions of bemusement or disgust. 'I shall be your prodigal son,' he says, smiling. 'I shall be the sheep that was lost.'

At Whitehall, little huddles of men, muttering, drawn into tight circles, their elbows pointing backwards as hands caress the daggers at their waist. And among lawyers a subfusc agitation, conferences in corners.

Rafe asks him, could the king's freedom be obtained, sir, with more economy of means? Less bloodshed?

Look, he says: once you have exhausted the process of negotiation and compromise, once you have fixed on the destruction of an enemy, that destruction must be swift and it must be perfect. Before you even glance in his direction, you should have his name on a warrant, the ports blocked, his wife and friends bought, his heir under your protection, his money in your strong room and his dog running to your whistle. Before he wakes in the morning, you should have the axe in your hand.

When he, Cromwell, arrives to see Thomas Wyatt in prison, the constable Kingston is anxious to assure him that his word has been obeyed, that Wyatt has been treated with all honour.

'And the queen, how is she?'

'Restless,' Kingston says. He looks uneasy. 'I am used to all sorts of prisoners, but I have never had one like this. One moment she says, I know I must die. Next moment, much contrary to that. She thinks the king will come in his barge and take her away. She thinks a mistake has been made, that there is a misapprehension. She thinks the King of France will intervene for her.' The gaoler shakes his head.

He finds Thomas Wyatt playing dice against himself: the kind of time-wasting pursuit old Sir Henry Wyatt reprehends. 'Who's winning?' he asks.

Wyatt looks up. 'That trolling idiot, my worst self, plays that canting fool, my best self. You can guess who wins. Still, there is always the possibility it will come up different.'

'Are you comfortable?'

'In body or spirit?'

'I only answer for bodies.'

'Nothing makes you falter,' Wyatt says. He says it with a reluctant admiration that is close to dread. But he, Cromwell, thinks, I did falter but no one knows it, reports have not gone abroad. Wyatt did not see me walk away from Weston's interrogation. Wyatt did not see me when Anne laid her hand on my arm and asked me what I believed in my heart.

He rests his eyes on the prisoner, he takes his seat. He says softly, 'I think I have been training all my years for this. I have served an apprenticeship to myself.' His whole career has been an education in hypocrisy. Eyes that once skewered him now kindle with simulated regard. Hands that would like to knock his hat off now reach out to take his hand, sometimes in a crushing grip. He has spun his enemies to face him, to join him: as in a dance. He means to spin them away again, so they look down the long cold vista of their years: so they feel the wind, the wind of exposed places, that cuts to the bone: so they bed down in ruins, and wake up cold. He says to Wyatt, 'Any information you give me I will note, but I give you my word that I will destroy it once this thing is accomplished.'

'Accomplished?' Wyatt is querying his choice of word.

'The king is informed his wife has betrayed him with various men, one her brother, one his closest friend, another a servant she says she hardly knows. The glass of truth has shattered, he says. So, yes, it would be an accomplishment to pick up the pieces.'

'But you say he is informed, how is he informed? No one admits anything, except Mark. What if he is lying?'

'When a man admits guilt we have to believe him. We cannot set ourselves to proving to him that he is wrong. Otherwise the law courts would never function.'

'But what is the evidence?' Wyatt persists.

He smiles. 'The truth comes to Henry's door, wearing a cloak and hood. He lets it in because he has a shrewd idea of what lies beneath, it is not a stranger who comes calling. Thomas, I think

352

he has always known. He knows if she was not false to him in body she was so in words, and if not in deeds then in dreams. He thinks she never esteemed or loved him, when he laid the world at her feet. He thinks he never pleased or satisfied her and that when he lay next to her she imagined someone else.'

'That is common,' Wyatt said. 'Is it not usual? That is how marriage works. I never knew it was an offence in the eyes of the law. God help us. Half England will be in gaol.'

'You understand that there are the charges that are written down in an indictment. And then there are the other charges, those we don't commit to paper.'

'If feeling is a crime, then I admit ...'

'Admit nothing. Norris admitted. He admitted he loved her. If what someone wants from you is an admission, it is never in your interest to give it.'

'What does Henry want? I am honestly perplexed. I cannot see my way through it.'

'He changes his mind, day to day. He would like to rework the past. He would like never to have seen Anne. He would like to have seen her, but to have seen through her. Mostly he wishes her dead.'

'Wishing is not doing it.'

'It is, if you are Henry.'

'As I understand the law, a queen's adultery is no treason.'

'No, but the man who violates her, he commits treason.'

'You think they used force?' Wyatt says drily.

'No, it is just the legal term. It is a pretence, that allows us to think well of any disgraced queen. But as for her, she is a traitor too, she has said so out of her own mouth. To intend the king's death, that is treason.'

'But again,' Wyatt says, 'forgive my poor understanding, I thought Anne had said, "If he dies," or some such words. So let me put a case to you. If I say "All men must die," is that a forecast of the king's death?'

353

'It would be well not to put cases,' he says pleasantly. 'Thomas More was putting cases when he tipped into treason. Now let me come to the point with you. I may need your evidence against the queen. I will accept it in writing, I do not need it aired in open court. You once told me, when you visited my house, how Anne conducts herself with men: she says, "Yes, yes, yes, yes, no."' Wyatt nods; he recognises those words; he looks sorry he spoke them. 'Now you may have to transpose one word of that testimony. Yes, yes, yes, no, yes.'

Wyatt does not answer. The silence extends, settles around them: a drowsy silence, as elsewhere leaves unfurl, may blossoms on the trees, water tinkles into fountains, young people laugh in gardens. At last Wyatt speaks, his voice strained: 'It was not testimony.'

'What was it then?' He leans forward. 'You know I am not a man with whom you can have inconsequential conversations. I cannot split myself into two, one your friend and the other the king's servant. So you must tell me: will you write down your thoughts, and if you are requested, will you say one word?' He sits back. 'And if you can reassure me on this point, I will write to your father, to reassure him in turn. To tell him you will come out of this alive.' He pauses. 'May I do so?'

Wyatt nods. The smallest possible gesture, a nod to the future.

'Good. Afterwards, for your trouble, to compensate you for this detention, I will arrange for you to have a sum of money.'

'I don't want it.' Wyatt turns his face away, deliberately: like a child.

'Believe me, you do. You are still trailing debts from your time in Italy. Your creditors come to me.'

'I'm not your brother. You're not my keeper.'

He looks about him. 'I am, if you think about it.'

Wyatt says, 'I hear Henry wants an annulment too. To kill her and be divorced from her, all in one day. That is how she is, you see. Everything is ruled by extremes. She would not be his mistress, she must be queen of England; so there is breaking of faith and making of laws, so the country is set in an uproar. If he had such trouble to get her, what must it cost him to be rid? Even after she is dead, he had better make sure to nail her down.'

He says curiously, 'Have you no tenderness left for her?'

'She has exhausted it,' Wyatt says shortly. 'Or perhaps I never had any, I do not know my own mind, you know it. I dare say men have felt many things for Anne, but no one except Henry has felt tenderness. Now he thinks he's been taken for a fool.'

He stands up. 'I shall write some comfortable words to your father. I will explain you must stay here a little space, it is safest. But first I must … we thought Henry had dropped the annulment, but now, as you say, he revives it, so I must …'

Wyatt says, as if relishing his discomfort, 'You'll have to go and see Harry Percy, won't you?'

It is now almost four years since, with Call-Me-Risley at his heels, he had confronted Harry Percy at a low inn called Mark and the Lion, and made him understand certain truths about life: the paramount truth being, that he was not, whatever he thought, married to Anne Boleyn. On that day he had slammed his hand on the table and told the young man that if he did not get himself out of the way of the king, he would be destroyed: that he, Thomas Cromwell, would let his creditors loose to destroy him, and rip away his earldom and his lands. He had slammed his hand on the table and told him that, further, if he did not forget Anne Boleyn and any claim he made on her, her uncle the Duke of Norfolk would find out where he hid and bite his bollocks off.

Since then, he has done much business with the earl, who is now a sick and broken young man, heavily in debt, his hold on his affairs slipping away from him day by day. In fact, the judgement is almost accomplished, the judgement he had invoked: except that the earl still has his bollocks, as far as anybody knows. After their talk at Mark and the Lion the earl, who had been drinking for some days, had caused his servants to sponge his clothes, wiping away trails of vomit: sour-smelling, rawly shaven, trembling and green with nausea, he had presented himself before the king's council, and obliged him, Thomas Cromwell, by rewriting the history of his infatuation: by forswearing any claim on Anne Boleyn; by affirming that no contract of marriage had ever existed between them; that on his honour as a nobleman he had never tupped her, and that she was completely free for the king's hands, heart and marriage bed. On which, he had taken his Bible oath, the book held by old Warham, who was archbishop before Thomas Cranmer: on which, he had received the Holy Sacrament, with Henry's eyes boring into his back.

Now he, Cromwell, rides over to meet the earl at his country house in Stoke Newington, which lies north and east of the city on the Cambridge road. Percy's servants take their horses, but rather than entering at once he stands back from the house to take a view of the roof and chimneys. 'Fifty pounds spent before next winter would be a good investment,' he says to Thomas Wriothesley. 'Not counting the labour.' If he had a ladder he could go up and look at the state of the leads. But that would perhaps not be consonant with his dignity. Master Secretary can do anything he likes, but the Master of the Rolls has to think of his ancient office and what is due to it. Whether, as the king's Vicegerent in Spirituals, he is allowed to climb about on roofs … who knows? The office is too new and untried. He grins. Certainly, it would be an affront to the dignity of Master Wriothesley, if he were asked to foot the ladder. 'I'm thinking about my investment,' he tells Wriothesley. 'Mine and the king's.'

The earl owes him considerable sums, but he owes the king ten thousand pounds. After Harry Percy is dead, his earldom will be swallowed by the Crown: so he examines the earl too, to judge how sound he is. He is jaundiced, hollow-cheeked, looks older than his age, which is some thirty-four, thirty-five; and that sour smell that hangs in the air, it takes him back to Kimbolton, to the old queen shut up in her apartments: the fusty, unaired room like a gaol, and the bowl of vomit that passed him, in the hands of one of her girls. He says without much hope, 'You haven't been sick because of my visit?'

The earl looks at him from a sunken eye. 'No. They say it is my liver. No, on the whole, Cromwell, you have dealt very reasonably with me, I must say. Considering –'

'Considering what I threatened you with.' He shakes his head, rueful. 'Oh, my lord. Today I stand before you a poor suitor. You will never guess my errand.'

'I think I would.'

'I put it to you, my lord, that you are married to Anne Boleyn.'

'No.'

'I put it to you that in or about the year 1523, you made a secret contract of marriage with her, and that therefore her so-called marriage with the king is null.'

'No.' From somewhere, the earl finds a spark of his ancestral spirit, that border fire which burns in the north parts of the kingdom, and roasts any Scot in its path. 'You made me swear, Cromwell. You came to me where I was drinking at Mark and the Lion, and you threatened me. I was dragged before the council and I was made to swear on the Bible that I had no contract with Anne. I was made to go with the king and take communion. You saw me, you heard me. How can I take it back now? Are you saying I committed perjury?'

The earl is on his feet. He remains seated. He does not mean any discourtesy; rather he thinks that, if he stands up, he might fetch the earl a slap, and he has never to his knowledge assaulted a sick man. 'Not perjury,' he says amicably. 'I put it to you that on that occasion, your memory failed.'

'I was married to Anne, but had forgotten?'

He sits back and considers his adversary. 'You have always been a drinker, my lord, which is how, I believe, you are reduced to your present condition. On the day in question I found you, as you say, at a tavern. Is it possible that when you came before the council, you were still drunk? And therefore you were confused about what you were swearing?'

'I was sober.'

'Your head ached. You were nauseous. You were afraid you might be sick on the reverend shoes of Archbishop Warham. The possibility so perturbed you that you could think of nothing else. You were not attentive to the questions put to you. That was hardly your fault.'

'But,' the earl says, 'I was attentive.'

'Any councillor would understand your plight. We have all been in drink, one time or another.'

'Upon my soul, I was attentive.'

'Then consider another possibility. Perhaps there was some slackness in the taking of the oath. Some irregularity. The old archbishop, he was ill himself that day. I remember how his hands trembled as he held the holy book.'

'He was palsied. It is common in age. But he was competent.'

'If there was some defect in the procedure, your conscience should not trouble you, if you were now to repudiate your oath. Perhaps, you know, it was not even a Bible?'

'It was bound like a Bible,' the earl says.

'I have a book on accountancy that is often mistaken for a Bible.'

'Especially by you.'

He grins. The earl is not entirely addle-witted, not yet.

'And what about the sacred host?' Percy says. 'I took the sacrament to seal my oath, and was that not the very body of God?'

He is silent. I could give you an argument about that, he thinks, but I will not give you an opening to call me a heretic.

'I will not do it,' Percy says. 'And I cannot see why I should. All I hear is, that Henry means to kill her. Isn't it enough for her to be dead? After she is dead what does it matter who she was contracted to?'

'It does, in the one way. He is suspicious about the child Anne had. But he does not want to press inquiries into who is her father.'

'Elizabeth? I have seen the thing,' Percy says. 'She's his. I can tell you that much.'

'But if she were … even if she were, he now thinks to put her out of the succession, so if he was never married to her mother – well, at a stroke the matter is clear. The way is open for the children of his next wife.'

The earl nods. 'I see that.'

'So if you want to help Anne, this is your last chance.'

'How will it help her, to have her marriage annulled and her child bastardised?'

'It might save her life. If Henry's temper cools.'

'You will make sure to keep it hot. You will heap on the fuel and apply the bellows, will you not?'

He shrugs. 'It is nothing to me. I do not hate the queen, I leave that to others. So, if you had ever any regard for her –'

'I cannot help her any more. I can only help myself. God knows the truth. You made me a liar as I stood before God. Now you want to make me a fool as I stand before men. You must find another way, Master Secretary.'

'I will do that,' he says easily. He stands up. 'I am sorry you lose a chance to please the king.' At the door, he turns back. 'You are stubborn,' he says, 'because you are weak.'

Harry Percy looks up at him. 'I am worse than weak, Cromwell. I am dying.'

'You'll last until the trial, won't you? I shall put you on the panel of peers. If you are not Anne's husband, you are clear to be her judge. The court has need of wise and experienced men like yourself.'

Harry Percy cries out after him, but he leaves the hall with long strides, and gives the gentlemen outside the door a shake of the head. 'Well,' Master Wriothesley says, 'I made sure you would bounce him into sense.'

'Sense has fled.'

'You look gloomy, sir.'

'Do I, Call-Me? I can't think why.'

'We can still free the king. My lord archbishop will see a way. Even if we have to bring Mary Boleyn into it, and say the marriage was unlawful through affinity.'

'Our difficulty is, in the case of Mary Boleyn, the king was apprised of the facts. He may not have known if Anne was secretly married. But he always knew she was Mary's sister.'

'Have you ever done anything like that?' Master Wriothesley asks thoughtfully. 'Two sisters?'

'Is that the kind of question that absorbs you at this time?'

'Only one wonders. How it would be. They say Mary Boleyn was a great whore when she was at the French court. Do you think King Francis had them both?'

He looks at Wriothesley with new respect. 'There is an angle I might explore. Now ... because you have been a good boy and not struck out at Harry Percy or called him names, but waited patiently outside the door as you were bade, I'll tell you something you will like to know. Once, when she found herself between patrons, Mary Boleyn asked me to marry her.'

Master Wriothesley gapes at him. He follows, uttering broken syllables. What? When? Why? Only when they are on horseback does he speak to the purpose. 'God strike me. You would have been the king's brother-in-law.'

'But not for much longer,' he says.

The day is breezy and fine. They make good speed back to London. In other days, in other company, he would have enjoyed the journey.

But what company would that be, he wonders, dismounting at Whitehall. Bess Seymour's? 'Master Wriothesley,' he asks, 'can you read my mind?'

'No,' says Call-Me. He looks baffled, and somehow affronted.

'Do you think a bishop could read my mind?'

'No, sir.'

He nods. 'Just as well.'

The Imperial ambassador comes to see him, wearing his Christmas hat. 'Especially for you, Thomas,' he says, 'because I know it makes you happy.' He sits down, signals to the servant for wine. The servant is Christophe. 'Do you use this ruffian for every purpose?' Chapuys asks. 'Is it not he who tortured the boy Mark?'

'Firstly, Mark is not a boy, he is only immature. Secondly, no one tortured him.' At least, he says, 'not in my sight or hearing, not at my command nor suggestion, nor with my permission, expressed or implied'.

'I feel you preparing yourself for the courtroom,' Chapuys says. 'A knotted rope, was it not? Tightened around the brow? So you threatened to pop out his eyes?'

He is angry. 'This may be what they do where you were brought up. I have never heard of such a practice.'

'So it was the rack instead?'

'You can see him at his trial. You can judge for yourself whether he is damaged. I have seen men who have been racked. Not here. Abroad, I have seen it. They have to be carried in a chair. Mark is as nimble as in his dancing days.'

'If you say so.' Chapuys seems pleased to have provoked him. 'And how is your heretic queen now?'

'Brave as a lion. You will be sorry to learn.'

'And proud, but she will be humbled. She is no lion, and no more than one of your London cats that sing on rooftops.'

He thinks of a black cat he used to have. Marlinspike. After some years of fighting and scavenging he ran off, as cats do, to make his career elsewhere. Chapuys says, 'As you know, a number of ladies and gentlemen of the court have ridden up to the Princess Mary, to assure her of their services in the time which is at hand. I thought you might go yourself.'

God damn it, he thinks, I am already fully employed, and more than fully; it is no small enterprise, to bring down a queen of England. He says, 'I trust the princess will forgive my absence at this time. It is to do her good.'

'You have no trouble calling her "the princess" now,' Chapuys observes. 'She will be reinstated, of course, as Henry's heir.' He waits. 'She expects, all her loyal supporters expect, the Emperor himself expects …'

'Hope is a great virtue. But,' he adds, 'I hope you will warn her not to receive any persons without permission from the king. Or from me.'

'She cannot stop them resorting to her. All her old household. They flock. It will be a new world, Thomas.'

'The king will be eager, is eager, for a reconciliation with her. He is a good father.'

'A pity he has not had more opportunity to show it.'

'Eustache …' He pauses, waves Christophe away. 'I know you have never married, but have you no children? Do not look so startled. I am curious about your life. We must come to know each other better.'

The ambassador bristles at the change of topic. 'I do not meddle with women. Not like you.'

'I would not turn away a child. No one ever makes a claim on me. If they did, I would meet it.'

'The ladies do not wish to prolong the encounter,' Chapuys suggests.

That makes him laugh. 'You may be right. Come, my good friend, let us have our supper.'

'I look forward to many more such convivial evenings,' the ambassador says, beaming. 'Once the concubine is dead, and England is at ease.'

* * *

The men in the Tower, though they lament their likely fate, do not complain as sorely as the king does. By day he walks around like an illustration from the Book of Job. By night he glides down the river, accompanied by musicians, to visit Jane.

For all the beauties of Nicholas Carew's house, it is eight miles from the Thames and so not convenient for evening journeys, even in these light nights of early summer; the king wants to stay with Jane till darkness falls. So the queen-in-waiting has come up to London, to be housed by her supporters and friends. Crowds surge about from one rumoured spot to another, trying to catch a glimpse of her, necks craning, eyes popping, the curious blocking gateways and hoisting each other up on walls.

Her brothers throw out largesse to the Londoners, in the hope of winning their voices for her. The word is put about that she is an English gentlewoman, one of our own; unlike Anne Boleyn, whom many believe to be French. But the crowds are puzzled, even rancorous: ought not the king to marry a great princess, like Katherine, from a faraway land?

Bess Seymour tells him, 'Jane is squirrelling away money in a locked chest, in case the king changes his mind.'

'So should we all. A locked chest is a good thing to have.'

'She keeps the key in her bosom,' Bess says.

'No one is likely to come at it there.'

Bess gives him a merry look, out of the tail of her eye.

By now, the news of Anne's arrest is beginning to ripple through Europe, and though Bess does not know it, offers for Henry are coming in hour by hour. The Emperor suggests that the king might like his niece the Infanta of Portugal, who would come with 400,000 ducats; and the Portuguese Prince Dom Luis could marry the Princess Mary. Or if the king does not want the Infanta, what would he say to the dowager Duchess of Milan, a very pretty young widow, who would bring him a good sum also?

These are days of omens and portents for those who value such things and can read them. The malign stories have come out of the books and are enacting themselves. A queen is locked in a tower, accused of incest. The commonwealth, nature herself, is perturbed. Ghosts are glimpsed in doorways, standing by windows, against walls, hoping to overhear the secrets of the living. A bell rings of itself, touched by no human hand. There is a burst of speech where no one is present, a hissing in the air like the sound of a hot iron plunged into water. Sober citizens are moved to shout in church. A woman pushes through the crowd at his gate, grabbing at the bridle of his horse. Before the guards force her away, she shouts at him, 'God help us, Cromwell, what a man the king is! How many wives does he mean to have?'

For once, Jane Seymour has a blush of colour in her cheeks; or perhaps it is reflected from her gown, the soft clear rose of quince jelly.

Statements, indictments, bills are circulated, shuffled between judges, prosecutors, the Attorney General, the Lord Chancellor's office; each step in the process clear, logical, and designed to create corpses by due process of law. George Rochford will be tried apart, as a peer; the commoners will be tried first. The order goes to the Tower, 'Bring up the bodies.' Deliver, that is, the accused men, by name Weston, Brereton, Smeaton and Norris, to Westminster Hall for trial. Kingston fetches them by barge; it is 12 May, a Friday. They are brought in by armed guards through a fulminating crowd, shouting the odds. The gamblers believe that Weston will get off; this is his family's campaign at work. But for the others, the odds are even that they live or die. For Mark Smeaton, who has admitted everything, no wagers are being taken; but a book is open on whether he will be hanged, beheaded, boiled or burned, or subject to some novel penalty of the king's invention.

They do not understand the law, he says to Riche, looking down from a window at the scenes below. There is only one penalty for high treason: for a man, to be hanged, cut down alive and eviscerated, or for a woman, to be burned. The king may vary the sentence to decapitation; only poisoners are boiled alive. The court can give just the one sentence in this case, and it will be transmitted from the court to the crowds, and misunderstood, so that those who have won will be gnashing their teeth, and those who have lost will be demanding their money, and there will be fights and torn clothes and smashed heads, and blood on the ground while the accused are still safe in the courtroom, and days away from death.

They will not hear the charges till they hear them in court and, as is usual in treason trials, they will have no legal representation. But they will have a chance to speak, and represent themselves, and they can call witnesses: if anybody will stand up for them. Men have been tried for treason, these last few years, and walked free, but these men know they will not escape. They have to think of their families left behind; they want the king to be good to them and that alone should still any protest, prevent any strident pleas of innocence. The court must be allowed to work unimpeded. In return for their cooperation it is understood, more or less understood, that the king will grant them the mercy of death by the axe, which will not add to their shame; though there are murmurs among the jurors that Smeaton will hang because, being a man of low birth, he has no honour to protect.

Norfolk presides. When the prisoners are brought in, the three gentlemen draw away from Mark; they want to show him their scorn, and how they are better than he. But this brings them into proximity with each other, more than they will allow; they will not look at each other, he notices, they shuffle to create as much space as they can, so they seem to be shrinking from each other, twitching at coats and sleeves. Only Mark will declare his guilt. He has been kept in irons in case he tries to destroy himself: surely a charity, as he would bungle it. So he arrives before the court intact, as promised, no marks of injury, but unable to keep himself from tears. He pleads for mercy. The other defendants are succinct but respectful to the court: three heroes of the tilting ground who see, bearing down on them, the indefeasible opponent, the King of England himself. There are challenges they could make, but the charges, their dates and their details, go by them so fast. They can win a point, if they insist; but it only slows the inevitable, and they know it. When they go in, the guards stand with halberds reversed; but when they come out, convicted, the axe edge is turned to them. They push through the uproar, dead men: hustled through the lines of halberdiers to the river, and back to their temporary home, their anteroom, to write their last letters and make spiritual preparations. All have expressed contrition, though none but Mark has said for what.

A cool afternoon: and once the crowds have drifted off, and the court broken up, he finds himself sitting by an open window with the clerks bundling the records, and he watches it done, and then says, I will go home now. I am going to my city house, to Austin Friars, send the papers to Chancery Lane. He is the overlord of the spaces and the silences, the gaps and the erasures, what is missed or misconstrued or simply mistranslated, as the news slips from English to French and perhaps via Latin to Castilian and the Italian tongues, and through Flanders to the Emperor's eastern territories, over the borders of the German principalities and out to Bohemia and Hungary and the snowy realms beyond, by merchantmen under sail to Greece and the Levant; to India, where they have never heard of Anne Boleyn, let alone her lovers and her brother; along the silk routes to China where they have never heard of Henry the eighth of that name, or any other Henry, and even the existence of England is to them a dark myth, a place where men have their mouths in their bellies and women can fly, or cats rule the commonwealth and men crouch at mouse holes to catch their dinner. In the hall at Austin Friars he stands for a moment before the great image of Solomon and Sheba; the tapestry belonged to the cardinal once, but the king took it, and then, after

Wolsey was dead, and he, Cromwell, had risen in favour, the king had made him a gift of it, as if embarrassed, as if slipping back to its true owner something that should never have been away. The king had seen him look with longing, and more than once, at Sheba's face, not because he covets a queen but because she takes him back to his past, to a woman whom by accident she resembles: Anselma, an Antwerp widow, whom he might have married, he often thinks, if he had not made up his mind suddenly to take himself off back to England and pick up with his own people. In those days he did things suddenly: not without calculation, not without care, but once his mind was made up he was swift to move. And he is still the same man. As his opponents will find.

'Gregory?' His son is still in his riding coat, dusty from the road. He hugs him. 'Let me look at you. Why are you here?'

'You did not say I must not come,' Gregory explains. 'You did not absolutely forbid it. Besides, I have learned the art of public speaking now. Do you want to hear me make a speech?'

'Yes. But not now. You ought not to ride about the country with just one attendant or two. There are people who would hurt you, because you are known to be my son.'

'How am I known?' Gregory says. 'How would they know that?' Doors open, there are feet on the stairs, there are questioning faces crowding the hall; the news from the courtroom has preceded him. Yes, he confirms, they are all guilty, all condemned, whether they will go to Tyburn I do not know, but I will move the king to grant them the swifter end; yes, Mark too, because when he was under my roof I offered him mercy, and this is all the mercy I can deliver.

'We heard they are all in debt, sir,' says his clerk Thomas Avery, who does the accounts.

'We heard there were perilous crowds, sir,' says one of his watchmen.

Thurston the cook comes out, looking floury: 'Thurston has heard there were pies on sale,' says the jester Anthony. 'And I, sir? I hear that your new comedy was very well-received. And everybody laughed except the dying.'

Gregory says, 'But there could still be reprieves?'

'Undoubtedly.' He does not feel like adding anything. Someone has given him a drink of ale; he wipes his mouth.

'I remember when we were at Wolf Hall,' Gregory says, 'and Weston spoke so boldly to you, and so me and Rafe, we caught him in our magic net and dropped him from a height. But we would not really have killed him.'

'The king is wreaking his pleasure, and so many fine gentlemen will be spoiled.' He speaks for the household to hear. 'When your acquaintances tell you, as they will, that it is I who have condemned these men, tell them that it is the king, and a court of law, and that all proper formalities have been observed, and no one has been hurt bodily in pursuit of the truth, whatever the word is in the city. And you will not believe it, please, if ill-informed persons tell you these men are dying because I have a grudge against them. It is beyond grudge. And I could not save them if I tried.'

'But Master Wyatt will not die?' Thomas Avery asks. There is a murmur; Wyatt is a favourite in his household, for his open-handed ways and his courtesy.

'I must go in now. I must read the letters from abroad. Thomas Wyatt ... well, let us say I have advised him. I think we shall soon see him here among us, but bear in mind that nothing is certain, the will of the king ... No. Enough.'

He breaks off, Gregory trails him. 'Are they really guilty?' he asks, the moment they are alone. 'Why so many men? Would it not have stood better with the king's honour if he named only one?'

He says wryly, 'That would distinguish him too much, the gentleman in question.'

'Oh, you mean that people would say, Harry Norris has a bigger cock than the king, and he knows what to do with it?'

'What a way with words you have indeed. The king is inclined to take it patiently, and where another man would strive to be secret, he knows he cannot be, because he is not a private man. He believes, or at least he wishes to show, that the queen has been indiscriminate, that she is impulsive, that her nature is bad and she cannot control it. And now that so many men are found to have erred with her, any possible defence is stripped away, do you see? That is why they have been tried first. As they are guilty, she must be.'

Gregory nods. He seems to understand, but perhaps seeming is as far as it goes. When Gregory says, 'Are they guilty?' he means, 'Did they do it?' But when he says, 'Are they guilty?' he means, 'Did the court find them so?' The lawyer's world is entire unto itself, the human pared away. It was a triumph, in a small way, to unknot the entanglement of thighs and tongues, to take that mass of heaving flesh and smooth it on to white paper: as the body, after the climax, lies back on white linen. He has seen beautiful indictments, not a word wasted. This was not one: the phrases jostled and frotted, nudged and spilled, ugly in content and ugly in form. The design against Anne is unhallowed in its gestation, untimely in its delivery, a mass of tissue born shapeless; it waited to be licked into shape as a bear cub is licked by its mother. You nourished it, but you did not know what you fed: who would have thought of Mark confessing, or of Anne acting in every respect like an oppressed and guilty woman with a weight of sin upon her? It is as the men said today in court: we are guilty of all sorts of charges, we have all sinned, we all are riddled and rotten with offences and, even by the light of church and gospel, we may not know what they are. Word has come from the Vatican, where they are specialists in sin, that any offers of friendship, any gesture of reconciliation from King Henry, would be viewed kindly at this difficult time; because, whoever else is surprised, they are not surprised in Rome about the turn events have taken. In Rome, of course, it would be unremarkable:

adultery, incest, one merely shrugs. When he was at the Vatican, in Cardinal Bainbridge's day, he quickly saw that no one in the papal court grasped what was happening, ever; and least of all the Pope. Intrigue feeds on itself; conspiracies have neither mother nor father, and yet they thrive: the only thing to know is that no one knows anything.

Though in Rome, he thinks, there is little pretence at process of law. In the prisons, when an offender is forgotten and starves, or when he is beaten to death by his gaolers, they just stuff the body into a sack then roll and kick it into the river, where it joins the Tiber's general effluent.

He looks up. Gregory has been sitting quietly, respectful of his thoughts. But now he says, 'When will they die?'

'It cannot be tomorrow, they need time to settle their business. And the queen will be tried in the Tower on Monday, so it must be after that, Kingston cannot ... the court will sit in public, you see, the Tower will be awash with people ...' He pictures an unseemly scramble, the condemned men having to fight to the scaffold through the incoming hordes who want to see a queen on trial.

'But will you be there to watch?' Gregory insists. 'When it does occur? I could attend them at the last to offer them my prayers, but I could not do it unless you were there. I might fall down on the ground.'

He nods. It is good to be realistic in these matters. He has heard street brawlers in his youth boast of their stomach, then blench at a cut finger, and anyway being at an execution is not like being in a fight: there is fear, and fear is contagious, whereas in a scrap there is no time for fear, and not until it's over do your legs begin to shake. 'If I am not there, Richard will be. It is a kindly thought and though it would give you pain I feel it shows respect.' He cannot guess the shape of the next week. 'It depends ... the annulment must go through, so it rests with the queen, on how she helps us, will she give her assent.' He is thinking aloud: 'It may be I am at Lambeth with Cranmer. And please, my dear son, don't ask me why there has to be an annulment. Just know it's what the king wants.'

He finds he cannot think of the dying men at all. Into his mind instead strays the picture of More on the scaffold, seen through the veil of rain: his body, already dead, folding back neatly from the impact of the axe. The cardinal when he fell had no persecutor more relentless than Thomas More. Yet, he thinks, I did not hate him. I exercised my skills to the utmost to persuade him to reconcile with the king. And I thought I would win him, I really thought I would, for he was tenacious of the world, tenacious of his person, and had a good deal to live for. In the end he was his own murderer. He wrote and wrote and he talked and talked, then suddenly at a stroke he cancelled himself. If ever a man came close to beheading himself, Thomas More was that man.

The queen wears scarlet and black, and instead of a hood a jaunty cap, with feathers of black and white sweeping across its brim. Remember those plumes, he tells himself; this will be the last time, or almost so. How did she look, the women will ask. He will be able to say she looked pale, but unafraid. How can it be for her, to enter that great chamber and to stand before the peers of England, all men and none of them desiring her? She is tainted now, she is dead meat, and instead of coveting her – bosom, hair, eyes – their gaze slides away. Only Uncle Norfolk glares at her fiercely: as if her head were not Medusa's head.

In the centre of the great hall at the Tower they have built a platform with benches for the judges and peers, and there are some benches too in the side arcades, but the most part of the spectators will be standing, pushing in behind each other till the guards say 'No more,' and block the doorways with staves. Even then they push, and the noise rises as those who have been let through jostle in the well of the court, till Norfolk, his white baton of office in his hand, calls for silence, and from the fero-cious expression on his face, the most ignorant person in that throng knows he means it.

Here is the Lord Chancellor seated by the duke, to supply him with the best legal advice in the kingdom. Here is the Earl of Worcester, whose wife, you might say, started all this; and the earl gives him a filthy look, he does not know why. Here is Charles Brandon, Duke of Suffolk, who has hated Anne since he set eyes on her and has made it plain to the king's face. Here is the Earl of Arundel, the Earl of Oxford, the Earl of Rutland, the Earl of Westmorland: among them he moves softly, plain Thomas Cromwell, a greeting here and a word there, spreading reassur-ance: the Crown's case is in order, no upsets are expected or will be tolerated, we shall all be home for supper and sleep safely in our own beds tonight. Lord Sandys, Lord Audley, Lord Clinton and many lords more, each pricked off on a list as they take their seats: Lord Morley, George Boleyn's father-in-law, who reaches for his hand and says, please, Thomas Cromwell, as you love me, let not this sordid business rebound on my poor little daughter Jane.

She was not so much your poor little daughter, he thinks, when you married her off without asking her; but it is common, you cannot blame him as a father, for as the king once said to him ruefully, it is only very poor men and women who are free to choose who they love. He clasps Lord Morley's hand in return, and wishes him courage, and bids him take his seat, for the pris-oner is among us and the court prepared.

He bows to the foreign ambassadors; but where is Chapuys? Word is passed forward, he is suffering from a quartan fever: word is passed back, I am sorry to hear that, let him send to my house for anything that might make him more comfortable. Say his fever is up today, day one: its tide ebbing tomorrow, by Wednesday he is on his feet but shaky, but by Thursday night he will be down again, as it shakes him in its grip.

The Attorney General reads the indictment, and it takes some time: crimes under statute, crimes under God. As he gets to his feet to prosecute he is thinking, the king expects a verdict by mid-afternoon; and glancing across the court he sees Francis Bryan, still in his outdoor coat, ready to get on the river with word to the Seymours. Steady, Francis, he thinks, this may take some time, it may get hot in here.

The substance of the case is the work of an hour or two, but when there are ninety-five names to be verified, of the justices and the peers, then the mere shuffling and the throat-clearing, the nose-blowing, the adjustment of robes and the settling of belt sashes – all those distracting rituals that some men need before they speak in public – with all that, it is clear the day will wear on; the queen herself is a still presence, listening intently from her chair as the list of her crimes is read out, the dizzying catalogue of times, dates, places, of men, their members, their tongues: into the mouth, out of the mouth, into divers crannies of the body, at Hampton Court and Richmond Palace, at Greenwich and Westminster, in Middlesex and in Kent; and then the loose words and taunts, the jealous quarrels and twisted intentions, the declaration, by the queen, that when her husband is dead, she will choose some one of them to be her husband, but she cannot yet say which. 'Did you say that?' She shakes her head. 'You must answer aloud.'

Icy little voice: 'No.'

It is all she will say, no, no and no: and once she answers 'Yes,' when she is asked if she has given money to Weston, and she hesitates and admits it; and there is a whoop from the crowd, and Norfolk stops proceedings and threatens he will have them all arrested if they do not keep silence. In any well-ordered country, Suffolk said yesterday, the trial of a noblewoman would be conducted in seemly privacy; he had rolled his eyes and said, but my lord, this is England.

Norfolk has obtained quiet, a rustling calm punctuated by coughs and whispers; he is ready for the prosecution to resume, and says, 'Very well, go on, er – you.' Not for the first time, he is baffled by having to speak to a common man, who is not an ostler or a carter, but a minister of the king: the Lord Chancellor leans forward and whispers, reminding him perhaps that the prosecutor is Master of the Rolls. 'Carry on, Your Mastership,' he says, more politely. 'Please do proceed.'

She denies treason, there is the point: she never raises her voice, but she disdains to enlarge, to excuse, extenuate: to mitigate. And there is no one to do it for her. He remembers what Wyatt's old father had once told him, how a dying lioness can maul you, flash out with her claw and scar you for life. But he feels no threat, no tension, nothing at all. He is a good speaker, known for eloquence, style and audibility, but today he has no interest in whether he is heard, not beyond the judges, the accused, as whatever the populace hear they will misconstrue: and so his voice seems to fade to a drowsy murmur in the room, the voice of a country priest droning through his prayers, no louder than a fly buzzing in a corner, knocking against glass; out of the corner of his eye he sees the Attorney General stifle a yawn, and he thinks, I have done what I thought I could never achieve, I have taken adultery, incest, conspiracy and treason, and I have made them routine. We do not need any false excitement. After all, it is a law court, not the Roman circus.

The verdicts drag in: it is a lengthy business; the court implores brevity, no speeches please, one word will suffice: ninety-five vote guilty, and not one nay-sayer. When Norfolk begins to read the sentence, the roar rises again, and one can feel the pressure of the people outside trying to get in, so it seems the hall gently rocks, like a boat at its mooring. 'Her own uncle!' someone wails, and the duke bangs his fist on his table and says he will do slaughter. That produces some quiet; the hush allows him to conclude, '... thy judgement is this: Thou shalt be burned here, within the Tower, or else to have thy head smitten off, as the king's pleasure shall be further known –'

There is a yelp from one of the justices. The man is leaning forward, whispering furiously; Norfolk looks irate; the lawyers are going into a huddle, the peers crane forward to find out what is the delay. He strolls over. Norfolk says, 'These fellows tell me I have not done it right, I cannot say burning or beheading, I have to say one, and they say it must be burning, that is how a woman suffers when she is a traitor.'

'My lord Norfolk has his instructions from the king.' He means to crush objection and he does. 'The phrasing is the king's pleasure and moreover, do not tell me what can be done and what cannot, we have never tried a queen before.'

'We're just making it up as we go,' says the Lord Chancellor amiably.

'Finish what you were saying,' he tells Norfolk. He steps back.

'I think I have done,' Norfolk says, scratching his nose. '... head smitten off, as the king's pleasure shall be further known of the same.'

The duke drops his voice and concludes at conversational pitch; so the queen never hears the end of her sentence. She has the gist, though. He watches her rise from her chair, still composed, and he thinks, she doesn't believe it; why doesn't she believe it? He looks across to where Francis Bryan was hovering, but the messenger has already gone.

Rochford's trial has now to go forward; they must get Anne out, before her brother comes in. The solemnity of the occasion has dissipated. The more elderly members of the court have to totter out to piss, and the younger to stretch their legs and have a gossip, and collect the latest odds on an acquittal for George. The betting runs in his favour, though his face, as he is brought in, shows he is not deceived. To those who insist he will be acquitted, he, Cromwell has said, 'If Lord Rochford can satisfy the court, he will be let go. Let us see what defence he will make.'

He has only one real fear: that Rochford is not vulnerable to the same pressure as the other men, because he is not leaving behind anyone he cares for. His wife has betrayed him, his father deserted him, and his uncle will preside over the court that tries him. He thinks George will speak with eloquence and spirit, and he is correct. When the charges are read to him, he asks that they be put one by one, clause by clause: 'For what is your worldly time, gentlemen, against God's assurance of eternity?' There are smiles: admiration for his suavity. Boleyn addresses him, Cromwell, directly. 'Put them to me one by one. The times, the places. I will confound you.'

But the contest is not even. He has his papers, and if it comes to it, he can lay them on the table and make his case without them; he has his trained memory, he has his accustomed self-possession, his courtroom voice that places no strain on his throat, his urbanity of manner that places no strain on his emotions; and if George thinks he will falter, reading out the details of caresses administered and received, then George does not know the place he comes from: the times, the manners, that have formed Master Secretary. Soon enough, Lord Rochford will begin to sound like a raw, tearful boy; he is fighting for his life, and thus unequal to a man who seems so indifferent to the outcome; let the court acquit if it will, there will be another court, or a process, more informal, that will end with George a broken corpse. He thinks, too, that soon young Boleyn will lose his temper, that he will show his contempt for Henry, and then it will all be up with him. He hands Rochford a paper: 'Certain words are written here, which the queen is said to have spoken to you, and you in your turn passed them on. You need not read them aloud. Just tell the court, do you recognise those words?'

George smiles in disdain. Relishing the moment, he smirks: he takes a breath; he reads the words aloud. 'The king cannot copulate with a woman, he has neither skill nor vigour.'

He has read it because he thinks the crowd will like it. And so they do, though the laughter is shocked, incredulous. But from his judges – and it is they who matter – there is an audible hiss of deprecation. George looks up. He throws out his hands. 'These are not my words. I do not own them.'

But he owns them now. In one moment of bravado, to get the applause of the crowd, he has impugned the succession, derogated the king's heirs: even though he was cautioned not to do it. He, Cromwell, nods. 'We have heard that you spread rumours that the Princess Elizabeth is not the king's child. It seems you do. You have spread them even in this court.'

George is silent.

He shrugs and turns away. It is hard on George that he cannot even mention the charges against him without becoming guilty of them. As prosecutor, he would rather it had gone unmentioned, the king's difficulty; yet it is no more of a shame to Henry to have it declared in court than have it said in the street, and in taverns where they are singing the ballad of King Littleprick and his wife the witch. In such circumstances, the man blames the woman, as often as not. Something she has done, something she has said, the black look she gave him when he faltered, the derisive expression on her face. Henry is afraid of Anne, he thinks. But he will be potent with his new wife.

He gathers himself, gathers his papers; the judges wish to confer. The case against George is flimsy enough in all truth, but if the charges are thrown out, Henry will arraign him on some other matter, and it will go hard with his family, not just the Boleyns but the Howards too: for this reason, he thinks, Uncle Norfolk will not let him escape. And no one has denounced the charges as incredible, at this trial or the trials that preceded it. It has become a thing one can believe, that these men would plot against the king and copulate with the queen: Weston because he is reckless, Brereton because he is old in sin, Mark because he is ambitious, Henry Norris because he is familiar, he is close, he has confused his own person with the person of the king; and George Boleyn, not despite being her brother, but because he is her brother. Boleyns, it is known to all, will do what they need to do to rule; if Anne Boleyn put herself on the throne, walking on the bodies of the fallen, can she not put a Boleyn bastard there too?

He looks up at Norfolk, who gives him a nod. The verdict is in no doubt then, nor the sentence. The only surprise is Harry Percy. The earl rises from his place. He stands, his mouth open slightly, and a silence falls, not the rustling, whispering apology for a silence which the court has endured till now, but a still, expectant hush. He thinks of Gregory: do you want to hear me make a speech? Then the earl pitches forward, unleashes a groan, he crumples, and with a clatter and a thud he hits the floor. At once his prone body is swamped by guardsmen, and a great roar arises, 'Harry Percy is dead.'

Unlikely, he thinks. They'll bring him round. It is now mid-afternoon, warm and airless, and the evidence placed before the judges, the written statements alone, would fell a healthy man. There is a length of blue cloth laid over the new boards of the platform on which the judges sit, and he watches the guardsmen rip it up from the floor and improvise a blanket in which to carry the earl; and a memory stabs him, Italy, heat, blood, heaving and rolling and flopping a dying man on to knotted saddlecloths, cloths themselves scavenged from the dead, hauling him into the shade of the wall of – what, a church, a farmhouse? – only so that he could die, cursing, a few minutes later, trying to pack his guts back into the wound from which they were spilling, as if he wanted to leave the world tidy.

He feels sick, and he sits down by the Attorney General. The guardsmen carry the earl out, head lolling, eyes closed, feet dangling. His neighbour says, 'There is another man the queen has ruined. I suppose we will not know them all for years.'

It is true. The trial is a provisional arrangement, a fix for getting Anne out, Jane in. The effects of it have not been tested yet, the resonances have not been felt; but he expects a quaking at the heart of the body politic, a heaving in the stomach of the common-wealth. He gets up and goes over to urge Norfolk to get the trial under way again. George Boleyn – suspended as he is between trial and conviction – looks as though he might collapse himself, and has begun to weep. 'Help Lord Rochford to a chair,' he says. 'Give him something to drink.' He is a traitor, but still an earl; he can hear his death sentence sitting down.

Next day, 16 May, he is at the Tower, with Kingston in the constable's own lodgings. Kingston is fretting because he does not know what sort of scaffold to prepare for the queen: she lies under a dubious sentence, waiting for the king to speak. Cranmer is with her in her lodgings, come to hear her confession, and he will be able to hint to her, delicately, that her cooperation now will spare her pain. That the king still has mercy in him.

A guardsman at the door, addressing the constable: 'There is a visitor. Not for yourself, sir. For Master Cromwell. It is a foreign gentleman.'

It is Jean de Dinteville, who was here on embassy round about the time Anne was crowned. Jean stands poised in the doorway: 'They said I should find you here, and as time is short –'

'My dear friend.' They embrace. 'I did not even know you were in London.'

'I am straight off the boat.'

'Yes, you look it.'

'I am no sailor.' The ambassador shrugs; or at least, his vast padding moves, and subsides again; on this balmy morning, he is wrapped up in bewildering layers, much as a man dresses to face November. 'Anyway, it seemed best to come here and catch you before you are back playing bowls, which I believe you generally do when you should be receiving our representatives. I am sent to speak to you about young Weston.'

Good God, he thinks, has Sir Richard Weston managed to bribe the King of France?

'Not a moment too soon. He is sentenced to die tomorrow. What about him?'

379

'One is uneasy,' the ambassador says, 'if gallantry should be punished. Surely the young man is guilty of nothing more than a poem or two? Paying compliments and making jests? Perhaps the king might spare his life. One understands that for a year or two he would be advised to keep away from the court – travelling, perhaps?'

'He has a wife and young son, Monsieur. Not that the thought of them has ever constrained his behaviour.'

'So much the worse, if the king puts him to death. Does Henry not regard his reputation as a merciful prince?'

'Oh yes. He talks about it a lot. Monsieur, my advice is to forget Weston. Much as my master reveres and respects yours, he will not take it kindly if King Francis were to interfere in something which is, after all, a family matter, something he feels very near his own person.'

Dinteville is amused. 'One might well call it a family matter.'

'I notice you do not ask mercy for Lord Rochford. He has been an ambassador, one thought the King of France would be more interested in him.'

'Ah well,' the ambassador says. 'George Boleyn. One understands there is a change of regime, and what that entails. The whole French court hopes, of course, that Monseigneur will not be destroyed.'

'Wiltshire? He has been a good servant to the French, I see you would miss him. He is in no danger at present. Of course, you cannot look for his influence to be what it was. A change of regime, as you say.'

'May I say ...' the ambassador stops to sip wine, to nibble a wafer that Kingston's servants have provided, 'that we in France find this whole business incomprehensible? Surely if Henry wishes to be rid of his concubine he can do it quietly?'

The French do not understand law courts or parliaments. For them, the best actions are covert actions. 'And if he must parade his shame to the world, surely one or two adulteries are enough? However, Cremuel,' the ambassador runs his eye over him, 'we can speak man to man, can we not? The great question is, can Henry do it? Because what we hear is, he prepares himself, and then his lady gives him a certain look. And his hopes collapse. That seems to us like witchcraft, as witches do commonly render men impotent. But,' he adds, with a look of sceptical contempt, 'I cannot imagine that any Frenchman would be so afflicted.'

'You must understand,' he says, 'though Henry is at all points a man, he is a gentleman, and not a cur grunting in the gutter with … well, I say nothing of your own king's choice of women. These last months,' he takes a breath, 'these last weeks particularly, have been a time of great trial and grief for my master. He now seeks happiness. Have no doubt that his new marriage will secure his realm and promote the welfare of England.'

He is talking as if he is writing; already he is casting his version into dispatches.

'Oh, yes,' the ambassador says, 'the little person. One hears no great praise either of her beauty or her wit. He will not really marry her, another woman of no importance? When the Emperor offers him such lucrative matches … or so we hear. We understand everything, Cremuel. As a man and a woman, the king and the concubine may have their disputes, but there are more than the two of them in the world, this is not the Garden of Eden. When all's said, it is the new politics she doesn't suit. The old queen was, in some sort, the concubine's protector, and ever since she died Henry has been plotting how he may become a respectable man again. So he must wed the first honest woman he sees, and in all truth it really does not matter whether she is the Emperor's relative or no, because with the Boleyns gone, Cremuel is riding high, and he will be sure to pack the council with good imperialists.' His lip curls; it might be a smile. 'Cremuel, I wish you would say how much the Emperor Charles pays you. I have no doubt we could match it.'

381

He laughs. 'Your master is seated on thorns. He knows my king has money flowing in. He is afraid that he might pay France a visit, and in arms.'

'You know what you owe King Francis.' The ambassador is annoyed. 'Only our negotiations, most astute and subtle negotiations, prevent the Pope from striking your country from the list of Christian nations. We have, I think, been loyal friends to you, representing your cause better than you can yourselves.'

He nods. 'I always enjoy hearing the French praise themselves. Will you dine with me later this week? Once this is over? And your queasiness has settled down?'

The ambassador inclines his head. His cap badge glitters and winks; it is a silver skull. 'I shall report to my master that sadly I have tried and failed in the matter of Weston.'

'Say you came too late. The tide was against you.'

'No, I shall say Cremuel was against me. By the way, you know what Henry has done, don't you?' He seems amused. 'He sent last week for a French executioner. Not from one of our own cities, but the man who chops heads in Calais. It seems there is no Englishman whom he trusts to behead his wife. I wonder he does not take her out himself and strangle her in the street.'

He turns to Kingston. The constable is an elderly man now, and though he was in France on the king's business fifteen years ago he has not had much use for the language since; the cardinal's advice was, speak English and shout loud. 'Did you get that?' he asks. 'Henry has sent to Calais for the headsman.'

'By the Mass,' Kingston says. 'Did he do it before the trial?'

'So monsieur the ambassador tells me.'

'I am glad of the news,' Kingston says, loudly and slowly. 'My mind. Much relieved.' He taps his head. 'I understand he employs a …' He makes a swishing motion.

'Yes, a sword,' Dinteville says in English. 'You may expect a graceful performance.' He touches his hat, '*Au revoir*, Master Secretary.'

They watch him go out. It is a performance in itself; his servants need to truss him in further wrappings. When he was here on his last mission, he spent the time sweltering under quilts, trying to sweat out a fever picked up from the influence of the English air, the moisture and the gnawing cold.

'Little Jeannot,' he says, looking after the ambassador. 'He still fears the English summer. And the king – when he had his first audience with Henry, he could not stop shaking from terror. We had to hold him up, Norfolk and myself.'

'Did I misunderstand,' the constable says, 'or did he say Weston was guilty of poems?'

'Something like that.' Anne, it appears, was a book left open on a desk for anyone to write on the pages, where only her husband should inscribe.

'Anyway, there's a matter off my mind,' the constable says. 'Did you ever see a woman burned? It is something I wish never to see, as I trust in God.'

When Cranmer comes to see him on the evening of 16 May, the archbishop looks ill, shadowed grooves running from nose to chin. Were they there a month ago? 'I want all this to be over,' he says, 'and to get back to Kent.'

'Did you leave Grete there?' he says gently.

Cranmer nods. He seems hardly able to say his wife's name. He is terrified every time the king mentions marriage, and of course these days the king mentions little else. 'She is afraid that, with his next queen, the king will revert to Rome, and we shall be forced to part. I tell her, no, I know the king's resolve. But whether he will change his thinking, so a priest can live openly with his wife … if I thought there was no hope of that, then I think I should have to let her go home, before there is nothing there for her. You know how it is, in a few years people die, they forget you, you forget your own language, or so I suppose.'

'There is every hope,' he says firmly. 'And tell her, within a few months, in the new Parliament, I shall have wiped out all remnants of Rome from the statute books. And then, you know,' he smiles, 'once the assets are given out ... well, once they have been directed to the pockets of Englishmen, they will not revert to the pockets of the Pope.' He says, 'How did you find the queen, did she make her confession to you?'

'No. It is not yet the time. She will confess. At the last. If it comes to it.'

He is glad for Cranmer's sake. What would be worse at this point? To hear a guilty woman admit everything, or to hear an innocent woman beg? And to be bound to silence, either way? Perhaps Anne will wait until there is no hope of a reprieve, preserving her secrets till then. He understands this. He would do the same.

'I told her the arrangements made,' Cranmer says, 'for the annulment hearing. I told her it will be at Lambeth, it will be tomorrow. She said, will the king be there? I said no, madam, he sends his proctors. She said, he is busy with Seymour, and then she reproached herself, saying, I should not speak against Henry, should I? I said, it would be unwise. She said to me, may I come there to Lambeth, to speak for myself? I said no, there is no need, proctors have been appointed for you too. She seemed downcast. But then she said, tell me what the king wants me to sign. Whatever the king wants, I will agree. He may allow me to go to France, to a convent. Does he want me to say I was wed to Harry Percy? I said to her, madam, the earl denies it. And she laughed.'

He looks doubtful. Even the fullest disclosure, even a complete and detailed admission of guilt, it would not help her, not now, though it might have helped before the trial. The king doesn't want to think about her lovers, past or present. He has wiped them out of his mind. And her too. She would not credit the extent to which Henry has erased her. He said yesterday, 'I hope these arms of mine will soon receive Jane.'

Cranmer says, 'She cannot imagine that the king has abandoned her. It is not yet a month since he made the Emperor's ambassador bow to her.'

'I think he did that for his own sake. Not for hers.'

'I don't know,' Cranmer says. 'I thought he loved her. I thought there was no estrangement between them, up until the last. I am forced to think I don't know anything. Not about men. Not about women. Not about my faith, nor the faith of others. She said to me, "Shall I go to Heaven? Because I have done many good deeds in my time."'

She has made the same enquiry of Kingston. Perhaps she is asking everybody.

'She talks of works.' Cranmer shakes his head. 'She says nothing of faith. And I hoped she understood, as I now understand, that we are saved, not by our works, but only through Christ's sacrifice, and through his merits, not our own.'

'Well, I do not think you should conclude that she was a papist all this time. What would it have availed her?'

'I am sorry for you,' Cranmer says. 'That you should have the responsibility of uncovering it all.'

'I did not know what I would find, when I began. That is the only reason I could do it, because I was surprised at every turn.' He thinks of Mark's boasting, of the gentlemen before the court twitching away from each other, and evading each other's eyes; he has learned things about human nature that even he never knew. 'Gardiner in France is clamouring to know the details, but I find I do not want to write the particulars, they are so abominable.'

'Draw a veil over it,' Cranmer agrees. Though the king himself, he does not shrink from the details, it seems. Cranmer says, 'He is taking it around with him, the book he has written. He showed it the other evening, at the Bishop of Carlisle's house, you know Francis Bryan has the lease there? In the midst of Bryan's entertainments, the king took out this text, and began to read it aloud, and press it on all the party. Grief has unhinged him.'

'No doubt,' he says. 'Anyway, Gardiner will be content. I have told him he will be the gainer, when the spoils are given out. The offices, I mean, and the pensions and payments that now revert to the king.'

But Cranmer is not listening. 'She said to me, when I die, shall I not be the king's wife? I said, no, madam, for the king would have the marriage annulled, and I have come to seek your consent to that. She said, I consent. She said to me, but will I still be queen? And I think, under statute, she will be. I did not know what to say to her. But she looked satisfied. But it seemed so long. The time I was with her. One moment she was laughing, and then praying, and then fretting … She asked me about Lady Worcester, the child she is carrying. She said she thought the child was not stirring as it should, the lady being now in her fifth month or so, and she thinks it is because Lady Worcester has taken fright, or is sorrowing for her. I did not like to tell her that this lady had given a deposition against her.'

'I will enquire,' he says. 'About my lady's health. Though not of the earl. He glared at me. I do not know for what cause.'

A number of expressions, all of them unfathomable, chase themselves across the archbishop's face. 'Do you not know why? Then I see the rumour is not true. I am glad of it.' He hesitates. 'You really do not know? The word at court is that Lady Worcester's child is yours.'

He is dumbfounded. 'Mine?'

'They say you have spent hours with her, behind closed doors.'

'And that is proof of adultery? Well, I see that it would be. I am paid out. Lord Worcester will run me through.'

'You do not look afraid.'

'I am afraid, but not of Lord Worcester.'

More of the times that are coming. Anne climbing the marble steps to Heaven, her good deeds like jewels weighting wrists and neck.

Cranmer says, 'I do not know why, but she thinks there is still hope.'

All these days he is not alone. His allies are watching him. Fitzwilliam is at his side, disturbed still by what Norris half-told him and then took back: always talking about it, taxing his brain, trying to make complete sentences from broken phrases. Nicholas Carew is mostly with Jane, but Edward Seymour flits between his sister and the privy chamber, where the atmosphere is subdued, vigilant, and the king, like the minotaur, breathes unseen in a labyrinth of rooms. He understands his new friends are protecting their investment. They watch him for any sign of wavering. They want him as deep in the matter as they can contrive, and their own hands hidden, so that if later the king expresses any regret, or questions the haste with which things were done, it is Thomas Cromwell and not they who will suffer.

Riche and Master Wriothesley keep turning up too. They say, 'We want to give attendance on you, we want to learn, we want to see what you do.' But they can't see. When he was a boy, fleeing to put the Narrow Sea between himself and his father, he rolled penniless into Dover, and set himself up in the street with the three-card trick. 'See the queen. Look well at her. Now ... where is she?'

The queen was in his sleeve. The money was in his pocket. The gamblers were crying, 'You will be whipped!'

He takes the warrants to Henry to be signed. Kingston has still received no word of how the men are to die. He promises, I will make the king concentrate his mind. He says, 'Majesty, there is no gallows at Tower Hill, and I do not think it would be a good idea to take them to Tyburn, the crowds might be unruly.'

'Why would they?' Henry says. 'The people of London do not love these men. Indeed they do not know them.'

'No, but any excuse for disorder, and if the weather stays fine ...'

The king grunts. Very well. The headsman.

Mark too? 'After some sort, I promised him mercy if he confessed, and you know he did confess freely.'

The king says, 'Has the Frenchman come?'

'Yes, Jean de Dinteville. He has made representations.'

'No,' Henry says.

Not that Frenchman. He means the Calais executioner. He says to the king, 'Do you think that it was in France, when the queen was at court there in her youth, do you think it was there she was first compromised?'

Henry is silent. He thinks, then speaks. 'She was always pressing me, do you mark what I say ... always pressing on me the advantage of France. I think you are right. I have been thinking about it and I do not believe it was Harry Percy took her maidenhead. He would not lie, would he? Not on his honour as a peer of England. No, I believe it was in the court of France she was first debauched.'

So he cannot tell if the Calais headsman, so expert in his art, is a mercy at all; or if this form of death, dealt to the queen, simply meets Henry's severe sense of the fitness of things.

But he thinks, if Henry blames some Frenchman for ruining her, some foreigner unknown and perhaps dead, so much the better. 'So it was not Wyatt?' he says.

'No,' Henry says sombrely. 'It was not Wyatt.'

He had better stay where he is, he thinks, for now. Safer so. But a message can go to him, to say he is not to be tried. He says, 'Majesty, the queen complains of her attendants. She would like to have women from her own privy chamber.'

'Her household is broken up. Fitzwilliam has seen to it.'

'I doubt the ladies have all gone home.' They are hovering, he knows, in the houses of their friends, in expectation of a new mistress.

Henry says, 'Lady Kingston must stay, but you can change the rest. If she can find any willing to serve her.'

It is possible Anne still does not know how she has been abandoned. If Cranmer is right, she imagines her former friends are lamenting her, but really they are in a sweat of fear until her head is off. 'Someone will do her the charity,' he says.

Henry now looks down at the papers before him, as if he does not know what they are. 'The death sentences. To endorse,' he reminds him. He stands by the king while he dips his pen and sets his signature to each of the warrants: square, complex letters, lying heavy on the paper; a man's hand, when all is said.

He is at Lambeth, in the court convened to hear the divorce proceedings, when Anne's lovers die: this is the last day of the proceedings, it must be. His nephew Richard is there to represent him on Tower Hill and bring him the word of how it was accomplished. Rochford made an eloquent speech, appearing in command of himself. He was killed first and needed three blows of the axe; after which, the others said not much. All proclaimed themselves sinners, all said they deserved to die, but once again they did not say for what; Mark, left till last and slipping in the blood, called for God's mercy and the prayers of the people. The executioner must have steadied himself, since after his first blunder all died cleanly.

On paper it is done. The records of the trials are his, to carry to the Rolls House, to keep or destroy or mislay, but the bodies of the dead men are a dirty, urgent problem. The corpses must be put in a cart and brought within the Tower walls: he can see them, a heap of entangled bodies without heads, heaped promiscuously as if on a bed, or as if, like corpses in war, they have already been buried and dug up. Within the fortress they are stripped of their clothes, which are the perquisite of the headsman and his assistants, and left in their shirts. There is a graveyard huddled to the walls of St Peter ad Vincula, and the commoners will be buried there, with Rochford to go alone beneath the floor of the chapel. But now the dead are without the badges of their ranks there is some confusion. One of the burial party said, fetch the queen, she knows their body parts; but others, Richard says, cried shame on him. He says, gaolers see too much, they soon lose their sense of what is fitting. 'I saw Wyatt looking down from a grate in the Bell Tower,' Richard says. 'He signed to me and I wanted to give him hope, but I did not know how to signal that.'

He will be released, he says. But perhaps not until Anne is dead.

The hours to that event seem long. Richard hugs him; says, 'If she had reigned longer she would have given us to the dogs to eat.'

'If we had let her reign longer, we would have deserved it.'

At Lambeth, the two proctors for the queen had been present: as the king's substitutes, Dr Bedyll and Dr Tregonwell, and Richard Sampson as his counsel. And himself, Thomas Cromwell: and the Lord Chancellor, and other councillors, including the Duke of Suffolk, whose own marital affairs have been so entangled that he has learned a certain amount of canon law, swallowing it like a child taking medicine; today Brandon had sat making faces and shifting in his chair, while the priests and lawyers sifted the circumstances. They had talked over Harry Percy, and agreed he was no use to them. 'I cannot think why you did not get his cooperation, Cromwell,' the duke says. Reluctantly they had talked over Mary Boleyn, and agreed she would have to furnish the impediment; though the king was as culpable as anyone, for he knew, surely, he could not be contracted to Anne if he had slept with her sister? I suppose the point was not entirely obvious, Cranmer says gently. There was affinity, that is clear, but he had a dispensation from the Pope, which he thought held good at the time. He did not know that, in so grave a matter, the Pope cannot dispense; that point was settled later.

It is all most unsatisfactory. The duke says suddenly, 'Well, you all know she is a witch. And if she witched him into marriage ...'

'I don't think the king means that,' he says: he, Cromwell.

'Oh, he does,' says the duke. 'I thought that was what we had come here to discuss. If she witched him into marriage it was null, is my understanding.' The duke sits back, his arms folded.

The proctors look at each other. Sampson looks at Cranmer. No one looks at the duke. Eventually Cranmer says, 'We don't have to make it public. We can issue the decree but keep the grounds secret.'

A release of breath. He says, 'I suppose it is some consolation, that we need not be laughed at in public.'

The Lord Chancellor says, 'The truth is so rare and precious that sometimes it must be kept under lock and key.'

The Duke of Suffolk speeds to his barge, crying out that at last he is free of the Boleyns.

The end of the king's first marriage was protracted, public and discussed throughout Europe, not only in the councils of princes but in the market square. The end of his second, if decency prevailed, would be swift, private, unspoken and obscure. Yet it is necessary to have it witnessed by the city and by men of rank. The Tower is a town. It is an armoury, a palace, a mint. Workmen of all sorts, officials come and go. But it can be policed, and foreigners evacuated. He sets Kingston to do this. Anne, he is sorry to learn, has mistaken the day of her death, rising at 2 a.m. to pray on the morning of 18 May, sending for her almoner and for Cranmer to come to her at dawn so she can purge herself of her sins. No one seems to have told her that Kingston comes without fail at dawn on the morning of an execution, to warn the dying person to be ready. She is not familiar with the protocol, and why would she be? Kingston says, see it from my point of view: five deaths in one day, and to be ready for a queen of England the next? How can she die, when the appropriate

391

officials from the city are not here? The carpenters are still making her scaffold on Tower Green, though thankfully she cannot hear the knocking from the royal lodging.

Still, the constable is sorry for her misapprehension; especially since her mistake ran on, late into the morning. The situation is a great strain on both himself and his wife. Instead of being glad of another dawn, he reports, Anne had cried, and said she was sorry not to die that day: she wished she were past her pain. She knew about the French executioner and, 'I told her,' Kingston says, 'it shall be no pain, it is so subtle.' But once again, Kingston says, she closed her fingers around her throat. She had taken the Eucharist, declaring on the body of God her innocence.

Which surely she would not do, Kingston says, if she were guilty?

She laments the men who are gone.

She makes jokes, saying that she will be known hereafter as Anne the Headless, Anne sans Tête.

He says to his son, 'If you come with me to witness this, it will be almost the hardest thing you ever do. If you can go through it with a steady countenance, it will be remarked on and it will be much in your favour.'

Gregory just looks at him. He says, 'A woman, I cannot.'

'I will be beside you to show you that you can. You need not look. When the soul passes, we kneel, and we drop our eyes, and pray.'

The scaffold has been set up in an open place, where once they used to hold tournaments. A guard of two hundred yeomen is assembling, drawing up to lead the procession. Yesterday's bungling, the confusion over the date, the delays, the misinformation: none of that must be repeated. He is there early, when they are putting the sawdust down, leaving his son back in Kingston's lodgings, with the others who are collecting: the sheriffs, aldermen, London's officers and dignitaries. He stands himself on the steps of the scaffold, testing them to see if they take his weight; one of the sawdust men says to him, it's sound, sir, we have all run up and down, but I suppose you want to check it yourself. When he looks up the executioner is already there, talking to Christophe. The young man is well-dressed, an allowance having been made him for a gentleman's apparel, so that he will not be easy to pick out from the other officials; this is done to save alarm to the queen, and if the clothes are spoiled, at least he is not out of pocket himself. He walks up to the executioner. 'How will you do this?'

'I shall surprise her, sir.' Switching into English, the young man indicates his feet. He is wearing soft shoes, such as one might wear indoors. 'She never sees the sword. I have put it there, in the straw. I shall distract her. She will not see from where I come.'

'But you will show me.'

The man shrugs. 'If you like. Are you Cremuel? They told me you are in charge of everything. In fact they joke to me, saying, if you faint because she is so ugly, there is one who will pick up the sword, his name is Cremuel and he is such a man, he can chop the head off the Hydra, which I do not understand what it is. But they say it is a lizard or serpent, and for each head that is chopped two more will grow.'

'Not in this case,' he says. Once the Boleyns are done, they are done.

The weapon is heavy, needing a two-handed grip. It is almost four foot in length: two inches broad, round at the tip, a double edge. 'One practises, like this,' the man says. He whirls like a dancer on the spot, his arms held high, his fists together as if he were gripping the sword. 'Every day one must handle the weapon, if only to go through the motions. One may be called at any time. We do not kill so many in Calais, but one goes to other towns.'

'It is a good trade,' Christophe says. He wants to handle the sword, but he, Cromwell, does not want to let go of it yet.

393

The man says, 'They tell me I may speak French to her and she will understand me.'

'Yes, do so.'

'But she will kneel, she must be informed of this. There is no block, as you see. She must kneel upright and not move. If she is steady, it will be done in a moment. If not, she will be cut to pieces.'

He hands back the weapon. 'I can answer for her.'

The man says, 'Between one beat of the heart and the next it is done. She knows nothing. She is in eternity.'

They walk away. Christophe says, 'Master, he has said to me, tell the women that she should wrap her skirts about her feet when she kneels, in case she falls bad and shows off to the world what so many fine gentlemen have already seen.'

He does not reprove the boy for his coarseness. He is crude but correct. And when the moment comes, it will prove, the women do it anyway. They must have discussed it among themselves.

Francis Bryan has appeared beside him, steaming inside a leather jerkin. 'Well, Francis?'

'I am charged that as soon as her head is off I ride with the news to the king and Mistress Jane.'

'Why?' he says coldly. 'Do they think the headsman might in some way fail?'

It is almost nine o'clock. 'Did you eat any breakfast?' Francis says.

'I always eat my breakfast.' But he wonders if the king did. 'Henry has hardly spoken of her,' Francis Bryan says. 'Only to say he cannot see how the whole thing occurred. When he looks back on the last ten years, he cannot understand himself.'

They are silent. Francis says, 'Look, they are coming.'

The solemn procession, through Coldharbour Gate: the city first, aldermen and officials, then the guard. In the midst of them the queen with her women. She wears a gown of dark damask and a short cape of ermine, a gable hood; it is the occasion, one supposes, to hide the face as much as possible, to guard the expression. That ermine cape, does he not know it? It was wrapped around Katherine, he thinks, when I saw it last. These furs, then, are Anne's final spoils. Three years ago when she went to be crowned, she walked on a blue cloth that stretched the length of the abbey – so heavy with child that the onlookers held their breath for her; and now she must make shift over the rough ground, picking her way in her little lady's shoes, with her body hollow and light and just as many hands around her, ready to retrieve her from any stumble and deliver her safely to death. Once or twice the queen falters, and the whole procession must slow; but she has not stumbled, she is turning and looking behind her. Cranmer had said, 'I do not know why, but she thinks there is still hope.' The ladies have veiled themselves, even Lady Kingston; they do not want their future lives to be associated with this morning's work, they do not want their husbands or their suitors to look at them and think of death.

Gregory has slipped into place beside him. His son is trembling and he can feel it. He puts out a gloved hand and rests it on his arm. The Duke of Richmond acknowledges him; he stands in prominent view, with his father-in-law Norfolk. Surrey, the duke's son, is whispering to his father, but Norfolk gazes straight ahead. How has the house of Howard come to this?

When the women strip the queen of her cape she is a tiny figure, a bundle of bones. She does not look like a powerful enemy of England, but looks can deceive. If she could have brought Katherine to this same place, she would have. If her sway had continued, the child Mary might have stood here; and he himself of course, pulling off his coat and waiting for the coarse English axe. He says to his son, 'It will be but a moment now.' Anne has given alms out as she walks, and the velvet bag is empty now; she slips her hand inside it and turns it inside out, a prudent housewife's gesture, checking to see that nothing is thrown away.

One of the women stretches out a hand for the purse. Anne passes it without looking at her, then moves to the edge of the scaffold. She hesitates, looks over the heads of the crowd, then begins to speak. The crowd as one sways forward, but can only shuffle by inches towards her, every man with his head lifted, staring. The queen's voice is very low, her words barely heard, her sentiments the usual ones on the occasion: '... pray for the king, for he is a good, gentle, amiable and virtuous prince ...' One must say these things, as even now the king's messenger might come ...

She pauses ... But no, she has finished. There is nothing more to say and not more than a few moments left of this world. She takes in a breath. Her face expresses bewilderment. *Amen*, she says, *amen*. Her head goes down. Then she seems to draw herself together, to control the tremor that has seized her entire body from head to foot.

One of the veiled women moves to her side and speaks to her. Anne's arm shakes as she raises it to lift off her hood. It comes easily, no fumbling; he thinks, it cannot have been pinned. Her hair is gathered in a silk net at the nape of her neck and she shakes it out, gathers up the strands, raising her hands above her head, coiling it; she holds it with one hand, and one of the women gives her a linen cap. She pulls it on. You would not think it would hold her hair, but it does; she must have rehearsed with it. But now she looks about as if for direction. She lifts the cap half off her head, puts it back. She does not know what to do, he sees she does not know if she should tie the cap's string beneath her chin – whether it will hold without fastening or whether she has time to make a knot and how many heartbeats she has left in the world. The executioner steps out and he can see – he is very close – Anne's eyes focus on him. The Frenchman bobs to his knees to ask pardon. It is a formality and his knees barely graze the straw. He has motioned Anne to kneel, and as she does so he steps away, as if he does not want contact even with her clothes. At arm's length, he holds out a folded cloth to one of the women, and raises a hand to his eyes to show her what he means. He hopes it is Lady Kingston who takes the blindfold; whoever it is, she is adept, but a small sound comes from Anne as her world darkens. Her lips move in prayer. The Frenchman waves the women back. They retreat; they kneel, one of them almost sinks to the ground and is propped up by the others; despite the veils one can see their hands, their helpless bare hands, as they draw their own skirts about them, as if they were making themselves small, making themselves safe. The queen is alone now, as alone as she has ever been in her life. She says, Christ have mercy, Jesus have mercy, Christ receive my soul. She raises one arm, again her fingers go to the coif, and he thinks, put your arm down, for God's sake put your arm down, and he could not will it more if – the executioner calls out sharply, 'Get me the sword.' The blinded head whips around. The man is behind Anne, she is misdirected, she does not sense him. There is a groan, one single sound from the whole crowd. Then a silence, and into that silence, a sharp sigh or a sound like a whistle through a keyhole: the body exsanguinates, and its flat little presence becomes a puddle of gore.

The Duke of Suffolk is still standing. Richmond too. All others, who have knelt, now get to their feet. The executioner has turned away, modestly, and already handed over his sword. His assistant is approaching the corpse but the four women are there first, blocking him with their bodies. One of them says fiercely, 'We do not want men to handle her.'

He hears young Surrey say, 'No, they have handled her enough.' He says to Norfolk, my lord, take your son in charge, and take him away from this place. Richmond, he sees, looks ill, and he sees with approval how Gregory goes to him and bows, friendly as one young boy can be to another, saying, my lord, leave it now, come away. He does not know why Richmond did not kneel. Perhaps he believes the rumours that the queen tried to poison him, and will not offer her even that last respect. With Suffolk, it is more understandable. Brandon is a hard man and owes Anne no forgiveness. He has seen battle. Though never a bloodletting like this.

It seems Kingston did not think further than the death, to the burial. 'I hope to God,' he, Cromwell says to no one in particular, 'that the constable has remembered to have the flags taken up in the chapel,' and someone answers him, I think so, sir, for they were levered up two days ago, so her brother could go under.

The constable has not helped his reputation these last few days, though he has been kept in uncertainty by the king and, as he will admit later, he had thought all morning that a messenger might suddenly arrive from Whitehall, to stop it: even when the queen was helped up the steps, even to the moment she took off her hood. He has not thought of a coffin, but an elm chest for arrows has been hastily emptied and carried to the scene of the carnage. Yesterday it was bound for Ireland with its freight, each shaft ready to deal separate, lonely damage. Now it is an object of public gaze, a death casket, wide enough for the queen's little body. The executioner has crossed the scaffold and lifted the severed head; in a yard of linen he swaddles it, like a newborn. He waits for someone to take the burden. The women, unassisted, lift the queen's sodden remains into the chest. One of them steps forward, receives the head, and lays it – no other space – by the queen's feet. Then they straighten up, each of them awash in her blood, and stiffly walk away, closing their ranks like soldiers.

That evening he is at home at Austin Friars. He has written letters into France, to Gardiner. Gardiner abroad: a crouching brute nibbling his claws, waiting for his moment to strike. It has been a triumph, to keep him away. He wonders how much longer he can do it.

He wishes Rafe were here, but either he is with the king or he has gone back to Helen in Stepney. He is used to seeing Rafe most days and he cannot get used to the new order of things. He keeps expecting to hear his voice, and to hear him and Richard, and Gregory when he is at home, scuffling in corners and trying to push each other downstairs, hiding behind doors to jump on each other, doing all those tricks that even men of twenty-five or thirty do when they think their grave elders are not nearby. Instead of Rafe, Mr Wriothesley is with him, pacing. Call-Me seems to think someone should give an account of the day, as if for a chronicler; or if not that, that he should give an account of his own feelings. 'I stand, sir, as if upon a headland, my back to the sea, and below me a burning plain.'

'Do you, Call-Me? Then come in from the wind,' he says, 'and have a cup of this wine Lord Lisle sends me from France. I do usually keep it for my own drinking.'

Call-Me takes the glass. 'I smell burning buildings,' he says. 'Fallen towers. Indeed there is nothing but ash. Wreckage.'

'But it's useful wreckage, isn't it?' Wreckage can be fashioned into all sorts of things: ask any dweller on the sea shore.

'You have not properly answered on one point,' Wriothesley says. 'Why did you let Wyatt go untried? Other than because he is your friend?'

'I see you do not rate friendship highly.' He watches Wriothesley take that in.

'Even so,' Call-Me says. 'Wyatt I see poses you no threat, nor has he slighted or offended you. William Brereton, he was high-handed and offended many, he was in your way. Harry Norris, young Weston, well, there are gaps where they stood, and you can put your own friends in the privy chamber alongside Rafe. And Mark, that squib of a boy with his lute; I grant you, the place looks tidier without him. And George Rochford struck down, that sends the rest of the Boleyns scurrying away, Monseigneur will have to scuttle back to the country and sing small. The

399

Emperor will be gratified by all that has passed. It is a pity the ambassador's fever kept him away today. He would like to have seen it.'

No he would not, he thinks. Chapuys is squeamish. But you ought to get up from your sickbed if you need to, and see the results you have willed.

'Now we shall have peace in England,' Wriothesley says.

A phrase runs through his head – was it Thomas More's? – 'the peace of the hen coop when the fox has run home'. He sees the scattered carcasses, some killed with one snap of the jaw, the rest bitten and shredded as the fox whirls and snaps in panic as the hens flap about him, as he spins around and deals death: the remnants then to be sluiced away, the mulch of scarlet feathers plastered over the floor and walls.

'All the players gone,' Wriothesley says. 'All four who carried the cardinal to Hell; and also the poor fool Mark who made a ballad of their exploits.'

'All four,' he says. 'All five.'

'A gentleman asked me, if this is what Cromwell does to the cardinal's lesser enemies, what will he do by and by to the king himself?'

He stands looking down into the darkening garden: transfixed, the question like a knife between his shoulderblades. There is only one man among all the king's subjects to whom that question would occur, only one who would dare pose it. There is only one man who would dare question the loyalty he shows to his king, the loyalty he demonstrates daily. 'So ...' he says at last. 'Stephen Gardiner calls himself a gentleman.'

Perhaps, caught in the little panes which distort and cloud, Wriothesley sees a dubious image: confusion, fear, emotions that do not often mark Master Secretary's face. Because if Gardiner thinks this, who else? Who else will think it in the months and years ahead? He says, 'Wriothesley, surely you don't expect me to justify my actions to you? Once you have chosen a course, you should not apologise for it. God knows, I mean nothing but good to our master the king. I am bound to obey and serve. And if you watch me closely you will see me do it.'

He turns, when he thinks it is fit for Wriothesley to see his face. His smile is implacable. He says, 'Drink my health.'

III

Spoils

London, Summer 1536

The king says, 'What happened to her clothes? Her headdress?'

He says, 'The people at the Tower have them. It is their perquisite.'

'Buy them back,' the king says. 'I want to know they are destroyed.'

The king says, 'Call in all the keys that admit to my privy chamber. Here and elsewhere. All the keys to all the rooms. I want the locks changed.'

There are new servants everywhere, or old servants in new offices. In place of Henry Norris, Sir Francis Bryan is appointed chief of the privy chamber, and is to receive a pension of a hundred pounds. The young Duke of Richmond is appointed Chamberlain of Chester and North Wales, and (replacing George Boleyn) Warden of the Cinque Ports and Constable of Dover Castle. Thomas Wyatt is released from the Tower and granted a hundred pounds also. Edward Seymour is promoted Viscount Beauchamp. Richard Sampson is appointed Bishop of Chichester. The wife of Francis Weston announces her remarriage.

He has conferred with the Seymour brothers on the motto Jane should adopt as queen. They settle on, 'Bound to Obey and Serve'.

They try it out on Henry. A smile, a nod: perfect contentment. The king's blue eyes are serene. Through the autumn of this year, 1536, in glass windows, in carvings of stone or wood, the badge of the phoenix will replace the white falcon with its imperial crown; for the heraldic lions of the dead woman, the panthers of Jane Seymour are substituted, and it is done economically, as the beasts only need new heads and tails.

The marriage is swift and private, in the queen's closet at Whitehall. Jane is found to be the king's distant cousin, but all dispensations are granted in proper form.

He, Cromwell, is with the king before the ceremony. Henry is quiet, and more melancholy that day than any bridegroom ought to be. He is not thinking about his last queen; she is ten days dead and he never speaks of her. But he says, 'Crumb, I don't know if I will have any children now. Plato says that a man's best offspring are born when he is between thirty years and thirty-nine. I am past that. I have wasted my best years. I don't know where they have gone.'

The king feels he has been cheated of his fate. 'When my brother Arthur died, my father's astrologer predicted that I should enjoy a prosperous reign and father many sons.'

You're prosperous at least, he thinks: and if you stick with me, richer than you can ever have imagined. Somewhere, Thomas Cromwell was in your chart.

The debts of the dead woman now fall to be paid. She owes some thousand pounds, which her confiscated estate is able to meet: to her furrier and her hosier, her silkwomen, her apothecary, her linen draper, her saddler, her dyer, her farrier and her pinmaker. The status of her daughter is uncertain, but for now the child is well provided with gold fringing for her bed, and with caps of white and purple satin with gilt trim. The queen's embroiderer is owed fifty-five pounds, and one can see where the money went.

The fee to the French executioner is over twenty-three pounds, but it is an expense unlikely to be repeated.

* * *

At Austin Friars, he takes the keys and lets himself into the little room where they store Christmas: where Mark was held, and where he cried out in fear in the night. The peacock wings will have to be destroyed. Rafe's little girl will probably not ask for them again; children do not remember from one Christmas to the next.

When the wings are shaken out of their linen bag he stretches the fabric, holds it up to the light and sees that the bag is slit. He understands how the feathers crept out and stroked the dead man's face. He sees that the wings are shabby, as if nibbled, and the glowing eyes dulled. They are tawdry things after all, not worth setting store by.

He thinks about his daughter Grace. He thinks, was my wife ever false to me? When I was away on the cardinal's business as I so often was, did she take up with some silk merchant she knew through her business, or did she, as many women do, sleep with a priest? He can hardly believe it of her. Yet she was a plain woman, and Grace was so beautiful, her features so fine. They blur in his mind these days; this is what death does to you, it takes and takes, so that all that is left of your memories is a faint tracing of spilled ash.

He says to Johane, his wife's sister, 'Do you think Lizzie ever had to do with another man? I mean, while we were married?'

Johane is shocked. 'Whatever put that into your head? Put it right out again.'

He tries to do that. But he cannot escape the feeling that Grace has slipped further from him. She was dead before she could be painted or drawn. She lived and left no trace. Her clothes and her cloth ball and her wooden baby in a smock are long ago passed to other children. But his elder daughter, Anne, he has her copy book. Sometimes he takes it out and looks at it, her name inked in her bold hand, Anne Cromwell, Anne Cromwell her book; the fish and birds she drew in the margin, mermaids and griffins. He keeps it in a wooden box faced and lined with red leather. On the lid the colour has faded to a pale rose. Only when you open it up do you see the original, shocking scarlet.

These light nights find him at his desk. Paper is precious. Its offcuts and remnants are not discarded, but turned over, reused. Often he takes up an old letter-book and finds the jottings of chancellors long dust, of bishop-ministers now cold under inscriptions of their merits. When he first, in this fashion, turned up Wolsey's hand after his death – a hasty computation, a discarded draft – his heart had clenched small and he had to put down his pen till the spasm of grief passed. He has grown used to these encounters, but tonight, as he flicks over the leaf and sees the cardinal's writing, it is strange to him, as if some trick, perhaps a trick of the light, has altered the letter forms. The hand could be that of a stranger, of a creditor or a debtor you have dealt with just this quarter and don't know well; it could be that of some humble clerk, taking dictation from his master.

A moment passes: a soft flicker of the beeswax flame, a nudge of the book towards the light, and the words take on their famil-iar contours, so he can see the dead hand that inscribed them. During daylight hours he thinks only of the future, but some-times late at night memory comes to nag him. However. His next task is somehow to reconcile the king and the Lady Mary, to save Henry from killing his own daughter; and before that, to stop Mary's friends from killing him. He has helped them to their new world, the world without Anne Boleyn, and now they will think they can do without Cromwell too. They have eaten his banquet and now they will want to sweep him out with the rushes and the bones. But this was his table: he runs on the top of it, among the broken meats. Let them try to pull him down. They will find him armoured, they will find him entrenched, they will find him stuck like a limpet to the future. He has laws to write, measures to take, the good of the commonwealth to serve, and his king: he has titles and honours still to attain, houses to build, books to read, and who knows, perhaps children to father, and Gregory to dispose in marriage. It would be some compensation for the children lost, to have a grandchild. He imagines standing in a daze of light, holding up a small child so the dead can see it.

He thinks, strive as I might, one day I will be gone and as this world goes it may not be long: what though I am a man of firmness and vigour, fortune is mutable and either my enemies will do for me or my friends. When the time comes I may vanish before the ink is dry. I will leave behind me a great mountain of paper, and those who come after me – let us say it is Rafe, let us say it is Wriothesley, let us say it is Riche – they will sift through what remains and remark, here is an old deed, an old draft, an old letter from Thomas Cromwell's time: they will turn the page over, and write on me.

Summer, 1536: he is promoted Baron Cromwell. He cannot call himself Lord Cromwell of Putney. He might laugh. However. He can call himself Baron Cromwell of Wimbledon. He ranged all over those fields, when he was a boy.

The word 'however' is like an imp coiled beneath your chair. It induces ink to form words you have not yet seen, and lines to march across the page and overshoot the margin. There are no endings. If you think so you are deceived as to their nature. They are all beginnings. Here is one.

AUTHOR'S NOTE

The circumstances surrounding the fall of Anne Boleyn have been controversial for centuries. The evidence is complex and sometimes contradictory; the sources are often dubious, tainted and after-the-fact. There is no official transcript of her trial, and we can reconstruct her last days only in fragments, with the help of contemporaries who may be inaccurate, biased, forgetful, elsewhere at the time, or hiding under a pseudonym. Eloquent and lengthy speeches, put into Anne's mouth at her trial and on the scaffold, should be read with scepticism, and so should the document often called her 'last letter', which is almost certainly a forgery or (to put it more kindly) a fiction. A mercurial woman, elusive in her lifetime, Anne is still changing centuries after her death, carrying the projections of those who read and write about her.

In this book I try to show how a few crucial weeks might have looked from Thomas Cromwell's point of view. I am not claiming authority for my version; I am making the reader a proposal, an offer. Some familiar aspects of the story are not to be found in this novel. To limit the multiplication of characters, it omits mention of a deceased lady called Bridget Wingfield, who may (from beyond the grave) have had something to do with the rumours that began to circulate against Anne before her fall. The effect of omitting any source of rumour may be to throw more blame on Jane, Lady Rochford, than perhaps she deserves; we tend to read Lady Rochford backwards, as we know the destructive role she played in the affairs of Katherine Howard, Henry's fifth wife. Julia Fox has given a more positive reading of Jane's character in her book *Jane Boleyn* (2007).

Connoisseurs of Anne's last days will notice other omissions, including that of Richard Page, a courtier who was arrested at about the same time as Thomas Wyatt, and who was never charged or tried. As he plays no part in this story otherwise, and as no one has an idea why he was arrested, it seemed best not to burden the reader with one more name.

I am indebted to the work of Eric Ives, David Loades, Alison Weir, G.W. Bernard, Retha M. Warnicke and many other historians of the Boleyns and their downfall.

This book is of course not about Anne Boleyn or about Henry VIII, but about the career of Thomas Cromwell, who is still in need of attention from biographers. Meanwhile, Mr Secretary remains sleek, plump and densely inaccessible, like a choice plum in a Christmas pie; but I hope to continue my efforts to dig him out.

ACKNOWLEDGEMENTS

I am truly grateful to the open-minded historians who took the time to read *Wolf Hall*, to comment on it and encourage this project, and to the many readers who have contacted me with family trees and snippets of family legend, with piquant inform- ation about lost places and almost forgotten names. Thank you to Sir Bob Worcester for showing me Allington Castle, once owned by the Wyatt family, and to Rupert Thistlethwayte, descendant of William Paulet, for inviting me to Cadhay, his beautiful house in Devon. And thank you to all those people who have issued kind invitations I hope to take up in the course of writing my next novel.

I owe special gratitude to my husband Gerald McEwen, who has to share a house with so many invisible people, and who never fails in his support and practical kindness.